.VILLAGE
IDIOT.
.PRESS

**PABLO D'STAIR** was born in 1981. At the age of 18 he composed his first novel *(October People)* for the *3 Day Novel Writing Contest* sponsored by *Anvil Press*. The novel did not win the competition but was published in the subsequent year - along with his second novel *(Confidant)* - by the infamous and now defunct vanity book-mill *Publish America*.

In the mid-2000's, D'Stair co-founded the art-house press *Brown Paper Publishing* with his colleague, the novelist, musician, and painter Goodloe Byron. Through this press and its literary journal *Predicate*, he released the work of more than fifty of his peers along with editions of two dozen of his own books (including *Regard, dustjacket flowers, Candour, a man who killed the alphabet, Carthago Delenda Est*, and the novella comprising *they say the owl was a baker's daughter: four existential noirs*).

Eventually shuttering *BPP*, D'Stair founded *(KUOBA)* press, continuing to publish work by his contemporaries. During this era, his own literary output remained prolific but largely unreleased, though several works were made available as limited-edition print projects and in various electronic mediums (including *the purse snatcher letters, the cigarette miscellany*, and the five novella comprising *Trevor English*).

Prior to composing *Lucy Jinx*, D'Stair spent several years as a cinema critic - primarily for the UK site *Battle Royale with Cheese* - and as an essayist/interviewer for the national newspaper of Sri Lanka's *Sunday Observer* (through which periodical several of his novella and a story collection were serialized). Also during this period, D'Stair began working as an underground filmmaker in the capacities of writer, director, cinematographer, editor, and performer - the cinematography of his first feature *(A Public Ransom)* earned an award in international competition at the *XIX Internacionlni TV Festival (Bar, Montenegro 2014)*.

*Lucy Jinx* was initially composed during an eight-month period, the bulk of the text generated during D'Stair's graveyard shifts as security guard for *Manheim Auto Auction* and during the day while he worked in a call-center for *Lancaster General Health*. A two-volume 'uncorrected edition' of *Lucy Jinx* was released in very limited number in May 2016. Final revisions to *Lucy Jinx* were eventually made during January 2019 and between July and August of that year. This edition marks the definitive version of the text.

D'Stair has also written several volumes of poetry, more than four dozen pieces of theatre, written and directed music videos, written and illustrated graphic novels and comic-book series, and produced audio essays. His work across all mediums has often been released pseudonymously.

Presently, he lives and writes in Lancaster, Pennsylvania.

# Praise for the writing of Pablo D'Stair

"The first thing that occurs to you when you pick up a volume of D'Stair is that it has no business being good. No credentials. None of the usual apparatus that tells you a book has appeared: publishers, agents, press releases. The industry didn't cough this one up. The second thing, once you start to turn the slippery pages, is: how the Hell can such good writing come from nowhere? Who the Hell is Pablo D'Stair, anyway? The final note, the one that makes D'Stair a little troubling, is that this writing is a voice inside your head. Nothing can prepare you for that ... Pablo D'Stair is defining the new writer. There is NO ONE else. As reckless as Kerouac's 120-foot trace paper, D'Stair's independence from all of us needs to be studied and celebrated ... This is revolution. Each word seems to want to wage war. Nothing is settled, nothing is as it should be - and we know as we read and it starts to sink in that this is how things are ... D'Stair's late realism needs to be included in any examination of the condition of the novel."

**Tony Burgess**, award-winning author/screenwriter
(*Pontypool Changes Everything, Idaho Winter*, and *People Live Still in Cashtown Corners*)

"[The work] is written by someone who cares about language - you'd be surprised at the number of novels written by people who don't. It takes a lot of daring and ambition for a writer to tease out a book like this in such minute detail, and D'Stair is committed ... you stop yourself from skimming because you start thinking you might be missing something - [the work] is too well written to skim ... Somehow again and again you're drawn in ... you get used to the rhythm and follow it because the work is obsessive. We find ourselves in a languid kind of suspense, bracing ourselves..."

**Bret Easton Ellis**, author/screenwriter
(*American Psycho, Rules of Attraction*, and *Lunar Park*)

"I knew he could write, and I suspect he can do about eighty other things as well - if our minds are hamsters on wheels, then Pablo has more hamsters than any of us ... D'Stair doesn't just write like a house afire, he writes like the whole city's burning, and these words he's putting on the page are the thing that can save us all."

**Stephen Graham Jones**, Bram Stoker Award-winning author
(*Mapping the Interior, Mongrels* and *All the Beautiful Sinners* )

"Over the years I've stopped being astonished at the multifarious things that Pablo D'Stair can do well. Let's just say it: whatever he puts his hand to he accomplishes and with a style and panache that is his alone ... Original. Idiosyncratic. Off-kilter. Strange. The slap-back dialog, the scenes as accurate as if directed by Fritz Lang. This is D'Stair's world. Welcome to it. I envy you if this is your first time in."

**Corey Mesler**, author/screenwriter
(*Memphis Movie* and *Camel's Bastard Son*)

# .LUCY JINX.

*a novel by*

Pablo
D'Stair

.VILLAGE
IDIOT.
.PRESS

Published by Village Idiot Press

*for my mother Catherine VanBrocklin*
*who told me the type of my soul*

Oh Hell no, she knows what the truth is,
'cause she says so, and she knows who her friends are,
so fuck you, don't get no closer,
it will only make her run far away

.RANCID
Red Hot Moon.


Oh and the things you can't remember
tell the things you can't forget
that history puts a saint
in every dream

.TOM WAITS
Time.


A woman's voice on the radio
can convince you you're in love;
A woman's voice on the telephone
can convince you you're alone

.THEY MIGHT BE GIANTS
Piece of Dirt .

# .LUCY
# JINX.

*The publisher asks the reader's indulgence for typographical errors unavoidable in the exceptional circumstances.*

*V.I.P.*

# .PART ONE.

# . I .

SHE WAS SITTING ON THE edge of the bed naked and could hear the mother prompting spelling words out to the child. *Teaspoon. Tea. Spoon. T. Ea. Sp. Oo. N. Teaspoon.* Had she slept? Maybe. Had she kind-of-slept? Maybe - more likely. The room was stale of a night of off air-conditioning and odd dreams, some of which still glopped behind her eyes and had her feeling weighted back toward sleep. *Archer. Ar. Ch. Er. A. R. Ch. E. R. Archer.* There was a melodious patience to the mother's voice. How many syllables could a single letter be given? The mother enjoyed breaking the words. Enjoyed breaking them more than was wholly necessary. Saying the words, broke, saying each part as its own word, own words, wanting to instill that magic nothing to do with the lesson or reality. So obvious the mother knew her child would learn to spell, with or without her.

What would Lucy wear? She looked on the floor. There was the dress and two pairs of panties - both of which she'd worn and discarded yesterday - and there was one sock and a glove that had been on the floor for a month. Yes. 'Glove. Floor. A month. Sure thing' she says, stretches, and still is not sat up, for whatever reason this morning rather liking her nudity though not regarding it. She liked the feeling of her nudity. This morning. The weight of it. She felt she was a presence. Though her toenails had gotten to be in that state there were not apologies enough for. She thought about vegetables that had gone off, but this was putting it too harshly. Anyway. She thought about a vegetable garden and a war going on someplace through the treelines around it.

The mother, downstairs, was now readying the child to go for the schoolbus. A hurry hurry sing-song, more pleasant than was needed - tone borrowed from popular cinema, moment borrowed from vague television. Or not. Maybe it was the way the mother sounded, felt, real, genuine, hurry hurry, backpack backpack, shoes shoes and all. The child was repeating some bit of babble - a lot of the neighborhood kids were in the habit of repeating this, now, Lucy heard them out the window all the time. 'What about it?' Lucy asks herself and, caught off guard, shrugs and lays down, tells herself 'Leave me alone, I'm thinking.' Then with emphasis adds 'You fucking worry about it if you're so worried about it.' Then more offhand, probably not even aware so much she added it, added 'Ha ha' and crossed both of her arms over her face, splayed legs, hiccoughed.

Had she drifted off? No. Nope. She could track her thoughts directly, it was just she had forgotten to pay strict attention, the mother and child had left the house without her remarking the close of the front door. Or maybe not. Unable to relax until it was verified and nowhere near in the mood to actually dress yet she decided if she heard no sound for the countdown of fifty it must, conclusively, mean that the downstairs - and therefore the house - was empty. By thirty-three she gave up. Hardly opening her eyes she looked to the coffee-pot kept on her dresser, the dregs of yesterday's stuff in it, enough for a good half-cup while she brewed something else. Or else downstairs. Glutton herself to the already, fresh brewed, hot stuff. She'd have to dress. A lie. Her habit was to roam the house nude until ten o'clock, easy, either showered or unshowered. It was just she had already - just now - laid back down. That was the issue.

What was it with this house? Where was this house? 'Where the fuck am I?' Lucy thinks, burps the words, whispers 'Excuse me' sits up and peeks out the window-blinds. Just a backyard. The same. Grumble grumble. Though Lucy tends to wish the word was *grumple* and did not know what authority to send the complaint to. With a lifetime of effort and enough celebrity achieved maybe she could work the change into the popular lexicon. Maybe. And on her tombstone they could say so. She thought about Socrates. She thought about subscribing to a newspaper, one that wasn't from around the area, the state even, tired of this rink-a-dink news, these rink-a-dink takes on matters of national scale. She thought about opening her closet to discover all of her clothes had been replaced with spider-webs and that leaves bitten through with tiny holes littered the webs, crisps, sharp enough to cut the strands if she breathed stern enough right against them.

*The room smelled of cinnamon.* No. *The room is cinnamon.* No. *The room is a cinnamon.* 'The room is a cinnamon' she tested aloud, liked it, but narrowed her eyes like she was not really being so strict with herself. 'The room is a cinnamon blah blah blah blah blah' - the five *Blahs* the placeholders for the rhythm of what the rest of the line of poetry would be. Sure. *A cinnamon* was good, that was real nice, she liked it as she started pulling on one of the two pairs of discarded panties, as she decided not to, let the fabric out of her hands, the things now just a soft loop around her left ankle. Nothing to write it down with. Well there is - her notebook, stray paper, several pens, and her computer. *The room is a cinnamon.* If she forgets it was it worth remembering? Or should she be glad?

The compromise was reached with herself to leave the room in a t-shirt and nothing else. The house, as always, sank away sharp from the edge of her door opening. Not that she thought anyone was there but there were many reasons the mother could suddenly return. The thing with this was: both of them were adults. A simple 'Sorry, sorry' would be enough to deal with that. In fact, chances were more it would be a perfectly fine breaking of the ice. Though Lucy knows the ice was already melted, she got on very well with the mother. But she should, if caught, be ready to act as though this was the first time in recorded history she had left her room without pants on. Oddly, she was more self-conscious about not being in a bra, even with the loose-fitted shirt on - a shirt which in fact made it moot that she had no panties on. Anyway. Why are we talking about this, Lucy? Dunno, Lucy. You talk about all kinds of things, who can keep track?

The piano was beautiful and untuned. So untuned. So glorious. Oh God, she could steal this piano, drag it up to her room, stuff it into her purse, ride it down the river and play it out-of-tune and sopping wet while the authorities scratched their heads about the clues she'd leave on purpose to keep them misdirected. In this scenario, she imagined the main detective was sympathetic to her cause and did not try too hard, knew the clues were bogus and had her number, easy as pie, but decided to let her get to wherever she was going where, yeah, she would be cuffed and locked away, find another out-of-tune piano waiting in the prison common-room, courtesy of the entire rag-tag crew that had chased her. The End. She played a few songs, the mistakes, the out-of-practice touch amplifying her asundered perfection.

Another matter was: none of this wonderful food was hers. Help yourself - we have to do a big shop every month, help yourself. But no one means that. Lucy, of course, would eat some toast, use some peanut-butter, drink the coffee - that was why a whole pot was brewed, after all, she got that, appreciated the gesture on the part of the mother - but could not cook up one of these steaks, make herself a burger, use pots for pasta. Unless maybe she made enough the mother and child would use it for dinner - the flaw here being that was taking things way too far. One, Lucy wasn't about to cook that much and two, Lucy herself, the roles reversed, wouldn't want to feel obligated to feed her child some weirdo spaghetti or tortellini some tenant spent the day, pantsless, preparing, unsolicited.

Also timid about using the television - this she knows is left-field insanity - she lays out on the sofa and stares at the art-prints on the wall, over in that corner by a bookshelf that seems never used, the shadows over there seeming dust-mote entire, such an unused, forgotten place, another dimension. Unlooked-at art-prints. Un-page-spreaded books. Air that went there when it was too sick to live. A lonely monster of a room-corner that, if the family moved, would only be packed up with a grudge. Or maybe it wasn't even there. This could all be a hallucination, Lucy. Like the start of some terrific adventure that will test the limits of your nerves and birth new imaginations from you, Oh such that you had no idea! That corner is all yours. Go into it. Join the dead air, the pictures no one painted and no one hung - think what treasures could be in those books written by no one and by no one ever yet read.

AT SOME POINT, SHE WOULD remember that this shirt was the shirt which never fit right and had the small stain on the righthand sleeve, tip of the elbow, beside. Though hadn't she, dressing, hadn't she checked, this time, this very day? Moot now - but yes she had, in just such a careless way she might as well not have, it seems. What's so terrific about the shirt, in any event? What keeps it from being scrap-heaped every time she realizes it doesn't fit, has the elbow-stain, there and then, down to the garbage, out the door of her otherwise well-mannered and all-in-order life? Is this on purpose, this shirt? Something about the lime green? Is there a memory connected to this shirt? Or maybe - new theory - does the shirt in some obscure way remind her base-brain of another memory, something that would defend it? The lime green, the stripes - that is what she focused on. What does that mean to Lucy? Lime green. Stripes. 'Lime green stripes' she says as she takes the left turn at the signal.

The sky is overcast the color of urinal porcelain - ashtray and faucet-tap stains and urinal porcelain. To her the day seemed languid, long, and hogtied. *Tongue-tied*, she switches this to, whether the day honestly seems it or not. *Tongue-tied* is the better thing to say, the weightier thing to say, the more of a maze. That is the day, today, but how would she describe herself? This is where her preoccupation takes her. There and to thinking about arguing with people's predictions about the weather. Or was that to avoid describing herself? 'Clever of me' she thinks and up goes the radio volume even though it's a commercial and she furiously steels herself to the endurance of such. A heartfelt, bought-and-paid-for endorsement of a steakhouse, one she's seen on her drives around every day she's lived around here. It was almost too late she pressed down on her brakes, stark halt, waited out the light feeling obvious, exposed, the volume turned down in a timid I've-learned-my-lesson.

'But what are we supposed to do about Eleanor? Because in the end it's her call' the woman preparing her coffee was saying to the man with her. The man had his soft-drink and was taking a bite out of whichever manner of sandwich that was, dark breaded, whiskers of lettuce, it looked like a children's film prop. 'Why's it Eleanor's call?' the man mouthfuled. 'Because Eleanor' the woman began replying, something had gone wrong with her adding sugar or something, though, an abrupt halt to the proceedings. Lucy felt she had stopped listening, but when the woman said 'Because Eleanor's Eleanor, she's always in it and she stamps the papers, man' she could not keep herself from straining in, wondering what the reply would be. Hurriedly, she moved to the other end of the gas station shop. There is her face in semi-reflection of frosted freezer-shelf glass, most of her not visible. There is her eye though, evident because of the thick orange of the French-bread pizza boxes. Wink. Smile, too, but that she can't see.

Then at the cash-register, very last moment sucker move, she got summoned over to be rung by exactly the cashier she did not want. The young girl who should not be there, who should not be allowed to speak to her. Even her feint of taking a beat as though uncertain she had her money with her did no good, the clerk she desired had ushered the customer behind her to that counter, a tiny 'Excuse me' and that voice, that perfect other clerk's voice going 'How are you today?' to not Lucy. Hell on Earth. The young girl was crisp and precisely gorgeous in that way young people were until looked at closer. 'What a sad little sack you are' Lucy thinks. The girl? The girl or you, Lucy? Didn't you look like that, ever? The thought is morbid, bread gone off. Even in her young pretty days she was not so nothing-else-but-pretty as this happy girl who told her, now, that she liked chewing the same gum as Lucy, zapping the barcode with vigor and smiling with no sense of self-consciousness.

'Write a novel' she thinks. How to go about it? Just make the character your mom. How's it go? She says 'Your mom is drunk, realizes she's gambled all the money gone. Run with it from there. It shouldn't take too long.' How would my mom get in to such a situation? This does clog up her thinking, but she gives the matter a squint while she wipes and flushes, takes up her plastic bag and goes to the faucet to wash hands. Maybe not write a novel. She unwraps the fresh pack of cigarettes but does not take one out, just gets the pack to her pocket so that it takes on the still stiff slouch, a slight start of crumple. This is an old superstition, to never smoke the first smoke straight fresh from a new pack, always from a pocket after walking, sitting at least once.

Has this music been playing the entire time she's been to the toilet? Well it could not have just this moment started, Lucy stalling, backpedaling, her hand already having begun pressing forward the door to exit. She tests - yes, the same music out in the store - then decides to linger at the mirror just awhile. What does this music even want? Why are there even songs for this particular Holiday? Certainly people, these people, these singers, are only singing these phrasings because they are being paid. The world can only have so many bent teeth, can only bristle in so many postures. Nowhere can there be human beings who look forward to this music, who sing along, unless in that awful way cat-food jingles are sung along to, remembered at night, treasonous minds mocking sleep and concentration with them. The bathroom door opens and in walks a woman dressed as though off from work at a buffet restaurant, just that sort of haggard, just that sort of dinge to the uniform shirt.

Though now she feels a little bit bad. There was no need to be so cutting in her criticisms of the clerk. Or there were reasons, but it was still an ill thing to do. Cliché. Lucy is sorry she was so cliché in it all. To call out the little girl for being such a little girl when of course she was. It's not the girl's fault she's had no time to be anything but a haircut and a way her shoulders look in a shirt. Now in this softer critique, she gets to wondering if there is an outside chance that the girl was still a virgin. Or if not, how did she feel about that whole event? When she told someone, honestly confided. Or did she? Was she the sort? Or did she not even confide to herself her feelings about such things, even give herself lines and evasions as people do? Less cliché is to wonder if that poor little girl is the sort who didn't tell the truth to even herself.

At the turn that leads to the long stretch of road, the final turn that will end her up eventually, ten or fifteen minutes, at her destination, she squirms around in her seat a bit, now wanting to be comfortable. The guest being interviewed is an aerospace engineer and never before has Lucy found this sort of thing interesting. This woman though - Lucy has not caught the name - is arresting in even the commonalities of how she speaks. In the obviousness that she has to talk way way way down to be at the layman level of the interviewer, who is, the interviewer, herself very erudite and with a wide store and scope of knowledge. Outside the window fields shoulder into houses nudge into buildings, a little town, the roads under her get more even, kempt, soon will slip away into fields again all the way until that forlorn, lowly traffic-light, no intersection, dangling and always set to a red-blink. 'This is the road into forgotten' thinks Lucy, listening to a beautiful woman speak wonders out of aerospace.

She parks, as she tends to, in the lot down the street from the bank and stares at the bank and stares and stares at the bank. The bank. What is it about? There's nothing, it isn't even in some little way like the sort of bank that could be photographed to look like something. What an uncanny draw she feels to it, because this parking space is not only random but inconvenient, in that she has to cross the street a few times to get where she is going and has to pass cafes that have tables on the street, the tables always full of people who are not like her and who look at her. Worse. She wants to howl, instead drags leisurely on her cigarette like a film much cooler than herself, blows the smoke at the inside of her windshield in a way that cinema would make iconic. Worse worse worse. These people think they are like her. She them. It's the loose tooth of a nightmare.

In the window of a ground-floor apartment there is a collared cat. No. It is a shop. A cat in a shop. Delighted, Lucy thinks she has been going about everything in life wrong and limply vows to turn it all around, to take in the flaws like graces and all of that. Who told her that? No one. Points to her! She has made it up and most symbolically at just the moment she is vowing to start anew in just such a way. Gears grind, but no need to be sullen. That is from a movie, Lucy. A grandmother tells it to her grown daughter. *Take the flaws like graces.* Lucy slumps like an aw-shucks and doesn't even realize it and something in her stomach gives way to a deep sense of distrusting everything about herself. A grandmother. An actress. Why did she have to remember that when she knows she has forgotten so many other things? And this would have actually meant something to her. Had the thought been her originality, just then, just there, today.


ARIEL WAS NOT IN THE office when Lucy arrived. No one was in the office, which is one of those things that is both usual and unusual simultaneously. The hours - which Lucy, and Ariel for that matter, refer to as 'the hours' - for the office - referred to as 'the office' - were loose and set by no one apart from Lucy and Ariel with the exception of Thursday and Friday - and the twice-monthly Saturday for setting the final files to printer - but Ariel had the more standard life out of the two and tended to be in by ten o'clock most days, hard at work - 'hard at work' - already by the time Lucy wandered in at eleven, twelve, three, four. The understanding between them, a tacit one, was they would obviously know if the other was not doing what the other ought be doing, so if Lucy wanted to show up at seven at night and work till the cock crowed it was alright. Ariel though, Lucy thinks, here, now, looking at the empty trailer-office under the buzz of the strengthening fluorescent track-lighting, was most often there, waiting, the coffee she'd have brought for Lucy cold, the breakfast sandwich the same.

Lucy was staring at the movie review in *Entertainment Straight!* sighing, thinking about a cigarette and about how she was going to invert the thing, do her review viciously negative to the orginal's obsequies lauding, when the office door opened and Ariel came in coughing, pointing back behind her as though with something of grave import to relate, immediately changing posture when the door closed, dropping a thump step while she said it, saying to Lucy 'Thank God you're here!' 'What's wrong?' 'Nothing. I just don't think I could have bore the thought of not seeing Lucy Jinx, today.' Lucy shrugged, squinted, said 'Are you being nice just because you don't have coffee and sausage for me?' 'Aren't I always nice?' Ariel points her fingers like a gun. 'Aren't I, bitch, always nice and courteously so - courteous to a fault!?' The telephone rang but neither of them moved to pick it up, none of their duties necessitating them ever to do so. 'What you're saying is you don't have coffee? Or sausage?' 'You want some sausage in your mouth, is it? Hot sausage?' Ariel changed her gun to a pantomime of smoking and Lucy got up smiling 'I want your hot sausage in my mouth.'

The trailer-office was at the extreme end of the parking lot to the flagship *Hernando's Grocery* and, as often she did, Ariel, voice a somber intimation, leaned in to say 'That's the flagship store, Lucy.' 'It's the starship *Enterprise*.' 'It is, Lucy. It's the starship *Enterprise* of Hernando's fleet. And we work in a trailer in plain view of it. Do you know why?' Lucy screws up her face good, little kindergartener looking 'Because we're lucky ducks?' Ariel knits brow, villainous suspicion 'How did you know that? Who told you that?' They both break the joke with an earnest, well-treaded laugh, Lucy's smoke out mouth left up, Ariel's out left down, Ariel punctuating the scene with 'We laugh, but it's true. It's true, Lucy. It's true.' And Lucy thinks that tree - look at it, there, the only one - planted in the parking lot where otherwise there are only lampposts is sublime and exists for a special, subtextual reason.

This edition, Ariel has asked to do the *CelebrInterview* feature because the television chef is someone she actually likes. 'It will give me a thrill in my nether parts' says Ariel, adding that she finds it a shame she isn't allowed to mock-up the answers while they are at it considering 'Who in Hell would ever know, when it all comes down to it?' A fine observation, yes, but Lucy knows that Ariel knows that Hernando, himself, has set super-strict guidelines on the *CelebrInterview* section based on - as had been outlined at terrific length in a memorandum filed in the top cabinet drawer - some news-magazine on television talking about libel and copyright and such things back when this publication of his had started. 'Why doesn't Hernando just get us on one of those lists that lets us get the actual, generic interviews like the websites get - the sanctioned ones?' 'Don't ruin my life, Lucy, please. Don't take this from me.' Ariel sighs tall as a church-door, following up with 'And we're not some chicken-dicked *website* baby, we're a *magazine*' Lucy bowing head 'Holy Ghost mea culpa sorry sorry sorry.'

It never does not astonish Lucy to find that the *Open Submissions to Poetry Corner* mailbox is always full. True, its contents come from all fourteen of the *Hernando's Grocery* stores, every two weeks a driver adding the pick-up and drop-off to whatever else this driver does, so the submissions don't generate overnight, but none of this gets away from the fact that these are physical paper-and-pen or computer-print poems submitted by actual human beings, things put in purses or on passenger seats while stores are driven to, expressions prepared, words written for the express purpose of this very submission to this very magazine. 'It's Lovecraftian' Lucy thinks, counting out - it's a horror of the Elder Gods! - thirty-nine, forty, forty-one submissions for the coming edition. 'It's like a lost chapter of *Charles Dexter Ward*!' she exclaims to Ariel who, typing, says, even-keeled 'You've no one to blame but yourself, Lucy - from now on keep your good ideas to yourself, right?'

Like this poem *An Ode To Dead Goldfish*. Like this poem *Desmela's Last Kiss*. '*Desmela's Last Kiss*, Ariel' says Lucy 'Desmela! The first thing a poet ought done is to've realized some names can't be poetic.' '*Desmela's Only Kiss*, more like it' says Ariel and Lucy, as she will do, likes this more than it needs to be liked and enthusiastically semi-guffaws about 'Yes, yes that would work, the one exception!' Now sure, Lucy jokes, these poems, their peevishness, their glimpses of more than she'd ever dared fear of the people around her, of their limits, of their photo-thin souls, sure Lucy shares some of these titles out with morbid smile and sarcastic playful batting to Ariel - but please know, Lucy we know, that her terror is actual, this feeling she has but cannot describe, the one which ties braids of her veins and could smother her outright in sack-cloth black dread were she alone in the room with the things.

'You just wear that shirt to show off your mountainous tits to me, don't you?' says Ariel, crumpling a paper and tossing it at Lucy, the missile going far right, Lucy just staring down at it with a disappointed-in-you shake of her head. 'I'm a C-cup, Ariel' Lucy smiles, shifting her shoulders around just to feel the off-fit of the shirt fit offly, watching how the second-to-last button up from the bottom is the one she replaced, the only thing she's ever sewn to anything by hand. 'To me, who has not had to buy new shirts since fifth grade, they are Kilimanjaro. It is imponderable, your bust' Ariel says, cartoon-face of awing despair - *Your bust* pronounced with foreign accent, one word like *Yabust*. Lucy, after return joke, some patter, after five minutes of Ariel back to typing, Lucy herself back to typing, covertly examines the thin edges of Ariel's shoulders pushing through the thin of her t-shirt, soft, semi-transparent brown, on the front some faded, cracked lettering Lucy'd been too shy to read.

They do their usual game of sharing *Traits Of The Office They Love The Most*. Lucy: that though only Lucy, Ariel, sometimes Hernando, and one man who certain days drops off supplies are ever inside the trailer, there is a cloth basket with a stack of the current issue of *Hernando's Highlights* in it, on this cloth stuck a handwritten sign, copy paper, green marker lettering, the word *Complimintery*, misspelling and all, proudly showing. Ariel: that a small bronze plaque has been affixed to the entrance-door - 'Right above the doorknob, no less' Ariel adds, this being her main point - with the sort of fine engraving one has to lean in close to see while holding a hand in front of to cast a shadow, the words *Publication Offices* upon it. Lucy says she wants to switch favorite things because Ariel's is the more hilarious, but Ariel vulgarly tells Lucy 'Better luck next time' and gives a motion like a man would make, a triumphal humping, then says 'Let's go smoke for my prize.'

Since the *Capsule Reviews* take the least time and since Lucy is prideful of her glorious insistence that they be labeled *Capsule Reviews* - because isn't *Capsule* such an exquisite word, one of the finest the language has on offer? - Lucy plows along through them, this week in a good mood and so not even troubling herself with taking different slants than the reviews she is cribbing from. The noia is her own that anyone would care even if she drew her versions of the reviews all from a single magazine - Ariel admits she and another man who had once worked there tended to do things that way - but it is jagged enough she is certain, even while good-mooded and lazy-happy like right now, to take each from a different source. Where do these movies come from? And all these people writing about them? Why? She knows why she is, she admits, but then again she really isn't and doesn't actually know why other than for the paycheck and it still seems so bizarre a thing to do. But these other people? These thoughts? What? And Why? And Why?

The telephone rings. They ignore it. They look at each other, ignoring it. They look at each other ignoring it. Ariel smiles and says, once the ringing has stopped 'We did that well' and Lucy says 'We've had practice.' Ariel complains how one girl - 'In college' she adds with a peculiar derision, self-referential and Lucy-referential since both Lucy and Ariel, indeed, are more than college-educated themselves - used to answer the phone despite being counseled that she did not need to, and this girl would always apologize after by going 'I know, I know, but I just worry it might be something important'. 'And thus this girl didn't last long, Lucy, and thus is why she was shit-canned with the rest of that land-lubbery lot!' Ariel says, giving Lucy a point, then a thumbs-up, then a hand gesture of *You're A-Okay*. Lucy smiles, a little bit blushing though surprised to be, and to hide this says 'Well, they don't learn about not answering the phone until the last day of college' and Ariel laughs, an ugly burst that is so beautiful it makes Lucy laugh, too.


THE LOT SEEMED LOPSIDED. BETTER say: the lot still seemed lopsided, the whole of it a lackadazic lilt to the left. Or the right. 'What do I care?' Lucy thinks and honestly cannot answer when she decides to treat the question as something more than a rhetorical blat. 'I honestly don't know what I care' she says aloud but barely, approaching the furthest out of the parked cars, consciously shifting her monologue entirely inward. She hadn't asked where Ariel had needed to go off to and was still nervous that her 'But I'll be back, an hour tops, just need to be someplace' was something that could be rescinded with a simple phone call. Or worse, with just a not-showing-up-again as Lucy, Ariel would know, wouldn't answer the phone, regardless. A man was singing a song to his child as he secured the kid in a car-seat, this man still singing as he stood up, gave Lucy a smile she pointedly did not return. Take that, Mister Smile!

So this is the inside of *Hernando's Grocery*. Flagship. This is it. It's homely. Comely. It is about as charming as permafrost for all of its banners and the café addition where sometimes - maybe every day, it strikes her - there is live music. *About as charming as permafrost*. She needs a goddamned pen. Don't lose that. Shit. *The vague charm of permafrost*. 'Can I use a pen?' *All the vague charm of permafrost*. 'Thanks.' Nabs a flier to write on. Nothing. Tries it on her hand. Nothing. 'Excuse me, this pen doesn't work.' 'Doesn't it?' 'Well, not on my hand or this paper, maybe do you have regular paper?' The clerk hits a button, some receipt paper extends extends extends is torn. 'Thanks.' She tries it. Squiggle scrag dash dash dash. 'Perfect, thanks.' 'Sure thing.' *About as charming as permafrost. As charming as permafrost*. Which? Those are two different statements. Where can she sit down? She has picked a table that wobbles and her shoe has stepped in something sticky because why not? 'Fuck you, Lucy' says Lucy and Lucy agrees, she agrees.

Her entire life - it's been awhile now, she knows how long but for sake of her feelings back-dates herself a bit - she has wanted to just take some candy out of the self-fill bins, eat it without paying for it, but never has. Not as a child. Not as an adolescent. Never. Perhaps now, when oddly it would be the most inappropriate, when it would be - let us not lie - the least excusable a time in a lifespan to display such behavior, she can. Perhaps she ought. Or else? Play it safe. Wait until she is elderly. When it will again have become specifically excusable, when it will have a context of specified appropriateness. Now is the time because now is the only time it is truly wrong and she knows, right this minute, this is what she has been waiting for. It is the Wrong she had desired. A kid, a teenage brat, a punk young girl, an old doddering woman: everyone knows they will take that candy and have charms in the cards for them when they do. But now? Lucy. Here you are. There is a gummy-worm. Take it. No? Then just stand there and look. But everyone sees you. They really see you, Lucy. As you are.

'How much is a pound of this?' the man in the Deli line is now asking for the third time, the attendant not at all put off, uncertain, or moving to verify from anything but their own memory despite the man leaning down, straightening, leaning down to look at the sign - that one, Lucy sees it, price clearly marked exactly the price the attendant is giving. 'How much? Jesus. For beef-steak?' 'Yes, sir' the attendant gives Lucy a smile which she returns but also doubles as her exit move still hearing the man talking but he dribbles off 'Wasn't it almost a clean two dollars less than that just last' by the time she is to the cereal aisle looking at toaster pastries. A box to keep at the office? Meh. They should sell single packs. They should. Strong self-assent. An approaching worker says 'Excuse me' from still a good distance off, Lucy not certain had he meant her so she freezes, only ducking to the side when he is almost upon her, he meekly saying 'Sorry' as he gets the empty palette cart by and then is gone through the swinging doors by the lobster tank.

'Haven't seen you around in awhile' says Suzette as she rings out Lucy's small purchase. 'I've been around' Lucy says. Though Suzette says she hasn't seen Lucy around for awhile every time Lucy comes through her line, at least - at least - three times a week, Lucy finds no cause to make a thing out of it. More than that though: Lucy likes this. How long has Suzette worked this cashier job? Well, look at her: that's how long. So long that to describe her, even nude, is to describe Grocery Cashier. She is a grocery cashier the way there are shadows burnt to walls by the Atom Bomb. 'Do you have a pen?' Lucy asks. 'There you are, dear. And how is the magazine this week?' Lucy writes and says 'It's coming good, good issue, good interview this time' - she writes *clerk the way there are shadows* - and Suzette says 'I can't wait' - writes *Atom Bombs*. 'You know, a friend of mine submitted a poem' Suzette says as Lucy is moving away, small voice, conspiratorial. 'They aren't allowed to write their names.' Suzette nods. Lucy, look at her! Look at Suzette! Come on Lucy, are you human!? Don't pretend you can't see! 'Well ...' Say it! '... do you know what it was about?'

Cigarette. Out under the main awning. Even from here it is plain: no Ariel's car. Though it has been all of half-an-hour. No less disappointing. Time has no bearing on disappointment. 'Hell, something can happen exactly how you wanted it to and you can still feel disappointed it didn't' she says, enough surrounding noise she doesn't even feel the need to whisper. 'Yep.' Lucy knows she just looks like someone smoking and having a little talk with themself. And there is a young kid pushing the rounded up shopping carts along, prim and vigorous, sure of the love of his first girlfriend. 'Yippie' she says 'yippie, young man.' And Lucy is decent enough to not sarcastically sing a *Beatles* song in his direction. How long did all that take? Another five minutes? She looks at the plastic bag she has set down only vaguely remembering what she has bought. Supposing with her discount it didn't matter. No different than having bought something she would actually want and far easier than going through that hardship.

The same clerk at the café kiosk gives her a 'You're back' and she agrees that she is and asks for a coffee. 'Coffee is now over there' points the clerk. An entirely separate café counter area, this one emblazoned with the logo of the local chain coffee house *Java Turkey*. 'When did that get here?' Lucy asks and is proud of herself, so local-person a thing to say. 'It's been there about a month. They kept it hush-hush all the way until two days before opening.' 'Did they?' Lucy asks, now genuinely intrigued. 'We all thought it was gonna be a *Toboggans*.' 'What's that?' 'Pizza and Ice Cream place. You've never had a slice at *Toboggans*? Or a cone?' Obviously not. Obviously not, sir. 'No. They're pretty smashing, are they?' 'Not as good as *Quincy's* over in Breadworth, but yeah. We all wanted it to be a *Toboggans*.' All she can manage to this is a nod. Enough for one day.

*The sky has curdled, all of its fingers in all of its mouths.* Lucy hurries, not regretting having two coffees to deal with, exactly, but wishing she'd only gotten the one for Ariel as this is all slowing her down. *All of its ears hear only all of it hearts.* No. *All of its hearts beat in all of its ears.* She discards her coffee, notices a woman giving her a pointless look of 'Oh no! Your coffee!' and because she has been observed so flagrantly is obliged to stop a beat, look anguished, and to not hurry off as sharply as she wanted - all in all her plan negated by random interference. *All of its tummyache from all of its swallows down.* Why is this car moving so slowly beside her? What could this mean? Don't look. 'Yes?' A woman rolls down her window. 'Is there a gas station nearby?' 'Nearby to what?' What the devil could this person possibly mean!? 'I am not the lot attendant, ma'am. I don't work here.'

At her desk, trailer-office lights not turned on, enough overcast through the window to have allowed her to write without making her feel back-on-the-clock yet, Lucy absently takes a sip of Ariel's coffee, curses, and carefully wipes at the lid opening, squinting to be sure she has left no trace of her mouth. Then to be certain of no further mishaps puts the thing over on Ariel's desk, a scenario playing out vividly of the following exchange: 'I got you a coffee' 'I got you a coffee, too' 'But I also got myself a coffee' 'I got myself a coffee too, but threw it into the street in a rush' 'I figured you'd done that, I just had a feeling' 'But you figured I'd not be considerate enough to get you one, too?' 'Why would I have imagined otherwise?' Stop. Yes, that could just keep going on. Just one more. 'You know me so well.' 'I do.' 'That was two more' Lucy thinks to herself, but then argues she had meant one more two-set, back-and-forth, one more unit.

If she had a camera she would take a photograph of the three young men all lounging in the back of their empty moving truck, smoking their cigarettes, drinking whatever that was, tin music playing - this would almost be seen in the photo - from someplace she couldn't determine. Why are they so happy? Where are they moving? Or had they moved here? One place to another? She levels some smoke out in their vague direction, whichever direction they are in vague. Why couldn't Lucy be a young a man, she wondered, helping a pal move, smoking a cig and feeling awesome listening to flat music? She'd be good at it, she promises. One day she could be one such young man, the next day another. This is a sort of way a life could go, why not? Couldn't that be the way an organism lived? Of the three in this lot she'd be the one without the beard, the one who did not have his long sleeves rolled up and who seemed to best know how to look while smoking, sat to the lip of the back of a moving truck.

SO HERE IS ARIEL, WALKING into the trailer-office and here is Lucy in just that moment returning a happy greeting, also realizing she has been staring into vacant space for at least the preceding five minutes, tapping her pen on the desk, sometimes giving it an elaborate twirl around her fingers, but staring into space, nonetheless. 'Everything alright?' Ariel asks, for whatever reason turning to look a peek out through the lowered blinds of the trailer. 'Everything's fine. How'd everything go?' Ariel sighs, to Lucy seeming oddly evasive - evidence: still no eye-contact to speak of, not having moved to desk, standing in an area of the trailer Lucy really has no memory of her ever standing in during the course of a day - when she says 'It all went fine. As fine as it can go. I don't know. Fine I suppose.' In a dreadful tension Lucy tries to sound nonchalantly jokey with 'That sounded like a little song.' By pure luck Ariel just then notices the coffee waiting for her, turns and mock-lovelorn coos 'Lucy' - the middle pronounced *ooooooooo* - 'you got me coffee. I didn't get you anything. I'm a selfish monster or some kind of emotionless crab-person.'

The two shared the curious mix of sensation that comes from realizing they'd been under the impression they needed to prepare the issue for print this week when really they had until next. How had this happened? Was it worse or better? Worse. Mutually concluded. 'We were stoked to do it, here and now - it will seem twice as dreadful by next week.' 'I wasn't stoked' admitted Lucy and Ariel admitted the same, both of them mutually confessing that even if it did have to go print this week neither had at all intended to do anything about it that day. This easily stitching to the further revelation that in reflection they likely never had been under the impression it was to go to print this week except for in the instant immediately before realizing it went to print next week. 'I think everything is dreadful, like the world's stomach has a headache' Ariel sagely imparts and, glowing, not to miss an opportunity like this, Lucy deftly whisks in 'Or the world's headache has a stomach' which gets the prize of the modern world for Lucy, Ariel going 'This is why you run *The Poetry Corner*!'

*The Poetry Corner*. So let's get to that. What had Suzette said her lamentable little friend's poem had been about? Oh God - Oh God Jesus, oh God - oh Christ's this cannot be the thing! Lucy feels a tremendous urge to belittle herself. Here is your humanity, precious girl! Here is your compassion! This is what it looks like, what it reads like! She got you, Suzette did, with her woe-mask of a face all tattooed up with mundane Hell - she got you! She isn't you, Lucy - Lucy, you aren't where Suzette is and took steps to never be. And this friend, too! You've let Suzette get the better of you with her maudlin show of being common, human, frail - you've taken such steps to avoid those things but they got you, too, rusty nail of them stepped on, poisoned sheets slept between. This is the poem!? *To My Beautiful Girl*. No. No! And it's about a cat. Who can make a cat seem hideous? This woman. This nameless friend of Suzette. This is how she dares malign both poetry and feline? Rhyming *Purr* with *her* is one thing - rhyming *meow* with the exclamation *And how!* is a darker complexion on a deader horse altogether! What about it, Lucy? Now you have a decision to make with direct repercussions.

Of course Ariel has noticed the war-torn brow of Lucy and has come to stand over her shoulder like three moons cooling the death of the Earth by an overstuffed sun. 'You look like your skin wants to strangle you, are you okay?' Lucy cannot even joke. 'I promised to publish this.' 'You promised?' Ariel says, not even having read it yet - that note of incredulity you heard in the question, the emphasis on *You* and the sing song to the second bit of *Promised* required not even an opinion of the verse, just a knowledge of Lucy, which even in her current state Lucy is glad to note Ariel has. 'I promised with my body. My face promised. Maybe she didn't notice but people like her notice things like that - they think things like that are real.' '*How comfortable your fur / no wonder you wear it all hours*' is recited by Ariel who tries to pretend like that might be okay as Lucy scans her face desperately for Let It Be True! but alack alack Ariel hands the paper back with a meager 'Lucy, I hate to tell you this but there is no balm in Gilead, there is no physician there.'

Lucy decides to just skip to the next part of her life. She accomplishes this as best she can by the following daydream while Ariel has to make some of the boring telephone calls, having lost three-in-a-row best two-out-of-three coin flip sets. Here is Lucy in a cabin apartment on a small boat. The desk with the typewriter is bolted to the stage boards of the room floor and a mirror stained off-bronze with time reflects her back like a drawing on soaked paper. She lives on this boat and people know only to come to her door with food, news of terrible coming weather - she doesn't like to be caught off guard, romantic penchant for sea-sickness if she doesn't brace - or to inform her there will be a showing in the ship's cinema that night. Not a month goes by that a guest on board does not know her by name, too shy to approach. Not a week.

This is better. A laugh with Ariel now about the nasal voiced woman who titters like a bagful of field mice at the prospect of having an advertisement in the magazine even though she always has an advertisement, full page, in the magazine. This time - no rarity, every third issue she gets this - the woman gets the reverse cover. 'Her daughter designed this one' Ariel says, tone of voice in mock of the solemn way this was expressed to her. 'Not her famous daughter?' hand-clasp-to-hearts Lucy. 'The famous daughter, known to us all' Ariel finishes the scene as they both, unrehearsed, take meaningful postures to hold as the stage lights remain full a moment, dim, turn them silhouette, extinguish, applause. 'This is for the bistro?' Lucy wonders aloud, knowing full well it is not, just wanting Ariel to say 'For the *Kidnasyium*' - because who wouldn't want Ariel to have to say that? 'The *Kidnaysium*?' repeats Lucy. 'The' begins Ariel, deftly catching on to Lucy's great trick, pivoting to a graceful 'Fucking writhe in Hell with your rotten onion of a mother, Loose.'

Taking a more casual gait of it, Lucy inquires as to what Ariel had been up to during lunch - referred to as 'lunch' - hoping that it's not entirely none of her business 'In which case, nevermind.' 'No, no' says Ariel, obviously not about to let out anything exact - mysterious, but something - and says 'I just had an appointment. Something. I don't know what you'd call it.' Lucy has nodded to this now fourteen times, Ariel not seeming put off by the silence, so this all indicates they both know there is a thing and Lucy isn't out of bounds, not unwelcome. 'You don't have an awful tumor or anything do you?' 'You could call it that' Ariel demurs - or Lucy inserts the word *Demurs* because it sounds beautiful, harmless, and she wants it to be the correct word, whatever it actually means - but she, Ariel, immediately overcorrects with 'I mean no no no it isn't a tumor or anything, it isn't any kind of anything like that at all, sorry' which is, just from being said like this in correction to so recently having so charmingly demurred, maybe the worst sound of a string of words Lucy has ever encountered.

The following is concocted by Lucy, on the spot, to weather what now seems an odd series of setbacks in mood and atmosphere. A story she claims, with forced animation she does indeed believe she pulls off without seeming forced, to be true and which she had meant to relate before. It happened, according to Lucy, that driving home of an evening, recently - short-handed as 'two weeks ago' - she had felt distracted and really wanted to listen to a particular CD. And though the road was empty, in a sudden fit of adult responsibility she had slowed the car to a halt - 'There is no shoulder to this road' she ad-libs for authenticity 'so just there in the middle of the road, putting on my hazard-lights' - and looked through the glove box. Then, inserting the found CD, she glanced ahead at the road, preparing to drive on, only to see in her headlights the - she says 'it seemed to me, then' - enormous form of a bulb-shelled tortoise there, directly in front of her, slugging along. Had she not stopped just when she did for such a random reason she would have destroyed this turtle, utterly. Good story, Lucy. And look: effect achieved. Remember Ariel as now, as that face, you did that.

The announcement is made by Ariel that the coffee Lucy gave her was all the necessary inspiration for this month's pen name for the lengthier, freelance - called 'freelance' - editorial on Digital Cinema, this cribbed mainly from an article in a major New York newspaper, a recapping of a documentary in the current issue of *Frazzle*, and an actual editorial out of *Out Of Focus: The Cinematographer's Magazine*. 'This will be written by a man, of course' Ariel zippily zips 'because women do not care to make such masculine distinctions as Digital and Not Digital, because women actually understand Cinema and Art unlike men who understand, at best, whether or not they like the shoes they bought that one time' - Lucy rolls her hands as though impatient which causes Ariel to extend her blah blah blah, sticking out her tongue, before finally saying 'It will be written by *Julio R.F. Zinn.*' 'What does that have to do with coffee?' 'It has everything to do with coffee, Lucy. I thought you of all people would get that.' Faux look of exasperation, a hissy pout, Ariel's lips a pretend-mean kiss. Bottle rockets and candy kissing the grass under the moon!

There's nothing to do in the room. Is Ariel staying longer than needed because Lucy accidentally seemed more worried than she'd meant to seem, earlier? Does Ariel want to maybe hang around with Lucy if Lucy were to ask? Because Ariel isn't doing anything and it's well past time she could have gone. Lucy is about to go, in just a minute. What if Lucy didn't go? Would Ariel not go? This job can be confusing like this because it's the sort of job that is surrounded by the tumult of every question that has nothing to do with the act of producing *Hernando's Highlights*. 'When's the last time you watched a movie, Lucy?' Was that actually Ariel asking that? Blink blink. 'Uh. I. Have no idea. Am I fired now that you've discovered what a fraud I am?' 'Yes. You're fired. I've turned State's Evidence. I did so without any consideration for you. I didn't even know what it meant and still don't. Your goose, Loose, is right and truly cooked.' 'When's the last time you watched an actual movie?' Ariel seems to not want to be able to answer when she instead has to say 'Last night. But I'd seen it before. I'd seen it a few times before. You know?' Lucy nods. She pictures a romantic comedy. Seen many times. 'I hear ya' Lucy says. She also pictures Ariel in the blue glow of the flickering romantic comedy and whoever else that is with Ariel. But whoever that is with Ariel is a different flicker of blue, the kind that a corpse gets before it disintegrates. Ariel is the flickering-middle-of-the-night of tired-eyed-cinema. The same as Ariel always is.

THIS TRAFFIC IS LUCY'S OWN fault. Though what Lucy really means by this is that the particular quality of its tortuousness is the fault of Lucy. In a general sense traffic does not even bother her. She will just sit in her thoughts - like that one there, this one here, that one there - and will have the radio playing - *Chopin, NPR, Rancid*, random station - and will be content as an unknown thing so far near the sea-bottom we'll never know it. But: she, on nearly her first day of work, had said to herself, or had thought, or something like that, how this particular traffic had the feel of a toilet queue and so now her stomach begins loosening as she sharp-tingles with the need to urinate every time she gets trapped in the clog. Doesn't she take precautions, know this will be the case and act responsibly? 'Of course I do' Lucy seethes. Of course she does. Always voids herself before leaving work. But it doesn't matter. No Lucy, it never matters: you brought this on yourself.

How she imagines it, the majority of these cars take the same winding turn off and plunge into the sour of a swamp, submerge limpidly, over the course of the night hours air pockets rise them back out, they pull onto the road, car-washes are kept in the black, and the life cycle repeats as it has since whenever the muck of this nowherescape first became what she grudgingly admits to be civilized - a word she pronounces in this case to sound like whatever jumble of letters would onomatopoeia the cringe of a slobbery tooth over a dry one. Listen: what's on the radio? Just that. And how many times has this same album cycled through in just the last week? Well there's nothing on the radio in the afternoon, anyway. Hearing well-spoken voices talk incisively about meaningful events elsewhere 'round the globe with full soul and understanding of their pertinence, well, that is just too much, right now. Every day, right now. Every day, around this time.

Lucy doesn't want to feel envious of war orphans and then later guilty for being so self-absorbedly awful.

There is a list of small responsibilities in her head. Simple list. Things that can be taken care of in three-quarters of an hour. Now she is talking to herself, but note: the traffic is moving. Now she is saying to herself 'I say three-quarters of an hour to make it seem longer. There's ways to say everything to make it sound awful, ways to make it sound normal, ways to make it sound pleasant. Three-quarters of an hour is dreadful. Forty-five minutes is regular. Not-even-an-hour is nice. Tada - Shakespeare, crown me something, stitch me by hand into a quilt.' Now she is boring herself, embarrassed that most of that is so malformed, not witty. What a brute, Lucy, such low class you might as well let your bra-strap show and always be pulling your hair up when people are around. Never put off till tomorrow what you can put off till the day after tomorrow. 'Who said that?' she whispers. Not you. Maybe Garfield. Anyway, it's not even that clever, little miss.

Rain is the most romantic thing that happens around this place. It makes even the *Countrytowne Buffet* seem there might be something going on inside. As Lucy passes now, not a whiff of rain, not even a thicking of ozone building up around, the overcast broken, sky through tender cloud cover, sunlight, ghastly *Countrytowne Buffet* is entirely void of beauty, even for its Joycean altogetherness, something Lucy knows is likely better attributed to a mistake or simple illiteracy than kindship to the pen of an Irish thunderclap holy soothsaying firecracker. The place looks like it could be peopled with slugs. Edit: the place looks like it could be filled with slugs covered under inches-and-a-half of dust. Edit. Naw, leave it. 'You get the idea' Lucy sighs. No point changing the CD at this point. Listens to the whir of it resetting for track-one, the dant dant dant of the first strikes of drum mixed with synth, something delightfully early-computer-game sounding.

What in Hell was she thinking of? When? Just now, before. Grind grind grind. Ah. Responsibilities. Get the bills into envelopes, good riddance. She will put off the telephone calls. No. Yes. No. Meh. She doesn't quite want to be home yet so this parking lot will do. Outside, car, leaned to, Lucy, light flame, cigarette, mouth, thick smoke, circle lips, kaboom. Smoke two of them, Lucy. 'Three.' Deal, but then you have to get home. No one argues it would be too early, now. So awkward to wend in while the mother does homework or piano practice with the child. Though you are welcome. Don't even need to quick step through like over just-polished floor, just-shampooed carpet, like dog tongue stealing half-of-bacon-slice dropped accidentally. Exhale. Long. Look at that smoke. A whore of a breath, that, a million dollars for one night, no doubt about it. Smoke three, Lucy. You do pay rent. And they both even like you. The child even drew that picture of you and on that homework said you were his favorite part of his house.

'Could I get a cig?' Who's this? Shit. He thinks he's handsome, yeah? Sure does, with that shirt he thinks he's got something one-size-fits-all in his wit. This will go poorly. 'This was my last. Sorry, man.' 'No worries, no worries. You always smoke here?' You're within your rights, Lucy, this is not okay of him - poor buggar might not know it, but like a gravedigger shouldn't eat cotton candy on the job is the same as how this guy ought know to be more prudently behaved. 'I do. Always. Where do you always smoke?' What are you doing? God. Just to see what he says? Okay. 'I used to smoke right here. Always. But I moved away and I guess you Bogarted in.' 'Where did you move?' 'To Egypt.' 'Like Cleopatra.' What are you doing, Lucy? 'I took her old smoking spot, come to think of it.' 'Birds of a feather, I guess.' You do know you want to smoke a whole 'nother cigarette, right Lucy? 'Birds of a feather, yeah.' 'Why'd you leave? Did she show up again and bug the shit out of you, too?'

Why put a sign up indicating a quarry is thirty-six miles off in that direction? There is not a sign, a mile that way, saying the quarry is thirty-seven miles nor one two miles that way or three indicating it is thirty-eight, thirty-nine. Could this be, some investigation unearthed, the spot where people on average first start to wonder how many miles away that quarry is? And what is the matter with Lucy's foot, now? Why are her toes sweating, all of a sudden? These are questions no one was asking until a moment ago. We are DNAs tip tip tapping along through some cycle until turning to nothing, surrounded by limitless questions that do not need to be asked. And here is the blinking sign for the *Shoe-Repair and Watch-Repair* which signals she is suddenly, abruptly, just about home. This sign, when it is midnight dark outside - it isn't now, but just to mention it - is so bold and deity-bright one can almost hear, even with windows closed and radio up garbage-truck loud, the contractions of the electricity prodding the light out from nothing in the itty-bitty bulbs of the letters.

To understand the swell of luckiest-girl-in-the-world Lucy feels when the mother's car is not present - even tempered by the outght-to've-remembered-it-wouldn't-be sigh because it never is until late evening, this day in the week - is not something Lucy even attempts. Cold like a shivering fish rush of joy over her, she just stares at the outside of the empty house and has not even undone her seatbelt. Incredible. And she will still have an hour. The bricks of the house almost seem yellow they are grinning so welcomingly. And her bones are hand-warmed putty done being played with, dropped to the floor, restful as the sleep after screaming into a phone for two hours. Somewhere a neighbor starts a leaf-blower and even this doesn't bother her - though it is wholly uncalled for, leaf-blower, the evening, no decorum to whoever that is. There must be something wrong with Lucy. What happened today? Why does any of this mean anything to her and where has this mood cockroached out from? What even in this mood, can she tell?

A message is being left on the machine and Lucy listens to it. So quaint this old fashioned answering-machine. Peculiar to have in a home that rents a room. But then the fax-machine in the mother's bedroom caterwauls, desperate feline yarl all hours, as well, so these people are obviously accustomed to their own sounds and think nothing of others knowing them. Those candy-bars have been on the kitchen counter all week. Is it possible they were meant for Lucy? Not wanting to risk it she writes a quick note that she will replace the candy tomorrow but was jelly-willed and could not argue with her sweet-tooth anymore, she had just given up even though she knew it no longer loved her. Smiley face. Weird. You're so weird, Lucy. Winky smiley face. Might as well give it a bow-tie. 'Stop yer flirtin'' she says with an off-brand country accent, getting the chocolate's first corner unwrapped.

So: here is your room, again. Here is Lucy's room. Anything changed? Not a thing, not a jot. She wishes she were more paranoid so that she could work herself into a tizzy, sometimes. There must be something about the room that could at least seem to be different were she unbalanced enough to really force the issue. Something malodorous in this home. *Malodorous*. Good word. She jots it down and while she does wonders if her just having thought the word *Jot* the moment before had made her think to jot it and so also jots the word *Jot* and sings a song that goes 'Jot jot jot jot jot jot jot jot' to the tune of the final notes before the chords of the first movement of the *Pathetique Sonata*. 'Malodorous jot' she says. Seems a good thing to call someone. That suave little prick who tried to pick up on her while she smoked. 'Fuck off, you malodorous jot' she tries out and her room stays empty and quiet after in a clear sign of approval. Also she tries, this done like as a line in a play not as like a scene in real life 'Petey? Petey, you mean? That malodorous jot!? Why would you think he'd been here?' If she were to lay down now she'd sink like something found weeks later in a motel pool by a wading kid's tippy-toe.

LUCY STILL ISN'T DRESSED BY the time she hears the front door opening downstairs. She had fallen asleep. Had she meant to? Had I meant to? Evidence to the contrary: her odd positioning on the bed, one leg half-dangled over the side, the thin sheet, orange, just vaguely draped to her. Not even draped. A wrinkled triangle of it sort of covers one of her breasts, the other breast long exposed, goose fleshed and tightened from the constant air-conditioning. Final evidence? The room door is not closed. Jesus. That quickly remedied - closed, locked, tested - Lucy gets her bearings, nude in front of the not drawn blinds of the room window, looking at some neighbors smoking and airing their dogs. They can't see you, Lucy, running fingers in scoops under your arms and painstakingly scratching the side of your hip, deep pressing skin, stretching up up so that your calves might cramp and feeling your toes go crick crick in the muffle of un-vacuumed carpet.

There is a soft tapping at the door as Lucy finishes with getting her socks on, the same socks as she'd been wearing all day. 'Yes? Come in.' The handle is tried but does not, of course, turn, the mother's voice starting but unheard because Lucy is already shaking her head at her silly self and saying 'Sorry' unlocking the thing and opening it a casual wide. 'I'm sorry, I don't mean to bother you.' What is her scent? Lucy always wants to ask but that just isn't a question Lucy has ever asked anyone and so somewhere in her feels she isn't the sort of person who asks things like that. 'It's no bother' Lucy's smile almost knocks off her ears for going big wide so hurriedly followed by an I'm-such-a-dork bleh face and a depreciating chuckle into 'I was just spacing out, I appreciate the jostle.' 'It's fine if you don't want to' the mother is whispering, leaning in, breath the same as that scent - could it be just a natural scent? - 'but Flynn wanted me to ask if you wanted to have some of the cake he got, he wanted me to invite you.' Stop smiling Lucy and say something. Nod nod. That works. 'Why does he have a cake?' Lucy whispers, stealthy step into hall, closing door like a diary lock while she does.

The child, Flynn - Lucy has known his name since moving in but doesn't like it as a name, though likes the child rather more than she tends to like children - asks Lucy what she does for a living, an obvious affectation lifted from somewhere to his posture and the pronouncement of the question. From the kitchen where she is putting slices of cake to plates and getting napkins and such things the mother serves as footnote 'They're doing Careers in school, this week' the child, Flynn, repeating right on top of his nodded approval of his mother's explaining him 'So what do you do for a living?' 'I plagiarize' says Lucy, same time turning to take her plate and flash a smiling 'Thank you' to the mother who is chuckling in response, asking the child 'Flynn, do you know what that means?' as she sets down his plate and then turns to retrieve her own from the kitchen. Flynn looks at his cake then up at Lucy 'What does it mean?' then back at the cake, obviously uncertain if he is supposed to wait for a fork or tuck in bare-fisted.

The reason the child has a cake is that he got a ribbon for a science project in school and the gaining of this ribbon was so unexpected the mother felt the need to grandiosely make a thing of it. Flynn using the toilet, the mother whispering

- Lucy realizes pointedly that when the mother whispers to her she gets a feeling almost like being drunken, giddy in her chest, listening to the hiss-hush - how 'I didn't even know he was working on a goddamn science project, knew nothing about it, and totally didn't know there was a contest! Since when does this punk like science!?' The mother fake growls and Lucy - aww - is smiling with her teeth pinching her lower lip. 'Are you sure he actually got a ribbon for a science project?' Lucy decides to act bold enough to ask, familiar tone and everything. The mother lets out one regular volume sound of a laugh, stifles, and says 'The first thing I thought! That's the first thing I thought! What science project!? But I wanted a cake anyway so figured I shouldn't be responsible, attentive, ask too many questions, risk ruining it all.'

Describe the child? Eh. A kid. Flynn. Has a surname, but not the mother's. Some story there. Hair about that length a kid in second, third grade or whatever has. The color, as well. Since when has Lucy ever had to describe a kid? It's like asking someone to describe their dog beyond its breed. A kid is a breed. It looks like what that looks like. But for sake of humoring: the kid has brownish hair and a tapered face and tends to either smell like bubble-gum - the scent of his shampoo or hand-soap? - or else that sweat that kids sweat that doesn't quite smell like sweat but more like soggy mulch. Right now: Lucy is looking at the kid - who is over there in the living-room, laid on the carpet, drawing in a notebook, talking to itself - while she desperately fights the urge to clear the dishes while the mother is out of the room just for the moment, having asked Lucy 'Can you hang out a bit or did you have to get going?' before having quick-quicked up the stairs, silence a moment, then some beeps of numbers on a fax-machine being pressed.

The mother is looking at the clock politely from time-to-time while they chat and Lucy knows full well this is the time the child usually is about to take his bath and what not, the final stretch of its night spent pajamaed and wet haired with comb teeth through it pristinely apparent. 'I wanted to let you know that you should feel free to use the shower in the master bedroom' the mother says, shake to her face, cartoon rabbit twitch of nose like she had whiskers to accent the expression of I-should-have-told-you-this-long-ago 'I know it can't be fun to share a bathroom with Flynn, exactly.' 'It's fine' Lucy says and says 'But maybe I will, thanks. I just wouldn't want to intrude with my showering all hours.' The mother shrugs like this renting a single room in the house, a room without its own shower, is just the most oh-so-absurd little world imaginable, seguing the resigned look of Ah-what-a-life into her saying 'Any time. It's a human right. Lord knows it must be awkward for you in the evening to always worry if you're bothering the kiddo. I don't think I thought this landlord thing through - and thank you for being so wonderful about it.'

A criss-cross of voice, water splash, room tile echo, overhead fan, the mother and child are singing a bath time song - more-or-less *Happy Birthday* but some gimmick of not saying *Birth* but instead inserting any other word in its place, funny scraggle of voice to whatever replacement. Happy *Blat* day. Happy *Comb* day. Happy *Zap* day. Happy - this done triple quick to approximately, though comically, keep the tune - *Caterpillar* day. Happy *Pillow* Day. Happy *I Need a Hamburger* Day. Lucy is at the piano bench, resisting the urge to start plinking the tune, the official tune, because oh God how psychopathic a thing would that be to do!? And after free cake? The mother with the kid in the tub, singing goes quiet, vulnerable feeling, exposed to anything, forced to realize the room is rented to a serial murderer? Don't do that to them, Lucy. Jesus. In the meantime - as though it's any better she'll realize in a pinch an hour later, panic-sick setting in - she has been absently playing the songs in the child's *First Funny Fingers* melody book, adding a few embellishments here and there in what limited way she can.

The matter at hand is as follows: so the mother is reading with the child, upstairs - not bed time yet, maybe homework, maybe just a thing mothers do with their children, who knows? - and Lucy is still in the living-room but unsure if it would be uncouth of her to head out without first saying 'Good-bye' to them both. Very tricky. Sure, Lucy would like to think she feels this sense of vagrant obligation just because they had all spent the last bit of time kind of together but she knows that isn't true at all. So is it this: Lucy rather wants an excuse to pop her head in, say 'Good-bye' to the mother? Why? She doesn't even want to think about this, obviously, because it doesn't matter, any reason doesn't make it less weird. So say she does leave - which statistically is how any other evening would go - would her not saying 'Good-bye' be particularly noted? If so, how? In what tenor? Damn it, Lucy. Would it be better just to say 'Good night' to the kid? No, Lucy. What's even the matter with you? But you better find something to do other than sitting at this table, that much is certain.

It's surprising that the child's homework still involves circling things since these vocabulary words are pretty tough. That's Lucy's assessment. If a kid knows what *Trepidations* are or what it means when someone says *Discombobulated* then they should be past the educational point where circling plays any role. The kid has circled the wrong thing here, though. Maybe as a protest, Lucy smiles, thinking, but of course it's not so. No, the kid did circle the right thing. Okay: idiot points to Lucy, read the instructions 'Jesus, someone ought to revoke my passport' she mutters. What terrific words. *Top Shelf Words* the paper proclaims. *Level Red. Nonchalant. Obliterated. Omnipresent. Sublimation. Cantankerous. Solicitous. Rankle.* 'These should be my vocabulary words' Lucy says, scratching lower back then, just a moment, left cheek of her ass. Upstairs can be heard 'Why do you think a lion would even want a typewriter?' 'It's just a story, mom!' 'You don't think a real lion would want one?' On the paper: *Cumulonimbus. Trenchant. Circumspect. Aplomb.* 'Aplomb' whispers Lucy and there are her teeth in her lower lip, again - what's that, five times tonight?

'Are you still here?' the mother asks, coming around the corner from just then descending the stairs, moving right to the cupboard for one of the plastic cups the child drinks from, the tone happy but genuinely surprised. For no reason at all other than, of course, feeling caught and ridiculous and shameful and scardy-cat Lucy answers that she was just about to leave, actually, a friend had sent her a message. That last part, the detail, was added to make things sound unassailably legit. Watch this quick pivot, though: Lucy asks about what had been so funny upstairs 'cause the mother and the child had been laughing like loons the past five minutes. And just like that, lickity-splitly, she has gotten out of a briar-patch. The mother explains, Lucy nodding and not listening, or listening but not getting the context. It was one of those odd things that happen which Lucy knows all about, having had some with other people now-and-then, that cannot be explained. 'I don't think I'll be out long and I'll try not to knock over garbage-cans and accidentally play the tuba when I come in, you know?' The mother smiles either because of or in spite of the preceding, possibly-most-idiotic sentence Lucy had in her life-to-date uttered, then tips the purple cup like a toast and tells her 'You have fun, I'll just hold down the fort.' The mother probably feels weird about saying that too, of course, but Lucy, when she tells herself so, argues that she doesn't see why she ought to.


TO UNDERSTAND WHAT HAS JUST happened just here - it really is extraordinary, Lucy isn't feigning that, anyone would agree, it has spooked her, moreover - we have to skip back just a few minutes. Here, Lucy is merely sitting in the front of her car, radio on - the song is irrelevant but happens to be *Come Right Back* by *The Honeycombs*, entirely by chance, random station set - and the thing has just happened. But just before: she had left the house a little while ago on the pretense given the mother, for no reason, that a friend had messaged her. Drove away, Lucy did, nowhere to go and certainly no friend had gotten in touch and she had no mind for much of anything, in general. She got out of the car to use the toilet inside a rather largeish gas station shop. Okay? There is Lucy, now. A minute ago now, after that set up. She looked at her phone and said 'Okay friend, now message me to meet you' and whap - bing whack, this is no gag - the moment she finished saying it, staring at her phone like a joke, the screen glowed that a message had come through from one of her few friends in the area, Katrin. And Katrin was asking to meet at a small restaurant, having some need to speak to someone. Lucy in particular. Yikes. This is Lucy's life. She sits here. Understandably terrified of Katrin and of everything.

But Lucy has decided that whole show of coincidence did not phase her. Aloof, she waited fifteen minutes then responded to Katrin how she would be there, straight away. This sort of thing is always going on, especially if one pays attention. In this case it would be a mistake to pay it too much mind because why wouldn't Katrin have sent her a message this evening, just then? That is about as ordinary a thing to do of an evening as Lucy can think. Coming down to it, in fact, it really ought to have been expected. It probably was. Lucy - she can't recall - had probably been wondering if Katrin was going get in touch all day, an undercurrent of thought set at simmer, and had likely checked and checked her phone, making the odds all but certain she would eventually be looking right when the message came through. 'And the fact that I'd lied to my landlord?' Lucy asks. 'I just answered that' she replied, turning left onto a road that will be more pleasant to drive along.

Finding herself subject to a delay based on a traffic accident or something, Lucy's fatigue catches up with her. 'I have been going all day' she thinks. Watches a policeman waving one car that way, one car this way, one car a third way - Jesus this will take forever. 'I have been going all day' she repeats, killing the radio, putting it back on. No. Killing it. It must be an accident, here. Construction on this sort of road is not likely and why would that take place at this time of the day? The evidence is bothersome because all Lucy has to go on at once suggests a minor accident and a major one, possibly with fatalities involved. Considering there are only two lanes, one in either direction, these with no shoulder, the one ending almost right on top of a treeline, the other square against the lip of a corn field, even just a slight bump and a car stalling could muck up this intersection where the jam is centralized. She wants to be angry, is the thing. Because the minor situation would be something to righteously be furious over - the whole thing a disappointment and stab of rage at this entire area. But if someone is dead she can't well be mad. That would just come off petty. Why isn't her radio on?

Katrin is tall, slender, and can most accurately be described in the following way: she looks awkward the way many women who later blossomed into exquisite beauties - actresses, models - looked in their adolescence but also clearly looks her thirty-nine years and so gives the impression just of being an odd-duck of a woman, not even of a close call, you-had-potential. Has Lucy said this to her? In fact Katrin said it, or something near it, and Lucy elaborated and this made Katrin feel just swell. Back when they first met. In fact, Katrin intimated at another time about how she has an exact photograph of a certain actress she admires - a photo of the actress at age fourteen - in mind when she thinks of herself, now. As Lucy arrives Katrin is loitering kind of in the condiment area but near enough the queue for the registers to make it seem she was holding a spot, another customer - a tad uncertain, but whatever - making room on the quivery assumption that maybe the two of them were there ahead of him.

Considering she was the one who sent the request for this meeting Katrin is coming off rather casual, an air to her of this is something she and Lucy do all the time. Katrin takes some of Lucy's fries. Katrin tells Lucy to take a sip of her drink and asks Lucy what Lucy is drinking. 'Iced Tea' Lucy says, not having enjoyed the taste of whatever fruit drink Katrin had passed across. And now the tang of this colors the delicate thin of the taste of her tea, enough to make her, hiding the edge of it, sigh and ask 'Is everything alright, Katrin?' 'I quit my job. And I don't know why. Except I felt like it was making me crippled emotionally. Spiritually. I just quit. I made a scene. I have no idea what comes next.' Lucy kind of thinks this sort of thing is cool despite she and Katrin both being full grown adults. But should she say 'Awesome'? Why not? 'Awesome.' Katrin laughs, beautiful, unrepentant, so fast it comes from her, the laugh, speed of the curve of a cat-food lid slicing through finger flesh.

Now smoking cigarettes and watching cars place orders at the drive-thru speaker - both complaining about the noise of it but not moving away - Katrin and Lucy come up with a handful of plans. The central tenet of all of them is that Katrin not get another job, no, not any time soon. 'You need to bamboozle some man, Katrin - don't look guilty! String some yutz along until that gets boring. Treat it like a vacation with the bonus that afterward you'll be able to ridicule the guy for letting it go on so long.' Katrin didn't look guilty, in fact, and the timbre of all the plans stay close to this, this is the kind of matrix for what Katrin wants her life to be the next two, three years. 'Or longer if I get used to it. But I'm not working. That is for suckers. I refuse to use this goddamned doctorate for anything else but a garnish to my honey-trap.' 'Hear hear' Lucy muffles, chaining a new cigarette from the stub of her old, continuing with 'I'd do it too, if I could, Rin-Tin, believe me.' 'Men still have your picture posted, is it?' 'Oh I've just got the scent on me. The price on my head doesn't even enter into it.'

'Do you want to come over and we can watch a movie?' Lucy was not expecting this question, certainly not the instant she exited the Ladies' Room at the grocery-store they'd wandered over to. 'It's cool if not' - Katrin is always so quick on the uptick of facial expression, booby-trapped the question like this on purpose - 'but this really has been a help and I'm a big brat.' 'I'll watch a movie, sure.' 'Yeah?' 'Let's do it!' Lucy, you have no intention of watching a movie with Katrin! How do you think this is going to play out? 'You're the best, Lucy-loo. Hey! You said *Yutz*, back there.' 'I did. But the trick is I say *yutz* all the time. It's just a ploy. I'm not very genuine, at all.' Katrin nudges Lucy's shoulder, again, again, then says 'I really should trap a yutz. I admit I've been loosely planning to nab some handsome, together person, but that would defeat the purpose.' 'Yes it would. You don't need to fall in love or be satisfied amorously - in fact, that's the worst thing you could do! You just quit your job, after all. Live a little!' Oh you vicious bitch, Lucy, you're a cat-scratch kept on ice - so that was your angle! And watch it work: Katrin laughing, one more nudge to you, but weaker, and her voice trails on the now repeated 'Yep, I just quit my job.' Deflation. You're a terrible terrible terrible woman, now arching one eye and asking 'Everything okay?'

Lucy promised to call. The illusion was all made complete with a few bolstering and a few concerned text-messages sent off while she just sat around in her car, still in the fast-food joint lot, both front windows rolled down, smoking though no longer remotely enjoying it. 'On paper I am an excellent person, magnanimous, giving, benevolent to a fault' Lucy alouds in the direction of the young guy taking haggard trash-bags to the dumpster. There should be something poetic about the sight of that young man, dumpster, all of it, but there just isn't. 'Hey!' The kid squints. 'Come here' Lucy encourages, padding softly at the air outside the car. 'Do you want a cigarette?' 'Uh ... yes. Can I have one, really?' Lucy hands over the pack. 'Are you sure?' goes the kid. 'Give me one more' she decides and the kid very dutifully, treating the whole action like turning in an essay he's worked hard on and he knows is already a day late with, gives her one. 'Do you want to smoke with me a minute?' 'I mean ... yeah, I really do' the kid says - lord knows where his mind is rat-in-a-mazing - 'but I have to get right back in.' 'Okay' Lucy says and tells him 'Thank you' just to watch him fluster one last time, tap dance 'You're welcome, uh, and thank you' and 'Uh, yeah ... uh ... yeah.'

Suddenly it seems as late as it ought to. It's one of those moments that come up. Lucy tries to take it in stride. Everything is dark, now. Civilized people are at least in bed if not already asleep. Her bones weigh their age. She sings along to the radio to bat away the questions that are starting to clamber inside the small tombs of her eyes. A dismal brew, questions. Louder goes the music, but it's too late. Lower goes her voice, acquiescing. This is the nighttime. Tower of Babble goes her identity, her sense, her surety, her joy, her understanding of being awake. There is nothing sublime about these awful questions. Questions are her night but they never are for anyone else. This is a fungus her mind grows on all corners, thickest right against the front bone of her forehead. This is the paper-tear of her insides, her being buried by everyone else evacuating. Yes.

'Fuck you all' she hisses, Paleolithic red clay of a hiss 'fuck you all.' That's just what is happening - a thought she has had before but indulges, liking the cleverness of this spite - everyone else is shruggingly dumping the burdens of their questions and they all are burying down Lucy, never even letting her have a last breath.

*Licentious.* She likes that word. She never learned what it means and now is terrified she's about to learn. Lucy is parked in her space outside of the house, again. Her room light is on and there is some indication of other light in the downstairs but also maybe not. *Licentious.* There will be no way of stopping the knowledge if it sneaks up on her. How could it sneak up? So many ways. Don't ask. Oh so many ways - all it takes is a moment, the definition lurking somewhere and her ignorance of this beautiful word is pickpocketed. Still in seatbelt she writhes against this unfairness and feels her nose welling with mucus for the crying she could, for all she knows, be just about to do. Why did she ever hear that word? Just for this misery? I'll bet, Lucy, I'll bet. It was a seed, it was a promise put in you long ago to grow, to be broken now. Why fight it? 'Licentious. Licentious. Licentious. Licentious.' Are you just gonna keep saying it? Licentious. Licentious. Licentious. Thinking it is the same as saying it. Pathetic. The knowledge is coming with the weight of a capsized boat, Lucy. Ready or not. Hell, you probably already know what it means if you think about it - and now you won't be able to help yourself thinking. The end of you's already in you, girl - and what good are your yesterdays when eventually you won't have any left?

THE MOTHER WAS SITTING ON the sofa, made a half-twisted corkscrew of herself to give Lucy a wave while Lucy was gingerly removing her shoes in the front hall. 'Can you not sleep?' Lucy asked, not speaking loudly but obviously not worried about being particularly quiet. The volume of the television was being tap tap tap lowered and lowered while the mother answered how she just needed to seep out slowly, things were 'not exactly going my way, across the board' and her brain would not shut up about it, her brain 'being quite the obstinate whiner.' 'I'm sorry. I hope you feel better.' 'Are you off to bed? You must be tired. Jesus. What time is it, even?' Lucy glanced at the commercial on the television screen but had her face done up like thinking of the time. 'Would you mind company?' Lucy asked 'I'm kind of restless, too. I can just hang out upstairs, though.' The mother straightened a bit, like bip-bopped where she sat one-two-three, and grinned that she'd be delighted if Lucy would hang out,

Lucy replying, an up-down on her toes motion 'Let me just get changed then, okay?'

Now this was a ridiculous situation. Lucy had not even considered this rascally dilemma. What was she supposed to wear? No pajamas to speak of, her habit to sleep nude, she couldn't seem to find anything but panties. Don't you have some sort of sweatpants? Lounge pants? Shorts? She has shorts but not lounging shorts. 'I don't own sleepwear' she whispers, loathe at herself for reaching this state of being, this fluxion of existence where such words were true with regard to her. All stop. You have no idea the hideous stop interior our Lucy. She stands topless, pant fronts undone, looking into the small drawer of the bureau that homes her socks and undies - there's a pair of suspenders too! 'Maybe I should just wear those' she tried out her voice, wanting to chuckle. 'Fuck fuck.' There is also the belt she thought she lost - why did she think she'd lost it? It's right there. Is that the belt? Focus, Lucy. Focus.

Lucy discovers the mother in the kitchen. 'I'm making hot chocolate because I'm at that point. Would you like some?' Lucy Yes-pleases and is relieved when she takes in what the mother is wearing: thin tanktop - semi-transparent, actually, semi-transparent green - shorts, yes, but such that they are no more concealing than the boyfriend-cut panties Lucy settled on and honestly if it came down to such things Lucy suspects that the material of her panties is thicker than that of the shorts. Both of them are wearing socks, Lucy's thicker, more meant-for-sleep looking, the mother's just the same athletic socks Lucy often sees her padding around in. Yep. You're right, Lucy. Letter-of-the-law, since you have the lumpy t-shirt going, you are more dressed than her. All above board. Yep - it's her house, you're right, she has every right to go around like that. Good on her - you endorse it, Lucy, let that be known. Even if the mother is in panties, too, since the shorts show no indication line of them it looks like your panties are still thicker than her both garments would be. But it is a good idea you're finding something else to look at.

The mother apologizes for just watching *Star Trek: The Next Generation*, mocks her bad habit and her nerdiness, which allows Lucy the perfect opportunity - still settling to the sofa - to lean over while she whispers 'I love *Next Gen*, are you kidding?' Lucy glances that it is an early episode, grins. 'Thank God' the mother says - touches Lucy, her upper arm, did you notice that Lucy? - while settling to place, herself 'I can stop thinking I have to hide it from you or you'll move out. You've no idea the stress. Honestly, it's why I couldn't sleep, tonight.' Lucy laughs - at this point the laugh is part earnest, part tarted up - and speaking into her mug as though doing so also helps cool the chocolate, there, says 'Tonight you just figured you'd put it to the test - chips fall where they will?' The mother laughs - genuine? seems it, though who cares? - and does a kind of impersonation of herself in an agitated mindset 'Not one more night, no! I must know! I can keep concealing this no longer, it must be tonight!' Lucy is sipping chocolate. She has to do something other than just sit there with her face.

Blonde hair, greying, brown hair, greying, they are colored bright flickers like an anxious hand sketching and resketching them while on the screen something is wrong with William Riker and Deana Troi looks stricken. It has been silent except for the program these serene passing ten minutes and now the mother goes 'We are both actually just sitting here watching the show.' The mother changes positions, moving her legs up and under her. Lucy makes a shushing sound and the mother - thank goodness she picked up the levity - goes all cowering and holds her mug up to her face with both hands, caricature of a chastised step-child. Lucy, for comedy's sake, lets the silence hold a moment then - yeah, why not? proud of herself, in fact - touches the mother's curled leg right on the thigh with her toes tap tap tap and says 'The pathetic thing is that this literally is the worst episode of this show ever' and her reward is the immediate - I mean instantaneous - leaned forward, gushingly smiley 'I know, I agree' and - that's exactly what that is, Lucy - hand gripped to Lucy's foot for an actual squeeze then an absent-minded finger flick.

Mid-breath, this being Lucy about to deliver another quip over closing credits - indications on the screen that another episode will be starting, the both of them already having hung heads shamefully, admitted they will be watching it even if it means dozing off where they sit - the mother holds up a finger, turns her head, keeps neck craned as though awaiting something, then says, softly, a balm 'Hey Flynnamon - everything alright, guy?' The child gives Lucy a three-quarters asleep wave as he rounds the sofa and lean-embraces the mother who has scooted a bit to allow the hug saying 'Miss Lucy and I are just watching our show - you have a buggy dream, bean?' 'Yeah' groggies the child, now looking at Lucy - she doubts he'd actually registered her when giving the moment-ago wave - and smiling, affect of about ready to pass right back out. Lucy mouthed 'Should I go?' but the mother did not seem to notice, caressing the child's face and touching him in feather light tickles over the ribs.

Lucy has an interval to compose herself. But does she need to? Not *compose herself* - that isn't what she means. She wants to have something appropriate to say when the mother returns. What is the thing to say here? She can't not acknowledge that the thing with the kid just happened but she doesn't want to seem more concerned than she is. What does that mean? Are you concerned, Lucy? 'He had a nightmare?' she whispers toward the commercial for denture glue. But why say that? 'Is he feeling alright?' No no - the mother said she was stressed. The mother just wants the child back in bed not to have his appearance color the night, give it its cues. Right? Say something funny about denture glue.

Except - Lucy glances toward the room ceiling - maybe kids coming down in the night isn't as annoying to a parent as it is to a Lucy sitting on a two-in-the-morning sofa with one. With this one. Anyway - obviously the mother will say something first. Just riff on that, let that be in the driving seat.

The mother is carrying a stuffed turtle and tosses it at Lucy as she comes back around the sofa. 'Turtle' she says. 'Yes' Lucy says. 'Apparently the turtle was looking at him. While he was asleep.' 'Jesus' Lucy holds the turtle to her face, giving it the hard glare. 'I've always hated that fucking turtle and now it's creeping on my kid, ruining our *Star Trek*.' 'Well' - oh go ahead, Lucy, push your luck, she can't just jump to hating you for it - 'I have to say I'm glad it was the turtle's fault. I was sitting here hating the kid for ruining our Riker date.' Slick - slick, Lucy, that last bit, you couldn't resist but used Riker as buffer, nice and innocuous, masterstroke that - but let's see how you fared: the mother is laughing and reiterating your statement with a furthering of her own. 'I'd have disowned him - he's hanging by a thread as is, Lucy, skin of his teeth. Barging in here in his underoos! He should be thanking the turtle, if anything, for giving him some excuse!' The mother then sighs and says she also wishes she could smoke inside, this in the same moment where Lucy kisses the soft fabric snout of the stuffed creature and coos 'Thanks, turtle.'

How tired are you, Lucy? Tired. Then why not drift off, too? You have every allowance to do so. Look at her, there asleep. Lucy knows she already is looking but tells herself 'Look at her' regardless. The mother has drifted off. She is laid is a semi-seated, semi-laying twist, head crooked to the edge of the sofa arm, knees bent and toes about a cat-hair away from Lucy's own. How long have you been looking at the tattoo on the mother's ankle? As long as you were at the mole on the side of her knee? Lucy touches all of the toes of one of her feet over all of the toes of one of the mother's feet, tip-tap-tip-taps them. 'I think you're asleep' she says but the first words don't even come out and the rest come out a gravelly gruff. Clears throat. Touches toes to the tattooed ankle and gives a nudge that doubles as the slightest caress 'I think you're asleep.' The mother stirs into a smile, eyes opening and lips rising all one and the same, doesn't even glance to the television or seem to need to get her bearings. 'I fell asleep. I'm sorry. What a terrible nerd I turned out to be.'

Lucy decidedly - pointedly, on-purposely as a thing can be on-purposed - did not watch the mother as she walked toward the stairs and made sure to return her eyes, hard locked, to Geordi LaForge explaining something urgent concerning the Warp Core - his concerned visage behind the vip vip vip of the Warp Core's blue lights reflected on windowglass - the split second she had said 'Get some sleep' in response to the mother pausing at the stair base to say 'I'm sorry, I had fun, I'm just zonked.' This all certainly, by the way, didn't just happen. 'No?' Think about it. 'You're right.' Yes I am. 'It didn't happen. Any of it.' Moreover: why would it? Moreover: why would you even think it possibly could have? When did you get in, Lucy? 'Dunno' a numb whisper, all of those questions, statements, answers. 'I don't know. Sometime.' She notices the odd evidence of two mugs on the carpet but deduces swiftly, with help of a simple algorithm of logic, that both of these are hers and she needs to stop being such a slob. 'I'm no way to be' Lucy says, knowing she'd meant to say something else while saying exactly what she meant.

*HER ROOM IS THE PLACE where a tooth used to be / but now where there's only / sometimes / a tongue pressing in, prowling around.* Lucy is hesitating about the word *Her*, there. It could be that she wants it to be *The*. Or even *My*. Or - no, she's dismissed the thought even as she thinks it - just *A*. For herself, she is in her room, lit only by computer glow. Years, decades ago she would have gnashingly bellowed or disciplinarian-trying-be-be-courteous intoned that a computer was no place to write poetry. She's writing this directly into the computer screen. She does that a lot. 'Piss off. I have plenty of notebooks and write by hand, all the time' she has defended herself, earnestly, often enough to not want to keep bothering herself about it. She daren't change out of the clothes she'd put on. *Daren't.* Good word. She also wants to say *a tongue is sometimes there prowling around* or *a tongue sometimes goes there just prowling around.* No: *Loiter.* She wants to say *Loiter.* That's what she wants. *Sometimes a tongue skulking in, loitering around. Loitering around* is nice. She could kiss herself though knows it was pure luck those words hitting.

She is self-conscious about the volume of her keystrokes. Diagnosis: she assumes the mother is awake and wants the mother to think she is asleep. Primal behavior, there since her own childhood. In this room she reverts oddly to daughterhood even more than tenanthood. Fatigue has thrown her blank, now, wrung her 'round into a coil she hopes will be used one-last-time as whipcrack before she's discarded outright. Something about how today - this day, this literal today, not some idiot general Today that is everyone's - had felt both like the first day and the very last ever. She doesn't want to just reword that she wants to say it. There has to be some trick of words that means that but her eyes sting in chalk spirals and her shoulders are growing broken fists like pimples. Why does she have to get tired? Now of all times!? *This is the worst time to get tired* she laments by typing it, erases it very very very quickly in horror that someone might have known she typed it and thought she'd meant it as part of a poem.

She takes far longer a pause than is necessary in the inside-out hallway, sounds of shifting in pipes, guttural whir of the vent fans though there seems to be no air-conditioning or heat happening, and her eyes hurt being open, trying to focus through the gloom at the mother's shut room door, stinging a bit more then the sting easing to comfort as she squints. To her immediate right is a poster for some violin concert once long ago in France - or maybe Spain, she just assumed France, now knows she really never verified - and to her left is a poster of frogs watching horses play hopscotch. This is just as it should be. On the floor is a washcloth from she and the child's shared bathroom, Lucy now bending to take it up, clammy and moist, deciding to leave it there, instead. Maybe if she breathes just a little louder. She does. And just a little louder. Does so. Why? She doesn't even understand this latest little sleepwalker game.

Lucy eats a slice of bread and when she opens the refrigerator the light is enough she can read one of the child's spelling tests that has been posted. Seven-out-of-ten. She's puzzled. Something in this strikes her funny, like the quirk that will make the dreamer realize the dream's about to be done. One-out-of-five of the Bonus Words is what lifted it to seven-out-of-ten, overall. Six-out-of-ten. She reads the words. The ones misspelled are *Tomorrow - tomoro - Lightbulb - lietbelbe - Shade - schad -* and *Toaster - toestare.* The Bonus Word the child had got correct was *Limpid.* So what? Something. She closes the refrigerator - verifies the blinds of the kitchen are drawn - then turns on the light, wishing it had a dimmer. One other spelling test on the fridge, more-or-less the same state-of-affairs. Math. Pictures. Blah blah blah. Why is this bothering her? Why are *tomoro lietfelb schad* and *toestare* anything to do with her? What are they drawing her to?

Automatic - or semi-automatic, she'd caught onto herself in process - Lucy finds the vocabulary list she had seen, earlier. The child gets the Advanced Word list but can't spell for shit? Okay. No. Those other tests are from long ago. Nothing so wild about that. Walk away. Because do you see the oozing disquiet coming over you like insects you never feel till they've bit you and bred in the puncture? Lucy. You know better than this. You're in the panties you picked earlier because they were your most modest, you're middle of the damn night in a kitchen reading misspelled words on a child's test and now you are looking at *Omnipresent Sublimation Cantankerous Solicitous Rankle* and you're continuing to glance down so - baby, baby - you brought it on yourself when now you see *Licentious.* Just like that. And it's already too late because you just read those words in less bolded print, defining it, after it after the dash mark. No scrubbing can do anything now, no fingers down throat, no amputation. Your world just did what your world always does, Lucy - and you've no one to blame but yourself.

It was the longest it has ever taken Lucy to walk up some stairs. Not remotely true. This doesn't even make the list of the longest-walks-up-short-flights-of-stairs. But it still takes a long time because she has to drag up each atom of her soul, one-at-a-time, and each one weighs as much as a potato. It's not even new that she stops and has to sit down though her mind is still alive with trepidation over being found that way - a light suddenly being turned up to reveal her there, a very soft, calmer-than-it-was-the-moment-before but still alarmed 'Is everything alright?' This is the worst sort of awake, where it is not even romantic to worry if you are, you just know, it isn't even romantic to know that you are, you just are. Lucy is a dreadful, absconded sack of plain reality - she feels little more than her bones, organs, the denseness of whatever she's eaten and is waiting to shit. Little more. And what that little more is she'd rather not name because the last thing she needs is to start crying on the rented stairs, too.

Naked to bed, the bed, and her face into mattress, and pillow pincered in the tense of her kneebend. If you sleep you'll wind up awake but it will be different. A disappointment that is even a day old is at least one that already happened and so the cinematic tightening of distilled image of it loses the always-been-now, forever-will-be-now bludgeon. Why in Hell does it mean anything? 'Be logical, Lucy' Lucy says - this very question thought-uttered not boding well for whatever syllogism might follow. You thought of a word, didn't know what it meant, knew you would find out soon, and then did. Is this the Horror of the Modern Age? Is this so sinister? What does it infect, exactly? Tell me what it infects! Tell you, Lucy? Go ahead and tell you. But you know you're all desperate questions because it means the same thing it always means and always has. From this moment onward all that was in today - try not to think about it but, yes, even that - is worm-ridden, rot-gutted, cankerous. Ask your questions, do what you will, but it was pure instinct the first thing you did when you came in this room just now was get out of those clothes and it was appropriate admission how they are already shoved, the lot, in that closet corner under the suitcase.

Lucy will not recall this but the dream she tried to coax herself into before she actually fell asleep ran along these lines. She wanted to dream about: her at a bus station, noticing a man who seemed to be pouring milk from a brochure but the milk vanished into thin air. And then someone pointed out how if one looked closer the milk wasn't pouring out from the brochure but was rising from the cavity of air into the brochure - either way, the milk had a Nowhere attached to it. Lucy ran her hands in the air over the brochure and under the milk, she ran her hands, motion like tracing an increasingly smaller ball or rubbing a shrinking pregnancy belly, in the space around the milk but refused to run her hands through it. 'What about your tongue?' she wanted a little girl to ask her so she could scowl at a little girl, only agreeing to lick the milk when the little girl's father had noticed her expression and looked disappointed she would behave that way when the suggestion had been so innocent. 'I know you were never intending to touch it' the man said, leaned in, face set apologetic for how he had a moment ago seemed so cross 'but she didn't know. Look at her. She's only that old. Can you guess how old that old is?'

Lucy will only for a few moments, and only in drunkard-legged snippets recall this, it being the dream that she actually had: ponderous building fronts in lemon yellow except for the windows which should be mint blue but are lime green are being dragged along as though they don't belong any place by an old woman in a cart pulled by five dogs and a half-dozen raccoons. Above board, this seems, and in fact the whole thing has a vaguely sexual demeanor, the way music does when it is a style one has never encountered and something has to be assumed of it: love, lust, something to draw flesh toward flesh. The ocean is only the size of a gallbladder and Lucy watches everyone in the township take turns seeing how far they can punt it. In the distance, each time the ocean is kicked, there are more and more birds choking on something and eventually it can be discerned that the choking is in individuated beats and each one sounds exactly like the elevator chime at a department store she's had other dreams about.

Lucy wakes in the irrevocable spread of the morning's light over her nudity. She feels as though she has recently orgasmed. Maybe she has. It's both early and late. She hears the shower running - this would be the mother - and though she doesn't hear cartoons downstairs she just goes ahead and acts as though she does. Lumps herself, laundry like, in the chair in front of her computer and blinks at the screen. *The day was the stone under the moss / not forgotten but not not forgotten.* She blinks. Noncommittal. But sees a variant, obviously built of the same thought. *Eventually we forget the graves / under the gravestones, and / anyway we are the / soil under those, never / thought about, once.* Meh. That is her assessment of the poetry she left for herself. As what? A clue? A prize. A consolation? 'Meh' she says again but is less convinced. Reads again both lines. Manipulates the things so they are now shaped into a verse containing them both, a few little alterations for visual aesthetic. Taps some keys to undo all of that, segregates the things. Since she is going to abandon them both she has no need to choose and no need to couple. Words are the same as anything: they wind up exactly the same as each other, in the end.

# .II.

THE MOON LIKE THE SONG *of a bloodied knuckle*. Hmn. *The moon is the bloodied knuckle of a song*. This is better - we're getting somewhere. Though after a moment looking away, watching someone return to their parked car from the eyeglass-store next to *The Postal Companion*, Lucy's destination, it is revealed to be all wrong. That's nothing to do with the moon. Either generally or the moon she is thinking of not exactly specifically but more exactly than this line is getting across. Don't cross it out though. No, she doesn't cross it out. Another tack altogether: *the moon hangs, an unwashed diner sign*. Meh. *Diner sign* is good. That's true about the moon. No one would go around denying it. They couldn't if they wanted to, it's there for anyone to see, every night. *The diner sign moon. The diner sign of the moon*. She tenses jaw, steels herself against this rotten disappointment. Why carry the notebook if this is all that happens? 'Anyway' she says 'it's obvious that the moon is menu print.' See? Just speak aloud. Lucky you did that. That's just what the moon is, exactly! It's more a fact than a poem and now it doesn't seem like she's just trying to say any old thing about the moon. *The moon is menu print, after my cigarette and thin in my hair*.

Never does this not happen. And by that we're not talking about just in this town. Not just since Lucy has been renting her room. Every time she has had occasion in her now several decades to come into a *Postal Companion* - whatever analog of the place - there is always someone like this bean-sack of a woman who gobbles the time and attention of the only employee with re-boxing something or ordering specific stamps or canceling a credit-card transacion due to some sudden muse grabbing her and she'll be back tomorrow. Anyway - off she goes, lawn-bag-full-of-wet-grass lady, finally off she twaddles, the day meeting her like a thing it has to struggle with again, resigned to her being something that's in it. Good jibe, Lucy, that'll teach her. 'You need your mailbox? Sorry. I didn't see it was you.' Well, thank you clerk, box two-two-nine-six. Does anyone buy these greeting cards? Does anyone ever want a greeting card? Lucy buys one but she wouldn't have if she didn't have three loose singles that having had been bugging her.

Cigarette lit, greeting card immediately slipped in the trash by the bench just outside of the sandwich-shop back in the direction of her car, Lucy sits and happily just looks at the envelope front addressed in the hand of Layla Nickle. Lucy still calls Layla *Layla Five Dollar Bill*, a nickname from - Jesus, was it grade-school? it was - grade-school when Layla had had a rough day of it and felt her surname made her puny. Lucy is honestly surprised that Layla didn't address the thing that way. She probably signed the actual letter that way though, right Lucy? 'Stop being a grump, you're just grumpy' she phahs with a breath out of ciggy smoke 'and you're a grump when you're grumpy.' Maybe Layla's finally forgotten about your stupid nickname, all the good it did. How long does she have to go by it just to make sure you never learn she never liked it to begin with? Be a grown-up about this. 'I will be' Lucy says, but nothing interior has changed. She eyes the trash-can, thinking of the sarcastic revenge simply sending that greeting card would afford her.

This is the way it goes. Firstly: Layla did sign the thing *Layla Five Dollar Bill*. Secondly: it's a nice fat long letter as it always is, Layla being a show off that way. Thirdly: because neither of these things give Lucy any grudge to begrudge she absolutely decides her entire reply to this thoughtful correspondence from Layla will be to send the damn greeting card with a succinct, preferably no more than five word - and generic - salutation. 'This is the cost of being my friend, friend' Lucy puts out to the no-one-around flatly. But fourth, most important, what is actually bothering her: this second letter - sealed and all - included with Layla's. From Gregory Chive. Her bowels almost start laughing from becoming so irritable at the sight of the name. The apologetic Post-it note from Layla whimpers in Layla's weakling voice 'Sorry - God sorry sorry - he sent this and left phone messages beside as he had no idea where you were, of course, me being the only connection to you he could recall and track down. I'm just sending it and will cut off my own head and send it in a separate box as penance for messengering. Read my letter, please. God I loviss you' - this signed with initials *LFDB*. Nice try, Layla. It will take more than sincerity and the use of our cute *Love Miss* combination and being generally wonderful to win me back. Bitch.

Maybe the moon is that diner sign she was thinking of. The day has turned doubtful with sour. That's a good line, see? Even that. But she doesn't trust it. So she won't write it down. Notebook goes in passenger seat, letter - letters - go in notebook in passenger seat, another cigarette - why not? - goes to Lucy's pristine puckered mouth while a humdrum of vague music goes from her radio at volume set not loud enough to hear. Further charge against Layla: this is the sort of thing she should have called about first, the trouble saved of this treacherous letter being sent. Defense: Layla has not been given Lucy's new number since Lucy lost that previous phone. Verdict: 'Fuck it, you're still guilty' Lucy jury-voices but leaves the identity of who she means by *you're* purposefully vague. Related charge against Layla: she knew right well Lucy wouldn't want any chickenpox letter. Write me to gain new phone number, call me to explain situation or put situation in letter! Yes. Further hardcore cross-examination to wring witness-box confession: 'Even if I did want the accursed missive it's not like I'd be chomping at the bit for it, eh!? Judge, please instruct the witness to answer.' Judge-voice: 'Please answer the question.' Bah. Fuck it. Guilty guilty. We're adjourned, pending sentencing.

What was this day supposed to go like? What was it supposed to be? Simple thing of going to work and all. That's even where Lucy was going and why she is in clothes and not in a bed. She pulls the car out onto the road but pulls in at the next lot, gets out, and walks into a secondhand bookstore to think. There is no getting past the fact that this all has not only affected her but afflicted her. A paperback novel will help but it won't be entirely curative. It'll be enough. Why would Gregory be writing her? And the envelope seemed as thick as Layla's letter and felt like it had photographs inside. Spatterings of what she imagines the photos could be - too many alternatives to bother explaining - long-train behind her eyes. He is aware that she hates him, certainly. He is not such a troglodyte as to have forgotten that. But perhaps mongrelesque enough to think 'Enough time has passed' or such dubious phrase that translates to 'He is permitted this venturing contact.' This effort. He's hunting her. That isn't even her being a sourpuss about it that is just, hey man, look at the facts.

The very fact that section with the tacked up sign indicating *Erotic Fiction* is not over some tucked away shelf - is right next to *European Theatre* and right next to *Early Philosophy* - but a regular and as visible-from-anywhere part of the shop wall as any other should be enough to make it no sweat for Lucy to go peruse. Should. Except: why doesn't the shop have blinds or windows tinted - why are there no posters on the glass or even displays in the window that could keep any passer-by from looking in? The very casual placement of the books among the other books, the non-judgementalness of the set-up is so normalizing as to make the trap obvious. This hickburg! This is awful. Lucy has no choice though, because she recognized some of the pale-pink-with-strange-brown-dots of some spines of a type of book she hasn't seen in forever. How long? Long enough, she smiles, giving interior her interview reply, that she never should have seen them in the first place, if you catch her lascivious, jail-baity drift.

The fact that they have the book called *Her New Sister's Best Friend* does not salvage the day but as she quickly reshelves it and catches her breath from not even believing such a thing possible she knows it is enough that the Gregory letter fiasco at least downgrades, the day set back to *Regular*. One last glance to the pink-brown-dotted spines, one last squinted reconnaissance of the whole shelf to make sure this is all of them - it is, or anyway she can't afford to dwell - and she snatches back up the illustrious paperback, palm contact with it jolting jazz right to her eye sockets, right to her now obscenely ticklish privates. She lingers in *Eastern Philosophy* until this seems stupid then goes to *Noir Fiction* and leafs through whatever. The book she holds concealed behind whatever she is pretending to read is an impossibility - why in the world would it be here and why now of all times? It is the one she did not read, back then, so this moment is not the same as if she'd found a copy of *The Artist's Retreat*, but anyway that one is surely the figment of a blistering fever dream. In honesty, though, even the closeness of her remembrance of that book, the one she did read, the tang of the thought of it so precise - really remembered, not offhand and vague - is nearly enough to transmute through alchemy this Gregory letter to heavenly father above me below.

It was a struggle, but her fear won out and she did the upright thing and bought the book. Don't worry Lucy, you didn't steal it. You should have! You're right! It belonged to you spiritually and in the properest sense of that word but it was best to pay the toll so causally and get out of there with your skin. She opens the book to any-old-where. No! Just the sight of the pulp, edge-blued pages, the thick of the print, the scent is too much - it's not even the same book, this is the other one, even, the one she didn't read! - and it goes to the glovebox and the glovebox closed with a genuine Whap. What're these other books she has? Well of course she didn't just buy goddamn *Her New Sister's Best Friend* and nothing else! Can you imagine!? No no, she also bought these two: *The Murder Clock* and *The Locked House*. Both by the same author. So there's that - she must have come across perfectly normal and her bit about the thin-little-naughty-book being a gift for a bachelorette party obviously had gone off without a second sniff given.

There is no way now to describe the air. Not in the car. Not in her lungs. The whole tint of each color needs to be reassessed and the world inventoried, all discrepancies finally reconciled. This day has turned into another day and then right into another day hard upon and Lucy is heading to work, still. That is, it could be said honestly, all that has happened, today. It is still happening. Lucy is going to work. Poetry about the moon might as well be on the moon. 'Har har' Lucy har-hars so disjointed and apart-rendered right now she isn't even sure if she likes the line or not. It's fine. Poetry about the moon should be on the moon. And the book in the glovebox jettisoned without another thought - to the moon or just to the moving road chucked. And the Gregory letter - why did she keep it? Well she decides for the time being that she did so because if she hadn't she wouldn't have needed to pull in at that lot, crossed threshold that secondhand bookstore. For the time being just say that, Lucy. Relax.

'LUCY JINX!' ARIEL LASER-BEAM fingered at Lucy the moment Lucy was through the door. 'Ariel Lentz' Lucy cautiously directed back with brow-raised meekness, producing from Ariel a theatrical 'Loooosssseeee Jiiinnnnxxxx!' and an embrace followed by a spring back to regard the startled mute Lucy. 'Have you committed an absurd murder with existential implications?' Lucy said, composedly moving to her desk where a coffee and a bag with some yummy or another was awaiting her. 'Why is that always what you think of me whenever I show the least moment's happiness, Lucy? Your cotton-picking mind leaps to murder!' Ariel came and sat to the side of Lucy's desk and Lucy - admittedly still recovering from the rush of scent she could taste in her skin from the physical contact so recently ended - did her best not to look up from blowing into her long cold coffee. Because there were some parts of an Ariel leg free from linen skirt, leg in stocking, plum and textured, and there the cut of an Ariel blouse. 'Maybe I'm not as much your friend as I thought' Ariel continued. Lucy, still not looking up, blushing and hoping her head tilted shadow and face over cup concealed it, saying evenly 'I just like to think that you'd kill someone, that's all.'

There was a scent to the trailer-office of having been recently spruced up and Lucy could not swear on a holy book that those two hanging plants had always been in that corner. Looking in that direction, though, an old obsession rekindled in her - namely: what in Hell is that folded quilt on that lower shelf? Who put it there? And would it be a punishable offense or even noticed if she put it out with the rubbish, one day? That quilt. It was something that gave an uneasy gurgle to the whole of the world. Any time she noticed it. It was the *K* after the name *Josef* as far as she was concerned, the bit that locked the whole thing to place. Ariel brisked back in from whatever her secret phone call out front had been and Lucy - good-girled about not even a causal 'Everything alright?' - opted for the non-sequitur approach, as thus: 'It's more unsettling to find an artificial leg on the side of the road than a bunch of baby photos in a lawn mower bag but both leave a bad taste in your mouth.' Ariel concurs. Says she'd always said so. Probably Lucy was copying all of her awesome thoughts and better knock it off.

'Have you ever had a craving for a particular food but you can't quite tell which food?' It seemed Ariel meant this as a complex question deserving of nuanced thought and incisive, skepticism riddled response but Lucy could not help but answer 'I think that's just being hungry.' 'What I mean is' Ariel went on, picture prim of unperturbed 'you can tell there is a specific craving you crave but the flowing saliva in your mouth, those pre-scents that rise, cannot quite get their finger on it. It feels like I-want-pizza but you know it isn't pizza but yet is something as-specific-as-pizza.' 'That was a long explanation - this question seems important to you.' Ariel gave a magnificent gesture of Go to Hell, swiveled a full rotation in her seat and then gave the entire explanation - it seemed truly verbatim - to Lucy, again. 'Yes' Lucy played back 'I have had a craving for a particular food but couldn't quite tell which food. On several occasions.' Ariel's volley: 'It sucks, right?' Lucy empathetic placation: 'It does. Yes, it does.'

In the scope of things this was the most meaningless of all the various types of days of work but the day they were both most required to be present. The latest edition of *Hernando's Highlights* had been sent to the local printer. The run would be printed and prepped for shipping some time by close of business but until they got the call that all was well and the printing had begun they needed to be on hand to answer any possible questions or respond to any issues the printer-staff might notice while prepping. Lucy had had to attend to such things exactly Zero times in her tenure. Ariel had had to deal with one minor typographical error that was not a typographical error but an example of that particular printing-staff person's ignorance of the English language and bullyish nature only once in her much longer time on the job. To Lucy it was like playing all day in a treehouse. She wished she had a bottle to spin and at least a tablespoon of guts in her.

Whither went Lucy's rotten mood? Lurking. She has no doubt. Distract yourself, Lucy. 'We could get a head start on the next issue' she says, knowing they couldn't. Ariel does not mock the suggestion, seems to think about something for real though there is nothing to think about. Lucy then says, with overacted demeanor of realizing her own silliness 'Or not. They haven't brought the box of the new issues of our Inspiration Material.' But Ariel still has a rather stern and reflective face to all this. 'I still don't understand' Ariel eventuallys, after smiling, after finally realizing Lucy had just been staring at her in the silence of the pause between end-of-Lucy's-statement and Ariel's *I still* 'why we can't pull from the same magazines, the same issues. It's not like we pick the bones clean. And by the time our thing goes to printer the mags we lift from are back issues, either way. It's an illusion that isn't illusory. What does that make it?' What is this tone to Ariel? No, that was words like she'd use but didn't sound like her. 'Hmn' Lucy goes, stranger currents in her mind now altogether. Ariel is staring like wanting a real response but a response, Lucy knows, from someone who has interpreted the tone Ariel doesn't consciously realize she'd had. 'We don't lift, Ariel' is all Lucy can manage and - that tone that tone - Ariel laughs and - in that tone, though, and turning to look at her phone on her desk - says 'Of course not, of course. I meant the mags from whence or inspirations come.'

There are things in the desk drawers which are not Lucy's. Whose, then? This was someone else's desk before yours, Lucy. But the thing is this: on what occasion has Lucy ever, in any capacity, used these drawers? She'd never taken anything out of any of them, never stored or filed or even put anything in. Your point? If Lucy has been here as long as she has and never used the drawers why would whoever worked here previously have used them - and certainly why so much? All excellent questions. Lucy wants to say aloud that she has excellent questions about desk drawers but doesn't quite feel confident enough in her ability to make it a charming thing to say out-of-the-blue. She has a vision of getting just a 'Mmn' from Ariel, not even Ariel turning in her chair. Or worse, a chuckle without a turn and some godawful, solicitous 'Oh yeah, right?' Are you glaring at Ariel, Lucy? Is Lucy glaring at the back of Ariel? She can see the clasp of Ariel's necklace right next to the thickest patch of freckles right there, anyway, shoulder base of neck. That skin in the smoothness of buttermilk. It must be the fragrance of oven kilned clay.

'Is *Slut* the word for a female horse that was not used for breeding but to allow the stallions to relieve themselves without siring?' That was the question. Look: Ariel is turned, she's on the floor, criss-cross applesauce. When did that happen? 'What?' Oh no no - Ariel is just swiveled around in her chair, has just tried to use a rubber-band to fling a paperclip at Lucy and failed, has head feeble drooped in admission of not being a suitable weaponry engineer. 'Originally' Ariel says, returning to normal posture. 'Originally?' Good work Lucy - when in doubt add question mark and repeat. 'Is that where we find the origin of the derogatory designation *Slut*? As it would be unkind to align a human female to such a horse.' Lucy thinks. 'It would be accurate' she shrugs, her thought containing more complex, elaborate reasoning she for whatever reason has left out. 'I figured you'd be the person to ask' Ariel nodded, then animatedly began work on what seemed to be her new idea for rubber-band and paperclip assault. 'I'm the one to ask. I feel gratified you were comfortable enough to come to me with your concerns.'

While they lit cigarettes Lucy tried to tell which way the garbage smell was coming from. It couldn't be those dumpsters clear across the road outside of the *Pal's Pizza and Pals* could it? 'Do you smell that?' Ariel sniffed, also locked in to where Lucy was squinting and squinted as well. 'That's ghastly. What do they have in there?' 'Do you think it's coming from there?' Ariel shrugged that if Lucy was trying to involve her in the start of a horror film then Lucy was barking up quite the wrong tree. 'Name me a day it doesn't smell like trash out here, Loose, and I'll win you a sweepstakes in gratitude.' What a wonderful thing to say! 'This is why you're my friend' Lucy says and Ariel smiles at her, blows out smoke in an appreciative extension of her genuine smile. Then of course the tilt to sarcasm Lucy was waiting for and is now kind of wishing had been left out, for once - but who cares, honestly? - Ariel taking another drag in and saying, voice odd from not exhaling through the sentence 'I do wish you didn't have to have a specific reason to be my friend, but I guess that is a good one.' Exhale. Lucy too exhales right then but just coincidentally. Just coincidentally.

And so Ariel will be stepping out to do something for lunch, if that is alright with Lucy - it was - but Lucy doesn't have to wait until she gets back to take her own lunch, though does have to wait until past the top of the hour, at least, Ariel having to go, now. 'Okay' Lucy had responded to all of this, watching Ariel stand - she'd smoothed her stockings, she'd leaned and adjusted at the buckle on those shoes - put things in her purse and look at other things, have eyes someplace else and move to the door. 'Am I allowed to torch the place while you're out since you'll have an alibi?' 'You can murder an Arab or you can shave your mustache, Loose Change, just be your absurd little self.' So that was okay, Ariel saying something like that on the way out. But if Lucy hadn't prompted it is clear Ariel would have just left. Still, it's okay because Ariel had said that, which was a really nice thing to say and indicated a lot. Still, it could have just been said to be weird or to seem nonchalant. But even still it was okay. Be her absurd little self. This trailer had never seemed more artificially lit or unvacuumed.

It's been ten minutes. Fifteen. All Lucy has to show for herself is this shameful bit of amateur verse: *Are you lonely like me? Are / you a tick or a flea? Will you / suck till you die or just bite / flit away?* 'You have to pronounce *Away* to rhyme with *Die*, obviously' Lucy explains to the person she imagines doesn't get that this is what makes the line motherfucking right on. 'Anyway, I did it in mimic of bad verse. It's going in next issue's *Poetry Corner* under the name of Suzette's little friend.'

Yes, Lucy will spread psychological mayhem. The best revenge is a dish served at the exact normal temperature but in a suspicious way and a little bit earlier than mealtime. Quote me. She sighs and would like a writer to write something really astoundingly human about her sigh but it's just a sigh, just human, and nothing about human sighing astounds nor is meant to. 'Why even bother to sigh, then?' Lucy says, fakes another sigh kind of to prove why not, mumbles something about real and counterfeit and thoroughly - so fucking thoroughly - scribbles out the measly lines she'd penned. And will tear the paper. And litter each piece into each a separate trashcan, besides.

UNDER MATTE FINISH OF SUNLIGHT speckled with odd staggered moisture, there is Ariel's car. So that is a curio. Lucy glances there and there - the funny thing is she is expecting to see Ariel's car in one of those places rather than Ariel proper, funny thing her jerry-rigged mind - then glances there there and there before shrugging and moving to the passenger window. Ariel's car, other than being Ariel's, is exceptionally uninteresting. It is obviously old but shows none of the dignified signs of it. It has not been recently cleaned - exterior or interior - so its state of emptiness, unlivedinness is off-putting. The car is like the sour in the gut from too much wine with a head cold. Try again: The car is like the sour in the gut from too much apple juice and cigarettes. Or: The car is like the sour in the gut from undercooked sandwich meat, stale bread, and a new brand of beer. Lucy dusts hands, shush shush shush of palms across palms, nodding at the short work she'd made of putting that vehicle in its place.

The performer at the eatery area of *Hernando's Grocery* is an overplump lady crooner, quite a set of pipes to her as the saying goes, at least enough to say she deserves better than a super-market. It's her looks holding her back. Hey, Lucy doesn't want that to be the truth but with other greater tragedies in the world we must be able to steel ourselves to these minor hard facts. Just today Lucy listened to a whole radio report about entire villages of children dying for lack of potable water, the men still insisting the women breed. That is the size of us all, in the end. We are no greater and no less than that. Lucy looks for a hat to give this plumper a few bucks, even a ten - Hell, blow her mind, make her think there is gold in her lead - but this seems to be a strictly-for-exposure gig. Lucy could glad-hand her when the song ends, slip the folded bill in wink-wink. Best to avoid the kind of insinuation that might make. Last thing Lucy needs is whispered rumors among the check-out staff of a fetish.

'What's the name of the woman singing?' Lucy asks this girl who is a pistol shot twenty-two-if-not-younger and who seems to have blinked into existence already wearing that barista apron with the strings tied in back, both bow-tie and kitten-tail. 'I don't know, sorry.' But you're arresting enough to dispense with the apologies - the shape of your phone in your back pocket can write you many an allowance, my girl. 'Are you new?' 'Yeah. This is my first time manning the fort alone.' 'I'll try to be gentle.' 'Oh no no, I have to get used to it, right? Have at.' My God. My goodness on high. 'In that case: you should already know my order, cunt, I work here, on the magazine - the fuck is your name?' And the girl just laughed! What sort of unholy prank is this? Nametag, sticker-style, hand pasted and caressed caressed to place exactly on left-side, hardly-there breast, decorative letters say *Charlotte*. 'Charlotte, do you know the origin of the word *Slut*?' Listen to that laugh! 'I don't! Please tell me - wait, what is your order? I feel bad even though I couldn't have known.' 'I take coffee black.' 'So do I' Charlotte says, like this is the only way - which it is. 'Now what were you saying about *Slut*?'

That took about all of Lucy's extant will to survive. It also didn't happen, obviously. There is nothing but nothing between the time of Lucy's curiosity over the balloon-shaped songstress and Lucy finding herself here holding a particular sort of frozen hamburger and trying to determine from the ingredients list if it is honestly just a plain burger, unadorned with some powdery false ketchup or onion glaze. Nothing happened. Lucy, you make things up and that is the short road to perdition. What about this hamburger? You going to eat these and burp afterward for imaginary Charlotte? What is the matter with you today, Lucy? 'Is something the matter with me?' For example: that was actually vocalized to a hamburger box Lucy is still holding. She physically answered her own question but has no idea of it never having wanted an answer to begin with. Drift through the cosmetics aisle. Drift through the shampoo. Drift past the men's razors. Drift past the glue. Smile that you just thought that last thing because you couldn't resist a rhyme to end the melody you'd got going.

This is a zone to which she never wanders. She is envious of people buying pet-food. They seem happier and more together than she feels herself. It's idiotic. She assumes this on the strength that they buy things called *Kibbles and Bits* and *Fancy Feast*. These are people who think that cats would be stupid enough to think *Fancy Feast* is fancy - they think this at the same time they insists cats are intelligent creatures. See that lonely man, there? He's buying pads to put on the floor to soak up dog urine. That is what is happening there, Lucy sees it with her own eyes. That is a regular part of his day. He's done that a lot. What have you done a lot, Lucy? 'No evasion or wit, give us an answer' Lucy thinks at herself, not without aggression. Shrugs. It all amounts to that. There are three full aisles of pet-goods and products in the flagship store of *Hernando's Grocery*.

This aisle has a refrigerator in it. Those are ice-cream sandwiches specially designed to help a canine's dental health. These are chew toys shaped like toilet bowls and these are shaped like pretzels and these are shaped like blueberry muffins.

Your excuse for walking back over there is that you had been assuming Ariel would be in the store? 'Maybe I missed her' Lucy whispers, nodding 'maybe she was in an odd seat of the café.' An odd seat of the café? This is the best you can do? Lucy has a flash of being able to, without a whiff of creeper to her, start right in with the foul language at innocent-pretending-to-not-be-innocent Charlotte. 'You forgot to remind me to get the muffin I like, you skank.' 'I thought I was the muffin you like - I'm just not off shift, yet.' No - you're doing both voices, Lucy? Sadly, Lucy knows she now officially ruined any chance - sure there was a chance, sure there was - that Charlotte will ever in reality say that now under any circumstances. Waste your chance on a fantasy. You're worse than a boy right now, Lucy. Stand and listen to the music, again? Charlotte might see you, have noticed you before, remember you had asked about the singer - is that the sort of association you want to encourage her to make about you? Take this opportunity of the Organic Food aisle approaching to end this tacky pursuit, this middle-aged stalk. There, turn into the aisle. Good work! You look sage. You look like you know what is best for yourself, ingredient-wise.

Since Suzette is working it is not a choice to not be rung out by Suzette. Alternately: Look how long Suzette's line is and it's not the Express Lane, today. Lucy watches the Express Lane fill three deep, empty, fill four deep, empty, fill one deep, empty. 'Hi Lucy, I haven't seen you around, lately.' 'I've been around. I was listening to the singing.' 'Oh it's beautiful, isn't it? So much better than the radio over the speakers - and they can't interrupt it with announcements and specials.' Such are the concerns and details of life considered by grocery clerks called Suzette. In fairness, that is kind of beautiful and sad - that thought superimposed on an image of past-her-prime Suzette. Suzette's complexion seems like it is a layer of powder make-up over a layer of beach sand. 'If my face looked that way, my arms' - but Lucy thinks no farther. 'New issue out tomorrow' Lucy says, giving this to Suzette without Suzette having to find a way to shoehorn it. 'I haven't told her yet' Suzette whispers in her famous whisper 'I want her to tell me like I don't know, already.'

There are times when bargains have to be made with Fate. Lucy's mind is not her fault today but the result of occurrences she has been subjected to. All philosophy starts somewhere and usually is the causal result of rash poppycock. Nothing that happened today is Lucy's fault - coincidence layered on bad luck on ill chance or happy happenstance - but despite that she has to negotiate it all, which is a form of making deals. She wants nothing to do with the events of earlier today but they are in her weed field to be gardened. Fine. So her deal is this: if she turns her head just now and Charlotte - who didn't exist before Lucy just on this lunch break concocted her - is there in plain sight and is faced either in profile or forward and not dealing with a customer then Lucy will consider it okay how imperative she feels the continuation of this vulgar flirtation to be. Further: she will continue it. With vigor. 'Okay Lucy, okay Lucy' Lucy prompts herself 'on the count of six, turn' and she counts six and 'Oh for fuck's sake' that settles that then.

The curling of cigarette smoke in her is something she rarely pictures. Same as anything in her. It happens, her mechanics are more her than basically all of her thoughts put together but her thoughts she understands visually, her innards as concept, ephemeral. Exhalation, she sees that Ariel's car is still parked there so figures Ariel is back from the café or wherever, they had probably missed each other, Ariel having been in the restroom or Lucy distracted. Or maybe Ariel is not back, is randomly roaming the store, making a phone call, the odds of them bumping into each other had been so astronomical as to be nil. 'Yeah' she cigarettes 'yeah. When I was a kid it took me forever to find my mom in a store - and that's even when I was actually looking.' Someone has left an entire sandwich on three napkins that had been arranged as a plate on that bench there. Not even a bite had been taken, Lucy wanders up to verify. 'Poof' she says and can picture the cartoon purple smoke that accompanied the poor fellow's prestidigitation. 'Poof.'

A breeze blew at her back that made her wish she was wearing a dress so she could feel fabric press to the skin of her leg backs, her thighs. 'Lousy trousers' she thinks and then repeats the think a good number of times just because it's jolly fun to think-say. Wait. Wait. Wait. There is Ariel, getting out of that car lulling in front of the trailer-office. Not Ariel's car. Wait. Okay - the image is clear as day and it's Ariel who has just closed the door of that lulling car. And it's Ariel - look for yourself, Lucy - moving around to say something in to whoever is in the driving seat. Meanwhile there is also Ariel's car - the one she drove to work in, the one she drives every day. These are images and impressions that clearly in tangible space-time have meanings and history coming before them and furtherences coming after. Having to do with Ariel and that car - sooty exhaust guffaw farting from it as it makes a wide awkward turn and heads that way, Ariel tip tip tip tip up the four steps to the door, dainty as the last crumb of pie. Ariel inside. Wait. Lucy. Lucy standing. A parking lot. Wait. Lucy waiting, but she didn't mean her.

**\*\*\*\*\*\*\*\*\***

ARIEL HAD BEEN PRETENDING TO play the piano on Lucy's desk for five minutes straight, Lucy, for the sake of seeing how it all would go, conscientiously pretending to be working on a little bit of writing, not looking up or indicating any betrayal of minding. Abruptly, now, Ariel ends with a few sloppish chord bangs and says 'I am having a hard time, can you pay me a compliment and I'll pay you back when my ship comes in?' This is a game they play: Ariel needing compliments which she cap-in-hands from debonair Mme. Jinx. 'My thoughts toward you are dirtier than the inside of a powdered wig' Lucy says and Ariel gushes a sigh as though scratched on just the right itch, relief beyond the erotic. 'You are a woman as well shaped as a Christmas carol' Lucy right-aways and Ariel says that that might be one of her favorite ones ever. That means you need to top it and double quick, Lucy. 'Not possessing you makes me feel flatter than a cartoon kiss.' Ariel's eyes actually betray emotion and she does not posture that she is awash in wanton indulgence. 'Okay. Two favorite-ones-ever in-a-row is too much. Now I actually feel bad.'

After an hour, Lucy is having a cigarette - Ariel to join her in a moment - idly thinking to rekindle her true life's passion of finding some way to make the word *Pubis* sound poetic. The same trouble as always is that someone, sometime, once told her that *Pubis* isn't an honest word and even now she has never looked anything up to verify the actual standing of things. Anything, anywhere, everywhere your mind goes when it's running interference, Lucy, you honestly must write it a Thank-you note! *Dear mind* you might begin. Ariel is out by now, three drags in and it seems the taste of her smoke is not up to snuff. The parking lot is littered with birds, right now. This happens. Common birds. Lucy and Ariel don't once get to stand smoking in the sort of place where grocery lots would be littered with pelicans or hummingbirds, no. 'Someone should warn those birds not to eat that plastic bag' Ariel says, poking Lucy right in the small of her back then polishes this moment off with 'I would, but then I wouldn't - because the fact is: I am a contradiction.'

Troublesome. Let's catch up. The thing is Ariel has now been speaking in a disgruntled way - not exactly disgruntled, that is what Lucy is trying to sort out - after the opening gambit of 'You do know that our livelihood is wholly dependent on the whims of a man named Hernando.' Not an unfamiliar thing coming from Ariel and something Lucy has assented to at least once a month. But - the rub, the rub - after twenty minutes a slurry of particular illustrations of Hernando's fickleness have been litanied and then a somewhat ramshackle list of various foibles Ariel feels the man has, little examples of her disagreement with his business acumen, on and on. 'Did I ever tell you about the woman who worked here before you?' Lucy nods. Ariel says 'Well, then about the man before that? The woman before that? And that? And the man before her?' It's crowded now, Lucy feels claustrophobic and to blame for something. No, no. You feel lumped-in-amongst-something and persecuted, Lucy - you need to start owning your feelings. 'You told me about the man who baked cupcakes every Saturday.' Ariel nods. Lucy nods.

'Did you really want to put in that awful *Cat Poem*?' Lucy blinks. Is this what is being talked about? Since when? 'The one the clerk wrote?' Ariel is eating a granola bar. There is another one still wrappered on Lucy's desk. 'The clerk's friend wrote it' Lucy corrects, looking up. 'Your behavior troubles me, Lucy. I guess that is what I am driving at.' Lucy can do nothing but start peeling the covering away from the granola bar - peanut-butter-chip in variety. 'My behavior?' 'You didn't actually want to print it - right? Did she threaten to raise a stink about things? Had she sleuthed you out?' Lucy shakes her head, drift caught, shakes faster then stops, abrupt. 'It was an anomaly. Perhaps subconsciously I felt caught. I was weak.' Ariel is so quick on this it is as though she said it five minutes prior 'Please don't leave, Lucy. But you're going to, aren't you?' Lucy eye wides, likely she is pale - is she? - and straightens, leans forward, forearms over desk front, raised from her chair. 'No.' Shakes head, shakes head. 'Wait - what do you even mean?' Ariel is chewing her tongue in her mouth. Lucy can tell. She knows just what the squish would feel like. What it would sound like from Ariel's ear's point-of-view.

It remains dubious to Lucy why she put in the *Cat Poem*. Yes. It does. Now she is so confronted with the fact that she shouldn't have her skin feels as though gauze over pickle juice. The situation with Ariel is diffused so she has a moment to think while Ariel is off to the toilet. Why did you do that? The purpose of the *Poetry Corner* was only ever to print Lucy's poems - every two weeks always under invented names. There is no one overseeing it. Lucy, herself, decided the format. The idea of making submissions open to customers was even her own, proffered to Hernando to make her seem a team player, the awful rot that shoppers submit just a laugh to line Lucy's cage with. The idea was spontaneous in conversation with Ariel when Ariel had first asked her 'The fuck are you always scribbling at over there?' Lucy feels she is sweating, as though her forehead is cheap restaurant garlic-bread. But Ariel knows she really submitted the poem, that it is even now going to print. They had obviously sat and put the proof together, days before. The toilet flush sounds like an airplane skirting in front of a bright autumn moon.

Unprecedented, there is a knock on the trailer-office door. Ariel looks petrified and coward motions Lucy to go attend to it. Lucy staunchly refuses by whispering 'You are the officer-of-rank.' 'Well, you are the sergeant-at-arms!' Ariel whisper-shout-hisses back and Lucy tells her 'You're whispering too loud!' 'So demote me - no one left to dock this vessel but you!' Lucy stands, moves toward the door, stops as the knock repeats, turns to tell Ariel 'I hope Klingon bastards kill your son' but Ariel knows she has won and so just shoo-shoos Lucy off, leans back as serene as a new roll of coins. 'Yes?' Lucy asks the extremely unofficial, no-business-being-there sort who is there. 'Is this the store office?' 'This is the *Publication Offices*' Lucy says, deciding she will confuse with a haughtiness and points to the plaque which is likely unreadable from the man's distance. 'I just wondered if the Deli was hiring.' Lucy hears Ariel laugh, not even bothering to be coy - why should she? 'Well, what are your qualifications?' 'I have worked at several Delis.' Lucy nods, finding this to be well articulated. 'I, for one, like the cut of your jib. Do you have a resume? Let me have my secretary here arrange the details with you.'

Lucy was delighted to learn of Ariel's work-flask, almost felt irresponsible for not having her own work-flask. 'Do you drink at work often?' Ariel was still amused by the man's resume, expansively criticizing his misspellings and slandering him repeatedly, certain the names set down as references were his pal's, the business names fake. 'Yes yes, not the man you want cutting meat, I concur. But how often to you drink at work?' 'It's for special occasions, only.' Lucy nods but Ariel breaks the put-on. 'It's not a work-flask. I just happen to be keeping a flask on me the past week or so.' 'Oh.' 'When did you get so establishmentarian?' Lucy watches Ariel swig a swig, watches the flask offered straight across in the same exact motion it had been removed from Ariel's mouth not even a half-second pause. The flask is in Lucy's hand. 'Establishmentarian?' 'You're such a scab. You're lucky I'm a scab, too, and that this ain't a coal town.' Lucy takes a drink. That might as well be the end of her. What does the world sound like when she takes her mouth away and watches Ariel take another mouthful? Who cares? All Lucy can do is wish her mouth hadn't gone so dry before her own swallow.

The call comes in that the magazine is being printed. Lucy says 'Thank you' a few other things, repeats the gist of it all to Ariel who gives her forehead a mime of Phew! 'It is true, though, that while Hernando has done this thing for almost ten years he could stop at any time. Or savagely reduce our wages. We are a bit elderly to work in a trailer in the parking lot. I sometimes forget the name of this town, even.' 'Yeah' Lucy says, numb-eyed and above-it-all. *There are songs to be heard / there are creeks to be the ones throwing stones and crabapples in.* Is that a poem, Lucy? 'There are songs to be heard, there are creeks to be the ones throwing stones and crabapples in' she says in her recital voice. Ariel says 'Exactly' having found this germane to her own point - Lucy can see that but worries it gives the impression of too much I'm-with-you, girl - and says 'It's part of a poem' and Ariel says 'Exactly' again, pointing this time. So that has made matters worse! What matters? What are you talking about, Lucy? Oh just the vein steady creep of impending horror I've been feeling awhile and ignoring so dutifully, that's all.

Dot-to-dot they go here-and-there and make little motions of ending the day. It's cute. It's like a valve of release: the issue completed, a thing neither one cares about worth a coffee-twitch yet nonetheless inspires them to seem business like, putting the room in a ship-shape of sorts, always what they do at this time. 'You never wear lipstick' Ariel says, Lucy darting her eyes up and making the sound 'Hunh?' with her curled lip and wrinkle-snout. 'Nothing. Nevermind. I guess I'm supposed to wear lipstick, you know?' Lucy contorts her face to resemble a good mix of 'Ugh' and 'Wha?' or maybe just 'Glegh' which covers all that territory, Ariel giving her a smile and another 'Nevermind. Fuck it' Ariel says 'there's nothing to retort to so Nietzschean a thing. Never mind.' Best move here, Lucy? A shrug! Good - as though you do not even see anything suspect in this at all and as though Ariel has pulled off her segue to casual putting on of cardigan as she seems to have wanted to. There is a coin on the floor. Lucy, a girl bred on fine old French novels, wonders a moment what it could mean.

'By the way, I didn't mean to be dramatic before' Ariel says as they exit. They stop. But neither move for cigarette and Ariel does have that stillness very indicative of continued motion, no eye flit toward her car but obviously picturing herself still walking that way. 'You weren't dramatic.' 'I was' Ariel says and breathes out her nose, gives Lucy's shoulder a playful jab, real stance like a boxer she immediately has to abandon to keep her purse sliding off her shoulder. 'It's just, you know? You're my squaw. I need you to getum firewood.' Some translators would agree that this is the most exact way to say the languageless thing Lucy imagines it to mean. 'Do you like Bob Dylan?' Lucy asks and would agree that this could seem an odd choice of words for the occasion but certainly she would agree that it could also not seem that way at all. 'I do like Bob Dylan, Lucy. Yes. And it's thoughtful indeed of you to inquire after that aspect of me, in particular.' They walk down the metal stairs together their combined weight keeping the usual ting of sound from joining each step. They touch the old asphalt of the gravel together. Lucy, soon at her car, is very careful not to look over, not to wave, self-conscious of her every bone.


MAYBE THERE IS NO TRUTH to saying it - really Lucy doesn't care - but the water in every shower feels distinctly different. No amount of science can change this. Water-pressure this, sort-of-showerhead that, it drivels to irrelevance when one is stood under the falling wet and heat - ah, it might be true that all cold showers, as showers, are the same but that is another matter, altogether - and can feel for themselves the fingerprint quality of the way the water new-contours each curve and divot of them. The shower in the bathroom she had shared with the child felt more powerful than this, more definitive, even more isolated - Oh much more isolated - while this shower, the mother's shower, feels curious, revelatory, but, above all, obedient. This is a poet's shower and in such it is the only thing for Lucy. And furthermore it is because of this that she turns the taps closed not even sure if she feels showered. The poem of an immediate shiver even before moving the curtain. A poem of 'Am I going to use that towel there or the towel I brought from my room? Am I going to use that towel or my own?' A poem of 'What if she notices?' A poem of 'What if she notices the next time, as well?'

'*The Gregory Letter*? That thing? I left it in the car' naked Lucy nakeds as she gets into her room and leaves defiant the door open. 'I have named it *The Gregory Letter* and it lives like a madwoman in the glovebox, unloved.' Lucy nods. 'Bwahaha' she says, broken into *Bwa* and *Ha* and *Ha* with a pause of a full second between each, and she then repeats 'Bwahaha' but with a diminuendo and a slow down like she has gotten bored with it as it is spoken. 'Liar' she then says, reeling around to point at the thing there on the desk, the air-conditioning from the floor grate hardening her nipples to raisins. 'So I'm a liar? And what of it? You are as much a liar and worse - a tattle-tale!' Lucy should be a playwright but whispers 'I refuse to be on the basis I would not be allowed to call myself a *Play Writer*. *Playwright* is one of the most obnoxious odors my mother-tongue ever issued, the bilge from its very worst crevice.' That she writes down, though - *the bilge from its very worst crevice* - while now the vent breathes the skin beneath her untrimmed pubic-hair to gooseflesh.

What is the content of the letter? Lucy is in her room. The door is closed. She is dressed because she will not read Gregory naked. She's even in shoes and under the covers because she won't make this the least bit dignified. If only she could be choking on a piece of angel-food cake or something too the whole time, scattering crumbs and spittle, wincing and in no real danger - but one has to draw the line somewhere. *You make me abandon accuracy* she suddenly has to sit up to scribble, vexation coursing all up her. She'll always know the line came from this. Anyway - looking at it now it's not so good. Still, she leaves it. What were we doing? Lucy is under the covers, shoes, yes yes. *The Gregory Letter*. What does it say? God Jesus she remembers it is long as she takes it out and the two photographs - three, four! - she does not yet at all focus her eyes toward slip out over her well protected belly. You don't have to read it, Lucy. But are you honestly curious? What would a friend say were they here to give counsel? I don't ask counsel from my friends - friends are there to deal with me after I take my own counsel, hence they are given that name.

The letter is an abandon ship, a later-but-not-now. Lucy is not for this, now.

Just his manure penmanship - he has not learned not to write in his own hand, has not recognized his handwriting looks like a kid trying to hide that it has wet its pants at the dinner table. These pictures? This one is obviously new - the color crisp, the image composed in all accordance to contemporary zeitgeist - and of what seems to be a five-year-old girl holding a frog and a grandmother of some kind holding what might be a jar of fruit flies and might not. Nothing on the back except a permanent marker jotted Roman numeral two. 'Is the letter going to be foot-noted!?' she can't help but blurt, almost wanting to look. She scoffs, can just picture the parenthetical *(see photograph II)*. This is one of her: Lucy in that dress she would always wear before it became a dress she would never wear. Lucy on a boardwalk. Roman numeral three. This one is just him. Gregory. As he looks now, she supposes. Like a step-dad who has raised a step-son who now is a step-dad, himself. What a grotesque thing to include. Are you rubbing you in my face? Are you showing me that if not for my well-honed paranoia I would have wound up entrenched and having-to-be-sometimes-touched by this you? Is this a threat, an admission, or an apology? 'Roman numeral one, at that!' She has to say this aloud and has to actually reach over to put it face down on the desk. One more. Wait: Lucy wants to guess first.

In an awful all-of-a-sudden it is on Lucy that she should not have let the unread letter, the envelope, or any of the photographs touch these clothes. No. These that she had worn after that shower and that towel, these were taking in a first time of a new scent rising from her and should have become her immediate favorites, worn and never washed past all reason except the kind had by the hero of a Russian epic. 'Shit' she shrieks and sits up. Well, Lucy does admit she had the sheet over her, nothing touched the clothes. But it's not the point. Her first sweat risen, pushing through the surface of her dried with the still damp of that towel, is sullied from being based on her disgust at these photographs, at this whole situation. This is Gregory's perspiration, usurping her, his way of touching some part of her she would never permit - his goblin way of reminding her of the virginity he owns because she gave it willingly like a subway token by a child, their first trip to the museum. 'I am being a bit theatrical' she says, mimic of the way she figures a therapist sounds, or would, barring that, instruct her to sound when she is alone and needs calming. 'I don't need calming!' she shouts. Stands. Door open. Hallway.

The whole thing can be quickly described. And it actually, symbolically, might even be better. But then Lucy has decided it is to be moved on from. She took another shower. She toweled dry again. She regarded herself in the mirror of the mother's bathroom and thought about trying on the necklace she saw, eventually did not, and returned to her room. All of this to her is self-explanatory. She is ahead another two hours, successfully not reflecting on it, so the matter is settled in a succinct way that time will continue to flush of any microscopic contaminant. A song, another, another on the piano. She keeps playing while the child comes through the door first, quirking its head in a smile while it kicks off its shoe and watches her, the mother entering at a hurry in the very next instant, touching the child, scooting it toward the kitchen and mouthing 'I'm sorry' to Lucy who smiles and continues to play mouthing 'It's okay' but wondering if it just looked like she was counting out her playing, trying not to lose concentration.

'Do they still teach cursive?' Lucy asks, having leaned over the child's shoulder - leaned way in, how intimate, Lucy - before moving to pour herself coffee, noticing the mother has just done the same. 'It is for extra-credit, eh Flynnagan?' pipes, amused, the mother. 'And what are you doing in math, kiddo?' 'What do you mean?' The child seems almost perturbed by the question. 'In math, you know?' 'For extra-credit, you mean?' What a snarl! Lucy wonders whether the bastard would be in trouble for that if she weren't in the room. Better not call him a bastard so casually, Lucy slaps her wrist in her mind - the mother might not dig that, having birthed him and all. Added to this: where's the father? Has the mother said? Now Lucy's entirely missed whatever was just said but laughs now because she sees the mother turning, rolling eyes and smiling at her as she moves to take a timid sip of the coffee. 'I hate math, Flynn' Lucy says, general voice, louder than needed but that to give it a pleasant, disarming tone. 'I gave up at long-division. Well, when we weren't allowed to use Remainders anymore, that is.' The mother is nodding and says 'I hate decimal-points, too. Are you doing division, Flynn-flam man?' The kid gives a long suffering 'I've done division since first grade mom, remember?'

Well, those two have to do something so Lucy heads up to her room. She looks at the open page of her notebook - *bilge from its very worst crevice* - and at the pages and photographs on the ground, some still on the bed. What else? 'I need to call Layla' she says, finger-snapping like a plucky kid-detective from a movie thirty years before her time. A new message on the phone. But from hours ago. Does Lucy not look at her phone? This would have come in while she was at work! Not a number she recognizes, but local. Good. Yes - good analysis, Lucy. Are you going to listen to the message? She gives herself the finger but in the direction of the bed, like she is lazing about there, tossing off snide commentary to earn the vulgarity. Katrin wondering if Lucy is free. Katrin saying *Or anyway, do you think you could give me a call?* Katrin saying what a wonderful time she had and hopes she wasn't a real bummer cause Lucy is *a solid gold star on top of an A plus plus plus*. Katrin repeating *Call me back*. 'Gosh, get a room' she pretends to say to Katrin but as though she is someone else, someone who was present when Katrin was leaving the message.

*You make me abandon accuracy.* It is a good line. Irresistibly, she adds under it *cursory glances become the whole storefronts* and also she writes *paragraphs shake their commas off and stare out of themselves far less perplexed.* She might be writing a bad poem just to avoid phoning Katrin. She might be. Might. She also writes *hands to mittens and roses to deaf mutes oh aren't you good at all sorts of things?* 'None of these lines are necessarily sequential here' she says under her breath, unable to leave the room with the impression that the opposite of this is the case, and she closes the notebook and puts two paperbacks on top of it to further be assured no wrong impression can be got in her absence. By the only step it takes to reach the bed she has already whirled around, tore open the notebook to random page, then decided - no no - to flip to the same page she'd just been on and furiouses down *the best trait I have is that I can in honesty say I never let you leave yourself on my face.* She is breathing hard because she doesn't want how she could bellow to interrupt the piano practicing downstairs that has just started.

Lucy saw the mother's eyes go soft with a question and unhidden, but not-on-purpose unhidden, disappointment at the sight of her moving toward the door - the mother counting aloud as the child hit notes - but gave a gesture meant to somehow indicate 'I won't be long blah blah blah just something blah blah.' This exchange ended with a wide smile from the mother who was repeating 'Three three three three three' waiting for the child to find the correct note. Why had Lucy said she'd left the letter in the glovebox? The letter had never been in the glovebox. She is sitting in her car, full well knowing what is in the glovebox - and using the word *Who* in the place of the word *What.* Yep: that's the madwoman in the attic darling, oh don't you know it! She gives it a tsk tsk of index-finger brushed over other index-finger two times but she also does open the glovebox just enough to verify the book is there and to in a hybrid, meaningless slang accented voice say 'You think I forgot you? You know I'd never do that.' Rolls her eyes at herself in the rearview. Starts the car and dials Katrin who positively and already tipsy Thank Christs! out of the speaker so that Lucy has to wince it away from her ear.


KATRIN WAS WEARING, OTHER THAN her clothes which do not warrant so much description - they are innocuous, to be noted only as Katrin-is-standing-there-I-assume-wearing-things-in-particular by Lucy - a phosphorescent pink headband. The quickest way to diffuse the monstrosity of this fact was for Lucy to blurt 'You are wearing a phosphorescent pink headband, Katrin - explain yourself, please.' Katrin alleged that she had found it amongst a box of remembrances from her University days. 'I wore this in University' she said, a can-you-beat-that? look of bloated-man-belly-in-barroom to her. 'If this is a situation where I'll need to prevent your suicide Katrin, I may not be up for it - I want that on top of the table from the outset, okay?' Katrin said she wouldn't mention what else she had found in that box and was wearing and Lucy gave an obligatory eye-roll - honestly not even picturing anything alarming. 'Wait - why wouldn't you be up for it?' Katrin stops her little dance to imaginary be-bop music. 'Is everything okay, Lucy?' 'It was until I realized that someone in your state would offer empathy and compassion to me. Do I look far gone?' Katrin gave an assessment, shrugged, said even if Lucy looked about to go overboard Katrin only had the one headband and she, herself, was the one who needed it more.

Katrin's apartment, now that Lucy was in it for the third time, had a distinct, perfectly named feeling to it. It felt to Lucy like this: what the apartment of someone who'd hosted a successful gameshow fifty years ago, endured a series of reversals and public scandals, attempted to co-host a morning show for awhile on a basic-cable station that no longer existed, and now worked as a hotel assistant-manager's apartment would feel like. Exactly like that. It's funny how particulars, when explained, seem insanely exact. Is a particular feeling supposed to be described generally? Lucy, you know what you mean. Should you tell Katrin? Why not. Lucy tells Katrin. 'This is why I summoned you! I needed to know just how my apartment felt. To me it felt haunted in the way a large house in a mediocre horror film from nineteen eighty-two would feel. That made me really uneasy. But you have put things in the proper relief.' How drunk was Katrin? Not so drunk, actually. Lucy wondered if she was drunk at all, in fact - maybe some residual from a drink or two some hours previous, the rest of this might just be sleeplessness, hunger, stir-craziness. Proceed with caution but not so much that you don't have fun with it. Katrin had called Lucy, after all.

Lucy's first suggestion, that they get Katrin laid, was peshawed outright as Katrin had tended to that 'thrice before the cock crowed' the day after she had last seen Lucy - also referred to as 'When this whole mess got juicy.' Lucy didn't puzzle at the math, briefly twinged a jealous knot, sobriety kicked in that that actually sounded miserable and ill-advised, got briefly jealous for one more twist, then asked if Katrin had been looking through old boxes or had she been packing. 'Please just assure me I should not be begging for my job back' was Katrin's reply. 'You absolutely should not be begging for your job back.' Oh shouldn't she, Lucy? 'What was your job, Katrin?' Lucy gestured that this was rhetorically posed then proceeded to 'Exactly. You are above such belows, my Katrin. Firing you is the thing that will squeak them into the pile of straight-down-to-Hell.' 'But I quit. Without ceremony. Like in a song by *The Kinks* without the excuse of a British mother-in-law silently breaking my psyche down.' Lucy had overlooked this. Solution? She deflected by flattery: something something something Katrin, who could make such obscure references off-the-cuff something something was too good for it something.

Out on the balcony - a very tight fit, they and the small chair-table set-up were like two shoes and one sandal trying to fit in the same shoebox - Lucy smoked and drank some very thinned-with-sports-drink vodka, listening to Katrin clumsily relate some things. The main thing was how when Katrin had worked in a booth, some vague job just out of college, she had looked through both the booth glass and the window glass of the wall just a length from the booth front, both things reflecting her oddly in the same size, and because when she sipped coffee she could always see the white circle of the cup lift right at her eyes, all day she had the impression she could see three of herself. 'Really, I only saw two.' Lucy probably was supposed to decipher this. She can picture it all well. Phenomenally. No third-prize ribbon for Lucy when it comes to picturing even the most oddly described thing. Lucy offers as response 'When I was seven or eight I am told I transposed the X from my last name to the place of the C in my first. I can kind of remember it. Even now when I think of my name that way there is a tingle of recognizing Luxy' - she pronounces it Lux Ee - 'as Lucy' - she pronounces it normal. 'However, I have never written it down as Luxy' - gives it that pronunciation, again - 'not since childhood, because I also kind of feel it would, in the physical world, look strange.' Katrin is nodding but admits she does not see how this relates to her own observation. 'Other than to say we're two different people, I suppose' Katrin adds. 'Maybe that is your point - who has anything in common?'

What about the fact that, Lucy, you cannot stay on all night? Well. Lucy knows she can stay on all night. If she wanted to. There is no work tomorrow. What does Lucy do when she doesn't work? Wake up at Katrin's house? Does that seem right? 'Maybe I should quit my job' Katrin sighs, seems confused by Lucy's confusion, catches the typo, quickly re-states 'Maybe I should try to wrest my job back.' So Lucy lays a rap on her about - using big-girl voice, using perch-of-experience and some jive about what she wishes she had done with her own life - the fact that liberation will always feel uncomfortable - resists saying 'Until a new cage can be found' - and that the Heraclitus-ian flux is something that needs to be used, regardless how rough-hewn and distempered it may make things. 'You want your life to be different? You are not of wealth or high standing? That means the change has to contain some likely later-regretted misadventures.' 'Like I fucked three people of an evening?' 'If you really did that, then yes - exactly like that.' 'At least I don't remember their names, right?' 'That would be rather pathetic of you, yes. Forgetfulness shows you have some sense of your God-granted pride.' Katrin frowns. Lucy sighs and flicks Katrin's knee, saying to her, eyes direct 'They were pads to test the pen-sharp with, scribble on baby, okay?'

By this point: the apartment seems like a cave that now has a gift-shop near it. By this point: Lucy briefly regrets having met Katrin - feels guilty, honestly recognizes she is glad to have met Katrin. By this point: that sorted, Lucy needs to find or manufacture a curtain-line. Lucy, you can't say this isn't what you had in mind when you drove over here, because it is what you knew would go down. Pound-for-pound, the course of the conversational night has been plotted by you as much as your on-the-fritz pal, here. What if you thought Katrin was more beautiful? Try that as an exercise. What if you were trying to weasel money from her or something? Wait - why did you change it to a question of weaseling money? Too late: Katrin is about to say something that will require the face of full reflection and some well digested response. Ready set Katrin goes: 'I'm not even upset about the job. Do you know why I really quit?' 'Was it for a different reason?' 'Well, yes and no. My sister died. And my mother didn't tell me. And so I quit my job and think I don't know why.' Lucy, this actually is the only important moment to happen so far tonight. Yes, you're doing good handling the appropriate Oh Jesuses to the sister situation, that is rotten beyond carcass, but you need to think about how that alters the main question you were brought in for. 'Katrin' Lucy put her hand on Katrin's hand, says 'Katrin - you really did the right thing leaving the job.'

Some weeping. Lucy prides herself on being good with friend's when friends're weeping. Private pride. She actually likes it when friends weep around or even on her. Katrin wept on her. Talked for five minutes when a tissue was obviously needed before the eventual 'Sorry, excuse me' then Katrin returning with toilet-paper, no tissues in the house. 'It's bad luck for single women to buy tissues' Katrin says, squashes and distorts and wipes at her nose, apologizes and says 'That is something I read out of a fucking paperback a co-worker once left laying around. Real trite. One of the only lines on the only page I read. I have never been able to forget it.' Lucy wants to say: The horrible truth is that might mean that you honestly liked that line. But Lucy doesn't say that. Lucy just lets Katrin mock the co-worker and a genre of literature in general before letting what she hopes is a natural, appropriate-seeming silence hang for five minutes. If Lucy had a sister she'd probably have reason to hate her by this point in life, would probably not be upset at a secreted death. Maybe. Really? 'Well, that's why I said *Maybe*' Lucy almost whispers.

But now Lucy finds herself outside of the apartment complex, walking to her car. It was unexpected, Katrin actually saying she needed to do something and had not meant to have Lucy over so long, but it did happen. And there had even been actual levity in Katrin's final re-tapping what had been the leitmotif of the night when, as Lucy stepped out the apartment door, Katrin said 'It might only have been two guys. I think I walked up to the third under the impression I recognized him from earlier.' Does this departure-prompt and good attitude mean Lucy's sagacity had been taken to heart? Or did it mean Lucy had been humored, found out for the fraud she is, ditched when it got to the hour a call to a more appropriate confidante could be made? The radio in the car comes on louder than Lucy remembers having set it to. She mumbles something about 'Goddamn it'. Then chuckles, thinking there must be someone in the world who uses the expression 'God, you need to damn it.' Well, if there isn't Lucy promises herself she will take on that role without qualm or hesitation. 'Just don't want to infringe on anyone's scene' she says, moving the car in reverse.

In a miraculously unlucky turn of events, Lucy has only now realized she has driven almost the entire way to work! In fact, unless she does something risky, the nearest place to turn around will be the intersection one intersection before the one that turns into the lot of *Hernando's Grocery*. She stops the car. How long will it take to make this maneuver? How far can she see in any given direction? Her telephone rings - by now she recognizes the number as Katrin. Still stationary she answers 'Did you forget I was just over there and how awesomely I already solved your life?' 'I figured I should tell you I totally love you.' Sleepwalker voice - maybe a bit more alcohol, maybe just end-of-tether, last dial before fast asleep. 'The word *Totally* makes that acceptable as a Platonic statement so I will not let my heart go aflutter. Is everything actually all right?' 'I have known you only as long as a hen knows an unhatched egg but I totally totally love you, you get it?' Headlights ahead - check to rearview: no headlights behind - Lucy nods while saying 'Get that you dig me above all other images Graven? Yes. Get the thing about the hen? Not as much. Do you need me to come back over?'

*Hernando's Grocery* exists and bustles in the unused look of the nighttime in a place like this. What to make of the place. What to make of Lucy parked, eating some fast-food from the restaurant that shares lot space? She normally shuns this place. All of the *Hernando's* folks do - on principle. We are a tribe. These are bad Europeans who think the best warmth comes with pox. But tonight Lucy should not be here to begin with so it's best to act like a savage, an unwelcomed. 'I am a disguise' she mangles her voice up to say. 'I am a villain the way only a xenophobic screenwriter can truly write one' she furthers and pretends to be gnashing her teeth and pretends to look like a Viking who also looks like a barbarian who also looks like a bounty-hunter from the dismal future but one sent to the past. Yawn. Oh God, two yawns. Lucy, in this moment, is in most precisely the last place she wants to be, thinking things she has no idea why, knowing so specifically where she'd rather be more than anything ever instead. Another yawn. Fake. 'But don't tell anyone' she growls as the last of her game.

INSIDE THE HOUSE. IT SMELLS like something had recently spent too long in the toaster. Smelt of things left standing in the sink. A trifle of bubble-bath mingled. The warmth of the heat having maybe five minutes previous been shut off - not likely, considering surrounding temperature conditions, but the world oft is odd. Lucy is still just inside the door, can hear the tin-can far-away of the television just around the corner - phaser fire 'Inertial dampeners are offline!' 'Mister Data, get us out of here!' - and recognizes the changes to the wall from the camera shots flittering, television spittle, even though the living-room light is still on. 'Hi Lucy' comes the mother's voice - Lucy still just inside the door, taking off her shoes. Enough of that, though. Why is she doing all that right there, like worried of tracking snow over carpet? 'Hello, hello' Lucy over-dramtics, sticking her tongue out, the mother already turned to comfortably regard her over the sofa back. 'What's up?' The mother is dressed for nighttime. Good. Obviously the mother is dressed for nighttime, Lucy. It's still good, though. 'I'll tell you in a sec. I just want to get changed.' The mother is a simple illustration of awaiting sympathy and solicitousness - she could be a drawing in a French textbook she is so representative of whatever that expression would be called in French. Lucy - admittedly without conscious thought, not even looking at the mother, just in front of herself at nothing - says 'Do you remember that world famous hot chocolate of yours?' And she needs not go on, hears the mother already standing and, for herself, first step up the stairs.

Lucy wants to make it clear: Lucy is not distraught over Katrin. Furthermore: Lucy is not distraught over herself. Moreover: she does not assume she is in for 'the same fate as Katrin'. Is this an admission she thinks Katrin is done for? 'Katrin is done for, yes' she snaps at herself, getting her pants off 'what are we? In kindergarten? Do we think there are enough pages left in that book to reverse things?' She means none of this. Let that be known. And she knows now that she is only mildly actually considering what she could wear that would seem alluring. Yes, you are. Come off it, how old are you? Lucy. Rented room. Classic casual: white panties, grey tank top. Nope. Green panties, slightly patterned, grey tank top. Nope. Well, yes. But only because this has gone on long enough not because the outfit is what you actually want to be wearing, Lucy. And all of the pundits here gathered get that. She wants to snap out of it because she knows she is about to go downstairs and be a bummer. 'Nobody will like my style' she says to the doorknob and it looks back at her like it's only thumbing a ride in order to serial murder her, obviously, why is she even stopping for it?

There are rice-krispy treats. The best kind: not made immaculately. Lucy wants to gush how there is nothing worse than homemade rice-krispy treats cut so perfectly into squares and nothing better than homemade rice-krispy treats that don't bother fronting off or keeping up appearances. But does she say any of that? Naw. Why? Two reasons. The first, and lesser: that the mother may be self-conscious and take it the wrong way. This is phantasmal, though, a feather-filled sack of boogey-man - I mean look at the mother standing there barefoot using the toenails of that foot to so exactly scratch a spot on the top of that other, she wouldn't care. The second, far more petty - but honestly, on reflection, the only reason, really: that the child might have been the one who made them, his inexperience and a series of moments doubly nothing-to-do-with-Lucy being what led to them being here, now, like this, in her mouth. 'Do you think we'd go to jail if we went outside like this to smoke?' the mother asks. She's making you look at her now? Mouth full of teeth-mashed sugar, no less! The mother just actually did a little look-at-me, really-look, turned around in place with her arms up like surrendering to the authorities and everything. 'Probably. I call dibs on being the cell bitch.' No no no, of course you never said that, Lucy.

Apparently Flynn had lost two teeth at school that day which had made him something of a minor celebrity to his classmates. The storytelling method employed by the mother to get this across was round about so that now both the mother and Lucy are starting second cigarettes, Lucy not as cold as she'd figured she'd be, the mother huddled tight to herself and tip-tapping tip-tapping on the balls of her feet while they move on with their conversation. Still about Flynn. Flynn had asked if the Tooth-Fairy bit - 'his words' the mother smiles, fake sarcasm - could be dispensed with - 'his words' - this time and straight up handed the mother the teeth and asked for cash money. 'I dig his style' Lucy says, venturing to rub rub rub at the mother's left shoulder and upper arm to generate some heat. 'Should we go in?' 'I am determined not to! Will you weather it with me, Lucy?' 'I shall.' Lucy clamps ciggy to lips, does the rub thing with both hands to both mother-shoulders simultaneous until this actually makes her feel winded then coughs on a bad drag and flounders about like this is the end of her, inelegant as a set of old shoelaces found in the corner of a motel room. But it makes the mother laugh, makes the mother say 'Well shit, you're just pure not good at anything!' and makes the mother give Lucy, doubled over with her own laughing now, a stab with her cold toes on the hip.

More hot chocolate. Where does the time go? Lucy lets the mother catch her up on the episode before it dawns on them that the hour has passed and this is a different episode. 'I hope they got out of that last debacle, alright' the mother says, nose sighing. Lucy nods, squinting at the screen, wanting to show off that she knows exactly which episode this is when she has no idea. 'I like it best when Piccard is in the blue shirt' Lucy says, the mother scoffing the self-evident nature of this observation, a face of recoil and an 'I thought you said you were smart?' 'I said I was smart but that doesn't mean I am smart. I thought you said you were smart, get me?' 'Hmn' goes the mother, giving Lucy the hairy eyeball up then down then up then down. 'Hmn. Touché, I guess.' The mother's favorite part of the Enterprise is Cargo Bay Four because she likes that they have so many big buckets in there, all the time. Lucy's favorite futuristic gadget is the thing they sometimes have to use to open the dividers when they are crawling in the Jeffries Tubes and for whatever reason the ship has lost power. This night could be long. Lucy looks at the carpet and sees an action figure, a rubber-band, and the wrapper from something inside-outed.

Before long they are ignoring the show without having turned down the volume. Lucy is all done explaining a version of what went on with Katrin. Some very high-handed elaborations. Some careful treading to get a feel for the mother's position on how the mother would have advised about the 'getting job back thing' before saying how she had insisted it was the right move until the bitter end. That story the mother just told in response was meaningless and off-topic - both the mother and Lucy know it, neither make mention. To be a proper person Lucy snapped fingers, right here, and says she forgot to ask 'Which two teeth?' the mother bored, shrugging 'Who the fuck knows? If he'd lost two fingers I'd have made note, right? Why do we ever tell kids that their teeth are important? What fools we are!' 'Ah Bartleby, ah humanity' follows up Lucy, the mother smiling but only in recognition that a quote has been quoted, no spark of knowing where from. It all is pile of stuff like this. The main room light is even still on. Everything incorrect, inconsistent, and not.

Whatever the mother went upstairs to suddenly have to do it takes awhile and Lucy has in that time decided to lay out along the whole sofa. That odd corner. That bookshelf. That picture hung. She waves twiddle-fingered, says 'Meow' just to seem generically confusing. Then stares at the ceiling, an old game from when she was a kid. Does she really know which room she is directly under? It's hard to think about the house as a thing around her that she could have the wrong perspective of, being inside. Is that her room? Doesn't feel like it but the stairs go up, landing, up to the side - there, already she's lost track of where that puts things! Her window looks out on the backyard, though - and that, she points to the door, is the back yard. She sits up. Hold on: she probably is under her room! That odd corner she thinks is right below her when she sleeps. Because on the other side of that wall is the neighbor's house and the wall at the side of her bed is the same wall. Isn't it? She is surrounded by she-has-no-idea interior and out.

The mother had to return a phone call, she admits. That's not why she'd gone upstairs. But she'd found a message waiting, it was one she had to immediately return. 'You don't need to explain where you go and why in your own home' Lucy says, rubbing her eye with a knuckle. The mother somewhere in the next bit of conversation uses the expression 'dime store severity' to describe the voice of someone - Lucy does not quite get who. What does that matter? 'Dime store severity' Lucy incants. 'What?' 'Dime store severity. Surely you know you just said that!?' The mother smiles, dubious - true dubious, or she's playing around? - and says 'I seem to recall that. Lester's voice. His dime store severity.' Ah, it was Lester - whoever that is. More important: 'Dime store severity.' 'Yes' the mother slowly-reaching-for-gun-under-the-tables 'Yes, that is what I said.' 'Can I have that?' Lucy says and her true self, the one from sixth grade she's never sprouted past is the one asking. The mother tentatively moves finger from trigger, lays gun sideways on thigh but still has tongue pressed between teeth, suspicious. 'Sure. You can have it.' Lucy's mind is already upstairs scribbling.

Before long it is three o'clock in the morning. This might be the second episode of whatever this other show is. What is this show? Is it American? 'What is this show?' Lucy asks, mock slaps the air in front of the mother's face and makes sound effect. 'You are the homeowner, I the renter. Explain this to me!' The mother finishes a yawn with the sound of a chuckle, wanting obviously to be certain Lucy understood her comedy styling were appreciated. 'I dunno. I used to sleep like a normal.' 'We all used to do something' Lucy retorts, snorting dismissively a little louder than she'd meant, the inside of her throat now scratchy a bit, first pawings of a coming head-cold. 'My greatest fear as a child wasn't very interesting. What was yours?' Lucy squints at the question. 'What was yours?' The mother shrugs and yawns, I'm sorrys, Neverminds. 'You get some sleep, okay?' Lucy says 'Isn't there school tomorrow?' 'School, drool' the mother says, patting her own head, big stretch on toes with accompanying rattle of various joint poppings, twist of torso this way and that, completely unselfconscious adjustments at the fit of bikini line, eyes three-quarters closed.

Lucy did the dishes. Scrubbed with lemon soap and a horrendous sponge - she did look for a fresh one but not too hard - then into the machine. Hoped that was the right amount and the proper way to put in the detergent. And hopes that was the right absolutely thoughtless turn of the setting dial. Rice-krispy treat. Water from bottle. One little piece of turkey. She has just gained forty-eight pounds and feels every gelatinous inch of each ounce of each one. Another bite of turkey. Swig of water. Who cares? Think pirates on pirate-ships cared? They were proud of how they looked out there, Seven Seas, plunder, captain's playing harpsicords and all of it. Lucy? Lucy is a pirate it's just that the world has changed. Lucy? Lucy is a ghost-story told as good luck when the sky in the morning shows signs of a coming squall. Lucy? Lucy is turning off lights now and reaching over the sofa for the remote - seeing the hot chocolate mugs she didn't put in the wash. Like a movie: lights out on scene. Darkness. Feel of hollow. Running of dishwasher. The house is the low hanging belly of a grumbly old bear.

THIS IS WHAT LUCY JUST typed: *You aren't going to read Maestro Gregory's missive? Are you feeling piqued? Kittinish?* She typed back: *I don't know what those two words have to do with each other. I don't know what Piqued even means. You misspelt Kittenish.* Nod. The room is saucepan dark except for the computer glow and silent apart from the tack tack tack and her breathing and the air from the vent. In other words: not very silent and, in essence, not dark. At a squint, she could read the spines of novels, if she gave the looking some gumption. She now types: *Misspelt is not a word.* She then types: *Yes. It is.* She now types: *Misspelt is a misspelling of misspelled.* And now: *I've giving you the finger.* And now: *No you're not.* And now: *The fuck would you know?* This is a very satisfying thing to do. If Lucy didn't erase it all, highlight, delete, every time she did something like this she would have a delirious, a delicious collection of these little chats. She wishes she had. So why not? Lucy, why do you delete these? *Saucepan dark* had she suggested the room was? Does that really work? Highlight. Delete.

Then we come to this box which she keeps under her desk with some books stacked on top of it. In this box are copies of all of the issues of *Hernando's Highlights* she has worked on. She does not keep them as a record of her participation in the bizarre, plagiarism based enterprise. She does not keep them because she is a keepsaker for the sake of keepsaking. In fact: this is not every issue of *Hernando's Highlights* she has worked on. Even here, she is reminded that she always thinks this and must always remind herself No. Take this one she is looking at. The main essay in it is by Ariel, under the name *Lenore Fenner* and is just a reworking, with opposite opinion slant and jumbled paragraph order, to an article from an issue of - Lucy honestly tries to remember, meh - *Cine-Zap!!* or *Entertainment Extra* or maybe even *Scope Weekly*. Lucy did the bulk of the rest of the text in the issue. Ariel had been sick? Something. 'At any rate' whispers Lucy, here, now 'it is also the first issue to feature a *Poetry Corner*.' The poem is called *Respite for Somewhat Beige*. It is credited to *Ruth Bledsoe, age sixty-four*. Lucy likes to include the age. She likes the look of her pseudonyms in the bold, small, italic font. Is she reading the poem, right now? No. Not right now. Why is she even awake?

*There are snakes of different air in every air.* Little glance down: part of the keyboard,

part of her breast, lip of the yellow wood table. *Your lungs are harbors for grief.*
Scritch-scratch at her hip, part of her stomach, the side of her neck. These
fingernails need trimming, for they are spreading tucked fungus into her,
planting furrows in her, braids of accidentally scraped up disease. *Your lungs are
harbors for grief?* She is aghast. Chewing her left hand thumbnail, repeating in an
obstructed way: 'Your lungs are harbors for grief!?' Sets the chewed off crescent
of fingernail tip with the pile of the five from her right hand. Nibble nibble, tit
tit tit, index-finger. Real ugly taste under there. Where in Hell have her hands
been? 'You are going to get rid of that, right? Right!?' she demands, sniffles, and
gets to work on the nail of her middle-finger. Some nights are not nights for
poetry - this is a thing Lucy hates to believe, but believes very much. Most
nights. And she is horrid aware of the dreadful paste that is the most of her
broken bird poetry. Her dreams are a ramshackle olive. 'Why not write that
down?' she chides. 'Best line you've come up with tonight.' And sad part, you
don't even know if you think so or not.

   This is one of the moments, sleepless and enormous and choking down her
spine, she moves about nude in her little room and points about to conduct
dreams out of the air. Little girl. Little girl. Lucy Lucy in her bedroom bedroom
doing this this while dad mom asleep and no one can see and she can whisper
fuck words too and often did. Summon a dream of your childhood - what dreams
did you summon, then? Who is that knocking on the underside of the ceiling!?
Look up and see that it's the face of a chickenpoxed moon, left eye running into
its right! Is it hideous, though? 'It just wants to eat me' Lucy mumbles 'and when
the moon comes down, especially when ill, to eat you, well, then you curtsey
in your best leather slippers!' Oh that was a little girl dream. Lucy in this room
in head-one-way-the-other, sluggish as the dong of a church-bell tonsil - Lucy is
in this room swaying until her grin slips off like lollipop wrapper ribbon. The
ache up her shoulders in a single line in the color lime and a single dime for the
phone that someone else is on. 'Fuck.' What was it? The fingers aren't fast
enough, Lucy - that was dream, not thinking. But what was it? She types. *The
ache up her shoulder was.* Breathe, just out one nostril. *Was. Lime.* Breathe, by forcing
out stomach all the way, hupping it all the way in. Lucy in the rented room dark.
Lucy putridly naked and unable to write what she's thinking, unable to think
what she thought.

   A soft tap on the door. All stop. First: animal eyes illuminated by about-to-
be-dying. Then: stove sizzle The fuck!? Then: oh Lord, wait - perfectly even-
toned 'Yes? One minute.' Through the door, the mother's voice 'I'm sorry - I
didn't mean to disturb.' 'No no' - a bit loud that, but now even - 'I just need to
- just a sec.' Where even are the damned clothes you'd been wearing? Silence a
second. Mother's voice through the door 'Really, I didn't mean to wake you.'

'I'm awake, just' - Lucy unlocks, turns the door handle, opens the teensiest crack - 'Sorry' - the mother's sleep-face in the tinge of the barely there hallway - 'naked. Not asleep at all. Writing.' 'I'm so sorry' the mother blushes in a radiant color of dark hallway 'I don't even know...' but Lucy cuts her off 'Please, I'm just up writing. One second - don't run off.' Still: where in fuck are the clothes you just took off!? The act of dressing is taking a distressingly long time from the point-of-view of the woman on the other side of the door, Lucy. By now. You do know that, yes? She's probably walked away and won't ever be back.

Lucy accepts points for her quick wit in putting on this soft grey blazer, no shirt, and explaining this is her normal writing apparel, though in throes she - the mother smiles, hand to face in order to keep the laugh from growing mature, perhaps waking the child - disregards dignity for unfetteredness, quite often. A ten minute conversation - no, Lucy, you aren't in panties, that's quite correct, though it has drawn no comment for it likely is not noticed by anyone but you, burningly, paranoiacally, giddily, disastrously every half-of-a-half-second this goes on - about what Lucy writes, for how long has she written. Lucy tarts it up in all lights and garish blinking colors, a really Christmas Eve whore of herself, as after all she was just caught nude and now is wearing nothing but a thrift store, men's sized, spring-weather grey blazer. She is a poet! She is one of the man-made mad ones! She is something unforeseen! She is the echo that precedes the thunder! The caterpillar too late to save accidentally trapped in a screaming skyward firework! Look at that face, Lucy! It's like the mother's damn freckles are fighting each other with no quarter to be certain they are the only fleck that you notice!

The spell breaks. Let's not even be fancy, cause it broke unfancy. Let's say something mundane - the spell popped like a soap bubble. But that's fine. The mother is sitting on Lucy's bed. 'I just heard you in here' the mother is explaining 'and noticed the light still under the door' this about why she had knocked 'and I could have asked any time really but' she shakes her head like as though to ask herself why she is being so roundabout, maybe at noticing Lucy's brow rising, now, a moment after her smile had. 'Sorry. And it's perfectly fine to say *No*.' 'Do you need a favor? Or is something wrong?' Lucy shifts, good pretend of regular curiosity. Double quick, the mother says 'No, nothing wrong.' Smiles with incredulous look and blow out her nose. 'Nothing's wrong. So, I have to take a trip to' - pause - 'I have to deal with some things with Flynn's father. And I wondered if you might be willing to watch him for the few days I'm gone.' It takes awhile - Lucy has already agreed, but has to wait till it's done to agree, proper - so to condense: the mother doesn't want to take Flynn, Flynn seems to adore Lucy, the mother could get another sitter but was awake, heard

Lucy, wondered. 'Sure' Lucy nods. Then, before she can give the assuring 'Sure' the mother has to get out 'He'll be in school all those days, so it won't be much of a thing - if it messes with your work - I don't know, nevermind.' 'Sure' Lucy says 'I don't mind at all and I'm happy to help.'

The mother whisper-chats from the mattress of Lucy's bed another half-hour. At one point, Lucy's computer went black from being idle and Lucy did not tap it to life and in that dark she wanted to undo the blazer's fake bronze textured button one-button. The details of the reason for the mother's trip are, frankly, such a bore Lucy stops listening. Because Lucy is cruel. Because she doesn't know how to care about things she's presented the first time and never has. She gets flits of ideas she might have to - secretly grits teeth - do Arts and Crafts things with the child, but then almost giggles and almost - in the dark, like she's only there just thinking about all of this, like a pretend dream before sleeping - whispers 'Why the fuck would you?' When it is time for the mother to go - 'Shit, what time is it?' the mother had asked, bleary, Lucy had tapped the computer - the room was illuminated, paltry bee stings of light against two sets of dry wincing eyes. And Lucy watches the mother move down the corridor. Yes. Lucy stares at that very thing - one side more rumpled-triangle, half-covered in rose cotton than the other - and the voyeurism feels symphonic and it feels known and it feels wanted.

The truth is forever unavoidable, despite the wide distance it keeps from everything, but one thing Lucy knows is that, when she wakes up, much of this will not have happened and what did will not in the manner this liar-night presented. Her life is a three-card-monte and she bets because she likes that the game exists. Yes. Some lose to perpetuate the myth, but they perpetuate the myth because they like to know that others will lose. This is ancient, the usurper nature in all of our blood. Lucy's pet theory is that there is no such thing as language, just a highly organized instinct, a magnificent engine of deceit in the brainstem that convinces everyone they recognize patterns out of babble, each person individually knowing they are only pretending to talk and listen, while an unconscious, perfectly calibrated balance orders the nonsense chaos of all others into niceties, euphemisms, Shakespeare, Albee, lists of places to visit this summer, and names for our kids. Yeah? Is that your theory, Lucy? No. Lucy is sound asleep. That isn't a theory, just buffer noise behind eyes as an actual dream finishes stewing.

Car crash awake, rattle rattle eye blinks of a cliché hubcap rolling further along from the shrug sprinkled blue glass of a broken out side-window. The room is bright. Downstairs the mother and child are singing a song of getting ready to go out for pancakes and bacon. The front door opens, it closes. Lucy pretends to hear the song continue, the vehicle door open, its engine start, grit grit grit of tires backward arcing, away. Lucy is upset at herself for having hung the blazer back up in the closet. 'Are you just trying to make yourself feel schizoid? Fuck sake, what a bone-rotten thing to have done!' She lets out a groan, allowing phlegm to rattle in the drain catch at her throat back. To make this all more pleasant, she is acting drunk. As though that is why she was up all night. 'I was two-fisting it, mate' she says in her world famously awful attempt at an Irish accent. Her belly feels like hardened porridge and her right arm has no sensation and seems to show no interest in getting any. 'If this was the end, would it be satisfactory?' she asks an imagined audience of herself. 'Is this the sort of moment someone, in seven hundred years, could use at the end of a play, make a soliloquy of it, a couplet?'

THIS MORNING IS INSIDIOUS, UGLY in that way a man past forty says 'Strawberry blonde' when describing some other girl on his daughter's lacrosse team. The cloud cover is a thatch, but arrogant, inaccuracy of brown-grey keeping all huddled to itself, pretending to have a secret just to get the goad of the rest of the sky. How could this be a day off? Asphalt glare recumbent for miles. Lucy had decided to drive and now is in some town adjacent by a mile or two from the area she regularly haunts - but that mile or two might as well be the difference between warm-enough-for-butter and burnt. There ought be mountains cordoning off the little elbow patch of world Lucy has made her habitat, her life the length of a Band-Aid. But why would the world's physicality do her any favors, make her feel in it correct? The radio won't even stop playing songs she doesn't like. Even this station - The Classical Station - seems to be making things up as it goes: sure, those are violas and that's a piano and whatever, but this doesn't seem something anyone ever wrote down. 'An approximation is good enough for us all' Lucy gripes. But, seeing the other side of it: if it was the point of the composer to sound just this way, he's struck the nail dead on into her head, nevermind on its own.

Why has no lover ever called her legs, her lope, *equestrian*? Do they think she would take offense? Are they so limited they don't know what bonuses she would have adorned them with and what vulgarities she's been bottling up since pubescence with which they'd be the lucky annointees? The best she'd ever got - and it was good - was 'the line of your hips is a sinful ruckus' and 'your thighs are a rumpus that emptied the churches of song.' Who'd said those things? 'I said those' says Lucy, smiling - this seems to put her in a better mood. As does the thought of what she'd ever do if she could get her own grubby mitts on her - look out! But too soon that too-often-empty-buzz, toy wasp that no longer winds but still rattles if you tap it a little. 'The proper declension is Buzz, bzz, zazz, zzz' she explains and all authors of children's literature smack foreheads and mumble mumble to each other 'Say, Lucy is swell! - Ain't she? - And how! - Surest thing you know, Lucy's the best!' A sudden cramp of thinking she'd forgot her wallet, but no, she has not. This is the sort of town they'd toss you in a cell for not having a license to drive. Because this is the last place it makes good sense to bother.

Where is this place called? *Lamont Plaza*. Never has there been a worse name for a place, a choice so inappropriate when dubbing. Perhaps the fact that there is a high clock right there, in a sick fit, gave the city planner a notion of so stately sounding a designation - but look down from that tower at tax joint, flower joint, closed down joint, pizza joint, nail joint, hair joint, toy store no kid wants to go into, Chinese joint, discount clothing joint, supermarket, ice cream joint, other discount clothing joint, tanning joint, miscellaneous greeting card et cetera joint, burger joint that will be something else soon and was recently something else, too. Yep. That should have sobered up the souse. 'The lush!' Lucy devil-faces, starting down steps to the five screen discount cinema that, along with a store selling stools and billiard tables, takes up the entire lower back side of the Plaza. None of the movies ring a bell. Ticket bought. Box of candy from a man old enough to be her father. A mom letting her toddler waggle the joystick of a Skill-crane. The odd refrain of a forlorn robot voice with its desperate enthusiasm coughing from a thick plastic chicken saying 'Take a chance, win a' - something indistinct - 'Bwrawk!' the whole mechanism of it rattling a spasm and a ping ping ping of rubbery-electronic fanfare.

Only person in the theatre. 'Mercy me, how old are you, Lucy?' She shushes herself and enjoys her candy, the defiance the Greeks liked to pretend they'd ever have against the Gods. It isn't out of line to question this scene. Nor to find it pathetic. Lucy has become one of those people, sometimes seen, who could, as they say 'go either way.' Alas, she would admit if she'd be honest, that she's gone so far as to become the sort who made the most sense anywhere she was if one were to assume a tragedy in her recent past. What's that woman doing in this theatre as the previews barf and prattle? Oh her? Her infant just died in a flood. Who is that woman, pondering the *Lamont Plaza* clock-tower with such a resolute expression of thought? That woman? That woman!? Don't you watch the news? The psychopath left her alive to deliver his message to the families of the victims. My God! How sad! Let's leave her be. Lucy munches the last of the candy as the movie, proper, begins. By the way, what was the psychopath's message? Hmn? Oh! That the dead would have been spared had they been as meaningless as this woman who had. Lucy raises eyes, thinks 'That'd be bittersweet for them, anyway' and then closes eyes closed.

Being a bitter pill is over. What a great movie! She never would have guessed that they'd never actually even stolen the jewels! That old fool got his comeuppance, that's for sure! He'll think twice before he sits so lordly - foist by his own self-important petard. Not at all a feigned enjoyment that Lucy experienced, it is clear. There is magic in having no idea what kind of a film one is sitting to - in that context and that context only anything in the world makes good sense and has gravity. But look here at the poster, Lucy! She laughs aloud and gets a smile from the passing employee. It delights her that she had just watched the film that this is the poster for - but lucky break she saw the poster, too, or she might actually have made the mistake of talking about this bauble with someone like it was the cure for streptococcus or something. She hopes she gets to pretend review it. Maybe she will proper review it. 'How long ago did these movies first come out?' she asks the old man at concessions. 'I don't know.' 'How long ago did these movies first come out?' she asks the young woman at the ticket window. 'Which one did you see?' Lucy names it. More than a year ago! But that, she is assured, is a real anomaly, even for this place. Lucy, the young woman tells her, could go buy a copy of the film for almost as little as she'd just paid on a ticket, by now.

By this time, here, Lucy is the most inelegant she could possibly be - hardly a thought to what she was wearing, siting outdoors in *Lamont Plaza*, eating a tuna sandwich, oddly postured because the bread was flimsy and the bench below-par. Now, who should casually stroll directly up to her but whoever this person is. 'Hi' Lucy says, swallowing tuna, bread, and the iced tea she was gulleting it down with, this in response to the young fellows faux-hangdog wave. He chuckles 'You don't remember me.' Do you? Lie. 'Not at all, right?' Lucy's lips are smacking because of the food, she moves tongue into lip crease, sniffles, all while wide eyed who-the-fuck-are-you-nowing with the slow shake of her head. 'Is there any reason on Earth why I would?' Why isn't this kid toddling off? Instead he says - listen to what he said, Lucy, what in the world? - 'I believe I owe you a cigarette.' 'Why do you owe me a cigarette?' The guy now does a foot scrape, like he is a cat indifferently burying a plop, smiles even wider, and says 'Can you just take my word that I do? And let me smoke one with you? You smoke one of mine, I mean. I like to pay my debts.'

Yeah yeah yeah, she supposes she recalls him, once she has gone through the entire ordeal of being here. And, anyway, she agrees to smoke a lousy, cheapo cigarette with him. Actually: 'Why do you say you just owe me one cigarette? Didn't I give you the rest of that pack?' The kid blushes, at first, then laughs and claps his hands, rubs them in the fashion somebody far more clever than he actually is would, goes 'Of course, you're right! In my enthusiasm, I didn't realize how much more of a debtor I am.' Oh Lord - he thinks he's being charming. 'So are you going to give me that whole pack?' Bonehead move Lucy, of course he hands the pack right over, and now you're encouraging this! Putting the pack in your back pocket is a nice touch - though what are you doing? because it's ten times as encouraging, too! 'If we keep smoking, now I'll have to borrow from you and this whole thing will become cyclic.' Does the kid see that was a silly play? Does he understand how to flirt? That he's just checkmated himself? Is he as dim as that, or does he have something up his sleeve to make it worth two minutes further of Lucy's attention? Don't be false, Lucy. You know you're having fun. Don't be such a stick-in-the-mud. Check: 'Then I guess we won't be smoking anymore, eh?'

'How old do you think I am?' Lucy gets down to brass tacks, five minutes later. 'Am I supposed to say a number?' She gives him the very Platonic ideal face of he's-boring-her so he, peace gesture with hands, names a number. 'You're exactly right.' 'Which makes me literally half your age' he says in honestly pleasant mock-tone of sagacity. Did you say *honestly pleasant?* Shut up. 'And what exactly is your endgame, here? With no art, young man, because you're about as clever as a slinky and about as state-of-the-art.' He does respond well to wit he knows is beyond him - that was a good candid grin. He's probably gonna pawn that line off for ages. 'I want to take you to dinner.' 'To dinner?' she huffs two breaths out her nose, giving him the benefit of the doubt he'll pivot or something. 'How forward am I supposed to be?' She stubs her cigarette under shoe toe, but he actually salvages with 'Don't get me wrong - it's just I know you know my endgame, already, so I'm torn between trying to be clever and trying to be forward. Neither seem like, really, to stand a chance, so at least lend me training wheels, here.' Lucy. Lucy. Really? 'You're supposed to be forward.' And now you have to listen to him be, Lucy. But, hey, it's your day off.

Lucy is much further along, now, but busy as she is touching a blouse in a store she honestly digs - this is back in her usual part of town - she might as well recap, because she guesses she'll admit it's vaguely still on her mind. What sealed the deal finally, at least tentatively, at least in the sense that she has that young man's telephone number in her pocket, inside that cigarette pack of his - Christ's no he doesn't have hers! and he thinks her name is Pricilla, and she explained curtly she would text-message, if anything, and likely nothing - was that the fellow's mother pulled up to the curb and he had to go, really quick, because that was his ride to his classes. Yes, okay fine: she'd taken the number before that, as part of the ebb flow of vague entertainment value, but that is the moment she actually considered some ethereal chance she might use it. His name is Calvin. Yes, he has a girlfriend. Yes, he knows this all seems weird. Yes, he does, in fact, have a general thing for older women. No, he's never 'been with one' has never done anything remotely like this before. No, he has no interest in 'dating her' or 'being called boyfriend.' Lucy would have arrived at the 'Do you live at home?' part of this lazy interrogation, but the mom pulling up - he straight up said who it was, points to him for candor - and his genuinely charming half-beat of 'Damn it' expressed by single to-himself eye-blink, rather drove that point home better than words ever could. Recap done. Now: more interesting is that these pants really are half-off the Sale price. The clerk says so, insisting when Lucy is skeptical. Lucy buys them without even trying them on, both pair.

There is no more joyous thing in all creation than five lanes of traffic all brought to a standstill by a long progression of jaywalking geese. Lucy could melt if she wouldn't rather explode from the sheer rapture of being party to this evolving gridlock. Please, never let this line of geese stop. A quick survey of the faces of other drivers restores some faith in her that if the world did, indeed, end tomorrow, like it was often supposed to, it would be kind of a shame. She sees no one upset. She sees many smiles. A father, there, leaning across passenger seat from driver's, still belted in, to, as safely as possible, give his children a good model for showing awe and humility in the face of purity, the sublime. The traffic builds behind her. And in front of her she sees it snake well along, the next traffic-light down backed up, the folks over there all likely cursing and dreadful boned. They are close to heaven and far. The difference between things is never more precise than the way geese show us it is. The one, there, who hasn't stopped cleaning under its wing is Lucy's favorite. Obviously the leader. This was all his idea. The ring leader protogoose. Lucy? You're crying.


WHAT IS IT, LUCY? AFTER the desert you've found yourself made to insect-size, under a cup, on a rock you cannot dig through? Is the sour so tart as that? Is there such a hideous length long of it left? Of what? Try: *Is there such a gibbonous crawl of breaths left till they turn to sawdust?* You like that? Or try: *Is there a toil to be debted even to the blood once it's mottled and dirted?* Why aren't you writing this down, Lucy? Do you ever feel the best of you is left for moments you can't find ways to record? Do you find, ever, a despair at seeing evidence of the best of you for the knowledge, the doubt, the terror it might just be residue? What is it, Lucy? Faster? Or slower? More? Or less? You came here, didn't you? Well: why? Where is it you were before the desert? You weren't the same - so what were you and what does that make you? Is the new thing that removes from the husk an escapee or some feces? Do you shed? Or does something, someone-altogether-else go on, you dead, the new thing too lazy to even think of what else to consider itself but you? Do you so much have a past or rather nothing more than no will to have a future? Want an answer? Lucy? Lucy?

Now, she had not meant to fall asleep. Blink. The parking lot. It's only been five minutes since she parked. A jolt, she turns the key to get the car started, looking again at the time. Settles. She does not have to be at work today. Blink. Her coordinates update within her, the entire topography of what she can see out the windshield goes from scribble-scrabble to set-piece. She had not meant to fall asleep. This is all the side effect of not sleeping. How much of her life goes on like this? Alack the day, she cannot fathom. But here - yawning and crick-rick-pop stretching, pelvis thrust into steering console underside, awkward kind of side-splay to allow her legs some semblance of ease, a hand reaching up over herself and vulture fingers down into the plump knots of neck and shoulder muscle - the feeling is pleasant enough. Wiggle. Wiggle. Left shoulder up - pop. Right shoulder up - pop. Listen to the rut-tut-tut-tut-tut of her rolling head around. 'Then you should sleep, ya dope' she smiles. 'Not now in your car' she adds, finger gesture that of a kindly Art teacher up in front of her as though at her 'but some time.'

Layla answers before it seems there was even a ring. 'My phone rang four times, actually' explains Layla 'I didn't think I was gonna get it before voicemail.' All fascinating. Lucy twists from where she is leaned to her car-side, sighs at the soot she sees glimpse of on her pant-backs and knows there is some on her shirt for sure, blows out the drag from the smoke she's just drug. 'It might be your phone' Layla says, aloof and mildly accusatory, holier-than-thou and prep-school elite. 'You might be my phone' Lucy zaps her chuckle chuckle. To it: 'Why in Hell are you siding with Gregory in all of this!?' But Layla, no chump, shows off how long ago she had braced for this: 'You owe me the apology - you're the one who ever did it with him or any of it. No one told you to do that. Now I'm the one having to deal with him because you've scampered. He's obviously diagnosable with something, so fuck you.' All cogent points. Lucy nods and is sure Layla can tell that she nodded. 'I'm in a parking lot' Lucy says, then with a tone of utter superiority 'where are you?'

The rest of that conversation is about what one would expect. Lucy always extends chats longer than they need to be extended for all of her reluctance to place the calls or whatever to begin with. In the space of this conversation she has watched a woman get arrested in the parking lot across from the parking lot where she was situated. Half-heartedly she narrated this in real-time but in a kind of mystique riddled way to jostle some envy from Layla who - she explained this to her - was 'a real bumpkin and does not even know what a policeman is.' They make the same kind of not-really-making-arrangements to see each other as they always do and like always Lucy feels a pang of want and a pang of guilt, entwined, a sterile emotion of stationaries. Hardly an emotion. 'There should be a kind of off-brand word' Lucy thinks. *Imotion. Enmotion. Ammotion.* She'll see what she can do about it. *Timotion. Lamotion* sounds good. The sky reminds Lucy of a television show with canned laughter. Probably just because it right then has the grit of decades-old haze to it. Not smog, just an effect like everyone in the world is as tired as Lucy is, everyone is looking at it at the same time, some of that feeling of worn-down rubbing off, imprinting up there.

Here is *Her New Sister's Best Friend.* There on the passenger floor are those other two paperbacks. But *Her New Sister's Best Friend* she pads with fingers, turns over. No description on the reverse. That is how she remembers these books. Yeah. Dorene. Dorene's mother had these slimmed between some thick other books on the top shelf of her bedroom library. Dorene's eyes when they would sneak the one down - not this one, the other - to read, not even giggling, rapt, unglued, single breath panting but silent except for the tink tink tink of twin eye-sets left-to-right. Dorene's eyes were the green of the whitest part of a celery stalk. Art class paintbrushes first touching dark green to water in clear plastic cups would tingle up her spine to her Dorene's eyes even years later, miles later, sixth and seventh grade later. Had they never read even a passage of *Her New Sister's Best Friend* together? Had it just been the other one? Lucy honestly is uncertain. *Her New Sister's Best Friend* though definitely isn't the one that she assigned taste to, assigned feel of fingers to. This wasn't the one she would sometimes hold spread open to the skin of her shirt-lifter chest. Lucy, you're more terrified you have read this one and will recognize, instantly. Lucy - oh yes - fearful a smile as can be, you are right.

The drive back to the home is leisurely. It's an ice-cube taking its time to melt since it's in a dinner glass that's been forgotten on the table overnight. It is almost like the wheels of the car have bones. That or they're thorn bushes. Lucy drives occupied with her game of stealing the lyrics from whatever radio song, adding new words to the same syllables and finding the difference inspired. This is a different route than she tends to take to the house. It cuts through a neighborhood where the streets are splattered with berries of some kind, purple-browns dropped from the ungainly tree branches which in storms would suddenly seem fiendish. Lucy wonders at the few houses whose walkways are not smeared. Who would clean concrete when they know doing so makes them seem alien? Well, those people would! What's it to you? But as soon as she is through the neighborhood she stops the thinking, doesn't care. She has to remember to take the turning just after the shopping-center, the odd turning which seems like it will dead-end into the lot by the pharmacy. If she misses the turn it's five miles until she can turn back around.

The mother's car isn't present but Lucy hides the paperback in the bag with the pants she'd bought, anyway. She had first considered she'd tuck it in her waistband, was actually a bit brought down when she remembered the bag in the back seat. Bring the other paperbacks in? Those? Don't even joke about something like that! Lucy greets the house from the outside as she gets her key in the door then gives another general 'Hello' with a quasi-tilt of a question sound to it. The house answers back in that way houses do. Upstairs. Tucked into her room. She's a false tooth in a beautiful grin. Hmn. Might as well. Takes a moment to wait for the computer to wake up then *She's a false tooth in a beautiful grin*. Tap tap tap. *I am a false tooth in a beautiful grin*. She decides to type both. She is far too tired for any of this. 'Poetry is a wide-awake racket' she says, beginning to undress. But wait: should she be asleep when the mother gets home? Oughtn't she be dressed and around? The mother, after all, had gotten even less sleep than she had and had been up with the child, early-worm. And had been busy all day. Is it important to seem like something? Probably. 'In which case' she must say logically 'it is important to seem like something you aren't.'

Lucy has always been a pervert when sleepy. Her current plan is to leave a pair of her panties on the door handle to the mother's room. Unfortunately she cannot think of a way to make this seem accidental. Unfortunately she does not even know what she specifically hopes to accomplish even could she. Hold on. No: she'd drifted off there. That doesn't count as a thought. She was more-or-less dreaming that and the door she was picturing was in some kind of subconscious cobbled-together-from-several-houses house, not this house. 'That was all a symbol, no doubt' she instructs the audience. 'Let's think what that could be a symbol of.' How did the cat get in her room? Shit - had it been stuck in there all day? Since last night? Stupid animal snuzzling in secret under her bed! That explains the odd scent sometimes and why she wakes with itching eyes! No. How long had she been out, just then? Was that cat an actual cat she had once seen in life? A cat with a sloppy stitched coat of colors the soft tones of print in the funny pages? The door closes downstairs, voices. Really? Or is she out, again?

'I hope you're just waking up' the mother says, unpacking this and that from the loudmouth plastic of grocery bags. 'Where's the' - Lucy fumbles, makes a gesture - 'the, you know?' Refrigerator suction of door opening, hum of cold, thump of cold. 'Is that' - the mother imitates, maybe accurately, maybe not, the gesture Lucy had just made - 'your symbol for *Kid*?' 'It's my symbol for Flynn.' This gets a snort-laugh and a 'Well, then it's perfectly fitting!' 'I am just waking up, yes. Because I am less industrious than you. Why do you seem actually awake?' Lucy makes no move to help put anything away - nor does she pay attention to what items are being placed where. The mother says 'I'm pretty sure I'm asleep actually and this is all a cruel dream just getting good and I'm gonna wake up to Flynn saying he's got an earache or something.' Lucy nods, wishing she weren't too tired to trust how she took that last bit. Wait - what was that? 'What?' Lucy asks. The mother had lips parted, breathed in to start speaking then hadn't. Pointedly hadn't. Had stopped herself. 'What?' Too long a pause for anything truthful, the mother lies 'I was just going to apologize for barging in last night, again.'

When the mother returns from upstairs dressed in a way to suggest she will have to be somewhere particular later that evening Lucy asks 'Was there ever a cat living here?' Lucy's just left-of-center phrasing and the mother's half-distracted affect of looking at herself in the bathroom mirror has the mother begging Lucy's pardon 'Did who live here?' 'Did you ever have a cat?' The mother and Flynn had had two cats. 'In this house?' 'Yes.' The mother looks at Lucy but nothing has changed fatigue-wise for Lucy so overall the equation of what-is-that-expression-the-mother's-wearing just nils out, again. 'Well, I think I dreamed about them. One of them.' The mother's eyes are softly welling and she is tensing her jaw but in the good way. 'Just now' Lucy continues, but making it expansive, doing up her confusion at herself, almost saying 'Sorry, ignore me, I still haven't slept' but remembers the company-line is she had been sleeping all day so instead says 'Right before I woke up. Sorry, I'm still a bit groggy. Ignore me.' 'It's okay' the mother smiles 'it's fitting, in fact. You know we only got you to replace *Lilybell*. You're in her old room.' They stand there like that. Like that. Like that. A few minutes later they move.

# .III.

HUNG TO THE TRAILER-OFFICE WALL far enough away from the desk where she sits that Lucy cannot see it is a framed page of *Hernando's Highlights*, this page in particular one with the *Poetry Corner* from two issues prior to this one which Lucy sits currently plodding on. *The Cat Poem* as it is only ever referred to by Lucy and Ariel - no one else, of course, refers to it at all. A small bronze placard in the black of the frame, solemn lettering stating *Never Forget* and beneath that imperative the date of not the issue itself but of Lucy's agreement to Suzette. Ariel, the puckish delight, had not even brought Lucy's attention to this decorative addition to their workspace and claims it took Lucy four full days to notice it. No way to argue, as she only noticed it when she noticed it, Lucy has to accept this claim though does like to think herself more observant than that. 'I am a poet, after all' Ariel had impersonated - more a mimic of the way Lucy carries herself, little half-strut half-loiter way of moving about, than of voice - on Lucy's first insistence of this while still staring at the slight reflection of her skin-tone on the bronze of the placard face, her grin immobile, a broken clock at three-forty-five.

Other than her first week Lucy had never kept anything like normal office hours. She is sitting. She is the only one in the trailer-office. She has not turned on any lights and only has one of the window-blinds raised. The sun is out there, if sulking. She is bathed in a kind of olive grey. That morning Flynn had told her a story about finding five dollars in the hallway at school. He had taken the money to the office, turned it in. His point to Lucy was that he became baffled at how it would go from there. 'Even if someone came in and told the office they'd lost five dollars how could the office know that it was really true - that this was the kid? Say the kid had overheard another kid say *I lost five dollars*. Say this other kid had no kind of outlook on life or was half-witted, just sighed and put it off to bad luck - or whatever, was just not the sort to go asking at the office? Then this other kid swooped in, opportunistic!' Lucy did the following two things. She first: 'Flynn, you need to just keep money you find, man. Don't be dumb.' She second: said the words 'I love you' to him for the first time and had touched his hair, laughing and thoughtless.

Is this what she does when she works in the morning? She recaps her morning as daydream? Lucy, you could have just told Ariel 'I'll tend to my lot at home this week, I'm watching this kid.' Hell, you don't have to, never have to, never have had to, tell Ariel anything! Do the work at home! Drive and drop it off in the mornings, sure, go ahead - but you're just sitting in the office alone doing nothing! True, that is your notebook. Shall we peek into it? Lucy closes it at that very moment, leaning back, listening. The toilet is running, an omnipresent - and Ariel insists also an omniscient - hiss all around the trailer-office. The sound is a glove. Lucy just now is a scab that has come off in it, has dwelled through the summer months, waiting to be found out, got rid of. Or maybe these are leather gloves and no longer to the taste of the wearer. Maybe she is laying in a rubbish-tip, never to know. Stands, lumps forward, back, probably in what is meant to be a stretch. Sits in Ariel's chair and spins then stands, tucks it to its waiting place as exactly-as-she'd-found-it as can be managed through meticulous micro-readjustments. A bit more that way. A bit more that. Pat-pat to the fabric top. Pat-pat. Caress.

Does Hernando read each edition of his little pet-project? Even still? Would he know if it was not following the guidelines - 'the Scriptures' as they are called in 'the office' - and if so what would he do? As though to Ariel Lucy says 'It's we who hold the power, girly. We could pull the plug on Hernando's little scheme!' Then as though Ariel to Lucy Lucy says 'It's not that I don't know that - but it's that he could just decide to stop doing it. Would we make him continue? How would that work if he had the option to just stop anyway?' Booming and general, the din of ten air-conditioners is Lucy's voice: 'Greed and short sightedness! He never read his Greeks! He probably never read his Romans

- the people or the Bible books, my beauty. Blackmail! Blackmail, dear Ariel!! We tell him to pay us double or we will turn him in - no matter that he could stop, we tell him if he stops that's when we drop our dime! You're too much the dreamer-variety anyway, Airy - you don't see things for the cynical dust-rags they are! There is no art, here! This is a functional thing - a shoe-bottom, my girl! We are the springs that make a comfy couch for his ad revenue, don't you ever think a second way about out poor swinish overbear and our poor rodent lot!'

Hour later. Lucy has a list of what *Capsule Reviews* she'll do and what mid-length pieces - mostly on television shows - she'll handle. Now she peruses the one mag they lift from that has anything more than cursorily to do with books. Still Bestseller, Book Club mundanity but with enough elbow-grease Lucy can pretend these things merit a tinker's damn. Hold it. You're being false, Lucy. What book have you read that is truly obscure? Some of those scholarly things for your precious degree, sure enough, but don't sidestep: what fiction? What author do you admire who isn't, cards down, the same as these you are hurling abuses at? How many would you have read had they not had the pre-worth granted to them by canonization, if - squirm all you want, false-heart, writhe the day long - you had not been told to? Ah! That's it? They weren't Bestsellers, you say? Weren't commercial!? Even if true, they have become so now and it is why you know them, why you sought them out - you weren't there for their virgin histories, are not part of their presence and assured continuance. And Lucy you are not a child so your continued attraction to these dirty things is no longer protected under the auspices of innocence, purity - of affinity, even! 'Fine. I'm sure these books are great' she says, flicking the magazine page. 'I'm sure they're real horrorshow.' Even there: that's your big obscure reference? You wouldn't even say that if not for the film - and the film fucking adapted an expurgation! 'I'm a whore then, a hypocrite whore - but please, just let me be happy.'

Ariel comes in, hangs head, mutters 'Oh goddamn it, Jinx' and then moves to her desk in stony silence. Back turned, still sotto voce 'And what are you trying to do? Intimidate me with your sense of professionalism? It won't work. You're after my job but you'll have to take my head for that and you don't have the right kind of pair hanging.' Lucy throws a magazine at Ariel. Ariel does not respond. Ariel is in a dress, again. Ariel is in boots and she smells like a melted candle left in a hot car all day. 'You'll never convince me of your femininity' Lucy proclaims, looking exactly at the yellow dot piercing at the top of Ariel's left ear. 'A few well-planned dresses will not overcome your unbecoming brashness, your brusqueness, or your bawd.' Was this planned? - it seems far too quick - was this planned? How in a blink Ariel turns chair full around, leans back, the sensual arc of a just dropped towel, legs unabashed apart with loose at wrists hands draped unpushing on the dress fabric one at each thigh and says 'You don't find my bod feminine?' Hold the stare Lucy. You're allowed. Okay, long enough. This is a moment for calculation and non-sequitur misdirection. 'I find it feline. But certainly tomcat.' Fuck! That face Ariel faces was not what you were going for and that laugh was a peal as the chair unspun to where it had started.

'How's the kid?' Ariel says, both of them irritated by the wind as they smoke. 'He's off my hands by the morning.' 'You two have not bonded?' Lucy shrugs, admits to her fondness for - her words - 'the tyke.' Street-sweepers and folks with leaf-blowers - though no leaves to blow so they must be up to something else - are bashing about the stillness of the lot-at-mid-morning, Ariel fed up enough to fling her cigarette away. Repentantly she lights another. 'What's up?' Lucy asks, because there is no punchline to the frustration then hangdogedness Ariel slouches to. But no response. The same no response. No real response except an expression to analyze. 'The fuck is this all, Loose?' Ariel finallys. 'The fuck is this all, El?' Lucy offhands, hoping the world will click to easy-levity. 'But I'm serious' Ariel looks *FH* sounding, lets out ten seconds of smoke, then 'You're okay with this?' Did you note the odd softness to that, Lucy? It was a down-comforter of an inquiry - a trick, though, seemingly same-subject when the reference point has changed. 'With working in entertainment journalism? With being a voice in the critical realm?' Lucy pulled that off tentative, Ariel can go either way with it. 'Har har' Ariel hars then long pauses. Then too-long pauses. Lucy has been too busy observing this to realize she's waited too long to stop it. Not enough cigarette left to do anything about it, now.

The temptation is there to go ear-to-the-bathroom-door. But the temptation is fought. That is not the sort of thing one does. Eavesdropping. Why is Ariel talking in the bathroom? And what if I had to go? Then you would knock, Lucy, not stand there listening. Blink. Lucy can find no way out of this point she has made and has never felt less proud of herself. In fairness, she could listen to as much as she could before knocking, perhaps be able to glean something from even that crumb. Ariel used to make whatever these mysterious calls were outside. Symbolism is symbolism - the distance is narrowing and Lucy knows the signs. Nature has a way of shrinking before the maul - no animal ever evolved to dispatch its prey from farther off. Something is lurking in these phone calls. Is Lucy attempting to avoid the obvious? The benefit can only be given the doubt if the doubt is not doubted. What? To Lucy this makes sense. 'It makes sense' she insists. What she means is there is no doubt so no benefit to give. 'You know I can hear every word you say when you're in there, you pervert' Lucy tries - a decent gambit - when Ariel returns to her desk. Note how wily is Ariel, how quick to disguise with a good humored 'I get two bucks a minute and I'm in there anyway, might as well narrate, you know?'

She reworks a review of a science-fiction comedy to make it sound a rollicking good time because she wants to unstabilize the world however she can. Does Hernando read this? Damn it - where is this mood coming from, Lucy? Who cares what Hernando reads!? Just this morning Lucy had eaten half-a-waffle in cherry flavored syrup and winked at Flynn when they'd agreed on another secret to keep from the mother. One secret for each day the mother had been away it seemed, now. A chocolate bar in his lunch bag. Pizza one night. Cupcake. Up until midnight to watch both parts of a movie on television. And so on. Lucy is coming to regret every last one of these. Indulgences. And for who? There would be consequences to these secrets and wee deals to silence struck with no one to no end. There was too much build up now because of them and the tension would have to ease elsewhere in life. If the kid didn't double-cross her then the deception would have to find another way to get her, make her pay so the world would balance. And the kid would not be the back-stabbing kind and moreover it is too innocuous a thing, no harm would come even if the mother were told. That was her mistake! She was old enough to know that all secrets are precursor to violence subtle, wide ranging, and irrevocable. Even now she stares at Ariel's up-done hair and sees nothing.

'Did I tell you I almost didn't publish that fucking *Cat Poem*?' Ariel scoots her chair all the way over to butt the hip of it to the hip of Lucy's while saying this. 'What do you mean?' It had gone thus: Ariel had produced a whole different *Poetry Corner* page for that issue with the file kept separate from the proof-pages she and Lucy reviewed together. It being Ariel's job to make the final send, Ariel had planned to upload the altered file in place of the one sullied by Suzette's friend - this person referred to as 'the interloping bumpkin' - and to not tell Lucy of the switcheroo. 'I know you, though' says Ariel here 'and I can just imagine how that would have gone had I gone through with it! You're lucky I have a grasp of the importance of good citizenship.' Lucy, in ten seconds of a pleasant smile, lives interior through the horror of what would have been had Ariel gone ahead with this ill-conceived gesture: she feels sweat, the clammy of when awoken by stomach cramps. 'Why are you telling me this?' Ariel uses her chair to bump Lucy's, again. Again. 'Pay attention to me!' she girlishly brats. 'Lucy, I do everything so you won't hate me, don't you know that?' Lucy has a specific question but now she can't ask it. Unasked questions are a kind of dizziness. Lucy's head is a hobo sack full of starving horseflies.

**\*\*\*\*\*\*\*\*\***

THE THREE, FOUR, FIFTH TIME now Charlotte has looked directly at Lucy while making the smoothie for the customer who'd been ahead of her in line. The one, two, third time Charlotte had rolled her eyes - and at a brag Lucy could say that time there'd been a wink too, though it was actually a strand, unseen, of Charlotte's hair has snaked her eye, brought a slight wince and back-of-wrist up to dab. 'I'm sorry, but it does give me confidence when someone can't stop watching my ass.' That was the woman-in-line. 'Sure.' That was Charlotte. 'I'm not asking for it but when you have a perfect heart-shaped booty down there you know people look.' 'Sure.' 'And I work on it, you know? Don't pretend you don't like it if you work on it! That's what I say!' Lucy gazes over at the two technicians who seem puzzled by whatever is wrong with the lemonade cooler. They seem to have had certain philosophical underpinnings removed from their life, are soullessly adrift, uncertain even of the possibility of the ether. 'If you work on it and don't have something to show maybe you don't want someone to look. That's another thing. You know what I mean?' 'I know what you mean.' Six! Sixth time! And Charlotte's eyes had so briefly darted as though to see where Lucy's had gone, the briefest warble of unwrinkled forehead shaped as question before the woman said 'It's still why you're working though, don't be a prude about it. I mean. I have a perfect little heart down there, people will look.' 'Sure.'

Daydream: print a set of poems. A volume. Ask Hernando if maybe he has a special price with the printer they use. Even of the same quality paper stock - Lucy loves the thin, pulpy, seemingly already discarded pages of the magazine. How the cover is the same thickness as the inside. Just print a thin volume to have. Daydream: the poems can all be about her. Whom? What? Lucy tests the coffee but the coffee is too hot. And Lucy is aware of the fundamental lowliness of even her daydreams. It's a bad habit, almost a vice. No imagination. Ambitious as a toilet-brush. Try another. Daydream: she touches foot to her and … But the world in Lucy's head seizes like a pinball machine blare. Spasmatic all stop! On the page she had managed when she first sat down *let's marauder our mouths / like we've stolen them from people / we loathe / let's jail our tongues above breaths in / to wanton to out.* So there isn't everything the matter with Lucy, anyway. Just something. Pen-tip down. Tense to let words. But there is no conviction. Whatever lust is in her has abated. *Lust like we call a room cold when we only mean there's a draft.* Look at that. Lousy, pimply verse there, but nonetheless accurate.

Then here: 'You said you work here but I never see you around.' Charlotte has just up and taken the seat right across from Lucy, is even peeking at the notebook page Lucy only just now thinks to conceal. 'I can't see that?' Good Christ, how does this Charlotte go pout-to-sneer like that? Christ! 'No, it's awful. Wait - who are you, again?' To describe Lucy's fluster now is to rhyme *hummingbird* with *hornet*. 'You know who I am. Are you a writer?' 'I really don't know who you are.' 'Oh. Well, then this must be peculiar. And it'll only get worse when I tell you I just came over here to admit that I spit in your coffee 'cause I know that's the sort of thing you like.' 'When?' 'Did I spit? Just now. In that. Are you a writer?' Lucy honestly hesitates. Nothing seems more dreadful than for she, a grown woman, to answer that question in the affirmative, in a grocery-store, right now, to this younger lady. Lucy is being blitzkrieged by the scents of shampoo and whatever brand of deodorant this obvious hallucination is radiant of. 'Are you a writer?' is all she manages back, finally. But Charlotte will have none of it. 'I'm never spitting in your coffee, again' she says 'And here I thought we were pals!' Standing - not breaking character and returning with a 'Sorry, be right with you' to her station where a moldy shaped man has now sloshed - Charlotte is gone.

Look what has happened. We're a little bit later but this has to be addressed. Look at this: Lucy has hidden herself in a grocery-store toilet and has already washed her hands twice. Why? She is looking at herself grim, proud, afire, and mortified. That's her reflection. The corridor leading to this toilet was rank with the brine of seafood and that is her reflection. There is no taking it back! But we're not caught up, so to explain - Oh but how to explain!? Hadn't she watched Charlotte go back to work? And hadn't she, Lucy, automaton, scribbled a verse on a page - finished a verse? scribbled a verse? there had been pen movement, hadn't there been? - folded that torn-out-notebook-page in half and walked right over to the counter area of Charlotte's work-space while Charlotte had been helping that customer, caught that exact Charlotte's eye and said to it 'Fine, you fucking win! It's all yours!' And then hadn't Lucy strode off? Yes. The reflection nods. So that had happened. So: what are you confused about? Why are you in a saltwater toilet in goddamned *Hernando's Grocery*? There are your eyes. And they seem confused but also seem more appropriate than they can remember ever being. Someone opens the door and Lucy watches her hands open the tap again, squirt squirt squirt pink eel-skin soap. Her reflection smiles forward over her actual shoulder at the person passing whose reflection is not looking at Lucy at all.

Lucy is considering purchasing this yogurt and wondering whether the two men over there could be considered athletic-looking. Her own opinion is that: No, they could not be called that. Not rightfully. But then she never has known about things like this. They are large. They are slender. They are - her mind turns over for a word - lithe. But they seem particularly unexercised. The shape of men. These two or any other. An untrustworthy shape. The conditions of their bodies are arbitrary and skirt to avoid precision. Which her own mind demands. No one athletic could have wrists so thin. No man. And shirts should hang differently on athletes, even those just casually having a chat by the processed, individually wrapped cheeses. And her sub-focus is: they are talking but she can't hear them at all. But she can hear the people further on. And she can hear those people, there. Are those two maybe-athletes really talking? Or is she forcing an oddity where there isn't one? Is she becoming cognizant of the method her mind is cobbling to distract her? Why isn't she ever anything? By this point she is flat out unbelonging.

'She's still beaming' Suzette unsolicitedly assures Lucy 'she carries a copy with her everywhere and I think she stole a whole stack to have at home and send to family.' Lucy nods, photocopy of the first time she had nodded, photocopy of the photocopy of that photocopy's photocopy. This is how interactions with Suzettes happen. Again-and-again, only different as much as this one technically isn't that one. Suzettes live life as a series of mumblings, rehearsals, half-moments. Suzettes have no more consequence than lies never told to suspicious questions never raised from jealousies never harbored by lovers never won. Oh you're nothing Suzette! And your friend is a joke on the wall of a trailer-office in a grocery-store parking lot in a town a Lucy has absently wound up in. 'I'm so glad' Lucy pleasants 'it's a big moment. Has she been a poet long?' That's the spirit Lucy! Same as it was the spirit last time! Suzette, Suzette, you are loved in exactly the same measure as a Q-tip is sometimes needed. No one has ever or will ever call you essential. 'Oh her whole life but this is her first time being published.' 'I find that hard to believe.' Look at you, Suzette! You'll be discarded like a saltlick from this world some day and not even a bovine will sigh.

A cigarette cures the world of its dropsy. Lucy is herself, again. She gladly hands a cigarette over to this young chap, delighted that he had used the word *Borrow*. 'Yes, you may borrow a cigarette.' The day has darkened in gradations of brown as though black decided to try to be yellow. It's a curious light. Lucy is a bold lungful, she says 'Yes, I am a bold lungful.' Maybe all she needed was a jolt to upright herself as so often the proper medicine will be. Even that fellow there who has nothing more to him than the speckled tone of the green of his shirt is a kind of display, pure, intricate dressage of humdrum doing its damndest. This crowd of loudmouth young men yawlping like ducks at the rapture, to Lucy, well, they might as well actually be ducks yawlping at the rapture, they move exactly in the rhythm of the engine of bibble babble that fills them brim to bottomside. A cigarette. Lucy. Nothing more plain. The world is now serene again, practically numbskull. A little scare and life is as simple as breathing asleep. The sun has undone its trouser front and leaned back from the table, burped, begged pardon, and chuckled at doing so even though it's in a room all alone.

You don't have your notebook, Lucy. Calm mama voice: Let's retrace our footsteps. Favorite teacher voice: How do we get from that to that? Mathbook equation voice, already frustrated: Solve for X. Then solve for Y. Show your work. But none of this bothers Lucy as she has the easy plan of acting like it had all been her big plan since the Prologue. The automatic doors shudder whisk wide, Lucy bows as she makes way for an exiting patron and soon is standing in the café area, matter-of-factly noting that those loudmouths are at the table where she had been seated earlier, no notebook to be seen. 'Hi, did someone turn in my notebook?' Charlotte is quizzical. 'Turn in your notebook?' Yes, Lucy. Actually go do that. Ask that question. And if Charlotte answers like that it'll just mean that nobody did turn in your notebook. 'Did someone turn in my notebook?' Yes, Lucy. Go actually ask that. 'Yes, here it is. Hey, I loved what you wrote for me!' Sure, that's just what she might say. Yep. 'Did someone turn in my notebook?' The grocery-store seems a tad larger now, floor to ceiling. Rather like a cankersore that's been nibbled and sucked on and patted all morning since you first found it, brushing your teeth.

Charlotte seems her genuine youngness. She wants to know if Lucy had written the poem for her specifically or had she just given her what she had been working on when she had come over to bug her. Lucy needs to find a way to ask 'What was written on the paper I gave you' without it having the usual tone of their patter because this is the first time she has seen this young woman acting sans affectation. The trouble? Lucy does not know what she wrote. At all. But that would be kind of difficult to explain, right now. 'I wrote it for you. I hope it's okay, I just wanted, I guess, to apologize.' 'For what?' Interesting that Charlotte asked this because it seems distinctly the second, less consequential of two questions she seemed to want to ask. 'For not being quick-witted when you came over. I've had an odd week.' Charlotte unconscious-upturns lower lip, sigh-breathes out nose. 'Well, you don't need to apologize for that, I just had to get that customer. Sorry your week is bad.' 'Oh it's not that bad.' 'I'm in love with the poem, if that helps - we're getting married tonight when my parents go out to the movies.' Lucy bashfuls a real-life downturn of eyes but can't maintain the honesty, says she'd gladly copy the poem out neatly if Charlotte would prefer, figured her chickenscratch made it pretty illegible. Customer approaches. Charlotte holds up Lucy's notebook for her from where it had obviously been all along just behind the counter and says - facial expression as she speaks already meant for the 'What can I get for you?' that follows - 'I could read it just fine.'

*Now the light is shaped like snakeskin.* This is fine. She writes it down. How long has she been away from the trailer-office? *And we all gloat over old skinned knees.* Passable - she keeps it, as she is already moving on. *We're braggarts of our childhood wounds.* But what else are we? A trouble with Lucy is she never wonders about anything. If we discount paranoia it's safe to call her uncurious. *It's safe to call her uncurious, yes, she's the taste of the ends of her hair that she chews.* See? What is the meaning of that? Ought she doubt it has meaning if she can find none for it? It makes one think about chewing hair only because that is what the words say. Does she want it to do something else? *We named the persimmon persimmon for no reason other than it gave us something to say.* Suddenly Lucy cannot help laughing. She has a burst of laughter and then an accompanying fit of giggling. She reads the line back and is delighted by it atrociousness. She looks up automatic to the trailer across the lot. Her first impulse to dash the lot length, slam notebook to Ariel's desk and Callooh-callay 'Look! Look!' laugh like an invalid's buttock 'Oh look at me, Ariel, read that and look at how stupid I am!'

ARIEL PUT IT THE FOLLOWING way: 'It seems to me the goal of man - all mankind, you know? - since the moment we became aware that we would die, since we have been conscious of that, should be to spend every waking moment trying to find out just what that possibly means. Consciousness. You know? Does death end it? If so: still, what was it? And I don't just mean some of us should be thinking about it or even that all of us should be passingly interested in it. No. I mean the whole of humanity should be engaged in the constant, uninterrupted exploration of the matter from all ends, angles, overs, and underneaths. There can be no purer pursuit. No more imperative expenditure. Even if you came to the end empty-pocketed, stress-browed, grasping for one strand of anything but despair it would still be worth it. Don't you think it would still be worth it, Lucy? That this is what we all ought to obsess and abandon over?' Lucy - old hand comic gem she is - hardly lets the last of Ariel's final *R* be pronounced before she answers flatly 'Yes.' The End. Raucous applause and laughter! They will consider this a classic moment of contemporary life, they will!

As Lucy sits typing her slight variants on the two-line descriptors of forthcoming episodes of popular television shows, these cribbed from a computer print-out of local listings - Ariel usually does this but this edition she had asked Lucy to on the strength of the plea 'I might not live anymore if I have to, you see my dilemma' - Ariel slowly moves the edition of *Hernando's Highlights* that features the infamous *Cat Poem* in front of her face. The position of Ariel behind Lucy, especially leaned forward, arms moving as though in a hug of the air just around Lucy's head, is so that a pulse of warmth and fragrance radiates into Lucy's hair from the skin of Ariel's abdomen under the thin of that dress she is in. Ariel slowly opens the edition to the page where the *Poetry Corner* is presented and Lucy, clearing her throat in play of irritability, typing louder - though just a mash of illegible keys - recited *'And as you catch scent of the tuna you give your chipper Meow! / as though to answer my Are you hungry? with a cheery And How!'* The edition now open, Ariel moves her finger to point at the poem in the shaded box. Lucy sighs, flicking a look. *There are no fewer cruelties than fingers lost count.* The loud typing stops. Ariel has just kissed the top of Lucy's head as Lucy's hands took the mag and she leaned forward before turning around.

But where had Ariel even found that poem? 'You don't remember?' The question is so earnest. Lucy blinks, at a loss. 'No. I don't.' 'You are a cold-hearted and absent woman, Lucy Jinx. I am regretting my gesture of high romance.' 'Don't regret your gesture of high romance, please! Really - where did this come from?' Lucy's eyes are warbles of wide awake REM sleep, engines casting oblong and hard-tugged nets through her memory, trying to find something. Ariel fishes through her purse for cigarettes, putting one to her lip - is she going to light it? - then tucking it behind her ear while she fishes out a lighter. 'You gave it me, Loose. Oh so many moon ago. You don't recall?' Lucy honestly doesn't. How can this be? 'I knew it was just an empty gesture' Ariel mock laments. Lucy laughs and says 'Give me a damn cigarette' because she is blank to anything more witty. Ariel gives Lucy the one from behind her ear - edit: the one from out of her lips - and says 'I actually just flipped through your notebook, once.' 'Oh' Lucy says, laughing, relieved and yet not. Ariel laughs, too, then sighs the words 'Man oh man' and follows with 'You'll just believe whatever the last thing I said is, won't you?'

Lucy has to do her best for the next hour not to just stare at the poem. She has closed the edition and closed the closed edition in her notebook but how long will that last? She has to not ask endless questions in twelve-year-old-best-friend tones about 'Did you have to pay for an entire run of this? How did you do this?' The paper stock is the same as any *Hernando's*. Lucy becomes kind of worried somehow that the *Cat Poem* was never actually printed and Suzette is hospitalized with shame and broken heart. Except: no no, there it is, framed and placarded on the trailer wall. Ariel lobs some casual comments around about how Lucy should publish a whole book of poems even if she has to pay for it herself, even if just a few copies. Lucy feels out-of-joint, sideways from her life of just earlier in the day, a terrible creep in her. The terror of encroaching coincidence. So she deflects and deflects. Such a strange breed of bitch you be, Lucy: here your friend does this good turn, is making all efforts to princess you and you are clawing the walls for a finger grip on your earlier bad mood.

'I like what you said earlier. About what we should spend our time doing' Lucy says, Ariel turns around, grins, says 'Well you're already doing it, aren't you? The word for it is *Poet*, I hear.' Lucy does a haughty impression of someone in regalia from abroad, mime-mouthing some grandiose blah blah blah, then musses her hair and goes 'Aw gee, Ariel, aw gee.' 'Or anyway, you think far far too much. Sometimes I can't even think myself this room fells so crammed with your head, my Lucy - you don't know the hard times I've seen.' This doesn't seem a moment for any somber intimacy - doesn't it, Lucy? - so Lucy uses her mouth to say something inconsequential while pummeling confessions against the inside of her eyes. Ariel is likely not joking about the room feeling coffined because of her. Lucy pictures herself in this room brooding or out in front smoking but tacit-toned and a river untold to Ariel so obvious in her postures and offhand remarks, her automatic chuckles. Things are off their leash inside Lucy, right now - the degree of agreement she wants to give Ariel, the roaring truth of the endless it-will-never-turn-off of her headfuck. 'Ariel' Lucy says - the word a precise falsehood, first syllable just enough to say *This is something true* second like a sitcom burp, third like a Silly-old-me - pauses, then with a shoulder shrugged to casually rub her ear continues 'I think you know me too well to ever really love me.'

It was Hernando himself on the phone. They knew this - and so Ariel answered - because a different line lit up and the ring was set to three quick little trills instead of the extended generic. After saying 'Hello' Ariel asked Hernando if he could hold for just one moment, covered the mouth-piece and big look of headache asked Lucy if she wouldn't mind taking a smoke while she fielded the call. 'Is everything okay?' Lucy asked, standing with her eyes at a worried squint while she got her pack and lighter. Ariel gave a twitch smile, said really quick 'It's fine, I just need to take this and thought he was going to call later' then right away returns to Hernando with a 'Sorry about that.' And here is the close of the cold panic down, Lucy having to strike and strike at her lighter to get it to catch. She can't hear a word of the call through the door but it's as though it is stage play in front of her. Ariel being chewed out. She'd done two print orders of that edition. She'd called the printer after knowing the edition was being produced to say 'Stop it' and then had sent them 'The correct file, so sorry.' 'Never do anything nice for me, Ariel' Lucy hisses while walking in slow, closed-down circles. She sees herself taking the phone from Ariel and screaming. In the stage play there aren't words when she screams just noises like war in a termite hive sent over the theatre speakers.

No. Barely five minutes and Ariel comes out laughing, lighting her own cigarette like nothing. 'Good gawd' she bizarre-accents, joining Lucy down on the pavement where Lucy'd fretted to. 'Everything okay with Hernando?' 'Mmn?' Ariel has to get her cig better lit. 'Alright? Yeah, yeah. Oh it wasn't a thing. Just about a time-off request.' How false does that sound? Very. But

Lucy, your nerves are frayed and trust yourself that the last person you should be trusting is yourself. 'Are you coming to the big *Cook Out Soiree*, by the way?' What? 'What?' 'Hernando just asked' Ariel laughs 'and told me to ask you. I feel like I'm setting you two up.' 'What is the *Cook Out Soiree*?' Ariel scolds Lucy for her appalling lack of get-with-the-program, gestures to the lot and paints with Victorian-era purple prose the scene it will be in a week's time: tents and two stages of live music, kiosks and portable restaurants, a Farmer's Market and starving-artist stalls, public hangings and urchin pickpockets - 'You'll cum so hard you'll get toothache!' Ariel finishes with obscene undulations. 'And Hernando wants me to go?' Lucy one foot ups, hands clasped, lips puckered. 'Well, he wants both of us. You know Hernando. That skeevy old coot.'

Though it has been the same thing each day she's been taking care of Flynn, Ariel does a character-piece of seething put-upon when Lucy starts closing out her computer and gathering her things. 'Aren't you the consummate part-timer. No no, I'll finish it up. It's fine, it's okay - hey, enjoy the day and your thriving domestic life, I'll just marshal things here in servile isolation and then go watch television. Really Lucy, it's fine.' Today, amused with herself, Lucy does not even show mock aloofness - no 'No, I appreciate it' or 'This is why we make a good team' - but does, in the end, walk right up to Ariel, thank her for the magazine, compliment her dress, and give her a rather hard kick in the side of her left boot. 'I've come to expect nothing less from you' Ariel says, though Lucy cannot fathom what this references. 'So, it's your last night with the kid?' 'It is. Why do you ask?' But Ariel seemed not to hear, these quizzical eyes now on Lucy genuine, only slowly changing to match her spoken 'Sorry, did you say something?' after a good two three four beats. 'I said *Yes*.' '*Yes?*' 'Or, I said: *It is*.' '*It is?*' '*It is*, why?' 'The Hell does that mean?' Lucy gives another kick - you're not going to kiss the top of her head, Lucy? Really? Do you not understand scenography? Where is your aesthetic for symmetry and symbol, today? - to Ariel's boot and says 'Don't worry. Back to normal, tomorrow.'

There is a message from Layla on her phone. There is a message from Katrin. Lucy sighs, the radio on, car parked, staring still at the outside of the trailer-office. Inside, is Ariel calling Hernando back? 'Can we do this later? I know, but Lucy is here and I'd rather not have my colleague present.' Inside, is Ariel regretting everything, begrudging Lucy, laying her every misery at her feet? She listens to Layla's entire message but immediately cannot remember it and has accidentally erased it. 'Fabulous' she clucks. Inside, is Ariel now in a room hollow with the ring of residual belittling, is she numb with agreement to make arrangements to repay? Or is she concocting a story to tell as to why she will not be there come next week? Time-off request? You need to ask better follow-ups, Lucy! Wait. 'Come on, man' Lucy groans, having just not listened to and then deleted Katrin message, as well. Space of three breaths. 'Jesus fuck!' she shouts, accidentally throwing her phone so that it strikes passenger window, the casing comes open, battery out. Most adorable chinck to the window glass, as well. About the size of the first baby tooth she'd ever lost.

'Aren't you supposed to be getting a child?' Ariel is just sitting there. Typing. Music is playing from her computer speakers. 'Why did I come back in here?' Lucy stops, pats herself, Ariel giving her the up-and-down while she does. 'Why did you come back in here?' Flummoxed, Lucy flop shrugs, arms noodle out, slap sides, dangle, and her fingers waggle. 'I think I need to get more sleep' Lucy decides to go with saying and Ariel nods, considers this a real gem of a thing to say and offers to make Lucy the official Office Sage. 'I really can't remember why I came back in here.' 'Was it to catch me watching porn? Do you want to leave and come back in?' 'Kind of' she laughs in as boyish a yuk-yuk as she can. Ariel has kept the confused face and keeps it until Lucy gives a final curtsy at the door. 'I truly am leaving this time' she grandstands 'and I am not coming back. Because of the child. My life is profound and you cannot fathom it nor plumb.' Ariel turns up her music a nod. And Lucy wilts backward through and watches the door close and her shadow looks wilted on the door that has closed.


THAT FATHER LOOKS LIKE A plum and a cumquat can't agree how best the other should be described. This father is the sort who whistles loud enough to draw notice, hands in pockets, in his secret heart believing folks who overhear are impressed and harbor desires toward him. 'They'll ask me to whistle in bed, oh yes they will!' she superimposes voice on his silent, milling form. And that father there is the cock-of-this-walk, almost handsome enough to go to the gym. This mother waits in pajama pants but the kind that show her deep fatigue and unwillingness to even bother. The foreign mothers keep their distance and rightly so. And Lucy? Well, Lucy is afforded the allure of being 'the woman who is renting a room with Natalie' and had fielded questions the first day just brusquely enough to keep people away without overstepping into the realm of standoffishness. If she weren't just left in temporary-charge she would never have waited out here. She is at a loss as to why these people do - the kids are all past first grade. There must be currents she is glad to not comprehend, some signs exchanged between these beleaguered middle-agers, propositions, communications to each other based on where they stand, which of their several stances they take.

In the door, Flynn thrusts backpack at the wall and makes a sound he has been making only for the last four days, one that Lucy has not asked for explanation of. He makes it again while she pours him a drink but then goes silent at the table while she prepares a selection of carrots, grapes, and a half-piece of toast with some abysmal brown spread she had never nightmared the existence of before her tenure as stand-in adult. 'Can I tell you something awful that I did at school today?' Flynn mumbles with his lips on the first grape he then sniffs before giving a nibble. 'What did you did Flynn-flam?' - this pet name she honestly thought she'd invented when first she used it, it took days to recall the mother used it often, as well - Lucy asks, never quite sure if she was being set up or if the kid was acting his actual head. 'I got a perfect Spelling test' he frowned, huffed, looked up with a scowl. 'A perfect Spelling test! Holy shit, fella!' Lucy held hand out for a high-five was high-fived and made a hoot noise of excitement. Flynn tried to keep his grimace through all of that, marginally succeeded while Lucy retrieved the paper from his bag.

The mother called while Flynn was drawing on the living-room floor. Lucy answered 'Hello' heard nothing, said 'Hello?' and was about to say it again when she heard the mother's voice say a testing 'Hello?' Then another. Then a more comical 'Heeellloooooo?' 'I take it you can't hear me?' 'Hello?' 'Hello.' 'Helloooo?' Lucy gave a wink to Flynn who had looked up to ask 'What are you doing?' 'Talking to your mom' Lucy answered, glib and fatuous. She dialed the mother back and the mother's voice said 'Hello?' 'Hi, I could hear you but you' - the mother's voice cutting over 'Lucy? Hello? - 'Can you hear me?' 'Can you hear me?' Lucy laughed 'I can hear you, yes.' 'Lucy? Hello?' Flynn had moved to sit on the arm of the sofa as Lucy, still laughing, hung up and said 'Fucking shit, man.' 'What fucking shit?' Flynn questioned. 'Don't say *fucking shit*, Flynn, okay?' 'You said *fucking shit*.' 'Yeah? Well, I didn't say *Lucy, don't say fucking shit*, did I?' 'I'm telling my mom' Flynn coolly threatened as Lucy's phone started ringing. 'Your mom doesn't care. Watch this.' She put her phone to her ear and said 'Fucking shit, Natalie! Flynn just fucking said I can't fucking say *fucking shit* or he'll fucking tell on me! The fucking shit is it with this fucking kid? Yeah? Oh I agree, I agree.' She winks at Flynn who has stiffened, tentative belief making him blush 'Is that really my mom?'

They decided to go out to a restaurant for their last hurrah. Lucy explained that the mother had left a message and would not be home until later in the morning, tomorrow, due to a delayed flight. 'She said I can keep you home from school if you want but I told her you wouldn't like that at all and so we're sending you to extra school, instead! And your mom'll see you next month.' Flynn nodded, unimpressed, listening to the radio as they drove and watching the dim roads wind to dimmer roads wind to harvested - or never planted, Lucy had no idea about such things - fields to eventually the shopping-center that had the local-owned eatery Flynn had been singing the praises of all week. Yes, it seems this was Lucy's way with kids. An odd stich-up of sitcom-moms and ingratiating-stepmothers from old television dramas. 'We'll come to love each other' she vaguely announced 'and then I'll steal your family's railroad deeds, you mark my words.' 'I already love you' Flynn replied, sniffing like a gnat had got up his nose, the next few minutes spent in odd snorts and pokes at his nostrils while Lucy sat rather relieved to not need to reply.

As the waitress left with the menus Lucy beckoned Flynn to lean forward. She stage-whispered 'I like this place because I'm not often the skinniest person in a room.' Flynn pulled his usual unsure-what-to-make-of-this face and asked Lucy why she had so much money. 'I'm just rich. Because some of us are and some of aren't, Flynn-mobile.' *Flynn-mobile*, Lucy? Where is all this going to end? 'You'd be rich if you were me. But you aren't me. I'm sure you have other things going for you, though.' At the buffet there surged an endless horde of lick and clatter, everyone in pant sizes which until this day Lucy assumed only existed representatively in Claymation films. Flynn asked her what was wrong and turned to look where she was looking. 'Do you see it, too?' she asked him while his head was still turned. 'Do you hate one of those people?' he asked, swiveling back around and leaning in to sip from the straw in his chocolate milk. 'I hate all of them, Flynn. They remind me of Hell.' Flynn was coloring a lobster orange and had colored a starfish green and an oyster's pearl purple. He stayed in the lines. Then he scribbled over everything in magenta making gnashing Kabooms!

Lucy tried to get the attention of a waitress, when she couldn't swiping one of Flynn's crayons, turning over her placemat to hastily write the line she'd just thought of but the words dismantled as soon as she was positioned to set them down. She leaned back, not even the numb of where the phrase had used to be in her head. They'd just escaped, those words. This barnyard was no place for verse, she supposed. Flynn returned from the bathroom and explained that it smelled like lemon cake batter in there and that someone had drawn a big penis on the picture of the baby on the changing-table in the stall. 'A big penis, eh? That's raucous, that is.' 'That's a vocabulary word' Flynn said, imitating the finger-point Lucy often gave when making similar pat observations to him. 'As well it ought be' she said and resisted giving him the middle-finger but in her mind saw herself doing it and felt serene. 'Someone called me a *faggot* at Science time, today' Flynn said after the waitress had come with his burger and Lucy's chicken fingers, the shared dish of fries, the words almost an aside as the lifted the burger bun and tapped at the patty. Lucy's swallow caught and she looked at him, shiver through her, but he was already reverse-engineering his burger and layering the toppings according to his own design, calm as a wish down a well.

A car swerved idiotically and then honked apologies to everyone, Lucy stringing expletive-upon-expletive and slapping the steering wheel repeatedly. 'The people in this burg drive for shit, Flynnt-mine! I hope you don't mind me maligning your town, but it's flat fact.' 'I don't mind' Flynn said and asked if the radio could be turned up. 'This is a commercial.' 'I know.' 'You know?' She gave head swivels back, looks of confusion and aghastment. 'You know? You know!?' 'I know.' 'You want the commercials loud and the music quiet?' 'I'm backward. And I assure you: you're just as weird to me as I am to you.' Lucy snorts. Then the kid says 'Music' with cartoon villain disdain, makes a raspberry, and looks off as though nothing exists. She turns down the radio when the music comes, expecting there to be protest or an 'I was kidding' said with rolling sarcasm but instead just gets a 'You're easy to train' to which she chortles. 'Flynn - are you going to serial kill me? I won't try to stop you, I just want to know.' He laughs and makes one of those sounds she has heard the neighborhood kids make. It sounds like a horse whinny. It sounds like the pull-cord of a lawnmower. It sounds like an old man who forgets to breathe when he sleeps abruptly remembering to.

While Flynn bathes Lucy tries to fix her telephone. This is overstating it. She removes the battery. She - for whatever reason - rubs her palms briskly together with the battery pinned between them. She rubs her thumb in the cavity where the battery will be replaced. Replaces it. Closed shut casing and then - again, what science she is drawing on, who can say? - wraps her hands firm around the phone, presses down, blows as though warming herself. Powers up. Calls Katrin - who she had texted to explain what was being attempted. 'Hello.' 'Hello?' 'I still can't hear you.' 'Can you really still not hear me? Hello?' 'Your phone still doesn't work.' Then Lucy says 'Gah' - or a collecting of succinct letters like that. Repeats, exactly, this process. Four times. Five. Six. 'What are you doing?' Flynn's voice and some vague slaps of moving water ask. 'I'm fixing my phone. What's it sound like I'm doing?' 'Oh. It sounded like you weren't fixing your phone.' She turns to the pillow at the head of the mother's bed - she is sitting on the mother's bed - and mouths 'Oh my fucking lord' with a strangle motion. The mother-she-pretends-to-see smiles back. When the mother-she-pretends-to-see pushes Lucy's shoulder with her foot it accidentally brushes Lucy's breast and the mother-she-pretends-to-see doesn't apologize. Just pushes her shoulder with foot, again.

Lucy lets Flynn watch another movie he is likely not supposed to watch and at the end swears him for the umpteenth time to silence. 'I don't know if you know this but your mother is cruel. Like a fairy tale from another country, you know? No telling what she'll do if she gets wind of this. I'll wind up a cake served to my own children or something - have to spend the rest of my life with a mouse laughing inside of and nibbling on my ear.' 'I don't understand most of the things you say' Flynn says, but adds that he's gotten used to it and figures the weird stuff is probably not all that important. 'Do you know that I'll actually miss you, Flynnima?' - she likes that one, hopes it's original, resists asking if the mother has ever called him that. 'What do you mean?' She looks at him. 'What do you mean?' 'You'll miss me when?' 'When I go' she says, automatic, but then realizes what she's said. 'No. Not *I'll miss you*. Sorry. I meant: I've had a really awesome time. I'll be sad when it's not every day.' 'Oh.' 'When it goes back.' 'Oh.' 'You know?' 'Not really - but sometimes I just don't get you, remember?'

Flynn is asleep by a few pages into the chapter of the book Lucy has been reading him but she reads to the end of that chapter and then reads the entire next chapter, as well. How far from herself is she, right now? Look at this room. What is it? She leaves, turning off the light, turning the little radio on - another habit the child will have to break the next night. Or who knows - maybe not. Who knows? Lucy moves her lips funny to squiggle the tip of the unlit cigarette she has just put in there around in a bee-bop kind of way and descending stairs she snaps her fingers like a jazz hound and beneath her shirt undoes the clasp of her bra gives a long scratch to the clammy indentation over her ribs, her back, feels some crigs and crags raked by her fingernails, little pig-squeals of tiny pain, the same as pokes to scraped elbows in childhood. She removes pants, folds them, sets them on the piano bench and leans, collapses, dropped sack, to the sofa, legs spread wide to cool her off. And the kid-finger-smeared television screen, mute and black, reflects back the most approximate semblance of this while she massages a raw inner thigh then leans forward to get off her socks with her hands when she can't manage to do it with only her itch-sweated feet.

IT IS UNNERVING HOW MANY people do not close their window-blinds or the blinds of their backdoors. Don't they know that with nightfall - unless curtains are drawn to every loiterer or passer-by - their lit living-rooms, dining-rooms, office rooms, bedrooms, become full blown diorama, pantomime scenes to take in at one's leisure? For her part, Lucy even likes to test from time-to-time that the blinds of wherever she's living do their job, that no curious angle or tilt of observer could allow their veil to be pierced. She is outside now, so knows she can be seen: as it should be. That woman, combing her dog, on her knees, television on the wall showing some news program, has no idea she is being observed: this is grossly unnatural. If Lucy were to go stand at the glass of those sliding doors, just wait there until she were noticed, her presence would not be expected, not pleasant or welcomed - it would cause recoil, tremors of violation, quakes that would follow that woman for the rest of her life. 'You'd better get with the program' Lucy warns sadly and dabs her cigarette against the brick of the house, moves to go inside, then decides to smoke another. See here - for example: Lucy has an itch just above her pubic-hair but will not scratch it because this is a time of exposure. This is wisdom. That young man who she can see in the window of that upper floor bedroom? That young man is unwise, unaware, deserves whatever invasions descend on him.

Lucy's habit in this time of being the responsible adult has been to wear these lounging pants she'd bought the day the mother left and an oversized shirt through the night. She doesn't mean to suggest the mother's choice of less modest apparel is not responsible - the mother is the child's mother, Lucy is the woman renting a bedroom, the difference is clear. The clothes make her feel unnatural. She has not woken nude this whole week - has hardly been nude except when showering and has not been able to find equilibrium with this. No, it has not been her lifelong habit, going unclothed, or hardly-clothed, as much as she has this past while. In fact, being dead sober with the truth, it is entirely new of her not to wear bedclothes and to spend any longer than necessary with any amount of skin exposed. 'Well, what of it?' she asks herself, looking at the bread, still not decided if she wants to have a sandwich or heat some of the leftover pizza she remembers is in the fridge. 'I'm just comparing myself to myself, that's all' she explains. Grimness. Disappointment. Disownership. Lucy, you shouldn't ever do that, silly ditz.

A text-message from the mother. From when? She brightens up - only ten minutes ago! *The flight has been delayed, again. Ugh!!! I just want to get home!!!* The new flight won't arrive until middle-evening meaning the mother won't be back from the airport until after dark. *How are you and Flynn? He hasn't forgotten me, right?* Lucy starts typing in a message - in stagger-steps, as she still uses the numeric keypad to do this, her phone antiquated as well as being basically non-functional as anything but a telegraph - but stops, discards the message when she realizes the tone was all wrong. Instead: *Flynn is good. He'll be bummed! He's staying home from school and everything.* Lucy wonders if she should have Flynn stay home, now. Probably not. Frown frown and 'Well, that doesn't mean I have to go to work' Lucy glowers. The mother suggests Flynn go to school. Lucy explains she was just thinking the same. Should she mention the Spelling test? She should let the child. *How are you? Are you watching Riker without me?* Smiling too widely *Riker's too much for me to handle alone, he's a tag team effort* - this followed by a winky-face and an exclamation point - Lucy is already five exchanges along in her daydreamed flirt dialogue, a little deflated to only get from the mother, a full five minutes later, the reply of *Ha!*

A glance in at the child. She still feels uneasy about doing this. Imagines the child there wide awake feeling her presence, stiffening to stay still, each breath feeling false, every little movement or tummy gurgle something that betrays its awakeness and will bring consequence. The child will never trust sleep, again. In her room Lucy sits on her bed lip and scratches at her neck. Most unpleasant. Why is her skin dry? Does she have a goddamn rash? Checks in the mirror of the bathroom she and the child share. Nothing. No sign even of off-color pink from how she had been scratching so vigorously. Comforting. Unsettling. Small things should be the most like they seem they should be. She scratches and watches herself scratch then douses the light and stares at the shifting approximation of her reflection, her eyes toying with the glass face, teasing out Lucy from the more-or-less pure dark as much as possible. A game of terror. This bruise-green, wax-melted, not-quite-a-face is the real look of her. Of all people, she believes. Our mechanism of recognition is in reality a mechanism to prevent us seeing ourselves, ever. That others don't see us, either? *That's just bonus* Lucy's mouth-darks, no sound uttered. 'That's just bonus' she says, the clash of her voice-as-expected over the phantasmal face enough to make her shudder, felt but unseen.

Whoever the previous owner of *Her New Sister's Best Friend* was they'd underlined and highlighted many a passage. See how, Lucy, you headlong to supposition? It could well be two separate owners are responsible for all of this - one underlined, the other highlighted. Evidence? In a few places underlined passages are highlighted, as well. Lucy is just flipping though, not under her bedcovers, propped into the crook of the room corner, knees up with wrists rested on them. There are also some ugly asterisks next to various blocks of text. 'I suppose those could be from yet a third owner?' Lucy cockily snides at her interrogator-self who has nothing to snide back. She scoffs, chuckles that she didn't even mark-up novels this much in her studies nor poems that she'd explicated to tatters. *Susie saw the pink twist of Gwen's asshole, more excited even than that first glimpse of her snatch one day in the basement, changing quickly before heading out to the car* is underlined and highlighted green. Lucy shifts a bit, lets one leg relax. Flips pages around more. Underlined, no hightlights: *Gwen closed her hand, gripping Susie's breast with a handful of the loose shirt fabric, pinning her to the kitchen wall. Susie's head bumped the wall, she gasped, giggled, but Gwen shushed her, two fingers of free hand pressing hard to her smiling mouth. 'Be quiet, my brother is right upstairs, still.'* Just then, a sound through the wall of Lucy's room: a television coming on - not loud enough to make out anything but muffled clapping, laughter, a music cue. Lucy has the book slammed shut, has hidden it without thinking under her shirt. A corner pokes stiff the awkward fold of her belly skin.

Oh why shouldn't she snoop in the mother's room? Just a bit, just once! Anyway, she's obviously already wandered over so what is she supposed to do, leave? The bookshelf is lush with titles recognized, others totally unknown to her. Knick-knacks on one of the lower shelves. And certain anomalous books that all must have been gifts or have curious backstories. She takes up a volume of Ocatavio Paz but seethes when she sees it is inscribed, puts it away. But was it inscribed to the mother? Or did the mother buy that particular copy because it had an inscription inside? Also: did you even read the inscription, Lucy? Forget it. Forget it. She's at the desk now, intrigued by a calendar that is several years out-of-date and not even open to the current month. No dates circled? Notations in the boxes? Hmn. The pile of envelopes are in plain sight - this is hardly even invasive! Well, your heart is invasive, Lucy, but go ahead and cling to letter-of-the-law. Bills, personal correspondence, but nothing that seems exciting. Then: under the pile of envelopes, loose papers. The first of these, top facing: a note. Lucy's own, quickly scrawled handwriting. She reads and feels numb then warmth fill her. *Alas, I ate this candy!! I have no excuse but my jelly-will! I have given up arguing with my sweet tooth, who no longer loves me ... yet still ...* Lucy is only the numb, forever-wide of her face. *I will replace this theft on the morrow.* She is a grin that has bloated to everywhere.

Are we smoking, again? There is such a thing as sleep! And if the child will be in school you should certainly be at work tomorrow. 'Tomorrow is horse-hockey' Lucy says, wishing she could come up with one of those childish euphemisms for the word *Shit* that she dislikes even more than this one, but really can't. 'Tomorrow is *caca*' she tries but kind of thinks that is actually a word for *Shit* in some language not just a silly expression. 'Tomorrow is *butt-mud*' she invents and the laughter catches her off guard, she stifles herself quickly. No way did you think that up, though. It's too obvious, the sort of thing every third child in a line would toss off. Still. She almost starts laughing, again. Out in the tree-line she hears sounds: rustle, scramble, thup! something like an ee-eepk! more rustling - the last of this clearly from the top branches of the trees as something brushes past them. She's seen owls around here. And hawks. Now she hears a car door close in the neighborhood back past there. She connects the sounds all into one narrative: the owl now pulling slowly out of the neighborhood, shifty eyed, mole still in its mouth, talk radio playing as it reaches the yellow blinking traffic-light and heads North to its hotel, pondering its next move.

Room door closed. Pitch black. Sleepless. Trying to decipher the still gurgling television sounds, hoping that this will drift her out cold unbeknownst to her. She has the impression it is a Western. Can swear she hears the kwa-ping! of sound effect bullets. There is no way the mother could return home by morning. The mother has not even boarded a flight yet. Even if somehow through a wild trick of zany Fate the mother had been told immediately on the heels of having sent that last text that a flight would be ready, right then - well, even then that flight would not get her in for eight hours, then the drive from the airport. Lucy stays in the dark. Pitch. Clothed. Above covers. Or are those the zchings! of Kung-Fu movie swords? Am I awake? You are, Lucy. There is no way you would be caught in her bed, Lucy. And even if you were would the proper word be *Caught*? 'Sorry - I just thought if Flynn had a bad dream it might be better to have someone in here. It seemed weird to be in my room where he wouldn't feel allowed to go.' Yes. Brilliant! Really? Yes! - and not even as deception, that is a very sensitive thing to consider. You should have spent every night in her bed, come to think of it! In the dark, Lucy's chest giggles and she too much hears the creaks of bedsprings and schuffs of shirt shoulder on top-cover.

Surprised to find it past three o'clock. The blue of the numbers fat on the oval pink clock. What book does the mother have splayed cover-down on the side-table with that little purse set absently on top? Lucy doesn't reach to see even though she would not even have to turn on the lamp - the clock light, blue, and the orange of the light from outside in the parking lot would be enough to read by, no trouble. She stares at three-thirteen closes her eyes for the count of forty-five opens and sees three-thirteen closes eyes the count of twenty-five opens eyes and sees three-thirteen. Paranoiac chuckle. She stares. No way does she count that fast - this clock is a deviant prankster! Stares. Three-thirteen. Stares. Three-thirteen. 'What is it, Flynn? Flynn, come on man, you can come in, it's fine. Those people just need to take the towels, okay? You can come in here for a second.' What? Dry breath in. Four thirty-two. She sits up. 'Flynn?' she tries to the dark. A bit louder 'Flynn?' She tries to hack some phlegm up for moisture but when she can't moves to the bathroom and runs the tap. Is that your face? Why did you ever do your hair this way? Why did you let it grow long, again? 'But see how if I tug it I can get the tips to touch my nipple? You see.' When is the last time you looked at yourself topless in the dark? Rough cough. Rough cough. Eyes make squishes when she blinks them. The clock shows four forty-eight.

Are we smoking, again? What else? Hardly enjoying it though, which makes all the difference as far as health factors. And when the stub is flicked out to the unseen grass Lucy lays down on the sofa and stares at the back of her hand which is at the end of her held-up arm's length. It'd be easy to guess how old she is from her hands, she thinks. The veins are a dead giveaway. The wrinkles between fingers depress her more than any on her face. Those - the face - those show refinement, the sculpting of indifference, rage, they show pertinence, irreverence, regret, and hard-won embitterment. These, between fingers? Frail. They are the single word *Frail*. The word sung, shouted, tried-to-be-joked-about, scholar-voiced, cartoon-toucan toned, bellowed, baroqued. *Frail*. So what if she falls asleep with her hand slipped for comfort under pants over panties? If she is nudged awake by the child, the child will not guess that the half-pencil length trace of middle-finger tip over the ridge under cotton - just gently, kitten nose light caress - is what she needed to do in order to drift off. And anyway, Lucy: what does anyone even care? She can hear breath loudening, evening, tightening from her nose. She can feel prickers of some few hairs which have found puncture through fabric as bicep quavers and finger stiffs, vibrates more tense. Oh nobody nobody nobody cares.


THE CHILD IS AT THE kitchen table eating a toaster pastry and reading a digest-sized comic-book when Lucy enters, rot mouthed and reeking, to her anyway, of cigarette smoke shoved out through the pores of her face. The weight of sunlight leaned dense against all the drawn blinds is enough that Lucy knows schoolbus has been missed so should not even go mentioned. The child hasn't even looked at her, thus she goes ahead and gives herself a good digging rub up in her left-side armpit. Waitaminute. 'Flynn, is that Jeff Goldblum on your pajamas?' Flynn looks up, down at himself, explains that he doesn't buy his own pajamas so maybe it's whatever she said. Anyway: it is. Goldblum with a rather unconvincing look of worry gazing that way, image of tyrannosaurus eye as encompassing backdrop. These aren't patched on images like pajamas were when Lucy was young - the image is as thin as the prickly, static laced fabric. 'Your mom won't be home till tonight, partner. So there's that. I think she's just dicking with us, at this point.' 'I wouldn't put it past her.' She likes Flynn. 'Nope. Neither would I.' Lucy uses two fingers to part the blinds a peek. 'She's probably in that house right there with her cute little binoculars just yucking it up.'

Lucy lathered herself twice in large palmfuls of this watermelon body-wash and would have used the mother's scrubbing-brush but could not get past worrying she'd mess up the bristles in such a fashion that would come off as she's used it some uneducated way. It's never good to doubt you can understand a scrubbing-brush but Lucy figures it best to play some hands safe. She doesn't linger long even with the indulgence of the twice-soaping, keeps thinking she hears soft little kid taps at the door. She waits to urinate until she is dry, clothed, out of the mother's room, into the bathroom she shares with the child. There are all manner of scribbles on the bathtub and the tile of the wall. Maybe she should have scrubbed those off every night. It really looks deplorable. She wets a washcloth now and gives scouring an earnest go. Marginal success. Shadows of the scribbles still there. And now her hands have a mildewed odor to them that even two washings with the apricot hand-sanitizing soap won't fully make rid. Look here: she's spit in the sink after finishing tooth-brushing and finds to her consternation that her spit seems off color - grey-almost-green? white-bile-brown-yellow? - because it doesn't match the white of the basin curve.

'What happened to your phone?' Flynn asks as he buckles in. Lucy doesn't answer until after she has closed his door, opened her own, and sat down, a view of him in the rearview. 'Well, your mom broke it. With her ghastly voice, you know?' Flynn doesn't respond but Lucy thinks this is just because he is having trouble getting his seatbelt to fasten. It does dawn on Lucy that she will have to admit to the mother that Flynn did not go to school. Notes will have to be written. Unexcused Absence updated in the master-file to Excused. 'That's fine' she pictures the mother saying. Because Lucy will employ strategy, tell her this first thing while she's still hugging the kid, over-hugging him, displaying the display of I-missed-you-so-so-big-and-much that is learned from anywhere but actuality. Come on, Lucy! - cynical cynical. She sighs. Coughs as she waits for an inexplicably long line of cars to pass. No, the mother will miss him. You'll give your update, Lucy, that will be that. Or what? You're going to volunteer for every day homework duty? Roomed and boarded for playing school-mistress, home-tutor? 'Do you think my mom's actually just been arrested?' Flynn asks, blinking Lucy to attention. 'We can't put it past her, Flynnstone, I'll tell you that much.'

There is a problem - one of those that is not explained to her while the sales-associate types and says meaningless half-phrases aloud - with her retaining her phone number when they do the upgrade. 'I have no attachment to the number - you can't just fix the phone I have?' The associate manages to extend the three syllables of 'Not really' across easily twenty seconds while tack tack tack tack tack poking with deliberate intensity the same key on the keyboard, three second intervals between each jab. Flynn needs to use the bathroom, the sales-associate directing them to the restaurant next door. There, Lucy buys a bag of potato chips - a requirement to get the kid allowed into the toilet. 'You can keep the chips' she tells the cashier when Flynn rejoins and the cashier holds them up, heroically reminding her of the purchase. 'I'm not allowed to.' 'Well, I'm just going to throw them away, man.' 'You can do that but I can't keep them.' 'Just throw them away, then.' 'You'll have to. I'm not allowed.' 'Eat them then, man - is this even happening?' Lucy wheels stage-comedy to the child 'Flynn: is this actually happening, right now?' Flynn shrugs but smiles as he watches Lucy ping and the clerk pong for another five minutes before Lucy finally tells him 'Kiddo, you better eat the chips after all this existential angst.' 'I will' he says, chuckling.

Having all of the features and certain methods of care for this ghastly new phone of hers explained - no, she didn't get to keep her number but all of her contacts and old text-messages have been preserved, brought over, so there's that at least - Lucy notices a display of pay-by-the-minute phones. She adds one to her purchase, the associate not shying from showing how perplexed this makes him but tendering the transaction and giving her a 'There's a Protection Plan' about that phone, as well. 'Telephones were our first mistake' she tells Flynn as they exit. 'Until then we'd done pretty much everything right.' 'People, you mean?' That's what she'd meant. And she lays a rap on the child about how even the slavery that built the pyramids could be kind of excused because 'It had never been done before so how could they know for certain how awful it was?' 'And we did get some pyramids' the child appendixes, Lucy wishing she'd said that and threatening to drop him off at school there and then if he doesn't mind his place as subordinate. 'Maybe I should be in charge, today' the child suggests, mentioning how Lucy looks like she might be hallucinating. 'How could you tell something like that?' 'Well, you are talking to me. And I'm not even here.'

Lunch is a calzone at a gas station eatery. Lucy is not one-hundred percent on board with this but the child says he ate there once with a friend and it was his favorite food in the world. 'You shouldn't spend your whole childhood lying to adults, skin-Flynnt. Because it's all you'll do when you grow up so now is really your only chance to be honest with one of us.' The child just blows on his calzone - which he eats with plastic cutlery - over and over and over, this habit semi-off-putting to Lucy in her admittedly not wide-awake state. She looks there at a woman finickying over the salad bar, removing some croutons into the waste bin, wiping her nose with the side of her thumb, the side of her thumb on the left-side shoulder of her light radish-red coat. Her own calzone tastes more like overdone turkey than sausage and the bread has an under-taste of garlic. 'Sometimes I think I'm not a very good poet' she tells the child and feels she looks like a purple-with-white-lettered, mostly-deflated balloon, still on a decorative string and still taped to a wall where there once had been a party. Or maybe she didn't say it. The child is chewing, looking at her, but not saying anything in response.

'But why would your mother want an umbrella?' Lucy asks when the child does not relent that this turquoise umbrella is the Welcome Home gift he would like to get for her. Point of fact: that he would like Lucy to get for him to give to her, all money out of Lucy's own pocket. 'I just have this feeling she likes umbrellas more than she ever lets on to anybody. She'll appreciate it.' Jesus, is this what an umbrella costs? Why? Do you have something else to spend your money on, Lucy? This was all your idea, after all. She hands the umbrella back to him without further comment, tilting her head that he should follow. Yeah, she wishes he'd interpreted that head-tilt as 'Put it back, find something else' but what does she really care? Umbrella. That's sweet, she guesses. 'Aren't you getting her anything?' the child wonders at her while they walk from the store they just left across to a smaller *Hernando's Grocery* - one Lucy didn't even know existed before they'd pulled into this shopping plaza. The child selects a cake shaped like a four-leaf clover and asks to have *Go get em' tiger!!!* frostinged on to it - insisting on 'three exclamation points, please' to the woman behind the bakery counter. 'Trust me' he explains with a bit of exasperation though Lucy made not a squeak of objection 'it's an inside joke, she'll get it.'

They agree between them that the mother wouldn't want them to have cleaned the house. 'It'd make her feel terrible, thinking of us doing that. She's lived here, she gets the idea.' Lucy lets the child play five-dollars'-worth of *Galaga* at a quarter-per-game in a drugstore she remembered having seen the arcade console in the entrance area of while she sends texts messages off to the mother, Layla, Katrin, a few other people, informing them of her new phone. Why don't you have Ariel's number, Lucy? She doesn't dwell on this. She watches the child whap whap whap the joystick stab stab stab the *Fire* button though the ship in the game can only shoot so many shots at-a-go, regardless. There is an elderly cashier, a woman, the sags under the eyes that exact sour stain of purple only old skin can get, some pigment indicative of at least one failing organ and general malnutrition. *She's the stance of a scrotum / her skin unalabastered / she's worth one coin / but not worth another.* Lucy text-messages this to herself. When the text arrives she opens and reads *She's the stance of a scrotum / her skin unalabastered / she's worth one coin / but not worth another.* The child glances over at her and smiles, tells her 'I'm winning, maybe.' She points her fingers at him - bang bang - he smiles again and tucks back in to it.

What do we think Flynn would have learned in school today? The child: 'About log cabins. Why they weren't such a good idea but some people still won't admit it.' Lucy: 'About Neptune - but nothing very interesting because it's just Neptune.' The child: 'We'd have just read a book about treasure hunters but they never would have found the treasure. Most kids would think that was sad but I'd have already stopped paying attention.' Lucy: 'Duck calls, but out-of-date ones.' The child: 'Things about the town where the teacher grew up because she'd be in one of those moods. She'd also pass out candy for no real reason from that big jar she has in her fat bottom desk drawer.' Lucy: 'That's exactly what I was going to say! Don't cheat, man!' The child: 'That octopuses hate the fact that they're octopuses.' Lucy: 'That sea urchins have never liked being called *sea urchins* - we've always known this but do it anyway because we, frankly, just don't like sea urchins and will do anything to give them a bad time.' The child: 'That one and one is two, yes, but that two, really, isn't all that impressive a thing to add up to.'

They return to the house talking about ghosts. Lucy carries in everything but the umbrella which the child twirls around and thrusts the tip of into the bushes like a musketeer. How is it going to go, now? Lucy? Lucy? She puts the cake in the refrigerator, no interest in thinking about that. How's what going to go? This was a favor. It got Lucy out of a month's rent. Yes. But just in a technical sense: how will your days go now? You can't stay hidden in your room, it'll be obvious. You don't want to invite yourself along on into the daily life because things can go from 'Thank you so much, I so appreciate your having done this' to 'You are the creeper who lives upstairs and is talked to only in increasingly I'm-humoring-you-because-of-a-favor-I-regret-asking' double triple quadruple quick. So Lucy concludes thus: her days will just go the same as they did before and they did before that and before that. How did they go before that? The child is practicing the piano and Lucy sits in a chair at the kitchen table and looks at her knees in these pants. They are knees. In pants. What are you looking at them for? The child is practicing trills. Lucy once practiced trills. So did a lot of people. And everyone has knees. Better knees than yours, Lucy.

THIS EVENING WAS LIKE LOWERCASE night - clouds had come on thick and burly so it was darker than it seemed it should be yet the grey was not brackish enough to seem nocturnal and there was the bustle to the neighborhood of kitchen lights on, cars pulling in, bringing home from work those who'd left too late to avoid traffic, the fields were still spotted with the organized play of some kids, the random wild laughs of others. Well described, Lucy, top marks. And now lights her cigarette, having just hupped from the kitchen and the consolidated bathroom trash up over the ridge of the dumpster. Five dead bumblebees on the ground, here. A suspicious tipped over can of grape soda. 'The game is afoot' she whispers, but then honestly wonders if the dead bees are a cause for concern. They are close in together. Had they died like that? Odd. But worse: did they not die like that but some one of the neighbors arranged the bodies all neatly, as we find them now? But: not so neatly as to seem a wholly unnatural lumping. Scan of the house fronts. She's never liked the look of the woman she's seen leaving that house, getting into that car. Decides there and then: this is the guilty party. Kicks the soda can and gets the distinct feeling she's being watched.

Lucy announces to the child that the mother is on the road back from the airport, starts to say, since it's late, how she's not sure about eating the cake tonight but before she even starts in on that it occurs to her: This, now, is nothing to do with me. The child is on its tummy on the living-room carpet drawing a comic-book about a character that is a thinly veiled version of the hero from the book series the mother reads to him, he reads to himself, Lucy had read this past week. Ah, photograph the two of these specimen, now: Flynn, exuberant youthful plagiarist in love pure and wide-flung - Lucy, the past-expiration model who'll do something-like-anything for a buck. Stands over him a moment, hoping he'll be annoyed. When he isn't she kind of is, moves to the kitchen and finishes getting dishes in the washer. Her phone vibrates. She glances. No number she recognizes, no name programmed to it. Vibrates. Lucy sighs. Vibrates. Stops. Pause. Vibrates. Lucy picks up to hear what was the message. Apparently someone else once had this number. They were being summoned by pre-recordings about debts that they owed.

The table is the neat little display, an hour-and-a-half already waiting. Cake. Umbrella. Gift box - interior: gift certificate for massage - from Lucy. Letter with illustration from the child. Envelope with poem from Lucy. Which poem is this, now? Hold on - which poem? Lucy had been writing it kind of awhile. For the mother? Eh, not really, she's told herself. That would be weird, right? 'Not for you' she's rehearsed explaining, emphasis *For* 'just a poem I've been able to write since I've been here, I figured Flynn wrote the letter so I should give something personal, too.' Yes, she knows that would be even weirder to say. Really: 'It's just a poem, no reason or anything, I just do that.' Good God! She calls up the stairs to the child to get out of the bath, to get ready because the mother should be there any minute. The child calls from the living-room 'I'm in here.' And he was. And the television was going, too. And she'd brought him a half-sandwich just five minutes ago. 'Did you take a bath?' she asks, the child turning off the television, hair wet, combed, pajamas tight to him as wrapped licorice, standing to reply 'I could really tell you anything right now and you'd have no idea, would you?'

The mother looks exactly as though she had been on an airplane, delayed, and had had a day she'd not planned for and enjoyed Zero moment of. Brave faced, though, she yip-yips like a lap-dog for the child and gives Lucy a beleaguered 'You don't have to do that' when Lucy immediately started carrying her bags up the stairs. 'It's fine. Hey - Flynn planned you a party.' 'A party?' the mother fake oh-my-goshes and proceeds to the kitchen as Lucy climbs the stairs. She hears, below her now, an uproarious kabang of laughter and a bunch of fake smooches - what the devil can that all mean? Suitcases lain of the bed, Lucy's eyes fasten shut, childhood diary-lock tight, the count of arbitrary seven because ten seemed too long halfway through. 'Do you have other bags?' 'Lucy, you don't need to get my bags - thank you for this.' Indication of table - cake, gifts, et cetera. 'That was all Flynn, I even tried to stop him.' 'Are you having cake?'

The mother looks like a corpse who woke up, stared confusedly, was briefly glad to be alive but then remembered how fucking tired it was. 'I will. Let me just get your things though - are they in the trunk?'

It isn't odd but Lucy is convinced that it is odd how she simply does not know what to do with herself right this minute. She cuts another piece of cake - or kind of forks off an oversized bite which she eats in a suck-gobble, cockroach, afraid of being caught - but that's the end of her inventive streak. Are you waiting for the mother? Why? Say you need to go! Jesus, that's your solution, right there! You've not only done your bit but you had not anticipated losing this entire day, as well - the child already narrated the day's events so the mother knows you've not had a moment to yourself - so it isn't as though she can be miffed. Miffed? Well Lucy, you should give her the recap of things and all, right? Then what were all those update calls for? What is the hold-up? If you want to go somewhere, just go! What is compelling you to loiter in a kitchen, sneaking bites of cake? You'll wind up making the mother feel awkward, let's not forget to pile that on! What do you think? Is she supposed to hang out with you? After this extra delay she hadn't counted on and her obviously frazzled state? Though: you should at least wait to tell her you're going. Though: why the fuck should you think you ought to do that? Though: Lucy has nowhere to go, so no hurry. Though: nor does she ever - that isn't the point.

'You didn't have to clean up, my friend, you are off duty' the mother bleary-eyedly yawned, getting herself a cup from the cupboard, setting it down, seeming to forget what she wanted it for or that she had taken it out, at all. Lucy it's-not-a-bothered, told the mother how tired the mother looked and how Lucy could deeply empathize about having travel days go bad. Reality: Lucy had never had travel days go bad. Still: she felt she could could imagine it - tired, crabby, that kind of thing, not as unique as it probably felt to whoever was suffering. Empathy. The definition of empathy: knowing it wasn't as bad as the suffering party was claiming but pretending it was to seem politic. 'You should get to sleep - why are you down here?' The mother had not changed clothes even, was staring at Lucy from some distance of centuries, finally blinked but only just to say 'Mmn? Sorry - what?' 'Go to sleep.' 'Flynn just needs a drink. I fell asleep on his floor, he woke me to ask for one.' The mother laughed, Lucy my-goodness-meed with a head shake, brow furrowed. Empathy. Still, the mother seemed confused. Lucy indicated the cup. 'Right' the mother said, replacing that cup and getting out a plastic one, filling this at the tap.

Another cigarette. Finished. But then just one more. Aren't you tired, too, Lucy? 'Maybe' she mutters with smoke for whatever reason not showing up in the dark. The mother had taken the gift box, envelope, umbrella upstairs after pinning the child's drawing-picture with a magnet to the fridge. That was something. The mother had said 'Thank you so much for this.' Dubious. Arms laden, cup of water also, eyes only as wide as cherry seeds, there was no certainty to what that statement referred. Likely: she'd been referring to the gift card. Or to Lucy having watched the child. Maybe the envelope too was lumped into the Thanks but it hadn't been yet opened. So: anyway. Anyway. It was a fine night - the fragrance of ozone, talcum, sopping leaves, and chill. Lucy's shoulders reminded her that they were on bad terms with the world and only had her to take it out on. And now she had an odd cramp in her wrist and her wrist also went clik-clik every time it moved half-a-twist. The door slid open behind her and she startled. 'That was the most beautiful thing I've ever read or even heard of. But I'm also tired so let me read it again tomorrow, okay?' The mother took Lucy's cigarette, gave it one drag, meeked 'Goodnight' - pronounced with an apostrophe for the *OOD*, no *GH*, and an *E* at the end - put the cigarette back to Lucy's mouth and drifted back inside. Or maybe that happened. It seemed that just happened. That probably is what just now happened.

Captain Piccard was aggressively quoting Shakespeare at *Q* when Lucy's phone vibrated. Obviously she ignored the phone. Obviously. The phone vibrated again just before the commercial, reminding her about it. Two texts from Katrin imploring the company of her voice - her company, proper, if possible - with a promise of 'No funny business' if Lucy responded and a threat of 'Burning your soul till it cinders to rot' if she didn't. *Burn till it cinders to rot* is good. Lucy should have thought of that! *What do you want?* she texted back. A minute later: *Why are you texting? Don't you speak anymore? I thought you had a new phone.* Lucy - to be her sensuously, bratty self - texted back the elaborate *LUCY: (sighing to self) My God, my God, this is a person I know (scoffs) Bitch! (mumble) Nothing and nowhere without me!* but all this got from Katrin was the message *How droll* and then *Fucking come to where I am!!!* 'But the crew are about to be hurtled across the galaxy to encounter the Borg for the first time!' Lucy wanted to explain. Would Katrin understand that? Lucy genuinely searched herself for an honest opinion on her friend, in the end just texting back *Fine. Where?*

She ate word *'Em*. Blue curly frosting. She stared at the word *Get* but let it survive. Was it only ten-thirty? Why did it seem a-hundred-and-twelve years later than that? Time left still to dawdle Lucy, since dawdling is your style. 'Dawdling is my style' Lucy said mostly aloud - just to show how well she could dawdle. 'This is meta-dawdling' she explained 'this is postmodern dawdling, the irony of hyperconsciousness in the character of Lucy Jinx explaining the meta-irony of Lucy Jinx's non-symbolic dawdling - the Act of Explanation itself a symbol for Symbolism.' She bowed then made a flippant hand gesture and sing-songed 'Ta-da!' Well! This is where the hands on her clock have come to, it seems. Is this back to normal, my girl? Say that it were: returning to normalcy will always carry with it disquiet but that will even out. Equilibrium. Severed hands in formaldehyde. Stolen paintings waiting centuries to find. Lucy? What? You still haven't left the kitchen. And you have that air of waiting around as though for someone else who said they were coming along or for a call to be patched through. Was it only ten-thirty-three? Why did it seem a languid adolescence later than that? She ate the word *Tiger* and three exclamation points. Blue curly frosting. She stared at the word *Get* but let it survive.

   The feeling was that of irresponsibility. Ridiculous. The mother was home, now. The child was sleeping. But the mother was dead tired - a fire wouldn't wake her! What would Socrates say Lucy should do here? What say the Chorus of the good people of Thebes? The sad grimace of realizing this was not so intricate a situation that Lucy was needed. It is regular life. An exhausted mother. A sleeping child. A night passes. The mother wakes short-tempered, the child maybe oversleeps. Or? The mother wakes fine because a full night's sleep had been had, sweetly Good-mornings the child who is downstairs before her - cartoons, chocolate milk, under-toasted bread with ugly brown spread over it. Still. Still. The car is on. The radio is quiet as though an inner monologue anxious not to wake anyone. The house is so dark - Lucy hadn't even left the porch light on for her return. The windows were coffins. *Coffinous. Coffinous. The windows were coffinous.* She rattle-tattles her fingers on steering wheel, sniffles a bit. 'The windows were coffinous, the brick's thin old lips all upturned.' Mmn. 'Maybe not the second bit' she says, car tip-toeing reverse. 'But the windows were coffinous. I will try to remember that.'


THE GIRL WHO HAD SERVED Lucy her drink just the moment before came back over to her and inquired shyly 'I'm sorry - your name isn't Emily, is it?' Red hair worn short. Glasses. Lines at the side of mouth from never wearing makeup. There would be a tattoo on this girl, somewhere. 'No. I'm not. I'm Lucy.' The girl apologized, could swear that someone looked just like Lucy, apologized again. 'No need for apologies. This Emily sounds lucky, whoever she is. What? Looks like me and is being looked for by you? Not bad.' The girl laughed, which was part of her job, but that there was a scratch less affectation than there could have been laced the moment in a kind of fragrance Lucy hoped the girl would remark, as well. Even if just internally, a quiver. 'Where's your tattoo?' 'I'm sorry?' the girl tilted head - the good way, genuinely pleased to hear a question worded just so. 'You do have a tattoo, yes? You have that air.' 'I have several. But the only one I'll tell you the whereabouts of is the one on my left hip.' 'Then that's the only one I'll imagine.' Jesus, where is Katrin? 'This hardly seems the night to be left to my own recognizance' thinks Lucy. 'Where's your tattoo?' the girl asks - finishing the second-in-a-row of those laughs. 'I'm my tattoo' Lucy answers. It doesn't much make sense but how Lucy said it made that not so much matter. And where in Hell was Katrin, anyway?

Abundant beg-pardons and a stuttering narrative of miscellaneous delays later, Katrin and Lucy find themselves securely situated in a corner booth. 'Are you drunk?' Katrin asks, opening her menu. This is whispered, the quiet of discussing an admired naughtiness. 'I just drank a little to work up my nerve to make that young lady unsettled' Lucy explains and Katrin laughs - cranes neck to see which one Lucy means - then gives a sophomoric gesture of approval. 'Well, I'm not drinking tonight but you carry on' Katrin says, Lucy waving dismissive, motion loose at wrist like clearing a cobweb. Katrin hopes Lucy will not remove her from the *Cool-Kids Club* roster but admits she did ask for her job back and was starting again the following week. Lucy knows this drill: no reason to give any opinion but that Katrin had done the perfectly awesome thing. What about Lucy's previous, repeatedly-stated contrary stance? Won't matter, won't matter. 'Did they give you a raise, at least?' Lucy asks 'in appreciation of your well-played brinksmanship?' Apparently they had given Katrin a raise just before she'd quit so since she had never been paid at that rate even once yes it was rather like they had.

Where this all came from had to be somewhere: Katrin asking Lucy if Lucy wouldn't like to stay with her awhile, rent free. But since Lucy can see no angle - benevolent or mal - she is on guard. 'It can't be comfortable renting that room and working that job. What does that job pay?' Did you hear how Katrin said that? How she said *That job*? 'It pays enough for the room.' Come to think of it: what sort of life does Ariel live? Is *Hernando's Highlights* her only income like it is Lucy's? 'It pays fine. And I'm allowed to work it right up until the day I die - I asked - so it's a pretty comfortable gig.' Katrin paused while their food was placed in front of them and while she asked a few additional things of the waiter then looked at Lucy and said 'Well, you can keep the job. But you don't have to. You can stay with me for as long as you like. Fuck - forever, if it so pleases you.' 'I think this is how horror films sometimes start, Katrin. I just want to point that out.' The waiter again, Katrin paused until she softly thanked him and he waitered off. 'Are you writing?' What's going on? What's going on? 'I am.' 'Yeah?' 'I've been writing great.' Katrin had a strange expression at hearing this - or so it struck Lucy - a kind of suppression of a smile mingled with a tensing to deliver bad news. They talked around the same subject for a few minutes then Lucy had to use the toilet.

There is something sinister happening here. Not traditionally sinister. Not underhanded. Some pieces have been moving that have something to do with

Lucy but Lucy does not know which pieces or what they have to do with her. Her eyes feel like swamps now and there is a sour she recognizes in the most buried of her blood - what does she recognize this feeling from? Or when does she recognize it from? What is coming? And can she do anything to pivot? Or is the world about to reveal she has made missteps and so things have been arranged to steal volition out from under her? In the immediate: How to get through this evening with Katrin? Lucy, didn't you feel you shouldn't have come out? Hadn't you dawdled? Hadn't you had grim premonition? Oh - you'd thought that to do with something else! There is the miscalculation - perhaps one of several! You need to understand that you are always more right than you know. Sensitive. Your sensitivity is there to blister you with warnings, Lucy. You may be nothing but scar tissue by now but even you can feel these boils that grow. You must stop ignoring yourself! But for the immediate: how to get through this evening with Katrin?

'Did you ever really quit that job?' Lucy extra point-blanks, Katrin's expression too awkward that her answer, so quick, could be a feint. 'I did. It was a real quit, not brinksmanship.' But that isn't what Lucy was insinuating, specifically. 'I got the funniest feeling that you never did. Nothing weird - merely that you wanted to test having said you did, really role-play it to build steam. That didn't happen?' Katrin takes this all well, just shakes her head - still a bit awkward-mugged - and admits she could see why Lucy would think that. 'Why can you see why?' Lucy asks, Public-Radio interview voice. 'Because I'm like you, man. If I could see you doing it I know I could, too.' Not at all what Lucy expected to hear. But it relaxes her. No. More. It paints Katrin in a much more pleasant light. Lucy - do you agree with Katrin, you mean? About the two of you being simpatico? 'I've always thought of you as a sister I'd sometimes think about kissing' Lucy raises her glass with a wink. Katrin laughs into her forkful of pasta 'Step-sister or biological?' 'Whichever's the sexier - sometimes I can't decide.' Katrin laughs a lot, manages to swallow, and tells Lucy 'Sorry' and tells Lucy she's going to make her pee herself. They eat for five minutes in kind of a silence, kind of a Katrin-still-stifling-giggles - there's something funny to her beyond what Lucy had said.

But leaving the restaurant, at Lucy's car, Katrin finishes asking if Lucy feels confident to drive - 'Yes, I had two measly half-glasses of house wine! Or no more than four! Five at a stretch but no one is printing the facts!' - then broaches the offer to come live with her, again. 'Are you asking me to live with you?' Lucy takes all levity from her voice, ends right on the borderline of gravity, a second-job-interview sort of tone. 'Yes.' Shit. Not just *Yes* - what's that supposed to mean!? 'Just *yes*?' Lucy asks. 'Yes.' 'Yes, you are?' 'Yes, I am.' Is Lucy broken? She is getting no warning whistles off Katrin. But this is not the sort of offer that could ever be so offhand - not because Lucy says it can't be so but because of the subject matter of it. 'Do you think I'm not all right?' Katrin is bleeding in her apologetics - she hadn't meant a word of that! And it's none of her business about Lucy's job if that was stepping over the line. Wait. Does Katrin seem to want to kiss you, Lucy? No. She really doesn't? She really doesn't. Or anyway if she does she can forget about it because if that is the way someone looks when they want to kiss you, too bad. Focus, Lucy! 'What are we talking about, here?' Lucy asks, unable to get her last fleeting train of thought back. And Katrin is smiling now. What about that Katrin is smiling now, then? Lucy has no idea.

How did that whole song-and-dance end? Obvious stall tactic: Lucy relenting to seeming merrily open to the option, as though she had just needed to be sure Katrin hadn't thought she was some alms-beggar twerp. Which is to say: it ended the same way everything Lucy is involved with ends - Lucy having taken a step-and-a-half forward when she should have just put her hands in her pockets and still been looking for her shoes. Say Katrin was serious? It's obvious Katrin was serious, Lucy. Well: say Katrin was serious? Lucy could take a few months off work, at least. 'I'd never stay without paying, indefinitely' she told the empty car around her 'but if for a few months you'd float me and then we just do a roommate thing, maybe.' But why not take her up on it, fully? Had Lucy ever done anything to suggest to Katrin this was something she wanted, needed, or was tacitly trying to arrange? 'No, absolutely not!' she said as though she were Katrin saying it, easing a doubt of Lucy's with energetic hand shushing. Still as Katrin: 'You never said anything like that - I felt weird even asking because I knew it would seem so left-field.' Lucy nods. Stern-father faced, elementary school principle first-time-a-kid-is-sent-to-the-office lipped. 'Good. You should feel weird.' That was said as Lucy. Nod nod nod. Lucy nodding in her empty, chillful car.

Red hair cropped short. Glasses. Tattoo on hip. Lucy at the bar, sipping house wine which red-hair-cropped-short-glasses-tattoo-on-hip just finished pouring. 'So, you're back?' 'I live here now. I'm surprised they didn't tell you. I'll chastise them on your behalf.' That's a good smile. That's the sort. Easily identifiable. Understandable. Smile equals: you talk in a way I find funny, Lucy, because it is how other people never talk and everybody should. Smile equals: I read Norwegian literature too and get your exact rhythms, Lucy. Smile equals: you can say anything, Lucy, and it will go just like a book, so have at. 'What's the best compliment I could pay you?' 'The best I've ever had?' 'No - the one you most want to hear. I don't want to waste my time so thought I'd just ask.' The girl does the obligatory thing about Wouldn't it not be the same since Lucy'd just be repeating it? and about how she's curious as to how Lucy would compliment her, unprompted. 'I don't know you so don't know how to compliment you. And anyway: let's just try it my way. Let me ask: have you ever just told someone how you would like most to be complimented and had them tell you that very thing back, straight away?' The girl hesitates. Perfect just-like-in-a-book-and-I-am-obviously-going-to-do-this hesitates. 'No' she says 'I never tried that.' 'Well, try it now. Tell me.' Book pause. Book grin. Book 'Alright.'

Lucy in her missing-tooth car. Heater on now, radio. She is not yet wound down from the drinks enough to drive but is glad it is only one-thirty in the morning. 'But I'm not even going to work, tomorrow!' she blurts out harried to her thought-question 'Shouldn't you get some sleep before work, tomorrow?' That settled, she keeps looking at the restaurant front. If you drive away now - you are obviously going to - it is exactly the same as none of that ever having happened. Exactly the same. This is how the world is controlled - deadfalls and misdirection, snares and hoodwinks. This was a well-played checkmate against Fate that you've played here, Lucy Jinx, provided you can overcome the enticement you left in the game, that delirious pressure to let your opponent win, see what those dogs jaws would do to you, after all. Well, it's a countdown game now, either way. You're too civic and noia-pocked to drive until you're certain your blood has unproofed and the girl only works till the end of her shift, like she said. Countdown game? Bullshit, little Lucy. You rigged the game to keep the danger rhetorical, knowing it was moot since the get. Secret weapon? Your terror! You know she might walk out, see you waiting like you said you might be. Terror on this: could you bear her never having believed you really would? Terror how you could tell just from her gait but would have to sit there until she got to your door to confirm it.

Lucy orders food from a drive-thru, eats in the cracked pottery lot. What a ghoulish place Lucy has picked. Is that establishment actually called *Fake Nails! Fake Nails!* There is a sound out there like someone bouncing a rubber ball against the high part of a wall. A red ball like grade-school Gym class. Lucy starts her second burger - but it's a chicken sandwich and slathered in sauce! 'Hell with it' she laughs, pretending she's a gruff old police detective in a B-grade thriller about smashing a kiddie-porn ring. 'Don't matter what we eat, we just need fuel, partner. Keeps us alive. These girls, they don't care what we had for supper.' She gets a fit of the giggles, a tantrum of hee-yuk-yuks - coughs on the chicken and coughs on the drink which taste so indistinguishable she can't tell if this part of her order was also got wrong. 'Oh what do we do when midnight just doesn't show up' she poets in exaggerant tones not even sure is she mocking herself 'and in its place just comes gangly four thirty-five? Oh what do we do when there isn't a May to be mad in and when February gangrenes to July?'

Some dogs start barking. Lucy starts her third burger. This one is fine. All the world is her unbridled applause.

IN THE DARK, THE OBLONG heavy of her head was made worse. She felt like her hair was getting in the way. Or at least this is what she mumbled - in between reminding herself to keep quiet - while she meandered in the space just inside the room door, foot-flat-to-carpet scoots, half-inch, quarter-inch-at-a-time, for fear of striking her toe against something. As she got her shirt from over her head and her pants undone the fragrance - just call it *Odor*, Lucy, or next you'll be saying *Aroma!* - the odor of her seemed egregious, bubonic. What a state! How did it get this way? A pang of regret for having been on the road - Lucy had driven in this condition! 'It's a bad habit' she told the nothing then giggled then shushed herself then was quiet and as immobile as she could manage, ears cocked but unable to actually listen. Why can you hear the trapped air round-abouting warm-over-cold in the attic but can't hear the end of the hallway? This is all viciously unfair, Lucy firmly believes, now onto her bed, the uproar of the mattress depressing despite all her efforts to be light, soft like an old dollar bill. Oh God, Lucy. You've only realized with one leg free of your pants and the other unable to free that you only took off one of your shoes, downstairs. She stays like that. There. It would be a picture if she could see herself. Her nose, the air through it, that all sounds outside of her.

If only one word could be used to described Gregory luck so has it that word would be *Gregory* - the only word, sound, stout-froth-of-phlegm odious enough to express him. True true, Lucy could list out a great many nice things she has said about him - even thought about him in private - times and places past, she could attest to there being a good stack of poems written *To* him or *For* him in terms of *He* being *Hers*. Gah, ghastlier! *Her* being *His*! But how long ago was this? In many senses: a lifetime it's been since. In a truer sense: several. Why is Gregory on my mind? Lucy wonders but only wonders a moment, eyes dislodging from their backward funk up inside her, the pages of Gregory's letter visible in the gotten-used-to-now of the dark room as they do. 'Have I read that yet?' she drunks to herself, heartily raking hard claw of all four fingers of right hand over hip just inside waist of panty elastic. Wait - has she? 'What?' Read the letter. 'Letter?' Too late, anyway. She's rolled on her back. She's laying on her fist turned sideways, thumb at a bent up spike, lower back writhing on it in search of her exact ache. Or whyever she's doing that. Must be a making a racket. All *Letter* reminds her of is the letter *R* because that's what the word

seems like it's saying when she says it aloud. 'Letter. Letter R. Let. Te. R.' And
*R* is pronounced *Rar*. 'Let. Her. Rar.' Then things go fuzzy into drool-bib
syllable strings.

Take a moment to appreciate the scene: Lucy - terrified of waking the mother,
of letting her presence be known despite she has every right - under the light
sheet of the bed - comforter on the ground someplace, probably - with the letter
from Gregory, pages well out-of-ordered, kind of all over her now greasy nude
flesh, using her chintzy cellphone for light. The humidity of her innards
revolting through her apple-peel skin makes her feel as though her entire body
is and resembles an ache in an ear from digging at an itch down it just a little too
forcefully. Why not write back to him? 'Who? Gregory!?' Well, why in God's
name not, right? Right, Lucy? Not write to him to respond to whatever garbage
is written here - she can't read it, at the moment, her eyes have the same glaze
to them as kids' unwashed hands after sucking the drips of dripped popsicle have
- but just to tell him this is to stop. Or better - look there. Under his hare-lipped
signature with its snaggletoothed *Y* is an address, a phone number, ways to
contact him over the computer. Phone number. She starts to compose the
message there and then, tacking it into the number pad while the enclosure of
bed sheet concentrates the blue of the tiny screen and makes her eyes sting and
water. Wait - what are you doing? Discards the message - Delete! Verifies no
remnant of it is saved in any of the menus she can navigate. There's no chance it
could have sent - she'd not entered a single digit of even the area code. Erases
all messages. Ever. To be sure. Turns off the phone. Turns it on. Double checks.
To be sure.

Now Lucy has moved to the floor. By the closet. She is caretaking illogic.
Here: even while she may have been drifting a bit her telephone vibrated with a
text-message from Layla asking if she was alright. *I'm worried now* the message had
made plain. Beseeched Lucy to call. So Lucy to-floored, over-to-closeted. Her
thinking: Lucy does not want to be overheard talking and a closet is enclosed.
Overlooked: the closet is much nearer the hallway and, thus, the person who
could be awakened to overhear than up on the bed was. Counter: she would be
closed-off, voice contained, and would be facing with her back to the room
door, hence away from the party who could overhear - whereas on the bed she
would be elevated and facing toward door, toward hallway, toward the mother.
Counter to this counter: she could face the other way on the bed as well and be
away from the door. 'Anyway, I'm already in the closet' she says and then asks
if she had put her socks back on or had never taken them off. 'Anyway, I'm only
wearing socks, now' she explains. But is this all inebriation? Or is she this tired?
Or does she have a fever? Or are you pretending? Lucy, are you pretending?
Sometimes Lucy pretends without even knowing when she began. 'I'm not

Prince Hamlet' she yawns, prouder than an autumn leaf 'but sure as fuck was meant to be, bitches.'

The conversation opened with pleasantries and questions of why Lucy was whispering. 'What's going on? Jesus - is everything alright?' Layla had asked, visibly shaken though not there to be visible and Lucy had her eyes closed. Lucy explained she was fine. Mentioned she was in a closet, but in a lighthearted way. 'Are you drunk?' Layla seemed put-off by the fact she could tell Lucy was. Not full on put-off - a tad of worry was left to one side in case the drunkenness had some compelling this-is-why-I'm-drunk to it - but enough Lucy picked up on it and la-di-dahed an apology, using a mock-up of fancy-pants speak to do so. 'Did you get my message?' Shit. Wait. Layla is upset, Lucy. Has been this entire call. Upset by something a priori. Fuck Lucy, focus! Too late, Lucy has already answered in her same cavalier, fun-and-games posture 'I got your message, yes, yes I got it - but something was going on when I listened to it so I didn't quite listen to it and then I erased it when I tried to save it or play it back or whatever I did. So actually no I didn't, but only in the complex way that I technically did. Does that make sense?' Silence over the line. 'Really' Lucy said, shifting where she sat as though verifying she had been giving the God's honest account. Could Lucy call Layla tomorrow? Lucy could talk now, Lucy assured. Lucy could get it together - she proved it by doing a very clear-as-a-bell 'I'm sorry - see?' 'It's okay' Layla allowed - that doesn't bode well - 'it's okay' - worse on the repeat. 'Just can you call tomorrow? Or can I call you?'

She had turned the doorknob and would have gone through had it not mortally shocked her - slow motion, delayed - that the door had not been locked, this jolt enough to snap her to awareness of her physical state: still undressed, molting soggy skin in flakes thick as cicada remains, her footing no more assured than a blind-at-birth pony's. The nausea elbowed around as high as the hollow where her throat first swallows but even traversing the hall to the toilet in she and the child's shared bathroom was too risky. And say she made an unholy racket in there? Glugging and glutting and hucking herself out! Say she forgot to close the door right and was discovered in action, face down the over her expectorant muck in the sullied water? She must be ill. This must be actual illness - disease even. The condition of Lucy could not be on account only of those drinks! Is she as welter-weight as that, puny constitutioned, no more to her than to a flimsy schoolyard *I love you*? No point in thinking about it too long, she snatched one of her bulky coasts from a closet hanger, kind of laid it out like kid-play over the dull point of the mattress corner, bunched it up a bit and tried to vomit into its diagram-center as quietly, precisely, and minute-an-amountly as possible. Again. Again. Just from the old orange-peel sting of the scent of the bile and the cold of some string over her chin - a slop she didn't bother with batting at or wiping into her - she knew this would not look as good in the light as it did in the dark, in the tense of allowing a fourth upchuck with her face not an inch from the dead fish skin, snot pool of it she has just assured herself doesn't look bad, hardly even noticeable.

None of this is real. These are slivers of the dream Lucy has for awhile. One sliver was her in a classroom, looking through a desk for a headache tablet and finding a turtle that no one had fed for two years. God, its face! So dry she could feel the sharp of being inside of it. Its mouth wouldn't open when she offered some of the bread she chewed mushy, first. Another sliver was her out-of-doors but no place distinct - at once a field and a crosswalk, a bench near a building and the gravel of a hill near a lake. Lucy dragged her toe until the toenail got tattered and she started to limp and regret it all violently. This is the sort of dream she might wake from with a throat drained of all wet, clay lizard scales the long of it, at the bottom a ball bearing with something rattling inside - but this time she did not wake. And another sliver was just her on the floor certain she was about to stand and her on the floor certain she was about to stand and her on the floor certain she was about to stand after awhile aware of the fake of it all, fatigued from waiting it out, just letting it run its course.

The only thing to do about the coat was to painstakingly fold it around itself tight, tying the sleeves in at least some semblance of a knot, and then to wrap two other coats and a large sweater around this and then the light bedsheet around that - this also tied, better than had been the first jacket's sleeves - the fabric tumor in its entirety left in the closet under all of the rest of her loose thrown in laundry. That all actually wasn't so hard to do. *Pride of a job well done* that's the caption under photo of ugly-in-the-dark naked Lucy-in-socks, right here. And are you better now, Lucy? Enough you are on your shipwrecked nude belly on bed top, skin of your back over you, seaweed in piles. And you're using the phone's light to read Gregory's letter? No. Just looking at it. Focusing on the ink of one handwritten word at-a-time - plink plonk plink plonk plink plonk, no order to which ones your eyes slathers to. *Around. The. Hollyhock. Do. They're. Pencilcase. Kindness. Olivia. Prattle. Me. Yard.* What is the meaning of this? She gives up on it. 'To Hell with this. Layla, I'm gonna gut you for this when I promise to remember to call you tomorrow! I hope you're sad about something! I hope you called for camaraderie so I can tell you *Stuff it!* You deserve it! Slop-bucket friend! Pox pox pox!' You're getting loud, Lucy. There is an ache in your eye, acorn tight. Is this still the same night as those other things that happened tonight?

Lucy has slid her side to the cool of the room wall but something is poking her in a rib and eventually she has to do something about this though she is certain she was almost asleep. A squashed cigarette box? 'Dear Christ, what else can go wrong?' she groans, cramps up at giggling at the inanity and disattached quality of this anguished call-out. Two cigarettes left. And a slip of paper. Quite distinct slip of paper. Torn. The name *Calvin* and a telephone number. Blink. Cough - it hurt to cough, licorice hurt - cough. 'Oh I know who Calvin is' she says, numb snapping her fingers thub thub 'yes, yes I know who Calvin is. Such a charming young lad, yes yes.' How long has this pack of cigarettes been in the bed? 'Creased all in between mattress and wall, good little seedling' she says, eyes rolling with mop wringer sounds - she would have passed out if not for another sour ache of cough, the cramp now in razor cuts to the very top of her shoulder where there should not even be anything that could cramp. She does not seem to have a fever when she tests. Or else she's asleep already. Her hand feels both on and beneath her forehead as though the semi-superimposed quality of her unfocused vision had become the truth of her physicality, at last.

*Do not write to me. Do not bother Layla again. Understand: I want nothing to do with you. Understand.* She has proofread this as best she can for the however-many-times-she-has-managed-to time. The good job is that her swallowing feels more appropriate now and the slithering down in her gut has eased off into a steamy, stove sizzle gurgle. Proofreads a last time and meticulously verifies she is using the pay-as-you-go phone - the last thing she needs is for Gregory to get her proper number, track her some clever modern way. One cannot fathom the will it took Lucy to overcome the paranoia that the temporary number of this little phone would allow Gregory to find the exact store she'd purchased it from and from there, via a few charming questions to folks who'd no reason to care, find her in this very bedroom. Message look good? But how does she have Gregory's number if the letter is all over the floor? Her eyes pad around down at her dark-room colored body. Paper scrap. *Calvin.* She confirms this is the number she nearly sent to. Undoes all that hard work and she's not doing it again! The ceiling is above her full of faces and goats seen in profile - shadow patterns, light-speck patterns, somehow the darkness has gotten almost bright and very nuanced. She notices the number is still entered, no message beneath it, so chuckles, types the word *S'up* types a question-mark and hits Send. Almost immediately - what could it have been? two minutes? - the phone does a beep and she is startled. A reply message? Jesus. *Nothing. Just kind of up. What are you doing?* She stares and knows she is comfy-cozy now, sweaty in a spitball on her bucknaked self, safe from all, home, and sleep coming. *Do you even know who this is?* she types. Not half-minute later: *This is Priscilla, yeah?* Sleep.

IT IS THE AS-ALWAYS SUDDEN blink awake after too much drink for Lucy, all of her senses Dostoevskianly nuanced. Hark that: way way out there is the chish-hshish! of the trash-truck pulling to a halt - meaning soon will come the onslaught of the dumpster tip. The very good news though is that if Lucy can hear this and if the room is as chill as it is - Lucy's wax-pilled nudity a harassed, goose-fleshed taut - it means she had the good sense to have opened the window sometime in all of the previous few hours' commotion. And there: that is the mouse titter of - from the other side of the top floor through several closed doors - the mother turning the tap shut on her shower. That? That is the child waking in the room next to Lucy's. Never mind, never mind - he would not have heard anything in the night, the beast sleeps like a cartoon hippo and besides Lucy has now sober-reflective doubts about whether she was as all over the place as it might have seemed. In fact, she proclaims inwardly that none of the previous night even happened. All evidences to the contrary are to be dealt with crooked district-attorney style, Lucy's own fragments of memory hearsay, inadmissible. Hear that? The kid going swish footed down the stairs. And that? The mother opens her bathroom door, shutting off overhead fan. This is all in order. Lucy is solid, she's solid.

Still, she keeps quiet, wants to be no more remarked than a spare button in a cup full of coins. The mother is incredibly bright and go-getting down there considering how bleak she'd returned from her travels. Good for her, good for her. The mother seems to be almost singing her conversation with the child. No doubt, it occurs to Lucy - and she tights even further where she lays now bundled under two blankets and in shirt and sweatpants - the child is relating several of he and Lucy's little adventures from the past week. Well, that's only fair, right? And the mother is humoring. Rather that than give the kid the scoop on what's up with his dad. It strikes Lucy, here: does the child know that's where the mother went? Noia: Did you say something about it to the child, Lucy? Noia: is the mother worried you did, hence being so sprightly and devil-may-care of it this morning? Lucy resolves never to leave the room again and can well imagine the turn-of-the-century Scandinavian novella that relates her saga in so attempting to keep that resolve. Noia: Why is it so quiet down there, now? And which of them is coming up the stairs? 'I still can't find it' shouts the child in the next room. 'Flynn!' the mother yell-hushes back and Lucy wonders if the mother is now cursing under her breath at the thought of the child's callousness waking her.

Once she hears the downstairs door close Lucy does her best to sit up and assess the state of herself. There is headache. There is eye-ache. There is a soreness from the underside of her left ear down her jaw into her collar-bone. Why did she ever sit up? She flops back, sudden, a discarded wet washcloth before hands move to cover a sneeze. And despite her best efforts a reasonably coherent narrative of her night forms. Meh. None so bad as she'd been bracing against - is any of that so terrible? She has to look under the closet laundry to believe she is remembering that madcap situation correctly - physical evidence supports things though she is certainly not about to peek inside. Gathers up Gregory's letter again, decreeing it to be got rid of in as once-and-for-all a manner she can manage. On the phone she is somewhat appalled to find she both wrote seven different, misspelling-laden, apology texts to Layla - *Go to sleep Lucy, it's fine, just I was worried and will talk tomorrow* was the only response, that to the third text - and had a far more lengthy and - to put the matter mildly - 'intricate' little text chat with Calvin than she has even the shoddiest recollection of. She is relieved when she finds she must have proofread, though. Thoroughly. Her smut is syntactically sound which makes it the smuttier. However: appalled at the number of winky smiles and occurrences of the expression *haha* she discovers, caulk between most sentences, first word of any of her replies to his salvos. Last message? Calvin to her. *Ok. See you then.* Lucy, Lucy. She sighs a boat capsized.

Then froze. Fuck. Sharp and hot breathed while getting back into the bed as weed-quiet as she can. The front door has opened, closed. The mother is walking up the stairs. Lucy goes full illusion and will not uncommit to it no matter what: she is asleep - eyes closed, deep, somewhat uneven breathing, lolls eyes behind lids in approximation of *REM*, here and there a twitch of foot or leg, this all a game she's known since forever - a crackerjack fake sleeper, that's Lucy Jinx for ya! The mother is just standing on the other side of the door, listening. But this is absurd! Oh goddamn it all, what could it mean? It isn't as though the mother can open the door even if Lucy had forgotten to lock it. But there! Did you hear, Lucy - she did try the handle! Which could have perfectly harmless even understandable reason for having happened - but it happened even if there could be no good reason. Locked. The door is locked. Lucy has moved blanket more over her, shoulders up almost down her ear canals. 'Lucy?' the mother genltys. But Lucy is asleep. She's nothing but a neuron of her lighting up in an image not really seen, a synapse going zap to dream whatever it dreams. One two three four gentle taps on the door. Lucy is actually upset now though some part of her knows she isn't, just terrified. 'Lucy?' a little bit louder, obviously a voice certain its heard some manner of movement. But Lucy is asleep. She almost wants to open the door to prove it. The pressure to lose the game on purpose rising. She's the last few old crumbs in the space between kitchen tile and cabinet base.

Unbecoming of a grown woman? Not at all, not at all. Lucy is sitting up now but still resolute in her muteness and stealth. It's the mother who has shown impropriety and ill breeding! Why is she home? Obviously she's just missed a week of work so Lucy really thinks she should be getting along, now - a joke's a joke but then a joke has to end. Why is she down there? For you, Lucy - waiting for you to wake up. 'Well, how long are you going to do that for!?' Lucy cannot help vocalizing, not a whisper but scarcely audible even to her, just a cotton swathed sound of breath in her ears. After awhile - Lucy has taken a seat in the desk chair and removed her shirt, the fabric of it had been making her itch due to the griminess of her flesh - there are sounds of distinct activity down there. The dishwasher is started. A closest opened, rummaged in, closed. And now - outside - a lawnmower cues up to lawn-mowing and Lucy cat-cowers in place, ears flat, whiskers flat, tail a coil the end of which gives a tense thump now-and-then. 'Lucy?' The mother is there again - used the noise as a cloak! Lucy's eyes can go no wider, her nostrils close no more, her mouth become any thinner a single pencil line. 'Lucy?' One two three four the little kindergarten best friend knocks. Then silence. Lawnmower. Dishwasher. Hush like upsidedown underwater. Clatter Smash Howling Clawing Mongrel Dogs of the silence of unheard standing still feet and turned ear and clenched jaw and closed eyes and hand waiting to one two three four a last time on the door's other side.

It is as unrelentingly anxious as this: okay, the mother is gone - okay, Lucy is out of her room - okay, it has been an hour but Lucy has not dared yet part the blinds even a tsk to verify that the mother's car is not still parked in front. Oh yes, make no mistake Lucy, the mother could just be out in the car, sitting. No, not because she is psychotic - no! and not even because she's trying to catch you out. Think about it, Lucy. Could she not have just left, found she was still worried - or whatever she was - and got lost in a long train of thought not even realizing how fixedly she is scanning constantly the windows for any sign of your motion? Sure - it could be! And without even going that far: she's there, blah blah, worried, lost in thought, not even looking at the windows but so exaggeratedly adrift in her thinking that without even knowing it the slight motion of parted blinds to fit the briefest flit of your looking eye cannot help but draw her attention. Come on - you think bugs on the ceiling imagine you'll be able to hear their little wings when they give them a shiver? But you always do hear it! It's like that, Lucy. Right now - this - this is like that. You're the bug and she's the you.

Enough is enough, though. Lucy figured she can at least act awake until she hears the front door - she even leaves her room door open to better hear down the stairs, concurring with herself that she'll have time to close it on hearing entrance below - it's not likely the mother will thunder in, come barreling upstairs full-tilt-boogie aha! I thought you said enough was enough, Lucy. Focus. She dials Layla, who comes on the line right away, friendly as a found coin. 'And what did they do with the drunken sailor? Feeling better?' Lucy says some charming things, still in a penitent tone, segues into relating the abysmal narrative of vomiting into her coat and the high-stakes-politics level cover-up that ensued. Layla reminds Lucy that this was not the first time that exact thing had happened. 'That's right!' Lucy blurts, happy for a moment then a bit crestfallen that she had not instinctively concocted that solution on the spot, in the thick of the crisis shown aptitude and the cooler head. 'Oh I'm sure it amounts to the same' Layla offers 'after all, you invented that procedure the first time, right?' 'I keep you around for the sagacity, Lay-Lady, yes I do. Oh and I also flirted with a barmaid and then sent messages a teenage boy that are lewd enough to make me even now blush and want to read them aloud to you while I do. So see? Let's not bottle me as glue yet, eh?' Layla dryly assents that, yes, Lucy has the world on a string, sighing in that way Lucy recognizes from about as far back as she has memory 'Lucy Lucy' pronounced in that way only someone who has said 'Lucy Lucy' ten zillion times to this exact Lucy knows how.

The reason Layla had left the deleted message: there was a particular stray cat who lingered around the premises where Layla worked - there were lots of strays there but this certain one was called *Delaware Bach*. Layla had no idea why it was called that but approved of the name. And like many others, Layla doted on the creature. *Delaware Bach* was, for an intact male outdoor, entirely domesticated, friendlier with humans than any housecat Layla had ever met, trusting and loving and beloved by all. It was always the talk from any of several co-workers that 'I'm taking *Delaware* home' and finally one day a woman called Henrietta did so, appropriate talk of getting the lover deloused and dewormed and de-everythinged proper. Not two days later, Layla overheard from in her cubicle two co-workers talking, the one telling the other she still could not believe that *Delaware Bach* was dead. Layla explained to Lucy how she had, on hearing this, been moving to speak over the cubicle divider that 'No no, Henrietta has taken *Delaware* home, that's all' when one of the two speakers said they had also gotten Henrietta's e-mail about what had happened. And Layla had felt herself begin to evaporate, she told Lucy, had felt herself somehow, irrevocably, become a little more nothing than she'd been the moment before. And Lucy, for her part, had been crying since she first heard Layla say *Delaware Bach* because Lucy could tell in some hidden tone lent the name already just exactly where this story of Layla's would all end.

Lucy was murder-violet, she was homicide-copper, slasher-kill-turquoise-gone-bronze. 'The neighbor poisoned the cat on purpose?' This was a point she had no language to comprehend, no part of her brain but that reserved for fiction would even allow this stuff in. 'That's what they said' Layla repeated the twentieth time, no sense of repeating, she and Lucy a wavelength identical, two things so lost as each other they might as well be the same. The garish hue to it, further, was that to everyone who knew the story at where Layla worked this outcome was somehow acceptable, timbre of natural, kind of said like 'Wow, what bad luck!' - as though a cat ought expect to be poisoned, surest thing you'd hope to hear. Even Henrietta - and this Layla said through tears singed with hatred rigor-mortised with hopelessness - said she 'had been a little worried about something like this' but didn't 'think it would happen the very first night, anyway.' Lucy felt such fangs jam shut all her veins, felt pleading in the slick inside of her skull-front to stop everything, to dead the whole world, to kill the dead world further - there wasn't Hell enough for any of this and she even hated Layla for telling her such sickness as she knew Layla hated her for being ears to spill the venomous unction down because in these moments there was nothing but to hate and comfort was useless and only made anything beautiful uglier uglier uglier still.

And now, a bit later, this is supposed to still be Lucy in this room? This is supposed to still be Lucy? There, with her face and her drunk-shakes and her eyes and something she may once have wanted? Yes. This is supposed to be the same human being in the same life, the same circumstances, and all of the commonalities of her are still to be there and common? And look, look outside: say the wall of the room weren't there and she could see as far as she forced herself able - well, all of that was supposed to still be all of that in its every texture and allowance *in its every cheapskate and charlatan in its every chortle and every pauper-paw in its every namesake and its every vestibule in its every look look look and its every empty carton and kid not reading a book and jar overturned and sour unburied* and Lucy is supposed to be leaking these words on this page in this hideous rush of still being Lucy while she's certainly not, as though pen and as though notebook? And poor Lucy Jinx - oh poor Lucy Jinx, right? Lucy who is the single most awful thing for feeling herself alive to write poems, for filling paper in a room she is renting while she's dead but is not but while *Delaware Bach* is and is and is is is and she can care all she wants and its nothing but words she can't stop scribbling - stop - and it's all the same - stop! - and she's too shy to even scream her face straight, too cowardly to even shriek two minutes a vengeance. Lucy is words on a slobbery-chinned page and that cat's dead and it's oh all her fault.

# .IIII.

THE SNOWFALL WAS AS MUCH an idler as the cigarette which had gone out in her lips. Viced on into this traffic we find Lucy, staring straight at the heat from the vent to the right-hand of the steering wheel. Talk talk talk from the radio. What is it? Yes, that interview with the writer-director of a small play which has done well, gone big, the writer-director now the toast of the elite spheres of this world, speaking warmly, abovely of his humble beginnings. Lucy hated this man. She was paying more attention to the sound of the heat just to prove this all in the realm of Platonic ideal: this - Lucy, here - is the Ideal of Dismissive, of Putting-Some-Blowhard-In-His-Place. 'But classy' Lucy nods to herself - no no, she'd not be the sort to get this writer-director aside, gruff by the lapel, and give him her say by the brute, box his ears, and leave him to know he's been seen through. No no no. Talk, John Big Shot Artiste of Our Age, of your play which is about as obvious as it is derivative - Lucy will just be within earshot and listening to the churning of air through a car motor out between some slats. And the snow, also. Noting the snow. The roadkill grey-brown of it already as it dusts down. Something the matter with it. Cancer is for flesh. Canker is for foliage. What is for snow that makes it tumor like this?

Still here: Lucy in traffic. Now she knows why she never leaves the house this early. Instinct. She's a cut above. And now she is not only a cut-above but is cursing Katrin and cursing herself for agreeing to pop by just to talk and to really give the place a look over. 'I've seen the effing place, Katrin' Lucy thinks with cutting eloquence 'goddamn you, I've seen it.' So why go, Lucy? Because Katrin is the kind of China you don't ever eat off, is specifically in existence to be careful with. The traffic is moving two-cars-through-the-light-at-a-time. Verified scientifically, the whole observational and re-observational process. But why is it? The light stays yellow longer that it stays green and stays red for - she's checking again - four minutes! Mathbook this: how long will you be sitting here if conditions do not alter? 'Well, how many cars back are you?' Lucy first-grade-teacher-voices 'Good. And so if two-at-a-time go through how do we figure this out?' But Lucy is distracted - maybe it's three-at-a-time? Maybe it could be up to five if someone wasn't turning left each time or if someone did not quickly turn left, opposite side of the road, just in the instant after their light had technically turned red. See? Maybe it'll be much quicker! Maybe it'll be only another minute. Maybe. There's no way to tell.

The frustrating thing is: Lucy, you can't actually be annoyed because your life is composed such that you can never technically be running late for anything. It's all perception with you, shifting standards and moods based on headache, stomachache, too much coffee, teeth feeling unwashed, pants riding funny while you sit. And you've made all efforts to arrange your life just suchly - no need to be at work at a certain time, no responsibilities else, no plans made out in advance any more than a few hours. To your credit: this perfect calibration is an achievement worthy of jealousy-laced libels. However: you need to admit that you'd better calm down - getting out of the car, heading toward the apartment building - because Katrin has not inconvenienced you by any stretch of the imagination. Here is Lucy, even taking her leisure with a fresh-lit cigarette just outside the main building door. Not even pressing the buzzer. Watching - there - that father curtly hurry that child along, the child playing a game of its sloppy track from dragged bootside in the quarter-inch slush-lick of snow. Watching - there - a dog having a shit while a woman dressed for jogging jogs in place and looks the other way to give the animal its privacy. Does that woman bag up the waste? She does! Disgusting. And jogs with it!? Lucy is watching but can't even believe the spectacle! The woman bobs at the crosswalk, crosses after a minute, is out of sight soon, shit weighted plastic bag shushing with each jostle of her lope.

Lucy straight-into-its how she has decided not to take Katrin up on the offer but wanted to show her face to say so and to have a peaceful, gratitude-based chat, to be certain all remained well between the two of them. 'You're an unstable person, Katrin - look how many lamps you have in just this one room!'

Katrin has to admit to this and goes so far as to open up about how, to her shame, at least seventy percent of them don't work. 'At least. I don't even know about some of them because why do I even have a lamp there?' She points at - Lucy agrees - an irrationally placed lamp, four shelves up on a bookcase, long line of books arranged one side of it, short line of books the other. Katrin lights a smoke, hands it to Lucy who reaches dubiously, asks 'Do I need to have an erudite opinion on this or you're testing it on me or what?' 'Just smoke the fucking thing.' Lucy does. 'Do you like it?' 'It's a cigarette. So it's accomplished that.' Katrin seems pleased, lights one of her own. What is the meaning of this? What is this all about? 'I was testing it on you.' 'You were?' 'I was. Someone gave me the pack. I figured as long as you're here, in case they're terrible, I can get out of taking a risk.' So amused by this is Lucy she jovially admits that when she is upset at Katrin she calls her *Latrine* in her thoughts. 'I used to feel clever, like I could say that's what your parents wanted to name you, just missed by one letter.' Katrin is relaxing to her chair, right with Lucy, easy. 'But then you remembered the *E* on the end?' Lucy lets a long drag. 'Yeah. Then I remembered the *E* on the end.'

Katrin shows Lucy the room that has been set up for Lucy to use as workspace. It is clean on the opposite side of the apartment from Katrin's own workspace - Lucy remarks to herself how sprawlingly long and thin Katrin's place is, like a sideways-tipped cereal box the size of a house - and is at least twice as large. 'This is in addition to your room-room - which has its own toilet, but there is only the one shower and we'd have to share that.' The shower was in its own room, not even a sink also in there - though there is a kind of cabinet-shelf one can sit on and on which, right now, Katrin has a miscellaneous assortment of piled books, most of them scholarly, unreturned to University libraries for years. Katrin was going to give Lucy a key no matter what Lucy did. That was the shot. Katrin considered the place to be Lucy's from that point forward even if Lucy never set foot in it. 'I am not going to use your two rooms for anything else and I will even leave the various wall-space in the common area I cleared for you clear.' 'You didn't clear wall space, did you?' Had she? 'I did.' She had. 'I don't have anything to hang' Lucy says, snapping for another smoke 'so you can put your stuff back up. It's very sweet of you, don't misunderstand me.' Katrin hands over a cigarette, laughing that 'It isn't sweet! I did that to creep you out, idiot - of course I'm putting my stuff back up the moment you leave!'

So: if every time anyone asks about your job at *Hernando's Highlights* you feel you are having to defend yourself why are you still working there, Lucy? Now: Katrin is asking and Lucy sits giving her same old company line, a spiel it felt years since she'd updated, the words unvacuumed, shabby, not even entertaining her anymore. But it can't have been years, right? 'It's just a job.

What else am I supposed to do?' She leans to one side, wondering if Katrin has become the sort to give that a straight answer. Of course Katrin is that sort. Were you looking for someone to do that, Lucy? Or are you dreading what you are about to hear? Both. Both. Tell Lucy the state of her, Katrin, go ahead - maybe another voice will rattle her into retreat from her retreated entrenchment. 'I can get you any number of jobs, Lucy, if you really don't want to just stay here and write - which you can do, I think you should. Jobs. You know? Fuck - I can get you paid to write - to research - while you do your own writing and research!' *Write. Research.* Stupid words stirring stupid Befores. Katrin is quick enough to pick up on Lucy's eyes, pivots to 'Or I can get you some goddamn work in an office, grunt stuff, mindless, but with real pay. I'm worried you've been make-believing too long. And I'm only being this blunt with you because I think you should live here.' Katrin lights a cigarette. Lucy does a posture that she's weighing whatever her next words might be. Theatrical pause. Katrin speaks, next. 'Look at us, Lucy. Look. We're old. And you're older than I am.'

Lucy can imagine life here. It would be quiet. It would be warm. It would be intimate. It would be books. It would be laughter. It would be being known and knowing. It would be lazy and silent and as by-herself as she wants. It would be conversations with every reference got and new references found. It would be exactly what food she wants, it would be exactly when she wants to sleep. It would be a kind of disappearance if she wanted to treat it as that, a kind of participation if her mood swung that way. And work? Maybe she should? But imagine not, first - imagine that a minute, at least. Live in these rooms until you die, Lucy. Death's a long time off still but how comforting to imagine having tucked in here, quiet and bookish and poeting for decades, the world around unnecessary and theoretical, something to bat at if bored, to forget when you're too busy and freefalling into yourself and your every idea, amusing yourself with yourself until exhaustion. The only despair would be boredom but it would be boredom alone under warm toast and buttery lock-and-key. What else are you doing? How is life supposed to go, else? Where did you even come from - it feels like it was somewhere but that was so long ago maybe it wasn't. You are certainly something the entire world could have forgot everything about, Lucy. Doesn't that still make you feel safe? You've been made to no one by pure disinterest. The perfect invincibility, isn't that how you look at it? Let yourself be snared to escape being unsnared.

Lucy does accept the key. Not that she had a choice. In fact, Lucy wears it now - by Katrin's hands just arranging it, forearms resting on Lucy's shoulders a moment - as a necklace. A thin silver chain, a common bronze-tarnish-tinted apartment key. Lucy holds it up by one finger, lets it drop, looks at it on her shirt front, slips it under the shirt, tap of cold instantly lukewarming in her cleavage. 'This makes it a symbol, you know?' Katrin says, arms at her sides now but not standing back from Lucy at all yet. 'And we know you eventually succumb to those, right?' Lucy has to chuckle, the way a cold pool makes you laugh when you first jump in, nothing else to be done. 'There is a syrupy history to evidence that, yes' she says and - purposeful or not, Lucy, this doesn't seem planned or expected - touches Katrin's arm, grips it, caresses it downward as she lets her own arm go slack. 'I'll certainly wind up here drunk sometimes, I've no doubt.' 'We can start with that.' Katrin finally takes a step, a wide one, to the side, looks around as though for something - a book on the shelf? the pause is now so long Lucy is intrigued - but then just moves toward the sofa and sits on the arm. Lucy says, after another look around herself 'I probably have to get going now' and she cannot even hide her uncertainty at the obvious question mark she unintentionally pronounced though on paper would have left period.

The snow has made strides since she left the car and shutting the door now she is ecstatically enclaved, cold glow to the dark of the still-bright crampedness, absolutely no hurry to so much as get the heat on. She closes her eyes and it seems, though it is not true, that the car now gives an echo to her nose breathing, that her speech would be amplified were she to make any utterance. Which is precisely why she decides not to. A nice, crisp illusion to defend, nothing to spoil with the sound of even a whisper. This is the sort of confinement that makes cacophonous the drizzle of even her timidest inner voice, gargantuans her bolder lashes of monologue, but which would dwindle the size of her physical voice down to the merest sniffle, a vibration of something else's vibration, just atoms rustling no more majestically than the pages of dried-after-wetted, stiff-and-sun-bleached coupon circulars, the ones that stay in the dumpsters or under them long after all of the other rubbish has been whisked, flattened, buried away. Her eyes open. It seems darker. But it probably isn't. She turns on the engine, jabs at the heat, and ticks down the lever for the windshield wipers, the first jutting arc of them revealing how godawful garish-silver the clouded sun has decided to be today.

Lucy cannot remember if this is her first winter on the roads of this area. It could well be her seventieth, push-come-to-shove of it. The landscape of her miniscule days, her penny-large activities, is such that she can picture her whole life here. Even memories she knows happened ages and miles elsewhere - well, why could they not have happened in that shopping-center she is passing now? See that local joint *Rondo's*? Why can't that be the setting of her first unrequited crush kissing their first giddy boyfriend? Why isn't that parking lot where she went to elementary school? Why isn't that Methodist cemetery where she got her degree? That check cashing joint where she libraried herself to exhaustion while she further-schooled? Now she laughs and thinks of the key she is wearing and how sharpshooter Katrin had her number. 'Now it's a symbol' she says quite loudly to hear something of herself over the uproar of the heater, doing her best Katrin-voice. And the Katrin-voice is fiendishly correct. Lucy's brain is already reordering all it sees into scritch-scratches found on some stones where villages anciently were, back when everything people thought and set down meant everything else in every way imagined or imaginable - eons before the unending suffocation of this world of specific-specifics wherein she must dwell.

OBSERVE: THAT RUNTY LITTLE CAR, again. Now it chugs out its waste, billows and billows coloring it the insulting sight of itself. Is it the same car? If not then what car it this? Lucy decides to have a cigarette while she observes. Ariel's car is parked there, snow-covered enough to suggest Ariel may have gotten to the trailer-office earlier than usual today. Or maybe not suggesting that but it has been there for hours, at any rate, the snow has been back to flurry awhile and there are no signs of the tracks where it pulled up. Yes. Good detective work, Lucy. Now what of the other car? Observe: in it some tuberculosis of a fellow, plump but not portly - you can tell by the face - strong enough but not fit, hair a kind of bushy that may have been attractive enough when styled on that head fifteen, twenty years earlier but now seems part afterthought part regret. Some of these observations are a bit of a stretch - the car window is iced and sooty, the glop of discolour to the snow even in undriven parts of the lot is not helping any favorable impression. Added to which, on unnamed - but come on, obvious - principle: you just don't like this man, Lucy. 'No, I don't' she admitted aloud, kind of sick-to-death already of having to make efforts at figuring him out. Yes. It all looks appalling, that car. It seems to be sitting there in its own, long shitted-in pants - or it seems pants with the man all shat in them, a seeping turd now matted-in, beginning to itch up surrounding arse-crack. Lucy - just go inside.

'You came in the split second before I managed to forget all about you and now I don't know whether I feel good or bad about that' says Ariel, tossing a plastic bag with a rather heavy paper bag inside of it at Lucy as soon as she's seated. 'When did you get in?' 'I slept here' answers Ariel with a yawn and an arch back, the phrase repeated after the yawn and an 'Excuse me' with tone of apology for being unintelligible the first time around. 'I heard you - did you really sleep here?' 'Yes.' 'But did you really?' 'Yes.' 'But did you really?' Ariel clucks her tongue in her mouth, a putrid slap slap of underside into the divot-pool of collected saliva beneath, sniffs loudly and asks what Lucy means to imply with her screwy repetition. 'Would it be weird if I had slept here?' The *weird* in this question is extended into seven seconds, at least, the end popping like a stubbed toe. 'Kind of.' 'Well, it so happens that I did sleep here. And I think that makes you jealous. And now you're being a bitter old crow.' Lucy does a look of polite consideration, nods, turns her attention to exploring the contents of the bag. 'Do you really want to know why I slept here, Lucy?' Lucy looks up, nodding - in the bag is a breaded chicken sandwich, long cold, and fries, cold to the point of having some of them soggied, some of them rock-hardened. 'I slept here because' - but then she breaks off, dramaturgical, as though she just cannot go on, and tells Lucy to stop being a busy-body prying old schoolmarm.

They play a game of braggadocio, blurting out what they feel has been their finest contribution to *Hernando's Highlights*. Ariel: 'I'm the one who made the *Hernando's* mascot a cartoon, rockabilly beagle - there was no Earthly reason ever to have done that!' Lucy: 'I have summarized every episode of *Law and Order: Criminal Intent* in exactly the same way for seven months, just switching out meaningless adjectives in key places - and no one is any the wiser!' They quickly scribble on scraps of paper how they score each other's response - *One* through *Ten* - take a pause to brace themselves then on Ariel's signal hold up the papers for each other to see. 'A *four!*' Ariel squeal-laughs-doubles-over. 'I'm scandalized, Lucy! How does the *Hernando's* dog only warrant a *four!?*' 'You've used that same answer at least ten fucking times, eventually you knew you'd be penalized for it!' Then they repeat the word *Penalized* to sound increasingly vulgar and then lasciviously threaten to 'penalize' each other and then just incoherently laugh for awhile until Ariel stands up, pats Lucy's head and tells her to get to work. 'Did you see the creepy guy out front, earlier?' Lucy decides to opportunistically snipe in but Ariel just expansively says 'Which one, right?' and heads down the trailer-office past the partition and into the bathroom.

Okay - Lucy touches the floor around Ariel's desk. Not wet at all. Ariel could not have come from that car. Lucy had already noted the dryness of Ariel's pant cuffs so this seems Case Closed. She steps outside for just a moment: there is the sloppy spot where that car had been, runny and plump, there are tracks of it turning and blurping off wherever it went and - okay Lucy, you see? - no sign of any footprints from there to the stairs up into the trailer. Door reshut, Lucy feels she should be convinced, once and for all. 'It wasn't even the same car, anyway' whispers Lucy to the vague of her shadow. But had Lucy actually slept in the office? You mean *Ariel*, Lucy. 'What?' There is the sound of the toilet flushing and Lucy feels suddenly flustered, like if she is caught out standing it'll be all the evidence needed to indict. 'Are we smoking?' asks Ariel - yes, Ariel has dry dry pant cuffs - patting her pockets with a where-are-my-smokes look before doing a light-footed kind of prance to retrieve them from her purse. Lucy pats herself up and down too, noticing Ariel looking at her. 'Do you need to have one of mine? What's the matter?' Snap to, Lucy, snap to! 'No no, I just left mine in my car.' Ariel shoulders open the door, seems to hesitate just a moment - does she really? - at catching sight of something then gives Lucy a smile and says 'Freak.'

Lucy asks Ariel's opinion on whether she should move in with Katrin. She was already committed to the impulsive question before she realized how little she wanted to ask it - to Ariel of all people - but the conversation went well so she was glad she had. Note: the conversation 'going well' meant that Ariel told her she should not move in. Nevermind that the reasons were no more compelling than '*Katrin*? What kind of name is that!?' because, frankly, coming from Ariel Lucy finds this a startlingly apt insight. Lucy doesn't mention that she already has the apartment key which in the most technical conversational sense is a peculiar omission but in this specific case makes a lot of sense to leave to one side. Or Lucy thinks it does. But obviously it was all just a long-game wind up for Lucy to say 'Or maybe I can just move in here with you.' Ariel chuckles - secretive, I'm-not-telling-you-ever brand chuckle - and tells Lucy that she can sleep over sometimes but she's not ready to take their relationship quite that domestic. Flutter flutter, Lucy-brains have gone mush and schoolgirl teehee. Ariel flicks her cigarette stub high and long out into the lot - Lucy wonders was she aiming for the now almost grey-whitened spot where that car had malingered but with the breeze and Ariel's ineptitude for flicking cigarette stubs there really is no way to know.

All of a sudden - this is two hours later, they had only just lulled into one of the quiet patches of doing the work that needed to be done - Ariel remembers that they are going to have to put out a special anniversary issue in two months and that Hernando is going to be sending them some specific guidelines for it. 'An *Anniversary Extravaganza*!!' Ariel pomps 'so the guidelines will likely explain exactly what that constitutes.' 'I thought every issue was an extravaganza.' But Ariel goes 'Naw, naw - every issue is a *Vaganza*, certainly, but this one has a little something more to it, you know?' Lucy - you just can't resist today, eh? - flirts back 'You're a *vaganza*' and Ariel smiles, holds eye-contact - no she didn't, not actually - does that charming thing where she closes her eyes to chuckle to herself and Lucy has had just about enough! 'At any rate' Ariel says but then stops - what? wait, that is not a fun expression, wait - takes a breath - now back to smiles - and says 'We'll have to handle this extra-*vaganza* together.' Then Ariel has moved to her phone - what is this about? - at which time she lets out a kind of throat clearing, fake few coughs and seems very phony in how she is sitting, constantly shifting, as though something just flustered her - something Lucy has no idea possibly what.

In the bathroom Lucy realizes she is staring at a Styrofoam cup with a toothbrush in it while she urinates. That hasn't always been there. Has that always been there? No. And there is a little carry-bag, the sort that inside will have make-up and various such things. Why this seems exciting or new - considering Ariel had not only explained how she had slept in the trailer but had done so on more than one occasion, no reason at all to assume she had been joking - is not something Lucy feels needs be addressed. That's Ariel's toothbrush. Ariel really did sleep in the office! Yes, Lucy - as Ariel has said she had done. 'Yes, yes' Lucy whispers, almost not managing to keep it a whisper 'but Ariel really did sleep in the office.' So: go ask her why, again. Don't beat around the bush! Be a normal sort! Go out there, say 'I thought you were joking - is that your toothbrush? Did you really sleep here?' But Lucy counter-reminds herself, tone of reprimand 'I already asked, she didn't want to tell'. But Lucy, you only *Lucy-asked* - you need to ask like a human being. 'I'm like a human being' she whispers. Okay - you need to ask As-a-Human-Being, then - as a friend. 'But what if I'm not her friend?' Lucy asks her reflection, not noticing the startled and pale look it has, the kind of fever in its eyes right now. On the count of three, then. Stop looking at yourself! On the count of three. Okay. Now. On the count of three. Don't just watch yourself tell yourself 'On the count of three' Lucy, but really on the count of three stop. Okay. On the count of three.

See? Now that Lucy claims to have finally resolved to get at the heart of the mystery we find Ariel has absented from the trailer-office. There is nothing to be done about this. It obviously means exactly what it means and Lucy will never so much as joke around the edges of this matter, again. All of it - sleeping in the office, that car, whatever else - that is all officially off-limits because Ariel has indicated she does not think it is any of little-Lucy's little-business. So a productive hour goes by. Lucy finishes making the interview with a sitcom editor - this stolen from *Yowza! The Pop Art Mag* - seem like a completely different interview. And she gets a good way along rewording a retrospective look at a television series she never personally watched into a far less exhaustive and ultimately substanceless overview of the series - this program's finale will be around the time this issue goes to print. Then she cannot take another moment of it and screams. She's surprised she could do it. Holy shit, Lucy! Now she is so worried that Ariel was just then walking up to the door - or that she was otherwise overheard - she does not even want to swallow. People aren't supposed to scream. She wets her lips, coughs into her hand, and returns to what she was doing.

But what on Earth is this now? Look! Is Lucy really manufacturing this mystery? See for yourself! Fresh tracks and a sploog of where some car had idled but meanwhile Ariel's car is still there, its snow-cover pristine. And Ariel has been gone out of the office for over an hour. Yep. Lucy smokes and nods and feels these facts speak for themselves. If she were a simple madwoman she would be more detail-oriented than this. Because it stands that the worst of it is this: there is a mystery but only as much as she hasn't been told something. This is like a Peeping Tom saying 'It's a mystery - hmn - where am I going to be able to get a gander from?' So Lucy gives herself a shivering, sober dressing down. Yes, I will stop this. No, I cannot get caught up in whatever this is. No! Sorry. I mean: There is nothing to get caught up in. Yes, I will stop this. Whatever it is it is none of my business. No - Lucy! Fine: There isn't anything. Yes. Yes, Lucy. Yes. But Lucy cannot help rapid-mouthed adding 'And even if there was it's nothing I am going to let myself get caught up in.' Lucy! Done, she's done - shakes her head and holds up placating, seriously-I'm-done palm-forward hands. Another cigarette and then into the trailer, the sudden surrounding of warmth making her face feel waxy and overlarge.

Ariel enters and immediately crosses directly to Lucy, hand to Lucy's shoulder to spin Lucy's chair facing outward, sits down in Lucy's astonished lap. 'I don't feel like I've been doing a good job flirting, lately. Is this better?' There is a heavy scent like vinegar - like crayons and vinegar - like crayons, vinegar, and a towel used two or three too many times. The thick of Ariel's perspiration held in beneath her coat is spilling up from the top of its buttoned-to-neck. The sensation of this as Lucy breathes it? Lucy wishes someone would explain that to her, as well. 'Is what better?' Lucy deadpans. A percussive slaughter of laughter from Ariel, a precise cut, the sound much like if every snap-sizzle from cooking bacon happened all at once and each trying to outdo the other. 'This this this' goes Ariel - bounces where she sits and roughs one shoulder to the side of Lucy's face and musses her hair aggressively. 'I am a terrible lout to you, Lucy Jinx. I don't deserve the love you strew me with but I take it regardless! So watch out for me. My cunt's a real sourpatch and I'm not going to dress it up different, you dig?' Lucy does not react to Ariel making a silly face, growling, then leaning in to fake bite her neck side. Then Lucy does nothing while Ariel abruptly gets off of her, kisses her own fingers and smooshes these fingers to Lucy's lips while she exclaims the sound effect 'Mwah!' And now Lucy watches Ariel unbutton her coat. Ariel obviously notices and does a kind of phony seductress-lower-lip-bite as she gets the coat slung over the back of her chair. Then Ariel says 'Lucy Jinx Lucy Jinx Lucy Jinx' is a spooky voice, waggling fingers between the two of them like sinister witchcraft.

**********

IT TOOK UNTIL THE THIRD 'Pardon me' for Lucy to register the *Pardon-mes* had been directed toward her. A woman - her own age but the worse for wear, looking her mother's age, in a dress that had the air of having been worn a firm thousand times, blue with some pattern that seemed to have forgotten what it was meant to be printed lazy, half-there - smiled, having been just about, it seemed, to have ventured to tap Lucy's shoulder. 'Yes?' 'Your daughter is in my daughter's class, I think?' 'No.' 'We didn't meet at the swap-meet after the tour?' 'I mean: I don't have a daughter.' Well, then Lucy was the spitting image of some woman who had a daughter in this woman's class! And oh but didn't this tickle the woman, so! This woman could have held her hand to God it had been Lucy she'd met. Was Lucy sure? 'I don't attend swap-meets.' A bit harsh that, but this bumpkin doesn't register the aggression, is just in the rhythm of her own cow-poke prattle. When the time came to Goodbye - one more 'It's really amazing! The spitting image!' - Lucy did a curt nod - she had earned this - and because that had been a waste of a cigarette she lighted another. It was colder than it needed to be. For snow. It only needs to be so cold for snow. This was colder. This was something personal. If she were an ancient race this day would be easy to make a myth out of - she could see herself spinning it, her skin inked crudely, piercings in odd places that had gone out of vogue, her body revered for the heft of its semi-lumpiness. Someone had lied to their child. A God? Naw, a mortal. One of those stories where this annoyed a God though, for some reason, and so they sent Cold as the bitterness the child ought to feel but knew not how.

The food aisles now had a tone to them of Katrin. Lucy would have to really buy her own food if she went there. Of course Katrin would 'I don't mind' in that way Katrin would but Lucy would have to keep her sense of superiority and feline aloofness, somehow. By having a vast selection of frozen dinners was her plan, judging by the evidence of how she is looking at them all. Or maybe buy a week's worth of the same frozen dinner. Or - better - a family-size, frozen lasagna that she cuts a square out of at-a-time, dwindling the whole to a series meagre meals lasting a fortnight. And a bag of potatoes which she would bake via the designated microwave button, eat without butter or any outward showing of joy! She would haunt Katrin's apartment, that would be her style. The morbid ghost of a peasant-folk. She'd walk around rubbing her hands, praying mantis, and blowing in them besides, her shoulder hunched around her, also praying mantis - insect with the sniffles, stick-bug moving from sofa to bedroom to toilet to kitchen to work. Blink. Blink blink. So, now Lucy is in the magazine aisle. She's never had a subscription to a magazine. But *Subscription* is one of her favorite words. *Subscription*. She smiles. Favorite words are as important as lungs.

'Haven't seen you in a little while.' 'I've been around.' Blather blather and transaction. Then, as she notices she has no line and likely none to come soon, Suzette lowers voice and asks if she could talk to Lucy a moment. Skipping past the preliminaries - what it came to was Suzette asking if she might be able to nudge Lucy in the direction of the poetry of a few of her friends. Transgressive Suzette, devil-deal logic: it's not like anyone would know and it would mean the world to them - like a secret little club. 'But Suzette' Lucy begins 'it's really not supposed to work like that. That was kind of a one-time favor to you.' But Suzette is a shrewd one - the guile that comes from years of living in neglect and mistrusting even her mother's tit - and says of course she understands but furthers 'It's not like there is really a higher authority than you and it's all your opinion, anyway - if you don't like the poems that's another thing - I'm just saying top-priority them, right?' It's not Lucy's final decision is the other thing, but someone else on the team who runs that aspect of the operation. Good work, Lucy - that should settle it! Suzette nods, getting the drift, certainly, but wink voices 'Well, I hear you'll be the one in charge soon, so maybe then.' 'What do you mean?' 'When the other girl leaves and whoever new comes on.' The look on Lucy's face. Yep. Suzette notes it. 'I just happened to be talking to Hernando - not a snoop - and he said the other girl was leaving, soon. A young man would be taking her place.' Lucy shakes her head slowly, her lips slowly part but seem too stiff to have parted. Suzette - again wink-wink I-get-it - says 'Well, maybe you know better. I might have misunderstood Hernando. You're the one who works there, you know?'

Of course it should have been obvious to Lucy that the staff of the flagship store of *Hernando's Grocery* would know Hernando. And these little po-dunks! Well, they like to busy their bodies right around all they can, don't they just! What treacherous old scheming bones in even so little a speck of the Earth, eh? Eh, Lucy? Here, on exhibit: a ratty old cow-patty of a grocery-store clerk, plotting Shakespearean to gain backroom control over the publication of poetry in a fucking newspaper circular! A divide-and-conquer gambit - it's almost hilarious! Lucy pictures a stew of these saggy old cunts, gabbing in full-mouth-still-chewing whispers and sucks at fast-food straws with each other about how they will angle their shadow-coup. What's the play? *Lucy's fucked* is the play! Obviously, if they are let-me-have-a-word-in-private with Hernando himself then they know - Suzette and all her caravan of cronies - they know it is Lucy and Lucy alone who does the *Poetry Corner* - or, either way, that there is no hierarchy of editorial say-so to the production. And if they know that, this was an opening aggression, not a favor-asked: we're giving you a chance to do it before we just go to Hernando and have him tell you to do it - but it'd be better for you, Lucy, if you just climb on board, if we know that you're with us, you see? This is a grocery-store! Lucy works in a trailer across the lot! Is no snippet of humanity free from such machinations as these? 'And besides' Lucy says, water just splashed to face at the bathroom mirror 'the *Poetry Corner* is mine.'

Initial rile of irritation now subdued to a seethe of bemusement and eagerness to share this inbred intrigue with Ariel, Lucy is passing through the automatic doors, cigaretting her lips and flaming the cigarette tip lit, thinking to walk straight across the lot. But she idles, moves off to the side because of how many cars are bumbling around just in that moment, her entire body slouching into the same shape and attitude of her grin. Quite without any warning or ceremony she feels a hard - a very hard - smack of open palm to her ass, contours her face to ready an ejaculate What-in-the-fuck!? but turns to see only a scarcely-able-to-contain-her-laugh Charlotte. Reset. 'Hi' said like some two dozen eggs spilling splat through a wet paper-bag bottom. Then blink. Then Lucy laughing and 'What in the fuck, man?' Charlotte moving prize fighter, biting lip, obvious aim on Lucy's unreddened flank. 'What are you doing?' Lucy says, only vaguely positioning herself to keep Charlotte from her target. But Charlotte doesn't answer until the second slap has landed - harder and with more of a grip down than the first - at which time she completely relents to a normal civil posture - about two dozen people have all watched this fine spectacle despite the fact it is all obviously a fevered nonsense of Lucy's imagining - and says with the bored lilt of customer-service-sort-on-break 'I figured we've reached that point in our relationship but maybe I should have asked, right?'

Charlotte, after a few minutes, goes shy girl. How can this be? Well let's examine, because it's one of those circular precariousnesses Lucy finds herself in - made all the more flustering as her attention does not wander from the too-fast receding sting to her rear flesh - the sort that seem reserved solely for her. The following has just now happened: By way of getting-her-bearings-back small-talk - Charlotte, the perfect flirt, had dropped all flirtatious airs after the physical - Lucy comically made mock of the sort of people at 'this goddamned *Hernando's*' calling them 'backwoods hoodlums and shysters, the lot - louses using all skullduggery their duggery-thick skulls could dredge to get what they wanted out of sweet innocent Lucys! You, with your perverse sexual assaults' Lucy had made J'accuse gestures which Charlotte bowed to 'and Lord knows what you're playing at there' - hurrying on out of fear Charlotte would retort to that directly - 'and some old ding-bat one of your colleagues trying to get me publish their poetry. Why in Hell do these dryhumps think they've got what it takes to be poets!? They just want to suck my city-blood dry and then mock my every bewilderment!' Okay - that all seems like Lucy just being fun and wordy. But why does this make Charlotte go shy? Lucy, have you gone too far? Noias explode and fornicate and begat thousands of others and spread to the ends of the Earths of her terror-sick mind. 'I'm sorry - I didn't mean anyone specifically! I was totally joking.' No. No, not that, Lucy - Charlotte seems to find what you said hilarious and your apology now ten times more so. What then? 'It's just I wondered if you would be interested in reading my poetry' Charlotte meeps, actual toe-drag to pavement and that chuckle off to the side, that touch to her hair: this was Charlotte more naked than dreams have dimensions.

It all ended well, have no fear - Lucy, in case you had not paid attention, have no fear. It all ended perfect except perhaps that Charlotte's pouted curtain line was 'I was going to smack you again, but forget it now' - but really even her saying that is more perfect than had she done what she said. And there are even five minutes of undiluted blankness of bliss within Lucy before she starts worrying what she will say if and when - likely when - Charlotte's poetry is vacuous rubbish. It's one thing to be Charlotte, Lucy think-smiles, it's another thing to be a poet. Is that right? It's probably not right. Lucy, you're never right about anything so keep the quotables to a minimum, they just reveal you to be nothing but an inwardly garrulous blowhard. But to the more pressing quandary: is there no way that Charlotte could be in on things, going halvsies with Suzette and her lot - the good gypsy daughter of some drunk-tank grandma with delusions of Gertrude Steinness? Lucy, look where you are: is it remotely possible that the answer to that question is *Yes*? Lucy looks where she is: *Hernando's*. Parking lot. Jesus Christ. She busts a guffaw till she cramps and draws a look from a man having trouble getting a cart from the line of them, there. She can't stop laughing, in fact. Picture it: Suzette signaling Charlotte 'You're on, phase two, phase two!' Charlotte signaling back Thumbs-up while deep-breathing, eyes locked pre-coquettish on Lucy's exiting ass.

Police sirens - or ambulance? that bitchier pierce must be ambulance - suddenly cloister the lot and area surrounding, ludicrous in their self-aggrandizing, shaking step-father abusive all thoughts from Lucy's head. Every patron in the lot seems dazed to deaf-mute. All cars stop their crawls for spaces. The teens jobbed with retrieving carts left in the lot idle - that one taking cigarette pack from back pocket, slapping it in hand, no cigarette extracted, replacing the pack back to pocket. Customers moving toward the store from their cars seem unsure if maybe they ought to return to their cars, customers exiting the store toward their cars seem unsure if maybe they should keep put back in the store. And there - look! - is the obligatory - actually toothless - old slack-jaw. This would be a delightful thing seen in silence but the noise really does Lucy in. Then zip - sirens always just silence, never seem to properly decrescendo - the world clicks back to normal, all motions resumed, and Lucy imagines any halted conversations pick back up mid-syllable, all trains-of-thought, too, except her own which has scampered off too bullheaded to return.

Lucy looks at her hands as though for something then at the ground at her feet as though for something dropped. Probably you thought you had a smoke going or you want one now, Lucy. Probably. But she squints off to the left, to the right, gives a glance over shoulder before deciding, getting the pack from her coat pocket. And she lights a ciggy, inhaling, certain that - no - this smoke isn't what she'd been feeling was absent.

Why don't you just let these women ransack the *Poetry Corner?* This is as good a time as any to take stock of yourself, after all. Certainly the usefulness of that idea has long since abated. Certainly it does not even give you a kick, still. If anything now it is just thuggishness, lording it over those you feel are the lesser-thans, those whose thimble-cup dreams you can keep unfulfilled. There are people - honest people, not people like you, Lucy - who see that *Feeling The Muse? Submit Submit Submit* line of text beneath each issue's featured verse, who see the guidelines and follow them, who craft and proofread, who go through old notebooks, who spend honest time - not time like you spend, Lucy - putting down words that mean more to them than ever words can mean to you, Lucy. And for nothing more than to see those words in print and to preen a bit, to pompadour around a day or two. What? What!? Oh can't you even admit it, Lucy!? Poetry? Hey, these may be sludge-bellied, three-toothed, booze-and-Chef-Boyaredee-sweating nobodies but the purity of their reasons for writing a bit of verse makes you, Lucy Jinx, seem like the Holy Ghost of phony-baloney! What is poetry to you? Would you ever painstake over an off-rhythm sonnet and submit it, fingers-crossed, into a slot in a grocery-store? No, baby, no. You'd never. So let's watch whose thinking their farts are the same stripe as Milton's, okay?

Lucy Jinx has walked to the exact opposite side of the parking lot than the trailer-office - all the long long lot away from it. In fact, technically she's walked off of *Hernando's* property, official, and is in the next shopping-center over - the parking lots don't join, one needs to get on the road to enter this lot here, *Hernando's* lot there, zealous demarcation of territory. 'Well, this is unprecedented' Lucy whispers, kind of proud of herself. It's one thing to loiter but a far more classicist absent-mind to by-the-books straight wander off! A flash of her elderly death: frozen to a bench somewhere or maybe huddled in the alcove front of a dry cleaners or a vacuum store - whichever is the more dismal to be found dead in front of by the time Lucy dies. The snow starts up as she crosses back and it is perhaps unavoidable that she remarks to herself that she really has no idea what to do with herself. Her molecules are only cohesive enough to loiter. That is the sum total of her. Something between liquid and gas, certainly no solid. She's an unmodern sort, a person several hundred years backward as far as being defined. There's a picture of her on a cave wall, no doubt. She's that first rendered humanesque figure - a scrawl that might signify man-standing-upright and might represent man-lying-sprawled-to-ground-dead.

'HOW MUCH MONEY CAN YOU lend me, Lucy Jinx?' Ariel in-a-turmoiled at Lucy the moment Lucy was through trailer-office door. Stammer stammer Lucy said stammers amounting to 'Not very much but - you need money, now?' 'By tonight. I gotta blow Lucy, things have caught up with me, you dig?' Lucy's heart unsomersaulting and she testingly, eyes narrowed, says 'But you aren't serious, right?' Ariel breathed hot out her nose once, buffalo-snort, then sat back down in a huff like a pencil snapped 'No, Lucy - but you could try to be fun about something, sometime.' Had any work gotten done today? The past two days? Three? Was this the week the issue needed to go to print? All good questions, Lucy is sure Ariel would agree. 'Take a poll: I'm more fun than you.' Lucy said that. Fifteen minutes had elapsed in kind of idle silence. 'Why do you always want to argue with me, Lucy? It makes me think you talk behind my back.' 'I do talk behind your back.' Then Ariel swivels around 'Oh!' and fingersnaps the air seven eight nine ten eleven times 'Oh I needed to tell you: I had a dream and in the dream I was you. And it was really cool. So you should be jealous.' 'What were you doing?' 'You mean what were you doing?' Lucy ponders the grammar, the symbol-swap construct. 'But you were me, so what were you doing?' 'But' Ariel says, tut-tut-tuting and spinning two full spins in her chair before finishing 'I was you - so what were you doing, see?'

Now Ariel claims to not be the least bit surprised that some swine would have their grubby minds set on taking over the *Poetry Corner*. 'Corners are big in the culture of these mouth-breathers, Loose - they fetishizes them. The only thing they lust over more are Nooks.' But in Ariel's estimation it would be better to raze the *Poetry Corner* to the ground and salt the soils of it rather than let these people have the slightest sway. 'It would be one thing' Lucy says - why are you even conceding this much, Lucy? - 'if every single poem in the submission drawer wasn't such burp-up.' After all, she allows, she did open it to the public and therefore is kind of flim-flamming everyone, tweaking their noses and all sorts of colloquial belittlings. 'You know, I have submitted a few poems just to see what you'd say, unfiltered.' That was Ariel said that. Lucy's face goes drained, her skin feels like a gutful of swallowed toothpaste froth. 'What?' 'I mean, I know you don't read all of them and I probably shouldn't take it seriously or anything.' 'Wait - wait wait wait, are you serious? I mean - I don't even read them all, you know?' Ariel holds the straight face for too long a beat rather than breaking into a smile, the effect the same, and Lucy throws a full cup of two-day-old coffee at her, she ducking out of the way barely in time and mouth opens as wide as her delighted shriek-cackling is loud, giant in-love-with-this-moment eyes turned toward the nasty spatter on the carpet and wall then turned to beam 'Oh my God, you're fucking awesome!' at Lucy.

Turning to matters after sobering calm - Ariel likely as headached from laughing, as gurgle-tummied and eyes-sore as Lucy - they are both a little bit disturbed to learn that Hernando is so chummy and free-to-speak-about their business amongst the pleabs. Lucy wants to interject that she might be putting too much blame on Suzette, in fact - that, in fairness, Suzette might just be at the mercy of peer-pressure, wanting to peacock a bit, give her dismal life some meaning. Ariel will, for her part, have none of this. In fact she can see no way around that it is all Suzettes idea and - hey, maybe Suzette doesn't have friends but writes the poems, herself, in a delicious bit of Swiftian irony! - bets Suzette approached her friends about submitting poetry, something that had never occurred to them, just to show off how she made the weather in her part of town. 'Put nothing past people who are going to die having accomplished nothing, Lucy-Loo. As counterintuitive as it sounds, these types of people will eventually do anything to have done something. Suzette: what scum!' Yes. 'Branded!' Lucy agrees and will never reverse positions. She sees it all just as Ariel says. 'How could I have been so foolish, Airy? Why do you even love me?' And Ariel points to the framed, placarded *Cat Poem*. 'Never forget, my girl. Never forget.'

Ariel tosses Lucy over half of her candy-bar - Lucy doesn't catch it, is thoroughly mocked, picks it up and says Ariel should not be such a superstitious honky - 'Floors don't do anything to candy' - when Ariel makes a dismayed-face at Lucy having a bite - then asks Lucy how everything is going with the kid. 'I'm not trying to pry, sorry if it comes off that way, you just hadn't mentioned him, lately.' Lucy big-breathes, blegh noises, shrugs and leans back sighing 'No, no. Not at all. The kid is fine, as far as that goes. No real reason to bring him up though, lately. I'm kind of out of his direct orbit, you know?' Ariel takes a hurried-up harsh swallow 'You didn't' - has to cough - 'Sorry' - sips from her water bottle - 'Did you break up or something?' Lucy waves this off, talking with quarter-mouthful 'Oh no, nothing so drastic.' And here the phone rings, theatre cue, and Ariel mentioned how it seems to have done so on purpose. 'We should answer just to teach it a lesson.' Ariel almost concurs with this but then gravely says 'Wait - what would the Greeks say? They warned us of such things, right?' And yes, Lucy is so glad this was pointed out. 'That fucking phone was counting on our hubris' - the phone has stopped ringing - 'but it did not count on you having retained so much of your scholarship.' Ariel has another rough swallow because she starts laughing mid-gorgedown. Lucy says 'Sorry' but Ariel glowers and grunts 'Unforgivable' and hisses 'You and your little step-bastard, too!'

Speaking of Hernando: has Lucy heard that the mag was going to start being done on glossy paper? 'No. Why?' Why: Hernando is opening three new stores - two of them in another state. Note: that sounds more dramatic than it is - the state-line is fifteen miles away so the stores across the border will actually be closer than some of the stores in the home state are, relative to the flagship. 'Hernando wants to jazz up the whole operation. Glossy mag but with less pages.' 'Because he has no sense of things?' asks Lucy. And Ariel gestures a Thank you! toward the Heavens for having a kindred around to get where she's coming from. 'This is my whole lament, Lucy - is there no such thing as legacy?' Yes! 'I want to be remembered for what I am not what I become, you know?' Yes yes, my God Lucy knows - she gush nods like a breakfast cereal mascot kangaroo might. 'What is the point in being this thing if this thing becomes that and that is what is known and this becomes just an early iteration? Lucy - do you follow me?' Do you, Lucy? Yes, yes. 'I will be an elderly sag when it comes time to die - that's what I will become - that's what becoming is! Call it *Glossy-Cover* or whatever - it's age and decay and not how I want to be remembered! This is who I am!' - Ariel voluptuouses herself - 'I am *Hernando's Highlights*, goddamn it! Chuck me in the bin unread but don't glossy-cover me and call my old-hag body the truth of the perfection of my past!' 'I love you, Ariel.' 'Well, obviously you do! Listen to me, after all! I swear if you remember me as an old woman, Jinx, I'll haunt you even in your Hellfire, babycake - and that's Gospel! Here and now is me, always - mark that!'

Lucy finds herself relating detail-after-detail of her time with Gregory. How they had met at a Taco joint. How Gregory had been the person to know this or that author's name. How there had been his fists to her, sometimes - often, oftener - here and there during their endless up-and-down, on-again-off-again always. How she would leave and he would wait her out like some ritualized suicide. How she would pen three-hundred line poems to him for his birthday and he would use how they made him feel as an excuse to lose himself, treat her like a bin being dug through when demanding a there-and-then screw. She told all about when she had learned how he had recycled the pet-name he used for her from a previous lover and then mocked her for being jealous, for being paranoid, for thinking that calling her *Sugar-pot* was the same as calling her *Samantha*. She apologized and apologized as she leaked this age-old stink out, this drip drop from the punctured trashbag of herself. 'It was so long ago' she would lace with the apology and would ridicule herself for using the fact that This Time wasn't That Time as an excuse. She told how she had actively 'tried to have kids with him' - let him fill her and would pillow-talk about how she couldn't wait for her belly to be this big, that big, and how she'd say 'Thank you' when Gregory would tell her he figured her belly would 'snap right back up tight how she liked it'. She spoke of delirium. Of buying and swallowing packfuls of daytime-cold-medicine after each attempt at family-making - how she still believed it was that stuff that had kept him from successfully mutating her insides in the shape of a person like him.

Now Lucy is calmer. How much of that had she said? More interestingly: having said it somehow none of it any longer felt true. Would this feeling last? Would this feeling be her now? 'We should fucking swap murders, you and I' Ariel said after however long, her both hands still closed around Lucy's one that wasn't touching to her sniffling nose, her woe-is-me eyes wrinkly-wet. 'We can do that' Lucy chuckled, clearing throat, pressing two fingers to forehead in circle circle circle 'Who do you need me to kill?' 'Oh take your pick. Throw a rock, Loose, you'll hit someone needs deading for me.' Lucy sniffled. Forced chuckle. 'Stop looking at me, Ariel.' 'I don't want to stop looking at you, right now.' 'No?' 'You look interesting, right now.' Lucy laughs, snorts saltwater phlegm, swallows it, clears throat 'Oh yeah? Well, I also decided I hate you now - so there's that, too.' Ariel stands, still holding Lucy's hand, but let's go with a quick 'I'll be right back.' Lucy alone, post whatever-the-fuck-that-was, in a trailer-office in a grocery-store parking lot. Lucy. Yep. That's about right. But soon, again, now, Ariel with a roll of toilet-paper and a quip of 'Figure you need this after sounding like such an ass, right?' 'Thanks, Ariel. But I was hoping you were getting a joint or something useful.' Lucy, here, trailer-office, blowing nose, saying to Ariel 'I guess you're just not as cool as I thought.'

In the new falling snow, heroin-brown in the parking lot lamplight now, they shiver, shoulders touching, upper arms touching, and watch some employees of the grocery-store shoveling the lot. One of these employees - a middle-aged, pot-bellied sort - must have spotted them standing and is now at something of a rush clearing a squiggle path through the lot over to them. 'Thanks so much' Ariel says with her best rise on tip-toes, leaned forward over the railing. 'You need me to clear your cars, ladies?' Lucy is in process of saying 'Oh no no, but thanks' but Ariel has already said 'That would be so incredible!' in the false voice she must use when wanting to get blubbery backwoodsmen to do her whimsical bidding. Ariel insists that the man take ten dollars, he refuses, she insists, he refuses, she says 'Please' and he - it's a dismal display, really, but Lucy cannot help being entertained and on the side of the villain - oh shuckses and does what he thinks is a comical stamping his foot while he says 'I guess you caught me with that - I can't say *No* if you say *Please*' followed by piglety nervous laughs that sound like he actually pronounced the words *Hyup-hyup*. Lucy calls a loud 'Thank-you!' when Ariel finally lets him go and they watch him reshovel the already part-covered path he'd just cleared as he goes.

'Do you want company tonight?' Lucy asks as she gathers her things up to go 'I could bring a mini-tv or something. Or we could light a campfire and tell spooky stories, you know?' Ariel turns where she is sitting, rubs her hands while smiling up in Lucy's direction, but eyes back tilted, thoughts someplace else at least halfway. When she breaks from whatever that reverie was Ariel explains she probably won't be staying in the office, that night. 'Or, you know, again, at all. Or I might. I don't know.' Lucy waits a beat - nodding - to see if there is anything further before punctuating the exchange with 'Okay.' She has the door open and has just stepped out when Ariel's arms go tug around her, clasping over her in an *X*. The warm of Ariel's mouth in the side of her neck, the garden of her unshampooed hair. In front of Lucy there is the cotton first-dark of proper night, there is the mangle of traffic letting her know she has stayed far later than she'd meant to. Ariel compresses tighter, moves her mouth, maybe saying something, probably not, lukewarm lip-spittle up-down on Lucy's feverish skin. A hand stays to shoulder and Lucy holds it a second. But you can't turn around, Lucy - you just can't, okay? You just can't. You just can't. At your car, though, you can look over. Lucy at her car. Okay. Big wave. 'Bye-bye.' Ariel there like an old-movie next-door neighbor. Lucy remembering exactly how that one of Ariel's leg looks crossed over that leg and that slouch and that sudden - it wasn't sudden, Lucy - closing door ruining everything.

Lucy sings along to every song on the album twice while frying herself in heat, her soggy head dampening heavy until she thinks she might just pass out. The scent of the inside of her nose is just exactly the same as she remembers the milk and sugar left over in a finished bowl of cornflakes or shredded-wheat smelling. The traffic luxuriates in itself as though showing its mommy I-love-you-this-much and straining arms out of sockets, imagining wingspans and talons. Boastful and well-feted traffic, plopped out with pant fronts undone. The snow is the most ruinous thing imaginable to the denizens of around here, it seems. Every traffic-light has people wrong-way left turning, honking irascibly, and the entrances to the shopping-centers before she reaches the country roads seem World War debris. The country roads are silent and uncleared. Houses along them already have snowmen and paths where sleds have been used and got bored with. Even the unlit houses, tenantless, seem warm and well-loved. Lucy could never fathom a life lived in any of these places, though. Those endless fields behind and hardly three paces from front door before road? It would remind her too much of the inside of her brain. That's it. That's what Lucy realizes. She knows the terror of these peaceful, decorated, lights-unto-themselves homesteads. They look peaceful. The way her face looks peaceful. But that's all they do.

'SO WHERE'S THE' LUCY SNAPPED her fingers 'the the' she rolled her hand expansively, the mother turning to give the cockeye 'the child. Your offspring. Whatever you call it.' And pat comic timing the mother holds Lucy's eyes then slowly lets her own drift down to the oven beneath the pot on the stove where she is stirring. The mother nods. Lucy winks 'Gotcha. And 'bout time.' 'Right?' grins the mother, just then a beep sounding, meaning something to do with the cooking and Lucy moves to pour herself coffee. 'In fact, he is having a playdate. A sleepover playdate.' 'Sounds like a hot ticket' says Lucy, coffee too hot, biting wasp stings to her lips 'I have to say I'm envious.' The mother's shoulders happy-shudder to unheard-from-Lucy's-angle chuckle, the mother's voice mingled with now bubbling - *brubbling* Lucy always thought the word should be, *brubbling* when bubbling gets to so unstable a pitch - whatever-is-in-the-pot 'Oh Jinx, you are incorrigible.' Then, horror-film-latch-lock-quick, the mother has turned and 'Wait - what does *incorrigible* mean?' Lucy, mock startled, uh-ums and holds up give-me-a-second-here hands. 'You don't know?' 'I might not. I have a picture in my mind. But it is of porridge. And that's because I picture you cooking your child and so am kind of - you know? - early Germanic Fairy Tale minded, just now.' The matter of the word dropped, the mother's brow goes that way it tends to go more and more, lately - Lucy has stopped trying to define it, specifically: *That Look* one Lucy likes and leaves unlabeled *That Lucy-Look* if she is feeling self-flattering - and hand to hip wow-oh-wow-whisper-head shaking asks 'Do you ever - ever - say anything ordinary, my old friend?' Lucy considers. Answers: 'I want to say *Probably* but that's probably because I just feel put on the spot, you know?'

Lucy had assumed the child being gone meant the mother had plans to be out overnight but was glad enough to learn the cooking had been meant for Lucy and her to enjoy. 'You don't have to' the mother obviouslyed 'but it just struck me odd that we've known each other this long and never shared an adult meal.' Lucy offhand offers to drive to get wine, the mother sighing in the manner those injected by villains in cinema faint, saying if she could it would be just terrific and then 'Wait, let me get money - my purse is upstairs.' You let her actually go upstairs, Lucy? You're not buying the wine? Lucy rubber-rubber face-shakes. Obviously Lucy will buy the wine. 'Though: why should I?' she whispers into the simmering pasta pot peeked into. 'Who are you talking to, Lucy?' she makes the sausage and farfalle say back but then just shoots it a stinkface, closes the lid, pulls the collar of her t-shirt forward and gives herself a sniff. Why would you stink? 'Why wouldn't I?' she alouds and the mother, descending the stairs, can be heard on approach asking 'Why wouldn't you what?' Caught talking to yourself! The first sign you are the murderer with split personalities! Were life cinema, suddenly all those at home viewing would know *This ain't ending well*. 'I was chiding myself for not telling you I'm buying the wine.'

Here's something about Lucy Jinx: firmly in middle-age she feels a sense of adolescent ill-belonging, an I-shouldn't-be-doing-this any time she enters a liquor store. She once spent days looking up statistics on how many liquor stores are in a general area on average, how much money such stores make, how many customers frequent them. And she'd been alarmingly shocked by the resulting knowledge that alcohol is quite popular and, indeed, she is far more on the outskirts of normalcy for only seldom entering a liquor store and way, way off angle for her feelings of pariah-were-I-to-be-caught-in-one. She has also, she grins recollecting, looked up statistics on how often people use the toilet in a day and whether it is normal to use a public restroom. In her defense: that does seem something only suspicious characters would do - no one strikes up a friendship in there so she was not so far off in having the creeps about being seen waiting in line. Her mental recap of that neurosis complete, now Lucy tenders the transaction, for some reason looks for a tip-jar to leave change in, laughs and tells the college-type guy giving her a curious blink what she'd been thinking. 'Hey - did I see you in *Trent Square*, earlier?' Lucy must look aback taken, the poor guy apologies and says 'Nevermind, I'm not being that guy. You just - sorry - you have a distinct face. It'd be odd to see it twice in a day on two people.' What are you going to do, Lucy? Bimbo grin - good choice. 'Might've been me' nose-chuckle. Brilliant. Why the fuck's this idiot blushing, now? Lucy: just leave.

The worst thing she can do is ignore the rising evidence that once again something is descending, surrounding her, that fissures and tectonics have arranged themselves just so - you'll be swallowed while you sleep, Lucy, and sooner rather than later! No. The worst she can do is listen to that. Do these few events even count as coincidences? Are you even pretending they don't!? The worst she can do is not resist if Fate is beginning its offensive. Fact: Lucy Jinx is still alive. Fact: that's because the world doesn't want you dead - it needs you, in fact, vital to keep jabbing at. You are some sick old religion's favorite plaything, Madame Jinx, and if you ignore the lessons of literature - if you again ignore your gut - then you deserve this. Hell, maybe you're beaten down to want it by now! No. 'No, no no' she says 'poo-poo to that whole psychobabble.' But the fever is on you, the first cold slick of it. You even sniffed yourself, earlier! All the world is unsettling yourself to yourself. 'So what can I do about it?' Lucy is honked at, she 'Fucking alright, super hero!' gives the finger to a carful of nice-honest family behind her, imagines the wifelet agahsting, the husband kind of turned on, the kid's 'What's wrong?' from the backseat, the husband and wife both starting to speak, the words a mingle of 'Nothing, just some lady' and 'Nothing, just this fucking bitch.' Lucy now has to take an extra, needless, backpedaling turn to get this lot out from behind her. See where this is going, Lucy? You're being shepherded to slaughter and you've bought the wine!

The kitchen table is fully set. The mother smoking a cigarette the sour-blue scent of which gives the entire lower floor a post-coital feel. Lucy is sorry she was late but it seems she has an impersonator going around making positive impressions on all manner of commonplace yokels so there had been autographs to sign and all of that. 'It's my lot in life' she says, then goes 'Give me a cigarette, can't you see I'm apoplexed!' The mother just gives her that look again, that look again, then a cigarette. 'Not that I'm difficult to impersonate' Lucy steams ahead after quick drag and forced piff out of pepper-grey inhaled 'just toss on any old fright-wig and some prospector pantaloons and you've got me spot on - but whomever this doppelganger is they're sullying my street-cred with seemingly civic-minded and home-and-hearth-centric attitudes and deeds, you know? For Christ's! Someone even thought I went to a parent-teacher night or some such thing? A swap-meet!? Have I become so drab? Am I no more than an office wall? You can be honest with me.' But the earnestness of this crisis was abundantly lost on the mother who now applauded and asked if Lucy could give her the wine now, she'd pour. 'This all looks amazing' Lucy said, blushing now - yeah, that had been kind of a scene, Lucy - 'and my God I think I need food.' Squeaky then plump sound of cork easily uncorked then duck-glugging-earthworm-unchewed-down-gullet sound of first pour being poured. 'You do the toast' the mother beamed, handing a glass across 'I'd just say something stupid like *To us.*'

Turning to matters of listening to the mother. The mother, by the way, has gained some weight and is resplendent, almost unlookatably pistol-shot, right now. Lucy is half-listening and frankly half-trying to not use the fact that she's had a bit of wine as excuse to tell the mother that. Not wanting to bore with too many details, the mother explains she'll have no choice but to take on some different position at the firm where she works. In fact, she's held this new position previously but it was years ago before a rather major upheaval in staff and workflow. All of this - the mother thinks she's boring, laughs in apology - the changes are the real trouble because the mother knows herself to be the sort who will want to keep saying 'When I used to work down here we this that whatevered' and is so ashamed at herself for becoming that doddering officemate who everyone is waiting to learn has left, miss for two days, then forget all about until someone tells a half-remembered anecdote at some party. 'I'll be the *Oh yeah - her! I remember*! It's the life cycle of an office butterfly, you know? Pupa, caterpillar, chrysalis, butterfly, corpse, dust, nothing.' 'You talk kind of like a poem, you know?' Okay - see that Lucy? That's called the-sort-of-expression-cannot-be-ignored. And this eye-contact held now a full minute in quiet? And you've watched her sip another mouth of wine and she's watched you at least dab the dregs of your own upturned glass to your lips and then tongue side-to-side? Good thinking - yes! - pour another glass and offer to pour for her, too.

Lucy Jinx: mirror of downstairs toilet. Lucy Jinx: mouth opened wide, examining the dulled sharps of her teeth all the way to the wretched lot in the back crooks. And looking at her nose and staring in her eyes. It's just wine and you aren't drunk. This is called being happy. This is called being warm. The only odd thing is this self-regard, here, holding up your shirt to look at the pale of your belly, turning in profile and gauging the width of your upper arm. Lucy Jinx: pasta-full and garlic-breathed. Lucy Jinx: lips stained the purple that red wine stains lips. Lucy Jinx: wondering if her face has started to grandma droop, that unholy tug floorward, starting in blubs at either side of the chin. What do they call these lines across throats? 'Come on' she berates herself 'are you forgetting your Colette!?' Lucy Jinx: closing eyes and putting face close to lightbulbs atop mirror - the same trick she did since her twenties. Earlier, earlier than her twenties. Lucy Jinx: imitating Dorene moving face toward bathroom lightbulbs. But Lucy's hands are beautiful. She's always said so. The one compliment given that had always stuck. Mrs. Pollop - such a beautiful name she would howl murder inside her head at the other third-graders for mocking - reading a poem Lucy had written and handing it back over to Lucy and saying 'Your hands, my Lucy dove - I hope you know how poetic those hands of yours are.' Okay? Breathe out. Lucy Jinx: fully regarded. That's her. She taps her glass forehead, her glass forehead tries to tap her forehead back - but look at it, it can't even get close. Glass finger to her finger touch.

The mother serves orange sherbet. Lucy learns for the first time it's not called *Sherbert*. You really just learned that? 'You really just learned that?' the mother cannot stop smiling. And the mother claims she'd never heard anyone call it *Sherbert*. Lucy is the startled party here - 'Everyone I knew called it *sherbert*!' she says, mouth full with half-spoonful, even saying this knowing that by *everyone I knew* she probably only means herself. The sherbet is very good and the mother indulges in three bowlfuls, as excuse each time pointing out that Flynn is gone 'So this kind of should be treated as a last meal, you know?' Lucy doesn't object but does switch over to eating some of the candies out of some bag the child brought home a week ago from some class party, poking through as though endlessly there will be one of the miniature chocolates she actually likes. 'I'm doing the dishes' Lucy says, timing this exactly as the mother takes a childishly large amount of sherbet at a go 'but only because I kind of have a domestic fantasy going, here' - she taps forehead - 'and really want to take it to the hilt, dig?' The mother swallows, laughs, says she'd never dare dream of stopping her but the backstory was appreciated. 'I'm telling you' Lucy tipsy sing-song expansive goes on 'I am going whole hog on this! I'm barefooting it and if you have overalls I can borrow it's just those, my skivvies, a ballcap, my utilitarian bra, and a cigarette to ash in the ketchup and then stub in a tater-tot at some point! That's how it's done around here, yeah?'

Lucy sneaks the last of the wine while she loads the dishwasher - no idea is this the best way to load a dishwasher, her physics seem off, but what does she know? Of course if the mother asks for more wine then Lucy is dead-to-red-handed-rights, but as she feels new waves of ease through her, well, what does she care? The mother is upstairs this whole time. And Lucy likes the downstairs lit just by the one kitchen light - the one over the sink area, two tones somehow, greenish on one side and then orangeish-brown on the other - and likes the only sound being her lazy, undisciplined, amateur-housewifey clatter. Provided she could be perpetually headful-of-soft-wine this is a life she feels she could live in perpetuity. But then she feels she could live a life of washing dishes in perpetuity if she could be kept medically besotted throughout. 'Besotted besotted' she sings and thinks this is an upward declension from *enamored* from *captivated* from *bewitched*. 'I'm besotted by you' she tries 'you've besotted me.' The mother could be sitting there, reading or having a cigarette. Lucy could turn and say 'You've besotted me - I find you besotting.' The mother is right upstairs. The dishes are done except for the last bit of the last wine Lucy is holding. It's easy enough to go up and tell her. Drink. Lights smoke. Should she start the dishwasher or just leave it loaded? The question in that question: is the mother coming downstairs or is Lucy meant to go up? 'What a besotting suspense' cigarettes Lucy then lets cigarette dangle and sponge-cleans the counters and wipes them with an already rather wet rag.

The mother comes down dressed in less than her usual nightclothes - or not less but it seems quite obvious those aren't the panties she's been in all day and just whatever tanktop had been on top of the laundry in the basket. Lucy watches her apologize and get herself some headache tablets, holding up a finger to keep Lucy from retreating as Lucy does a wincing I'm-going-upstairs face and starts to over-pantomime tip-toeing away. Swallowing the pills fast with a gasp and a sour expression like a dog yawn after, the mother says she is fine, that she just over-ate. 'As those on Death Row, I mean, should' she adds. Is this the first time the mother's not worn a bra? Lucy knows the mother knows she is thinking that. Proof? The mother asks 'You're doing alright yourself, right?' Lucy can't meet her eyes. 'Yeah. Though I'm a lush from way back, just ask around.' Then, camaraderie tactic, Lucy asks if she might have some of those headache pills, too. 'Preemptively' she says as she tries to act nerdishly bashful, moving by the mother - who does not make particular room, whose bare arm Lucy's shirted shoulder is pressing against, not just brushing - to get the tap going, water into cupped palm, pills into mouth, that brief candy-coat taste to one pinprick of her tongue before she swallows, the always heavy-gut feel of tapwater and pills. Lucy fakes a sniffle to have excuse to move to the bathroom, to tug a short length of toilet-paper, to blow her nose and sniffle again while the mother leans there, cigarette now a mess of scribble, a long lick of navy blue over one side of her face.

THE MOTHER STOOD OUT BACK with Lucy, each with a small blanket draped over shoulders, standing on a third shared blanket, but after a few drags from her cig the mother went back into the house and just smoked through the open door. 'Why are we smoking outside, anyway?' the mother wanted to know, Lucy reminding the mother it had been her idea, all along. 'I should not be listened to. Next time I ever suggest anything reference this by way of telling me *No*. Aren't you freezing?' Lucy's teeth were chattering, her body tensed to the point of cramp. 'On record: this is not the most uncomfortable I have ever been, but on that smiley-face doctor's office chart I am definitely making an odd expression.' The mother tugged Lucy's blanket, the whole thing slipping off, then tugged her by the back of her t-shirt, rather tersely, inside. What about the blankets? Should Lucy remind her about the blankets? 'We left the blankets out there.' 'You left your blanket out there' the mother poshly corrected 'and you'd better sort that out - I'm making some tea is what I'm occupied with.' But neither moved as there were still cigarettes to finish. Ash now sprinkled visibly on the carpet some places where passing feet had smeared black of it already into some almost letter-*Ms*. The mother noticed Lucy noticing that. Lucy watched the mother's toe dab in the thickest of an ash-splotch and watched it trace something - letters? a shape? a symbol? - but Lucy could not tell what, nothing really appeared, the ash not spreading so well. So Lucy just told her she was for shit at foot-carpet writing.

Lucy felt waterlogged by the time the tea and the floor-heater got rid of her shiver. The wine lullabied even the most coursing of her blood - which Lucy knew there was much of. Under same blanket as the mother, flesh of thighs even causally touching, Lucy could not tell if she regretted the coming of sleep. She'd not be able to stave it off. This was like when she drowsed in the passenger seat of a moving car - try as she might, twist or chit-chatter or anything to keep her going, her eyes built their own weight, a gravity, a collapsing singularity, blackhole in her head-back sucking all universe into it. Or was she glad? This was perfect - as perfect as anything, more perfect in certain analyses. Here and now it was one thing, but say she were a story: how would she be interpreted? Now say she was a story written thirty years ago: how different things would seem. And a story forty years before that: what would she make of reading this scene of her here, the sitting resulting one way or the other, sleep or remaining awake? Four-hundred years? Two-thousand. More. There - that was the first genuine nod off. The die has been cast - why point out lack of perfections even could they be found? The mother's left hand has drifted onto Lucy's inner thigh. Lucy tenses then eases then with eyes shut as though drifting ever so bit-by-bit allows her legs to open. Fingers there, hand there. Inner thigh, light-downed with hair in that crease. Steady. Staying. Her breathing is false asleep. Beside her - she just checked - the mother's head in back-tilt and soft whistling from nose.

In this interim Lucy regards herself. Lucy touches each knuckle of the mother's hand where it carelessly drifted in sleep to end up and Lucy traces the bulb at the wrist-edge and the length up to the elbow-crook where further tracing - because of positioning in physical space - becomes too difficult to continue. Lucy watched herself do that. She is fiercely awake now though the moment the mother's eyes open she will shut her own eyes and power down, lickity-split. Until then: she regards. She touches little-toe to little-toe, bit-more-of-knee pushes bit-more-of-knee. Really she sees only blanket when she looks down - technically, technically, in moments *technically* is not relevant. But these aren't things you even get to see with your own eyes still, Lucy, look how your real-world keeps itself partway dream rendered! Why not pull the blanket away? Yes. Close eyes when you do so. Do so in motion so controlled, so miniscule, it will seem only natural if the mother wakes, finds you sleeping, the blanket to the carpet, innocent rumpled to its pile. But Lucy can't. She regards herself: can't. Look at Lucy, Lucy, look how she can't. And then shiver shiver Lucy thinks: the mother might be awake! Lucy, she might be wondering 'Oh what is all this now?' And even had she been waiting through the first slow indulgences - waiting patient and rapt as you, Lucy - by now she is just confused, by now she will not open her eyes just because it would be awkward. You've rejected her! And now her genuine sleep seems feigned and her sleep if feigned is trying to be made genuine. The mother will either wake with vague pleasant sensations of *Was that a dream?* or will wake wishing it had been.

Or has Lucy been asleep? Is this how you had been sitting? The hand on your spread-to-permit thigh - yes - but feet aren't touching and you can tell by your warm thick mouth you've been sleeping. Have you been asleep, Lucy? For how long? The television is on still all but muted and Lucy has no idea what program she is looking at. That is not how the mother had been positioned, either. Lucy opens eyes. Again? Had you just woken up right there, before? Or is this the first time? No. The mother is kind of side curled, knees up. Lucy is twisted kind of the same except full sitting up - her knees pressed together, foot crossed over foot. 'How long have I been asleep?' she wonders. The television is on still all but muted and she has no idea what the program is. She nudges the mother's hip through the light blankets - tip tip tip - no response. Pats it - taptaptap - and still nothing. If Lucy were to stand she doesn't think the mother would stir. So? The thinking is to go up to her own bed, behind closed door, fall asleep. If the mother had been asleep awhile she would wake and assume this had been agreed on by way of some half-awake *Goodnights*. And? Or - yeah, Lucy rolls her eyes - maybe not upstairs to bed, maybe just go to the kitchen. The mother would wake, feeling the absence of Lucy - not Lucy specifically, that sort of thing just wakes people, someone next to them, someone not - and soon appear with still sleeping eyes to say 'I'm going upstairs' and Lucy - who would be busy with coffee or last cigarette she'd apologize for - would say 'Me too, as soon as I'm done this.' Goodnight. Goodnight.

'Lucy?' A little last flicker of dream, misshapen: there is a carnival in the distance, someone is throwing rocks - Lucy thinks maybe she should tell Dorene about this, Dorene who is arguing with that person, still. 'Lucy?' And Lucy understands she is being gently rocked awake, opens her eyes with a sound effect Mmn? and then an eye-pop, big nostril-breath in, sits up some and 'Sorry, what?' The mother is smiling, telling her 'Sorry, I didn't know if I should wake you, you were twitching a little.' 'Twitching?' Lucy is now swiveling where she sits, pressing the butt of one palm to first this eye and then that. 'Do you want to come up to bed?' Lucy yawns through that question then on the exhale sits up even straighter and again says 'Sorry' then 'I must have passed out. What time is it?' The mother has been sleeping, as well. 'Is it morning?' The mother seems so particularly amused, smile deepening, widening, contouring, everythinging, enough that Lucy is self-conscious. 'Shit - what time is it?' 'I don't know. Are you okay?' 'I'm fine' she yawns again and then laughs on the out breath with 'Jesus, so sorry.' 'I think you need some sleep.' 'Then why the fuck did you wake me up?' Burst of stifled chortle. 'Because I'm a wicked bastard - did you want to come up to bed?' Lucy is making her face ghastly, scraping her tongue against her upper front few teeth, going 'Blarg' as though every speck of her is sour. 'I think I need something to eat really quick - or just a little more tea.' 'Do you want me to make it?' 'I got it.' The mother gives her shoulder a gentle punch, sound effect Poof with a puff of lips. 'Okay. I'd join you but I don't think I can keep my eyes open. Then come to bed, okay?' Lucy yawns again, head nodding 'Yeah.' Finishes the yawn into the bend of her arm around her face.

Question: Had she been told when the child would be home the next day? Answer: Yeah, probably. Question: But she doesn't remember? Answer: No, she doesn't remember. Question: It's not likely the mother would have not aired out the house if the parent of some other kid were dropping off, first thing, right? Answer: Well, it's neither likely nor unlikely - that could go either way. Question: But it feels more probable that the mother would be going to pick up the child - no one wants to be dropping off other people's overnight visiting kids at the damned crack of dawn, right? Answer: I see what you mean - yeah, that makes sense. Question: So you think that's what's going on, here? Answer: What? Question: What? Answer: What do you mean by *going on*? Question: Nevermind - my point is 'Do you think it's fine to have another cigarette, right now?' Answer: In the house? Question: Obviously in the house - where else? Answer: Down here? Or in my room? Question: Are you sure you even want another cigarette? Answer: Because I'm talking to myself half-naked in a kitchen at almost three-in-the-morning? Question: Is that so odd to assume? You think the question is indelicate? Answer: Gah. Question: What? Answer: *Gah*. Or *Bleh*. Or *meh*. Something like that. Question: You're not feeling well? Answer: I'm just tired. Question: Go up to bed - or did you actually want that cigarette? Answer: I should just smoke in bed. Question: Are you still here talking to yourself? Answer: No. Question: You're not? Answer: What? Question: Goddamn it, just go to sleep. Answer: Fine. Fine. Fine.

Lucy does have a smoke. Another two actually. She is certain she'll feel such a fool in the morning. 'Her night was ruined' Lucy cigarette mutters 'I'm sure she didn't mean to get drunk with the tenant and wake all hungover.' But like such nights, Lucy had the best intentions. It's just in her estimation she'd had too much wine. Or not even too much, just too-much-too-quickly. Now the mother would wake up regret-laden, shower and think 'Fuck, gotta get Flynn' and think 'Is that really all I did last night?' Lucy opens the dishwasher to put things away, closes it without doing so. She figures she shouldn't go to sleep closed in her room because she should at least face the music, offer to drive to get fast-food breakfast or something. Sleep on the sofa? Is that what the mother will want to come down and see? Drunk-bellied Lucy Jinx, beached-whale of Lucy Jinx, sour nicotine-sweat of Lucy Jinx warmed all night into the sofa upholstery? Well, it's not as though Lucy can be expected to stay awake! And they both got drunk! 'Besides, I'm not really feeling hungover - we didn't drink that much, anyway.' Nod. There is a lot of truth to this. Lucy opens the dishwasher again, closes it again. Better to sleep on the sofa. She'll just lay a blanket down under her because that can be washed. Lay down two. If the mother is upset Lucy was obviously just sleepy and never quite got to her room.

How heavy would Lucy call her limbs as she tries to oh-so-stealthily pop into her room, takes up the sweatpants where they are left on the bed - just in case the child is dropped off early and has a doorkey, never too careful, never too careful, the mother might well oversleep - grabs her phone when she sees it on the desk, tries not to let out even one breath until she is halfway back down the stairs? Her arms are scapegoats over slave shoulder. She's getting her breathing even and swaying to how much she likes that phrase, still, into the sweatpants, sat to the sofa. *Scapegoat over slave shoulders.* Might be the sort of line she'll dismiss once awake but for now she figures she'd ought to remember it. Moving to text-message the line to herself - no way was she going to stand up again, other than to arrange the blankets she just remembered about - she finds the phone screen indicates messages waiting. And that this is the pay-as-you-go-phone - not what she'd thought to grab. Three messages. One: *Hey - you flaked on me tonight.* Two, just a short time later: *Sorry, that was stupid. Haha. You probably didn't even think I'd show up haha.* Three, just two hours ago: *But I am still mad haha Grrr. Not one of those idiots though, I won't text after this. But I was waiting haha Ok. Don't know why I typed Ok. Haha Bye. You're awesome. Bye.* She smiles despite herself and says to the phone 'That's all certainly cute, anyway.' Texts to herself: *Heavy as scapegoat on slave shoulders.* Send. Oh! Texts: *Her regret was the mouth of a tunnel, her joy heavy, a scapegoat on slave shoulders.* Looks at it. Won't like it in the morning. Delete.

This is what Lucy dreams - she's asleep before a handclap could echo: there is a large wall, on it a painting with windows in it. The windows are lighted in a way that seems sinister. Not a pattern. Like each room has an invader, each invader terrorizing each rightful occupant in exactly the same way. In this moment she is aware of the music in one room and of something in the ceiling corner following everyone with its eyes. In this moment she is aware of the shower running in this other room. Nothing else. So close to the shower-head it seems insulting. Face forced to it. Jaw locked with the thing in her mouth, doorknob thick, doorknob pustule, the water flowing a pimple burst, only air in her which belches into the flat closed bronze of the door she's gotten her mouth struck around. Gags. Awake. She sits up in the dark and her phone tells her that all must have only been dreamed in five or six minutes. The feeling is that her throat had been violated. A man's hand had gripped hard her hair, forced her back-and-forth back-and-forth on his stiffness. 'It's the heat on from the vents' thinks Lucy. The vent is right above her. Her throat had been dried out already from the drinking, the heat pouring down her open gullet had been too much. Dry throats always lead to nightmare.

'Lucy?' She opens her eyes abruptly. It is night - she can see enough through the slats of the blinds mostly closed over the backdoor - but the living-room light was on. The mother has hand to her shoulder. Moves it to the side of her face. 'What's going on?' Lucy asks, the words coming out rather pasty. 'I think you were having a nightmare. Are you okay?' The mother looks so oven-warm, new-bread warm, kitten-sleep warm, such concern on those eyes. 'I'm fine.' Shit. Wait? What's going on, Lucy. 'Shit - did I wake you up? What time is it?' 'No, no' - the mother makes a shush sound, hand still on her face, now touching hair at the top of her forehead, around her ear - 'I just came down to see if you weren't feeling well. I wasn't sure where you were.' 'Okay' Lucy says, nodding, not with it, really. 'Okay. Yeah. I get really shitty dreams sometimes.' 'I could tell. Was it my cooking?' Lucy blinks. 'Oh' - yes, Lucy, that was levity - 'no, no. When I sleep with my' - for some reason she can't find the words, knows from the feel of her nose that her face must be a rotten gnarl of confusion - 'my mouth open' - there, Lucy, you've managed it - 'I get weird dreams. On my back with my mouth open, I mean.' 'Do you need some water?' Lucy touches the mother's hand, moves it over her face, holds it over her face. Holds it over her face. Moves it back to her forehead. Eyes on the mother's says 'Don't think I'm awful, okay? Because of tonight.' The mother passes hand - deliberate, slow - over Lucy's face, down cheek, across shoulder, and tells her she is getting her some water.

THE CHILD IS EAGER TO show Lucy a dance move, the mother saying 'Flynn, can you give poor Lucy ten seconds to just be!?' Lucy, stepping down from the final stair, waves the mother off - shared, silent-mouth 'Good-morning' from the one 'Hi' from the other - and says 'Poor Lucy is fine. Let's see this alleged dance move, Flynnov Flynnonovitch.' Lucy shrugs when the mother goes What-on-Earth? faced to this Russian-novel-protagonistesque nicknaming here and claps, holds hand out for a high-five after the little be-bop, spin-and-slide motions of the child are complete. 'Where'd you learn to dance like that?' 'From my friend Nikki' the child answers offhand, moving off into the living-room to rummage through one of the bins of toys. 'Nicholas is the sleepover friend' the mother explains, Lucy pouring the last of the coffee and prepping the next pot. 'Do you work today?' the mother asks, very casual air to the question, preoccupied even with whatever the content was of the mail she had just opened. Does Lucy work today? No. 'No, not today. Some weekends but not today. And anyway' she sighs 'fuck that place.' She does a jaw-clench look of Sorry-sorry, eyes darting in the direction of the living-room, but the mother doesn't even notice, might not have heard, might have heard and just not given half-a-shit. 'And what about you?' Lucy flicks the paper the mother holds. Again. Snatches it - very very very careful to not go too far by actually seeing what it was, this little snatch of hers totally catching her off guard if she's being honest, a line she feels she might have crossed - and says 'Focus!' snaps her fingers 'Hey hey!' points with two fingers first at the mother's face then at her own 'Focus - I'm asking you a question, you see?'

The music in the car is appalling. For a minute Lucy regrets agreeing to come out to eat but when the mother reaches over and pats her above the knee one two three four times, hand lingering before moving to steering wheel, she understands this is a shared torment and therefore one more endurable. In fact, it's fun to make snide comments that go totally over the child's head. Or not so much over the child's head. They aren't even directing the comments at the child after the second song, just trying to one-up each other with making vulgarities out of word combinations that would come off innocuous if the child suddenly showed interest in what the grown-ups were talking about - 'or if he was just one of those wily little bastards' thinks Lucy 'the ones who make it a habit to seem to not be listening, spring shit on folks later.' Like you were, Lucy. Maybe. Maybe. It wasn't a question, Lucy. Well, fine. She chuckles at her recollections and the mother catches her eye, makes a question mark of her nose in a wrinkle, the tip tap of a one sided smile the dot underneath. 'I just remember what a sneaky little bitch I was as a kid' Lucy leans across to whisper. 'I was always trying to get the goods on everyone. Figuring out how to use them against themselves, you know?' The mother turns her face from front in Lucy's direction before Lucy has time to move back her head. Their eyes locked and Lucy knew the mother could tell she had slowed down to let their noses just barely miss touching right then.

Lucy Jinx has embraced this all. Why in Hell not, Lucy Jinx? So she'll go out to breakfasts and she'll let the child bond. She'll even offer to give the mother 'nights off' with all eager claims of enthusiastically wanting to spend some time with the lad! It's becoming more and more expected of her. It's becoming more and more self-aware. Yeah? Could she imagine reverting to 'I live up in that room and we sometimes kind of small-talk?' From this point, could she backtrack to that? Not without implosion. Not without all of the things that reversion would mean and would make people feel who had done nothing wrong. Not without causing self-mutiny inside of people she has nothing against. Lucy has let this happen and now she will let it happen to her. Fair is fair. Fair is fair. 'Isn't fair fair?' Lucy asks across the table and the child gives her a huff of 'I don't know what you're talking about' and she says 'That's because I wasn't talking to you - you're nothing but a pipsqueak!' and the mother goes 'I've never thought fair was fair but if you say so.' 'You never did?' 'Naw - I get the short end of that, every time. But I guess somebody always does.' Lucy has to nod without showing she doesn't follow. She has to nod without showing she's not certain what is being implied. Was that meant to be something she'd pick up on? Was she meant to smile in some way, to touch feet under the table, to ask 'What do you mean?' or to laugh or to scoff or to say something sarcastic about 'Your mother this-or-that' to the child? Jesus. What fun.

This is the third time she has caught the woman washing her hands at the bathroom sink flick a look at her in the mirror - the third time she has pretended not to notice. What could she want? Fourth time. The woman turns. This is a toilet! I'm waiting for the stall! Are you really about to speak to me!? 'You get your gas at the *Sullivan's* off of *Dorchester*, right?' Lucy goes 'Uh' because the anger has drained from her at the specificity of the question, she is a kid caught off-guard by a question mid-story from a teacher who has no doubt she'll know the answer straight off. 'Sorry - yes, accosting you in the Ladies' Room, I'm sorry' the woman deprecates. 'It's fine' Lucy says, subduing her blush as best she can manage, full recognition by now of who the woman is. 'I do get gas there, yeah.' 'I thought so. Okay - since I've already broken etiquette can I say one more thing?' The background is the sound of toilet tissue being applied, sniffles of nose - Lucy can only imagine the look on that person's face in their stall listening out. 'Sure' says Lucy, blinking some images gone - it kind of seems the woman remarked the sound and is ridding herself of the same image - and when the woman starts to speak there is a Kablamo! of toilet flush, two second later the stall door opens and the occupant timidly scurries to sink, washes hands, tugs paper towel, and is gone by the count of thirteen. Lucy quickly glimpses to herself in the mirror while the woman is still looking that way - Jesus is that what I look like? - then disguises the glimpse as a wince, rubbing that eye with a knuckle.

It does feel awkward continuing the meal, now. It goes without saying Lucy doesn't mention the toilet adventure any more than Lucy mentioned anything else - yet still. Yet still. It's just the presence of the child, really. That funny-bones everything. From a distance, Lucy knows they look all-together, little family, inseparably linked since mankind's dawning. Or is that not it? she wonders, attempting to be honest. She didn't see where that woman - Amelia - was sitting but if Lucy and her companions were somehow observable by her it would be just as likely things looked like this: mother, child, good-pal-from-work. Or: mother, child, sister. Or: mother, child, wife-of-husband's-friend. See? Any number of things. 'How's it going?' the mother asks - Lucy is now wary of mind reading, needs to come up with something to say - and seems to unconsciously reach a bit across the table but to restrain at some headless-horseman line. 'It's nothing - sorry - something. My friend.' She makes a gesture of she-knows-she-shouldn't-be-bothering-the-mother-with-it but the mother does that head tilted Go-on-I'm-here-to-listen thing that in this highly particularized, wholly there-was-no-way-to-have-expected-to-even-have-to-expect-it circumstance Lucy truly, gutturally despises so she has to press on. 'My friend quit her job. Which was good. But then asked for it back and got it. I told her it wasn't a mistake. I need to tell her it actually was.' 'Let me know if I can help' the mother says, voice well-versed in knowing when to trail of and attention changes to 'What's that you're coloring there, Flynnima?'

If Amelia happens to wind up passing the table or happens to wind up at the cashier station in front of or behind them - if Amelia happens to be standing out front smoking when they exit - the best move will be for Lucy to just give a brief wave and say 'Hi' making and immediately breaking eye-contact. The *Hi* will be a bit confusing, sure, but will also get the proper message across. Now: if Amelia says 'Well hello, again' - oh God, that's exactly what she'll say! - or something, if Amelia talks first - Lucy can't fathom particulars, they make her brain double over, just now - then Lucy will have to behave as though she has known Amelia longer than just exchanging names and mutual 'I've always wanted to ask you your name' 'I've always wanted to say *Hello*' in the toilet, twenty minutes ago. She can't make her voice seem to be trying to give off a drift. Just 'Oh hi Amelia.' Should she add 'What are you doing here?' Hmn. Or does that run the risk of Amelia's face betraying some little blip that might give something away? Hmn. But if Lucy goes 'Hi Amelia' then introductions of the mother and her child, well, that could lead to actual polite conversational death-traps forged straight in the last inch of the bowels of Hell! Or just play it off with the truth? 'We just met in the toilet - she works in the gas station I go to.' Sure, easy. No. Nope, not so. Then why wouldn't you have told the story right when you got back from the toilet? Lucy. Lucy. How could you not have taken a moment to at least have made note of where she is sitting!?

The child has already climbed in his seat and in the moment when the car is closed - Lucy on the one side, the mother rounding to the other - the mother asks really if everything is alright with Lucy's friend. 'You seem really worried. And I feel bad, now.' What? 'Why do you feel bad?' 'I kinda forced a night of drinking on you. I didn't even care if you had stuff on your plate.' Neither move to open their car doors - though, Lucy, you really should at least get hidden in the car. 'I wanted to spend the night with you - please don't worry' - but this is a good opportunity, Lucy, to go - 'And I may have been a bit of a drag there once the wine got me, yeah, but believe me there was nothing that could have been better for me than non-crisis-management time with someone.' You're a crackerjack liar, you almost believe that yourself it's so just-left-of-center! The mother nods an *Okay*, pauses, smiles, pauses, and says 'I wasn't really sorry, anyway. Fuck your friend.' You need to smile at that, Lucy. 'No interest in that' - wait? Why did you say that, now? - Lucy says then rolls her eyes while saying - this is all going to cause you real headache in about five minutes when you have time to think, Lucy! - 'no need to worry on that front.' Lucy! The fuck with you, fella!? I mean - what are you doing!? The mother opens her car door, head downturned to chuckle, to chuckle, looks up to find Lucy still looking at her. 'Then I won't worry, then.' Lucy, Lucy - how do you explain yourself, now?

But Lucy assures herself it is not part of an elaborate, ever expanding cover-up operation that she decides to say 'Sure' she's keen to come along while the child gets a hair-cut. 'One of those clip-joints' the mother says and Lucy wry smiles at the groan-joke 'shouldn't take too long.' And sure enough they are able to take the child to a chair, straight away. The mother has to go give some likely - knowing the child - painfully and meticulously itemized instruction for the trim - in the meantime Lucy sits breathing in the smell of the place. She adores this smell, associates it always with wet hair, combed, snipped with soft blades of scissors. She notes, each at-a-time, the various, age-faded posters of hairstyles mounted around the waiting area. How long have those been there? Is that a thing with strip-mall, franchise hair-cut joints? An industry-insider thing, a time-honored thing, the drib-drab equivalent of the Barber Pole? And why do these woman always look the same, these shopping-center hair-dressers? Does the entire establishment come as a set, ready-made? This one and that one and that one. Lucy can almost guess which will have what anecdote: divorce, ex-boyfriend whose band was once on tv, finishing classes at night, just doesn't want to be her sister but knows she's coming to understand her sister's choices, auditioned for a sit-com and so on. The mother sits down and sighs 'Jesus Christ - even if it was real immortality, immortality isn't worth dealing with Flynn's goddamn hair.'

Lucy lets the child have her compact and kind of watches his reflection in the car's side-mirror looking at himself and looking at himself and looking at himself. 'Don't tell him he looks good' the mother leans in, a rush to the words as though she cannot believe she had not already mentioned this. 'Just' - Lucy makes a formless gesture in response to the mother's desperate eyes - 'not a peep.' 'What are you two talking about?' 'We're talking about ways to reduce belly-fat, same as always. God Flynn, I told you, didn't I!' Lucy doesn't even have time to register amusement or to wonder what the meaning of this is before the child, all of a sudden an unselfconscious throttle of frenetic voice flung in all directions, says 'My mom told me that all those magazines are always about belly-fat because that's all women talk about. Is that all women talk about?' 'Belly-fat? Goddamn straight that's what we talk about' Lucy full turns in her seat to say. 'Do you know how fascinating belly-fat is? Can you even begin to imagine it? Do you even have belly-fat?' And the child grips his belly, pressing and pinching at the skin. The mother mutters some curses under her breath, Lucy alarmed - had she crossed a boundary? - but turns to see the mother's bile is directed at a long line of bicyclists who are using both lanes of the road ahead of them, causing the car to dramatically slow. Face all a bitter-lime scrunch, the mother tells Lucy 'Norman was a bicyclist, you see?' Holds a dagger of eye-contact, breaks it with a wink and a flick to the side of Lucy's neck.

Okay: now Lucy safe and closed and locked back in her room. Below her the mother is clapping hands and directing the child to piano practice. God in heaven, this just keeps going as long as it wants, doesn't it!? And how long, Lucy, can you continue to be you before you find out what it's like to be limbless in unmarked luggage left outside a bus station? She laughs at how easily she can picture this and laughs at how she always imagines one is still alive when one has died. Why do you imagine that? 'Because death is supposed to be awful' she says matter-of-fact as though for the umpteenth time. How long has it been now since you've written? Look. Seriously. This is nothing to glibly gloss over, little girl. When is the last time you sat at that computer, penned in those notebooks? Do you even have any verse in your head now? 'I must' she says but doesn't try to verify. She starts to say something but doesn't. It's true: the notebook looks untouched to the degree it has become infectious, it would make her untouched to part it open. And the computer seems a remnant of something ancient and not-very-interesting, a lost city those digging up figure they must not be the first to yawn at and immediately rebury.



WHERE IS LUCY JINX OFF to? How exactly can Lucy Jinx answer that question? In some cases, completely exact. For example: Lucy, if going to work. Lucy, if at work, going to *Hernando's* on her break. Lucy, if on her break at *Hernando's*, going back to the trailer-office. Those all only count as one answer. Lucy, if coming back to the rented room. Lucy, if in her room going down to the kitchen. Again: only counts as one! And what is meant by the question is 'How specifically can Lucy answer, if leaving the house?' Lucy, if going to Katrin's. Lucy, if going to a restaurant. Ah - is that specific? Which restaurant? Lucy, if going to see a movie. Wait. Lucy, if going to a bookstore. Is there always a specific bookstore? A particular movie? Where is Lucy Jinx off to, right now? It isn't enough to name endless places she's not off to - France, Cordoba, the Hague - and it isn't enough to name places she might want to go to - Italy, Ireland, the birthplace of Ezra Pound, the grave of William Wordsworth - and it isn't enough to name places she could readily go to but isn't - no need to give examples of those - none of that will get us closer to an answer. She isn't going to work. She isn't going to Katrin's. So where is Lucy Jinx going, now? How specific can she be in answering that, having now been in the car, driving, for fifteen minutes, already?

Here is one place she winds up: a strip-mall she has never been in before. Technically she is still just in her car, though, smoking a cigarette, looking at the storefronts. There is *Rio Tacos*. There is *Ali's Discount* - the sign says nothing further. There is the small grocery-store called *Ample*. There is a travel agency - 'Why do those still exist?' Lucy wonders not aloud but vocal by way of a dramatic squint, snarl, smoke out harsh and up-angular - though it also has a sign on the window that says *Copys or Faxes fifty cents*. This transfixes her. What a mysterious sign! What a use of language! A rune hidden in plain sight, an Aztec swear-word no one knows is an Aztec swear-word, people would think is just invented-on-the-spot gobbledygook if ever they heard someone utter it! She doesn't even mind the misspelling of *Copies*! This is a glossy, full-colour, professionally-rendered sign so she supposes the typo is purposeful, likes how this supposition adds to the thing's mystique. What she is more focused on is the choice of the word *Or*. Why not *And*? Why not just the two words, nothing connecting them or setting them at arms to each other? And why *fifty cents*? For one fax? One copy? What size? How many pages? Lucy could suppose that one would find out if they went inside but prefers to believe the sign has no desire to lure in all general comers. Those words - that set of words - mean a specific thing to someone properly initiated in something. And only someone who knows the meaning would go to that travel agency for whatever the real reason to go to it is. This is an impenetrable hieroglyph in her contemporary tongue! Yet at the same time she is to believe scraps of sheepskin with ancient ink on them can be figured out if just thunk about long enough!? Harsh puff out, car in reverse, she mutters 'We're idiots, man.'

Here is another place she winds up: another strip-mall she has never been in before. One more posh than the previous. More posh, in fact, than any she has been in around here. A still under-construction building promises *Luxury Apartments* are coming, even gives them a name: *The Lofts at Stoneridge Manor*. A gas station and a row of the usual shops - the glaring exception here being a comic-book shop, obviously well-loved and owned by a dedicated and lonely fellow, this judging from the fact that the sign's letters are genuine vintage and the joint is called *Knick-Knack's: Funny Books and Bubble-Gum Cards*. Maybe that doesn't mean anything vintage. Lucy, who knows nothing of comic-books or their history, perhaps should not allow herself hasty conclusions. But she fixates on the restaurant on the lower-level of the already completed but seemingly unlived in second building of *The Lofts at Stoneridge Manor*. Will that place survive because the tenants will frequent it? Or will the tenants of luxury apartments shun a fake Italian bistro beggardly proclaiming its clearly phony authenticity? And what if no one ever moves in? Was it all an elaborate hoodwink to get the restauranteurs to ruin their lives? To die in their never visited bistro at the heel bottom of an unlived-in-by-anybody rise of glorious living-rooms? This is your day off, Lucy! Why are you sitting here? Why aren't you writing? She sniffles and wonders if the at-least-few-day-old coffee in the cup in her cup holder is drinkable. And, if so, would it be ghastly? Or would it just register as slightly sour water?

Lucy drove with more purpose to the secondhand bookshop where she had found *Her News Sister's Best Friend*. She's smoked her obligatory cigarette and now, wishing she had some gum or breath-mints, has entered the place and moved with purpose to the section of dirty books. Of course most weren't honestly dirty, were the contemporary, perfectly polite little stuff of above-board, purely-for-maintenance orgasms. 'Nothing wrong about that, all on top of the table' she thinks and smiles at her entendre. Certainly none of these are smuttier or more explicit than either *Her New Sister's Best Friend* or even than the object of her search - she'll know the title when she sees it, can't understand how could she not recall it, even still! - that pink-with-brown dotted spine she had traced thumb-tip along endless times, its pages spread, its pulp yellowed musk giving each word a taste as her saliva thinned, pooled, was swallowed. 'Are these all of the titles you have?' Lucy is pointing at the section she had been perusing - not too prudish to name it just not sure whether to say *Adult titles* or *Erotic titles* or what, each phrase seeming both silly and to not give the correct impression of her query. 'Not at all. We have a stock-room a mile long. Is there a particular title?' Lucy - your heart is racing like the time on that morning you'd realized you'd dressed by mistake in one of your lover's blue socks! 'Can you look up by publisher? Or type-of-series?' The man - obviously the owner - seems to consider, a look of *Maybe* to his lipstick-thin moustache. 'Or is the stock-room arranged by type? I could just look through there, myself.' Yes, Lucy, yes - you really just said that.

It seems impossible - why is this man still back here!? go tend the store, goddamn you! - but Lucy swallows the rising shaking in her hands, turns the book back to its wordless reverse cover, hoping this will stabilize its actuality. There had been only a small trove of these pink-with-brown spotted books. So few it had seemed ridiculous to even hope. There had been *Her First Secretary* and there had been *Her Favorite Secretary*. There had been *Candy Kane* and there had been *Eliza On Beale Street*. There had been *The Bride's Twin* and there had been *The Babysitter's New Job*. There had been *Aunt Stacy's Dalmatian* and there had been *Replacing Mommy, Again*. But that there is - turned to hide the cover - right now, in Lucy's hand, *Claudette, The Bashful Girl* seems impossible beyond scope. What is going to happen is this: Lucy will turn the cover again and it will be one of the other's she's just seen - she's picked up one of those accidentally and in that moment has finally recalled the title she has been searching her buried soul for and trick photography has been performed to lead to the slap of disappointment - of dismemberment - she is about to endure. *Claudette, The Bashful Girl.* Why is this man still standing here!? Slash him dead where he stands and flee Lucy! Take your crown back with you to rule in the forest, running forever! 'I found it' she says, comically holding it like a trophy as flimsy as a day-old caught fish. 'Did ya! Terrific!' And they move back into the main room of the shop. It isn't in her hand. Of course it's not. She is smiling so hard at the joke she is playing on herself. 'What a thing - us having the very one' the man says, bagging it up 'when I was a younger lad there must have been hundreds of those titles - my older brother, his friends passed them through each other's hands.' Her manners keep Lucy pleasant chit-chatting fifteen minutes. And stepping outside she is still afraid to look down and of the weight in the brown bag in her hand.

The book in the trunk of the car, Lucy drives aimlessly in a bliss of half-singing along to a song and half-remembering a half-remembered Dorene. Is Dorene half-remembered? 'Yes - be honest for once, Lucy' Lucy laughs aloud breaking off mid-word from the refrain of *Piano Man*. Her memories of that girl are the equivalent of a dream described in the text of a stage play. Oh she can say it - she can even recite it just like the actress or actor she saw do it on stage, verbatim to the sigh like how the actor, the actress did it in the film version - but it's not her words, her dream. A specific to prove Dorene is a mere memory-cobble? Here: The bedroom she is remembering could never have been Dorene's - she is thinking of the bedroom she had lived in with her first roommate in University. That is the bed the two of them - not she and Dorene, she and her roommate - would sit against, smoking joints and reading James Joyce, pretending the skunk weed made the prose unmuddy itself like a defrosting windshield. Dorene is feelings under her arms and tensions in the backs of her calves. Dorene is the word *mouth* and the fingers moving *Come here* and then coming there. Then this reverie breaks and - what an odd intrusion! - Lucy recalls that her actual first kiss had been at the rehearsal for a play. She had not known there was to be a kiss. She and the boy - Victor, she no problem remembers - had come to the stage direction, both she and he had paused, Victor asking the teacher - Mrs. Cordone - 'Do we really kiss?' Mrs. Cordone, like nothing, almost rolling her eyes Oh Jesus saying 'That's what it says, right?' She doesn't remember the kiss. Just remembers it was her first.

Lucy is now pulled over in the lot of a restaurant called *Pitts!!* Her phone had vibrated, she'd quickly glanced - it was Layla - the phone had vibrated, vibrated stopped, a pause, vibrated. And so Lucy had pulled over as soon as she was able to. Which brings her to here: dialing Layla, not bothering to have listened to the message which she immediately admits. 'What are you doing you could call back but couldn't answer?' 'Use your imagination, Layman - we were in the same classes together, you're as clever as me.' There is a pause which after-the-fact could be fairly called *a dubious pause* as the voice Layla used when she asks 'Why do you sound actually happy?' indicates, primarily among a few other things, dubiousness. 'Because the sky is as weightless as a discount envelope, Labiya, and is sure to contain something of as much value, you know?' 'Oh God' moans Layla in a manner Lucy can't help being able to see her face from 'why are you talking to me in half-assed poetics?' Note: Lucy actually liked that line but she has enough dignity to allow her friend some bad taste, moves on to 'All poetry is half-assed, Lay, I am going with the flow. What'll be crammed in that discount envelope? A shitty anniversary card with a shitty sentimental couplet by me, that's what!' Layla makes another wisecrack, Lucy does too, then Lucy asks if there is something the matter or anything. 'Don't ask me that, you dick! You're the one who always has something the matter! And it's all always bullshit! God, when I think of the sugar-pills I've had to suffer to keep you in even passable spirits and now you're just fit-as-a-fiddle over nothing!? Fuck you!' Good comic effect: Layla hangs up.

Back on the line. Picking up about here: Lucy says 'You aren't paying for me to do anything. I will just drive, okay? It's not as though I couldn't have just said *Yeah, I have money to fly but I can't leave till next week* - I'd get there the same time.' 'Yes, Lucy - you could have lied but instead you are shooting down a kind and earnest offer. If you're going to start driving tomorrow just let me buy you a ticket to fly tomorrow. How do you have time to drive out here?' But Lucy has no time to explain how she has time for anything she wants. Lucy is the world's whimsy turned back on itself, she is the better punch the audience thought up to a line, still laughing at the comedian but not without a tinge of pity. 'Fine. Buy me a plane ticket.' Long silence and Lucy watches a man employed by *Pitts!!* walk out the front door with a bucket, toss slop water into the handicapped spot, then light a short cigarillo and pat his belly, his buttocks, his belly again, all while kind of tip-tapping the bucket with first the toes of one shoe then the heel of the other. 'Really?' Layla's voice finally comes on. Yes, Lucy - really? 'What do you mean *Really*? Are you withdrawing the offer?' Tone of now-I-know-you're-just-being-a-dick Layla point-blanks 'Are you actually going to come out? Be serious.' Actually be serious, Lucy. Try to think ahead more than abstractly. 'I am serious, Layla. As even the least serious of diseases. Which any good physician will tell you is still serious - one cannot be complacent about matters of health.' It is likely, Lucy knows, that Layla hates her more than she loves her but Layla hides it admirably in the even-keeled way she condescends to say 'So, are you actually coming?' one more time.

Lucy had been about to pull into *Lamont Plaza* when the sight of the clock-tower reminded her this place was quarantined, totally off limits. So she drives around the perimeter - exterior the lot, a wide outline of it and the adjoining shopping plaza - four five six times, not sad but bittersweet melody-like, it could be said. There is a packed parking lot in front of the place that sells billiard tables but the half of the lot in front of the rear entrance to the movie theatre is barren. She risks entering the lot, risks pulling up slowly by the entrance to the billiard joint to get an idea what could be happening. Even through still rolled up window she can her the muffle of live music, singer and all - discount grunge rock, tinny and produced locally - but no signs or posters naming the band are posted up on the doors, the walls beside the doors. Is it a concert? Or are they some sort of entertainment for a tournament in there? Such bottomless riddles everywhere she looks! Things that only participation in could answer! 'Is Lucy Jinx interested enough' she asks aloud in a voice she also gives to narrators of lousy-novels-that-win-major-awards when she reads such things 'to leave her vehicle, to venture in, to sate her curiosity with as simple an act as looking, nodding, and leaving?' Were she a lousy award-winning book she would say *Yes* approach the door but then cower and then - 'Then something!' she bangs the steering wheel gruffly - go to the movies or something symbolic like that. But she's not a book of any variety. So she just stares another moment through the car window, honks her horn long five or so times, laughs like a dime noir and drives off at perfectly appropriate speed while imagining herself doing so erratically and leaving black marks to grey pavement.

Where has Lucy wound up, now? Lucy has wound up having driven down a very long road that dead-ended at a farm. For a good five minutes she is stumped - because it can't be possible that an almost twenty-mile-long road would wind up dead-ending at a farm! No? No. It seems an aberration. It seems like an audition reel to a world that obviously struck no one's fancy and so was shit-canned. But there is no through-road - really there's not! And hardly a way to turn around since the gate is shut fast. Lucy drives backward with such caution she feels her teeth growing lose in her gums, the enamel tasting the slick of saliva. But soon stops. Growls. She'd thought one of the turn-offs she'd passed by had been only right back here a short distance, but turning now - twisted, seatbelt off - to squint long-distance out the back windshield she sees no indication of it or the mailbox she'd remarked - a silver one shaped like a cactus. Puff puff pops of lips, lower-lip turned out in the way lower-lips turn out when parents are mean to children. It takes Lucy six-and-a-half minutes to complete the maneuver to turn the car around. That's how thin this road is. Six-and-a-half? 'Well' she explains 'the clock had gone from oh-eight until fifteen, the fifteen clicking just as I finished the turn-around - but I know I had not started right at oh-eight because I didn't see oh-seven turn to it.' So she thinks the half-minute shave is fair. It's important to be accurate even on absurd roads that shouldn't exist.

KATRIN IS NOT THERE AND the apartment smells like clean laundry but looks like used laundry though perhaps Lucy over-romanticizes. She has lit one of the cigarettes she finds in the pack on the counter before even thinking about it, finds herself taking out her own pack a moment later. What's this? Why am I holding another cigarette? She puts it straight down the sink drain, runs the water, hits the disposal, opens the fridge and eats a piece of the cooked bacon she finds on an uncovered plate. Katrin has retained that habit from - what? - childhood? Lucy has known about it these twenty-odd years, at any rate. 'Katrin?' she says, quite loud, just-in-casing, as she had not done any sort of prying peek into her friend's unlocked, ajar bedroom. She pretends to be startled by Katrin suddenly being behind her, holds up her hands as though Katrin is ghoul-eyed, babbling froth and advancing on her. Drops the game just as quickly as picking it up and takes another piece of the bacon. 'I'm not living here' she broadly makes known, dusts her hands, feeling the matter settled and shook on, lays out across the sofa. This place is good, like living in a house made of moonrocks would be. What does that mean? Lucy doesn't care. Now is a time for not caring about explaining herself, she's done far far too much of that already. Sits up, moves back to the kitchen to finish her smoke, feeling she's being polite even though she knows it only occurred to her to do so after she'd ashed several times on the living-room carpet.

Here, you would not have to worry about your room being snooped in. Katrin and you share mutual blood gladly offered each other in toasts to mutual health - she can look at things but only with eyes as much not hers are hers are also Lucy's. Proof? Lucy drops *Claudette, the Bashful Girl* unbagged to flat center of neatly made bed and will leave it there, the room door not even locked when she goes. The book holds her in its magnetic mesmerism. This would be the place to read it - you do know that Lucy. You'll never read it in your rented room - if you keep it there you will end up burying it in a riverbank. And you were right not to keep it in the car - what if there was an accident or the vehicle were stolen? She cringes at the thought of the book being found there, chuckled at by strangers, flipped through, touched, pages turned by male-fingers increasingly having been cleaned of their gunk and going to be again.

Ceremonious, she leans forward and kisses the bedclothes on either side of the book. No, she can't put her lips to the pen drawing of Claudette, herself, on the cover. Polka-dot-panties Claudette. Topless-pen-and-ink Claudette. Vague-scribble-as-background Claudette. Those eyes like not-eyes of Claudette. That thumb of ink-drawn left hand hooked under side-elastic of ink-drawn polka-dot panties Claudette. This isn't the same copy, Lucy. Her mouth never would have touched it. It's safe. You can kiss it without exploding. 'But no no' Lucy says whoever is saying this doesn't understand. 'That's exactly why I don't kiss it.' And she says it like she's famous for having written that line in the Portuguese.

Snatches the book up and hurries to the kitchen where she had left the bag, forces the book inside, leans reeling to the counter. Had she said *Katrin*? Why had she said *Katrin*? She is glancing kind of in a fever now around the room. Katrin shares mutual blood? Lucy had meant *Layla*. Leave the book out like that on a bed in Katrin's apartment? She has to fight panicking as though this already happened - she panics that it happened even only as much as it had. How had this become Layla's apartment? How Katrin Layla? And the refrigerated bacon, even! This seems not to bode well, that looking around this still feels like Layla should live here. Lucy rubs at her forehead as though to cut off the opportunity for the one name to permanently tape over the other, scribble its letters in ink atop the typeset of the proper printed original. Her mind is graffiti, is some crude middle-school doodle she'd done feeling listless and too unknown to care. But you need to calm down, Lucy. Lucy. Focus. Nothing happened. And the last thing you need is to create this into some dreadnaught symbol of looming demise! 'Jesus' she whispers, terrified - now she's thinking the word *Symbol* in this same room where the key around her neck and been given and labeled *Symbol*! One person becoming another person, she becoming several elses, given false names, repeating repeating repeating, locked in a set of events which eventually have to stop being the same set and only know how to alter by violent uproar.

Better now. That wasn't so bad. Lucy is treating it like a dress-rehearsal for how she'll eventually be mauled, maimed, mince-meated. The problem is deciphered: it was just bringing the book in. There are ways to set the world at balance, once more, it just takes vigilance and avoiding certain contacts - this-to-that, her-to-her or her or her. 'To anyone, really' she says, sighs like it's all a lame joke that translates in a way it's funnier to read in her language. That book can't be in here. Now it's not. Now it is in the glovebox of the car - which is risky in its own right but the least risky place. Obviously, Lucy could not have kept it on her, even in the bag. One: it needed to be removed, immediately, the way cursed talisman need to be torn from necklace chains and flung oceanward, not necklaces taken off casually and ho-hum put out of the room of the sickly into the one just adjacent. Two: say Katrin had come in and somehow conversationally it had gotten awkward not to say which book after easily having to say *A book* in response to *What's in the bag*? 'Or even if I had said something else was in the bag' Lucy blows smoke, batting at it like it has teasingly just called her a ninny. Non-sequitur: she says 'Bah humbug' and considers the matter resolved. Her mind feels like she's tried to use porridge as waffle batter. 'Or bananas and bread as banana-bread' she says, last drag. Well, last drag before lighting another.

Not reacting at all surprised to find a Lucy Jinx there, Katrin enters, sets down on the kitchen floor two shopping bags and tells Lucy 'Come here' while she proceeds to pull her shirt over her head, covering her braless chest as she turns to point her bare shoulders at Lucy. On the clockface-white skin is a bit of plastic-wrap taped to place, blood smeared, a new tattoo not quite viewable under it. 'Should I peel this off?' Katrin goes 'Hunh?' but then shakes head, now recalling, says 'Yes, please.' What is revealed is the name *Polina*. Lucy admits this is awesome and drinks in the leisure of knowing she will not be asked 'You know what that means, right?' because if nothing else Katrin knows that Lucy knows what *Polina* means. 'How long have I said I would do this?' Katrin glowingly asks, tone of still-astonished self-triumph. 'Since you actually got that young man to jump off the *Schlangenberg*?' Katrins trills with lunkhead laughter at the remembrance, pulls her shirt back over her head - after a fruitless effort to twist enough to see her own mid-shoulder - and moves in, giving Lucy a very brief embrace. 'I'm just trying here out' Lucy says 'I can't write at home.' This seems to have been the perfect thing to say because now Katrin wry smiles, kisses Lucy's cheek, turns to get a bottle of cold water from the fridge while asking 'When are you getting your tattoo?' 'I'm my tattoo' Lucy answers with lazy flit of hand but - and Katrin notices it - has another rise of anxiety when she realizes that response was not improvised, here, the first time. Lucy - you need to be careful, now you're repeating yourself from elsewhere in these rooms! Katrin is a better person than to melodramatic up a 'What's wrong? What is it?' as Lucy gives a more cryptic utterance befitting the both of their dignity: 'Do you ever feel you'd bleed snake-oil if you were cut in the right place? Well, I think I'd bleed snake-oil, cut no matter where.'

Katrin tells Lucy she'd forgot to mention earlier that she often uses an electric typewriter when working on essays. 'Or poetry' Katrin furthers, now barefoot and a vague pile of herself - upside-down from Lucy's angle - on the bed in her bedroom 'but mostly the essays. If it bothers you, move out - but since it won't bother you what I'm actually saying is I can type out in the living-room when I use it, that way you can enjoy the scent and the clittler-clatter of it more as it was meant by the musician who first invented it.' Lucy doesn't see the typewriter but doesn't bother to ask where, in specific, the thing is hid. Plenty of time for that. She does ask 'If I spring for ink-ribbons can I use it sometimes?' 'Lucy, I can steal another whole typewriter, easy - you don't even have to figure out my name's Rumpelstiltskin first.' Lucy is jealous that Katrin has a life where she can steal electric typewriters. And she's jealous that Katrin, in just the past hour or so, had gotten *Polina* permanented to her napkin-white shoulder. And Lucy is just jealous of Katrin. 'I'm jealous of you, Katrin.' 'I'm jealous of me too, Loose. And hey - I'm jealous of you because you get to be jealous of me from over there.' Lucy lays on the floor and looks at the side of Katrin's foot. She's jealous of the side of Katrin's foot. Then she looks at the ceiling. 'To be aggressive, I'm going to forever tell you that you really should paint the ceiling a different color than the rest of the room. It'll get to you, eventually.' Lucy can hear Katrin scratching her belly under her shirt while she chuckles and says 'You don't have the guts to make a play like that - you're a powder-puff.'

Lucy goes to her room while Katrin has to make a few phone calls in hers. Only Lucy doesn't name her room *Her room* she labels it *Her Room At Katrin's Place*. If she does move in it takes awhile and some half-dozen or eight specific rituals to make the room *Hers*. Right now, though, she just wants to let her head go blotto, empty, a defective peanut. She wants to be inconsequential the way moonlight pointed away from the Earth is. A special, revered kind of worthless. The technical same as something poetic but something that always will be nothing but *technically the same* that expression always used, the derision imbued in it always well-apparent. Leak out, Lucy. Leak. *Milksop*. 'Milksop.' What is this? *Milksop*. 'Milksop?' she says, hoping just saying it once will rid her of the word. *Milksop*. 'Milksop.' She cannot get clear of the word. She says it a few more times. It's all because she never learned just what it means! All these decades on it's a springe that has been waiting to noose her! And of course it happens right now, during this first attempt at Katrin's apartment! Of course: Katrin comes home with *Polina* and from there it's just the merest hop-skip to *Milksop*. Blame Constance Garnett all you want, Lucy, because she could have chosen another word - doubtless she could have! - but that was her translator's preference and it was your pleasure not to look it up or ever inquire. And so it comes down to you, yourself, your past lazy moments, your uncurious parts, that this room might not work. 'Milksop.' Your life grinds to a halt over the word *Milksop*. Jesus, Lucy. Just Jesus.

Katrin knocks on the door. 'Lucy?' Lucy has been asleep. She shambles her way to the door, opens it with a puffy eyed smile. 'I passed out. What time is it?' Katrin tells her - that was hours, then! had Lucy dreamt? she feels heavy, bloat-mouthed like she had - and says she did not mean to wake her. But Lucy had not meant to fall asleep and actually cannot stay the night, had only meant to come and hang 'round, get the lay of the land. Katrin had made some dinner though if Lucy was hungry before heading out. Was this something Lucy was allowed to decline? Sure. Is it something Lucy wants to decline? Certainly. 'What did you make?' 'Rice and sausages. Which sounds batshit, I know, but it's clinically sane, I assure you.' 'You know a clinician who can provide an affidavit to that effect?' 'I know several.' Lucy nods. She begs off by way of tummyache which Katrin can see right through. 'God's blood, Lucy! Do you think I am easier to be played on than a pipe?' 'No no, I knew you were brighter than most school nurses, I'm sorry.' 'I didn't even want you to eat it, dolt! I only made enough for me but was trying to be a good pal. Screw you in the shabbiest of Hells, then.' They hug again at the door and Katrin tells her to at least move some things in, too. 'Just let me believe that you're here, now. I'd rather be eventually heartbroken than just blandly disappointed up front, you know?' Lucy waves, realizing she's still pretending the tummyache and is still acting as groggy as when she first woke.

Lord, why do her bones feel quill sharp? And why do her hands on the steering wheel feel more claw-like than usual? Just because they are so cold? Does she even own gloves or mittens? Her whole skin feels the way her ribs feel when they cramp, speckled and ready to cough, pricker-bush and centipede. She catches herself drifting a bit into the adjacent lane and shakes her face, gives it a ham-hearted slap. The old fear of continuing-past-empty is on her. She must have dreamt something she's not remembering! This physical revolt came from somewhere and her brain hasn't always felt nothing more than a dollop of ketchup gone crusted! Maybe she has run out. Another string of words will never come. Verseless, forevermore. Or if the words come it will be by some formula, some mechanic of her old soul she'll tinkersmith until she finds. There will be some algebra she'll discover by pouring over old poetry and she will just get a list of words and play cut-and-paste, slip this sort of stanza here, that sort there, concoct her desperate attempt-at-herself out of what she used to ceaselessly, boundlessly, fightlessly be. Goddamnit Lucy, what could you have dreamt!? Why do you have to always be dreaming? Why can't this be the dream - this right now? Her gut doesn't kick at chastising herself, though. There's nothing to beat herself for. Split milk is one thing - go ahead and cry. Milk drunk, filtered, and pissed out? That is, in the end, what you wanted to happen to begin with.

The windows of the house are crayon-lemon. She stares at the not perfectly aligned blinds for any indication of motion but either sees none or doesn't know how to decipher whatever subtle tell would be there to note. Lucy has no sooner decided she will sit there until this last song plays out completely - a random song, radio dial just tapped at and tapped at while she drove until this station was where she'd lost focus or had had to put both hands to the wheel or something - then the thought of such a wait fills her with noia. People have seen her pull in. The mother might have heard her while out smoking a cigarette - or seen her from maybe the upstairs window where Lucy had not been keeping a watch-out. 'Am I not allowed to be alone, ever?' Lucy says, trying to mock herself with an image of Bible-times mourners rending their garments but the emotion is too actual to so easily cow. Come on, Lucy. *The night is corkscrew / its eyelids supine / and your throat as sore as / last nights untasted wine.* Dismal. Try again! Try something else! *You are a pavement square / and I'm a Holy Book.* That's okay. Anything else? *I'm a latecomer and you / a busted straight.* Lucy shuts off the car, hisses a kind of bitter repentance. Always the need to apologize in you, Lucy. Always the need to be what is wrong.

WAS LUCY THE ONE WHO had left this window open? The question isn't stern - she would not mind at all, in principle, if the mother entered the room in her absence. Truth be told, as talented a paranoiac as Lucy was she assumed the mother entered the room at her leisure, assumed there was no point hiding anything. Here: even *Claudette, the Bashful Girl* is being left smack-there. And look: its set right atop *Her New Sister's Best Friend* so obviously Lucy is not putting up much of a fight for her perfect right-to-privacy. The question of the window is just a point-of-order: did Lucy decide to open it before leaving? She just didn't think so. That's all. Also: she is wondering what it would signify to go downstairs in her sweatpants. Because she's going to, that is decided - she just wonders if it needs to be addressed in some direct way or if some well-placed surrounding phrases can contextualize it down to an innocuous act. Anyway - she will wear just a cotton camisole, her thinnest, to take the curse off of things. But maybe something else? What else? Tiptiptiptiptip she clicks with just the very tip of her tongue to the extra-moist gums behind her front teeth. What else? Some offering. Something to stave off suspicions. A gesture is needed here. A token. She takes a pen, testing the tip on the skin of the back of her hand, nodding definitive, turns to go but then stops. Five minutes of flipping through her notebook - she settles on nothing, waits a moment for her computer to warm up, scrolls through her file labeled *Sketchbook*. There. That. She takes ten minutes - seven maybe, it feels she decided ten was too long - to be sure it is memorized. Downstairs.

The mother is in the kitchen, leaned to counter, half back-faced to Lucy, one leg bent, foot crossed behind it and a bit wrapped around to the top of the stable foot in front. The mother at that moment is rubbing her shoulder with arm crossed from right side to left, looking down at a magazine of some kind. The mother: a tangle of herself. Lucy almost hates to interrupt the image but does. She takes the hand that is rubbing the shoulder, lifts it upward - the mother, because of this, turning rather as though first-time-student being taught how to be twirled in a dance class. Lucy tightens her face to mean 'Stay quiet' when the mother chuckles and breathes in, readying to say something - and so the mother stays quiet. Lets Lucy extend her arm forward - maybe for the first time noticing that Lucy has a pen sideways in her mouth. Another face from Lucy means the mother is not to lower the arm while Lucy upcaps the pen. Understood. Then the mother's arm is given a quarter rotation, allowing the inner soft of upper arm to be the most presented surface and Lucy, after one more brief test - a scribble next to the already there scribble on her own hand - and not looking at the mother at all begins to write. *The hounds stopped baying, the moon for a night is its own forlorn jealousy and we in the scream of its hideous light fallen down.* Lucy caps the pen and she - well, first she reads the line four times for proofreading then stares at it finding it nothing near as nice as she thought, but too late - lets go the mother's arm and moves it to hang slack. 'That's all' Lucy says and then 'So how are you?' The mother is trying to read her arm. Lucy is watching that one vein in her neck raise those few darker-patched freckles, there.

Lucy invents a *Poet's Superstition* about reading back words that were invented on the spot to beg off of reciting the mother's arm. She likes when the mother reads it, though. 'I wish I could write you a poem' the mother says - Lucy is glad at how casual, in fact is glad that mother is speaking while also opening the cupboard for a plate, not finding one, is opening the dishwasher and selecting, Lucy guesses, the least dirty one - 'but it'd be dreadful. The best poetry I ever managed was good enough for winning a prize in fourth grade - I doubt I've improved. Something about a Panda bear, that poem. Something about Mother Earth. You probably want to disown me about now, right?' Poems in fourth grade. Poems in fifth grade. Poems in sixth grade. This all flipbooks inside Lucy's head like a beetle has laid eggs that are soon-hatching there but all she says is 'I'm sure you didn't want to write something so bullshit sounding - in fourth grade or otherwise. I consider you victimized for having to, if anything.' Laugh. Laugh. 'Gosh thanks.' 'But never mention Pandas or Mother Earth again or we're quitsies, capisce?' Laugh laugh. Laugh laugh. 'It's because you're a poet you're so superstitious?' What? 'What's that?' 'I mean, I can see that. It makes sense. I never put that together.' 'Do I seem particularly superstitious?' Laugh - snort-laugh. Laugh along, Lucy, come on! Laugh. 'Do you know the first thing I ever noticed about you?' the mother asks, still smiling but this an earnestness apart from the laughter. What? No. What? 'What do you mean?' But too late - the mother has Neverminded in that way that prying at will only make awkward.

A little too much blush on the mother's face like she had almost said something that would risk a little further than she was willing to fall.

On the sofa. Geordi LaForge mutely shaking his head in disbelief at this Romulan's stubbornness. The mother, unblanketed, foot on Lucy's foot, toes up under the cuff of Lucy's sweatpants. Each has a mug of hot chocolate. There is a plate with the last crusts and one whole unbit bite of sandwich left on the mother's open-turned thigh. 'What time is your flight?' Lucy says it's not until the afternoon - and she doesn't have to affect the searchingness at trying to remember just when, she's drawn a blank - then says she is going to head to the airport early, though, because that is just what she does. The mother seems sated, seems there - the roots of a tree stump, just there, the deeper earth beneath the caskets buried down a cemetery lot. 'I don't want you to pay rent this month' the mother says after having let silence stand awhile and staves off Lucy's protest by slipping her foot further inside of the sweatpants, entire sole now the length of Lucy's shin, heel in the bend of Lucy's ankle. 'You should stay as long as you need to and your room will be here and the last thing you need to worry about is money having to do with that. Just be with your friend. Please.' Should it be shameful that though this is all deceit Lucy doesn't feel shameful? She touches the foot on her leg through her pant fabric. 'Just do come back, okay?' Lucy sniff-smiles, squeezes the foot and lets go. 'It's nothing so bad. My friend. She'll be fine. She's always just very dramatic.' The mother nods as though in deep empathetic concord with this utter and abstract fabrication. Lucy's eyes dart a little to the side as some boulders fall on the Romulan and Geordi gets him up and into a cave.

The child lurches, sleepwalk topple, into the room, a lump into the lap, wrapped around, of the mother, the mother trying to adjust to move the plate - which has shifted to the sofa cushion, between her legs - rolling her eyes at Lucy while patting the child's head and asking 'What's up?' The child doesn't say anything but snuzzles closer to the mother, the mother having to tilt head side-to-side to keep hair out of her mouth, Lucy giving a kind of mocking smile and a shrug by her two hands turned over, palms up. 'Did you have a bad dream, Flynnawhile? What's happening here?' The mother's tone is a perfect tuning-fork quaver between exasperation and mortal concern. Lucy pinches the mother's big-toe between forefinger and thumb, gives it a waggle, then stands and moves to the kitchen, taking the two mugs - Lucy's empty, the mother's with a third of now-room-temperature liquid left in it - with her. She rinses her own. She drinks the last of the mother's. Why? No reason. For aesthetic. For completion of symbolic sequence of the subterfuge. This needs to be done to drive the whole thing home. This has to be done unwitnessed except by the invisibles who watch and decide which Hellfires to dole to those who misstep.

She even taps the remnant slick in the mug-bottom with index fingertip, rubs it dry on other index-tip. These ceremonies are invented on the spot but each tick assures her a continued - if only for a moment - stability.

The child looks heavy. Lucy almost wants to help or something. Simultaneously the mother looks ten years younger and thirty years older - a vision from the other world she lives on, only as half-true as something glimpsed through a telescope, noted, and guessed at. Lucy traces the length of the mother's lower back as the mother starts the - it must be - precarious climb to the upstairs and also touches the back of one of the mother's calves even though in retrospect she imagines this will have seemed absurd. 'Why did she do that?' the mother is obviously now thinking, perhaps thinking also 'Lucy had tripped - as how else could one explain how her hand came to be on my leg?' Lucy to sofa. Another episode on? The same. No - another. You don't need to eat that last sandwich crust or anything, right Lucy? Good Christ no - that would be grotesque! But yes - Lucy does bus the plate, gets it and the few other dishes into the washer but does not yet start it. Almost lights a cigarette. Five minutes. Ten. Lucy goes out and has a smoke in the cold. Only when she has to tend to an itch over her ribs does she notice that there is a half-coin-sized hole in this camisole, that much of the skin of her left breast - just outside the shade of her nipple - is exposed to the air. How can this be and what does this mean!? Are you embarrassed, Lucy? She is. Even hunches herself around as though to hide this exposure from peepers who might happen by. But does it indicate anything? Have you miscalculated this entire night since leaving the parked car? Since before? How does this exposure of intimate flesh - which will seem a calculated accident - retro-continuity your whole precarious circumstance tonight, Lucy?

The breathing lilts to a snore - or not quite, is deep then suddenly seems shallow. The way the mother is arranged on the child's bedroom floor is bizarro in only this bit of mint-blue from the night-light - this light itself half-obscured by a pile of books with a sock and a toy cheetah or something on top of them. There seems to be excess of the mother - she's spilled ink and a paper-tear, both. The child's hand is still at a dangle over the bedside and it is well evident from the lay of the mother's arm they had both slipped off into sleep with hands held. The mother's arm will be numb - it cannot have blood-flow like that, crooked and part beneath her. And though the heat is on the mother will soon tighten with shivers and her throat will be infected with dust-mites and all manner of cretinous flecks from the carpet fibres. You're allowed to just stand and look, Lucy. No need for analysis or to think of what it is you are to do here. Nothing. You've nothing to do. Watch her lay there - as you are allowed - and feel your arm getting sore at the bicep where it leans in the doorframe. Now: Lucy wetting lips to speak the mother's name at half-volume. But doesn't. Goes to her knees - feels crumbs, cracker corner, dig up into her skin - goes to hands and knees - feels a small bit of fabric, maybe the discarded cape of a superhero-figure, under one palm, a poke of ticklishness - goes two motions of crawl with the feeling of her belly and breasts hanging plump and stress at her elbows insides asking her to flatten to floor, to curl to other body. The mother's ear is there near Lucy's lips, a twist of the mother's hair curtaining its whorl.

The mother apologizes as she yawns down the corridor to her bedroom with Lucy. 'Flynn has been having these dreams about walruses. Fucking walruses!' Lucy isn't sure if she should laugh, if it is just fatigue, half-awakeness that is mashing the tone of the mother's voice indecipherably into both bitter and bemused. 'Well, walruses are cocksuckers' Lucy offers, patting the mother's back - but she isn't drunk, Lucy! you are patting her like she's blitzed and are speaking to her in that condescending tone as to a down-and-out friend on a post-break-up binge - 'I'd be at my wit's end same as him if I dreamed about walruses every goddamned night, you know?' The mother - most of what she is saying effaced by the sounds of her roughly bending her way into bed and beneath covers - says something along the lines of agreeing that walrus are 'pointless' or that walruses are 'punk princesses.' Something. 'They are' Lucy says, giving the mother's head a pat, saying 'Goodnight' and moving to stand. 'Hey' the mother's voice, the mother's four pressed-close fingers brushing Lucy's forearm to wrist, staying there like holding her from going. There isn't light enough for them looking at each other, the silence is black and kind of smells musty. 'Oh you have to pack' the mother says - she has drifted, she's not even awake, Lucy, don't worry - and Lucy says 'Sorry' - which is silly to have said - but the mother - yeah, she won't even recall this - says 'No, no I'm sorry' and Lucy figures she needs to stay sitting there until the mother's hand betrays limpness enough to be considered no longer exactly in contact with her. Lucy's swallows sound far too loud in her ears. She's horribly self-conscious when something in her stomach shifts with a small pfft like air slipping from a closing plastic bag. She tenses but it only makes her notices the volume of her breath out her nose and the squish of her mouth when her lips part and the squish again when they close.

Now Lucy does have to pack. No, not necessarily. You aren't going to pack, Lucy? Not really - she is going to see Layla, what packing for that is necessary? Now though - if only for effect - hadn't you ought to? Yes, yes - it feels so burdensome, all this this-and-that for effect, but a brief little trip someplace isn't going to change anything fundamental so what is the point of huff-and-puffing over this, rebelling your stand here, tonight? Socks. Panties. T-shirts. Pants. 'Presto alazakang!' says Lucy, a What-else-could-there-possibly-be? kind of gaze down into the suitcase. Yes. That is the size of it. She leans back and tries not to consider the implications of this. It's an oddball corner you've gotten yourself painted in here, Jinx, but at the same time if you were generally more stoical this could all be avoided. 'Fuck the Stoics' Lucy says to the room celling and takes its haughty silence as sign of its picking a fight. 'Just because you're a ceiling doesn't make you fucking Stoic!' she bullies. 'You have no choice. You trust to Fate. You thank your very existence to caprice!' Well, the ceiling has been put in its place. And the door-jamb and closet-handles could not have helped but overhear so Lucy can rest assured her room won't get back-talky again, any time soon. No. She feels bad. 'Sorry, ceiling' she says, flimsy-wheeled bicycle feeling 'I don't even know what Stoicism really is. I just have things on my mind.' Is this playacting, Lucy? Does Lucy know she doesn't need to say these things to the ceiling and that no one is listening, forming opinions, deciding their take on her from afar? 'Even if you are' she sits up, dusts thighs and nonchalant 'I don't care what little weaseling hide awayers think of me. Voyeur yourselves fat, boys! Peep yourself into any ill opinion of me you fancy!'

Of course Lucy sleeps. Precisely because she'd decided not to. It's the correct decision but nonetheless one she can berate herself over the next day when it becomes convenient to do so. If she had to call herself anything Lucy would call herself a *Nesting-Doll*. Mainly because anyone can call themselves that - it's true because it means nothing, a profundity to use on morons, an easy go-to ready-made symbol for filmmakers and authors too insipid to consider that symbols ought to confuse not pigeonhole. In her ideal world Lucy would call herself a *scratch in the painted number fourteen on a resting roulette wheel*. Sleuth that out, symbolists! Bask in the meandering, specific-only-to-widen-to-infinity impenetrableness of that! Her life, as anyone's, should be in finding the symbolic expression of herself and then harrying her every sigh until she manages to explain it. How terrible were she really a nesting-doll! How inhuman to see yourself as a jig-saw puzzle or a ship's compass! The truly unimaginative see themselves as animals, see themselves as seasons, or see themselves as bumps on logs! Lucy wakes. Was that sleep? Was it? What do you see yourself as, Lucy? She knows she was thinking about that but has no idea what she'd decided. Hadn't decided anything. Part of that had been her trying to sleep, part of it had been her asleep - and this part might be her awake but she's drifting and it's another dribble of her life snuck away from her - this is a confusion she won't remember by morning, like so many other confusions she tries to convince herself she should be glad not to be burdened with memory of. The way a deaf-mute should be glad of how unburdened they are, how dreadful they ought to feel for still having hands and eyes when they've come so far. She thinks that. Is asleep. That pitch of bitterness is gone now too - though if she could remember it come morning she'd be furious it was.

# .V.

IT TOOK LUCY A MOMENT - still sucking the side of her left wrist where she had cut it fifteen minutes before - to realize what was different about the poem she had used her fingers to trace in the soot of the rear windshield of her car when she had - before her departure eleven days earlier - parked it here in the corner of the lowest level of the Long Term area of the airport carpark. That question mark had been added and that *D* effaced - *find these hores at distance a delight?* should be *find these hordes at distance a delight* - the exclamation points and the effacing of the *M* the *N* and the *E* - *refuse the penis! refuse them stories to tell!* should be *refuse them pennies, refuse them stories to tell* - and this other question mark - *send their mouths down creekbed with the stones?* should be *send their mouths down creekbed with the stones* - had been added by some chucklehead's crumby mitts. Ah! See here, Lucy - less easy to tell at first since you'd kind of scribbled it to begin with - that also the *CY* of your first name and the *JIN* of your surname have been effaced leaving on there *LUX*. What could be the meaning of it? 'Lux?' she says, as though speaking it aloud will decode it, remove it of foreboding accursedness. 'Lux. Lux.' Different pronunciations tried. Does that mean some slang vulgarity? *Lux?* She thinks about her name - can any vulgarities be made out of the letters removed, reshaped? Inspection of the rest of the car: nothing of note. She decides to leave the poem there. She even takes a photo with her phone in a happy way, sends it to herself with a text-message as though sending it delightedly to a friend. Who could be watching? Dunno. But they could easily be there, there, or there. Lucy has seen movies.

Gosh, hadn't Layla looked terrific? Well, hadn't she Lucy? She had gained twenty pounds that Lucy wishes she could gain to look just like her! Lucy would do it, too - except Lucy's body carries weight at different vantages than Layla's. Lucy's body is incapable of sublimity. But Layla! Her neck, the side of her face, that daredevil way she just walks calm down a corridor or across a bookstore café and might have to blow her nose or wipe a spot off a table before they sit! Tremulous. Likely not the correct word at all but Lucy is beyond caring. 'I have a tremulous friend and that friend is called Layla' Lucy could tell any passerby, shaking their hand a comical, foreigner-doing-things-wrong *Hello*, the passerby at first feeling accosted but soon laughing at the genial unselfconsciousness of the gesture - and that passerby would take away this: Layla must be one terrific and tremulous person to stir such a thing! Oh Lucy - you like sitting in a parked car giggling. Even as you shiver a bit and wait for the heater to really kick in you miss Layla and think of the length and size of her in that red pea-coat and that polka-dot dress and those leggings. And how she had said 'This has been just what I needed' to Lucy right as they were hugging *Goodbye*. They were some sort of two shipwrecks that over time had become brambled into one.

Something must have happened here on this road. What is the smell? Turpentine? No. That medicinal wash for horses? No. Something medicinal though. Like a cube of it covered a mile of highway road. But no sign of bother. This does put Lucy in mind of the fact that she is driving back to the *County Of Dead Skunks*. Remember that, Lucy? Who had laughed when you admitted aloud you called it that? Stumped, Lucy now tries to recall. Not Ariel. Or was it? You want it to have been, Lucy, but not likely. Who then? In what context? To get around the problem sneak-like Lucy thinks: Well, how would I explain it to someone? If I can remember exactly how I explained it context should tell me who I told it to. Could it have been Ariel? Focus down, girl - try the plan. 'Every time I go driving around here - to work, wherever - I pass - what? - five dead skunks. Fresh dead and long dead. The squirt of their demise is like pepper in smears of steak sauce on the plate of this damn rotten burg!' No. She could have said that to anyone! They never clear the skunks away! You hit the city limits there should be a speed bump of dead skunks to mark the occasion, refreshed daily! Now: highway and highway and highway and idle thoughts about this all for ten minutes of highway. Some poet, locally, must have noted the phenomena, some Willa Cather will make it a well-beloved quote for some future generation. 'There we met - the *County of Dead Skunks* as I had heard a debarking passenger mention it was known' Lucy pretend-recites in a voice that is like no one but she is pretending is that of Kate Chopin.

In the dark, the first sight of the area further on - rising above the horizon-line to reveal the dots of the city, the suburb lights - is like the first tuck of louse found by meticulous comb with gloved hand. It really never is beautiful. It's the only place light at night isn't beautiful, maybe. A profound place. Lucy has seen a flashlight dropped outside of a parking lot portable-toilet and even there - with no sign of anyone in the lot so even with the undercurrent of horror at hand - that light was beautiful. How can you have lived here, Lucy? 'Well, consider' Lucy says, yawning, not finishing the thought aloud. But the thought would have gone along these lines: Consider wherefore I came - consider how this place with regard to that might have seemed opiate exquisite, how the purgation which had been endured by me previous would make this seem monastery. 'Then time makes it monstrosity' she adds aloud, high-five to her intonation. Well, Lucy you are on a roll. Layla, who is not sitting beside you, would have British guffawed and pointed out her guffaw was pronounced *Guh-fuh*. Layla, who isn't sitting next to you, would have called your country-entire 'the same as this glory-hole county of yours' and lamented how she herself dwelled in it - the country, not this county - would have called herself 'wrest from her homeland, bereft of nepenthe except for in quaffs of Lucy Jinx - Lucy Jinx, the tattered jewel of the world when 'twas holy!' Look at those lights there - like stitches that won't be removed, like chickenpox on a grandmother's lips. Look at you driving home, Lucy. Do you feel it already? You do. That's your first smile you have to try to smile before smiling. Welcome home.

Lucy settled on this joint to eat in. The vague feeling of having been in it before. The vague feeling that this same waitress had already taken this same order. If Lucy said 'Have we met before?' this bone-thin but plump-lipped woman would say that they had. In some fun, colloquial way. And Lucy would remember. And the two would have a down-home laugh of it and when the check came some of Lucy's items - but not all - would not be on the ticket, a wink from the dame as she handed the receipt to her and said 'Pay up there, sweetie - need anything else, first?' Lucy blinks. What? How tired are you? Airplanes knock Lucy's mind out of its plate. Even the other passengers can tell. The attendants likely whisper about her to the pilots. Lucy blinks. Is she drifting where she sits? What about the waitress? What about this place? Ah. It has come back to her. And prideful chest she decides to try it out. 'Excuse me?' 'Should be just another minute, hon.' 'Oh that's fine. I just wondered: Haven't we met? I could swear but can't quite place you.' Big obvious confidence in Lucy's delivery and the way she now peruses the woman's face like a favorite Chagall.

196 / PABLO D'STAIR

But - wow, she looks to really be trying, though! - the waitress is drawing a blank. 'Have you stopped in before?' That was, Lucy explains, what she had been thinking, too - only she hadn't done, she's sure of it, she insists. 'It feels like it had been somewhere else.' Had Lucy lived in the area long? 'For ages' Lucy says, figuring this gave the best odds. The woman knits brow in a cascade of *W*s, perturbed now by the lack of remembrance, bewildered, a little determined whistle to each breath out her constricted nose.

A couple, together, come bum cigarettes off her. An interesting approach. 'I've never had two people come rip me off some smokes at the same time' she says as the two of them light up. They laugh, jolly sorts. 'We do it all the time. It was my idea' the woman says and explains in a long-winded way that it was based on something she'd learned in a Psychology class. 'You're a psychologist?' She isn't. But studied it. 'Where?' Names a community college. Lucy is far less enchanted by them, suddenly: pictures domestic abuse or at least slow, encroaching, irrevocable estrangement. What does the man do? 'What do you do?' Lucy is going to make them earn these cigs - no need to worry about that, ladies and gentleman! Showcasing wit, though, the man says Lucy should have a nighttime variety show - actually says *Variety Show*. 'And my next guest is' Lucy says 'the man who bummed a fag and then won't answer my goddamned question.' Presto: the man laughs heartily, the woman does one of those louder-pronounced ffffttssss of smoke out and suddenly acts interested in something over there. 'No, no, though' the man says 'I am a teacher. I teach physics. In high school.' 'Well, it's good you don't put on airs.' The guy is doing well - what's his game? the woman is stepping her cig out and heading inside, he just noting her doing so but not hurrying to follow, she not turning to nod - in that he picks up on Lucy's gist here, too. 'Nothing worse than someone who says they teach physics and lets a silence suggest they mean at a University. Sin of omission. Can't lie to ourselves, right?' Ask for his number straight out, Lucy. What do you think he'll do? Is this where he'll become predictable?

The radio promises coming snow. How do these people on the radio manage to make everything sound like it is the first time it has happened? And that it will all be swinging and pleasurable, to boot! Lucy almost wants to drive to the hardware store to get some salt and some de-icer for her windshield. And for her car locks! This man is full of good ideas. But how long has this man been on the Air? Is this the first and only town he has ever worked in? Is there an archive of him? Of every word he's ever said over whichever airwaves? There must be. What a mountainous waste that would be to behold, the room where he stores it all - she is certain he and all radio hosts keep copies of themselves for themselves. How long is he on, each day? Say five hours. Then remember there's something like nine-thousand hours in a year, twenty-four hours daily.

Would this man accrue a year's-worth of his own voice telling people of coming weather and recommending hardware stores and 'While you're out there try some local steak place and if you've got kids then visit so-and-so's ice cream, so-and-so's candy shop?' Fuck, Lucy! Fuck! 'Fuck!' she yells. Jostles steering wheel. 'Fuck! Fuck, fuck!' Outburst done. Ears feel muddy, head ruined, she's shoes after walking in beach water. 'Anyway' she says 'it'd take him something like five years. Something like forever.' There's that billboard, Lucy. You aren't away anymore. You're back. This is now *back*, not *away-from*. There's a commercial for ear muffs. Someone right now is thinking 'I need to get ear muffs.' Some idiot girl. Will have her boyfriend go with her. Feel so smart: the girl with warm ears.

Stop here. She doesn't. Stop here, then. She doesn't. Stop here. She should, but doesn't. Stop here! She doesn't. Why not? Finally she pulls in here. Closed *Gardening Shop*. Closed chiropractor. Closed drive-through bank. She gets out and lights one of the last two cigarettes in her pack. Peers in at what she can see of the *Gardening Shop* and has the urge to steal one of these birdbaths. Always has had the urge. Lucy is going to steal something. But not a birdbath! Why not? She looks at it, finds some inane reason, some point of rhetoric or something. But if you are going to steal why is it you won't steal this, specifically? Price tag: is that what a birdbath costs! Put out a mixing bowl - the bird doesn't care! You want birds so bad you can get birds in water in your yard for free! How can this be something an adult human being considers - buying a birdbath? It'll look nice? 'It'll look nice!?' Lucy actually bellows and - fun - her voice claps in echo three times - her shadow is also in triplicate - there there and there, a wonderful cinematic moment, such pizazz and depth. Is this what you are proud of, Lucy? Your shadow and your echo? Yet you go mocking people for wanting a birdbath in their yard? 'Fuck off, Lucy' Lucy says to Lucy and stands there leaking cigarette, head bowed and ginning at her three shadows and the memory of her three gun-shot It'll-look-nices!? just a minute or so old.

*Oliver Cromwell lay buried and dead, hee-haw, buried and dead.* Lucy. Parked car. Stolen garden hose on seat. The following memory and the following still unanswered question: in grade-school Lucy had heard that song in a Music class. *Oliver Cromwell lay buried and dead.* She can remember it all, actually. *There grew an old apple tree over his head, hee-haw, over his head.* The teacher, being a teacher, had asked 'Who is Oliver Cromwell?' Lucy thought it was a terrific thing to ask and really was curious for the answer. No one answered. 'What is Oliver Cromwell?' the teacher had rephrased. 'Aha!' a little boy seemed to think, for this little boy, from that clue, said 'A donkey!' 'That's right! And why do we know that?' 'Because donkeys go *hee-haw*' Lucy whispers, shaking her head in shame at the words. *The apples are ripe and they're ready to fall, hee-haw, ready to fall.* But: is that song really about a donkey? Or is it about Oliver Cromwell? Does it have some interesting history? Was it sung during Cromwell's life? After his beheading? What do those symbols mean? What is the song? *There comes an old woman to gather them all, hee haw, gather them all.* Lucy hates that teacher. Hates learning that boy's ignorance had been rewarded. More? Hates she has never proven it was ignorance. To this day. Are you waiting here to get caught with this garden hose, Lucy? 'Hee haw, garden hose Lucy' whisper-sings Lucy, difficult to fit those words to the tune.

Back on the road, Lucy has driven a loop of a few neighborhoods. Twice. Again. Fourth time. Have only fifteen minutes passed? 'Okay' she sighs, deciding it is time to make a decision. Obviously she is putting it off because she understands what is lurking. 'If I've survived this long' she knows the fool always thinks 'it means I have done more things right than wrong.' The fool thinks 'I must have!' Lucy: not a fool. Lucy: wiser than the boots she is laced in. Lucy has had a long life - she knows exactly how long - to get wind of what the world is, how it operates. Something is coming and it has already peeled the bark of Layla from her with its breath. Lucy needs to be shifty - because it's about to come. Still: you just have brought yourself to think this! Still: people have been right who have told you the world works other ways! Still: if you could learn to think different you'd feel this all schuff away! You could believe them, Lucy. You could believe that a rhinoceros could shed its skin like a snake, too - it isn't that it can't it just doesn't. Aren't you a poet? Aren't you meant to disbelieve? Lucy: Do you feel like a poet? 'I don't feel like myself' she sighs. Lucy: Not what the question was - do you feel like a poet? Aren't poets meant to transcend? 'Oh sure' she says 'a poet. I'm a poet like this: *repent all ye sinners for the end was sometime last week.*'

NO KATRIN. THOUGH IT TOOK Lucy fifteen minutes to feel sure of this. The door to Katrin's bedroom was open so it should have been a simple matter. But what, ever, is a simple matter? Simple matters are for the simple minded and they are the lever which flushes the world off axis. Lucy first intrudered into the apartment as though with a shrewdly pickpocketed key. Then she whispered various *Hellos?* which were empty formalities not meant to be heard but to give her an air of being innocent of something. She ventured the kitchen light on, from there passing Katrin's open door the first time - dark inside but quite obviously vacant. Except: the comforter and blankets were all an odd pile. So, Lucy turned on the light in *Her Room At Katrin's* then the light in the shared bathroom - note: this all done on tip-toe, expecting to be come upon and hush

Sorry-sorrys she was trying to be as quiet as she could - so the corridor was now more than illuminated enough to make Katrin's room practically the same. Empty. 'Katrin?' Lucy tested in a voice like 'I am saying your name because I'm sure you're not there and if you are the tone will indicate I really did not think you were.' Lucy petted down the comforter et cetera and for good measure looked under the bed and in the closet. Pranks did happen and Lucy would rather not be caught in one just now, however good humored - she'd take it with contempt and no need to make Katrin feel bad. Then the rest of the apartment explored. Then 'Katrin?' Then standing there, silent apartment, head nodding. Silent except for refrigerator sound and some intermittent clicking from behind that corner - whatever it was. No Katrin. Certainly. She's sure.

Then for awhile instead of sleeping - or really instead of anything - Lucy put her mind on blink, put her limbs on blink, floundered her way to the sofa and stared around. An unruly tension broke in, almost immediately. It was quite evident that now - right now - Katrin would come home. Yep. The moment Lucy settled honestly there would be that scuffle of lock-to-latch and that long breath of having lugged in grocery bags to an apartment one expects is empty and then the chirp-chirp of greeting and then it would go from there. Each minute Lucy waited was a minute it would be closer to the one where it was just about to happen after which - 'Because this is how such things work' Lucy said to the room - it would happen. Now it was - what? - one o'clock. One-thirteen, to go by the clock on Katrin's Cable box. That was the sort of time someone who wasn't home already would get home. End of a long day. Slug slime of them left, only. Last-scrape-of-jelly-from-a-sickly-smeared-jar only left of them. And then 'Hi Lucy!' Or 'Lucy, you're here - oh my God!' And if not by one-twenty certainly by one-thirty. If Lucy started to watch a show, certainly Katrin would come in by the top of the hour, just at the episode's denouement, the greetings cutting off Lucy's enjoyment of even that which would have been the last little hump to hump before she truly felt ready to retire. So: going into the bedroom and head to pillow is out of the question, Lucy? 'Are you fucking kidding me!?' she all but chokes on her breath saying to herself. 'Don't you know what would happen the moment my head hits that pillow?'

So easily - on her first real snoop - Lucy found Katrin's pornography. It hadn't even been a challenge. Just there - bed-stand drawer, little thing of personal lubricant and a small cloth purse with drawstring Lucy knew the contents of though had never owned one, herself. Aren't you going to look at it? The pornography? She is looking at it! No - the contents of the bag! Decidedly not - this would be a turn too far. Just to see what it looks like? It's one of those that just goes on the fingertip, to judge by the label - Lucy knows because she's seen them at stores. Anyway: she had hardly expected Katrin's material to be so old-school! Delightful! Printed magazines - obviously the same issues lumped around with Katrin for ages. Well, two are relatively newer ones, to go by the cover dates - interesting! Lucy does a Hmn! on noting this - but the others, well, one can tell just by the look of the women are an era-and-a-half backdated, at least. 'We have similar taste, Katrin' Lucy oh-hos, presumptuousing that this certain woman called *Carolina Tate* is Katrin's personal, most thumbed-to favorite-gal - her belle of the ball. Or this woman simply called *Cade.* 'Wow' Lucy actually unthinkingly blurts 'Hello, who are you?' Lucy stares at one picture in particular, one of the photos set pre-getting-down-to-it: Cade at the mirror, nude except necktie, grinning her satisfaction at how good she looks to herself. Slightest discoloration of bruise to her backside, another high on the back of her thigh. Lucy touches the picture. Says 'Cade.' Thinks she looks a bit like Cade. Thinks Cade would give her the same pleased expression Cade is giving her own mirrored nudity. Thinks she might as well be a mirror. Lucy's lips part, groaningly audible, from the settled film of saliva-all-day and unwashed-teeth behind them. Lucy? Yes? Lucy, it's time to leave Katrin's room - put the magazine down.

She finds the station just as the music swells on Doctor Crusher's face and the scene fades to a commercial for a local furniture store. Large spoonful of Katrin's mint-chocolate ice cream. Straight from the tub because Lucy Jinx is Lucy Jinx! 'You invited this snake in, you snake-charmer, so let this snake charm ya back' she says by way of making defense of this theft. No one can be mad at a miserable, sleepy-faced Lucy Jinx! 'Would you deny me this, Katrin? Isn't this why you invited me here? Don't let's speak falsely - I'm eating your ice cream!' That settled, Lucy also tosses the flower-print pillows onto the carpet to lean better to the stiff of the sofa-arm's shabby inside. Now even the Captain and Data are not sure who Doctor Crusher is referring to when she says certain crew members' names. Has Lucy seen this episode? Seems her cuppa, but she doesn't think so. A rare treat! Without much thought to it she sets ice cream tub to carpet, retrieves her phone and texts the following to the mother: *They have Trek in my hotel! It's one I haven't seen! Yay! I can't wait to get home, tomorrow.* Before she sends she wonders if anything in the message betrays her overall deception. No. The mother will get it, she knows. Type back something like *There's one you haven't seen!? We can't be friends anymore, you phony! How could you do this to me!?* Now: a commercial for a type of cinnamon-bread at some restaurant which seems the same as cinnamon-bread at any restaurant except this kind is 'Sizzlin Hot, baby!' according to the voice-over and rock 'n roll music. Lucy almost texts the words *Sizzlin Hot, baby!!!* to the mother. Catches herself. Where Lucy has told the mother she is wouldn't have the same commercials! Sleep-headedness is turning Lucy almost accidentally-honest.

Lucy strips in the shared bathroom rather in the way a bag of mulch sometimes tears and litters one's shoes. That's what you look like, Lucy. In this orientation or that. Were you under the impression you were beautiful? Still? You were, for awhile. Once. But looking at herself now Lucy knows she is not. Objectively. Subjectively. There is a gummy drag to her as though she's something treacly and partially solid that makes someone's steps stick to a floor just a little. Leaned forward, pale skin made bright-paler by these lightbulbs. No Cade. Had you really thought that? Thought that girl with her perfect bruised thigh was you? Thought that when Cade looks at Cade's belly in the mirror she sees your cottage cheese and hashbrown skin, lumpy as cat-sick and colored of restaurant mops? Lucy submerges in the bathwater, trying not to care. Her nudity is as welcome as a dog fart, she knows it, knows it as the surface of this slightly bubbled water settles to stillness and little cracks of collected suds in her pubic-hairs sound in radio-static hiss. Stale meat. Lucy is stale meat with gone-off honey glaze. But regardless she drifts a little and manages to reverie someone there washing her, dipping hands underwater - slursh slursh they go around, looking for the washcloth Lucy doesn't tell them she's sitting on. Who is it? Who is it in the dream? Not Katrin, anyway - though Lucy stirs, now, expecting Katrin to be standing there, grinning the way Katrin would be were she there. Lucy would grin back. But nobody is there. Has the air-conditioning been on this whole time? Or did it kick on just a few moments ago? Either way, Lucy shivers a bit, working up the will to back-and-forth one-two to stand. The chill has given her a runny nose. And it has brought her skin to itself fiercely. Her breasts where they blurp, mostly unsubmerged and dry, are sickly-tight, shelled, slush-centered, crabapples too long on a late autumn sidewalk.

Why hadn't the mother texted back? Since when would she be asleep? Lucy made a circuit of the apartment, a drunkard meander through all of the rooms, sitting down, and bounced - bouncing squeaking hop hop hop - on the lip of Katrin's bed each time she went through there. She smoked some of the cigarettes she found in one of drawers in the kitchen, clicked through the television, aiming smoke at each not-interesting image that flickered, shut the television off and without thinking flicked her cigarette, orange arc of it splatting and leaving ash in the shape of an almost-lowercase-letter-$Q$ on the wall, drizzle of embers firecrackering. She took up the stub, smoked a last tip tap, flushed it down the toilet, wetted a tug of toilet-paper and dabbed at the mark on the wall but the mark would not rinse off. She tried a sponge with soap but this didn't work, either. But a little bit of carpet cleaner on the sponge did just dandy so Lucy considered this a learning experience and a burden well met. 'But now what am I going to do?' she asked, checking the phone again for a message from the mother. She's asleep, Lucy. It's three in the morning. But it wasn't three in the morning when Lucy had sent the message! Why wouldn't she have been watching *Star Trek*? Just because Lucy isn't in front of her does it mean nothing has meaning? Is it fair to go that far with things, Lucy? She has a kid, the kid has school - she has a job! 'Or maybe it's too sad to watch it without me' she interjected, underlining the thought in the air thrice and gesturing *Duh!* to her bare feet on the kitchen tile next to a curved black something - an old piece of some sandwich cookie which Lucy kicked under the fridge.

So: she'll try to sleep, now. The room is locked. No way to surprise Katrin she'd been there when they both wake up in the morning. So: she'll try to sleep, now. The room is locked. It might be a good idea - 'good' in the sense of 'polite' 'polite' in the sense of 'decent' 'decent' meaning 'what a kind person would do' - to write a charming little note letting Katrin know she is there. Katrin will know that I'm here. So: she'll try to sleep, now. The room is locked. Wait: is it? She stares at the door uneasy for not knowing how to tell from the barely seen knob if so. One of the first things she likes to learn about a door? How to tell just from looking is it locked! This room doesn't seem to trust Lucy, yet. It's making itself unedited, the idea there but not quite coherent. So: she'll try to sleep, now. The room is locked. Of course it is. Katrin must be out. Lucy chuckles and tries to think of what Katrin might be up to. She blanks but then smiles and remembers Layla tugging her into a dressing room and making her try on that green suede blazer. Making her take off her top and try on that green suede blazer. Layla taking off her own top, removing the green suede blazer from Lucy and trying it on, herself. Making Lucy look at the two of them in the mirror. Look: Lucy topless, sublime, exquisite as rainclouds next to Layla, green sueded, holy-book paper, ink for her eyes, so much of it that page one can still be seen seeped through to page two-thousand-and-ten. Layla had said 'We're why prisoners wish they were painters' shuffling the blazer off, bending to take up her shirt. So: she'll try to sleep, now. The room is locked.

Lucy tries the old trick of pretending she had just been asleep is the same as having slept. Her codger old body is a bit too unsenile for that, though - it lets her sit up, even stand, but tilts her head forward, cauldron-skulled, and the whole of her is a door out of its jamb. She wanders into the apartment, naked. Looks in Katrin's room and goes 'Well, hey there' to nobody. 'Katrin? she says as she paws around in the dark of the kitchen. 'Oh shit sorry!' This man - who is this? Lucy doesn't even cover herself and just leans in to try to see what he's eating - something like a chicken spread open as though a book spine, fingers slupping up something like custard out of it and sucking from two fingers fused together with a vein around them like a vulgar cartoon penis. 'Katrin left with her sister' the man says and Lucy says 'Okay' and is kissing him and letting him pat her ass - pat it way too much, too particularly, as though he's trying to get the flab of it to warble in just some ultra-specific waveform. She is on the bed blowing air, seeing if it can reach her knees. Was that sleep or just wandering thought? It felt like a dream at first but then like something she was composing. The man had seemed like someone, though. No one she knew but like someone. 'Like - like. Like' she says, increasingly imperative. 'Like. Like! You know what that means!?' Tap tap tap at the door. 'Sorry' she says. 'Can you be quiet in there!?' 'I'm sorry' she's screeching and the slicing ping of violin of her sorethroat rupturing wakes her to a fit of sneezing, sitting up, turning the wrong way to leave the bed and flatting her nose right to the cold wall.

But Lucy does sleep. She does. She decides to skip past all of the other interruptions and now finds herself under the shower water. Using hypochondriac amounts of scented soap and a professional-grade facewash she knows from having always gaped at in grocery aisles costs a virgin's-head-per-ounce. She regrettably has no choice but to wear the same clothes as the previous day. Rather: she decides to because she'd have to put them on anyway to go out to get other clothes from the car and by then what is the point in not wearing them? It's not as though the world would start being fair to her if she wore a different t-shirt Wednesday than Thursday. Cigarette. Another. Maybe she'll live here and maybe she won't. It gives her a kind of reckless feel but one she knows would diminish upon Katrin's arrival. She takes out Katrin's naughty magazine to look at Cade, again. At that photo - and Lucy's as human as the next person so a few of the others, as well - and at that photo and at that photo. Cade. You have yourself a little crush, Lucy? 'She looks like me' Lucy says not believing it now, anymore. She looks like Lucy thinks Lucy looked some indeterminate number of years ago - however many it would mean made her think the word *Young*, a number she's not up for arithmeticing just now. Funny thing, Lucy - Cade actually looks like you, now. Lucy touches that bruise. Winces and says 'Ow.' Really fine play-act. Loves how in the photo it is the reflection looking out over Cade's shoulder not Cade herself deigning to turn. That's how Lucy would do it. That's who Lucy is looking at.

She sends a text to the mother - glad she thought to, just in time, just in time. *We're boarding! Oh God, finally! Remind me to tell you about this guy, just now - holy shit!!!! Miss you and tell Flynn he'd better have my money.* Giddy giddy Lucy - most of that means nothing and the rest is another lie you'll have to tell. What man? Lucy isn't going to make up the story now! Just some loser, obviously - some dryhump of a twerp doing his dryhumpy twerepery in her direction. Blah blah. A guy, you know? Something to say. Twenty minutes. The mother hasn't written back. The shakes. No. Not the shakes. A slight ping third bump down of Lucy's spine. What's going on? If the mother had seen her since she'd been back, somehow, it would have had to have been in the last half-day. She had gone on a trip. 'I did go on a trip!' Lucy says, kind of affronted at the imagined accusation she hadn't. How else could the thing have been figured out? How could the mother know she'd been lying? 'And so what!?' Lucy shouts. Calm down, Lucy. She's just at work. She's at work, right now. There is no possible way she saw you someplace. And if she did: the result is she stops answering texts? Did something in the demeanor of your texts while with Layla give it away? Did one of your texts to Layla get sent wrong? One of the photos you snapped? Your phone is pure horseshit! Lucy? 'What?' Lucy? 'What!?' She breathes heavily for ten minutes. Fifteen. Types: *Hey, taking off, phone shutting down. But I'll see you this evening, okay?* Almost sends it. Don't send that. Cigarette. Cigarette.


WHO'S THIS? HE'S LOOKING UP. Pleasantly. He just said 'Hello' to Lucy. 'Hi' Lucy limp wrist flaps back, wondering *Who is this man sitting in Ariel's chair?* 'Are you Lucy? Right?' Lucy? He is standing in that courteous and disarming way, making an obligatory handshake situation seem like something he has been warmly looking forward to. He looks like he wants an autograph. That's what he looks like. Who is this person? 'I'm Martin Penn.' Martin Penn pauses after releasing the handshake, little cutesy look of waiting and smiling. 'It is Lucy, right?' 'I'm Lucy, yeah.' 'Well Lucy, I have done my best to look after the place these last few days. Hopefully it's none the worse for wear.' What did you say to that, Lucy? Lucy has no idea how the next minutes of conversation went. She then excused herself to use the toilet but didn't use the toilet but flushed the toilet because appearances must be maintained. Martin Penn is still standing there, hands in his pockets now like he's a preppie about to give the grand tour of daddy's trophy-room or something. 'Martin?' 'Yes, Lucy?' Martin says in what Lucy is certain he thinks is a charming, satirically businesslike manner. 'Where is Ariel?' He tilts his head like a robot processing something and Lucy more than half-way expects him to go 'Error. What is an *Air E L?* No file matches this in our record-banks.' Instead he just told her that Ariel's last day had been Monday - a little mouth shrug, scrunch this way, scrunch that way, smile.

Now: Lucy is letting that process but it's one of those awful almost comical situations. The rules clearly state that she betray no sign of alarm. Her legs - yes, it's all just like you would expect and as it's often depicted - are numb planks and send dull thud-shivers up her as she gets to her desk and of course there is something odd about the chair that has never been odd about the chair before, as though the chair is bent on making her aware of it, today. Martin Penn had gotten most of the run-down from Hernando of course all of the broad strokes and - Martin Penn has a bad habit already of saying *Of course* after and before almost everything - of course Ariel showed him a good amount of the practical, end of last week, and got him passwords and whatnot on Monday of course. But of course Martin Penn is a graphic designer of course and of course a keen film and pop-culture enthusiast of course in addition to having completed his degree - two of them but of course he does not say that to mean anything of course - and so of course something like *Hernando's Highlights* is a bit of a cake-walk of course. 'Anyway - Hernando liked my pitch to do the thing as a standard size, glossy magazine - no more of this pint-sized kinda coupon-looking thing. Of course we got a bit of a budget increase, you know? Mostly for the thing though of course - the different format.' Martin doesn't know how much Lucy gets paid but he can tell her how much he gets paid to make sure she and he are on equal footing - or that she got a bump, if anything, cause that seems the fair way to go of course.

'Oh!' Martin Penn swivels his chair around, twenty minutes later. 'Hi' he then chuckle-apologizes. Lucy has been holding her eyes open but does not know what else to do to indicate she is waiting for him to say whatever he is going to get at. Tactfully - big time politic - Martin Penn scratches the bit of his goatee above his lip, under his nose - for effect avoiding direct eye-contact except in dips and dots to be certain he does not seem aloof while he says this: 'I pretty much do normal working hours. Of course Ariel was very cool about explaining that that in no way has to be the thing - of course Hernando said so too, of course - but I do. Just in case.' Just in case what? 'Just in case what?' This man is horrendous - his breath has hives, she is sure of it, and his teeth look fake, so fake they seem stolen! 'Oh' Martin Penn's eyes go up like he is shocked his drift has been missed 'Oh I thought, just in case - I suppose I meant: in case you want to sync up of course. Of course I don't know if you and Ariel synced up. It doesn't matter of course.' '*Synced up?*' Lucy repeats as a series of letters that are those words, probably lip snarling. 'Your schedules.' Now he is humble-pie, Martin Penn is - lookit there at that humble-pie farm boy with his artiste gee-golly eyes and all - 'I can't really stay on later - on print days of course on print days I can of course - so didn't know if you and Ariel did that for work reasons or just because it was something you could do.' Did what? 'Did what?' What is this man saying!? 'Synced your schedules.' Lucy has followed all of this. Yet there is something else because look: Martin Penn right there, still. 'What?' she says. 'What what?' he smiles and whatever impression he has of how he is coming across that face of his betrays just there is so wrong he should be flayed.

There is the lot of *Hernando's Grocery*. The flagship store. Little known fact: Ariel had once told Lucy that this specific store - the flagship store - was built on the site of the shopping-center where Hernando's father's shop - *Hernando's Grog* -

had been. The shops were demolished to build the flagship though the flagship wasn't the first of Hernando's - the son's - stores. Here is Lucy Jinx, in rather a mottle of cigarette grey-blue and air-blank and the general washed-out grit filter over everything this time of the early afternoon. Lucy might well be wondering what she is thinking. She is not in a good head, this much is evident from her inhuman posture - inhuman in that she distinctly seems to not be rendering her body in a natural way - and the fact that she is actually very deeply inhaling. Look at her inhale! It is a marathon runner's cramp of an inhalation! In her gut the smoke jingle-jangles and it comes out her mouth the consistency of the first steam of a just coming-to-boil spaghetti pot. There is, apparently, a man just through the thin door to the trailer-office behind her who claims his name is *Martin Penn* and that Ariel left work forever on Monday. Just this past Monday. Just now Ariel took it in herself to leave - just now. Lucy suspects murder. Serial death. Why isn't she running? Because she also pictures just-recent-abduction. Trunk of Martin Penn's car: Ariel. Ariel: already bludgeoned to her maker but the body not yet moved from the trailer's rear-door out to the dumpster. No. No. Lucy doesn't think that. She only just kind of wants to.

A series of questions: Why not just call Ariel? Why doesn't Lucy have Ariel's phone number? Why not just go see Ariel? Why doesn't Lucy know where Ariel lives? In there, there must be a number on file - right? Is that right? Or ask Martin Penn, maybe? Ask Martin Penn!? For Ariel's phone number!? Why would Martin Penn have Ariel's phone number!? Because Ariel had trained him and Martin Penn seems the conscientious kind who would want something like that? Okay? Except: why would Ariel give it to him? Why wouldn't Ariel ask him what he was playing at? Why didn't you know Ariel was leaving on Monday? Did Ariel know she was leaving on Monday? Why didn't Lucy know Ariel was leaving, at all? How had Suzette and that rabble known? Why hadn't Hernando informed Lucy of this? Had Hernando assumed Lucy knew? Had Hernando not brought it up only because Lucy had said that her imaginary sister had died and she needed a week or two to be with imaginary family - leaving out the imaginary part, of course? Certainly Ariel would have told Lucy had Lucy not left - yes? Wasn't that it? Wasn't it that Lucy should not have left? Hernando would have Ariel's number, yes? Is Lucy going to ask for Ariel's number? Is Lucy some freak, some stalker - what does she need Ariel's number for? Couldn't she just say she had lost her phone - her phone had been damaged, she'd lost her *Contacts* and needed to touch base with Ariel about something? Wouldn't people want to know why she doesn't know where Ariel lives? What does this make her look like? Does it make her look like exactly what she is? Is she the only person who didn't know Ariel was leaving? Was that because - obviously - Ariel hadn't known how to tell her - obviously - and - obviously - would have done, face-to-face, had Lucy not suddenly been gone? How could you do that to Ariel, Lucy!? Can you think what that must feel like? Would it feel like this? Do you think she felt hurt like this as she left?

Martin Penn tries a new tack pretty much as soon as Lucy is back through the door. He gives her a rap about how much he thinks about time-travel. He's no physicist of course - deprecates that he doesn't even know if physics enters into time-travel of course - but he thinks about it all the time. Lucy listens. This is what listening would feel like on an autopsy table. This is what listening would feel like, waking up without a head. 'They say of course if you go into the past and make a change it'd change the future. Sure. Makes sense of course. But considering time - on a line, right? - what is *past*? Here's Point $A$' - Martin Penn demonstrates with a poke in the air - 'and here is Point $C$' - again demonstrates - 'so if $C$ goes back to $A$ it'd change $B$ of course. But what about $B$?' Martin Penn does a big wind-up and Lucy does a physical gestures of assuring him he's brilliant and she is following him studiously. 'Well: say one guy at $B$ goes back to $A$ - that changes $B$ and $C$ of course - but at the same time' - air quotations - 'another guy from $B$ goes forward to $C$ and does something: wouldn't the future-change to $C$ - which is the present to $C$ - change the change caused by the first $B$-guy changing $A$?' 'I think so!' Lucy enthuses and Lucy is an ace at the face of mock doe-eyes. Martin Penn says he has never really met someone who digs talking about time-travel. Lucy agrees - but to keep Martin Penn from catching on to that she goes 'Right!?'

There is a man, likely still prattling in his inner monologue about time-travel - likely imagining possible responses from Lucy - sitting less than three arm-lengths from her. Instead of Ariel. Eventually this is going to hit Lucy, fully. But meanwhile: she is feeling the other developments tide-swelling against her back. The ground-shifts, the subtle changes to air currents - superficially apparent to anyone - but also the subtle, even impossible-to-know-for-certain things that she will have to watch for signs of and modulate behavior due to accordingly. How much is going to go wrong? The actual question, as Lucy well knows: How far along is the wrong she has brought down already along? She feels staggered without having yet gotten toe-hold on the slipperiest particular. 'I'm going to plummet down this well' she thinks 'and at the bottom is something that fell before - that has survived but is nearly dead - and I will be there, it padding pruned Martian-fingers on me while it expires!' Lucy just stood up. Abruptly. Martin Penn glanced back, now is holding the glance. Lucy asks him if he has ever forgotten where he was, one second to the next, in the same breath going from familiar to far-flung? First he says 'I really like the way you talk - Ariel said you were a poet.' Then he says 'No - is that what just happened to you?' Lucy answered. Something. Does it matter what? Maybe. Or anyway, it'd be helpful to know because Martin's face if bland and unchanged in affect and it has asked 'Is that a good thing or a bad thing?' What? She's not sure if she said *What?* or not. Too many things are hitting her. Talking to Martin Penn is dangerous.

By the way: Martin Penn actually watches most of the movies they write up of course and is going to make efforts to watch them all, now that he has this gig. By the way: if Lucy ever wants to, Martin Penn and some friends of his - oddly, Martin Penn adds 'And their girlfriends and stuff' - watch movies most nights and she's welcome to stop by of course. By the way: Martin Penn thinks it'd be cool to start doing everything under their own names, make a selling point that the articles are *Original To Hernando's* instead of the vague explanation that the articles are *Submitted from various freelance sources* that currently can be found in the *Credits Section* of each issue. By the way: Martin Penn knows Ariel found that part fun of course - and he hurry hurry hurries to get in 'And it is of course it is' - but maybe a whole-new-thing to go with the whole-new-look? By the way: Martin Penn figures it could make them mini-celebrities - or anyway, it could and would be neat to put on a *CV*. By the way: Martin Penn has written film essays for years if Lucy ever wants to read them - he has a website of course - he is writing the address on a card. By the way: Martin Penn says Ariel said that Lucy owned the *Poetry Corner* and Martin Penn thinks that is awesome of course and he won't muck his way into it of course. By the way: Martin Penn's ex-girlfriend was a poet and got published in this mag and that zine and even had some chapbooks out that did pretty well and though nobody really read it of course she also did a really cool long interview once - maybe Lucy would like her stuff.

What had caused this? Not the trip. Lucy doesn't think that was it. If anything the trip is part of the consequence, part of this Rapture she is in the torrents of. But she needs a causality. She needs to know when she was handed her Guildenstern-letter, set into her Rosencrantz-boat. But right now, anything she starts with seems to be a miniature of the larger maw she is being gnawed in. She can't even focus, decides she'll come back to the question. Later. There's later for that. Martin Penn asks her what she is working on. 'I haven't been able to write for awhile' she says. Then, kind of amused at realizing she can say it, she says 'My sister just died.' Martin Penn had been nodding - happy to indicate that he liked how she'd misconstrued his question to be about her poetry not whatever bit of *Highlights* she was doing that day - but then went ashen. 'Shit' he said. Jesus - he looks the pink of remorse! 'I'm - shit - I'm sorry of course. I didn't mean to be - I've just been blathering at you.' But Lucy doesn't want to deal with this. She puts on cheer. And she 'Oh no, not at all.' If anything she's glad to have something else to think about. And she'd been having trouble with the poetry before her sister had snuffed it, she added, Martin Penn so much the gentleman he only gave that kind-of smile that indicates I-know-you-are-sad-and-I-understand-that-joke-is-a-defense. So: all's well. The briefest of awkward silences. Martin Penn has turned around feeling a greasy twat of himself and Lucy the magnanimous champion of the day! Or something. Sure. Whatever Lucy says, why not?

The phone rings. '*Hernando' Highlights*, Martin Penn speaking.' There is a phrase: *the living daylights*. There is a phrase: *the horror, the horror*. Martin Penn is actually speaking to someone and Lucy has not the zaniest concept of what it all might be about! He is talking on the phone he just answered! And Martin Penn is taking notes. This is not something Ariel taught the tyke, no no. And Martin Penn signs off, thanking whoever it had been for the thought and assuring kindly how he'd bring it up with everyone - gave Lucy a kind of eye-roll at that bit, at least. 'I thought you said you'd been to college' Lucy says, giving it a go at making paly. 'What do you mean? Yeah, college.' 'And you graduated?' 'Yep' he says like he is honestly unsure - Lucy can see him thinking the words *Did I not tell her about my two degrees*? 'Did you not pay attention on the last day?' she asks. Okay: Martin Penn is at least picking up that there is some joke going on he might be supposed to be getting. 'I guess not enough' he finally does a you've-lost-me face saying. Lucy gives him a look of ancient pity, the kind a God might've given the animal it'd made love to as it turned to leave. 'Who was on the phone?' Lucy has changed tone and so after one last kind-of-shrug referencing the previous miscue - or whatever he might think it was - Martin Penn does too, answering her 'A reader.' '*A reader*?' 'A reader, yeah.' '*A reader* was on the phone? Is what you said?' Now he tries the tactic of saying 'Ariel said you would haze me but she didn't say it'd be this shrewd.' Lucy can't help the smile. But tempers it by saying 'Either you're lying and she never said that or she certainly said it'd be shrewd.' Immediately from his look Lucy regrets this further mistake. She's bringing Sodom down on Pompeii down on Rome down on Alexandria's Library down on her, now - even Fate is starting to blame itself on her.

TREAT THIS AS A REGULAR lunchtime walk across the lot from trailer-office to store. Lucy ought to be proud she is not denying anything, not putting herself off to dreamscape or hallucination, not going in for any strand of hope at all. Nor has her fatalism curdled to morbidity. No knot becomes entirely solid. She can only tug and be left unraveled or be left a never-to-untighten mess. The lot is full and there is a harangue of live music - rock music - coming from the store itself, gulping louder out each time the automatic doors skirsh open but always loud enough she can even make out the lyrics from this far off. What is it? Two o'clock in the afternoon on a Thursday? This seems the worst time for a rock band and exactly the time one would be playing at a *Hernando's Grocery*. The reviews are mixed: that customer comes out shaking in just the way a cartoon dog flooding a room with its dry-off-after-bathing would while that other customer is honestly grooving and mouthing the current refrain as they get to their van. Lucy takes normal position for her smoke. Perhaps this is the last song. Perhaps what sounds like the lead singer telling people to check out the deals on produce and frozen pot-pie is a witty way to bow out, not a sign of his puniness revealed. 'Nothing is less rock 'n roll than deals on frozen pot-pie' says Lucy in the direction of the empty bench. 'Sid Vicious puking a frozen pot-pie in Siouxie Sioux's lap can't even make deals on them rock 'n roll.' She winks. Who at? At anyone. No. Just at the bench. She makes a point of putting her cigarette out on it to the throb of the band's next number.

Hidden in the frozen-food aisle, the churn of the coolers at least gives her some peace. It sounds more like her own head, anyway. See, though? Just moving around is a good distraction. In the brief stint she's been away from the trailer-office she has gotten the outline of herself back, at least - unsettlingly empty seeming, though clearly her, she is an illustration-in-a-coloring-book version of herself, but at the moment this suffices. Now to the seafood: the rotten scent of it all, the lobsters waiting to die at the hands of amateurs. The woman working back in the butcher area gives her a nod like they're in on a heist together and she returns it - the connection immediately broken by knives being slathered the one over the other. Lucy can't hear the sound of the knives. Lucy loves the sound of the knives. She hears it in her mind. The lead singer says 'Kleenex are buy-one-get-one-free' then laughs like as though he is gesturing to a funny face the drummer made, says 'What's that?' then laughs heartily like something was said to him off-mic and goes 'Too right - Kleenex are Bogo! Now that sounds a bit more like it, yeah?' And then the singer - as though his manager held up one as example and pointed at it urgently, gesticulating - furthers the announcement 'Oh yeah - and forty-nine cents off of any bulk candy purchase over five dollars - so get on yer mums, kids!' Electric guitar sting. Blah blah blah and the next song begins. Lucy looks at the lobsters with no sympathy. She clicks her hands like pincers, like that is how lobsters talk and she is telling them something they need to hear, would find solace in.

She isn't going to buy anything. There isn't room in her for food. She'd go comatose over so much as a Hydrox cookie. Always the rattle of noia about leaving with nothing, though. She could buy something just for her piece of mind. Peace of mind. *Peace. Piece? Peace?* 'Peace, Lucy' Lucy mutters, this distraction not as charming today as it would be any other. What does it matter?

she thinks, since she'd only thought the word. She'd seen how she'd have spelled it and that could not be ignored. What if someone could tell by some sound in her voice that she was reading that spelling when she spoke, those the letters her mind saw? Yes, this time - this time - she had only been thinking it but say she had been speaking with someone!? Does Lucy ever wonder if people are picturing the proper spellings when they speak? Does Lucy - do you, Lucy? - truly believe that folks picture any spellings at all when they speak? To most people words are as devoid of letters as the world is of scientific fact! An odd coupling - aligning lack-of-letters with overzealous-religious-convictions when, she knows, quite the opposite is true. Those religious zealots: they like their letters, they horde their words! Lucy should be religious. She already is, practically, why not ride that boar proper bareback? Is this what you're thinking about, really? In a supermarket on your lunch break? Today? Now? Is this the distance you will go to keep shut of yourself? Jesus Christ, Lucy Jinx - fucking Hell, now!

This needs to be explained. First, look here: Lucy moved in the direction of the café, thinking to get a coffee which would settle her trouble exiting the premises. Simple solution - at her best, that would have been the first thing to occur to her. Funny thing: Charlotte had been nowhere in her thoughts. Look: Lucy spent a minute thinking which was the best route to the coffee-café area, considering the band traffic - they had fans, it seemed, or else people had some other agenda for watching attentively - and took a route which would bring her up angular to the coffee station from in back. Had she come the normal way she would have been right in his line of sight. Whose? Just a moment. As it stands: she stops short and has time to duck further behind some people and back-pedal - though she doesn't move further than that. Calvin was standing at the coffee station, leaning on the counter where once before Lucy had leaned - several times before, where Lucy had leaned, often. That was Calvin. It was, right? She comes to look from another angle - from in back - and sees - no - she's not certain, she can't say she's certain it's Calvin - Charlotte grinning a giggle and leaning forward on tip-toe to kiss it-might-be-Calvin before turning to a customer. It-might-be-Calvin does not move but watches - Lucy can tell even from her difficult to describe angle - Charlotte's ass and the sides of her breasts and her cleavage while she goes about preparations Lucy cannot see. Now look: it-might-be-Calvin just said something and laughed and did a slapping-your-face motion at whatever was said back to him - obviously by Charlotte. He'd said something about her ass, the side of her breasts, or her cleavage - obviously. This needs to be explained: Lucy - Lucy Jinx - just happened to see all of this just now, right here, in just that way.

So exterior. Cigarette. Will it-might-be-Calvin - it was certainly Calvin,

Lucy, you know that more and more and more and more - stay until the band is done? Until Charlotte is off shift - she wouldn't be off shift soon, would she? Or would he be out soon? Also: Lucy can only suppose he will exit through the main doors, that he will not pay for something and go 'round the doors on the other end of the store, for whatever reason. Why would he? Well: look how full the lot is! He might have had to park over there! 'There are lots of reasons, shut up' she hisses. The point being: Lucy are you concealed enough, here? Would Calvin - because it was Calvin - be picked up by his mother at the curb? Wait. Wait, Lucy. If it is Calvin - you're sure it was Calvin - why are you standing here? To verify? Are you really unsure? Anyway - moot. There he is. Lucy instinctively hides her cigarette behind her back as she ducks behind the brick pillar. That is Calvin. Calvin moves at a hip, musical jog to that car there. Of course he'd have that car - that's exactly the car he'd have now that he's not being chauffeured by mommy. Lucy almost wants to go tap on the window. So do it! 'Hi, Calvin.' Kiss him. Had she never kissed him, she'd ask. Let me do it, now. Okay - so do it! She almost wants to just open his passenger door, sit down, smile as he registers who she is and then guide his hands to fondle her while she undoes his pants front. The car - that young-man clunker with its I-don't-give-a-shit rattle as it gets warmed up - still has some carbon-blacked snow in a tumor over the rear wheels, a bit of which falls away now, the bit Lucy goes and gives a kick to after the car is well away. It wasn't mushy, the soot-snow. It ice-balled along the pavement five distinct blinks, the last one hitting some dent or divot, bouncing high with a brown trail of itself chipped to mist.

Idle. Idle. Checks her phone. Nothing. Idle. Idle. Cigarette. No - this idle isn't correct. This leisurely sit to the bench she had been talking and winking at earlier is most out of character. What is Lucy doing? What are you doing? She sits in oh-so-precise a way. Regard: knees touching - almost knee-tops touching, feet as wide spread as can be, considering that about her knees. So, kind of a triangle. Regard: leaned way way forward, almost folded in flat half - by which we mean that her head if forward past where her knees are in space. Regard: her wrists are crossed over each other, the top of one forcing upward into the underside of the other - the other not pressing down just kind of slumping to the up-pressure - and her chin is pressed exactly into the space between the index and third finger of the lower hand. Mark that! The lower hand! Meaning to say: her head is kind of craned forward and wrapped around. And she holds that position. If a hat were in front of her it would be filled with coins and dollar bills. Tourist would take endless snapshots of her but then when looking at them later be creeped out, wish they hadn't. Every visual cue of the wrong of the moment! Her body is processing everything because her mind is refusing. That is the theory. That is even *Her Theory* while holding that position and ignoring an itch inside her ear canal. Ignoring it. Pointedly. Ignoring it as a kind of fervent thing to do. And she knows it. And thinks it. And thinks this. And does it all anyway and kind of pretends she is being interviewed about it and that the interview is often reprinted in textbooks - as an example of erudition, sometimes, as an example of vaudeville, some other times.

Still. Still. Still. The build-up is there. She is not oblivious. It is just she feels it is not quite the time. It is not the time to show her mind has caught on - that is what they are watching for! Her body can goblin itself all day long, it means nothing to them. Even now they would think 'Well there, you see! Lucy is back to normal. That's Lucy Jinx, walking back toward the trailer-office after her lunch break. Who knows what that was on the bench - Lucy Jinx is a complicated and multifoliate bough, we cannot snap to judgement based on the quirks and mishaps of her physicality.' But once Lucy shows where her mind is? Well! Then she'd better be ready to draw down without quarter because it's her or them, at that point - and no softer tones to put it in. Maybe this even is just Lucy walking back to work. So what? Are you thinking about Charlotte and Calvin? That's fine. See? Thinking about that is fine. Who cares? Lucy does not care. No. That isn't it. Watch her think about it, now - parking lot, moving at a toddler-toddle. Calvin was Charlotte's boyfriend. Charlotte had a boyfriend. See? Calvin had meant *Charlotte* when he'd said he had a *girlfriend* - he had been in-front about that and, of course, would not have thought to have said *Charlotte*, that day. None of this can affect Lucy. These are facts. Kind of funny. 'Mighty funny' she says in a sing-song voice like a character in a movie she enjoyed.

Can you imagine, Lucy, if you had walked up? Don't. Can you imagine if Calvin had seen you and Charlotte had seen his face seeing you and then saw you and your face seeing her seeing him seeing you? Don't. Or if he had played it cool, just waved you over and you had had to go over? Don't. 'You know Lucy?' - can you imagine Charlotte having said this? Don't. 'You know' - a pause - '*Priscilla?*' Don't. Or if Charlotte had seen you and hopped up-and-down and introduced you as her *Poet-Friend* all giggles and 'This is my boyfriend?' Don't. And if his face had betrayed something!? Don't. And there's nothing to betray! But there is nothing to betray - that's what's worse! There is something that is nothing which is so much more sodden and pathetic! And how old are you, Lucy? And who are you supposed to be? And you can't even think a fart of poetry anymore, can you!? You said *Don't*, Lucy - so don't! Stop. What if Charlotte already knew about it all - can you imagine? Don't. You're a game to them, Lucy - can't you see? Don't. Why else would Charlotte be like that with you? Don't. Why would Calvin have been like that with you, come to think of it? Don't. All of it - all of that? Don't. Had it ever made sense? 'So what if it hadn't?'

- she is just talking aloud now, moving to her car - 'So what if it made sense or not - nothing depends on making sense!' Can't you so easily imagine it: they had seen you at some point before - Calvin had 'That's the old dough-belly who sex-chatted with me - that's her! Look!' and then Charlotte had 'Oh my God! She was that weird old bloat I told you wouldn't stop looking at me at work and gave me a poem!' Stop it, Lucy. But you do see how that's more likely? Stop. Than what? Stop! Than what, Lucy? More likely than what?

She enters the trailer-office for two reasons. Her car keys are there. There - on her desk. 'Do you think we should try to get some actual interviews? We can't keep doing this fake stuff, right?' That was Martin Penn who, in the meantime it seems, has gotten a head of froth up about nothing. 'Ariel and I used to talk about that' Lucy either said or didn't say. Probably did, because now Martin Penn is saying 'Then let's do it! A whole new thing, man. Revamp. Rejuvenate! Things happen for a reason - for all kinds of reasons, of course! But: the good thing? You know what the good thing is?' The other reason she entered the trailer-office: to take the framed *Cat Poem*. Is that something you want to do, Lucy? You want to take that? Or is that a mistake? Lucy: they're definitely watching you, right now. This will determine a lot - what you do right here, right now. Martin Penn ventures to chummy-chum-chum her a tap on the side of the arm, having scooted his chair from his desk - which was once Ariel's chair from Ariel's desk - 'You know what the good thing is?' 'What is the good thing?' Do you want to steal the *Cat Poem*? Ariel left you, Lucy. And before that, Ariel made this. So: this belongs here, doesn't it? What are you asking for if you take it - what will you deserve? What are you agreeing to if you don't take it - what will that result in? 'We get to choose the reasons!' 'We do?' What is this dolt on about? The fuck are you even saying? What reasons? Lucy probably didn't say that. Martin Penn is rapping his fingers, piano trills and then piano arpeggios and floppy fish chords on his desk, now.

She promises Martin to be back to it one-hundred-percent come morning. 'I should have taken today, too. My flight got in late and I slept poorly.' Martin Penn says it is nothing to fret over of course and he looks forward to it even if she takes off until Monday of course - even recommends she does since it's so far along, this issue, already. 'I can do this printing of course, you know? If you want to skip it.' Wait. Wait. Wait. 'Who picked the poem?' Lucy suddenly knows she needs to know this but definitely also shouldn't be asking: this is something to let lay that she cannot let lay. 'For the *Poetry Corner*?' Martin Penn's eyebrows go up then he gets it. 'Oh - Ariel, of course. Or - of course - she said you had them sorted out in advance of course. She did the one you had picked out, already.' This is never going to end, Lucy - you know this is never going to end. 'Well, okay' Lucy says, knowing it is never going to end and attempting to move for the door. 'She has that laid out if you want to see - from before she left of course so it was done to your specs, she said.' 'I'm sure I've seen it, already' she says, weakling, stopping, standing, doomed. Martin Penn laughs 'Obviously you've seen it of course - obviously, right? You're obviously the one who picked it - obviously.' Are you going to verify, Lucy? No. Because both outcomes are worse than the other - they are one-and-the-same and the only degree of either is *Worse*. Martin Penn is pulling the file up. You need to leave, Lucy - now. Martin Penn is turning to say 'There we go!' and doing Voila! hands. Are you going to look, Lucy? It's worse if it is that one. It's even worse if it isn't, though. It's even worse if it isn't - this is what Lucy can't take - because then she'll never know - but it's worse if it is because then she'll never know somehow more. 'Just please tell me how it starts, okay?' We must understand that Lucy does not look at all like Lucy honestly is now - she just looks like Lucy Jinx, standing there and asking that question. Martin Penn says 'Oh just a sec' because that is how this has to go 'No, shit - this isn't the file, just a sec' and he tack tacks at the keys. He tack tacks at the keys. Lucy watches. Watch Lucy. Watch Lucy, watch. Watch, Lucy, watch. Then Martin Penn's voice - reprehensibly not Ariel's - his blowhard recital-at-bookstore-café voice goes *'There are no fewer cruelties than fingers lost count.'*


THE INSIDE OF HER HEAD needs a specific description. Imagine something like a child trying to find a way to imitate a growing rainstorm. First: tapping one finger of each hand tip-tip-tap-tap on the wall of their bedroom. Then: a nice one-two-three pattern done evenly - one-two-three one-two-three - three fingers of each hand keeping pace with the other. Then: the pace starting to lilt uneven - not one going faster than the other one slower, just each three-set going gooey and unencumbered, its own random one-two-three. Then: one hand starts using all five fingers while the other just uses three but the one using three goes deliberately slow - hard-hard-hard, hard-hard-hard. Then: all at once both hands are going as hard as the one which had until that moment just been doing one-two-three - and both hands are careening with all five fingers in a slop. And then? The child moves both hands from the wall, eyes closed and - keeping the force and franticness - is thudding this rhythm over both ears. And then? Really suddenly has plugged each ear with the butt of each palm and the hands are drumming as hard - with all five fingers - on the top of the child's head while - pump-pump, pump-pump - the palm-butts move in-out in-out to give a hollow, disembodied whoosh whoosh to each ear. And then? The child opens its mouth and begins making a loud, long, droning sound - how loud the child is unsure because of ears clogged and pulsing from palms and the sound of fingers rough on its head, but it must be pretty loud, the droning. That describes the inside of Lucy's head. Keeping in mind: she shows no outer sign of it. And is driving. And is even able to sing along to what is on the radio. If someone described themselves suffering this headspace to Lucy, Lucy would feel terrified for that person. No. Not *For*. Of. Lucy would keep far, far away.

Point: Didn't Katrin come along out of the blue saying how she wanted Lucy to stay there, no need to pay even? And therefore isn't it true that dropping the job at *Hernando's Highlights* is more-or-less not an active obstacle? Response: Yes. Counter: This would - as it always would have - absolutely necessitate leaving the rented room which - however handled - would be an upheaval of sorts. Lucy had entrenched there, carelessly. That was a place she would need to extricate from, job or not. Point: But here - hadn't Katrin offered to find Lucy work? Any manner of work? And in such case could Lucy not take a job and kind of shunt between the two places? Continue to pay rent for the rented room but balance time between Katrin's and there? Response: Yes. Counter: This ignores the writing on the wall. First of all: so precarious a balance would be difficult to maintain without questions - and questions are what would further unbalance everything. And - be serious - the mother is obviously on the verge of asking Lucy to just live there, proper. She is. She certainly is. Things got out of hand there because Lucy had been stupid. Further point, end of it: Eventually, this would lead to a blending of worlds. Somehow. There would be no way to avoid it. Lucy would show some sign of something and information would spill out. Katrin. The mother. There would have to be an integration. Integration leads to explanation. Everything would come out and Lucy would have no control.

She almost walked right into the store smoking her cigarette, had had her hand on the handle before stopping herself, wheeling away, hopefully before the proprietor had noted the almost mistake. 'Had had my hand on the handle' Lucy mutters, simpleton. Giggles. Simpleton. 'Had had hand handle.' Enough. She isn't even certain if she has in fact ever stopped in this shopping-center. That dismal fast-food joint with the one dumpster all wrapped up in a bright, thick, blue plastic? It seems familiar. But at the same time: so much so as to make Lucy doubt it was in this set of shops she'd seen the phenomena - maybe just a dumpster like that someplace, maybe confusing that thought with *I have been here*. 'Seeing a dumpster in a blue bag is not' she Confuciuses 'the same as having been someplace.' A truth. Something that no one can argue with. See how long that lifeboat lasts! If she were to describe herself it would be with the word *tentacled*. She cannot lose the word. Pictures a mop-head of slimy legs beneath her as she walks to the far end of the row of stores - glances at the poster of a decorative cake, sniffling as she does - and then back to her car through the parking lot. Lucy, the ungainly Daddy-long-leg. The word *tentacle* seems to apply to those creatures. She has now checked both pockets and no car key - is about to collapse is anguish before she checks pockets again and it's right there. Right there.

This place. This place where Lucy Jinx is. This whole area. It is untenable. It has cumbersomed up, bulbous-labyrinthine. Regardless of trying to choose a hidey-hole the place will get fat fingers around throat and throttle you, girl! Think: even if you forget about Katrin's, maybe get a job, stay on at the rented room, just sometimes hang 'round and visit with Katrin? What about it? In effect: you choose the mother. Just say it, Lucy. 'If I choose the mother' Lucy says and the matter aloud makes her feel pusillanimous. Never mind that! Say you choose the mother - say even you cut out having to deal with getting a job from Katrin, full stop - you just choose the mother, find your own job. Say that. Now: will you be able to hide in that house forever? Of course not! You will be dragged about more and more and any move of free-will against such tugs will put things at odds, ruin the point of having made the choice to begin with! So: you're out-and-about - you don't think that leaves you open to all fronts of exposure? Bumping into this-and-that person who might know you from such-and-such place or 'Hey - didn't I see you at someplace or some other?' or here is Calvin or Charlotte or Suzette or anyone! How many of these shopping-centers - for example - are off limits by now? How many infected in ways you could never know!? All it would take is being pointed at once - even if Calvin didn't approach you - by Calvin to some one of his pals, then that pal - or those pals - see you someplace then the mother wonders 'Who is that kid looking at you and why?' or some crazy noise and the whole scene is misconstrued and someone actually accosts you - some young idiot - right with the mother there and all!

Lucy - here, now - is sending a text to the mother. It seems that now is when the flight would be landing, right? She looks at the time indicated on the screen of the phone. Even if not, what does it matter? 'The mother doesn't have my blankety-blank flight number!' Lucy said that aloud, courage-voice, used the silly phrase *Blankety-blank* on purpose to make the matter seem diminished - though instead of that her false braggadocio has collapsed on her and even having said such a ridiculous thing makes her feel on edge. And even if this seems a bit early, so what? *Just waiting for luggage. Is it cheesy to say I missed you? Probably, right? In that case, I didn't miss you.* She stares at the text. Seems long. But when she moves to alter it all she does is add the sentence *Well, obviously I do because apparently I'm still typing, right? Think you're clever eh? Haha Loooooonnnnngggg flight. God! I'll have to tell you.* Jesus, Lucy! Did you just send that!? She lights a cigarette and gives a demolishing look to this old man who came within an inch of hitting her as he puttered his car past her own. 'I'm in the middle of the goddamn lot! I'm in the middle of an empty goddamn lot, you corpse!' Lucy feels better. That was insane. Cigarette. Ten minutes. Cigarette. Why isn't the mother texting back? Lucy verifies the number - double-verifies by matching it up with *Dialed* and *Received* calls from some time back, with old texts which were responded to. She sends a message to herself. Receives it. Reads it. *S'up Lucy?* The sight of that *S'up* makes her start to double-check everything again but she halts herself. No. That was a different phone. But obviously it's not good that you wrote yourself that word, just now.

And let's not forget Suzette! Leave the job at *Hernando's Highlights*? Madness! And that is you - cut off at the knees at the pass, Lucy. Try to leave that job, why don't you - just try! Consider: isn't it a true fact that the moment you do Suzette and her coven will get nose of it? And then the gossip starts up. They will ask that infant Martin Penn what happened to you and he will think it prudent to relate that entire day you worked with him. Today, you mean? He'll describe today! Exactly! And oh the 'Hmns' and the 'Interestings' that will come from that! She can hear him now in his shit creative-writing class voice pondering out aloud 'And she stood a long while remarking this framed poetry, here. She seemed - unless I am mistaken of course - on the verge of taking it - which means of course - we now can surmise - on the verge of taking it with her, wherever she knew she was going.' 'What's in the frame?' Suzette would ask. 'Well, gee howdy!' It's that *Cat Poem* by Suzette's simpering mongoloid friend! 'Why is this framed? *Never Forget*? What does that mean?' Oh even if Suzette is flattered a moment that inbred mind of hers is antennaed for insult and it won't take long to feel she's been made mock of. And then that word spreads. And who knows who some toadstool like Suzette knows! And how vengeful! 'Where did Lucy say she was, Hernando? Dead sister? What ho! Lucy has no sister!' Suzette had seen Lucy talking with Charlotte - but even if not Suzette, somebody. 'Where do her paychecks go?' Or worse, mortal, the end: Some kid is in the child's class - the mother of this kid knows a friend of Suzette who has recognized the mother's address and who asks 'Does a woman named Lucy live with you? Her sister died?' 'She was out of town until Wednesday?' Yeseterday's date will be sleuthed. 'Wednesday? Dead sister? She came back Thursday.' Today's date will be verified. 'I have the texts. What sister?' Then Lucy will come home, unsuspecting. 'Hi, Lucy' the mother will go - kiss kiss to set Lucy at ease, Lucy sees it all now - 'I had the strangest conversation, today.'

But honestly: Why hasn't the mother texted back? Should Lucy risk calling? Voicemail. Right away. What could it mean? Lucy doesn't leave a message, just eats some more of her hamburger. Should you be eating a hamburger, this close to home? Home? To the mother's house. 'I'm not close to the mother's house'

Lucy says as though reigning herself in with a simple 'Tut tut, now.' Still: this does reflect a general sloppiness. To wit: why had she decided to spend an extra night at Katrin's and then to go to work before returning home? Home? Returning to the mother's house. Had there been a reason? The burger is unnervingly tasty. She is eyeing the front of the joint, wanting another. Had that been for a reason? No. But yes, it does seem a sloppy move. Surely that could have ended badly regardless of any further subterfuge or anything. What Lucy means is: that is obviously why the mother is not returning texts! Had the mother - perhaps not even with any bad intent - poked around and found Lucy's flight number? Checked it out. Wrong day discovered. Played along with pleasant texts, just because? What in Hell is it to her!? Well? Lucy genuinely ruptures with a bit of chagrin - feels as though Gregory is sitting across from her, his tongue draped from his jaw, unraveled all the way from over there on the opposite side of the booth to tap at and dampen the zippered crotch of her pants. The mother had been happy-happy and responsive right up until yesterday, hadn't she? There is one-thousand-million-percent no way to ignore that! The mother only stopped responding when your flight touched down! She only hasn't responded to you since then. Another burger? She blinks. 'Yes' she whisper-disguised-as-a-belly-pat sighs 'yes, why not?'

Lucy in a fast-food toilet mirror. At this point that sounds more like her name than does *Lucy Jinx*. A family name. *In* was her mother's beloved aunt. *A* was her father's father. *Fast* was the name of her mother's other daughter who died at two months. *Food* was a favorite teacher who had set her father on the right path after years of delinquency. *Toilet* was the man who had sheltered her mother's great-grandmother during a war. And *Mirror* was the surname, nothing intriguing about it. She is letting her eyes focus, unfocus. Focus: she mostly notices her nose - how much she has always liked it. Unfocus: well, that's the smear that she feels like. Focus. Unfocus. Why all this fuss over Lucy? She is hardly a looker! Because she's so charming? So just be her friend! Enjoy her idiosyncrasies! You know who would laugh at all of this? Layla would laugh. Lucy is sure of it. She almost wants to call her to get giddy, all-embracing counsel. Except: why would Lucy have needed to lie about coming to see Layla to anyone? Lucy had mentioned nothing of this place she had been living - nothing at all - in the time she spent with Layla - and definitely none of this multi-tiered intrigue. 'Who is this woman you're living with? She has a kid? *Star Trek*? Well shit, Lucy!' Layla doesn't even know Katrin. Lucy in a fast-food mirror toilet. Staring. Layla would never be upset with Lucy, though. But, see? Layla is wholly uninfected. You shouldn't even be thinking about Layla in conjunction with any of this. That's going to cause something - a stir, a sub-breath, a coincidence, a gaggle of them, a murder of them, a shipwreck - and

Layla will, joking but with a little bit of a serious-face, say to Lucy - as Lucy is saying to herself in unfocused glass now - 'Lucy, do I even know you?'

The solution epiphanies and it is the same solution as always: let the situation sort itself out. No one can keep the world from wresting its control back. So give it - give it back by giving in. It isn't as though, Lucy reminds herself, she'll wind up headless or barren-wombed. Besides: Lucy is meant to be the eternally fallow sow - cudding the growth of this field or that is all the same to her. 'You're being udderly ridiculous' she giggles, letting her mind free-associate itself into a stupor. All Lucy needs to do is drive home now. Drive to the mother's house. Jesus - if the mother does suspect her of something but goes a day without letting on then the mother is a psychopath! And doesn't the mother creep Lucy out, just a bit? Hasn't she seemed rather forward? Oh is Lucy supposed to pretend all of that is her imagination? Pretend she is so left-field if the mother starts making hurt faces and 'You've been keeping things from me.' 'Because I don't know your deal, man!' Lucy says, forehead smack of triumph. 'You're mad I didn't tell you what I was doing in my life with people I've known forever - and you want to rake me over the coals for it, make me kowtow!? Fuck you!' Lucy, you're still talking. Lucy keeps talking. Finally settles into a seethe. But are you actually upset or just prepping? 'I'm not actually anything. I don't have that luxury, right now. We'll see what I am. But whatever it turns out to be: I am allowed to bite!'

She circuits the nearby neighborhood awhile, keeps a few miles off - just needs just awhile, yet. Last consideration. What? Consider: There is a normal, nothing-to-it explanation for why the mother hasn't texted. Yes? You get back - no bother - she's just happy to see you. Yes? What do you mean *Yes?* What of it? Listen Lucy: you haven't figured anything out. You can't stay. Or so you say. You can't go. Or so you say. But you cannot do both. And you cannot do neither. And by *Stay* Lucy means it in any sense of the term. *Stay*. You exist, Lucy. You have the look and taste of a canker sore, you exist so much! 'I know I exist' Lucy has dawdled the car to scarce-motion-if-any and that woman is giving her a friendly nod like about to come over 'but what is the point in saying *I exist*, right now?' The closest, her thoughts remind her, she came to a decision was more-or-less to *Let the mother's reaction decide*. Yes? That woman is now walking over, dusting hands of garden mulch, smiling. 'Well' Lucy's thoughts say 'that doesn't really make sense. For any number of reasons but most primarily: what if she not only asks you to stay but you stay and she doesn't give a shit about any of that other noise - just thinks it's hilarious and so ever-much-more adores you for the rough-hewn brouhaha it all is?' Lucy does not like the sound of this. 'What about it?' she think-asks in response to her thoughts. That woman is at the window. Lucy smiles back to her smile but reacts no further than that. 'What about it!?' her thoughts incredulous. 'Well, Lucy - how will you ever get out of it, then?'


THE MOTHER IS NOT THERE. And the note from the mother is simple, but not as simple as it could be. Written at a rush and not exactly - fast, but faintly lingered over. Ridiculous as it was to say - the mother keeps a forced tone of good humor over the page front, over the half-a-page back - she had dropped her phone in a bathtubful of water even as she had been about to call Lucy to explain things. Timeline: this had been written yesterday morning. The mother had to gather up the child and head out, because the child's father had been in an accident and was in a rather grave way. She would try to call as soon as she could, but also could not promise anything, immediately, because there would be a headful of noise awaiting her in the shape of the child's father's relations and she just might not have the time or wherewithal to remember to take care of more pleasant things. There was other stuff in there, too. Other stuff - an air, a feeling, words that seemed excess for the sake of intimacy. Perhaps it was just Lucy's lean in thinking, but the mote seemed almost too smoochy, laid here like this - a bit presumptuous, even. And the child had drawn a picture, as well, but it didn't seem his heart had been so in it, just colorless pen lines in kind of the shape of an owl looking at kind of the shape of a barn - a wolf? - drawing never one of the child's strong suites. Lucy decides the note makes sense. Is almost annoyed. Shouldn't this have been the first thing to occur to you, Lucy? Maybe not the particulars, but also maybe so. Things always go like this. Now, here, Lucy. A house around her. Lucy something like a flea in the discarded trousers of a giant.

She plays some things on the piano. Goes through most of one of the books of television theme songs, a few things from memory, even improvises something formless and using mostly just black keys. Then just sits on the bench. Then plonks some keys. Then just sits on the bench. 'The world is so anticlimactic' she says, tonguing around the inside of one cheek in an innocuous way she then decides to turn lewd. It's easy to believe this is the way it has turned out for Lucy. It's easy. Some people, they might find themselves on a piano bench in a house where they rent a room from some woman, thrusting their own tongue into their own cheek like the blub of an unwanted, mulch-flavored cock and think 'Well, how did this happen? How is this life?' But for Lucy, this was in the cards since day one. She goes to kitchen and does the dishes that the mother had not had time to tend to, even eating some of the fleshy steak fries off what she knows was the child's plate. Then re-reads the note and sticks it and the child's picture to the refrigerator with magnets, opens the freezer and eats one of the two popsicles she finds there - not knowing it was a green one until it was opened, the plastic white and impenetrable until the thing burst through. She only eats half, even though green is her favorite and she'd been so thrilled to see it. She melts the rest with hot water from the sink tap, shatters the stick down the garbage-disposal.

Had the mother been sleeping in Lucy's bed? Or is Lucy now inventing noias and seeking out incredible things because she had gotten feverish from the day, could not accept herself back into a normal flow? Had the mother been laying in her bed, even if not sleeping, reading from *Her New Sisters Best Friend*? Because *Claudette, the Bashful Girl* is exactly where Lucy left it, but hadn't she left the two books on top of each other? Lucy undresses, but nothing else. She feels the weight of cloth over her feet and has the sensation she can feel the whole length of the shirt - it's the shirt - and since the shirt touches the pants can feel the length of those, too, like the way she is aware of a finger and more aware than she is of her fourth toe. She sits at the desk, looks at the drawn blinds of the window. Maybe she, herself, had left *Her New Sister's Best Friend* on the bed like that. Spread open, face down? And the bed not made? She never made the bed. But is that how Lucy tended to leave the sheets bunched up? That doesn't seem like her - though at the same time, she doesn't seem the sort to leave the sheets any particular way, just however they wind up left. Had the mother, perhaps, wrapped legs around the sheets in a bunch, a simulation of Lucy, a simulation of skin-to-skin, or mouth-to-skin or tongue-to-skin-down-there, this side, that side, tongue flitting in, tracing the unparted lips? Lucy is breathing heavy, looking at her own mattress. But honestly, she doesn't know why. 'So what?' she manages to say and to feel pithy and erudite for having said. If this is the state of her, imagining passionate, unabashed, erotic intrusion out of the sight of a bed only she has slept in and a book only she has read, well, then Lucy has doubts about herself, she really does.

Well now, this: she's botched the chance to have found the house abandoned and just leave things untouched, make it seem she never came back, got waylaid a bit longer in the affairs of her friend, and then keep moving back the date of her return until she just never did return. That would have been the best way to handle things. You had that chance and failed to note it, dope. Now: Lucy has been back. And even if she hadn't done dishes and moved notes and drawings, she had now sent at least a dozen messages proclaiming her joyous, longing, yip-yip-yippie return. Messages all the way to claiming to be driving to the house. So, when she leaves now, it will be after having come back. The mother will return to find the empty house and an almost angry curiosity at Where could that Lucy be? Why angry? She'd be expecting Lucy as balm, Lucy as friend, Lucy as way to let off some tension from the mess of the father of her kid being - whatever it was - mangled by a thresher or whatever it was, flung from a riverboat onto hard rocks, never to walk or speak right, again. No Lucy will be there, though. But eventually a fixed phone will spit out happy messages of impending return. But no Lucy that night. Or next day. And it'd be a bit thin for Lucy to send more messages, now - messages that something else has come up. Maybe if the mother doesn't return for several days? Then Lucy could leave her own note like the mother had. No, Lucy. It'd have to be a week. A further complication from the same friend? Something she would have told the mother about, first thing, had the mother been there when she got back - would of course have told her, first thing, in person? All such a bore. Why not just stay? Why not?

Lucy still hasn't dressed. She showers. She lays showered in the mother's bed, drifting off and shivering. Why is it only now, prickle-skinned and splayed on an empty bed in an all alone house, that Lucy considers this she does not know, but she thinks it interesting the thought only comes, here and now. She's been only imagining any interest on the part of the mother! 'Any interest' she says. 'You know?' she says. 'Interest' she says. And if there is no interest - she is sitting up now - other than being friends, being close, knowing each other, then doesn't that make it nothing to worry about? 'Alle, Alle, auch sind frei' Lucy says, then says 'I said Ollie Ollie oxen free' then says 'That means Come out come out, wherever you are!' and sits waiting. Then lays back down. She's just renting a room. People who rent rooms do not come from rented rooms, they just rent them. Lucy can go on to whatever life she wants and remain perfectly fine friends with this woman. This might have nothing to do with the salivating of the world's tongue, the dribbles of hunger wet over its chin for Lucy's skin and bones. Maybe this house and the mother being gone can be read as a symbol for This is Safety. This is Okay. This part is nothing to do with it, this is just where you live. The ceiling is where the ceiling is. Lucy is where she is, looking at it. Car doors open and close outside and she tenses, but after half-hour she is relaxed so much she is drooling. Knows she is. Doesn't even wipe it.

Asleep. One of those ten minutes which seem a whole week. The feeling of having had a hideous dream but no memory of it. To her, the room looks like she just blinked and unblinked, but there is a numb feel of excised time to her body. She moves around until she is under the covers. Imagines, well awake now, the mother returning, all of a sudden, to find her there. But this doesn't stay pleasant or even knowingly-imagined for long. What if the mother was actually on the way back? It could be she had impulsively dashed to take the child to the dying - she hadn't said *dying*, Lucy - father, but got a phone call telling her 'Don't you dare come here or bring the child he never wanted a sniff of!' And then maybe the mother had stayed at an airport hotel, overnight, not wanting to overly confuse the child, and had been having whisper arguments with ex-this-or-that-in-laws, finally, recently, just gave up, headed home. On the way. Almost here. 'Arguing with relatives how?' Lucy says, mouth to the pillow she has let her mouth dampen 'she dropped her phone in the toilet or whatever.' Good point. 'Well, something like that is still possible, though.' Good point. Lucy closes her eyes, the part of her that understands reality really - really, really - wanting to sleep, warm and soft and on fabric that smells like this fabric smells. Eyes open. 'Stop telling yourself things that aren't true' she says, shin-kick toned. Had she just fallen asleep? What was that said in reference to? What things that aren't true?

Is this one of Lucy's notebooks? Lucy has moved to the mother's desk, one hand rubbing her stiff neck, the other massaging a numbness in her left buttock. Then she sits, scratches nose, pokes at the notebook, green-covered. The mother is using the exact same variety of notebook as Lucy uses and in it are attempts at poetry. Terrible poetry. But it seems the mother knows that it is terrible poetry. Scribbles. Strike-throughs. Stanzas circled and Xs Xed through the circles. But still, there are thirty-one pages of it and a few indications of where some pages have just been torn out. If Lucy looked in the waste bin her toe is now wraggling against, she'll find those pages, she's no doubt. How bad is the poetry? Is any of it good? Lucy imagines it must be heartfelt. It is. Lucy, Lucy don't be cruel! *There didn't use to be sunlight at midnight.* Gah. *I remember a summertime, but this is all winters.* That's okay. Yes, that is okay - accidentally it is okay and it goes bad in the next line, but that is okay. *Is it allowed to name you? Is it permitted to have found a name?* She shuts the notebooks. Well, that is quite catastrophic. For starters. The poetry itself is catastrophic, but being found now reconfirms this is linked and causal and one and the same as the rest of today. The notebook, closed again, puny offering on altar. No matter that Lucy was maybe never supposed to see it. And there on that wall? Lucy squints. That's okay. That's quite good. That's a torn page tacked there, quite good. Lucy squints. But that's what you wrote on her arm, isn't it, Lucy? You can't even remember, can you!? 'I wrote on her arm?' Lucy asks in a voice of little girl feigning forgetful to get out of hearing a big big angry voice.

She still isn't dressed, but is eating a sandwich in the dark at the kitchen table. Some neighbor has a lot of people over and they all are in a chittering herd in the parking lot and out in the field. Lucy peeks out and finds there are even some dregs of sunlight left - the last slather, milk lacing the bottom of a cup, seems like it'll be a swallow's worth, if small, but tilt the glass and it all joins up into nothing but a droplet. *The last of the sun is the lick of beer left that hisses the cigarette stub.* Yeah. *The last of the sun is the lick of beer left that hisses the cigarette stub.* She flaps on a light, rubber-armed, dog-mouthed, finds a pen on the counter and turns over some of the child's old homework. *The last of the sun is the lick of beer left that hisses the cigarette stub.* Anything else, Lucy? She traces the letters 'round and traces the letters 'round and recopies them regular - regular seeming faint - underneath. But: anything else? No. Nothing else. But the feeling of even these words makes her spine millipede up and down her back, coil her throat and stiffen her loins into the bulb of a hornet. She goes up to her room, expecting computer or notebook, but those are packed in the car, still. So she folds the paper, after seeing what was written on the front: a flier asking for volunteers for a community night and on this the mother has signed her name and listed phone number and e-mail - 'Oh Jesus' whispers Lucy - and crouches, tucks it into the rear pocket of her earlier discarded pants.

Had she really run out of cigarettes? What a terrible time for that to have happened! And none she can find in the mother's room or anywhere. Now dressed, she pats all her pockets again and again, shrugging that she'll either find some in the car or go buy some. If the mother had been home, right now, Lucy would be waiting downstairs on the sofa, nervousing herself into a funk about something, all sensations in her draining to the numb pings of peg-legs to floor. That's how that would go and the progression that had been progressing would progress a bit more. But look around: that's how it is. If ever in doubt, look around again and it's still how it is! But right in this moment, as true as that might be and whatever Lucy might have been up to had the mother not been gone, Lucy does not feel the least bit bad. Isn't it funny, how calm one can feel in the moment when things are most tempestuous and ungodly? The tricks the mind can manufacture, mass produce, the chemical-packages of There's-nothing-wrong that can mix in and be circulated with clean blood and brought back with dirty? Lucy can almost believe, this moment, that all is well and that her bones sometimes get silly, that she right now is just feeling something akin to the way she is sometimes jealous of strangers over things that they don't even have. She can believe that life is no more complex than a business card. It seems so evident that she should just be like everyone else and that by being like everyone else she'll get to be like everyone else. It really does. It feels that way. But it feels that way exactly like teeth imagine they'll never fall out.

Maudlin. This was the house where Lucy Jinx lived. There is no one in it to say goodbye to. Maudlin, she isn't even moving herself. Could be a good sign and could be a bad. It's as though she isn't in physical space at this juncture, is the static that holds eyes moving left-to-right left-to-right over printed text, a gravity utterly pretend but a gravity, nonetheless. She has walked out the door. She has tested it is locked. She has tested again. Then she checked the back door from outside, because the stupidest vision of an invader getting in, a worry about the mother having left with the child, not thinking to check this door which had been opened, earlier, and closed but not locked. And another pat for cigarettes and a fizzle of memory but not of any memory having to do with here or now, even vaguely. But does that surprise you, Lucy? Is leaving this house supposed to fit to some aesthetic? It's a house. The same as always. Do you know how long it was here before you were? And how long it will be, again, now you're gone? You're leaving as your remnant a slight irritation for the mother, a headache of what to do with your things and all, little more. She'll be a tad bit confused, but then she won't be. And then the next day after that. Lucy has already started the car in a gummy old false-numb of running away like she's running to.

IF THERE IS ONE THING Lucy Jinx has wished for in life, it would be to suddenly understand Latin. There have been people who have claimed to her that there have existed situations where, suddenly, with no study, a person finds they know how to play the piano, or become mathematically genius, and there have been cases, she has been told, where some trauma has led to a language - intact, utter, understood - being thrust into some unsuspecting head. These are stories to doubt, of course. Even when she has read in some book of Case Studies about something like this she has done so with great skepticism. There is a reason case studies leave everything anonymous: it leaves the writer the ability to flagrantly invent. Oh the more formalized their Case Notes, the easier the trick is to pull. And that there is the tacit agreement amongst people in the field - which field, Lucy? - that anecdotal evidence is not anything conclusive, well, because of this agreement these madcap sprees of invention can take place. It's likely a game, a sport played on the layman. Obviously, no researcher or talk-doctor fools another with their silly stories, but people like Lucy eek toward believing more and more. Especially when desires are teased at. You might be part of a gigantic control group, Lucy, part of an experiment you must be unsuspecting of and never know the result. 'That's fine, if I can have Latin out of it' she says, flicking cigarette out, unlooking, across lot.

Are you going in there, Lucy? The excuse is Supplies For The Road. Cigarettes and water, a large coffee to let get cold in the cup-holder, drank over the course of two days. Candy. Mass produced pastries. Sports drinks - she always gets sports drinks when going on long drives, but then is always miffed when they get warm before she can drink them, each particle of their fake color coating her tongue like glass shavings shived in the pink sponge. And candy. Candy. And candy. Lucy, in front of the gas station shop, trying to get a look at the register area. Crowded. You're waiting for it not to be? Yes. She checks the time on her phone. Winter always askews her sense of time. She has plenty. Why did it seem so late at night, moments before, and now she feels almost silly for being where she is at so normal a time? All of these activities she is now engaging in were meant to be cloaked under witching hour cloth, she realizes, though they would be impossible by such time. The mechanism of her automatic brain is catching up with her - Lucy is equalizing. This is where she is and what she is doing. A gas station. Not late at night. Here. Now. You're regular speed and alright, now. You're out already, this is just you being militaristic and savvy. 'This is me doing something right' Lucy says and feels the cold of the brick just beneath the lip of the frame of the window she is leaning on digging a good line into the skin of her ass center.

'Can I have one of those, you think?' 'No' she says. What a look! 'What do you mean *No?*' Lucy blows smoke right at the man - something she has always wanted to do. A stranger, no less, and an uncouth, grease monkey sort! Scratch that off the list, Lucy, though terror is sour milking your middle, girl, stay brave! 'I'm not sure how to rephrase it to make it more simple, guy.' Oh he is mad at you, Lucy! He's actually mad! This random shmope in front of a gas station is giving her eyes intent on ill. He's probably thinking of who he can call to post bail after what he's about to do - these swine, Lucy, the ones you have been living amongst, they don't think of life in the same dulcet tones as you or those of your tribe. 'You the Prince bitch is it?' the man says, sticking out his belly though he might have meant it to be his chest or just him straightening up. And while Lucy likes that - *Prince bitch* - she reminds herself it is not actually wit, charm, or wordsmithing that led to the pronouncement. No Lucy, that enchanting phrase is the result of genetic dullardry. 'I don't think it, guy' - why do you keep calling him *Guy?* - 'I know it. I'm the King Cunt, babe. So how about you piss off?' And she's blown smoke in his face again! Has that really happened? 'I'll see you later, hunh?' he says as he opens the door like as though opening the door is the one thing Lucy forbade him and he's giving her the what for, but good! Lucy wants a retort, but none of the ones she thinks of make sense. She mills there through a whole nothing, smoking, trying to word one before finally giving up.

Amelia is behind the counter but has not seen Lucy. Lucy is behind a salad bar and then in the corner the opposite side of the store. Here she stands next to a man saying 'We need to just get Clark out of the equation, but Clark's always up in it' and next to a woman - not connected to this man - saying into a telephone 'You just called, I'm calling back - you've vanished in the last twenty seconds?' On purpose, Lucy accidentally bumps into the man who, looking away from the other man he is speaking to, says 'I'm sorry' to which Lucy replies

228 / PABLO D'STAIR

'No, I'm sorry, you were just standing there.' The man she bumped merely nods - it is the other man who gives her the letch eyes. But now they are talking again and Lucy is making sure that it is feasible to approach Amelia, that she is isn't stuck jockeying the register solo, that some throng of whoevers aren't going to move to transaction all at once. Did Amelia just see you and not betray the notice? It looked like Amelia had just gazed straight down the barrel of Lucy, staring. But no reaction. How far can Amelia see? Lucy holds, quite on purpose, the stare, a few patrons moving around her in bob-steps, one giving her a side glance as they do but she doesn't break focus-eye to flit that she's noticed and annoyed by this. Amelia looks up. Right in her direction. No customer even. Amelia yawns. Moves wrist to mouth to cover it. Hands to counter. Stares just right at Lucy and nothing. Lucy raises a hand. Nothing. The blindness endears her, but Lucy wishes it didn't.

'Amelia' Lucy says, seizing the opportunity of Amelia having stepped away from the counter, over here to the two frozen-food standing coolers. Amelia turns, general drib-drab turn of going-to-have-to-tend-to-the-public then glitter-lashes when she sees that it's Lucy. 'Hi.' 'Hi.' 'Hi.' 'Hi!' Oh how adorable. Oh how easy this all is - Lucy is cold-blooded and razing-to-earthed and field-salted. 'Hi' Lucy says just because that was fun to say one more time, stage segue, repetition based on camera edit. 'I know you are at work, so I will make this quick.' Amelia gets out part of what Lucy is sure would have, if completed, been 'Please don't worry about it' seems to be restraining pawing at Lucy's forearm, but Lucy is over top with 'I want to take you out tonight. May I? May I take you out tonight? For a drink.' Amelia is blushing in the way a blush can turn someone pale. 'You' Amelia says, then goes twittering-bird 'Uh' and can't seem to hold eye-contact 'may. Yes you may.' Lucy waits for the eye-contact. That. Sting. That. Stab. That. It hurts Lucy and thrills her. That. 'What time do you get off?' 'Not until late.' A pause. 'Not until. Unfortunately.' Lucy likes that: *Not Until Unfortunately*. Lots of accidental things said around here that are just swell. 'Can you smoke a cigarette, now?' Lucy asks. This had not been part of her plan, but she just heard herself ask it. It's obvious Amelia cannot, but she says she can if Lucy gives her five minutes. To which Lucy says she will give her 'Exactly five minutes and not a penny more.' Amelia already hop-glancing there, there, and there, at certain other employees.

How much do you smell like cigarette? It's a rather meaningless thing to consider, seeing as Lucy is smoking a cigarette and will soon be smoking another, but still she wonders. Diagnosis: Lucy is a tad out-of-body. There is a this-is-happening-yet-not vibe. Diagnosis: Lucy is attempting to appear unerringly rational, right now, and questions like 'How much do you smell like cigarette?' are as close as she can get. This is all obvious to Lucy. It's just obvious. There are avenues Lucy needs to have cut off, before she leaves. She needs to unlimb some of this place before she goes. It had occurred to her not so much in those terms and not so much as an idea, but more of a feeling. An inertia. There are things within Lucy's power, even as she feels herself ragdolled by circumstance, doggy-chewed and slobber-bleached, and if she tucks tail out of here without acting, without doing, without attacking that will be the final victory of a world that she does not want to cow to, not listen to it crow. She knows this is the explanation. And she knows it us hurtful, what she intends. To whom? Well, for example, to Amelia, in a way. But she needs to balance the uncontrolled hurt, the lashes she has so cavalierly passed around without intent, with some calculating lacerations. She needs to be deserving of the world whipping her in order to defang it. In this case, she needs to be the conscious, calculating cause of discomfiting - or, better yet, of plain hurting - some people to balance her scales. That makes no sense of course. 'But of course it doesn't. Of course it does doesn't make sense' she says, like this is a sour look given from one schoolgirl to another in the second their mother's aren't paying them mind.

And here is Amelia, all fake-breathlessness and over-apology. Well, the breathlessness seems real. Why is Lucy worth this trouble to her? 'This is the last time I'm ever going to be nice to you' Lucy says, holding across a smoke even as Amelia starts to take her own pack out. Look: hesitation sits on Amelia's face. How should you be, Amelia? Lucy holds blank-face, not telling, doesn't even keep the cigarette held out, her arm now limp at her side. Good. Amelia put her own pack away and stammers a bit, Lucy holding the cigarette in such a way that Amelia has to reach for it as though for a stolen thing back. 'I'm teaching you a lesson' Lucy says as though in general 'about talking to strangers. In toilets.' Amelia lights her smoke and Lucy wonders does Amelia have the guts to say whatever flirt goes with that smile she has on, lit click-orange click-orange held-orange, flare-snap-orange. Naw. Amelia just puts lighter away, blows smoke, coughs into the raise of her shoulder and says 'Excuse me.' Lucy likes Amelia's turtle-green jacket. 'I like your turtle-green jacket.' Amelia touches it, smiles, repeats 'Turtle green' like she is verifying, and tells Lucy 'Turtles aren't really green.' Good for Amelia. She getting her sea-legs? What are you saying, Lucy? Why are you acting like it's your place to say? 'What color would you call my eyes - and I warn you, your answer had better be clever.' Lucy is poorly lit, but won't move, so Amelia leans in. Scootch. Scootch. That way something in eyes tightens to show looking more. Lucy just kisses her. Tongue to closed mouth. Tongue to parted mouth. Pulls away and says 'What color?' See, Lucy? Kissing is as simple as that.

The trouble? Lucy is not certain what this all indicates. She was until just then. The trouble? Lucy had even expected that to happen. Her to kiss Amelia. Amelia to accept it not only no problem, but eager and butterfly tummied. The trouble? Despite having expected, even predicted, even imagined the moment would go so pleasantly off - imagined it by way of daydream, not even strategy, this as recently as sitting in her car while also thinking about Latin - Lucy does not know what it indicates that this has actually happened. You should know what something indicates when you are right. Now: Lucy knows what it indicates for Amelia. Look here: Amelia doesn't even resist this other kiss, this kiss with its three quick tongue snakes and a touched nose before pulling back. It's obvious what it indicates for Amelia. But Amelia had indicated that already, which is why Lucy had thought to come here. You do see that, right Lucy? Amelia had indicated that when you learned her name was Amelia. You could have kissed her, even then. You see that, right? The trouble? Lucy is not certain what this all indicates for Lucy. What are you supposed to do with this, now it has happened? Why did it happen? Why did you make it? This is supposed to be destructive? Of what? To whom? Now triumph, even, now this play of dominance and taking steps to leave carnage or whatever Lucy had just been on about, is thrown into vagueness, fog, riddle-rhyme.

'I have to go in' Amelia says, more than long after she very obviously - she's a clerk at a gas station - had to have gone in. 'Amelia.' Lucy lets the name hang. 'I am going to be in the chintzy little restaurant of that hotel' - she points to the franchise hotel that kind of shares a lot with the gas station - 'having a drink. When you get off. Tonight. Late. Okay?' Amelia nods, a slight question on her face but one she smothers while Lucy also says 'And you also owe me two cigarettes. I have been keeping tally. Now get back to work.' Amelia holds the moment. Look at you, Amelia. Look at you! Like a part of the world-ordinary made cutie-pie - a plush stapler, a stuffed alarm clock with whiskers! Amelia tries to make Lucy change the expression of her eyes by attempting to equal the intensity, but in the end seems almost adrift, dissolved, it's even bashful the way Amelia leans forward and pecks a last kiss, one that Lucy only returns with a smile, her mouth closed the whole time. And to cap it: Lucy does not even watch Amelia go, but is already moving across the lot to her car. And in the car and under closed eyes, Lucy wants to drift out of herself, loiter like in front of a drug store she knows has just closed but she kind of hopes will open the door for her if she is noticed, then drift back into herself and wake up uncertain that any of what she just did had just happened. She wants to be less real than she is. Malleable. The way how if she were nothing but an idea being written then a new idea could change her in just a few words. Words like *Of course, that never happened*. 'Of course that never happened.' She says this. Of course that never happened.

This is something you wanted. And now it's something you did. But is it something you wanted to do? Yes. Wait. We're lost in semantics, Lucy! When? When what? Did you want to do it? I don't understand. You wanted to do it before? I wanted to do it, now. But you wanted to do it before now, as well. I wanted to do it before, too. But is what you wanted to do before the same as what you just did? Kiss Amelia? Is that what you just did? Isn't it? Let's go back a step. Okay. Before: you wanted to kiss Amelia. Yes. Why? Because I wanted to. And why did you want to kiss her, now? I still wanted to. But that isn't why, exclusively, is it? It isn't? You said you wanted to hurt her? I said that!? It's why you did any of that - had you just been saying that? Wait. Where are you going now, Lucy? What are you asking? You do know that Amelia will be at that hotel restaurant. Tonight. No, she won't. She won't? No. She won't actually go. I'd just be sitting there. Waiting. She'd not show up. And then what would I do? What could I say about it? Lucy: where are you going? Right now - where are you going? I'm leaving. And isn't that why you told Amelia to go to that restaurant? Because you knew she would, would look for you, would be confused, would be hurt, would look for you every day, after, would never know, never understand why you didn't come and never came to her work again? No! No? She wouldn't come - she won't come to the restaurant. Even if I waited. That's why I'm leaving. That's why you're leaving? Yes! Oh Lucy. Lucy, Lucy. Why are you leaving? Lucy? She'd not really show up - I'd be the fool, the one left wondering, then wondering if I should ever show my face again, then never showing my face again, forever. This was a mistake, then? This was a mistake. I am such a mistake. I'm not confusing anyone, just letting them know they were wrong about me.

LAME-BRAINED, HARE-LIPPED, JUG-BELLIED, LUCY SITS within the parked car outside of the trailer-office reciting 'So rudely forc'd Tereu.' Then she makes some weird sound with tongue movement like a wishing well, pulpy-walled and swallowing. 'It is quite cold, let us say' she says aloud, but her breath does not yet show in front of her. She does expect it to. Any moment. The parking lot of *Hernando's Grocery*, by this time, in no longer packed, but busy enough. The traffic encircles everything in tittering goggle-eyes, putting Lucy in mind, as it always does, of the underline of an eye starting to well with tears, a lip trying not to bawl as a voice scolds it. It is odd how short a time ago Lucy was in there, yet now she treats herself like she is ill-belonged. A memory of stealing from a grocery-store, once: Lucy at fifteen-years-old, being caught, giving name and waiting for parents to be called. She'd been told not to go into the store ever again, but of course she had. Of course she had - not even a few days later. Yet that feeling of not belonging, everyone looking at her, scouring her, and with rights to her to do that and even more. Belts coming out from belt looks. Hands coming away from threating pretending-they-needed-warming breaths into fingers laced, fingers clawing, crack-knuckling, fisting. Everyone. Is that how Lucy feels, right now? At the mercy of whoever catches her, if someone were to catch her? No. It never even felt like that. Not so dramatic. People looking at her, sure. But no one would touch her. Wo ever touched Lucy? They might shoo her away with a mop, but mostly would just use words, remind her she was unwanted. Thins unwanted are not even worth belittling touches.

The exact thought on Lucy's mind as she enters the trailer-office and flips on the light is nothing to do with what follows and is truncated, mid-word. The appearance of light, despite she being the one who hit the switch, startles her. She feels exposed and douses the boxed office-space back into darkness - in front of her eyes floating green swirls and colorless-white swirls that seem to crackle like soap-film dissolving on bathwater top. In the film version of the following moments: Lucy proceeds to set the place on fire, chop-frames, cut cut cut, frenetic-editing, then suddenly a long shot of her outside, just looking, then abrupt cut to behind her, the flames already blunderbuss loud and brazen and high. In the novel version of the following moments: she finds Ariel's toothbrush still in the bathroom, wets it ever so slightly, then sours teeth, gums, tongue surface, swallowing the taste of old residual mint and the blank of her own spit pretending it's Ariel's. Here, in reality: Lucy sits at her desk and opens the drawers and closes them and wonders why she came in. She is so boring, here. That's what she had been thinking. How hectic, even thrilling she had felt. But now just feels like she has been thinking about herself. She's the voice that is prattling and no one is listening to and she'll still be talking to herself when everyone has gone, as though now that they've left they are bumping into her, later, and picking up on some interesting subtext in what she'd said, before, something they had been heatedly waiting to comment on. 'Jesus, I'm boring' bores Lucy in the dark.

Then: Lucy is out front. She observes the parking lot, the sky, her parked car. Describe the sensation? The sensation: that time between incidents has lost all meaning. It still accounts - she's not gone insane - for the majority of her life, she knows that. But while, just days ago - certainly months ago, certainly years ago - each speck of time between this point and that point in her life had seemed fascinating, now abruptly they all feel the same. Elaborate on this description? Elaboration: Details, nuance, the meat, the flavor, the in-the-moment of a moment no longer has currency. Lucy isn't what Lucy is doing. She isn't what she is doing and only sort of is what she has done - only 'sort of' because she was not even hardly there when it was done because she isn't what she is doing. Never has breathing felt so not only arbitrary, but laborious. Is that the word? She doesn't even care. The sensation? That she is loitering in and cognizant of moments of life that neither she nor anyone else will ever remember. This is what the moments the mind flushes from itself, constantly, feel like. This is awareness of being forgotten. No word latches to object. No feeling carries even atomic weight. 'I'm like a goddamn science fiction story' she says, then tries louder, but then can't get up the guts to actually exclaim, to scream. Funny, because no one would hear. Is it you don't want to prove the point, Lucy? To scream while you're inside Forgetting, to consciously scream while being conscious of forgetting you've screamed would be just a little too harrowing, is that it? Forgetting doesn't end, does it? It seems it should, because forgotten seems gone if you move past it, but forgetting, forgotten, it doesn't disappear, it just stays.

Picking up here: Lucy - dismantled and expurgated a Lucy as she may be, yammering to herself, internal, though she may be - is striding the length of the *Hernando's Grocery* lot, gamecock chest forward, on the lookout for slippery patches after - just before - having almost lost balance on one. A shopping cart there, wind easing it to the bumper of that stumpy car. Bump. Lucy could have prevented it, could move the cart away from the car now, but she doesn't. This is the acceptable form of revenge. There: at least those two people saw the whole thing, too, and now share grins with Lucy. Grin. Grin. Yes, we're in this mess together - right now Lucy and two others are chuckling the same, are the same. Hop up the curb, lean to brick pillar. You hadn't even noticed that old woman on the bench, had you Lucy? Well, she hasn't just materialized, this instant! You walked over here, even shook your face like a deadbeat dad dusting your hands in long swishes over thighs, and she has been there, perfectly visible, the whole while. Looking at you in that elderly way. 'I suppose you've seen me before?' Lucy might say. Impenetrable blandness of elderly face. 'I've seen you before' Lucy says. Old woman shift in place motion, leaning head in, that obnoxious old-person pause as though sound travels slower to them and then they have to remind themselves they have to speak by thinking the sentence 'I am going to speak' then the words 'I have to speak now before speaking.' The old woman says 'Oh?' Is that all!? 'Oh?' Lucy says, almost slapping her knee and hyucking some bounce-belly guffaws. 'Oh!? Oh!? Is that what you say: Oh!?' The old woman tilts her head either like a cockroach or like Lucy is a cockroach, it's tough to tell.

Charlotte noticed Lucy approaching, setting down the container she had been wiping the deepest interior of with what seemed to Lucy a cartoonishly filthy-stained washcloth. Before any real pleasantries could be got off, Lucy went somber faced, took a preface breath down nose, punctuated by stopping her forward approach, up-down on her toes, click-stop on the touch of her heel to the tile. 'I need to talk to you - are you still working working? Can you step away?' There was, Lucy assumed, at the very least a brief tick of question mark to Charlotte's feature, but she could not actually say, had already turned and was, here, taking a seat at one of the nearby café tables. Hands folded in front of her. Decorum. Clearing her throat into curled hand, then again into nothing, no one there to notice these things or to remark the brief scratch to the itch in her ear or the rub of the fingertip of that same hand, just after, to the fabric just at the top of her sock. Lucy kept that hand there, by way of scratching a make believe itch. Now she looks over and there is Charlotte, setting a little notice on the counter - a Be Right Back sign inside the curve of a hard plastic standee. Charlotte fairly trots over, seems to be trying to work something out from between her teeth with tongue squashed just there, gives it up as she sits down. Lucy has given up her adult-person pose, so it's like it never happened. Now? She's leaning hard to the point of one elbow to tabletop, other arm dangling unneeded beside her, little finger absently tapping the pants over the side of her calve. Charlotte's eyes roll and she goes 'Just a sec, sorry' exactly as Lucy was all set to speak. Trot trot canter canter, goes Charlotte, muffled sound of her taking the order of the plump little foreign fella who'd ambled up to the counter.

This is unrehearsed, keep in mind: Lucy says 'I saw your boyfriend in here the other day. Can I ask: how long have you been seeing each other?' No hesitation from Charlotte in replying, but if Lucy was keen she would notice, moreso than the no hesitation, the clip to the words meant to indicate their subject's lack of gravity 'Calvin? I've been seeing him for about, something - eight months or something.' Wait - what had that change in expression, lizard-quick then lizard-quick back, there been? Too late, Lucy is already pressing on, here ad-libing: 'Okay. This is going to seem peculiar, abrupt, and out of nowhere' - Charlotte kitten smalls, all ears, nose atwitch, faking anxiousness poorly, seeming excited - 'but I've been sleeping with him' - the smile on Charlotte's face should be enough to pause Lucy, but Lucy is invested in her scene - 'I've been fucking him for awhile now. While you two have been an item' - *An item? Really Lucy? Are you Charlotte's step-aunt now? her assistant principal? An item?* - 'but I had no idea he was your boyfriend, of course. Though I did know he had a girlfriend - I asked him when I first approached him and he told me, so' - Charlotte briefly straightened to full, now has settled back and her left shoulder wiggle wiggles, then her right shoulder wiggle wiggles, she seems captivated and chomping at the bit to cut in - 'But, now, seeing you were that girlfriend, I decided I needed to tell you this' - Charlotte is fairly bursting to interject but is of good breeding, it seems - 'because I think he's bad for you. And I really think you should drop him and forget about him and never give him another chance. And you should tell him why, too. I don't care. He's a piece of shit and you're better than that.' Done, Lucy? Done. Why is Charlotte smiling at you? 'Why are you smiling at me?' Charlotte sniffs, flicks Lucy's hand, and says 'First: you are fucking awesome! Second - and far less important: he's dropped. Okay. And you are so fucking awesome.' Pause. Charlotte flicks Lucy, again. 'Now can I tell you something?' Charlotte asks. That finger that flicked, Lucy? It hasn't retracted. Now Charlotte is sighing 'Gah, be right back!'

Lucy has sat chewing the inside of her mouth. We are to assume this was based all on a similar impulse as the earlier Amelia debacle? Lucy chews the inside of her mouth. Or is this really as impromptu as you tried to make it come off, Lucy? Lucy switching to chewing the side of her tongue. Do you even know at this point? Charlotte keeps making comical faces over at Lucy from where she is stuck tending to a short line of patrons. We are to assume you are returning these faces with some expression, Lucy? Lucy waves, anyway, at this latest Charlotte-face, the one accompanied by a gesturing of sit-back-down or don't-go-anywhere. Had Lucy been standing up? Yes, she had. The impulse - keep in mind how muted and redundant reality and spatial-relations have become to Lucy, please - in that had been to go out front for a smoke. To test if Charlotte would follow? No. Charlotte wouldn't follow - she'd expect you'd be back, Lucy. 'And if I didn't come back?' Lucy asks herself - she has not entirely sat down, legs are still tense enough to stand - but immediately afterward goes right out loud a Pfft sound, rubbing side-to-side her index-finger beneath nose as though in imitation of a moustache whisking beer foam off. You should be thinking of a plan or else leaving, Lucy! What bearing could what Charlotte has to say to you now have on anything? Had you said that stuff about Calvin to hurt her? To hurt him? To finalize something? Whatever - you said it. What else was this visit for? Lucy - can you report on your current operating conditions? Optimal? Standby? What are you, right now?

It turns out Charlotte made the decision to move the conversation to outside ground before any more customers could gum up the works. She and Lucy walk out the skirting open-shut automatic doors into the chill - Charlotte had not put on even a sweater, was still short-sleeved and aproned - and then around the corner a ways, stopping just here. Lucy has been removing a cig from her pack as they walked, has just settled it to lip when Charlotte looks at her, rolling her eyes in a giddy, nameless kind of playful. Charlotte takes the smoke from Lucy - look, Lucy, it's there, Charlotte is holding it right in front of you, look on her face of 'Do-you-see-this? Do-you-see-this?' - and snaps it in two, huffs as Lucy takes a breath like to talk and then, forefinger-tip to thumb-tip, a circle holding

Lucy's chin, steps forward and kisses her, holds mouth to Lucy's the count of five, then steps back and shivers. 'What about that?' Charlotte asks. Lucy blinks. 'What about what?' is what Lucy had started to say, brat stance of one hip struck out just begun, but only got as far 'What abo' before Charlotte, hands to each side of Lucy's waist, gripping - clawing, actually - kissed her, again, this time Lucy's mouth opening to allow it. And the next thing she knew she was still kissing Charlotte, only had her back pressed against the brick of this bit of the side wall of *Hernando's* and the fingers of her left hand were around Charlotte's throat. In fact, Lucy is now pushing Charlotte's throat, getting her to step back just long enough to see her starved-hound face's mouth panting while teeth automatically chatter, just long enough to hiss - Lucy hisses at her - which makes Charlotte's eyes go impossibly wide and then Lucy drags her throat back, her mouth with it. They kiss with eyes opened until they can't.

It could be characterized as awkward - and it would be understandable if Lucy convinced herself that none of that had just happened - but after however many minutes - and it winding up with Charlotte's back against the wall, but no kissing, not anymore, just smoking cigarettes in speechlessness, Charlotte's back to the wall, Lucy's smoke breathed out not a half-step in front of Charlotte - Charlotte said she was freezing and that needed to get back inside, too, to work. Lucy probably nodded. Obviously Charlotte went back inside. There might have been middle moments, caulk to those facts, but anyway: Lucy is outside, now, by herself in *Hernando's Grocery* parking lot. She smokes a cigarette and another, then realizes that this is an odd place to pick to smoke, as, right there, inside that caged, locked compartment were propane tanks the store either rented or sold. She scoots away. Back inside. Expected to see Charlotte with customers, but Charlotte is back to her cleaning. 'Did I just make out with you in the parking lot?' Lucy asks, timid, side-slinking up to the counter as though in fear of the back of Charlotte's wrathful hand. 'No. Make out? Nope.' 'I didn't?' Charlotte bunny-noses, eyes pointed upward tick left, tick right 'No, I don't think so. Or if you did I don't remember, you know?' Lucy lumps elbows on counter, breathes out nose - again, again, some kind of breathy ellipsis - then doesn't go Phew! but just says the word 'Phew.' Charlotte puts a napkin on the counter - tap-tap-taps it - and gives it a slide toward Lucy. 'That is where I am. Tonight. How about you be there? Where I am. Tonight.'

It takes Lucy five minutes or so of aimless frustration, squint-faced in the lot, to remember she was parked over by the trailer-office. She coughs and feels the carpet-tinge of sore throat, her face warm with headache rising up the tubes inside her wet nostrils. Oh she feels a frayed knots under a coat button. Her ears clog as she gets in the car, just exactly in the moment the door slams. Thunk. Muffle. She swallows but it cannot set her hearing correct. She grips her hands to the steering wheel, tightening them, relaxing them, ratatatatatating first the left one then the right one then both. Coughs and the cough shake her around, chicken bones down a dry garbage-disposal. She opens the door to spit out some phlegm that she takes five minutes to hock into a real mouthfuled pile, putrid little fetus of it splatters there on a spot of white parking lot line, and a thick dangle from her lip bulb to the pavement she gingerly pinches off - delighted that it all seems to fall, none of it but the teensiest fleck left to either finger-tip. Closes eyes and slumps back. Before too long is shivering, a bit from the cold, more from trying to keep still so as not to cough more. Lucy - you seem oddly unthinking, right now. Lucy? But Lucy isn't thinking or listening to herself thinking about how she isn't thinking. Her head is filling more with physical things, sinuses shuttering closed like boardwalk shops or token booths, eye pulsing and dry, a raw feel to them - they are apple cores bleeding worms out through mealy brown white. Lucy turns sideways in the driver's seat, eases herself into a stiffening, seering-sore neck, as this is the position that seems to make her head the quietest and least flotsamy. When she yawns, her ears grind like a bag of greying teeth and fungused toenails. When she closes her eyes, they feel as though stitched shut after having been stuffed too plump with her tongue.

SHE'S ORDERED 'A CUP OF coffee and a chocolate doughnut' having decided she is in a movie, now, this the cinematic thing to do. Placed that order in the way the order would be placed were this cinema. Quick glance to the menu, then shut it, tap it to tabletop, hand it up almost dismissively while saying 'A cup of coffee and a chocolate doughnut.' Minimal eye-contact with the waitress and then set to her own contemplations. This was an acceptable thing to do, it seems. The manner of ordering was even smiled at and there is the waitress, brisking thataway to enact. What are Lucy's own contemplations at this point? Very minimalist. For example: When the waitress comes back I will say 'Alka-Seltzer and a glass of water, could you?' like some actor she likes would. Like - she screws-up mouth, twist pout of Hmn - Ed Harris would. Or Dennis Weaver. Other than that? Well, along the same lines: Lucy wishing she knew a more generic name for Alka-Seltzer. Tangentially, she wishes she was suffering indigestion so she could ask for Pepto-Bismol by the generic name. 'Some Bismuth, please - some pink bismuth, if you have any!' But, Lucy, does Alka-Seltzer not do the same thing as Bismuth? There. She's stumped! You want something for the head cold, right? Yes. Lucy wants something for the head cold. That isn't what Alka-Seltzer is for, she decided. Here are her coffee and a doughnut. Look there: chocolate doughnut, in this establishment, means plain cake doughnut with chocolate frosting. Not what Lucy had pictured, but as it turns out this is exactly what she wanted. Has taken a mouthful before she remembers to, napkin to lips, blushing, thank the waitress and answer, still chewing, still napkin-to-face 'No' when the waitress asks 'Anything else?'

This is the same diner as before. When? Earlier. The diner on the way from the airport? Yes. So now the diner on the way to the airport? No. Lucy is not going to the airport. But she's leaving. You are leaving, Lucy? Lucy? 'Yes' she says through bit teeth and eye-stabs like 'Keep it down' into the steam of the coffee she is tilting - sting sting - to her chapped, sore-with-dry lips 'I am still leaving.' She gets the waitress' attention and asks to borrow a pen. 'You need paper?' 'I'll use a napkin, thanks.' 'Okay, let me know if you need paper.' 'I will.' Always good to have a pen. Even if all she does is twirl it around fingers. Tap it. Test it is scratch scratch scribbled-downward-warble on the face of a napkin she then crumples and adds to the crumpled napkin on her plate of doughnut crumbs. It's gotten stone black out there, black as an underside. Lucy can tell by how much the inside of the window is nothing but a crisp, too precise mirror of her sitting there. Reflected over there? Just a young couple. She images them slightly high on marijuana and bored with each other, less enthralled than they'd figured they'd be on this night, at this time. That young man is proud of how he looks in that shirt. Those boots were a real important thing to the girl when she'd found them - she'd have felt like an honest-to-God dame, a photo from the cover of a rock 'n roll album, magical in the way such photos are when one is fifteen years old. Now that girl - what is she, twenty? - is already learning how people older than fifteen look at photos on rock 'n roll albums: they don't. This might be first time she's ever had to sit with a fella and realize her boots don't mean anything and meanwhile he is quite proud of his shirt.

*Life's fairly simple - just because you are in love with someone doesn't mean you aren't in love with somebody else.* That's what you've written, Lucy. In this napkin draft of what is meant to be a letter to the mother. But what could be the meaning of it? Is this statement - true and cryptically self-contradictory in tone - germane to this letter to the mother? How can it be? Because if you write that - especially just after the salutation - much import will be given it. What import? She will think you're saying you're in love with her!! No, no: it will simply read as a preambling, pleasant, casual-but-intellectually-astute sort of way of leading into an apologetic - but only somewhat, Lucy will not go too far, as she has to make allowances for her own appearances in this, as well - explanation of why she had to leave so abruptly. Under cafe lights, this honestly makes sense to Lucy. Lucy who is getting to a point of fatigue and mild-fever where all considerations seem incidental. When in truth she is not even settled on leaving. Hours ago she felt prodded and poked but now a familiar sense of bearing shame is defensively kicking in, balming her state-of-affairs down to a smoothness. Why else write this letter or any letter, if you aren't leaving? Are you thinking of not leaving just because this letter is a burden to pen? She's losing her train of thought. Lucy is some kinda cartwheeling scatterbrain! What does that mean: why else write this letter? Why else what? Why are you writing this letter, Lucy, and why does it start that way? But Lucy just reads the words and finds them beautiful and true. Why strike them out? Meaningless or not, who wouldn't like to get a letter like this?

It is not the waitress who refills Lucy's coffee, rather a man who can be best described thusly: he clearly uses the word *cooter* - possibly the word *yammy* - when referring to a woman's vagina. How can one tell? What physical description gives away this lexiconal-preference of his? See the plump folds of the alcohol eyes, like warped carpets waiting to cause stumbles? She the beard growth, not thick enough to hide the freckles? The freckles not enough to hide the liver spots? See the paunch he forgets to consider he has in his masturbatory fantasies? All of that speaks to his linguistic attitudes. Lucy can size him up in the space it takes him to pour her more coffee she didn't ask for - she might not even say *Thank you* she thinks while she says 'Thank you' - and as he rather snot-rags away thinking filth of her. Lucy feels highly perceptive of the world in this moment, so much so it troubles her. As a man stands noosed on a scaffold, he must think himself pretty observant - novels have taught her this, as well as notes in prefaces to novels explaining incidents in authors' lives or accounts they based their work on. Hyper-perception is a sign of being hunted. That man who filled her coffee? He is not being hunted. He's the sort to be surprised each time he sees his feet have shoes on and that the shoes have laces. But Lucy: be careful now. Ear to the ground, girl, because this café is not going to last forever.

The mother deserves honesty. *You deserve honesty.* The words stop Lucy. *I can't think of how to be honest. I can't think of how to be honest*, she reads. That is true. 'End of note, eh?' she attempts at levity. The truth of the matter is all that Lucy wants to reveal is nothing to do with the mother. Isn't that true? Isn't this letter just absurd? Honest about what? Lucy had liked the mother's figure - almost exactly Lucy's own, though more flatteringly carried. Lucy had gotten on relatively well with the child. Lucy was lonely. *I'm lonely.* But she only writes this because she knows she will tear this particular napkin to rubbish - the fifth she has written on - rend it to smithereens, add it to the pile - right there, five napkins-shredded high - and then dunk all of these wretched little scraps into the coffee which will stand tepid by the time she leaves the booth. Does being lonely make her obligated to someone? Does it mean she is attracted to someone and ought kid-glove around it and become subject to this person she felt close with, awhile? 'I didn't do anything wrong' Lucy surprises herself by saying, aloud, tone of voice malicious in its curt. The waitress come over, not hiding the look of 'Everything alright?' in the ten paces leading up to her being there and actually asking 'Everything alright?' I'm feeling guilty about something. Try it, Lucy - say that to this woman. What harm would it do? This woman is a waitress, after all, and in this she might have keen insights into the minutia of your psychology, Lucy. 'No.' 'Okay - let me know if you do.' 'Sorry - can I get some chicken?' 'No chicken. Chicken didn't come, today.' 'Roast beef?' 'Roast beef sandwich?' 'Sure' Lucy shrugs and the waitress is still looking at her but the waitress also looks at her own reflection before walking away - looks at her own reflection, touching her own hair, a little longer than the regard given Lucy.

Lucy Jinx had rented a room and come to like someone. And now she is leaving. Say that woman, right there - or that one, right there, since that one has a kid with her, a better analog - ate a meal here with Lucy and took a liking to Lucy and even knew Lucy had taken a liking to her, but then had to go home to things nothing to do with Lucy - should Lucy expect a registered letter, dripping with rings of existential wits end? It would be appalling! And even if the woman left with nowhere to go, so particular! It's the same. Even if the woman did nothing but go to some shabby cold-water flat and opine for Lucy, it's the same as if she went home to loving, waiting arms and secrets kept. So fucking what? Is Lucy bound by some propriety to stay around until she can explain some third-party-approved hard facts that absolutely necessitate her going? Does she have to fend counter-arguments from someone who might want her to stay? Must she weigh the delicate soul of any person who sits on a sofa with her, who might see in her some new chance or something better-they-have-always-wanted, something they want now, selfishly do not want to feel gone from? It's absolutely arbitrary that anyone comes to like or want Lucy. Arbitrary. Anyone not nonchalant about Lucy Jinx going from Here to Gone has overlooked a lot, both generally and specifically. Lucy needs neither wet-nurse some whomever nor be adjudicator of her own responsibility. She has none. Any more than would have the mother were the mother to have told her she no longer wished to keep tenants or be friends or live in the same country, even. Would the words 'What of Lucy?' come into it? Doubtful. And if they did, they would be easily dusted down with 'She's a big girl - a goddamned adult - and one cannot concern oneself with her when one has one's self to think about.' Or if one day Lucy said a thing wrong that turned the mother sour-hearted toward her, if she became something maligned in the mother's - or anyone's! - eyes: should Lucy alter, beg pardon, feel she had done wrong for being herself, stating herself, naming who and what she is? Well then: this is the same! This leaving without word - or some bumble-brained letter - is just a method of speaking, is just a mannerism of Lucy's, a quirkiness: socks in bed, yawning after a kiss if it's too warm out, never liking to eat standing under a tree.

The entire point is mooted, thusly: Lucy cannot remember the address of the house she has rented a room in! No fake-out about this. No address. It lives not in her memory. She pays her bill and moves into the cold dark of the parking lot. Had she ever had occasion to write the address down? Perhaps she did on some paperwork for the job at *Hernando's Highlights* - or for those other little jobs she'd had, just a few weeks, before she'd answered the *Hernando's* ad? No. Or maybe, but it seems unlikely. She'd used her Permanent Address - her parent's home - and her money all went directly into her bank. 'My address is' she says, but can go no further than that - or rather, she can name many addresses just not this one. Which both seems to make the absence of the words genuine and highly suspect. Evidence: you have a memory for addresses, it seems. It's true. If Lucy knows one thing, she knows where she's lived. The development where the house she rents the room in is called something. *Potter's Glen. Dancer's Glen.* 'Dancer's Glen' she nods. That is something she recalls from an image of the sign on the road she drives down to get there, though, the icon of houses and hill in somewhat the form of a calligraphic ballerina. She has to relight her colded smoke. It tastes off but she sucks it down. Now calm is beginning to fissure. This is like stepping out of her bones. Even if she had forgotten - or never known - the address, fine - 'That's fine' she even right-out-louds alongside an exhale - but why does she have to become boot-toe-in-the-ribs of it now, here, set to go? Why does the point of Forever about this motion, this leaving, in particular, keep insisting it be looked at direct and bowed low to? 'I get it' says Lucy, head thick like Gregory has just bellowed in her smacked ear 'I get it, I get it.'

Imagining: the mother is just there when Lucy arrives back. And Lucy walks in and they hug lightly and laugh. Imagining: they will talk in the morning, because 'Christ's it late' the mother says, and the child is just kind of there, half-asleep with nothing to add. Imagining: in the morning, well, the mother does have to get the child to school, but then they breakfast in the kitchen before Lucy goes to work. Lucy, here and now, in this car: there is a notebook open on her lap and she kind of is starting to think she is just trying to extend this all out as long as she can manage because it's what she always has done - there's just a principle of making decisions torture. Lucy's the coin that went into the slot, caused a clunk, but no matter how hard the buttons are slapped nothing is given out. And another coin is returned to the buyer. And the buyer goes away, content with that coin and content to not have what Lucy would have bought for them. She looks at her face in the flapped open visor-mirror, is rubbing an eye the entire time she looks, so comes away with no real impression of herself. Or, more correctly, she comes away with exactly the correct impression of herself: this has nothing to do with wanting to stay, this has to do with not knowing where exactly she's going - and nothing more than that. This is not a book or a rhetorical train of investigation - departure implies Some Place and that is a blank and however symbolically attractive it is to think otherwise people go Somewhere when they go not Nowhere. Lucy doesn't have Somewhere. She cannot have Nowhere. The pressure to stay is mechanical, syllogistic. But Lucy is not young now, and choosing places to flee to is a game for the young. Lucy, by now, should know how to go without choosing.

However lowly Lucy Jinx may be at a time like this, she has her pride and will not find herself beholden to so simplistic a cliché of: here is an intersection, left leads home, right leads away. There is something more metal about her than that, thank you! As point of fact, she turns left, but there is nothing deliberate or secretly telling in that, she only does so to more easily get to some turn-offs that will wend her around to someplace she'll have to find her way back from or out of. It amounts to the same - yes, she knows that - but in this moment she is demanding, diva-footed to the gas pedal, of this indulgence, this terming the world in her way. Once she has made up her mind on where she will go, she will then sleuth her way to it from wherever she winds up in the next blind-hour's drive. Or if you decide to go back, Lucy? She doesn't respond to her prying as it seems counterproductive to the exercise. It is a free person who can play around with the elements like this. Lucy has that much to show for herself! Which, silly as it could sound, is calming her, right now, as she notices her gas gauge is relatively low and as topography has gotten murky and outlandishly rural. She's not some vagabond, hobo, self-deluding nobody! She has several easy places to go, she just hasn't chosen. She's not a mess. She has the last nibble of her youth left, an education, health - a fine specimen, actually, just at a nexus of several elements of herself. Life is the process of running out of choices and she has kept stolid enough not to convince herself she's bereft already of them. The world has got her head lost, so she gets her body lost - and onward from there!

What is growing out there? Or is this just tall, unweeded grass? Country grass grows tall. Maybe all grass would, though she doesn't think so. Lucy, here, smoking a cigarette in this someplace. The moon at its distance from the field is as brazen as a debtor, the house over there is so dark and still it seems the face of a playing card. Lucy is writing this down. *The moon, brazen as a debtor, the house / dark, still / a playing card's face.* Other things she has written are already scribbled over. And soon Lucy doesn't like these two things, either. Tears out the page, lights it on fire, then spends an extra five minutes stamping it into the grass, scuffing her foot, stamping, rising fear of a wildfire that would not flare up for hours, of some lick of curled, charred, oh-so-invisibly-orange ember igniting the world, flames cackling and sharp as the letters of the word *Zig-zag*. Then, like that, she knows she is going. And where. No place so astonishing - Lucy will drive back out to Layla's, stay on there as maybe she always should have done. What she came back for is gone, anyway. She stubs her cigarette out in the base of a windshield wiper, wonders how she could have forgotten that the start of the day is always what informs the end of the day, the one always a straight line to the other. Even the radio agrees, by offering nothing wise or alarming - no certain song, no interview, mid-sentence, that in some tangential way contradicts her - just a public service announcement brought to her by a local tire and auto shop, ending in a tin-sounding, decade-old jingle about how important tooth brushing is.


LUCY GASSES HER CAR AT an automatic pump, a desolate station with a café affixed to it, signs in the window proclaiming *For Lease* but everything inside as though the joint could have, five minutes ago, been shut down for the night, an illusion that if she looked over there a line-cook and the waitress he lovelessly rooms with would be smoking the smoke they smoke before heading home in their grudgingly shared only car. Lucy knows how almost asleep she is, but will not stop for the night for at least another hour. Two hours. She is in no particular hurry to get to Layla, is not going to make this a sprint of any kind. Indeed, now that she has gotten a reply of *I certainly don't object, but still should probably ask what gives? And Are you okay?* to her text of *Oh for goshes Lay, I'm coming back to you, no more of this mobled burg!!!* Lucy feels definitive, a sensation in her blood akin to have just gotten paid back fifty dollars she never expected the debt of to be honored. She can drive until sun-up. Knows the highway is just a jaunt down this way and can make a good leg of it in the early morning blank. Then she can just drive through night-times, come to think of it, avoid any semblance of being among normal folks and human commerce, skirt along wall corners the whole travel long. One minute she turns the car heater up. Then it is awful. She shuts it off and the skin of her fingers go cold but the bones still feel warm, as though she is some meat somehow cooking backwards.

She reconsiders at the sign - mark it, that sign, that is the sign she see, just here - for a fifteen-miles-off *Starlite DeLux Motel*, that she might just stop, might just. Why that insistence, Lucy? Why did you so particularly note this and shift with a kind of attention? Something about that name - it recalled her to something. It brought an imagine of too much sunlight off some parking lot asphalt, a paint chipped yellow word *Photos*. What is this memory? She has it in mind the next five miles, hunched over steering column, eyes held in tight squints but not really focusing. And a creep glazes her back, her shoulder begins to itch to the point that she just has to scratch it, removes one hand from wheel, reaches around - and there! there Lucy!! - and she screams before she knows she is screaming, it seems even before she sees the two perfect green circles of light reflected off the cat's eyes above its mouth opening just barely - she's sure she saw that, the expression on its face! - and feels the amusement-park dip-wobble of her car slightly juddering, nothing more than a hiccough bouncing tummy flab. She slams the brakes to papercut images of the animal still pinned beneath halting rubber, smeared like obscene lipstick across the split-and-scabbed-pucker of the road. Lucy, not hardly just halted, opens door and tipsy-flops out from the car, stands swaying in the road facing two wrong directions before she finally turns and sees the lump just past the prune-red of her rearlights.

The animal is still alive. Lucy? Lucy! Lucy!! The animal is still alive and Lucy is walking a circle so short it might not be a circle, her hands, unseen in the dark, in front of her and shaped as though poised to each catch a ball and now she is back pedaling, gaining momentum, has fallen, roughs one palm all over the road - it might be spelling a W mixed with a G if this were a canvas and Lucy had paint on her hands - before standing, losing footing and falling so that she knows skin has torn on her knees under her untorn pant fabric. Lucy is no longer Lucy. She is no longer Lucy No one screaming like this can still be themselves. Screams to the lip of the road, screaming left, right, across field, across field, screaming back to where she had been but teetering off-angle and into the grass screaming. Now: here is animal - unseen mound and it is making a noise and Lucy screams louder and imbecile and just cannot hear this, she just cannot hear this so screams. She is too unsteady to easily shrug her coat from herself - tugs it, peels it, titling herself that way, tipping over to elbow which rattles her jaw into biting her tongue. She recoils when the animal yowls as she applies even the tiniest pressure - had been trying to kind-mother-lullaby 'I'm sorry' when it yowled and she was repelled and struck herself hard in the face - bashed herself in the head, again,again, gargling sound no longer screams but just sounds - as the animals hideoused and yowled out to her how it was dying and Lucy's touch was the tough dying it and Lucy's scream was the scream dying it. But here: hovering over it - such images in her mind, of it being smeared so into the ground it would stick when she attempted to lift, of it being Velcroed there, embedded, a parasite, a burr - Lucy listens to its now subdued, but constant tea-kettle, whine, to that and the chug of her door-opened, dialogaled car - and burbled 'Sorry sorry sorry sorry sorry I just need to I need to I need to' in time with her hands hesitant and pulping and wanting to make the scoop elegant and one-time the space around it until she tensed, lifted, screamed 'Fuck oh fuck sorry I'm sorry God I'm so fucking sorry!' not loud enough to drown out the dismal, hating yarl that renamed her very soul Fucking Bastard.

Then she had set it on the floor of the passenger seat, having thought the seat itself would be unsafe in case she slowed too inelegantly and caused it to slide off. Lucy incoherently gives explanations of herself, wanting to express to the animal how she wants to hold it in her lap but cannot, wants to express that she has to drive, wants to express that she didn't put it on the floor because it is like the other garbage on that floor, not wanting it to die thinking it was garbage on the floor, that that is what death was - Lucy Jinx screaming her pathetic I'm sorrys while its nose touched a candy wrapper or a gas station receipt or a Kleenex she'd cast away some random time. She sucks in mucus from over lip into nose not wanting it to die while it's dying. *The Starlite DeLux* appeared and she promised the animal she was not slowing down just to slow down, she just needed to slow down not because she did not care to hurry but just to turn into the lot without jostling it, but as she executed the turn it let out a sound something like the thought of a cardboard corner across her wide open eye. She promised - promised - she would be back, she wasn't leaving it and as she turned, as though unable to help it, unconsciously stopped to regard her monstrous face in the rear passenger window and spit at herself reflected for stopping to see herself, then slapped herself for spitting, then slapped herself for herself and went dog-hobble to the lobby doors which startled her by opening themselves, but not swiftly enough to keep her shoulders from slamming into them, this spinning her, tumbling her into the second set of doors that stayed closed.

Why on Earth this mongrel attendant thought telling her to calm down and that he had no idea where there might be an Animal Hospital and telling her to 'Please sit down' and pointing to where water was on offer while clacking keys on his goddamn computer was helping she had no idea, but look: Lucy in hotel lobby, mute as the womb, in lobby light, lobby heat, lobby music piped in too loud for the emptiness of past midnight. The clerk said something about how there was an Animal Clinic with an energy line, that he was dialing it, but that the place was thirty miles away - at least thirty miles away. 'What's wrong with the cat?' he asked. 'What's wrong with the cat?' but then said 'Hello - yes, you're open' and Lucy figured she could stop listening and stare at these two green-patterned chairs with a circle table and a fake purple flower and a magazine between them. 'What's wrong with the cat?' she heard, again, wheeling around, all of a sudden at the desk and motioning for the phone which the clerk relinquished after blurting into it, informing whoever was on the line that 'The woman, the woman with the cat' was asking for the phone. 'Please' - her voice burst, she had no control, the clerk made no show of hiding that he was unsettled in how he backed away to the corner of the work area behind the desk Lucy was almost drapped the entire way over, now - 'I hit a cat and it's alive and I just need to come to you and I can leave right now just can I take the cat there please? Please!' She stopped abruptly and now the absence of her voice seemed ominous, she felt warmish, felt as though she'd just make pork-squawks over the lines and was being mocked, hung up on, having eyes rolled at. They were asking where she was and she was saying 'I don't know where this is' and next she knew was half-fainted looking at the ceiling mumbling not into any phone 'A hotel a hotel' the clerk taking the phone - which she was holding out to him, then, infant-plea, still saying the 'A hotel a hotel' - and giving the name, road address, and another name, looking at Lucy, looking away from Lucy. And Lucy wondered why her teeth, so sharp as this and down pressing, hadn't snipped the tip-inch of her tongue clean off yet.

The clerk kept clapping his hands wkhenever he saw Lucy swivel to leave. 'Listen to me! Listen to me!' He was willing to believe that Lucy wasn't drunk - the fuck does this snot think he is? what is happening? - but she's fucking obviously in no condition to drive. 'I need to go.' Hand clap. 'Listen to me: they are coming here!' Hand clap - why hand clap? Asshole! Lucy hadn't been moving - 'They are coming here! Even if I gave you directions, you wouldn't get there.' What? 'What?' Soft face from the clerk 'Look, listen to me. Hey.' Soft hand clap. 'Hey.' What? 'What?' 'What if you got lost - if you missed the turn, whatever. You hit the cat with your car?' 'I'm going out front.' 'Just' - hand clap - 'hey, hey. Fine. Look, they said they'd come out, okay?' Lucy knows she is sneering at this man, the clerk reacting but - she thinks - maybe trying to temper his reaction. What do you look like, Lucy? 'What?' 'Do you need anything?' She might have said something to warrant that question, but is now in what seems maladjusted cold, outside, her car's both doors open and two people are laughing on their way to another car, over there, one of them wooting. She turns and tries to shriek but coughs, hacks, doubled-over 'What!?' as she thought she'd heard the door opening behind her when really the door was closing. On the other side of it, she saw the clerk on the telephone, darting eyes toward her. Raised his hand. She raised hers. Coughed, again. His eyes now down to the desk as his body turned, the urgency of his speaking increasing.

Lucy forced herself to look. She required it of herself. Her hand felt like faucet knobs as she moved the fabric of the coat aside and her ribs were tightened as though from recent liquid-cementing. 'I'm just going to look at you' she said, listening to the hikhikhikhik of the cat's breathing. There: its lacerated side, a whole flap of skin displaced, something like a magnet on a fridge door in the shape of a continent that could be moved entire, slid, lifted, flopped down. This flap and the almost lemon-wet pink of the flesh she could see breathing thukthukthukthuk out-of-time with the sound of the breath from the cat's mouth or nose mingled with growl mingled with wheeze, the effect something rather like the deflated rubber of a balloon covering the drain of a bathtub, the water only exiting in belched glugs under it that bubbled it up, the force of its expanse then flatting it back down. The fur was a marmalade orange - or that is how Lucy called it, the word *marmalade* always associated in her mind with a cartoon cat of this color, marmalade something she had never seen nor tasted, a thought she despises herself for having as, still under fabric, the cat's rear leg suddenly spasms enough that its head lurches and grease brown bile bubbles big from its nose and then burst while a squirt also issues in a long arc from its mouth. Lucy looks. She wants to touch. Wants it to bite her. But the terror of the cavity where it had had an eye until her pierces its gaze through her, the gore there neon, fuchsia, magenta, something like salmon and bone-grey, a mat of mud, torn fur, skin and grit from the road surface in an almost shimmering glop. She holds her face close to it and can no longer apologize. It moans and flops viciously once, as though a kid playing sock puppet snake, lurching snake high to bite then retract.

The clerk has brought her coffee. She does take it, not intending to drink, but drinks and it is almost as though she owes him a few minutes of speaking in his tone of voice, her gut swamp-sour with resentment for his presence there. 'Someone should be here, soon. They said they needed to gather some things together, I guess to be ready for whatever, right?' Lucy managed 'That makes sense, yeah.' And she can tell in his face that he hears the shallow crinkle of all the animal can manage, now, the last of the high pitched punctuations of balefulness it had in it seemed ages ago, by now. She knows he thinks this is idiotic and that there is nothing anyone coming can do for this cat she's destroyed. She knows what people do when they drive and strike cats is drive on, lower the radio or say 'Shit' and few times and tell it as a story to their spouse or pal or lover, obviously expressing they feel bad and man-oh-man and all and then put on the television and then something to eat and then nothing and then 'I once hit a cat, it was awful.' 'They know where this is?' Lucy asks and he is so-matter-of fact in his 'Yeah yeah' Lucy is reminded that she isn't actually nowhere, but in a place where people are and people live and all of it, where a cat would still be alive if she hadn't come along, hadn't noticed a sign, hadn't had some memory to think of, hadn't rented a room or ever met a girl or ever written poetry or ever been birthed out to blemish every surface she brushed. 'I guess this is somewhere' she seems to have said, as the clerk - fuck his chuckling, is that supposed to be empathetic? - says 'It is, this is someplace.' And over top of that she looks at him and tells him 'I hate myself' and he - chuckle, warm eyes, face like he'd touch her shoulder but last second thinks he oughtn't to - says 'Come on, don't do that.'

A dot of light appears way way over there. Lucy's head pricks. The clerk is gone, he left some time ago. The light is obviously moving but does not seem to be getting larger. Has it stopped? Why would it, Lucy? She starts to say 'They're right there' to the cat, but doesn't want to lie. The cat is now a crumbling sound, wet cloth-slipper filled with marbles twisted in a mangle by some child's pretend-monster hands. 'They're right there. They're right here, they're right here!' She has knelt. 'Please, they're right here, please, hey okay?' She touches the cat and it tips its forehead, that bit of forehead there, just there where Lucy touches, the tip of forehead right at the end of the strip of soft above the nose a quarter finger-length, the lowest of its tabby $M$, it tips its forehead into the slight touch of her finger and gives a purr, telephone underwater sound, thirteen pebbles dropped in a handful down a well sound, and Lucy feels all breath choked from her, hyperventilates and puts two fingers, three fingers, the cat pushing pushing, kneading kneading its head into the touch of her shivering, palsied three fingers and it purrs two more sounds of fingers pretend-plonking slow trills of piano keys on surface of bath water while Lucy wails and watches a ruddy brown van slowly crest through the parking lot, stopping an odd distance off, as though it is bashful and needing to take a last bracing breath down its nose before actually showing up.

Lucy sits in the passenger seat of the van, unseatbelted until the third time the driver tells her to buckle, this time explaining he will stop driving if she doesn't comply. The scent of throat lozenges and the paper of grocery bags lacquers the cabin, the heat making her eyes sting, but she says nothing. She had passed out, woke to his touch at her shoulder, was told the cat was already inside and she could come in to wait. 'I'm sorry' she said but he had already moved away. A little boy sits with an empty box on his lap, what seems to be a handful of grass tugged from a field in it and Lucy makes and meets eye-contact, even hears herself whisper - from a smiling face - 'Hey' and the little boy gives back no expression but then looks up over in some other direction as though something important were going on there. A woman at the desk seems to have been waiting for her, motions a tentative wave and Lucy approaches. 'You about the hurt stray?' Lucy blinks. 'What?' 'Intact male tabby - you called from that hotel?' Lucy had started yes yes yes nodding during the question and over the end of it says 'Yes - but it's not a stray, he's not a stray.' This is met with no skepticism, the woman just changing a notation in the computer. 'He's my cat' Lucy says and her jaw clicks audibly and her eye winces down. 'He's my cat.' The woman types some more and begins to ask her to fill out a form she is handing across, then stops, regards Lucy with a patient gaze, says 'Nevermind' moving the form away and readjusting herself at the computer. 'What is your name?' 'I'm Lucy Jinx' Lucy says, spelling it while giving a feeble glance around for a stool or something, then leaning to the counter, then feeling awkward about that,

standing back, swaying. The woman types a bit more. 'And the animal's name?'
'*Lucy Jinx*' Lucy says. The woman chuckles, looks up over the rims of her glasses
without lifting her head, scent of peppermint from shampooed hair pulled back
tight. 'And the name of the animal?' the woman repeats, tender as sponge-
wetted clay, eyes still over glasses, smile felt but not seen from Lucy's vantage.
'*Lucy Jinx*' Lucy says. 'His name is *Lucy Jinx*.'

# .PART TWO.

# . I .

BUNDLED UNDER ELLIOT'S COAT, LUCY felt as though the shiver set to her bones was perversely unfair. The coat itself was grotesque on her and smelled - of course - of those godawful cigarillos - the pockets which she had her hands down in, currently ungloved, were poxed with flecks of tobacco from the things which Elliot could not lose the habit of carrying pouched about without wrappers. She pinches a good pellet of tobacco together, grinds fingertips to it. Lucy - isn't that just encouraging things? Isn't that letting you in for some wiseguy pointing out 'You don't seem to mind?' The wool cap - not Elliot's but not Lucy's either, just some hat that had come to be found in their apartment and this-day-on-Lucy and that-day-on-Elliot, whatever questions one or the other wearer had kept quite to themselves - was sodden and crisp with where the freezing rain had most gathered. Why it takes longer for some ice to melt than other ice was quite beyond Lucy - just one of those facts there was no arguing with. Oh yes, she knew - even two hours on, even after being inside - when she picked up the hat there would still be a collected mash of ice clinging to at least some of the twines of maroon fabric. Her shoes were worthless. You

254 / PABLO D'STAIR

need new shoes, Lucy. 'You need new shoes, Lucy' she heard herself mock-mimicking back to Elliot as recently as the previous evening. Well: you do need new shoes, Lucy. 'I know I need new shoes' she says, now yawning into shivering into lips achatter into ears popping and promising headache.

Lucy Jinx also smells like pizza grease. She imagines her face spongy, like the remnant crust left on plates she watches moisten, dampen, pulp, lose cohesion, get ransacked down the industrial disposal when she taps the blue button always thinking the word *Bwahaha* as she does. Other scents have got her clobbered in their bruises, too - the powder soap and the liquid soap, the stale steam of dishwashing hot-water, the slime of buffet salad-bar juices, the raw meats and must-be-sick-causing mushrooms and olives-she-cannot-believe-diners-request. The grease, most off all - ovened into any exposed bit of her face, forearms, neck, top of chest, and in through all of her torso-flesh no matter her shirt, her camisole, her brazier. A terrible thing: to not only visually consider one's nipples uncooked pepperonis but to have undercurrent olfactory kind of lean in supporting the thought. All of this scent pinned now in Elliot's jacket and only two more stops left on the Metro. That man still giving her eyes. She's a target because she'll seem to be sporting an ex-boyfriend's coat - Elliot had explained this when first lending her the thing, an obnoxious warning since she hadn't asked for the garment, had just complained-for-the-sake-of-liking-her-voice-in-complaint that she froze to death daily and that even discount winter coats were outside of the financial grasp of this lifestyle she'd settled on. For fun: she smiles at the man. Or: she thinks she did. Is that what you call a smile, Lucy? Whatever it was, he's looking at his paperback now, intimidated and fluffed, simultaneous. He's imagining he needs him a wicked good stratagem to woo that girl in her ex-boyfriend's coat and that Lucy will be thinking of him even if he doesn't get up the sack to approach her.

This station. The worst of it. So ride until to the next station, idiot! 'You're the next station' she would flippant at Elliot were Elliot the speaker but to herself she just whisper-jabs 'Don't called me an idiot - have some vocabulary, you trollop.' But what's this now? What could this mean? Her pass has insufficient funds to let her out? Consulting the wall map and the *Information Board* is useless but she will not let this pass unaggressed, will not just hang head and pony up the thirty cents the read-out on the turnstiles demands. 'Excuse me' she bullies the attendant in the booth, who discourteously finishes chewing the bite of that whatever-it-is - *mustard sandwich* is the only phrase Lucy can conjure, repellently thought, because look: the man has a nose like a kidney stone and likely figures his overweight is an allowance written him to play-life-on-his-own-terms - before also taking a sip of his transparent soft drink through a straw that looks as if it has been reused for more than a week, this as lead up to saying

'Can I do you for?' That's his voice!? Lucy likes him even less for sounding so down-homey! What a disconcertingly poor pairing of physicality and aurality - if Lucy wasn't so bitter-pill she might pity him now instead of detesting. 'Why doesn't this card let me out?' She brandishes it like a beaver pelt. 'It's the same card I get for the same amount for the same trip every day.' 'It's past the thirtieth' she gets as response, the man rubbing his eyes with hands unwiped from the sandwich. 'Yes. It's the second, you mean?' He points up. Lucy ups her eyes. Then he indicates with a shoo-shoo motion how Lucy should back up then with a pause motion how she should stop then points up again and when he then sneezes Lucy notes his eyes have the consistency of dishwasher detergent.

This endless escalator. It gave her vertigo - almost - the first time she rode it - she avoided this station completely for two weeks because of it - and now it is her favorite part of the days. Clunk-clunk-clunk, clunk-clunk-clunk she just walks the whole up of it, all the more glorious in this ridiculous Elliot coat - this *Salvation Army* monstrosity, burlap and soft-lined, heavier than a corpse being hurried out to the trunk of a waiting car. She - never slacking pace - ascends past other riders who are finishing crosswords and magazine articles or sending text-messages or - the young couple she passes, just now - seeing if they can both fit hands into the same set of gloves. Losers. Think they invented the couch-quickie, proud of each orgasm like they should be keeping a list for a retrospective! Bitter bitter, Lucy gets to the fresh air, decides to stop those two for a cigarette but chickens out when they don't kiss at parting. Why did that spare them? Lucy watches the girl go. She watches the boy light a smoke and start to place a phonecall. Anyway: Lucy isn't bitter. Her description of them was factual. They will come to laugh at their coital habits in twenty-year's time after first having come to long for them in ten and forlorn for them in fifteen. This isn't bitter, Lucy? The young man is laughing into his phone - breath out with cigarette out and eyeing that homeless for reasons she hopes are artistic or something.

Once she gets a day-and-a-half in without eating - double this sensation if these two days were spent partially at work - the thought of stopping for food feels a weakness. Why waste the luck of having beaten the game!? She could not help but lose weight if she just held out now: nearly forty-eight hours will have burned through anything she had eaten whenever she last ate - it was two sandwiches and then a sleeve of cookies, not yesterday morning but middle-of-the-night before morning, also one-spoonful-the-size-of-two-spoonfuls of cookie dough - so if she gets through this evening, can sleep without having another bite, and can exercise tomorrow she'll be ahead of the damn game, for the first time below where she wants to be below in ages! Weight conscious? At your age? I thought you'd just last week told Elliot your goal was to look like a pushing-fifty fella who did his own television spots for his discount furniture warehouse? I thought you thought 'What does it matter?' and 'What do I care?' and 'Hey, fuck the people!' as the dirty punk rock 'n roll Elliot first got high with you proclaimed with zest enough to become your motto. Well, in fairness that was before this opportunity presented itself. Think of looking down at that scale and - bing-bang! - it's a pound-and-a-half lighter than you were last time! Wowza - you'd be lighter than damned thunder clouds, Lucy Jinx, all would gather 'round to grope ya and gander ya, you'd be quoted and then misquoted for ages for this! And think: if you look at that scale and you're not lighter? Oh you'll feel awful remembering this moment, this chance you have to carpe the diem by denying yourself sustenance - the master of your slavish toad belly, a horse taught the true value of straw!

Ritualized bookstore visit. Ritualized look at herself in the toilet mirror. Ritualized look vaguely through the *Biography* section for something to magically be interested in. Like an immune system, trust yourself, Lucy. One of these biographies is what will do it for you. Has Lucy Jinx ever once read a biography? Negative. But rattling around in her always has been the title *The Lives of the Great Composers*. A ghost in six words her mother left to her. Was it one book? A series? Go ask a damned shop-clerk! But Lucy does not want to read about composers, really, for fear of regretting the languishing parts of her soul - the parts untended to so much so the weeds have all wilted and no one even drops cigarettes there or spits while they pass. *The Lives of the Great Composers*. She can name Chopin, Bach, Liszt, Rachmaninoff, Schubert, Schumann, and feels like she could manage to name some others if she really knuckled down. 'Hayden' she says, just as someone comes around the aisle and smiles. 'Hayden?' they say. Quick once-over: college-girl, tells anecdotes about attending soccer games in Ireland, too proud of the fact that she's been drunk before to have been drunk more than two dozen times in her twenty twenty-one twenty-two-at-a-long-shot years. 'I'm sorry?' 'It's so funny - I just had to read a book about Hayden.' This is obviously not true. 'Yeah?' 'Are you a musician?' 'No. I work at *Stella Tom's Pizza*.' The college-girl laughs and says her husband once worked there. 'On Loam Street?' 'No' Lucy says. The college-girl is not wearing a ring but might wear it as a necklace or just have a husband who thought it cool to let her think not wearing rings was where it's at and nothing to do with he had an unmarried piece on the side who laughed and laughed with him at her ringless, college-girl paw.

Coffee down the street. Have to ration cigarettes until payday. The hardest thing Lucy Jinx has ever done? Broken the two-at-a-go cigarette habit. Giving the things up, wholly, would be easier - smoking one-at-a-time was like coming to unbelieve evolution. Payday is when? she ponders, hurrying like all the others through the now loitering drizzle. Could it be just upon her? It's impossible to enjoy coffee in the rain so she chucks it at the bin by the nearest crosswalk. Could she be just about to get paid? She ducks into this alcove - in front of a maternity clothing joint - to get respite from the wet to her face, it pummeling her ability to think. Why had she thrown away that coffee!? How much of it had she even had to drink!? What a ridiculous fruit you are, Lucy! You hadn't even had but those two drizzle-laced sips, taken at harried-down-street-with-pedestrians pace! Your mind is all over because it's not supposed to be raining right now. Rationing cigarettes? Is this the order of your life, now? Will you stand for it? Look at those mothers-to-be in that shop, Lucy. They're the ones who can't smoke! You are just playacting that because you're a pauper you're supposed to have a plan all day long - when everyone knows that paupers are supposed to go hungry rather than hang-about cigaretteless. 'I can't even be destitute in the proper fashion' Lucy says and wonders if a belly like the one that thin woman has grown makes that thin woman feel taller or shorter, if it makes her feel more of a unit or a thing split into three - 'Top, baby, bottom' Lucy says, faking a cigarette and faking a smoke down her nose.

The mats into the hotel lobby are being rolled up so that the attendant can get at the grime-brown, grime-black spew underneath with the mop. Other than that the place looks pristine and Lucy, in her coat, feels quite anomalous. She is like the personification of that lousy murk from under the tongue of those mats. Yes, she knows it. But what of it? 'Ms. Adroit? How are you!?' Lucy turns, gives a little 'Eep' kind of excited sound to go with the Oh-my-gosh face she makes, as though bumping into this front desk clerk, Melinda, was a happenstance unprecedented. 'I'm just getting off, I thought that was you!' 'It is me' Lucy says and immediately seizes the opportunity to go 'Melinda, between you and I, I will murder a prostitute if someone does not give me a cigarette. I believe I have witnessed you with such a thing before, yes?' 'You want to kill my prostitute!?' Melinda phony aghasts, emphasis over-placed on *My* and Lucy is surprised at the precision and quick of this wit. 'I'm not beyond that, Melinda, but I'd hate to rob you of the solace you find there - and I am too perturbed to continue this banter so can I just have a motherfucking smoke? I'm a derelict with no prospects my own, so please help me!' Melinda just thinks Lucy Jinx is hoot and touches Lucy's coat-burdened shoulder saying 'I'm taking a quick one myself, come on.' Lucy feels obligated to return the second shoulder touch - this one a nudge - with a fake jab to Melinda's arm by her elbow. Then they exit the lobby in silence except for Melinda coughing aloofly 'Hello' to another guest who gives her an I-have-a-question smile while raising a finger.

It's always something like this for Lucy, these days. She doesn't keep track. Hasn't kept track for ages. This conversation? It's automatic patter. This

Melinda? She's some person. She works in the hotel. Everything gravitates to a Lucy Jinx so Lucy Jinx just lets it all flock and behaves like a character in the first act of a play, all day, every day. Perpetual tourist, perpetual instant-best-friend. Someone says something? She laughs. Unless she's supposed not to laugh, in which case she does whatever it seems is to be done. Cuts in on people with requests for cigarettes. Inserts non-sequiturs with the air of assuming her drift has been caught. Invite her someplace? She agrees to come and then doesn't. See her again later and ask what gives? She says something about 'an ex' or something about 'her sister's kid' or something about 'I honestly forgot, shit I'm an asshole.' That bit? The 'forgot' bit? Oh Lucy never forgets. She knows everyone before they know her. She recalls each incidental glance as though her bloodflow red-whited and bones calciumed with them. Try to find a forgotten thing in her head! Try to find some unremembered, tiniest interaction! She remembers so many Mclindas and college girls-who-lie-about-Hayden-for-some-reason and men-trying-to-get-up-the-guts-on-trains she has scales over her eyes and lungs like a belligerent muffler. And how does this make you feel, Lucy? How is it, having this chit-chat in front of the hotel with this woman who thinks you're called Ms. Adroit - Ms. Stella Adroit - this woman who wants to call you Stella and will likely try that on by the time this cigarette is done? 'How does it make me feel?' Lucy non-sequiturs aloud into the last exhalation of cig, and Melinda, who had been mid-sentence about something else stops everything and side-glances, ear-cocks. 'It makes me feel like you should call me Stella, Melinda. It's not my name, I'll let you in on that. But we're close enough you should at least think of me more familiarly than Ms. Adroit. How about it?'

Elevator or stairs? Stairs, always. Lucy takes her time up, lightheaded by the time she is on floor seven. The corridor is propped open and the garish tangle of whatever this pattern is on the carpet seems particularly musty. She slows down as she approaches the housekeeping cart by an open room, vacuum going, light outside the room seeming less shining for the din. As to the cart, Lucy moves this draped towel, here, just so. And yes, indeed! Assorted little wine bottles! So they hadn't been a fluke that one time - the housekeepers are responsible for supplying the complimentary two-in-each-room. They keep the things hidden from prying eyes while they cart up and down. Which means the bottles are likely counted before the housekeepers head out on their duties. Lucy passes the door slowly: no person visible, the vacuum sound over there. She pockets five bottles, down into Elliot's coat pockets they go, replaces towel and now hurry hurry - Lucy hurry! - hurries down hall, room key obtained yesterday out and into the slot and door opened and closed and back to closed door and laughing. Now, just hope you weren't on camera. Which you bloody well could have been, Stella Adroit! Naw - not in a middling joint like this - but Lucy will certainly check later. One bottle out, unscrew-topped, little pipsqueak bottle neck raised, toast of 'I've earned this!' and the same survey she always gives of whichever little room - her bag on the bed already, left overnight. 'Ritual' she says 'ritual. Life is so difficult' she sighs, empty wine bottle back to pocket of full others.

THE HOTEL ROOM IS THIS: now on the bed are the drug-store-blue notebook Lucy will write in and on it the graphite-grey pen she will use to write - this was gifted her by a previous subject, a woman called Nadine, Lucy had been covetous and had her greed casually rewarded with 'You like it? Please, it'd be my pleasure for you to have' - and now laid out next to these are the clothes she will soon change into and now stowed in the bottom drawer of the bureau are the clothes she had just been wearing, all day - from outer to underwear, hat down to socks - and now in the shut entrance closet, up with the extra pillow and the stubby ironing board on the high shelf, are Elliot's coat, folded as neatly as can be managed, and also the duffle bag which contained the change-of-clothes, journal, pen, and which still contains some various other this-and-thats. And now on the bathroom counter are two more empty miniature wine bottles - this is three more than you meant to drink by now, Lucy - and beside those a pack of cigarettes and the Zippo on which is engraved *fucking loiterer* and beside those is not Lucy's normal phone but the phone she uses on days like today. That phone has now vibrated once and Lucy Jinx, full-nude, pauses with unlit cigarette to over-moistened lips, double checking the time on the display. Is - she momentarily blanks on the name though she had been just rehearsing a greeting - Heather early? There should be an hour still. *Stella - I am soooo sorry. Something has come up and I cannot make it for six. Shall we reschedule? Or is later tonight - say nine? - something that works for you? This was completely unexpected and I apologize breathlessly and to no end!* Lucy gruffs though doesn't really care. Don't you, Lucy? It isn't a drag? 'It is a drag' she mumbles while she types *Nine is perfect. Or whenever. As long as it works for you. I'm just here.*

By the anonymous water of a hotel is the cleanest she ever feels. This is a nonsensical speck of superstition but she believes that the heat and pressure of such water is fundamentally different than that found in apartments or houses. Just as she believes the cakes of handsoap, though they dry her severely - almost seem to paper her and give her tears, something like pages unsuccessfully pulled from notebooks along perforations, repeated diagonal nicks made all along - do a better job getting her clean than the gluey and moistening body-wash on the shower bar, at home. Savage soap, barbarian soap - Lucy is cleaned the way sun bleaches things felled on battle fields, animal, human, or cloth! This hotel - the one she is coming to prefer though has only used on three previous occasions due to the slight uptick in price from the others she's patroned - also has a complementary vial of perfume next to the five-set of Q-tips. Vial. Right on the label is says: *Vial. Parfum Mint Berry. One vial. Not for resale*. At home, Lucy has the three vials from previous rooms, though she keeps these in a small purse in the drawer at her bedside as though they are artifacts from some time long ago passed and by now only blandly sentimental. *Mint Berry*. Here she sniffs Mint Berry. It smells exactly like a vial of those two words, sparing no energy to be scented anything else. The coffee, which she prepares in the four-cup maker plugged in next to the sink and next to the toilet, is the only off thing about the room, though in this perhaps is the key to the romance. It has an undercurrent odor of cat urine to it, perhaps an undertatse to go with that - she tends to think so but has no experience to judge by. If, however, a vial the size of the *Parfum Mint Berry* were filled with feline piss and tilted - bloop! - into a cup of regular coffee-shop swill she would take odds that - yep - it'd taste like this *Colombian Terrifico Blend*.

Oh and now a wretched suspense! Lucy doesn't even have to bother dressing yet because of this latest response. This Heather has, here, said she promises to text back no later than seven-thirty if something gets *cocked up* - Lucy approved of this phrase which is perhaps why she replied in such fine spirit - and even still has not settled on definitive nine o'clock, ten o'clock, later-than-that. And you have agreed to this and said it was *just dandy either way*, Lucy, so no space to complain, is there? You have a voice! This is your show, girl! You want to reschedule, reschedule, then - you want to tell this Heather to take a walk, nevermind even making new arrangements, then do it! You can do it, even now, if you feel like, as simple as a few little taps to a keypad! Oh there will always be a reason not to, won't there? 'But I've paid for the room' Lucy whines aloud, kindergarten tone of mocking herself. 'But I made the arrangements and shifted my oh-so-unwieldy schedule!' What a puttering old-crone you are, Lucy, and what stings of noia you're spiking that this message string is all some wholesale rejection of you. Listen to you seethe: This Heather should just cancel if she'd lost nerve or interest! 'No reason you ought to have' Lucy explains toward the heavy drawn, stain-proof-slick room blinds, but saying this only makes her more certain of this being a blow-off. No one has yet not shown up, Lucy. 'All the more reason isn't it, Heather - you wanna be the first flake little time waster?' Lucy is spit-hissing, snake sizzling to death in a buttered pan. Up tilts the next glig-glig-glig sounding mini-wine. Blown goes the brown-grey of this cheap cigarette smoke to the shirt she might not bother to iron, after all.

Sharon asks her why she is drunk, Lucy demanding that Sharon either apologize for this libelous slur or explicate 'How the fuck you cans tell I've been drinking!' Well, Sharon's explanations are quite sound, Lucy cannot find false with a one of them - so she, embittered, has her revenge by pointing out how she had lied about liking that 'damned tweed coat' Sharon had 'worn that one time to be too-cool-for-school.' 'I don't have a tweed coat, Lucy. Alex has the tweed coat.' 'Then I hate Alex's tweed coat - it amounts to the same! You and Alex and your coats and your love-birding! You make me want to take the vows, my former-friend, you make me want to commit to the Holy-alone and jilt the wide world!' When Sharon points out that Lucy has well attained, already, the Holy-alone Lucy changes her tone, fluffing up her feathers and remarking her thanks for the flattery. 'And I've done it without God, mind you - that is something!' Yes, Lucy has accomplished a feat not usually seen outside of retirement homes - she is alone and might die in the company of strangers, any day. 'Is there some reason you're calling?' Sharon eventually asks, polite strain to the voice - mark it, Lucy, you're not drunk enough to side-step civility, Sharon has company to return to - and after a final barb or two Lucy hangs up, upset at herself for having placed the call without first dressing or leaving the room. Now she's still here. Nothing has changed at all! And has it only been twenty minutes? Hotel-rooms and Time, they are terrible to each other, soon-to-be-ex-spouses just not quite vicious-pitched enough to dig the final claw.

What does Lucy wear to these meetings with women the likes of this Heather? As simple a uniform as can be. Regard: this brown, once-upon-a-time-fitted suit-coat which has become somewhat large for her, now hangs something-she-begged-off-her-brother-like, wrinkled at the seat but the sort of garment she does not brave putting hot-iron to for fear of damage she should know better than to cause being caused. Regard: this green shirt with a faint pattern of small black and grey dots - her daguerreotype-green-blouse she calls it in her thoughts of it though never has tried that phrase out on anyone, vaguely concerned they would poke some hole in it or worse - and more likely, Lucy, more likely - would whisper some jokes about 'She likes her wrong words fancy, eh?' behind her back, become fast friends over an agreement to spare Lucy her undeserved dignity. Regard: these brown, slightly checkered pants which are not a unit with the suit-coat and the brown of which doesn't quite sync up, either, but which also have become slightly-too-large, enough that at least there is that kind of consistency to the set. Regard: this blood-purple tie - the clerk had called it that and Lucy had taken that clerk out to dinner, twice - thin and worn so that the kiss of its tip just brushes the bronze of her thrift shop belt buckle which has since been engraved *fag*. A bracelet she found with, also engraved, the home address and required medications of some person called *Neville Barton Longfellow* on it, chipped in places and peculiarly weather worn for something she assumes is stainless steel. Her cloth shoes, terribly having been through the worst of it, laces impossible to unlace, gnarled clots Lucy leaves intact, pulling the things on like reluctant bed-slippers, prying them off like debtors-at-beg.

Now we find Lucy wandering the seventh-floor corridor, the eighth-floor corridor, the seventh-floor corridor, again, the sixth-floor corridor, all the while rather self-consciously smoking. So much of her life is these boring betweens, now. Good Lord, just the commute from work to apartment is almost a highlight of any given day - Oh by Saint Catherine! the sublime summits of nothing Lucy achieves even when making an effort at event! Aren't these moments Lucy is frittering on begrudgingly-chain smoking down some stale-aired hotel halls and stairs-ups and stairs-downs the kind of moments normal people would fill with bric-a-brac pleasantries, indulgences, decompressions - isn't this the time people would fill to bursting without effort only to have an appointment suddenly, intrusively upon them? Though this really isn't your fault, Lucy, that you have nothing but these empty corridors to walk merciless on yourself, right now - if that Heather had shown up you honestly would have been feeling rushed, hardly enough time to have washed and dressed, gotten your face together and your manner settled on, you'd be pacing the room in practice preamble after preamble, nerves coiling and thinking you ought to end the whole thing off by not answering the soft knock when it came. You still might not. Lucy: in a hotel corridor, thinking another guest is going to tell her to stub out her cigarette. Lucy: ready to comply and slink off. Go smoke in the lobby if you so need to be scolded, if you need to feel spanked to go sulk in your room! Now Lucy: in sudden defiance stepping out cigarette right on the floor. And then hurrying back to her room. Styrofoam cup of now lukewarm swill to her mouth, a choked swallow, a spit into sink.

Now can this Heather *do ten o'clock*? This Heather is *so so so sorry*. 'Goddamnit.' But Lucy caves immediately that *ten o'clock is fine*. Then adds in *I apologize, but the room might be already quite smoky by then*. This Heather - almost too quickly, like the words had been pre-prepared, so much so Lucy squints at them and tries to fit them into the brief conversation in some way other than a response to her last send - says *Smoky is the thing, honestly! Leave the window shut please?* Still baffled by this - on several levels, more with each key she taps - Lucy, smiling the way Lucy always smiles while typing, pretending the letters are jotting down as fast as the spoken words would be, types *Perfect, then. I'll give you a real jazz dive to jive in.* You sent that message, Lucy? Jazz dive to jive in? Lucy stares at the screen until - again, so quick the pop! this all seems too uncanny to be altogether spontaneous! - this Heather hits back *Ha! Perfect. God, thank you for being so patient! You have no idea!* and then wants to relax - you had not come off an idiot, Lucy, a bullet dodged! Yes, the insistent eager-beaver tone to these messages is taking a toll. What exactly is this Heather thinking? This delay - no, it's not paranoid to think so, Lucy - is starting to feel more like it had been a well calculated ruse, that some endgame is being arranged nothing to do with Lucy's own intents. Think, Lucy - had there been any odd indications in the correspondence with this Heather? Had she seemed to be playing to some other agenda, her own? No, no. No. This is just the blotchy feeling of limbo. And when had Lucy last slept? When had you last slept, Lucy? It hadn't been last night, certainly, so when had it been?

Checking her regular phone, a message is waiting from Carlo at work. Can Lucy come in the next morning? He'll pay her time-and-a-half even though it won't be overtime for the week. It's just that Gretchen is sick, again - Gretchen, Jesus Christ, Gretchen! - and there is some motherfucking Little League thing going on - 'Not kids' Carlo promises desperately to Lucy it is 'not a bunch of kids' rather is a 'thing for the parents' and that it should get her good tips on top of the time-and-half. Carlo leaves a long message, doesn't he? What a pathetic display, being honest. Lucy is tempted to let him down, let him wallow in it, but in the end she calls him up and asks 'What time?' without even identifying herself first after his 'Stella Tom's Pizza and Ribs, is this for delivery or carry-out?' And Carlo all but vomits his gratitude in a sputtering rush. Lucy has saved him! Lucy is a godsend! 'Since when are we Pizza and Ribs?' Had Carlo said that!? He finds this hilarious and has no explanation! 'Well, good job it was me then, or you could have caused a tremendous chain-reaction. Ribs? Can you imagine having to tell the dregs we serve there aren't ribs when they've heard through some grapevine there are?' Carlo laughs and Lucy knows he is ignoring a patron to do so. 'Do you just want me there to open? Or can you not spare that much overtime?' Lucy is to do whatever she sees fit - if she wants to be there at open, if that works better, he will not clear his nose at her. 'I'll see you tomorrow, then' she sighs and even as she does he hangs up. 'Hello?' Nothing. Lucy blinks, a little perplexed. He just hangs up? What does it matter to you, Lucy? Why are you just staring at your phone? 'It matters, I think' she says, retuning the phone to the duffle bag after checking the ringer is still off. 'Shouldn't it matter, anyway, even if it doesn't?'

Now that she has opened the blinds, she wishes she had stood at the window nude for awhile, earlier. She can see right into those offices, there, especially now that night has fallen, everything extra-dark for the swinish weather still snouting around out there. A meeting room: one man excitedly scribbling something on a dry-erase board while one colleague sits bloodshot-eye postured and another is cavalierly checking his phone. An empty office. An empty office. And in there, a woman sitting on the point of her desk lip, speaking on her landline, working her fisted knuckles into the skin of her lower back, dress shirt untucked and tie unloosed wide but still knotted. Lucy raises a hand. Lucy taps the window glass. Lucy wets her lips and kisses the glass, then, surprised at how temperatureless it is. Come to think of it - she considers this while remarking how unseemly the spittle streak her lip pucker left appears, how malformed the shape of it - aren't these windows irregularly thick that she cannot hear a bit of the clearly blustering wind out there? The flags are threadbare strangulations, the trees down on the pavement outside the hotel entrance tantrums of bare branches looking to pierce their laments into flesh. Lucy takes up her notebook, turning it to the page already titled *Heather* and dated today's date. She writes *and how your threadbare strangulations and your laments looking for fleshes to pierce.* Stops. Is it okay to allow this? Can it have to do with what Heather elicits even though Heather is not in the room? 'Heather should have been in the room and gone, by now. And it's not as though Heather-in-the-room is to do with it, really' she points out 'remember not to start believing the company line, yeah?'

She has typed out a rather long message to Elliott before realizing which phone she is holding. Laid on the mattress but tense. Wine-tired thicking the back roots of her eyes. Television on but nothing of interest found on the one round through the thirty-four offered channels so she chose to settle on this show she despises and now reads the insipid dialogue miswritten by the Closed Captions. 'Just send the message, Lucy. So what, right?' she tries to coax herself. 'Tell Elliott you borrowed a friend's phone because yours was out of battery.' She taps the message erased, yawning, eyes watering, knows her clothing has become unfit from her laying. 'Time to get into character, Stella' Lucy says, willing herself to stand, then not standing, closing her eyes. Why had this Heather been so insistent on sending photos, as well? Lucy had had to tell her not to - what had it been, don't exaggerate, now - four times? Five. 'Three, Lucy' Lucy says 'and you just got done saying Don't exaggerate.' Why these misgivings? If you're so pussy all of a sudden, don't answer the door. Leave. Go to sleep. 'Your options are endless' she expansives, making the word last ten seconds, wide arc of arms up while she still lays and with fingers wiggling like tittering stardust, tone for putting toddlers to sleep, the wine sweating grease into the wrinkled crags under her eyes along with the wet from these yawns she can't stop.

FACE WIND-PINKED, SHIVERING - ONLY A light coat and mittens quite sopping, as though they had been ruined at the start of the day, had only got worse - Heather apologies 'Hello hello' and how she is sorry and 'Hello' again, holding out sodden handshake with another, sniffling 'I'm really so sorry.' 'There's nothing to be sorry for - thank you for coming, at all!' What a nice burst of giddy-up! Our regular Lucy, as she always is in the moments of first reveal! 'No, I know it's late. I just had no idea when I could reschedule and really wanted to do this.' Lucy - no, she doesn't take these women's coats - does up the room latch-bolt and that secondary-lock devise she's no idea the name for - having quickly verified the *Do Not Disturb* tag still nooses the outside doorknob - says 'The thing with poetry? It's whenever the Muse strikes. You, being the Muse, make the weather, you know?' Heather, giving the squat room a nodding appraisal while she removes her mittens and stuffs them in coat pocket, laughs and says 'Oh I'm not the Muse.' 'That's just what you are. And I am grateful for you.' Making a gesture that Heather should sit, stand, whatever, Lucy indicates the small room fridge where she has bottled water and the two non-stolen freebies of wine that come proper with the room, saying Heather should help herself if she's thirsty. 'Or if you're cold - you're obviously cold, right?' - Lucy makes a *Duh* face, boinking comic her head-side with butt of her palm - 'there's coffee that's probably overdone now and tastes like cat piss, only a little. You want it? Have at!'

Heather asks if she should undress, now. Lucy shrugs 'As long as you're ready, but, well, yes - as long as you're ready.' Heather is a perfectly ordinary, modest enough sort and Lucy, therefore, much prefers her to many of the others, who have been models - professional or amateur or 'semi' of either variety - and so see this all as nothing but run-of-the-mill, some even likely mark it a yawn and an if-not-for-the-money-complete-waste-of-time. As Heather begins to disrobe, Lucy lights a cigarette, hardly paying her mind. 'When you say I should just do whatever I want?' Heather asks, clammy-cold skin with deep marks, there, from just unsnapped bra - bra placed beside turquoise with burnt-orange stripped turtleneck sweater at the foot of the bed. 'Unless I ask you, particularly, to do something - but I don't usually - yes, just be. Pretend I'm not here, if you want. Unless I tell you not to, you can talk to me. I might not respond, sometimes' she chuckles, trying to seem warm 'but you can still talk. Whatever. You're perfect - just be.' Heather has unskinned herself from the dark jeans, inside-outed them and folded them still in that state, now lifts herself from sat-on-the-bedlip long enough to get butterscotch colored - with bright-pink trim and small bows at each hip - panties under and off of her, chuckling 'I'll try not to yammer at you - but I wanted to be sure it'd okay if I stood in the shower?' Lucy is transfixed a moment - her angle of Heather is from behind and beside, three-quarter angle at her leaned forward to get off the sock of her right foot - by the splotchy skin so slackenly tired, end-of-day moan to it, three thin but still radiant scratches over the outside heft of that thigh. 'Of course. You just can't close the door. I get to watch anything you do - I make only the exception of your using the toilet.'

Lucy Jinx looks at the few lines she'd written on Heather's page before

Heather had arrived, regretting them. But it seems they have to be allowed, now - and being allowed, they seem to direct, dictate, influence. Look: Lucy has even struck them through, but not scribbled them over. Why not tear out the page? After a few more women - Hell, even after the multiple pages you might well fill tonight, Lucy - you won't even be able to tell something has been removed, will you? And certainly no idea what! Heather laughs about how it's kind of fun to shower without the curtain drawn, oh-my-godding at the flood of the bathroom floor, saying 'My mother would be fucking strangling me right now!!' She says this while lathering in a kind of specific method: above, and into just incidentally, her untrimmed pubic-hair, then all over her inner thighs - legs lifted, wide, one-at-a-time, up so that Lucy imagines at home she would rest feet on the bathtub lip - then a quick shake-shake-shake of sudsy hand over vagina, immediately sloshing washcloth over everything, erratic, then, now, holding washcloth like a bag collecting falling rubies, splashing this onto her privates and scrubbing with even more force, the washcloth then discarded abruptly aside, back turned to shower-head, skull-base as close to it as she could manage. Lucy has thought of several responses to Heather's comment about being strangled. Strangled. Smiles. Recopies *how your threadbare strangulations* and as Heather sings a few bars of a song Lucy is unfamiliar with then continues with *conjure mother's old watery bones, gardens left unplentied, bellies left overstarved, books unread at bedtime you listless imagined.*

Here: Heather smoking cigarette, peeking out window-blinds. Also here: Lucy wishing 'Please open them - and I'll say Stay and I'll move in to stand with my chin at your shoulder.' Written: *constant are the glances lost, constant are the mourning moans.* Here: Heather saying 'I should have brought a coloring book' and then quickly 'I didn't mean I'm bored, I was just thinking!' Heather laid on bed, ankle crossed over ankle, cracking toes in tense grabs-at-nothing, blushing now that Lucy hasn't responded, smiling as Lucy holds her look, impassive, and is writing something Lucy's not paying attention to. Also here: Lucy holding her look, impassive, blank, basking in the uncomfortable-but-almost-not fidgeting of Heather, knowing the worry - that the apology for her remark had not been needed, the worry that it had been - and the weird pressure behind her eyes, the feeling of unsettled in her tummy, just then. Written: *nothing. Really nothing. I'm just moving a pen to look at her, ankles linked logs, her legs unshaved, knees ash grooved, odd darkness of white here and there.* Here: Heather regarding herself in the chintzy room mirror. Also here: Lucy, on purpose, moving to be reflected as well, resisting - resist it, Lucy - the desire to look up, to catch Heather's reflection trying to make eye-contact with her by Heather's eyes gazing at Lucy's reflected head looking down at Lucy's reflected notebook. Side note: Lucy is not usually bashful, but in this moment cannot let her eyes linger on the rear figure of

Heather, cannot tell Heather 'Stand still' while she painstakes her eyes over every divot, small bump of red prickle, counts the darker moles, moves in like she will almost touch the scriggles of stretch marks curving-over-hip. Heather would say 'You can touch me' and Lucy would say, as though only half to Heather 'Oh no no no no, I just wanted to see my shadow on them.'

As has become her habit - Lucy pretends the women's responses indicate something to her, that she can read something in the words they choose - she tells Heather 'It's eleven-fifteen, now, so only an hour left. Or we can just go to midnight, even - I won't hold you to it over pennies.' Heather had been leaning on the bathroom sink counter, sniffing a bit of the coffee she had poured - repulsion-face of uncertainty at taking the measliest tap of taste of the stuff - when Lucy said this, now looks up, shaking her head tightly but imperative. 'Please. There isn't any rush. I put you out, for hours. I honestly don't even want you to pay me. You have no idea.' There's that again, eh Lucy? You don't have to check your phone but Heather had said that in the one message, too. *You have no idea.* Maybe impolite, considering it is obvious Heather was trying to intimate something there, Lucy decides to ponder this turn of phrase, disguising her lack-of-response as serious-concentration, writing the phrase *an ellipsis of you short legged with cola and no more coins.* Why did this woman come here so late? This woman, ordinary as a grocery bag. She writes that *ordinary as a grocery bag.* This woman, beautiful as a glove lent by your sister. She writes that *beautiful as a glove lent by your sister.* Does she not want to leave? Now, Lucy holds blank eyes over Heather's breast on the front of her unstraightened back. *Slouch shouldered Heather* she writes *uncurious as a cat.* Why is this woman here? So late. Looking back at Lucy's stern glare, now. Looking back. Lucy - have you seen this woman before? Eyes avert - no, not at all and don't start with thinking some rubbish! 'Well, I might keep you awhile, then. But I'm definitely paying - and don't be such a doormat, alright?'

'How long have you been writing poetry?' asks Heather. Heather is sitting now on the bed, knees together in front of her, leaned back, elbows tight to her reposing sides. 'For only five years or so' Lucy lies from the bathroom sink, rinsing her face and then roughly drying it with the mildew smelling hand towel. She has noticed this about the rooms at this hotel - not the other hotels - that the towels get funky as soon as they are wetted, one that starts fresh-scented, applied just after a shower, will have a sour tinge to it by the time she has completely patted herself almost-dry. Lucy hears Heather removing a cigarette from - she thinks - her own pack, which she had discarded on the bed. And can tell by the labored quality of the words that Heather did not sit up when striking the match - certainly from Lucy's own booklet - and taking a first drag before saying 'Did you go to school for it - or do you, now?' 'No' Lucy tells-the-truth-kind-ofs, now in the room proper, arms crossed - notebook in on the sink counter still, though Lucy has the pen in her hand and twirls it slowly, automatic - one leg crossed, shoe toe of it scratching at the ankle of still-straight leg but not alleviating the itch. 'Sometimes I think that poetry is the only thing that matters' says Heather, very in-referentially, someplace else 'It's funny though, because I used to think that about sculpture and now I can't for the life of me remember why!' They both laugh, Lucy deciding to tell her 'Please don't move your head' and Heather freezing, tensing teeth into a Grrr and going 'Shit, right here? Like this?' Lucy gives little dips and daubs with fingers in the empty air, directing Heather before finally moving in - only leaning, not going to knees - and, holding eyes, says 'Sorry, may I?' hands both held in slow-motion approach. Heather breathes 'Sure' down her nose the same moment Lucy touched her fingertips, as gently as she could manage, to Heather's hairline, one Lucy thumb-tip, on purpose, touching the outside of the low end of one Heather ear.

Various things Lucy has written. This: *I arrived here only yesterday, ill belonged morning greeting me with cold lips smacking.* And: *you would taste like watermelon, you would taste liked roots to water.* And: *photography matte, dust you, dust you, you let the bed sheets deceive you, you let the pillows explain.* Lucy does not know what do with any of this. But she judges it. In fact, it should be understood that Lucy has the atrocious habit of telling herself 'This is just about free-thought, scribble anything, this isn't composition, this is stimuli and response, this is drag-net to ducks of unconscious somethings, there is no need to judge this, it is all to use later, the moment is irrelevant until after and altered' while at the same time snarling and scoffing whatever she writes. Oh yes, Lucy tells herself wonderful, artiste, poetess things - but, fuck, how she labors over her impromptu. And how she judgementals! Immediately! Hounds the most meagre crumb of scribble thought! She lacerates it, internally, belittles it, as though ashamed of the unformedness of herself without form. The pressure, when writing, is beyond suffocating - she is in a coffin, ready to suffocate, growing frustrated at how she is still able to breathe! Just let it happen, just die! Just seize up! Make it impossible to judge - a death rattle has no elegance, it is taken for truth, isn't it!? That is what she wants - the unselfconsciousness of finality, even a faked no-choice. But every chirp she manages to get to page without first filtering she ridicules, hurls epithets at, knows these are the line she will immediately efface and compose something entirely other in their place, later. The women is the room make her self-loathing worse, her anxiety - this song-and-dance, painter-and-model, is supposed to make the words come out more desperately, but tends just to make her attempts to bludgeoned them, pistol them down the more desperate, instead.

Does Lucy ever let the subject read the poems? This woman, Heather, is asking. 'Do you ever let your subjects read whatever the final poems are? Obviously not the notes - though I imagine those are even more beautiful.' Lucy responds 'My Subjects? Yes. I like that. Subjects.' Heather lets the redirection take, but only a moment, laughs-in-time-with-Lucy's-laugh 'What do you call us, then? Oh - your Muses, you said. I like that, too.' 'I just call you my Women' Lucy says now, flatly, then cannot resist 'though, originally, I thought of you as my Tarts.' Heather trills laughter, sits at attention in bed center, crisscross-applesauce 'Your strumpets! Right?' Lucy, not able to help it, says 'Even better. Yes. And' - to get to it before Heather asks, as she is obviously about to - 'no, I don't let them read the pieces. Everyone eventually asks.' Heather does a pouty, lip-twisted frown 'Well, call me a tart if you want but - gah - don't call me *Everyone*. I will say good night to you now, sir!' and she pantomimes, more-or-less, standing, grabbing a suitcase, and storming off, but does this all just as a series of twines where she remains seated, and by her face set this way and that way and thusly and thus. 'I don't give a knick, a knack, or a goddamned paddy-whack about ya, baby' says Lucy - look at this! - venturing to give Heather's shoulder a shove and Heather letting herself be shoved but then growling her shoulder in a retaliatory swipe, Lucy already moving to the chair in the room corner. 'You're just fodder to me.' Lucy crosses her legs. 'Now dance for me' she says, burgundy-voiced and hands folded like some lascivious millionaire - Heather, instead of obeying, in a series of hops winds up laying flat on her tummy, chin rested on hands, feet in the air and crossed up behind her.

It is past midnight and Lucy is still in the chair, Heather now rolled to her back. Heather has one knee bent and the foot of the other leg plopped on the thigh just under it - wouldn't you call it *under it* from that angle, Lucy? Lucy knows that Heather is not going to ask about the time. She'd stay in the room all night. Even if Lucy fell asleep here in the chair, Heather would stay. Get herself cozy under the comforter. Sleep. No funny business. She won't leave until you tell her to, Lucy. Which makes this oddly unique in your experiment, so far. Not so much Heather's obvious subtextual arousal - Hell, it isn't even subtextual, here. Not so much Heather's neediness for attention and wanting to milk this adventure she's found for every drop of eye-contact, even peripheral gloamings of even her own reflection, her shadow, in the same room as someone dressed while she's nude - Lucy, in truth, wonders if the nudity is even necessary for Heather. Why doesn't she want to go? She had been so dead-set on not rescheduling - had this night really been the only night she'd ever be able to find for this? This? This was worth effort? Why bother? Had she had to arrange this even before contacting Lucy, initially? Now, thinking of it, it seems perhaps so. What fantasy is Lucy fulfilling and which aspect is she falling short of? Where do you go now, Heather? Ask it! Ask her. Jesus, don't you know she wants you to, Lucy? Where do you go, after here? Ask her. And tell her you've never wondered, before. Show her how sad you find her humming now, how silly her desire for your puny, anonymous amour. Where do you go, Heather? What are you doing here? 'Would you mind staying another hour, Heather?' Heather curls around, her chin on the formless large of her right breast. And just Yeses by rolling back, doing a wobble-wobble of foot, limp rubber-chicken, at ankle. Heather, you'd stay even if I left, wouldn't you?

Lucy opens the room fridge and hands one of the wines to Heather. 'This is a privilege - I usually keep both for myself.' Heather, such clear purple of fatigue to the skin beneath eyes and lakeweed of veins uglying her off-milk eye-whites, does a play of being struck speechless, then giggles when Lucy gently tosses the miniscule cap at her forehead, the thing dropping straight, rolling over the foremost part of Heather's breast, tinking off her big-toe and, now, there on the well-rumpled covers. 'You are my exception' Lucy says, drinking her bottle at a go, while Heather sniffs hers and then gives it just a touch to her tongue. 'I am going to send you your poem.' Suspicion - Lucy knows suspicion, she knows - for a beat in the set of those used-tissue eyes of Heather's, but a quick conceal by way of 'Really, you don't have to, I was just being a brat.' Get this over with, Lucy - I think you're the one who is tired, by the way, because this is pointless and you're letting yourself in for such a slog, such a weary-old bore - take a breath and then say 'I want you to sit for me again, will you?' Press on! Before she can answer. 'I hate to even ask, because this isn't supposed to be creepy.' Don't let her cut in! 'But I just am asking, okay? Can you sit for me, again? Can I write to you, again?' Should you push it a tad further? Assure her this is unique - or should you let the earlier *Exception* remark stand? Yes - this conversation is one Heather will obviously go and obsession her nest with, padding over of every detail, so the less said out blatant the better. Why isn't she answering? Lucy, soft eyes, grins, tilts head. 'I don't know when' Heather finally manages - *manages* really the only word to name that tone. 'Okay' Lucy says. Touches Heather's knee. 'Okay.' Moves hand from knee. 'But you'll let me know what you think of the poem? I'll send it next week, okay?' Suspicion and something in Heather's eyes. Lucy holds the gaze. 'Really?' Heather barely gets out - does she know there was two minutes of silence, before? Smile, Lucy. Get this woman out of this room. 'Really.'


THE VERY LAST SUBWAY. UNDER coat and duffle bag, corner seat, nearly asleep. 'You should've stayed in the room' she allows herself to grumble one final time, sniffs off another dismissal. 'Terrible idea' she says, deciding it better to stand so she doesn't miss her stop. The last thing Lucy needs is to wake way out somewhere on a train car that won't be making a return trip. She is the only one in the compartment, which seems colder, like all the others would have been heated, this one the anomaly avoided by those in the know, and the light is particularly harsh. She has seen nearly-empty Metro-trains from outside, this late, sometimes from cab windows, sometimes from being out with a pal, flasked and cigaretted. She knows she'd look washed out, grainy in a minty green light - lonely and deadbeat, she'd be one of those people she's seen and thought pity for. Lucy: the overworked single mom. Lucy: the night student who must know she's getting nowhere. Lucy: the girl who regrets at least the past two years but not enough to move on from them. Well, that last one almost describes you, actually. Lucy sighs in acknowledgement of this. She knows what the muted rattle of this train would sound like and how fast it would be gone from her sight were she outside of it, looking. She knows how long she would keep watching the rear window of the full train proceed before losing interest, finding something equally snide to remark about a sign in a window, a pile of murky slush, the grin of a clothesline set out the window of a fifth-floor apartment. 'We're a bunch of bump in the night' she whispers, getting a cigarette ready. 'We'd make ourselves cry if we weren't ourselves, wouldn't we?'

There is a young guy playing a guitar by the enclosures where buses will no longer be arriving. The lot is deserted. In the four-level parking garage the yellow-orange klaxon of the security cart whimpers, casting hiccoughing shadows. Lucy gets two dollar-bills ready and to be polite stands listening for the remainder of the song before dropping them in the empty guitar case. The guy nods his head but says 'I'm not playing for money, just waiting for my ride. Take it.' She doesn't answer other than a purposefully cryptic movement of her shoulder - could be she was just moving her duffle-bag strap to be more comfortable, the guy will spend the next hour thinking, or was it a kind of flirt? What did her eyes look like? Was I meant to do something other than calling after her 'Thank you' as I did? That's what he'll think. Lucy Jinx: spreader of middle-of-the-night romance - Lucy Jinx in high style. A car passes her even before she is to the end of the station sidewalk so she quickly moves around the corner into the stairwell of the garage, climbs half-a-flight and leans to the wall. Last thing she'd want is the guy to be able to glimpse her again, be telling his buddies about her and them coaxing him to hop out, approach her to say something banal she'll have to say 'No' to. New cigarette. Not sure she'll hear the car from here as it exits. 'So I guess this is where I'll be for the next fifteen minutes' she groans.

There: a fallen over shopping cart, soaking wet linens strew out from it, a pair of jeans tangled around the push bar as though someone tourniqueted a rat tail, no way could those have gotten that way by accident. Children's jeans. Children's blouses. A pair of child-size earmuffs with the price tag still affixed, though sodden and part ripped and the ink mostly made indecipherable. Lucy is careful not to pause, of course - tenses in case she is being observed - but does give glances around for signs of anything else amiss. A broken bottle, here. And there: a sandwich, ruined with frozen rain that had thawed then refrozen, on top of that sour-pulped, unfolded newspaper sheet. She doesn't so much as hesitate at the crosswalk indicating *Stop*, though this is hard for her - she feels herself being commented on from one of these bleak windows, keeps her eyes down so as not to notice the marijuana smoke from exactly which one, knows doing so would earn her a catcall or at least mark her as a face-to-remember. As she gets up the opposite curb she notices the parked police car, cabin light on, cigarette-lipped officer upping and downing her like an eel. He's going to stop you, Lucy. No, he isn't. Yes, he is! Keep walking straight - make a loop of the block, don't let him see which way you would actually walk. She can't help but look back over her shoulder - the officer still watching her. Shit. For the whole block long she is certain she hears the cruiser skirting, lightless, behind her. Only relaxes when she's turned and gotten the length of the whole block, that way.

No one is at the counter of *Deneven's Doughtnuts* when she enters, the sound of the *Ms. Pac-Man* machine abrasive, the quack sound of the Game-Over screen mixing with faint radio playing music in, she thinks, Russian. Takes a stool, back leaned to the countertop. Sees her apartment building, there. Looks up to the colorless curtain of the bedroom she knows would be green were the light on or Elliott still up with the television going. 'How long have you been here?' She limply rolls her eyes at Clarke, telling him he's got a shit business savvy and she intends to leave without purchase for being so neglected. 'Never neglected, Lucy. In fact - I want to ask you something.' 'Do you want to get me coffee and a plain cake, first? Or do I not count as a fucking client, anymore?' Clarke gives her the finger, tells her the only plain cakes, at the moment, are the stales from last shift. 'You aren't written up in the trades often, are you?' In fact, Clarke has assumed a lackadaisical posture, slumped-to-elbow on counter, leaned in her direction. 'And I notice' Lucy continues despite his lack of seeming antagonized 'you are the only - the solitary - coffee-shop in this city without at least one *Vincy Gazette Best Of Award*. Is that even allowed?' '*The Gazette* is a rag. And I don't need accolades or word of mouth. You want a free stale one, or you wanna wait?' 'I wanna wait' Lucy says in mock of Clarke's dim-wit slur. Clarke chuckles, throws a sugar packet at her, and tells her she's a bitch for not even mentioning his haircut. 'Get me some coffee, okay? Then I promise I'll make a point to tell you your hair looks like shit.' He does so - obviously the dregs of an overcooked pot, setting it on the counter but at a distance from her before returning to the backroom where he'd come from.

'Did you still want some night work?' She did. 'Is there something available, now?' There is. 'But it'd just be the Tuesday-through-Thursday, overnight.' Would she like that? 'Those are the nights you aren't even open!' 'It's not to work the shop' Clarke explains. Lucy would just have to do a bit of cleaning, maybe a bit of paperwork - since as long as she'd be there he'd have to give her something to do - while the main thing would be she'd take care of accepting some shipments that come in, sign for stuff, making sure the orders are right. 'That be okay?' 'Absolutely. Is this something you normally do, yourself?' Clarke shrugs and Lucy doesn't know why she's pressing so redirects to 'Is this temporary? Or would it be a thing? Either way I'm in, I just wondered.' Clarke assures her it'd be a thing, regular, and the check would be proper, not some under-the-table cash-in-hand gig. 'Unless you prefer it that way, but I'd rather it be official.' Lucy takes the last bite of her doughnut, chewing thick, her hand gesture meant to indicate she's right with him, she'd prefer it be official, as well. 'Then if you ever want, you could work days, too - but I seem to think you have a gig, yeah? You'd just asked about night work awhile back - this came up, figured Why in Hell not?' 'When would this all start?' 'This coming Tuesday.' She takes another dreadful swallow of the coffee, some grinds in the shape of a horsefly apparent in the now revealed cup-base. 'I'll be here Tuesday, then. I appreciate it.'

What a bit of luck! She's a bit too draggy to feel giddy, just now, especially with having to be at work in six hours, but it is a bit of terrific good fortune! And even as much per-hour as she earns at *Stella Toms*! Which doesn't make sense and she's certain there's something shady to it, but she'll take it. Here: she even lets out a laugh, still thinking about this, as she sets down her duffle to get her key from the pouch in her wallet where she keeps it. Then in through the lobby door to be met with the chlorine smell of the forever damp carpet, those patches still torn up to reveal mouthwash-blue tile under a layer of sepia grime. Checks the mailbox, though obviously Elliott already would have. 'Jesus' she says softly, noticing that once again Elliot has written *Not at this address - RTS* on four five six of these envelopes made out to this mysterious *Sylvester Town*. As usual, Lucy chucks them in the - right now overflowing - garbage bin outside of the shuttered Lobby Office, gingerly moving some other rubbish on top of them in the off chance Elliott happens to check the box and wonder why it is always empty before the postman even arrives. 'Sylvester Town' Lucy says, drama-voiced, then repeats it, over-zealous mock rock 'n roller. She adores the Lobby Office sign - the elegant calligraphy of the script, the tin rust stained like mold has got hold of it, three shades of brown, two of black, an odd squiggle of purple bisecting the *L O B* of its *Lobby*. She kisses two fingers, pats the fat *O*, and moves on past the *Laund-O-ry* placard, looking in at the cartoon-dog nightlight, half-obscured by the dryer-unit nearest the far wall.

Places her duffle bag on the floor against the corridor wall a pace down from her apartment door, giving a paranoid glare around at the other silent five doors. Then she quietly gets the door open, making certain Elliott at least isn't there at the kitchen counter or the dining table, keeps the door propped with foot while reaching to take the duffle up, hurrying on in into the pitch black to her desk in the corner, duffle stowed beneath, then back to the closet just inside the door where she, coughing on purpose, starts to remove Elliott's borrowed coat. No sounds except for refrigerator hum and that click from the toilet which has run of the joint every night. What is that click!? It haunts Lucy! Haunts her! It does not start until past ten and then has stopped by six in the morning - but between those hours looms audible in every cranny of the apartment and it, every four seconds, click-click-clicks obnoxious sets of three rickety threes. From the pipes? It doesn't seem so. From the bowl? No. But it is louder in the bathroom, certainly. As though the air just prestidigitates it, ex nihilo, dark magic of the very worst kind. Lucy listens at the outside of the bedroom door. Elliott's snore. She moves to desk, unpacks the duffel of notebook, and returns the clothing, one piece at-a-time, to the laundry basket against the heater by the room window - removes some of the folded clothing from the basket, first, then setting each of the things she had worn in the hotel underneath something different, putting the towels back on top last. And - per usual - lights a cigarette after. Heart racing. Giggling. Rapscallion, Lucy. Robber-baron and rouge!

Rather mute light - brown of used mop water - above the stove flipped on, Lucy begins boiling a pot of water and crunching the packet of thirty-cent noodles, squinting her eyes as though at Elliott remarking this behavior odd. This is how noodles are eaten! Before Elliot, she had never seen anyone just put the noodles in the water, un-broken-up, had never seen them slurped long - had never even imagined them to be noodles of full length! Wait - is this pot still dirty? 'Fuck' she hisses, noting the goddamn sauce hardened in a ring. It's only been sponge cleaned and put in the washer, the washer not started. Is there anything can be done for this, Lucy? 'No Lucy, there is not' Lucy says, though while she does so she - deciding she will begrudge every last of Elliott's sighs from this point in time until Kingdom Gone! - moves the pot to the sink and squirts in some soap and gets to work scrubbing it hard with the green-dirtied-grey-brown rough side of the three-week used sponge. There are other sponges. But Lucy has her pride. She is not the only inhabitant of planet Earth who can open a new sponge - let the record reflect that, please! She is burdened enough, just here, and would feel belittled to take on this task, as well - it'd feel like admitting some subservient state. To make up for lost time, she lets the tap water get as hot as it can before returning the pot to the coiled orange of the stove burner. Takes two of the snack-sized candies from the plastic bowl next to Elliott's gloves, then moves Elliot's gloves into the one kitchen drawer, the cord of the wall phone getting tugged and the receiver unhooking, hitting the counter with a crack and the floor with a louder one, tip-tip-tipping the wall as it dangling twists, a hollow Bong! of it striking, once, the thin-metal side of the water bowl down there, as well.

She eats at her desk in the dark, hot bowl of noodles on a towel over her now bare thigh, turned to look out of the window. What a view. The sloppy brick of the side of the Dry Cleaners. *Zilch's Dry Cleaners.* Jesus, what a beautiful sight is that unlit neon sign shown in the chalk-orange streetlight from below it. And the letters only light up during daylight hours. The place closes at three o'clock except on Saturdays when it closes at two. A masterpiece Lucy never grows tired of. *Zilch's.* The sight refreshes her - she pictures herself as a pencil sketch being filled in by pen-strokes as she eats and regards it. And now Lucy feels Lucy Jinx swatting at the back of her calve so makes kissy sounds but Lucy Jinx does not come out from under the chair. So Lucy, steadying the noodle bowl, lowers one hand down, slouching to get fingers as close to the carpet as possible, rubs thumb pad over pads of index and third finger in a swish-swish-swish-swish sound, the cat crackling its reptilian meow as it slathers its always wet mouth against her wrist side. 'Did El not leave you food, baby-boy?' Lucy whispers only vaguely in the direction of the cat, concentrating on keeping the bowl balanced in the groove of her now together thighs, attempting to get a spoonful to her mouth without spilling a drop of the broth while Lucy Jinx crackle-mews, still louder, running the length of his side, now, over her ankle fronts.

Lucy adds a folded piece of Elliott's lunch meat into the bowl where she's just emptied the pouch of Lucy Jinx's dry-food, lightly grips the base of the cat's tail and pulls her hand along its length as she stands. 'Feed the fucking cat, Elliott' she whisper-Fuck-yous in the direction of the closed bedroom door, giving an angry hump or two to the counter edge. 'Fuck' she then hisses 'the Fuck' she then gutterals, throat clearing sound without throat clear, just after. How long can you sleep now, Lucy? Is it worth it to get any? Not really, eh? Not if you want to shower. And it's a good idea to shower if you're gonna have to pull this busy shift - you'll be on the floor, not in the back, remember? She situates herself on the sofa and gets the television going with the remote, lowering the volume to nearly mute while the screen warms up to showing a commercial for a miraculous product - something that, by manipulating the girth of a lady's ass, takes *Ten Years Off Your Look* or so some brackish yellow letters appear to cock and to crow, four blinking exclamation points after them. Next channel: pledge drive. Next channel: detective interrogating hoodlum. Next channel - hmn, Lucy goes, hmn - some movie she has certainly seen but does not remember the name of. 'But I know you gonna die' she says, pointing flippantly at the woman on screen, this woman speaking into a cellphone while looking up and down crowded streets. Watches this another few minutes. It might not be that movie. 'Well, you still gonna die' she says, making the words more slangy this time. 'Yuh. Stull. Gon. Dheah.'

HERE IS SOMETHING LUCY DREAMED: there is a veritable ocean of coat-hangers, the plastic kind, spilling from a house on a neat-and-tidy street, the sort she supposes she once grew up on though in the dream it is not meant to be her street but somewhere she is with a man who cannot get a cigarette out of his pocket. 'You're going to break it!' Lucy tells the man but isn't looking at him. There are people in that house, the one the hangers burst out from - one of who she sees, quite distinctly, as though now in there with him for a moment, shaking a heavy rug like he is trying to get it produce a satisfying Crack! 'I'm not going to break it' the man says, having slowed and lost his balance. Focus shift. Still on a street. Maybe the same. Set on a long hill, severe downward sloped. A vertigo, stomachache, headlong feeling, the curve evening out into a view of a bay of some kind - a prison with flags and the sizzle of cooking meat coming from it. The view is hazy, an over-warm summer day. Her mouth feels sloppy, as though she'd eaten an ice-cream sandwich and had nothing to rinse her mouth with. Now - different place - more people around and her hand is trying to pick a coin out of a bucket with three lobsters in it. She's laughing. The glint from some old woman's glasses is bronze and piercing and in the moment it distracts her Lucy feels herself cut but looks down to see that she isn't, that one of the lobster's antennae has just brushed her - now that she sees this, the pain turns to ticklishness. She looks up and goes 'Let me borrow it, okay? Come on' and a sneezing, tissue-to-mouth - squirting a quick bit of phlegm into it - oldish man just jiggles his grape-red face and goes 'Oh no no no' like she's joking, obviously asking of him something patently absurd.

Elliott's finger is on Lucy's forehead as she slowly groggies to awake. 'You don't get into bed?' Elliott says, her breath the peach warm it always somehow is, first thing in the morning. Lucy scrunches, unscrunches, scrunches her forehead, but when Elliott does not take the kind hint she bats at the finger and tells her 'Okay, come on, man' a real lemon-tasted snarl and her lips gummy as they smack. Then bang: 'Shit - what time is it?' No - Lucy, calm down - it's still even dark, nothing to worry about. 'It's not quite seven. Why are you even here?' Elliott says, lifting Lucy's legs and then laying them over her lap as she sits. 'I live here, you know? Why are you here?' But Elliott puts her finger back on Lucy's forehead and demands 'Seriously.' Lucy wriggles to sit up, her feet still in Elliott's lap. 'It's seven?' 'It's almost seven' Elliott says, then continues 'I thought you were having a night of it with Deb?' Lucy clears her throat, chews some phlegm - Elliott saying 'Lovely, Jesus Christ, Lucy' - then swallows it and says 'Deb met some louse and so I came home. Oh! I got a new job. And I have to go to work - so let me shower first, okay?' Elliott asks 'No joint shower, either? I'm thinking I've miffed you, fella' but Lucy flicks Elliott's chin - which seems to pacify her - and says 'Business shower, work work work, I'm a little buzz-saw, don't ya know?' 'You got a new job and have to be there already?' Lucy cartoon moans 'Oh Christ, keep up will you? I gotta work the old job - got begged in and caved to my better angles. New job's an overnight. Don't you know anything about me, you fop?'

Preparing a new pot of coffee, Elliott calls across to Lucy to please not feed the damn cat any of the meat. 'You want to go fuck yourself?' Lucy replies, tilt of genuine curious in her voice. 'That's fine with me - I won't stop you if your heart is set on it.' But Elliott does make the valid point that the meat not only tends to make the cat vomit but gives it the blood-shits - and that they are well and truly screwed out of the deposit, already, because of the carpets. 'Aren't we going to live here forever?' Lucy asks, getting her shirt off and tossing it toward the dirty clothing pile by the space-heater in the bedroom, remarking to herself that's either a bad place for a heater, a bad place for the laundry, or both, then does nothing about it. She does not hear Elliott's reply. Then after a moment hears Elliott go 'What did you say?' 'What did I say, what?' Lucy overlouds back, remembering her towels are all out in the basket by her desk, hanging her head and then putting her just removed shirt back on, inside out. 'What did I say, what?' she repeats, entering the main room to retrieve her towel, Elliott adding creamer-powder to her coffee and indicating with her head that she's poured Lucy some, too. 'What? Coffee? I'm getting in the shower! Why'd you pour it, now?' 'Because I don't like you, obviously' Elliott says, then asks 'How can Clarke pay you that much to do nothing?' Lucy takes two hurried, irritating mouthfuls of coffee, flicks, hard, Elliott's belly and says 'Shrug!' while turning to leave.

The toilet in the apartment upstairs flushes as Lucy brushes her teeth - she's sneaking some of Elliott's *Cherry Bubble-Gum* flavored stuff - and so the two working lightbulbs over the mirror dim and the toilet right next the sink starts to hiss. Sigh. Big sigh. 'Will the water be over-hot or under-cold?' Lucy mouths to her reflection, then makes the reflection give her the cock-eye and mouth back to her 'You mean *over-cold*, right?' She smiles and the reflection smiles and

Lucy Jinx is pawing at the outside of the closed door. The proper expression would be *over-cold*! This must be the fiftieth time Lucy has asked her forlorn question when having to shower after an upstairs-toilet flush, yet she is only just now, the first time, noting this typo. She turns her back on her reflection, rests ass on wet counter lip, pinching and jiggling her blotchy Sneetch-belly, the crumbly look of the skin like children's book porridge, her belly button cavernous, enough to lose an ear-plug down. Whips around to reflection, straights shoulders and regards herself. Nothing to be done about the vein-work that has loused-up her breasts - this new thick bastard, she hopes, is just due to she's chilly and a trick of light, what a hideous bit of map-work that vein! - but is her belly as bad as that? Even after the weight loss? Or is it because of the weight loss she looks so sack-of-liquefied-potato? Has she reached that stage where numerical weight-value means nothing and she'd be better off learning to cut her losses and wear Portly like a peacock fan? 'Not so bad' she tries out saying and almost believes it until she turns profile. It's like three bags of coins are buried in a lump just over her pubic-hair - this paunch seems a part that should be able to disconnect! 'How can a body even be that?' she demands, full voice aloud.

Over-warm and towel-wrapped, her face seems like a ceiling that's just had asbestos removed. She cuts off Elliott's solicitous grin with a bitter set to her eyes, Elliott moving to speak some compliment but stopping and, instead, leaving the room. Lucy closes the door and dresses at a rush, sitting to the edge of the bed and noting the scalp-stained look of her pillowcase. The room is like being in a pox scar, she thinks. Who paints walls this fever-slick yellow? And who lets walls painted like this get these mysterious, liver-spot smears near electrical outlets. 'We should be dead, in here' Lucy thinks, truly feeling it true. The paint on the window? What about it? Well: look! Lucy's most hated thing. It's bumpy! It's prickly! It looks like it has eczema, for Christ's sake! How does that happen to paint? Or is it some kind of rot to the wood? Really, Lucy thinks it is termite feces - that they have shat all under there, gnawing the sill and the pane wood, their anal excretions have piled, petrified, pressed up and prickled the dry skin of the paint. And the heater makes the dust weigh more - cooks it. The drifts caught in sunlight aren't even beautiful but look like the shake from some used, let dry, used, let dry, used invalid's handkerchief. Elliott taps on the door and opens it before Lucy can say not to. 'I wanted to tell you that' but she stops midsentence, stares, pauses a beat before asking 'What's wrong?' Lucy gruffly stands and says 'Nothing' running handback over wet eyes and getting to the bathroom door while saying and kind of not saying 'I'll be right out, okay?'

Question: Isn't Elliott going to think something amiss? Response: No. Or, yes. But she'll think it has something to do with last night. Question: Isn't that dangerous? Response: No - wait, why would that be dangerous? Question: Why are you crying in front of Elliott? Response: I didn't mean to cry in front of Elliott! But wait - I asked 'Why would it be dangerous?' Question: You don't think she might think there's something going on with you and Deb? Answer: It can be easily proven there isn't - and never has been - something, anything, going on with me and Deb. Question: Not the point - don't you see that's not the point? Answer: No. Question: You know you need to go explain why you were crying and give some excuse for not getting into bed when you got home, right? Answer: I didn't want to pass out too hard - because I have to go to work! Question: Tell her that! But what about the crying? Think about it - isn't it too much, not getting in bed with her and then crying - all on top of you said you would be out all night and then you came home, middle-of-the-damned-night? Answer: Fuck Elliott. She doesn't even know Deb! What's she gonna do, ask Deb if something happened? Why would Deb even have such a chat? Deb knows what the shot is with Elliott. Question: Exactly! Right? Answer: What? Question: Can't you just go smooth it over? Why were you even crying, anyway? Answer. Because. Question: Because? Answer: Yes. Question: You don't actually know, do you? Answer: Fuck you. Yes, I actually know!

Lucy takes the magazine - stolen from one of the neighbors - from Elliott, curls it into a tube and softly baps first Elliott's left shoulder and then her right with it. 'I suppose I deserve that' Elliott says, holding her jellied English muffin up but not moving to take a bite. 'You don't, actually.' Lucy sighs. 'I'm so fucking stressed, man.' Elliott takes a bite, chews as she drinks some grape juice, swallows fast and leans back, giving Lucy's shin a little kick with her still-just-in-socks foot. 'You're always stressed. Come on.' Committed, though, Lucy shakes her head like Elliott is missing the sincerity of this moment - this is the best way, Lucy feels, to seem sincere, lacing in some petulant bristling - and goes 'I was so excited to get this job, then realized how even with this job - the new one, you know? - we're still so bent over with things and now I'll be at the fucking doughnut shop three nights, all night, and it's stressing me out because it's like I do nothing to help and then what I do just seems to cause there to be less of us.' Too much? Did you overplay that, Lucy? Maybe. Anyway: Lucy takes Elliott's muffin and tears a bite, unsure what to make of her silence. 'I'm going to get a second job, too' Elliott finally says and she cuts Lucy off before Lucy can make the objection Lucy gives the appearance of having been about to make. 'Just - I am. Okay? You're not the only one who has to do things, okay? We're Us, not You-and-Me.' But Lucy has to maintain that her line of thinking is that Elliott has much better things to do and, besides, already brings in decent money with her gig. 'It's not decent money, Loose. You're right. We're fucked. I don't want you to think I don't know that. I know it, okay?'

The better plan, retrospect, would have been to have pulled Elliott onto the bed. You had time, Lucy - you don't need to be at the fucking store to open! You could have made it look to Elliott like you were fine with showing up for work late on account of just needing to vent via a rough, clawing tumble with her. Quick fix, that would've been. And now this is about saying you're stressed about money!? Fuck's sake, here! What does Lucy care about this place or this money? Lucy has a goddamn degree and can go someplace legitimate! Lucy, frankly, is having trouble even remembering what is what, these days - aren't you, Lucy!? Elliott? Who is she? But same time: Elliot - what are you supposed to do, leave her in a lurch? Look at her there: she's mincemeat on her own! She'd shack up with the first guy who showed her a card trick or told her 'Hey, your short stories are as good as any man's' and who'd claim they knew someone at a journal who would run one. Imbecile. Elliott is just shy of an imbecile, admit it! Not that - be honest, Lucy - you can exactly be claiming the moral high ground, here. 'At least I don't want anything from her' Lucy defends herself, mumblingly, watching Elliott through the bedroom door: Elliott removing her tank top and tossing it right overtop of the space heater. 'I'm keeping her from being taken advantage of - I'm keeping her from dealing with people who'd want to use her.' Look at Elliott: she's about as sturdy as a Saltine cracker, man, she's about as self-possessed as a coat-button! Elliott catches sight of Lucy and smiles. Whisper-mouths something to which Lucy gives a blank, one-size-fits-all expression and to which Elliott smiles wider than she had been and bites her lip, shy-lass, turns around and purposefully lowers her panties off - sway-and-tug left, sway-and-tug right - looking over her shoulder as they puddle in a soft tuft around her crossed together ankles. Lucy shakes her head, mouths 'Fucking exquisite' and tight-claws her one hand in front of her like ringing Elliott's slim little neck.

This pudgy workman, skin like a Styrofoam cup, is scrubbing the tile of the torn up lobby-rug with some steel wool, oppressive thick of bleach rising from the floor and from that bucket, fumes that warp the view of the glass of the entrance-door. He makes a gesture that Lucy should cover her mouth and she gives him a scathing look, he idiot-grinning and then lifting the top of his t-shirt over his nose and fanning the space between them. Outside, Lucy shoots him in a last snarl, trying to figure out why he didn't have the door propped if he'd be so damned concerned about tenant's health. Ought not Lucy to go point this out? Isn't he stuffing toxins down himself, as well? She pictures returning home, later, to find him dead. No one will move the body though someone will slosh the bleach water out on the sidewalk in front of the building, leave the empty bucket out there to get filled with rain water and then, over time, this water soaked up by cigarette butts. Yes - Lucy has a pristine vision of this! As her own breathing starts to feel less queasy she even rather longs for it to happen. It'd be worth it - to watch the carcass bloat, leak, maybe one day find it had been robbed of shoes or belt, maybe one day it had been moved to the corner and vaguely covered in a tarp. How much sleep did you honestly get last night, Lucy? Two hours at most? You need to stop thinking, today. You need to start over. Fix this. This day is wrong, already.

Where she waits for the bus, this same guy - Patrick - as always chums over and offers her a cigarette out of the copper case he is so proud of having. She, as always, accepts. 'You ever go down and see the street artists?' he asks just as Lucy gets her cig lit from his held across lighter. 'Which are they?' 'At the park' Patrick says, little nose gesture in some direction, probably not the direction of the park. Naw, Lucy hasn't even been to the park. 'Geist Park?' Patrick says, as though bowled over by this news. Lucy apologetics her face and puffs cheeks like holding her breath as she shakes her head. 'Oh! Well, every weekend - and sometimes just random evenings - they have all kinds of them there. Artists. Selling stuff. Or showing. Musicians just out performing.' 'Yeah?' Lucy tries not to overtly be looking to see is the bus coming, just casually - she is at a bus-stop after all, meaning she has her mind on places other, is allowed to not seem devoutly attentive to Patrick. Who, right now, has just said 'I used to play there, sometimes, actually.' 'In a band?' 'Piano. They used to, in the pavilion, have a piano out. Got to know a guy, he'd let me play. Had to pay him twenty bucks the first time' Patrick laughs - how long has he wanted to tell you this story, Lucy? - 'but then he just let me. And he couldn't stop people tossing me money, you know?' 'Sounds awesome' Lucy says, kind-postured, cigarette hand using its thumb-knuckle to rub at her temple. 'He made me split the take - because I wasn't supposed to be playing, let alone earning. Anyway' Patrick shrugged, make-believing he's suddenly shy. 'Anyway' he repeated, chuckling, nodding his head, shoulders raised and then drooped.


CARLO - THIS IS THE FORTIETH time, at least - tells Lucy he would marry her if it would make her know how much he knows he owes her and wants to be sure that she knows the only reason he hasn't proposed is he knows she would find the idea appalling. 'But still' he says, sympathy-face at Lucy like she has just lost both legs to some fiend-strain of plague, she - slamming the cuts into this newly-out pizza - mentioning that she's getting time-and-a-half for the hours that Benny should be working, too, so it's all good. This had not been agreed on but now Carlo just says 'That, too' seeming thankful for Lucy's smile. 'Worth far more than a marriage, Carlo - a marriage to you, anyway' she says, pizza moved to serving-tray next to the three others. 'Don't forget they want the pretzels' he says, knowing to return to sharp business tone or Lucy will get sick of him. Pretzels! She has to search through the fridge for five minutes only to definitively discover they are all out. 'No pretzels!' one of the men at the table announces to the others, moans and growls - both mock and too genuine - rising up in a chorus. Then this other man says 'How about those cinnamon sticks? You have those?' Nevermind that these cretins are your age, Lucy - older, some of them - and are asking for cinnamon sticks instead of pretzels at noon on a weekday as though making a concession, taking a blow with dignity. Nevermind that, Lucy! If there was some way to prepare these things wrong, you would do it - but they just go into the cook-tray and onto the conveyor belt-oven. Send them through twice - send em out brunt! Lucy grins, sees another two men enter and a chant she cannot understand shot toward them from those seated.

Something about a thunder cloud. Lucy jots down this new order and wonders why this man is actually asking her about coupons from another shop he does not even have with him. *A thunder cloud.* A thunder cloud? You should have written it down, Lucy! *Storm cloud?* But it wasn't about the cloud. 'If I had the coupons, though - you all used to match competitors, right?' 'We match competitors, yes' Lucy says - catching the eye of another man who is just then realizing his coffee is empty and that he would like more, holding the cup up, dainty ting-a-ling-a-ling motion of it, winking when Lucy meets his eyes as though all is acknowledged. 'What I mean is - don't you know that *Horton's* has those coupons?' 'Which?' 'Buy one, next one half-price, third one quarter-price.' Lucy has heard of this deal and says so and tries to politely pull away to tend to the rest of the order on her pad. *Thunder cloud*, she sees written. You just wrote that, Lucy. The line, though, was about a woman. A woman. In reference to a thunder cloud - but such an interesting, random phrase sort of comparison. Something. *Storm cloud.* 'What?' The man does not relent. ' So, in essence, why not let us use the coupons?' 'Which coupons?' 'From *Horton's*! The ones we both admit we know about!' Big fat man, little league father laugh. 'You need to have the coupon' - she tries levity in her tone - 'which isn't asking so much, right? Throw us a bone, right? Gotta be some rules, eh?' The man grunts - oh God at large, he is actually serious, this gooey-shaped prune! 'I can ask' Lucy finally says, wresting herself away. *Thunder cloud.* Something about the word *mutinous*. Her neck is tense. *Her neck is mutinous.* You should have written it down, Lucy! Though: why are you trying to write something, today of all days? *Thunder cloud?* Forget it.

While using the toilet, Lucy finds a waiting voicemail from Cami. She calls back, right away, doesn't even listen to the entire message. After Hellos, Lucy laughs and explains she is calling, middle-squat, from a toilet at work 'So don't mind if I sound a bit preoccupied.' Laughter. 'Where in Hell are you? Are you in town?' Cami says she just got into her apartment and was hoping to be able to speedy-delivery a Lucy Jinx to her door. 'Why in Hell are you in a toilet at work? At the pizza place, you mean? Why are you there!? It's the daytime and I just got home!' Lucy apologizes - and then has to say 'One minute' when the bathroom door is jiggled, Carlo's 'I'm sorry' coming through the door genuinely repentant, though at the same time he knew right well Lucy was in there, was supposed to be keeping an eye on her tables for two minutes! - and says she got pressured into working the extra shift 'by society and all of the billboards aimed at her, as a woman.' 'I don't accept it' says Cami 'and henceforth do not love you and will pick another old codger as my hobby-horse. You had your chance.' 'No, no' - Lucy is standing, having awkwardly wiped, and is trying to get her pants closed with one hand - 'I'll come by, right after. I'm just here until' - she doesn't know when, it occurs to her - 'sometime.' Cami is just kidding - 'Calm the gosh down, Jinx!' - and is going to pass out 'until Christ-only-knows, anyway. But I do demand Lucy: beck-and-call, next time. Or else!' Pinned-phone to shoulder with head, Lucy gets shirt tucked, button fly shut, is getting apron loop over her head promising 'Yessir - you won't regret it, sir - thank you, sir.'

'I'm sorry about a lot of these guys' says this one father-of-however-many who has come to the counter to explain how, eventually, the bill is to be divvied. 'They don't get out much and I think they think they're cool mobsters or something.' It's okay that you actually laughed at that, Lucy, this man is nice, it's fine to be pleasant. 'Are you the only one here?' 'People had tummy-aches and dead relatives, you know?' The man laughs, leveraging the fact he has kids to get in chummy that he knows all the tricks - though his daughters have not gotten around to claiming the demise of family-members, just yet. 'Tummy-aches, though, yes. And Cara - my oldest - she can do something to the thermometer, I just haven't figured it out.' Warm memory - unexpected: holding the silver bulb of the glass-and-mercury thermometer up to the bathroom light, shaking it, shaking it, gently, gently, to get it to seem she's just-feverish-enough to stay home in bed. 'In my day, it was easy' Lucy is now saying 'I'd have thought parents'd got together to fuck that up for kids, by now.' He laughs. 'Parents are a punch of smarty-pants, yeah. But Cara does something - I dunno. She can get around the digital!' The man's eyes flick when the phone rings and the brief stick of 'Goddamn it' in his expression is cute enough that Lucy gives him an 'Aw well' shrug before answering. He is smart enough not to linger there - 'Small mercy' thinks Lucy, laughs and now gives the usual greeting into the phone, realizing when she hears an uncertain but slightly put-out

'Hello?' that she had lifted the receiver and not said anything while watching the man move away.

She motions for Carlo to come over to where she is hastily prepping. 'Look in there' she says, venom in the tense thack she makes her head gesture. Carlo opens the fridge-unit and exclaims 'You're fucking kidding - who closed last night!?' 'I was here until three' Lucy says, getting a pie into the oven, her face held in a seethe - 'and it was not like that when I left.' 'I know if wasn't' says Carlo, defeated, sighing before giving the door a feeble shut instead of a slam. 'I will prep new crusts' he says, touching her arm to be sure she's listening. 'It's fine' she says, anger welling. 'No - seriously - I will prep them.' 'No, it's fine.' But she is at bursting and cannot help it and now is going 'Why the fuck does she still work here!? Come on, man!' Carlo is holding up placating hands and insists it was not her - meaning Claudine - who closed, but Lucy knows it was and Carlo's lack of vigor on the point proves it. 'I will prep, Carlo. Once these goddamn soccer-dads fuck off, okay? But then I'm out.' And though it is a bitterness Carlo doesn't deserve, she snipes at the end of this 'And these hours better go on this fucking check, man - I don't need this shit' - she jerks head to indicate the fridge-unit - 'on top of coming in and not getting my check straight, okay!?' Poor Carlo! Lucy - come on! Say you're sorry. No? No!? Why 'Fuck him' though, Lucy? He's never screwed you over on a check. And he did offer to prep! 'I'm not going to let him hold that against me' Lucy sotto voce declares. 'Fuck Carlo and fuck Claudine.' And then Carlo's melting-popsicle voice timids 'Lucy - can I get you a sec?' She shuts eyes like they're a mouth screaming, a head wild flapping-on-a-hinge clattering bang bang bang but then breathes steady and says 'Just let me put this in. I got them, I know what they want.'

What is it like? This sullen, gone-off, thawed dough, these guts of canisters of toppings and sauce left to warm too long, a scent of the maggots that will grow somehow already on them as she drags the deadweight of this second bag to the dumpster - what is it like? Someone eviscerated. The bag is ghoulish, obscene. It's like jizz mixed with soured milk and heavy as a sack of baseball gloves with hands severed inside them. Lucy has to let the bag drape on her knee and then get her hands under it - Oh doesn't this feel the same as she imagines gripping the ass of the carcass of a sun bloated grandmother would? - getting the right hold of the bag bottom, its contents sloshing around her - thin plastic not enough to keep the fresh-dog-shit-warmth from her skin - and then do some ridiculous pelvic thrust motions to up-and-over it into the enclosure. Right into a cigarette, Lucy whirls. Carlo can handle the patrons for the time it takes to actually enjoy this cigarette - don't rush, Lucy. What else could those men possibly want? She bursts laughing, having just asked herself 'Can you imagine if we served beer here?' Laughing is all she can do is response to even contemplating that monstrosity of a notion! She shivers but somehow feels odors and perspirations trapped in her instead of feeling refreshed by the biting chill. Try. She tries. She tries to let the cold be a relaxant. No good. It'll take a soak in the bath and a night's sleep, at this point. And what does she picture when she thinks the words *night's sleep*? Herself. Alone. A bed. Alone. A room. Alone. She thinks of sleep as nobody-can-touch-her. She wants nobody-can-touch-her. But it's just that she's tired. 'The money, though' she says. The shift will be worth it and she just lets the sensation of her headache, front-and-center, serve as the calculations she is too beleaguered to cogitate, right now. Yes. That headache is a number worth all of this, surely.

'Carlo, I am sorry about what I said before' Lucy says, here, gently patting his shoulder, touching her forehead to where her hand just touched, moving past. 'Please don't be sorry, okay?' 'I'm obviously not actually - but I did think I ought to say I was.' Carlo laughs, relieved, throws a filthy paper towel in Lucy's direction and Lucy mocks him when it just limps nobodyish to the filthied prep-area floor. 'I am doing the dishes' she says before Carlo can try to make some further noble gesture. 'I am starting, now' she adds and Carlo makes no objection, it well understood he can handle whatever remains of the gathering-of-fathers' needs. It's astonishing how many dishes these mongrels have generated already! True, there is a restaurant-worth of them - the lot all being clustered around tables dragged to the dining area center illusions it away from the fact that there are at least three-times as many of them as a typical busy-shift would harbor, and all of them there at once - but this still seems kind of appalling, like evidence of a civilization that is only grudgingly included in history texts. 'Yes' Lucy says, separating cups and glasses out from silverware and plates 'this People technically meet the criteria - buildings and a social-centers and all - but really should not be mistaken for the Incas, let's just put it like that.' This fork! Evidence! A grown man used this, don't forget! Observe: a kabob consisting of a small bit of pickle, a mushroom sliver, a bit of a straw-wrapper, a mash of crust, a soggy sugar packet, and capped with a bit of cinnamon stick with mayonnaise on it and - look here! - it was then scribble-scrabbled through salad dressing, likely while trying to pierce that last bit of lettuce, as well! 'Jesus' Lucy says and just tosses the thing entire - utensil and all - into a garbage-can. No way to clean such an object.

She looks up from her daydream about sharing a cab with a woman she is certain she recognizes and who is certain they recognize her - neither able to place the other, warm lust, regardless, rising between them while they 'Hmn' and shyly giggle, calling it, speaking simultaneous 'Distressingly absurd!' - but does not quite get what Carlo has said. 'Two things' he repeats, seeming to find it jolly how obvious it was she had retreated to fantasy - what is showing on your face, Lucy? he's smiling very pointedly! - 'first: they put a bunch of the tip on cards - but I am cashing it out, right away.' 'You'd better if you value, you know, breaths beyond these ones, right now' Lucy says, unable to be pleasant, her eyes held, she knows, very very wide. 'I got it, I got it' cows Carlo 'and two:' he continues after pausing as though waiting for a further whack of snark 'one of the customers asked to speak to you.' 'I don't want to talk to one of the customers - Jesus! - let them use the coupon or whatever! I don't fucking care! Whatever they say, please let them just do it.' Carlo is perplexed, Lucy, so it's not that. 'What do they want?' she exasperates, lifting foot to stamp it, splish of a puddle from the unmopped spillage of the last several sink loads. 'I don't know. But I can tell him to beat it - he's out front smoking.' Lucy knits her brow and Carlo rolls his eyes in illustration of having no idea about this turn of events, being on Lucy's team, solidly, and 'So, are you going?' at the same time. 'They already paid?' 'Yes' Carlo says, dramatic of head hung. She hiss-sighs and Alrights.

This man, again! Lucy reeks of crime scene carpet, she's no doubt, and her face feels like a rash on a callous in the crook of a pack-mule's knee. Lucy is bleghing her way into her cigarette as he gives a happy wave and does a cross between a gentlemanly approach and a shumble. Which, she admits, he looks fine doing, now that he is closed up in his suit, properly - yes, she will allow him an audience because none of those other slobs had dressed nice and he has. He begins: 'I should state, in front, how I know there is no way you can be looking forward to whatever some asshole Little League dad who was just in there and chatted with you once, already, is likely to say' and then pauses for her to acknowledge. 'Correct' she says, but is already crediting him one easy smile. 'I assure you I am far too aware of my homeliness and far far too aware that you know I am married' - he holds up his ringed hand - 'to try anything creeper. Okay?' She gives him an even once-over, nods her head 'Proceed.' 'If I am incorrect, simply say *No idea what you mean, dickwad, piss off* and I shall.' Pause. 'You are a poet, correct?' Lucy cannot hide the acknowledgment in her surprise - nor the wariness. The man chuckles. 'And your name is' - he rolls his eyes, gestures at the nametag she is wearing - 'well, obviously Lucy! But it's Lucy Jinx, right?' Now it is mostly alarm. Why alarm? Well, she had been thinking he maybe saw something she'd scribbled while taking an order, hence the poet question - this knowing her name is another, altogether more unnerving animal. 'How do you know that?' The words are a recoil and the look on his face - the pure I-will-leave-right-now-I-am-sorry - is the only thing that keeps Lucy from flicking her cig at him, there and then.

In the end, though, that was not unpleasant at all, was it Lucy? No. Sure, it has taken Lucy ten minutes to get composure after the chat - the man, Leonard,

would have thought she'd had composure the whole time, of course, Lucy good
enough at seeming unphased - but it had all been very nice, actually. And now
she is recapping in her mind - are you kind of glowing, Lucy? - not listening to
Carlo as he prattles away, over there. The man had seen her read a poem at
some random Open-mic, more than a month ago, and the two - she now
remembered clearly - had even briefly said 'Hello' while smoking, but she, as
always, had hurried away just after stepping hers out, the man recalling to her
how abruptly she'd done so, the both of them laughing at the memory. She looks
at the slip of paper with the man's telephone number on it. 'I am in here often,
but I've never seen you working' he had said. 'I just work prep, today was a
favor.' She looks at the paper and smiles. He had introduced himself and
explained he was a high-school teacher, had hoped she might come and either
read for his class or - what he honestly hoped - meet with them a few times to
discuss poetry. Was he a skeevy sort, Lucy? How had he struck you? Now that
you are thinking back, what sort do you peg him as? 'I know it's odd - but you
made an impression. Your verse. I can still - at least I hope - recite some of it.'
And he had. Recited it. Or something. It had sounded like her. 'That sounds
like me' she had said and he had laughed 'You don't remember you stuff?' She'd
made a Pshhh! sound and spit cigarette and he'd said 'That's fucking perfect.'
Lucy you had honestly blushed! 'This is me. Just if you're interested.' And he'd
handed her the paper she is looking at, unsure - you're still unsure, Lucy - what
she'd made of him.


IS *WEARY* THE CORRECT WORD? Words are important to you, Lucy. You
say that. Or have you ever said that? What do you think of words, Lucy? Are
they important? Do they mean anything to you? This one moreso than that one?
Do you honestly see meanings? Your own? Those given? Do you value either?
Or are they both arbitrary and, for being arbitrary, the same? Don't you
sometimes wonder if this love of words you claim - you've said it, Lucy, you've
said you love words, either way, regardless of if you do - is just something stuck
in you, without your will, the same as anything about you you would undo? A
grease stain from an odd dribble from a sandwich or an elbow that dislocates
due to a harsh tug, once, for misbehaving in childhood? Or not even so dramatic.
Just: is the love - if it even exists - your own? Or is it imprinted? Do you love
words the way you love grape-juice or rice-with-sausage or this-brand-of-
cookie-over-that - simply because it is what was served you in times formative
- times you could not have known were any such thing and that knowledge of

their being so would have done nothing to change them being so? Or in spite of how it was? Is there a difference between your alleged love of words and your inability to forget some flicker of a passing television screen - some odd glance, once - or a look from a child - an odd glance, once - in some department store? Come on! Think. Concentrate. What do you think of words? You can give such grand speeches, but do you really think you need them - that you are them? Fine. You do - you are. But which? Any? All? The ones that haven't betrayed you yet, only, or do you obsessively claim your heart scoops the whole spread? Is *weary* the correct word, Lucy? Are you *weary*, right now? Here? Here? Or here? What word are you? What does that word mean? Do you mean more than that word? Less? Aren't you only it if it means you, exactly, and can't it never do that? *Weary*? Anything. Are you any word? And if not - what?

To escape this pitfalling mind, Lucy pretends a conversation. She pretends she has been famously remembered for explaining *Hamlet* thusly: 'It is as though claustrophobia is wrapped in vertigo buried beneath paranoia.' She sees herself, fat and smug for having said this - Oh a real doll, above it all and with her photo in miniature adorning anthologies and the walls above certain desks where certain women studiously go at their pursuits. Lucy has said more than this about *Hamlet* - much much more - but pretends herself seated on a wide stage, spotlight on her, spotlight on her equally renown - even more renown, let's say that - interviewer, these spotlights tinged a little bit green. The audience is students and some random sorts who have paid to be present - the students are there for free, the lifeblood of this imaginarily prestigious University where Lucy is invited. They applaud as the quote is recited and Lucy mock-humbles as though she had not been expecting the response. 'Well, isn't that just what *Hamlet* is?' she as-though-obviouses and laughter is gifted her, copious splats of the stuff. Now: Lucy knows how to fantasize - she takes her comments no further than these deprecations after being quoted. To start - even just to herself in her head - an attempt at expounding some original and silver-tongued expression of how she feels about *Hamlet* would reveal the mundanity of her view. She'd start disagreeing with herself, even! This happens. Lucy knows her mind the way one can tell this matchbook is cheap while this other is quality. She needs this train of thought to last just long enough to distract her from her previous bother. 'Complicated little Lucy, Lucy' Lucy says to herself - claustrophobic, vertigoed, paranoid, proud.

Though the main branch of the library is only ten minutes further on the bus route, ever since Lucy found this smaller annex she prefers it. It seems like it used to be the stockroom of a shoe store or else the space behind the mailboxes one can rent at a Post Office. Thin and long, one of the first whittles from a stick being shaped, it has an invisibility - the three people who work there always the same, always seeming surprised to have a patron, never giving her any particular notice. Even here, now, sitting, Lucy has the impression that if she decided to not get up at closing time they would, without even aheming, go about their business, douse the lights, except the one over her table, leave for the night with her locked in. It'd be a mistake - Oh they'd learn that - because she covets and plans to rob that old tape-recorder with the heavy headphones - what is it? forty years old? it seems it could be her twin sister! - and would burgle the micro-film viewer, no matter what the consequences might be! This is her ritual: always sitting, removing her coat, preparing herself as though for a long bout of study before moving to her actual business. Every other patron here is foreign and elderly. She must seem foreign to them. And elderly. The young must look far more bizarre and horrific to the old than the old do to the young - there must be something garish in seeing the form of even Lucy's patchy middle-age. Never the same people, other than generally old and foreign, they are never the same. This is striking. She comes at, usually, the same time and there are a handful of littered patrons, always, but never the same ones. Have any even once repeated? Probably. But this is the sort of thing Lucy would rather leave unverified, unadmitted, a thing to make her seem the oddest for winding up there again and again, a filthy-grey penny always in the pocket of some laundered pants.

*I hope it isn't intrusive or corny, but I wanted you to know that last night meant more than the world to me. I know it was business as usual for you, but I wish you hadn't paid me - you have no idea.* Lucy blinks at this, pops in a breath-mint from the pack she has found left on the table by the computers, figuring odds are they are not poisoned - and if they are, it'd be interesting to fall victim to such a milquetoast murder plot. *Anyway blah blah blah. I do hope you meant it about sharing the poem! And if you really meant I could sit for you again, really do let me know when and I want to. If I sound weird, I'm sorry. It was for me.* Then Heather had typed her name. *It was for me.* What word is missing there? 'If I sound weird, I'm sorry. It was for me.' Aloud, this seems to mean *It* - the time in the hotel - was weird for Heather. But that goes against what seems to be this clingy, solicitous tone. Is the punctuation just off? Lucy tries a few breakdowns. Nothing makes this make sense. Was the last phrase a new thought? Okay: so then what word is missing? Or is Lucy emphasizing it shoddily, accenting the wrong beats? 'It was. For me. It. Was for. Me. Itwasforme.' The fuck, eh Lucy? 'It. Was. For. Me. Fucking proofread, Heather!' Lucy berates while tapping front teeth on mint, not hard enough to break it. The message had been sent, likely, as soon as Heather had returned home. Or not. Middle of the night, it shows here. While Lucy had been at the doughnut shop. Just a bit later. 'Where are you now, Heather?' Lucy wants to get her reply out of the way, but thinks fatigue should rule out doing so now. *You have no idea.* 'What's that - your goddamn catchphrase?' Sitcom applause. Or sitcom silence. Lucy notes Heather's e-mail avatar is a child's scribble of a cat face. Wishes she hadn't. Sitcom solemn applause after silence.

One new taker, only. Lucy doesn't rush to open the message. Subject Line: *Interested in modeling for your poetry?* 'Is that a question?' Lucy sighs, looking over her shoulder at the librarian who will let her have some coffee if she hauls herself over there to ask. *Perhaps you need to put the ad in another publication? Or try the free online message boards* - what in Hell is the difference? Well: the whole enterprise has a ring of classiness as a boxed advertisement in the rear pages of *Haute Sequin* or *Hilmouth's Review.* She hasn't gotten one goddamn response, though, from what she considered the fanciest ad - *Poets and Madhares Quarterly* - so maybe she should open it up to the pleabs and the groundlings! Does Lucy really think it doesn't cross the minds of the people who read the ad, no matter where, that there might be something illicit in the set up? Come to think of it - this is an interjection of thought, immediately moved away from - where had Heather come across the ad? Lucy tries to remember without re-opening Heather's initial e-mail, cannot, doesn't care, stands to go ask for that coffee. Forgotten. Heather. 'Hi' - the woman makes her face show familiarity but does not smile - 'I know I'm such a pest, but you were so great to let me have some coffee, once before.' The woman touches her glasses and sits up, rubs her side with her elbow while saying 'You need some coffee? I can see if Dennis brewed some. If not, can you wait?' 'Of course I can wait - it isn't a bother?' The woman does a motion indicating it is not a bother but doesn't say anything, moves off through that very oddly placed door - is that even a room? Lucy scratches her ear and wants to steal the stamp and the stamp pad - that one, those ones - right there.

*Name: Victoire Elan.* Wonderful name. Lucy has fallen haphazard in love. *Age: twenty-eight.* And types out the word *Twenty-eight?* 'Marry me, Victoire' Lucy says. No image icon when she scrolls over the name. Before reading further, Lucy opens another browser, types *Victorie Elan* and searches images only to be assailed by the usual too-plenty-a-plenty. Some *Victoire Elans* - if indeed that is who the images are of - Lucy would murder to so much as brush past in a soup line, others are hum-drum, others are book-covers without that name on them, others are images of streets, other are obvious advertisement images, and at least half-a-dozen are actresses with names nothing remotely like *Victoire Elan.* 'Peh' she pehs and shuts the browser. So ask for photographs, Lucy! Instead of insisting they don't send any! You are a pervy old dirtbag-dame, so why hide it? 'Yes, yes' she rolls her eyes at herself, sips this miserable coffee - do they brew it with fucking sea water!? - and returns to business. *Are you a professional model / have you modeled before? No. With a name like Victoire Elan!?* Lucy feels should have been the next line of the questionnaire *Are you goddamn serious!? Are you a writer: I am not, though I have started four novels and once wrote a long letter to someone, which I burnt after putting in the envelope.* Lucy, are you aroused? 'Shut up' Lucy whispers. It's a name. And a vaguely interesting response. Victoire Elan is not merely 'a name' and that is a plenty great response to *Are you a writer!* So get a room, already. 'Maybe I will, Lucy' - she sticks out her tongue, her eye catching the bottom line of the form as she scrolls. *Do you have any questions for me: When do I start?* Stop chuckling, Lucy - that isn't even very clever.

In the restroom, she closes her eyes after finishing, not pulling up panties, not standing or straightening. It's just your fatigue that is making you not feel excited about that man's offer earlier, Lucy. 'Why do I want to talk about poems to kids?' They aren't kids. 'Yes, they are. I could be their mother! No one wants their mother to spout off wise about What-makes-a-poet. They would all know better than me!' How's that, Lucy? 'Poetry belongs to the young. They sit there: poems.' And people like Lucy? 'We sit there: lumpy and writing and sad to take in.' They? 'They speak and are poetry, move and are poetry, obnoxious and are poetry, be-what-Lucy-once-was and be poetry-she-isn't-and-never-got-proper-to-be.' How's that? You weren't ever young? 'I wasn't ever poetry.' She flushes, not standing - something she never does - mist under her, cold feeling and tension and regret. I thought youth had no choice but it was poetry? 'I wasn't young' she yawns 'I was Lucy Jinx.' This is just tiredness. That man heard you read, wanted you there! 'He didn't think twice about me until he saw me, scullion at a pizza joint. Figured I'm good for a one-off, figured make nice about I'd struck him as a poet, thinks I'd never heard that, all I'd ever done was be old and serving pizza to people like him.' Jesus, Lucy! He made a good show of things, if that's it! 'Well, did you see him?' Even you said he was handsome! 'He was. That's my point. Handsome men don't go asking gully-gutted pizza cooks to read poetry because they think they are poets.' Your logic eludes us, Lucy, explain. 'I know him. I know him exactly. He thinks I'm a scab to pick, give a lick, squirt some ointment on.'

It has started snowing and Lucy is unsure why she is back outside. Is it time to go home? She thinks of Elliott showing up in just an hour or so. Hadn't Lucy said she was going somewhere, tonight? She is blank. Then: Aha! No. Elliott is going to be out, tonight. At her thing. Her peer-review thing. You should pop in there, Lucy - don't protest! - it'd be a good way to smooth over the awkwardness of this morning. 'Oh that' Lucy says and in her mind I-guesses she'll go. But that gives her hours. She cannot go home, because Elliott will go there before heading to her group - and that would ruin the whole showing up, Ms. Spontaneous-magic-trick. Would it have the same effect to be at home, ask to go? Gah. No! That would be awful. That smacks of patching it up before the kid's school play! Lucy actually shudders. 'And since when did I start calling it *Home?*' she finds herself blurting after lighting a smoke, not bothering to stand in the empty bus-stop enclosure. Hadn't that been how you'd thought of it for awhile? 'Home. Home!?' she hopes not, but now her eyes make slopping noises whenever she blinks them and the cigarette tastes like the residue of stale bread in her gums. For a moment - but it passes, she's got it - she forgets where Elliott's group meets, then - shrugging when she can't think of what could be done about it - wonders 'What if they have changed venue or are meeting someplace else, tonight?' More pressing: Lucy does not even need this bus, but almost stepped on. 'Sorry' she says, stepping backward down the stairs, telling the driver not to worry about returning her coins. 'When does the Orange come by here?' The driver - handing her back coins equal to what she just deposited, different denominations, though, from a little cup on the dashboard - tells her and points to some schedules in little hanging pouches just inside the bus door, one of which she takes, now feeling obligated to.

A flabby-but-well-put-together sort milling in front of a secondhand clothing and record shop asks a cigarette off of her and she obliges, deciding to smoke one of her own. 'When did I start hating rock 'n roll?' the guy asks. 'Last Wednesday, you said. After dinner at Pete's' Lucy deadpans, not missing so much as a tick to his tock. 'That's right, that's right! Well, that's when I said it, anyway, that's when I let on. But I think I realized it a little before.' 'Get your stories straight, mate - you sure took pains to make it seem a sudden and organic realization.' 'I'm such a liar' he chuckles, snaps his fingers '*Mate*' he says, Lucy staring '*Mate* - you said.' She blinks, nods. 'Yeah - Oh I see' - she pretends like she finds this a thing of interest as much as him, something she ought be ready to explain to all loiterers who query - 'yes, I say *mate*. I'm not British or anything. I dated an Irish guy, is all. That made an impression. Mate.' This guy - sniffling, a bit of mucus he needs a tissue for but does not have one, is terrified of using his sleeve to deal with, instead - gives a knowing Mmn-mmn and a head nod. Take pity Lucy, take pity. She does - turning away as though giving a serious glance down the way she just came from, as though wondering where a friend who was supposed to be catching her up has got to. Okay - enough time, he better have dealt with it, wrist or shoulder or whatever. 'Hey, if a guy comes down this way and seems confused, tell him I got in a car, okay?' 'A car?' the guy asks, grinning like this little deception gives him a shot with her. 'Yeah. I like lying to him, confusing him, really unsettling him.' The guy nods, eyebrows positioned to Cool and I-get-it and Will-do. 'It's the fun way to make him know I don't like him, you know?' And she holds this guy's eye-contact for another five seconds. 'Oh you poor bastard - you have fun with your girlfriend tonight' Lucy thinks 'see me in your dreams, mate.'

The snow gets more impatient so Lucy takes refuge down in a subway station, joining many others just lining the wall by the pay-telephones and the two automated ticket kiosks. There isn't even an attendant booth in this station. But somebody must be employed around here, right? Why are you concerned, Lucy? Say I had a heart attack or something, a slip-and-fall! She glances around: at least there are cameras. But there must be an attendant, some booth - there always is. This is honestly unnerving her! And the more she sees how many of these people are betraying no intention of boarding a train - of even purchasing a pass - the worse it gets. Moments like this make the world seem like teeth where there shouldn't be teeth - on the palm of a hand, down an ear, a row of them clotting a vein. Should you ask someone if this is a working station? If it wasn't, wouldn't somebody be smoking? How many people are around her, exactly? She makes a sneaky estimate disguised as working out a cramp in her side. Twenty. At least. Because of snow? No - if it was rain this would be justifiable. But snow: you walk through snow as it falls - before it can accumulate! It makes no sense to wait out the snow because the snow doesn't go anywhere it only gets worse and then stays put. She is jittery. Maybe you should smoke, Lucy. Maybe that will summon an attendant. She wants to move, to peek past the turnstile, see is there evidence of anyone, but also doesn't want to betray her sense of out-of-joint. Who are these people? And why is Lucy one of them?


IN THROUGH THE DOOR, REPEATING it to herself as her steps thunk - one slipping a bit in the brackish grey-brown utterly oceaning the worthless *Caution Wet Floor* stand - because if she says it she can both try to remember the phrase and to remember 'What was I whispering?' the more cues the better. *I'm her lover the way a thundercloud is cotton.* 'Her lover. Thundercloud is cotton. As much a thunder cloud as cotton.' Are you allowed to bypass the line, Lucy? Damn it! Civic-mindedness at a time like this? 'I'm terribly sorry, can I have this pen?' The cashier seems reluctant but gives-in at Lucy's second, much-harried 'Please, may I?' But Lucy does not seem to be able to write on her hand. 'I'm your lover the same as a thunder cloud is cotton.' Napkins. Does this pen not work!? Scrape. Scrape! Scrape!! She tears a bit of a paper placemat from the trashcan - there! - gets a good blue scribble, returns to the napkin. *I'm her lover as much as a thundercloud is cotton.* Not it, exactly, but she can work with that. Now in line, churning the words around, pot simmer. Lets out several Phew breaths, as though needing to show those present she is relieved, each individually. Couldn't you have just used your phone? She never likes to do that - always feels so sure the clunkiness of having to peck the number keys over and over will lose something fundamental, sabotage the soul. *I'm her lover as much as a thundercloud is cotton*. It bugs her. But the core is there. She wins. And now orders two hamburgers as well as a milkshake she knows she doesn't want but will not tell the cashier to forget about because of how it might make her seem.

So, Lucy, what is the sentiment? What is the crux of this? *A lover the way a thundercloud is cotton.* That doesn't seem poetic enough. Yes: thunderclouds aren't cotton. Yes: thundercloud are. Grade-schooling it, are you? *Only as much as.* This always hits false. Now is no exception. The burger is delightfully overcooked, the bun day-and-a-half stale. Heavenly father, if only all food were like this! Focus. Yes, it will be a shame if the second burger is fresher - but focus. *Only as much?* No - you just dismissed that. 'I am your lover. I am her lover.' Why not *She is my lover as much as cotton is thundercloud?* Hey - that was an accident but she writes it down and it seems an utter improvement. An entirely different thought than the one she had been excited about to being with, but perhaps that is for the best. But she does not want to barge all over herself. Two more bites. Tries to chew, to savor, but it is of such perfect texture her gullet wants to swallow it, unbroken, finger long, wants to choke and have to peristalsis it down, aided by a drink of water. *She is my lover and cotton is thundercloud.* A good line, but that is straying too far. Why? 'Because that does not beg an argument' she mutters. 'This poem is a cackle - it is angry.' Is it? 'It is now' she says, plain-aloud, and those kids there are giving her the look-up-look-away-look-up-look-aways in a pattern of each other, one-by-one, two-at-a-time, one-by-one. Give it something else to start. *We live in a sealess autumn* she jots *and she is my lover only how cotton is thundercloud.* Last bite, taken without noticing, already unwrapping second burger, eyes rolling upwards and hand touching to brow.

The shit of this? Now Lucy has to do something for each of these beginnings she's tried and is obsessed with making this a repetitive klutz of a profound type of thingy, this poem. How many beginnings? Five. *We live in a sealess autumn.* And here - already this is a problem - *We are an autumnless leaf* is terrific but now it has got this damned Autumn shtick to it! Just these two, though, the other bits nothing to do with autumn. Quickly decided: one is first stanza, the other is final. 'Okay' she says, kind of feeling like she should be walking around outside, but then knows she will not have the freedom to jot at a moment's notice - outside is sloppy and flip-chill and craggy of brick. Breath. Breath. *We live in a sealess autumn and she's only my lover as cotton is thundercloud.* Circle it. One. Are these all two-line deals? Anyway - the first and last are - move to the last. *We are an autumnless leaf.* Stare. Breath. Hold. Breathe, Lucy. Breath. Stare. What? 'We are an autumnless leaf. Blah blah-blah blah blah-blah blah blah' she says, trying to groove into a rhythm. Is that the rhythm of the first bit? Does it need to be? Don't check, Lucy! Nope. Not at all the same rhythm. Does it need to be? It does now! Lucy has noticed it, thus Lucy has made it so it must be so! No - it can be the shorter rhythm. It's the end. 'If I think of something for it right now' Lucy says 'it can be the shorter rhythm.' Go. She says: 'Go.' She says: 'Go, go.' She says 'Go go-go Go go-go go go.' But nothing. Where is her food? How long ago was that?

Here's the solution - simple. First line: *I live in a sealess autumn and she's only my lover as cotton is thundercloud.* Last line: *She is an autumnless leaf.* To start. And now to end - she gestures, gestures, gestures - it will go: *whose tax is a* - something - *in the sand.* Tax? 'Yes' she insists 'tax.' Her tax? 'What does that fucking mean?' she whispers then whispers 'Shut up, Lucy - you're an idiot, leave the poetry to me, you go plumb with the Mario Brothers.' Whatever that means. 'Shut up, Lucy.' Focus. Whose tax is a blah-blah-blah in what sand? *Whose tax is a shore without sand.* Awful. *Is a grave in the sand.* Appalling. *Whose tax is a gravedigger's hand.* That's okay. Something, anyway. She takes a moment to scribble out thoroughly all of the obvious misfires, to tear the napkin and litter it in her gloppy milkshake cup - has to drink some of the lukewarm puss so there is room to deposit things - and to whit-whit-whit three more napkins from the dispenser and to recopy first verse and start-of-final. *She is an autumnless leaf and she's only my lover as gravediggers mend.* Pause. *As gravediggers end.* Looks. *As gravediggers.* A sigh of dejected bleak, she crosses this out and decides she'd better see what time it is. Only that? Fine. It's become rotten luck, remembering that bit about thunderclouds! And to think how happy you had been at first, Lucy! What a reeking buboes that remembrance turned out to be. Ooh - there: *And only my lover as plague cares for graves.* That. 'That' Lucy says. But is it That? Or are you settling on anything to give a spectral satisfaction? No, it works. Move on. Move on. Move on. *She is an autumnless leaf and only my lover as plague cares for graves.* 'Something like that' Lucy somewhats 'move on, move on.'

How long has this been going on? Time is in one of its shiver-stints. It feels more awful than it is and seems to go on for far longer. Rejoining Lucy: we find her still in midst of the poem, polishing off the center of the piece. All need has dribbled from this. All desire and necessity and stabbing and give-me is gone. She's spent it - it's spent - things are written she already does not remember and so she knows she is empty of what was there and cannot go back, this bit of her razed. What is this poem for? Usually a stupid question - as what is any poem for? But she knows this one serves a purpose. It cannot be read to or given as gift to Elliott because Elliott is too scardy-cat to recognize it as a love poem. And: because Lucy is not in love with Elliott. And: because it is not for Elliott, full stop. Well - hold on. Hold on. Lucy can easily give love poems to people she is not in love with - modus operandi, Lucy Jinx, truth told. And she can, without compunction, give poems to people they are not meant for - that is where nearly all of her poems eventually find themselves. That clarified, Lucy does know that this poem seemed meant for something. Heather? Yep - though Lucy agonizes at knowing this. You can't mean it, Lucy! You can't give this to Heather and tell her you thought it up watching her nude in some hotel room! 'Then she shouldn't have asked to see it!' What is Lucy supposed to do? Fill a jewelry box with maple syrup and wrap it in bubblegum silk? If someone wrote something like this from Lucy's nudity Lucy'd go mad with rape in her bones! Well, is that what you want, Lucy? 'What?' For Heather to react that way? Pause. No - Lucy means it'll make Heather feel troll-titted and worm-fleshed - Heather wouldn't know what to do with this! 'That is my point' Lucy says, confused. Antsy. What is she on about, here? Shit. Time to leave.

This snow has truly made the city look toothless, a grin of sore gums. How scurvy-yellow the sidewalks outside of shops look, how coffee-piss-brown the light against apartment-above-shop curtains. The inelegance has its own sort of merriment, Lucy supposes. If looked at as a game, there is a simple mechanism to this downplop - now slowed to mere flurries, adding snickering to abomination - just an inside-outing the flesh of what winter is normally. Lucy moves along, wanting to hurry but also not. She thinks she has the rest of the walk timed, except she fears her worthless discount-shop shoes will have her socks burping moist and feet tight in half-spasms if she takes that long of it. Ducking in this place or that won't help. Maybe you should just abandon ship? What are you doing? Going to see Elliott for some reason? Resigned, Lucy trudges on. She needs to resettle things - needs to make a week, two weeks of easy stability. Elliott is going to start figuring things are amiss for herself, soon - and why have her have to go through with that? Lucy ticks off what she has going for her on fingers as she sloshes. New job. Victoire. What else? You can go talk about poetry at that school! No - she doesn't lower the finger, but doesn't count this - there was something else. New job. Victoire. This poem you just wrote? Maybe you should give it to Elliott, come to think of it. Make a thing of it - call it 'A mature work' and stitch on some business about how it is a 'Poetry of exposure' or something. 'It's not so much about you, El, or about us - it's about me, something I know I need to start showing you, giving you.' That, she had just whispered. Normal voice, she tries - though panting from having picked up pace - 'I need to let you know me.' She slows. Meh. Maybe.

Coming upon an *Ace-On-The-Case Checks And Cash*, Lucy enters, nuzzling the air in front of her uncertainly. At the counter. 'If I am a member but use another location, can I do stuff here?' The attendant nods. 'You're a member?' 'I am.' 'Or you just need to cash a check? You can do that even if you're not a member.' 'I'm a member' Lucy says, getting out her Ace Card and letting the guy scan it. 'So you are' he says and asks if she would like to redeem her points. 'What are my points?' It seems *Points* are accrued that can be used to bring down the percentage taken out of a check cashed - enough points and a check can be cashed without anything taken out. Lucy had no idea, but thanks the fellow for letting her in on this. She actually just wants to put some cash on to her Debit card, though - can that be done here? 'Of course.' 'No fee or anything because I normally go to another location?' The clerk seems somewhat scandalized at the suggestion. 'No fee for putting money on. That's your money' he says, real point-of-pride to letting her know this, she can almost feel him visualizing himself patting her head, to-the-rescue. 'Well' Lucy says - adding it was a long time ago in another state - 'I belonged to some place that charged for every little thing.' 'Absolutely, you want to be sure - I wasn't blaming you for asking.' 'No, no.' 'But we aren't shady like that - that's why we got the Loyalty Points and all, keep people out of other shyster joints. Treat you right.' She's nodding - has been holding the money across - is nodding - the guy is tip tap tip tap looking at stuff on her account. 'Everything okay?' 'Your name Lucy Jinx?' Her eyes narrow. 'I'm.' Narrow more. 'Lucy Jinx - what do you mean, why?' Tip. Tap. Tip. Tap. He's nodding, tongue pinched out, squirming, between teeth and chapped lips. She says 'Everything' but before she can get to 'alright?' he shakes his head like a sneeze has passed, apologizes and says 'I just need to see your I.D., sorry.'

No. Yes. No - don't even get thinking about it. Yes - there was something about it, something went iffy there. But: no - don't even start wondering. The guy thought he recognized your address? No - because he would have asked 'You live at...?' not inquired about your name. Yes - that's right. He can't have known another Lucy Jinx. Or been another poetry fan. No. But: did he know that guy from earlier - is that it? That guy had said the name Lucy Jinx, earlier - said it to this clerk - and now it had rung a bell 'Weird, that same name'? Yes - I mean, no, but yes, that could be it. 'Your name Lucy Jinx?' Had he pronounced the surname oddly, unsureness in the delivery? No - he had said *Jinx* just like that, just like *Jinx*. Yes - but had he said it correctly, luck of the draw, yet with expression on his face of he wasn't certain? No. Lucy is certain the clerk's *Jinx* hadn't been mongoloid sounding, he hadn't been some oaf idioting about something. No. It had been recognition? Yes! It had been some phylum of Recognition! Had he, himself, recognized her? No, no. Why would he have made such a glazed over, ominous play of it? 'Your name Lucy Jinx?' 'Your name Lucy Jinx?' Lucy now not-even-mimics, just says. Lucy - simple: you are thrown off because, only early today, you were recognized by someone else. Yes! There would be nothing odd about that Check Casher's tone if not for the earlier guy knowing your name, your poetry. No. 'No, you're right' Lucy says. 'Yes, that's right.' She has been watching only the ground at her feet, looks up now, disoriented. Why? Did you need to go deposit that money there, then?

No. Don't you know: never do anything different? Yes. 'Damn it' she says. Which way from here?

'Sharon, thank Christ' Lucy says, jaw-shiver into her phone. 'Why? What's up?' 'I just need my mind someplace - anyplace. What can I do for you?' Sharon laughs, puts on a deep-purple tint of dubiousness to her tone as she says 'You can stop talking like that, for starters. Is something the matter, seriously?' But Lucy has gotten herself inside of a pet-food store, uses lower tone and makes out that it's just she is freezing because she's decided not to take the bus. 'Do you want to come over here? That's all I was calling to ask. Seriously, if not I can just hang up.' 'Come over when?' 'Now!' Lucy is about ten minutes out from where she is going to meet Elliott - but is forever away from Sharon's place and not even sure about buses from out here to there. 'I want to.' 'Oh fuck you, Lucy Goosey. I'm calling someone else. Someone cooler than you are - someone who you don't even know about and who wouldn't like your style though you'd worship theirs! That's who I'm calling.' 'You're just describing yourself!' This remark gets an affectionate - soaked damp with sarcasm - 'Aww' from Sharon, who deems it, as far as responses go, worthy of two more minutes of her exceptionally valuable, commoditized, and publically traded time. Lucy - yes, she feels herself getting a sore throat, regrets ever having made a snowball or thinking the word *Winter* in anything but the most morbid and rust-barbed tones - asks Sharon 'When you say *Your* with that silly accent you have, do you feel it ought to be spelled with a *U* or with two *Es*?' 'What accent?' 'Your impediment - your slur - whatever you like to call it. The defective way you speak.' 'Flirty flirt flirt, aren't we? What's going on with you, really? I want you over here if you're this flirty! I'll spell words however you want.' Lucy catches sight of herself in a mirror lining the wall behind some fish tanks and wonders if she actually looks as great as it seems she does or if the cold is just screwing with her perception.

Lucy has left the store with a heavy bag of a brand of cat-food she has not been able to find since moving to this city. She can hardly believe it and it takes two blocks of the bag straining her arm for her to regret the purchase. She also bought a - is it burlap? - pouch of catnip with the letters *TNT* stitched on it - or maybe it is an iron-on patch made to look stitched - and a bottle of a spray that is supposed to discourage cats from urinating, defecating, or vomiting in any area it is spritzed. The Description and Instructions use that word: *Spritz. Spritzed. Spritzing. Liberally spritz your carpeted areas with solution. Once spritzed, discourages your feline from soiling the area. When spritzing, avoid soaking any patch too thoroughly - carpet should appear glistening, not damp.* The purchases had all been a compulsion, one she has now deciphered. She needed to do something with the money she'd put on the Debit card - some of it, at least - in an entirely random place in order to make the random act of going into *Ace-On-The-Case* not seem entirely isolated, make it seem paired with something, not only connected to that attendant's odd interrogation. It's an interrogation now, Lucy? That this food turned out to be in the pet shop she'd gone into seemed a good sign - a balance of Random Places, one yielding negative result, one yielding positive. That she had been amused by the word *Spritz* seemed to even out the roughness left by the spoken words of the clerk. She had set things right. And Lucy Jinx, feline, would eat well tonight and wrestle silly-girl with cat-nip bomb! And Lucy Jinx, human, would soothe Elliott, thank her for reminding her about the state of the carpet, the rental deposit - all of that - and would sleep. And would reset. And things are balanced. Like nothing's nothing. She is nodding. Nodding. Nodding. Nodding.

THE CORRIDOR IS GREEN-TILE SMELLING, dim overhead fluorescent light - only every other rectangle turned on - giving it a community pool, an aquarium, a public-school-after-hours feel. The hum from the water fountain, the over-littered bulletin board, the stale murk of the wet mats on entrance, the heavy, milling heat from the unfiltered wall vents. Lucy. Lucy, here. On this bench, the cushion of which has been cut and sealed with duct tape in two places. Lucy perplexed. Why? See this trashcan - inside the corridor, right next to this bench? It has an ashtray on top. But clearly - she can still see it from here - on the door is the icon indicating *No Smoking*. Further examination: no sand in the ashtray, yet there are evidences of butts having been stubbed, long set-in blackness of ash, a general shabbiness suggesting use. Well, you can't smoke Lucy - you can't smoke in here. Leans back and stretches legs out in front of her. A cough emanates from somewhere. A crinkle like a plastic bag being rummaged through. No signs of life. But the building is not empty. For example: just at the end of this corridor, behind a blue painted door, is Elliott's writing group. And behind each of these other doors some other group, some evening classes, some workshops, some somethings. The ring tone of a telephone - did you recognize that song, Lucy? kind of? or just recognize it as a ring tone? - and a voice answering, laughing immediately. See? Just around that corner: life. Now being able to hear the one side of the conversation is an irritation. She spits. No one will notice. Footprints piled on footprints, some stained, some dirt-based, some slush melting. The floor is a mess with haphazard footprints in mishmash.

What sort of things are Elliott writing these days? Lucy, you could be sitting in there listening if you're so curious. That would make Elliott anxious, it would make her self-conscious - she'd appreciate the gesture, initially, and then, over the course of the hour-and-a-half or however long, she would come to find Lucy's presence oppressive. Elliott has never asked you to attend these sessions. Elliott regales you with the ins-and-outs, you know the names of these other writers-so-called whom you have never set eyes on and likely never will, you criticize them based on Elliott's prompts - even taking the lead sometimes - and Elliott digs all of that - but she has never asked you to be here, Lucy. Likely: that's why you haven't gone in. Even to nod your Hello. To let Elliot know you are waiting out here is the same as you being in the room, smiling unsolicited as she reads and takes remarks. Why are you here? Elliott would say that. Elliott would keep a happy tone and a glad-to-see-you, a what-a-surprise face but would mean the face like 'What are you doing here?' Lucy, you don't belong here. Don't you think if you were wanted an invitation would have been extended, at least once, before now? Think. You linger outside in this corridor in a building you are grotesquely purposeless in - why are you here? Do you want to know what Elliott is writing? Has Elliott ever asked you to look at something, in progress? Lucy sets her features stern. Wait. Has Elliott done so? 'No' Lucy says, standing, head going clogged, moving to the door, getting cigarettes out. No. Exactly! Elliott gives you finished pieces. Lets you see things crafted and commented on and pawed at by these others whose names you know and whose faces you don't - these might-as-well-be-made-believes see what they see and Elliott shows you what you see, what she wants.

Now: Lucy in the corridor of the floor above the main - standing, it could be, maybe even exactly above the room where Elliott could be, even then, reading. Feeling like a space where there used to be a tooth, no memory of how long it has been gone. The window at the corridor end is open so Lucy allows herself an indoor cigarette. Down there: young man annoyed at his bicycle lock. Or at his cold hands unable to work it. A toddler tramp to how he eventually climbs on the machine, starts to ride, decides to get off and walk the thing awhile, the courtyard too much a slop. Well before being through, Lucy sees herself discarding her cigarette - flick, spin, wind-took, lost-from-sight - out the window, winces, starts to take out another, but instead just grumbles away. Her plan: act like she has just arrived as Elliott's thing lets out. 'I needed this cat-food' she slightly lifts the bag now as she rehearses this scene 'and when I saw how near the only store with it was to you, figured I would come by.' How would this be recieved? No. Grim. A creep up Lucy's back, her shoulders feeling long-sweated and itchy. She can picture Elliott coming out of the door, in conversation with someone - is this a jealous tinge? are you angry, Lucy? - standing close together, papers held, remarking something, nose-to-nose, shoulders casually touching as they move down the corridor, not even noticing Lucy until Lucy says Hi. And there it will be. That look. Caught. Immediately turned to curious - but caught, a flash of caught, first. The air will change. The introduction to whoever-that-is will seem offhand but will show slight touches of being truncated. That person, they will linger just a breath too long, walk just a beat too slow as they exit. 'Did you have plans?' Lucy will say - will she be able to hide the aggression, disguise it as innocent sorry-I-know-I'm-butting in? - and Elliott will say 'No.' 'Oh no?' Lucy will try to be so very affectionately casual 'Why don't you have plans?' And Elliott will shrug, adjust her bag or something, and will say, no eye-contact 'I thought you'd be at home - aren't you tired?' Lucy can hear Elliott asking that. And Lucy knows what it means.

In fact: this is why Lucy came. In fact: it is her medicine-headedness of late, her always-fatigue that has put her thoughts off on herself. In fact: isn't this the impression you've been getting, for some time now? In fact: isn't this why Lucy has been feeling away from Elliott? In fact: isn't it just Lucy's commonplace guilt-laden persona, her complex of everything-is-my-doing that has made her feel in a place to do penance, today? In fact: Lucy knows where Lucy is, every minute, but listens to Elliot say Elliott's wherever. In fact: right? In fact: take this morning - Elliott had been so half-hearted in her squeaky little 'I'm getting another job, too.' In fact: Are you, Elliott? Are you? In fact: Had Elliott even slightly protested to Lucy's self-sacrificial 'Don't do that - you have your gig blah blah blah?' In fact: No. In fact: What do you do all day, all night, Elliott? In fact: Well, what? In fact: Hasn't Lucy had every right to wonder this for such a long time, but not - buried it, put it off to her being a bully, tried to make sure that Elliott is left to her freedom, her writing, her time to herself? In fact: Yes. In fact: Goddamn it, Lucy is a fool. In fact: But Lucy will not be treated like one. In fact: that time Elliott had leafed through Lucy's notebook and had asked 'Who are these women?' - what was that about? In fact: thinking back honestly, it was evident Elliott was lingering on phrases, looking for something, though trying to make the page turning casual. In fact: it had been searching, suspicious. In fact: can't every moment of Lucy's time be accounted for - work, transit, time-with-Elliot? In fact: other than the brief time she says 'I'm out with Deb' or 'I'm with someone else I know.' In fact: But Lucy has introduced these people, at least once, to Elliott - Deb, Sharon, whomever. In fact: But Elliott never shares. In fact: Because she knows Lucy won't ask? In fact: Yes.

All of this was while pacing in the restroom - single occupancy, door locked. Lucy comes out into the corridor, now. There is a frayed knot of nausea all the way into the curl of her throat, a pepper-sour waxiness to her forehead and her under-arms. Fever? Maybe. But fever does not discount logic! And the facts stand that Lucy has wound herself up here and now has no reason to slink away. Let facts speak for facts - let Lucy verify. She is always quick to admit if she is in the wrong, especially about some assumption. But Lucy, you cannot go back from a period of suspecting only to learn - eventually, suddenly, not-on-your-own-terms - how correct you were to suspect. That cannot happen, anymore. So Lucy moves down to the main floor of the building and takes sentry where she imagines she had earlier heard that telephone ring, that one-side-of-some-blather that had shook her from her lazy waiting. It is rather evident - who can disagree, who? - that all of that conspired to keep her from being witnessed, from catching out Elliott in an environment she would have no grounds to voice her concerns in, from which Elliott could escape, lucky-me, and know to be more careful. Because of course Elliott would suspect Lucy was there for some reason. And if there was a reason, she would just assume Lucy had sniffed it out and would double-down to keep Lucy off the scent, going forward. A flash: Elliott, all out-of-the-blue, inviting Lucy to hang around with this or that person, inviting this-or-that person over, muddying the waters, dare-deviling her secret liaison right under Lucy's nose, baiting her to make some accusation, writing herself excuses to say 'Is something wrong - you're acting odd around me lately?' 'Am I?' Lucy would retort. And be forced into retreat. To apology. Or into action as though she was the transgressor - her retaliation recast as aggression.

There is Elliot. Exiting the room alone, coat slung over her arm, scarf over shoulders but not wrapped, backpack limp and almost-off her left shoulder. Elliott lingers. Lucy can see this from where she is positioned now, out in front of the building - her coat muffled around her, collar up, stood in profile, unrecognizable through the reflections on the glass if inside. Elliott lingers and other members of her peer group exit - she gave a general nod to those two young women, who are now approaching Lucy, but only did so because one of them touched her shoulder and delivered an in-motion remark and a gesture that seemed enthusiastic though non-intrusively so. Elliott lingers, sets her backpack down, leans to the wall, and takes a tin of breath-mints from her still slung-over-arm coat-pocket - or two mints, Elliott always takes two mints - returns the tin and slides down to the floor, knees up for a second, then legs out in front, then quickly knees up again when a few more people come out of the room. 'Who are you waiting for?' Lucy thinks, breathing grey to the window glass, obscuring her view, watching her view reform, no change to Elliott's position. That young man? Elliott seems pleasant and responsive to his over-acted mannerisms, whatever it is he is pantomiming. No. The young man exits stage-left while Elliot does nothing but wrap her scarf once around and stays seated. How about this woman? She looks like you doesn't she, Lucy? Does she? Lucy has forehead to glass, thumb-knuckle rubbing up into one nostril. Elliott stands and the two of them chit-chat - nothing of gravity, it seems - and then a man joins that woman and those two head off while Elliott gets into her coat.

Backpack up. Looks right in Lucy's direction then back down at herself, pulling telephone out of pocket - looking at screen, lingering look, intent bump to brow and lips piled. Meanwhile: time for Lucy to move away. To wait. But to wait differently.

Lucy almost doesn't notice - over the rattatat and skirshes of the street, the crisp static of her bag, her labored breathing to keep up Elliott's pace, and the dull-thudness caused by the tromp of her feet rumbled-up through her body, clothing shifting shift-shift over her skin - that her telephone is vibrating. Wait - is it Elliott calling her? Elliott has her phone out - Lucy had just seen her dial - and to her ear. 'Hello?' 'Hiya.' 'Hey, beauts.' 'You aren't sleeping?' Ah - that is the first question, because of course it is, eh? 'Naw - actually, I passed out a bit, yeah, but I'm out to get cat-food.' 'Don't we have cat-food?' Lucy explains how Elliott had been totally right about needing to be better about Lucy Jinx's diet, so had gone out to the one store around that had this certain food she used to give the cat, keep his insides regulated proper. 'I didn't mean anything, Jazzy' - Lucy's least favorite, most not-understood petname given her by Elliott, cringes at hearing it every time - 'and Jinx can have all the lunch meat she wants. Anyone who has a problem with her shit stains can take our deposit and go fuck themselves silly with it, seriously.' Lucy chuckles. Elliott is heading up the stairs to the outdoor Metro-station, there - what do you do about this Lucy? 'Well aren't we cute - both apologizing after our tiff.' 'It wasn't a tiff' Elliott says and then calls herself a crab, a gremlin, a dolt, and a pinhead. 'You're more a dunce than a dolt' Lucy genuinely warms as she says, immediately purr-toning 'How did your thing go, tonight?' 'The same' Elliot nose-sighs and the connection goes crackle from it 'the same the same - le sigh.' Lucy chuckles - wonders does the connection crackle for Elliott - then starts up the stairs to the station, slowly, abundant caution necessary as, easily, Elliott could have to double back for something, catch Lucy out, or Elliott could have not moved very far down the platform, see Lucy as Lucy ascends. 'Le sigh, le sigh' Lucy repeats as she slows, unsure, halts, starts up again 'I totally understand.'

Obviously, Lucy is starting to feel idiotic - not bad, not unjustified, just idiotic. Here she is: the train compartment next over from Elliott. There is Elliott, dutifully looking over her papers, likely railing against but beginning to relent to the notes she'd taken from her peers' comments. Here is Lucy: watching Elliott as though Elliott is going anywhere other than home. Meantime - good thinking, Lucy - taking the receipt out of the pet-store bag. Yep. Address right on it. Little panic of 'Anything else?' No. Nothing else. Elliott has tilted her head to the train window, seems to hold it there, hold it there - is she asleep? Lucy moves from the compartment-door window to have a seat, herself. Her resolve? Wilted. But don't let it tumble, entire! Jesus, Lucy - you have committed yourself to this much suspicion, you have to see it through! So, Elliott is heading home - or so it seems - but we have learned, however, that she had a text-message waiting on her phone when she got out of the group. So what? 'So what?' Lucy mumbles. So check her damn phone - what was that message? 'What could it have been?' What could it have been!? Oh I don't know - a message like *I can't make it, so sorry - fuck I miss you* or *Sorry I wasn't there, I couldn't slip out, but I tried and I'll make it up to you* or anything like that. What? A message from whoever she usually meets! The cause for this glumness she's exhibiting! Aren't the likely imbecilic remarks from her half-wit peers she is in the car - there, just there - reading over what likely caused this glumness? Sure - Lucy chuckles mean-spirited - on top of that fact that whoever-it-was had not been there to listen to the story! A story likely written for whoever-they-were, that much is clear. And now - oh poor poor Elliott - Elliot is having to wonder if it was for the best that whoever-they-are had not made it, if maybe these dumbfuck comments were right, if she would have embarrassed herself in from of her erudite paramour! Back to the window. There is Elliott. Now facing profile - pouring over those page, once more.

Because it cannot be avoided how suspicious this is. Elliott walking ahead, stopping in at the drug store, slapping fresh pack of cigarettes to palm when she exits, shooting off Lucy this text *I'm almost home - you back yet?* and now trundling on. But no hurry, no hurry. Stopping entire to read Lucy's reply *Had to make one stop, but be there is twenty minutes or so. Let's go dancing or take a shower together or something, okay?* See? Elliott read that but then walked another five minutes before stopping to text - just down at the apartment entrance-door, Lucy watching from way over here - *I will be waiting. Let's go to bed untoweled. Fuck it, right?* See what, Lucy - see what exactly? See: of all nights, this night - this time, not any other time - Elliott goes to her group and then comes home, straight after. 'This time' meaning what? 'The time I am there to see!' Has Elliott never come home, right after? Well - it has to be granted - Lucy does have a point, there! No, in fact. Peer Group Night is Elliott's night - always out after, often home late. Hell, that is why, whenever possible, Lucy arranges her hotel stints for those days. But now, of all nights, there Elliott is, finishing a ciggy and heading upstairs to unclothe and wait for Lucy to join her. It is suspicious. Yes, we admit that Lucy - it is. 'Or it's odd' Lucy whispers, now knowing Elliott is up there causing her to relent, a trifle, in the industriousness of her accusations. 'It is odd' she nods, concurring. Ask to read the story? Head tilts, considering. It's elegant, that plan. Kind of perfect. Goes with the whole apology thing. 'Hey, you seem crumby' - say it right after the shower - 'I want to read it, what you wrote, what you read tonight.' How would that play? 'Tent her to the quick' Lucy smiles. Closes her eyes. Scoffs a wet breath down her nose meaning 'Isn't enough of this enough?'

'I mean, who even cares?' she says, looking up at the apartment where it seems, as always, to be bowlegged and humpbacked.

Lucy - yes, a good idea, little Jane Paranoiac - takes a moment to erase any record of odd numbers from her own phone as she slugs up the stairwell. Inquiry: doesn't this action prove that even if Elliott did erase messages, they might not be indicative of anything untoward? Response: What? How do we reach that conclusion? What chop-logical numbskull would so consider? Lucy is erasing *Suspicious* entries in her immediately visible phone record. *Suspicious*. She is not erasing messages from Elliott, for example. Or calls to-and-from work. Or various innocuous messages. Or even messages to Layla - and those could always be given the raised-eyebrow, content-wise, yes? regardless of how well and often Layla has been mentioned and explained - those are all being left. On the other side of things: Elliott got a message just tonight, coming out of her group. If Lucy's messages to Elliott are still on Elliott's phone but no messages from just before them, it is proof this mysterious message was erased due to content. Inquiry: What if your messages - even the most recent - are gone, too? What if the message record is totally blank? Response: Well, that is just self-evident, isn't it? Who on Earth does that!? Counter: Lucy does that. Response-to-Counter: From time-to-time. Counter-to-Response-to-Counter: Regularly. Redirect: But tonight, of all nights? Within twenty minutes of my texting her? Assent: Fine! Lucy stops, shoots Elliott a text now. *Start the fucking water - be inside - I want to find you there.* Not thirty seconds and Elliot responds with *Ha. Okay - how far are you out?* Lucy writes: *Imminent. Don't cross me, El, you're in trouble enough as it is!!!!* No reply? Lucy lights a smoke - why no response? - as her phone vibrates. Elliott has sent a photo of herself - nude - under it the text *I don't want to waste our tiddly amount of hot water. I'll hop in when I hear the door. Haha - took three tries to get a good angle!* then a wink face with tongue out - semi-colon uppercase *P*. Taking a drag from her cigarette, Lucy puff-hisses a percussive exhale. Lucy - look at Elliott. Look at her. She took multiple photos, wanting to send you a flattering one. Stop this. You need to respond - and positively. Text back an exclamation point - three, four exclamation points. Look at Elliott, Lucy. There she is. Waiting. A giddy, waiting, good-girl. So stop it, okay? Okay? Just stop it. Lucy - okay?


LUCY AND ELLIOT LAY, POST-COITAL, listening restfully to the argument taking place in the apartment above them. 'It's not up to me - your sister has to pay this! I'm fucking serious.' That is one of the male voices. Elliott repeats it - mock-masculine, caricature - and while she does, as she always does, traces her fingers through the rough of Lucy's pubic-hair - caress, caress - absentminded strokes with one finger, with two, with a slow trill of three. Lucy can smell her own body odor, decipher it from its mix-in with Elliott's. Upstairs, another of the male voices is, harder to hear, saying 'If you told her that, why did you tell her that? You have to tell her different.' Lucy and Elliott giggle as the woman - she'd been quiet for awhile now, obviously this explosion a long-brewing one - breathlessly ejaculates 'You said we had the fucking money so don't pretend you don't because now you forgot my fucking sister! She's my sister. And what the fuck do you' - referring to one of the two men, or maybe to another, silent, member of the show - 'have to do with it? Why are you even here!?' It carries on up there. Elliot tip-taps a finger on Lucy's belly button then returns fingers to Lucy's pubes - Lucy feels the skin under the hair irritated but rather likes how Elliot pets her, doesn't want to say something that might make her think she oughtn't to, in future - and pretend aggressives, whisper-sized 'What are you doing here?' to Lucy. 'What are you doing here?' Lucy snoots back as some clustering bang-bang of feet moving around, loud, softening, the arguers moving to another area of their apartment thunder-grumbles above her. 'What do you think they look like?' Lucy asks, very absently, and Elliott doesn't answer but does kiss the thick skin over Lucy's left hip, sniffling, gently also rubbing her nose, there.

'How did it really go, today?' Lucy, returning from the toilet, asks Elliott, who is pulling on her thick orange socks, Lucy leaning to pull off a raggedy Band-aid that has gotten stuck to the bottom of one. 'Whose is that?' Elliott asks, face made hideous at the sight of the thing. 'This is true' Lucy thinks but does not say then does say 'You're right. Do we even have Band-aids in this house?' 'This is a house now?' Elliott's eyes make giant, ludicrous question marks. 'Oh I've lived in houses before, Smelliot - just because you haven't.' Don't always remind me of how low I've been brought to hovel here with you.' Elliott makes some non-verbal indication of I-approve-your-quip while meticulously going over her socks for signs of other horrors. 'But really' Lucy gets a random T-shirt from the floor on over her head, trouble getting her left arm through that hole 'how did it go, today?' 'How did what go?' 'Tonight, I mean' - Lucy is distracted, looking for her panties, remembers she'd undressed in the kitchen while having some grape-juice and looking at the mail before joining Elliott in the shower - 'at your reading.' Elliot stops with the socks. She is looking at Lucy in a highly particular way - her one knee is up, her wrist draped over it, her front teeth pressing on the wrist, her pinky-finger twitching in some odd rhythm. 'Why are you asking?' Don't let on you remark anything in her tone or how she is positioned, Lucy, keep it inconsequential but sincere sounding. 'You seemed in a mood.' 'In a mood?' Elliott makes a face clearly meant to ask if Lucy meant recently - recently as in 'while showering or fucking or laying pleasantly, listening to the neighbors go at it?' 'When we talked on the phone' Lucy says after letting Elliott's look loiter its stay. 'And you still kind of do. I can just kind of tell.'

Now Lucy is in the position of having a glut of information to decode. She had Elliot have moved - no more clothed than they were when the conversation began - into the kitchen where Elliot is preparing one of her sandwiches and Lucy is eating some sugar cereal straight from the box. Since the bed, Elliott has been, in detail, at length, explaining some of her current reservations as to her talent as a writer, her anxieties about the worthwhileness of the group analysis - 'It seems some weird personality club, though I could just be being sensitive - but I've noticed, though, over time, drifts, teams forming, things homogenizing with me left out, the odd lump' - and how she's been spending a lot of time thinking of just stopping it, half-convinced she is one of those idiots 'Who isn't a writer but who thinks people who aren't writers can learn to be them by processes and making pals with people.' Obviously Lucy cannot give Elliott her ill impressions of all of the slime-balls, the obvious-talentlesses she saw leaving the room - and obviously she cannot point out how it doesn't speak well of Elliott to even lump herself in with that lot. What Elliott is saying seems actual - it seems like maybe this is intimacy, truth being shared - but Lucy has to allow in that they'd just had sex for the first time in almost two months so all should be viewed through that aperture: the talk could be accidental, chemical based, Lucy's finding it non-evasive, Lucy's not-questioning-it could be effect to the causal numb I-don't-care of orgasm, the rolling rise of coming sleep. 'Can I read what you wrote?' Elliott shakes her head. Lucy moves in, shoulders arched away, fingertips touching Elliott's hip skin, their bellies just-oh-so-gently brushing. 'Let me read it, okay?' Elliott won't look up, is pushing her tongue into her cheek hard, Lucy hearing the squish of Elliott's teeth chewing the prickly wet one-two-three one-two-three.

The result: a lousy story. That is all. What's it about, Lucy? What was it about!? It was about a woman who finds a package, just left out randomly in the grass, with the return address impossible to read. She takes it home, leaves it on the counter. Over the course of a few days, the woman hears a telephone ringing inside of the package. Eventually, the woman opens the package and discovers and examines the phone - which is the only thing in there. Even as the woman meticulously regards the thing, it rings, so she answers - thinking to explain the situation to the whoever-it-is-calling. But the woman - named Quinn, by the way, fucking *Quinn* is what Elliott named this woman! - discovers the caller is speaking a language she doesn't at all understand. So after the call terminates, the woman thinks to send a text-message to the number that just called, this message aimed at explaining just what is going on. But here, the woman notices that all of the text-messages on the phone are - of course, though Elliot writes the woman as 'startled to discover' this - in this other language - or in some other language, though Elliott, narratively, does write 'the very same strange language the voice had been speaking in, quick and drawling, tuning-fork then well-hollow.' So the woman next makes an effort to look up some of the words, thinking to compose her message in the same language - with computer aid, of course, just very simple phrases - only to discover that none of the words are real - this the woman 'over-verifies, increasingly alarmed, as not a single word from more than twenty messages registers in any online translator or yields linguistic results from any Search Engine.' Meanwhile - this needs to be mentioned, the story being thirty pages long, double spaced, this needs to be known - there is another narrative thread going, this one of Quinn - gah, *Quinn*! - starting up a relationship with a man who teachers piano in the same building where Quinn's office job is located - 'office job' is a phrase that is used fifteen times between five hundred words, by the way. Anyway: eventually Quinn sends a message on the found-phone, in English, telling the recipient that she will be at such-and-such a café at this-certain-time and to please meet to retrieve this phone - why this plan makes any sense is beyond Lucy's capacity as an analytic reader, but Quinn does not even poke holes in it, does not seem fleetingly interested in entertaining the nonsensical nature of it, despite the abundance of nuanced thought good ol' Quinn gives to all other aspects of the phone. And then on the day she is waiting in the arranged place - well! What is this!? - the man she has been seeing shows up. Quinn first thinks it is coincidence - which, yes, is the name of the piece, *Coincidence*, Heaven forfend our forgetting that! - but the man seems perplexed, says 'No, you asked me to meet you.' And he shows her a text-message, evidently sent from Quinn's phone. And it was sent at the same time she sent the message to the other phone but is nothing like the same words - just a simple message asking the man to meet her. The End.

Lucy is almost annoyed at how nothing there is to interpolate from this. At a stretch, she could cobble up something to feel is revealed, some betrayal of whatever is going on with Elliott she let slip in, but frankly the writing - the prose itself - is so unctuous she can hardly make herself focus on rereading little bits to give praise to, let alone work herself up into a lather of suspicion, ferreting subtextual clues in the syntax, the specificity of adjective choice et cetera. Elliott had given up seeming timid and by now - Elliott knows Lucy is coming to the end of the story and Lucy knows Elliott knows - has taken up an almost flippant posture, seated in Lucy's desk chair, while Lucy is laid out on the sofa. Throughout the read, Lucy has been saying things - using the notes in Elliott's own handwriting but attributed to certain of her peers - to seem engaged. Example: 'This Veronica has no idea what she's talking about - did she actually say *ambiance*? I think she meant *atmosphere'* to which Elliott had considerately responded, admitting she was not sure if Veronica had said *ambiance* or not. 'Anyway: the remark is off-base - so we'll assume she used the wrong word, too.' This sort of thing is likely why Elliott is more bucked up, now. How to interpret that, though? Could be: Elliott is glad that Lucy, specifically, is finding positive things to say - that Lucy, Elliott's lover, appreciates the story - as in to say that Lucy liking it, valuing it, is of tantamount importance to Elliott. Also could be: Elliott is just bucked up, generally, at having any voice say nice things after the pecking-party these comments littered throughout every free spec of margin - top, bottom, side, and side - indicate. Or could easily be: Elliott is using Lucy's defense as what whoever-it-was-Elliott-had-been-wishing-had-been-there-but-hadn't-been would have said, that Elliott's currently sleek, definite, self-possessed demeanor over in Lucy's chair is meant for that person, is daydreamed in their direction - all Lucy's comments just kindling up licks of flame, redoubling desire to learn what this other party would have to say when they finally got together.

As it would be uncharacteristic of Lucy to give nothing but praise and defense, the following conversation does take place, back in bed, Lucy joke-pretending to find Band-aids in Elliott's hair, on her ass after she's been under the covers awhile, in her armpit, and so on, Elliot pinching Lucy or threatening to flick her breasts through her shirt - Elliot's common flirt-threat - if she doesn't knock it off. 'It should not end with the girl' - Lucy will not say the word *Quinn* - 'being surprised that the man shows up.' 'Why not?' 'She shouldn't be confused the whole way through - not start-to-end.' 'No?' 'I was reading it, right? I was with her doing the tick-by-tock investigation. I had my questions - sometimes the same ones she had, sometimes others - but I was with her.' Elliott chews on the fabric of Lucy's shirt shoulder, making Mmn-hmn sounds as Lucy proceeds. 'So when the guy shows up and she is confused, I think it doesn't deepen any mystery - because my position, as reader, has not changed. Because her position has not changed. The guy should show up' - Elliot bites Lucy's earlobes a little nip, hardly felt - 'and he, the guy, should look harried or something. The girl' - 'Her name is *Quinn*' Elliot says, kissing the moist spot of Lucy's shirt, snuggling next to her - 'yeah yeah. The girl, she should perk up and raise a hand like she was expecting the guy and the guy should be confused.' Elliott is rubbing her feet-in-socks both over one of Lucy's feet-not-in-socks. 'It should be clear the guy does not understand why he has been summoned and I - the reader - should flit to his confusion, siding with him now, the girl seeming foreign because the girl is now acting like she had been waiting for him when I know she wasn't.' 'I love you' Elliot says - Lucy marks the tone, the timbre, the when-is-the-last-time Elliott said this?, the Elliott-has-never-said-this of the words - and hooks two fingers around Lucy's panties just at the bulb of her hip. 'But do you see why the story would be better? That's the thing here, right?' Elliott kneads middle-fingertip inside the panty fabric to thumbtip outside and nuzzles her nose to Lucy's biceps, giggles a sound like a half-said 'Yes, ma'am.'

Somewhere here, both Lucy and Elliot fell asleep. Their bodies, per usual, asleep moved away from each other. Nothing to sleuth out from this, both are just hyper-particular sleepers - Elliott needs that pose and her legs wrapped-around-pillow-and-bunched-sheet, Lucy needs to be very close to the edge of the bed, legs in the shape, more-or-less, of the number Four, only one shoulder covered by blanket, pillow faced so that the open side of its pillowcase is pointing toward Elliot. Lucy had a brief dream like this: Elliott had gotten up to fiddle with some device, like a thermostat but not a thermostat - not anything real - on the wall, had gotten annoyed, pounded it, Lucy asking her, groggy, if those men were still downstairs with the flags, Elliott banging and telling Lucy 'That's what I'm trying to see!' Lucy had popped awake. Or grimed awake, maybe. Or, maybe best to say, she had stained awake, as that is what she felt like, a stain that had started small on something and spread over time - she feels flat in the dark, a sullied piece of it but still it, dimensionless except for the sensation of seeping, expanding, becoming a larger smear as her thickness diminishes. When she wakes up again, she realizes that Elliott had not been sitting up in the bed, looking down at her - that is what had just startled her, Elliott doing that, but it must have been part of another dream. Now Lucy writhes in the desire not to go urinate. Mostly because if she stands she does not want to come back to bed - but if Elliott hears her using the toilet, flushing, opening the door, but then she does not come back to bed, well Elliott will come out and join her, the purpose of staying awake beaten dead.

There is the sign for *Zilch's*. Why aren't the streetlights on? It took Lucy a moment to realize what was off with the image. The lights across the street are on but none of the lampposts she can see on the same side as *Zilch's* are lit. She pointedly drags on her cigarette, as though making the orange glow of it violent can correct this aesthetic infraction. Turns out she just makes herself cough and sneeze at the same time - too much smoke down her lung without preparation, sneaky slip of smoke up her nostril causing her to shiver and her brain to prickle, haywire, achoo! Lucy looks at the things she has taped up on the wall in front of her desk. What are these things? They seem like they might as well belong to someone else - though it can be said, more and more, that everything she has seems that way. A symptom of continuing to age? At a certain point, she thinks, the mind stops seeing The Lucy Right Now as Lucy - the mind has chosen the Lucy Of Sometime Previous as the Lucy Proper, the template from which things started to deviate, mishap, unbelong. 'When was I Lucy, then?' she asks the postcard photograph of the poster for a movie called *Tenebrae*. She pretends the postcard says 'I'm not talking to you - you haven't even seen *Tenebrae*!' 'Oh yes I have' she says, knowing she hasn't, then asks the notebook paper with a doodle Elliott had done, one day - Elliott had taped this up, not Lucy - 'When was I Lucy, then?' She makes the doodle say 'I thought you'd always been Lucy - but that's because I've only known you awhile - what else will I think you are?' She looks down, trying to find the cat, to ask it 'When was I Lucy, then?' But the cat isn't there. Still, she pretends it says something funny and she chuckles and tells it 'Fuck off.'

Why did you look? Lucy! Is this why you woke up? Defensively: 'Maybe it is! Part of me knew not to let this pass - and now we see!' Come on, Lucy - why did you look? 'Doesn't matter.' Elliott's phone. Middle-of-the-after-fuck-after-story-after-I-love-you-night: Elliott's phone. Calmly: What about it, Lucy? What about it? 'What about it?' she says, chewing the side of her fourth finger, getting a nibble of dead skin off that she chews with odd precision, keeping it pinned a hump over the top of just her left-bottom front tooth, teeth above eye-lash-light tapping it, not-quite-chattering-fast. 'There are my messages' - Lucy thinks, just barely not muttering the words. 'Then, the one right before mine is more than a week old! Sent more than a week ago from whoever's number that is' - Lucy will figure that out later, rest assured! - and below in the list are more of Lucy's messages, that number, this number - a few more from this same number-in-question - nothing to them! Calmly: Seriously, Lucy - what about it? 'Look at that message! From a week ago from whoever: *haha and she still got there late!? She knows she's being fired, right? Hahaha* Lucy. Lucy. 'What!? Are we to believe this is the message Elliott had been reading, reacting to, staring down at so knitted and concerned?' Lucy explains to all gathered how she is even trying to give Elliott the benefit of every single doubt she can dubious up - anything! 'But look: Elliott's phone is a piece of crap - it doesn't get e-mail, it can't do anything' - Lucy says these words 'Do anything' in a sarcastic spit-bubble-pop hushing-aloud - 'and' - this is the absolute proof of Lucy's generosity of investigative spirit - 'there are no records of Sent messages except those to Lucy, this evening, and no drafted messages where maybe Elliott had jotted something down to remember, been reading back over!' Well - hold on - she still could have been doing that! 'After she'd been sitting in a fucking writing group? In a room with pen and paper out! She made some notes into the Draft folder of her cheap telephone!?' Lucy can't believe anyone could even suggest that as an interpretation, as a chance-in-a-million, even! Scoffs so harshly her mouth fills with phlegm she pushes noisily through cooed lips into that green cup in the sink basin.

Lucy, from the bedroom door, listens to Elliott breathing. Listens. Lucy removes her clothing and tosses it, wherever, into the messy dark of the room. Immediately, her skin tightening, goose pimples everywhere. She caresses herself to enjoy the sensation, though soon is annoyed because her nipples - sore from teeth and still laced with settled-in sweat - begin to feel irritated, sharp, stung, and any touch she gives to them is raw, causes the base of her neck to tense, the muscles in tangles, creaking like the bough of a ghost ship. She climbs into bed and, lovey-dove, lumps her almost-nude body into a cuddle hard up against Elliott's nude-except-for-socks one, burying her nose in Elliot's hair, tightening to resist pulling away from the discomfort of some of the hair getting up in her nose and the stab of a strand of it had stuck her eye palpably, singed her, winced her shut fast. Elliott - Lucy knows she is awake, fakery, fakery - reacts with a warm wiggle, making grherm and hrrigh sounds of comfy-cozy, of I'm-asleep-but-know-your-touch, still. Lucy traces the knuckle of her thumb up along the side of Elliot's thigh, back down, back up, puckers her lips and pecks her head forward by straining her neck, placing a dry, formless kiss into the hair and the scent of recently perspired scalp. 'Are you awake?' Elliott - why the game, why the pretend? - does not answer, except another sleepy sound, gravel in bottom of nose breath, a portion of a generic sound-effect snore. Lucy sniffles, makes dry suction sounds of wetting her mouth, repositions her head on the skin of Elliot's arm-side, giving a drool-thick kiss, the saliva breathy at issuance but almost immediately after seeming fever-brow cold, then holds mouth just above the skin, slowing her tongue to it, not letting the tongue shrink back from the pinch of saline it tastes. Lucy has a thought that the salt is how freckles taste, is almost annoyed by how pleasant, how sweet that thought seems. 'Are you awake?' Same playtime sound and now a phony leg twitch, a miniscule shuffle of pelvis forward, ass back-and-a-bit-to-the-side. 'If you were awake, you'd hear me say *I love you*. Are you awake, now?' No movement. No sound. No response. But that isn't sleep breathing - Lucy knows all the sounds of fake. 'I love you' Lucy says. Stares at the silenced dark - the dark that only sounds like not-asleep breathing. Lucy's and Elliott's. That is how it is, a full two minutes. Then it's Lucy moving from Elliott to take the shape Lucy sleeps in every night, again.

# .II.

LUCY WAS IN THE BOOTH, second from the end. This one caught the most illumination from the parking lot lights, was really the only tabletop lit. Her notebook spread open, when she wrote it would be through thick shadows of her hand and of the pen itself moving. No matter if she sat on this side of the booth or that. Something about the light's angle made dense murk of her shadow - she could not even see the words as she wrote them, which gave the whole endeavor of setting things down a dream-world quality, it was a gimbal as like playing make-believe of writing only to have the make-believe made actuality in the end. A magic wand tapped the empty pretend, it yawned, blinked around, then it danced or it went back to bed. There are her words. She reads them, forgets them - they are there though they are not. Of course Lucy had the option of sitting all manner of places, the shop being closed - she could not turn on the lights in the front, true, but in the back area, in the office she could be perfectly lit up. Also, she could bring her computer, the glow of its screen eliminating any concern or effect of shadow. But the booth was where she wanted to be. The always sooty windows - most nights she had worked also dribbling rain-streaks, these shadows freckling her and her paper in a million places, some of the shadows seeming to cast second shadows their own, afraid of the dark and willing themselves into their own company. If she could get enough light at the counter she would station there. In fact, she had tried: by turning on just the dim lighting inside the cake display the counter was bright enough she could work, not so bright as to give any impression that the joint was open, attractive it to the midnight-to-four-am vagrant crowd. This was one of Clarke's concerns - and it seemed aimed at her safety. She doesn't get it. But the booth. The booth, either way.

Now - her head is humming electric agitation, the good kind, the sound of something broken just about to start working right again if long enough is waited or a palm is struck, just so, to chug-chug the mechanism stable - Lucy paces the dining area. And loops back behind the counter. And sits there. Still. A kind of loop of its own, this, inside of the other, an extra around of a shoelace. She looks at the paper sign - see it there - above the sink, oh it always so fascinates her. Try to describe it, Lucy. From a distance, due to the way the slight light catches its textures, it seems a cloth, a rough, craggy cloth that is taped to the tile, that the words instructing *Wash Hands. Twice. Thank you.* are penned on to wrinkled fabric - almost seems like the wrinkles themselves, through odd chance, have formed avenues, fingerprint whorls the shadows of which only almost make the shapes of these letters. Dreamscape, corner of one's vision. But: this is a plain piece of paper - ordinary stock, taken from the office, out of the printer, ages ago, affixed to the tile. Over - it has to be years, years and years - years of being posted it has gotten spitter-spatted with mists of water, everyday again-and-agains of dribleting lifted hands, daubs of thick wet from a cup being overed - never enough moisture at-a-time to soak the paper, really sully or ruin it, never enough hitting the thick marker ink to cause it to run, dissemble - and the cumulative impacts of these waters has shaped it to seem so soft, talcum-papyrus - like a tissue that has gone through the laundry, remaining intact, coming out in the semblance of a wrinkled and faded and slightly-stained-from-dyes-in-other-clothes dress shirt. Dress shirt? 'Yes' Lucy affirms 'one that has shrunk a bit, been washed many times and never ironed, its creases permanent, its surface almost the visual-same as bulbous, grey shaded clouds threating rain.'

The man arrives with the soda order. Lucy lets him in. She props the door so that he can go to-and-from his truck with the handcart without any trouble. With. Without. Never talks. Seems in a hurry. Seems near to suicide, a cynical night-owl might hoot to seem trenchant. Just one more irk will be the end, poor fellow! He's pummeled to the point of only needing a nudge to be nothing! Lucy signs the form and it is with a resigned, fatalistic resignation that the man removes the yellow and green customer portions, taps his pen shut, pen shoved - really shoved, that is a shove - back to breast pocket, pulls handcart out behind him, tosses it - heave-ho! - into the back of his truck and then absently pulls down the back shutters - Lucy wonders if it's illegal for him to drive off, as he sometimes does, with the truck-back partially open - and then headlongs away, the truck having been lulling and seeming instantly in motion once he climbs inside, no build of acceleration just Go instead of Stop. Otherworldly. Lucy considers him an alien. Or a rarified virus that has procured a human body but has little imagination. It's always difficult for her to focus to writing or even give attention to specific thoughts after these interactions with company in her otherwise all-alone-nocturnalness - so she no longer tries. This is usually when she takes a bit of a nap. Fifteen minutes. Enough to let the engine of her shut down, cool off, but in the instant it is legitimately cooled to start up, again - as refreshed as can be without actually being. Tonight, this morning, though? No - no, no. Tapping tongue against gums behind upper teeth. Nerves nerves and regretting she's agreed to go to the school, later that morning. Sighs and forced chuckling and pathetic-so-she's-glad-no-one-can-hear repetitions of 'I have nothing to say on the subject of poetry'. 'I have nothing to say on the subject of poetry' she has just said, umpteenth time, this time pretending she is apologizing to the man, Leonard, rather than, as most of night she had been, pretending in various tones of voice to be starting her speech to the students with the words. 'I have nothing to say on the subject of poetry. Neither does it. Look at it. Look at us. Look.'

Re-entering the dining area from the back - she had taken a piss, wetted her hair over and over, afterward, no good reason for it, none at all - she finds that Elliott is smoking outside the front door, leaned to it. Lucy regards the way the contact of pant fabric and ass looks to the glass, how the light plays with tones and shadow, how the flat-press seems perfect circle - circles, they move, the spots of Elliott's ass in her pants to the glass, like the flecks of two drips of water on eyeglasses passing beneath streetlights, bip and bop, gone and back, visual and nowhere, based on some whimsy - rounder than the flesh, in one sense, absolutely unround in another. Then just watches the back of Elliott's head. Probably she had shown up almost just when Lucy had gone to the back. 'How do you deduce this, Lucy?' Lucy needles herself, grinning. 'Well: observe how Elliott has not once given a glance through the door, these five minutes.' Aha - good point. 'Yes, thank you, yes it is - see: Elliott would have been facing the door in the first span of time she had been there, then would have started pacing with her back to the door but still giving glances in during the next phase of waiting.' Now? Now Elliot, Lucy thinks, is to the point where she knows Lucy will see her when Lucy comes to the front - knows Lucy will walk over, tap the glass, unlock the door. Which, eventually, Lucy will. Right now, Lucy looks. Look. Elliott. Parking lot beyond. Sidewalk beyond. Buildings, other shops - what are they again, Lucy? a tailor and a storage unit rental joint? - beyond.

Beyond beyond. Gargantuan yawn - tarantula yawn - 'Tarantella yawn' Lucy says, free associating. Her eyes grease-watering, oozing the stringy tugs of sleepiness and the leaked juice of undreamed dreams - a smear it is impossible to clear with just fingers or towel. It is also the hour by which Lucy's armpits feel rough, rash pickled, the hairs in them bristling like a cat giving warning or a cat just being a bitch for no reason. She sees Elliott drop her cigarette, half-bend to pick it up - shadow and light of pressed-ass to grime-pocked glass taking denser presence, leering, the only bit knowing Lucy is watching and voyeuring right back - decide not to, take pack from coat pocket and get another one going. Smoke sent out away. Not even a casual glance in to check for a Lucy.

'You don't get to work the doughnut machine?' Elliott asks, Lucy having let her inside to smoke, lighting a borrowed cigarette, herself. 'Doughnut machine? He doesn't bake the doughnuts here. Or fry them. Or whatever.' Elliott looks gutted, honestly to have gone pale, in need of a Victorian-era brandy to get back her cheek. 'What do you mean? Don't tell me things like that.' 'They are delivered from another bakery.' 'No.' Elliott is almost desperate for this not to be true, takes a stabilizing position at a counter stool, one leg kind of raised so that she is not sitting on it, exactly, but is supported by it, anyway. 'Yep. Sorry, man. This is not the classy joint it appears to be' - Lucy raises and editorial finger - 'though we aren't hillbillies, either. We're a breed in between, at *Deneven's*. We're an illusion, kiddo, and I'm sorry we are.' Elliott gestures Lucy to stop, declares she will put this last speech down to Lucy's morbid comedy-stylings and go forward under the impression that all which she just heard was treasonous slander, the sort ladies of good-breeding - as herself, Elliott notes with a tug to her crotch - are taught to ignore. 'It is pure folly to listen to you, Lucy. You're the blasphemy that led to science. I have to remind myself of this.' 'Suit yourself. But your world will come crashing down in an hour when the truck with the first batch of the day pulls up.' Elliott, involuntarily, shoots eyes where Lucy gestures - the lot is empty, Elliott's breath still catching as though some spectre, some ghoul is shambling there, moaning its delivery of from-elsewhere doughnuts and pastries. Lucy almost remarks at how nicely dressed Elliott is, how put together - how *alluring*? or what? what other word could she use, here? - but then doesn't. Does Elliot expect to have sex in the shop, right now? Is that something you're not going to try for anyway, Lucy? Look at her! Those pants! How they catch tight the wide of Elliot there and there perfect - make her seem the sturdiest surface, oh don't they just! So set in stone one just can't help but try to topple down the legs of, the surface, with deadweight. And that shirt? Stop looking, Lucy. Or don't. But if you keep looking, just get to it, alright? You're behaving like a child.

Elliot explains she stopped by just because she wanted to wish Lucy luck, for later. 'You don't need luck. I'm just proud of you, really.' Elliott is so bashful - she is fragile as a peppermint, just now. 'I feel so funny telling you I'm proud - is that odd?' Lucy makes a considering face - really doesn't know, she supposes though doesn't say so, just leaves the face on. 'It's funny, right?' Elliott presses, as though pleased the matter gums up Lucy a moment - yet, look Lucy: confusion on Elliott as well, as though stroked into purring by what she is taking as honest response, not just some rote 'No, no, of course it makes sense you'd be proud of me.' Lucy gives curt nod - it seems bad to do nothing, now - mouth a twist of Well-hmn-hmn and another nod, softer, leading into her saying 'It is funny. Why do you think that is?' Elliot has a working response ready - Lucy finds this all so cutsie, but seems in the mood for cutsie, startling herself most of all - and clears her throat, taking orator, student-debate-captain position before starting - tone of Cicero, Lincoln, Kato the Elder or a telethon guest: 'You are the one who does things. You're real - the real one, between you and myself. There is an actuality to you. While I am partial. No, there is no need to contradict. Is it a weak thing to say? Perhaps. But true, nonetheless. See: I am not formed, myself, rather I need to be in relief of something else to be whole, to make sense. Need you - yes, I just said that, shut up. So: as you have the stature and I the station of supplicant to you, to feel Pride - the current in direction me-toward-you - seems out-of-whack, drain whirl in reverse. It seems an impossible thing for the lesser to offer the greater.' Lucy has put hand to chin as though somberly, biblically weighing the rhetoric, the interpretive import. 'That makes good sense, yeah' she eventually says. And not being soulless, giggles, kisses Elliott, full mouth, full tongue, for at least a minute, fake slaps her face, genuine tugs her hair for a last smooch, beak-lips, jab to the nose.

All well and good. Even pleasurable. Not only because it shows how things are simultaneously maintaining order and could-be-totally-coming-apart, but because it gives Lucy an excuse to shut her notebook for good. Shut. Bang. Flop. Lifted. Dropped. Slapped with palm. Lucy's notebook. All of that interaction, all of that Elliott Elliotting, will make it impossible to get back into the roiling mire of 'What am I going to say to some teenagers?' so Lucy is free to idle about, penless, until the next delivery comes. Sometimes - in times like this, she means, she means Sometimes sometimes, in a sense - she would mop. Sometimes, in fact, she mops more than once a night because the actions of it are therapeutic, she's found. Yes! By heaven if she could bottle the feeling of mopping a closed-for-the-overnight doughnut shop - or if she could make it injectable by needle, capsule-snapped-inhalant - she would! And would keep it all to herself! Live and die blissful and blissfuller! But now, she doesn't feel like it. Mopping. Something about having to open a new box of the soap packets. Clarke doesn't insist on mopping, so nothing to fear. She makes a broad meander, hands out in the manner of an airplane trying its darndest at walking a balance-beam, trill-taps the counter as she comes along, trill-taps this part of the wall, this cooler, this booth table - having to lean hard right to do so - then gives a kick to the air, laughs at how feeble her physicality is. Yes. She is old. That is how she kicks. It has been demonstrated and so cakes with the hardness of fact. It brings laughter to her, though. The idea of viewing, from a documentary remove, her nude body in motion. Split screen. Her nudity kicking, pacing, making what she figures are passably elegant motions and stances on one screen, on the other a ballerina, a gymnast, a stage actress. Even in just the most banal postures, the mundanest movements - lighting cigarette, scratching neck, looking down at belly while breathing in - Lucy's version is illuminatingly meager, scrubbed down, hardly human, hardly human.

It's Elliott, again. Her tapping wakes Lucy from having just drifted. No. Lucy is soggy-head - are you certain this isn't a dream? She closes her eyes, counts down thirty, feeling herself a cloth left in undrained bathwater. Elliott there. Still. Proving awake. Smiling. 'Hi you, what's up?' Elliott grabs Lucy's face - a hand to each side - and kisses her. This is called *passionately*, Lucy. 'I know that' Lucy snaps at herself, getting around to opening her mouth so that Elliott's tongue stops just mashing against the front of Lucy's teeth. Okay, here it is: Elliott moves hand beneath Lucy's shirt, but not in any pawing way - one palm flat to the skin between the wide-set breasts, the other gripping the fold of flesh at Lucy's hip, this made prominently grabable due to Lucy's not-stood-straight-yet-not-crouched-really posture. The kiss takes awhile. Lucy honestly a bit impatient, as she has her line ready for the kiss's terminus. But Elliott talks first - her lips not even fully away from Lucy's yet. 'I didn't want to leave what I said before on a joke or anything. I want to show you how I feel more.' Elliott takes a steeling breath, Lucy touching her face - hoping this will allow her time to snipe in a remark - a touch Elliott acknowledges but gently moves from. 'You intimidate me very, very much. But I am proud of you. And I know that today is something important to you. And I want you to know I know and that I know you will do amazing and that this is something you deserve and I'm proud.' Elliott got ahead of herself, has to swallow awkward, seems to let this blip be an allowable cue for Lucy to speak. 'It's just me talking to some whelps, El. I really' but before Lucy can get out 'appreciate' or 'it' or whatever was going to follow that 'I really' Elliott cuts her off with a kiss - all of this getting a bit theatric for Lucy's sensibilities, though she plays her part and the kiss is swell, sure. And now Elliott says 'They're not whelps. I'm a whelp. They're not. And the things you want to say to them will be amazing and I'm so glad you get to. Now - you don't say anything else, got it?' Another kiss. Try to just kiss, Lucy - let Elliott have this, it's darling.

Now there are two young men out in the parking lot. They aren't waiting for the shop to open, just are crittering, totally self-contained, seem deeply invested in whatever is their conversation - the one is smoking, the other drinking from, Lucy supposes, a large beer or malt liquor. Now they swap - cigarette traded for drinking, swig took, drag took, items traded back across, the socialist commerce of good pals. They are walking unspecified, almost-circles in the center of the parking lot, one of them all spill of jittery energy and slashing grand motions - stage gesticulations, feet raised high, body arced left-and-right like an elephant's trunk bathing leathery body in dirt flings - and the other moves only in tense-coils - hand-not-holding-can riveted to pocket, funeral-stitched there, walking with knees hardly coming apart, a kind of bent-backed waddle - equally excited as his partner, just more miserable to the chill. Likely because of where she will be in a few hours' time, Lucy finds herself trying to pinpoint their ages. Are these still children? Or - what do you call them? - adolescents? Could they be in their twenties? Certainly no further along than that, right!? Are they supposed to be at home at this hour, parents, each set, thinking the one is staying with the other, their jig not up provided they manage to get to class on time, come sun-up? High school? Community college? Have they ever worked? Or are they at the age where thought seems a thing in itself, important labor, allowed, necessarily leisurely and long boned, lackadaisical in order to be sublime? Could you be their mother, Lucy? Good Lord - what a thing to realize! - that is almost certainly possible! The word *Young* scarcely needs be applied any longer to people you could have birthed without even having done so at scandalous age. 'No' she whispers, wry grinning - happy, you're happy watching these guys out there, Lucy - 'no, they'd still have to be young if they were mine - let's not lose our heads, here.' Her eyes rather sparkle at the math she stands doing, the one guy clapping, the sound of it almost nothing with distance, cold, and glass muffling the smack, the other guy seeming very pleased at this applause, shivering too much, though, to bow anything more than his clenched-jaw.

She eats the plain cake doughnuts in quarter-tears. Or almost. More-or-less. In four pieces, anyway, broken off, one-at-a-time. Always manages to eat at least three entire doughnuts before regretting it. It always seems less until that twelfth bite is swallowed down, when - sharp as tugging the wrong sized pants up - her belly seems full with budding dough, gaseous to the point of rupture. The mash of doughnut slop is a very certain kind of weight down her. It seems to last, linger, bloat the way other food doesn't. These doughnuts, worst of all! The sort of snack one cannot help but figure out something to feel blameworthy of before downing. This week, the exact place where the sun rises has been a real headache - like the thing is egging her, being a churlish lout of itself. 'Yeah.

Fuck you' she says to the light angling in so that it hits window and table top in a way to make everywhere pinch to look at - and the not-red, not-orange, not-pink color, the color of an off-brand fruit juice, sickly-sour looking, almost a taste to it, makes matters all the worse. Oh the sun this week is rude, the sort of pimple bellied husband who would use a toothpick in bed, figure ten-years of marriage excused his unabashed bratwurst farts while his wife does crosswords or reads a novel she is actually interested in but he assumes is just some book and assumes books are just some objects that wives have because they have nothing and are too comely to be allowed to buy dildos. 'Sun sun. Rising today. Oh sun, oh sun - piss off.' Clarke waving from where he approaches - science fiction in his bundle of winter clothes, cinema poster mutant who turns out to be sympathetic when the film is actually viewed. 'How was it, tonight?' he asks, locking the door behind him, slapping his cap to his tummy and hips - slap-slap-slap - as though clearing it of snow though there is none - Lucy pictures fleas or other such louse clinging to the aged knit of it, hissing. 'Fine, except for the sun' Lucy says, wincing even as she does, Clarke coughing and his stature now past Lucy, no longer obscuring the full hemorrhage, the protuberant bleed of the thing, dawn guts everywhere.

LEONARD HAD A FRESH HAIRCUT, shave - his suit seemed recently store bought or at the very least as-of-yesterday dry-cleaned. 'Don't you look fine' Lucy said, giving an awkward smile and tap of head nod from where she stood by the coffee-maker in the faculty lounge which she had entered, sheepish, feeling intruder though Leonard had assured her she should make herself at home upon arrival even when he was not readily around. 'Have you been here long?' Leonard first asked, then blinked, then turned eyes down, giving himself the once over, straightening with a hiding-embarrassment sort of jaunt and said 'Oh thank you - I guess you've only seen me in civies - we teachers have to be kempt, you know?' 'Ridiculous' Lucy said 'I feel underdressed now - or that I'm getting the celebrity treatment. Admire the coke-fiend, she's won an award!' Broad laugh and non-affected nonchalance, Leonard rummages a particular coffee-cup out of the cupboard - Lucy stepping aside from the pot - and as he poured himself coffee, took a mouthful of it, black, he explained 'Not at all' - laughed - 'not at all.' Now the one bashfuling, Leonard admits 'There's some parents of prospective students coming in and I am one of the designated liaisons. Which is not at all as sexy as I thought it was going to be.' 'You wouldn't have volunteered if they hadn't used that word, though' Lucy laughed, over-chummy. Leonard was drinking so could only Mmn with a pitch like a chuckle by way of response. And when Leonard didn't say anything for another ten seconds - not drinking anymore - and when Lucy understood, of course, she could not light up a smoke, she said - now even flirtatiously, but just from antsy-noia - 'Are you sure I'm allowed to be left in the room alone with them? I feel' she looked for a word 'fake. And somewhat illegal. I feel, put most favorably, *deceptive*.' Leonard laughed again - it was like a canned recording but somehow not pretentious, the same laugh, a button pressed. He told Lucy he would try to pop in, but it was all above board. 'You're official - you're a goddamn Artist-in-Residence, girl.' And he chuckled in a way that indicated he felt he'd gone a bridge-too-far with the familiarity, maybe had overstepped into misogyny with the *Girl*. Lucy did a cute pout to hide her glum - that had been the first time she'd actually felt eased.

The truth of the matter being that this situation was - the very slapdash of the phrase *Teaching A Class,* which was the only one that felt correctly descriptive to Lucy, verily proving the point - promiscuously absurd, her being allowed to *Teach A Class.* No. Lucy has not adopted that phrase - despite Elliott's insistence and her endlessly ass-slappily calling her *Teacher Lady* or *Mrs. Jinx.* Lucy was *Supervising A Workshop.* She was - what's better? - *Proctoring A Workshop.* That's worse, she thinks, here sitting in the empty classroom, sound of shuffle out in the corridor. Not a class. That's just the truth, by the definition. A selection of students. Electing to be there. Signed for. Bonus. 'I'm bonus' Lucy steeled herself. Or tried to. Really, she feels a fraud. That she will be caught out the moment she speaks - the moment she has eyes laid on her, everyone bloodhound snouting her out with her imperfections. It is almost miraculous, in some ways, that she actually showed up for this! Why did you, Lucy? What are you going to tell complete strangers about poetry? Are you going to read your stuff - oh God, you're not, are you? - to these young men, these young women? Are you here to see the blank stares they give you or - maybe worse - the look of being-impressed some will give? Those looks - the horror, the horror - predicated on assuming a legitimacy you don't have, Lucy! Oh those looks that will change later, in private, after reflection, not be tendered across tomorrow, again. 'Hi. I'm Mrs. Jinx' Lucy says - damn it Elliott! Lucy feels lascivious saying that now. 'I'm Ms. Jinx.' That's better - and you're not a Missus anyway, Lucy. 'I'm Lucy Jinx. Hello. Hi. Everyone. So. I'm Ms. Jinx.' There are words on the chalkboard, this whole thing the establishing shot of a porno scene. Lucy grins. To camera: 'Hi. I'm Ms. Jinx. I'm your substitute, today. Let's see what I can teach you.' Giggles. Then clams up. The fuck are you doing, Lucy!? She blames Elliott. Blames herself. Blames pornography. Blames women for being so desirable, generally, especially in roles of authority so deliciously turned to roles of transgression or subservience! Focus. Jesus Christ already, Lucy - what if someone had been watching you, just then?

'Poetry is an absolute liar. It is the art of nothing-has-cohesion. It is the fact that every letter is, in fact, every letter and every word the bursted innards of an atomic shell that has been split. It isn't lies in the sense of the opposite-of-truth - it does not deceive. God no. It is above all such petty things. And it is well-deep beneath them. It is the Platonic ideal of Lie - you know about Plato? Good. It is the perfection of untruth, the whatever string of sound you make to yourself to feel exactly how you want to feel or say exactly what you want to say in any given moment and that you know you will not remember - not at all - next day, next moment, anytime, ever. It is the thing you forget and never even try to remember - the thing you say perfectly so that even exact repetition takes from it, depreciates, loses. There is nothing more finely untrue than poetry - it gets at nothing because it allows that certainty lasts only as long as it takes to be made uncertain - technically more than an instant, yet demonstrably not. You can say anything, write anything, bleed anything, reveal anything, meticulous anything, screech anything, confess anything, swindle anything, sandbag anything, blaspheme anything, beg of anyone anything - poetry poetry, anything anything! - and more than anything else, ever, you can be assured you will not be heard, understood, regarded for what you did - your poetry! - and that you, yourself - if you are honest - will stare at the product of words as baffled and disengaged as anyone. Oh yes - if you do it right you are someone else's broken toe in a wilderness you'll never know! You are an extortion of a kiss from the bottom of a lake! You cannot learn poetry anymore than you can learn to lie. Oh yes, oh yes, anyone can not-tell-the-truth - anyone can misdirect - but you have to know how to lie. Outside of anything! Lie with every letter you are, with every portion of every syllable! You have to understand that only dishonesty can ever be truly, logically sublime.'

The class likely did not know what to make of any of that - not *Class*, Lucy, *Group*, *Collective*, *Gathering*, not *Class* - but it knocked them dazed and giddy and stumbling over each other into conversation. 'What if I do understand a poem?' 'You don't, man - I just gave a whole speech!' Laughter. 'What if the poet says that I do - theoretically?' 'Then they're not a poet. Aren't you listening!' Laughter. 'I thought they sent me the smart kids!' Laughter. 'What if I am moved by a poem, though - haven't you been moved by a poem?' 'Sure. But I didn't say you can't be moved by a lie. Surely - how old are you lot, anyway? - surely you have been moved by lies by now - some of you anyway, yes?' Nervous laughter and one girl says 'Fucking awesome' and goes onion-purple in hiccough blush, hands to mouth, not knowing what to make of Lucy's gun-pointed fingers at her. 'You have been, though - getting back to the question - right?' Assent,

assent. 'In fact - be honest - in one way or another, all of the things that have moved you most in life, they have been fabrications, untruths!' Assent, assent, vigor, heads nodding Yes-yeses. 'And even those that maybe weren't lies - they were things you didn't understand at all, beyond you-were-moved. This is maybe most important. Do you' - she points to the blusher - 'understand everything that moves you, that does something inside you, coaxes response as if, at times, against your will? You know it happened - you might even know, abstractly, why - but do you know Why-for-you? Why-to-you?' The girl's eyes have widened and lips thinned to pencil-underline so Lucy picks on someone else. 'Who here has ever written a poem?' Bold-girl, front of class - Lucy immediately hates her which makes her certain she adores her - prim proper, smarty-pants, everything-girl answers 'I thought I had before right now!' Laughter. Lucy holds a gaze hard - the girl meets it, no sweat, composed as a petty-coat, elegant as a grace-note played by a pinky before a mezzo forte - 'Now you know better, though - now your path is arighted. That's why I was summoned.'

'By the way' Lucy is sitting on the front lip of the desk - I thought this wasn't a porno, Lucy! - ankles crossed, feet going flap-flap 'I'm Ms. Jinx.' She points to the board. Everyone laughs generally, one boy saying something she doesn't catch that receives a raucous follow-up laugh - Lucy does not ask to be told what was said, just points at him and says 'Exactly, sir.' Now - wait - was that wise? Lucy's adrenaline is going at such a pace she is not doubting every action, not doubting any action. For all she knows, she just agreed with something inappropriate, lewd. No matter. If so, the class - the *Assembly*, the *Gaggle* - will assume she did not hear or misheard. Or something. Lucy can no more control herself, now, than a brick wall can slouch. 'Have you been published?' comes a question as Lucy is twisted to take up her coffee. 'I have been, yes. I wish I hadn't been, though.' 'Why?' 'Because it makes my cynicism seem less pure. It's the world's way of undercutting me, giving me pages in print.' Some chuckling - from shy-girl and head-of-the-class mostly, Lucy smiling directly a sliver to each - but the boy who asked the question follows up 'What do you mean?' 'When I'm bitter and contemptuous - *cantankerous*, to put it better - toward Art, Culture, Basic Human Interactions, well now people can assume it's because I'm resentful at not having succeeded - or that I'm jaded from having gotten some recognition, trying to Lord it over those waiting for table scraps. It's nothing major - just a personal pet peeve.' Head-of-the-class chirps 'You don't want people to assume you're a cunt for any particular reason.' The air drains from the class. Lucy - Lucy! - Lucy, do you realize how wide you are smiling? Now the class is making sounds appropriate to they-can't-believe-what-was-just said. Lucy - you're staring. Blink, for Christ's sake. Okay, settle down.

Coffee sip. Compose yourself. The class settles. Now. Pin-drop. 'To answer your question' cliffhanger tension in everyone's shoulders - everyone except head-of-the-class' - 'you're goddamn right.'

Obviously it was a terrible idea to have let Lucy around impressionable people - of any age, but Young Adults was a poison waiting to dissolve. She will have cost Leonard his job and reputation - that might snowball into his marriage, his custody, his sobriety if movies and television can be trusted to have taught Lucy worldly things. She might as well just claim she got this gig because she fucked him and blackmailed him into it - that would save him a bit of face, at least. Yet the rush, the frenetic pops of jazz, of rupture-punk all in her as the group files out of the room - some still applauding, random 'Bye, Ms. Jinx!' yelled in the general din along with louder-than-shout-whispers of 'Oh my God' and 'Did you fucking hear' and so-and-such - has her not giving a sour-mash damn. Will they all go straight to their other teachers, to their parents, to administration with the laundry list of What-the-fucks? they must have? Or will it be a thing that rises quiet, bandied about, this group telling students who were not even present, the tale filtering upward, capillary action, until the class is made to give proper specifics in some center-lit inquiry room. Lucy Jinx: banned from the property. Had you said anything so bad, Lucy? My God - Lucy has no idea what she just said, at all! Shy-girl is still in her chair. 'You okay?' Lucy asks, just milling at the desk. What is Lucy supposed to do now - wait for Leonard, she thinks, go to the lounge or something? Shy-girl does not answer, just stares. 'It's Petra, right?' The girl nods. 'What's on your mind, Petra?' 'You' Petra says, quick grin like the hiss of a just opened soda can. 'Well that's okay, then. How did I do?' Lucy is not asking with timidity or with reference to the burgeoning certainty she has of being arrested any moment. Petra swallows, ducks upper lip down inside lower, bell-rings her head side-to-side. 'I fell in love with you - so, I guess there's that.' This is a time an adult would do something responsible or even make an easy joke of it all - so, of course, Lucy sips her coffee and says 'Yeah? That's better than I thought, anyway - cool' and really wishes she had a smoke to light up since she's never coming back to this place, anyway, Hell frozen over, million years, what have you.

The buzz begins to subside when she is confronted with an overstuffed Faculty Room - everyday postured, actual teachers eating their motely lunches and having their familiar, well-earned comrade jibes and guffaws. Lucy gives a pixie wave, eye-roll, half-curtsey. Nope. Not a one of these educators has the slightest idea who you could be, Lucy - you'll have to explain why you've come through that door or else scamper. 'I'm Lucy Jinx' Lucy begins - oh-thank-goding when this crisp-wrinkled lady stands up, still chewing, extends a hand, mayonnaise breathing 'Of course' - the words muffled-pronounced - 'you're our poet' -

swallows - 'sorry, the poet Leonard netted us.' General noises of 'Oh' and things et cetera, the other staff mostly returning to what they had been doing after a few pleasant-enough nods. Another woman joins the wrinkled woman - honestly, Lucy is struck by the texture of the skin! like a three-times-used plastic baggie now full of graham cracker crumbs, one thick mole like a raisin down in there, as well - around Lucy, this woman younger, dressed stylishly but clearly on-the-cheap, and also a middle-agedish man kind of loiters in the general vicinity but, technically, outside - or at the extreme outskirts - of Lucy's presence. 'Did you meet with them, already?' Wrinkles asks. Lucy nodding and giving chipper affirmative gushes about the students as a whole. 'Leonora was so looking forward to it - she's known she's going to be a poet since second grade. Did you meet her?' Oh but Lucy is a mess with names - she doesn't understand how you all do this - hand gesture, all inclusive of staff-in-the-room - Lucy had hardly been able to keep standing, let alone make articulate noises like speech, let alone get anyone's name right! 'There was Petra - I got Petra' she says, as though Sherlock Holmesing a memory up, tapping a finger in the air to emphasize. No one says anything particular to that, but Ross-Dress-For-Less says 'Simon will give you a hard time - I bet you and guarantee. His dad's a writer' - she does a voice Lucy supposes is an impression and the other two belly laugh, Wrinkles wiping her eyes - 'and he never fails to let us know. He's all bluff though - don't let him get to you. Sweet kid.'

Here comes Leonard - quite a brisk, happy-go-lucky he has to him, must not have gotten wind yet of his dead-man's sealed letter - giving an expansive shrug down the corridor until he is near enough Lucy to be certain she will hear his stage whisper 'Are you planning a coup? A coup d'etat?' Lucy playacts *Wha?* with her posture and flashes li'l-ol-me? eyes, real bo-peep like, Leonard clucking tongue and telling her 'You have gone and got yourself a fan-club, I will tell you that. Good start of it, I'm taking? So sorry I couldn't be there - this was all supposed to be more hand-holding based, I feel you were just left to it!' Lucy demurs 'Naw naw, it was an absolute thrill' though she is sure she came off a genuine yammering cow-poke. 'Or, at best, perhaps I was the world's most erudite polecat.' Leonard seems to not know if he needs to actually bolster her or show that he gets it. 'I desperately need to smoke' Lucy lets him off the hook by mentioning 'is there someplace?' She regrets the question, though she knows Leonard smokes, because he has to so shamefully tell her 'Sorry, man, I left out the *No Smoking* stipulation so you'd take the gig. This is not the environment for any truly living being, I'm sure you've gleaned.' And yeah, Lucy notes for the first time this is an honest, exquisite, Bristol-fashioned Private School - the air seems imported specifically to keep the poster frames from streaking. 'I think I might have gotten you in trouble' she blurts. There are his eyes, pleasant Oh yeahs, two of them. Oh just warn him Lucy. Yes. Yes. Lucy is hit now with the guilt. Fuck. Leonard raises an eyebrow but it is only mock-concern. 'Seriously. I'm not a teacher, man' - she punches his arm, plaything - 'and I just got talking and there were just weird things I was saying. And bad words' - she puts her foot down, holds up a hand like Wait, stamps her foot again - 'actually, I didn't say the bad words - not first, anyway - but I did not disencourage some from the kids. They ran roughshod, fella. I think I fucked you over, but proper.' Leonard is looking at Lucy. What's the look, Lucy? 'What bad word didn't you discourage - just so I can plan my escape?' She deep breaths. Face scrunches. Breath out. Pause. 'Cunt.' His laughter blitzkriegs the corridor.

Okay. This is okay. The headmistress - who terrifies Lucy as much now as she had on their first meeting, this candelabra elegant, double-Doctorated, painting-of-her-behind-hered Valkyrie - asks Lucy if she got through it okay and says that she had chatted with the students, who were raving, falling over themselves with superlatives. 'Maybe even too much!' the headmistresses breaks character to chortle, returns to crisp-posture, hand just having brushed Lucy's shoulder-side. 'They have already enshrined you in folk-song and tapestry, Ms. Jinx. Whatever you slipped them, congrats, it was well mixed.' Lucy - you know you are blushing and have been struck dumb, yes? - is chuckling, no-noised hiccoughs of tension leaking from her. 'I need to apologize, I think' Lucy begins and Leonard chimes in 'She let someone say *Cunt*' and Lucy solemnly nods 'Yes - I let someone say *Cunt*. Enthusiastically. But' - she holds hands up as though having to calm a savage room of disgruntles - 'she was talking about me, so I figured that was, you know, pedagogical-prerogative. And all.' The headmistresses says she can well imagine the students who were selected for the workshop - see, Lucy!? *Workshop*! - are all thick-skinned and bullheaded enough to roll with a little bit of coarseness. 'And Leonard didn't say he was sending us Betty Crocker, even though he didn't say he was sending us Debbie Dock-Worker, either' - the headmistresses smiles. 'In earnestness, it seems to have made quite an impact - as long as they weren't too much for you.' Wind to her sails, Lucy now big shoulder shrugs, scoffs scrape of shoe-toe to carpet 'They're whippersnappers to me, you know? I's a rabble rouser from way back, don't worry on that account.' This little meeting then breaking up - it seems sudden to Lucy, but what does she know? - with handshakes and Leonard holding the door open for Lucy and then shoving her, familiar, when, as soon as it shut, she got flustered and started apologizing, again.

Assessment: that didn't happen. Any of it. Opium haze, Lucy is skid row, pond-scum waiting to be crime-scened somewhere and this, say, was just the last hurrah, a shebang of her dying synapses firing off a last salvo, a narcotic ease into the void. She drove as far as the parking lot of this liquor store before pulling over and lighting up and is now on her fifth cigarette. Had that happened? Maybe some of it had. She'd just spent time somewhere. That headmistress, though? Lucy's shoulder still simmered from where it had been touched. Hallucination that, no doubt there. She tries for the third time to get Sharon on the phone. Layla. Dolores. Finally tries Elliott and leaves the briefest possible message before sinking deep into her unreclined driver's seat, body almost too tight from giddiness to inhale the cig her lips pincer. Assessment: No, that certainly didn't happen. That? How could it have? Because you're a poet, Lucy - why else are you a poet if not for things like this to happen? And yes - yes! - she doesn't want to argue. Not now! Let her not argue just for this happy once, this solitary chance, just for this hour in the immediate aftermath. Lucy Jinx: deserving of this. Lucy Jinx: swimming the waters of home, striding the stage where she belongs and from which only cruelty, envy, vindictiveness have kept her. Assessment: that just fucking happened! She screams cigarette and slams a fist to steering wheel - expecting the horn, but the horn not sounding even a squirt - and thumps fist side to window, realizing only then it is still shut, she adrift in the exhales of all of these cigarettes, engulfed in an ether of celebration sucked into her lungs and expelled. 'Because I'm a poet - fuck you! Fuck you! Fuck you!!' she directs at the rearview and it grins back. Every glint in those eyes a fiend. Every tooth in those lips a fang slick with tasted bloodshed.

AS THE METRO-TRAIN SURFACES, LUCY - mobbed stiff, standing amongst a slurry of commuters - checks her phone to discover a new voicemail from Elliott, a text from Sharon - one of their many in-jokes, all capital letters extolling Lucy to remember to take her tumor medicine because tumors are unsightly, quadruple exclamation-pointed - and another text from a number she does not recognize. *We're still on for that drink tonight, yes?* Who could this be from? Lucy is momentarily titillated, chest flushes warm at the thought that this message might not even be for her. Why is that exciting, though - specifically being misaddressed by the words of a stranger? Well: to Lucy there are endless daydreams of wrong-number texts leading to impromptu adventures, one-offs, daring-dos with illicit twang. But this message is from Melinda. 'That's right' Lucy mutters, not disappointed but less-than-thrilled. Yesterday, checking into the room to leave off her bag and stuff, they'd chatted, smoked, Lucy had shared her number and accepted the invitation. And then, par for the course, promptly forgot all about it. 'As is my wont' she says, suddenly self-conscious, having noticed the whisker-flick of that hunched-over man's eye in her direction. Like being watched by a larvae feeing on the insides of a dead turtle shell. She feels like whispering *Bastard* - or even uttering it aloud - as the bum in his long-soiled raincoat would know the word was meant for him, never stand up for himself, sit stewing in his unspoken cut-downs of her. *Cut-downs*. Lucy hasn't thought of that expression since childhood! *Cut-down*: adjective. To Insult. To Diss. To Roast. To Serve. To Own. *Cut-down*. Lucy had never been good at cut-downs, herself - or never in the moment, aloud - but remembered well how Barbara had been, the unquestioned champeen of those playground circles of venom. *Barb with the barbs* some clever girl had dubbed her. And Dorene. Dorene had called a girl's mom a *Fluffer*. Then had told Lucy what exactly it meant to be one. Then had shown Lucy her first pornographic movie. A *VHS* Dorene's brother kept hidden. They'd had to rewind it, scared shitless, back to the exact frame they'd started on. Fingers wet with each other. Lucy's shirt used to then wipe the *VCR* buttons.

The library annex is locked fast. The lights are on inside - what's going on? - clearly the place is functional. Lucy knocks, an immeidatly put-out thud-thud of her palm-base. Nothing. She puts cheek to door next to the square of glass she can see through. No one, as far as that goes - but the appearance, no doubt, of open-for-patrons. And the Hours back Lucy up - olden looking as the fleck-red lettered placard may be, it is still there for all to see. She primly descends back to street level and has a cigarette, figuring only one staff member came in today and they were using the toilet, locked the door in the off chance that someone would show up, never believing anyone would in the minute or two it took to void or change tampon. In fact, Lucy staunchly resolves to stay outside smoking for at least fifteen minutes - no desire to mortify, scar irreparably the poor worker. Dear God! Think on it, Lucy - the spikes and voodoo pins the poor neebish would feel if they found a Lucy Jinx, face pressing on glass or trying the door, someone showing up after no one all day in the one instant they needed to be indisposed, pants down. Might as well burst in, threaten them at gunpoint, pistol whip them but good, the trauma would amount to the same, down the line. Lucy is still quite giddy, anyway - no hurry, no hurry. The cold outside is doing her good. Milling in the library just to use the computer for no real reason might merely agitate her. Now, she is set to just press on to the hotel - look, has even taken a step - but now thinks the better. She is here. 'I am here' she says. Across the street a car is being ticketed - thing looks it has been there a long while, the iced snow almost melted from the roof and the windshield revealing purple, white, black splotches of bird shit, rust thick. That tire is flat. Lucy can see through the driver's window that the passenger window was broken out, once upon a time, several plastic bags and thick tape the only replacement. What a sight. Like an art project, that. *City malaise* there might be a title etched somewhere. *Urban ennui.*

It turns out there were three employees working when Lucy re-entered - now she's already at the computers - so she decided not to bother even a half-hearted inquiry. And just where have you all been, eh? They wouldn't tell her the truth, she'd not be able to glean any sordid specific - if Lucy, for example, worked in a library and locked the doors, well, good luck to all comers unzipping her lips on the wherefore. Pulling up her e-mail she concludes, even this spoken with a perfunctory air 'They'd say they had been having a meeting in the backroom and what would I say to that?' Nothing more smug than bookworms in their habitat! Then Lucy has trouble recalling her password - realizes how much it is muscle memory she depends on for it to work. Your password is *Tackwhickthimble* right, Lucy? 'Right' she says, rejected again. She types it carelessly - as always, that might be the ticket - rejected. Types it slowly a few times, absolutely certain her finger is not rubbing ever-so-gently a technical-strike to some excess letter key. Nope. Rejected. Then what is your password!? 'It's *Tackwhickthimble*' she blurts, excellent pronunciation to the gobblyde-term. It used to be *Hackwritetremble* which she morphed to *Truckwhitetumble* when - who had it been? Georgette! - someone had spied her typing it and then jealousy-mined her correspondence, finding shit to be angry about pre-dating their liason, utterly - then had changed it to *Tackwhickthimble*. Which is what it should still be, goddamnit! Did you have occasion to add Zero Six Zero Six, in your McGoohan homage, as usually winds up an extension to your passwords? Nope. Rejected. Just Zero Six - no thought to the repeater security? Rejected. *Whick*? Or *Wick*. Rejected. Rejected. She turns around and gives the eyeball to the man at the desk - the other two employees have vanished. Had someone gotten into her account and changed the password? Elliott? Had someone - wait, why do you assume Elliott, Lucy? - at someplace she's had to provide her e-mail to somehow gleaned it and dastardedly upped to shutting her out of herself? *Tackwickthimble*. The e-mail opens. What had she typed!? Slowly turns, controlled breath. The man at the front desk in the exact same position. The other two nowhere, still.

Pitter-pat, a new message from Victoire. *Just writing to let you know if you can do two Thursdays from now I am so fucking game. Look, I'm even admitting I'm not jerking you around and you have no idea how hard it is for me to not just take advantage of how desperate I know you are, how pompously lost in delusions of utter rejection-haha - But really: that work, Thursday not next but the next?* Just singed *V.* What's ridiculous is that Victoire is entirely correct in her joke that the cancellation and now week-long silence after promise to reschedule has been a torment. What's double-down ridiculous is Lucy trying for one minute to believe that Victoire doesn't know that, Lucy trying to wrest it so that the joke was coincidental levity not on-the-nose call out. *You're a sassy fucker - gonna take this outta yer hide!* Lucy types, immediately deletes, closes out of the message, checks the Drafts folder and the Sent folder to be sure there is no trace, types the word *Thunder*, highlights it, cuts it, pastes it - yeah, Lucy, you have obliterated all trace, settle down. Breathe. Good. She types off a more measured reply - not business-woman, but not too familiar, either. Only notices after pressing Send that the message from Victoire is only forty-five minutes old - 'So, I'm pathetic' she sighs - though in the case of Victoire, she somehow does not mind. Reads the message from her a few more times, in fact. Reads a few of the old ones, on top. Grits her teeth at the imageless icon where there could at least be some weird photo, some still from cinema, something to give her a more nuanced imagination of utter perfection to go with the general picture she has of this woman. 'Lucy' groans Lucy 'it's a name and you don't even know how to pronounce it! Not even you can be this lovelorn over a funny spelling!' This reminds her - she takes a moment to change her password to *lovelornticktock*. Remember that, Lucy. She exits the mail programme. Types the password to reenter. 'Lovelornticktock' she nods, memorized, lock-and-keyed.

Now what is this? Lucy finds it in the Spam box, but is intrigued enough to open it from the Subject line: *Poems xxx*. Obviously - yes, obviously - she had been expecting some sort of advertisement for pornography, imagined some scholarly algorithm had Sherlocked how often this account corresponds about poetry and so had generated a targeted hook to offer Lucy some lookie-loos. But no! Another animal altogether discover. *Hi Ms. Jinx. I didn't want to wait until tomorrow because these aren't for class, okay? I just couldn't keep from writing and threw away all my old stuff and this is what I have now - everything in the world - and I want you to have it. But it isn't for class. It's for you. Can we have some coffee after school or on the weekend one day?* The thing is signed *xxx ooo xxx*. Lucy looks at the attachment, which is a single document entitled *XXX*. No signature. The e-mail address is *illegiblesparrow* and when Lucy rolls cursor over it no proper name of owner comes up in the information box - just *Illegible Sparrow* spelled out like first and surname. Two things. First: Lucy wishes she had thought of the name *Illegible Sparrow*. Holy cow, don't she painfully wish it! Briefly daydreams legally changing her name to that and aloud says 'Illegible Sparrow.' Second: 'Who the fuck are you?' she says, honest tone of exasperation, clicking the document open and discovering - giving it a quickest possible pass through - that no name is there, either. She closes the document after a brief, disapproving scoff that the author had chosen to use an imitation typewriter font - but you've done that before, Lucy! - and re-reads the message. Petra is her first assumption. But she doubts it, just as quickly. It's whatever girl had called her a cunt, more likely. Maybe. Or someone else altogether. Probably. The trouble being, she feels aroused right now and is not certain she can put this off to her still thinking about Victoire. 'Which I am doing' she says. 'I am.'

This is what she needs to change track - and anyway, don't worry about it, Lucy - to snap out of - what? - whatever she is thinking about. Lucy has been staring blankly, no idea wither to her mind has flitted - seems subjectless, her thoughts not sluggish, exactly, more like legs laying down after a jog. Heather. 'Heather, Heather' she says, looking at the Subject line *Hiya hiya*. 'Hiya, Heather' Lucy sighs, doing the work like she's just done a karate kick more than she's just done a doff of a cap. She leaves the e-mail program open and moves to the main counter, asking the man if she could get a cup of coffee. He is delighted to oblige, as he just brewed some and explains as he broom-whisks off to retrieve some 'It's Swiss.' 'Delicious' she exclaims after one mouthful of the stuff, a taste she can distinguish in no way from any other coffee she has ever drunk - seriously, she hopes it is not Swiss at all, that the man feels he has duped her with the power of suggestion, this stuff the same swill as always, squirted through a discount filter into a two-years unwashed plastic pot. She writes down *Victoire* and asks him 'How would you pronounce this name - it's a woman's name.' He squints, but straight away, hardly a glance, claps his hands and says 'Victoire.' *Vic. Twah.* Lucy repeats. This is how she had been saying it, already - just exactly as he does. Or almost exactly. He more French than her more drawl. *Vic. Toi.* 'Toi' she says, noting, yes, the slight crispiness to his *Oi* than to her *Wah*. 'My sister's daughter is named Victoire. Victoire Lorette Menghail.' That is a fucking terrific name! 'That is a terrific name' Lucy beams. 'Say it again.' He does so and she claps at him so doing. 'Your sister is basically the best mother in the world. But her daughter will grown up only to tempestuously disown her. She knows it though, you sister, she must - giving her pup a name like that. She will just smile when the rift happens and hardly be able to suppress the chuckle. Named her well to foment familial revolt.' The man is glowing at these remarks. And Lucy is sure he is jotting them down - that's what he is so hurridly scribbling on the scrap-paper he grabbed after she said 'Thank you, again' and moved off.

Like the mysterious Illegible Sparrow, Heather is benefitting from the radiation leak of Victoire - and the still surging look-at-me-look-at-me of the high off the earlier time at the school - but even still this is getting to be more than a fractional slog, this Heather. Now, though - this is Victoire backfiring on Heather - Lucy's mood takes a slight warble down. Not much, but she notes it. She is the same note played - Middle C - but now marked in the Bass clef, left hand taking over from the Treble high right. What? What is it? The following: it has irked Lucy since the second of Heather's post-modeling correspondences that Heather has reassured her that Heather is her actual name. Heather Tracee. Not a bad name, in itself - but it had led to Lucy spending a whole commute worrying she had accidentally assured Heather, reciprocally, that her name was actually Lucy Jinx instead of Stella Adroit. You'd never do that, Lucy. And no, Lucy had used the correct not-her-name-really, she knows it. Yet the bitter tension had never entirely uncoiled - as why in heaven Lucy is still in touch with the woman at all she cannot exactly articulate. If Victoire assured her 'My name is Victoire' well, face facts, Lucy would cat-out-the-bag Lucy Jinx!!! in three-eight time. Returning to the present: Lucy is now actively, for the first time, considering that Victoire might be a fake name. And finds it stupid she didn't immediately think this before becoming so attached to the nomer. But also thinks maybe it means something - means, specifically, that it is a real name - that she never suspected it: this lack of her normal way of viewing the correspondence of a Subject illustrative of the factual nature that there is going to be something as profound to this woman as Lucy cannot quite explain what she thinks there will be. And that her name will, because of that, really be Victoire. Yes: Heather, the actual writer of this still not fully read correspondence, seems twice as feeble a sort, all negatives fanned, all positives wet-blanketed. And now, of course, is when Heather is asking if they *could maybe have a bite to eat, just hang out, nothing to do with the poetry*. 'Sure, Heather' Lucy resigns-herself-to 'let's hang out.' You don't have to, Lucy. 'I know' she says, voice still dripping-wet, mucus-scented breath down her nose 'but I should.' Pause. 'Yeah, I should.'

As she is getting back down the stairs, pausing to close up her coat to the chin, her phone vibrates. Still indoors - when had it gotten so windy out? listen to that high-pitched blade, it sounds like a papercut out there! - she finds it is Melinda's reply, confirming she is, indeed, working the Swing Shift and so will be ready by nine. Lucy tosses off some nonchalant blah in response - *yeah yeah lovely and all can't hardly wait as they say* or something like that - figuring it best to light a cigarette while still sheltered. She braces herself for the assault of the pelting air but then, out the door, finds the day windless, silent other than the typical prattle of the only semi-busy city block this is. She steps back inside. The sound of the street is present, nothing else, silencing abruptly as the door gets nearly closed and then - alakazang! - in the same moment the door clicks and the street is silenced this high pitched wheeze starts up, afresh! Lucy pigeons her head around but there seems to be no source of the din other than Everywhere. She changes her orientation - squats, tip-toes, spins slowly in place - still the sound, as though omnipresent, around her. No, it doesn't seem to be in her head - she is clearly hearing something exterior her. Yes - she tests like a good skeptic - hands over her ears lessens it exactly like anything else. 'A phenomena, indeed' she laughs, more amused at her interest than the actual oddity. The joke is, she kind of knows she is standing here exploring this curio to keep out of the wind she knows doesn't exist - Oh Lucy's mind, Lucy's mind! What of this development, though? There is something more than natural afoot, here. She takes a step up the stairs - the sound is gone. Stays gone at two steps. Does not return at three. Still gone back at two. Still gone at one. Presto! Foot down to Step Zero, there it is - instantaneous, not even gradual, as certain as water to flopped belly bang! Her back to the wall? Still there. Back to other side wall? Still there. Back to the door? Still there. Up the one stair? Still gone. Step back down? Back. What of it, Lucy? She brushes her sarcastic-self off with a shoulder shrug. 'Try some romance for once' she says 'try thinking something might be something for a lark, it won't bite ya.' Depresses the door handle - and it stops! Slowly lets the door handle back to rest - suspense! - and there it is.

Without having made the decision, Lucy discovers she is walking to the hotel rather than catching the bus. Fine and dandy, though she ought to get a solid grip on where her mind is. Ditzy and derelict, it unbecomes her. There are appearances to up-keep, after all! She cannot, as some others might, cavalier herself in daydreams and wistful fancy, not concerned with each little elements of her habitat. Good humored as she may be now, she is well aware, basecoat, the homeostasis she had maintained for quite awhile is besmirched. Oh yes, surface tension has been broken, ripples are revealing that there is an element with a distinct above and beneath, the All of where she dwells merely a portion of the All where she actually exists. Perhaps she is only not panicing, here, because she is reinforced with random good fortune. Though some of the fortune, who knows if it is good!? Foolhardy girl she still is, Lucy Jinx can confuse interesting-developments for what-she-actually-wants. Occurrence for Appropriateness. She can treat a mistake as an inevitability - not only Can-Treat but Has-That-Bad-Habit-Of-Treating, in fact - a penchant she focuses on quite wormwood when things south-turn. Oh she could save herself bruises and buffeted soul with a daub of caution, here or there. What is it, Lucy? It's simple! She doesn't feel like finding a thread to tug trouble from in an unravel. Doesn't. Feel. Like. It. Why should she? She is a poet and a headmistress touched her arm and was fine with the word *cunt*! She knew she'd been pronouncing *Victorie* correctly, if with a bit of a cottonmouth tone! There was Illegible Sparrow, for goodness sake - and here she was going to write in the presence of the nude body of some woman called Tilda Mauve! Tilda Mauve. Victoire Elan. Illegible Sparrow. Lucy Jinx. What wrong could there possible be with names like those set in play with each other?

Where has her lighter gone, though? That's a tactile ill she can begrudge. 'What the devil?' she says, going methodical through each and every pocket, again. Cigarettes, there. Wallet, there. 'No bag right now' she subvocalizes, slowly, seeing the words added to her list and crossed off. You had - yes, you're right, Lucy - just been smoking. She does a pantomime - has stepped off the sidewalk proper, is in the area between this bank and this franchise café - of her having lit up at the base of the library annex stairs, but all it does is verify that, left to rote, her lighter should be in coat pocket, here. Where it isn't. No hole in pocket. No extra pocket she'd never noticed. A cigarette is at dangle in her mouth, the unfiltered end of it already a tad soggy, the front end a bit rumpled, enough she doesn't want to light it reverse. Even if she had a light. 'Some-a-one's alighted with-a my-a lighta' she Italianos, hoping that is all the world was after, some comedy, and now would, still giggling, return her property to her. Then - there, look Lucy, but waitaminute - on the ground at her feet - in this exact space between this exact bank and this exact franchise café - there is a booklet of matches! A full booklet of matches. Even without having flapped its roof open she can see, profile, that the tips of these matches are mint blue, not Beelzebub-red or past-prime-apple green. The matte cardboard stock, the embossed letters. This is one class-act booklet of matches that portends something! And surest thing you know, they are for an establishment called *The Falsetto Note Corporation*. Everything is up to something right now and she knows it. Lucy looks up, suspicious that the sky can't resist squinting at her, gloating, proud as a waitress' hip, over having snared her in whatever new strangled-veins avenue this was all going to course her down. Wet sullied end of cig back to now wasp-wing dry lips, she strikes a match right on the bank facade brick - and even the sound of its combustion seems to be spelled the way a child would imitate it in old world French.

LUCY CAN RIGHT AWAY TELL that the slender brunette, skin as taut and precise as a model-house countertop, clothing outlining her shelter-tight, is her Tilda. There she is, early-bird loiterer, reading from - maybe not a loiterer actually, that isn't the word for someone with a book like that - a textbook of some kind. All less romantic than what Lucy was hoping for. A corner-torn edition of *The Notebooks of Malte Laurids Brigge* would be more the ticket, or at least befit the term *Loiterer*. Oh these student types - they certainly do not trouble her, don't make her life a burden, but seeing them so set to their own pursuits and knowing that sitting for Lucy's poetic-kicks is an idle quirk, only indulged in because it can also help with tuition, diminishes the punch. Nothing is left unformed - young women, cement exact, young women, latitude and longitude set. This, here, seeing Tilda at work - who knows, maybe she arrived two hours early, specifically to have time to work on whatever that is she is so concentrated on, notations to spiral-bound pressed briefly over book-face, then eyes double-squinted back to the again revealed page - makes the matter more slouch postured. Lucy feels the size of her pouting lip. Sure, be a student! Be doing it for tuition or rent or to save for some trip - but do you have to be doing that, here, also!? In forty-five minutes, when that young woman disrobes, Lucy will know that she will have, only just five minutes before doing so, looked at the time on her phone, puffed cheeks to blow breath, momentarily considered not going up because her mind would be on the good progress of what she had been working on, that her eyes would stay drifting an extra few moments over the page, book and notebook would be packed, ordinary as laundry, backpack shrugged up over shoulder and the elevator approached, summon-button pressed already with thoughts of Will she be able to keep to her schedule of whatever she is going to be doing, after. Stop staring at her, Lucy, she'll notice you back! So Lucy turns, starts heading to the front desk, but remembers she already has her key. Pivots toward stairwell. One last glance back.

In the shower, Lucy resets by first daydreaming that Tilda will simply study, nude - Lucy would let her, of course, would not instruct her to any pose, would even go about her own business quietly, verse guided by feeling Tilda forgetting she is even there - then by trying to come up with ways to suggest doing just this to Tilda. Couldn't you insist, Lucy? The soap bar caresses her, dries her, her fingers slosh through the filmy grease of it almost feeling as though they are affixing to her, her skin prickles moist to the pose it will take after towel, the scales it will become. You could insist - yes - yes you could. These are powers Lucy Jinx has. Within these rooms. She is still thinking this while she applies deodorant and smokes a cigarette, only her unbuttoned shirt draped over her body, only her bra on beside that, body still warm-wet from the shower though her legs are starting to feel chilled. If you wanted to, Lucy, you could lay down beside her, your notebook of poems open beside her notebook of whatever-it-is, shoulders touching. You would know she would be trying to resist glimpsing at what you write and you would be tense with wanting her to and to be impressed - to feel her trying not to comment, the tension to her skin, aching like with anticipation of a kiss. Lucy closed up her pants. And could tell the young woman to do anything, really, and could do anything in her vicinity. It is not like that hadn't been discussed. Provided Lucy does not cross any obvious lines - and some obvious lines likely could be crossed, but only so far as to make them seem murky, seem Were they though? - these women are her malleable, temporary property. They aren't resistant to her, they don't not-want-to-be-there. This is a choice. Tilda isn't a model, used to this. If Lucy made her behave in some way that seemed casual, insisted she do something that would keep her from focusing on her being Object for Lucy, wouldn't that make it all the more pulsating, the desire, the want to connect - wouldn't it cigarette scar this in

Tilda's mind, make it a recurrent scene of fantasy even if it otherwise would not have been?

By now, the knock comes to the door. Lucy has convinced herself she will do the most natural thing of - after the trifling Hello-Hello - telling Tilda she saw her in the lobby and really does insist that she continue with studying. Yes. Casual as can be, no bully-pulpit abused. Tilda might resist at first - just out of generic courtesy - but over the course of two hours - or is Lucy paying for three? no, two, Lucy, just two with Tilda - her shyness will lessen, she will 'Are you sure?' and Lucy will have what she wants, all-Tilda's-idea seeming, sweetening the win. Who is this? 'Can I help you?' The woman looks startled, eyes moving up as though a room number is posted there then, realizing it will be on the door itself, trying to look over Lucy's shoulder. Why did you say 'Can I help you?' by the way, Lucy? 'Are you Stella Adroit?' the woman points her thumb and head tilts to ask. Finally catching up, Lucy realizes she is staring perplexed at the actual Tilda Mauve, but is not quite able to readjust her demeanor, immediately. 'Yes' she says 'sorry, so sorry, yes.' Tilda - Lucy has seen her, but mind has not registered a description of her other than not-the-Tilda-from-downstairs, certainly has not adjusted to that-was-no-kind-of-Tilda-at-all-down-there - darts eyes, but not with lack of confidence, leans in as though advisor to a king hearing hobgoblins and says 'Is everything' dramatic pause 'alright?' Now Lucy recalibrates, Yes-yesing and concocts from nothing a half-explained excuse meant to sound too meandering to be paid mind, Tilda acting as though she got the gist as she crosses the room threshold and lights a cigarette, straight away. You just feel like an idiot Lucy, that's all - like a schoolboy who asked out the girl he thought he'd have to settle for only to have his crush sit next to him on the bus and abruptly hold his hand. No. Wait. Or like the opposite of that? Tilda is asking you something - Jesus, Lucy - focus! 'Yes' Lucy manages to get in without seeming out of step 'I'm glad you like it. It's a step up from my usual dives. Thought I'd spare you the bedbugs.'

What about this woman, then? She does not look like her name? Is that it? Well, Lucy has to consider that. Maybe she does look Tilda maybe she doesn't. Meanwhile, here's Lucy writing the phrase *we traded licorice for cigarettes and walked the frozen woods sharing sucks from the only breath-mint was left* though completely unaware these are the words, doesn't read them back. Maybe the woman does look precisely the name Tilda Mauve. So the girl downstairs didn't, then - is there a syllogism here to uncouple? *Coins for scorn-lips coins for plump-hips.* Maybe that girl didn't - no. That is more plausible - especially with the evidence that this woman is definitvely what Tilda looks like. Lucy is internationally famous for being a muddle, for whirligigging her head with expectations borrowed from fancy, pawned off as reality, scraped at to seem fake, cleaned up to assume realness again, discarded offhand, and left half-remembered. They both look like Tilda - easy enough, magnanimity all around. Lucy, you've had other things on your mind - stop being so hard on yourself. Look at this Tilda: this Tilda has lopsided breasts set at extreme distance from each other - really lovely, not that Lucy is here for that - the push of bone through skin, full finger-length between left and right. That is something that, in photos or on video, Lucy never finds attractive but here in person is rather hypnotized by. *Underscore the key turn with some remark about her pinstripes.* This happens often. Lucy has been taken by cellulite scrags and by skin pilled on elbows too much, by thin-skinned necks, almost translucent ones, by thick hair on arms, by none on an elderly crotch. Not that she mentions it. These are internalized appreciations. And she only looks at these visions if her pen is moving, so her eyes are resting, drinking in, seem lost-to-purpose, fixated on words plucked, for whatever reason, from the female form, from intimacy created of unacquaintedness - or whatever Lucy explains her philosophy as if a Subject happens to ask. *The candles know they are melting, they judge you for what you do while they die.* Flips the page. Settles to a lean in the room corner's wall. Tilda is - Lucy thinks - trying to blow a smoke ring and wriggling her index-finger between big-toe and neighbor-toe, rubbing like there is an itch that needs friction not scratch.

So, what about this woman? She looks the way a customer in line in front of you - returning something you would never buy, wearing a sweater that seems hand-made by a not-often-seen relative, trousers that seem too short but are actually the appropriate length for that out-of-vogue style, socks an odd color considering the shoes and the trousers, insisting to the clerk who is offering cash back that she really needs the money put back on to her card - would look. Exactly. And right now the woman is text messaging after grin-chuckling at whatever the response to her previous text had been. And now? Look for yourself: putting the phone back into her purse. Lucy supplies a narrative to this. This woman looks precisely the way a woman - fully clothed, coming to meet her husband and to say Hi to her kids at the community pool, just there to drop off rental car keys before walking home to load up the family car, which she would rather take on the trip she is about to leave on, with three bags of her things and some mail to drop off before actually exiting town - would look. See? Wearing a ball cap and sunglasses she has owned for four-and-half-years. Exactly like that! You know the sort? Oh you know the sort. Lucy is really looking for words to complete a certain turn of phrase. Tilda is now standing and waggling her leg like its foot had fallen asleep or the toes had begun to spasm - yes, that is it, *spasm*, because now Tilda is, face in pain, pressing the foot hard to the carpet, leaning weight, and lamely relaxing it only to press it down, again. Charley-horse fury blues her veins in the dim light, blues them grey-almost-brown. There is a way the shadows are sponges in the open-book fold of Tilda's spine, the gully of it as it mingles to the small of her back - the demarcation of her ass cleft is severe, magic-marker instead of mechanical-pencil line tracing, off by a half-stroke, a line suggested by dashes. The tendons - are those called *tendons*? - at the back of Tilda's knees suction into piano string bridges as she tenses foot, untenses foot, tenses, untenses, and the veins varicose up the back of that thigh, giving that meat the appearance of a just-dead fish held by the tail-fin while the owner holds a too-happy smile for his drunken pal playing photographer.

'Do any of your models ever do drugs while you watch them?' This is the first thing Tilda has said since the session began in earnest. Lucy doesn't even mind being interrupted mid-scribble - though it is a good scribble, look, it goes *you're remembered for your hammer gouge, your curious taste in where to stroll, those lukewarm gloves of yours and* - and for the pure pleasantness says 'Which was it?' to get Tilda to have to repeat the question, which Tilda - no apology, still, for the interruption or even eyes set to Is it okay to talk? - does by the slight rephrase 'Have any of the women or the girls who model for you smoked a joint or shot up while you have written?' Lucy hears the - not unhappy, but still - pop of disappointment in her answering - lips twisted silly into the word - 'No.' 'Would you let them?' 'I ain't their pops, you know?' she says 'I ain't Pastor Jinx and am sure thing no narc.' This pleases Tilda - it is visually apparent so. As it is that the two are now talking, full on, Tilda sitting up as though Lucy has no writing or, indeed, business of any other sort to tend to beside idle prattle. Tilda now asks 'Do you ever want them to?' 'I think about it, sure. It'd be swell if someone did something offbeat, at least. It is usually a very button-downed thing. When I thought up this project, I figured it'd make a good documentary. It still would, but not an exciting one.' Tilda has lit a smoke and offers it across, Lucy giving it the eyeball and cartoonishing 'Is this some drugs?' Tilda only winking at that and then lighting her own cig. In this light, Lucy sees three small scars on Tilda's left temple, like three shaves of smooth wax have been tucked under the textured surroundings. Lucy takes up her notebook. Tilda - who seemed about to start speaking - holding very on purpose the pose of the non-pose she is in, eyes moving to note she knows what Lucy is writing about, expressionless mouth slowly letting go expressionless smoke.

How long has Lucy been doing this? Is it an ongoing - as into say interminable - project? Or does it have a specific mortality? Is there thought to publication - either piecemeal or in toto? Are any of the poems scraped, or is this a kind of what comes is the point so is kept? Tilda admits she had researched Stella Adroit a bit and had not discovered anything - or no poetry - so wondered 'Is that your real name? I wasn't going to ask, but now I'm talking so I guess I am - is it?' 'Is

Tilda Mauve your real name?' 'Yes.' 'Stella Adroit is not my real name.' Did Lucy pick this phony name, particularly - as in to say Is it referential to anything? - or just make it up on the fly - or, maybe more interesting, was it one of several options, winning out after some thought? 'The false name is entirely arbitrary' Lucy explains, then asks 'But is Tilda Mauve really your real name?' Just a wink. Lucy likes being interviewed this way. She can hear the sound of the whipwhipwhip of the footage being replayed in eight-millimeter black-and-white, separate soundtrack so delicately glued to the film with meticulous fingers. Lucy likes that Tilda has not asked her real name and can tell Tilda is not going to. 'Are you a poet other than this?' 'Or is this just my way of seeing naked girls?' Lucy ribalds, sticking out her tongue, pronouncing *Nekked Gurhls*. 'It would be a good way.' 'That's why I do it. And I'm a poet otherwise, into the bargain - to confuse the ditzes, you dig?' And from the amount of wrinkles added to Tilda's face and the clasping around of her shoulders and legs up to Indian-style, this was the best answer to anything the woman had ever heard. 'You aren't famous, are you? I'm a terrific sycophant if you are - I'm credentialed.' 'I'm internationally famous for being a muddle' Lucy answers, now pretending to be writing and jotting down the halfway decent line *constable your dress and wait on the laugh with my cigarette*. 'I'm wanted in Portugal for perjury' Tilda immediately replies, Lucy almost certain she should be getting this as a reference to something, so playing it cool by just one-side-of-face big smiling and writing a bit faster as though 'Yeah, I get ya - but that reminds me of something'. Really, she just writes it down. *Wanted in Portugal for perjury*. 'I like that line - is it from something?' Tilda blinks. 'Line?' '*Wanted in Portugal for perjury*.' Tilda blinks. 'I don't think so. Why? Oh gosh - are you stealing it?' 'Naw, I'm not stealing it' Lucy says, standing and - to make this seem natural - moving to the bathroom sink for some water.

'What is the strangest thing a Subject' - Lucy has corrected Tilda to use the word *Subject* not *Model* now for the third time, tone of a stern schoolmarm to the one student she puts up with - 'has ever done while you've written?' Lucy feigns thinking, waits a good suspense then at-a-losses 'No one has done anything strange. I feel like I'm doing this wrong, when you keep saying things like that' she fake laughs and Tilda maybe-fake-laughs, maybe-reals in return. 'One woman, knowing full well anyone could see in, stood at the open window and spoke to - or so she told me - her relatives almost the entire time. In another language. That was interesting.' 'But not strange' Tilda amendments. 'No' Lucy dots, comfying herself better where she is now situated at the head of the bed. 'Have you ever fucked any of your Subjects? Not elsewhere, not above-board afterward, this-is-just-how-you-met - I mean during your sessions.' 'Yes' Lucy says - elongating the word, at least seven eight nine *E*s and four *S*s - 'yes, I have done.' Tilda blats a laughing 'No you haven't - Oh I can tell!' So Lucy throws her pen at Tilda who takes it and lobs it gingerly across the room. 'Go get my pen' Lucy finger snaps, Tilda going phony affronted. 'Go get my fucking pen, man, I'm not even joking with you.' 'Get your own pen - I'm not your pen-getter.' 'You do what I say - I am your damn purse strings, Tilda. If that is your real name. Which I admit I think it probably is - but still I'm going to taut you by saying it might not be, the implication being you are a low-down deceiver!' But Tilda tells Lucy she doesn't have to pay her, then, reiterating, gallows proud, she is not going to get the pen. 'Because you lied to me' she explains with a third-grade eloquence. Lucy resorting to the only tactic left, which is to, light-at-heart-and-in-step spring-sprong over to the pen and laughingly ask while picking it up 'What makes you think I'm lying?' 'You don't seem the sort. I could see you not-fucking a woman who wanted you, I could imagine you telling her to sit for you, instead - but I don't see you fucking a woman who was there to sit.' Lucy shoves Tilda down - tugs one ankle to move her limp, splayed body nearer the drop of the bed lip. Stares. Smiles. Points. Says 'Stay. Like that. While I write. And no talking. Or get out.'

It has gone a sight past the allotted two hours but Lucy waits a moment before mentioning it. Then broaching the subject, pure business-woman, by insisting that she is going to pay extra for the time the session ran over. Tilda points out that Lucy isn't going to do so as a favor, but because Tilda stayed extra and is owed it. Lucy sighs her best sarcastic and holds the cash across, insisting, oh-so-put-upon, that she had 'not said' - this word pronounced as though to a mental invalid, slow motion - 'it was a faaaayy vorrrrr' - again, slow, for an elderly dementia case - 'I was just pointing out how above board I am because you're a jump-to-conclusiony sort.' 'Am I a jump-to-conclusiony sort?' 'Yes. Yes you are, Tilda. A jump-to-conclusiony sort. I marked you as that, dead bang, miles back, and almost didn't let you in the room because of it.' Tilda changes tone and says 'I imagine, Stella Adroit, that many a subject has wanted to sleep with you.' 'I imagine, Tilda Mauve, you are absolutely correct' Lucy says with a hand rolling stage bow. 'But you cannot be tempted with such sully' Tilda says, politician hand punctuating the statement, proctor giving the correct declension or the proper square root. 'It's like you are my long lost biographer, Tilda. I'll forward all inquiries on to you from now on, save myself some time.' Now Tilda asks if Lucy would ever be interested in reading any of her poetry. And here we find Lucy saying - prefacing with she is 'not about to start being dishonest' - that she does not read very much poetry these days, so cannot promise she would get to it if Tilda gave her any. 'Which is fair enough' Tilda says and, adjusting the strap of her purse, remarks - head nod of *Really* before - how much she likes the room. Lucy gives it a glance over, nodding as though seeing it with fresh eyes, makes a foppish gesture of expansiveness, arms thudding to her sides. And Tilda says 'You have a good evening' and has already gone when Lucy turns to warmly say 'You do the same, it was nice meeting you' obviously not getting all of that out, watching Tilda just a moment before watching the closed door just the next.

Yawning, she sips at the first of the two wines and leafs through what she wrote. It felt there had been more - hadn't it felt there had been more? - and something specific. Well, it certainly had seemed that not so many of the lines were this illegible. What in Hell does this say, here? *Jumping off something something sandpaper?* It clicks. *Juniper thrush, your knees chaffed sandpaper.* 'Whatever that means - chin-chin' Lucy raises bottle, downs the liquid, tosses it at the room telephone. What about this? *Temperamental as sundown, miserly as a just emptied dumpster.* That's terrible. Oh God - that is awful. 'Well' Lucy raises a finger, sharply, pausing the critique from the empty room, holding the finger at threat while she opens the second wine and undoes three of her shirt buttons, has a sip 'Well, let's hold on, guys! I can admit, together, that these words is some vile bit of rubbish - but each of those phrases, used in isolation, coupled with some kind of elsewhere stuff, would be fine. They'd be fine.' She reads it again, aloud. *Temperamental as sundown.* Yes. That is fine. It evokes how geezers with Alzheimer's - or early onset dementia or what have you - get antsy when dusk comes. That's good. Crackerjack. 'Hey! Good for me!' She finishes the wine. And what's so bad about *miserly as a just emptied dumpster?* 'No' - she holds up hands defensively, as though a lover were about to scold her with a pillow-whack - 'no, no - that's bad.' *Miserly as a dumpster,* though, that is okay. 'A dumpster is miserly' she says, chest gesturing, thuggishing her imagined detractors. That's right! Tosses the bottle where they would be, wriggles and undoes her belt buckle, the front of her pants. Five minutes. Five minutes. Five minutes. Glum look, but now it passes. Head shake. 'You could have said you'd read her poetry, Lucy' Lucy feebly berates herself. Shrugging - hands open, wrists together, butterflies - 'But I wouldn't have, man.' Nodders head, bip bop bip bop bip bop. But you could have said you would. She sees Tilda had left the cigarette pack on the bed. Takes one. Throws it toward the door. Takes one. Lights it. 'Yeah. I coulda. You're right. Happy, now?'

TIME WAS FEELING, TO LUCY Jinx, in increasingly abstract ways. The world - the things in it, herself especially, words and events - were as pages from a book left out in the rain, soaked on and through each other, pulpy, thin cartilage, difficult - no, impossible - to remove, one from another, without tear.

The words of this page could be see through the words of that. Words from the page behind, in fact, sometimes showed bolder, thicker, more-there than the words on the surface. This isn't unpleasant nor is it disquieting - Lucy welcomes the feeling, it's a kind of transit, a stasis while she is shunted from here to wherever. This feeling rising up her while she showers and while she dresses back in the clothing she had worn before Tilda - everything except for the bra which she just cannot stand, it feels particularly unwashed, or rather it feels as though covered in tufts of fuzz from being laundered, hair from the cat sleeping on it. Something. It felt off. Now she is at the window, thinking of time in terms of various insects, various condiments crusting plates, various odors left to her skin after this or that activity. She sometimes believes time has its own sentience, sometimes a physicality, that it is a field with density and girth - Time as a phase, the other one, the one that liquid can, solid can, vapor can undo or tight more to. That is important, she is thinking. It is not a progression - say Solid, Liquid, Gas, Time - the physical state of Time can suddenly be transitioned to, immediately, as though without momentum, from any of the others. It's a comforting thought. Lucy likes to believe that everything is a tick of physical states, that super smart physicists will one day be able to explain moods the way they can explain budding yeast or the speed of a falling coin versus a falling fountain pen.

The room phone rings. So that's what it sounds like! Not like any kind of telephone at all, really - the sound of a shambling robot-cat from a low-budget sci-fi film from decades ago heard through a wall from a television turned up too loud while the neighbors argue. 'Hello?' 'Stella?' 'Hi, Melinda. Are you off, now?' Lucy looks to the room clock - as always, the time she expected seems like it shouldn't be the time she expected or the time that it is. 'Not yet. I just wanted to see if you were in.' Why does Melinda still calls her Stella - does she have to because she might be overheard by a co-worker? This makes sense and is backed up by the fact that Lucy can only think of Melinda calling her Stella while at work. Maybe it's not even to do with being overheard - maybe it's just out of respect, just because it is what Lucy calls herself, here in the hotel, Melinda thinking it best to do as the Romans, that it would make Lucy most at ease. 'You know you can call me Lucy, right?' Melinda knows, says so with an embarrassed laugh, tacks on how she likes the name Stella but surely will call Lucy *Lucy* if Lucy prefers. 'I have no preference - really, I was just wondering if you had to, for work.' Nothing like that. Melinda will call Lucy *Lucy*. And they hang up - Melinda having to tend to a client - and will see each other downstairs in forty-five minutes. And then what? What is this thread of you, Lucy? Do you feel it? You do. You feel it, Lucy. Things are being orchestrated - hummed - you are being written - mapped out on index cards, shorthand - that creeping sense of this-fits-to-that-and-this-to-that-to-that-to-that. Melinda had seemed a deviation from concoction, untill now, a free-roaming variable - now she seems the next groove of the vinyl the needle arounds. Not liking this thought, Lucy chooses to mock the metaphor. The needle doesn't go around - the needle stays in the same place! The record goes around. Which are you in this though, Lucy? The needle? The record? They both kind of seem the same, symbolically. 'I'm the tune' she says, laying back. But then regrets it. Because that seems the worst of the three, by far.

She has fallen asleep. The dream seems to go on for days - illusory both in that it goes on for no more than fifteen minutes and that the content of it, the following conversation, is even shorter than that. Here it is: Lucy there - standing at a table, there, refusing to clear some coffee grounds from a chair, sure there are ants mixed in, and a woman, there, with a man, there, who is peeling an apple, nibbling bits off the skin and then spitting them sloppy and loud, a thick stream of tungsten colored liquid coming out of his mouth each time he does, over-wet and muted-out raspberry sound then smeck-smeck-smeck-smeck while he eyes the next nibble. 'We should never have to have a radio.' 'They don't have one.' 'I asked everywhere.' 'It doesn't matter.' 'No, it doesn't.' 'Have you asked them in the backroom?' 'I'm not allowed to and there are rooms in there I don't know about and they won't let me near.' The other woman is moved in close, hand touching the small of Lucy's back: 'Don't tell him that I love you, please.' 'I never told! Why would I tell him!?' 'He doesn't know how I hate him so - he doesn't know - and I don't want him to tell everyone - that's what he'll do.' Now: they are in a different place, by a bench, but it's all the same except the man doesn't have an apple and is tugging at his hair like a game - quick tugs, spring-like, mousetrap, a game Lucy played with her own hair as a child, proud of tufts that had a sniff of scalp to them. She tells the other woman. 'Don't do that!' The woman is upset. 'Leave me alone' she says to Lucy when Lucy tried to follow. The man tells Lucy, when they are alone 'I'm going to give you some of my money. You can give it to her. She just wants to buy you something, anyway - don't think about it. But you have to pretend! You have to pretend it's fine!' Lucy puts the money in her back pocket and the man pokes at her throat and gives it a flick which makes her cough. Which is how she wakes - feeling the flick and her body reacting as though righting itself from a fall. Stares at the ceiling above her. Eyes slurring with oily weight. Has to kick-start herself with violence to stand, throw water on her face, the eerie vibe of the dreamed conversation difficult to shake - throat like it has been papercut, she even looks in the mirror for a mark. When one isn't there, she fingernails one to make her feeling feel normal.

The only way Lucy could think to describe the color of Melinda's coat - it was a very cool coat, the cut, the pockets, the buttons, it seems patterned when Lucy squinted but not when she didn't - was to say it looked like a game show. 'Which game show?' Melinda asked, indicating with her nose her intention of stepping out for a smoke, Lucy falling into easy step with her. 'Not a particular gameshow. You know the way colors behind a contestant look? The reds are that certain red, the greens that certain green, the purples that certain purple?' 'What about the blues?' Melinda lights up, scratches an already inflamed-from-scratching spot on her right cheek, looks at the fingertips at the scratches termination, frowns, wipes the tips on her raised knee. 'Those look that certain blue' Lucy explains without missing a beat. But Melinda doesn't follow - seems occupied with thoughts of her cheek, maybe? - until she abruptly perks up 'Like powdery? Grainy? Old film color?' Lucy is confused, points at Melinda's coat and asks 'Does your coat look powdery? No, Melinda. It doesn't. Any fool can see. The question is rhetorical.' Melinda doesn't even answer, blows smoke with a head arc like to make it a *U* or maybe a smile. 'You know what I mean' Lucy sniffles 'color like photos in an old *Social Studies* textbook.' '*Social Studies*' Melinda says, chuckle down her nose, shoving Lucy and telling her 'Smoke, you shirk-a-day!' So Lucy lights one of the Tilda cigarettes, telling Melinda 'These are drugs.' 'Are they?' Melinda rubs her hands, lecherous pervert style. 'Naw.' Melinda's head slumps, chin a dribble-drabble in under her coat's folding lapels. 'I don't do the drugs - and even if I did I wouldn't tell you.' 'Because I'm a representative of the hotel? You think I'd kick you out?' 'I certainly don't trust you not to, if that's what you mean - yeah. Because you'd kick me out if it suited your weird fancy - what do I know about you other than the best you can manage is to work in a hotel?' Melinda wistfully explains how she misses drugs. Tells a story about how one time she did drugs and fell asleep in the fallen leaves, slimy matte of them that was the whole floor of the woods she played in as a teenager. 'A man walking his dog woke me up. Said I'd made his heart stop. That he'd thought I'd been raped or strangled or something.' They simultaneously blow smoke, both grinning, titling heads so the smoke collides, commingles. 'That was actually the first time I'd ever heard the word *Rape* - no idea what it meant till my sister told me, later.'

Lucy has not asked where are they going. Kind of because she assumes - does not quite remember - that this had been discussed at length, agreed on, enthused over, and kind of because she would almost prefer walking - walking, walking - doesn't matter where. It's Melinda or whoever, freezing cold city walk, in chatter with someone. It has stirred her to some memory of decades before, something she can't place but which is otherworldly pleasant to feel in her head. A memory of a place she - in that place, that time - never wanted to leave but now has no face for, no name. So tell that to Melinda, Lucy. Say: 'Melinda, I just want to keep walking, there's nowhere we need to exist, the best places already happened.' Or maybe just tell Melinda the first part, eh? Or not. Be civil, Lucy. Remember: Melinda just got off work and could well be hungry. Let her say that to you then, Lucy - don't just imagine she might! It would be rude, wouldn't it? Melinda might keep walking to be polite, hating it, confused the whole time. Let her be, Lucy - so what!? And if it gets to be she's annoyed enough to say so, let her be annoyed and just don't get annoyed back. Tell her, Lucy: Walking is all I want to do' right now. Tell her: I'm reminded of something. She'll want to know what? And so tell her you don't know! Why would I do all that when I can just walk wherever we're going? What do I care about something I don't really even remember? Anyway - Melinda'll press, try to help me figure it out, and that is poison. No, Lucy - just tell her not to. Tell her you just want to walk and talk about whatever and anything, that this walking and talking with her - make it seem she is essential - is what is stirring the memory, whatever dust of it is left. Tell her that talking about it would dissolve it, foot to last crinkle of brittle stem of dead leaf. This is easier, though. I'll enjoy it while she talks. Maybe it really is Melinda - her voice, anyway. Maybe the air in wherever we go will carry the memory further! It might be her voice! Or the exact height of her next to me! It might not be the walking at all, but the exact dimensions of her presence, you know? She might somehow, to scale with my body now, be the exact duplicate of whoever I'd walked beside before. That might be what I like about her.

Clink - it's a cliché sound, but the sound nonetheless - go the shot glasses before back-tilt go the heads and harsh velvet go the bee-stings of bourbon down throat, numbing to warm rubber as the swallow ends. Lucy fakes her harsh reaction, thinks Melinda's might be genuine. 'You certainly were giving that young lady in the lobby the thrice over.' Lucy, who had been about to say something she often says about bourbon, is stopped up by this remark, ponders it, Melinda interpreting this, it seems, as Lucy feeling caught, biting her lips as she turns to order another two shots from the bartender. That bartender! Jesus, what a crumb! How does he have a job at a nice place like this? He looks the way a mildewed sponge smells. 'Not that I blame you' Melinda says, now facing Lucy again, eyes swimmingly pleased with themselves 'in fact, now I ache - ache with someone kin to my plight.' Had Lucy really be ogling? 'Was I really ogling her? Was it obvious?' 'Ogling? Obvious!? To say the least, dearest Stella' - the drinks come, Melinda paying and telling the bartender 'Keep it, again' meaning the change was his tip for these two, the bartender politely nodding but not showing any real gratitude, merely doffing bartenderyness - 'you were agog and making it no unapparent thing to multiple onlookers. You looked the way I figure a man's face looks when he is refilling the condom machine in a toilet.' '*Agog* is a good word for it' Lucy concedes. Then explains how it is a vocabulary word she still remembers from seventh-grade, how it had been defined. '*Wanting to see or hear something, very urgently*. I also remember *Benevolent - kind, nice, charitable, doing good deeds*.' Melinda remembers *Recalcitrant* - the word, but not exactly how it was defined. 'And I love the phrase *Recalcitrant rebel*.' 'Is that a phrase?' Melinda shrugs and indicates she has been holding her shot glass this whole time and Lucy needs to get with it, hold hers likewise and drink of the contents, immediately.

Two more drinks in, Melinda tells a longwinded story Lucy does not have the heart to interrupt though she despairingly needs a piss. The story is about how police were roaming the corridors of her apartment because a suspect to some crime had some connection to the building - 'Or something along those lines' Melinda blahs, admitting she wasn't quite sure the shot on that really, maybe made it all up out of media-induced paranoia over crooked coppers - showing a photograph and asking for information, however scrapy in nature, about the man. Now, Melinda had talked to an officer when she entered, then had made a telephone call, during which time she lingered in the stairwell. Then, this same officer had been up in the corridor of the floor where her apartment was and had shown her the picture again, and she had - 'Like verbatim' Melinda explains 'down to the gesture, the pauses, the eye squints' - given it a look and her response again, the officer making note in his little pad. Then Melinda had gone inside, but remembered - 'After taking off my pants, so I had to put them right back on' - she needed to feed her friend's cat. So Melinda had gone out and up two more floors where, obviously, the officer now was. And he held up the photo, again! And Melinda did the same thing - said the same thing, gestured the same way, the whole rondo - again! And the officer wrote it down, again - 'His handwriting was probably even the same, you know!?' Melinda exclaims then waves the importance of this observation off. And then she fed the cat and played with it for awhile and ate some of her neighbor's cookies. And when she left to go back to her place, the same officer was in the stairwell again, stopped her again, showed her the photo again, and she went into her thing, again. 'Only this time' Melinda camp-fire-storys her voice 'part way through, the officer said *Have I spoken to you before?*' Pause. 'No, officer' Melinda acts out to Lucy exactly how she had put on a confused look. And says the officer flipped through his pad, saw the previous time he had recorded her remarks, got a look in his eye, flipped back a page, another, the whole matter dawning on him. 'Why didn't you tell me you'd already spoken with me?' Melinda sneezes, shakes her face, repeats that line. 'Because I just thought you really wanted to know what I thought' Melinda shrugged to Lucy, turned to the bartender to order more drink - wine, now - Lucy meekly saying 'Cool. Be right back' and off to the toilet she goes.

Are you having a good time, Lucy? 'Yes.' You seem not yourself. 'Do I? Do I not? In what way? I am drunk by now, you know?' It isn't the drink. You seem like you feel something closing in. You seem like you are feeling plotted. '*Plotted*?' What does Melinda represent, here? 'Oh Jesus!' Lucy snaps that bit full volume, unselfconscious, no one else is in the bathroom though it is suitable for three occupants at-a-time. 'Melinda doesn't represent anything.' She isn't an element in a story? That's what she feels like, right? Otherwise, what purpose does she serve? 'She serves no purpose. She's just Melinda. That is her purpose as far as purposes go - I mean, I guess it is. As far as it concerns me.' Who is Melinda? 'The front desk clerk at one of the hotels I sometimes go to.' So why are you at a bar with her - why does she know your real name? 'Why not?' Lucy demands, the third and fourth drink - shots, before the switchover to wine - obviously twining their way up her vertebrae, bang bang atop each other into the base of her brain. 'She, Melinda, is a woman who I met and with whom I get on with well. And who is nothing to do with anything.' Has anyone in your life - other than peripheral, background people - ever had nothing-to-do-with-anything - or anything-to-with-nothing for that matter!? 'You're drunk' Lucy announces, then clamps down, the bathroom door opening, the sink being run, a cigarette lit. She had been referring to her interrogator and gets the giggles when - it is a genuine revelation - she realizes that this is actually herself and so the statement is, in a way, twice as accurate. Why isn't this woman using a stall or going anywhere? 'She came in to smoke' Lucy is whispering into her hand over her mouth. The bar allows smoking. You're avoiding the topic, Lucy. 'Which topic?' Melinda. 'I told you: Melinda isn't a topic.' No? You do feel it, you know you do - don't you know you do? You must! Because I know you do - ergo, as they say. 'You're not me' Lucy ever-so-louder whispers. Regardless - you know she is buying you drinks like breathing down your neck in the dark. Lucy tunes herself out, but knows she is continuing. Look out, Lucy. She's right behind you! That's her breath on the window, her warm prints on the doorknob. She's inside the house, touching your things while you sleep.

Now a man is sitting on the other side of Melinda, the two of them talking. 'I thought I'd lost you' Melinda seems to bellow, looking over from the man, who does that tentative thing, half-standing like inquiring is he allowed to join in talking with both of them now or is he summarily dismissed? Lucy tests by giving him a wave and a tiny drunk 'Hiya, I'm Lucy.' 'You're so drunk' Melinda goes, then to the man goes 'This is Stella - who is obviously drunker than I thought' then back to Lucy goes 'Since when are you Lucy? Why wasn't I informed?' Lucy gets it. She's hip. She winks the insider-wink, Melinda is doing her a solid or something. What a Protector-figure. By way of appreciation she plays along 'You were informed, shugah. Obviously. I am Stella - but why can't I tell him

I'm Lucy? Who are you, anyway?' Lucy at-the-mans, overplaying the part of the drunk - which is as easy for her as the Word Search on a Kid's Menu considering she's sloshed and knows it, less acting than merely following her nose. The man is so-and-such. 'Ah' Lucy says and pats him. 'You are my Lord such-a-one who praised my Lord such-a-one's horse when he meant to beg it, are you not?' '*Hamlet*' the man says, seems pot-bellied in his pleasure of knowing this and Lucy points at him, calls him '*A-ok* in my ledger' and then tells him that Melinda is actually *Mary Marelene*. 'She told me she was *Cathy Catholi-ca*' the man says, pronouncing it as though sung in the song being referenced. Lucy giggles but the man ruins it by saying '*Donovan*, you know?' 'I just drunkenly quoted a peculiar bit of old goddamned Billy Shakespeare cause I'm so cotton headed with booze I didn't catch your name - and you think I didn't recognize a *Donovan* lyric!?' To Melinda: 'This guy's a ponce. Tell him he's a *ponce*. See if he gets the film reference, eh?'

Now they have moved to this corner booth. Better, more verdant. Just Lucy and Melinda. For a moment, Lucy thinks another woman is joining them, but it is just the waitress. 'Do we have money for all of this?' Lucy generally asks, not listening to the response from Melinda due to her attention is caught by the decorations on the wall, framed black-and-white photos of - what are these? - 'What are these pictures of?' she demands of Melinda while Melinda is still placing an order. 'Are you ordering food?' 'Who are these pictures of!?' Lucy now insists of the waitress, who says she thinks they are just patrons of the restaurant from way back in time when it first opened. 'Oh - way back in time. Gotcha. You're very clever. Because even if that isn't true, I can't assail you - it's a clever answer. You're so tricky I'd feel smarter voting for you particularly because I know you're not on the level.' Melinda gives apology-eyes to the waitress, who seems amused to the hilt, shaking her head 'It's fine' doubling down by asking Lucy if she would like anything edible. 'Food-wise, you mean?' 'I mean food-wise.' 'I am a poet' Lucy explains, feeling she needs go no further, but when the waitress just smiles and chirps 'Awesome, okay' she horse sighs, jowl warbles, and says 'So a hamburger with bleu cheese and some steak-fries. Like, I dunno, Yates ate. Or. Whoever. Fucking Ezra Pound!' 'Or like May Sarton' the waitress goes. 'Yes!' Lucy claps, but adds 'Only without any pickle even on the plate at all - May Sarton differs from me in exactly that respect. Which is why I'm better than her. The difference between Good Poetry and Imperative Poetry can be decided on a scrimmage-line that thin.' And done with it all, Lucy sniffles and shudders and announces to no one that it is 'Colder inside than outside - like physics gone wacky!' Now - though it's likely a bit later: Melinda is sitting closer to Lucy and seems to be complimenting her but also hoping she doesn't need to be anyplace. 'You're quite an easy lush' Melinda says. Lucy might have kissed her, just then. She's not sure. Later, now, here: Lucy is obviously scraping excess bleu-cheese off her burger and Melinda is laughing, so that may or may not have been - that kiss - what she'd done.

THEN SUDDENLY: WHERE IS THIS? Christ alive, Lucy Jinx is gnashing waterlogged and her eyes close, back. A period of time passes - one of those maybe-twenty-seconds, maybe-half-hour, maybe-however-longs. Suddenly: awake. Suddenly: awake. Suddenly: awake. Gradually the word *Suddenly* seems not to apply despite retaining its accuracy. This is the common way it goes after a black-out drunk. She is awake, it seems immediately, though if she could be outside of herself she would see how not-immediate it is. It is as though she comes awake ex nihilo and is energetic, focused, somehow the alcohol coursing through her the previous hours is gone, residue flushed from blood through pores, all better, all better. She feels ready to go and is laying on her back, the room fighting to remain twilit but the sun on the other side of the blinds more than enough to make it soft yellow-lit - or at least beige-lit, khaki, the tone of the most generic daytime. Where is this? A good first order of business, discovering that. Obvious: this is her room at the hotel. Which is a relief - see how with it you are, Lucy? - as if she had would up someplace else she would need to make her way back there - here - to gather her things before heading home. Or do you have work today, Lucy? Do you? Do I? she wonders, silently, no idea how long it has felt she's been supine and noting the way the room is lit, the probable time, figuring out where she is, praising herself for her state-of-affairs. No. 'No' she says and it comes out of overinflated-tube lips from up a scaly, chapped throat, hardly a sound, a combination of letters nothing to do with the word *No* - something more along the lines of Kyrizghtr - but which she knows is her saying that she has no work today. Provided she has only slept the one night and is not forgetting more than she figures she is.

Lord holy God, but Melinda is beautiful! Look at her, Lucy! It is within reason to figure you have already looked at her - amongst other things you have to her - quite a bit, but in this new state of fresh sobriety, please, take a moment to regard her. That is a perfection of nudity! Honestly shocking! Which is not said as any kind of disrespectful dig - it is only that Melinda is not in any standard-fare way a person one would expect to look this church-ceiling resplendent unclothed. She must have noted you awake Lucy, but it seems is more interested in walking over there, then back over there, not exactly facing you. Which you don't mind because - this not said in a lecherous or base-minded way - you have never seen shoulders into lower back into ass into reverse thighs into lower legs quite so astonishing. And you have to, Lucy, be wondering: Did you leave those rakes of red-scratch on her? Lucy decides to think so and thinking so is the first time her head feels less than one-hundred percent, the oven of piercing arousal garroting up her, eyes wincing dehydrated headache and brow revealing its waxy, perma-creased state. Yes. Yes, please. Let Lucy have violenced Melinda in such a way as to leave those specific discolorations as evidence. If it turns out not to be so, the depression will be too severe, too absolute. Lucy does not even care if they made love - she cannot trust her body to be sensationing correct, the booze has wrecked her ability to know just from her own physicality what she got up to, how wantonly, how sated, how tamed, how unbridled - she needs only to have moved fingers in the fashion to have produced that ramshackled pink. She feels the same as these sweated sheets she only now realizes are sweated soggy and pungent - her scent, Melinda's, they, both. Lucy tries to raise a hand - one eye closed - to trace Melinda as though painting her on to a flat canvas. This is an old habit when waking, regarding a lover. Right now, though, Lucy's arm is disobediently unable to lift and her fingers are clammy and fish-stick feeling, at best.

Melinda crawls and then flops to belly beside and a little on top of Lucy. She says 'Hi bully' and Lucy smiles, asking if her breath reeks of chewed diaper. 'Yes' Melinda says, kissing Lucy's tender lips - Lucy makes a little hiss sound from the contact, knows there is a just-starting-to-heal cut there, this hiss causing Melinda to giggle and give a bit of a suck, ending in a pop, before pulling away and, beaming smile, soundless laughter, say 'I don't want to hear it from you.' She kisses the severed lip again, then taps teeth like a nut-cracker jaw on Lucy's chin. And this is the first point Lucy has mustered enough energy to move, manages to get propped mostly on to her side, awkward elbow-to-bed, awkward wrist for her chin to rest on - gives this effort up and slumps herself over Melinda, inelegantly, the contact of both body heats not especially pleasant but the skins warming to equilibrium while Lucy drapes a leg over Melinda and Melinda arranges to have one arm back above head, bent, forearm under pillow, giving her a comfortable rise of chin for Lucy to get top-of-her-head in under. Lucy is curious as to the time and Melinda tells her 'It's early.' But Lucy insists on a number value, because the more awake she stays the more it feels she has lost a long while of herself. 'How can it only be seven and this much light is getting in through the blinds? Is a lamp on?' The question quickly becomes immaterial, as Lucy becomes conscious of the fact that she is tracing a tattoo above Melinda's left breast, not quite able to make out what is it from the angle, the proximity, her shadow off Melinda's pale skin muffling her vision to charcoal blur. 'What is this tattoo of?' Melinda just goes 'Mmn' and though Lucy is annoyed - she wants to know - but her own eyes have closed and she is far too sodden to raise head, by this point. Then she thinks Melinda has actually drifted off which, though she won't remember so in a moment, makes her happy, makes her press lips in a long, flattening, inarticulate, and slobbering kiss to Melinda's upper chest.

They shower together wordlessly. Going on for a long time. The water. The chemical taste mixed with unbrushed teeth. Mouths, here and there, finding each other, here and there. Water goes from unnoticed-seering to unnoticed-lukewarm. Their fingers lace. Lucy absently sucks some of the water collected in Melinda's hair from it, dribbles it out down over her breast, over her belly, listening to the pitch of the stream hushing in her own hair. Melinda has her back to Lucy's back and uses the hotel shampoo, the heavier gathers of water and the weight of the falling lathers buttery warm, coffee-stir warm, snuggled-blanket-warm all down Lucy. Melinda leaves the shower first - not abruptly, but without any specific last gesture indicating she is about to - and though Lucy means to follow immediately she remains with the water streaming into her face then on to her very-top-of-head, wondering if Melinda is dressing, even partially. Willing herself to break out of the spell of the water against her numb, hungover body - as she wants to see this, watch Melinda, be there for that flesh being covered. Here: Melinda is still nude and back on the bed, smoking a cigarette with another waiting on the shower-pinked skin of her tummy for Lucy to take. In fact, Melinda chains this other smoke lit from her own and beckons Lucy over from the random spot Lucy is merely regarding her with it. 'I look about how I look, gawker - come have this with me.' Melinda continues to call Lucy things like *Bully* and *Thug*, *Strong-Armer*, *Bandit* and *Lout*, and says Lucy had better come up with a right clever way for Melinda to get out of the hotel, unseen by staff, after so uncouthly having her way with her. 'Was I uncouth?' Lucy purrs, skin going goose-pimpled at the thought of rough-and-tumble, of thoughtless and indecorous forcing herself on Melinda. 'You certainly weren't *couth. Anti-couth*, might be the better term. Why Stella, it scarcely felt it had anything to do with me, you cad. You were doggone *discouth*!' Melinda makes a huff and then does a slow motion slap gesture to Lucy's face, lips pushing the sound effect Pesshhh out into a kiss as she does.

Lucy: alone in a room, now. This hotel room. The same one as before. No Melinda. This same hotel room. Remembering how just five minutes prior she had, shy girl - both of them whisper oh-good-definetelying - said how they would do this again, only do it in right minds. Had Melinda been so sober, throughout, as she this morning had insisted? Or was saying that just to enjoy seeing Lucy teased, to drink the hungry, give-me-details look Lucy knew she was wearing any time Melinda would let slip some remembrance of what had gone on? That's just the sort of trickster Melinda was, eh Lucy? Maybe Lucy had done, in fact, very little but burp and pass out, beached whale, and this morning was Melinda's chance to implant suggestive things she desired for next time. Yes - those perhaps were all things Melinda wished had been done to her - by Lucy or anyone - and she was seeding Lucy, making her think she had been so notoriously forward as that and so was expected to double-down on it, in future, without blush or any preambling Is-it-okay-if-I talk. Well, Lucy is as far as her panties pulled up as high as her knees sunk over mattress lip, but can go no further - teeters until she tips to her side and squiggles herself, only approximately, into the comforter, cannot get it to cover her proper from shoulders-to-feet - one minute choosing shoulders, next minute feet, the covered portion always immediately starting to itch - finally leaving both out, opting to bunch more between her legs because that eases the now prickling nausea. You never did verify the time, Lucy. And when had you asked about that? It could be hours since then! Melinda. Jesus. 'Jesus' Lucy says and goes flush and in love and feels like a simp but doesn't stop herself feeling that way. In fact: go ahead and feel in love. Be in love, for all you care! Who is Melinda? Random, whomever, Melinda: who now you are in love with, Lucy. Why not? Wasn't she wonderful? Wasn't she all the more for her not having anything to do with anything and her asking no questions and obviously being gung-ho about taking advantage of women named Lucy who go drunk to the point of viciously leaving circle reds of mouth to someone's stranger-skin in at least half-a-dozen places ranging from hip to the cheek-near-to-ear?

A voicemail from Elliott as well as this text: *There is kind of an emergency with Kate. Blargh. I might not be back until late or till tomorrow - we have to go into the city. You can call though. Love you.* That last thing - *Love you* - is not something Lucy is comfortable with seeing spelled out, yet. She is able to say it to Elliott - either instigating or responding - no problem, but the letters have an uncanny and warying tactility. Yes, okay - Lucy can say it. She tries it now 'I love you' as proof. There. Though she will admit to herself she - even though only in her own estimation, would not even be able to notice, herself, if listening back to a recording of it - puts sway and dodge to the words, as though they do not, how she pronounces them, mean - nor are meant to be taken - what they readily denote. Do you have to write it back? Have you yet? What implications are here? She thinks about this while listening to the voicemail - which, though different words, is, in tone, verbatim to the text-message and also ends with 'I love you.' The spoken version seems girlish and timid: Gee, giggle, gee okay, well I love you, giggle, bye. The typed version seems emboldened, stately, well-regarded and not to be considered as less than a command. Lucy types *Aw - luv you too El-bot. I hope everything is ok. I'll call in a bit. Just getting up.* She regards the message. Is there a way to diminish it a bit more? She types the word *Smooch* at the end. What's the matter, Lucy? 'Nothing' she says, throat clearing while hitting Send and then busying herself with getting her duffle down from the closet shelf, looking through it far more thoroughly than is necessary. What's wrong, Lucy? 'Nothing.' She sits. Still isn't dressed. 'I said *nothing*' she says. Then says 'Yeah, I heard you.' She just stares at her knees, now. She stares at her feet. She switches focus, like a cinema camera, between knees and feet, knees and feet until she loses the ability to do so and her headache becomes more pronounced. 'Shut up' she says with a play stammer sh-sh-sh and uh-uh-uh and with real slam to the puh.

Melinda's panties - plain green, unadorned - are by the sink, near some sopping wet hand towels. All in a rough bunch, they are - Lucy does love how a panty is pluraled when regarded with language 'The panties are' never 'The panty is' loves it even if that doesn't technically indicate plurality - soft wrinkled, like water-half-become-paper, when she straightens them out and gives them a pat flat to the counter top. *Plain* is not the best word for the green. Do better, Lucy. Nothing common, now. Green. But not *grass* or *Kermit* or *shamrock* or *envy* or *moss* or *burnt* or *forest* or *autumn* or *arrow-frog*. *Melinda* green. She feels the synapses carving a new pathway for what this shade is named and will be forever recognized as. *Melinda* green. Her instinct will be able to choose the color out of the brush like it's snake scales. If you never come back to this hotel, does Melinda have a way to get in touch with you, to connect? 'E-mail' Lucy says 'phone' Lucy frowns. Had you hoped not? 'I'd hoped so!' Lucy insists and snaps at herself demandingly, asking what she had meant to imply by her question. What had you meant to imply by your frown? 'That wasn't a frown, it was just me frowning!' Well, fair being fair: Do you want the trouble? What trouble? 'You're with Elliott' Lucy explains, pulling t-shirt over her un-arced body 'would you leave her, deal with that hassle?' Retort: 'I don't think Melinda would be so picky as to make me leave anyone.' Scoff at retort: 'You think that'd be any less of a hassle? What are you - gonna fold that into all of your other subterfuge? Or would you just give up the poetry sits for some skin-to-skin with your bellhop? Be serious, Lucy!' But Lucy is serious. And she says 'I am going to see her, again.' Who? 'What?' You're avoiding the name, Lucy. 'I am going to see *Melinda*, again!' Ah, but here now: isn't saying so - especially forcing yourself to name the name - rigging the world against it happening? You should keep your mouth shut, Lucy! You should enjoy whatever happened and accept that there is a reason you can't remember it. 'What reason?' But Lucy's phone vibrates and her train of thought is broken. Then she is just disappointed to see that it is only Elliott texting back *Smooch* with a winky-smile following the lowercase *H*.

Actually, the panties are a bit of a problem. She can't leave them. 'Eh?' part of her mind asks, cheek in a scrunch to match the sound. Because there is every chance Melinda will return to the room before housekeeping gets to it. The part of her mind that Ehed is no less scrunched at this reply. No, Melinda wouldn't have told Lucy she was going to come back to the room - it would be an indulgence for her, a secret that she'd admit next time. So? Well think! If her panties are still there it will seem odd! Why - this is Melinda asking, see? - would Lucy leave them there? But Melinda knows Lucy cannot keep them! She'd have to find someplace to squirrel them away in her apartment - which, while possible, even easy, is inconvenient and, just principally, asking for bother. Melinda wouldn't expect that of Lucy! Or would she? 'Oh goddamnit.' And Lucy cannot well envision herself discarding them into some street-side rubbish bin or dropping them to the floor of Metro or bus - no no. 'No' she snaps, shaking her head, gesturing sharp as though to drive home for the television audience how serious she is about this, how it is inconsiderate that she would treat this garment, of all garments, in so callous a fashion. 'Well, Lucy my friend' Lucy sighs to herself as though from across the room, only concerned as a confidante to the scenario and its possible fallouts 'you have to pick one - there are only so many options.' She decides. Leave them. But, hedging her bets, she replaces them where they had been - no way Melinda could recognize the extract bunch she had left them in, don't even fret about that, Lucy, this is reality, after all. This decision, Lucy insists, speaks well of her. The other two options would be either - in the case of discarding them - too hurtful, or - in the case of hiding them away - too creepy at this juncture. 'Yes' Lucy nods her head, now quite pleased with that conclusion. And imagine it: Melinda returns to the room with it mind 'Shit, I forgot my panties' and then cannot find them and then thinks 'Did Lucy fucking take them?' Nod nod. Or imagine: I know I left these on the counter - why are they on the floor over here, what was Lucy up to with them? Nod nod. Lucy has rather forgotten what she's even on about. Nod nod.

Opening the blinds fully, she discovers it had been raining. Must have been during the night. The view she has of the street, the puddles seem stale, walked through, driven through many times, the sidewalks already taking back their normal complexion - the roads, too, though slower than they would if the sun was out and there wasn't the tremor of wind Lucy can tell exists by the mist-not-quite-fog in front of those lulling taxi headlights. The street looks like the tile in a bathroom after throwing up and sponging clean a debauch: the same, except for what you know. Oh! It had been last night, the rain - yes yes. Was that when you'd first kissed her, Lucy? A flash of memory - the two moving at a choppy lurch along from where they'd eaten back to the hotel, the rain tormenting down its abysmal brandishes, Lucy had grabbed Melinda and pulled her in under a brick awning by an appliance repair shop and pushed her against the seldom-washed window glass, grabbed her face with both hands and gone at it. Yep. Succulent, ozone scent, sting of nearby dumpsters, that sweet made so thin it is sharp. That had happened. Had she put her hands down Melinda's pants, there? Somewhere, right? Out in public. Both to each other. 'Right?' she asks the view from where she leans forehead to glass. Maybe. Maybe, maybe. That business might have been in the hotel stairwell. No - it had been out back of the hotel! By those dumpsters - not against the dumpsters, or had it been!? She blushes and loves herself for being almost sure it had been. She remembers a shoe moving through a glue thick spill of something like soured-thick creamer. Anyway - all of that is well and good, but Lucy ought stop rehashing this escapade as though an adolescent who snuck a grope from a first girlfriend when mom and dad were never thinking that even a thing to consider guarding against while sitting up at the kitchen table paying bills and chit chatting. You're a grown woman, Lucy. This is all quite unbecoming, if you put it in the appropriate relief. You do know that? And Lucy does, she knows - though, defeating the purpose of knowing, she kind of titters at the thought of being unbecoming. 'I have unbecome.' Almost takes out notebook to write those words, but just doesn't feel like doing anything so in particular, so outside of this neverwhere reverie.

And left from the hotel, the cool air and the moisture imp her horrendously - the walk amongst people, the waiting at crosswalks, the sounds of passing traffic all lashes to her, makes flatulences of cupped hands in armpits squeezed by chickening bent-elbows, is sticks prodding her along, callously. It is an empty day. One that, though it should not have, has come on her unexpectedly. Of course, it is only Elliott's being occupied that causes it to be formless - she relaxes at this realization - or otherwise that is where she would be. With Elliott. How would that have felt? This should be considered, Lucy. Is Elliott's absence - and therefore the entire lack of choice in how you act toward her upon your return home - a good thing or a bad? Yes, it does have to be one or it has to be the other. In between? There aren't always those - even physics will eventually admit that! Does Elliott not being there leave this adventure incomplete or is it what gives it fair-copy definition? Put it this way: how would it have gone? Certainly, you would have given the usual vague fabrication of what you had done with Deborah - but that is to the point it is scarcely a shrug. And would you have fucked Elliott? Smeared Elliott on top of Melinda? Blended the two together? Or would you have done some measure to make certain that could not happen? A shopworn feign of stomach cramp or few-days-early menstruation to keep it out of the question? Would you maybe have left it up to Fate - Elliott's fancy the factor to decide, though she would have no idea the

implication of anything, this way or that? Lucy pauses at this option. Leave it to
Fate? Isn't that what Elliott not being there is, though - so nothing to consider
about if she hadn't been? Does it, de facto, indicate something that Elliott is not
an option, that this decision cannot take place? Maybe. And if so, if that is
something - well, Lucy? - then what is it? What something is that something?
Should it trouble you that Elliott is occupied or should it please you? Should you
perhaps not be so indifferent? Should Elliott's name, which you have brought
into the matter - too late too late to ever make it otherwise now - have been left
out, after all? Should you just be thinking about Melinda, right now? Why are
you thinking of Elliott? How is the one going to affect the other? 'Why think?'
Lucy sighs, difficulty lighting a smoke as she walks but refusing to stop walking
'Why bother?'




UP THE STREET FROM HER apartment, Lucy sits to a bus-stop bench - no
bus will be coming, she's just having a smoke, the plaster beneath her with a
give like stepped-in bubblegum - and watches across the way some police talking
to a man. Obviously the victim of a crime, that fellow - poor thing, all hexagon
stood in the world's square with distress. How many times a day would you say
you say the word *Obviously*, Lucy? 'Say it?' she under-breaths. Say it, think it, use
it in some capacity. She shrugs. The fellow truly looks shaken, to her - so Lucy
is trying to determine from the body language of the officer if the officer thinks
the victim is milking this all a bit much, just needs to buck up and sally forth.
Impenetrable, the policeman - water on the floor reflecting the water on the
glass ceiling above it reflecting the water on the floor at itself reflecting the water
on the glass ceiling back. Now Lucy daydreams: the victim suddenly freezes
upon seeing her - the officer turns, following the man's quaking, outstretched-
in-violent-accusation finger - Lucy stands, her duffle bag dropping from her
hand as she wheels to run - the officer in pursuit, drawing weapon and speaking
into the radio clipped to his shoulder like on television - the world a cameraman,
image shaking more than natural through its lens - Bang bang! she ducks, but the
shot she doesn't hear gets her! Oh Lucy - oh no! Point-of-view: she watches the
world go grainy, sepia, black-and-white, her blood in an amateurish dribble, a
half-uppercase *Q* from how she staggers around the pavement, collapses, lays
there breathing, undead, waiting for someone to approach so she can utter her
last words to them. Lucy, Lucy - speak to me! And what words are they? Well,
they are the sort would be reported in the news! Cryptic. Who had this woman
been? Tragic twist: the victim had looked at Lucy's corpse, astonished. 'It's not
her!' he had said 'She isn't the one!' *My God* the news will print *who was this woman?*

*Why had she run?* Her final words worldwide reprinted. A code? Prophecy? Random balderdash just spouted by a brain as it wheezed locomotive heavy, malfunctioned? Poetry, some will say. Lucy Jinx had run, gunned down, innocent as unpurchased socks, and died proclaiming the poetry of one who ran to their gibberish death with no cause.

Does Lucy want a doughnut? Or will her gut revolt? Surely the residuals of the previous night's drunk are off her back - if she is sagging, beleaguered now, that's just how she is. Or else she's a faker, plain and simple - which is fine and dandy with her as well, for whatever that's worth. Clarke gives her a wave as she enters and joins the dust-motes caught in the barely slanting sun through the hip-to-ceiling windows of the otherwise empty shop. 'Does your mother know the lowly grub you've become?' she asks, sitting, snaps her fingers in the direction of the plain-cake on display in the main case. 'I own a doughnut shop, part-timer. Outright. What do you own?' Lucy concedes the point and polishes the little exchange off with 'I guess I shouldn't suppose your mother has done any better for herself, you're right, you're right - it's safe to imagine that this' - she indicates her surroundings - 'is palatial Shangri-La in her eyes.' 'Exactly' Clarke nods, tossing her doughnut onto the table with the jaunt of a seven-year-old hocking a loogie. 'I have your check' he then says and Lucy, saying nothing because her mouth is full and she is as conscientious of propriety as a funeral parlor doily, perks her shoulders. You'd forgotten you get paid today, Lucy? Or not so much forgotten as are just not used to the kind of freeform issuance of checks from the night gig, here. Either way, this is wonderful news. Lucy actually hardly counts the income from this job as real, as part of what-she-has-to-live-on, yet - so this feels like a windfall, bank heist in its scope. 'Do you want the night off?' Clarke asks, so absently Lucy is put on guard, thinking if she says 'Yes' it will give him allowance to segue into telling her the job is kaput. Maybe sensing this - or maybe something else, based on the content of the statement - Clarke looks over, sighs, and explains he kind of wants to be out of his apartment at night - 'For awhile, you get me?' he says as confession with false-heart bravado - so figures he can do the shift if Lucy isn't hard-up. 'Yeah' she says 'I could get use an extra night's sleep, this week, if it's for a good cause.'

The truth of the matter is as follows: Lucy Jinx should in no sense be feeling she has this sudden glut of free time, just now. Yesterday into today was supposed to be bulbous with busy-work that was not to abate, was to make her normal schedule all the more difficult, this week and part of the next. When in Hell is the next time she even needs to be someplace, now? She isn't on at *Sella Tom's* until tomorrow afternoon and then she's not there again until the following afternoon and she doesn't have to be to the school again until Friday. Is Lucy not-busy this entire weeklong? That's just preposterous! She enters the apartment building lobby, feeling nervous, disemboweled even. Don't go upstairs, Lucy. Why not - what does upstairs have to do with it? It's just something - just don't. All of this time freeing up, coinciding with a walk home, is a sure sign of an interloping doomsday. Flash: Lucy Jinx finds Lucy Jinx, feline, dead on the kitchen tile. Flash: Lucy Jinx finds Elliott waiting on the sofa, stern faced, eyes scummy from crying, real glower, junkie-just-shy-of-an-overdose look to her scurvy beige skin. Flash: an intruder, immaculately dressed enough to be confusing enough to her she fails to react as he bludgeons her with Elliott's iron! But no - as Lucy gets further up the stairwell she knows it will not be like that. However, look here: still the tug of resistance. It isn't that something will happen in the immediate Lucy, it's the return home just serves as the punctuation mark on a death sentence - a sentence that, in theory, would have meant nothing, morphed to its opposite, if only a dot of ink hadn't named it all done. You're closing a phrase. You're ruining the length of a thing that could be lingered. Well: here is the door, Lucy. Make up your mind. Tricky, certainly. There is the door. The apartment will be all yours until who knows when. Is that something you can handle? Behind Lucy, in another apartment, is the sound of children's programing on television and a blender going and then a woman's voice in elsewhere-in-the-world tones - the voice sounds harsh to Lucy, but likely does not to those it is addressing - calling from whomever and whomever to come to the table to eat.

Lucy Jinx, feline - very much not dead - is, in fact, interior the kitchen sink basin, licking mustard yellow and ketchup not-right-red off of a paper plate with four cigarettes tombstoning it there there and there there. 'Obviously' Lucy says, setting down her duffle 'that's just where you'd be and what you'd be doing. Predictable as a cough during church, eh Jinx - you and yer one eyeball and everything, eh?' She coos all this, extending her hand with fingers rubbing - if the motion were said aloud the word would be *Wubbing* - to attract the cat, the cat not paying her even a perfunctory beat of acknowledgement. Paper plates in the sink: Elliott. Lucy has grown to love the paper plates and the Styrofoam bowls, but Elliott's penchant for putting them in the sink sits on Lucy, decidedly irritating, a corn cob down a bowel. If the dishwasher worked, Lucy would load it, day-by-day, with the disposable cutlery and dishes Elliott puts in the sink, run it just to prove a point. The point? 'The point is to show you how easily you can be mocked, darling' Lucy says to Lucy Jinx, touching the animal's tail, he still not stopping from the rough lapping of the plate. How old is the coffee? Lucy tries to mathematic herself into the here-and-now. Too old to drink, even the bookies would caution her that. Even if she microwaves it, the pit-boss would come over to whisper addendum discouragement. 'Health' she tells the cat 'is important. The viruses build up in coffee if it remains

out more than thirty hours, you know? Between thirty and thirty-six, anyway.'
She coughs loud, the cat not responding. Shush shush shush goes the sound of
the ridges-on-coin tongue to the soggier-and-soggier cardboard - the cheapest
kind of cheap plate, not even wax coated! Lucy claps and the cat does not pay
her mind - sure, he stops licking long enough to sneeze and yawn, in quick
succession, but that's nothing to do with Lucy and then it's straight back to the
licking. 'You can't convince me I'm not here, Lucy' Lucy says 'and it's a dick
move to play at it. Passive aggressive little wench.' To prove her point, she turns
on the faucet - but even still, the cat continues what it is doing, now under
water-fountain steady trickle of wet. Lucy shuts off the tap in an admiring
goddamnit. Opens fridge. There is a slice of green-icinged cake in one of the
regular bowls - one of the two of those green ceramics Elliott snuck out of that
diner - under a not-very-well-applied tear of plastic wrap. Stiff as a board, Lucy
bets without checking. Sighs.

Never yet has Lucy been afforded such a leisurely time of it, unpacking her
treacherous hotel bag. Remark, for example: she had left the duffle, here, just
outside the kitchen the entire time she changed into sweatpants and a camisole,
brushed her teeth with some of Elliott's paste, thought about flossing but once
again thought better, cut an English muffin - poorly, as always, a trick she cannot
get a mastery of - and depressed the toaster mechanism before taking the bag
up, moving it to her desk, and even there she has done nothing but unzip the
thing, lit a cigarette she hardly wants yet, speaking around in semi-too-loud
voice to nobody, not even herself. She is saying *Toaster. T. Oas. St. Er. Toe. Stur.
Toaster.*' And she is swaying her body much like it is a noodle being utilized as a
conductor's baton, hips in absent-minded sashays while she gets the cigarette
relit from a flick that somehow expectorated its whole cherry - there it is,
blackening dead on the carpet, nothing to fear. '*T. Oh. Ss. Teh. Er. Toaster.*' And
clumsy kl-klunk of a broken spring sound - the exact sound of a Jack-in-the-box
bolting up through its lid after a crank turning when the music bit is broken -
there is the, overcooked of course, English muffin. 'Goddamn you Elliott!' Lucy
says and gives Lucy Jinx, feline, a slight caress with her big-toe, the cat drinking
plib-plib-plib from the water bowl plib-plib-plib the bowl moving with a
gravelly sound from the rippling. It is Elliott, even when she's not around! This
and that - Jesus Hell! Grumble growl gnash! 'Why set the toaster to this setting,
El!? This setting should not even exist - it is like setting the thing to *Burnt*. Why
is it even an option!? And why do you choose it!? What other idiot things do you
do - set the *ATM* to *Tagalog*!?' Lucy demands answers, poking the cat a tidbit
more venomously. 'Which is a good point' she now Ahas, pointing where she
means 'even the visual icon on the toaster-dial is just an entirely black circle! It
tells you in plain pictograph! An Egyptian would get the point, man!' This

toaster debacle really seems outlandish in an entirely Lucy-is-actually-right-about-this-this-time way. 'Black toast, indeed' she says, shoving the crisped muffin down the sink drain through the rubber diaphragm which is long sick-glazed with various oozes, most visually with the orange-sauce of the microwave bowls of little-kid pasta which - again! - Elliot is still so very fond of.

Hanging her Adroit-clothing up in the closet, Lucy gives a quick once-through the pockets of all of Elliott's things - her coats, they seem so stubborn, almost rulers, at shoulders but droop at such imprecise dangles, don't they? She starts with, as always, the most daily-used of the lot, then moves on to the folded pants - does Elliot even wear a sixth of these? - then to the pockets of the things in the hamper. Nothing doing, as usual - this whole noia has become routine, like post-nasal drip. On a whim though, she decides to go through some of the pockets of these never-ever used heavier coats and things, these things on hangers - yes, in fact the sturdier hangers - but just kind of shoved toward the wall, packed tight into each other. Nothing but old tissues - a pack of tissues never opened, which Lucy puts in the droopy pockets of her sweatpants, hunter-gatherer instincts aflame - the usual coins, some receipts for nothing of any probative value, a little toy birthday-present, entirely purple-plastic - Lucy has no idea the meaning of it, likely it had none, the rubbish of Elliott, the rubbish she sometimes picks up and pockets - and blah blah blah. All quite boring. Yes. Elliott is always good for a tedium. Good lord, even these receipts are - what? - three years old? Four! This perks Lucy up a moment though, as she checks them all, hoping one will be sore-thumbingly dated just-last-month or at least from-this-calendar-year. But - alack the day! - the pockets all only contain history, pre-Lucy-Jinx. So she stares up at the two boxes of Elliot's keepsakes - boxes Lucy has meticulously gone through on several occasions and found nothing to get worked up over in, not stopping her, though, from getting worked up over that photo of whoever that bastard is in his military fatigues - thinking to give them another look, maybe to discover something new has been added, something not borne of time between she and Elliott and therefore proving some insidious goings-on. 'Elliot, I'm onto you - you're a small shard of purple wrapper exactly a condom in shade!' But Lucy does not look in the boxes. Though she does - no thought to it, just kind of does it - pat at a few of the hung dresses - the old, were-they-ever-even-once-worn ones, the ones right in line next to the four-years-gone-since-last-wear coats. And she feels the rectangular firm. Mark that. Mark: *And she feels the rectangular firm.* She feels the ridges, under speckled mint-blue cotton, of the spirals of a small notebook. Her breathing goes fish-cold and affect drains from her face.

Why upset though, Lucy? Had you not expected, quite precisely, to find something - and, regarding that something, had you not expected it to be something just like this? Ah - but that is it, eh? You had not *expected* - you had only *desired*! Those words, any second grader can see, are spelt differently - though second graders might only include one *F* in *Diferently*, eh? Well, here it is. Lucy! Look! Generic pocket notebook from any-old-drugstore - though you are certain it is from the *Scott's* on Plume Street aren't you, Lucy? - the front cover phony-bird yellow, a bend to this cardboard, just here, having taken on a fleabag look, some scrapes of pen-on-the-back, blue, red, black, from various times a scrawl or a dash-dash-dash had been tested before writing down whatever. Nothing better to do, Lucy scoffs at that, ridicules Elliott for - well, for some reason! - never having a pen that just works, right away. Because - lo and behold! - some of the notations in the book and in red, some blue, others black. And all so obviously coded. Obviously - obviously to the extent it is clear one would have to be oblivious not to notice and that *Oblivious* should be spelled *Oblivyous*. This is something you just needed to physically keep, Elliott - a notebook!? why not use your computer!? or your phone!? - something that carried the requisite tactile thrill of being hidden-someplace? But just letter abbreviations - Lucy can't outsmart them. *H.H.* there and *O.Y.* there and *V.W.* there. And did you think someone like Lucy Jinx, Elliott - like Lucy Jinx! - would not recognize that the runs of numbers here and here and here are telephone numbers - extra digits added in front of and after area code, likely between first three digits and last four, a few more after that? There are some area codes Lucy knows, off the bat. Local! You even kept local area codes in! Some kinda Enigma machine, ain'tcha? And did you think - this red entry! - Lucy would not know this was a User Name and a Password for something on the computer - exactly the site or the program or the et cetera Lucy can't sleuth out, no, but something! Something. All so painstakingly made to seem haphazard scrawls of no consequence. Pages not used in order. Writing not centered. Crossing blue lines. Upwards. Sideways. Bravo, Elliott! Even scribbling this out and that out to make it seem nothing-is-nothing when everything-is-twice-as-much-everything for being obscured.

'And to think' Lucy positively crackles with the thought while sat to the toilet and then while turning the shower taps - tugs, were the taps children's wrists there would be explaining to do to teachers, doctors, and authorities - and while moving into the bedroom where she has meant to undress but meantime has only just paced a lot and flicked a few times the rickety discount-stock window-blinds 'that I had been attempting to convince myself that coming home would lead to something bad! That it was a death march from the bed with Melinda' it took her a moment to remember the name but she does not dwell on that, if anything puts the bloop off to momentum, inertia, her mind a chug-a-lug of sprint-ahead-unbridled and obsessive repetition of single words to let herself catch up 'when instead it is this!' Wait. What? Wait - Lucy: isn't *This* bad? *This* is a bad discovery, would you not say? 'No' Lucy explains, impatient-to-say-the-least - coming home, this day, on a wave of time-off, to the room, all alone, had afforded her leisure for this search. 'Oh come off it' she counterpoints. Come off what!? 'You explored this apartment, alone and unencumbered, on multiple occasion, man - what are you even on about, here? You're loopy! Think: you could have discovered this notebook anytime - this day in particular wasn't required!' What an annoyingly correct and centering comment! Fuck. 'Yet still' Lucy nods and nods, repeats and repeats 'yet still - yet still - yet still this had happened, this time, and with a chunk of free time gaping wide still before me.' Are you meant to do something? What exactly? Keep searching. Use the time to call these numbers, crack these codes? Do you even want to do that, Lucy? 'I don't know' she says - the shower is still running, she looks at the almost shut bathroom door, full well knowing the hot water is out. 'I don't know. I think maybe. Something.' What? 'Something. I can't remember what you asked - repeat it, please.' Repeat what?

Lucy will later on buy her own exactly-the-same-sort-of-notebook as the one Elliott is hiding - and she will hide hers in exactly the same way with all of exactly the same things written in it in exactly the same way, just hoping for Elliott to find it in one of her own exactly the same, no-doubt common searchings of the premises. But for the time being, Lucy copies everything from Elliott's book on to loose pages, pure white. Note, however, how Lucy duplicates the style of how things appear in Elliott's book - same orientation of letters and all of that, same color inks, though she does not have red so indicates Red by writing *Red* in the lover corner of the large page - and jots down, circles, traces, numbers corresponding to the page-numbers in the original document, too. The thinking, here? In the off-chance Lucy does not get around to making her Exact Duplicate today and, in the interim, Elliott gets rid of the original. Gets rid of it, mind - not just rehides. Rehiding will accomplish nothing! If the notebook is not in the dress pocket, if somehow Elliott can whiff it has been discovered and therefore knows Lucy knows about it, Lucy is under no illusion that Elliott will not bother about secreting it, further - naw, just chuck it away, litter each page, in shreds, to a different storm drain while having a put-upon walk, planning her next betrayal! Lucy? 'Yes?' Why wouldn't you get your exact copy done, today? Isn't that what you are going to use the rest of the day for? 'No' Lucy snaps. And additionally - to keep the question from having to be asked - she explains that she certainly, as any fool could see, needed to do the copy on to notebook paper, in the event that she had gone out to buy a notebook, Elliott had returned in her absence, and - because things line up that way, times like this, every Tom, Dick, and Harry knows that much, especially when it comes to Lucy Jinx! - gotten rid of the thing. Then where would Lucy be left!? 'Exactly!' Knowing the truth but unable to verify it and no clues to kid-detective nor revenge-noir about town with.

She sends a text to Elliott inquiring after how things are. Elliott says *Things are fine, please and thank you.* Then Elliott sends a text saying she will not be home until night, but misses Lucy *very much and actually finds the whole thing with my friend a bit of an overdramatic slog.* Lucy texts back her most sympathetic support, making an off-color jab at this *alleged friend* of Elliott's, using the word *Turd* because both she and Elliott tend to use that word a lot lately and so using it here will come across as a nonchalant I-miss-you-too. Smart, Lucy - smart. Elliott texts back *Oh - Lucy caught a bug today - a fucking monster - a stick bug! A fucking stick bug on our mattress! Crawling out of our mattress!* Lucy wonders if this is true, as it seems kind of overtly particular, but then reasons with herself that were she not getting the story via text, if Elliott were present and just telling her - say just as Lucy walked in the door, returning from the hotel, today - she would believe it blindly and do nothing but say 'We need to buy her a trophy!' And so that is, now, what Lucy texts - except at the last minute changes *Trophy* to *flute of champagne or whatever cats think is good like champagne.* Tack tack tack, tack tack tack - each message takes Lucy some time to compose, the numerical keypad always pausing up if the word she is typing reaches the end of the phone's screen. Elliott texts her - apologizing for how random it is to, just here, say so - that she won a door prize, just today, when she and her friend went to some oddball supermarket where there was some manner of special political event taking place. And so now, Elliott's message goes on, she and Lucy both - *because the prize covers two people -* have coupons for *five-months' worth of free tanning at some sort of a place but a kind of hinkey one.* Lucy is typing that Elliott should give her part of the prize to whatever-her-friend-is-named-again, but then - really in her own not-understanding-how-adrift-it-is orbit - smiles, giggles, and types *Perfect! That's what we can give Lucy for saving us from the bug! Only don't tell her it was a prize, because we want her to feel we went all out.* And Lucy waits - waits - annoyed, finally, that the response from Elliott is nothing but *Ha! Purrfect!*

OBSERVE: THIS PAPERBACK BOOK. DETAIL: Lucy Jinx is not even interested in it. However: the fact remains that stealing a book from a bookshop is not something that even requires, particularly, much effort. Further: not any effort. Now: is this Lucy's fault? Details: she sees no security measures whatsoever - no protective, magnetic tab inserted anyplace that the clerk would deactivate by laying it thusly or thusly on a special part of countertop. Some background: in her twenties, Lucy had worked in a bookstore and certain books were tagged - she is certain that books of this or that variety still are tagged, to this day - and some person, she cannot recall whom, who had worked at another bookstore had told her that all books in the store where they had worked were tagged - 'The lot' this guy had said 'even the remainders, they stay tagged till they're stripped.' Yes: this had seemed ludicrous to Lucy. Yet: it had stayed with her - is with her, even here and now. Investigation: where would the magnetic-whatnot even be on this paperback? Built right into the binding? If not there, then the book is defenseless. Now: are you or are you not going to theft this off, Lucy? Consideration: it is to be a gift, after all. Question: What does that have to do with it? Answer: it might be better, cleaner, more appropriate to purchase the thing - as it is going to be given to somebody else. Jesus: will paying for it change the words in the book, the heavy of the font, the amount of times it is read or recalled? Well: that might not be the point, philosophically. Coming to the point: just steal it - you aren't going to get caught, simp. And moreover: you are a forty-some-odd-year-old woman who will be given the benefit of every doubt even if you are caught - though you will not be caught, please remember. But waitaminute: if committed to stealing, should I not look for a better gift? Point of order: is this the best I can purloin? Sigh: Lucy, that is quite another matter - by all means do better, but let's just get on with it.

Lucy has not stolen anything in quite some time. This surprises her, in that she cannot even put her days of unlawfulness firmly in the distant past, dub them *Youthful* and so rightly over-and-done. She's even stolen since moving to this exact city - though not so much. 'Adults kind of want less' she thinks. Wandering the second-floor of this bookstore though, Lucy is in a wave of wondering why she got out of the habit. Stealing is exceptionally pleasurable and harmless! People had to invent the whole concept of *Law* just to justify telling people not to do it. Lucy is a thief of books - an elegant thing to steal, those. Yes, yes! An illustrious thing to abscond with. She has, admittedly - she can admit it even now, pursuing this shelf of photography books, these which she cannot steal for they would have protective measures in place, or better say: Which it would be somewhat trickier to steal, though not so much so - stolen things other than books, but what she means is that now - Lucy Jinx, now - will only steal books. 'That is what I mean' she says to this photograph of a destitute sort from a South American country, posing humble-proud for the camera, never in their life ever occasioning to imagine an image of Lucy - or any prim city-woman - in a store like this, looking at their visage, their posture, judging them a wonderful composition. To this photograph a Lucy Jinx standing here is a science fiction - the poor bum can no more conjure an idea of her than she knows what tunes were hummed by women carving on stone in Qohaito. If women carved on stone there. 'Lullabys they fucking hummed, then' Lucy rolls her eyes, putting the book back. Irritated she has lost track of what she was thinking. What had it been? *Prim*? Is that what she had called herself? No - that was a side note. Ah yes - you had not stolen in some time, Lucy. Blah blah blah, right? She nods, moves along.

Out. Paperback in hand. Air and a few paces. Lucy is the very tulip of a great success. And now that she is officially around a corner and thinking about how she needs fresh cigarettes she is not even considering her theft. Over and done. She lights her last cig, crumples the package, deposits that in this over-full rubbish bin and moves on. A bit later: she is ducked into a drugstore and considering purchasing a gift-bag for the book. Odd how a gift-bag would be the more difficult thing to make off with. But this is, after all, for Sharon and so it should be dolled up a bit. Lucy selects a decorative bag - and striped tissue paper into the bargain - then looks at cards for a bit but figures one of those would be silly to include. A book should be inscribed. Are you going to write an inscription? Only if one occurs to her. She will toy around with one, yes - she needs something to do, as she will arrive at the café well in advance of Sharon - but vows not to worry her pretty little self if nothing occurs. Lucy Jinx's head is water left standing too long. Her brain feels gummy, like the veins of it are peristalsising gelatin in order to get her to function - each thought, word, decision of movement, voluntary or involuntary, is a physical glob making its termite way in a gnaw to her brain core. Outside. You forgot the cigarettes! Inside. 'Which brand?' asks the woman who seems elsewhere in a most pleasant way. 'Oh you please pick' Lucy cutie-pies just to break the woman's reverie. 'I don't smoke.' 'I know. But I'm trying to quit. Just pick a kind and hope I hate it - you'll be doing me a favor. I trust you to have shit for taste.' The woman chooses a really lousy brand. Outside, again. Lucy lights one and desires ill toward the woman and her stupid decision.

That is always lovely to see. The world is fairy-dust someone didn't bother to brush from the universe's sleeve. Those designers working on window displays, right now? Just two young women in a big empty window, a single nude, armless mannequin in there with them, large sheets of paper hung with notations on them - grand ideas, ambitions well out-of-scale. Lucy is sure it will be lovely, in the end. Her whole life, Lucy thinks of women like these - or men, so maybe best to say *Workers* like these, *Employees* like these 'People like these' she tries aloud but then reverts to *Workers like these* - as Artists. Trained sorts. Done up in schooling for this. Satisfied - grandiose in their air of having arrived at destination, fulfilled their potential, achieved a station to last their whole lives long. These workers could brag to Lucy and Lucy would fall mesmerized and ready to wed them - they could relate the details, the mundanities, the travails of their every workday and Lucy would see constellations, Sistine Chapel in their brows, scent perspiration of Caravaggio in the underarms of their pulled-over-head t-shirts. Of course, this proves what a chump old Lucy Jinx is. 'You're a sucker' she says, blocks away, still thinking about the workers, the women. God in heaven, think girl! Think how many a dope has come under the impression that Lucy is some honest-to-Betsy poet, officially titled - capital *Poet* - and based the impression on little more than she might have said so and been able to show them an issue of some magazine she once-upon-a-time found publication in, direct them to a website. These window women? No different than this windowless Jinx. 'Life is cobblestoned of all tints and tucks of meaningless ideas' she says. Doesn't like that she said *Tucks* - because what does that mean? - and gets morose when she cannot immediately come up with something nicer sounding. 'Forget the whole thing, then' she clench-jaws, hears in the roots of her ears teeth, wet, grinding to teeth.

A flier left on the corner table Lucy takes - before anyone else can - asks *Do you have caregiver fatigue?* A sad picture of a woman laying next to a toddler - or is that still an infant? If one does have caregiver fatigue, Lucy doubts this bulleted list of *Tips For Survival* will help. In fact, the word *Tips* seems quite preposterous, here. *Survival* is not something you should give someone a *Tip* about, is it? That seems rather cavalier, if genuine survival is on the line. 'Looks like yer tryin' ta survive there, guy - lookit: whyn't try this out, might be something, hey?' A *tip*, Lucy feels everyone would agree, is closer to being an annoyance than something of life-or-death value. Braggarts and boast-faces give *tips* about this or that - the father who is always out on his lawn in some neighborhood she once lived in gives *tips* on this and that. *Tips* are intrusive jabs, aggressions. 'Let me give you a *tip*' Lucy seethes, just sponge-twisting mockery and belittling sour from her in the words. Well done, Lucy! Hear-hear! You have put that word - and this flier - in its place and it won't be so cock-of-the-walk, in future. Coming to other matters: are you going to get a coffee? The gift-bag should be enough to save the table for you. And regardless, this place is not so busy. How long until Sharon is to arrive? A text-message from Elliott is waiting when Lucy checks the current time. *I think I need to stay here tonight. This is getting bad. I will try to call in a bit, just wanted you to have the head's up.* Lucy stares at the words. An hour old. So Lucy doesn't bother texting back, as that seems to be the conceit of the message to begin with. Lucy slumps in her chair and, phone away, has already forgotten the time. The light in this place looks like a cobweb. This café is like a billboard seen through the fog. It is like a telephone number for a taxi in another city you've memorized, roaming your current city, wanting to already be home. This café is a glove when what's needed is an ingredient.

All at once, the inscription for this gifted book to Sharon comes to her. As she writes it - something between a scribble and a smart second-grader's best penmanship - she wishes she'd stolen a better book. That's just how aces this inscription is! Sharon doesn't even deserve such an inscription, but this is the only book Lucy has and Sharon is the only person she's giving something to and Lucy Jinx may be many things but one of those things is not so-far-gone-she-would-hold-off-on-using-an-inscription-until-later. Also: she wishes she had had the book gift-wrapped. But then you couldn't have inscribed it she points out, this sagacity making her feel prescient. What a good mood Lucy is suddenly in! And so effortlessly - she is only now realizing the winged extent of her joviality. Yes - Lucy is good at thinking of pleasant things to think. She has, when she does not fight the open valve of it, quite a delightful current to her, can well see why so many men, so many women are attracted to her all the time. Considering her mannered-aloofness alongside her charm and all the world is hapless in her orbit, nothing but a face straining toward her lap. But - did that really happen? - right there that woman full on slapped that child! Jesus - did that just happen? Lucy has stiffened and the breath in her throat has curdled, lungs geriatric thighs, scabbily bed-sored. Her eyes dart to the customers waiting in line right with the woman who has now grabbed the child's face, pressing enough to leave marks - it looks like it, anyway, if the woman's nails are long the skin could be broken! - curted something at it and is now stood, facing away, acting composed and ready to bulldozer anyone who gives her so much as an eyebrow's worth of disdain. And nobody is. The other customers made sure to look that way, that way, that way - one of them, coincidence or not, actually holding open their coat pocket, twisting, and trying to peer in there at something - even while the assault took place! Maybe you should do something then, right Lucy? Look at the kid. Look at her. That little girl is resigned to it, already - resigned to the fact that the world is conditioned to, lickity-split, pretend her away.

Lucy doesn't even notice Sharon waiting in line as she passes - is, as a matter of fact, about to respond viciously to having her arm hooked and her body turned in a jerk. 'I nearly killed you, Sharon! What a foolish thing of you to do, knowing my temper!' 'Do you already have a table?' Sharon asks, craning head around, and then says 'Okay, but can we smoke first?' when Lucy points to the corner booth and explains 'See, I got you a present and everything - and you treat me like a dowry you want to be rid of!' Sharon hesitates a moment, though, about the cig - seems to think maybe it would be prudent to order food first, then dismissively Naws and tells Lucy 'We might go someplace else, in any event, mightn't we?' 'We can do anything you want, my pet' and to that Sharon turns her light grip - unmoved from Lucy's bicep - into a harsh claw, the pain enough to draw sharp gasps from Lucy, even water her eyes - because it was unexpected, her eyes wouldn't have watered had she been braced - which seems to give Sharon much pleasure going by the grin she blurts just before moving off toward the café door. 'Your trouble is that you're too isolated - too much time by yourself, these days!' Sharon accuses toward Lucy, flush from getting her smoke going and giving a phony sort of cough. 'These days?' Lucy quizzicals, having trouble with Sharon's borrowed lighter. 'You've only known me These Days, Shar - what could you possibly know about it?' 'Regardless - you are too alone all the time. Your head doesn't seem the best bet for a faithful, constant companion. You seem like a jewel thief who would settle just as well for some Tupperware.' This judgment is spot on, no doubt about that, but Lucy treats it as, if only mildly, debatable and defensively indicates all of the people within eyeshot as to her reasons for hermit-crabbing as she does. 'Your noggin' can't be any better stead than them, man' Sharon chuckle-exhales then wipes at her nose with the side of her thumb, rubs this on Lucy's shirt shoulder. 'You always forget that I know all about you, man, however only-a-little-glimpse I have gotten, so far. You're the picture on the puzzle box and you think you're the pieces - you think you're the task.'

Sharon is thrilled to learn that Lucy had stolen the book - she glowsticks at Lucy, turning the book over and over and caressing it like every part of it is the tuft of a snoring kitten's belly. The two bond for awhile about the joys of stealing and Sharon tells the following story: 'There was an Arts and Crafts store in the shops near where I grew up and I would steal the living fuck out of it. Especially around Halloween time. Other times, I would just steal something - a sketchbook, some charcoals, a fold of fabric, some iron-on letters - just whatever anything as a kind of base-line This-is-what-I-do-when-I-walk-over-to-the-shops - but around Halloween it was a different animal. Oh a real, howling compulsion come Samhain. I was only in fifth grade, of course, so I didn't yet understand things like fuck-lust - but if I had known about such headspaces it is the sort of obsession I would have compared the Halloween bandit-mindset to. One day, I stole a bunch of liquid latex - for making phony wounds - and a whole bottle - beautiful bottle, kind of in the shape of an inkwell but made of a thick plastic, like it had shampoo for horses in it - of fake-blood capsules. So, unable to restrain myself, five minutes out the door of the shop, walking on the train tracks, I start biting the capsules, the fake-blood pooling in my mouth - minty and iodine or alcohol tasting, mouthwash, but more hospital a flavor. The waxy outside of the capsules collected and - a spasm - I took a hard breath, a sudden sneeze coming on, and all bang at once the mash of these pill residues got lodged down my throat and I just started choking up a riot. I mean wheezing and whistling and trying to even say *Help!* I will always remember being brought to the point it seemed instinctively reasonable to say *Help* only to find I lacked the ability - if I were an actress portraying illiteracy, this is the memory I'd method from. No one was around, see? It was the makings of a real catastrophe - train horn in the distance for texture, all of it, all of it, Lucy. I remember trying to call for help, the word changing to *No!* - how instinctual that part of my brain lit bright - *No! No! Wait!* I knew it could be the end of me - and how! Obviously it wasn't - not to kill the suspense - but I pelted the rest of the capsules, bottle and all, at the train as it passed and it wasn't until I walked all the way home and happened to need to piss that I realized my whole front was a mess with dribbled blood - bright red, like an old kung-fu movie! That's how in a daze I'd been - how close to death - that I'd walked home in that victim state, unawares.'

The sandwich Lucy had ordered was too much for her to believe. Where the restaurant had come across these particular long rolls she could only speculate and would be mad to share her suspicions with outsiders. And the way the ground beef had been shredded - she wanted to only ever eat ground beef like this again and would betray orphans to gulags to be the only one allowed the privilege. Sharon insisted this enthusing was a result of the crumby wine they had each had a glass of, but Lucy did not allow that and proved she was still discerning in her taste by having some of Sharon's pasta and proclaiming it absolutely revolting, bottom-shelf drivel that likely would make culinarians weep piss. Sharon fought back by taking a bite of Lucy's sandwich, spitting it out in an all-chewed-up gore onto a napkin, leaving this uncovered while she demeaned the thing. 'It's oily, Lucy - that meat is oily and the bread tastes like a freshly contracted allergy.' There was brief moment wherein Lucy considered eating the pulp of slandered meat, bread, and cheese - but only just a moment. Instead, Lucy covers the napkin and unsightly slosh with another napkin and slides it all behind the napkin dispenser, pins it with that to the wall. 'How long do I have you for, pup?' Sharon point-blanks, looking up menacingly from reading Lucy's inscription for maybe the fifth, sixth time. 'You just have me, Cinderella. I'm done with it all. I'm quitting my jobs and everything and you can raise me like a guinea-fowl to slaughter, for all I care.' Sharon cartoonishly lascivioused, rubbed her hands, and let her eyes turn upward as though she were lost in a delirium of delicious slaughterhouse limericks, vulgars so intricate they could only work as animations. Oh how Sharon's every freckle had a psychopathy as Lucy again met her eyes.

The walk, aimless for a little while and then in the direction of Sharon's, was the sort of jawbone a goblin would preen over and polish, a bauble of cigarette smoke twined around cigarette smoke, a hand-over-fist ransom bag emptied of giddy, unreflective joy. Sharon's coat alone was a sea-craft to escape Hell's most obscure waters on, the artsy stitching where the sleeves met with shoulders, the pockets each made of different fabric - the whole school-kid-art-projectness of it, toddler-coloring book style was intoxication, let no man defame otherwise. This - if ever anything other than an actual story book page was - was a storybook page, illustrated in pristine detail of shaggy minimalism, each oblong seeming straight, each straight bent to double-crookedness, each word speaking outward to God flippantly and too-big-for-britches in its certainty of the whole universe it contained. That Sharon was some groovy cat, no doubt about it! Lucy propelled along, regretting each and every moment she so often decided not to spend with her, any tock she behaved as though Sharon were ancillary, featureless, of no more individual importance than a motel doorknob. But she's Sharon! Her face is the color of a bird-plume used as a pen and the veins in her ungloved hands are the best lines of an illuminated manuscript set behind glass for scholars to gawk dissertations at! Lucy, Lucy - how do you manage, for a single moment, to forget about Sharon!? She is a veritable century all her own, a time-and-place, a combination lock cursed at for your forgetting its click. 'I like you a lot, Sharon' Lucy tells Sharon. And Sharon relates how if Lucy weren't such a wimp she'd kick her in the shins for saying something so groundling, but as it is she doesn't feel like dealing with Lucy cry-babying off and tattle-taling to her step-mommy. 'Then I'll say it, again - I like you, really a lot.' 'I like you too Lucy, Jesus' Sharon says, mock gripe, overplayed exasperation, putting her cigarette out on the blinking apostrophe of the *Don't Walk* sign the two are just passing.


SO SHARON'S FELLOW - SHARON HERSELF clucked-tongue at using the term *Boyfriend*, claiming it seemed weak juvenilia, while to Lucy the term *Fellow* seemed bald-facedly absurd even beyond its olde tyme jaundice - was miles and miles less attractive than Sharon was and this curio always occupied the first half-hour, forty-five minutes of any time Lucy spent with them, together, the three. Yes, Lucy had only spent two handfuls of hours in the man's presence, but it had amounted to enough to note how he had some ongoing rotation of facial hair - he would shave to smooth, let a full bread grow out long, shave this to a goatee, then trim the goatee, let the sides grow in a bit before shaving to smooth, again. This was off-putting and Sharon always quite enjoyed Lucy's tactless mockery of it in private, but it was a burden on Lucy that the line of derision could not be folded into the general communication-trio. The fellow, Arthur Something, went by the nickname *Pops*, for some God-unknown reason - likely too horrendous to contemplate long without delirium setting in, gut rusting with sully of distaste - and according to Sharon had self-esteem problems because of some stuff when he was in middle-school. All-in-all, his shared orbit with Sharon was a mystery pit and Lucy had never bothered to probe or plumb the subject very far, preferring to show a gracious acceptance of the toad, treat him as an interesting tagalong, at best - a fixture or odd extra appendage, more often - a stained shirt she knew would be replaced eventually or just never unpacked from some moving box, one new city to come. Not that Lucy thinks about him much. Lucy assures herself, doctor toned, she doesn't do that. Not that Lucy busies herself with bookshelves or refilling glasses if they happen to kiss or if she sees Sharon letting the fellow take casual, glancing liberties with touches to the backside of her jeans or hooking finger in belt loop to slow her progress away. Not at all. Not at all.

Grudgingly, Lucy find herself wholly engaged in with some statements the fellow Arthur is making about his past and how he came to realize that it was little invasions of his privacy by people who he never would have thought would transgress in such ways that had led to some bad headspaces, ones he claims dictated many of the jobs he's worked and the apartments he's decided to dwell in. He begins with examples from romantic relationships. Some of his e-mails gone through, some covert telephone calls made to get information on some of his activates, nothing altogether nefarious but certainly nothing that anyone would condone, despite however much - right, Lucy? - one might do such things, themselves. 'It got to the point, though, when my sister had kids and I was living with her that I came to understand how imaginary privacy always is - how much of a make-believe construct it is, right? It's a version of things presented by adults to children - no different than saying *This is a wall* but not mentioning an ear can cup to hear through one. My sister's kids, she would always tell me - and I witnessed as much myself - would obviously, at times, think they were not being overheard - or that their little hiding places for things were sound, not easily discovered - and they would move, on faith, through life as though these things were absolute. Privacy was a thing like a star-scape - you can't doubt it because you can just look up or straight ahead, you know? But everything was overheard, wasn't it? I'll tell you it was! By us. By neighbors outside. And so everything from my youth must have been, just alike - that's what I realized - from mine and from all youth. As one gets older, it is so evident how little time one has alone, unobserved, unknown - and how all of these moments are only obtained by built defenses, by purposefully keeping other out. Privacy is a lie from parents to children - it's a deal that All will be known but only certain things acted on. And the postscript is Other things - anything really - can still be acted on, but only in clever ways, made to seem accidental.' Lucy could not help chiming in when Arthur took a moment to refill his glass with whiskey and to stick his tongue out at Sharon making blah-blah-blah motions with her hands like a duck puppet. 'Yes' Lucy eagers 'Yes! Nothing is accidental. People are everywhere. People-looking is like air, like water filling every crack it can find with the fluid of I-know-what-you-did. Eventually we're just wet with how people know-what-we-are - we are, they know, their stains!'

Now Sharon and Lucy are out on this patio. Not *patio*. What is the word, Lucy? Sharon is talking but Lucy wants to know what to call this. Not a *deck*. This is an apartment. They are high up. Outside. What is the word? 'What is the word for this?' Lucy finally just has to ask. 'For what?' 'For where we are standing.' Gesture, gesture around - show befuddlement on your face, Lucy. 'Outside?' offers Sharon, triple ellipsis between the two syllables. 'But this thing we are standing on. It's Kingdom is outside, it's Phylum is fill-in-that-blank. Not a *patio*. You know?' 'What is this thing we are standing on? The balcony?' Is that right? *Balcony*. Is that it, Lucy? Why is that not sounding right? 'Why doesn't that sound right?' Sharon has eyes between amused and pretend-concern. 'Is that what you mean? We're out on the balcony?' 'We are out on the balcony' Lucy slow-motion statements, the deceleration of the syllables doing nothing to make the word seem appropriate. 'I feel like a word has been cut out of me!' Sharon Oh-nos and does a caricature frown, big flip-flop of lower lip. 'Do you know what I mean?' *Balcony* is the right word, Lucy assures herself, but still demands Sharon provide her with synonyms for *Balcony*. 'Is *Portico* a word!?' Lucy desperates and Sharon bursts a snorted laugh and gives calm down hands, rolls them, and snap-fingers and Uh-uhs and Ums before saying '*Veranda, Balustrade*' Sharon seems uncertain of that second one 'maybe - what? - maybe *Terrace?*' Lucy's face has betrayed something. '*Terrace?*' Sharon repeats, a bit of a playact of backing away in shy trepidation. 'Does that sound right? Are you going to rob me or something?' 'Terrace.' *Terrace*. 'Terrace' Lucy agrees. 'That is what I was thinking. *Terrace* means *Balcony*.' Sharon thumbs-ups but does not relent on the act of anxiety and for the next five minutes won't lose the imitation of talking to a senile-gremlin even though Lucy multiple times tells her 'Oh fuck off with that, already.'

New cigarette. And while Arthur has to run out to buy whatever it was at the store Lucy tells Sharon 'I think Elliott is cheating on me. Well, as a matter fact - not to tell tales out of turn - I have become aware of the fact that Elliott is cheating on me, definitively, but I am polite enough to speak of it in terms of a general uncertainty - a kind of I-don't-want-to-jump-to-conclusions, you know? I am well-mannered, like moot court, even when dealing with a rascal.' Sharon - as Lucy knew Sharon would not - does not throw on a concerned face, a Golly-gosh! or anything, but seamlessly gets in step with Lucy's mood, right-awaying 'You just don't have a name yet, is what you mean? For who she's perpetrating with?' 'Exactly. Bitch uses codes. This is that math thing from World War Two, all over again - I remembered the name of it before, about Nazis and submarines.' 'Yes' Sharon agrees and admits to being of the persuasion that codes are really annoying. 'Can I ask - aren't you cheating on Elliott?' Lucy shrugs, lying that 'Unfortunately, no' and illiciting 'But that was where I hoped you could come in - we'll bedroom farce this up, matinee style, you know?' Sharon curtseys and says she serves at the pleasure of the President but does think there ought to be no shortage of waiters-in-the-wings to snipe at Lucy's trim. 'I think it would be more potent if it were a straighty I was going to the ledger with, you know? Really get in ol' Elliott's craw, that would!' Sharon sees the logic, but this magical moment - of course, Lucy, you should have known - is ruined by Arthur-forgot-his-wallet and has to show up and stick his nose into the room to say 'Goodbye, again' at which point Sharon - not mean spirited, Lucy imagines she thinks she's being a help - says 'Can I have sex with Lucy if it's for a good reason?' to Arthur, Arthur giving it a beat of Hmn before saying 'Can it wait until Monday, at least?' And they all laugh and Sharon tells Arthur to get lost and Lucy says 'Hurry back - nothing to worry about or anything, just saying' and they all laugh some more. But now Lucy cannot return to it and has to boil in a vile cannibal pot of 'Did Sharon change the subject with humor on purpose, or as a way to indicate she would actually be up for it?' - as in: if Lucy were to kiss her, kiss Sharon, right now, would it be stratosphere or would it be tripping on parking lot pavement and broken brown beer-scented glass cutting knees, cutting palms?

By a little while later - are you even going to check in with Elliott, Lucy? are you going to return either of those two *How are you?* texts you know have come in this past hour? - the television is on and the conversation is general humdrum, repetition of classics, repeated riffs on these repetitions, and Arthur has overcooked a pizza and seems to have no intention of going anywhere. So Lucy's patience with everything is thin. And she acts a bit on the blink, blaming a cold she thought she had beat. Why is Arthur here!? It's inane. And Sharon had given no indication he would be present when they had met up, when she had asked Lucy how long she could keep her. Sharon had not said *Keep*, Lucy - Sharon had said *Have*. And not in the sense of *Have* you wanted *Have* to have - not by halve. 'Well, you know what I mean' Lucy snaps with an eye wince, words breathy into an uptilted glass that has been empty for the past fifteen minutes. Maybe Sharon had not known? Had brought back Lucy thinking Arthur would be elsewhere. Fucking stowaway, Arthur, busybody and knob-purple as ever! Though Sharon hadn't seemed surprised, hadn't done any of that stuff a couple does when they do not expect to see each other, when one really hadn't wanted to see the other but cannot let on that's the shot. True. True. And beyond that: Sharon has had every opportunity to intimate to Lucy 'Sorry about him being here' and there's been nothing-doing of the sort - not even in a stenographer way, some facial set or otherwise-innocuous gesture. Hasn't she, though? Lucy, you would have noticed, right? 'I would have noticed' Lucy says to Sharon while opening the freezer for ice. And Sharon gives two little punches to the empty air in a 'Rah-rah, you tell em!' kind of way. Does Sharon let Arthur touch her? Does she bring him to climax and then sit with him after, like in the bask of hard won accomplishment? Does she listen to him when he is concerned about whatever it is he is always on about - his job, his mother's ridiculous cosmetics addiction and her hand-crafted jewelry line? 'What?' Sharon asks - a tone, a look, but maybe just because of Lucy's face. What is your face, Lucy? 'Sorry. Nothing.' 'You okay?' 'I am. Yep.'

Bathroom. Toilet seat up. Lucy sits. Not undoing pants. Then moves to the sink counter, doesn't even care it is wet. She texts back Elliott. Elliott will not be back until tomorrow and is apologetic. Lucy explains how she is currently hanging around with Sharon and Sharon's boyfriend *who is a halfwit but who will not leave because he probably thinks he'll finagle a threesome out of the bargain*. Why did you text that, Lucy? Now: Lucy standing. Now: there you are in the toothpaste-speckled mirror glass, Lucy - the mouthwash-blue speckled mirror glass, Lucy. *Hahaha - you totally should, just to confuse him forever - think of the trouble he'll get into later in life if led to believe such goings-on just go-on!?* If Lucy still liked Elliott - if Elliott was somebody else - Lucy would smile at that text, think it charming, a reason to be enamored, something that showed an appropriate view of the humor-sick world that this - all of it! - is. But being as Lucy despises every cellular trace of Elliott, all Lucy does is spit in the sink and mutter 'Why the fuck did you put a question mark in that sentence?' *Some writer*, Lucy then thinks, glad she just thought it because that seems more reductive than bothering to have muttered. Opens the medicine cabinet and touches at one of the four five six - six! - neatly displayed rolls of medical gauze. And a jar that just says *Wound Putty* and has some characters in Chinese or something below that. What in the holy name of Lord Jesus could all this mean? She unscrews the putty and it almost seems fluorescent beige - if such a color is possible - and it is scented something like milk and fabric wetted by stray dog urine then sun-stiffed. There you are again, Lucy. In this mirror. You don't look like anything you feel. Good? You think that's good, yeah? That's good - how you can seem so blank, how you could readily have a career as a discarded throat lozenge wrapper? But you are unsettled. Unsettled at how even your eyes are hiding you. Even from you. Look at them not looking back showing how you aren't looking at them not looking back, either.

Someone - she's guessing Arthur - has turned on music. Nothing Lucy recognizes. Modern. Glazed-doughnut sounding. The voices are antiseptic in their nondescript. Woman, man. Man, woman. Yes, Arthur chose the music because there he is a-boppin away to it while he makes himself yet another lettuce-and-cheese sandwich in the kitchen. Sharon is outside. Lucy joins her. They both light new cigarettes. 'My friends who have kids' Sharon exhales widely as though giving a wash to the furthest can be seen of the skyline 'they look at me like I incorrectly grew tits or something - that I have an extra knee, you know what I mean? Like my appendix actually must do something.' Lucy doesn't understand this so stays silent, not wanting to make it a joke. 'I guess what I mean is: they jab at me whenever they get a chance. I used to figure they didn't do it so much - but they really do.' Lucy says this sound annoying, but offers that people with kids need something to do, same as anyone. They're like celebrities who sometimes have cars that need gas and the photogs are there to regale us with the proofs. 'Teams are important' Lucy segues to 'otherwise we'd have no wars and no one would accomplish much of anything.' Not the right tone, Lucy. Shit. But good recovery with 'Sorry, man - I am just trying to indicate my ignorance, to let you know it's safe to talk, that I'm with you, no matter how feebly.' Sharon smiles and - maybe non-sequitur, maybe dead-hard-on-point - she then says 'I have a nephew. But a nephew is like a pet turtle you forget you have most of the time, I guess. No harm comes of it. It's only a turtle.' Yes - this is out of your league, Lucy. Time to leave? What is going on? Why is Arthur here, anyway? Jesus, Lucy! Don't you get anything? Oh - that was a tactic of his? How is it meant to have worked? Arthur doesn't know how to leave - there's a spat on and he is unsure if his departure spells something specific. He doesn't get it. He's literate, technically, but he's memorized the books from listening to the teacher at Circle-Time, you dig? 'I dig' Lucy says, though probably not really, but honestly feeling she does.

'Is Elliott really cheating on you?' This perks Lucy up - ping! There had been smoked cigarettes in two minutes silence before that. 'She is.' 'And you really aren't cheating on her?' Lucy acts red-handed. Lucy acts Oh-what-does-it-matter. Lucy rolls her eyes and stretches her legs out in front of her, a perfect diagonal plank, hardly in the chair, just against it. 'My defense is this, Sharon: I think I've known longer than I have known. And I have, I feel, been blaming myself just because I think Elliott is a putz - so why pin it on her? That is my defense.' Sharon kicks the side of Lucy's foot - again, again - gently, like a shoulder pat from a favorite teacher or someone snoring but you don't mind. But why doesn't Sharon offer any words? Is she waiting for more? Okay then, Lucy tried: 'I would break it off with her if I didn't feel like her guidance counselor, nowadays. She wants to be a writer. She says that like it's a thing one can walk to or build a door into the side of. She actually still says things like that. Like that is a want - like it's a goddamn Maslow's need. Like life is really a selection of an apron, the execution of a recipe, a taste, a weight in the belly awhile, and then the letters spelling *The End*. Or *You Win*. Or *You've Done It, Kiddo, Atta Way!*' Still nothing from Sharon. Fuck you, Sharon! Well, you're the one who keeps talking, Lucy, and you don't need to stay on this subject - and why are you being so candid, so unguarded? 'I mean, I guess it's like you say: a nephew is like a pet turtle you forget you have a lot of the time.' Sharon chuckles. As does Lucy. They discuss making this phrase famous and point out how it fits all occasions. The plan they settle on? Get it to be a catch-phrase on a sitcom that will be nuclearly loved for a year, spawn merchandise like an unchecked yeast infection, then be despised by even those most prone to nostalgia. 'That is my dream' Sharon says 'To be something everyone loved, once, only to have them all, one voice, realize - No! - they never loved me at all.' Lucy grins. Lucy says her dream is 'to be the spiders that hatch out of the eggs is some little girl's teddy bear.'

Doesn't Lucy have to work? 'No.' Do you want to stay over? 'No.' Are you sure? No. 'Yes.' No. Lucy explains she needs to get going. Promises she is not in a bad head over Elliott. In fact, downplaying it now, claims she thinks she might be overreacting. Arthur is laughing at some movie everyone has seen ten million times. Yes, Arthur is just that sort. He feels if he laughed the first time he is duty-bound to laugh again! Covers all his bases in case the auditor knocks. God, all Lucy wants to ask Sharon is if she really cares for that person, Arthur - that wart - does she really, at all? There is no way the question can come off as funny, though - not here, leaving, lingering in the door. Anyway - Sharon couldn't possibly. Look at Sharon. Look. Look, Lucy! But Lucy doesn't want to look. 'Do you want money for a cab?' 'I have money. I'll walk. Nobody will bother me. Cabs are boring.' 'Let me give you money then, just on the strength of I didn't let you cheat on your girlfriend with me.' This is the saddest thing Lucy has ever heard, but she has to roll her eyes and just say 'Don't make fun of me! I already said I'm overacting. And I already said cabs are boring! Whose side are you on? Mine? Cabs? Hers?' Sharon breathes out her nose and makes eyes in the shape of Are you sure? 'I'm going' says Lucy and begins taking walk-backward steps into the dingy, milk-gone-off colored light of the corridor. 'Can you call me or text me when you get back?' 'Oh Jupiter - yeah, mom. I will.' 'You're like my nephew, Lucy' Sharon says and - torture - bites her lip while she silly-smiles. 'Yeah yeah - that joke is old, now. You've lost your touch.' Lucy turns and is almost to the elevators when she hears Sharon's door clicked shut. But this is not how any of this was to go! And what is this? Where? An elevator? And Lucy inside it? And what? What? She shakes her face exactly how she imagines a bat does, hung upside down, still asleep, stifling a sneeze it thinks it is dreaming.

This area of the city has always seemed odd. A suburban toast crust. Shit. Lucy is sure she'll remember that! *A suburban toast crust.* In reference to the city. To a part of the city. No. No, you won't remember, don't buy into that malarkey like the others do - memory is something we say we have while we forget that we don't and we never did! So, she texts it to herself. Nope. That didn't go to yourself at all, Lucy. Five minutes later her phone vibrates and someone is asking *What's a suburban toast crust?* Lucy laughs. Deb. Decides not to respond. Then to send the message to fifteen other numbers, just to see who gets back to it. Within a block, Sharon does. Within two blocks, Sharon and Julia. No one else. No! Now Carlo does! Good for Carlo! Though he just types four question marks with two dots between each. *A suburban toast crust.* Well, the poetry has been sink-soaked off of that phrase, by now. The garish hue of microwaved orange-sauce has been untwined from the pasta and it sits in a watery bloat much like chewed up scar tissue would, like a body sweating through watermelon skin. How drunk are you, Lucy? 'No, I'm not drunk a little bit' Lucy explains. And this seems true, logistically. She tests some eye movements and some speed-up and then slow-down and then move-normal things. Lucy: in total physical control of Lucy. She recites some Lewis Carroll and is able to admit she does not do it perfectly, but probably never does - and, moreover, is just noticing this deficiency now because she is being hyper-critical due to her vague uncertainties toward her sobriety, at the moment. Which proves, is her point, she is the-rock-the-church-was-built-on unsloshed! There are no cabs to hail around here. 'Due to the suburban toast crust of things, dash it all!' Lucy stomps and fist-toward-her-chests. This hardly even feels like the city. But by another block it will all even out. That steep hill down into the drug store Lucy has waited out rain in and thrown up in the toilet of and lingered outside of not wanting to go home from - it will feel like the city by there. There is always some building just like that. The sentry. The outskirts. The place waiting to make you feel you are not so lost as you think you are, not so far from home - at least your current one. A place waiting to let you know those thing in order to make you feel miserable. Sunburned turnip peel.


IT HAD BEEN HALF-AN-HOUR AND there is no sign that Clarke is in there. Lucy has traced the following in the dirtied window next to the window she is now peering through: *take the last grief from my last sigh and leave me wherever I'm dragged.* She has also signed it *L. Jinx.* She has also - now, with fervor - roughed it out. But immediately wished she hadn't. It doesn't matter, probably - a blank pane or a sooted pane Lucy had traced fingers around on, the same. What if she had written it down? Can she objectively think of any difference it would make? To anything? Is she to imagine that had she simply never written it, never conceived those words out in that order, the world would be any different for it? Even as far the window edge, what difference to existence? It's an event, so it must have had some impact! It not having happened, if somehow it could be undone, must, of necessity, lead to an alteration in things! Why? 'Why?' she asks. This is something she always wanted to know, to have it explained without speculative, moralizing fiction attached. The world would be so different if one were to go back and shoot Charles Dickens dead! Oh it would be unrecognizable - that one life, the impact of it! 'Bullshit' she says and puts fake gun of her fingers to temple, depresses thumb like hammer ka-bam! If Lucy Jinx died, would that be the eventual cause for some whomever to have never read whatever and therefore lead an army insatiably into war? What if she were to turn gunfire wide on a whole twenty, fifty, one hundred people on a street - does the future suddenly become unrecognizable? Does everything that would have happened without that outburst now not? The whole world undone due to an aberration that is not even aberrant? Nonsense! Just because someone heard a song does not mean it affected them, even if they were thinking of it during a crucial time, even if they felt it inspired them. If not it, something else. Really: just them. Just them: inspired. Lumping in whatever randomness was around them out of some unconscious magnanimity. The superstition of inevitability. The horse pride of My-every-sniffle's-significant.

Very philosophical that, Lucy. 'Thanks, Lucy.' But I mean it! 'No, no, I know you do - I take the remark graciously.' You should be a philosopher. 'So should you.' Well, I suppose that only makes sense and I have to agree - but please don't shift the focus from yourself even if to yourself. 'Which one of us made that joke?' You I think. 'But it was you!' Was it? 'Wasn't it?' Can't we swap out? 'Swap out?' Zing! - I'm you, you're me! 'Oh - you mean since we're just talking to ourselves.' I'm just talking to myself, you mean. 'You're just talking to yourself, you mean.' I'm just talking to myself, I mean. 'I'm just talking to yourself, you mean.' You're just talking to myself, I mean. 'Which of us is it, now?' I don't think we switched. 'I think you're right - so how can we tell which one of us said it?' Said what? 'Which one of us asked which one of us made the joke?' How can we tell, you're asking? 'How can we tell, I'm asking?' You're the philosopher! 'Am I?' You must be! 'Well, I cannot philosophize a method to figure it out - how to get back to that point, considering we've lost track.' If we knew how many steps back it had been asked, then we'd know - mathematics would gather us home. 'But we can never know that - we have no record.' And no manner of recollection can ever truly concretely know? 'Do you think one can!?' I admit - it seems unlikely. 'And so we'll never know which one of us told the joke.' Alas. 'And see how little it matters - I even think we could figure it out, but what would it matter?' We're entertaining ourselves. 'It's how philosophy began.' People who didn't like exercise mouthing off while watching the athletes. 'That's how it was explained to me by Mr. Stumpf.' The acropolis and what have you - Mr. Stumpf, yes. 'We go to the games to chit and to chat and to feel better than everyone else when we're demonstrably not - at least not at what's going on there.' So we become what's going on there - the athletes are now what's going on around us, like grass dying and the flight of geese. 'And why in Hell not - who made the athletes boss?' They don't need us, we don't need them - we just evolved to want them to think that they do need us. 'And why in Hell not!?' Why in Hell not? 'Let's focus here, bring it back to roost: if we're both the same - try this on for fit - we can both be Me or neither be Me or there might not even be Both-of-Us to begin with but none of that nullifies the fact that we can't know which one of Us - if you catch my meaning - asked the question.' Hmn. 'Hmn.'

Is Clarke just not in there? Or is he sleeping? Why this has become Lucy's fixation, there's no point in going into. Fact: Lucy is not interested in going back up to the apartment, just yet. There is a pall over the place. The rooms will smell like an eyeball, nose right in close. The bedding will smell like a dead insect that smells like dust that smells like the heat from a heating grate. But Lucy - as much as she likes shivering in this parking lot - cannot wait out here all night because she is relatively certain she works tomorrow. No, she cannot just quit - reality holds a grip on her biology and the market has spoken as to what nourishment costs. Needs some sleep, certainly. This was all supposed to be terrifically different. Life. She recalls reading books when she was young, re-feels those first turnovers inside her of 'This is perfect, this is where it's at!' She remembers going to a bookstore with her father for a Children's Poetry Workshop thing. Had it just been an employee of the store leading Lucy and the other kids through some poetry exercises? Or some volunteer girls from the high school? Well Lucy, and so what if it was!? But Lucy had not been asking this to sound or seem dismissive. 'To the contrary, to the contrary' she to-the-contrarys - walking in the direction of her apartment now, though not really knowing it. It makes her feel sublime to imagine it was just some girl who worked at that slip-shod franchise shop. Maybe the girl had been nervous about even volunteering - or maybe the entire thing had been her idea! There are nuances and wrinkles in the world just so graceful as that - looking back on your life you find grandparent creases and crags in what you once thought was buttermilk silk. Some delirium had made a young girl who fancied herself a poet want to sit with shy-as-the-devil Lucy Jinx, to try to enthuse her into acting more like a Leopard in order to write about a Leopard - to do it more playfully, more explanatorily, just as the other children were. Lucy remembered being bashful as a tortoise-shell but also certain she was right: a leopard would just sit there, hardly moving, looking around, maybe yawning just as Lucy had pretended to yawn - maybe just how Lucy had then yawned, for real. And Lucy had stayed steadfast in her certainty. Had Leoparded herself into illiteracy, not a jot scribed.

Now look at this: Lucy has bypassed her apartment building door and is proceeding, dishevelledly ashiver, all the way down the block, the next block, the next. Why is this happening, Lucy? It has got in her head: someone is following her. She feels eyes on her shoulders, her thighs, eyes lacing her ankles around. Now, it could be pointed out how this is likely a symptom of the events of the evening leading up to here, her - causality showing itself as causally as always. To wit: Lucy had been suspecting Elliott of something and had snooped all around and found evidences and then Sharon's boyfriend had ranted about privacy and then Lucy had looked through the medicine cabinet and then Lucy been wondering why Sharon's boyfriend was around and had been trying to decipher what Sharon saw in the lout and then Lucy had sent text responses to Elliott in a deceptive way and then Lucy had on purpose texted that line of poetry to people to needily goad some response and then Lucy had been peering in the window of the *Deneven's Donut's* trying to get some idea where Clarke was and wondering what he was up to - so obviously she will get it all over her, now, that maybe someone is keeping an eye on her. Not to mention: Lucy had just spent a drunken night, ardorous and scratch-leaving, with Melinda! But now the rub becomes this: do you feel like someone is watching you, Lucy? Or do you feel that you ought to feel like someone is watching you? What drivel! What drivel!? Why is it drivel, Lucy? You're addicted - maybe, at least give it an ear - to feeling ill at ease and about to be found out. You protest and whinge about the fact that your life is suspiciously made up, like an arc plotted on purpose, yet it is you - you, Lucy - who never relaxes and just lets a moment be. Don't you know that nobody cares about you, Lucy? Don't you know, to most, you might as well be fictitious - that, Hell on Earth, you'd mean far more to most of the world if you were!

Take a moment. Take a moment. Here is Lucy. Lucy Jinx. There is the sign. The sign for *Zilch's Dry Cleaning*. These are the very lights admired by one Lucy Jinx. There? Just way up there? That is the window Lucy Jinx so nightly admires these orange lights, now above her, and this unlit sign from. Just take a moment and enjoy knowing that you, Lucy, are currently an object embedded in an image that so often gives you peace. Amaze, my girl! Amaze at the somewhat paradoxical ability to - due to the fact that you look down on this very spot you are in so often - see yourself when you do not actually. Doesn't it feel like you can see yourself from up there, Lucy? And from down here don't you feel, though darkened, you can make yourself out through that stiffed-syrup pane? And isn't it peaceful to see yourself inside of the image you would look to to feel peaceful when you cannot sleep for a head that won't stop tensing and twitching, a brain that is gun-shy or can hear it is surrounded by conspirators, surrounded by double-crossers, surrounded by guessing-games about to guess against it? Take a moment and just be here. In fact: stop thinking about all of that! Stop it! Forget it all! Just be here. Look at the sign for *Zilch's*. It is how many times as big as as-big-as-you? It weighs how many times as much? Relative to you, how old is it? Relative to you, what will happen to it, eventually - what is the death of a thing like the sign for *Zilch's Dry Cleaning*? What is the death of a thing like you? Smelted, it - cremated, you? Scrapyard, it - Potter's Field, you? If you had to give it a voice, what would it sound like? A personality, how would it feel on a night like tonight? Grumpy? Fine. But at what, grumpy? Or no! No! Stop with all this. Just be here, can't you? Can't you simply be? You once were - yes? Have you forgot how? Have you forgot you ever once were? Just be standing here. Lucy Jinx. Here is Lucy. Take a moment. Take a moment.

So fine - the world wins and can whir gloatingly it axis around - Lucy has come back to the apartment and she entered it exactly like a tooth chipped by a bite on a candy cane and that chip-of-tooth then chewed by the rest of the tooth and the other teeth along with the candy cane and swallowed and followed by worry of 'Will that jag of tooth cut up my insides?' Just inside and out of coat and turns up the heater obnoxiously high - she's a roach needs fumigating, she plays at. Cigarette. Plumps herself to sitting on the counter and looks down to see she needs to feed Lucy Jinx but doesn't yet want to. The cat will be asleep. As always. The damn refrigerator magnets are awake more often than that cat! A cat not asleep is more like an *Asleep* briefly *Cat*. So a few minutes pass. The cigarette finishes. Her ass hurts to the pitch she decides to move. And by then the apartment does not seem so bad and she is more than glad to be returned into it. She lays out on the sofa and crosses her ankles over each other and closes her eyes and starts counting down from sixty - repeatedly losing count - hoping to fall asleep in her clothing and to have some sort of vivid bad dream. She hopes to wake choking on a dry throat, wants that water so frost-sharp and desperate to be down her it feels out-of-body. Did she ever actually lie to somebody about how she used to induce nightmares by sleeping in multiple layers of clothing, under two comforters, after taking a gut-load of cold and flu medicine? Or had she just used to think that would cause nightmares and maybe thought about prattling about it being something she had done to whoever even listened to her at that age? What a mongrel you were, Lucy Jinx! And her own name and the word *mongrel* - apologies all around, she begs pardon, insisting - remind her that the feline Lucy Jinx still needs feeding. So up she goes and tends to that. Holding the dish and calling the cat - giving the dish tilt-tilt-tilts to send the sound of the hard morsels out through the murk of the kitchen-lit rooms. Kiss noises. She walks through the living-room, the bedroom - tsk-tsk-tsk sucks-in made fast-as-she-can as though an attempt at mimicking the viola legs of a cricket - holding the bowl and hoping for a sight of the kitty. Nowhere. Asleep. Nowhere. To a cat, that's the same. Asleep. Nowhere. And both are the same as Everywhere. And as Awake. Lucy yawns and rolls her eyes at the fact this is the mump she's become.

Warmth spreads out to-and-fro and wafts down on her nude body like a spray from an aerosol canister, she shishes her legs over the still-cool-but-not-for-long bedsheet and tightens her headlock on the bunched up blue-green-stripped blanket that also drapes over the bedside a little. What is she thinking as she drifts, semi-dissociative? Nothing out of the ordinary, for her. She wonders if she would be the sort who could bear doing something unforgivable. If she was wired like the sort - like the doubtless many millions - who could honestly go through with whatever heinous action and not only show no outward sign of being ill-used by Fate, but honestly, in their hearts, feel no burden, though intellectually acknowledging the wretchedness they've enacted. She thinks she could pull it off - she might even be well tailored to it, suit and tie and shot cuffs. Part of her sure it would not even be difficult. And that part laments - in a way one, or that part of one, can only lament when exhausted and not yet asleep but in the state where one might as well be - that she is not an individual in a position of power - or even with access to someone in a position of power - as, were she that - or had access to someone who had it - this ability, this trait she is certain she possesses, would be an asset. It would be the thrilling foible that would tease a playwright to their pen-sword. Even those who would satirically chastise her, who would immortalize her as an exemplar of Flawed would not help but have to admit their awe, their envy, their jealous loins at her imperfectness. Then her thoughts, abrupt, turn giggly and self-indulgently clever. Lucy Jinx believes *Flawed*, the word, should be officially spelled wrong. That the actual spelling should be wrong. 'Do you see what I mean?' she asks, but will never remember she'd asked. She means it should be, for example, spelled *Falwed*. But said *Flawed*. 'The pronunciation is *Flawed*.' And even though that is the correct spelling - *Falwed* or *Flaewd* - the correct spelling is incorrect. 'You should have let me invent language' she says, turning on her side - she might, if only somewhat, if only peripherally and one day, recall having said this, have the feeling she had when she one day comes up with the sentiment again - 'because only I understand it, only I would make it as flippant and never-stale as it ought to be.'

If she remembered the dream, it would only disappoint her. The feeling of being at odds with herself, lacking, would shroud her the entire next day - she is judgmental of her dreams, judgmental of her talents as dreamer. As it stands, she dreamed it, but woke not able to recall even a shaving of detail, only had an uneasy feeling and a mouth thick with standing saliva, churned to a thin froth, so is able to believe she would like the dream could she recall it. It went like this: she saw a sign that read *Mail Room* but did not see the entrance to the room. Though the lobby she stood in was small - and the sign clearly was not referring to the lobby, itself, as the Mail Room - she looked around and wandered the stumpy circle of the place and could not find anything anywhere. Then she was outside. And it was a dream of the scent of passing a dumpster or an unlidded trashcan when she had been just shy of adolescence. There had been no dumpster in the dream, and she, herself, had reduced to an abstract kind of fuzz, nothing more than the sound of a pop of static in a radio not tuned into anything in particular and set far too loud, but still could smell the odor. In fact, all she could do was smell it. The smell defined her pop, her absence. That vomit tang, a taste to the fragrance. It was the ether and her marrow and her heartbeat and the juddering rough of her brain pulsing out words and instructions - a perfume of what to do. She woke not long after that bit and lay in a state of trying to summon back anything but sensation, unable to. All the lights in the apartment were still on - or enough that to say so made sense. She's wound up underneath of the blanket, except for her feet, and so sweated and shivered at once, her whole body the pilled tickle of a sore throat.

There is nothing on television except for whatever this was and the feeling that someone is watching her, still. But this is a bleak and comforting noia, by now. Being watched out-of-doors makes her feel vulnerable - indoors she feels a caged thing, beloved even if wrongheadedly. Were she to choke, someone would burst in and save her! And Lucy takes a moment to reassess, generally. There had been a point, today, where things had seemed wonderful. And certainly there had been, yesterday. And so things likely still were. There is no percentage in trying to disabuse her current head of any notion, as only sleep then a return to endless and to-no-end business will do that. Or at least will dilute the poison. Her current agitation: the result, merely, of her hands being given too much time. An idle Lucy can never think of anything else to do but become her own enemy. History bellows the truth of this. The only thing Lucy - past *X* point of fatigue - is capable of is in-no-particular-order dismantling her happiness. Now, she is eating a sandwich. Now, she is finished. And eventually she will seem to suddenly be waking up - and within an hour's time of that won't remember that feeling as sudden, really, at all. A commercial, here, makes her wonder how long, specifically, it has been since she spoke with her mother. Is that how you picture your mother, Lucy - how you are picturing her now? But that is not up-to-date - and would you know her voice from a distance? The bitter truth? Her mother could well have died sometime recently and Lucy would not know at all. She'd know what movies were playing in a theatre she doesn't even know the name of but has kind of walked past sometimes more than she'd know of her mother's health failing. Where her mother would be buried. If she would be burned. If there was something to do about it. If it pertained to her, at all. See there? Had that been thought or dreamt? Lucy is awake now, but knows she had not just been. Had not just been, when? That is the unknown thing and around it ripple other ciphers, eh? They drift until thin enough to no longer bump anything and that's when things feel fully actual, not until - the sea-face calm until the shore-line. Lucy Jinx, feline, is on the sofa, next to Lucy Jinx, now. But the same thing is on the television - it doesn't even seem the plot has proceeded very far. Maybe all of that happened at exactly the same time. Maybe. Lucy opens her eyes. She'd been asleep. How many times? How many times?

Here is a dream she will remember every detail of for years. This is the sort that functions the same as a memory, creases the brain in just the same folds and squiggles. This: Elliott emerged from the bedroom holding a shoe and asking Lucy whose it was. 'Whose is this shoe?' 'What?' 'Whose is this shoe!?' 'What?' Was Elliott joking? Lucy knew how she was caught and had no defense. And the two had screeched and Lucy had pulled Elliott's hair hard enough that some had come out and she had run to plunge her hand, fist full with hair, into the toilet. Then depressed the flush lever, feeling the water inertia around her wrist, sink, fill back only enough to cover her knuckles. Uprooted strands still, like melted wax thinned, gooey under her nails. And Elliott had been waiting on the couch, unlacing the shoe she had first brandished. No. It was a boot, now. And not unlaced. She was whittling it down with a box cutter. Long thins of it were coming loose and scribbling the floor like a wailing knot of centipedes. 'Is that supposed to mean something? Is that supposed to look like hair? Is that what you're saying!?' Lucy had demanded and found, just like that, Elliott was at her throat with a hand up under her shirt, fingernails raking over her ribs and drawing a twang of cramp that made her cough. The coughing woke Lucy. It was a coughing she could not stop but also made no move to alleviate. The hurt to her ribs felt so real. And she heard her 'Is that supposed to be your stupid little hair!?' residualing in the television lit apartment around her. The cat wasn't there. No - the cat is right there. She sees the look on Elliott and can taste her thin with thirst angry mouth on her mouth. She feels she had just been entangled with Elliott's specific flesh. That some of the dryness her body feels strained under is the left over salt of Elliott's evaporated sweat. Her eyes ache as she blinks them hard enough to cancel out the television flicker informing the black. Closes them so tight her hearing goes high-pitched and the black she sees is a kind of silver like the sound when accidentally striking one's nose, silver then tin-warble green.

# .III.

IT SHOULDN'T BE THAT ONE can so clearly hear the vacuuming going on in the hotel room the floor of which is one's room's ceiling. Especially, Lucy particulars, what with this being a rather up-done establishment. Is this something physics just conspires to keep impossible, soundproofing the Above from the Below? It does not seem this can be. What would it take? A thin wafer of concrete? Or less than that, right? Some sort of foamy insulation. The miracle of asbestos? We've discovered it's venomous so we have to suffer the horrors of the goings on upstairs? Lucy can hear each crick and snap of whatever miniscule debris the vacuum is up-sucking. Also of interest to her, but side-noted: though the sound is way over there, just now, she can distinctly hear the louder and softer, the intensifying and diminishing of the vacuum itself as whomever is working moved it forward, back, forward, back - but why doesn't the fact that it is above and far off remove this quality? No, Lucy - what are you talking about? Why would it? It is still, relative to you, altering its approach or retreat, its side-to-side nature - and sound is a physicality that travels according to rules. *Upstairs,* Lucy concedes, has nothing to do with it. She'll deal with this for now, but if she hears the feminine hush of heavy pissing or the shebang of a flush - let alone the ablution hock-splats of some man at his flab-gutted mirror - she is demanding a reduction in daily rate! And so she paces, unshirted but pants done up and belted - she will not tuck the shirt in, today - and hopes that the business up there will be done in the next forty minutes. Seems it ought to be. Relax, relax. But are you going to light a cigarette, Lucy? You don't want to keep the crispness of the room awhile longer? It is a fair point to mention how, since you have resisted smoking thus far, what is a bit longer? Fair. But: are you going for some kind of posh, healthy, prestige-edition thing? Are you not supposed to come off as a smoker? Are you supposed to be elegant, Lucy? Or what? Because not smoking is an obvious and somewhat deplorable posturing, considering how false-hearted it is. What are you hoping to achieve by this abstinence? You're a stain trying to dress up as a brush stroke, man.

Lucy is mistrustful of the partially stocked kitchen area. She is meant to be able to eat the food, certainly - that was clearly explained when she booked the room. But is there really no individual charge-per-item? The hotel must count those apples, those bananas, that pear. There'll be a reckoning for each one, oh she'll be itemized right into the fabled Debtor's Prison her mother would spin yarns about when Lucy was young. Certainly, Lucy, you will let Victoire Elan eat and drink freely! 'Of course I will' Lucy says, unbelieving she has to answer this charge. But are you hoping Victorie won't eat or drink? To the contrary: Lucy chose this room to seem less pauperesque than usual. But look here at this kitchen: vodka in the freezer, wine in the fridge, a bottle of whiskey next to the toaster for God's sake - this placement still seems weird, Lucy cannot believe this is not an oversight, that the whiskey should have been arranged someplace else and that housekeeping had goofed in their last pass through - surely the entire contents of those bottles aren't covered in the room charge. Though: come on, sure, why not? How much did Lucy spring for this room, all accounting? For two hours' worth of this room, to be exact - what'd that run her? Yes, you paid for two days to use it for two hours! This room. Why, Lucy? Because of the name, some name you like? Lucy takes her shirt up from where she'd left it on the bathroom sink - note, this bathroom is almost the size, itself, of the entire room she takes out at other establishments - and gets to buttoning it. Then: there she is in the grand mirror. Well, not so special a mirror. Pretty par for the mirror-course, really. But: there she is. And blazer brought around - you've put on some weight Lucy, not that you weren't certain before, but now there's no doubt - but not center buttoned because that seems to make it all too taut under her arms and around her shoulders.

More evidence. Look: a fresh notebook. Not just fresh, but bought especially for this session. A fancy number, catcalls and two-fingers-in-mouth whistling. Green faux-leather cover, hot-cha! One of those ribbon bookmarks built in to show a nod of I-don't-give-a-crap dandyism. And here? Yes, that is a new pen. Nothing special, Lucy's normal brand, but bought just on the walk over, yesterday. The first page will be blank. Ceremonial, blood borne, Lucy could never have it otherwise. The second page will have - delicately, tiltingly written - the name *Victoire Elan*, all capital letters. As though this entire notebook will be the home of one single poem by that name. What airs, Lucy! The things this all indicates to those keen to observe - fanning themselves with newspapers, they are. You might as well have bought a cigarette case while you were at it and an antique flask that shuts with a squeaky quark. Oh ho! Here it is! When the damn breaks it does so suddenly and without having ever heard the word *opposite-of-irrevocable*. Lucy Jinx is lit up and sighing into a long exhalation in the shape of the first time someone formed a letter that everyone agreed on the meaning and sound of. And then immediately: a short glass from the cupboard - should you use a mug, Lucy? mix it with the fresh brewed coffee? no, perhaps not - and some whiskey right into that and gulped down without quarter and hardly with a sniff. Lucy winces but is certain it would be delectable if she'd bothered to savor it even a little. Another bit of the stuff and then a pour of coffee, too - yes, now a mug - and this coffee too magma hot to bother drinking so was, in a sense, pointless. The smoke will cover the booze breath, anyway. And anyway: you're goddamn Stella Adroit, Lucy Jinx. Be drunk as a sailor's wife on a night out with her best friend the substitute teacher! Lucy looks at the bottle. At the notebook. No, no. Focus! This needs to have some semblance of suave, alright? 'Suave' she concurs. And she pointedly walks the room to spread the cigarette smell. And purposefully opens one window slightly and stubs her finished cig on the sill, leaving the bent-in-five carcass of it there next to the black smear of its blotting.

Lucy feels she's in some piece of cinema she'll watch and only remember certain images from - not the shots used on the poster, the cover box, but the images she would choose for the poster, the cover box, had she been asked - which she should've been. There is a movie she feels she is in that her experience of watching can sum this all up, perfectly. Generally: it is the sort of movie that is languid, long-limbed, that seems to dwell while at the same time covering much ground. The colors are rich and distant. The light, especially, seems to be the meaning of all things - script, performance, music, all just aspects for the light to touch on, round over, or shape past. It feels like a film that is good but not as good as it seems it ought be. The sort one never wants to speak anything but fondly of, but that one never, when mentioning it to another, gets any particular enthusiasm in response from doing so. What are you driving at, Lucy? The sort of film that seems less-than-the-sum-of-its-parts, as they say? No. Not that at all. More individualized a thing. She cannot get her mind to articulate proper, not now with it being any-minute and then all-at-once Victoire -

Victoire, at last. She knows whatever this moment feels like - cinema, corn stalk, well-thumbed directory, faded turpentine label, other - will irrelevant itself without fuss and some other patina will go over things once Victoire. This is the minute, the kind with nothing to it but to notice it - in all its specific components - to feel the grains of it pass, know each uneven of its suede. Whole days in childhood pass like this, don't they? And in adolescence, if not days, certainly some evenings or late-at-nights do just the same. By now - by Lucy, here - it is only minutes, here or there, that are so tactile and nothing-to-do-about-them, no way to color or fill or shorten or elongate. This minute, this lasts. She has to just pace and smoke and feel and then will not even recall having done. Stop. Wait. Everything stop. Like the first beak strike of a cramp in a center rib, there is a tap tap on the door. It either sounds soft - the type of door blurred with the type of hand - or else Lucy is buried too much in not breathing to hear right.

Ah. Now. Here. Here. Well. Here, ah. This is something that perhaps should pass quickly and without comment, that perhaps should simply display, real-time, as though it has been a mistake not to have known this was rounding the bend. No, no. Even in the moment Lucy is having trouble processing how she understands the moment, let alone how it will be explained in moments come after. The door has opened. That went as planned. This woman looked at Lucy - Lucy who had been smiling, ready to do some bit of her usual over-apologizing-though-there-is-no-need for taking so long to get to a door she had got to, straight away - and had blinked - had blinked, had eye-cocked and laughed - and Lucy had clay-to-a-wet-riverbanked, had unshaped to silt in drifts in a creek bed and - Lucy was absolutely not seeing this correctly - the woman had done this or that and Lucy had been this or that and then this woman, Victoire, had said to her, plain bang 'Lucy Jinx?' 'Ariel.' That is how Lucy had responded. And not a question. And Ariel's response of 'Lucy Jinx' - in stern, sober-tone mimic of Lucy - was also done up as statement-rather-than-question. And then it went kind of ping and pong of 'Lucy. Jinx.' 'Ariel. Ariel.' 'Lucy. Lucy.' 'Ariel. Ariel! Ariel!' 'Lucy!' 'Ariel.' 'Lucy.' Until they both got the point but stood saying it - still just there at the door, saying their names like the first things to breathe outside of the water - the sounds pawed so that syllables lost distinction and the names flailed like the mud on two kids' filthy hands as they shivered from being outside too long, ignoring the rain, playing some handclap rhyme they were inventing as they went, concentrating on too hard to know if they were even keeping coherent. Ariel is the first to add in the ripple of giving Lucy a poke - like Are you wax? Are you apparition? - with her face, meantime, done up exactly in the expression What the fuck, eh? Lucy lets herself be poke-poke-poked on collar bone and holds the eyes of Ariel's expression with likely an expression of her own, but her whole face, her everything, feels about as solid and describable as the clear of a diner-greased napkin - so who knows what she looked like.

Coming at this moment another way, because it bears this distinction: Lucy had been expecting Victoria Elan who - she just saw - turned out to be Ariel - that Ariel - and Ariel - yes, from before, Ariel Ariel - had been expecting some woman named Stella Adroit, who'd turned out to be Lucy Jinx. Lucy understands this. And it is azurely obvious that Ariel understands this, the same. And then they acted appropriately surprised to see each other, because it was not only surprising on $X$ level, but also, to say the least, on $Y$ and $Z$ and other alphabeticals that they should be doing so. This was a surprise, so they acted it - that's what one does when surprised, one acts. There: Lucy. There: Ariel. It's really quite simple. But the rupture of it speaks volumes that kept anything other than repeated names from being said. The moment passed, of course, and Ariel came into the hotel room - doing nothing still but looking at Lucy and saying 'Lucy' and sometimes saying 'Lucy Jinx' and sometimes adding liberal pepper-shakes of the word *Motherfucking* before, between, or after those options. And Lucy - more blushed than Ariel, let's point that out - kept just out of arms' reach of Ariel as she back-pedaled toward the kitchen and toward her cigarettes - a superstition to this distance-keeping retreat, the sort of thing her over-active brain had trained itself to do since first being terrified of spooks in her little-girlhood. Lucy offers, wordless, a cigarette to Ariel, who responds 'Well, yes - did you even have to not ask?' as she takes it and helps herself to the lighter which it had not even occurred to Lucy to lift in giving. Ariel hands lighter to Lucy. No. She doesn't hand it. Ariel strikes lighter. And Lucy tips head forward and, apparently, that lights the cigarette she took up, just before. In that moment, things return to an agreeable normalcy. For example: Lucy says 'There is also alcohol here that came with the room' and to that Ariel goes 'This is all so fancy it feels like eventually I get clubbed over my head and wake up somewhere less regal - just so you know that I'm on to you. I almost feel bad I didn't wear my nice boots you could rob - if I'd know it'd be you I'd have made sure there'd be something in it for your trouble.'

Free admissions of not having expected each other are made. 'At some point' Ariel is saying, her coat removed and third cigarette going 'you decided to re-enter society, I discover, but under the guise of Stella Adroit - and for the dubious purposes of luring women to hotel rooms? I need this correct for my, you know, biography of you in five volumes in the original Danish.' Lucy, leaning forward across this cat-on-back-luxuriant island-counter, seems to consider this. 'That's about the size of it, yeah. And - in conjunction, let me now mention - you apparently now pseudonymously agree to denude yourself in front of strangers for a modest fee? This is where your plot arc has trajectoried, eh?' Lucy gives a shrug of bland disappointment and Ariel laughs. 'It's a bit derivative, yes I know. But no one was asking me to take off my clothes when I'd just do it for free so I figured it must've been my cow-patty name. I am easy to explain - at least I have that virtue.' Lucy is wondering what Ariel meant by 'decided to re-enter society' as it had seemed not not-casual but to have a certain ring to it, Lucy coming at it from where she did. No better way for it than to be blunt, Lucy says 'What did you mean, I'd *decided to re-enter society?*' 'You're the one who left.' 'I'm the one who left?' Ariel has gone honest-tint, leans the way Lucy is leaning from the other side of the island. 'I'm the one who left?' Lucy repeats, a challenge. 'Yes.' Lucy holds eye-contact, proudly, much longer than she can really bear and her brain in going drips of sausage fat curdled in cold sink water, is going dirty-fork-but-the-only-fork-left. 'Yes. You are the one who left.' Ariel nods. What is it? What could this be? By the way, Lucy: have you noticed that's Ariel standing right there? Look - you can see her if you look! Do you see the grey-speckled white of her face in the shade of this hotel? 'I suppose that is true' Lucy thinks she says and, whatever she said, Ariel nods. Smiling. Obviously choosing not to say something and Lucy not either.

'The hotel comes with this stuff - or you bought it?' 'I know, right?' 'I've never been in a hotel that comes with a stocked kitchen. With a kitchen, sure, but not a stocked kitchen. It even has Ziploc bags!' 'It isn't actually that much. Kind of paltry, really.' 'There's vodka in the freezer, so it can only slide so foul on the paltry scale before I come mad-dog to its defense, Lucy. Vodka. In a freezer. Can you imagine if you had rented this room and not known this was going to be here?' 'I cannot.' 'It'd be, more-or-less, Saul of Tarsus, as far as I'm concerned. Vodka in a hotel unexpectedly? I'd change my fucking name to *Paul* over that - try and stop me!' 'Indeed. Though I cannot imagine anyone renting this room, full stop. I only did it to show off.' 'To show off for whom?' 'For you.' 'But you had no idea it was going to be me. Do you fucking treat all your whores this way? Are you that lousy at this? A wad of sweaty fives and tug me by the hair into a gas station toilet, babe, all the trollop I am.' 'I actually used to run an ad for that, but it painted me in the wrong light and I lost my sponsor at the croquet club for my trouble.' 'That's just on account of you said the pervy shit about wanting to write poetry about it. That's kind of sick, really. That puts a lot of pressure on someone - to know they are going to be obliquely described by means of clumsy metaphor and, I dunno, other poemy terms like *Trochaic* and *Volta*.' 'Wow - you got caught up at the community college, did you?' 'Naw, I'm not a sucker - they just let you look at books in the shop without buying them when you're as strumpet as me.' 'I only use the sexy poetry terms though, m'dear. *Diction. Assonance. Enjambment. Chiasmus.*' 'Very nice.' '*Explication.*' 'Ooh.'

'*Anapest*.' 'Stop now.' '*Spondee*.' 'I'll *spondee* you good if you don't settle down, I promise you that.' 'Yeah? You'll *sestet* my little *couplet?*' 'Oh I'll *dactyl* you right in your *blank verse*, honey-pot - watch me now.'

Lucy watches Ariel open the blinds and both of them politely applaud as though someone else had done it when she is through. The view is nothing of consequence, but the visual difference to the room's dimensions with the light added in is almost psychedelic. Lucy wonders aloud, not aiming the question directly, what the specific reasoning behind a name like *Victoire Elan* would be. 'Perhaps it came from somewhere? Perhaps it was a reference to something? Maybe? Yes, no?' she says, and she says 'I wonder if anyone could ever know about something like that? I feel like an Atomist even asking - fumbling at the very first thread ends of philosophy, well before it became cumbersome, back when it seemed it was all about to be cleared up, you know?' Phrasing it as merely a guess, tone-of-voicing it to keep it mystique-ridden, Ariel offers that 'There seems a chance - one could call it a chance, certainly - it is the name of a female soccer player.' But then also says 'Though the surname *Elan* sounds like a certain discrimination of mosquito.' 'But then' Lucy butts in 'everything in the world is up for debate, I suppose - up for debate and resale for less than quarter-price if you wait long enough. *Cheapskate* is just another word for *Buddah* is just another name for *money-in-the-bank*.' 'I suppose' refrains Ariel and knock-knocks on the window glass, then turns and smiles - directly, it feels like the first time, at least the first time this unselfconsciously - at Lucy. 'I am very glad you are, in fact, you. Here, I mean. Even though I am certain none of this is happening. This does seem like the sort of thing that isn't happening - or are you going to argue? I suppose you bump into me like this all the time.' 'No, not at all' Lucy says, Ariel shaking her head like she is being patronized. 'No, I agree it has the earmarks of unreality.' And Lucy, for herself, well she knows she is waiting for this to end, to be drifted from, for the other side of it to come on the down of an upped gulp. How long will the sensation of it linger when she is stirred by needing to urinate from wherever it is she has dozed? She's even looking around the room, wondering when she is, really, where exactly she passed out.

Lucy watched Ariel fold a piece of the wheat bread in half, press her fingers into it hard - so that the sides rather mash and hold together - then fold this folded piece, again - watches Ariel frown when, here, the bread tears and comes apart in two pieces. 'You're miserable at bread folding.' 'I never said, Lucy Jinx, that I was anything but lowest rung at it. Don't think your persnickety shit can drag me down, though. You're a real bully, if you want to know my personal opinion - when they publish my diaries eventually everyone will know that I think so.' 'No one is going to publish your diaries, El - I've told you that about

two-hundred-and-thirty times. Jesus. Your diary? The kind someone, even
were they looking for it, would be glad had a lock. *That's a symbol* they'd say *I'll
respect that* they'd say. And they'd go Phew, after - bank on it.' Here there is a
pause and the entire room is the pause and in the pause Ariel touches Lucy for
the first time since the kindergarten chest pokes, which did not count. Ariel's
hand, Lucy, is on your wrist. Do you see? Ariel's knee is practically touching
yours - though, yes, you are angled away from each other a bit. Do you see? Do
you? 'So where did you go?' Who asked that? It was Ariel. And it really
happened? The question? Ariel is holding Lucy Jinx's hand - holding it, holding
Lucy's middle three fingers by the tips. She has asked it, Lucy. I left. Say it,
Lucy. But that is no kind of answer! Do you have something else? I left. I left.
That doesn't make sense! 'I left' she says - and is aware from the change in the
touch of air against them that something distinct has happened with her eyes.
'Okay' Ariel says and she also says 'I left.' I left. But it's not a repetition. Was
it, Lucy? 'I left' Lucy says and Ariel says back - back or in response? - 'I left.'
And the conversation, as far as that goes, is all finished and, as far as things go,
the building Lucy is in tips headfirst, wakes up too deep underwater to bother
struggling much as it drowns. Ariel lifts Lucy's held hand up - two quick twin-
sister kisses to the knuckles of the three fingers specifically held - and casually -
the same sound as the turn of the page of a restaurant menu after selection was
made and you were looking a bit more but not really, or an envelope with an
Electric bill inside torn open while sighing - says 'I missed you I think, Jinx. You
know?'

'SHALL I GET UNDRESSED NOW?' This said offhand. Business returned to.
Lucy shifts where she has taken a seat on the room sofa. Stands. 'What?' 'Is it
time for me to get naked?' 'Oh you don't have to' Lucy says, brushing one hand
with the other, absentminded, flummoxed, doing her darndest to not seem so.
Is Ariel asking because she had been counting on the money? This was a cash
proposition, Lucy. 'I'll still pay you, you know? But there's no need to strip or
anything.' Ariel grins at that. Why the grin? 'You don't want me to undress?'
But it isn't that! No, no. Lucy explains, for example, it has already been an hour
out of the two hours and they've just been caught up with catching up and la di
dah and just the surprise of seeing Ariel - are you going to ask Ariel what exactly
she is doing here, by Here referring to In The City, Lucy? - is more than Lucy
had hoped for, if she's telling the truth. 'I never thought I'd see you, again.'
Ariel seems to regard that remark in a meticulous way, is chewing the inside of
her left cheek like it's it. 'You don't want to write poetry about me?' she

eventually asks and Lucy, so curve-balled by the question, stands hapless and vaudevillian Well-er-ing. 'And are you really gonna kick me out if it goes past two hours?' Lucy nothings. But Ariel, so far, is not beginning to undress, Lucy finding mild balm in that fact. The situation is still up to her. 'I just' she begins some abortive statement then laughs and asks Ariel if she would find it awkward. 'For you to write poetry about me?' 'To take off your clothes in front of me' Lucy is unable to hide the prudish blush - though where one of Jinx's ilk found anything prudish is beyond fathoming. 'Do you want to write about me, but I stay dressed?' Lucy gives motions as though to say she'd be fine with that if it is what Ariel wants. 'Or is it I'm supposed to do whatever I feel like?' Lucy has to admit that is the general thing - that's what Stella and Victoire had discussed, yes, technically, yes. 'Because unless you tell me not to, boss' - here Ariel winks in a flashbulb that will forever float in Lucy's field of vision, bauble of bulbous off-green - 'I'm taking this off.'

Lucy has not looked at Ariel yet. She can hear - not much - the sounds of her removing her clothing and folding it, the sounds of that duffle bag being unzipped, zipped, set on the sofa, lifted up, set on the floor, then set back on the sofa. But Lucy has moved back to where her notebook is set. And is testing the pen on the back of her hand, the skin clammy, the raised veins as though covered in condensation, drinking glasses left out, ice melting inside them, caterpillar hair trying to sprout from underneath. Ariel sneezes. Again. Again. Makes a Gah! sound and Lucy hears her say 'Be right back' and then sounds of Ariel opening the bathroom door, tearing a length of toilet tissue, blowing her nose. Coughing. In a moment, Ariel will be moving toward Lucy Jinx, nude. Meantime: Lucy is not caught up to the fact that Ariel still exists. No Lucy, this would not be your state of mind had Victorie - even all your most literate dreams of her - been the one about to approach you, naked. You would have watched Victorie unclothe, seated with you leg crossed mannishly and notebook on knee. Are you bothered that Ariel wants you to write about her? That she doesn't know how you have always wrote about her, for her? Wait. Have you? Maybe not. 'I don't know' Lucy says. I don't know. Tell Ariel that you are uncomfortable. No - not that. Tell her that, honestly, the project requires the women to be anonymous! Yes! That makes excellent sense! There are whole reasons Lucy is called *Stella* and there is payment and timetable involved. Ariel cannot be used - the ecosystem of purity and all, maintained, blah blah - but of course they should hang out. And what are you doing in this, of all cities? Don't forget to ask that. 'Looooooossssseeeeyyyyyy.' 'Yeh?' Lucy quick chirps, still looking down like some petulant toddler at shoes it could lace but just won't. 'Why aren't you looooooookkkkkiiiiinnnngggg at me?' The sound of Ariel plopping down on the sofa, shifting, clearing her throat. 'Be right there' Lucy calls across, movie-line loud, not quite the correct delivery for this situation. *Be right there*, Lucy? Is that what you just said? Do you know how you are coming across - sweet Jesus, man!

To now, Lucy has written the name *Ariel Lentz* three times and made some squiggle lines and turned the page. Ariel is now clearing some ash from off of her belly - is now rubbing thumb-tip to tips of index and middle-finger, clearing the soot, sniffing them, wiping these on her just wiped belly. In the years since seeing her last, Lucy notes, Ariel has gained a good amount of weight, seems shaped quite different - still very much herself, but more of a neck, more of a torso. Her breasts are certainly larger - not that Lucy had seen them, plain presented, but had enough times seen Ariel is thin fitted t-shirts without brassier and had joked often enough about her boy-chest that Lucy can safely assume these current breasts are a development between Then and Now. Or you are hallucinating, Lucy? Doesn't it kind of seem that this is Ariel but with a body closer to yours superimposed on her - Ariel locked in cloth of your flesh? Kind of. *The hard place of her skin against the unassuming olive of the sofa - are there words for it?* Lucy is making notes more like that than like poetry. Lucy writes *She has three freckles that somehow do not seem like straight lines can be made between them, these in a loose cluster on the side curve of her knee - it would be ugly if it wasn't also impossible, but it is and so it's quite lovely*. 'Do you live in the city?' Ariel looks over but it is clear she is enjoying the game of having to keep a pose - though Lucy has told her she needs do no such thing, in fact quite the opposite is even preferable - so the look is just a click of eye, lower-corner-of-socket. 'In this city? No.' Then nothing further. Ah - a guessing game. *Ariel is playful, tonight* Lucy writes *and yes, I know it is not night* she writes after, then writes *and yes I know I am writing this whole conversation with myself even as it loses cohesion and becomes a conversation about me having a conversation instead of a conversation about how Ariel is there, coy, plaything and playthinging with me*.

Now see that! Ariel has lugubriously reached to the table for her cigarette pack while singing to no real tune the words *Ennui ennui, Lucy Lucy, ennui and Lucy and me*. Needless to say what this has done to the drool shaped insides of Lucy's skull and chest cavity. What is important, though, is there are further tattoos over Ariel's ribs - Lucy of course noted the key tattooed above her left breasts, but nothing else. 'Don't move.' And Ariel obediently does not, despite the absurdist pose she was in when the words were handclapped at her, lighter lit but not near enough to get smoke going. 'I mean, you can move - sit up.' 'Yes ma'am' Ariel snipes but chuckles right afterward and asks if she wants as cigarette. Lucy has set down her notebook and walked to the sofa, taken Ariel's hand to make her stand and moved her arm - the one not holding the smoke - out of the way to examine her side. 'Touching costs extra, kid' Ariel brats and Lucy yeah-yeah-yeah faces and says 'Shut up - what's this?' Ariel twists, as though Whatever-could-you-be-referring-to? then raises her cigaretted arm to show there is writing on her other side, as well. 'That's my Dylan - I am temple to him, you see? I'm his old tile flooring.' Of course Lucy knew it was Dylan - Ariel's left side says *I ain't gonna work on Maggie's farm no more* and her right side says *You're gonna have to serve somebody* - and she stands, hands to hips, and tells Ariel as much. 'I mean who wrote this on you?' Meaning that Lucy has noted the lettering is some person's specific handwriting, not fancy script or design-book lettering as with many tattoos, not some approximation of cursive script et cetera. This was someone's pen-tip and this is Ariel's skin and there need to be answers, now. Ariel doesn't say anything until Lucy looks up and their eyes smear into each other's unable to move. 'Who wrote it on me? Are you jealous, Lucy Jinx?' 'I am. Just who in fuck wrote it!?' Ariel bends a knee and pushes the front of Lucy's left thigh with it, Lucy without-heart batting at the knee, hand going nowhere near it. 'It's my handwriting. I wrote it on paper and they transferred it.' Ariel bumps Lucy with knee again. 'Don't ask me anything so idiot again or I'll call you a bastard.' Lucy is looking down. 'Hey - we friends again?'

In fact, Ariel has had the Dylan tattoos for years - for decades, really. Further exploration of her body - pretense of poetry-project and eye-on-the-clock, at least temporarily, has been set all on one side - shows that Ariel also has the word *Revision* inked to her back, between shoulder blades, a reproduction of an illustration from the children's book *There's No Such Thing As A Dragon* - the dragon with its head poking through the leg of Billy Bixbie's pajama trousers - on her lower back, and down the back of one thigh is a bit from Dante *her changes change her changes endlessly*. Having Ariel display herself, rotate, extend, turn around, turn around, has gotten Lucy more at ease with things. She hardly notices her own gooseflesh at the scent of Ariel so close up and her general sense of fever has moved from prickle-of-anxious-arousal to medicine-head-full-on. Lucy's vision is a hand too big for a glove, her thoughts are the chill on the floor under the underside of a wine-bucket. This is not happening anyway, so she embraces the unreal of it, resistance broken the same way as a cholera-brow accepts clammy. Or it is happening - it seems that it is - but in such a way that her immune system is acting to delete the memories of it as they form, readying Lucy to wake, amnesiac, whenever it all ends, her inside filling with formalin and grain alcohol, intoxicating her and preserving her senseless. She knows Ariel has noticed her letting her eyes linger on the untempered pubic-hair, there, the lashes of it in thigh creases - darker red, almost pure brown, than elsewhere - and to loiter on the spread-beige of her areolas to the side of the eraser-stub bumps of her nipples and the dot-to-dot few-days-old animal scratch beside the left one. Remember, though, Lucy, that Ariel knows she is modeling for you. Remember that. You are allowed to look anywhere - you have looked the same way at dozens of other women, dozens of other times. Or no, maybe not exactly the same way. But similar - you have looked at other women, similarly. And you are only imagining Ariel can read your mind - the truth is she is just there, a bit as surprised as you, and many times over less bashful, is all.

Lucy hides back behind cigarette, back behind notebook. Still not a line of poetry written. But that is not even a consideration, really. Is she expecting herself to write? Under these circumstances? She dares anyone to write, being her, being here, being her, here, now! Isn't it more the case that she feels were she to start crafting verse, give in that this is just a screwball coincidence, happenstance that has crossed Lucy's and Ariel's paths - as opposed to Lucy and Ariel's path - one time more before never again, it would signify her acceptance of it all being nothing more than that? It's impossible that Ariel is here and if Lucy disrespects that, treats it as not only possible but as appropriately mingled in with her pointless exercise of these shenanigans in hotels with strangers under the poor guise of le artiste ambition, the bubble will burst and she will have this thing taken from her again. Well, Lucy, that is some heavy talk! Ought you not to verbalize some of that? Can you think of nothing to say to Ariel? What's that? Why isn't Ariel making more of a to do of it? Look: Ariel is naked, right there - unabashedly yours to do with as you please. Ariel has small-talked and flirted and insisted on presenting herself and is likely curious, confused at your quietness, wondering worse wonders than you could wonder in your most ponderous downs. And you aren't writing anything! You need to say something to her if for no other reason than she is going to ask you to read something you wrote - or to read it, herself - and you will not have the strength to tell her 'No, I don't let people do that.' Why aren't you letting this be heavenly, Lucy? Why aren't you letting it fantasia you true-believer? Who are you trying to convince that this isn't all you've ever wanted? Trying to sematic out of it with 'No, I've never even imagined this once, never daydreamed it, so it can't be something I can be accused of desiring' - come on! You're caught, Lucy. Caught. So relax.

Think, think. Here's somewhere to start: Ariel has been corresponding for over a month as *Victorie Elan*. Not over a month. A few weeks. Sleuth this out. Why not just ask her another question? How long has this silence been going on? That is Ariel, right there, and you are refusing to speak to her and barely even looking at her, anymore! Anymore? It's been a few minutes, only - it's only been a few minutes. All Lucy is doing is trying to think of something to actually write - she is doing, truthfully, what she liared she was doing in a room with those other women when she wasn't. Ariel has walked over, poured a drink, drunk it, walked to the window with a cigarette. Ariel thinks Lucy is writing, Lucy assures Lucy, and Lucy writes *Ariel thinks Lucy is writing, Lucy assures Lucy*. Why is Ariel here? How? She must live in the city. Why then would she say she didn't?

Ask her. I'm not asking her! Are you really in this much shock? or are you just playing, stuck in a dent of this-is-how-one-should-act-when-surprised and you'll spends the next two months yowling curse-words at yourself once you've let Ariel leave with - what? - another hay-penny nod, a wooden-nickel hand-shake, a here-is-your-cash *Goodbye*. Ariel won't leave that way. This isn't nothing to her. See Ariel, there, by the window? Allow that she must, in exact tender to you Lucy, be spinning in her head about how it could be you two have wound up like this. You two want to squeal and to bounce up-and-downing and Jesus Christing the insanity of this. I want to. And she must have wanted you to see her, all of her, her her - she's liked it when you've known she was watching you looking at her - she said so exactly by not saying so. Wait out the clock, see what she does. Or are you imagining that if you don't speak neither will she and this hotel room will go out as long as a church ceiling or a pillar from a fallen colosseum? How long has it been quiet? Honestly, how long? 'I am allowed to talk, right?' Ariel asks, just then. Just then, Lucy, just then. Do you mark that?

'I admit - and keep in mind I don't admit shit - I am having a lot of trouble writing. Ariel. Ariel! Come on! What the fuck are you doing here!? Why are you keeping so mum - do you think I'm honestly able to write under this circus stand!?' 'I did think so. I didn't want to throw off your groove. But if you aren't even doing anything, let me point out: you double-crossed me, if anything! You're the one who's here!' 'I know, I know. And I feel just toadstool about that. But I feel bad how I can't write - I'm just making you smoke cigarettes, naked in a hotel room.' 'You really can't write? I put the whammy on you good?' 'Not like that - yes - but not like that. Okay?' 'Okay.' 'Okay?' 'Okay.' 'Ariel - I cannot believe I am seeing you again! There. Are you fucking happy!? Does that put the jolly in your holly?' 'Am I happy?' 'I said that part aloud?' 'Yes. You did. Right out loud. And Yes, I am happy. And I'm in shock, man. I just have always been more of a damn grown-up than you so am trying to be classy about it while you mope or whatever it is you are doing. You're so bratty, man - and at a time like this!' 'What are you doing here!?' 'I just answered an ad to pose nude, man - I'm all explained. But if you want - never mind.' 'No - don't shirk! - if I want what?' 'Never mind.' 'Come on - tell me, goddamnit!' 'Where did you go, Lucy?' 'I don't. I don't know. I just. Went. I just went. I can't even remember that time. To be honest. Something happened. This one day. And I snapped and got in my car and drove away. That is all I remember and I never thought about any of that place anymore. I broke or something. Something wasn't me anymore and I left.' 'Okay.' 'I can't explain it.' 'Okay.' 'But you were gone! Too, I mean. You left first, didn't you? And what did you just mean *Never mind*? What did that mean?' 'I mean I never forgot about you. And I know what you mean. And I left, too. And I never thought about it anymore except that I did, all the time. You know? You know what I mean?' 'I do. Yes. I know what you mean. No. I can't write. Why are you here!?' 'Did you start hating me like I started hating you?' 'Yes. Did you start hating me like I started hating you?' 'No. Did you start hating me like I started hating you?' 'No. Did you start hating me like I started hating you?' 'Yes.' 'Liar.' 'Liar.'

The plan becomes to take-five on things but to start again after going out for a meal. Ariel has nowhere to be and does - she insists, she insists - want Lucy to let her pose, for real, and wants to be the subject of some sublime work of art. 'So, you know, make it sublime for a switch.' Ariel shrugs about how the money is not a thing but lets Lucy pay her - as agreed between Stella and Victoire - for the more than already two hours that have passed. And Lucy tries to argue 'You'd better not use that to pay for the meal or whatever!' but there isn't really anything Lucy can do about that, as Ariel says the money is now all mixed in with her money from before, so Lucy will have no way of knowing which money is which. Side note: watching Ariel put her clothes back on is making Lucy swoon, she knows, far worse than the first sight of her nude and far far more tremblingly than she would have been had she watched Ariel undress - my God, my God, Ariel has just put her hands in pockets to tug right their insides after buttoning her fly, sweet Hell!! 'Well, then we'll just split the check. See? I'm smarter than you.' 'You're dumber than me - you think I'm not gonna make you pay for me, to begin with? Look at you, Jinx - worm on a hook! I wish I had overdue library books I could bat my lashes you'd buy me - our meal is on you, nitwit, and that's Church.' Did you just chortle, Lucy - is that what that sound was? 'You do have the room all night, by the way?' Ariel asks, one eye squinted more than the other also-squinted eye, finger pointing in a tentative gun. Blink. 'Yes.' But why? 'Why do you ask?' 'I told you - I really don't live in the city, man. So I'm gonna have to stay over. When you were only Stella I'd have been on my way back, by now.' Lucy nods. Ariel finishes buttoning her shirt and sniffs the back of her hand as it mashes upward her nose and - oh look, Lucy - wrinkles flit from her left harsh-closed eye, luminous as fireflies. And now Ariel is staring at Lucy staring. Smiles. 'I really like your blazer, by the way. Can I try it on?'

And so that leads to this. Lucy Jinx, Ariel Lentz, hotel corridor, Lucy checking that the room door is locked and then deprecating herself a moron for this. 'It's just something I always do.' 'I do that, too. I don't check my house door, but I always check the hotel.' This is what is happening and there is no explaining it and Lucy is now letting Ariel nudge her shoulder with her shoulder and is reacting more than needed, bouncing from the corridor wall back into another nudge into Ariel. There is some static blip in the communication, the otherwise round circle crumpling, half-squaring, snapping back round. They are sonar in their communication, at best, down the stairwell, both waiting until fresh air to light cigarettes, Ariel the one bringing attention to this with 'The last thing we want to seem is pedestrian, Lucy - you spent a lot to put on airs for me and we do not need to be at the wrong end of a nose looked down through. We need to be on guard and smoke like swishy barristers. We need impress the rabble - rouse them, as they say.' Like school kids, they paddle back and forth the expression this place is run by snoots 'They're snoots, this burg' 'Snoots' 'Snoots, Lucy' 'Snoots, Ariel' 'Snoots whose lips purse like the pucker of a cat's ass at things so crass as cigarettes - and lord help us if they just heard me say *Pucker of a cat's ass* they'll add on some surcharge and draw it out in court if you protest just out of spite!' Fresh air. Cigarette. Sweet mercy, it's colder than it was before and Ariel finds a hat in her coat pocket and takes Lucy's scarf without asking or making a quip, wrapping it one two three times around her and tucking the excess down her coat front like a landlord would a love letter in some bedroom farce. Is there somewhere particular they are going? Does it matter to mention that Ariel used her lighter, put it in her pocket without sharing, Lucy reached right into that pocket, lit her cigarette, put the lighter then to her own coat? And does it indicate anything to anyone how, meanwhile, the two of them smoked wordless with noses together beginning to run? Maybe? Perhaps. No? Not at all.

THE TWO OF THEM - LUCY and Ariel, both the singular of plural, still bundled up in their coats though the other bar patrons were down to shirtsleeves and cardigans-draped-over-chair-backs - were taking breaths between tight teeth, jaws clenching in shiver-interrupted one-two-threes and the drinks they had ordered remain untouched, rippling in impatient glaze, while they fidgeted. Ariel made a face at something behind Lucy, met Lucy's gaze, furrowed brow to Look-over-there-but-be-sly-about-it and Lucy - pretending she needed to cough and so needed to turn away, decorum's sake, from her companion - did her best to find the offender but does not see anything. Pause. The thought through her mind now: should I fake a sardonic chuckle of some kind, roll my eyes knowingly but in a way that commits me to nothing? Or else shall I admit I have no idea what the matter could be I was entreated to give a looksee to? Fake cough, again. *Squeeze the Universe into a ball.* Turns back to Ariel and gives eyes like 'I dunno, mate, what gives - is it still there?' *Roll it toward some overwhelming question.* Ariel huffs, silent, and chicken-pecks a flaring squint 'Look, look!' *Say I am Lazarus, come from the dead!* Lucy opens mouth a little as pout of protest and does another polite turn, this time with bar napkin to faux-blow-

and-wipe-nose - though she really does this, easier than faking, surprised at how wet the napkin comes away - still coming up nothing. *Come back to tell you all! What could it be? I shall tell you all.* Inventory: blobbish men drinking - but nothing ghoulish to them - a woman about as descript as a garden rake, the bartender, Platonic representation of Bartending. What? Something on the television, reflected on those posters? Now Ariel's voice in her ear 'I told you to be cool - what are you doing?' Both turn to regular facing and wriggling and freezing and Lucy saying, growly-growl kissy-kiss whisper 'What are you even fucking talking about?' 'You don't see those two guys have fucking swastika tattoos?' Lucy's eyes dinner-plate and she turns, no subterfuge at all. Holy smokes! Not two - three! Four! Back to Ariel 'Where the fuck are we, man? Where have you brought me? Do we have our papers!?' Ariel chatters her teeth and seems to be warding off a sneeze, mumbles about how Lucy had picked the place and 'I'm just a tourist, man - never trust you again, you miserable bigot.'

'I have to piss like a nightmare is teething on my snatch, man - but I'm afraid if I let you out of my sight you'll vanish again!' Lucy slaps Ariel hard. On the arm. Pretending the left cheek. 'Hey!' 'That's what I think!' Ariel little-girl's you're-not-my-friend eyes at Lucy while rubbing her hit arm 'What's what you think?' 'I have to' Lucy sarcastically I'm-sorrys but then condescendingly Oh-grow-ups Ariel about Ariel still rubbing her wound 'piss but am terrified of losing you, again!' And it is agreed they are just the most pathetic things, between them not tuppence of pride. 'I was gonna Knut Hamsun this, man - just eventually piss!' 'I was gonna Knut Hamsun this, too!' Well, aren't they both just high-falutin' literate copycats. 'Let's go piss together.' 'I'm scared if we do it'll be eerie - like we'll piss for the same length of time at the exact same velocity - water impact in stereo.' Lucy points out that Ariel tends to fear ridiculously complex things that aren't even scary in the legitimate or traditional sense of the term while she absent-mindedly takes a sip of her whiskey, the sting rising the alarm bells that she needs to get to the toilet, no shriving time allowed, now. It's a one-at-a-timer, so Lucy triumphantly is able to further mock Ariel's previous worry-warting, but Ariel pays her back by speeding up and going into the room first, likely trying to emphatically bolt the latch, though over the din Lucy would not know whether this was successful or no. 'Go ahead and piss then, Ari - but you know you'll just have to live with the fact that you'll know I smelled what it smells like in there after you after! You've victoried yourself into shame!' Is there honestly a chance that Lucy will wet herself? Yes. She already has, a little bit. A headache of fop-sweat sours her forehead and her shoulders feel itchy, as though worming underneath of a three-days worn dress-shirt, neck pin-pricking, tingle of ring-around-the-collar grime enflaming mild eczema, and she has her legs twined around, good, the heel of one foot pressing down hard the toe of the other. She bats her palms on the door and hears Ariel laughing, hurling some epithet at her, knows she is leaking a little more as she smiles, certain she has just sealed her doom. Ariel will be in there, all grins, deciding to wait a vicious extra five minutes before leaving. To let her scent dissipate. Lucy played her hand, too soon.

It's Ariel's decision to stay. 'Because of the Nazis' she says - though they have moved to a booth, this maneuver having cost them a twenty dollar bribe - 'because Nazis don't necessarily indicate anything. We don't want to seem paranoid, you know? Say the rest of these people aren't Nazis at all and they see us leaving and the rest of their night is ruined because they assume we assume they are over-the-hill Hitler Youths? Would you want to have to live with that - would you? Because I wouldn't, Lucy. I like to just go with the flow. Even when the flow is Nazis-in-some-bar. A bar which, I should vigorously re-point out, you chose.' Lucy defends herself by way of explaining she tends to take it for granted that everyone is a Nazi so doesn't give it much of a sniff if it turns out they are. 'You're just naïve, Ari - that's how I see it. You're the sort who never understands rock 'n roll songs are about drugs and homos and stuff.' 'Which rock 'n roll songs are about drugs and homos!?' Ariel clutches-her-pearls and Lady-Macbeths her hands. 'Well, *Crocodile Rock* is, anyway. That I know about. I assume it's not the only one, though. I'm just saying: watch where you step when you're down on the farm. And know what's funny, speaking of that? A farmer didn't think up that advice, because a farmer doesn't bother! You see?' A burly, middle-aged waiter - who they share looks of He's-also-a-Nazi about - asks if they want food and Ariel orders a plate of small hamburgers and some mozzarella sticks, explaining to Lucy after the waiter has gone that she has no intention of eating any of the food but figured if they didn't order anything they'd be put on some list which circulates amongst God-knows-who. 'I'm looking out for you. Even though you ridiculed me, just a moment ago. Why? Because I am basically a better human being than you are. Why? Better stock, Lucy. My mother and father were better than yours. Which I realize might be offensive to say, but I figure you're too much a doormat to get in my face about it - again on account of watching yer folk's dilapidated marriage go to foreclosure.' And she gives Lucy the finger and downs her drink and pours Lucy's drink into her empty glass and gives Lucy the finger, again. Oh flutter flutter, eh Lucy? Oh where-has-this-person-been, eh? Oh put her in a pumpkin shell - nothing makes more sense than that line, here and now.

Lucy gives the run-down of her current jobs, tarting it up to seem very down-and-outer, very gutter-poet, all a grand joke - a ship she is steering on purpose over the sharp lip of a flat Earth. Yes, Lucy grandioses herself up, milking anecdotes and descriptions of job duties out to such high rococo extremes she almost believes in the version of wild, Joycean word-mash she is peddling - expects to find herself returning home, Ariel in tow, the walls of her apartment building moss covered and sweating martyr's blood, her apartment carpets a forest of junkie needles, each stab containing another letter of a new and much improved alphabet. Lucy is making herself a hieroglyph. She is making herself an equation scrawled in a demented mathematician's suicide note margin. Carved goes sarcophagus goes her skin. Ariel is appropriately in hysterics, caught up in the thick malt of *Stella-Toms-Pizza*-as-Rimbaud-would-express-it-no-better, of waiting for deliveries of doughnuts and soda all night in a perfect shape of *Guernica*! There is a goddess sprawl to this unpacking, a gymnastic-gone-bad, careening sort of giddy - Lucy, now feeling, feels sure she a moment ago would have felt gone from here forever ago. Oh Lucy! Look at you, girl! You aren't, as you've feared, a chalkboard eraser-clap posing as a raincloud! You have dimensions and exaggerations waiting to demolition derby from you if given the proper stimulus! That last thing you said, for example? You're fully aware what a complete fabrication it was! My God - that never happened, even in part! But it was funny! It was funny and Ariel is saying 'Goddamn you' about how the laughter is going to make her piss herself, for real now - that she doesn't have the bladder control she used to and this is a treasonous, underhanded vengeance-for-earlier disguised as jocularity and caring for the glee of a comrade. Lucy Jinx is talking better than she has in ages - the inertia of it is all that is important - she's a novel page without a single word spelled properly but no one reading cares because they are turning the pages so fast, just wanting the thump! of the book closed and the cockswelling pride in their strutted chest that Yes, yes they did read that whole thing! Fuck, they want to believe it is the pace of their eyes and their fingers doing the whisking pages one after another that is causing the words to misspell!

Ariel tells a story - horrifying - about her apartment being broken into. The story is related, just like this: 'It was cliché - that is the scariest part of it all. The unoriginality of lived horror. I am, verbatim, someone else's same terror. I was in bed. I was alone. Now, I always kind of drift off thinking a killer is already in the apartment, anyway - and thinking I am drugged from something I ate or drank in the previous hour or two and can do nothing about it - so of course I'm thinking that when I hear the door jimmied open. Now - let me tell you, since you don't know, Lucy - all of those sounds you hear at night that you think might be somebody sneaking around or you think might be someone trying to get in the door? Well, they sound nothing like someone trying to get in the door. That's a sound that is not exactly possible to not hear - nope, that sound is unmistakable. And there was no *Oh I'm sure tis nothing* about it. I heard it, I knew what the fuck it was, I froze. And of course my telephone was not in the bedroom. And of course the bedroom door wasn't closed. And of course I wasn't wearing anything because, well, I don't. Cliché, see? I don't make fun of scantily clad victims in the movies - most women don't, it's only men who think they thought up that idea to be symbolic, we gals really just get it. And I admit this following thing with a mixture of fascination and shame: I did nothing intelligent. I listened to them out in the apartment, ransacking. I didn't hide. I didn't even cover myself up. I just sat in the damn dark, naked in bed - didn't even get my blanket from the floor or right my sheet to obscure my skin. I just lay and heard every little thing they said to each other and knew exactly which drawer or whatever they were going through. I just lay there. Doing nothing. It didn't even occur to me to do anything. No plan formed. I didn't think *I'd better hide!* or bother to come up with other options which were shot down by panic. There was just nil. And also: I didn't think anything bad was going to happen! Not like when you only think you hear sounds and fantasize about all manner of horror-show stuff, right? Nope. I was listening to honest-to-Christ people - they were quite crude, I will say - actual people in my actual apartment and I just lay and listened and nothing at all went through my head about what they might do when they found me there. I still don't think about it, to tell you the truth. Never have. I have never pictured a single worse way it could have gone. They left without ever coming into the bedroom. I didn't even call the police after. Ever. And I never told anyone about that until now.' Ariel points at Lucy's glass, lifts her own and says 'This is where you says *Cheers* and I say *Cheers* and we down these.'

Back on the street: Lucy berating Ariel for being a souse. 'I am supposed to write a poem - ideally a heartfelt one - about you - and now here you're just flouncing around like some scallywag!' But Ariel will not stand for it. She insists that she is not even drunk - or that, if she is, it is within acceptable levels as far as pay-by-the-hour Muses go - and vehemently objects to the character assassination Lucy is peddling about her. 'If this alleged poem of yours turns out to be libel, I am a litigious sort - mark my words.' Lucy is hardly listening, though. She just keeps tugging at her scarf - Ariel still in possession of it - ruining its meticulous tuck, Ariel growling and flapping hands at Lucy as though she were a swarm of bulbous, stingerless wasps, each time stopping abruptly, undoing the scarf entirely, redoing it, tucking it tight, only to have Lucy tip-tap-tug it loose within another few paces. Is Lucy drunk, though? Are you, Lucy? Well, Lucy doesn't know what she is, drunk or otherwise. She is something stitched together from purloined parts, now. Whatever bunch of things she is, she is certain it's transient and does not trust its sensations - and she felt drunk even back in the hotel room, knows she didn't feel drunk at all on the walk to the bar, knows she must have had a good bit to drink inside not-so-long a period but - I mean, come on! - the sun is even still out - barely, but that still counts - and so everything remains up for debate but left undebated. She has noticed her mind is on another speed - true - that she is not slowing things down, noticing particulars as she often might. It's as though the world is a snake, one still coiled but ready to strike, a thing she must be on the obsessive, mesmeric vigil concerning but only for that spit-pop that will come too late - after fangs have struck, any observation preceding will jettison as soon as it arrives.

Ariel drags Lucy into some fast-food restaurant or another and they make their way to the restroom. 'I'm not making you come in the stall with me, but go no farther than there.' 'Are you going to throw up?' 'I'm only just somewhat, yes. So there's another term for it. Yes, I am, is what I mean.' 'I can hold your hair or something, if that's the aesthetic you go for at these times.' Ariel scoffs and says Lucy is exactly what Holden Caufield meant by people always wind up doing something pervy. 'Wait there. And don't think about my hair - that will make me throw up lousier, I need to concentrate on one thing at-a-time.' Lucy takes a posture of sentry, leaning against the stall door, mortified that a child will come in and need to go potty or something - petrified when this morphs to the idea of a child and its mother coming in, then for some reason it becomes even more bone-chattering when this side-steps to it being a child and the child's teenage older sister. 'Teenagers intimidate me' Lucy over-loud-voices back over her shoulder as though hoisting the words over the stall door, them landing in a plopping sack on the tile beside Ariel to be rummaged through. 'Though' Lucy adds 'I think one is kind of in love with me, right now, in an entirely inappropriate way. Which makes me a little bit less scared of them, on the whole.' 'That sounds like a hot ticket.' Ariel's voice is muffled and echo-toned, Lucy picturing her face over the chilly toilet water, wonders how stained and with what colors in what thickness the porcelain of the bowl curve is. 'It is rather hot, yes - there is no denying it has a specific centigrade to it. Did I mention that I was doing a *Poetry Workshop* at this posh high-school and some girl is hot for my goods?' 'Nope' Ariel says and then spits - twice, three times - makes a bubbling Grah! sound and spits a last time, likely futilely 'You said you were waiting to tell me about that until I was puking at *Taco Bravo*, remember?' 'This is *Arby's* I think.' 'Well' Ariel spits, spits 'then you're not keeping your word, are you?' Spits. 'Typical of you, Lucy.' Spits. 'I thought we were pals until just about now' spit 'and I was even going to paraphrase something sweet from a movie I saw' spit 'so it would be special when we watched the movie together, years from now' spit 'but all things considered you can suck my dick instead, how about that?'

The thing Ariel apologizes the most for is referencing *Catcher In The Rye*. She apologies with such conviction that Lucy feels compelled to shamefully admit that she has referenced the novel at times, herself. 'Mainly just to say the only good thing about it is that he spells *Crumby* with the *B*, but I still do it. So you don't need to feel quite as bad as maybe you should feel if you had done it around someone else.' 'Thanks, Lucy. But we both know I'm a leper, now. You once thought I was cool, but now you've got the straight dope on me and I'm reptilian.' But Lucy tells Ariel that she is cool - 'Cool like some kid who can actually hit the one-hundred-point hole in *Ski Ball* - like, every time!' 'No one does that. I might as well be cool like *Beowulf* as long as we're La-La-Landing this!' 'Except' Lucy points out '*Beowulf* is not cool.' Ariel concedes to that point and feels shabbier than ever. 'Remember when we used to know each other and I'd be the one to say all the cool things and you always seemed so dumb in comparison? What happened to those times? I preferred that, I have to say.' Lucy shrugs and says a phrase in French, the wrong phrase, but - either because she was not listening or didn't know better, herself - Ariel does not correct her, just announces she is sober now 'Because that sort of thing is all a matter of charisma and misdirection, anyway.' Lucy is glad to hear it. 'Speaking of which' Ariel says - now very animated, tug-tugging Lucy's coat sleeve - 'if I were a magician, I'd exclusively do tricks for drunk people. I'd get so famous so quick! Nobody would remember to tell people they were drunk when I did my tricks, you know? Drunks are goatishly prideful - don't you find drunkards edit that part out of most of their stories, because of human psychology and stuff like that?' The fact is: Lucy can't meet Ariel's eyes. She wants to do something bold but cannot think what. Or she can, of course, but - no - she won't do that! Jesus. Maybe, at best, she'll take her scarf back. Maybe. Though probably not.

In front of the hotel, they smoke cigarettes. 'We could smoke these inside but we aren't going to.' 'I know.' The doorman seems quite amused by them and Ariel whispers that she dares Lucy to ask for his telephone number. Nudge-nudge, Ariel prods Lucy's hip and seems to mean the dare was to be put to the test, posthaste. 'I'm not asking some doorman for his telephone number.' 'You're stuck up.' 'You're stuck up!' The doorman opens the door, as doormen do, and does a head doff to some other guests as they exit, as doormen do, too. 'Aren't they supposed to give you a tip?' Ariel asks, the guests only just barely - or even not, maybe - out of earshot. The doorman shakes his head slowly, trying so obviously to forge a deeper human connection with the movement than he is managing to. 'Look how awful his life is, Jinxy! Ask him out or something.' 'I'm not asking out the doorman. You're making a mean-spirited echo of me.' Ariel smokes her cigarette slowly and her eyes have a dark hue to them, akin to the compacted purple of the circle of wine that hardens in the base of a glass left out overnight. 'Do you need to get going?' Ariel blinks. She bristles, seems genuinely hurt, drops her hardly smoked cig and steps it out, moving to the door - the doorman opening it, dipping his head for her, dipping his head for Lucy who follows quickly behind. Ariel does not answer Lucy's 'Hey - hey' or her 'Ariel' or her 'Are you actually mad at me - wait' as the two make their way over to the elevators. Ariel stabs the summon button just once and crosses her arms, demon in her stance of this-machine-is-not-speedy-enough. 'You just seem tired, that's all I meant' Lucy tries now, the two closed in the elevator, Ariel just leaning to the wall, neither of them hitting a floor button. Soon enough though, the elevator starts rising and Ariel steps off on whatever floor it was where it stopped, pushing past the folks waiting to get on with a mumbled 'Excuse me' in the shape of the blunt stab of an unextended switchblade's hilt. Lucy lets the other people into the elevator before slipping out and catching Ariel up, flicking her ear. 'Give me back my scarf if you're going to be some sort of brat, okay? I didn't even know you were going to be here today!'

In the stairwell, Ariel lights two smokes and sets one in Lucy's mouth when Lucy doesn't reach to take it when it is loiteringly offered across. 'I didn't leave, you know.' 'What?' Wait - what is this? Lucy is off-footed - something is going on and she is in another volume, entirely, not to mention not on the same page. 'What?' 'I didn't leave, Lucy.' Hold on - Jesus, wait just a sec - this isn't a joke, anymore. Or it never was. Had there been some undercurrent of this coming, all evening? 'What do you mean?' 'You left. You left!' Lucy hasn't taken a drag yet but now does, in mimic more of Ariel doing so than because it is something she wants to do. 'You left' Ariel repeats when Lucy sets the smoke back to her lip, still not having made a reply. Why aren't you saying anything, Lucy? Just out of curiosity. Lucy blinks. She takes another drag. 'Don't ask me if I *need to get going*. Okay? How about you knock it off asking me that - retire some words, for once, you don't need to mouth off everything you think of forever, you know?' Is this real? What is this? Wait. Look at Ariel, Lucy. This isn't a game. She's drunk, though. Do you see her eyes? Meanwhile, Lucy has said 'I'm sorry.' 'Just if you want me to go, I'll go. I thought we were coming back, together. Do you want me to go?' Lucy swallows. Mind blank. Takes a drag. 'I just. Thought you looked tired. I was saying something because I had nothing to say. So I said that.' Ariel sighs out a scrawl of blue-grey, wet-hisses the last of the drag and thumbs in the direction of a posted *No Smoking* sign. 'I guess we're not supposed to be doing this, anyway. Scofflaw. Criminality is all you breed.' Lucy manages a chuckle. Are you drunk, Lucy? Is that why the drag in your reaction time? What aren't you processing? Because Ariel seems to get something you aren't. 'I just feel like you've been trying to get rid of me.' What? 'What?' Lucy swallows hard, again, and furthers a 'No. No. I don't know what you mean.' 'I never left. So let's fucking know that, okay?' 'Okay.' '*Okay*? Say it! You have to say things, Lucy.' 'Okay.' 'No - say it.' Lucy nods. Swallows. Steps out her cigarette and follows Ariel as Ariel turns up the stairs. 'I thought you left. But you didn't.'




OF COURSE LUCY REMEMBERS IT. She has not thought of it - never had specific reason to before seeing Ariel show up, for one thing, but also never had even in the most general way - but now it is quite clear. *Poets and Madhares Quarterly*. It had been - what? - her third day at *Hernando's Highlights*. How many years ago is that? Her mind comes up with a number, but she shunts it off the tracks before its horn can announce it, hears the bang of the cars wrecking, the remains a harmless, indistinguishable mess. She'd hardly peeped a squeak to Ariel, by then - Ariel, intimidating waif of a twig in her chair with a back turned and those sudden spins around with snap-crackle comments or odd conversational prompts - could hardly muster up a dignified 'See you tomorrow' when awkwardly gathering her things to leave. But that day - third, fourth day - she had made the drive in with the copy of *Poets and Madhares Quarterly* in her passenger seat - driving so carefully, irritable at each fleck of inertia that so much as moved the journal a tit or a tat in any direction, even if it was inertia returning it to its previous position from the earlier movement caused by a rather sharp bend in the road. She had wanted to show Ariel. She had wanted to show Ariel, who she could hardly speak to or regard. It had been her first thought when the author-copy had arrived: This is how I can talk to Ariel, talk to her, this is what I can show her, show her, this is how - I can use the excuse of my excitement! *Poets and Madhares*. 'Can I show you something?' Oh Lucy of course remembers that exact moment, standing there like some five-year-old in galoshes with a wildflower - no idea it was dead - protected in bashful cupped palms, presenting mommy with a gift, imagining it put into a vase of water and adorning the dinner table forever, hierloomed, growing taller by the decade, filling the house with its smeared, old-woman yellow. Ariel had been sucking on that cut on her lower lip she had had from the first day Lucy had shown up at work. Smiled. 'Are you a poet? Is that why you're so goddamn quiet over there?' The dam burst with 'This is my white whale, you know? God, I have wanted to be published in this journal since' blah blah blah 'Mina Loy' blah blah blah 'Bogan' blah blah blah 'this is like being part of a thing that only exists in a movie I've seen - you know what I mean?' Of course Lucy remembers. That's how they'd met. How they'd really met. Look at me look at me look at me! is how they had really met, always.

Ariel is saying: 'I bought a copy of that stupid journal and I went all out and subscribed - that discount postcard inside - the whole nine. Why would I have told you? I figured I couldn't ask you for that copy you had, you seemed so peacock-fanned about it - I figured you had countless others to parade it around to. I went to some bookstore - you know the one by the fabled University? They had all that shit, man. All those fru-fru lit journals and things, those periodicals that so put the stars in your eyes and that I always thought were kind of pretentious circle jerks. I felt like a real lady-of-the-world - didn't I just? - purchasing it and - you bet - I even told the cashier - some poser dope, you know the type, the kind who would say *I have a first draft, but still need to kill my darlings and stuff - but I always have the Stet to save what I can't part with* that sort of shitheel - that *My friend has a piece in here.* Oh he seemed so impressed. Figured I must be telling him because I thought he was a Venus-in-Blue-jeans or some such - probably wrote me into that week's short story for class, right? I still have the copy, man. Well, I have every issue since then, too. I don't know where you went, man - I don't know why you suddenly weren't anywhere - but I kept the subscription and also subscribed to a bunch of the other ones you'd mentioned - I'm not gonna name them, but you know the ones. Oh I've become painfully versed in the current clime of American verse Lucy Jinx, I will tell you that. I was superstitious. To the point I became a dork! That's what's funny - about this, Ms. Stella Adroit - what's funny is that I would read the fucking journals - especially *Madhares* - cover-to-cover even if your name wasn't in the Contents listing because I figured you might have been writing under some disguise. I'd cross-reference your weirdo *Hernando's* aliases. Obviously those names were never there. I'd think of some and such name, though *Oh that sounds like a Lucy Jinx name, there* but I'd read the poem and it was nothing like you. I was the blush of the fervent fan-girl, Jinx. Oh golly, I sleuthed for you, I sleuthed - my hobby became not finding you.'

The sound of Ariel removing her shirt is nothing. Had you remarked she had not put on her bra, before? When the two of you went out - when she had re-dressed, back then? No? There it is - by the way - on the kitchen counter. Maybe you had seen her holding it at some point and assumed she'd put it back on? And the sound - this sound - of her unbuttoning the fly of her pants, sliding them off is rumple-shish-shish is rough-rough rumple-rumple like it always is with pants, especially those fitted and not wanting to come free from the hook of the foot to the ankle, legging themselves, at least one leg inside-out and up through itself. And now Ariel's panties, again. See them? They are there - those, those right there. What is the sound? The crackle of disappearing suds in a kitchen sink? No. A drop of coffee percolating and hitting the warmer while the pot is briefly removed? What is the sound of them down before the butterfly quiet of foot up, foot down - foot up, foot down - Ariel bending and whisk-flicking them onto a sofa arm? Never mind. It'll come to you, Lucy, the sound. Ariel must be so self-conscious of the sound of her swallowing - it's always like that when you have a bit of a runny nose, right? The mash of gurgle-plud that seems to congeal in your throat sounding compressed and cacophonous, like the embarrassing peal of false flatulence from sinking into the over-polished chair of some fancy dentist's Waiting Room. That's Ariel, scratching the purple and over-red dryness curving the plump of her left hip - a twin irritation afflicting the other hip but no fingernails raking through that just now. The sound of Ariel saying 'Really: write about me this time - I only forgive you being lazy the once, my self-esteem is on the line, now. It better be good, too. I better feel beautiful. I'm going to critique how you're able to make me feel sublime.' What did that sound like? Those words? Not much like words - that's for starters, right? And you don't need to answer so don't and you even shush her with finger to your lip. And Ariel turns her back, crouches to go through her dropped-to-the-floor coat pockets for her cigarettes. Lighting one. Still crouched. Twisting creak-creak around her axis on popping joint tip-toes when she stands and some lines of skin along her tummy are whitened by her tallness making skin taut and these spot settle into crinkles like shrink wrap when she relaxes before her movement obscures the particulars of these markings to the natural shift of shade, shadow, here to there.

What are you writing, Lucy? How are you writing it? Thoughtlessly. More unawake than you have ever been. Refusing to let your eyes even assure you that letters are forming in shapes even related to themselves - letters, for all you know, so mutant to their ancestry it'll take Ice Ages and rebirths for someone to be curious enough to be brilliant enough to understand what they purport. Lucy, Lucy: worrying as you flip pages that when you look down it will seem syrup drizzle from forkfuls of oversoaked pancakes on some diner countertop, sticky, nothing-to-be-done-about, but indecipherable, meaningful to no one. What is it you have to write about Ariel - Ariel Lentz - nude and there in your hotel room, scheme of artiste-at-work with model and some project of import? Do you care to know? Aren't you terrified that this moment - in a moment - when Ariel will say 'Read it to me' - no, she will just say 'Read me' she will just say 'Read me, Lucy, Lucy, read me to me' - is the moment - this moment, here, writing - that either whatever talent you may have had, whatever skill at producing words in some arcane order to express something, will fail you utterly - the last slurp of shit sucked down a gulping toilet gullet - or else be revealed to never have been there to start? Aren't you thinking that - aren't you, just a little - just now? Aren't every line you ever wrote numbly, unpronouncibly, processioning by in the blood behind your eyes, suddenly seeming cockamamie, suddenly malforming caricature of ham-fisted oaf fly-swatting mitts across the octaves of some delicate concerto? And the moment you read, Lucy, the moment you read Ariel to Ariel - because she is going to ask you to - and some codswallop drools on to your dribble-bib, don't you know Ariel will have those poems - your conjoined past, that time you first met and that first time she'd told some clerk you were *Her friend* - fizzle to blur, reconstitute themselves to you, to Lucy Jinx, buffoon long and hand cupped in arm pit, chicken-winging farts and giggling? Won't that be who and what you will reveal yourself to be? What are you writing, Lucy? Why are you? Shouldn't you look? Shouldn't you stop?

*Those tears, sumptuous, serpentine, clementine coloured.* That's on one page, up angled - it looks like a stumble-bum failing at thumbing a ride. *There are wagless tongueless waglessings all-outing in auditoriums, clamour, oh clamour oh claptrapping pirouettes of you.* That's very miniscule, you see? It's invisible from how hard one has to squint will only lead to their giving up. Lucy, herself, will eventually have to only guess at some of it, probably. *Rogue you are you let the summer simper, you limp with symptom of leg asleep with siren song of last night while last night isn't yet yesterday.* That is on the back of one sheet - Lucy had dropped the notebook and Ariel had called her 'All class, baby' and said 'Wowee' - and next to it Lucy wrote the word *Wowy* and underlined it five or six times. *There's a cauldron of you and a long button of you and long tail from an uncertain animal of you and your hindquarters bruise in the colors scarlet, white wine, and blue lips of old books' top edges.* That is rendered neat and tidy, as though Lucy was starting something new, just there - that definitely meant as an Opening, proper, with a Roman Numeral One above it - this is circled and traced, the circle traced, too. *The map I forgot to write the wax I forgot to light the daytime that forgot to night the brackish that forgot to foam.* This is underneath the previous, either just as neat or neater, depending on how you're feeling. It has a Roman Numeral Two over it, but each word *map wax daytime* and *brackish* have lines from them indicating these other phrases written at ends of these lines from them - indicating Lucy had had something on her mind, structurally, but that was pages ago, so by now she no longer does. *I can pronounce your every stare, even the ones you regret.* That is recopied and recopied - but Lucy puts her typical squiggle circle around it, that symbol of hers, that not-quite-shape meaning 'I love this, just now, but feel it not right - which means it must be perfect and I must remember that I should not tinker with it, should either just discard it or use it as is - and I must never discard it, because it's a line I will remember, no matter what, even though I feel uncertain of it, now, and will always, more and more, for how much I love it.'

It's all very funny. Lucy is talking as she writes, as Ariel roams the room diligently. Sometimes Lucy follows Ariel like a cartoon accountant giving some Lordship the updates on what this is all costing the kingdom - or as though a tailor trying to take measurements from some spoilt brat toddler Prince-of-men. Well, Lucy is giving short responses to what Ariel is saying, likely these not matching up cleanly to what Ariel is saying. It's all very funny - it is. Ariel had seen Lucy's ad for models since two editions of *Madhares* ago - yes Lucy, you've been doing this that long - and had wanted to participate from the moment she did but had not seen any way to swing it. 'Why not?' Lucy had asked, this remark from Ariel coming in a rare moment Lucy was not writing but just gazing at Ariel's shoulder and breast and other shoulder and short of her hair. 'I wrote to you once before, Stella - I don't remember what I called myself - and you said that this - the illustrious city in which I am here so nudely lured - is where the modeling took place. I had imagined it would be local, for some reason. Broke my thirsting heart, you did - the facts have a way of making desire seem a moon away.' Yes Lucy, haven't you been listening? She still lives back there - back there, where you first found her. She lives basically where she always had. Pay attention, man! It's all very funny, this - yes? The suspense Ariel had felt, the odd rattle of relief when she saw the ad in some other journal - more than a month on since she'd seen the first - and the somersault in the belly when the ad was still in the next edition - this most recent edition - of *Madhares*. Oh all that back-and-forth correspondence, that forever-long to arrange the time to meet. The machinations on Ariel's part to find an excuse to get away. To sit for this Stella Adroit! 'And then it had just turned out to be you, all along! Anti-climactic to say the least, man. I come for a Stella Adroit and find nothing but some gone-off-all-rancid-and-clotty Lucy Jinx, crising at middle-life!' Ariel poured herself some of the vodka. Told Lucy 'I don't know if it's poetic, this, but I always figured you were the taste of cold vodka thinned with rain-warmed seawater.' She downs a gulp, breathes heavy. 'You can use that, if you want.'

'Do you think if we ordered Room Service they would be the sorts to act awkward and all, bringing the cart in while I just nude around and you scritch your poet-scratch, leering at me so intently?' 'I'm not *leering*. I'm *ogling*. It's how poetry works. Dante did it. They all did it, really - at least the ones who understand ogling is necessary for good penmanship.' 'But - posh place like this - I could open the door - you figure? - tits and all and it'd be par of the course, they have a training video covering it, yeah? They'd have to just act like this is normal, assume I'm from another country and nothing about what I do is to be frowned on - it's all forgiven due to customs and religions far scarier than their own and related things?' 'I'd think so.' 'This is an orgy hotel, right?' 'I think so.' 'That's why you rented it, right? What fleabag do you usually slut around in, Jinx?' 'Some real rat holes, I'll tell you that much. Fuck, Ari - if I'd known it'd been nobody but you was gonna show up we'd be at an off-ramp *Econo Lodge*.' 'Frankly, my heart sunk when I looked up this place. *Oh what a crock* I thought to myself, Jinxy. *And here I thought this was gonna be something bed-buggy* and *Hmn, maybe I'd better see my general practitioner today, just to be on the safe side.*' 'I'm posh, El. I always was. If I got jug-bandy in even the slightest freckle it was on account of your influence.' 'I can see that. I don't take offense at that, because truth is beauty, beauty truth. I am the set-in stain in the crotch of those overalls on the clothesline outback - you know the ones?' 'I know the ones.' 'Do you want something? I'm ordering.' 'Get me something - but under penalty of torture don't tell me what.' 'Okay. But you: get back to work. I'm gonna stop talking to you if it makes you lazy. And I'm getting dressed in three minutes, so gawk while the gandering's good, you know?' 'You're on my dime, darling. Or had you forgotten? I'll gander till you droop more than you already droop.' 'Lucy, Lucy - do you think I don't know that I control the room, girl? And you're just a light-switch in it, a knob on a cabinet! I'll get dressed now - right this instant - if you're not careful. You can keep your two nickels, rub 'em against each other for all I care, baby. See: I can be naked anywhere, no Lucy Jinx required for that.'

Here it is. Lucy. 'Lucy?' Ariel has just asked Lucy to read something. No, Ariel hadn't said 'Read me' and - no, no - she hadn't said 'Read me to me, Lucy.' But she did just ask Lucy to please read something she wrote. And she preempted any excuse by saying 'I'm preempting any excuse you have that you won't by telling you I truly don't give a fuck and you know it. Read something to me - I don't care what and don't look for anything good.' What? Did Ariel think Lucy would stammer and chin-wag some Um-but-uh-you see? Not at all! Nothing could be further from the truth. 'Sit down.' 'I'll stand.' 'I said sit down - right there' and Lucy points at the floor by the window - which must please Ariel, because she complies without further sass, new cigarette fresh lit, knees together at the top of bent legs, arms wrapped around and cheek rested on one, cig smoke let out most-of-the-way uninhaled, thick as cab driver dandruff. 'Good audience' Lucy obedience-trainers and Ariel maybe takes and extra second with smoke-in before smoke-outing. Lucy reads: *never enough twilight to lessen your wails, you're tomorrow that forgot it was ever not yet.* Lucy reads: *something like the March recalled by a years-later February, shiftless girl, gallop when you ought trot and trot when your ought gallop faster.* Lucy reads: *the gloves are the skin of your bones, your scraped knees the kisses not coming, the tone of the room is the claw of the color, the sky's sour the sour-sky's scamper.* 'Fuck you, anyway' Ariel interjects 'Read something else!' Lucy reads: *buttonloose you, crow caw, cat in the window across - little finger you, minus sign, growl at my face, growl at me, face bruised from you.* Lucy reads: *I remember the autumn better than you can, the autumn is more my sized coin.* Lucy reads: *you could rhyme nocturne with anything when your mouth is this close.* Lucy reads: *poor pleas are the only ones worth giving to first loves awayed.* Lucy glanced up at Ariel, but she shouldn't have - she should never have. Oh why did you do that, Lucy - how do you go on from that? Look down. Look downer - be punished. 'Should I keep reading?' Ariel doesn't answer. Because Ariel cannot? Don't look up again, Lucy. You can't. Just read.

As it turned out, Ariel wimped out of dealing with the person who knocked with the Room Service and Lucy just shook her head, piteously, after they were alone again. 'I thought it might have been a guy - and by *guy* I mean *fellow*.' 'That's your excuse? How many ways could you have worked around that?' 'I don't think well on my feet. You distracted me, anyway. I wasn't supposed to not remember I was naked - it was supposed to be a Billy-club, you know? Cold-cock the bugger!' 'Come on - just cop to being a chickenshit and we'll move on without further remark. I'd entirely forgotten about the food, honestly.' Lucy was a bit surprised that Ariel started eating, immediately, and admitted aloud she thought the food had been ordered just for the excuse to show off her devil-may-careishness in front of strangers. 'Oh don't be so haughty - you didn't even ask out the doorman. And that was outside! -So I don't want to hear it from you.' Lucy took a handful of the steak-fries and ate them as she walked to the kitchen. What do you feel like right now, Lucy? Anything? 'No' she says, opening the freezer, closing it, deciding on wine over vodka. 'I don't feel like anything.' You don't feel like anything? 'You don't feel like anything?' asks Ariel, loud voice, over-shouldered. 'Stop eavesdropping!' 'I thought you were talking to me! Shit, man - are you over there talking to yourself? Are you talking to a ghost in the freezer? Is this night about to go in that direction?' And Ariel says something else into a mawful of hamburger and from the sound of it drinks from her soda right into the still being-chewed mash. Lucy is here, staring at the clock on the mounted microwave. So what? Is there some time it should be? Lucy shakes her head - listens to Ariel over there, chewing, drinking, sloshing thick swallows - but keeps staring. Do you want it to be later? Earlier. 'I don't want it to be' Lucy says. And Ariel mouthfuls some vowel-smeared approximation of 'Goddamn it! Stop talking to yourself, psychopath - you're freaking me out!' 'I was talking to you, that time' Lucy says. Stares at the clock. The time. 'Go away' she mouths. 'Go away!' she silents. A blue four at the end turns to a blue five, snide little flicker of *Fuck you*.

'I don't want to sleep.' Lucy didn't want to sleep, either - but did ask if Ariel was tired. 'Even if I was tired, I am not to be allowed to sleep.' 'Well, did I ask you to sleep? Stop being such a prissy agitator Ari, it's quite unbecoming.' Time had hobbled and see-sawed and now seemed kind of leaned to the walls of the room like a wet banner from some lamppost. It crosses Lucy's mind here to ask if Ariel would like to listen to more of the poetry. But there is now a cold-stone of hollow inside her - you've been excavated Lucy, there is a cavity, here, where there was whatever all that verse built up had been. Indeed, a ten pounds, twenty pounds lighter gait strides Lucy to the window - when had they opened it? - to close it against the draft. She catches herself in time to turn how she would have said 'I think I'm done writing' into a cough and a rough throat clear. Don't be done! Her eyes flashbulb with a squirm of fatigue when she tries to focus on some phrasing, though. She blinks in sets like smacks to an ink cartridge blacking grey. Ariel excuses herself to the bathroom and for a moment Lucy thinks she did not close the door - but when she glances over she finds that it is shut and the buzz of the overhead fan sags lumpy throughout the old tin can room. The lost boot room. The hungry hand room. The whining dog room. Are these attempts at verse? 'Ariel?' Lucy shudders, but completely by accident - just happens to catch a chill that rubbers her step, there, nothing more. 'Ariel?' she calls again, louder. That door. The hum. Cancer dot, cancer dot - larger and larger! 'Ariel?' Even if she is still there - she is Lucy, get a grip immediately - whatever happens now is cantering toward the end of it all. You do know that - you do know that, are at peace with it, not flailing with admission of how soon you are to a corpse. How has so much time been wasted that this seems like the first blink, that everything else just flimsys of flittering thoughts while pacing and waiting for someone to arrive? 'Ariel?' The vibration of the fan vanishes. Silence. 'Ariel?' 'Are you calling me?' Silence. 'What?' 'Are you saying something to me?' Lucy lights a cigarette and makes a baffled face at the closed bathroom door, drawing her posture back mockingly. 'Saying something to you? No. Christ, you're paranoid! Just finish whatever you're doing in there!' The overhead fan goes back on. Lucy's ear cranes. Ariel said something, just now. But on purpose - a game, a jumble of noise to make Lucy say 'What?' But Lucy just smiles and doesn't and waits.


'AS I'M ON THE CLOCK' Ariel says, positioning Lucy there - just there, exactly in front of her, no place in particular, the middle of the wide room floor - 'and as I understand from your charming e-mail demeanor' Ariel centers Lucy's face, her shoulders, Lucy falling to Ariel's beats, letting herself putty to Ariel's whims, here 'that I am not only permitted to but supposed' Ariel nods a punctuation, eyes locked to Lucy's - does it seem Ariel could not hold the gaze Lucy, are you imagining that? - 'supposed' Ariel repeated 'supposed to do whatever I want while you ply your trade, well I - here - shall do as I please.' Ariel finds the clasp of Lucy's pant-front and gently cleaves button-fly down - slow one slow two, quick three four, slow five - then this-side-that-side this-side-that-side gives tugs, jiggles, until the fabric drags over Lucy's sleep-aching hips. As Ariel goes to knees to finish Lucy's pants down, the tug also insides-out and only inch-or-two pulls down Lucy's grey-and-green panties, as well - this noted to Lucy as a touch of room air warming the curve into the cleft of her buttocks. Lucy tightens a half-breath, thinking to right the underwear - not out of shyness, but in case Ariel would have wanted it that way - but then stays as she was positioned, only giving one click of eyes down, this seeing nothing but odd blur of Ariel's head-top while she feels Ariel lifting her left foot and working the pant-leg off then removing the sock from that foot. Ariel sniffles and the sound of her wiping, annoyed, at her nose with the side of her hand. Then the feeling of Ariel, with thumb and pads of index and middle-finger, pinching the bottom center fabric of Lucy's panties - some of Lucy's pubic-hair incidentally caught in the pinch and tugged, pinprick - tip-tap tip-tap pulling them down. Suddenly the full warm of Ariel's cupped palm over Lucy's whole inner thigh while the panties are taken down half-trunk of right leg, palm removed, panties easily slid down bannister of left leg to slow-motion dancer land over the roots of Lucy's sweating tops-of-barefeet.

That is Ariel Lentz. Exactly what Ariel Lentz - in this hotel, tonight - would look like. Those are Ariel's eyes over Lucy Jinx's bare shoulders, neck, down over Lucy's breasts and the heft of her exhausted-from-all-day-long tummy. What kind of expression would you call that? Ariel moves in uneven half-circles, absent-minded, around Lucy, now or now or now giving her a little touch, lifting an arm - Lucy self-conscious of the tricking bead of sweat from her underarm over her finger-length ribs - or touching the side of a knee like as though a child ever so delicately hoping a music-box would just start to tinkle again after ages of standing broke. Ariel's hands through Lucy's hair - no complaint of Lucy's muteness and no betrayal of enjoying it. Is Ariel as numb as you are, Lucy? Every limb asleep? Does Ariel's every breath feel like the peg-leg of some pirate, still-framed from a silent film? Is this more a game for her? Or the fulfillment of a forever-long-even-as-your-own desire? More important, maybe - only maybe - is to note that Lucy is fully aware she is not retaining this. Ariel's eyes pour over her and she wonders if the input is falling unread to the floor the same as Lucy's regard of Ariel pawing her, turning her, face now close-ing now far-ing. What was the first part of you Ariel looked at? And for how long? And does Ariel seem daring, willing herself to braggadocio, to linger on the parts of yours that have either most allured her always or those which she finds, suddenly, ex nihilo, transfix her now? This is awake what sleep feels like. This is coma. This is a word trapped inside a sound not at all like it. What was it? What was it that Dorene had asked you, that first night, that time? Her question: 'How would you think, Lucy - think - what would thinking feel like if you didn't have any language?' Lucy's answer then: a long breath out - still unbelieving those were Dorene's lips there, the question so near her shoulder -

and then 'I don't know, yeah, I don't know.' Lucy's answer now? 'You wouldn't. And *like this* - it would feel *like this*, Dorene.'

'Do you know that you have this patch of freckles, here? Or is that something about you that only I have the secret of? Maybe they were never there before, you know what I mean? What are they? Look at them. I mean you can't, but here - right here - where I'm poking you - poke poke poke - did you know you had these freckles here? I think if no one else specifically told you about them, I am claiming this unprecedented discovery. Besides - admit it - nobody's looked at you before me. You're like some grandma's house sofa I'm the first one to open the cushions of, pull out the stuffing. Little brat, little brat. You don't even know if there are freckles - poke poke poke- do you, old girl? Maybe you think I even mean moles. Maybe I do. Or maybe you assume *Well, even if no one told me, they must have always been there.* Maybe you're thinking *Freckles don't just materialize when stripped by some former co-worker in a hotel room one night!* But I posit you're wrong, Jinx. That's just exactly what they do. These ones. I'm responsible. A new part of you. Say I were to disappear, right - I won't, shut up, don't worry - say I were to disappear - I mean, I might, who knows, I can only promise for so long, you know? - but say I were to disappear and then you were to have someone else look just here - poke poke poke - or to take a photograph yourself, right here - poke poke poke - and they were to say there weren't freckles, the photo would just be your pasty, blank skin, maybe a blemish or a rubbed-raw from your walking that day. Well, you'd still think I saw them, now. As much as you think maybe I'm making it up. You'd think *Maybe those were just there because Ariel was looking. Maybe that's scientific. Maybe it's something out of old mythology.* Maybe you'd go to libraries and look it up or write it in some poem. This is what I do, Lucy-cat - I make you a mystery for you. Only I can ever verify this part of you was ever here right when it was here.'

Wait. Is any of this happening? How is Lucy here, now? Last-warmth-of-bread-center eyes opening and a corner of crust in them. Ariel there, talking, across the way in the kitchen. This is a sofa. And Lucy Jinx is asleep. And Ariel suddenly is cursing and telling someone over the telephone to stop calling and that there isn't anything she can do about it and is laughing and saying the words 'Oh God' over and over and over and over and they are getting larger and larger like a head with a fever and spots breaking out across it and hands too gummy and thick to properly scratch at the dryness scaling the outside of her neck just up the center, hair growing from it, follicle, tangle, nest of spiders cracking open like a salamander egg and the things spilling out, carbonation of legs and glugging whine of a wasp caught inside of her ear under her hands clamping out the noise they are clamping in. Lucy wakes. Blink. Says 'Yes' rather loud, in precise response to a question and shaking her face. Ariel laughs a peal and says

'Are you asleep over there, godaamnit!?' 'I'm not asleep.' Lucy looks across the sofa, over the length of her nude legs, ankles crossed, and can tell she has been squirming herself more shoved into the corner-crook of the sofa-arm and the crease at the base of the back cushions. 'Then what's the last thing I said?' 'You asked me why I don't have any tattoos!' More laughter. Ariel is pouring the coffee that is responsible for this new aroma everywhere - the scent seems part of the sleep-glaze in the creases of Lucy's brow and the slick that won't rub away from her eggplant purple under-eyes. 'That is so not what I asked at all, fiend - fuck Lucy, stay awake! But as long as you bring it up: why don't you have tattoos?' What? Blink. 'What?' Ariel is right here, now. 'I'm not letting you sleep. Sorry.' How long were you out, Lucy? Lucy smiles and says 'I'm awake' while she watches Ariel dip her fingers in the coffee-cup and flick the liquid onto her already brown-speckled-with-it breasts.

Lucy Jinx: hereby deemed worthless, nothing more than a stumble-bum nuisance, C-list gadfly at best. Ariel dusts her hands and explains that, for the benefit of all, she will take the reins. 'My first order of business is to reduce you to the lowly role of me' - she finger zap-guns at the now standing and limply drinking from coffee-mug Lucy - 'and to take over the previously dignified role of Lucy Jinx, myself, in full hope of returning it to its previous place of stature and envy in the socioeconomic strata. All in favor?' Ariel *Hear-hears!* and *Carrieds!* And the matter is resolved. Lucy watches as Ariel sits in the armchair and puts on first Lucy's discarded socks then, still sitting, pulls on Lucy's - still inside-out - panties, then - noticing the inside-outness - pulls off Lucy's panties, calls her 'An old gummy bitch' a 'gin-sot' and a 'square-head' while fixing the things, pulls them back on, sifting her ass side-to-side without ever completely lifting it from the sofa cushions at all. Lucy remarks that the panties do not quite fit as she watches Ariel wedge her way into the pants and struggle them closed, the plump of Ariel's belly in all kinds of offshoots and the two segmentations of the flesh of her sides turns three when she doubles over to lift up Lucy's shirt, flattens to nothing as she lifts arms to get the fabric over her head. 'I'm not going to wear you clown-shoes, but give me that bracelet you have.' Lucy relinquishes it and is about to explain it - Ariel taking a moment to read the likely very-odd-to-her inscription - but doesn't when Ariel just slips it over her thinner-than-Lucy's wrist and starts patting herself as though for a cigarette. 'Can I have a drink?' Lucy asks, the words coming out cartoon villain rasps, old sound effect of windstorm in grainy sepia-grey from late night Horror Feature. 'You' Ariel says 'can do whatever you want, Ariel.' And Lucy hears - now at the kitchen, pouring some last-two-mouthfuls-at-most of the white wine - behind her a cigarette lighter scratch scratch scratch light up and then a soft thunk of it tossed to the room carpet.

Lucy opens a window and immediately her body bristles and tightens. There is snow falling outside when she focuses right - one can see it in oversized shadows cast from flakes passing in front of streetlights just off camera. 'It's snowing. Sorry. Do you mind if I talk?' 'Not at all. Act however you would act.' Now, maybe this is an invitation to do some cutsey impersonation of Ariel, to show some of the things Lucy remembers having heard Ariel say so long ago - or a chance to make a monkey out of her, act all like some lurching old inbred, hoot and chest-thump in the manner some frat boy drunkard so sure of himself before getting the test results back would. Lucy just lets her back be chilled frozen by the draft from the window, rubs her eyes and again takes in the size of this room. There is Ariel. Is she really writing? What is she writing? Make believe garblemouths of consonants, twenty-five to every one vowel? Penning dirty fantasies or crude limerick? Whatever it is, Lucy can tell Ariel is actually concentrating. There, dressed now in Lucy's blazer as well - it fits Ariel even worse than it fit Lucy - is Ariel, hardly even looking up from the page. What are you writing, Ariel? How long does this game play for? Or is it your turn to decide, Lucy? You could, you know? Yeah, yeah - Lucy knows. But in this moment of not being Lucy she is honestly imagining her body is Ariel's and her blood is Ariel's and her memories are Ariel's and that Ariel, the real one, is only full of pretend memories of Ariel and a perfect understanding of Lucy. It's a complicated thought, all noted out. More: it's as though Ariel's body only has memories of the times it shared with Lucy and other than that has mere confirmations of this or that of Lucy's assumptions - all assumptions correct. But it is not like this is odd. Is not like the body went into a hibernation between Then and Now, but is rather as though there is only Then or Now. Lucy-as-Ariel wonders if Ariel-as-Lucy only knows what Ariel knew of Lucy and what she assumed and what is going through her head, now, here, in this room.

Read it. Ah, Lucy you almost said that! But how can you resist? Go on. 'Read me to me, Lucy.' Ariel looks up. Ariel - at least it looked like - was about to quip something witty, but lost the charge even as the head of steam got full. 'Just a second' she said and returned to her writing, holding up a hand as though to stave off another immediate interruption. But Lucy just took another drag of this - what is it, the eighth-in-a-row? - cigarette, the smoke forming something like letters in the way the light catches it and the previous breaths of it, the thicknesses mingling in swirls with shadows and changes in vantage from Lucy drifting her head along shoulders. Ariel turns the page and keeps writing. 'Do you want some vodka?' Ariel does not answer, so Lucy - also stuffing, hardly a chew, two slices of bread down her throat, wincing contractions slowly dragging the mash to her belly, bruise-feeling all down her numbed only by some tap water and a full tug from vodka neck throat - brings her a glass of it anyway and just sets it on the sofa arm. Was that piff-breath a *Thank you?* Lucy flicks this cigarette out into the chill before closing the window. And the room, shut and stale now, seems to contain only the sound of this latest swallow - squish squish in her ears - and the mouth-breathing of Ariel as she turns another page and goes 'Okay.' 'Read it.' Ariel huffs. 'Naw. You can, though.' Pouty, Lucy insists. 'I hate my voice.' Lucy does hate her voice. 'Well, I like your voice.' Lucy imagines Ariel is thinking 'Well, that's true - I do like your voice.' 'Just fucking read it. I want to hear it!' 'That's what I'm saying' says Ariel, pointing at herself and then at Lucy - who is Ariel - then flip-flop, flip-flop between them as though the game has become Mephistophelean in its complexity. 'You read it, Lucy.' 'You read it, Ariel.' 'You.' 'You.' 'Me?' 'Me?' 'You?' 'Me.' 'Me?' 'You.'

Lucy-as-Ariel recites Ariel-as-Lucy. Part of it is this: *commonplace as dry ink, my rare letter girl.* Part of it is: *I found a new page for you and wrote nothing there.* The trick is to not let this strike you, Lucy. Do you have any idea how tired you are? Imagine a world in which the distance between the continents as we know them is three times as long - got that? - now imagine it ten times as wide as that three-times-as-long - got that, again? - now imagine the distance between one bit of land and another - the world as we know it - three hundred times as wide as even that ten-times-as-long-as-three-time-as-long and you have some idea of how far you are from yourself, right now. On such a world as that - invention being as pressing as it is, passion as coalfire as always - it would not matter, the people of Here would never reach the people of There - even if they in their sometimes-dreams felt so sure They would find Them there. Lucy-as-Ariel recites Ariel-as-Lucy. Part of it is this: *gravebellied, you, and your trunks undug thick of books you borrowed and phrases you stole.* Part of it is: *I'd steal the coins from your eyes just to spend them on cigarettes to smoke in your now long cold sheets.* It is only coincidence of landmass that even allowed dreams of reaching each other. If the horizon was forty feet further on, would anyone even have cared how curved the world was? If the nearest star was even another half-the-distance-further-on than it is now - and the ones past that further on in equal measure - wouldn't we have given up thinking to touch them before we had even begun? Come on - there are spaces between things so vast that even the absolute knowledge of something beyond breeds nothing but 'That is what we mean by *Alone.*' Lucy-as-Ariel recites Ariel-as-Lucy. Part of it is this: *I'm a thread reminding myself to remember to lose a loose tooth.* Part of it this: *You're the last sound of the last piano I never learned to play.*

While Lucy kept reading - Lucy, you aren't even trying to hide what this is doing to you anymore, you're a wreck! - Ariel has downed that there vodka and gotten some more - yes, too far away to hear Lucy reading and, anyway, the suck of the freezer door and the yawn of the coolant blown would drown it out

- and she returns, again empty-glassed and holding her duffle, her own second-time disrobed clothes dumped in a pile on the sofa. Mid-phrase, Ariel takes the notebook from Lucy and says 'Stop reading that. You're messing it up, anyway.' Lucy is a wet-nosed whelp - it's embarrassing - and she has the headache of unstopped tears and unsucked-up mucus and just chuckles in a shrug of *Yeah, sorry*. Ariel holds one of Lucy's grimy old arms out, shoulder high, and gingerly gets the sleeve of her shirt around Lucy's wrist and her arm length all in it. Has Lucy drop the arm. Bends Lucy's other. Un-inside-outs the other shirtsleeve and wrangles Lucy's arm through. Then slowly, seeming to lose track of what she is doing once or twice and dusting at the fabric of the shirt shoulders, instead - at one time licking her thumb and then wiping a spot, maybe in some attempt to press out a wrinkle - buttons the thing. Ariel gets her pants straightened and ready, jokingly says 'Jesus, I wish I'd worn a skirt - but that would have entailed stockings and could you imagine having to deal with that, right now? With you blubbering and everything?' Lucy snorts but feels less ridiculous - hey, at least you're not crying anymore, right? - than even the minute before and asks if Ariel wants her to get in the clothes, on her own. 'No' Ariel says, lifting Lucy's left foot up to get the first circle of panties in under it, ankle-arounded 'I don't want you to do anything but to let me do this.' Ariel's panties seem to fit Lucy fine and the tingling heat that catches her breath as Ariel snaps the fabric, flirtatiously, at the hip before turning to the business of getting the pants on to Lucy now is maybe the last she will ever know of whoever else she once may have been.

There was more than enough light from the main room to light the bedroom, but as they entered - neither leading the other - one of them - yes, it's funny, Lucy really doesn't know if it was her - flicked the switch on and the ceiling fan overhead started up too, the slat shadows thin to the room paint, seeming so wrong for nocturnal movement, as though this room just had no conception of what else the world was up to, what place it held, how to comport itself with any appropriateness. Anyway - Lucy, why are you thinking about ceiling fans and shadows? - the two, in each other's clothes, lay down on their bellies like they are going to read the same page of the same magazine, shoulders touching and hips touching and Ariel smacks a pillow and the clap echos like a split block of concrete. 'That's one loudmouth pillow' Lucy points out, Ariel nodding. 'I'm going to go to sleep now. I think with the precautions we've taken we can be certain not to either of us run off. Agreed?' 'Agreed' Lucy agrees, assuming Ariel is referencing their mutual state of dress-up and, indeed, can see how confusing it would be to wander off, slink away, only to be covered in fabric that amounts - in this case, very cuttingly - to some unrequited other's unrequited skin. 'Lucy' Ariel says, very seriously - the game of you-be-me is broken, that is clear - rolling on to her side, yawning twice without giving Excuse-mes to either 'listen to me.' Lucy takes a similar pose to Ariel's, but by no means a mirror image or even an attempt to be so. 'Yes?' Pause. Ariel sighs like something in translation. 'I don't believe you're real again, yet.' Then a pause. 'Okay?' Lucy nods. This doesn't seem to be the sort of thing Lucy needs to understand to agree with - it seems that the point is to not understand and not care. 'Maybe if I wake up in awhile or something I will. But right now I don't.' Pause. 'Do you think I'm real, right now?' Ah. This needs to be answered Lucy - this calls for honesty, but it seems you already know that. Here - and as simple as that - Lucy says 'No.' And - as simple as that - Ariel says 'Goodnight, okay?'

This was sleep and this wasn't sleep. Not at all. Look: Lucy Jinx. Look: Ariel Lentz. Ariel's breathing - not that Lucy notices - is much heavier than Lucy's. There is some tartness not present in how the various alcohols mix in the scent of Ariel's breath on Lucy's. Yes, Lucy's breath is more childish. She has even noted this to herself, at times. How when she wakes - while her mouth feels gummy, spittle thick, a paste like microwave oatmeal - it never strikes her that her breath is any sort of flavor, just light, almost not there. Lucy wakes now and again and each time it seems to her she is conscious far longer than she actually is. Maybe it is the same for Ariel, maybe not. For example: when Lucy's eyes slug open and she notices the bent curve of the color of her shirt on Ariel, she thinks she is looking at it quite some time, making comments on the fit of shadow to shadow, crease to crease - comparing it to a broken vulture beak, a bent-wrong toe after the webbing of a frog's foot, a dog-eared page that had been so for so long to touch it would snap the triangle away clean - but the fact is she only thought the simple recognition of the sight of the collar, hardly even considered it was on Ariel, and all the rest of that - and much more - she dreamed and would eventual wake, proper not remembering a dent of. They touch at times, though mostly not. Their knees touch most of all, as they maintain their original positions, give-or-take, of slumber for the majority of the night. Eventually, near waking for good, Lucy has rolled over completely, perhaps some unconscious reset, the typewriter of her slapped after reaching the Ping! of an end line of text. She is upset at herself. Dreadfully hopes that Ariel never woke once and found her with back turned. Not a moment of jealous asleep for Ariel, please! And Lucy, you need to forget this slap of guilty just-awakening.

So, that was sleep. And a little while later it was not. And it still is not. They are laying and looking at each other and smiling. Are you each pretending to be drowsier than you are, Lucy? Or is it just you? You are hyper-caffeinated, practically - you feel like jaunting about town in the style of a jangle-nerved dope-fiend and going into secondhand shops and buying the things you like the least just to have the pleasure of finding a lake to chuck them in, Ariel sidekicking beside you and laughing hang-jawed at what a galoot you can sometimes be! 'I'm not really tired.' 'I'm not really tired, either.' 'You're a big fake.' 'You're a topaz bitch.' 'That's better than mine! Fuck. You're a topaz bitch!' 'You're a copy-cat.' 'I am - jealous?' 'Yeah. I wish I were a copy-cat.' 'You could be.' 'But I mean I wish I'd thought of it first. Though I guess I'm an even better copy-cat if I do it second.' 'Fuck! Stop cheating.' 'Stop whining.' 'Stop making me.' 'Stop goading me.' 'Fine.' 'Fine.' 'Jinx.' 'Goddamn right' Ariel says 'Jinx.' Ariel rolls over on to her back and gloriously stretching with creaking bones and odd gurgle breaths of settled phlegm in the cup-bottom of her throat. 'I can never remember. Who did we decide was older - you or me?' 'Me.' 'Me, you? Or you, me?' 'Me, you.' 'Which one is that?' 'Me.' 'Me, you? Or you, me?' 'You, me.' 'That's what I thought: me. Why didn't you just say that?' 'I did. You're just confused.' 'You did, I'm just confused, I did, you're just confused? Or I did, you're just confused, you did, I'm just confused?' 'You're confused.' 'And I'm you?' 'That's right.' 'And you're me?' 'That's right.' 'So you're confused.' 'That's right.' 'So I'm confused.' 'That's right.' 'This is going to get very fucking complicated. We're not even out of bed yet, you know?' Ariel sits up a moment, then flops back down. 'Oh Goddamnit it. What time is it anyway?' Lucy shrugs, terrified there is some specific reason Ariel is asking. 'I thought you were a clock!' 'I am a clock.' 'You're a clock, I'm a clock? Or I'm a clock, you're a clock?' 'I'm a clock, I'm a clock.' 'Aha.' Ariel flicks Lucy's chin. 'You're tricky. Fuck. That was a good one. Cause I'm you, right?' 'That's right.'

It happened kind of quickly, in retrospect. Ariel had mentioned how she had not imagined she would be staying in Stella Adroit's room, overnight. This oddly surprised Lucy, but in the laughing way. Oh Lucy - how you had a headful of romance about Victoire Elan, eh? And fact, Lucy girl: you did just spend the night with her! Even got into her pants, ha ha ha. But: Ariel has a whole other hotel room where her whole other stuff is. The point - though Lucy supposes there is also a larger point - in bringing this up being that Ariel has no toothbrush or toiletries or et cetera and so commands 'Lucy, I will be using yours - and your motely lot is to deal with that.' So now Ariel is in there, froth-mouthed with Lucy's toothpaste and the worn-bristles of her well-overused brush. Ariel will take a mouthful of the small bottle of mouthwash. But what had happened fast - Lucy was reflecting on - was Ariel had removed Lucy's clothing. Ariel is naked in there and - did you hear the groan, the hiss, now the steady shush? - the shower has been started. A pile of Lucy's clothes. How does that feel, Lucy? All things end and that was not something you ever imagined even starting. It means nothing negative - and certainly the dress-up was not just the result of sleepyhead, warm-sloshy-style drunk. Is it an invitation, though? Ah. The questions, the questions! Does Ariel expect you to undress and to join her? Are you supposed to be unconscious simpatico? Alternately: does it matter if Ariel meant for you to consider that? She doesn't need to invite you, after all. Invite yourself! What do you think, you will be rejected? Lucy sits on the edge of the bed in the hotel room. Ariel had not expected to spend the night here. She had expected to be in another room. There are thoughts in Ariel's head Lucy doesn't know. 'Best not presume, Lucy' Lucy thinks at the same time as she goddamn well presumes.

They dress together. Ariel says it is unfair that Lucy has a change of clothes. 'But I'm not using it!' 'You still have it, though. Don't do me any favors. I don't need you philanthropy!' A friendly shove - Ariel is only dressed to the waist and Lucy only in stale socks, sitting on the sofa arm. Lucy wants to say something to Ariel about how much she liked the poetry Ariel wrote. But she doesn't want to deal with deprecation. Which will come. She doesn't want to be dramatic, not have a little moment, nothing like that - she just wants to say it without having to hear Ariel say 'Oh I was drunk' or 'Gawd, I don't even remember what I wrote - please just burn it, okay?' Lucy's head feels like it is fillinged with the penny taste of blood, the lining around her skull shrinking in that way a stomach feels sour after upchucking to dry heaves and only having citrus around to drink. I really liked the poetry you wrote. There. I mean, you didn't say it - but you could. It's progress you aren't imagining it'll just kablam! up in your face, Ariel careening, bone hurt, out of the room and disowning you to every person she passes. I really liked the poetry you wrote. *You don't even remember it!* What if she says that, Lucy? Would it be true? It would be true, wouldn't it? Recite, quietly - while Ariel twists her now clasped bra around and arranges herself - one line of it, just here in your head. 'You don't need to remember something to like it!' That's what you said aloud, Lucy? 'Well' Ariel smiles 'anyway' the wrinkles around her mouth a sharp pucker of considering and a nod 'I suppose that's true. I'd like that, for example, even if I don't remember it.' Lucy chuckles. Ariel gets her shirt over her head. 'But I will try to remember it' Ariel roughly scrapes fingers up-down, left-right, up-down, back-forth through her still-only-just-barely-towel-dried hair. I really liked the poetry you wrote, Ariel. *Thank you.* It could go like that, Lucy. Or are you afraid it would only go like that and no further?

'I am going under the impression that you have already slyly deduced from my tits that I have - you know? - birthed offspring, to put it colloquially.' Lucy is drinking coffee and Ariel is drinking coffee and both of them are eating plain bread, Ariel's toasted just a bit - Lucy touched it suspiciously and gave the hairy-eye to Ariel, unable to tell the slightest difference between it and her own untoasted, backing away as though from the killer revealed as the-last-one-you'd-expect in a film when Ariel had told her 'Oh piss off' - and they both sigh, in unison, before taking a simultaneous swallow, here. 'A son or a daughter?' 'A daughter.' 'What's her name?' Ariel drinks. 'I'm not telling.' 'Why not?' Calm down Lucy, tame those butterflies - you think Ariel named her daughter *Lucy*, is that what you think? Ariel isn't a lovesick psychopath, no matter how hard you squint to try to make her so. 'Really - why not?' Ariel sets her coffee down and crosses into the sofa area, bringing what's left of the cigarette pack back over to the kitchen, giving one to Lucy and telling her to start smoking. They smoke. 'Why can't I know what your stupid daughter is called?' 'Oh you can. I'm just nervous you won't come and visit.' What? Wait. 'Are you even fucking kidding? Are you even fucking kidding me, Ariel? Of course I'll visit.' Ariel sighs and whatever the elsewheres in her eyes are Lucy doesn't know - and it's a nightmare not knowing, because it seems the best part of a song that she's the only one who doesn't know the melody of. 'Ariel - do you know that I'm in love with you?' 'Yes. I know that.' 'That I've been in love with you for like however many millions of years it has been?' 'Yes' Ariel says. 'Do you know that I am, quite to the marrow, pusillanimously in love with - even right now, while I never thought I'd see you again and blah blah blah - you? I love you.' 'I know that.' 'Okay.' In case you're not caught up, Lucy: you did just say all of that - it exists in physical space-time and nothing undoes it and those were Ariel's actual responses. Same as, right now, Ariel is saying 'Her name is *Kayleigh Ylajali Moor*. I only chose the *Ylajali* part, though. Okay?' 'Yeah' Lucy says. 'I love that book.' 'Do you?' Ariel asks, sarcastic chuckle then cigarette drag. Long, long breath of cigarette out from Ariel, then. Some of that grey must have come from somewhere else, some of the no-color just barely blurring the empty air, too - no cigarette breathes out so long as that, none that Lucy has ever seen.

If Lucy has forgotten anything, well, that's just fine. She doesn't care! She is more concerned with the fact that Ariel's sniffing has increased exponentially since they exited the door, a moment ago, and that Ariel has burned through that length of toilet tissue she'd taken as snot-rag twice over, already. At the start of the stairs, Ariel waves off Lucy's offer to double back to the room to get more, even when Lucy says there are paper kitchen napkins and - come to think of it - there will likely be a box of actual tissues in a room so well-kept! - and explains about how the difference between someone-like-herself and someone-like-Lucy is that someone-like-herself knows there is a front desk, downstairs, that will be more than accommodating. Sniffle. Snort. Hack. Sniffle. They trundle and bump bump their way down the stairs, Lucy's duffle adding extra bass beats and sounds of strain like a poorly designed bridge going to collapse those in transit to water-clot doom. 'Did you like the poetry I wrote?' Lucy spins on Ariel - right there on the stair - bullies up to her and says 'Fuck, Ari - I adored the poetry. Stop making me feel so shit-heel for not saying so until I did! You can take such things for granted, okay?' And Ariel slow-pokes and sniffles while Lucy thunders ahead, pivoting at the next landing to stick out her tongue, family-friendly brat sort of glower. 'You saw me fucking cry, Ariel - so you're just being a prick!' Now Ariel seems to consider the matter through that aperture. 'In that case - I adored the poetry you wrote, too.' 'In that case?' 'Yes. It was conditional. That's why I hadn't said anything. But you did cry at mine, after all, so you've painted me into a corner.' And here, abruptly, Ariel snorts loud and stamps inpatient foot in a one-two-three bang. 'Now, are we going to stand in the damn stairs all day long having a spat, or what?'

How about this? Snow. Oh Ariel and Lucy - the both of them - trade remarks about how they despise the sort of people who make a big deal out of snow - adults, those who know better, who whore-paint themselves like they are enthralled to the romantic nostalgia of white laden drifts and all, who go I'm-cute-kiss-me-toned and hang to their boyfriends' and husbands' arms as they get pink-nosed and pale-cheeked and pretend suddenly they love looking in windows at retail workers hating their lives. 'My husband makes a thing out of the snow. I tell myself he does it because of the kid - that's what I tell myself - but she - the kid - is smart enough not to care and he's just still in the throes of thinking being a dad requires something particular of him.' 'He sounds like the pick-of-the-litter, El' Lucy says and the high-pitched, surprising-even-herself musicality of Ariel's laughter and 'Get to fuck, man' and the shove into the oncoming pedestrian's path - 'Excuse me' Lucy embarrasses and on-purposes Ariel with a smack as she falls back into pace beside her - makes Lucy proud as the last crow on earth that she said it. After the next crosswalk, Ariel slows her pace a little so that she is not breathing so hard. Lucy assumes Ariel knows where they are walking - or did until this moment, to be honest, in this moment absolutely sure they are just trajectorying aimless-like - so that she can talk in an even sort of way and can be certain Lucy hears her. Their heads almost touch and their shoulders are pressed hard to each other. 'Lucy - of course I'm in love with you, okay? And I have been not since I first saw you - I'm not an exaggerator like you - but since pretty quickly on I-first-saw-you's heels - and it's only gotten worse and worse. I don't want you moping around or anything because I didn't say it.' Can I mope because you did? Say it, Lucy! 'Can I mope because you did?' 'You're so predictable, Jinx. You're like a spec script I could write and discard as derivative.' Ariel stops - dead stop - quickly holds Lucy's eyes, says 'And yes, you'd better' then presses on in the make-believe of having a destination.

Lucy wonders how this all looks from different vantages. It is happening. And things that happen happen multiply. Vantage One: a customer in there, looking out. They cannot even see Lucy - or not inasmuch as they can consider her *with Ariel*. And Ariel is, to them, a mostly-obscured-by-the-reflection-of-the-inside-of-the-store streak on the glass. Maybe from that vantage neither of them can be seen. Let's say that, Lucy. And Vantage Two: one of those office windows, up there. Someone looking down, not specifically. There are a lot of people on the street, so Ariel and Lucy both are not distinguishable as a damn thing. They are just portions of the way a view from above always looks - beautiful and unique, though somehow - more and more - normalized. Above never goes completely normal - Lucy doesn't believe that it does - but it does eventually become unique only in the way seeing a new postage stamp design or one from another country is unique. Yes, you know you've never seen it before but have seen many things like it - so there's that. The brain categorizes it *Stamp*, some sketched-in details of color and a question of *Is this still useable?* and then more than half-way forgets, right away. That's Vantage Two. Vantage Three could be from someone on the opposite side of the street. Able to tell Lucy and Ariel are walking together, giving them a story, deciding subconsciously they - Lucy and Ariel - are sisters and have just been to a concert. Or are going to one. Have rode the subway and - at some time during the ride - Ariel had whispered to Lucy - or Lucy to Ariel - about some obviously vagrant passenger doing something with their mouth and coughing like an important businessman as they rattle the three-day-old, stained-from-use newspaper they hold like some Napoleonic saber and whistle down their nose every time they breathe out. A squeeze toy of poverty and ill mental health! Yes. That's Vantage Three. Lucy is sure of it.

They have gone into a diner sort of restaurant and Ariel has answered the hostess 'Two' when asked 'Just the two?' Weird. This is the first time it's dawning on Lucy that it is morning. She double checks over her shoulder. Yes - Jesus - it is that dark outside. Night dark. Okay. For a moment there, Lucy feared this was the beginning of the unraveling - Ariel about to dismantle into a collection of geometric shapes and typewritten numerals, spill to the diner floor in a puddle of sleet, Lucy handed a mop and told 'Clean up, it's your mess!' blink her eyes and suddenly know she had been an employee in this shithole all along, an aged old hag, droopy-dog pussy-lips all rubber black as unpolished shoes, scuffed in tears like unruly facial hair. 'Hey, talk about something - I'm thinking this is all hallucination. You. All the things you said. I'm not doing so good, Ariel.' 'Who's Ariel?' 'Talk about something other than making me want to strangle you like an unruly streetwalker, okay?' 'Fine fine' Ariel sighs, putting down her menu and rapping her fingers like piano trills on the still-slick-from-the-wet-rag-the-bus-boy-had-been-circling-around-on-it-before-they-sat edge of the table. 'I think we're very Pythagorean, you and I, Lucy. I really do.' 'In that we are triangular?' 'In that we threw ourselves into a volcano to convince our followers we were gods.' 'Or in that we believe beans resemble the gonads and therefore are unclean?' 'Beans do resemble the gonads! He was right about that!' 'Except we're both thinking about Heraclitus' Lucy says with a double finger-snap, pronouncing the name *Her-Ack-Leh-Tis* 'except for the triangle bit.' And Ariel says 'Oh you're always talking about Heraclitus' - pronouncing it *Her-uh-Clit-is,* the *Uh* and *Is* said softly for de-emphasis - 'or as you like to call it the *Triangle Bit.*' Lucy's eyes in that moment inhale all the air in the room and Ariel lets them, waits politely a few seconds before rolling her own eyes, and then says 'Yeah, you're not clever enough to hallucinate that. I'm just sitting right here - boring and undramatically actual, pal.' Smile. Smile. Okay. This is good.

Ariel sends back her omelet twice - the second time she does, asking for 'a French Dip sandwich, too - just in case.' The server is profusely apologetic and Lucy wonders if she is worried for her job. 'It must be awful having to serve someone like you' she tells Ariel. 'Oh it's the worst. Some people collect - what? - *Pogs* or bubble-gum cards or old issues *Mirabelle* magazine, but I - I? - I treat people shitty in diners for the most nitpicky reasons.' 'Ghastly - you're the very worst sort of worst.' 'Yes Simba' Ariella deep voices 'but let me explain: when we die our bodies become the grass and the antelope eat the grass and so we are all connected in the great Circle of Life.' 'When you put it that way - and with such a spot-on *Mufasa* - I admit I've one-eightied from *repulsion* to *all-moist-like-new-melted-butter.*' The third omelet seems fine and the server says 'We aren't going to charge you for it, since the trouble.' 'What about the sandwich?' Lucy asks. And, in asking, did you just make Ariel's eyes smolder? Or is she just stifling a cough? Either way, Ariel is sitting - rapt audience - and so you better get on with the show. The server says 'The sandwich?' 'Are you charging my friend for that?' This is a stumper it seems, so Lucy goes double-down. 'I mean - take it back, if not. The only reason she ordered it was she was certain you'd fuck up a third omelet, right? I mean - you do see that, right?' 'I can ask the supervisor.' Lucy scoffs - loud, theatre scoff, scenery chewer blunt - and Ariel's eyes pop wide and the color goes from her lips, leaving them the beige of a long healed scar. 'Why don't you not bother? We'll pay for the sandwich. And you'll get your tip - no need to worry!' The server starts to say something but Lucy leans forward and just starts talking to Ariel like returning to a conversation - mid-word of midsentence - something about not needing to take guff from some dork who works at a carwash. Even when the server leaves they continue this nonsense line of chatter. 'You're better than that, Ariel.' 'I am, aren't I? I mean, screw him! I told him I needed to have that weekend to myself! He should have remembered! Why's it my problem that now he's got to change his plans?' 'Idiot' Lucy says, sucks some saliva in like that's the sound of this imagined lunkhead. 'And did I tell you he had to ask his mother for his half of the rent?' 'What a hump.' 'God, I can do so much better - you're so right, man, absolutely right.'

OH BY NOW WHAT'S LIFE? What is it, Lucy Jinx? Try to tell me. This morning - let's start with it. See how it's trying to anonymous itself? Or if not anonymous, to confute itself with night - you've yourself said as much as that! Yes, let's say the day attempted it. People like you, Lucy Jinx, you believe days can attempt things. Ruin in well-metered strophes and iambs comes hard-toes-over-hard-their-own-heels when this is ignored. Stop believing the days think and have will - that life is composed of desires all its own - and you invite whatever slaps want to redden you and, indeed, let them pick where! Back to this morning: describe it, explain it, make someone understand what it is. *This* always wants to be *That* and *That, This* - and the definition of each is the lust it has to be the other. This day reads like Camus but is proved to be Borges. Or it's Sartre on-purposing itself in some cadence of Ingalls Wilder. Right? Like a good book given a bad cover or a book-you-aren't-supposed-to-be-reading hidden in the dustjacket of a book-anyone-who-knows-you-would-know-you-never-would. But how if you had to explain it best? The morning itself, Lucy, not you in it - you're nothing to do with the day, you know that. 'The day is a *W* that sulked until it looked like a lowercase *D*.' And what in Hell is that supposed to mean!? 'Well, explaining something doesn't mean that someone will understand, eh? If we limit ourselves to such strictures we'll ignore more truth than we could ever boggle at! Because that's it, exactly - the day is exactly what I just said, no word more-or-less to it. And it has no synonymous statement! What? Now you want to know what-not-quite-exactly the day is like? Like anything else - like anything but the specific thing I said! Throw a dart, grope the floor blind and pop what you find in your mouth, swallow it whole.' And what about life - I asked *By now, what is life?* 'Life is this day, once and then never again - and that happening over and over and over and over.'

Lucy waits while Ariel has to duck into this fast-food joint to piss. Aren't they near to Ariel's hotel? Yes. This must be as urgent as that, then. While Lucy mills, she smokes - and while she smokes she sees that there is a panhandler, just there, who has no legs. Her brow moves - she is struck into deep consideration. Ariel comes out and nudges Lucy, who points across to the legless person and both of them are silent. There is nothing for such a moment. Any version is incorrect. Do they change demeanor and walk in somber discussion of the world

- which is no different than it was just before, after all - and the stakes of things and the connections of this to that and the blessings of themselves and their stations? Say yes - say that is what they do. Well: for how long? And in what manner do they break from that to normalcy - when that is normalcy, or so they have just been saying, and really that very fact is what they are steeling themselves against. Isn't it just as commendable to say 'So what?' or to mock a little bit, spin a wisecrack while pressing on. You'll forget it, Lucy and Ariel, by the time you are two blocks on - don't imagine you've never seen a legless man before. Or something worse. Innumerable. Maybe your memory keeps a few such pitiables at the ready to access in moments of self-indulgent maudlin, but just a token selection of what you have seen or heard of, a flake from the total heap of humanities mold. Lucy - you know whole peoples have been irradiated and that women have birthed things the fictions of their people had not yet dreamed up as horrors! You know this - you read a book a whole book about it, felt comatose still three days after, for God's sake. In fact, you are mentioning that book to Ariel, now. That book. That irradiation. Those women. Why? To defend against this current sight? To honor it? To turn the plight to *Woe is you to have seen what you have seen*? To allow Ariel a chance to share something - there - and you will link, you will agree that suffering is a drag and press on with some self-inflicted I-know-I'm-shitty comment like 'I guess we could've given him a buck or two - God we stink, right?'

Eh, too much of that. On to this. The hotel lobby - Ariel had picked a posh joint, too! 'Well, I thought I'd pamper myself' she says. And this does make sense, after all. 'A trip to the big city, golly!' Lucy hee-haws and raises a knee to give a good smack to as she pretends to fire a tobacco bullet from cheek into some nearby spittoon. 'In the years since you left, Loose, the area has seen a renaissance, so your jibes just show you to be outdated. Oh we have three skyscrapers now and a movie theatre that plays porno. You can't imagine the things we have! Some restaurants are two-restaurants-in-one, Jinx - Pizza and Tacos. Think on it! And there are some places that do Doughnuts and Ice Cream! Oh can you imagine? You can't - you think I'm all shuck and jive, but I speak the truth.' 'So this room was a step down then, not pampering?' Lucy tried to shoehorn in, wiseass, but Ariel is wittier than Lucy and spins this to her advantage with a delightfully timed change in demeanor from Proud to Broken and a 'Well, I live in the same shit part of town. Fuck, our Free Clinic just closed down and so I have to get medical advice from the people at the discount pharmacy. No - this hotel is a big step up. And I made my husband pay for it all.' By the way, Lucy - are you going to ask Ariel what her husband is under the impression she is up to, right now? 'And what does the hubs' - Ariel snorts at that expression and whisper-repeats 'The hubs' under Lucy while Lucy goes on

- 'think of you taking trips out of town to do nudie shows in private for strangers? He's the enlightened sort? Figures that sort of thing makes him a feminist, is it?' 'Oh he's a feminist, that's no trouble. Give me some credit.' 'It's him I'm not giving credit. If I give you some credit on that point, de facto I'm giving him some. And stop avoiding the question.' 'No' Ariel says primly and tap tap taps the button for the elevator, it ping-sounding and opening by the second tap, wafting out a scent of artificial strawberry.

Lucy leaves her duffle bag right against the closed room-door, once in the room, contemplates bum rushing Ariel and pushing her on the sofa, the carpet, or choo-choo-training her, weird sounds of chug-a-lug to the room bed, but can't quite find the nerve. 'How many days are you staying?' But instead of answering, Ariel turns around and says 'Do you want to know why I haven't kissed you, ever?' Lucy's immediate answer 'Yes' coming out of her like the bubble of a cartoon mouse's drunk hiccough-burp. 'You do want to kiss me, right?' 'Yep.' Lucy is sure this is happening but does not resist being reduced to monosyllables - it seems if there ever was a time for them, now is good. 'Anyway' Ariel seems to return from a flashback 'I have to leave in about, I don't know, an hour or two from now. To answer your question.' 'Oh' Lucy nods 'so you just got away for the day, then?' 'Yes.' 'How old is your daughter, again?' Lucy asks - had she ever asked before? probably, certainly, probably - and Ariel answers as though for the goddamn half-billionth time - 'She's three, one of these days. Coming up. Her birthday.' The two of them aren't very far into the room. The room is irrelevant the way a stain to the inside of someone else's sock they themselves never learn about is. 'And I haven't kissed you ever because there was too much else - and I'm not kissing you now for those same words but meaning something totally different. You're Here and I'm There, right? Like a bookshelf and a horseshoe crab or something, right? Different things. Different places. Those things don't kiss each other.' Lucy nods. She is going to say something that she thinks she shouldn't but that makes her want to all the more. 'I never kissed you ever because I thought you might not have wanted me to and I wasn't sure I could shatter into enough piece to deal with that. You know?' Ariel calls Lucy an idiot. And tells her she really needs to do something smart, for a change. Lucy agrees. And Ariel coughs and says 'Hang out while I pack?'

Part of Lucy wishes the last bit had not happened. A common thing, in life. It seemed like it was still in rehearsal but had to be rushed to the boards. Though, she admits, there is every chance she will feel quite differently upon reflection. It is bad luck to trust a first impression. Lucy's main curse - the proto-curse - is that she too often does. This is a complex thing - she is smart enough to know better, but is so smart she thinks she is smarter than that, too. Knowing you are going to catch a cold does nothing to prevent it, but that doesn't mean she'll wear a coat when she doesn't want to. Since she was a kid. Add into all of this the fact that the tragic aesthetic of trusting a first impression only to have it upended is an allure her sensibilities are drawn to. In the end, no one wants to be the novel in which things turn out well for the imaginary whomever. That keeps them imaginary. Imaginary and Immortal is not a good mix - that is another way of saying *Consigned to being forgotten in hellfire*. And though Lucy revolts and writhes against any thought she is being written - or has to bow down to these currents she obsessively tries to identify, to navigate - part of her truest soul wants to sink deep into as many snares as she can because her despair will be immortalized, the humanity of her scream being screamed silently in the heads of every endless reader whose eyes pass over the words of her wallows and unavoidable abuse from the Fate she saw coming and was too weak to resist! In summary: she wishes Ariel had said all of that and then kissed her. It still would have been torture - because then Ariel would be gone - it would just not be imaginary. Wouldn't it though, Lucy? Ah. There. You don't give your friend credit enough. Her lips on yours? Why, that would be too-make-believe. Eternity is colored the hue of your untouching.

What's Ariel's husband's name? Leopold. Really? Yes. What is his surname? Moor, obviously! And it was he who had chosen the name of Ariel's daughter? It was. For what reason? He actually had a good excuse based on his family, the death of this person called Kayleigh. But Ariel's husband had been gracious and let the middle name be Ylayali? Yes. He knows what that is, Ariel had explained it? No. Is Ariel being truthful about this? Yes - though, fine, he had wanted it to be something else - Jeanette, who was another person, though more obscure, who had died. But he had relented - because fair was fair or what? Ariel theorizes it is due to the fact that the backend of the pregnancy was complicated and it was obvious she would have a high spike of depression - the middle-name seemed to make her happy. It's on the Birth Certificate and everything? It is - and Ariel explains so with a laugh, also telling Lucy she has every right to hate Leopold but no right to make him so sinister, if for no other reason than it kind of makes him more appealing to her. When did Ariel marry? Ariel had been married the entire time Lucy had known her. What? Yep. That isn't true is it? It is. Why had Ariel never worn a ring? Ariel isn't wearing one now either, she points out. Does Ariel's husband wear a ring? Yes, he does. Does he know Ariel doesn't? No. And the two of them live together? Yes they do. And does Ariel share a bed with the man? Yes. And does she share herself with the man? Sometimes. And how is that? Snort. 'Seriously, how is it?' 'You should see your face, Lucy!' 'Did you or did you not just tell me that you love me?' 'I did.' 'Then don't you think this is the face you should expect?' Ah, Lucy - Ariel would never have expected anything less. 'Are you going to give your husband any warning of his impending murder - or just let it be a kind of surprise-party thing?

They recall the man who did not have any legs. They sit on the sofa and talk about it. And Lucy turns on the television. They watch some commercials and then both start taking bets on which will be the last commercial before the program is returned to. There were fourteen commercials! Lucy wants to watch through the next segment of the show to see if there are always so many. Ariel checks her phone - there is something there - and she then turns to Lucy and says 'I need to call home. Does that make me legitimately awful?' Lucy makes a curt shushing hiss and points violently that she is watching this. Now: Ariel is the background, talking in normal-sized voice - she has no reason not to, but still Lucy thinks of it in terms of Ariel pretending-to-speak-normally - and Lucy is doing her best to not listen in. Her best is irritatingly good, considering she wishes she knew every word and the words from the other end of the line, as well. The television show is *Law and Order*. It is McCoy and Carmichael, arguing about a legal tactic. The accused is a rapist, allegedly. Carmichael is taking some issue with the alleged victim. Now: Ariel is talking to her daughter, the change in tone is the difference between a refrigerator hum and a piano heard through an apartment wall on a rainy morning while drinking coffee. Oh it is clear to Lucy that Kaleigh is hardly holding the telephone and that Ariel knows it and wants this part of her daughter's life to go on until all else has been long forgotten. Lucy doesn't dare turn to look, to see the exact shape of Ariel's posture, her pose, her doubled-over, instinctual head pointing downward where her daughter would be in space. On the television is a commercial. One. Another. Two more. Ariel's voice goes back-to-her-husband-toned, though spiced with some laughter at how great a talker little Kaleigh has become. Commercials. Five. Six. Ariel's hand touches through Lucy Jinx's hair - a long pet, on purpose - and then her voice re-crosses the room. Commercials. Seven. Eight. Nine.

Let Ariel tell Lucy about something Ariel read: 'It was an article about memory and how people can be tricked into believing things - even outlandish ideas - if shown doctored photographs they are told are snapshots of them as kids. I know the article had a point - a real heavy-duty point - but it just made me think it would be funny if it was all a gag and that everyone was conspiring together to make the researchers think that their research proving people could be convinced of fallacies by being shown mocked up photos from their childhood was true when really it was not! A bunch of fakers wanting to let the researchers feel groundbreaking! That would be a cool experiment! That's something that I would fund. People spend far too much time thinking about if things are true considering people can be tricked or lied to, anyway - or that's my platform.

There is research all the time about Why People Lie, as though we don't all already know why people lie - as though we don't, ourselves, lie and can easily explain it damn well enough. It's a scam to get grant money, I guess. They have to pretend - what? - the research will help come up with a way to stop people from lying? Like a cure of diabetes? Or make it easier to tell when someone is lying! Considering how easy it is, already, that would be a feat, indeed! Like improving a wheel by making it rounder, right? Such respect is given to liars by the scientific community - Oh they treat them like goddamn super-villains. *He's good at lying - study him! Let's get the best liars in the world in here!* There's the flaw in their research, after all. No one would know the best liars! That's why they're the best! Recognition in that field kind of proves you're a turkey. And if you're studying the folks who were once good liars but now admit to everything, that's another matter! And if you're studying people you've figured out are liars who are still fooling other people, well, you're only fooling yourself that you're not wasting your time!' That was Ariel telling Lucy about something Ariel had read. This is Lucy remembering every word Ariel had ever said to her, alphabetizing them and then trying to put them in order by which ones she liked the most.

Ariel's suitcase is still there on the bed. The top in flopped open. How many outfits had Ariel brought? How many times had she changed before heading over to see Stella Adroit? Lucy peeks in. Maybe two, three alternatives, at best. Then again: if her husband was a snoop she'd have been limited in how many changes of clothing she needed for wherever she'd said she was going. 'Give me a hint: did you say you were going somewhere he'd be the least bit suspicious wasn't where you actually were?' 'Who, Leopold?' 'Yes, Leopold. Stupid name - it sounds like a bad flavor of gum or a condiment no one regularly chooses.' 'He is not the least bit suspicious.' 'So there is some legitimate reason - other than a penchant for anonymous nudity - that would bring you to this city?' 'Yes.' Lucy almost - as though she has *Gotchaed!* Ariel - blurts 'So why haven't you visited me, before?' but at the last moment gets why that doesn't make sense. Still, you could have said it, Lucy - it would have been cute. 'I'm not cute' Lucy says, and Ariel nods, enthusiastically, concurs, concurs. 'But why do you choose now to announce that?' Ariel asks. 'I do what I want' is Lucy's reply. And to prove this point does a duck-looking dance and says 'This isn't duck-walking but nobody can duck-walk like Joe Strummer can duck-walk, girl, so I don't bother myself with trying.' This does nothing to impress Ariel, who takes pains to body-language this fact to Lucy, zipping shut her suitcase and dusting her hands, job-well-done. They drift back over to the sofa and sit back down. And Lucy turns the television on and it's another episode of *Law and Order* - now Detective Briscoe is saying something to Detective Green about how Mr. Such-and-such has three alibi witnesses so Green needs to drop whatever Green had been insisting as the screen is warming into life. 'You know' Ariel sniffs 'it just occurred to me that my alibi doesn't know the half of what she's alibi-ing and never will.' Lucy blank-faces at that because it makes her too giddy to grin.

'Where are you actually supposed to be, right now?' Lucy finishes her drag, takes another before saying 'In which way do you mean this?' Ariel explains that, firstly, obviously Lucy was not planning to be in Ariel Lentz's hotel room - nor walking the street with Ariel Lentz, nor having breakfast with her. Ariel furthers that it is conceivable that Lucy would have, herself, planned to stay in the hotel, overnight - where she had been with Victoire Elan for a couple of hours - and that those couple of hours Lucy would have planned to be there was time arranged out, in advance. 'So what is the question?' Lucy blows smoke while swaying her body so that her head traces a rectangle - or a rhombus, anyway, something four-sided. 'Are you seeing anyone?' is the question. 'I could believe Stella Adroit was just a way to be generally anonymous, but if you were on your own what could be more anonymous than you? You weren't her just to be her. So - that leaves me with the question: Where are you actually supposed to be, right now? In the sense of: according to what you told whoever it is who wouldn't know you are here when you are places like this with people like me.' Lucy holds her cigarette delicately over the cup of water she and Ariel have been using as ashtray, lets it go, watches the carcass of it cough a last grey line, soak, bloat. Then Lucy looks up at Ariel and shrugs. 'I was supposed to be at work a few hours ago.' Ariel nods. 'Where do you work?' 'At a pizza joint.' 'Are you going to get fired?' 'Probably not.' Ariel lights a new cigarette and hands it to Lucy and then lights a new one of her own. 'What's your favorite part of me?' Lucy's eyes both go to the top corner of a right-triangle and stay there while she considers how she's going to come at this question. The thing is, she doesn't know. Yes, she does! No. She truly doesn't know. But she's not supposed to be commonplace and say things like that, true as they are. 'It's okay if you don't know' Ariel mind-reads into Lucy's ages-long pause. 'I just want to be sure I don't know.' The pause continues. 'Ariel. I don't know what my favorite part of you is. I just checked. And I don't know.'


THERE IS SOMETHING AGAINST THE rules about sitting so quietly. There must be. Though other people waiting on the platform are waiting as quietly. Or quietly, but not so quietly. Lucy thinks Lucy and Ariel are the quietest - and in that they are, there is something rather scofflaw about it. In her view of the world, Ariel confirms, she thinks this, too. And the game has become who-can-stay-the-quietest between them. Ariel's Current Strategy: assume Lucy will become so excited realizing there is a game being played that she will ask 'Are we playing *Who Can Stay Quietest?*' and so be foisted by her petard, there. Ariel knows Lucy's tragic flaw is impatience. Or rather - quite obviously - Ariel incorrectly assumes impatience in Lucy's tragic flaw. Lucy's Current Advantage In The Game She Is Sure She Is Playing: to Ariel, Lucy is mistranslated Greek. Oh Ariel, silly Ariel, so long away from your scholarship! 'If you don't get that first word, Ariel' thinks Lucy 'that first important, theme-setting word of the Epic, then you are adrift and leave yourself open for sly abuses' like that which Lucy is here winning with. Possible Deft Move On Ariel's Part: can it be proved that Lucy's thoughts are louder than Ariel's? Why, this is a science Lucy knows nothing of! Say Ariel can prove its existence and is, in fact, counting on it. Your thinking is getting loud, Lucy. That is your tragic flaw - loud thought! This is the first this has even occurred to Lucy, truth be told, but it certainly seems correct. Yes, Lucy - you have a sea-at-tantrum way of thinking, it's a wonder you can hear yourself think through all the thinking! Sometimes you can't! Lucy takes a moment to make certain her physicality is quiet, at least - a bit hard to tell in the underground of this station, but she thinks it is normal volume, at least. Possible Way To Defeat Ariel's Clever Little Strategy: make Ariel think louder. But how do you do that, Lucy? How do you do that?

By the time they are packed into the Metro-train compartment, standing in the aisle, arms raised, Lucy and Ariel converse like make-shift walkie-talkies - now Lucy leaning to whisper in Ariel's ear, now Ariel nodding then thinking then leaning to whisper in Lucy's. The sound of Ariel's whisper is as unique as the feeling of scraping one's knee the first time, that time when you didn't even know that was something could happen to skin and stare disbelieving a part of you is missing. The sound of Lucy whispering, or so she fancies, is something like a roll of tape being tugged just the right length, snipped quick down diagonal over the teeth of the dispenser, and the ruffle of paper wrapping held in place with one hand while the other hand smooths the tape down. Ariel is the joker of the two while they mill. Lucy is the one, probably, more intoxicated by the scent flowing from under the other's raised arm. 'What kind of deodorant are you wearing?' Lucy uses her turn to ask and Ariel quickly - cheek touching - moves to answer with brand name and specific type of scent. 'Why are you so proud of that!? Christ, that seems like the most important thing you've ever said - have you been waiting this whole time for me to ask that?' Ariel answers just by making the sss-sisss-ssss sound of little kids' pretend whispering and - this is true, Lucy swears enthusiastically it is true - Lucy insistently whispers 'I knew you were going to do that! I totally knew you were going to do that!' Ariel's hand smacks Lucy's jaw - the side of Ariel's palm, karate chop - and Lucy bites the inside of her mouth - all of this the result of some doofus who just has to suddenly start moving toward the exit while the train is in motion. 'You paid him to do that' Ariel whispers, new tone - what is the tone? mink and chocolate and the color of fresh hissing soda - 'because you thought it'd get me to kiss your cheek! Not gonna happen, shyster - I know all of your goddamn tricks and known associates.'

Maybe this delay will make Ariel late. That is what Lucy is thinking, the train stalled mid-tunnel and she and Ariel in a sternly agitated clot of people who suddenly feel bitter enemies with the Fates. The two play a tip-tap tip-tap game of Lucy bending her knee exactly enough to gently bump Ariel's, Ariel doing the same in reciprocity - neither of them looking at each other, each putting on airs that they are sly, getting away with something. Tip-tap. Tip-tap. Here's a daydream: Lucy knows how to pickpocket and pickpockets Ariel and Ariel is so impressed she makes eyes at the person standing on Lucy's other side and Lucy knows what this means and - Presto! - picks the man's pocket with finesse and zazzle, Ariel taking the thirty-two dollars cash and the snapshot of some girl - the man's daughter - and then Ariel hands the wallet back to Lucy and - the real challenge - double raises brow, blinking to emphasize Yes she is serious, Lucy is to replace the wallet not in the pocket of the man she stole it from but in the backpack of the college girl standing on the other side of that man - Ariel not even watching, studying intently the photo of the man's daughter - which of course Lucy does - even with everyone there who could witness her - and then Lucy does an exaggerated eye-roll meaning *Knock it off, you should be impressed by now* and Ariel smiles and mouths something about the girl in the photo, though Lucy doesn't quite catch what. Yeah, maybe this delay will make Ariel late. Maybe. Is there a way to delay the train further? Well Lucy, surely there is - but I suppose you mean something that doesn't indict you, personally. 'Yes' Lucy thinks, wiggling tongue against her wounded inside-of-cheek, something ingenious - 'the sort of thing I am famous for coming up with in the clutch.' Ariel smiles at Lucy, wrinkle nose, knit brow like an *N* and a mirror-image *N* trying to stand really close to pass for an *M* - the exact expression of *What are you thinking about?* big - big long - long emphasis to the *You* - letters uppercase and italic enough have not been made to denote that emphasized *You* justly, no sir.

'Oh shit!' Ariel whispers - the train moved a bit, but is stalled again - 'I forgot to tell you' - but she goes no further. Lucy asking 'What?' Ariel shaking her head and saying 'I mean: I didn't forget to tell you - you didn't exist to tell you.' Another pause from Ariel. 'Can you tell me, now?' Lucy whispers - purposefully like a flirt, lips just-almost-but-not grazing the lobes of Ariel's ear. 'Sorry. Suzette got arrested!' Lucy's eyes holy-fuck-are-you-serious and Ariel is already nodding, knowing she will have to defend the claim with energetic gestures before verbal communication can continue. 'What did she get arrested for?' 'Assault.' Lucy does the silent face of a cartoon *Wha!?* with ten *A*s after three *H*s and Ariel, again - this time in tones of defensive-but-knowing-the-defensiveness-is-there-to-add-humor-and-nothing-else - nods over and over. 'Whom did she assault - for the love of Jove, out with it, man!?' 'Some customer.' 'This was at the store!?' 'In the parking lot.' Lucy gives tight pout mouth and tilts head to indicate disappointment that she now knows Ariel is just messing her about, but Ariel makes innocent eyes of *Naw-naw* and then rolls those eyes like *Alright-alright, I'll tell you more* leans in - her lips actually do touch Lucy's ear, but not enough Lucy can count it as her successfully tricking Ariel into that kiss, after all - and says 'It was some guy she knew who worked there, who she called her cousin but who wasn't related to her, you know?' Lucy knows, she knows all about that - never figured out why people in that area did that, but they did it enough to make up for the fact that nobody anywhere else ever on Earth did it, too. 'But wait - do we know why?' 'He owed her money - that's what she said.' Lucy's eyes narrow. 'How do you know all this? You don't still work there, do you?' Ariel makes a sourpuss face and seems a bit queasy at the suggestion. 'It was in the *Police Blotter* section of the local paper, man. It's a hot bed for transgressive, immoral stuff, our little town. Hernando's own son was accused of date rape, but the girl recanted.' Lucy nods, kind of impressed with the town now. Ariel shrugs, nonchalant but boastful, like Yep, I've got awesome things to say, don't I?

They are out on the street - all the way up that escalator - before Ariel, midsentence, stops gabbing, her eyes fixing on the Station sign then flitting around while she says 'This is the wrong station. Why did we get off the train?' Lucy does not know why they did. Wait - you didn't get off the train on-purposely-early, Lucy? Some gambit? No, Lucy just followed Ariel! 'You're the one who got off, in any event' she now says, smarty-pants, and Ariel has to admit this. They find a map and discover they should have rode for six more stations. 'This isn't even a little goof up' points out Lucy 'it's a straight up *boner*, wouldn't you say?' 'Oh yes' Ariel allows 'it's a real ding-a-ling.' So: are they going to walk or are they going to pay to get back on the vile machine? Does Lucy understand the map, Ariel ponders aloud - if Lucy were given trust and authority, would she be able to get them, walking, from where they were, at present, to where they needed to go? The funny thing is - Lucy, you're grasping, this is pathetic - Ariel could have gotten a cab, could get a cab now, so maybe this mysterious *Why did we leave the train?* is a bit of a put on, a bit of something designed to make it seem organic that she needs to stay on in town, awhile longer. Yes, Lucy supposes - Ariel would think like that. So how to best play along? 'I can get us there. This is my town, right?' Ariel gives a tentative look before saying 'You're never particularly good at anything sensible though, Jinx.

And don't look hurt! I can't be the first one who's told you that.' Lucy is not the least bit bothered by the remark. 'No worries, no worries' she assures Ariel 'but let me prove you wrong then, compadre - after all, it's been ages since you've seen me and for all you know I dated a survivalist in the interim due to some weird kink of mine you knew nothing about and through this torrid liaison picked up some know-how!' Tentative look, again. 'No one would date you, Lucy. Not someone who knew things about surviving.' Oh har har Ariel, Lucy expresses with noodley posture and fingers, all ten of them, waggling. 'Say they did it to test themselves, wisenheimer - I'm a fucking merit-badge if you last longer enough, pal.'

When it is surprisingly easy, though, to navigate city streets on a grid with very clear labels, Lucy has to make a choice. What's in store for her? How to play this hand? Is it better to just ask Ariel if it's possible for Ariel to stay another day - either straight out or through some sideways approach such as 'What if we miss the bus, how much does that stitch you up?' - or are the odds better that Ariel will actually bring it up herself if they get all the way to the station without it being broached? Like a reward! A reward for Lucy being so civic and selfless! Why, not a thought for yourself, Lucy - nothing but big-hearted concern for your long lost pal! Good for you - we thought we could trick you, we couldn't it turns out. The reward for self-restraint is a pile of Ariel to indulge in for a whole extra day! But before Lucy can lull herself into this, she realizes how outlandishly happy that sounds. And while the world can be happy, it seldom is outlandish in its affecting that bent, especially about bus schedules and the ability to stay extra days in some city because that is what Lucy Jinx wants! That's never happened once, some last, right-thinking part of Lucy's mind gasps a dying breath to point out. Maybe Lucy should say something like 'You must miss your family, right?' Oh God - that would fool no one! But of course there is the chance that it being so comically inept a strategy to get at anything might make it, counterintuitively, the perfect move! Ariel will think Lucy is being her usual silly self and will then - deus ex machina - say 'I think I'll stay on another day.' Focus, Lucy. Focus. The bus station is coming up and this pleasant conversation with Ariel is showing no signs of changing timbre or anything - the pressure is building up and it is all on you to say something. Remember: it's supposed to be as much a surprise to you as it was to Ariel, the two of you bumping into each other like this. Lucy! You could inadvertently have become the one setting the pace, Ariel just following your lead. If you seem ho-hum about this upcoming parting-of-the-ways then Ariel will seem ho-hum so as not to make you uncomfortable. This is hopeless! It's like two shadows arguing about how to gain weight.

The bus station: Lucy, haven't you ever been to one? The bus station: an amalgamation of dated science-fiction set-design, the colors from three-decades ago middle-school textbooks, and the cast of a cruise ship production of an original adaptation of something lesser by Charles Dickens. The bus station: if there are cockroaches here, they know how to work the light-switches. The bus station: did Ariel have to ride a bus to get here - how long does that take? The bus station: a restaurant there - this is the big Central Station - and a bookstore where everything is discounted but when you look at the prices it doesn't really seem that can be true. The bus station: something like a song no one danced to at Sadie Hawkins - one of several, but the one everyone most of all didn't dance to, you know? The bus station: Lucy Jinx and Ariel Lentz, somehow any mixture of the letters of their names spells this place. The bus station: all of the extra buttons that come with blazers bought at *Wal-Marts*, more useless than those from an actual suit-store because these ones will likely have to be used. The bus station: Ariel has arrived well early, because she is the responsible sort who has a child that requires food and picture-books read to it and pages held open longly and lingeringly so that the most important parts of the kid's mind can form without ever knowing they did. The bus station: if you remembered you had a caramel in your pocket, you'd realize it had been there for a month and the plastic has kind of fused with the soupy thick sugar. The bus station: if you take what your eyes feel like in a motel room - exhausted after the drive, neck-ache and medicine not kicked in and television flickering extra hard in the extra dense dark - and you lash it with three-pronged whips for awhile then you get the idea. The bus station: air being churned by vents and fans until it becomes butter - and this sitting around long enough to become beeswax. The bus station: the bus station, named exactly correct.

'Do you want to have a drink over there?' Ariel points to a smaller little nook of a café, one that hardly seems legitimate. 'We have forty-five minutes until I have to be over there' - she points - 'to board. But only if you want to, you know?' Lucy sighs. 'Drink? With you?' 'On the bright side, you'll be drinking - which should make it easier.' Lucy admits she has always had to admit that Ariel has sagacity when she is being clingy and needs her Linus blanket before a big trip, so - making sure it is known how much the action is begrudged - makes a noise like Merghtre and tugs Ariel's sleeve to get the two of them moving. The man who tends the bar is some sort of wannabe actor - or maybe an actor who is a wannabe magician, it's hard to tell - and he has a practiced little quip for everything Ariel or Lucy say. Lucy tells Ariel she admires this little fellow, when the fellow in question is out of earshot, as she imagines him to have an entire rolodex of comments and off-the-cuffs memorized and at the alert - likely can go three whole weeks without recycling a single one. 'You know how people like you and me still have poems we memorized in third grade in our head?'

'Yes' Ariel nods, she knows about that. 'Well, this fine fellow is that times more than a kabillion!' 'What poem do you have memorized from third grade?' Ariel queries. Lucy recites: *If all the tress were one tree / what a great tree that would be / And if all the seas were one sea / what a great sea that would be / And if all the axes were one ax / what a great ax that would be / And if you took the great ax / and cut down the great tree / and it fell into the great sea / what a splish-splash there would be.* Oh Jesus, hooray! Ariel can't stop oh-my-God doubled-over clapping, Lucy had been so dramatic! Ellipses held long and the tone rising into a Herculean fit of tornado third-grade dramatics! 'Now your turn' Lucy says. But 'No, no' Ariel says - absolutely correct - she can't follow that act, she'd just fop sweat and stagger and wait for the hook!

Suddenly: Lucy is in the Ladies' Room and giving herself the *Do it, what's the matter with you?* look that accompanies the confident swell in her self-assurance the wine had brought on milliliter-by-milliliter. Ariel will be at that nook, hidden away. 'Okay.' Lucy leaves the toilet after getting fingers wet and rubbing her eyes, clearing the moisture with the ache of this rough brown paper towel - the stack splotched wet, dried, re-wet all over. She makes her way to this ticket counter and wonders if things really work like this. 'I am so late, but is there a still a seat available on the such-and-such bus?' Ariel is still at the nook - stop worrying, Lucy, it's been four minutes, tops, and why would she come looking for you? You could just tell her you're doing this, Lucy! Christ with you, already! 'The such-and-such bus?' 'The such-and-such bus - that very one, you've got it!' 'There are seats on the such-and-such bus, yes.' Well, what did you think Lucy? Reservations from There to Here are made months in advance so that the exactly correct amount of finger-sandwiches can be prepared for the doily-kneed bourgeoisie of travelers? 'How much? Is that it? I'll take two in that case' Lucy jokes, but then makes this into a reasonable thing to say because she explains blah blah blah she means a Round Trip, she is just accompanying someone and then coming right back - is that a thing that can be done in real life? What? It is! Splendid! 'In that case, I'll take two' Lucy says again, double wink-wink voiced but full-bloomed of the knowledge that this woman is not the sort to get it even were it clever. Money changes hands. This is what a bus ticket looks like. 'You and your companion will have to be at that' - the clerk points, but only just hardly - 'terminal in the next fifteen minutes.' Lucy: now back in the toilet. Lucy: in the mirror, back where she started. Lucy: breathing. Surprised. Yes, she'd remembered to be doing that too, it seems.

'You're such a goddamn stray!' 'Well, I'm not staying!' 'Why aren't you staying?' 'Because I haven't been fixed - that's what a stray is!' Ariel makes a snip-snip then a third very-hard-snip gesture then demands to actually see the ticket, again. 'Where did you get this?' 'Does it matter?' 'Well, I thought the fact I was going to have to get on a bus was my way out of this mess - you know I've just been being polite this whole time, right?' 'You make yourself seem so complicated.' 'To be my friend Lucy, you have to be a certified forklift operator. I am complicated!' Lucy snatches her ticket back and points out that she will be sitting next to Ariel, too - so there's that. But Ariel makes a smooth tone of voice and easy-going eyes when she now says 'Lucy, this is awesome, but I feel bad. You won't get back until - when do you get back?' 'On the next bus' Lucy says, last word lilted into a question mark. 'But when is that?' 'I'm just staying at the station - they told me this is a thing people have done before and it worked just fine.' 'Look at you, Jinx - they'd tell you anything if it meant you'd get out of the line.' Lucy seems to dwell on this very somberly, then to be silly-over-on-purposely-giddy she says 'Hey, isn't it cool we'll get to sit next to each other on a bus? I've never sat next to anyone on a bus before!' 'Neither have I!' They drain their drinks and give a last look to where they seem to both have expected the barkeep to be - no one there, to which Ariel gasps and says 'Was he ever there to begin with!?' - then take their bags and move into the stale din. To Lucy, the station seems the gums of a woman who has suffered the decay of every tooth, one-at-a-time, but there is something comforting in the thought. Her breaths all seem breaths out and to start at the very last of the tip of her nose. Ariel holds her hand for a moment. More than a squeeze, more than a touch. She holds it just for a moment - a moment no longer than a squeeze or a touch. But still the hold, Lucy knows it is one, before the hand is let go.

THERE'S THIS THING LUCY JINX thinks about leaves. Leaves in autumn. They hang there and are forced to watch each other's skin change shades. And as they do they know their grips to the tree that sustains them are weakening. They will fall soon, tumult to the floor below. She imagines forest floors. The still-branched leaves watching the other leaves fall in a brittle-then-pulpy carpet over the soil. They wait their turn. And they know that if their brethren below could moan - could scream, could Hell-howl - they would. Mashing into each other bit by bit, animal-step by animal-step, rot-rise by rot-rise - now these two, this one, and these three-at-the-same-time and then all of them a single thing made of individuals glopped indistinguishable from and yet still each other. And the forest floor begins to devour them. Makes them a fused organism, a paste of consciousnesses in which each particular identity can feel the dissolve, the pain of the consumed others. Leaves hang on trees and see below them the monsters of their childhood, the very Earth itself an endless now-lush-now-barren-cold gullet and gut waiting to take them and turn them to its out-belches and feed the whole of itself with their carcasses. The cruelty of coloring them so enflamed and resplendent, as though they become most glorious mere hours before death when - no - they will not be dead for ages, still. And their colors will be gone - syruped and one-toned, drained, rubbished, nothinged - that indistinct mildew of a muddy, woodland expanse. How miserable the crisp-rustle of first winter air is, how horrific the unconcerned honks of the geese taking wing! All the world - in all its types and nuances - is the endless slasher-film the leaves watch, listen to, hang within for no other purpose except being painfulled and forgotten other than - maybe - by humans. By humans who like them least and mock them most with the indifference of calling their final, desperate moments - colored and hung-up, forlorn - their most memorable, beautiful - that charnel-house a human's favorite aspect of them, the entire reason for them to be there. Autumn, autumn, Lucy Jinx thinks.

Just at this time, Lucy has something occur to her and cuts off Ariel with asking 'Did you really think you could pass for twenty-eight?' Ariel blinks. 'Victorie!' Lucy accusations. 'Victorire Elan! You said you were a twenty-eight-year-old!' Oh yes - she most certainly had. But there had been no reason for it and certainly no thought that it would be a trickster sort of thing. 'But did I put twenty-eight, really?' 'You did!' Maybe Ariel doesn't recall while at the same time not denying - the look on her face is as amused at herself and as fascinated, if not far far more, than Lucy's about the matter. 'Why do you think I chose twenty-eight? I could have said anything, I suppose. I don't even like that number.' Lucy presses the antic tone of this conversation by pointing out it was quite lucky Ariel turned out to be Ariel, because if she had been Victorie Elan, actually, but looked as aged as Ariel did - without also happening to look exactly like Ariel - there would have been a real to-do and litigiousness would have reared its raccoon little bits and reheated-bean eyes. 'I can't be the first of your bitches to lie about their age.' Maybe true. Is that true, Lucy? 'Well, you'd have been the most egregious, the most flagrant case - I can vouch for that!' And Ariel suggests maybe Lucy had been hot over the idea of seducing a twenty-eight-year-old, positing the hypothesis 'You like them young, I'd wager.' 'Oh you have no idea' Lucy says and the hair on her arms practically all somersaults and she tingles with the thought of illicit delights while Ariel says 'I bet and simultaneously don't want to know and crave anecdotes to vicarious through.' 'You'd think less of me' Lucy says. 'I know I would. The question is: How can you resist me thinking less of you, girl?'

Lucy, the bus is really moving. This is not a circuit ride, you get off where you came on in a trice - consult your ticket, this is ten hours on the road, stops added in. Eleven - be better at math. Math. Say ten of those hours are straight highway driving and the bus moves the speed limit. Word-Problem me that - solve for the sum of how far you have gone away from Ariel. Can that be right? More than five hundred miles!? The planet seems only half as long as that and - really - how can you have gotten so far away and still feel the breath of that shitburg down your back and cringe as though you're still smelling its aftershave and the things it heated for breakfast? Lucy knows she is turning right around upon getting there, but her roundaboutness and lack-of-this-is-why for winding up in this city, at all - mixed with thoughts of an exact figure of how many miles away, Point-*A* to Point-*B*, it is - gives her some kind of rubbery fever. Ariel made arrangements to take - what? - three days off from work in order for two hours in a room with Stella Adroit? And Ariel had her mind made up well before that first e-mail - the correspondence after it was nothing that sealed the deal. Who is Ariel? There she is. We see her. She has physical mass and can be easily, lyrically described - but who is she? Who is she that she would go to such lengths? How long had this daydream of presenting her body to a poet for penning existed - and why? And why? Why? Stella Adroit would never have asked Victorie Elan, so maybe Lucy Jinx should not ask Ariel Lentz. Despite this moving bus. Despite that all of that is very odd. Let it be odd, Lucy, it can just be - most everything is. If you let it mean something, it will - and things that mean something, you stand warned, always spell *I-will-be-taken-from-you.*

'Where did you meet your hubby?' 'Do you want the awful, mundane answer? Or can I come up with like a *Mad-Lib* version?' 'Give it to me straight - I want to question my association with you.' 'He worked in the store where I had to go to get prescriptions filled for Kaleigh.' 'What was wrong with Kaleigh?' 'A sinus thing. And another time she got covered in spots. And another time her eyes got gunky and closed up like how I always pictured that scene in the Bible.' 'Which scene in the Bible?' 'Jesus and the blind guy! Don't they say his eyes were funky - like scaly or something or chicken-poxy or something and Jesus scraped them open like clearing away crusty clay?' 'Doesn't who say?' 'God, I suppose. Anyway - and another time she got a weird thing with her gums - teeth that weren't teeth, it's hard to explain.' 'Until that last thing, this list of maladies was just making me think you're a shit caretaker - now I'm kind of thinking about Larry Cohen scripts.' 'Right? Well, he worked there. And he helped me when there were no thermometers on the shelf - went to the backroom and got another batch.' 'That's a terrific story.' 'I think so.' 'What does he do?' 'Now? He works in a bicycle repair shop.' 'I don't know if it's more fascinating to me that he does that or that that is something that someone can do.' 'He's very into bicycles. He is an advocate. Don't look at me like that! For biker's rights. Definitely don't look at me like that!' 'What does it mean? You've started speaking like I also come from planet Neptune or wherever this jabberwocky you're slinging makes sense.' 'He attends rallies and stuff. To advocate for stricter punishments for drivers killing bikers. For funds to go to bike paths.' 'That's very admirable.' 'It is. Thank you for recognizing that. I'll tell him you said so.' 'What did he do before - you said that's what he does now.' 'Well, he worked at that store. Obviously. Honestly, Lucy - I thought you were smart, but I think now you just stole the Teacher's Edition or I've only ever asked you the odd-numbered questions.'

By the way, Ariel had this dream last night - maybe it means something. This was dreamt, she explains in a tone of you-are-to-blame, while she had worn Lucy's clothes. The dream: Ariel's husband had been going through a lot of suitcoats in a closet - not at Ariel and her husband's place, but someplace they were staying, a place they had never been, actually. Ariel said her husband had been very insistent that one of the coats belonged to him - he just could not quite tell which because of something he had eaten which was making it hard for him to talk. So Ariel's husband had tried on all these suitcoats and then settled on one that wasn't a suitcoat at all, but a thin trench, green, for springtime wear, and wanted to go out immediately to show it off. Then they had been unable to find a telephone to get someone to bring up a room key - they could not leave until they had a key, this was the thing and there was nothing to do about it! In the dream, Ariel complained of stomach cramp and there were things like veins on the outside of her skin, growing in the necklaces-of-Venus along her throat. She'd peel them away like decals from toy cars - or like single strings from some shirt in the laundry that wound up squiggling, half-embedded in one of her daughter's burp-cloths. Eventually, they were in a car - Ariel and her husband - and she was trying to get him to understand that the radio was responding to what she said, but he insisted - without ever letting her finish her sentences - that what she was proposing was impossible. She proved it over and over to herself, but he scoffed - did nothing but scoff! And when she woke up she felt very muddy and dry mouthed. In the dream she had just been tearing at her husband's clothes and they had been going at each other like teenagers against the glass of an old telephone booth. She felt his hands all over her ass when she woke, she said, and it felt weird, like she'd just woken up from morphine or something.

Lucy Jinx - crackerjack dream-understander - was into her fourth, maybe fifth, detailed analysis of what all of that yakitiyak could have signified when a young guy timidly leaned across the aisle and got both she and Ariel's attention. 'You two look like you smoke cigarettes.' 'That's because we do' Ariel said, after dramatically making sure the coast was clear and beckoning the lad to scoot in closer. 'I think the next pick-up is in a few minutes - could I get a few smokes off you?' Ariel wheeled around to face Lucy, really almost bumping Lucy in the nose with her forehead as she did. 'Do you have some cigarettes? I really think we ought to give him' - she thumbed in the young man's direction - 'some. I think this is like a scene in a myth, you know?' 'You studied myths, so I will trust you. How many cigarettes does he need?' 'I didn't just study myths, Lucy - I got a motherfucking doctorate in myths, so you're damn right you'll trust me! Eight is a good mythical number - give him eight.' The lad asked 'Why is eight such a mythological number?' And Ariel gave him some rap about Quetzalcoatl which Lucy doubted the veracity of - a doubt she kept to herself while she got out eight cigarettes and tendered them to Ariel - the guy not knowing what to make of it and saying 'Are you sure I can have all eight?' 'I'm not sure. No. And you and I both will have to live with that uncertainty. Don't you regret asking?' The guy - did he think he was being flirted with, toyed with, made a laughingstock? it was hard to tell - admitted it would make him anxious the whole time how he could never be certain she wouldn't ask for them back. 'And even after you're done with them, you'll never know if I'll irrationally demand their return, in whole! Unhinged usury throwing interest atop! It'll never end. Nothing ever does.' Lucy said 'Quetzalcoatl is that flying serpent, right?' Then she snapped her fingers and told Ariel 'In seventh grade I wrote a rap song about Teotihuacan' and Ariel demanded to hear it, immediately - the young man, somewhere in all this, taking the hint and replacing himself back in his seat, well dismissed.

They shared some stale *Coffee-Cake-Crumb-Donet-Minis* from the vending machine at the Rest Area. They shared two packs. Ariel had never heard of the brand, nor had Lucy, so they spoke of their shared wonder for off-brand products. Specifically: Lucy liked to think about the people whose job it was to come up with mascots for store-brand cereal or generic candy only sold in certain states. There must be a moment - perhaps blink-and-you'll-miss-it - where these designers come up with a knock-off *Count Chocula* or decide that *Fruity Pebbles* are now *Ruby Chips* or that *Jujubes* are now *Joli Bees* and that their cartoon rendition of *Joli "Bimble" Bee* is going to mean something - anything - to anyone - someone - somewhere - anywhere! They also share a soda, even though Lucy doesn't like the variety. Ariel tries to throw the can away but misses by three feet and a civic minded little boy picks it up and slam dunks it before hurrying back into the grass to wrestle with his brother. Then Lucy points and they see that the replacement driver is taking over from the driver who had gotten them this far. 'Where does he go, now?' Ariel shrugs, but Lucy envies the man this marvelous life. 'Does he have a quarters, somewhere nearby, where he will sleep until the bus makes its return trip - will he, when the bus backs this way, resume his driving? Could the world really work this way?' Ariel picks up on how Lucy's intrigue is genuine and good-pals into the investigation - they come up with the fact that there must be a box on the application that says *Are you willing to exists as more-or-less an abstraction for the duration of your employment?* Though Lucy prefers the wording *Are you really, really, really keen on self-abnegation?* with a few lines below it prompting *If box is ticked, please elaborate.* Ariel says she wants some more of those doughnut things, but when they arrive back at the machine an *Out-of-Order* sign has been taped to it. 'Try anyway' Ariel barks at Lucy. 'You're the one who wants them - you try!' 'But you're supposed to be the one who likes doing frivolous things for me!'

This time, they sit more toward the back - even though it makes them acutely aware of the fact that the bus has a toilet. Lucy says 'I feel like I'm on a field-trip. I feel like I'm already bored by the zoo before getting there, you know?' Ariel ignores this, but dares Lucy to go into the bathroom and chew a stick of gum. 'That is absolutely revolting! What sort of skevy mongrel would even think to say such a thing?' Ariel presses, saying if Lucy has the guts to do it she'll get a new tattoo. 'Nothing you say matches up to anything. You're like a book with the pages bound wrong. Though, saying that aloud, I think it made me fall in love you a bit more. Though saying that aloud made me start to think maybe I don't like you at all, have just described you really well to myself, all these years.' 'It's a good thing you bother taking the time to be you, Lucy, your head seems like the grey-matter equivalent of a glove someone finds in the bushes one winter. You know the kind? It's a glove, but it's not anymore?' Right there, Lucy more fiercely wants to kiss Ariel than she has anything her whole life combined. 'If you were a spittoon, I would polish you.' 'Aw' Ariel Aws 'if you were a chamber pot, I'd leave you for the staff.' Then all attention has to be given to the lout who is clearly making his way to the toilet. They move shoulder-to-shoulder while the galoot galumphs past and don't even know what to do when he lets out a creaky-church-door-in-a-horror-film blat of flatulence before the door closes, sniffs like shaking beer-foam from a moustache, and goes, to himself 'Boy oh boy, right?' Ariel's face makes it plain she sets this experience negatively in the ledgers of she and Lucy's friendship, but warms a little when Lucy says she wants to make a porno mag for philosophers and call it *Syllogism.*

That hopeless sort of falling asleep begins. Lucy - you know you cannot stop it. It begins from the middle of the spine - something has compacted. Squirm as she might, it is like the conscious-thought is being twisted out of her. Look! Lucy even does some song-and-dance about faking a leg cramp as an excuse to stand, shake her limbs around, generally hoping to juke-out whatever blockage this is that is deadening her - but when she sits again she is still dwindling, the last rounds of a roil. Maybe Ariel won't notice, as they do seem to both be getting a tad more contemplative - or maybe not *contemplative,* that might be going too far. But wasn't Ariel looking at her phone and probably sending a text-message to her husband and then suddenly clamping Lucy's leg and opening Lucy's mouth to tug on teeth one-at-a-time and go Tthth thtth thtth as though trying to communicate the exact way each one was supposed to be sung if Lucy was going to be singing about them? Lucy snaps awake. Yes. Hopeless. And you'll be asleep again soon, in just a moment - you likely already are actually, Lucy. Too bad. That's what it feels like - finally, finally it has caught up and this dream is about to end with you on a sofa someplace. It'll take you awhile to remember where. Just fits from eating too much and not stopping at one glass of the room-temperature wine, Lucy. All this while you've shambled awake a few times and stuffed some crackers in your mouth, hoping to fall back into the same dream - which you have done a few times, but this time when your eyes open it will be different and you won't even feel tired anymore, just top heavy, like someone tied a doorknob to your nose and you forgot to use mouthwash after eating that glue stick. Lucy snaps awake. Crick-rick crick-rick goes her neck as she side-to-sides it and closes her eyes extra hard, hoping to make a loud enough squish that the sponges of them will feel wrung and she'll get back to things.

'My arm is asleep and you're asleep on it.' Ariel is whispering this. Lucy opens her eyes. Ariel. The outside of the bus is evening-just-came-but-isn't-quite-settled. 'I'm so sorry. Shit. I fell asleep.' 'Well, we didn't really sleep all that much, you know?' Ariel does take this opportunity to scoot and free her arm, tick-ticking the fingers while Lucy imagines some sharp pains of returning circulation and some fade-ins-and-outs of vision assail her. 'How long was I asleep?' Ariel says she cannot be sure, because her theory goes that Lucy was not technically awake for the larger part of a whole conversation before finally going silent. 'What were we talking about?' 'You'd just be embarrassed if I told you. It was sweet, but I don't want you to make a big deal out of it.' Wait. Is this Ariel ribbing you, Lucy? Ariel who is now opening and closing her fingers like she's finally got the right feel to a new pair of leather gloves. What had you said, Lucy? 'What did I say?' 'All kinds of things. And I meant everything I said back to you, too. Though I wouldn't have said any of it if I thought you'd remember.' Oh she's just joking. 'Oh you're just joking' Lucy confidents and changes the subject. They talk about a television show they both only saw one episode of - different episodes - and try to cobble up a larger storyline and critique the program's overall quality and cultural cache just from the portions they can recall. Ariel yawns and Lucy stares as far down her throat as possible, wants to chop off and bronze the bob of her tonsils, thinks the exact symmetry of the hues of pink and black of downward-her are the perfect resemblance of a split peach, probably what a peach would be if it was its Ideal. 'Did you watch me yawn?' 'Yes.' 'Cool. Were you impressed?' 'I was.' 'Wanna see me sneeze?' 'Yes.' Ariel pauses, hangs her head. 'I'm such a shit person to love. I can't even do that for you.'

AND ANOTHER THING, JUST IN case Lucy wants to know, is that Ariel hates it - and does not believe it - when some artists - writers, mostly, but the principle applies across the breeds - say *If not for such-and-such writer, this-or-that book, I would never have started*. 'That was the book that made me want to write' Ariel fairly blanches as she impersonates 'I owe it so much. You owe it nothing!' There are people asleep, but Ariel keeps breaking from loud-whisper into actual-speaking-volume and - just there - clapped her hands to mark the exclamation point. 'And it is no sign of something's quality or meaningfulness, either. You would have read another book or would have written, anyway, without some specific Inspiration. People want to reduce their lives into such bric-a-brac, just trinket themselves into easily told anecdotes meant to convey oh-so-much. But you cannot express your true expanse by foreshortening - and you won't know yourself by making yourself something that can be understood with a quick finger-slide down the reference section!' Not that - maybe - Ariel cares about that, but Ariel wants Lucy to know. 'Why would someone feel obligated to Nothing? Is it a kind of guilt? Or is it just some humblebrag trick? Things don't come from one thing, anyway' - Ariel tries to stay on her main point - 'and the big trick, Lucy, is if you unravel anything enough you see nothing was the direct cause of any other thing. That's the bizarre part of it all! Nothing touches - you look a little closer, a little closer, and all of those little closers add up to *Nothing Influenced Anything*. And nothing is even so complex when you think of how infinitely more complex things can get! We're more than an amoeba, man. Imagine something that much moreso than us! We're the amoeba, the other thing is - you get me? - that much moreso than we are now - is relative to us as we are relative to the amoeba. Or whatever way that works - you get what I mean.' Lucy gets her, nods to make this officially noted in the transcript. 'Well: think that thing would find it so startling that a bunch of books got thought up, nothing to do with each other? Hell, we think there is life in outer space! I'd like to think we can think things happen on this planet without ping-pong cause-and-effect.'

And honestly - Ariel is dozy and Lucy does not try to keep her chatting, might even be hoping she'll sleep past her stop, sleep all the way back the return trip and Lucy will pretend she fell asleep too and they both woke up at the same time and 'Oh rats, guess we have to stay' - Lucy wonders if she agrees with Ariel on all of that business. She wants to. And she feels like she does. But well, Lucy, you feel like you agree with everything Ariel says. Especially if you hear it aloud. And if you got it second, third-hand, you'd feel like you believed it, just to be safe. And there is an allure to this. There is. Nothing does touch. Ariel is no nihilistic debutante, nor some sophist schoolkid trying to be smarter-than-the-average-bear. She might be on to something - that was all said with passion. Why not? Why can't everything be a self-contained, entirely-whole-to-itself accident? Or not even accident! That indicates some sort of way it should go. *There are no accidents* some philosophies say, and maybe they are righter than they think - or it's what they meant all along and some dunces who did the first critical analysis dumbed it down to dullardry. There are no accidents. Not because everything is connected and so - it follows - because each thing is the reason for another thing and the result of something previous - no! - but because there is no connection - nothing is connected - and nothing is the result or cause. So: nothing is accident. My God, Ariel is right about outer space, isn't she? We can talk about Infinity, Lucy thinks, and then try to dismantle the concept of Infinity, and then reinvent Infinity from an argument of the method that dismantled it - but we cannot believe in the complete absence of touching, of connection? Lucy is furious with all of us! How did the earliest philosophers miss this! Zeno even went the whole *Everything is all really one thing* route, but none of them remembered to suggest there are just infinity circumstances and bits and pieces and they are in a random pile and none are anything but themselves.

Though, much more important - this terror is like choking to death on talcum powder after falling into a bathtub full of shirt pins: Ariel would have said if her husband and child were going to be at the station to fetch her, wouldn't she have? Of course, Lucy - this went without saying. But - Lucy has to run this thought into the ground to be sure - Ariel would never spring that on Lucy, right? The facts: Lucy had talked about Ariel's daughter and husband on this very ride. The facts: Lucy had talked about Ariel's daughter and husband back at the hotel. The facts: those things had happened before and after Lucy had gung-hoed herself onto this bus, slapdashedly, and so it was a pincered surety from both sides that Ariel would have said 'Are you going to hop off and meet them?' - or something like that - at least once if they were going to be there to perhaps hop off and meet. Yes. Of course. Ariel is an upstanding and extremely civic sort of person. That is another of the facts. And Lucy had professed love and Ariel had and they both got what the other was saying and meant the same thing - and so all matters attaché to that is not to be ignored in moments like this. Because: Ariel had not been glad-handing. That was all the way it is. And so it would be unforgivable to then say 'Hi, this is Leopold' and 'Leopold, this is Lucy' and let Lucy hold Kaleigh - taken maybe directly from Leopold's stupid arms - and have to endure that and then get back on a bus and watch Ariel and Leopold kiss and watch them walk away together all having missed each other and joined by lived-life and DNA and difficult-to-untangle nonsense! 'Yes.' Lucy just says *Yes*. It's an answer. Somewhere in that was a question and the answer to it is this simple *Yes*. And this *Yes* is indicative of calm. You have considered things and reduced it to *Yes*, Lucy. *Yes*. You can untense and stop adding details to a thing there was no point in make-believing, because Ariel would never do that to you. Nor would she wait until last minute to spring it. Even if she might do it, you'd be warned. Even Ariel isn't as vicious as that.

Closer and closer and closer. Now it is even feeling like that. Water in flickering tornado down long-since-scrubbed bath drain. Water through hair clogging that drain. It's starting to feel like how dry that stain will feel around that drain after the water is gone long enough. However, though: Ariel is awake and the conversation Lucy is having seems innocuous, enough - sure, it's a scent that technically doesn't belong in the room, but not one anyone notices so nobody names, let alone fans away with their hands. 'Do people still say *Wisenheimer*?' That was Ariel. 'If they feel like it, I guess - I believe I said it recently, for example.' That was Lucy. 'I mean, to denote a class-clown type, an instigator sort.' 'It's a matter of taste - it depends on their frame of reference.' 'But no one without a kind of dated, I'm-using-a-funny-old-timeish-word-on-purpose sort of style would say it?' Lucy nods, the affect of only-just-now-catching-the-drift. 'No - I think it's something that is mostly said in quotation, repeating it from other sources.' 'I do know what a quotation is' Ariel says. Then - because she's so witty - adding '*Wisenheimer*.' Closer and closer and closer. Lucy honestly had not thought about this part. And hadn't, just recently, the bus ride seemed long enough it could technically be called *interminable*? That was hours ago, unfortunately. And the ride was, while interminable, also only hours long. Lucy should have thought of that! Things end. Some things. Things like this. All the time. Everything does. But things like this, the most. And Lucy always forgets that. And Lucy is always at fault for Lucy - and nobody seems to notice that in time to point it out. 'Are you going to be okay getting back?' Ariel asks, rabbit-nosing due to, Lucy thinks, trying not to sneeze. 'I'm an adult, El. It's a bus.' 'You're an adult?' Ariel jaw-drops and disbeliefs and then inches away from Lucy toward the window. 'That's yucky' Ariel now sniffles and finally does sneeze. 'What kind of pervert are you? An adult - buying a ticket and riding on a bus with me?'

Here is Lucy Jinx insisting on carrying Ariel Lentz's bag from the bus across the bus station. For a moment, it is all so confusing. As though Lucy must have been here before. She has to insistently badger her chronology to herself, while also smiling and walking casually while Ariel sends some text-messages - which:

couldn't Ariel do in just a damn minute or something!? No - Lucy did not arrive in this area by bus when she lived here, nor did she leave by bus when she left. Yes, she'd been in airports. Airports. But had not arrived to this area - when she had lived here - by airport, nor left that way. When had she been here? There is Ariel. When had this been where she just - in her every breath - felt she was and had been and had been awhile and was going to be for awhile and for forever? And when had it felt like the only place and that it was where all pieces would have to fit around and lock themselves because she wasn't going anywhere else? There is Ariel. Bus station. Two bus stations in-a-row has scrambled Lucy's very soul. She and all aspects of her are like the things scraped from breakfast plates into overfull kitchen trash-bags. Snap out of it though, Lucy - is this really what you want to be doing? Is this really when you want to be doing it? There is Ariel. You have a job. There are rules. You are beholden to the way you are supposed to be. And there is Ariel. She is a pristine thing, maybe someone still unsullied by you. Not untouched, certainly not untouched - you have that! But maybe there was part of you you'd never seen that was clean - and maybe, by pure chance, that is the part where you brushed against her. Maybe that is why everything! Why Ariel thinks you are Lucy Jinx the way Ariel says *Lucy Jinx* and not that you are Lucy Jinx the way Lucy Jinx is.

'Forget the combination to his bike lock, did he?' There you go, Lucy! Levity. Reward: Ariel shoves you. Enough to unfoot you, almost. Nice. 'This was a personal thing. I figured I'd still be in some sort of post-Stella-Adroit rapture. I insisted that I would get myself home and kind of scheduled this all so it would be inconvenient for Leo, either way.' There are cabs, right there. Ariel is going to take one. The kind with set rates from things like bus stations and airports. Do the sensible and friendly thing and don't drag this out and don't make Ariel be the one to have to demarcate The End. 'You're taking a cab? Or you have someone besides Leo' - that was hard to say, but it came off with ease and normalcy, good job Lucy, good job again! - 'coming to ferry you?' 'A cab.' That's what Ariel just said. 'A cab.' And this is an excellent cue, Lucy - it does not get better than this. 'A cab' Ariel had said - and then, Lucy, you say? You say? Lucy - what do you say? 'Let me pay for it.' Ariel dog barks a laugh of what-an-idiot-loverboy-thing-to-say-Lucy, snorts and starts walking over, having picked up her bag from where Lucy had set it down with her duffle. There's your mistake! Shouldn't have done that, Lucy! Now there's no stopping her! But, I'm not trying to stop her! 'I'm not trying to stop you' Lucy says while a cab driver opens the truck - Ariel resisting, as there is no real reason to put her single bag in there, but then releasing it to the fellow - to which Ariel gives her a nudge with her shoulder and demands a book recommendation. 'I don't know about books - you're the smart one.' 'I didn't say a good book - one of those

*Texas Millionaire* things you read, or *I Married a Navy Seal* or something.' 'Read *Nightwood*' Lucy says right on top of Ariel's snarky bit. But Ariel rolls her eyes. 'I read that already. Remember?' No. No, Lucy doesn't. 'Then read. I don't know. No - don't read. I recommend you don't read.' Eyes held. Ariel nods. 'Agreed. Then I won't.' And Lucy begins a smile but wilts and at a rush - because that cannot be right and just in case Ariel really wouldn't - touches Ariel's hip and says 'Read *Detruire, dit-elle*.' Ariel rolls her eyes again, but says 'Je vais. De nouveau. Tout de suite.'

It's been an hour. It's been almost an hour. It's been half-an-hour. Nearly. Since Ariel left? When did Lucy mark that moment? When the cab door closed? When the cab pulled away? When the cab was out of sight? When she finally stopped pretending she could still hear it? Yet? Really, yet? Regardless, this analysis has to be tended to. So lovely, that last little bit of French. But dangerous. Lucy is being thorough in combing her memory, double careful not to overlook things on purpose. It's hard to concentrate with a mind this swollen, but she does. Lucy's Theory: The most beautiful things are meant to end in French. Had she ever said that to Ariel, though? Concentrate, Lucy - this is maybe the most important moment of your measly life! Gut reaction is 'No, I would have remembered that'. Why the Duras recommendation? You could have said anything! Did your mind treat this as The End? Yes. But, Lucy insists - her mind toddler arm swinging, foot stamping - only of this encounter! Not of the thing! Not of everything! That French had been an accident! And Ariel's reply? That was only because Lucy had said the title in French. It was playful connectivity. It was 'This is continuing - I am agreeing to more by agreeing to read something from before.' Ariel was not acquiescing to 'This is the end of us'. And she was not doing an End Scene in French to make it beautiful - that would have been nice, of course, if she were ending it and was doing so in French to admit it was deserving of being considered beautiful, which it would have been. Sure thing - that sure would have been swell of her. But that isn't what happened. Ariel doesn't know that theory, Lucy. She doesn't know everything about you. Or even very much. Analysis complete? Jesus, is it ever? Why did you pick the Duras? Did you know if would make her speak French? Were you testing her? Did you want her to? Stop it, now - Lucy, this is indecent! It's only been an hour! Almost an hour! A half-hour. Nearly.

'When is the soonest return for this?' Lucy's manhandled ticket, there on the counter. Laid flat, in essence, but too wrinkled and curled to ever really go full flat again. Three hours! Is that all? Well, to go by the attendants tone, this should not be so astonishing, so let's just peel away from the kiosk and mill over here, shall we Lucy? It isn't that Lucy had wanted it to be longer. Nor shorter. Lucy was not going to set foot outside of this station even if it was three days until the return bus - the only reason she'd gone as far as the sidewalk was Ariel had been with her so it was sanitized, the air, the place, this, here. Lucy shuts down the insistent thoughts being bratty and rattling her sense of composure. She has to whisper-talk or it won't feel addressed, so she seethes 'When I come back, it will be another thing - because that will be what I am doing. Right now isn't then, so it has different poisons and different ways to set off alarms and drift my scent downwind of predators.' Inside, Lucy will stay. No one was trying to make you go, Lucy. 'Regardless' she mutters and thinks about how long three hours will be. Not three hours, really. Time is always less than itself, in cases like this. She will be able to board the bus by two-and-a-half hours, probably. And the fifteen minutes up to that will be a poof-and-its-gone. And fifteen minutes hardly feels like anything, especially when one is anxious about departing. So: it's basically two hours. This is how good Lucy is at understanding the venous workings of the world. She pays attention. This intersects here and That there and much can be worked to one's own whims with experience. If she wanted to - and she will - a few other clever moves will shave off twenty minutes, which is basically a half-hour. And when someone has said 'Three hours' and it already feels like half-of-that, that half feels like less-than-half, so call it fifteen minutes. Which brings it to one hour and fifteen minutes. Which is basically just an hour, as anyone would agree. Lucy can do this with time. When a rabbit is tangled in the briars, it knows all kinds of things.

   Someone sat down. Right behind Lucy. There is a bench there. Despite the fact that there are special allowances in Hell for halfwits who set benches back-to-back - do they even understand the concept of *bench* or of *having-a-seat-to-relax*? - there is a bench right beside hers and this - Lucy will not dignify them with specific malice - someone-she-refuses-to-look-at has sat down. Her guess is it's a woman. Right now a woman seems capable of anything. Get up and move? It's worth considering. There. There. There. One two three empty benches. That this Other could have chosen. And had not. What is the hope, Lucy? That this Other will grow irritated that you are where you are and so slither off? How can you retain faith enough in humanity at a time like this to believe anything so wooly-lamb? A person like this Other is the soul of a bus station like this - they have no other role but to wraith and emanate the rank legion of the coming grave! Is that giving them too much credit? Lucy pretends someone asked her that. And pretends she is considering. What is Lucy even talking about? She should just go to another bench! Or better - this is what she does - she will walk around for a little while and then decide if she wants to sit back down after having a cigarette over where those people are having their cigarettes. That's why cigarettes were invented. To give you a reason to stand someplace else. True. And also to give you a reason to stay exactly where you are - but that's just the point. 'That's just my point' Lucy sighs, lighting up and kind of - just for a bit and without true gravity or relevance - wondering if this is really what this is like. Cigarette in. Cigarette out. It probably is. And if it isn't it might as well be. Cigarette in. Cigarette out. This isn't anything. But it doesn't feel like nothing. Nothing ever does. Things that disallow themselves go on forever. Cigarette in. Cigarette out.

So there's not much for it. Now isn't the time to reminisce or anything. And Lucy does not feel like making punchy observations or remarking on the insidious minutia or the verdant mundane. Lucy Jinx is allowed some moments of nothing and it is best to reserve them for times like now. A time which she does not want to name itself more elaborately than that. If someone were looking at Lucy, they would see her - here - on this bench and drinking a soda from out of the vending machine she is still in eyeshot of. Or if someone else was looking, they'd see the indistinct back of a head of her hair and no idea of the soda, nor of the duffle bag on her lap, which the other person would have also remarked. This isn't the time to leaf through what she'd written in that notebook she'd picked out so specifically for Victoire Elan. It certainly isn't the time to read what Ariel had written in there. Briefly - though she shouldn't be - she considers the commonsense of burning the journal, utterly utterly gone-ing it. When will you ever do that, Lucy? Don't bother with melodrama, here. Now isn't the time, remember? This is Lucy Jinx: in wait of return trip at bus station. And she wants just five minutes even without all of this business of her being her and having to even dance about to not be her those five minutes. Don't other people just get time when they aren't themselves, when there is nothing happening? Other people have heads that stop and minds that blink, automaton. Right? Everybody else gets that. They can summon it, at will. It gets on them when they don't mean it to. The strangest phrase in the world to Lucy is 'I've forgotten myself.' Certainly she has done that, herself, but only while remembering every ounce of every half-second of herself, too. Forgetting yourself is the easiest thing to remember, Lucy - you're doing it right now. You did it just before - what do you think this whole day, two days has been? And you'll be doing it right after this. 'Then I'll try to remember myself' Lucy weak-kneed tries to bravado. But - come on - when all you've ever done is forget yourself, that's all that remembering yourself will accomplish.

# .IIII.

THEN THERE'S THIS TOMORROW. LUCY has to rotate her shoulder, should not be trying to write laying down, pillow-propped to wall like this. '*Then there's this tomorrow*? Did you write that?' she asks, accusatory and embarrassed at once. A strike-through is hastily scrawled, even as she supposes maybe she had written it and it wasn't so bad - in fact: it wasn't, as she now recalls what she had in mind before the shoulder rotation. It's too late now and she'll leave it lay. To explain: Lucy writes as she is positioned - here in this pencil-thin twin bed - because the desk in the room seems to be facing the wrong way no matter how she has tried to move it about. She can't lose the feeling of someone sitting right next to her, glancing over her work, but doing so in such a way as to never seem like it. Because they are not glancing to see anything, in particular, their image of Lucy would remain out-of-focus, entirely. They'd just be looking to look. Something perverse. Maybe hoping Lucy would notice, while at the same time going to such pains to keep the distinction between seeing-her and not-at-all no thicker or more substantive than a half-paper-leaf slice of water. 'Understand?' Lucy asks. Lucy does. But she means does the person she is picturing in the desk chair - scrunching befuddled-nose in her direction - understand. She would write, sometimes, during the day, out in the apartment at the green dining table. Actual wood, though she doesn't believe it because it doesn't seem dyed and no way can wood seem naturally green - not that green, practically Sin-green - all the way down into the grain - a green to every imperfection when her pen bumps if only a single sheet of paper is set down at-a-time. But not often. Not out there. On that table. Once, she had written in the large corner chair, facing the window - facing the brick of the side of the building, next-door, the brick and that odd, disused air-conditioner that juts straight out from the brick as though there has once been a window that got smothered in some rising lymph of brick streptococcus.

All effort - now, here - to refocus. *Dawn with its distempered jowls, it can only render up these can-souped disused tomorrows.* Lucy is fond of scratching the - she's sure of it - very top, the center-top of her skull against the wall as she writes. The sound here, head to regular-old-painted-wall, is luscious, like it has horded all the good fruit for itself and will gloat while it goes bad. Use that. What was it? *This tomorrow is a novel just eight pages long.* That wasn't it. 'Fuck off, Lucy, it's getting there' she mutters while pressing on with things. *The one page luscious, hording all the good fruit for itself and will gloat while the pile goes bad.* Still she presses up and skrutch-skrutch-skrutch sounds her head, the noise of it deep in her, wholly interior like she's six-years-old and has mittens on and its freezing and she's covering her ears but only because the side of her face is stinging from being struck hard by a too-fiercely-packed slush-ball. Physical sounds. Grains of sound, one-at-a-time, under-foot, rolling as slowly as possible to articulate each tone of gravel it can. *Three pages made of cottonmouth another two rash-bellied cats that don't know the word mangy and* - head stops moving, she stares. *Don't know the word. Mangy.* 'Don't know the word *Filth.* Let's make this plain' she insists and imagines a gathering of physicians watching her dissect a Saint, all of them nodding and trying to not to smile while they nod. *And other pages twelve pages but all of them none.* If this weren't poetry, Lucy would think of what the other two pages would be - she promises - but now she is sick of this describing pages and moves on to *The music from the floor in the morning no more no more no less no less than teeth which make the sound of long vacated insect husks sat down on in attic rooms by children who covet such noises.* A little bit more of the head motion. She wonders what her hair thinks of that. What her scalp thinks. She wonders. And there must be things living in her hair - she's seen science documentaries - so she would like to know is she's affecting their mating, their feeding, their migratory patterns with her lolling around?

Ah! Speaking of sound - of noise, of such things - Deb and Curtis are at it, proper. Again. That needs to be added - *Again*, they are at it *again*. Hasteningly, it is pointed out that Lucy does not mind the sounds of the two of them, the aggressive, arrhythmic percussion and the slips of words that almost make it through the wall at full articulation. At times, she can even become aroused in a detached way - no scenario to accompany - just at the knowledge of what it means that she hears what she hears. Something like listening to erotica being read in a foreign language, Lucy? She considers. Supposes it is along those lines. And now, for example, she goes kiddishly curious at how their bodies are positioned to get that pitch, that dull slap, more-or-less certain that - as she is only able to concoct rather up-done positions, clever things that anatomy might not play-out so well - her guesses are landing absurdly wide of the mark. No - it'll just be Deb with belly flat to towel on carpet and Cutis like a pinstripe right atop her. She can always tell when Deb is on her knees - or positioned however she may be, but hard at such work to which knees are always associated, bent and growing warm with pierce-hot soreness - because of the pucker-pops which trail a curmudgeon slurp. Lucy giggles, always picturing Ebenezer Scrooge before his visit from old Marley - that or some Scottish rebel soggying crusty bread in meat drippings and glumping the more-than-mouthful into throat before having that throat slit in a sudden slathering choke like a duck swallow. If Lucy were to guess: this time had started slow, gentle slit tracings through bedsheet by coy-wiseguy Curtis, Deb at first mildly resistant before oh-what-the-Hell when he lingered just right on the bulb of an up-trace long enough to make her have to tighten and then be annoyed when the pressure alieved. Is that what you would guess, Lucy? It is. She also pictures the egg-speckle line of dark black moles that she knows march the length of Deb from center of breasts around swirl of her left hip and then more dribblingly ellipse into the hook of dimple above that buttock.

But Lucy seldom listens for long - untrue! she often listens through the entire act and strains to catch baubles of whatever the after-chat is - and now is in the kitchen, having forgotten her notebook and unsure if what she is thinking goes with the poem at all. Either way, there it is, on this napkin from the collection of napkins from various fast-food joints - a brown napkin - written in purple ink from the dry-erase board marker magnetized to the fridge door. *I've forgotten you as easily as the four of clubs.* Or how about: *I've forgotten you no more so than I have the four of clubs.* She lights one of Curtis' cigarettes - the ones with papers in all different color, like smoking a box of kindergarten crayons. Or how about: *I've not forgotten you, exactly as I haven't the four of spades.* 'Something like that' she exhales, coughs a bit, shakes the match she'd lit to get it to finally extinguish when her breath out had failed to accomplish that. And now: a quickly bent and mostly swallowed, unchewed, slice of this cinnamon bread that she swears she tastes chocolate in though the package takes pains to contradict her about it. She reads the ingredients, again. No. Nothing like chocolate. And no bizzaro chemical concoction type words that could be letting it in through some technical, scientific side-door. But there - there, Lucy! trust yourself - in swallowing she damn well tastes chocolate! 'If it isn't chocolate, what is it?' she demands of the empty rooms. Notices the television has been left on, the screen to its Sleep mode - the word *Video* blinking first at this corner, nowhere, that corner, nowhere, dead center, nowhere, again and again. Exactly like a television would look if really asleep. The way cartoon letter *Z*s or saliva bulbs would bubble from its drowsy lip creases. And the cigarette smoke seems asleep, too. Or just real homebody. It keeps close to the kitchen, like waiting for somebody to ask it to bring out another drink or to call out 'Almost!' when its lover whines from around the corner, supine still 'Is that pizza done yet - I'm hungry!'

Enter Curtis. Lucy is a fixture by now, so he is not embarrassed to find her there. No, he doesn't even shy up at his obviously just-unerected - or even still semi-so - bulge pushing against the ill-fitting brown-with-blue stripes and hot purple waistline of his athletic cut underpants. Lucy quite likes Curtis - the way he looks, most of all. There is something about him that makes him - no matter his appearance or affect, in fact - seem he is just about to step into a tuxedo he rented an hour ago. His teeth rather look like tuxedos, in themselves, and his eyes an undone bow-tie waiting for a pal to show up to tend to and even then not-sure-how-it's-supposed-to-go. Curtis ducks past - ardor-musked but not a lick of sweat apparent in the green-hue of the over-stove light - opening the fridge and taking out an already open can of *Ginger Ale* that rattles like the pop-tab was purposefully dropped inside. 'Lucy, my love' he says, his accent always more subtle than she is waiting for 'we didn't wake you with that undignified racket, did we?' 'No, no.' 'Or distract you from your work?' 'Not at all. You two are like a smooth jazz station I just have on in the background - hardly notice you're there.' Curtis half-chuckles into his last tight-lipped slurp of the drink before pressing his foot on the release of the trash-can lid, tossing the thing into the overfull-in-there, rubs his belly and then full chuckles. 'Is that it, eh?' 'Oh' Lucy says, tone she shouldn't be so insensitive of the pride of others 'that sounds bad. I'm sorry, Curtis. It's like whale song or womb noise. Sarcastic whale song or womb noise from a fetus already disowned.' And now Deb enters and tells the two of them to stop planning their wedding, snaps at Lucy and tells her 'You are coming over yonder to smoke this joint with me' - the joint in question, magic trick presto, pulled out from the silently opening far kitchen drawer. 'Am I disincluded from these festivities?' Curtis whines, and sulks off when Deb says 'Oh I'll smoke your joint when I get back, make it up to you, cry-baby.'

Deb - after two drags, one pass, two more drags - glares accusatory at Lucy. Lucy does her best to put on the air of not noticing - or at least not caring - while she takes another long drag, but finally gets genuinely unsettled. 'What?' Deb gives her shin a kind of rub-cum-kick. Again. Again - Lucy looking down to see if maybe there are ants there Deb is trying to slosh off. 'What?' 'I told you: you are not paying me anything.' Lucy raises up on her toes and begins to speak but Deb kicks her harder. Lucy tries again, Deb kicks her harder and makes the sound Ppbbt! or Pfst! - some harsh Shut-up-or-else sound, at any rate. After a pause and a few more shared drags, Lucy shyly tries 'Can I just pay you that one time and then not anymore?' 'No.' 'Deb, I need to feel I am contributing.' 'No! And don't start doing my laundry or anything perverted like that either, or I'll put you out like all the other goddamned waywards that wind up here.' Lucy argues: 'You're letting me and my cat stay here.' Deb counters: 'I'm letting the cat and his you stay here.' Lucy acquiesces to this, taking a drag. Then she clevers: 'Will you let the cat pay you?' But Deb seems ready for this and is scoffing even as Lucy asks that, says 'The cat is permitted rent free under Federal Statue - and you, as its ward, get to come along. Same as its shit-box, you know?' Lucy could easily believe that Deb does prefer the feline Lucy Jinx to her, if she is being honest - and likewise that the cat feels it has finally arrived home. To the manor born, she is informed kitty-Jinx always wedges between Deb and Curtis, post-coital - and Curtis even slept on the sofa once when Deb insisted that kitty-Jinx would feel like he had to move from the pillow where he drowsed if Curtis even gingerly tried to lay down on a return from the kitchen with Deb's cup of *Tummy-Mint Tea*. 'Added to which' Deb waves the offered joint away - thinks better, takes two tip-taps from it, offers it back, takes another long drag and two shorts to kill it when Lucy declines, drops the thing in the rusted can by the dead potted plants - 'you don't even want to pay me. So stop being such a liar. Jesus - you are lying! You're a truly awful person, Lucy - but regardless, you don't have to pay rent here.'

Lucy returns to her room and reads back what she had been writing. Of late, this has always lead to the thin-stomached feel of disillusionment in her talents, but she may be over a hump of some kind because much of this current stuff seems quite good. 'Or maybe you're glad you got that two hundred bucks back' she snides and to the snide she gives a clearing of her nose and a cold shoulder, sitting down and reading back: *three more times I called you and it was thumb tack on rust wall on telephone ringing, booth empty*. This summons to her a memory that also feels not a memory because at the same time it summons an exact scene from a movie she cannot recall the name of - something she caught on television, late night, only-just-technically teenaged and three hours after the first time she had been brought, third-party, to orgasm. Oh her eyes against the television light just then - she could feel the purple under the brown-red of every vein, eyes were pennies that had confused themselves with prunes! But what memory did the line bring to mind, Lucy? 'Not that?' she asks. But no - she is correct to question.

Isn't that an interesting little phenomena: the poem brought on a distinct memory which also brought on the memory of that movie scene which in turn brought on thoughts of first sex and bedroom floor alone. And now the memory the poem brought on is gone! Is it really, Lucy? *three more times I called you and it was thumb tack on rust wall on telephone ringing, booth empty*. Yep. What a dirty trick this is. Now she stands in the room and wants to know what that reminds her of, but all she can think about is that she had switched socks with that girl and they had said 'I love you' to each other in whispers, noses touching and both wet from how they had been crying from laughing at having to be so secret and silent while her dad watched television two rooms away. The poem reminds her of something. But now all it reminds her of is that it had reminded her of something it now doesn't. And that movie scene. And the fact that she spent an hour in the bathtub that night, counting and counting and counting the seven crescent-moon, last-of-the-bourbon-red fingernail marks she'd found left under the soft hair of her left wrist.

Of late, this is how sleep comes for Lucy Jinx - let's have a look: She thinks about how Deb is plumper than she is, but far more attractive, the difference in degree that as between Exquisite and Wax-Sculpture-Left-To-Neglect - she thinks about the word *Plumper*, awhile, and wonders when exactly it had become something negative sounding to her so that, even now, she feels awkward or edgy or around-the-curve-from-normal to think of it in positive, envious terms - she thinks about envy and tries to come up with rhymes, her favorite of which is one day *Trilby* is another day *Excellency* is another day the Norse name *Denby* - she thinks about a time she needed some fast cash-in-hand and, though the plan was idiotic, she had deposited an empty envelope in an *ATM* and told the machine the envelope contained five hundred dollars because she knew the machine would immediately let her withdraw two hundred - and then had panicked terribly, after spending the money, at how much trouble she would get in when the bank discovered her fraud - she thinks about that more - specifically: How had you gotten out of that Lucy? - she thinks, seriously, how had she gotten out of that? as she recalls - no, none - not the slightest consequence when there must have been - she thinks 'Well, that is where life goes and there's no getting it back' - she thinks about the outside of some certain apartment door she had lived in, twenty-two years old, and how the sounds she'd heard on the other side had belonged to a man she'd convinced herself she was in love with and who had turned out to be the worst abomination she had ever encountered - but she doesn't think about that much - then she thinks 'I wonder if Curtis and Deb try to hear if I'm touching myself' and tries to arouse herself at the thought, tries to imagine kissing Curtis, kissing him without Deb knowing, tries to imagine the blank of his saliva - though to him hers would be vinegary with forbidden heat of stolen sex and pepper guilt of his eyes welling with the lies he thinks he will have to tell Deb and the ones he thinks he should tell Lucy.

Sometimes, now - this night, now - she wakes up and realizes she had forgotten something that now she remembers. No - Lucy - that was a dream or the memory of another day. Who are you? Lucy Jinx. Where are you? Lucy Jinx. How did you get here? Lucy Jinx. And are you allowed to be here? Lucy Jinx. No. What were the questions? She's already falling asleep. In the dark she says something by way of apology that no one hears and she won't recall having said. What's the truth? The truth is sleep has been bad since getting here. Dreams are like this: sitting in front of a table in an apartment she is not familiar with but that is not this apartment and knowing they will rummage under the correct rug eventually and she'll never be able to explain why she has all that old skin hidden there and no matter how she cries they will not stop berating her and tearing it and giving it nibbles just to mock her. She'll help someone - with a paperclip, she'll help - when they cannot get a little fleck of the skin out of the bump of the tops of one of their teeth. Eat it! She has to! In her sleep she'll taste bile which when she wakes is just citrus and she blames Deb's apple-juice for the whole thing, the whole inside of her sweating, skin dry as landfall, eyes the aches of the sun off some part of the sea no one's ever seen. And when she goes back to sleep it is still bad: each day she has convinced herself it will be better and that something is wrong with her. Both things seem true. But seem they go together. They don't. The opposite of both things actually are true. But seem not to go together. They do. Look, right now: Lucy Jinx is staring at the ceiling and is making amazing images out of the shadows and daubs and gashes and microbial forms that float in the space in front of her eyes and over the glazed curves of their surfaces. She wants to remember, to tape record how fast her mind can make the connections, write it down, call it a poem. Just do it when you're awake, Lucy. But she only thinks this after she's fallen asleep, the buffer noise, the body-catching-as-though-falling, the dttzzz sound that fumbles a numb wave from the base of her skull over her skin and makes her a mass of pill-bugs before she's out cold.

'Lucy?' Who is that? Slow awake, then startle. Deb. Her eyes are half-written and under blank pages - is she even awake? Are you, Lucy? 'What's wrong?' 'Do you have any Ibuprofen in here?' 'What?' Deb is caressing what at this close a distance in this much a dark seems a horn halfway grown from her forehead but is just the up-down of the brow hard knit and being pulped circular and tense in. 'Ibuprofen?' 'Or anything. Acetaminophen?' She wants to know if Deb is okay, which Deb says she is, except it feels like something has been chewing on the very front of her brain and it's bleeding lead paint down her throat, post-nasal. 'What? Are you okay, Deb?' 'I'm dying, Lucy.' Deb has crawled up into the bed - which means Lucy is now standing, except she can't so she sits on the carpet, then gets to her knees and is rubbing Deb's arm. 'I don't have any Ibuprofen. But that doesn't mean I'm glad you're dying.' The sound of the 'Aw, Lucy' in the dark is confirmation of that-was-cute-and-funny so Lucy is glad and feels accomplished. Except: What's wrong with Deb? 'Lucy?' Who is that? Slow awake, then groggy gum-eyes. Deb. Deb speaking, midsentence: 'been for about twenty minutes, can you come listen?' 'What?' 'Come here.' Deb helps Lucy get unsteady on to her tingly, one-of-them-asleep legs and they make their way to the living-room where Curtis is standing on one of the dining chairs, head titled as though to hear deep into the canal of the ventilation shaft. 'Do you hear anything in there?' Is this happening, Lucy? Lucy is unsure. She is tensing her foot against a cramp, pressing it hard into the ground. Awake. Yep. You're awake, Lucy? She gently tap-scoot-shoves Curtis from the chair and stands on it. Imagining the tone with which she will say 'I don't hear anything' and at the same time trying to guess what she'll hear - a rattle, a scratching - not prepared at all for the steady-timed, repetitious 'Help me. Can you hear me? Help me. Mommy? My mommy fell down. Help. Help me?' The monotone making her skin crawl, the voice hocked out of context and resembling, most perfectly, the look on both Curtis and Deb's face that accompanies Deb's 'That's a television, right?'

HOW IS IT, TODAY? CAN you be certain you are not somebody else, Lucy? Couldn't you be, by now? Think about how without-effort the switch might happen. What would you use as evidence if you wanted to protest that you are who you have been, who you were, and that there is no difference between that and who you are? You woke up, now, and have in your head what is in your head - but does it belong to you, based on anything? How much of you has changed and which memories are obsolete? Can't they be shed like hair, skin, clothing, attitudes, aesthetics? Put it this way: you are the sum of your memories of your experiences, but only of some of them, yes? Say the ones you actively recall were shunted out of you and replaced - replaced not with nonsense or with randomness, but by conscious focus on other things that happened to you. What about it, Lucy? That which you are conscious of now - which you preen over, stress over, define yourself with and consider *You* - say that is now the background hum, the unconscious of you, only the things that pop up, suddenly remembered from time-to-time, the things you say 'I forgot all about that!' to. And here is the switcheroo: all this stuff that was you but that you forgot is suddenly front and center - are you at all the same? Have you been ignoring yourself? Are you ignoring yourself, now? Jesus, Jinx - you can't be the sum of all of you! There is Dominant and Recessive in life - and there is choice-to-keep and choice-to-discard! Well, what governs that? Ethics of some kind? What are the ethics of your own memories if they're only regarded by you? Or does someone else remember your memories, Lucy? Is that it? Come on! Aren't you allowed to forget? Aren't you allowed to remember-this-instead? You are a pile of what you have observed and the prickles of sensations that have snuffled against you, jolted you, carried you away - so why do you say you are just whatever got its claws in most, better or worse? You are yourself, but cannot choose yourself? Or if you do choose yourself, you are obligated to keep certain parts, deemphasize others - or else be told 'You are avoiding yourself, denying yourself! You are a liar! This is not you!' You are lying to yourself with yourself? You are lying to who-you-are about who-you-are with who-you-are? So what about it, Lucy? How is it, today?

Lucy cannot answer herself, but how it is today, for example, is this: Lucy is not yet used to this new commute - by weird instinct goes muscle-memory from where she used to live always down the wrong block because it reminds her a bit of what used to be the right block. A too sunny morning. The too-sunny of it made even more by the remnant of the marijuana salivated over the saliva of her mouth, haggardly there. Today it is: this is kind of a big day, Lucy - why were you smoking last night? Why has that become a habit? 'Piss off, mom' Lucy smiles at herself, knowing full well she is fine with having smoked and that she is just avoiding the real issue at hand. How it is today, for example, is this: Lucy Jinx, bus-stopped, watching this old-timer read a newspaper as though the words in it still pertain to things from two, three decades ago. That's a lovely thought, Lucy! Top marks for gloominess but bittersweet! If Lucy had a pen and paper, why she might write a whole essay about this, or least make a note - it's too garish to write poetry about, of course, a sadness meant for prose and reflection. Yes. That old man, always with his newspaper. No sense of time except what it says happens each day. In her imagination, Lucy has the old man scanning the pages for his own name, every day, wondering if life will ever have any place for him, even if just a name in a caption listing all the people in the photo above it. How it is today - since Lucy seems to want to avoid the matter with these school-girl digressions into 'Ah me, such is life' - for example is this: there's the bus, Lucy gets in it, wordless, Lucy sits at a window and knows the young man who is spit-humming a drum-rhythm gave her the once over when she turned - this young man taking it quite as read it meant she was presenting her back meat for giddy inspection - and Lucy sitting wordless, despite herself, wondering with an attempted-to-shape-back-to-normal paperclip grin if she had gotten high marks or low and, if high, what the kid figures she'd say as he undid her pant button, pop.

Deb has been sending updates. This one is: *Oh my God - that kid had been in the room more than a day with the body*. Lucy is not soliciting these. She'd gotten the scoop. She wonders why Deb bothered keeping up on it once it was clear other neighbors had also figured out something was amiss and that authorities had been called to the scene. Deb is getting updates fed to her from Curtis and so in turn is pelleting Lucy. Lucy has been told: *The kid was only four! Jesus, I can't imagine*. Lucy has been told: *At least he didn't know - or are you old enough to know, by then?* All of this, frankly, wrecks Lucy's ability to pretend that the horror had been just something out of one of her dreams. But it does not clobber her ability to feel the creeping surety that it is all to do with her. Dot-to-dot. Lucy was a new element to the building and Lord knows what happened to that woman. Are you really trying to wrangle this around into something to do with you, Lucy? Deb sends an update: *Curtis says a neighbor is arguing that the kid shouldn't be allowed to go with his dad! Something about something with him*. It would be a simple matter to not read these texts. It would be a simple matter of texting to Deb *Just got here - give me the full story, later*. But Lucy is a good friend, in abstracto, and her dial is set to long-suffering. Not that she has suffered Deb long, but the principle is the same. The truth? 'What truth?' Lucy sighs, but knows full well what she means. The truth is, Lucy: you are blaming yourself because you don't give a shit about that kid or its mother or any of that - and you don't like that Deb does because it prods you with obligation to be something you aren't, to be full-bloom as ugly as the something you are. Why should you care, Lucy? That's fair. That is fair. It really is fair, Lucy. Agreed. It's a good point. You can stop agreeing, you're right.

Unfortunately, by the time Lucy is having her coffee at the café where she is in love with the Lithuania barista she has no sense of doing anything but running away. That is her plan. And on point - unavoidably - Elliott's text-message is what she sees just when she's about to finally text Deb *Stop telling me about this, it's honestly freaking me out*. Elliott: *Can you please call me? Please?* The barista knows Lucy's name. Already. First and last. 'Lucy Jinx - you have the most beautiful name. You should be a character in a novel my daughter will grow up to love.' Lucy can do nothing but smile and lust and want to belong to this Lithuanian and her daughter. That and say 'How do you pronounce your name, again? I'm sorry I'm such a swine.' The barista laughs and pronounces - in a way Lucy cannot repeat - 'Rozalija.' *Rozalija*. 'You will call me *Rosie*' the barista laughs somewhere between a question and a statement, hand touching Lucy's hand on the counter in a don't-worry-about-it, but Lucy just focusing on the use of the word *Will*. 'I will not call you *Rosie*. I'll butcher your name every day before I do that - don't let anyone call you *Rosie*!' That laugh - it coats Lucy's eyes like gingivitis and is a tight like chewing stale popcorn in her jaw, in her belly. And her phone rings with maybe more Deb and probably more Elliott. 'Lucy Jinx' says the barista, handing Lucy her coffee and Lucy hacks at saying 'Rozalija' hues like a clown-nose and says 'What is your surname?' stammering, but glad she'd stammered - as she only had done so to keep from saying *Last Name*, to sound fancy, to give her time to say *Surname*. 'Surname?' 'Say your whole name' Lucy cannot-stop-blushings. '*Kavaliauskas*' the barista laughs and blushes a little at herself - wouldn't you blush if you knew you had a name as beautiful as you had two eyes and a mouth and hands with fingers nine days long? - and tells Lucy 'You will call me *Rosie K.*' And Lucy holds the look and says 'I will never call you *Rosie K.*'

What was going on? Ah. Elliott, three messages in quick succession. *Please call me, Loose. I don't know what to do with myself and I just want to know where you are, okay? I hate myself but please don't do this to me.* Lucy sips the coffee and tastes the caramel Rozalija puts in, the caramel Lucy doesn't really like but gushes for and even once went back up to ask for when it hadn't been added. She texts back: *You don't need to hate yourself. And if you do, that's really something you should be discussing with your girlfriend, okay? Stop texting me.* Did you send that, Lucy? No. Not yet. Do you want it to be harsher or less harsh? Why are you still here - why still this city, these people? What is the purpose of your not having left - have you forgotten how to run away? That can't be it, eh Jinx? Have you forgotten how to run toward, then? *I never knew how to do that* she adds to her text to Elliott. Reads that back. The whole of it. *You don't need to hate yourself. And if you do, that's something you should be discussing with your girlfriend, okay? Stop texting me. I never knew how to do that.* She puts her phone back to her pocket, coffee in mouth, coffee in mouth. How something arbitrary and accidental can link to something bitter and form the unadorned truth! Now some defensive mockery at how you are making today a day full of insights that should be committed to quote books! And Rozalija - Lucy cannot even think the proper pronunciation of the name - says you are something her daughter should read - or fall in love with, or read and fall in love with! - and now what you are writing by accident is who you honestly are. Don't show how terrified you are, Lucy. You haven't run - you know it - because you're caught in the snare again and the only thing keeping you alive is the spider's web didn't jiggle enough to wake it. You're just waiting to die. Which is far different than dead. You're just a good idea. Which is not at all the same thing as a book permanently written, possible to close, possible to summarize, possible to forget.

Her phone buzzes. Elliott writes: *I don't want you to feel that way. I was the one lying. I know that I hurt you. And I cannot make it better but please just call me.* For a moment, Lucy wonders if she is on the wrong page of the wrong volume entirely - and it is almost a feeling like relief, like she heaved a breath hard enough that when it compressed and her lungs emptied out she was past it all, where she was supposed to be, had corrected the world with a last hesitant steeling-herself-against-facing-it. Then it street-muggings in her head what had happened. Yes, indeed! She had sent her previous text! There it is - holy smokes, eh? Oh Lucy, it'd be funny if it wasn't you and you didn't feel the tug at the stitching of your life where the puppeteer click-clicks the strings with his jitterbug fingers. 'Goddamn it.' Well said, Lucy. And be proud of yourself that there was soft humor in the remark, even if it's just because Rozalija is there - maybe looking at you - and you cannot have her see that you are a creature who knows distress, because something like a Rozalija will be able to tell how plebian and how self-inflicted and how petty your aches and pains are, will recant her inclusion of your name in her daughter's - does she have a real daughter? Focus, Lucy! - future literature, will instead just offer you two tablets of Aspirin, no more to you than that. Lucy puts everything out of her head except the memory of Rozalija saying her name. But it's a memory she does not have. And all her poetry, all her trying to insist that she does have the memory, that there is more to it than the sound, the pronunciation - that her memory is the feeling, the weight of the light in the air, the sensation that will never away from her, ever - does nothing to truly dispel the fact that she is just incapable of remembering the sound - the name - is so artless that her mind cannot conjure that melody, but can recall exactly the mop-bucket sound of a stray cat in the up-chuck in an alley some time when she was a child.

'What do you want, Elliott?' 'Why are you yelling at me?' 'Because: why are you calling me? We're done - have you not picked up on that! Look left, right - see me anywhere?' 'Why are you talking like this?' 'Because I'm sick of your crazy messages and don't even know what the fuck that last one meant - so here's my voice telling you *Get past it, we're done*.' 'I want your face. I want your face, not just your voice, to tell me.' 'Aw, well that is just too bad. You have your girlfriend's face, Elliott. That's whose face you have. You had mine and you're the one who lost it so how dare you ask to see it, again!?' 'I want to explain about that. You really don't understand.' 'Don't fucking tell me I don't understand - Oh you're a charmer today, aren't you? Is that what you want to call me to say, Elliott? That I don't understand?' 'I want you to look at me - I don't deserve it, but I want it.' 'No - you don't deserve it.' 'No - I don't. I know. And I don't think it'll matter, but you know my face and I want you to see my words on it. Because you'll know they are true. Even if it doesn't matter.' 'Elliott, it doesn't matter. Okay? It doesn't. I can tell you that from way over here. Stop texting me, stop calling me.' 'Fuck you, Lucy.' 'Ah - well golly, there we go! Very nice!' 'Why should I be nice?' 'You shouldn't be, Elliott. I'm hanging up.' 'Then fucking hang up, Lucy. Christ, you wouldn't even touch me anymore! And it killed me! And I'm not even seeing her, Lucy - and I know I did what I did but fuck you, man!' 'I'm hanging up, Elliott.' 'And you're gonna screw me with rent? I can't pay for this place myself.' 'Shucks, Elliott - why didn't you just tell me that's what you were calling about.' 'Please, Lucy.' '*Please, Lucy?* - you sound like an idiot, you know that? What do you want? Few bucks for the rent, is it?' 'I just want to see you?' 'Well you can't have either'. 'Go to fucking Hell!'

But a cigarette fixes everything. In the end, it's good that Elliott called, eh? 'Well, I called Elliott' Lucy corrects as she leans to this wall but then decides it really is time to get walking. This area of town - already - seems so much more appropriate. If Lucy belonged somewhere, this would be where. Or someplace like here. Or something. Nevermind that Lucy knows she has not sorted out anything about the rent, really, anything about the lurch she honestly is leaving Elliott in. One would think by the time one had lived as long as Lucy has lived one would know better than to sign one's name to an apartment lease! But, in fairness: Lucy had known better. She had just been in a different head and the idea of all of this current bother, when seen from so far away - the vantage of time-will-never-proceed-to-here taking the curse off of everything - had seemed romantic and desirable. Sigh, sigh, Lucy - abstracts and Platonic Ideals are always so desirable, even those that spell heartache and doom and endless ring-around-the-collar malaise and it-feels-over-while-it-never-ends. Lucy had known she would get to do these scenes of pure self-serving, slash-and-burn heartlessness - but what she had known so long ago oddly seems unknown and unknowable now that it is happening. You knew you wouldn't enjoy it, Lucy. But that's not the same as not enjoying it, is it Lucy? If only you'd known you can, from afar, enjoy not-enjoying but, in up-close, cannot enjoy not-enjoying-not-enjoying! Oh Lucy, you're a circular ruin of a cartoon of a balderdash wordplay! Can being done with Elliott be as simple as that telephone call? No. Well, Lucy - it could. But you won't let it! Can Lucy get her name off that lease? Had Elliott beaten her to this punch and removed her own name? Aren't you meant to be leaving anyway, Lucy? 'Meh.' Here are some fine, suddenly tall buildings and here and here are some, right after those, sink-on-the-floor low ones that will lead her to the last left turn she needs to make this morning. Lucy chooses to focus on only that right-now. And if she were writing that choice, she'd have spelled *Chooses Choosed* and not corrected the typo when she'd noted it.

Something compels her to stop in this small pizzeria and to break five dollars into coins and to stand there playing *Galaga*. The grease in the air, invisible thick on the wall-paint and windows, invisible thin in her hair, invisible smeared on the joystick and the *Fire* and the *One* or *Two Player Start* buttons she taps. The scent of in-the-corner-stacked Styrofoam cups in shed skins of paper-soft plastic packaging, waiting to be filled with half-melted ice and always-almost-stale fountain soda. The smell of cardboard and used napkins, of plastic cutlery dropped by one customer, kicked by another, ignored in some wall crevasse by the staff when it's time to mop up at night. Oh - and Lucy, the tile! Look at it! Mostly bone white tiles, but then some red ones, some blue and - rarest of all - a green one, bespeckled with stains of shoe-skid, one there, there, and one there. If you took pen and paper, Lucy, and took all day could you decipher the overall design, the way the room would look from above if denuded of tables and countertop and child booster-seats - shit-grey rough plastic and stacked in the corner with their some-of-them-yellow and some-of-them-blue-grey buckling belts? Lucy has her quarters all lined up and is seven-years-old again and has a best friend named Susan and Susan's mom is in a chair over there and reading from a paperback novel that, for all Lucy knows, would turn out to be *Rubyfruit Jungle* if she looked. These *Galaga* bees suicide with such tenacity, trying to explode Lucy's spacecraft with that cotton ball, powder squeeze, stifle-sneeze sound effect Boom! Which, if spelled, would be spelled with overlapping *oughs* and *cks*. Everyone knows Lucy Jinx does not belong here - the college girl who had been studying when she'd handed over to Lucy the quarters got the entire idea and could whiff Lucy's desperation as easily as Lucy could whiff the scent of bacteria on the Salad Bar lettuce. Here, in this place, things are what they are and nothing needs to seem anything but: college girl, grease-in-the-air, sometimes-green-tile, desperation, *Galaga*, and quarters lined up like-as-though-a-kid when certainly not a kid anymore or ever again.

So silly, all the effort it now takes to move the day from one aspect to another. In the last twenty minutes, abundant things have happened - yet Lucy is still stuck in the sub-heading *Leaving For Work*. Instead of her life, all these incidents are intrusions on her inertia and trajectory. By what right does the world assert itself into her life? By what right is she accosted and blockaded from leaving the apartment she is staying in and going where she planned to go, thinking what she planned to think, feeling what she planned to feel? Here is Lucy Jinx: in a pizzeria toilet, no reason for it! But this pizzeria toilet seems a thing out-of-time and a place under the subjugation of nobody. Is this the only sort of place Lucy can ever just be? There she is, in the mirror. And here, sitting down to urinate - but really only just doing so to prove she can and that here it is meaningless and no tissue of event connects it to anything else. That trash in the bin? It will get emptied into a larger bag, that to a dumpster out in back, that to a dump-truck, that tipped into a pile and buried under the Earth - and in all that travel, the tampon Lucy just tucked in a long twine of toilet-paper - and hid under two paper towels she'd used to dry her washed-without-soap hands with - will never been singled out, noted, never be seen as part of the progress of the trash in that can. This toilet is a sanctuary that sends little vessels of unremarked peace all glissando to their burial without ever having to be named, gazed on, known, anything. Lucy can leave the room freely, but never as freely as trash. Her tampon is less at the whim of the Fates than she is, herself. It carries her blood to sanctuary. She carries her blood to someone else's tumult. Funny, funny - Lucy can wake without even meaning to and keep herself from staying in bed though it is where she would always rather be, but has to damn well hoist herself out of this toilet even when she honestly wants to move on.

'NOBODY CARES WHAT THE POET thinks, what they are saying. The intent is irrelevant. Do you think the people involved in making that intersection on that hill did so with the intention that that intersection on that hill at that time of night with the traffic-lights on-the-blink and the woman crossing the street and the young man taking forever to make a left turn would remind someone who peacocks themself a Poet of a lost-love-in-wartime or the futility of charity in a world defined by starvation and flitting attention span? No. No, of course not. And so a poet thought that about it? So what? If we read the poem as saying anything, we need to know we are hearing ourselves - what we say when looking at someone-else-saying. The poet thought this? Thought that? The unfortunate residue of them-personally is left on the page, yes, but it needs to be wiped off, same as a toilet seat someone else pissed on! You don't sigh and sit down without cleaning the thing! Listen to me - if you ever listen to me about anything - poetry is very simple. It is one thing. A person running and screaming. That is a poem. The sound of someone running and screaming. Ugly and pointless and lost in a dark they know doesn't lead anywhere, choosing a path and scrambling on gangrened legs and screaming at the top of their lungs until they hit a wall and don't have the will to turn around so just stop. Poets only scream for other poets - and if you are a poet and hear the scream of another it makes you run a step faster and scream hoarser, makes your voice give out a nameless second sooner. That is poetry. If you are writing the smallest, quietest observation you're still gangly and untouchable and blind and hand-scabbed and have no idea why you chose the turn you chose and your chest is gelatin with exhaustion and you keep going. You keep going. There is such unknown in you and such desire to accept it and screech it to a Heaven you don't believe in to any degree except it has overlooked you. If you think you aren't those things, if you think you are at peace, calm, that you are well and are someone who has arrived someplace and can see things, relax, have things, relax - well, if you think that, write a poem.

And try to keep thinking it. Until you can't. Until it dawns on you that you just fell asleep running and screaming and now have woken up to learn you still are. You are screaming and running until you are nobody and the last thing you scream is the same as the first: *I am somebody, please, I am somebody*! It's what we all scream because we all eventually are nobody. A poet just knows it, first.'

The usual awkward few students kind-of-clapping and a smattering of So-do-you-means followed Lucy's address. And, as usual, now that the words were out of her she both regretted them and forgot what they were. In this case, there was the added distraction of Petra's seat being empty. Should be simple enough for Lucy to ask 'Has anybody seen Petra, today?' Should be. Except for Lucy is Lucy and the risk of asking so simple and understandable a thing was in that students might hear the question and for the first time understand Lucy was Lucy and that it was Lucy who was asking. As in to say it would not be Ms. Jinx asking. One of the young men in the class - while Lucy had the others reading to each other in three-sets - made his way over to her desk and shyly asked if he could talk to her. 'Of course.' Petra's seat still empty. The room door still not suddenly being opened by Petra. Unsurprisingly, the young man just had some questions about where he might submit some poems of his - scholarship contests and the like - and moreover wondered if Ms. Jinx might be willing to read over his final drafts of them before he sent them. 'This class has really meant a lot to me' he said, the look of earnest I-think-those-words-carry-definitions that probably only adolescent young men who want to send poetry to scholarship contests can have. 'Roger, I wouldn't be surprised if you grow up to be a billionaire, you know?' He smiled and tick-tocked his eyes like *Wow, golly, thanks* and Lucy of-coursed she'd read his drafts and any-school-would-be-lucky-to-have-you-there-for-freed. Petra still wasn't there. Which should not trouble you, Lucy. Why does it? Lucy looks at the clock and figures she'll have to stop the groups reading, their voices triangle-circles of chalk dotting feverish on slate-board. She figures she'll have to listen to some things and say some things. And one of those things will be final. This room was a *Goodbye* the moment it was a *Hello*.

Let's take a moment to explain this girl Leonora. What of her? She is a girl the way a stick is not quite strong enough to be a wrist. Her clothing is nice, always, and she wears it very much knowing science means it will outlast her skin. She is the most talkative in the class and - pound-for-pound - is better read than Lucy. Not that Lucy is troubled by this - Lucy quite prides herself on being not-so-well-read and feels by now enough time has elapsed since her education it is good to be reminded she mooted it into superficiality. Leonora carries herself very well and will obviously succeed. She refers to herself as a Poet and makes bold-statements then humble-pies, always - a bit of a princess who

realizes she walks everywhere on a carpet of slaves. Lucy cannot help but feel
tart-mouthed envy toward the girl, sometimes - and reminds herself she is
allowed to. Lucy is not a teacher, not really. So this young thing who will likely
not grow out of being a surface - but will be a surface given enough polish to
reflect back an eternity-of-distance some might confuse for a depth - can be
something of a nuisance. How is Leonora's poetry, Lucy? There is some on the
desk in this room you have been allowed to play in. The poetry is not bad at all.
It sounds like interesting words. It reads like a quote in Latin, but one that was
first written in English and translated. The girl Leonora makes one of the teeth
of this school, this room, this all, seem wrong - one too many, something, one
a shade more off-white than the others but stuck in the back so not obtrusive.
Lucy is staring at the girl because Petra is not there. And because of the vague
fear that she is wrong about Petra and wrong about Leonora, as well. Maybe
nothing would make Lucy happier than to think Leonora could be Petra could
be her - could be Lucy's course if that course had not once-upon-a-time been
corrected wrong and then all calculations made from that first mistake, the
vessel coasting long-lost past continents all of which would have poured out
their bounty to the crew and to the captain, most of all. Stop staring, Lucy. Stop
watching Leonora smile. Stop wondering if it looks true or false. You'll never
sort it out.

Will Lucy be teaching this workshop again next semester? Or next year? Lucy
does not know, she tells this group as she sits among them, their reading to each
other less imperative than these as-though-off-the-cuff questions. Will Lucy be
coming to graduation? 'Yes, certainly' Lucy says and this gets an appreciative
Phew from the girl who'd asked - she had mentioned once that her older sister
was in charge of some poetry website and Lucy had looked into it and had been
rather impressed but never brought up the matter again. Will Lucy be coming
to graduation? Lucy says she will - this time the question asked amongst another
cluster-of-three and this time Lucy wonders if she is saying this to be nice or
saying it to be distant or saying it because she wants to or saying it because she
knows it won't matter by then. 'Do you ever read anywhere?' Leonora asks and
blushes - or faux-blushes, who ever knows with Leonora? - saying how she had
meant to ask this for awhile but was always too intimidated. 'That's how I got
this gig' Lucy smugs, too-cool-for-schooling it, surprised the students didn't
already know that. 'Oh yeah' she lays it on 'I was discovered in some dive. Bailed
out of lock-up after a fist-fight and puking down the front of a lady-cop. Judge
took pity on me, said *Is there anything you can do?* so I said *I can teach poetry to kids,
prolly.* That was that.' Leonora is looking as close to drunk as a teenage girl who
probably puts on gloves before kissing can look and yet Lucy still feels it a
playact. The other two are already turning to relay the details of this tale of

Lucy's to their pals in other groups. 'Have you seen Petra?' Lucy asks Leonora since the two of them seem to inhabit a cauterized pocket of silence and Lucy needs something to gain a sense of self and place. 'Petra?' Leonora turns to look at the empty seat. 'Oh shit - she was here, earlier.' She turns back to Lucy, who must have a quizzing look on her face. 'I mean at school. I didn't notice she wasn't here in this class. Petra's really quiet, you know?'

One student reads: *the summer like a stomach unplumped and the only part of the book that the author forgot.* One student reads: *what do you say, roach? Would you rather choke on a dandelion or a bent piece of cork?* One student reads: *you're all weary with upside-downedness, a lake no one is glad to have seen as the car passes by.* One student reads: *What would I call mom? A fork without prongs. What would I call mom? A piano without sing-a-long.* One student reads: *the room has an extra corner, the one so ugly we refuse to call it itself.* One student reads: *a child with a face like a stolen bag of marbles, a woman's leg with veins clustered in kneebacks like the sticks that once had green-grapes.* One student reads: *you don't have a soul, just a pile of maps.* One student reads: *graveyard mouthed, cold toes for bedtime kisses, life is better off if not rhymed with anything.* One student reads: *forever it's Tuesday but one underripe and pale next to the other ones so devoured.* One student reads: *his past tipped its hat like it was the first time it'd worn one.* One student reads: *in his house songs electrical in his house books in triangular vinyl.* One student reads: *she died before she was old enough to know if she felt lonely.* One student reads: *milk from my brain down my eyes down my hands in my pockets too shivering to shake.* One student reads: *the sea is choking on the shore which chokes on the shore as well.* One student reads: *kiss me, bottle of Port wine, whatever that is, kiss me, you're my mouth like a cigarette was my grandmother's.* One student reads: *she seems tarantula exhausted, wasp spined, paint-thinner boned.* One student reads: *all I ever wanted from you was when I told you my dreams that you'd ask me to spell them.* One student reads: *love is the last room in which one should bat an eyelash.* One student reads: *Escape me. But remember. I know where you've been.*

There is a small discussion about whether or not they should be trusting all of Ms. Jinx's praise considering Ms. Jinx's more outlandish and controversial pronouncements as to poetry and posterity and intent and that business. It's all in good spirits, so Lucy explains that she does not know where she would be without poetry. She tells a story about a certain volume that had been on this bookshelf in her house all growing up. How she had thought it was simply the ugliest book she had ever seen. How she had detested the photograph on the cover, which she figured was a portrait of the author. It seemed gaudy and Look-at-me-aren't-I-artsy-and-special and young Lucy's blood had boiled and she had memories of sitting in the dark of her bedroom some nights, randomly simmering in a kind of shit-can disgust at that book. 'No' she says now, the students all rapt 'I never so much as flipped through the book beyond enough to see it was poetry. I sort of knew what it was called, but - gah!' - Lucy mimes spitting on the floor - 'I hated, despised what it was called - what it was called was as garish and fake-bellied as the photo on the cover. What was it doing in my house!?' 'What was the book?' Of course Leonora is the one to ask, but Lucy holds her off. 'More than twenty years since I first saw the thing - at least twenty, who knows when I first saw it - I was at the lowest point of my life. You're too young to even know that there can be lows like that - you all, no disrespect, still think the world is flat when it comes to things like that. I read a poem and it rebuilt me, starting with the scabs at the back of my eyes. This one poem. It didn't it even have an author's name - it was part of a print-out someone had left on a city bus - a packet from someone's night class or something. When I looked up the poem by title, I learned the author's name. And what book it came from. The one I'd slandered and hideoused since there was a thought in my head! It had been waiting for me. Waiting for me to get drenched enough to understand it. To need it. To make it make me!' 'What was the book?' Leonora asks again after what seemed like a somber enough pause. 'You and your questions, Leonora. You and your questions.'

If this same room, these same young men and women - even all the same surrounding events, all the situations she is in - had happened when Lucy was twenty-five instead of now, would they feel so weighty? Would she even care that Petra was not in the room as these last minutes wend down and the chatter plinks and skittles along into irrelevance and everyone readying semi-prepared, adolescent I'll-miss-yous and this-has-been-so-amazings and all? Maybe not. But maybe you would have been wrong or missed something if twenty-five and unaware of what it was. Or maybe not. As maybe, back then, it would not have already been too late. Things can be overlooked before things are at the final toll of the final bell's final echo. Much can be overlooked and cast aside. It would be wrong, maybe, for this not to feel so weighty, now. To treat it as a replica of something someone younger has - to treat yourself, Lucy, as a youthful-you with choices and a history still in front, not so much mostly already behind. Are you going to cry? Because Petra isn't here? That young man whose name you are already forgetting - you've forgotten! you're calling him *Tomas* just to be a snot about it because he looks like a *Tomas*! - is talking to the class, in a general way, about having finally seen a movie they all had already and how it was weird to already know so much about it but still to feel the same way everyone else did at all the big moments. Let this mean something. Stop them! Say something! This may be like watching a ghost sing its own murder ballad, Lucy, but you don't have to just watch. 'Guys' she says, voice a melodious-on-purpose-up-tilting-sigh and the students all go silent as though the switch that controlled them had been swatted 'I don't think you understand how beautiful I think you all are.' She smiles. 'I mean, don't get big heads. I can think of things more beautiful than you - I just don't think you know - you know? - the exact, peculiar way I think you're neat.'

On exiting - which she does quickly, obviously with places to be - Leonora hands Lucy an envelope and says 'I wrote that for you. I don't need you to say anything about it.' Just as simple as that. Lucy watches as Leonora flits away like a commercial break while a conversation drifts into the adjoining room. She has another little chat with Roger, who also hands her something, though far less exotic: an index card with his email address and telephone number on it. 'I wrote my phone number, too - just in case' Roger says, clearly some thought process that there is something transgressive about the ten digits being there and passing from his to her hand. Lucy gives his a good-buddy punch on the shoulder and tells him she will keep her eyes peeled for his stuff and will get back to him on it. He mills like he really feels there ought to be a more-clever curtain-line, unaware he is a character to her about as much as a vacant seat in the orchestra pit. Look there, Lucy: knotted muscle of students being massaged smooth by each other's passage - five seconds, ten, then the ease and warm butter of a fully massaged empty-corridor, nothing but the vague scents of motions left and the ephemeral presence that feet have recently been here, the floor not yet readjusted normal after the intricate work it had in rendering the proper passage of shadows and smeared reflection, the oily swirl in inchless depth of the dimensions above it. 'Such rough work, the poor floor' Lucy thinks, sighing, shoulder to open door and feeling she actually has a reason to be here when, officially, she has none whatsoever. She is about to move, when the public address system does its three little beeps meaning *All at attention*. And she tries to find the nearest speaker before the voice starts, but cannot even once it has. Eerie. She hates that. Has to look at the doorknob of the room across the hall and pretend that the voice is coming from there. 'There is a Chess Club meet later' the knob tells her 'and the Chess Club would love it if folks would attend. This should have been announced in the morning. Apologies.' 'As you were' she imagines the doorknob saying after a minute of silence and her still there staring at it. She smiles and re-goes into what until just then had been her room.

Lucy: 'Where are you Petra?' Empty Chair: 'Shouldn't you be one your way?' Lucy: 'I'm waiting for Leonard. I have a meeting. I said I'd wait here.' Empty Chair: 'What did she write?' Lucy: 'Whom?' Empty Chair: '*Whom*? Did you say *Whom*? Your secret-admirer, there!' Lucy sits at the desk, leans back and taps Leonora's sealed letter - or poem, it's probably a poem - a slow snarl, devoid of meaning, to her lips. Lucy: 'Why weren't you here, today?' Empty Chair: 'Why? Was that big speech just for me?' Lucy: 'That big speech was just for you, as a matter of fact!' Empty Chair: 'I know. I heard you practicing it on the way in.' Lucy rolls her eyes away from the chair. No, she had not rehearsed the speech. But yes - yes, so what? - she had wanted to say those things for Petra, in particular - had known she would say something like that on her last day. For Petra. Empty Chair: 'That's what I meant. About rehearsing. That bit about blind corridors and screaming, you said that to yourself a week ago - gave some rough draft version of the whole bit in the shower.' Lucy: 'Oh. That.' It was true, she had. Lucy: 'So what? You're making fun of me?' Empty Chair: 'I'm not even here. You're one paranoid lady, lady.' Lucy: 'And just where are you?' Empty Chair: 'What did you say?' But Lucy hadn't said it, had just thought it - a bitter-fruit, sarcastic growl of 'Busy slitting your wrists or something?' Lucy: 'I'm sorry.' Empty Chair: 'You didn't even say it. Sorry about what?' Lucy: 'It doesn't matter. You can read my mind.' Empty Chair: 'No. I can't.' Lucy: 'Of course you'd say that'. And she's glad the chair sounds like Petra, again. Or how she imagines Petra to sound. That she doesn't really imagine Petra sounds like her - interrogating and haughty with snide disinterest. She turns and remarks the board. Wishes she had written her name on it so she could erase it, now. Empty Chair: 'You still could. I won't let anyone know how lame you are.' Over her shoulder she flips her middle-finger and hears the Empty Chair chuckle and fidget and be a teenager in love.

Only now, Lucy notices that it does not say *Ms. Jinx* on Leonora's envelope. *To my friend*. She gives the words a suspicious sniffle and carefully opens the thing, tight shoves of her index-finger, ripping it open a centimeter at-a-time. Out come three heavy-stock pages. Linen paper. Did Leonora use an actual typewriter? Or is this just a computer font? Pages backsides examined - a real typewriter! How about that! Lucy inhales the unread letters, but they don't really smell much like anything. They smell the way they sound, she thinks, momentarily feeling clever, then confused by the statement, shaking her head and announcing to the room 'Nevermind - you know what I mean.' *Look there at the taxi-exhaust of her bare shoulder*. That is an entire stanza, in itself. The next stanza separated by several blank lines. Lucy has difficulty moving past it, as she had been half-coiled to do nothing but snark the poem, top-to-toe. 'Shit' she says and sits down properly - in some whichever-student's desk chair - hoping that Leonard is caught up in something and will not suddenly pop in. *I don't recall the song / but recall every foam mouthed Q / of I forget the song! / Every stab of / I lost track of something sterner / than my disdain / for the thick of my throat*. Honestly, Lucy, you need to stop reading this. Yes. And she does. 'Fuck off, Leonora.' Lucy feels like old, tinny music in a movie that wouldn't scare anyone anymore except her. *Don't you want to be the skirt of my shadow? / Don't you want to be the Violeta / of my broken English / forgetting Purple just now?* I thought you weren't going to read it! Leonora didn't write this, Lucy insists, seeing through the game, putting the pages back in the envelope but then taking them back out. She drums her fingers on the desk and looks up for Leonard to be there. Then pokes her head into the corridor - poem held hidden behind her back, tapping against the rised-curve of her shoulder blade. No one there. Which is why she feels someone must be. Someone can see her from somewhere. There's no other reason for this.


LEONARD SAID THAT IF THEY kept by the window, they could go ahead and smoke. 'The headmistress won't mind?' He heartily chuckled at that, slapping pack to palm, cigging his mouth and unlatching the holds of the window. 'She'd tell us not to bother with the window.' Lucy takes the smoke he tenders and they lean on walls on opposite sides of the opening window, sounds of cars and students filing out from end-of-the-day. Leonard has the air of being the overly good host. Likely, he imagines Lucy feels put out in some way at having had to wait all day for this audience and now to have it delayed, again. See here? Now Leonard is offering her the too-too-insider scoop as to what the headmistress is dealing with. Some parents of a lad caught smoking a 'joint of marijuana' - Leonard's term, perhaps not even said to be cute - during school hours and on property are throwing a fit because they'd like it brushed under the rug and are aghast that the twerp is being made an example of. 'They pay big bucks to keep the kid an entitled pratt, you see?' Lucy nods, smoke out of her nose, and says 'The headmistress is putting the hard word down because he didn't share with her, or what?' Now: Leonard bursting out laughing, cough cough like a comedy father played by an underclassman in a high-school play whose son is played by someone in the graduating class. 'You're going to get on famously here' he finally gets out. 'That's actually it. Fucker wasn't paying his landlady' Leonard is now defenses-down, no more act-for-Lucy's-sake 'and is lucky he didn't get croaked.' And so on like that. Lucy knows Leonard is flirting, knows Leonard is aware of the grain of each breath he takes with her. 'Poor sap' Lucy says, meaning Leonard, and Leonard says, fitting her script nicely 'He really doesn't get the writing on the wall, see What for what What is, right?' 'Right' Lucy concedes and wonders, scale of one-to-ten, how much more attractive she honestly is than his wife.

The headmistress is even more astonishing today, done up in the apparentness that she has either just been yelling or had been holding her tongue and finding perfect-syllable amounts to valve her invectives out with calm even-headedness. Christ, Lucy hopes she had been yelling. But Lucy - Lucy! What? You need to stop picturing that. Why? Why would I ever have to stop picturing that? Look: Leonard and she are through with their tete-a-tete and you need to sit down before everyone sees your stiffy! 'Is he telling you how we smoked in here?'

Lucy says the moment she can tell for certain the headmistress is finished with her private word with Leonard. 'It was all my idea. He, in fact, was wet-palmed and squirmy through the whole thing. Said he didn't want you to get your switch out.' The headmistress sits. 'But you did? Want me to get my switch out?' Be very careful, Lucy, because that wasn't said in reality. No. It wasn't. 'As long as I don't have to put out the cigarette.' You didn't say that either, Lucy - so don't go thinking you did. Leonard blah blahs something to join in on the camaraderie and Lucy thinks she gets a half-second look of the headmistress being as irritated by his presence as Lucy is before the laughter becomes three-way and all is ordinary. Well, the headmistress gives the official account of what she is sure Leonard was blabbing about. And how she may have made an enemy who will, in later chapters, turn out to have been a bad one to have made. 'But, ah well' the headmistress says. 'It would have been fine if I hadn't used the term *dope-fiend* - but I did. So there will be payment due on that one, fair's fair.' 'You said *dope-fiend*?' Leonard I-can't-imagine-its and Lucy gives him the side-eye. 'Of course she said *dope-fiend*. Look at her! That's exactly what she'd say just from looking at her!'

Due to the nature of the scene, Lucy cloisters herself into a small space at the very back of her left eye and chooses a pre-programmed sequence of facial gestures and verbal responses to whatever turns out to be going on. It passes in a curious way, the conversation, like a dream about a television getting unplugged in the dark over and over, the person plugging it in always thinking 'This is finally fixed' only to have their foot tug the cord from the wall again, impossibly, even after they have already sat down. What happened? Lucy was offered a job. Or - to flesh out the intricacies - she was offered, long-term, a full position, short-term, a kind of semi-position, as she was not credentialed to teach on the full-fledged level. 'Is teaching something you ever considered?' Pre-programmed Verbal Response Number Seven is given and a facial expression of eyes big open and mouth made little to denote the seriousness of the thing it is saying. The headmistress and the school would help facilitate things - even find money in the budget, as perhaps Lucy is in no position financially to pursue further education, just then - and in the meantime they have discussed having her give another Workshop, like she had these past weeks, and to also participate in Leonard's class in a not-technically-a-teacher way, but as a Permanent-extra to the course. 'Basically: we just want you here and will find clever ways to make sure we can give you money and not have folks arrested.' Pre-programmed Verbal Response Number Twenty-nine is given and a pattern of head motions that incorporate eye-contact with both the headmistress and Leonard. 'If you were able, after the break' the headmistress just said and it seemed to be in response to the words Lucy had uttered. So she nods and says

'I'm able. Anytime.' And then she figures she should toss in some levity, so she says 'I guess those kids keep a pretty tight lid on things, eh? Good for them.' That smile! That Christ-is-dead-and-gone headmistress smile! 'Oh no, they told us everything. We're just into that kind of thing, here.' That smile! That do-you-want-to-kill-or-do-you-want-to-watch headmistress smile. Not that that last thing was said, Lucy - not in reality. But, yes. 'Okay. I can do that.'

Taking a step back from everything, Lucy wants to place her attraction to this woman. It is brimstone soaking in leaked battery acid? It is oils that actually mixed with water? Lead-paint robbed of its sweetness but more irresistible for its sour? Does she remind Lucy of an actress? Of an old crush? Some image from a dirty magazine seen in middle-school? There is something so tangle-veined about it. Just the authority she wields? A figment of Lucy's once-desired future-self? Maybe. Maybe. Did you want to be this woman, so now mesmerize yourself with her? Because what has she done? Sat in a room with you a few times? Been marginally witty? She turns Lucy's limbs to cake batter soaking in sink water, her loins into a full hamper of used towels from the gym swimming pool! What's the best word? Take your time, Lucy - the world has stopped for you to sort this. Does she look like the mother of that girl in college you had kinked it up with, pretended to be sisters with? What nerve is she hitting? It's deliciously curse-word inciting! Lucy Jinx: writhing in something too obvious to see. Her voice? The exact series of blouses she's been seen wearing? Hey! Maybe that's it! Some coincidence of she is wearing, in-a-row, some garments you have seen elsewhere and your brain is just bristling at the alignment of synapses that should not touch but now are. Why would that feel erotic? Why wouldn't it, though? Just an overwhelming sense of deja-vu coupled with a flattering figure and a well-proportioned face - that little extra quirk making a perfectly ordinary woman seem unnervingly exotic. Is that what she is, Lucy? *Unnervingly exotic*? Yes. The headmistress is *unnervingly exotic* - all the moreso for not being obviously-who-wouldn't-say-so so. Do you know her? Lucy: do you know her? Could that be it? Is she imagining you are sharing the knowledge of your acquaintance and keeping it secret for some low-smoldering reason? Lucy. Lucy! What? Are you trying to figure this out or just daydreaming, man!?

Now Lucy has wound up alone in the office with Leonard, again. Note: she did just touch the headmistress' hand and her eyes had felt like two asterisks with nothing to indicate at the bottom of the page of her. Leonard is handing her a cigarette. She takes it, but wonders if there is a symbolic cleverness to the gesture. Does she have a pink flush to her, freckles more pronounced? 'Do we have to go to the window?' 'I'm sure she'll understand. And she doesn't have any other meetings, I don't think.' Lucy takes his light, but narrows her eyes a little thinking 'Then why did we have to stand at the window, before?' Leonard:

putting on the bravado. Leonard: fresh swagger from having bought a new suit at a discount department store. 'I'm a little bit overwhelmed' Lucy obviously-I'm-obligated-to-says 'and I don't know that I took all that in. Was that an actual job offer?' 'It was' Leonard nods. 'And I hope you take it. The students bloody adore you. They have a surprise I'm forbid to give away, but if you aren't already sold on joining us here, I hope - and they hope - it'll do the trick.' 'What surprise?' He laughs. 'I'm forbade' he reiterates, rolling hand gesture to proper emphasize. 'By whom? Children? Dope-fiends?' 'Not that kid - your kids.' 'My kids are all dope fiends! Or I didn't do a very good job of things, did I?' But Leonard won't tell so Lucy just says 'I absolutely accept. Can you let me know, now?' 'Absolutely not! Especially if you accept. Now I can use that information to keep them in line - right? Keep them wondering and manipulatable.' Lucy actually likes this wit and plan well, says as much, instructs him to press his cigarette briefly to hers like the clink of a thin champagne flute. Then she opens her mouth to say something, but is glad Leonard had been turned in the other direction, apologizing for a sneeze into the hook of his elbow, as she would have regretted saying it and would not have been quick enough to have come up with any substitution if she had said 'Nevermind' and he had gone with 'No, please - what is it?'

As they walk - Lucy had demurely wrinkled her nose when Leonard had gestured at the light-switch, as though to ask did she want the honor of closing the lights on this last day of her first jaunt, so Leonard flapped the room dark, instead - Lucy says 'Do you know any reason that Petra wasn't here, today?' He is as surprised as Leonora had seemed. 'Where was Petra? What do you mean?' Lucy tries to lighten the tone of the chat, now fearing she is bringing trouble down on Petra's head. 'It's just she wasn't in my thing, today. Otherwise she was in class?' Leonard nods, no-big-deal to the gesture, says Petra had been in Morning Assembly and in his class, offers that maybe she had had an appointment and signed out - they could always go check. Lucy Naws that suggestion aside with a puff of breath. 'It's hard to imagine her missing you for anything short of a gunshot, though, so it must have been something.' 'Yeah?' Lucy makes a face as though this is of passing interest, but only in a moot-court sort of way. 'She seemed to like the class - or whatever we want to call it? I'm glad.' Leonard, face one big you've-got-to-be-putting-me-on, explains that Petra had, by all evidence, only just started living and breathing upon Lucy's arrival. 'We figured you'd spiked her punch or something, man. One minute' - he holds his palm open - 'the next minute' - he snaps his fingers, the whole visual example a curiosity Lucy refuses to bother trying to plumb. 'That's terrific. She's really quite the little poet.' 'Is she?' Lucy makes an expression meant to convey this is so obvious to her she cannot imagine it is the first time Leonard is considering it. 'I admit, we had no idea about that girl for a long time. The poetry stylings of Lucy Jinx were the medicine, it seems.' Leonard holds the door open - overly slacker, overly boyfriend - and nods to a group of other teachers off at just a distance, all of whom look over as though acutely aware and pleased by the existence of Lucy. She checks. No. She recognizes none of them from anywhere.

The campus is a damned booby-trap! No sooner is Lucy free from the encircling small-talk barrage of faculty than she rounds this corner and has to duck back because there is Leonora. Wait. Are you hiding from a teenage girl, Lucy? 'So what if she is!?' Lucy imagines a gallant voice coming to her aide. It seems odd, is all. 'It doesn't seem odd, not even a tiddly bit' her defender protests. 'Lucy has a lot going on in her head. And that Leonora has some sycophantic tendencies that would flare up like allergies if Lucy strolled by and seemed to be unencumbered, to have even five seconds to spare!' Now, in truth, Lucy doesn't feel precisely that way about Leonora - yes, she believes what she just thought is accurate, but not that it equals the full measure of the girl. Not that that is why you are avoiding her, Lucy. 'Leave Lucy alone' Lucy's defender now grit-teeths. 'Yeah, leave Lucy alone' Lucy says, eyes placating the shadow at her feet and the same shadow where it sharp-angles up the wall, there. The door to the building won't open here - so she is trapped, has to weather this out. So out comes her phone - the easy excuse. It takes a full minute to start up - she doesn't remember having shut it off, but cannot argue with presented reality - and starts vibrating with messages that came in since whenever. Glance over her shoulder: is no one in there who can open this door for her? Life is never like a generic film script when one most desires it to be! Where is a generic-janitor-sort to see her and friendly-nod-shamble over and politely bow his lowly-sort *Thank you* for the privilege of aiding out his better? The real trouble is: Lucy feels it would be in bad form, just now, to speak admonishingly of the world, to call it *Shit-pants unfair* or whatever else. Yes, technically a number of positive things had happened to her today. And so she has to mind her pints and quarts, she knows she knows. Even though she knows there are many other shoes still to drop and a piper to pay for the tune someone else had called.

Message from Elliott: *I'm very sorry I yelled.* Message from Elliott: *I just don't know what to do and I don't see why we can't meet and talk.* Message from Elliott: *Where even are you? I'm honestly worried. You don't work at Stella's anymore, either?* Message from Elliott: *I will stop texting, I promise, but I'm not going to stop trying to find out where you are. What are you doing, Lucy?* Message from Elliott: *Do you hate me this much? Really?* Message from Elliott: *I'm sorry.* All of these messages have good blips of time between them, but still Lucy reads them as a consecutive ranting. Which is not out of line. Elliott would have seen what she had written previously and would have known how long it had only been since. And when Lucy says *good blip* she means *interval of twenty minutes, half-hour.* She shakes her head, returning to the messages. To the one not from Elliott. The one from Melinda. *Are we going to celebrate, my official compatriot? So glad it worked out! I'm at your disposal, Madam Adroit.* What a world, right Lucy? She puts her phone away and isn't sure she should light a cigarette. Though, hadn't those other teachers been smoking? She is on campus, but after hours. Or she thinks so, anyway. And she had just smoked in the headmistress' office, so can always claim confusion because of that - wrong assumption, be let off with a warning. There is the cigarette pack in your hands, Lucy Jinx. And there you are, putting it away. How neutered of you! The weight in your head is five corpses high! But at least, when you do peek out, Leonora is gone. Best to wait another few minutes. So you might as well respond to Elliott. What is the best play? Certainly, Lucy isn't afraid she will relent in her stance of aloof cruelty just at the sight of Elliott, so what harm in seeing her for coffee? Do it like a One-Act, right? Write your script in advance and stick to it, even if Elliott's lines seen non-sequitur. Eventually, she'll be overpowered into compliance. Verbalize her into a whelp, eh? Lucy texts: *If you'd like to, I can do coffee tomorrow. Around two. Let me know and I will tell you where.* That's good? It's fine, Lucy. Nothing given away, no clues. You keep the advantage and haven't committed to anything that could stoke up your guilt.

Observed from one block away, the school seems like it could be anything, really. The palatial off-world quality is absorbed into the environment around it, sopped up like sausage grease by a mildewy sponge. Part of Lucy is walking so slowly because she is spooked she won't be able to find the place again if she passes out of natural eyeshot. It will be revealed that she had been sadly mistaken for a special sort who can see extra angles in reality, the sort who would be able to identify this institution most mortals overlook due to poor evolution in the lobes of the brain in charge of observation. Lucy might have only by accident become temporarily magical or science-fictioned. If it could happen in a story, if could happen in reality - that is the tacit deal between those two things. Maybe she had had a particular stomach flu and her body immune-systeming it off had increased the count of some chemical composition flowing around in her blood and when Leonard had seen her at work he had instinctively offered her a way into the company of his kind. All had gone well, because being around - touching, breathing the same air as someone rife with this state - had kept her infection at bloat - then she had breathed the concentrated air of the interior of buildings and touched papers and read words written by all sorts of fellow-afflicted, her body almost accepting its influenza as baseline. Now, though? She would be away a good while. Night sweats and hydration would rid her of the connection! Her lymph nodes would return to paper-flat and the extra words in her language would wither like office-party balloons! These are the fears of Lucy Jinx on a day like today. Maybe even her draw to the headmistress was just some imperative tick of needing to mate, but the draw anchored in the reproductive organs of the bacilli her every fluid is currently swimming in. Her sick attracted to a more fertile home soil - a seed that knows it is surviving in a fallow place and had better run to the first new verdant. Yes. Lucy Jinx thinks this. This is exactly how it goes.

Now a cigarette. Now a cigarette. How many times? How many many times? That phrase, that gesture, it is more common than wine to Lucy. Now a cigarette. Like a capital at the start of her every new sentence. And like every comma, hyphen, period, too. Or rather: not like any of those things, but like every lowercase! Her life, if she were keen to argue, could be seen as a series of Subjects controlled by the Predicate *and then a cigarette*. Nothing to the particulars of the lead-in except it gets to the punch. Look at all that had just happened in the last four hours and she is honestly able to all but summarize it: *Now a cigarette*. The title of her autobiographical novel! The name of the actress that gets the lead in the film! What her barcode rings up as when scanned! How many turns it takes the can-opener to cut a circle 'round her tin! *Now a cigarette*. Remember Petra? *Now a cigarette*. Remember Leonora? *Now a cigarette*. Remember all those things all those kids read that they never would have been able to write if it hadn't been for you - you - Lucy Jinx - you, Lucy Jinx!? *Now a cigarette. Now a cigarette!* Is that the rest of it? The headmistress? *Now a cigarette*. They are offering to pay for you to become an actual educator? *Now a cigarette*. You have been asked back and are a word on the lips of students and faculty at a place you'd not even heard of three months ago? *Now a cigarette. Now a cigarette!?* You don't even like the taste, Lucy - and have you ever? It was always so much persona, these things, so borrowed, so other people's much nicer coats you covet from afar and try on by pretending to shiver at some outdoor party. *Now a cigarette*. And now and now and now. She looks at this one and her emotion snaps in the other direction. It seems so fitful and timid. A kitten mewling, soaked by rain, a thing that would die beneath a parked car if not for her coaxing it out, giving it a soda-capful of coffee creamer she takes from a gas station. Deworms it. Makes it her own. *Now a cigarette*. Long inhale. Longer exhale. Again.

COFFEE-SHOPPED NESTLED, LUCY FEELS quite the scofflaw. There is a sense of escape, underserved, from crimes she does not know the exactitude of. Good word. She writes it down on a napkin. *Exactitude*. Obviously something somebody trying to sound smart made up one day and carried in to practical use on the strength of their pure audacity. *Exactitude*. Scholars and smarty-pants, every one of them, must still cringe at it, do contortions to avoid it, hope - as they teeth-chatter with sheets pulled up past their chins abed each night - that it isn't *Exactitude* they hear, skulking its way, skeleton horror, up their darkened stairs - or else there already, that shadow they cannot quite account for lurking on the wall, opening like a millipede mouth every time a car passes on the street and the headlights animate all darknesses arc-wide across the room! *Exactitude*. 'Yep' Lucy says and also, for that matter, likes the word *Scofflaw* but does not write it down. What's the plan, Lucy? 'To do nothing' she says, disguising it as the blow into the overhot - still - of the coffee in her overhot cup. Nothing at all. Work tonight, certainly, but that is not technically until tomorrow. Just a gaping day, the space left from the flesh Lucy gored away with hacks at her obligations. She has none, now. She is powerful. Rhinoceros! Gush of an open hydrant! And deserving to be, she thinks, taking a sip not the least bit pleasant of the burnt-toast smelling brew. That is maybe the most interesting new glaze over things. *Deservingness*. While it could be argued that Lucy did not so much accomplish anything - but rather simply decided to explode the world she had built and shook hands to be a component part of - she, for the first time in a long time, does not feel she needs to induce that argument, herself. No one is arguing. Not even her in her head. Lucy Jinx in agreement with Lucy Jinx. The only-just-so-recently earlier of so much jostling, rising fear over how she might be in the process of being railroaded into some new condition she'd find herself locked in has settled to the assumed and permanent calm of the silt-bed at the very bottom of the bottom-of-the-sea.

That woman, there, being shown to her seat by a patient waitress and, in turn, patiently helping her not-elderly-but-certainly-old mother out of a too-warm coat and into the booth seat. That woman takes the chair at the other side of table, but obviously wants a cushioned booth, too. Her face, this woman, smoothed around the eyes and mouth from there-is-no-point-really-in-saying-anything-to-her-mother - too smooth, eroded to something perverse, like a glass shore long lapped by a freshwater ocean. Lucy once had a mother. Or always had, is the better term. Always had a mother. In her case, the expression carrying a sour poetic - the *Had* permanent past-tense, Lucy's mother a thing existent but no memory of Lucy ever feeling in possession of. It is this soft weakness of feeling free for ten minutes that is making Lucy watch and observe. To align herself to this and find succor in it. Those two cannot have anything to say - and if they do, something is askance. It is the natural progression: away, never closer. Lucy, the most natural of all. Never close, nevermind closer. Her coffee has lukewarmed twice, as she seems incapable of drinking it down more than a third or so - just enough the waitress always tops it off, just enough top-off to make it all seem warm again, not hot. What a little poem, eh Lucy? See how your thoughts and that mechanism of coffee refills go together? Actually - no, Lucy doesn't see that. But is perturbed, because when she thought the question it felt like she'd hatched a really dynamite correlation! The woman, there, seems to wish the mother would just admit they have nothing to say and release them both from this - what? twice-a-week? - contracted ritual. The not-exactly-old mother wants to do it. But doesn't want the daughter to want it. And can see in the smooth face - the face she has smoothed out of all its possible earned imperfections - the want. 'The want' Lucy toasts them, coffee lukewarm. Down a third. Waiting for a top-off.

'Ms. Jinx?' Lucy turns. Petra! Who seems to have been standing there shyly for some time. But Lucy is too 'Oh my gosh, Petra!' and scootching out of her seat, arms already opened for a hug, to feel self-conscious, voyeuristically compromised. Petra keeps one arm crossed and her limp other hand up in its flag-at-ease wave until Lucy insists on the hug, a straining wide of her arms and a 'Petra!' said with gleeful, stubborn stamped foot. Petra holds the hug long, though - in fact, Lucy is not sure exactly what to do about it - and after the second casual attempt to step back - resulting in a tightening of Petra's arms and head above Lucy's right breast - she decides to tighten her portion of the embrace, as well. This goes on for some time. No sign of tears - either having issued or swelling-having-been-tamed - when Petra does remove herself, abrupt, and plops herself down in the booth opposite a slowly-getting-to-place Lucy - but no words are said either, and that, maybe, is as much an indicator of the suppressed waterworks as the waterworks unsuppressed. Not that that matters - why are you focusing on that, Lucy? Had you expected tears? Lucy speaks first - now - the basic, most apparent salvo to open with: 'I am so glad you bumped into me! I was worried sick when you weren't there - I asked everyone where you might have been! Everything okay?' Petra nods, expressionless, then breaks into a smile the terms of which are difficult to place. 'What?' Lucy asks. 'I didn't bump into you' Petra says this while tucking some hair behind an ear, hair behind another, untucking both, scratching the back of her head 'I followed you.' Lucy Hmns, appreciatively, and gives Petra a raise of her coffee-cup. 'Even better, then. Though you did miss a good speech. Or were you at the door, cup to your ear?' Petra shrugs, admits she was bummed to skip the class, figured Lucy would say something hugely important. 'But I can't deal with goodbyes in such a pointless setting, you know?' Lucy does know. She doesn't say so beyond sighing out her nose and giving Petra a knit-brow, but Lucy does know.

Lucy can see that Petra is writing something on one of the napkins - can see Petra was annoyed to discover the napkins had the logo of the coffee-shop printed both front and back, smiled at the agitated growl she could not hear - while Lucy is at the counter getting the hostesses' attention after she doesn't see her waitress, right away, giving a point to where Petra is, saying 'My friend showed up, if you could send someone over.' The hostess nods, cubby cheeked, and Lucy returns, Petra still scribbling away. 'And what is my Illegible Sparrow illegibling there?' she asks. Now: this is the first time Lucy has called Petra this - the first time either of them, outside of e-mail correspondence, have made the slightest admission of their knowing each other other than as *Ms. Jinx* and *Petra*. Now: Lucy is butterflies tangled with moths about this and is rather staggered - yet oddly still uncertain - when Petra - not missing a beat - chuckles back 'No, no - I'm sparrowing this one, it's perfectly legible.' Petra had not looked up. That chuckle could have been just about what-a-weird-thing-Ms-Jinx-just-said and the return of *Sparrowing* to *Illegibling* could well have been Petra exercising quick wit - wit made double whip-smart due to attention being caught to a task. Snap: Petra hands the napkin across and Lucy knows she is hoping to recognize it as something previously sent to her over e-mail, straight away, but she doesn't. And while it seems to fit Illegible Sparrow's style, Illegible Sparrow's style was rather all-over-the-place. As was this bit, here - it seemed offhand, referential to this very sit down at this very coffee-shop. Lucy is unsure how to respond, so reads it twice and sets it down. She looks at Petra and smiles. 'You're a better poet than me' she says. Which succeeds, visually, in unfooting Petra at least - and so Lucy doubles down by silently folding the napkin and putting it into her wallet, air of there-is-something-I-see-in-this-more-beautiful-than-you-meant, something that to ask for further comment on would make Petra feel small.

Within five minutes, Petra motions for Lucy to lean in close, coy eyes grandfather-clocking as though to make sure the two of them are utterly in confidence. 'What's up?' 'Since you're not my teacher anymore, could I have a cigarette?' Lucy is unable to stop the laugh, pulls back her head to let it blat, then gets herself composed and hunkers back down over the tabletop where Petra is still slouched. 'Have you ever even smoked a cigarette?' Petra nods a smooth-as-silk 'Oh yeah' wriggling two fingers meaning *Therefore gimmie-gimmie*. 'Then why don't you have your own?' Lucy brats, Petra ready with the play-along 'Because I'm just kid and have never met any cool grown-ups. Until. You.' The *You* is just mouthed and a finger-pistol shot off to emphasize, little Pop sound to an extra mouth-open made after the unpronounced word. 'You're so artful, aren't you?' Petra shrugs. 'But it just betrays the fact that you're full of shit and now I think you're merely working some bamboozle - nothing but a cheapskate.' 'Maybe I should have gone with *Cheapskate Barn Owl* or something, right?' Petra blusters, not relenting in her you-know-you're-gonna-give-me-the-cigarette stare. 'I don't know about you, Illegible.' 'Well, that's the best thing to know, right?' 'What is?' 'That you don't.' Lucy has to allow for a pause to give the gal points on that finely built contraption of back-and-forth fun, does so, then changes tactics to 'I don't even have anymore cigarettes, kid. You've been watching. You saw me chim-chimney my way over here.' But Petra ain't buying it, Lucy, and gives you an admonishing tsk-tsk to which you finally bend. Last trick: 'You can have the smoke, Sparrow, but I've been asked to stay on at the school. So it's not *Goodbye*. Meaning: you'd better be able to keep a secret. That something you can manage?' Petra opens her mouth, tentative, then quizzes Lucy's gaze, eyes warming, softening, resetting indecipherable. 'I can keep pocketfuls of secrets, Ms. Jinx. And I have others buried under the porch.'

Petra lets Lucy light the smoke and they have agreed to smoke out back of the shops, at least, Lucy taking the hit by straight up admitting - yes, yes - she was not quite ready to just strut and stroll down Quaint Street with her underage Joe Camel cohort. 'Who's *Joe Camel*?' is the first thing Petra asks once they have had a few drags. Lucy blinks, it taking a moment to remember she had made the reference, only five minutes ago. 'That's the big question on your mind, these days? *Who is Joe Camel?*' Petra explains how she has always been curious about Camels and defensively accuses Lucy of trying to put down on her by making it seem silly - to which Lucy put palms together in obsequious bow-gesture of begging one-thousand pardons. 'You talk to yourself - a whole lot' Petra next tosses out. 'You've met me - wouldn't you talk to me if you were myself?' Petra takes a moment to dubiously mouth back this question, giving it a palm-down hand wobble iffy-at-best sort of critique. 'Yes, I talk to myself. I bet you talk to yourself, too. If you manage to still keep it all internalized, currently' - Lucy touches hands proudly to her chest, right about collar bone - 'well, may I present *Your Future*. The hands on your clock will come to here, my friend, I've no doubt.' A car rounds the lot and lulls at a distance, Lucy instinctively ducking her cigarette behind her back, it taking a moment to register that Petra is not doing the same. 'Don't worry' Petra smiles, noticing Lucy's noticing 'I'll tell them I gave you permission if they get gruff with us.' Then Petra yells 'Busy bodies!' and zaps a vulgar gesture, but the car - windows tinted - doesn't seem to register it - or, if it does, doesn't care. 'What do you talk about?' Petra asks Lucy, flicking her stub at the wall, stepping it out where it lands after bouncing. 'But give me another before you tell me, yeah?' Lucy watches the car pull away while she gets out her pack and tosses it at Petra, who obviously had not been expecting it, the pack hitting her chin and dropping to the floor. 'Asshole' Petra says, crouching, snatching pack, popping up straight. 'You're very different, today' Lucy says with a long slow out of smoke. 'Am I? Than what? This feels about the same?'

Lucy has fallen into Petra's lead. By twenty minutes into the stroll, she has no idea where she is. Nor does she care. She sees, as they wait out a traffic signal, a secondhand bookshop called *The Mahogany Pawnbroker* and takes out her phone to text herself the name. Obviously, as soon as the light turns, that is where Petra leads her. 'We can't smoke in there, because though it is a bookshop they don't understand books - but you can't come in unless you promise to keep lighting me up.' This bravado, Lucy - you do know it's all insecure puffery, yes? Petra is about as substantial as the nuance of a six-year-old's very neat picture of a house - yes, it's fantastic that it is drawn to portray inside and out simultaneous, but that's only because the child understands the object and not how to accurately depict. 'At least you're not resorting to blackmail, already.' 'No' Petra proud-of-herselfs 'not yet.' Lucy extends a hand and they shake - and, child Lucy is, in her head she hee-hee-hees that she did not propose an oath so can, on technicality, wriggle out of handing over anymore smokes if she feels like being an agent provocateur. The bookshop is wonderful and goes the full three stories up. Lucy gets peeks in at the bottom of the stairwell, at the second-floor landing - the place getting warmer and the vinegary tang of so many musty volumes growing thicker as she and Petra ascend - but does not get to take in a room proper until they reach the top and Petra leads her to a corner section marked *Discount Theatre*. Petra says 'This is my place' and does a kind of embarrassed curtsy and head-tap to indicate the signage 'Come in.' All smiles, Lucy moves in to the narrowing cranny - something of an optical illusion about how dark it gets, as though walls close in on approach to the shelves at the rear-wall though nothing actually physically indicates this is so. 'How long have you lived here?' Lucy asks, picking up a copy of *Oleanna* - watersoaked, notations from a previous owner leaked all over the faded text on the pages - priced at ten cents. 'Oh I don't live here. This is where I came to die.'

'Can I kiss you?' Lucy honestly didn't register the question, immediately. 'Nope.' See: Lucy is reading *Rug Comes To Shuv* by Duncan McLean and Petra has been sitting, quite in her own world, reading *Best American Short Plays of nineteen-eighty-seven*. So, Lucy rather assumed Petra was reading aloud. That the line would either be followed by another or that, in a moment, she would admit to Petra she did not know the context, which play it was from, and so apologize for not responding with appropriate style. 'Please?' There is Petra. She is actually asking the question, Lucy. With the look only someone exactly like her and exactly that age can have as accompaniment. And now she is moving closer, obviously having assumed the *Yes* - obviously meaning *Why the fuck wouldn't she so assume, Lucy?* On your toes, now! Lucy doesn't say anything. Touches Petra's shoulders to stop the forward momentum. Touches her chin to stall. Touches hand over her - Christ, lips are that soft in youth, aren't they? a mix of ether and the meat of an orange - lips, three fingers, feeling the - steady now, Lucy - strawberry-half moisture and the never-been-so-dry dry. 'I can't kiss you?' 'No.' 'Why?' Just like that, Petra asks *Why?* Lucy! What are you supposed to do with that? What am I supposed to do with that? Tell her, Lucy. Just explain why - explain why not. 'Petra.' 'Sparrow.' 'Sparrow.' 'Illegible.' 'Listen.' 'Okay.' 'There is nothing I would rather do. Than kiss you. And I will write that in tattoo on the town charter, okay? But I think it might not be a very good thing for you.' Petra seems uncertain - no, what? disappointed? what? - looks down a moment, then up. 'I'm a Poet' she says. 'You do know that?' Lucy presses her fingers back to Petra's mouth, harder than before. And closes her eyes. And this time her fingers are pressing down, in fact, on to Petra's teeth, lips parted, Petra tensing jaw to make the pressure constant. 'You don't need to let me kiss you to know that, Petra.' Petra bites. And holds Lucy's wrist. Hard. Bites hard Lucy, who now has her eyes open. And who watches Petra - Petra's eyes closed - bite, eyelids squirming with ruptures of ell-over-eel-over-eel-over-eel of thought underneath.

Sidebar: This whole thing seems rather derelict, Lucy. Argument: Why? Evidence: You followed a student to a bookstore-corner and fed her your eager hand! Argument: She's not a student. Scoff: Isn't she? You just got a job offer and she's gonna be on the roster another two years - three? two? do you even know!? Argument: Well, look. Prosecutorial sneer: I think we've all done more than enough looking! Plea: You're railroading me. Further: And besides - I didn't take the offer. I'm leaving. In that case: Oh are you leaving? Oh that's still definite, then? Pointing out the obvious: What else would I still be doing here? And before you get sassy, I mean *Here* as in *Here with Petra* not - which would be silly to have said, I agree - *Here* as in *Here, still in this city*. Returning to the point: This is exactly why this derelict of you! You had been doing so well with the not kissing her - odd you felt compelled to add you wanted to - but then you ceded control to her teeth! Expansive gesture: But they're her teeth! Even you have to concede to that point! Further evidence: You don't feel this will, in future - recall, Lucy, time continues and moments tend to link to one another - swing 'round to some detrimental effect? Put upon: Come on. Piling on: You don't think she'll think something that isn't happening - and likely shouldn't be - is happening and then be sideswiped by your lack of still being anywhere around her? Counter: Or she could have just experienced a formative thing in her life! As she said - she is a Poet. What am I? Grime? Plague? Infection? When did I compact with society to not affect her the way I did? And to not be affected the way I have been? Eye-roll: And what way is that? Chest-thump: However! Final evidence: Look next to you, Lucy - you're walking and smoking in some flagrant city street afternoon with a teenage girl and have just of your own volition bumped her shoulder with yours and called her 'A real poison pen' - whatever exactly that's supposed to mean! Final argument: Just let me walk with her. Just let her walk with me. Jesus, who fucking cares?

So they walked and walked and eventually ran out of cigarettes. Then had to walk awhile, nothing to occupy their fidgets but hands to pockets and bodies a bit closer and a time then wide-hinge apart to point out this or that with their noses. It could seem quite otherworldly if addressed in certain languages or if it all happened under the stale sun of a resort hotel in a novel written in dense Scandinavian more than a century ago - humidity drenching all like poor lyrics to an otherwise addictively pleasant melody. Finally, we get to the part where Lucy goes in for cigarettes, her spine a loosening shoelace of 'Is Petra going to slip away, was her *I'll wait on this bench, here* a ruse?' And the part with the hurried-up transaction, impatienceful and snapping at the clerk 'To the left of those - over, over, yes, no, yes, that one!' Oh that is all fine and amusing! And then Lucy and Petra walk with a few more cigarettes gone through, between them. The universe is finite. Even infinity is finite, named, and one infinity is neatly tucked into another, pulled out of another - a bucket dumped into a bucket dumped onto a floor mopped up and rung into a bucket dumped into a bucket and spilled on a vaster floor! 'Hey' Lucy abruptly says, knowing full well she is going to end this all at a forthcoming Metro stop now that she recognizes the area she is in from - when? when does she recognize it from? - sometime. Petra stops. And Lucy cranes her head awkward, sideways - her ears gasping as though just cleared of public pool water - her lips finding Petra's whose seemed to have been opened and tongue at leisure waiting between them. The kiss goes on and has an undertaste of watermelon and mint. It goes on and Lucy let's Petra put her hands to her face and then into her coat pockets. Then some half-dozen lip tappings, just blink-touching each other. Petra's teeth chatter. Lucy's teeth don't. And Lucy says 'So you know I meant it when I said I wanted to - in case you thought it was a lie.' Petra's nose touching Lucy's - both noses running a tad - she is saying in that absent doodle way a young girl can, so indiscriminant to the warping expanse of the real world 'I don't care if it was a lie as long as you meant it.'

HOW MUCH LONGER IS THIS? From then to now? Just so that we may situate Lucy, first of all. How much time has passed? There is some *Zeno's Paradox* to this, some *Bootstrap Paradox*, some *Plato's Divided-Line*. Well, where is Lucy, then? Look: here is Lucy. On a Metro car and well aware of all that has gone on. The train is fatigue having at her head and trembles of sleep are rising and lowering up along the staircase of her. It has been an exhausting day. And she understands it has been. She is antsy - paranoid as a lake looking up at the sky, as the sky looking over its shoulder at the sky further on to another sky it is but which, to it, is called something-behind-it. More in particular - considering this only five or six Metro stops - it cannot be more than fifteen or twenty minutes. Since Lucy boarded the train. But since the kiss, how long? Let's imagine up a number so gargantuan it would take forever to express it. About that long. Or a number so infinitesimal it would take forever to express it. About that long. Noddering, noddering, all these things seem so simple to Lucy. Large-beyond-measure takes up the same space as small-beyond-measure. As in to say each, on paper, would contain the same amount of Zeros - so many that by the time they are read the fact that there is one One at one far end and one One at the other far end of the first Zero becomes irrelevant. Eventually a list of numbers flips itself over. That's math. You can only look at something so long before you aren't. Atomically. See? Stare at the same person for seven years, they have changed every atom. Freeze one moment of them and stare at it for seven years and it doesn't matter - you're not looking at anyone. And Lucy believes every atom of a photograph changes in seven years - or however long, the point is it changes - that some magnetism keeps atoms of the same color and size and import attracting to each other to bump out and replace. That's what Lucy thinks. Lucy Jinx: all but asleep on a train.

Let us not beat glibly around this: Lucy is in crisis. It could be avoided, saying so - she could avoid admitting so - as there is so much else of her to observe - let alone observing her-in-the-physical-world-around-her, let alone her-in-the-psychological-or-the-representative - and much fun could be had abstracting all of those things down to pleasant-to-poke-at renditions. But: she is in crisis. She can only feel her lips and her suddenly too pin-tip-heated awareness of herself. The scope of her crisis: imagine you are told the color of the exact moment you started down a wrong path - the color, but nothing else - and it was a color-name you had never heard. Say, for example, *Mirle*. The color *Mirle*. Then you look around for a picture of *Mirle* but no two pictures are of the same color, not exactly - and most of them appear to be *Vermillion* to you, anyway. And in saying that, you admit how even each *Vermillion* seems different. But you are told 'The moment was exactly *Mirle*. The color *Mirle*.' Even if you could never track down the moment this knowledge would titillate and then haunt and then torment you - and then the lack of specificity would come to define you. Because until being told this - and you trust it, it is told definitively, as by a God speared to your forebrain - you had no inkling of any specific of the moment you took the wrong path but now you at least know what color it was! Even if you don't know what it means 'The moment was *that* color' - what it means to name a moment's color

- you still know something definitive about the definitive wrong step which has become the definitive step, full stop, of you. This is the crisis of Lucy Jinx. Imagine: you are eventually shown an example of *Mirle* and it no longer looks *Vermillion* - enough dissimilarities to *Vermillion* exist that your brain now births the registering of *Mirle*. But *Mirle*, like *Vermillion*, in each instance you are shown is a slight little spec off - an atom, two, some weight of color - no representation exactly the same. Then enough *Mirles* line up, as did enough *Vermillinons*, that your brain differentiates another color - not *Mirle*, a nameless one. Still, no specific *Mirle*! The focus on it unfocused it and now you are left with the most indefinite, unnamed thing. You could name this new thing, but it already has a name. You think it already has a name - most likely it does. But nobody else you meet can think what to call it. They say 'Mirle' 'Vermillion' - they say any number of colors with mouths all Maybe and you say 'Thank you' as best as you can. You've forgotten what else you were doing. You care only about the name of this new color you are not even certain is new. This is what we mean by 'Lucy Jinx is in crisis' - no one is taking it lightly.

Lucy debarks from the platform and the spell of her woe is broken by her inability to clear the cobwebs of her half-asleep, her inability to smoke down in the station, and the realization that - beyond this large-bloomed crisis - her diddling with Petra for hours has led to the more irritating matter of she does not have her clothes for work with her. Because, Lucy, you had meant to return home. After the class. To nap. Maybe nap in the bath. To change at your leisure and get to the graveyard shift in plenty of time. Is this an impossibility, now? Oddly: no. Looking at the time - setting her distrust of clocks on one side - she finds she could get home, change, get to the hotel in plenty of time still. If she sprung for a taxicab, she could even likely still nap - or at least waste all the hot water in the shower on a single tense point of her neck, not even lather her body, just let the scalding massage that one sore spot into overcooked gruel. Why did you kiss Petra? 'That's the least of my troubles, right now' she retorts in her head. And she wonders: is it? Lucy doesn't think Petra is doing anything but living like the expanse of existence around the first wet shaking of a hatching's fluff. Petra is not souring to Lucy - quite the opposite, she's coming into normal dimensions and recognizable shape of Petra-in-time-and-space maybe for the very first time. So what Lucy kissed her? It was actually terrific. Leave it at that. And now Lucy is up an escalator and deciding if she will cab home or buy a new outfit. See? Her faculties are admiringly intact! Solutions upon solutions like apples budding grapes abound! That is quite exactly what Lucy Jinx will do. Her instinct of avoiding Home at a time like this kicked in, nick-of-time, and she can see a franchise clothing store, there, humble as a cloudless dawn.

Had Lucy asked herself why she had kissed Petra? As in - what? - why Petra as opposed to anyone else? Why Petra, specifically? Lucy has kissed many people. Why is there such a difference here? And don't feed me nonsense about age - don't let's pretend the world is so finite and that we actually become keys jammed in the wrong doors as we age. Isn't the distinction between Now and Then the exact same as Then and Now? A direction works the same as another and time moves backward at the exact same pace as forward. Oh stop talking in riddles, Lucy! Stop it! She crossed up the curb and decides to smoke before getting an outfit. And she isn't talking in riddles. But she will stop, because she has nothing to defend. She wants her head to be someone else's so she can have the pleasure of bashing it in, stomping it fractured with sharp-heeled tap shoes. In fact, instead of begrudging her her every happiness, why doesn't life just piss off and not crowd around her like the last street-lamp all the billions of moths want to die upon? The pressure of keeping a running tab of her is draining. And it is nothing to do with Petra! Lucy is bludgeoning her pleasures in the defense of the things that truly are upsetting her. Why had she said she would take this job? Is that it? 'That is it' she cigarettes, hiss thin as a number line. That was a mistake. It was all a mistake she should have seen coming. Why had she let the idea of something accomplished and permanent get all over this perpetual impermanence she had made up her mind so firmly - once-and-for-all - to take on forever? She feels like bark, mushrooms in dingy mustard half-circles up her lower lengths in an eczema, twines of poison sumac tighted around her upperest branches like frayed ropes that are really worms covered in carpet-rubbed cat hair. She flicks her cigarette and it hits right against the window of that parked car. In that window she sees only a bizarre half-cow-lick of her fun-housed reflection. But out of the tail-pipe, she sees rising exhaust.

'I don't think this is the place that had that jingle' the woman in the blue says to the woman in the pencil-grey - and the woman in the pencil-grey mostly hums, though does include a few words, of some partly-remembered television commercial song for this shop. 'You're definitely confused' the woman in blue says. The woman in pencil-grey tries to get the full jingle - evident how she is trying to force-feed the store name into the melody line - gives up abruptly and asks the woman in blue 'Whatever happened with Jeremy's kids? Did they get into' but Lucy doesn't pay attention to the rest of that, now holding a skirt against herself, observing her length in a tall mirror mounted to a pillar. Of course, the garment will not fit her like that. This is something Lucy would mock: some woman trying something on as though a paper doll that just needs something as flat as herself pancaked atop. She sets the skirt down, choosing the same style in herringbone, and gets some textured tights from a display - *Ruby* the color says - which she puts down immediately to take up another pair - *Carrot*

*Wine* the color of these - and decides to let one of these bored-to-tears sales-associates pick her out a blouse. 'For an occasion?' 'First night of work. Which sadly is nowhere near as sinful as it sounds.' The joke is repeated through overwide smile to another sales-associate who passes - this associate proclaiming 'That's so funny!' in a tone of high-and-mighty, not having even paused in her passage as the thing had been related. 'Where do you work?' 'A hotel. *The Elizabeth Bishop*.' The sales-associate had once dined in the lobby restaurant. 'With a man I didn't marry' she adds as though supplying the perfect brushstroke of context. 'Good for you' Lucy says - the blouse the woman is holding against the tights as though to satisfy herself the colors go well is atrocious, but Lucy stays herself from saying so - and the woman perks to the first real-life attention she's given all evening, most likely, saying 'Thank you! You're awesome. Everyone always says they're sorry, first.' 'Idiotic default' Lucy somber nods. 'Men have the charm of dry floors around *Wet Floor* signs, you know?' And the woman says 'Exactly. Exactly!'

As usual, all it took was one ordinary interaction to set things back unaskance. Things like that - purchasing an outfit - are the abundant regular of Lucy Jinx's life. You only needed to remind yourself of how common you are, Lucy. As rare as a lucky penny, right? Normal as thinking face-down is bad luck. And it cannot be denied how if Lucy took all of the moments of her life she thought transgressive or unfit for display - the curios, the one-offs - and listed them on paper, it would only take up so many sheets, while if she listed her moments of ordinariness - even just all the occurrences of any single one of them - it would take reams and reams. Odd things only seem so volatile when they are new - because when they are new they are exploding. After awhile, though, they have no impact - they are just places where something once exploded, now the most uneventful places of all. Lucy Jinx: you go to shops. Lucy Jinx: you drink coffee. Lucy Jinx: you wear the same socks for years. Lucy Jinx: you squint when you pass Laundromats. Lucy Jinx: you memorize phone numbers only long enough to dial them, surprised every time if the proper party picks up the line. Lucy Jinx: as a kid you spread white glue with your fingers instead of a Q-tip, like shown - as everyone did except the friendless schulb at the one table that always seemed in the part of the classroom where overhead lights were not lit. Lucy Jinx: you chew your fingernails. Lucy Jinx: you often love reading the synopsis more than watching the shows. Lucy Jinx: you never honestly have a favorite drink, you just name different ones to say something. Lucy Jinx: you hate the same thing about your shoulders when you look at your back in the mirror, every time. Lucy Jinx: you never resist using name-tags as an excuse to see if flat-chested clerk-gals are wearing bras. Lucy Jinx: the last of the syrup stays in the fridge, unused for months on end. Lucy Jinx: when you wake up, your foot cramps. See all these things, Lucy? You are less fancy than a spit-shine. Uncommon as a broom bristle.

Now Lucy texts to Layla - double and triple-checking the phone is only sending the message to Layla - the following: *If hypothetically I just made out with a sixteen-year-old, would that be enough to bar me from Parliament? Margin-of-error: say she was fifteen, say she was seventeen?* Send? Too late, already have. It's best to get advice from someone amoral on such matters, promptly - Lucy should have texted Layla hours ago! Has it been hours, Lucy? 'An hour ago then, sheesh' she says, lingering in the space between a nail salon and a closed-for-the-day stationary shop. Preferably a soulmate. Who are always amoral. It is a requirement. No one wants a soulmate with an actual soul! There's some more dismal designation for that. Lucy can't think of anything witty, just at the moment, but pretends everyone has smiled, a few of them even privately smirking at something the remark stirs in their memories. Lickity-split, good old Layla, already vibrating Lucy's phone with response. *There's no way you're cool enough to have done that before me. Trick question. You owe me fifty quid.* Lucy starts a reply right away, then decides to light up first. Then she sends: *Did I mention I'm her high school poetry teacher?* And Layla replies: *Since when do you write poetry?* And Lucy writes: *You're being a turd.* And Layla writes: *You're being a paedo!* And Lucy laughs aloud and writes, cigarette stinging her eyes the whole time: *Just give me my fucking high five, already!* And Layla sends back five exclamation points to which Lucy decides not to reply. Yeah. Let Layla stew in it. Make her ache. Wonder why Lucy isn't continuing. Even let her start to wonder if it was a gag as it cements on her it was not. Lucy's phone vibrates. Layla has sent twenty-nine more exclamation points - Lucy counts them twice - to which Lucy writes back: *Why not thirty?* She steps out her smoke and lights another, something in her neck starting to ache, deep, and that vein she sometimes feels under her right eye standing up tall and grease slick. Lucy's phone vibrates. Exclamation point.

Lucy Jinx stops at a cookie shop - a franchise she had no idea still existed, one she used to frequent daily, fifteen years ago, sometime - to buy a coffee. Winds up buying a half-dozen semi-sweet chocolate chips, though, because the place has such an unstopped-in-to air to it, the proprietor - foreign, hangdog like a torn belt-loop - smiling in such a way as to let on he knew it was the only chance he had - smiling, smiling enough to hope this person will actually buy a cookie. 'You aren't hiring are you?' Such a brusque head shake! Lucy throws the cookies away, her only regret that there had not been a trashcan just outside the shop-door to use. And the coffee? Well, she needs the coffee. It was the cookies that were a charity case - charity once again nothing but a button-nosed pickpocket, it turns out. There is a paltry thin to the cold of the evening as it darkens enough that everyone will start, without exception, parting company with 'Good night.' Lucy looks up, surprised that she cannot see stars. There's the moon. Behind clouds no more substantial than fogged windshields - the glow of the circle a just-soured-milk tone, squiggles of the lunar surface visible in the way weed specks are in the first stirs of dark tea. And Lucy looks down, wondering what to do next. There should be something. But more than two hours until work. Today seems weeks ago. The traffic on the street seems a postcard on a guest-house refrigerator. You can get changed, Lucy. And yes, she nods, says 'Thank you' aloud, because that is a very good idea. She'd feel conspicuous if she changed at the hotel - the improvisational zeal of her outfit purchase would take on the pallor of I-want-to-impress. Today still seems weeks ago, though. Today feels like yesterday, actually - yesterday stuck in her throat like the thick drool of a slowly sucked lozenge.

Lucy had never been more incorrect in her judgement. The blouse the sales girl had chosen is a goddamned thunderclap! Briefly, she plays out a scenario of calling the shop, asking for the girl - the phone number and associate name are right there on the receipt - to gush her appreciation. Because that would be jolly to do! Big of her! Lucy Jinx, everyday-do-gooder! Theme song and everything! Against the color of the stockings? Lordy, the thing is like someone broke a Bible verse and it bled a perfect twist of licorice! This she feverishly taps into her phone. Oh she needs to write a whole poem, call it *Anna* - the associate's name - and deliver it to her semi-anonymously. What does that mean? Lucy explains: 'It means I would give it to a co-worker of hers on a day she did not work, not leave my name - I'd have been seen, so could be described, but would do my hair differently and wear a lot of mascara so those two things would be the most stressed elements of the description of me given. Semi-anonymous. There's lots of ways to do it!' And the stockings and blouse with the skirt? Lucy should be going anywhere but to work in this! This square mirror in this single stall toilet she has to stand against the wall of cannot do this outfit justice, of course - but even in these precise dimensions, in this spilt lemonade of fluorescent uncovered bulb, Lucy is nitroglycerin photographed a millisecond after being combusted. She needs new shoes and panties! These clothes are a new tongue in her neck! She needs a bracelet and a wedding ring to take off and leave on some bitch's bed-stand! Of all the times to look this resplendent, of course Lucy Jinx manages it when there is the least at stake - nothing to gain, as much purpose as lipstick kissed to chimney brick. *Anna*. It's even a good name for a poem. She stands looking at herself as she hears the door behind her tried, hears a sigh and can just picture the woman out there, shifting weight from foot-to-foot, wondering 'Would there honestly be trouble if I just used the Men's Room. Lucy Jinx: narcissus in reflection, chewing the knuckle of her thumb with her smile.

Lucy's personal theory: the number of stars is set. New ones only appear when others burn out. In the same moment. Based on nothing in Science, just based on the will of symmetrical aesthetic. The universe can be exactly halved, the same configuration of stars on each side, each side an odd-number. She doesn't know which number, exactly, but the last digit is Three. A boggling number, but write-downable. One could write it in a lifetime - less than lifetime, maybe it would take a decade at most, including time spent not writing. That the universe does not end, no, does not mean there are endless stars, endless planets - it, in fact, demands that those things have perfectly measurable quantities. Just Lucy's personal theory. And walking now, she feels so assured of herself she indulges in this reiteration of such a long held belief. She has never altered the way she articulates it, either, not since speaking to herself in the top bunk at Dorene's house that night. Looking at the crags of the stucco ceiling's face. Lifting her toes to snag along the sharps. Feeling Dorene's feet pushing up through the bottom of the mattress in cat-kneads then suddenly both feet, toes-at-point, prodding. 'I don't even think there is a Universe' Dorene had said. She had told Lucy that Lucy believed too much. 'But you believe in stars, right?' And what had Dorene said? What had she said? Lucy? What had she said? Lucy opens her mouth. Sees the image of the halved universe as she had first envisioned it - and the stars in a freckle pattern, spatter symmetrical even if not pictured distinct, more and more space between each as they got further from center, the most wayfarer ones the dimmest, blue instead of rose-white, the blotched clots overlapping the centerfold cinnamon-cracker brown. Lucy sees that same Universe. But what had Dorene said? 'She'd said' Lucy says. 'She'd said' Lucy repeats. 'I had said *But you believe in stars, right?*' Lucy says. Nods. 'Fuck.' What had she said!? It was nothing about stars, Lucy remembers that. But she doesn't remember what not-about-stars it was.

LUCY HAD BEEN SHOWN HOW to adjust the volume and how to select between several stations of the radio that pipes over the lobby speakers, but now she just blinks multiple times at the control panel and images from films about submarines dot through her head. It is not that Lucy is shy - she would press a button if it even seemed the least bit reasonable to do so - but this is matter of punching in a code-number to get to a little digital display-menu and then to scroll through low-tech display-letters with various pointillist icons adorning them. Just now, the lobby music is set to *International Mix* which, to Lucy's unrefined middle-of-the-night palette, seems to be one long song where the same male singer passes off a baton to the same female singer over and over, both of them trying to avoid huge bear-traps of a sudden brass ensemble, never able to do so, blundering headlong into the things and soaking in them as though they were cobwebs made of silk the consistency of maple syrup. She blinks. You need to sleep more, Lucy. You keep forgetting that. Much as you may like to think otherwise, you cannot go days-and-a-half-at-a-time without rest. You feel like you do, all the time. Fact: you don't. Lazy bones, an untouched garden rake, prongs thick with last year's leaves - that's Lucy. She sits and looks at the lobby doors. Automatic, most of the time, but on her shift will only open if she presses the button affixed under the desk where she sits to make them do so. Great button. Mobster-calling-for-backup button. Setting-the-magnet-to-the-roulette-wheel button. But going by the Check-In forms left on the back counter from the previous shift, she will have to press the button only four times, at most, tonight. Her gut tells her only once. Two of those supposed to arrive will be no-shows she'll file, at seven in the morning, in the stale, beige-metal bin where such things go. The other guest will show up past six, the doors by then back to automatic. The breakfast crew? Lucy doesn't let them in. They punch a certain code into the vestibule phone. Fancy.

Sometimes, Lucy thinks about feeling a Twick at her chest, looking down to find she has been impaled by an arrow. In reality, were she struck through the heart, would she even register the moment? Grasp the stiff of the arrow length? Go to her knees and have time to swim in a spill-of-milk-warmed-from-being-out-all-night feeling such like she believes a last thought would have. Or would that be it? No more Lucy. Instantly no more Lucy. All the commotion of her body falling and splaying and bleeding and all would be nothing to do with her. If she were struck in the belly, of course, she would live far too long. What a drag. And most of that time would be spent waiting for another arrow to finish her off. Headache of a death! Irritated and disappointed to the end! She would complain that it wouldn't even be a waste of an arrow - her assassins could come take it right back! They were just being lazy! They were just jerks, no way around that. And such indifference did not allow for her to believe they would wallow in even a shade of remorse. At least her death ought cause someone crisis. Especially considering the someone who had killed her had killed her with an arrow! All cards shown, she'd prefer - if she couldn't just snuff out instantly or have the brief eye-wide, knees-fell-to 'Is this the end?' eyes rolling back, jellyfish tendrils last gurgle of life scenario - to have some sadist porcupine her mercilessly, get off on her screams as arrows perforate gut and biceps, crotch, one through her jaw - but that one at an angle so that it doesn't ruin her throat, right away - one into her foot, maybe while she slowly drowns in herself. Yep. The monster would then watch as she tried to get some peace of mind, gather her thoughts in the belief the attack was over, and just as she was relaxing into something profound to think about as she finalizes, as she slips to radio static - ssssswwwwppppp - he'd brain her, special color arrow right in and out.

Now: Lucy is watching an animated paperclip look at her as though wondering what is the matter - it's hips out sassy, question-mark above its head, pointing at its wristwatch. The timer - which she has been told by management she can ignore - to this portion of the *Elsinore Corp Third Shift Training Module* is rolling up and up like the price at the pump if one were soaking the joint, ready to set it aflame. Really: it is a fancy little clock icon - like an old-fashioned analog thing, each place value number rolling as though printed on a rotating dial. A lot of work went into the ancillary graphics in these training modules. Lucy appreciates the hard work. No, she is not pretending that it is admiration for all of the various stances and expressions the perplexed paperclip takes in between word-bubbling hint-hint suggestions at her that is leading to her just sitting here doing nothing - it is just fatigue. 'It's laziness' she says, leaning back 'I can admit it' her fingers intertwining and shoving out above her, mouth gawping a most lustrous and enviable yawn. Tap. She chooses the correct answer! And blurts a 'Ha!' when the paperclip wipes its brow as though genuinely relieved. New question: *A guest can use a temporary State Issued ID or an ID issued by their work place at Sign-In. True. False.* The paperclip has reset to calm. Lucy thinks its vexation and wariness over her being employed by the company, as displayed in the previous question, should carry over, even just a little - the paperclip should seem willing to give her the benefit of the doubt - as though it has said 'Oh she could have gone to the toilet or been tending to an emergency call and just not been able to get right to that last question' - but should not look at her with naiveté, bosom-buddies anew. *False.* The paperclip tadpoles its way center screen and enlarges, word-bubble proclaiming *Terrific! While a temporary State Issued ID is Valid, a work place ID is not an acceptable documentation.* 'I know that, smarty' Lucy hisses 'that's why I chose *False*! Fucking paperclip' she cartoon panel mutters 'gotta be some show-off like I'd be nowhere without you!'

Sometimes, Lucy thinks about how it would go if she got hit with a hallucinogenic dart in her shoulder, but one that was coated so as to guarantee she would not feel the impact - and one that had such a concentrated dose of drug that even if she did register it hitting, her nervous system would be awash with the crazy-sauce before she could even scratch, as though only a mosquito bite. She thinks about it happening, now. Her face would warm and bloat like a cookie held dunked for too long, her eyes glugging under then blooping to surface while continuing to soak and slowly submerge, again. She'd have no idea, no idea - to her brain, this would just be the next thing that happens in the sequence of events that is Her. One moment: answering a paperclip's questions. The next moment: watching the automatic door give a Hellfire sermon about the bacteria-ladenness of ivory piano keys, the mat on the floor becoming a tongue that grows whiskers which, quick-as-a-wink, become coffee-cups filled with honey-bee legs more enormous than a kid thinks a whale is! Oh the blimp shaped mound of her heart would capsize and before long, for all it mattered to her, the skin-rash behind the shrink-wrap separating her from the sky will have been rendered in pastel and whole new children would be made out of gravel and come begging at the feet of their mothers, tears the exact size and flavor of potatoes but made out of hemorrhoid ointment and spread over the newspapers she'd be using to smother some cockadoodadooling grandmother with! As her blood became accustomed to the new juice that flowed through it, words would each take three generations to say and letters would revolt halfway through, only reconciling when it was far too late - and anyway, by then silence would be in vogue and so languages would be rendered of no more value than a dog biscuit would be to a deep-sea blob-fish. Never would she fear any of this! Her life would be like an overturned bookshelf, all the pages like flash-paper vanishing as they inelegantly pile, the screaming ghosts of each blue-bang giving Lucy just enough time to read them, but they'd be too loud - like the sound of cats knocking over pans downstairs - for her to understand a single word.

Still four Check-In forms. She reads them. One is already marked *Canceled*, so she pulls up the reservation on the computer. Tears up the sheet once this and that is verified. Hotel work is ludicrous. This guest is a regular - twice-a-week - but, at this hotel, most guests are regulars. During her paired training days, her supervisor had given her a brief synopsis of every person who entered or exited - Lucy had trained partially during normal hours, so there had been a lot of that. In fact, hadn't you been mortified that you were retaining none of it and worried you'd be booted out, sans ceremony, after two days alone, Lucy? Yes. But no one is around, overnight. That soon became clear. And clear it has remained. Lucy feels more like she works in the corner of a closed briefcase no one uses anymore than a hotel. That would, she nods to herself, be the profession she is best suited for. A piece of mechanical-pencil lead, snapped and left in a briefcase a businessman transferred everything out from into a new one and left on the top shelf of his bedroom closet. She'd be swell at that. Come to be known as the best in the field! The telephone rings. The ring indicating a *Room-to-Desk* call. 'Front Desk, this is Lucy Jinx, how can I be of service?' She still kiss-shivers at saying this, almost giggles a spit bubble. Hesitant voice 'You do wake-up calls?' 'I can program a wake-up call for you, sir. For when shall I?' 'They always work?' She smiles, leaning over the counter in a way that would be pleasant to observe from any angle, and says 'The phone will certainly ring, alright - I can guarantee that much. The rest is up to you.' Bah - humorless mope just abrupts 'Yes, of course.' Where'd the timidity go? And they settle on six twenty-five. He hangs up without so much as a *Thank you*. But: he's not a regular. 'That's his problem' Lucy down-her-noses while programming his call. The phone - *Room-to-Desk* - the same man, again. 'No, no sir - your room number comes up on the phone. I assure you the call is set. You have sweet dreams' - but the man doesn't hear past *Set* as he is too busy coughing his room number and hanging up.

By middle shift, the air in the lobby - especially behind the desk - seems to pressurize and stale - sort of humid and sort of dry, like full-to-the-brim with powder flecks of shook-around tissues. Swallowing starts to taste like it must in ones sleep. Lucy becomes pronouncedly aware of every time her fingernails touch against something and of the weight of whatever grime is in underneath any of them. Many quirks of physiology in a hotel overnight, sequestered to the front desk! The hum of the two fax-machines and of the juggernaut copier become physical, exactly how a sweater does when first put on. Her palms take on a wax-seal quality like old-fashioned candy, feel moist but are hyper-specifically dry when she curls her fingers around to rub along them. She stamps the hotel address stamp on some scrap paper in the same spot the same spot the same spot - after awhile is suspicious that no more ink is coming out, as though the stamp has caught on, refuses to waste itself at some madwoman's whims. 'You won't last a week, anyway' the stamp nana-bo-boos at her and she gets back at it the only way she can - by pressing it just once on many different sheets of paper - its teleological end does not let it resist if it is pushed to blank paper each time! 'Yes, Stamp: ontological argument demands this of you - I am educated, whereas you know nothing but this hotel name, address, telephone number, and how to be a wiseguy!' Stamp! Stamp! Stamp! The label says this stamp will stamp over ten-thousand times and Lucy wonders how many times that had to be physically tested, prototype stage, to be sure. It's a bold enough assurance - quite the proclamation - she does not imagine it was left equations on a page as proof - no, no, Laws-of-Nature, physical properties and all is one thing, but when it comes to a stamp, one will get down and dirty because the customers will demand proof. 'Proof!' Lucy bellows, giving the stamp a last Stamp! Her voice distinctly does not echo. The moment is weird. It's like she is the inside of the inside pocket of a coat realizing for the first time that that's what she's supposed to be.

Probably the overnight shift at *The Elizabeth Bishop Hotel* is the safest place for Lucy Jinx to be. If someone had thought of it, this is where she would have been put since the very beginning of her. Look, Lucy, at how many hours have passed and you have been wide awake, doing nothing, victim of no torment and not rubbing your poison out into anything else. You're better off here than most anywhere you've ever been. You should work out a deal where you sleep in a room all day, then come on shift. Kenneled. Quarantined. For the greater good! Hell, Lucy - you could probably convince them to let you if you say you'll sleep on the floor and not even use a bed pillow. You can bring your own pillow! And will even vacuum up after you wake! Lucy looks at the current *Vacancy Rate* - seems pessimistic to measure it by *Vacancy*, eh? - finds it to be forty-percent - well, not really, it's kind of motivating, in a way, going by *Occupancy* would make one complacent or fatalistic, like there's no foe to be trumped, just abstraction to war with - and looks through the records of a few days, jotting the numbers down to do a calculation before she sees a tab that will give her all of this information and much else. On average, the place runs at only thirty-percent *Vacancy*. But why had you wanted to know this, Lucy? Her eyes go left, go right, go left, look at the *Thirty Percent* on big display and some of the breakdown beneath it, then close. Why had you? 'Why had I?' she demands of life in general. This is certainly the best place for you, Lucy. No bones. You don't even need to know why you want to know things - you could flit around like a goose beak plumping rainy fields for worms. She adds up the few numbers she had jotted down, divides the total by the number of numbers. Forty-nine. 'Whatever that means' she mutters while writing out the word *Forty-nine* beneath the digits. Discovers she wrote *Forty-none*, instead. 'Exactly' she says. Tapes this to the desk to confuse the day-shift workers.

So that she can step out to smoke, she sets the lobby door to automatic - tests it a few times, still kind of scared when she takes the final stride outside - and tells the phone 'If you ring while I'm gone, tell them I'm in the shitter, okay?' It has rained and the world still being there at all is surprising. If it weren't still dark, Lucy would feel ruptured out of all continuity and might even start crying. A few taxies are already lining the curb, over there. The drivers mostly smoking their own cigarettes behind windshields, but some of them huddled together, there, in a conspiracy. *Conspiracy*. Lucy thinks that should be the official word for any group of cats. A *conspiracy*. Crows got *murder*. Geese got *gaggle*. Cats should get *conspiracy*. Or *treason*, she thinks. Some animal should get *treason*. Maybe it could just be a degree thing. Two-through-five cats is a *conspiracy*, while six-plus is a *treason*. Why Lucy does not have a position of esteem in linguistics is beyond her! Why she works at a hotel when she has such wisdoms to litter is a mystery! She tests the door. Still opens. Pauses. Closes. In which case, she will have another cig. Like a taxi driver. She wonders if she would bond easily with the one lady driver she sees or if it would be awkward - like that one hillbilly security guard she had humped up a big crush on but could never seem to get to cotton to her. A hillbilly security guard, Lucy? 'Goddamn right!' Those prison-ink tattoos on her forearms and the way she bad-postured everywhere and seemed to think saying 'Shit, I don't know what' to everything was always the best bet.

Lucy had wanted to shampoo her hair. Brush it. Slap her bare thighs with the brush back. Be ravaged amidst her nicotine-sour chest sweat and lay catching her breath in the heat of her underarms. She smiles. Calls herself weird. Steps out her second cigarette. Take up the stubs. Carries them inside and throws them in the pedestrian trash off the dining nook.

When the breakfast-crew finish up, one of them tells Lucy, tickled pink 'They found where than one plane crashed, you know?' Lucy nods as though she does and is glad that whomever can now have peace of mind. This man is a very interesting sort. On a subway, she would fear him - but on the walk home, she'd feel bad she did. When she saw his picture in the paper - underneath it a caption reading *Before taking his own life* - she would be both not surprised, relieved, and kind of happy - like the story had ended all according to his desires. The breakfast-crew is such an oddity - but then, they are never meant to be seen by the public. Because the staff of the restaurant proper are blue-blood dynasty inheritors with estates in both Essex and Yorksire. That place has a chef in charge who has been on the television. Lucy, you are as out of place here as the breakfast-crew. And this guy at least knew there was a missing plane! She watches him and the rest of his crew comrade out the door, all pausing the exact same seconds to light their cigarettes, milling a moment, then going off in each of them a different direction. Overhead, the lobby music volume diminishes. It takes Lucy a moment, still, to note it has also changed to the *Classical* setting. Someone would recognize this melody. She just imagines it must be Chopin or something. Not Bach. 'To many chords' she yawns, returning to her workstation. And then she Bachs the next few keyboard strokes, hearing the printer behind her start chugging, and says 'Bach didn't like chords - nope - learned that at school.' She collects the print-outs. Signs where she needs to. Pulls up the one screen she has to in order to jot down the numbers which display into the appropriate boxes - it had seemed so stinging to the man who had trained her that whoever had programmed the reports had not made it so that those numbers automatically print to the page! - staples the sheets and opens the stately entire-length-of-the-room cabinet - from afar one would never know that it opens at all - slipping them into the faux-leather divider silver-lettered with the name of this month.

'Good morning, this is *The Elizabeth Bishop*. My name is Lucy Jinx, how can I be of assistance to you?' The line breathes. 'Hello?' Not very professional, that, but Lucy cannot think of a fancy way to do a follow-up to her prestige-greeting. The line cuts out. But in a minute - if that - the phone rings again. 'Good morning, this is *The Elizabeth Bishop*. My name is Lucy Jinx, how can I be of assistance to you?' The line breathes. Breathes. 'Are you calling for *The Elizabeth Bishop Hotel?*' That's better, Lucy, make that your usual thing. The lines breathes. Cuts. This

time Lucy doesn't set down the phone, just taps the release to get a dial tone -
this all she can think to do to verify the phone headset is functioning. And she is
doodling a toss-away phrase she might put in a poem, thinking to herself how
she does find it kind of odd that anyone who calls the hotel always lets her - or
whoever - get out her entire mouthful of what amounts to just 'Hey, hotel,
what?' never speaking over her or seeming impatient - or overly impressed -
when the final question mark hits. The telephone rings. 'Good morning, this is
*The Elizabeth Bishop*. My name is Lucy Jinx, how can I be of assistance to you?' The
line breathes. Now Lucy feels she's been saddle-stitched into a short-story.
Atmosphere unleavened. 'Are you calling for *The Elizabeth Bishop Hotel?*' The lines
breathes. 'Hello?' This *Hello?* seems appropriate - anything else would seem
unhinged. The line cuts. And the front door opens, Lucy first startled at seeing
nobody there, then seeing the big brown dog, then the dog-walker catching it
up and pulling it away from the door, waving in at Lucy an *I'm sorry*. The phone
rings. She lets it go on a moment. Points at it in a friendly I-get-what-you're-
up-to, as though perhaps doing so will end the cycle. 'Good morning, this is *The
Elizabeth Bishop*. My name is Lucy Jinx, how can I be of assistance to you?' The
line breathes. Lucy just listens. Hoping that whoever is on the other end of the
connection is just as confused by her exactly repeated, no-change-in-demeanor
greeting as she is by their silence. 'Who is this?' She is too startled to feel startled
by the voice in her ear. 'This is *The Elizabeth Bishop Hotel*. Is that who you are
calling for?' The lines breathes. Cuts. And that is the end of it.


THIS IS THE THING: THERE is nothing unfounded about any of Lucy Jinx's
noias. On this train, here and now, she drowses and points this slumberingly
out with half-snore vehemence to herself and those she pretends are listening.
Things are always nearer than they seem, can be touching when it seems there
is no reason they ever should. No one knows how things are being moved and
manipulated. Sure, Lucy Jinx - or anyone - might try to put this out of mind,
but this reality is programmed into life from language - language from the
alphabet on up! The letter *B* is told it is part of the alphabet and has the alphabet
explained to it - it is always the letter *B* and in the alphabet is always just-so-far
from the letter *T*. The alphabet works like this: left-to-right. And even if one
could go past the end and - as if by magic - skip backtracking and start at the
front again, *B* would, in that sense, still always be just-so-far from *T*. These are
*the principias of the physical alphabet. B should feel entirely secure that it does not have
to be* confronted by *T*. Then suddenly: *Debt* has *T* right up on it, mouth this close,
practically teething. Or there is *Doubtful, T* there again, barring advance. There
is *Obtruded. Subtheme.* There are *Misdoubt, Unsubtle,* and *Bobtail.* 'How can this be?'

*B* will demand, hair-pulled out, fistful and graceless. 'Because of Language and Spelling' the letter *B* will be told. 'Your world will constantly be fluxing, this part to that - Before after After and After before Before. Not to mention foreign-tongues! And misspellings!' All the letter *B* can know is that no force can keep *T* from getting at it. So if Lucy Jinx thinks *This Moment* has no bearing or connection to *That*, *That Event* will not lead to *This Consequence*, she is going to find that the world will machine all manner of contortion to show her she is in the wrong! Life is the alphabet made into atoms and piled up tetterously. And who knows what words are being come up with, what their spellings will be! If whoever is writing will get the spelling right, even! Hell, sometimes language just slaps two words together to bring on the confrontation: *Dirtbag, Catbird, Outbred, Tidbits, Nutbrown, Lastborn*. 'And if words can do that' Lucy drifting-offs 'imagine what the World can - Life can. Fucking imagine it!'

The sunlight and chill are something Lucy has gotten so used to that now the sunlight and mild makes her feel medicine-headed and bee-sting limbed. No, she is not overdressed - but the fact that all of these folks out and about and clogging the streets keep tank-toppedly looking skyward and cargo-shortishly slinging to each other in lover-hugs makes her feel brown-bagged and filling with her own overwarm smell of brought-from-home-sandwich. That, and there is the pestering nag in her head she has forgotten something. At work. The feeling exactly like being certain she had left pornography on display on a computer screen - except mixed with the absolute certainty that it was not that, specifically. But what else feels like that, Lucy? Oh lots of things feel like that! If it was only one thing, this wouldn't be a mystery, would it? Three women over the course of the next five slow-walked blocks compliment Lucy's outfit, which is swell and makes her feel less that she is being focused on by passersby for nothing more than smart-alec remarks to each other about the moisture she knows is making circles of the shirt fabric nuzzled up her underarm. A man compliments her skirt when she peels off from the sidewalk flow to light a cigarette and this spoils everything. No, Lucy does believe he is not flirting - as he bashfully explains - does believe he just wants to get something for his girlfriend - even believes that his girlfriend has Lucy's 'exact figure' and that this is why the man is so pleased - believes the whole 'She is so picky and I understand fits of clothes on ladies for shit, so you are the perfect visual example to give me confidence' - and even thinks it is downright cool the guy does not ask what her exact size is, just 'Where did you get it?' Then what, Lucy? Then what, what? Why does the guy complimenting you ruin it!? Because Lucy just doesn't like him, is why. He looks like part of a hotdog a kid chewed when its mother insisted it try at least one bite, spit out, and put under a napkin. The entire rest of her walk, that is what she has to think about. Kids teeth! Chewed pink slurry! Veins!

Gagging! The squish sound of lips puckered, anusing out something hardly nibbled!

Curtis is home - seems to have just treadmilled, down there in the communal work-out room on the third-floor of the building - but Deb is not. 'I thought she was off today' Lucy says, pouring apple juice, sniffing it, pouring it out and rinsing the glass, getting another, pouring water, instead. Curtis nods approvingly at all of that and Lucy, thuggishly wiping her dribbled over chin with handback, says 'What? It's warm out, for some arcane reason. I need to hydrate and those apples seemed poisoned - I've read Fairy Tales, man.' After a brief explanation of where Deb is, Curtis says this: 'I often wish I could be one of the characters in a drug-store novel, you know? One of the killers the pages of whose crimes are always written first-person. That way, my life would always be blocked out so overdramatically - to denote my confusion. I'd seem sinister, but kind of pitiable in my man-childness. I like those parts of the books. The Prologue murders, especially.' Lucy asks for an example. Curtis says 'My life would be:' then in recitation tone 'There she is. I knew she was there even with my eyes closed. I always know. Her. Always.' Lucy is smiling, so Curtis presses on. 'I say her name: Georgette. Georgette. But something is wrong. *Please?* - that would be in italics, right? - *Please?* What do you mean, Georgette? Oh. You are just playing! Are you? Something is wrong.' Lucy nods emphatically that she is all in, Curtis should pray-continue - says she will think of Curtis like this, now, and must read some of these stellar novels of which he speaks. So he does a finale. 'No. This is not Georgette! How could I ever have thought that!? I let go of the fragile neck and it lays obediently not breathing. Soon. This wasn't Georgette. But soon. Outside I see the first thaw of the coming spring. This winter has ended. But, Georgette, there will always be another.' Lucy claps 'And that's just the Prologue!? Wowee!' Curtis is guffawing in his somehow high-society way. 'Oh yeah. First five pages. Then we skip ahead a year and Georgette is arguing with her kid while they drive or something. Yelling at her agent. I dunno. I'm not in that part, of course.' Lucy says she would just skip to his parts. 'Well, it all gets pretty racy, to forewarn. I describe Georgette's nipples as *beige rounds* and when I spread her legs I say I *breathe in the strong of her chocolate moisture.*' When Lucy stops laughing, she says she stands warned.

Notebook on nude lap. This written: *You're south prayers turned easterly.* Scribbled through. *Southprayers* made one word. She writes this mash alone to test. Naw. Now: *you're south prayers turned east.* But this, while fine, is wrong - it will seem like an evocation of Hell corrected by something like Taoism. It'll seem to stand for something, skirts too close to standard symbols. *You're south prayers pried east.* Better. But spell *Pried Prised. You're south prayers prised east.* Prised west? Even worse. Lucy yawns for the seventh time consecutively, now has to cough as she hardly swallowed once between yawns four five six seven. With animation, she flaps over on to her belly, scrunches around until this feel comfortable - irritated by how long it takes - yawns one more time and writes *You're southern prayers prised east*. Except she had very much liked the phrase *South Prayers*. That had been the whole thing, the germ of it! - that is unassailable! So she decides to be reckless and go with *You're south prayers prised southern*. Ah! Ah! *You're south prayers prised souther!* She rewrites this without the exclamation point. Presses her groin hard into the mattress, cricks her shoulders and hears squeals of released air chimney up the tubes to her ears. Now, all she has to do is avoid making the other lines about *North prayers* and *East prayers* and such and this will be a spectacular success! Rolls to back and scratches an itch around the sullen once-round of her left breast with the pen, knowing she is scribbling on herself, wanting to be. *You're two-plus-two wormwooded to gravy.* Scribble. *You're two-plus-two gravied to wormwood.* Scribble. *You're gravy two-plus-twoed to wormwood.* Not scribbled, but still: *you're wormwood two-plus-twoed to gravy.* Scribble. Then, with triumphant teeth-chatter and then turning to bury her face in the pillow, pretend kissing - large tongue a lashing out paintbrush, teeth tugging nips to triangles of the fabric - she writes *you're wormwood gravied to two-minus-two.* Who is Lucy pretend kissing? Writhing loins to bunched undersheet - blanket on the floor - pretending to grab hair of while she is too almost asleep to finish or remember any of this? She says something, someone. Doesn't care what, who. And even if she did care, she didn't.

Here is what Lucy dreams first: She is working some job she's never worked, sat on the floor of a busy clothing shop - two stories, at least, she can hear bustle up and down stairs and associates calling up-down, down-up, up-down, down-up - pulling pantyhose on to lower torsos of mannequins. Then just sheer knee-socks to just mannequin single-legs. Then just sheer ankle-socks to just mannequin ankles. Then she is chipping old polish off of mannequin toes until she cuts her finger and sees that doing so broke off, also, a fake toenail entire, the underneath of the mannequin revealed to be clouded up mirror glass. Here is what Lucy dreams second: She has to find which of these old advertisements she had meant, or else none of these people will stop ridiculing her! But she cannot concentrate until they stop! But they will only stop if she finds the advertisement! And to do that she needs to concentrate! 'This one!' she says, brandishing it like a hog picked up by one haunch. And she laughs so aggressively before they can even look, face hot with tears. And when she glances down her belly looks like a deflated decoration birthday cake. She stops and - in horror - sees those little pricks of light are staples and they are in her flesh, her belly shirtless though her breast is sweatered, her throat turtlenecked, her ears muffed, and her hair wet and gritty with the sand of a beach-water swim. In between the first dream and the second, Lucy had woken for fifteen full minutes and felt for her lubricant in the bag she kept under the bed, slathered her hand in the mint of it and pinched both of her nipples awhile. She won't remember that. This is what Lucy dreamed third: 'I know all of their songs' she insists, she insists, but the guy keeps playing just five seconds or something of each one. They aren't even the songs by the band! He's a tall guy, as long as someone forever blowing their nose in the same tissue because it's the last one around. 'Don't give me that shit' he says, embittered to the point a colloquialism could be invented comparing him to some certain variety of fruit. And it would catch on, the folksy abbreviation of him. When he kisses her, she guides his fingers up her and he holds the back of her head while she sucks his held-tight-together three center fingers, his cupped hand jostling her head in a hiccoughing rhythm she, after a moment, starts to exert control over, herself.

It feels like she has been looking at the ceiling awhile, unable to shake the sudden tug that woke her. And it seems as though this is not the first time she has listened to her phone vibrating on the bedstand all the way through the length of someone listening, on their end, to five rings before hearing her voicemail. Lucy is answering. 'Okay, you exist. Is everything alright?' Elliott. Elliott's voice. Toned between pissed-off and concerned. 'Shit!' Lucy flapjacks to sitting, stands, teeters, sits back down. 'Shit, shit. What time is it?' Elliott, now pure concern, asks again if Lucy is alright. Lucy only hears this as though from a distance due to she has moved phone from her ear to check the time. 'El, I'm fucking sorry. I passed out. Are you there, still?' 'I am still here, yes. Sorry to have called so much.' Lucy isn't really listening to that and overtops 'I just passed out and didn't even wake up. Is it already two-thirty? I'm coming.' 'We can forget it, Lucy, if it isn't a good time.' 'It's fine' Lucy says, more snappish than she wanted - though she doesn't make any statement of apology - 'I just need to get ready. Or do you need to go?' 'I have nowhere else to be.' What a cheery Elliott you are, bravo. Do you think this works to your advantage or something? 'Okay. I just need to get ready.' 'Long night?' Elliott better-friends-than-we-ares. Lucy just Hmns? stretching out her back. 'You seem shagged out' Elliot laughs-in-not-a-jealous-ways. 'I just got back from work later than I thought. Fuck off.' She hears Elliott using her goofball 'Sorry, sorry' - pronounced *So-ree* like *Story* said by a curmudgeon catfish with a head-cold - which is one of Lucy's least favorite of Elliott's cutsienesses. 'I'll be just a bit. Or would you rather do later on?' 'I'd rather do now, Lucy - I'll just be here. Take your time.' Lucy blah blahs something and finishes the call. Rolls back into a coil on the bed and only luckily wakes up when she shivers enough to snort, jarring herself. 'What was it?' she says. 'Yes. Elliott. Fine' she tells the room. 'Fine.'

After showering, Lucy comes-to-think that she will wear the outfit she had purchased the previous night. The sinister benefits of that being - one - she looks fantastic in it - two - Elliott has never seen it - and three - it will leave it in the air where exactly Lucy had slept after work. Why this matters, mainly, is not to goad Elliott with the idea of trysts and tumbles, but because Lucy has no interest in sidestepping - again - having to say where Deb lives. Elliott won't bring this up - won't bring up Deb at all, or even Lucy's current living arrangements! - if she sees gorgeous old Lucy, rumpled new clothes, who had just previously said she had only just woke up from after work. She waves general goodbyes to the empty apartment - quick glance to that vent, pauses ten seconds, straining a listen - then is out and bumps smack into her own cigarette which she slowly sucks down. This pause is important. This is where Lucy will develop her strategy for whatever it is this conversation with Elliott will be. Yesterday and all of that business is so far off that now it seems marked on her calendar as not to occur for another fortnight, still. So she can, without fear of betraying a snag of uncertainty, tell Elliott she is leaving the city for good. 'Which' she says, idiot facing 'is exactly the thing you do not want to do, babycake.' The truth: Lucy will probably stoke a bunch of false hope in Elliott, depending on what ensemble Elliott, herself, is wearing. Lucy knows the roughed up primness of her own clothes will raise the specific lust of I-want-that-too in Elliott - and while Lucy won't give her the actual pleasure, she might let it tease out awhile that it is being considered in the tentative. This is what you call a plan, Lucy? She discards her cigarette and heads for the bus. She doesn't even remember what possessed her to agree to this meeting. This is dour obligation, at this point - the Invoice for Petra being paid before late-fees are added. Something like that. Lucy is wary. She's wary. Not alarmed. But she is definitely wary.

All of these buses. All of these trains. All of these walked times the same crumbs of the expanse of city - walked, bused, trained so many times the same spot is enormous and the city around it seems miniaturist backdrop, set painting, suggestive patter from magician about to vanish something but not really, of course. This one. The last one. The last one. Of course, all the same one. The same bus. The same driver. Maybe the same driver-or-two. Likely all of the same passengers - in varying combos with a few guest-star alternates who will, themselves, eventually repeat. Lucy will one day just think of this as *The* bus. The *bus*. *The bus. The bus, again.* Boastful of the fact she still feels it's a different one each time she rides, she gets off and starts down toward the *Café Driscol*. Oh there is Elliott of course. Look at her: done up like a lark-wing in her plain-as-a-faucet-knob girlishness. Lucy cannot help but feel aroused. Shorter hair than before! And black - Elliott hasn't done black for ages! Good trick: it feels both back-in-time and that it has been longer than it has. Elliott doesn't stand on noting Lucy's approach, but Lucy knows Elliott has stiffened and is second guessing everything about herself - from her kneecaps to wondering if she lost her soul when her appendix was yanked out. Lucy, unthinking, says 'Stand up and hug me.' And then quick-thinks, while Elliott gives an actual look of What-is-this? to add 'Let's do all the appearances of civility so muscle-memory might take over, keep me from cunting off, alright?' They hug and only after hugging Elliott says 'Since you put it that way.' Yep. Bang. There was Elliott's too-young-to-conceal-it and too-young-to-know-it-had-been-noted up and down of Lucy's outfit, figure scan of all exposed neck skin for marks. Lucy pivots to sitting, over-friendlying 'I am so, so sorry to keep you waiting' as though this was just a set-thing they did and she knows the apology is stupid. 'Where are you working, now?' Right in with it, eh Elliott? 'At a hotel. But I won't tell you which one. Just because I know you so adore phonebooks and the word *Quixotic*.' 'I don't even know the word *Quixotic*.' 'Well, then think of Horton and all of those clovers. Same thing. More your grade-level, too.'

'I have tuberculosis' says Elliott - this is a few minutes into the chat, both with fresh coffee, first-few-minute airs removed - and Lucy says 'That's not something you could have given to me, is it?' 'I don't know, honestly' honestlys Elliott and snaps her fingers as though the jig is up. 'Even if you did, I take all the medicines from all the commercials and so the side-effects will cancel it out, anyway.' Elliott quips 'Ah, if only they had had such opportunities on the Oregon Trail.' And Lucy: 'But didn't they die mostly of typhoid?' Elliot: 'Listen to you - *mostly of typhoid*? Define *Mostly*.' Lucy: '*The majority of instances. The biggest amount of.*' Elliott, hang-dog, pout lips - Christ Lucy wants to bite those and choke that pale neck under that just-yesterday ink-blacked almost-shaved hair: 'Oh. Then, yeah. Probably.' And Elliott ten-year-old shy eyes 'You're really smart.' 'Hey, you know people died of diarrhea on the Oregon Trail. Think of that! How terrifying that word must have sounded when it was a thing you actually died from!' Elliott, Elliott - it would be harder for Lucy to get herself eating out of her own hand. The best Elliott can try is 'There must be a horror movie called *Die-arrhea*'. But Lucy even purloins this by one-upping 'You mean like *diorama*? Those cardboard box things you make at school?' - note: Lucy used the word *Make* in the sense of suggesting that Elliott is still in grade-school and Elliott knows this, gets the flirt - 'or do you, I'm thinking, perhaps mean something like *Die* hyphen *O* hyphen *Rama*? Like *Shop-o-rama* or *Fun-o-rama*. *Die-o-Rhea*.' Elliott does gain back some adorable ground by deadpanning a mumbled 'I truly and very honestly thought *Diorama* was spelled like those other two - and does it really not have an *E*?' But Lucy is still winning. All she has to do is not originate any nice statement or fall for the honey-lure which is so rapaciously set. Lucy squints as though more aloof than she is and says 'I am thinking of the word *Rapacious* - but only because there was another smart word I wanted to use, today.' Point to Elliott: 'Oh so you're going to be talking to someone else later, I see.' Elliott, stop doing so good! 'Ah - *Subaltern*' Lucy says and lights a cigarette and repeats it. '*Subaltern*.' Elliott smirks. 'One: I know what that means - and that's a long way to go to take a dig at me!' 'Oh it was never a dig, I just wanted to say it - I totally forgot you are it!' 'And two:' Elliott lights her own cigarette 'your words don't intimidate me because I can always say the sentence *Lucy, you don't know if my panties are green with blue alligators on them or blue with green alligators* if I have to. If I have to, Lucy, I could say that.'

And the chat continued for more than two hours, actually. Elliott won - in case you're wondering, Lucy. Not in the sense, obviously, that you have been wrought breathless and plied to her trade - but she did not break, did not ask you anything beyond that one *Where do you work?* which, retrospectively, seems as casual as it wanted to come across. And now you have your doubts, don't you, that it ever wasn't just casual? And she made you leave first and stayed seated while she watched you walk away. Clever girl! It's like she's spent time around you or something, Lucy! And what is this we find in Lucy Jinx's hands now? The true reason Elliott won. A copy of *Lindenwood*, that journal you showed her one of your poems in. And golly, well if that isn't Elliott's name right smack on the cover - not front-and-center, just in the list at the right corner, but still! See, Lucy? She waited until you were getting up to leave to give it to you so you would not really peruse it until, at the earliest, here on the bus - and immediately on the bus, of course, just as Elliott had known you would! So that you would be alone when you scanned the Table-of-Contents and see Elliott's name and the title *Coincidence*. There. There it is. The story. And it's changed in just the ways you had said would make it better, isn't it Lucy? Specific down to the whisker! And Elliott knows you will be looking at this right now, on the bus, while she has black hair and is the better part of two decades your junior and has whichever panties she teased you with on - though you'll be picturing her sans them and the way she looks bleary in the aftermath. She knows you'll see this and think 'What else is different, though?' Something. Something sticks out. Well, Lucy, obviously. There. Look. Read. *Lucy*. Lucy is your name. But it was never here before, eh? It was *Quinn*. 'Fucking Quinn' Lucy hisses even now, smiling and beat broke. 'Fucking Quinn' Lucy says and feels transparent even though the name isn't changed because Elliott had known about Lucy's distaste for the name. Elliott had known something else. Something else altogether. Elliott knows you how she shouldn't, Lucy, and - what's worse! - she knows she knows you how she shouldn't. Oh Lucy - Oh Lucy - how did you ever let that come to pass?

*********

WHAT LUCY JINX NEEDS IS time in a library. A moment or two ago this was how she'd diagnosed matters and now - without consulting anything but her own, at best, whimsical memory - she is moving down the street in the direction she believes one to be. A real library. Hadn't she passed it a few times since bunking with Deb? Tied to some satellite offices of a University? There is a chance it was a museum - and she decides if it turns out to have been a museum then a museum will do. There is a gangliness to her walk. She's spaghetti strands doing their best impersonation of an escapee. And Elliott sways in and out of the vision of her thoughts like a reflection in the rolling wheel of a truck belching past. Today has all only been one day. That alone is astonishing and worthy of scholarship - as much as always and more - but that today, in particular, has all only be one day - this day - that this day has all been one day is something other. A fish feeling chagrined for the first time. Lucy doesn't know. A floor finally deciding if it is eternally face-up or face-down. Yes. Library. She needs the singular closure of a library. She'll borrow paper and sit and write. All very simple. Lucy, you have been overloaded, but let this be why you have been: to get you to the juncture where nothing but a library will do. Elliott. Elliott. Lucy does not trust her impressions but is not yet in full possession of why not. Maybe you want to touch her again, Lucy, but that isn't the same as giving her adulation. Cigarette? None left. So a detour is necessary in the exact shape of that discount *Food Markete* - spelled just that way! - with bold words on the outer wall - not quite straight-lined - proclamating *Keno Beer Chips Ice Milk Groceries Wine Cigarettes ATM* is just exactly that hypnotically casual order. Another sign? *We now have PXs!!!!* Ominous. But wonderful. It almost makes Lucy forget everything she is underneath of.

'You tell me which kind of cigarette you want, I will see.' The proposition is confusing. The man is clearly pronouncing *Cigarette* as though it is spelled with only one *T*. 'Any kind, really - you can just pick.' The man shakes his head. Something, he explains, about the exact license his shop has does not allow the open display of cigarettes, so he needs to know which kind she wants and he can check to see if he has it. 'Fine' Lucy says and goes 'Uh' and 'Um' and 'Well' and then she says '*Spotlights*.' 'What are *Spotlights*?' 'They are a brand of cigarettes.' 'I don't have those.' 'You didn't even look!' 'I've never heard of them. I don't have them.' Lucy wants to challenge this man - tell him to name every brand of tuna fish in the store, of bread, of canned beans or olives - but instead she offers this helpful chit of advice: 'Why not have a piece of paper that lists all of the types of cigarettes you have, then customers could just point?' Full blown liar, the man said he tried this but it just led to headaches. 'Which headaches?' 'I don't have *Spotlights*. What else?' '*American Clovers*?' 'I ran out.' 'Then just a pack of *Camels*.' 'Never carry *Camels*.' Yep. This is an olde British comedy sketch repackaged for the actual ennui-entombed crowd! This is the reality of what wouldn't be funny about actually being in the situation of some irreverent sketch comedy! 'Do you have any cigarillos then?' 'Yes.' 'I'll have those.' 'What kind?' 'Do you have more than one kind?' 'Yes.' 'But do you really, is what I am saying - do you *actually*?' 'Yes.' 'Prove it.' Good try, Lucy, but now you're the one extending this scene. The guy is just a cipher - this might be all he was bred for, he might have this same conversation with anyone - not interested one way or the other in your money or if you get what you want. 'Do you have *Lucky Strikes*?' 'Do you want *Lucky Strikes*?' 'Yes.' He stares. Lucy stares. Ah. Yes. She gets it. Nods, as though sharing an I-getcha wink with a pal. 'May I have a pack of *Lucky Strikes*, please?' And that is how that went.

And Lucy knows the library, if there is one, is someplace around here. So she starts dental flossing the streets - up this way a block, two, three, back to where she started, cross one block over, down that way a block, two, three, back to the start of that, cross to one block over and so on. The streets are a grid, but she doesn't trust them to continue being so if she trusts them to be. An oddly placed Pawn Shop catches her eye. The thing stationed there - between to-the-left-of a building that seems to contain fairly pricy and well insulated apartments for classier older people than she is and to-the-right-of a three-story Spa - seems like a flaccid dick hung out of the unzipped fly of the street façade. The windows say *Pawn Sell Pawn Pawn*. So that is something to distract herself with! Why so much emphasis on the *Pawn*? And is three *Pawns* to one *Sell* the equivalent of one *Pawn* and no *Sells*? Lucy shakes her head roughly at this, calls herself *dolt*. Obviously they want to let on that they *Sell* - they merely want to downplay it. But would it be the equivalent to - say on a slightly more windowed shop - have six *Pawns* and two *Sells*? Another cigarette, Lucy is thinking not. That - while the same in proportion - nonetheless would indicate an attempt to honestly point out the *Sell* - lest it get lost in all those *Pawns*. 'So' Lucy says - she can speak aloud, she's going to the library with her damnable ex-lover's literary journal getting finger sweated wrinkles on its cover - 'is it safe to go as far as saying that no matter the number of *Pawns* only one *Sell* is appropriate - the multitude of *Pawns* do nothing to alter the statement, like Zeros to the right of a decimal?' Alternate theory: there is only one *Sell* to emphasize it, not to diminish - like a blot of orange on a room-size canvas of white. That orange isn't the least important part. You're over-thinking this, Lucy. 'No' Lucy counters 'the world is just more artful than I give it credit for, I think.'

Here is an observation: Lucy should be more agitated than she is. And here is another: she is agitated, but in that way wherein she does not know how to portray it. Here's an extrapolation from that: Lucy is always agitated - her calm ought never be seen as calm, but rather a deaf-mute attempt at learning a language based solely on sight. And here is another observation: this is some swaddle-cloth that Lucy infants into when her faculties are overwhelmed and she actually has to think in order to act. Meaning: her body is at trot, but nobody is actually trotting it. Another thing one might venture to say: Lucy Jinx, adding up minutes into two columns of two different types, would have to be said to 'Be most Lucy when she is not Lucy' - or, more simply 'Lucy is Lucy by never being Lucy.' Confusing? In an effort to make things more articulate, but not quite precise: Lucy has spent most of her life not feeling as though she 'Is herself' - so the most common state, the Normal Her, is her feeling 'She is not her.' Less confusing? The two most common states of Lucy are, as just explained 'Not feeling like Lucy in a conscious way' and 'Not feeling like Lucy because she is, technically, not feeling like anyone.' If her minutes were lined up and sorted. Right now, she is in-between those two states. But nowhere near to feeling like Lucy. Whatever that means. Even this - and even though she is aware of it - is a subconscious thought - felt instead of said - in the sense of spoken internally, words in the brain. Along this street, looking for the library, she is aware of the words that are not words enough to say them, conscious of her unconscious thoughts. But see: she, as most people are, is always conscious of her unconscious thoughts - but then the thoughts are erased, thumbed to infinite pinhead-sized ants on a countertop getting too near your sandwich. Here is an observation: these are the lengths Lucy is going to to avoid thinking about she-knows-what. Yes. Lucy is agitated.

The library! And it was a library, after all. Big push for Lucy's self-confidence, as now that it is all over with she can admit she had grown increasingly certain she had been thinking of another town she'd lived in, entirely. The sight of it - and it's a stately library, with front-door plump as a prized hog - brings on a curlicue of relaxation and some specific things to do fall into slots of her future, coaxing out of her a sigh. The sky now wraps around things, settled in, the long deadpanned actor in an otherwise raucous old vaudeville. Lucy reasons it is good luck to have found a library she had grown doubtful of. *Library* had ahemed its way insistently into her thoughts, she had wrested up the vague idea of a library she had never been to, she had basically drifted along - systematic as the drift may have been - until she came upon it. And now will go in. Left to Chaos, Order came! Library. Lucy - you need to trust more that your base programming works and that all seas are not choppy and colder as they go down. Even the option of a rotating door! A *Carousel Door* somebody had once called those and Lucy had given them a bad time for it. Who had that been? Who had it been, Lucy? Nevermind. Because here is a long, needless antechamber. And when is the last time Lucy had been in a room, palatial and unnecessary as this? And a library! Arrogant book bin, pompous and grand as a grandma boastful of her most whorish night! If anything deserves mawkish opulence like this entranceway it is a library. This room is designed for one purpose: letting you know you have left one place and entered another. This room exists the way lightbulbs kill insects. Lucy slows on approaching the first human she encounters, a woman her own age, sitting at a front desk - books all hobnobbed around, some clean stacks some stacks not yet straightened up, that stack as undone as pant fronts after a quickie in the corner - really almost cartoon tip-toes by, because eye-contact would feel like getting caught or like falling in love or like both at the same time.

Quite packed, this place. Mostly with young men. Studentish. Lily-livered, the lot. Hoping upon hope that being able to prove an equation or quote a passage and give an interpretation of it will be all that is ever asked of them. Lucy sits and is - it does feel *At last* doesn't it? - able to let go of Elliott's literary journal. There it is. Perfect bound. Matte-finish cover. Squatter than a magazine but not as svelte as a paperback. Slender volume. Slim. Elliott's name. Once-upon-a-time, Lucy Jinx's name. And, in a way, Lucy's name this time, as well. But: Lucy does not want to open it, now. She wants to make these young men uncomfortable. To sinister their insides and ill-fit their pants in their thigh creases. Lucy, you were as young as these. Lucy, you made love to many. You met two of those ones in libraries. Warehouses of the sorts. Cute-haired and unaccomplished, pimples convinced they are acorns. As concerned with the lengths of their fingers as the pens they hold. As unaware of their postures as of the age of the words in the books that they read. Oh Lucy. How you envy the youth of men. That pocket-turned-out gait to even the most well-dressed of them. The togethered way they are isolated. It had been your dream to be one, something blood-borne wishing to grow up into a fever. They were so not you, Lucy, and all of their locks didn't seem to need keys. Wouldn't that have been darling to be, you'd thought and thought and thought. Picked this or that to sit astraddle and still not know the selfishness they selfished. Yours wasn't that. Those boys and their ways of reducing the world to food wrappers and wherever they wander to next. They're the polished front of a furnace. That's what Lucy had thought. While the best Lucy could manage was to be the word *Heat* with none of the details - no, neither the brightness, the curvature, nor the stab of the flame.

Not roaming the shelves for more than ten minutes, this young guy asks Lucy 'Do you work here?' She shakes her head and says 'Sorry, dude.' The guy takes this in, then says 'Are you, like, familiar with the library?' She chuckles and smiles a bit wider, explaining she had never been in it before, had only been here for less than an hour. 'I can be of no help' she shrugs. 'That's okay' he sighs and heaves his shoulders the way a slug dreams it could, rounds that aisle there and is gone. Lucy does not trust that wasn't a flirt. It was even if it wasn't. Everything is notoriously Schrodingerian if it happens in a library. Especially between boys and girls. Women and men. Women and boys. Girls and men. Boys and boy. Women and women. Men and men. Girls and girls. And then say that again and then that twice, backward ordered - because libraries make uncertain the everything of everyone and so all bases have to be covered and some invented to cover that base, as well. These winks and flecks in the air - unavoidable - aren't dust-motes, but normal microbial virus-scrags made bloat enough to see. Books do that. They are pitri-dishes, bound pages are - the longer they go unread, the more potent, like barreled whisky waiting to brown, browning, browned-waiting-to-sting, stinging, seeping-in, waiting to use a body for plunder, then plundering. No one knows the results of what residue-from-this-page-of-this-book mixed with that-page-of-that they are breathing - and no idea how that will chemically interact with their own physiology. When in a library, the infection is this: breathing becomes the same as reading. You are not doing it, you are it. And the eyes of others feel that way on you because you are a word and they can see how you are spelled while you can't - a paragraph they can read and dissect that you can only be. And they are the same to you. In a library what you become is Reading reading Reading - a pile of drowning last breaths that just keep never drowning.

Curtis had done a spot-on impression of these thriller novels. Now, Lucy hears him in every single word she looks at. Uncanny. She even dwells in the area longer than she'd meant to - not the sort of place she can be seen for long, my goodness! - as this, in her opinion, fortifies her with an excuse. 'My boyfriend does the best impression of this kind of writing, oh my God!' No, no - you don't think Curtis is your boyfriend and don't want him to be, Lucy, and you don't have to worry about explaining that. It is the sensible way to say it in the fantasy of someone for some God-knows-why asking, looking at you queerly for being in this area where you are hoping they note you do not belong. If you said 'My friend's boyfriend does the best impression of these books' - now that would seem odd! That would give people ideas! Wait. What are you talking about, Lucy? Lucy has lost the thread. Give people what ideas? That you had aims on your friend's boyfriend! 'Yes' Lucy says, closing a book, taking up another 'I get that.' But: why are you even thinking about that? Lucy blinks. Stops reading to be confused. You hadn't been worried what other people would say if you stated the actual reason you are here - who cares about that? - you had been worried that you, yourself, were saying Curtis was your boyfriend because you thought it might mean, just because you said it, that that is, even in some modicum, true. Lucy blinks. 'Yeah?' she says. That makes sense. That sounds like Lucy to Lucy. 'But that's so ridiculous' she says, starting to read again. You need to stop thinking like that, Lucy. 'I agree' she agrees. Shh, she shushes. 'Fuck off' she whispers. 'This is a library' she still-in-the-tone-of-shushes. 'So you'd better be quiet, then' she retorts. 'I'm just reading.' 'Christ, you're so fucking weird' she under-breaths after a pause. 'Shh' she shushes. And this time she smiles at the shush like her best friend had done it, both of their eyes aching with heat and pretending to read.

Now here is Lucy Jinx: pillow-forted behind sixteen books of various types. She has the copy of *Lidenwood* open to Elliott's piece and has borrowed a pen and been lent a good stack of blank paper from a roaming attendant, as well. She is blocked out from the world. The most anonymous anyone can ever be. Aware of every cough, shoe-drag, carefully kept silent wind-passing, hair tousle, page turn, bag rummage, shirt tug, knuckle crack, chair strain, whispered chit-chat, fan-blade rotation - aware even of the sub-molecular creak of a shadow being made darker or lighter by motion or by change of electrical flow. This is what it must feel to be a toothache. Enamel protecting you as you madcap your mayhem within it. Lucy fits here as exactly as the bottom of a sock. Succulent nowhere, the citrus of the-last-place-anyone-could-ever-find-her. She has out maneuvered the world, herself even. She is a bedbug fornicating in a dystopia. So many bodies have dropped so suddenly in this apocalypse that the maggots bred enough generations to evolve a belief in God by the end of the first week. Or something like that. Lucy, you are practically giggling. So at ease you forget how to even spell *Shoulder*. The only thing lacking is a cigarette, but that is okay. Something has to be lacking. A cigarette is not so much. If the reward is to never have to look up. To hear all and be a synapse through which the daydream jostles - to see nothing and be the signal that finally gets to tell the body you're asleep. You could be a story right now, Lucy. Yes, a bit lame to think in a library - but nonetheless true. You could have become a word in a book. And that book could have been burned. And the one person who remembered the book remembered every word but you when they rewrote it. Every word but you, Lucy. You could be that free. And it's okay that you're starting to cry. You've cried at less, Lucy. And at more. Maybe now you finally get to cry at just-this-exact-much.

Elliott's story gets better on each re-read. How many times has Lucy read it, now? Four times. It's not long. Reading it over and over again is like breathing in wine from a glass being tilted circularly with a barely tightened wrist. Is this really how you feel, Lucy? Elliott's story is that good? It is. In an entirely non-showy way. It is actual writing. It is honest, now, whereas before it seemed hogwash and manufacture. Just because your name is in it now, Lucy? No. Or because Elliott's hair is now black? No! Or because while Elliott's hair is black, other-of-her-hair is far from black? Grow up! Can't Lucy just like the writing? Sure - condescendingly, as though doing Elliott a favor. That is how Lucy 'likes

Elliott's writing.' Isn't Lucy allowed to be genuine? Well sure. Is that what Lucy is being? Yes. The story is marvelous. It is out of the reach of having anything to do with Lucy. The way Elliott's slouch in that chair had been without Lucy's gravity. The way Elliott isn't hers. Lucy wishes she had read this and then met Elliott, but that would have been impossible. Because - and here we are - that is what you see, Lucy. Elliott took you, processed you, made something out of what you said but didn't make what-you-said. You are reading the result of you. And the result of you is: now you are not needed, anymore. Is it a pleasant feeling? Further evidence of your impact in the world? Well, Lucy now cannot even tell if she is being sarcastic or not! What *impact in the world*? Your name in a book, Lucy. A journal, anyway. A story. Is that my *impact in the world*? Isn't it? Sure. Lucy doesn't care. This is all library drunk. This is just a moment in a dream. A hot piece of water in a fat cask of wine. Fuck - Elliott's story is beautiful. And that's right. That's just how Lucy told her to end it. And that's just how it ended. And that's what you're reading - the actual end written before the actual end.

REMEMBER THAT? YOUR FRIEND IN fifth grade, Lucy? On the way back from the shops - you would take that back way, closed in between treeline and fence separating those apartments from the business park. Remember that period of two weeks, three - it seemed longer then, as everything seemed longer then, it is funny how short it seems now, like it hardly had time enough to happen - when the two of you would buy those bags of *Extreme Sour!!!* candies? Now - well now you know, Lucy - they are not so sour as that, but the two of you would tense yourselves into strained panics of anticipation and shove two three four five into your gobs. 'You have to last thirty seconds!' 'You have to last a whole minute!' And the squealing placations to Jesus and God and to all the Holy Saints! Remember when you had so many - laughed so hard, worked yourself up so much - you bent over and vomited candy-smeared bile, just leaked out that violent heat, just the spit and the dye you had sucked - because you also spit the candies out - while she boomed her laughter around you and could-not-believe-it the entire walk home? Yes. Yes, Lucy remembers. And remember the lover you had - that woman Cynthia - in University? The mathematician, the theoretician, the adjunct professor. Remember how she would make you lay nude and would cover your flesh with equations - with number, letter, symbol - each and every pen-stroke meaning so much to her - all with precise explanation, definition - and all of it meaning nothing to you but at the same time more than it meant to her - concepts with no words, no numbers, no letters, no symbols, equations that meant to you, Lucy, the-exact-explanation-of-everything, the Universe as simple as a lost rubber-band? Remember her? Yes. Lucy remembers her. She can remember whispering to Cynthia 'You have no idea how smart I feel, right now.' And Cynthia smiling back 'Well, I know exactly how smart you look.' But that is Lucy's trouble. She remembers everything. She truly thinks she does.

Lucy Jinx looks up. You haven't written anything yet, Lucy. Just borrowed pen-tip on given-to-you paper. Isn't it eerie - isn't it? You can control your thoughts, but more often than not you aren't. Where does your thinking come from? Why this? What that? As soon as you start thinking, you decide to own it - you in effect blame yourself for it. Stop thinking about that! Why am I thinking about this? I just need to stop thinking about this! Why can't I think about what I want to think about!? 'Yes - fascinating, Lucy' Lucy comicals at herself, under breath and still looking down at the paper. 'Highly unoriginal, all that - and you still haven't written anything.' That was your point though, Lucy. It feels like you're waiting for a thought. Waiting. Then - laser zap - you'll be writing. Writing that thought. So why can't you do it, now? Thought doesn't care about time! It doesn't need to formulate in seconds, minutes, to warm, defrost, wind-up-and-the-pitch. If you want to think something, well think it! What do you want to think? Don't you know? You have a pen on the paper and want to write - what, in abstracto? Something compelled you: I want to write. This. This. This. And then you bus-stop impatient for This to show up. Why not write something else in the meantime, then? Because terror! Because fear that while you are choosing what to write, what you would have written if you had just waited will have slipped away! And that's what you wanted to write! That specific thing with no qualities, yet. That thing to which all chosen thought will be forever vastly inferior. Nothing. And nothing, still. Lucy cracks her neck, goes 'Hmn, good point.' Looks back at the pen on the paper and writes nothing with it. But also does not set the pen down. Carefully, she leans back and the pen is going twirl twirl. She is ready, nothing else to her, until this thing happens. This thought that isn't enough to even be thought yet but is there. Disappointment begins to well in anticipation of larger disappointment. No matter what now - no matter what - she'll never trust the words on this page.

Nonsense. Look how far Lucy Jinx has come. She, with a heart that is fifteen poor copies of the word *Rattlesnake*. She, who is milk denied to pauper's kids. She, who is limbs for the coffins. She, who is immediate and long as a nosebleed. The library is busier now, but quieter. Surprising even herself, she is writing all of this with people surrounding her on all sides. Across and across, left diagonal, right diagonal, the table - and one person sat next to her and another person sat other-next-to-her. *You don't know my music, darling, my records can't learn how to crawl.*

520 / PABLO D'STAIR

*You don't know my red meat, darling, you're the outside after the wall, after the wall, and after another wall.* Lucy does brackets to note to herself which bits are to be segmented off separate in the fair copy, circles for emphasis large chunks that she decides will stay definitively together - not trusting herself to keep to that insistence if she doesn't put in these precautions to reminder herself that those odd longnesses are meant to be odd-long. Only one of her surrounders is a pest, at all. Everyone else must be with her on this! That guy, with his coffee he keeps blowing on and his throat-clears which he must believe he is doing quietly enough to be polite. Oaf-thin, this man, reading a book on maritime law - which is distracting to Lucy, because now she's got the word *Yardarm* stuck in her head and it seems to want to Bogart its way into every stanza. *Yardarm*. She writes it and circles it in a margin - little cage for it, the word has to stay there with her false-hearted promise to let it out as soon as she has found a safe place for it. Lucy presses on. Presses on. Look: now she is doing out the fair copy. She is writing this part: *you need kisses bigger than that, ferocious as fingers slammed in a drawer, you need to set Wednesday alight just to watch it from Thursday too late to save it. You need to be too late to've ever bit the taste you now long.*

What needs to be explained here is this: in all of that writing, there was a subset of Lucy that was working out 'What will I call this piece?' And somewhere in the running of various alternates, that quest exhausted itself and she just knew it would go without title but it would be atopped with *For someone*. But not just *Someone* - she'd have to choose someone. And as she wrote, ex nihilo suggested to her that *someone* ought be Heather - and so the poem has at its head *For Heather*. It all happened just like that. Like Lucy Jinx in a filling library after a long pause writing. She has now made a fair copy of the fair copy - a few tiny alterations to lines - the first thing set to this fair copy being the words *For Heather*. An official dubbing, just to cleave all doubt from the matter. And as things go for Lucy Jinx, she decides: I will give this to Heather, in person. Just like that the thought came, no effort, and that was the decision and that was why this poem was here. Lucy wanders a bit with the poem and finds that the open-to-the-public computers are all occupied, only a polite bit of signage to enforce the one hour limit. In the meantime, Lucy confirms that no library-card is needed to use the things - not that this would have been something she'd have raised objected over, she intends to get a card before she departs. Lucy goes to the toilet and when she returns there are several vacancies, as though a group all had left together, the empty chairs in a tidy row. This is how all of this happened. Lucy has a tingle of happiness thinking of Heather. She imagines how nice it will be for Heather to be told that Lucy wants her mailing address, wants to send her something not over the damned computer anymore. She imagines Heather cautious-flirting back. Wouldn't Lucy rather meet her in person? And Lucy agreeing to go to where Heather lived - if not her home, the town, anyway. Lucy is content, as though elsewhere. Lucy is heavy chocolate lungs, breath serene as though sculpture.

The Inbox is glutted. Some messages as recent as yesterday. Subject Line: *Modeling*. Subject Line: *Interested in posing*. Subject Line: *Poetry model*. Subject Line: *Muse?* Smiled-lips, tight and colorless, Lucy lurks her eyes down, hardly focusing. The entire first page of the Inbox is unread-these-sorts-of-messages - plus some pornography Spam and some offers for discount business-card printing that started showing up back when she was active with this. The second page, too. She opens a few at random. Just to see the women's names. *Julia Birch. Selena Cauldwell. Melanie Fiske. Ermalina Este-Fernandez.* Then she makes her self-satisfied gutful of feeling oh-so-adored unblob, pointing out to herself that this is no more interested-people than usual. In fact, considering how long it has been since she's opened this e-mail account, this may be far less! Then she sees Subject Line: *Jiiiiinnnnxxxxxx* - quick flit that, yes, the sender is *Victoire* - and almost slobbering click-click-clicks it open, annoyed that this computer runs lazy and the words take a moment to load. *I still love you. But I have realized you are ugly. P.S. You actually aren't ugly. 'Victoire'.* Lucy shuts the message and backs out of the mail program full stop a moment and her head swims heavy, a wasp trying to fly while dragging a half-full bourbon bottle with it. She is not mad at the booby-trap at all. This is why you came to this library, dope! This is why all of this flit-flitting and memory games and needing a reason to find your way to the computer. Victoire - no, she can't bring herself to think 'Ariel' because that would come with a scream of the word - had written to her. Even only - she had looked and now opens the mail program to verify - three days ago! Even after you've not, Lucy. Even after you've not! The world made you come to find her saying *I love you*. Lucy cannot read the message, again. But can scroll through the e-mails. *Victoire. Victorie. Victoire.* Bold black Subject Lines. Random mashing of letters like *lwkfhlkfw* or here *Never Forget* or here *I know why you stink* or here - this is the first one - *I miss you. Already. Victoire.* Right after she'd gone.

Here, in its entire, is the text of that first *I miss you*: You know how some twats go on about the Universe being indifferent? Some blather that it's cruel in its indifference, some that it is benign? We won't waste our time talking about mongoloids who think it has no personality, because I don't know enough ways to spell *Fuckwits* to keep that interesting. My thinking, Jinxy - I love you, by the way - is that the Universe is too interested. Not in a wrathful, jealous-God way. And not just in individual things. It is too interested. In everything. The Universe is an overzealous fanboy about every atom. It collects rare editions of all of them and quotes the liner-notes of every frog or nebula. It knows where the printer of every poster was located and how much scalpers charged to see this live show and has - mint-condition! - some of those tickets which were fake, to begin with! It doesn't want to talk about the shows in a fun way, you dig? It wants to nitpick who was Executive Producer that season or how you can tell it's a new set and talk about how there were different versions of scripts but this scene was cut due to that and this actor wanted a higher salary and that's why they became more of a supporting role. The Universe loves the word *Auteur* and to say *This was the very first time that* and *But if you think about it*. Over every scrip and scrap, man! The Universe doesn't know how to leave anything well enough alone. It collects when it should enjoy. It obsesses when it should collect. It display-cases when it should obsess. You know what I mean? It does everything wrong because it just can't stop being interested. Not just in me. Not just in you. Nothing more here than there. The Universe is a terrible person who is terribly boring in their terrible enthusiasm for everything, terrible and not. We are stuck in its fawning paws and made greasy by its inability to ever stop staring. Nothing is individual to it or perfect - everything is just so goddamned interesting and has to be talked to death! I just got home. I can't think. I wore your clothes. I didn't kiss you. Go fuck yourself - but like, for me okay? Enjoy the bus ride, idiot. And by the way: take wooden nickels. Trust me. I love you.

And gee, Lucy - wouldn't it be just jolly if that had been why this day had gone as it has? If that had been all and then Technicolor *The End* under swells of tinny old orchestra fanfare? But that would make Lucy Jinx not Lucy Jinx. And Lucy Jinx is Lucy Jinx. And a sweetie-pie message - and the obvious saccharine of whatever is in the not-yet-read ones to come - does nothing about that. Here is Lucy Jinx, curious as to how many messages exactly there have been - wanting a number in her head before she starts digging into the nougat of each - and so meticulously tapping the screen, finger touch to each unread up from that first one from Victoire. One. Two. Three. Four. Victoire messages smattered in with the others, in with Subject Line: *Available to model* Subject Line: *Nude Poetry* Subject Line: *I would love to have you write me*. Seven. Eight. Nine. Mixed in with these others through the weeks of all being abandoned. Then: right here. Right. Here. Subject Line: *DESIST*. Lucy knows it is something. Because first she counts it as Twelve. Then realizes it isn't one of the messages she is meaning to count. Then Lucy loses count - was it Eleven or Twelve? had she said Twelve, again, because she'd realized Twelve had been the previous Victoire-message number and this was not a Victoire-message so didn't want to confuse herself? - and just the largeness of the capitals scream masculine in a sea of comfortable only-amongst-women. 'Desist' Lucy says and wonders, for a moment, what she must look like right now - black-and-whited after a moment ago fluorescent tangerine. *You will immediately cease contact and interaction with my wife. Your corrosive presence will not be permitted in this family*. Nothing else. Nothing else. No signature.

Just those words and nothing. Not that Lucy doesn't immediately understand who is being referred to. As the writer of this knew she would. As the Universe aligned to make her certain of. As Ariel - Lucy uses the name now - appeared so graciously to remind her of the Universe's endless over-interest and never stopping it fiddling fiend-connoisseuring. And gee - wouldn't it be just jolly if this hadn't been why the day has gone as it had?

Lucy gathering her things. Lucy putting the fair copy and drafts of *For Heather* into the *Lindenwood* atop of the spread open *Coincidence* by Elliott with now Lucy's name in it. Lucy making her way, dresser-drawer legged, through the to-capacity library, a screech in the otherwise-silent. Lucy through the still cathedral-empty entryway, its girth twice as booming, the walls seeming to squirm 'round and 'round, termites defending their invisible queen. Lucy as though breathing for the first time, rebirthed back into who she'd gotten away from being just moments before, a shuddered inhalation in place of a bawl and a      find-a-bench-to-sit-on-because-walking-won't-work-any-more-for-awhile instead of some head being handed to a welcoming breast. 'Heather' Lucy says. Heather. But why did it have to be Heather? It clearly is Heather - Lucy is not under illusions, but just thinks it might be less demolishing if this was explained. How would the man have discovered anything? Why would Heather have told him anything if he had discovered? 'And so what!?' Lucy cannot help but tense-jawing, the words coming out a grumble-loud Susuhcht!!! She repeats, calmer, normal mouthed 'So what? I said So what?' And her first anger - it's not so terrible, Lucy, just forget it, perfectly natural that it would be - is toward Heather. Heather for being such an idiot! For all of it! For needing to nude skin and playact at being paper and words! And Lucy can feel the hard palm of her accusatory hiss across Heather's old bovine-teat cheek, can feel it again and again as she unrelentingly asks Heather 'Why the fuck did you write to me if it was such a goddamn problem!? And just keep your damned mouth shut if you didn't get your permission slip signed!!' Lucy standing but only getting a few paces before realizing she has forgotten her things. Lucy looking at them on the bench, wheeling away and pressing on. Lucy stopping and - now trying to put on a la-di-dah gait - just a tad bit of a hurry, silly-me, going back to the bench and gathering the things up like a bird that wants its unhacthed egg to go bury.

Not that the message could be real. That couldn't be real. 'That couldn't be real' Lucy, Metro-seat cuddled, says to the apple-juice thin of her window reflection before it gets obscured by various forehead grease and residue of sneezing-turned-heads as the train enters the first of the short tunnels. *You will immediately cease contact and interaction with my wife.* Nobody wrote that. Who would? *Contact* and *Interaction*? What person would not even contextualize such a statement - just e-mail it without signature or shame? *Your corrosive presence will not be permitted in this family*. She has to repeat that, hiccoughs a fake giggle. 'Your corrosive presence' she switches to cartoon-dad voice, mid-recitation 'will not be permitted in this family.' *Corrosive*. 'Young lady' she adds, giggling more genuine but stopping genuinely just as soon. *Family*. She sits up and tries to give it all the brush off, even dusts the top of her thighs and twists at her belly left-right, right-left, creaks from around her ribs sounding. 'He showed me. Put the wifey back in her place. Bodies are Heavenly, again - String Theory unknotted! Yep.' Lucy nods. 'Hubby has massaged the cosmos back into harmony - harder on him than on her. And' - this is most important - 'it is nothing to do with me' - so she says it twice - 'and it is nothing to do with me.' *You will immediately cease contact and interaction with my wife.* 'Fuck you. I should have fucked your wife! Your! Wife!' Lucy laundry dumps herself backward now, the hieroglyph of inelegant surly. The train out-of-one-tunnels right into another, the hill more pronounced and her ears clogging, popping to a swallow, ringing an extended Eek then clogging cotton-swab again, her next swallowed gulp echoing, trapped in her head. *Your corrosive presence will not be permitted in this family*. My *corrosive presence*? Who would write something like that? Lucy now just wants to understand. There is nothing she can do about doing anything - the message is weeks old now and so the author is assuming his point was well made - she just wants to understand. Or she doesn't. 'Or I don't' she says, closes her eyes. 'And she's not your wife either, fella. I mean you can have her, but we both know she's mine.' Closed eyes and smile. And ears clogged and heartsick as mottled as sunburnt freckles.

Now off the train. Now random block this way and random block that. Nothing new. New as anything else. 'There is special providence in the fall of a sparrow' she Hamlets. But then, as always, bungles the rest of the lines. That odd progression. *If it be now. If it be not now. If it be not to come. Yet it will be.* Again, she tries to discard *Lindenwood* and *For Heather*, this time at a trashcan in front of this tattoo shop. But doesn't. Can't. Her hands are not hers, right now. She's a goddamn thought not quite been written, not yet a goddamn thought that suddenly will have been. Then - because why not? - she says 'There's special providence in Illegible Sparrow.' And just stands there, wondering for the next time in the same sodden sequence What-is-the-matter-with-her? Is she just a jukebox that only one person likes one song on? Is it a simple matter of waiting for that person to die and then taste in her will vanish, the tune of her forgot, an undercurrent of relief to every person on Earth's next five minutes they will not understand or even ask to? Oh yes, even those hard asleep! Especially them! Dreamers will remember those five minutes, will wake wishing to re-dream just that part of whatever dream it was even long after the memory of even the sensation of the slumbered life has expired. The tattoo parlor smells of decaffeinated tea and overused typewriters and the two people in it stop their conversation just long enough to say 'Hello' - both in unison, almost in harmony - before returning to it as though Lucy is only there to give them reason enough to have done that. So she mills and looks at the large wallfuls of designs. Sighing, she sets *Lindenwood* on the counter, opens it to the place held by *For Heather,* and glances over the first stanza, immediately shutting the pages back in. About to ask for a pen, she notices one, takes it without asking - the conversation over there continues, continues - and flops her forearm, belly-up, to the counter. She writes on the flabby, middle-aged white with the blue-ink *You will immediately cease contact and interaction with my wife. Your corrosive presence will not be permitted in this family.* And then Lucy turns. And as polite as she can says 'How much would this cost?'

# . V .

LUCY CONTINUES HER DRESSING, WONDERING how long that tag has been around the handle of the suitcase. So long that, in essence: always. Button. Button, button. Shirt done up, pantless, pantyless, socks she has been wearing all day and needs to change. Next: that bracelet of hers goes on. Next: cigarette to mouth and she sits in that starts-smoking-very-stage-theatrically way, staring at the luggage handle. How very-stage-theatrically? She sees the mock-up of the bed, the only thing lit, the smoking and the staring is the whole scene for almost a full minute - so: very very-stage-theatrically, to answer the question. It has to carry things into the viewer's impatience. The audience would be sitting, waiting for the first sound cue - it would be of a taxi lulling up, door opening and closing - and then Lucy is still to not move, to not stop staring, to not stop smoking. Next sound cue? Knock at the door. Light goes on over set-piece room door - audience can see another character waiting there, coat tugged up overhead protecting them from pretend rain. Lucy's stage direction reads *She continues to stare. To smoke.* How long has that tag been on the luggage handle? Lucy is wondering. Now. Now, in earnest. A long time, yes - but it could not be twenty years, could it? Well, it could be eight. Easily. And just as easily it could well be passing ten. This is something. Ponder, ponder. How many times has Lucy looked at that tag? Yet she does not even remember which airport it is for, what the abbreviation is on it? Were she a character in a story, some author would make it a point to have her remember all of the details of the tag, a way of driving home how long it has been there and how often Lucy has lugged the luggage around - would make a point to put the words *Lugged* and *Luggage* together, you see? The abbreviation. The sequence of numbers under the barcode. Some other odd minutia. Some kind of intricate things proving she is oh so familiar with it. Real Lucy, though, is not interested in any of that because she is real. She has lugged the luggage around for she's-not-sure-how-long and has absolutely no idea what that damned tag says, no matter how many times she's thought all of this fine stuff, here.

Best detail of this room? Look at that mouthwash. See what it says on it, Lucy? Just the word: *Mouth*. Amazing. The cake of hand-soap, there? *Hand*. The little bottle of lotion, there? *Face*. All of this Lucy wrote in a letter she will send to nobody the moment she made a circuit of the room upon entering: the mildew air of the place, the unvaccumed-forever-and-ever carpet growling at her before deciding 'Eh, fine, come on in' the windows, curtained, which look out - this is true - across the way to the toilet doors on the outside of the gas station. In the shower: cake of soap larger than the hand one is labeled: *Body*. And the bottle of shampoo? *Hair*. This makes Lucy wonder if it is shampoo and conditioner, combined - she may be overthinking it, she knows. And - she is not sure if this ruins things or somehow makes it better - the packet of coffee has on it the single word *Gourmet*. To be fair, what could the coffee be labeled other than that? No need that it ought keep with the leitmotif of the personal care products. What would a tampon be called? This makes her grin even though she has thought of it twenty times, by now. What does the wrapper of a fresh roll of toilet-paper say? Ah. *Sophistication*. Lucy is fully dressed and roaming smoke circles, smoke squares - smoke polygons of all kinds - the room. Most of the time with her hands in her pockets. No reason for that. The smoke does not seem to dissipate, at all. No breath of it has vanished. Now there is some tussle, one warble of grey-blue to another, an overcrowdedness in the back of a show house, standing-room-only. The walls and ceiling are sponges so over-used they cannot take in another dribble - solid, liquid, or gas - and are so impermeable they have no other side. Ceiling? Lucy pictures it a mat - up and up and up - of collected tobacco smoke and sex-scents and middle-of-the-night coffee farts and odors of toilets left drunken unflushed. Layer and layer and layer. Ancient mythos. 'Turtles all the way down' Lucy says. It's gross, the actual image she has. But she cannot describe it. Moss growing on tumors growing on buboes growing on the foam of a yeast infection gone rabid. Miles of it above her. If she keeps smoking, she'll wind up pinned to the ground in another decade. Paint layers, paint layers. Lucy Jinx: she'll wind up a cheap, seeping moist hotel room floor.

Lucy walks over to the room door and gives it a timid rap. She waits a moment, gives it another. Then opens it and - flushed faced, rushed - says 'Oh my gosh, I am so sorry. You caught me just getting out of the - never mind. Come in.' And here, Lucy wilts her posture and slips into the smarmy corridor, taking steps over the threshold back into the room, giving flit smiles and nodding, darting eyes around as though not sure of this, not sure of herself. Note: Lucy pictures this Other Her's hair long and brunette. She pictures this Herself in glasses bold and round and green framed. 'Did you find the place okay?' Lucy said that but was acting the Other Lucy part of nodding and standing there. Lucy re-latches and chains the door - for a moment considers commenting on this to Other Lucy, but that isn't really part of it. The specific room isn't part of it. Lucy, you're just so complicated! You don't need to explain yourself to yourself! So: Lucy has sat down on the corner-point of the bed - it sags a clean mile down - and takes money out of her matter-of-fact-pocket which she then acts like she is taking and puts into her shy-pocket. 'You can get undressed now' Lucy says, whisking off to the toilet area mirror and pretending she is looking over her shoulder at the Other Lucy who is unmoving, looking at her back. 'Is everything okay?' 'It's okay if' - and she trails off her voice. Lucy squints at the part of the reflection where she is pretending to see the seated Other Lucy - in reality, she cannot even see the bed in this mirror, at all. 'What's that?' 'Nothing' she timids for Other Lucy as Other Lucy does not move. Lucy turns and reenters the room - as though reentering the room, never mind the continuity bloop, as though she had been watching Other Lucy in the mirror but now had actually been unable to see the bed - and she leans to the room wall, looking at the empty mattress. 'What's wrong?' Her smile rises, quavers, falls. 'Is it okay if I'm not very pretty?' Lucy softens her face and looks at the bedspread. The bedspread is a green that could only be sold on discount - green the way one would picture the eggs of a termite - and it has patterns in it of nothing, as though whoever had designed it had been instructed 'Make it patterned' but had never heard that word before in their life.

Lucy on her knees at the bed. Now at the center of the mattress. She unbuttons her first button. Her second. Smiles and giggles. Smiles a different smile. 'Okay?' 'I'm okay.' Third button. Fourth. Fifth. She glances down as though at the cleavage she knows would be presented were she really on her knees before herself, then she pulls her chin in and looks down at her cleavage, actual. 'What?' she shy-fidgets. 'Oh just so far so good' she confidents and gives a flick to her own shoulder, hardly a touch. Sixth. Seventh. 'I'm going to take this off now.' 'Okay.' 'Or would you like to?' 'Okay.' Lucy doesn't move. Doesn't move. 'Okay, I take it off? Or: Okay, you do?' 'You do.' And one shoulder slow, two shoulder slow, elbows to sides, palms rotated out, Lucy shurgs herself out of the shirt and it goes quietly over the bends of her knees, the tendrils of her legs, probably covers one foot. She looks up. She makes a face as though never more certain and never so How-do-I-breathe? 'Would you like to take this off?' That face. That face. 'You can' Lucy barely-outs. Tick. Tock. She lets the bra hang, unclasped. Her face does the curve and the straight of a question mark, her head-tilt dots it. 'Do you want to, the rest of the way?' Swallows as though her lips with it. Does not answer. But that not answering is *Yes* and she touches her palms over the loose cups of her bra, not pressing in at all, and leans to loose the straps from her shoulders - and the thing comes away, set aside somewhere but nowhere. 'Can you stand up?' Lucy stands - now that discarded shirt is annoying, it was over one foot, she heard a strain to the pulled tight fabric as she got her balance and started to up - and while she does shylys 'Are all of your models this much trouble?' Lucy pucker-lips tsk-tsk 'No trouble' uses thumb to undo belt buckle 'No trouble at all' in, as much as possible, one extending of her arms - gets the whole snake of the thing off. Kerplink sounds the buckle as the leather rumples on the carpet which likely lets spoors up in a multicolored spritz.

'Can you read to me while you write?' 'No.' Lucy is naked and belly down, the comforter removed, the bedsheet prickly, like hair coming up through a grandfather's undershirt. Lucy has just written: *clever as winter grass, the ink that wasn't dry when I brushed it.* 'Why not?' 'I don't read. And you don't get a copy, either. Stop being a pest.' 'I don't get a copy?' Someone in a nearby room had ordered a pizza and Lucy had heard the entire payment transaction and now can hear the slaps of slices on paper plates and can smell the mixture of vegetables and grease and something advertised as cheese that just cannot be. 'Can't I get a copy?' 'You've already been trouble enough.' 'That's what I mean! It'd be fitting, right?' Lucy has just written: *I never believed the sound of the radio, it could not have been what it said that it was, what was told me.* Four pages full, Lucy turns to the fifth sheet. Quickly scribbles *Lucy* a colon, then *Five* at the top, underlines it, winces, circles it, trying to make the underline part of the circle, then circles it circles it circles it until at least the mistake is indistinguishable, itself, from the general sloppy. 'How many women have you had?' 'As Subjects? Two or three.' 'Oh. Honestly?' 'No. Not honestly.' 'Then how many?' Lucy has written: *There again! That sound. A dog pants the corridor long but when we look we see nothing and call each other hearing things.* This line is drawn from how Lucy swears she hears animals out in the hall - right now, she swears! Wolves, she thinks - but that word seems too fraught with symbolic to work in this poem. This poem. 'Do you think that sound is wolves?' 'What sound?' 'Listen.' Lucy has just written: *Do you think that sound is wolves? What sound? Listen.* 'I think it's just the vents. I kind of figured I'd be dead by now when I saw this place, to tell the truth.' And Lucy makes a face

Hmn-hmn-hmn, head in jots left-right-left 'I can see that. But you came, anyway?' Lucy has just written: *Want to learn how best to lie? Study the face of a clock. Want to learn how best to come back to me? Show me the split of your lip.* 'Well, yes. I had to see what my murderess looked like. You know?'

Lucy explains to Other Lucy that it has been two hours, though Other Lucy seems to utterly disbelieve it. But it has been. And Other Lucy should get dressed. So Lucy sits up and has Other Lucy say 'I could stay awhile longer.' And Lucy admits she got everything she needs. Here, of course, shy Other Lucy would take this the wrong way despite the rapport they have developed so Lucy is obligated to act out all of that bit, as well. Reassurance. 'There are only so many words. Poetry is tiring. My brain cannot keep up, necessarily, with the stimuli of the body being presented.' Other Lucy says to Lucy that she could always stay the night. 'There isn't any rush. If there is more to write.' So desperate that phrase! *If there is more to write.* But Lucy cannot lash out and so has Herself say 'Man, there's always more to write - you're volumes, Lucy, you're shelves.' But: does Lucy want Other Lucy to stay? 'You don't have someplace to be?' 'I do. But it's not where I want to be.' Lucy is disappointed with that exchange. She corrects it, principally, in her thoughts, but does not come up with actual better dialogue. Then: Other Lucy offers Lucy the money back if she would just be allowed to kiss her one time. Lucy notes here that she is still nude, meaning Other Lucy said this without even getting dressed first. 'Shouldn't you get dressed?' Ah, but that comes off harsh, doesn't it? Lucy, Lucy - it's so hard to fantasize! You know this isn't actually a live performance, right? You can pretend something wasn't said, change it, alter it. So literal, Lucy! Just kiss her if you want! Have her kiss you if you want! 'You don't want to do that' Lucy says. 'Do what?' Lucy says Other Lucy says. 'Kiss me.' Then after a pause, unbidden, Other Lucy says 'No. You're wrong. I do want to do that. I don't want to get dressed.' 'This is hopeless. You're a pest - just get dressed.' 'Is that from the poem?' Other Lucy wouldn't be so sassy, Lucy - keep to character! Well, maybe she would if pushed this far, thinking she'd gone so out of her way and was being shooed off. 'If I kiss you will you go?' 'If you don't kiss me, can I stay?' Lucy slumps to the bed and lights a cigarette. Everything just goes on and on, doesn't it?

So for awhile Lucy is lost to self-inflicted throes and despite her fatigue - and the fact she cannot get fully comfortable with wetting the hotel pillowcase with her tongue-lather - she manages to orgasm multiple times. While she does, someone is honking at the gas station. So much so that it's funny. While she does, she is picturing cinnamon-red hair tangled around her forearm and she knows the tugs hurt more than she means them to - but all there is is loud breath and no sound of Stop. While she does, two people pull jittery baggage down the corridor and talk in singing-in-the-shower voices - Lucy can fairly well still hear them even after the echoing spring of their room door slamming behind them. She pictures Elliott with chest to carpet, arms triangles, chin on crossed hands used for some slight comfort. She pictures that skirt Melinda had worn, thin enough it could only be written about in cursive and soft pencil, the tan of her legs seeming to instinct against the linen grey. She lays exhausted between one bout - high-note trills of odd embarrassment, knows she had been overheard but that no one would be picturing her soloing it. Laughs aloud and begins again, third finger and index caressing either side of her over-sensitive-still clit, thinking the family who'd order that pizza are having to cover their children's ears while at the same time mom and dad cannot stop giving each other lascivious eyes. Maybe she is asleep, because it doesn't make much sense, a moment when she finds herself arguing how she has only been parked in a spot for twenty minutes and the sign doesn't even say there is a time limit - or maybe she is wide awake and just lolling after her cum. That had been to a woman who she had just invented, someone who had asked her for help at a library only to make a bold pass at her back in the stacks. Breathing heavy. Aware of her chest so much she would not be surprised to find a rash when she goes to the mirror. Cannot spread her legs wide enough to not feel sticky and tangled. Then she says 'You're still taking the money.' And then she laughs and says 'I know.' And she says 'You fucking suck.' And she says 'Are you going to read me some of it, now?'

Lucy does not put back on her socks - cannot even find her bra - or her panties. She tears out the pages of the poems she just wrote and folds them in three as though to slip in an envelope. Over to the door she moves - and she opens it as though to let someone else out. Note: she glances up and down the hallway, gets a bit self-conscious, closes herself back inside. She has the now re-timided Other Lucy give an interrogative look, makes up the excuse that there are two troglodyte sorts in the corridor she gets a bad vibe off of. 'Here' she then says and makes as though handing the folded poems across. She takes it. But acts unsure. 'You don't need to copy it?' Lucy shakes her head. Gesture of handing it back and 'You don't need to give it to me - I really hope that didn't make things weird.' The poem still held out in the air in front of her, she leans to the door, rolling her eyes, and kicks as though the air there is Other Lucy's ankle, which - incorrectly - she pictures nude - though this glitch is understandable, as her whole scenario has gotten mucked in her head. Lucy is picturing herself as nude, frankly - which, while it makes sense due to the fornication and all, does not make a shave of sense considering she just opened a hotel door. Anyway. She says 'You didn't make it awkward. I want you to have it - all of it, unedited, unadorned, likely meaningless. And I want to always wonder what it said.'

Hesitant still: 'You don't have it memorized?' 'No.' 'Any of it?' Just an expression is given in answer to that, but she acts Other Lucy relenting, nodding a solemn 'Thank you' or a solemn 'Okay' tucks the pages to the left pocket of her pants. It's time for Other Lucy to get going, though Lucy doesn't have either of them say it. In fact, most of the remainder plays out solely in her thoughts as she listens to the crinkles of the poem in the pocket and tries to use the lips of the doorframe to work on an itch she cannot quite reach with her arms up behind her. She does picture watching the rear of Other Lucy walk away, but as though the blinds are spread and she can see that out the window. A different view. Still the gas station, but more of it. Can see a blinking red traffic-light, another blinking yellow. Sees that Other Lucy is waiting at the crosswalk even though there are no cars anywhere. She finds it interesting, that. Interesting that she would do the exact same thing.

After three minutes, Lucy understands the water will get no warmer than it currently is. She mulls the option of having a bath instead of a shower. They must clean the tub. It doesn't look so bad. She runs her hands along it, though, and the consistency of the porcelain - or the water this is made of - is Gila monster. Nothing comes away to her fingertips - there isn't sediment or anything like that, nor are there signs of scrapes - but the thought is that the already-abused-by-cheap-sheets bare-skin of her bottom would not come away the better if she were to soak, there. Something would get in her. There's an ecosystem, she's sure of it. Something symbiotic. Something crash-landed, crawled into this tub at some time, and lies lurking. Lucy Jinx as opening passage in a dime-magazine science-fiction! Yet: the water has gotten no colder, either. Perhaps it stays one temperature. Modern girl she is, this take a moment to compute but seems feasible when it does. If she were to build a cabin house, string pipe from the well, the water would issue perpetually the same. If one doesn't heat water it's just the temperature of water. Or if one doesn't cool it. Wait, though. Again: modern noia. Water isn't, left to itself, icy - is it? But in most showers, water has the following declensions: *scalding, perfect, hot, hottish, warm, lukewarm, not-quite-warm-but-not cold* - yes, that is different than *lukewarm* - and then *cold* and then *suddenly-goddamn-freezing.* 'Yes.' She nods. She has tested water or stood in it and recoiled from the mean spirited slice of it. This water - still the same - isn't like that. Lakes she has swum in, many were mild, room-temperature margarine. This is just like a glass of tap-water she'll still be able to taste conflicting minerals in. Why won't it get cold? She lets it keep falling, knowing she is stuck in a classic philosophical conundrum. To wit: if she does not get in the water, it will stay this temperature - while if she does get in, be it now or fifteen minutes from now, it will always get cold, right after. Some would argue sentience. Some would argue pH balance or something. So you aren't going to shower, Lucy? Lighting a cigarette, she holds up a hand like 'Don't be impatient'. 'We'll see' she nods, winks. 'We'll see. I just need a plan.'

This luggage. Always, always. The zippers on the widest mouth of it never seem to open anything. See! Look! She has moved it all the way from one side around to the other and the bugger won't open! That's when - always - she sees this second zipper, just below, seemingly sharing the same track - and that opens it, right away! What's the first zipper for? As always, she does not investigate. Merely: Lucy hates this particular suitcase. Also: the wheels don't work. And there is a special sort of incompetence that makes a wheel not work, that's for sure! One thing she is certain of: that. Onto the comforter which has been haphazarded - draping more over that side than this - across the bed again, Lucy tosses jeans, t-shirt, bra, underpants, socks. Regular her. Lucy Jinx. Only now does she see how well the colors go together. Even the wash of the jeans - her lightest pair - gives such a pure, lighter-than-air effect. Mint yellow panties. Almost-pink socks. Antiseptic-rinse green of the shirt and the pattern on it in tongue-after-lollipop blue. 'Smashing' she says, and workmanlike gets out of her pants, folds them - if you can call that folding, Lucy - and her shirt, too - unbuttoning only the three top buttons, pulling it over her head, balling the inside-outed thing and lobbing it at the television. When she lets out a long breath, head slowing ceilingward, it pulls something in her neck, for the next ten minutes her mind feeling machined to place wrong. Yes, Lucy - you have to get dressed. If for no other reason than you have to get something from the vending machines. If there are vending machines. You don't want to wake up after a night in the wheezed air of this room with nothing to eat but tap-water! Order in? There aren't even menus in this room! Call to the front desk? Fine. Fine, Lucy. She pulls her t-shirt over her head and tells herself 'Stop pouting.' She had just been pointing out the nuances of the world. There is always more than one thing to do. The multifoliate splendor of options, opportunity. 'Before us stretches Valhalla' she says 'behind still burns Tlalocan - before us apexes Folkvangr, beneath us under-hills the Fields of Aaru - to our backs, long devoured, is Vaikuntha, in our fore-eyes writhe-drumming comes Elysium - yes, to our shadows has all consigned the cold and bones of Cockaigne, yet our arms know they will fling wide and be brought un-asundered to Tir Na Nog. Weep, we travelers, yes - but, while weeping, press on!'


SOURMALT. SHE SHOULD'VE THOUGHT OF that before. Her eyes are raw, fingers-too-long-in-bathwater, sudsy crackle to her attempts at focusing. Sourmalt. She has nothing further, just needs to remember that. For the a-billionth time she reminds herself 'This is why you need to carry a notepad.' Deftly countered: having a notepad would keep these things from occurring to her. Statistically, she gets more out of not having a notepad to capture these randoms. Yes, anguish unfettered for how many she has to go through the sensation of having, losing - numb shapes missing from her, holes that tingle asleep when poked - but more in the long run, come along. Lucy. Lucy? 'What?' What are you talking about? In front of her: vending machine. Typical set up. Chips atop. Candy at mid. Pastry things, cookie packs toward the bottom. Little appendix of mints and chewing-gum. How long have you been standing here? She doesn't care. What was the word? *Sourmalt.* She uses it in a sentence: 'His scent was a rupture, the *soulmalt* of an overturned bin.' You'll never remember that, Lucy! That's a lyric! Use it in something normal-prosed. Oh! *Normalprose.* That's another thing she'll want to remember. The mood of soldering words is strong with her - and so far both are spectacular! Regular sentences, Lucy - focus! 'Give me a *sourmalt*, please!' Good. Now, tie it to an image. Image: kid in soggy gloves, wiping his nose, sitting at a café counter, dinner served to him on a piece of newspaper. *Sourmalt.* There is nothing in this machine she wants. Magically, even, all of the candy is just exactly the sort she is never in a mood for. All of the chips either flavors or brands she does not like. Who buys almond-and-white-chocolate-chip cookies out of a vending machine? For sixty-five cents!? She nervouslys a look around, this joint she's staying at now seeming foreign, like a landfill full of terrorist's bones or a Deli that says it only sells magazines. *Sourmalt. Normalprose.* She makes a pugh-pugh-pugh pugh pugh-pugh-pugh rhythm through kiss-lips a few times, rubs her eyes - hard to stop, hitting just that spot and the sound like deep tissue massage uncracking muscle fibres - and gives the machine the finger, the cold shoulder, all of that, everything negative she can.

It is exactly this sort of young man working the front desk: backwoodish but city-raised, too young for the saggy-drunk pox of his cheeks - he will have slept with the girlfriends of at least three of his pals, which gives you the exact portrait of them too, he being the more-attractive-one to the girls in the circles he mixes in. To flesh this out further: if you ask him local directions, he will know eight different routes and will weigh them like variants in manuscript drafts by Kafka, but ask him about Kafka and he will indubitably picture a slice of American cheese. The long and the short: Lucy is not going to ask him anything. As she exits the office - cup of the free coffee in hand - she does ruminate as to how he might have arrived at this job. This, you see, is not the sort of job anyone *tries for.* Counterintuitive as it may seem, one must know someone to get this employment - and once it is obtained one is fundamentally tenured, at least until the eventual warrants are executed and the bailiffs arrive. She has little to go on.

The name of the hotel is just *StayWell*. To Lucy it seems foreign-run, but that guy is no more foreign than an imperfect pavement stone. 'Eh' she says, hoping there is enough force in the sound to get her to drop this futile detectiving. There is. She kicks this plastic soda bottle - relatively certain it is filled with urine - and likes the hand-clappy sound of it pocking brief ricocheting echoes as it checker-jumps down the night street. Rather desolate this night. The moon above is a tooth if a tooth were the ready-to-peel scab of a scraped elbow. This neighborhood, one of those that seems in an actual corner - as in it seems there really is nowhere further to go in that direction, the only way out is the way that one came. In that, the streetlights - though certainly orange electric - seem shirt-covered gaslight, the shadows just light in an uglier shade. Something nice about it, though, all things considered. This is what the end should look like. She walks like drifting in outer space, not needing to breathe or live or die or anything - the kind of place in a city where forgotten things go to forget they're forgot and remember they aren't remembered.

Gas station attendant is no better. Describe him? Lucy has a go, as such: his eyes are the color of the most crusted part of a tissue used to stave a nosebleed and there is always a spot of wet wherever the tip of his dick touches his underpants. She buys a candy-bar and a bottled water, rather reluctantly - mainly because it will stave off the most droolish of his leers as she exits - and then - why not? - asks for a scratch-ticket. Lucy, you should play more scratch-tickets! It is something Lucy always thinks of buying as she idles at a shop counter but has holier-than-thoued herself out of the pleasure of ever doing. 'Three of them, please' she says. In front of her mind dances piles of fortune, a field of grass mowed and ninety acres long and then her brand new front door, freshly installed! And outside, she chooses a coin to scratch with though has the feeling she ought to be using the tab of a soda can. Scratch scratch scribble scribble scratch. Loser. Same with the second. So into the store and she buys that soda can and she goes back outside and she takes off the tab - sets the can down, moves to kick it then halts short, remembering physics and all of that - and has at the final ticket. Lo and behold! Lucy Jinx has just won a hundred dollars! I do declare! And the mistake of her every impulse floods her brain like heroin pudding. She spent not three dollars, won one hundred! And it's true - no mistake, she isn't sleepyheading herself into delirious untruths of better-life: the ticket means she has a cool hundred smackers. 'I won' she tells the clerk. He is suspicious - deadly venom, his envy, careful Lucy, he's raped and killed for less! - but admits it is a winning ticket. So, Lucy does her best at politely preambling 'I guess I'll take one hundred dollars, please.' 'I haven't got it in the till.' There is something malaligned, here. 'I can wait. Get it from the back.' 'Gotta wait for the boss.' Oh Lord, of course. 'But it says *Instant Win*! I can't redeem this

here?' This oaf is cesspit with deception - four-flusher just doesn't want to face
up to the sorry of his lot! 'Is there somewhere else around?' *Someplace with class*,
Lucy doesn't add - because that would allow him to honestly say 'Nope'.

If Lucy could be something other than a Lucy Jinx, she would be the inside of
a coffee-pot curve. Or she would be the last of the cough medicine left in the
container after the final useful dose is poured. Or she would be the fur of dead
insects on the top of a porch lightbulb. Or the tone of voice when someone
corrects someone on the pronunciation of *Aficionado*. Her mood is starting to
gather around her like the palm fabric of a larger hand's glove. Lucy does not,
in the best of worlds, want to be walking these particular avenues at night - even
if there is a police car parked there - to redeem her first scratch-ticket winnings,
but she also doesn't know where she does want to be walking, in the best of
worlds. Or she does. You do. She does, she does. But moratorium on those
thoughts! Let all sleep until she is awhile in her new runaway life. Then she can
do whatever she wants. For now, this walk is enough. One hundred dollars. If
she could be something other than Lucy Jinx - this is how she is enduring this
walking, breathing just a tad heavy, feet thunking down a bit harder than they
need to be to metronome the pace she is wanting to keep the words to - she
would be the pause after the last note of the Jack-in-the-box tune, the silence
before the crank goes all the way 'round, the silence that could be ongoing if
someone so chose. Or she would be the mercury in a thermometer. Or she
would be the taste that won't leave a kid's mouth when they decide to bite off
a pencil eraser. The street looks like it should have rained recently. The quiet is
the kind reserved for closing up retail shops on a night when the weather kept
customers away but no one could leave early because that's how it goes. It
strikes Lucy that there are people who live for years in streets like these. The
thought feels exactly the same to her as realizing things have been written on
walls down in some sewer tunnels - or the thought that someone has, at least
once, choked to death on an orange.

A regular convenience store. Look at it! Beautiful and open twenty-four-
seven. The automatic doors part before her uncertainly, like the first step after
a stubbed toe. Overhead: innocuous music. Lucy listens, wanting to get the feel
for is it just an instrumental song or a song that originally had lyrics, this just a
wordless version of that. Can't place it, Lucy? She gives up, anyway, when a
prerecorded announcement comes on informing her of the great deals currently
being offered on napkins, instant coffee, and Greeting Cards if the cards are of
a brand called *Quality Expressions*. 'How can I help you?' This is how a human being
is supposed to look: a little bit too smallish, beard overgroomed and
unimpressive, eyes longing for instant assurance of best-friends-forever, just sad
but in the way it seems there's no reason he should be. 'I'm hoping you can'

Lucy flirt voices, able to tell she is the first at-least-semi-normal sort this man has encountered in weeks. 'I am not from around here' - points at herself, gestures outside - 'and, on a lark, I bought this scratch-ticket - but the liar at the gas station I bought it from said they had no money to make good on it.' The clerk is softly gesturing he'd like to see the ticket, not vocalizing the question, though, probably not wanting Lucy to stop her fatuous monologue. 'I was told you were the law in this part of the territories, though, and so am throwing myself on your mercy. See' - she finally gives him the ticket but he doesn't do anything but flit eyes to it split second and then just hold it, looking at Lucy again - 'I am putting a lot on you, man - because you could screw my faith in things, here. First ticket I ever bought and a big winner, you can see that yourself! Pretend I'm Virginia - you know? - and don't tell me there's no such thing as Santa Claus, dig?' A head nod and head nod in return worth of pause, the clerk ever-so-tactfully says 'I just need to show this to my supervisor - do you mind if I step away with it? She's in the office doing the drop. Or we can wait and I'll call her in fifteen minutes.' All of that is so specific, Lucy just grins and says 'I trust ya. You don't look like you want the blood of a broken heart on your conscience. I'll just be here.' And to period the point, she picks up a gossip magazine and immediately takes the stance of loitering.

Not even eleven-at-night and one hundred dollars the richer! 'Ninety-seven dollars' Lucy's wet-blanket prissy-pants, but even still: not even eleven-at-night and ninety-seven dollars the richer! Lucy distinctly left the store right away, before the impulse to spend so much as a dollar could get her, diminish the high which would dew-drop by dew-drop amount to nothing, soon enough - now, though, she rather wishes she'd asked where some action was. Up, down, left, right, thither, hither, she sees the same corkboard storefront streets, nothing open for business except for all night taco joints and what looks like a tax preparation office but could really be anything. Not someplace flush-Lucy can luxuriate, anyway. Are there no corner pubs!? Are there no dismal clubs where people know they've all slept with each other but still go to anyway and manage to formulate new grudges, regardless!? Back to the hotel, Lucy? Get some rest? One more block up and she is about to concede this seems the best bet. She will pen a humorous essay on the Emptiness of Wealth and then go to sleep watching whatever Basic Cable channels her room can hairball up. This is what the last strand on a balding head must feel like: Lucy tonight. Or the first whisker in an otherwise appropriately bare ear. There are some last roils - faster than all the others - at the very termination of a slip down a drain and Lucy has always liked those ones the best - plucky and obese with wrong-indeed pride at their vigor and quickness, thinking there will be time, at least, for one more round of applause before the slurping abyss makes them part of the not-there-any-more.

Wrong! Silly last twists of a tub drain! The same as the over-eager shimmer of water refilling a toilet bowl. That poor water, shivering and bristling of refreshing life. Lucy has deep affinity for it, too. Before it blinks and puts together how two-and-two ain't Heaven. 'And it ain't' Lucy says, smacking her lighter harder than she needs to and hissing the first drag out with unmetered disdain. 'Soon you'll be begging to get dunked right back down where you were!'

Here. A more proper gas station. With *Lottery* signage. Why hadn't she been directed here, in the first place!? There is her hotel - right there! - and if she could see at even a slight little bend there would be the gas station that had toddled her off to all the far reaches. Portly woman, shirt untucked, is pushing a mop and singing along to the show-tunes coming from the two-decade-old radio on the shop counter. The woman does not stop mopping - stops singing but continues to hum, as though this is Tourettic - and Lucy backpedals while the woman slap-slurshes onward, asking 'Do you know if there is anyplace social open, at this hour?' '*Social?*' the woman says, either confused or else voice toned to intimate she is giving the matter her most affectionate concentration. 'Like a bar or a club - just someplace where one might hang out.' 'Hang out, yes, yes' - the old woman cannot help singing *It is the music of a people who will not be slaves again!* giving the notes a tremendous over-clatter of voice, obviously feeling the composer did not ask near enough the proper emphasis of the singer - 'you mean tonight?' The question slipped so out from the singing that only Lucy's fond familiarity with the tune enables her to know it was not a part of the rising refrain. 'That would be ideal.' Now mopping stops. To counter. Button struck with old-crow finger, cassette stopping with an offended bang. The old woman tells Lucy there are a few options. About ten minutes walk in such-and-such direction there is a bar called *Imperials.* 'Not the nicest place, but they never close.' Down some other direction is a slightly cleaner bar - but the old woman laughs, says she shouldn't even mention it because the stupid place closes at midnight. 'Or then, if you don't mid something a bit fancier - not like you need to dress up, just jazzier - there's the, the' - she repeats *The* a half-dozen more times, snapping fingers on top of the last four - '*Falsetto Note Corporation.*' Lucy blinks. The old woman is witch-cackling how she can never think of that weirdo name, but it's a nice place. She went there once for an anniversary, the old woman did. 'What was it called?' The woman blinks, now broken from dreams of a happier, mopless, radioless times. 'Sorry, hon?' 'The name of the place was what?'

There is no way to forestall the crawl of her skin. Let the facts stand in support of the sallow gut Lucy is burdened with as she steps along - one cannot call the way she is moving *Walking* - and let it not be said there is so much as a wink of overreaction. Here - this final night, packed to leave, more than four-fifths asleep to begin with - Lucy had ventured from her pimple room, hoping the vending machine would sate her. No luck. Then she had entered the lobby office to perhaps ask what place nearby might deliver some food, but had encountered that loathsome young man and so pressed on to the gas station. By that time, Lucy was outside and so the first thought of 'I'll actually stop someplace to eat' had entered her mind, but then she had seen the lummox there - his eyes bake-bean greased in pervert wrinkles - so had just bought her candy and water. Then that damned impulse for scratch-tickets - where had that even come from!? - and of course she had to go ahead and win. That should have clued Lucy in! It was the obviousness of lymph-bloat and she had ignored it! Walked the plank for not-quite-one-hundred-dollars, Lucy had. Oh and the pathetic short-story symbolism of it all! Three tickets bought, two losers, then she had gone back in for the soda can tab she had - again, where had that thought come from!? - thought up to use - and because that was the device that scratched up her fortune her mind had been made pliable, amenable to believing that Fate would ever stoop to playing a kind hand to her. Winner, winner! And the lout won't pay. If only he'd paid! Oh but Lucy - come now, come now - there were so many points to turn back. So many If-thises and If-thats. And the letch then sling-shots Lucy out a good way so she can encounter good spirits at the drug store, put her at ease, fill her lungs with the desire to go on as she's already ventured so far. And this splotchy back-page of the city, no place to go, so flat and cold and nowhere! And you would have given up, Lucy, if not for that gas station! Beacon of sooty but welcoming almost-midnight neon white. At the very end of it all - the night before you are to escape - an old woman all but voodoos at you that there's still a jaw left to bite you. You've been set up! You've been seasoned! You've been stuck to the spit and given a turn! Oh Lucy, poor you - oh Poor, Lucy you! What good is whining at the history that led you here? Just because it's nothing but five minutes old doesn't mean it hasn't been waiting forever.

So don't go. 'To *The Falsetto Note*?' Yes. 'Don't go?' Don't go. This part of Lucy Jinx's brain is the first on her list to carve out. Does some part of Lucy truly understand so little it would think not going would keep her from going? She already didn't go, first of all! Whatever is waiting there, she had avoided it once. And so it - petty and bitch-hearted - decided to wait until just now. Not go? Lucy knows it is where she will wind up, anyway. And if she avoids going now, she will walk into consequences far more dire. To not go - well! - that is to step outside of the auspices of the governing laws, to badland herself and have no recourse to justice, however unloved she might be in its eyes and however certain to be abused by its agents. Not go? And bare-chest herself to the ungroomed curs of the superstitionless wilderness? There, where every voice is a gibber and kissing tongues turn vultures seeking access to foolish throats to pluck right out the organs while they still beat warm and course-pulsing? Oh it is certain she is going! She is going, right now! And she can look back miles and see the straight line she has walked. Lucy Jinx: idiot. Lucy Jinx: Cassandra's Casandra, destined to tell herself the future but to disbelieve herself when she tells. Don't go? 'Why would I be here' Lucy alouds 'at the *StayWell* - have picked this place on this night to squirm my getaway if not to be told where to go, instead?' This is punishment for something. This is to let her know she has been found out, in the fabric of things, even if she manages to hoodwink every innocent she cons into thinking her possessed of a soul. The world is smarter than you, Lucy, and you'll never get out of it! You've chosen the cowards path and have read enough books to know where that ends. Not go? Fine, Lucy. Don't. And then press on - get on with life, find your next grave to croak in. But: *Poet?* Dare to tout yourself *Poet?* This night is your crucible, little miss. Poetry isn't play-pretend and stringing saps along with false posture. Poetry is being the swallow down a throat you don't know the belly of.

One last stop: this alleyway to smoke in. Lucy can see some faint movement behind that window blind. What do you picture, Jinx? She pictures herself at twenty-two, when she had that typewriter and would sit writing, overweight and unclothed - her boyfriend, runner-lithe and stab-nosed, would be practicing darts at the other side of the living-room. Darts. Or teaching himself some sleight-of-hand with coins. Is that really what Lucy is picturing, firing squad cig erection-stern in her dry lips? It is. Oddly. Memories of that, now? And the more she stares and wonders if the movement is anything more than an oscillating fan that vibrates on reaching either extreme of its arc, the more the youthful sheen of that young man's body shapes in front of her and the more she can recall him overlong telling her how gorgeous each freckle by her lip was, how puddled-paint her shoulders, how carved-but-unpolished-marble her eyes. The sound of him had always been like a television set. The look of him had been the crisp gloss of an architecture magazine. Lucy stares at the blinds and wonders if she would be at the table, dunking cookies in milk and waking up with cramped stomach, despicably thirsty and sucking down cartons of limeade. If she would be able to let him insist on her reading what she was writing. And hate him. 'I want to hear it now, when it is rawest - when the iron is most heated, even if the sword is not shaped.' Vile. Lucy stands in this alleyway hissing. 'What does that have to do with this!?' she horror-mouths at the window. No change to it. No one in there to get nervous, wonder what is that yelling. And she'll have the answer to that question - soon enough and finally - she supposes. Or that will just be another whap and jangling light-up and Bonus Points in the pinballing of this last night. A calm now, though, as she chains a new smoke lit. *Horrormouths.* That's fine. *Horrormouths.* And *Normalprose.* And a whole night of graves raked up to assure her she'll never forget the word *Sourmalt.* A little poem that. Perfect. *Sourmalt normalprose horrormouths.* She gives her window a burn-victim smile of a bow.


EXTERIOR VIEW OF *THE FALSETTO Note Corporation* on slow approach: patchy building, part of whom's charm is its façade of unkempt. But Lucy marks it right off for what it is: exactly the fancy where lusterless suburban-type infidelities go to eat - fathers taking out mothers of their kid's one friend from that other school, mothers dining late with the office-mate who is always kind enough to stay on to meet the deadlines. Its own parking lot has no lights, just the perpetually dim, salmon pink word *Falsetto* in the one window, that light nudging through cobwebs made funeral-veil with car exhaust, grown thick as though thumbs had over-stroked a drawing of them in charcoal. The perimeter: across that way - where most of the light comes from - is a closed-by-this-hour pizza joint called *Julia's Pie* - the slogan of which is *Pizza so good you want to lick it* - all of this innuendo made more obtrusive by the fact that immediately after the slogan is the triangle - point down - icon of pizza with an exclamation point slitting it centerwise. Adding to the remarkable ambiance of that place is the fact that the lot trashcans are two days' worth of overflowing and there is a faded zipper of crosswalk - diagonal across the pavement - a ghost of some other time, making the jagged yellow of the already-difficult-to-decipher parking spots all the more bewildering. And across the way is a large shop, warehouse like, a door on one side of which says *Hunan* in lit green - the *N*s on the blink - and on the other side a door beside which is a scrolling sign of electric orange letters forever jogging the words *Hockey Supplies* left-to-right, every third swipe flashing the them in orange, red, yellow, then holding them red the count of ten before the pattern recycles. Lucy imagines these piles of cigarette stubs - see them on the pavement, as she approaches? - are not there by accident of nature - a pile there, a pile there, a pile there - but are the handiwork of some employee of *Falsetto* who wants the lot to seem spruce, just not at the expense of bringing along a dustpan. Lucy Jinx finishes a cig and crouches, extinguishing the last heat of it in the cartilage-goo of this one pile - a scent of chicken bones left out overnight, stale neighbor's dog, and mulch that was fresh yesterday.

A piano lounge, at that. And swank! You should've dressed up, Jinx. In fact, Lucy is expecting to be given the bum's rush or a jacket to borrow while she is asked to leave or else to be only begrudgingly admitted. There is something science-fiction to her entry: the interior temperature, coloring, attitude, volume of all noise - mix of piano, chatter, cooking, drinks being poured, two televisions on behind the bristle-fashioned bar area - the heavy of the second door after the as-inauspicious-as-the-parking-lot sub-entry seem some sort of portal, Time and Space bent to allow this illusion. She holds up her hands, fearing tentacles. Touches her neck, surprised to find it hasn't become broached or scarved in mink. There are posters on the wall of past advertisements for entertainers who have performed here - right up to contemporary names Lucy knows - and there are photos of individuals of note - black-and-white though as recent-as-this-Thursday - stood at the bar, seated in this or that booth - one of these a Newswoman Lucy recognizes, frowning while waiting in queue for the Ladies' Room. What in Hell is this place? 'How many, ma'am?' This woman glissandos over, menus bound better than first-edition Cervantes held in her arms like freshly asleep infants. 'I'm just here for a drink.' Good work, Lucy - don't play into their hands! The woman smiles, recommends some drink whoever-the-name-of-the-barman-on-duty is famous for and walks Lucy over, personally, making sure she gets her preference of available barstools. Nothing so plush has been beneath Lucy's ass for at least half-a-decade as the pouffe of this stool! A napkin, a glass of water, and a small espresso are set in front of her by a sous-barman, Lucy protesting 'I haven't ordered yet' the man - in some accent resembling a kind of mock-Transylvanian - explaining 'Complimentary' before turning to make some notations on a slate board that takes up a portion of wall next to the cash-register. You should probably leave, Lucy. Any minute now, the drugs you've been dosed with are going to wear off and you'll find you're bound upside-down and armless, listening to a madman explain the uses he has for each one of your thighbones! Naw. Lucy pigeon-pecks a sip of the expresso, then lips a full taste. The napkin, she notices, has this written on it: *Staunch meter, great song, it is yours, at length / To prove how stronger you are than my strength.*

Does any of this put Lucy at ease? No. But has her panic increased? No. Yet, is she in the exact-same-state she was in before she entered? No. We can say this is Lucy sideways-in-time, not the same and not different - a clumsy way would be to say she feels alternative, replica in all but a few atoms, but those enough to salt the taste of wine and to unblue each shade of blue as though all always are in slight passing shadow. So, we're sticking with the science-fiction motif? Yes. Lucy in a pulp-mag, dime-magazine - *Tales of Astonishing Worlds*? Yes. She has entered another dimension - and what happens to her will not exist once she is outside the doors? Yes. Look at this clientele! Only a few blocks from the *StayWell* and the exact spot she scratched a lottery ticket! They are unbelonging to this part of the city as much as Lucy is to their midst, yet already she has received pleasant smiles from several. But let's not go too far. Is it so otherworldly, in here? No. Look: aren't those people ordinary enough - like the mop-woman, maybe just out here on a splurge, once-in-a-lifetime? Yes. Could it be the majority are such and it is just the sore-thumbedness of the others which makes them seem the appropriate sort for these environs? No. Maybe, Lucy, the ones smiling at you assume you are one of the grungy entertainers you saw photographs of! Shit. Why did you have to think of that, Lucy? Are you only allowed in here because of some superficial resemblance to a daytime talk-show host or a rhythm-and-blues singer on a come-back tour? What do you look like, right now? No! Idiot - don't look. And don't get up to use the toilet, either! The only thing keeping you safe might be you holding your ground, no one daring to approach you out in public lest they wind up looking the classless whelp! If you move, they can huddle in and trade misgivings, send envoy in to sleuth you out. And they'll likely find you agitatedly chatting to your reflection, knowing you! Just drink the espresso. Sip the water. And you need to order a drink! They might assume you are waiting for someone who will give your bent-cardboard presence the laminated sheen to excuse you - they'd be loathe to shoo out some upper-cruster's trollop! But when nobody comes for you, Lucy? When they find out you're water drained through the bilge? Get loose, Jinx! How long have you just been sitting here?

Of course, though: to the toilet. Lucy can only withstand the blitzkrieg of nobody bothering her in the slightest in a restaurant she's never been to for so long, after all. Only human. Only Lucy. New problem: it seems smoking is allowed in the lavatories. In fact, there is a damn pull-lever cigarette-machine - there, underneath the free feminine-product dispenser! 'Brand name' she remarks, giving it an appreciative wink. And there is a leather - mark you, leather! - armchair, right there. This bathroom seems as large as the entire joint, outside, and so the kaleidoscope of this night takes another mischievous twist and things only just recently patterned before her unbelly themselves, turnabout, reticulate, splay, symmetrical, and present in this new configuration. No, of course Lucy Jinx isn't actually dreaming. Or going Lovecraftian mad. Oddly, paying in coins for a pack of *Lucky Strikes* slaps her just the right way in the face to grip her back down to Earth. Here: a whole altar-bowl of those match-booklets one of which foreshadowed this establishment to her, so long ago. But why are there no other women in here? Lucy blows smoke in all directions - ah, a vent working soundlessly aways the smoke whisk-whisk straight at once, likely poofs it in rings out a cute little chimney, to boot - and squints into each of the stalls. The toilets, anyway, are just stolid and to-their-purpose, no more - the porcelain not even free from the encroaching liver-spots of constant blown waste. The stall doors do go floor-to-ceiling - Lucy notes that, appreciatively. Finishes ciggy, flushes it, lights another. Could it be this place means no harm? Oasis? Eye-in-the-storm, at least? Could it be you were led here to give you a bolster, to reconsider your plan from the most comfortable vantage? Look around you - remember what it was like out there at the bar? - and honestly say you can claim to understand the world if this is here. It's not what you were so certain - on approach - it would be, Lucy. Is this the world's way of telling you you're being too limited - of apologizing without admitting fault? Lucy gives her mouth a squirt of the communal binaca and then behinds-her-ears two touches of the oil perfume labeled *Rhodesia*. That's your face in the mirror, Lucy. In there is your brain, which might be leading you wrong.

Handsome man - thus far unnamed - who had been waiting with a drink-bought-for-Lucy watches her drink it and is pleased that she gives it an approving 'Mmn, yes - quite nice.' Side note: Lucy cannot distinguish between one alcohol and another any more than the spit she leaks Wednesday is different than the spit she leaks Wednesday-next. 'Good, right?' 'I am pleasantly surprised' Lucy says, just to keep him on his toes. Seems it was the bell-ringer to say that - the man's pose goes more chummy, less I'm-trying-to-flirt, and he dives into a pre-recorded bit about the 'bourgeoisie's preconceived notions of flavor'. 'You do know' Lucy has to finally disappoint him 'that I am not a countess out among the pleabs in disguise, right? I look like this. And while I can spell *Proletariat*, I nonetheless am it.' Unnamed man bows all Victorian-novel and changes track in a way that would unsettle most but which Lucy prefers to the bore of his previous angle. 'If you were told, today, that a race of people were being systematically wiped out - which they are - shown evidence, facts laid out in front of you, but they were a people, a race, a type, a sort you had never even heard of, would you be moved to action? If so, which sort? Sign a petition? Donate a few bucks in the checkout line? Watch the documentary and give its director an award?' He shrugs. 'I wouldn't do anything' he says as though what-a-ludicrous-but-alluring-bastard-is-he. 'I wouldn't, either' she says 'I already don't.' Prize-lights go off in the unnamed man's eyes, riches mounting fist-over-fist-over-claw. 'Exactly!' he too loud proclaims - look, Lucy, even the barman showed a chip of keep-it-down in that Vermeer of imperturbable. The man touches her arm, fish flops the touch away - instantaneous and all-apologies - continuing to speak the whole while. 'Fucking exactly, man. I learned just the other day about how a tribe of people died out - and with them a whole language that will never be translated or understood!' 'I heard that, too' Lucy can genuinely say. 'And they walked on all fours, right?' 'Right' says the man. Lucy motions the barman to refill her drink as she says to the unnamed man 'They sounded like good-for-nothings, really - an entire language-worth amounting to *We haven't figured out what legs are.*'

Unnamed man says '*Hamlet* fan, are we?' Takes a sip from his refreshed vodka, pointing to Lucy's forearm as he swallows. Lucy glances down at the ink in her skin. *We defy augury.* 'We defy augury' she says - the room now incrementally vicing, she notices, she notices - and raises her own drink, forcing the unnamed man to have another mouthful. Everything looks like a page to her, now. A notepad with the name *Lucy Jinx* scribbled and underlined, bullet-points listing this and that of what is necessary to flesh her freefalling one line at-a-time underneath. But no fangs are barred yet, no black gummed lips even up rippled, snouts leaking rotwood steam of ready-for-a-kill. 'I was going to get something else' Lucy says, feeling scripted, hand-forced, needing to be easily analyzable 'quite a different thing, actually. I think I changed my mind so that I could be more easily analyzed.' The unnamed man 'Indeeds' rolling his hands she should go on. 'In a classroom, you know? By people who aren't so bright. The sort that think *Gatsby* is well written, you know?' Is that guilt in the fellow's next chuckle-swallow? He who had so railed against the Haves, just two drinks ago! 'What were you going to get before?' 'Something much more personal. Something far less Shakespeare.' The unnamed man - predatory sensing her discomfort - gives an obvious head-cock of steering the conversation into a side-street - clever, he knows not to barrel away too fast or she'll get spooked - and says he always wished he had a tattoo, but never just went ahead and got one. He even knows what he would get. Nothing fancy. An illustration from an old comic-book. Formative to him. He shrugs. Now pivots into a territory of Lucy is free to cleave the new path forward or to tell him 'Well, nice meeting you' - or any whatnot she might whatnot. 'Do you think there is such a thing as blame?' she asks, editing the question to 'Of being deserving-of-blame, I mean. That one can be at fault for something?' Who is writing you now, Lucy? Who are you meant to sound like, here? The deplorable fumes of an overworked pulp scribbler, fighting against plot-logic for deadline? 'I do' the man says. Did you expect him not to, Lucy? To act as though you are a pity-case to be set outside the well-established norms of ideas such as Guilt, Blame, Action, and Fault? 'I do, too' she says, finishes her drink. The man - this is a middle-school short-story, my God! or a rom com script that never got greenlit - decides to introduce himself at just that moment - he's Ewan - then to listen to her say 'I'm Heather' and not know her cringe at the turn this has taken.

The hostess comes over and lets Ewan know that his booth is ready, Lucy surprised at her sunk heart over their coming parting of ways. 'Will you have a bite with me?' Careful, Lucy. 'Sure' she not-a-second-thoughts. And like that is being led through the dining floor - feels to her like a circular blade cutting the correct length to a carpet. The hostess - she knows Ewan well - and Ewan have some small-talk, and once she has gone Ewan explains to Lucy how this is his 'regular booth' and that he's 'in here, all the time'. Wait. Wait. 'Do I know you from someplace?' Lucy is laying a napkin - lady-like she can be, you see? - over her lap while she asks, then reaches for the wine-list to seem she is not gauging every click to Ewan's eye-wrinkles for signs of the game. 'I don't think so. And I could commonplace flirt that I'd certainly remember, but frankly you seem the type too complicated to ever be sure of.' Both Lucy and Ewan make *Wait-what?* faces at that and - gosh Lucy, how goo-belly of you - share an exactly equal-length laugh and both blush. 'Can we both assume that came out fantastically elegant - like the epitaph Dante would have written for Wordsworth or something?' But this, before being replied to, suddenly reminds the man that he thinks headstones are a fat waste of time! That he hates how people know where great poets are buried. 'There should just be rumors - such burials should not even be recorded in ledgers. Oral tradition alone to keep track - and after not so very long, nobody really knows. *I hear Picasso is buried here*, someone will say. Folks wander over. No way to tell!' But seeing Lucy's not-so-enamored blink, he drops the line and admits he is trying to impress her and thinks he is falling far short. 'You are' she says. 'But everyone does.' 'I honestly don't know who Dante or Wordsworth are' Ewan so-blatantly lies 'and I only know about Picasso because of a magazine I read at the dentist.' Lucy lets the scene fall to silence after a curt little Hmn. Reads wine without prices. Words she cannot pronounce meaning tastes she has no idea of. Long enough, she decides to say 'You regret asking me to sit with you, yet?' But - too quick for you, Lucy! - he doesn't look up from setting his silverware in a line and says 'Yes.'

Meals like this are the worst, the most ponderless things. Lucy should extricate herself, but to do so seems like admitting to a typo she's too stubborn to not insist that she loves. Are you expecting this to go somewhere, Lucy? To date: every expectation of this adventure has be undone. And now you are sitting with some hipster dullard who is just staring-contesting you out of spite! He eats here 'all the time' for God's sake! He has a regular booth! He doesn't care if you make this interminable, he'll likely go home and use it as fodder for his novel. Oh ho! Perhaps he is the orbit you've fallen into - his influence making you some *Cliff's Notes* chapter, take-home-test due tomorrow. Maybe. Or maybe you should have just gone to sleep and now booze is oatmealing your faculties - and that oatmeal has been left to harden to elephant-hide in the sink, overnight. Say something to him? But what? He's a drip. A sackful of Subjects that match Predicates. A person who thinks a symbol means what it means. But nobody brought you to this moment but you, Lucy Jinx. There are no bogeys and are no gremlins who set up the scenes beforehand. Your biggest fear, isn't it? You and your decades-old body, you and your past-prime brain, always fallen short! This is where you have brought yourself. Based on aren't-you-so-clever and there's-art-where-you-say-there-is. Well - there isn't, Jinx! You are no more a poet than a corkscrew is a hummingbird. You're just a patron in this café with no one to meet - a lonely, mealy-worm bellied woman who this-where-you've-come-to-tonight. Do you need to believe the world has screwed you? When did it? When did it, Lucy!? Someone hurt your feelings? Someone didn't say just exactly what you wanted them to and so that means the Gods of Old must have thundered their armies to stop you up, that Mythos came strangling to keep you from being the holy-spark you are? You're here because you're here, Lucy. This meal is the worst because you're in it with you.

Here is the speech Lucy gives Ewan: 'I'm running away. If you want to know. I know that I'm terrible company. I am running away from everything - I am staying at a shitbag hotel and only wound up here because my head is a gargle of paranoia and I find sickbed belief in my own bed-time stories. I run away because it seems ethical. Or so I say. But I think I warp the world until it seems the only way to fix it is to remove myself - and then I do. So: I came here, to this place, thinking there was going to be something awful waiting. Because I found a match-booklet months ago, right when I needed a light. And then someone said the name of this place and so I slavishly made my way here expecting to encounter - I don't what, exactly - some coincidental being, a representation of how right I am about being constantly drowned. Sorry - I've obviously also had too much to drink - but this is who you are sitting with. I asked you, for example, if I knew you because I thought maybe that's why you were talking to me. You'd recognized me, knew I hadn't you back, and were coiling me around into your intentions. Even now, I think that a little. Even now, saying this to you, I think that I only am doing so so that when I play into your hands you'll know that I know that I am and so at least you can never be smarter than me. I'm barking, my man - barking! I'm the tall grass where the *Mad Hatter* lays his eggs. All I know how to do is dodge, you know? All I know how to do is convince myself I'm staying one step ahead and so my brain has hardwired to invent broken-mother's-backs out of everything. Somewhere, when I was young, I made the mistake of thinking I was smart or beautiful or clever or something. I made the mistake of having pride and thinking myself better - and so now mop-face myself in yuck-water strides through I'm-worse-all-the-time. But I'm good at being this. I'm terrifically good at this. Ewan, you should see the people who I have made trust me and who shower me with themselves, in their every gesture such aplomb! When you look at me now, for example, I bet you don't just see a skeleton who has borrowed every creak, every clatter of its bones - but that's all I am. No. I tell you: it's all that I am - that's all I am.'

Wait: before you go too far Lucy, remember you don't actually remember what you said. Right now, Lucy Jinx is in the toilet again, vomiting. And thinks she's crying, as well. Either way, she's spitting and sucking in nostrilfuls of acrid string that must be coloured lime-yellow. A woman in the next stall is asking her - for the fourth time - if a cab has actually been called and Lucy is - her voice as though trying to disguise all the retching up goings-on she's engaged in - says 'Yes, they should be here soon - but I really could walk.' A train-crash of the toilet colliding its flush. Lucy probes fingers down her and gets a good gurgly-heave-ho of liquid and cigarette smoke from the barest scrape of the lowest bottom she has out, hoping the two noises combined into one perfectly appropriate one. Someone is smoking out there. A staff member? Wait: someone called a cab? 'Is someone there?' No one answers. 'Is someone there!?' Lucy says, now sitting on the floor with her arm propped up over the cavity of the toilet mouth, a chill of the water hissing below, nipping at the skin of her elbow. 'Hello?' Someone is smoking, though. Lucy lights up her own. How long has Lucy been in the toilet? Factually? Not long. How long does it feel like for her? *Drunk*. It feels *Drunk* for her. Like the dial turned the color from white-to-green and now what was white never happened. *Drunk*. Just this hanging coat of worry that she'd said something silly to some man. But had she? 'Name one thing that you said' she demands of herself. As though if she cannot she has proven her point! As though if she cannot she isn't! Just isn't. 'Isn't' she says. And of course this night ended up drunk. The night, itself - she just a bleach odor in it, the ache of a cold hand pressing on toilet tile too long. You're leaving anyway, Lucy - who cares what you said? You think this night is any more formless than any other? This is just a person named Lucy Jinx on a toilet floor not being answered by whoever is out there smoking. Are we really to pretend that's so singular? Even Lucy knows not to pay Lucy much mind.

THE SOUND IN LUCY'S HEAD: blade of an ice-skate, clack of a roller-skate, long of a knife across a sharpening stone. She isn't asleep. The sound in Lucy's head: the up-down-up-down of a record needle across a childish cardboard mock-up of a record, the fip-fip-fip of a grade-school film projector done with the feature, waiting for the lights to come on. There - out the window - that looks like an upside down Q. What? Lucy's eyes aren't even open. The radio is going on about Chantilly lace. The sound in Lucy's head: two pennies rubbed against either side of a nickel, forefinger and thumb pincering down on the sides of a palm-sized beanbag, the foot of a stuffed rhinoceros filled with something like uncooked rice being ground under heel. Where is this car going? 'You shouldn't be driving' she says, maybe doesn't say, and the response she hears is griddle spit, her unopened eyes crinkle as they roll away from it. The sound in Lucy's head: the shuffle of a caged rabbit skittering over newspaper, chalk dotting *J*s on barely-dry-after-drizzle sidewalk squares, the skid of hopscotch in last year's shoes. 'Are you doing okay, back there?' 'Mind your business' Lucy says and with the retort she feels his handback smack window glass, opens her eyes long enough to notice she is lain out on the rear seat, one hand now up over seat-back, the other dragging through rubbish on the floor, something sticky. 'No' - laughter laughter, kindly molasses paced - 'you just threw up.' 'What?' 'You threw up.' 'I didn't spill a soda?' - laughter laugther and she feels something slip over her knee and away. The sound in Lucy's head: stem of a leaf - the meat of it crisped and broken away - stuck in a bicycle wheel, the slow-as-you-can bridge of a deck of cards and the shushing push together of the parted halves, a ball-bearing loose in the wooden bottom drawer of your favorite aunt's desk. Lucy tries to sit up, but the inward grip of her skin around her face is too much. Crabapple eyes, she wilts and snorts something long out of her nose which she wipes at and hears herself snoring. 'Lucy?' Lucy? 'I didn't' Lucy says. 'I know you didn't - I just needed to hear you, you'd gone really quiet.' 'How long is this suppose to take!?' Lucy demands. Laughter - peach-furred and duckbilled. The sound in Lucy's head: change in a pile in a pocket that is hupping left-and-right, left-and-right in pace with a skinny girl's jog.

'Where's here?' Lucy asks, being helped to walk and watching the dangle of her hand. 'What's your room number? The key really doesn't say.' 'What key?' 'Your key. Sit down a minute.' And then Lucy is sitting on a stair and can smell it has rained some time recently. 'Where's this?' she asks, feeling like she's squinting but also like she's widening her eyes and certainly really doing neither. 'We're at your hotel. I hope.' 'The *StayWell*?' Whoever it is claps once and she can see the *Hooray!* gesture in the sound of his '*StayWell*! So we got that, eh?' Whoever it is. Well, who is it? 'Who are you?' Lucy asks. It is brick she is leaned to and her shoulder is bruise-cold from the contact, her leg beginning to cramp from the foot-top up, veins in a strangle and toes pulsing to spread wider than a mile-long. 'I'm Ewan. We met earlier. We got on famously.' 'Did we?' Lucy seems astonished by this. 'I thought we did' Ewan guffaws. 'You're not the best company for self-esteem, you know?' 'Where did we meet?' But whatever he just said Lucy obviously marked as irrelevant, having to stand and press her weight down against this Charley-horse. 'What's wrong?' 'What?' 'What are you doing?' 'My leg is cramping?' This seems to go on for an hour. Finally, she had leg bent like she's tying her shoes and is smoothing her cupped hands over both rounds of her ankle. 'You look like an idiot - let me.' She makes the sound Pfphfst and says 'Fine' starts rubbing her eyes while Ewan's larger hands firmer her ankle, grip all the way down the calve. She pictures herself used like the club of a cartoon caveman. 'Does it tickle?' 'Gah! Don't stop!' The pressure returns, the cramp momentarily abiding again. 'You're a fucking asshole, Ewan or whomever!' 'Sorry. I've never had someone with legs this rickety.' 'Was that your car? That we drove here in?' 'Yes. You said you don't have a car.' 'I don't!' Lucy has had about enough of Ewan. She yanks her leg from him and wheels around on him menacingly. 'I wasn't accusing you of anything' he laughs. Now she is sitting, again. The cold at her ass right away lets her know if she doesn't stand up her leg will go off again. 'I need a cigarette and to stand up' she petulants. 'Which one are you going to help me with?'

She hears the room door close - sea-legs attained as they got to the interior corridor and her vision now passable - quickly puts to place the chain and downs the bolt. And as Ewan says 'Do you need me to get you' she grabs him by the face and kisses him full on - then her hands moving down his sides, clawing cloth, and thumbs wind up hooked in his belt-loops. But he pushes her away and - debonair and curtsy in affect - says 'We don't need to start that, now.' Lucy is removing her top and Ewan is saying 'Hey' a lot. '*Hey* what?' she blithes and moves chest-strut back toward him, his hands gripping her arms enough to stop her, maybe enough to bruise if she's as fragile as she usually is. 'You don't want to kiss me?' she pesters, making kiss-bites in the air like a snapping turtle being held back by a gingerly pinch on its tail from taking a chunk out of a teasingly-in-front-of-it leaf. 'I don't.' 'You don't?' 'Nope' Ewan in his oh-so-pleasant tone oh-so-pleasants. Lucy is backed up, sat now to the bed. 'Because this room looks like the word *Jism*, is that why not?' Big blurt of *Ha!* from Ewan, then 'No, no - the room is just my style, actually.' 'Because my mouth tastes like vomit, then? Because if it's only that, there is a bottle labeled *Mouth* over there that can fix it - seriously, go look.' Lucy points and tries to stand and sinks back to sitting and Ewan has been saying, palms up 'Yes, I quite believe there is a bottle labeled *Mouth* - but it's not that, at all.' 'Because I'm old - you don't like old tits and stuff?' 'No, Lucy.' 'You do like old tits and stuff?' She emphasizes the *Do* in that question. 'I like them just fine.' 'Because I have a few of them - you don't need to say you do if you don't.' 'Well, I do - hey, can you put your shirt on?' Ewan likely says this because - and she realizes she is - Lucy is unclasping her bra. 'You're a prude, man. You don't understand squat!' And over her head goes her shirt. 'It's inside-out' - Ewan's face in front of hers now - 'so you look cool, don't worry.' She kisses him and he lets her a moment, then he just stands up. 'I'm sorry I'm kissing you. I don't even like you, so don't worry.' And now she feels a warm wet cloth across her neck and her shirt moved aside a bit so it can get at her shoulder. Ewan is asking her is she's okay - or does she need to get to the toilet, again?

In the corridor, she can hear that outside it is raining a kettledrum. 'You're terrific' she explains, slung to Ewan 'and I am going to get you the Keys to the City for this or something.' 'Am I terrific?' he asks, tone in his voice like in the movies where one buddy is carrying another buddy along through a blizzard and the buddy being carried is not long for this world. 'What's so terrific about me?' Lucy gets to her own steam again and manages a meek chug-a-lug of a few paces before realizing how best it is for her to take Ewan's offered support. 'You didn't just rape me. That's one. And probably the bulk of it.' The by-now-familiar sound of Ewan chuckling down his nose, almost like the sound turned sheets of paper make when recorded by a discount brand Dictaphone. 'It didn't seem proper - you seem pretty stuck on some girl, actually.' Lucy makes a face indicating she is emphatically pausing, but Ewan - faced as he is, thataway - does not do his scripted part to this, instead reiterates how he really could have walked to the vending machine and brought stuff back. 'Or I can drive someplace - you can even fall asleep, I'll let myself in and leave the key.' But nope, Lucy isn't letting the sly dog away just so. 'What girl? What do you mean? What girl am I hung up on?' When he doesn't answer, she protests by limping all of her weight to him, he responding in his normal good humor but halting and leaning her against a wall she then slides down. 'I'm serious' she eyes up at him. 'What girl? Was I really going on about some girl?' 'You were' Ewan says, almost drowned out by the slap of cigarette pack to his palm. 'Are we having a smoke break?' 'We are.' 'Fine. Give me one, then.' And Lucy spoilts her hand up, fingers will-o-wisp gimmieing. 'Some girl called *Elliott*'. Lucy lights her smoke and burns her finger when she fails to shake out the match flame. 'How the fuck did you know Elliott is a girl? She's not named one!' Ewan gathered from context, he explains, from much belabored context. Lucy makes a kind of Smumf sound, smokes a few long drags and says 'Well, that's stupid. Because I don't even like her, man. You must be wrong.'

But Ewan will not help Lucy undress - even out of her shoes - even though she explains it's just to get in a shower. And Ewan won't hang out while she showers, no matter how paranoid Lucy calls him. 'I clean up good though' she whines, her eyes sluggish in spit bubbles. 'I saw you clean' - Ewan is sitting on the side of the bed, caressing Lucy's forearm how one might the much-needled arm of an invalid at the end of visiting-hours - 'and I honestly prefer you dirty.' She nose-whistles and knows she is speaking in a slur. 'Well, you're either tricking me in to not showering, which is mean' - she makes a flap of her free hand meant to be a pretend smack to his face - 'or else are flirting, which it seems a bit late-to-the-party to be starting.' Whatever is in her ear is having trouble being got out - and something as wide as a falcon beak in being used to prise the canals open and she can feel the adolescent fumbling of fingers all squabbling like turkeys and making her sweat. 'Hey' she says, jerking awake, finding Ewan midsentence stopping and looking at her, dubiousness mixed with concern. 'You need to throw up, again?' 'Why were they here?' 'Whom?' He humors her with a move of eyes left to right. 'Nevermind. Fuck. You're making fun of me. The people who brought all those little books, you know?' And her face is to the wall and the smell of grass is gargantuan - whoever is patting her back starting to do it too hard, like they are paying more attention to whatever is making that squealing upstairs than her - the feet get heavier and the pig gets her whole hand in and she can feel the sores under its tongue, pearl-big and rough like sour-gumballs, exactly like her cousin was saying. 'What's wrong?' Ewan blinks. Has any time even passed between that dream and awake? 'What do you mean?' he asks, using his shoulder to wipe at an itch on his nose. 'You're just looking at me.' 'I asked if you need me to take you over to the toilet.' 'I don't know what you're talking about, anymore' Lucy sighs, arches her back and thinks she is giggling and unbuttons her pants while she yawns and her ears go high-pitched then pop.

By later, Ewan left the room and it's been however long that Lucy has been awake and not thinking anything. Really not thinking. Really. Really not. Not even a sound to describe, not even the always-there burble of numb that comes with even her quietest head. Maybe this is a moment she won't remember. Realizing that she was not thinking. She has no other memory of such a time, but maybe one or two moments like this go by every day, every night, and the mechanism of the brain is to flush the memories without quarter. She hopes this one stays. Already her head has filled with the ruckus of thought and the sound of unformed words, the rivulets of unconscious streaking the curve of her skull's inside. And already she cannot explain what it felt like to not be thinking - so that's gone and she knows it. Soon she'll sleep and not even remember there was something to miss. Haven't you thought this before though, Lucy? Maybe. But the trouble is, she could think something like this - think this exact *This* in fact - without ever having to even have caught herself thinking absolutely nothing. Rendition. Rendition. She says aloud '*Soultmalt.*' '*Sourmalt*' she says aloud. '*Ss. Ow. Er. Maul. Lt. S. Hou. Er. Mmm. All. T. Se. Our. Mall. Teh. Sourmalt.*' And with that Lucy has sat up and is checking the door to the room. Unchained and unbolted - but what was Ewan supposed to do about that? 'Now you're just picking on the putz' Lucy says, long sharp scratch to the back of her head where there seems to be an eczema patch that has ruptured and discharged something colorless and clammy-cool when agitated. '*Putz*' she says. '*Puh. Tuh. Zee. Puh. Uh. Tuhz. Putz.*' Big yawn that candy-wrapper crinkles her eyes - and her eyes are grease pools when she opens them - and the world rather purrs how it's time for sleep and rather cautions it, too. Lucy to the room protests that she had been trying to sleep, so needs to be given credit for that. And walks in a seesaw way to the bathroom sink, looking for her toothbrush. Where is her toothbrush? Hmn she makes as the sound of her stumpedness. But it is no matter. She moves to the toilet, undoing herself of all lower garments, sits and tries to lean back but finds the bulb of the toilet-tank too cold, standoffishing her. And bends in half, forward. And between limp belly-skin and skin of her together-knees where it piles, she feels gurgles of hunger and soon-to-hiss-out-from-her squeaks.

Lucy Jinx's body, to the water's tumble, feels open all along itself in mouths the size of safety-pin pricks. Her jaw remains clenched as she adjusts at the dials, shivering in the sameness of the stream. When she turns her back, the multitude of lashings she feels, though each microscopic, make her screech out and burp, which itself rises acid reflux up her throat. What a dismal old shipwreck ye be, Lucy Jinx, what a fallen apart log! The duration of this shower is what a dried-stiff piece of blue-edged paper from an old paperback must feel like when incinerated. She is surprised to find the room clear of smoke when she finally turns shut the tap and ventures out toward the bed - no way will she towel off, look at those things! But is this the worst night of her life? Hardly. In fact, it is only her on-in-years that is keeping it from being hotly enjoyable. Yes: back her up two decades and this would be a boast for the next eighteen weeks! She'd embellish up all of it. And Ewan would have bedded her whether he'd desired it or no! Oh yes, let the record reflect how Lucy had been a feisty one! False-alarm red and papercut orange, she'd wilded the hours until the hours'd tried to disown her! Remember? Remember, Lucy? *Bloast!* That had been the word! Layla had coined it but had shared the honor with Lucy since it was coined at the tail end of one of Lucy's verbose debauchings. 'We are bloated with boasting! Bloat and boast!' 'We are *bloast*, Lucy Jinx - we are tinder-stick violet and purple pastel disemboweled!' Oh if only Layla were here! They'd have stashed a body in the ice machine, by now. Ewan had been a nice guy, but he'd have had seen too much and could never be trusted to keep such buxom secrets safe-housed. Lucy becomes too shivery to look for her phone though, just bundles up in the five-o'clock shadow of the bedcovers and figures all there is to do is wait wide-eyed till dawn. Or it might be dawn. Her nipples stand stiff, which only makes the touch of the covers the worse. She shirks them off and - looking down - sees how many slashes her scratching fingers have raked to her heavy-down-breast's white.

This is one thing Lucy dreams: her hand gets more mannish, then thin-manned, then ashen-skinned as though kept out gloveless too long at winter, and patterns begin emerging on it she almost recognizes. And the idea of patterns makes her feel she is talking in a strict meter. She knows she is, in fact - and starts saying things to everyone to prove it. But she's faking it, they insist. 'You're doing that, just stop. You can stop. Just stop! And her left hand fists almost all the way and she can't angle right to get the thumb out from under the other fingers, so scared that if she tugs wrong it'll dislocate for good. 'Just put your gloves on!' Someone is upset. Slamming a book shut they have been trying to study from for a long time - and Lucy knows she has seen them trying - out of the corner-of-her-eye - and now is sheepish with regretting she's waited until they finally had to raise their voice for her to just shut up with her nonsense. This is another thing Lucy dreams: to the refrigerator she returns, but the egg cartons are all empty. One has an egg, finally, but it was kept to the back and had frozen, is half-cracked beside. Rather than throwing it out though, she picks at it with a pin she takes from her hair - which cascades down her back to where a cat, tall as the sofa arm, bats at it, tangling its claw and limping along after her on three legs as she gets to the front door. 'What do you want?' Through the door comes a reply. Lucy can't hear. And the knocking gets louder. And she can't get her eye to the peep-hole correctly to see out, always comes at it from too far above or from under in such a way that her nose casts an obscuring shadow. That dream she wakes from, feeling uneasy about. Outside the drawn curtain is the sound of a street sweeper and of the radio on inside of it. She listens until the sound seems to reach the end of the parking lot, to stay put in one place - figures the driver is smoking a butt. Yawns into her bent elbow which smells so salty she gives it a lick, tongue-tip shrinking as though to the frost-bit snap of a clothespin.

Next thing Lucy knows, that is housekeeping knocking, trying at the still chained door. 'One moment!' Lucy nudes as she ups her pants, snagging some thigh skin. Impatient old woman - all of four foot tall - half-Russianing at her how it is past time to check out. 'Then I'm extending my stay' Lucy still-blearies. But this only grows the aggravation of the woman. No, the broad will not hear any of Lucy's polite voice and calm body - no no, the shrew just foreign-tongues at a sheet of paper, tapping the clicker of the back end of a pen against this point and that point and that point. 'Well, Jesus!' Lucy finally can't-take-its 'What in Hell do you want me to do!? Tell me, man! You want me to just leave!?' Lucy makes a rushing gesture, shoulder in and arms with elbows to waist as she twists her torso, laughing. 'I can skedaddle, man - but you're gonna have to shut up to make me!' That seemed to get at something raw with the woman. '*Shut up?*' the woman hotheads and then mangle-speaks about how she is doing her job but Lucy is not doing hers. 'I don't have a job, you goon!' This is really quite hilarious - if not for the broken-dish hangover, strict between the sides of Lucy's knit brow, she would be struggling to memorize this to relate it later just exactly. Now the woman is making - both hands, like big waves of fanning smoke, arm-length swings leaving her short of breath - gestures that Lucy should move out of the doorway. So Lucy does. The old woman makes a circuit of the room, parting the blinds and gesticulating at the bright of the afternoon. You're in the world's most violent beginner's language course, Lucy! If you wanted, you could almost see the bright yellow of subtitles beneath this hag's haggish fingers as they stab. 'I get it! I get it!' Lucy says, approaching - but is no sooner over the threshold than the woman, arms above head, waves her to stay out. 'Are you goddamn kidding me!?' But the woman, it seems, is not. Continues her harangue another five minutes before shutting the blinds and muting entire, exiting past Lucy without meeting her eyes. Now that it's quiet, Lucy kind of feels bad. What had that all been? Is this poor woman now forced to stay on shift, late to pick her children up from daycare or something? In penance, Lucy moves her suitcase onto the bed.

There you are, Lucy. Mirrored. Moth-mouthed and eyes rhododendron. What a state of you! Arms feeble-crotched, veiny and muscleless, worm-titted and goose-honk for tummy. You're a broken knee shoved in a tap-shoe. How have you come to this? How? Keep in mind, as Lucy looks at herself she is not saying this with gloomy pangs any longer, only with a curiosity akin to a dog with a snout under the sofa ruffle. Lucy Jinx: a volume roughly thumbed and lick-fingered. Lucy Jinx: this moment inevitable as a bad glass of wine. Now has it all been upturned? Or are you just procrastinating and playacting how your features are so in need of your dander-tongued poetry? Here's how it stands, Lucy: you need to decide what you are doing. Last night was a fine time and only you drifted it anyplace nearly to nightmare. Ewan? Fine chap. Look around - he didn't even leave contact information, nothing to link you to that. File it all as a fever dream, a bleed from a fleabite on your brain-tip. But it is midafternoon now and your options are dwindled and there is no longer Fate to blame for your ushering. Do what you want. Do you know what that is? Nothing is gun-barreling you. People are waiting in some directions and vastness rolls out in the others. People there, too? Maybe. But that's as much a figment as last night's carnival tent was. You are the only attraction. Your own shrunken-head on display. The world's largest pig, Lucy. The world's smallest horse. You are the broken forehead of a mock replica of Goliath's skull. But who is paying for ganders at you? Nobody, Lucy. The interest of even the most insensitive and obsessive Fate has worn out and you are discarded. Or freed. Which are one and the same. But you have survived. You have survived the miasma of your life until now, gotten this far along by telling yourself you're a kick-mule to Destiny - but now you have nothing to answer to or to blame but yourself. And there you are. Mirrored. What a state of you. Heart a pulse as much as the stammer of a radio between station and static.


SAME SKY AS ALWAYS, FLAT-CHESTED and up there. Right now, Lucy is sure that it is looking up rather than down. Yes, Lucy understands the physical universe, that the world is a spheroidal thing and the sky is round all around it - what she means is: vantage from the ground, looking up, we find the sky, Lucy

being certain it is looking in all directions but at the Earth. The too long a laugh
of her hangover is faded, somewhat. She steps down from the bus, sick of her
suitcase and of feeling she deserves whatever odd looks it is earning her. What
a rigamarole this has all become. *Rigamarole*. Alternative spelling: *Rigmarole*.
*Rigmarole*. Synonym: *Lucy Jinx*. Oh well. So she has to bout with this luggage a few
blocks longer - the pestering refusal of the wheels to turn proper, to instead
start stubborning and digging their toes into the pavement as they are pulled -
but then she can stand in a proper shower and lounge on a proper sofa and sleep
in a proper bed while she makes up her mind, finally. *Incremental* is the method
of Lucy! Perhaps if all her life she had moved only an inch-at-a-time - instead of
not-at-all then panicking she should be further along and so blind-blunder-until-
breathless - she would have made the exact, straight-line progress she believes
most people do. Because Lucy Jinx does believe that. No. That the average
person moves like an unarced stream? No. That they melt like popsicles, exactly
just right? No. Most people don't wonder who they are - or if they do, they
mean so rhetorically and to front-off to lovers, to con hands under blouses, or
as a way to live without needing a paycheck on the regular. Lucy spent too long
actually wondering, throughout her life. Spent too much time actually looking.
Then all those sophomoric games that pleased her awhile - those Who-I-am-is-
I-am-searching-for-who-I-ams. Gah! What rubbish and pat-a-cake games of her
identity! What else could it have been, Lucy? Just 'I am this, I want that, here I
go, there I went, here I am?' But no one gives awards for that, do they? No one
lavishes perfume on those bones for centuries, right? It is the questioners and
the abberants who are monumented and Iconed - the singulars who become the
alofted! Ah, Lucy - if only that were true. But sadly, it's the most-ordinary who
are remembered - or anyway, the most-ordinary are the ones that the most-
ordinary pay the most attention to.

Try this: shut up and watch. Don't think. Sit at this fast-food booth and eat.
No poetry. No analysis. Over there? Two school-aged girls, whispering and then
suddenly laughing pots-and-pans loud. What about it? Nothing. Is it necessary
to point out the ceremony of their Shh-shh-quiet-quiet only to lead to their
squeals and the Shh-and-shoves when they know eyes are to them? Must you
sigh and think 'If you want to have secrets, you're doing it wrong'? Need you
draft off commentary on the betrayer impulse that will turn on itself if there is
no one else to back-stab - criminals all eventually confessing not out of a need
to be known, just having run out of anyone near enough to them to one-over?
Answer: It is not necessary. Though of course - very clever - you just did just
that! And Oh turning it into a commentary about self-betrayal whilst betraying
yourself - what do you want, Lucy? A Nobel Prize in irony? How about we go
kid-game on this? Who can win a prize for being quiet the longest - by which I

mean in-their-heads-as-well? How would you fare there, smart-guy? And as Lucy will argue, of course, that if it really were such a contest there would be no way to judge - as one can blank-face but have bucket-of-explosives going off verbally, philosophically, klaxons and whistles of tumultuous thinking and no tick to betray it - we will just say 'Honor System' and leave it at that. But needlessly we answer! Obviously too late! You've lost again, Lucy. And have you even tasted your meal? What do you take away from all of this thinking? Meticulous you. *Metus* - Latin root of *Fear*. *Metum habeo*. Remember that, Lucy? Not 'I am fearful' but 'I entertain fear.' Another tattoo, perhaps? Lucy looks at her ink-free forearm and knows she ought have a pair. *Metum habeo* or *I entertain fear*? This may be a case where the English outclasses the untranslated. Lucy. Lucy! Yes? You're just supposed to be sitting. Looking. Like the rest of this lot. You see that scruffy-jawed one, there? That nothing but a complaint about his job, a kidney, and some bowels? See him? Yes. Good. Now: don't think anything. Don't call him *vanitati*. Latin for *Meaningless*. Root of *Vainglory*. Again, English winning. Don't say that where he should have a soul there is just a wet sock alive with inchworms. Just look. Just look at him! Are you nothing but comments, Lucy? Do you even need eyes!?

A bit later and Lucy has drafted this by hand - on the backside of a page in her notebook, this the symbolic thig to do to assure herself it doesn't matter what she writes because the words will go no further. She has written: *Hi Ariel*. As a salutation. The conceit is that this is the draft of a letter. And then Lucy has written: I rather agree about the Universe. You probably know that. And what else bothers me - and will probably you - is how people think there are really ways to fundamentally make things different. Let me make this clear: if there had never been rock 'n roll, the world would look exactly like it does now - there would just be different music playing, is all. I know we like to believe otherwise. That if somehow jazz hadn't caught on we'd look around and recognize nothing - blink-of-an-eye and everything in the whole of history has changed! That's all just so much hogwash! That fatalism will get you nowhere! Look at a photo from six decades ago, five, four - and so on, do I really need to write *three two one*? - and a lot of things happened between those photos but the world is not so unrecognizable, is it? And anyway: what changed would have, anyway. We dropped atomic bombs, Ariel! We did. Decades on, is the world otherworldly? Maybe the relatives of those who were instantaneously undone will say 'Oh but look! In this era people played music on vinyl and in this era cassettes and in this compact discs! That explosion fundamentally altered the face of the world!' Maybe - but I doubt it. At best, they can say 'That day made the world ugly.' But someone - a *wisenheimer*, right? - will always be there to point out some atrocity far past. Then some other clever-head will say 'Maybe that lead to the Atom Bomb!' And then another 'That doesn't look much different though, does it?' The most astonishing development will lead to something just like it and which will yield the same result. Even cells know this. Replication. Replication. We don't want change, just continuation. And we want continuation-of-the-same. It's just now we've discovered iron ore, the printing press, denim, digital - so the same looks just the tiniest bit different. Give it awhile and it won't.

Well, what a terrible letter! Go on, Lucy - critique it. Other than a generally good thesis about *the Atom Bomb not having changed much of anything* - implicitly saying 'If that didn't change anything what, really, did rock 'n roll change?' it's all so much flash-powder whingeing! Some love letter! Here Lucy balks, though. Had she said it was a love letter? Can't she just share some thoughts with Ariel? All of a sudden her every interaction with the woman has to be about love and being-in-love? Lucy's more even-keeled side points out: every interaction? You've had none! And even this one you on-purposed to the back of a notebook page! Lucy closes the book then, refusing to finish the letter. Her thirst-for-justice makes her point out, though, that it was a direct response to Ariel's e-mail about how she saw the Universe as a perverse fanboy. She even said so in the letter! That's loving! Saying 'Ariel, I am interested in the things that you say and want to discuss them.' Then - maybe toward the end - Lucy would have added in *I love you* or something flirty - but if that is true, anyway, why should she have to say it all the time? Again, even-keeled: *All the time*? Name a time other than this! 'Theoretically' Lucy snorts - actually snorts! - and now is over-aware that she is still sitting here. There is a worker - just there - spraying down vacated tables and doing their politest to put off the other tables near Lucy till last. Assessment of those tables: they don't even need to be wiped, right now. Lucy would sit at any of them with Zero complaint, well assuming they had been recently wiped. She demonstratively picks up one of her remnant French-fries and gives it an eat, proclaiming her right to exist here! More irrelevant than a table-wipe? No, not she! And the tables don't even need to be cleaned. Tell them that. Say it, Lucy! It wouldn't even be weird. Open your notebook, look like you are concentrating, say it in a tone of Can-you-please-do-that-later? and they will! All you have to do is say it. And then write *I love you* at the end of your Ariel letter. To prove you can. And because you aren't going to send it, anyway. Do it like you are pretending to do it. Like it has to do with vinyl, Atom Bombs - all of that. Writing it will just be the most recent replication of not saying it, eh? Just like saying it was. Write that in your letter.

Gah! Foul-minded Lucy is on the street again and pestilent in all known dimensions. Her physical state has reached the post-debauched description of something like a three-quarters-filled vacuum bag. Press the button, she will still strain skin with hot air and the long settled, moist feeling dirt within her will have room to mist and hothead around. Her skin feels dry, like covered in that stuff. So, for sake of this description: her skin feels dry, as though she has been digging around in herself. And the realization that she got off much further away from Deb's apartment than she'd intended to does not help matters. What is the point of making definitive decisions if they are this much trouble!? This doesn't feel any less like aimless wandering. Lucy Jinx is not suddenly buoyed with purpose and focused determinedly on tomorrows-to-come in centimes-at-a-time. It is all a transaction, though. That is Lucy's attempt at making this all a swell worded epiphany, because that makes the acting on it go down less bitter. It is a transaction. Happiness is a fortune amassed nickel-after-dime. Soon, her pockets will be weighed down with the monies she has slaved for and those monies are moments of *Joy* she punches the clock of her life for and she trades them in for *Contentment* and *Happiness*. The same as the choice of a new suede coat! Yes, yes! Now, it may sound bitter to put it this way - but is anyone truly claiming *Choice* and *Happiness* are something else? A bit disingenuous to build your house by hand, to labor away at it for ages, and then sit there in it, comfortable and aged, toasting till death by your by-your-own-hands-stacked stone fireplace saying 'It sure was fun to do all that - not annoying at all!' Lucy's new deal: no more cockroaching-when-lights-come-on from here-to-there, this-to-that, as though some mad dash will accomplish Paradise. No, sir - no, ma'am! Lucy is fox-holing in. This is where she has dug. Her grave above ground until she's under-ited. This is where she will insist on *Happy* from the elements, till her water from the soil. Which may sound bitter. But why shouldn't it? Does *Happiness* preclude *Bitter*? Does *Peace* disavow constant, browbeating *Strife*? Lucy will experience every experience, here! She will not expect less-from-more or cleave-from-cleave.

Up we go. The elevator, even. Lucy wears the air of someone who hadn't left-for-good less than twenty-four hours ago. It's a shame she doesn't pass someone. If for no other reason than she has what she will say to them ready. They: 'Oh were you on a trip?' She: 'Yes, just got home.' Not very fancy, but she has it exactly prepared. And has dozens of faces to go with the words, depending, in part, on who does the asking, what their tone is, and how near to Deb's door Lucy is when asked. All variables taken into her accounting, Lucy estimates she has nineteen different expressions she might wear. Add in tones-of-voice she is prepared to adopt and it can only be fairly said there are *Umpteen* ways it can go. She even has a secondary-script prepared, in case *They* don't just say 'Oh were you on a trip?' but instead go with something like 'Welcome back!' or 'Are you staying with Deborah?' or 'I don't think we've met, I'm so-and-such and this is my husband such-and-so.' Her secondary-script, if *They* say that, is 'Hi - I'm just getting back from a trip.' Again: plain-Jane, but functional. Less faces to go with that one. She'll want to seem not to be trifled with, jet-lagged and not-over-a-recent-misfortune. Let *Trip* stand for something like *To bury my sister* or *To see my kids the one time of year I'm allowed to*. And here is Deb's corridor. Where Lucy is choosing to go. Twelve-step-program of foot-then-foot all down the hall, aphorisms and thoughts of how good it will be to feel she is constantly winning! Some people have to struggle to do what is regular. Lucy is like a drunk. But sadder, because she isn't a drunk. Still: she can say things like 'I realized something in me was broken, but didn't let that break me.' Yes. You will be an inspirational person to know, Lucy Jinx! Your every day shall stand testament to the importance of *Staying*! When others are down, you will be their Madonna - their if-she-can-do-it, their at-least-I'm-not-her. Here is the apartment door, Lucy. Stand there. Stand there. If nothing else, the cat will welcome you back. It will know your dark insides and how humbled you are. It will look at you and feel nonplussed that you didn't abandon it. There's that. 'Lucy Jinx is already in there' Lucy says in a whisper, key to the lock, treating it all like a sign.

So far, Lucy has accomplished putting her luggage back in the room she uses and paranoiacally unpacking it so that neither Deb nor Curtis can suspect she either left-and-has-come-back or is going-to-go. Stasis. She has accomplished: Pause. And making a sandwich. And setting it and some chips on a plate and turning on the television. The crunch of the chips in her head is as though she has earplugs in, the chew of the soft-bread-and-meat, too. Tilt-tilt like after a swim goes her head. Still, the rumbling-inside feel to the sound. Hangover symptom. Must be. If she were to look at that letter she'd wrote it'd likely have dozens more misspellings than it would have under normal conditions. This sandwich is probably more sloppily made than usual and she probably left more of mess on the counter than she'd realized. Also: the television volume is likely louder than it seems. She was merely drunk, last night. Perfectly normal. And another good sign: she is feeling uneasy that Ewan didn't fuck her. Kind of him - gallant and all - yet what was the matter? It must have been his plan to. And it was only when she went on about Elliott that things had gone change-of-heart for him, yes? That just doesn't make sense, though. He'd taken her back to her place with the intent to leave her senseless and full with him - so why would Elliott make any difference? Wouldn't he have already assumed her to be involved with someone, as charming as she had been? So: what was the matter? He'd known she was drunk when he took her back, so it could not have been that. All part of the fun - that would have been an attraction! Feature, not bug. The entire point, even! And there had been the opposite-of-resistance - Lucy had likely grabbed the bloke's joint at least a few times, the amount of kissing and pawing she recalls suggests at least that! So why had he just hung 'round with her? He could've paid for a cab. Or let her out at the hotel. The End. Even walked her to her door! He had stepped into her room. Right? 'Yes' Lucy says, the commercial she doesn't even register she is watching flailing in front of her. So: what was the matter with her, to him? She'll never know, of course. But it's a good sign she is curious, worried even - shows she is nothing more than recently drunk like a normal person, wondering about last night, today.

Then, in her room, Lucy undresses. Here. Now. Here, now. 'Here, now' she says. Then says 'Herenow.' Writes that down. Beautiful. Letters make everything glorious! Side note: now that Lucy has the one tattoo, it seems she has a subprogram dedicated to 'What ought I pair it with?' Two forearms - so: two tattoos. It's like leaving the last line of a sheet of paper blank when you could wring out one more phrase. How about: *Herenow? We defy augury - Herenow.* Oddly apropos. 'If *Apropos* is the right word' Lucy says, deciding, it seems, to sit naked and then to lay on the floor with the bedpillow plopped over her tummy, her groin, and her together thighs. Then, her eyes are open and the fear it has been longer than the minute or two it turns out to have been. Then, relaxation. So: what had been the fear? Well, for a moment Lucy was convinced that she should be gone without letting Deb know she was going. But that isn't so. Deb will be back any moment now, anyway. 'And I need some of her pot' Lucy says, underlining this all. Or maybe the fear had been some falling asleep quirk to the thought that unpacking the luggage was a way of tricking herself into this room making this room where-she-was-staying - now she would not have the strength to go, ever. But no, no. The unpacking had been to reset things from yesterday's failure of a flee. It would indicate to the world the wrong things were she to leave with the same packed bag. The meanings would smear. Smeared-meanings are bad. This is the start - here, today - of what will be Definitive Lucy. That was resetting the stage for tonight's show, refilling the prop-guns and all. What Lucy - Definitive Lucy - needs to start allowing is: Maybe the fear had been phantasmagoria - been nothing - a thought she can dismiss, one with domain over nothing. She'd merely drifted off, her body had startled, she had sat up. Lucy Jinx is sitting, Indian-style, on the floor of her room at Deb's, hugging her pillow. See? That's all. And that's okay? It's fine, Lucy. But it isn't anything! No - no, it's not. And it will stay that way for awhile. And you will survive.

Computer plugged in brings Lucy her next test. She ignores it - she'll get to it - for a moment to delete all of the responses to her model invites, not even opening them to read the names. That is a sub-test, as Lucy - before striking them permanently deleted from the *Trash* folder - wonders if some were cute put-ons from Ariel, teases to see if Lucy would this time suss out a topaz Victorie Elan. Anyway: now she cannot ignore it. A new e-mail - look - from *Illegible*

*Sparrow.* The subject line is just: *Ms. Jinx.* And here? Well: a new e-mail from Ariel. The subject line is just: *Lucy.* This is exactly why Lucy's new plan will fail! This is insurmountable! Both barrels at once! And today of all days! And right now of all times of today! See: if Lucy had checked her e-mail earlier, there would have just been the Illegible Sparrow missive to contend with. She wouldn't have, she'd have done nothing. But still! And not for another two hours would this Ariel e-mail have appeared. Which - 'Yes, yes fine!' Lucy swats as she uses putting on a t-shit as a method of procrastination - would have led to the even worse situation of having ignored the Illegible Sparrow e-mail, then discovering the Ariel one added in 'On top of that' - which Lucy knows is how she would have taken its appearance, as a second, vicious twist of her arm. Though - she relapses to as-of-yesterday Lucy Jinx here, feeling the return of the old course of her blood, knowing she is soothing herself in oblique commentary rather than being alive - in a way, it is even worse to find them both at once, because that means she found both at once and is still aware of how she would have reacted if she had found them one-and-then-the-other - so truly has to suffer both fates, now! And also: she can imagine having checked her e-mail an hour before the Illegible Sparrow one, feeling safe, then happening to feel like - say, just for argument - looking into if some of the model invites were really Ariel only to then find the Illegible Sparrow one, freaking out, to only now discover the Ariel into the mix when she got a grip and returned to be brave! Discovering it all now is the most abysmal, though! *Ms. Jinx. Lucy.* And all she can think seeing those Subject Lines is *we defy augury herenow*, so that idea is sullied - which brings to mind Heather, which brings to mind why Lucy can never - never, never ever - change! Because trying-to-change is what led to trying-to-change is what led to this!

So thank God that was the door! Lucy opens her room door a peck and says 'Deb?' in a semi-urgent, semi-just-curious way. And Deb rounds the corner then rolls her eyes and mockingly tiptoes as she asks 'What's up, man?' 'Is it just you?' Faux scardy-cat, glancing around, Deb stutters 'Wuh wuh whuduya muh muh muh mean?' Huff huff goes Lucy, real *Fuck you* to the breath. 'Is Curtis with you?' Deb dramatically pauses, moves her face almost lips-to-Lucy's, whispers between unparted teeth 'No' then long pauses 'Why?' 'Is he coming back, soon?' Deb pretends to be trying to see further into Lucy's room. 'What's going on in there? Are you vivisecting, again?' 'I just don't want to put on pants if I don't have to.' 'Oh' Deb deflates for comedy then thinks of something peppy for comedy 'You don't need to wear pants for Curtis' sake. He kind of likes naked chicks, you know?' Impatient eyes from Lucy. 'No' Deb Christ-Jesuses 'come out - without your pants. Curtis isn't here. What's going on?' 'Can we smoke some pot?' 'Can I take off my pants, too?' 'Oh Lord yes!' girlfriends

Lucy, bumping her bare hips to Deb's who mumbles 'Meh, you'd like that too much - I can't enjoy it if you like it that much.' 'Yes well, my loss' Lucy chirps and asks one more time about Curtis. 'I'm telling you, Lucy - after this I'm gonna make it my mission in life to get him to catch you out naked. Hasn't he seen you naked, yet?' But they soon agree, no, he once saw Lucy in a towel, once in just panties and a bra, but never nude. 'Okay - then it is my mission. So trim up and all. Or whatever you do. We don't want it to be traumatic for the poor duck.' 'Are you telling him it's your plan? Or is part of your plan making it a special surprise for him?' Deb bird-ticks her face as though considering all options. 'I should make it a surprise. But it's more important to make it actually happen, so I'll tell him. You look stellar with no pants, by the way - but what the fuck is going on, honestly?' Lucy splays on Deb's bed the count of ten, then sits up to see Deb already lighting a ready-rolled joint. 'I like your jaw when you concentrate, Deb. You look like a reptile.' And Deb goes a long 'Aw' - Lucy holding up fingers, old game between she and Deb, to indicate counting the *W*s - takes a drag, says 'You are just the sweetest thing when you're nervously breaking down or whatever you're doing' passes the smoke-scribbling joint over to Lucy.

LUCY JINX IS FEEDING LUCY Jinx some bits of a chicken nugget, the cat batting each morsel around a tap or two before suddenly lapping them up and seeming to swallow each by the very motion of shutting its trap. Lucy assumes the cat needs the nugget-portion to seem like an insect. Something. There is heat rising from the white flesh of the chicken when she pulls each nugget in half. This probably makes the cat think the meat is still alive. The pats at it are first verifying, then verifying the verification. A few more taps of that. Lap. Gulp. Tongue windshield-wipes the dots where the whiskers come out from. Ready for new morsel. Let it be known: Lucy is explaining these theories aloud. Curtis, who was so kind as to bring the food home for the trio - quarto if cat is counted, there had been, earlier, a debate on this and no absolute consensus had been reached, Curtis thought *Quarto*, Lucy thought *Trio*, Deb was in a pensively-semantical mood and kept wanting to go over and over things, refusing anything as absolute except that nothing was - now puts the query forward 'What do you mean by *verifying the verification*?' Lucy means: the nugget bit seems dead, except for the heat, suggesting warmth, suggesting animal-perhaps-wounded - 'Guts would issue heat' Lucy explains 'a slashed shoulder would issue heat' - so the first tap - 'Or *ver-if-i-ca-tion*' she slow motions the word, mostly to be a dick - is to - 'like like like' she says, snapping her fingers - see if the nugget is alive at all.

'But' Lucy sits up to indicate to Curtis - and less so to Deb, who is doing something with her toe - 'the tap, the *verification* makes the thing move. So: *it then needs to be verified: Wait, was that it moving, or me-moving-it?*' Curtis, getting the drift, picks up saying 'Then the further verifications are safeguards and due to *It could be tricking me, realizing what I'm up to.*' 'Exactly' Lucy thumbs-ups. 'And then he just says *Fuck it* and eats it because, in a kind of intellectual shame, he realizes *That's all I was gonna do anyway, so what am I tapping it for? How verified does this need to be!?*' Curtis fake bellows, mouth full, gesticulating existential crisis with two fists brandished at Heaven. 'Why does he do it every time, though?' Deb finally snaps to - is also scratching kitty-Jinx's middle-back while she asks. 'Cats rest, Deb. After everything. It's why they're able to do so many of the things they do, you know? Evolution.'

The symposium moves to: Curtis with ice cream sandwich, Deb finally eating her chicken-bacon sandwich, Lucy with a bag of microwave popcorn she realized she does not want but which Curtis bullied her in to having to suffer with because otherwise she'd be thumbing her nose at a lot of hard work from the manufacturers. The subject comes around to - as history indicates is the usual course - *Love*. And to this, Curtis is outlining - anxious-eyeing the new joint with each over-fast swallow of his ice cream - the following - based, he explains, on memories pulled from his own youth. 'There had been a span of time' - he believes second-through-fifth-grade, or at least several months of two different school years - 'where the boys would all say to each other *I love you* but then tack on the addendum *Like a friend.* They would say it at all' Curtis posits 'to say the *like a friend* part. And they did this over and over. *Pete? - Yeah? - I love you … Like a friend. - Oh cool. Tyler? - Yeah? - I love you … Like a friend. - I love you too, man … Like a friend, you know? - I know. Yeah. Like a friend.* And then the boys would all break down how friends can love each other, but it is a kind of love different from romantic love - which they would call *Boy-girl love* or sometimes *Real-love* or sometimes *Regular-love.* Then some clever person' - Lucy suspects this person was Curtis himself, Plato to his storyline's anonymous Socrates - 'said *Well, can't a girl be friends with a boy and so say 'I love you' to a boy but mean it 'Like a friend'?*' Much mutterings, it is explained, went 'round the school kids. 'Yes. That followed, syllogistically. But oddly: the girls didn't want to say it like the boys did - not about boys or about other girls. And now' - this was Curtis' point - 'it was left to divine the reason behind that. Which the girls incisively explained - after the boys got through debating for another turn or two - was because' - Curtis spake this Zarathustraian - '*Girl don't say things for no reason and would only say they love someone if they do.* It so happens that these girls were friends with each other and with the boys, but not to the point of love. So to say it - *I love you* - would be so much twaddle. And boys could twaddle, but girls were loathe to. The boys said it, but didn't mean it: Tyler did not love Pete, Pete did not love Steven and so on. It was just words. Girls were actual, not verbiage.'

Interim of Lucy explaining what it would feel like to taste words instead of hearing them - or, she tries to better explain, if the process of cognition were olfactory and not synaptic. She admits *Synaptic* might not be the right term. What she means is 'If understanding words was done physically, not intellectually.' She is upset at having to explain herself! 'We're right back where we started! I mean what I meant the first time I said the first thing I said: this is what it would be like if we tasted words instead of hearing them.' 'What would be?' Deb wants to know, Lucy glaring used-needles at her for so flagrantly admitting how she had not been paying attention. 'I haven't explained yet!' 'She hasn't explained yet - Jesus, Deb' mitigates Curtis. But Lucy won't have it and declares she will not explain. 'Which is fine with all of you, I daresay - as you don't think that I can explain it, to begin with! Fine lot of friends you are. I'd feed you to Lucy if she wasn't already full and so pacifistic.' 'I think you can explain - and very eruditely' Curtis says. 'Well, I don't' bitters Deb. 'See? Your girlfriend doesn't, Curtis. Your nest-mate reckons I'm a Sophist blowhard looking to make some quick bucks rather than a legacy for myself.' 'You are!' insists Deb, long drag from the joint she has discovered beneath a napkin. 'I refute that' Lucy nonchalants. 'Anyone who uses the word *Refute* in reference to themself is always certainly full of hot air' is Deb's conclusion. And this time Curtis sides with her. 'How can you two think that?' They explain: historically - going by their anecdotal, personal history only, they admit - the word *Refute* does tend to only come up in situations when what is refuted eventually is revealed to be true. But then there is confusion, because Deb swaps out the word *Alleges* for *Refuted*, quickly corrects, but Lucy has already pounced that this shows a give in their consistency, a sag to the bridge of their proposition! 'I just misspoke.' 'I should say - but that's just the point!' Lucy says - meaning, she explains, that she meant Deb's entire argument could be labeled a mistake and thus 'something misspoken' and Deb resorts to a sarcastic 'Oh is that what you were saying?' and a posture of crossing her arms and turning out her lip, saying she is only appreciated for her mistakes and that - while it sounds like it should - this actually doesn't feel good, at all.

Outdoors, Lucy tells Deb again how she is unholy jealous of her body. 'You're plump and I want to eat you or parade you through town like a trophy kill!' 'I'm *fleshy*' Deb corrects, saying *Plump* is a word she lets Lucy get away with too often. They settle on *Ample*, Lucy explaining the word *Fleshy* makes her think of the character description for Martha from *Who's Afraid Of Virginia Woolf?* - 'Ample, but not fleshy' Lucy says. Deb is staring. 'Have I said that before?' 'Have you? Yes. But I'm more astonished at your lack of self-esteem - always having to point out you've read Edward Albee just to feel you've got a nostril above the surface, man.' How often does Lucy mention she reads Edward Albee? All the time. '*All the time?*' All the time! Whenever someone mentions the word *Goat*. Whenever the conversation is about Mr. Rodgers, Lucy will mention his sandbox out on the back porch and from *Sandbox* move on to Albee! The name *Sylvia* - obviously that gets things going the same as *Goat*. It just on-and-ons. 'You even pointed to three women who weren't particularly tall once and just said *Albee!*' 'I sound insufferable.' 'You do sound insufferable - because you are, Lucy - because you are.' Deb has slung her arm over Lucy's shoulder, let her weight go and says 'Pretend I'm an ample feather boa.' Laughter, laughter. Deb compliments Lucy's body back, finally - making sure it doesn't sound like an afterthought. Specifically, she says Lucy wears age on her face like most people wear tattoos on their hips when they are nineteen. 'I still wish I was *fleshy*.' 'You're *plump*, anyway' Deb says, shoulder nudging Lucy and pointing to something in the distance Lucy doesn't look at but goes *Mmn* about because she knows it's something Deb doesn't care if she actually looks at or not. 'Do you ever play arcade games, Deb?' 'Well, Lucy. I do. I gotta tell ya. Sometimes. Yes. Do you?' 'Sometimes' says Lucy. And she asks Deb if there exist any circumstances under which Deb would be amendable to Lucy taking over her life and Deb Lucy's - sweetening the pot by saying Lucy will keep Deb's life as it is but Deb can run roughshod with Lucy's, soil it, and dump it in any old donation-bin when she's done. 'You really wanna be fleshy, eh?' Deb asks, one eye squinted because it really has something in it but also because it looks cool. 'I really want to be fleshy, yes' Lucy nods. 'So - just sleep on it. The offer is a standing one.'

Deb asks: 'Don't you want to go over, first - just test the waters?' Lucy answers: 'No.' Deb, connectively, says: 'You can come get Lucy, whenever. Or I can bring him over.' Lucy says: 'It'll only work if I just go. It's still my apartment, you know?' Deb nods. Lucy says: 'I am just trying to decide if I want to just go - time it for when she's not home or for the middle-of-the-night - or if I want to go when I know she is there and so have to explain myself, too.' Deb asks: 'What's the appeal in each?' Lucy thinks, then responds: 'In the first case: I guess I daydream I can just, wordlessly, twine myself around her, still asleep - or, as that might be too creep-show, she will find me asleep on the sofa and so cuddle up with me - and when I wake I can just be back. It'll just go - not be a thing. In the second case: I know the first case is childish and insane, so it'd be best to not have to kind of be come upon - *What are you doing here?* - and explain myself from the vantage of *I'm already back, like-it-or-don't.*' Deb, to show understanding, offers, only the slightest lilt of question-song to the words: 'That would feel aggressive?' Lucy points at Deb: 'Exactly.' Deb shows insight: 'But - part of you wants to be aggressive.' Lucy points, again - three times: 'Which is why you pose the question *Maybe it's not a good idea to go back?* right?' Deb presses, also slightly redirects: 'You do know you have every right to be aggressive - you get that, Lucy, because it's true, right?' Lucy slumps a bit: 'Is it? Do I?' Deb imperatively moves on this: 'It is. And you do.' Lucy feels like a weakling: 'I don't think I do.' Deb goes: 'She cheated on you!' Lucy goes: 'I cheated on her. A bunch. And intricately.' Deb goes: 'And good for you - that's allowed to be good-for-you! I mean - don't get me wrong - you, to an extent, gotta let her slide on the whatnot, but not to the point you don't get to be jabby about it, sometimes.' Lucy sighs, long, and then: 'I know what you're saying is right. But I'm not supposed to do that. Because I'm in love with her. So it's fine.' Deb flicks Lucy's thumb-knuckle: 'I'm not sure you're in love with her, man.' Lucy grins, flat mouths, watches Deb flick her knuckle again: 'I am, though.' And Deb looks at her with good-friend in every fleck of her eye color while saying: 'That's stupid, then.'

Now Lucy is soaking in the bath. And she can hear Deb and Curtis animaling each other, metronomes her relaxation to the melee. You've only had sex-while-high twice in your life, Lucy Jinx. And those were your favorite times! And they were both with fellas - fun fact. She submerges her shoulders more at the expense of her knees rising out through the bubbled surface another chilly inch. She wonders if the slaps are Curtis to Deb's ass or Deb to Curtis's face. Or Curtis to Deb's face. The bubbles cicada they are so numerous and boom-boxed by the harmony from the overhead fan. She concludes, just from the low pitch, it is Curtis smacking Deb's hind-side - and can rather she the hot-red, less-redding to still-stinging pink of his hand print. Or maybe Deb's is the sort of ass that immediately soaks handprints up in its original color. Lucy imagines Deb's ass to be buttermilk pale. Deb's nudity would be bikini-lined precisely, her tan torso downing, her tanned legs upping, that perfect pallor of female flesh in the places where teeth could most favorably sink. Oh you made a rule, Lucy - no getting off to Deb while a houseguest! 'But I'm leaving' Lucy fidgets and aways and on purpose sits up a bit to feel room-temperature padlock tight her nipples. Then back into the warm. And fills the tub a bit more. Like when she was eleven, she coats her palm long with an amount of suds, holds it at her face and lightly flits tongue to it as though testing the rough of a real, unshaven snatch being offered her. Snap. Pop. Pop. Her whole body tingles with nostalgia-arousal and she laughs, slipping herself as completely under the water as she can, some of it splashing over the tub side to the tile and the over-used mat there. The laziest woman on Earth invented the bathtub, Lucy has always thought - in her single moment of inspiration and effort, she concocted and fabricated the thing and then sank to its blissful embrace. Posthumous, all others get to soak in endless versions of that first lazy dame's deathbed. If Lucy was as bold and brave she'd soak herself past death, as well. The world's most comfortable copycat. Bathtubs were such a remarkable idea.

Lucy cannot coax Lucy Jinx out from under the bed. 'Infuriating' she says, now going flat to her belly, giving up. '*In-purr-iating*' she then says, hoping the playful tone will get the cat to snap out of its coiled-ball-of-terror - or whatever that pose is supposed to be - but no. '*In-fur-iating*' she tries, but it makes no more noticeable an impression on the cat. 'Fine. I can simply move the bed, Lucy. To you it will seem magic, because you are inferior in your grasp of the actuality of the physical world. You'll think whatever the Greeks would have actually thought if gods ever actually came down from on high to do whatever it was they're alleged to have done in those stories.' The cat yawns, settles itself in, at least now seeming relaxed. So Lucy busies herself with the last of her packing and with prepping the cat carrier. You hadn't already done that, Lucy? 'Fuck off' Lucy says, half-speaking, mostly thinking, that she had not imagined Lucy Jinx, feline, would be giving her any resistance, as the bastard never had before. At least you're not taking this as a sign! Am I not taking it as a sign? Oh God - are you? Am I? You tell me, Lucy - you seem to have me so cover-to-covered. Lucy calms herself. You could never be cover-to-covered. You aren't bound. And you're the whole library in pages come out of their books from different chapters in different rooms over the course of ten centuries. You make about as much sense as re-spelling the alphabet. Lucy returns to her belly and point-blanks at kitty-Jinx 'You make about as much sense as re-spelling the alphabet!' To which the cat mews a mew that would be spelled like a frog croak. Wait. Was that a direct response? A symbol? 'Was that symbolic?' Lucy asks the cat. 'Why did you do that?' Nothing. Not a peep. Kitty-Jinx's one eye is doing its reflective yellow thing, taunting Lucy, the only coin its got and the one thing she'll never. 'You want me to leave you here, creature? You want to be Deb's pet? Roommate with Curtis?' Another mew, more regular-cat in timbre. What in Hell is Lucy to make of this!? 'Good luck without me, Lucy' says Lucy. 'If this is your idea of Destiny, you haven't been paying much attention to how you wound up here!' And Lucy wants to stand abruptly, for emphasis, but that would take an effort beyond her, just now.

List Of Reasons Lucy Will Change Her Mind - ongoing. It will be raining. She will see a sign for a brand of sherbet she recognizes. She will see a sign for a brand of sherbet she doesn't recognize but convince herself she might recognize. Someone on the bus will insult her cat. Someone on the bus will be old and make her sad. Someone on the bus will be reading the exact book she will happen to be thinking about and she will only notice because she and this person on the bus will have sneezed at the same time. There is a moon. She will remember a description from a short-story about something like someone's nose being as large as the knob on the front door of a giant's house, thus getting too annoyed to go on. She will meet a stranger who will allure her into following them - and by morning it will be too late for us all! A radio will have an *equals* sign painted on it. She will see a sheet-music store she did not know was there but that will have been there, in that same location, for the past thirty years. Someone will catch her chewing on her fingernails. Someone will see her scootch in her seat a little bit and assume she had farted. She will be arrested, wrongly. She will be arrested, rightly. A flier for a lost dog will have almost exactly her old phone number on it. Something interesting will be happening to the telephone lines. She will buy a new dress, instead. She will try to buy a new dress only to learn it was tagged incorrectly and the boutique won't honor the mistake. It will be snowing. She will fall asleep and wake up feeling different about everything. She will steal somebody's wallet and need to hide. She will Raskolinkov that wallet under a rock and walk around expressionless like she's something out of a Bresson film. A street vendor will have a radio on but she won't quite be able to hear the interview over the sizzle of whatever is popping on the cooker - will be too shy to ask for the volume to be turned up. Lucy Jinx will get sick and the vet will have to be rushed to. Lucy Jinx will run away, having managed to unzip the carrier just enough to make this possible. She will think she has two pulses but not know if it always feels that way when one tests in two places at once.

After knocking on the door and being admitted, Deb sits on the edge of Lucy's bed. 'I tried to have sex with Curtis really loud for you - did it work?' 'It did. And I could feel how it was all for me. That was a terrifically faked orgasm.' 'Thanks. You don't think he was wise to it though, right?' 'Boys think that's what they sound like, you're safe.' Now, Deb unzips Lucy's suitcase - look! Deb has no problem doing it! but Lucy refrains from remark - and takes out a shirt, unfolds it, tosses it back in, re-zips the thing - again, first try! - shuts and moves it from bed to floor. 'Lucy.' Serious tone. Deb serious. Lucy immediately postures to show she understands the coming address, whatever it is, is to be taken with gravity. 'I meant it when I told you it's stupid to be in love with that girl. And I want to say it again. I don't think you should love her and I don't think that you do.' Look how Lucy is not objecting. Look how Lucy is listening and taking it in with appreciation. Look how Lucy is not falsifying any of this and likes how Deb is her friend. 'Why is it stupid?' Lucy asks, more just to hear more of Deb than because she wants genuine convincing. 'First of all, she's a young girl. Second of all, she's not an interesting young girl. Third of all, you've never said you even liked her before today when you say you love her. Fourth of all, you're Lucy Jinx and she's just some dumb kid who isn't.' Look how Lucy nods. Look how Lucy even agrees and takes very even breaths, not giving further prompt, not anything. 'Do you have other reasons?' 'I have many other reasons.' 'Tell me the reason you feel the strongest about - or the one that's most compelling - or maybe those're one-and-the-same.' Deb very contemplatively sits. But look, Lucy, she already knows exactly what she is going to say. The exact words. She knows them in her blood, so pay attention. Why the pause? Just because it's important and most people give important things a proofread before publishing. 'Because you don't have a lot more parts of your life you can waste.' 'No?' Lucy says, the word hardly getting out. 'Maybe one more. One more part you can waste.' 'But I'll just waste it' Lucy says, half-whisper half-nothing. Deb looks like she feels bad, but she doesn't feel bad and Lucy knows it. 'Yeah. You will. But find something better than this to waste it on. Please.'

And then, after awhile more, Deb has left the room. In the cartoon version of this, Lucy would now be going 'Oh! I see! Now you're in there, huh?' at the sight of kitty-Jinx suddenly calmly sat in his carrier, waiting to be zipped in. The cat would purr louder than the news of airline fatalities. Here, though, Lucy takes off her socks and puts them back on and says 'There.' Because that is sometimes something that happens in life - and out of a sense of dutiful display of agency, Lucy chose this time to be one of those times. Back to the floor, she tries to coax out the cat, Lucy Jinx, but the result is the same. She wriggles in under as much as she can and makes her prodding more aggressive, desiring nothing more than to hear the cat hiss - but when it hisses, Lucy feels pathogen with guilt and tries to settle things back. 'Lucy, come on' she good-buddy coos. Hiss-hiss. 'Lucy, you're being prissy.' Spit-hiss. 'I'm just trying to pet you! You've heard of it!? You can stay here, if that's all you've ever dreamed about, but I will pet you, again - hook or crook!' Hiss. Spit. Simmering yarl. 'You're as poisonous as Laertes, you know that!?' You should write that down, Lucy. 'Stay there' she person-in-changes and the cat grumble-mumbles something like a vacuum-cleaner going over spilt staples. Same trouble as always with unzipping the luggage, Lucy wrests a notebook out, a pen from the pouch. Notebook opens to some scribbled page top-labeled with her own name. She adds into the scrawl there, a bit cleaner writ *You're a cat, poisonous as Laertes.* Underline. Underline underline! 'Underline' she says, closing the book. Wait. Opens book to page-at-random and *You're my cat, poisonous as Laertes.* Moves to underline. Stops. *I'm my cat, poisonous as Laertes.* 'I'm my cat, poisonous as Laertes' she recites. Circles. Closes the book. In the cartoon version, she would now look down - and there would be Lucy Jinx, sheeshing and putting out a cigarette before climbing into the carrier. 'That's all I was waiting for. Poets - oi!' the cat would say. In the sitcom version, there would be laugh-track. The cat would be a puppet filmed to seem almost-real-but-still-clearly-puppet. Lucy would wait

LUCY JINX / 571

for the laughter to die. Pause. Deliver the usual catchphrase retort: 'Oh Lucy - *Mew so crazy*!' Applause. Here, though, Lucy just says the poem again. And thinks about sitcoms and cartoons.




THE WORST PART OF DYING for Lucy Jinx will be that there will be no more talking. In fact, Lucy could bear perfectly well being dead - provided she could go on prattling. Just be ignored, left to herself to chase word with word with word. It'd be fine for that to go on forever and nothing else. Not even Lucy. Lucy wouldn't need to be Lucy, just Lucy's words. Or not even her words. Someone else's? Sure - anyone's. Or no one's! Words without ownership - originated of no mind, no voice. And if there is a chance that she could be allowed to sneak past dying - technically she could be dead, she promises, she needs none of the trappings of life - with the condition required being that she could not be words, but only letters never connecting to form language - that would be fine, also. Letter to letter to letter to letter, the suspense of 'Which will be next?' and 'What will no language sound like, forever?' Or not even *sound like*! Just *look like*. And even if she cannot see the letters - she just is the letters and cannot see herself - if she could just be them. Just know that is what she is. A letter. Even only that! Only one! Which? It doesn't matter. Lucy doesn't even have to know which one. And it could be all alone, the letter, just knowing itself. Not even knowing which letter it is - but knowing it is one and forever wondering which and what it looks like and sounds like and if it is the only one. All alone. All alone and a letter that isn't sure how alone it is. That would be fine with Lucy. Of course, it would be terrific if things didn't need to reduce quite to that, Lucy admits - but still she would be satisfied. Though isn't even that reduction all a trick on your part, Lucy? A way to con-artist you back to being language - you being you, talking full-on? Cordoned off, lonely letter, not knowing itself but getting to - even interior, even without words for it to use in the sense of 'words it already knows' or 'words anyone does' - guess and guess and guess at itself. A long, unknown conversation, forever. Ignored and forever. Those two ideas which should go together but for whatever reason never do: *Ignored* and *Forever*. Or Lucy can die, proper - fully die - and then come back. There can elapse a billion years in the meantime, if only she could reincarnate as a declension in French. Phoenixed as the subjonctif! *Lucy Jinx* could be that mood always followed by que or qui. *Lucy Jinx* que nous partions. *Lucy Jinx* que tu le fasses.

Not the best idea for Lucy to fall asleep on the Metro, just now. Cat in the seat beside her, one side, luggage, the other. That's it, Lucy - a cough into your hand and a look around like 'Ah, that nod-off was on purpose, a business strategy I read in a book.' There is Lucy's reflection, probably wondering why it has to wake up, too. Probably still sleeping, just looking like it has opened its eyes. Wait! Lucy! Look at that! Graffitoed on to the cold metal trim at the base of the window is: *arguing that religion is the opiate of the people is the opiate of the people*. Did you write that, Lucy? It sounds like something you'd say - something you've said. It has that cadence of you, don't you agree? Lucy does agree - and though the handwriting could never be hers, she does her face up like there is a chance, hard squints, look of its-nebulous, hard-to-tell because of the thick of the lines. Either way: cleverer graffito than one tends to find. A good point, even! Lucy agrees and likes the wit well. Though: Lucy is never one to trust those who dismiss religion, out-of-hand. 'Which is the only way to dismiss it' Lucy now pretends she is explaining to a radio interviewer. But she does wish the graffito were phrased a bit nicer, the more she looks at it. There should be more an elegant algebra to make of it. This seems smart, but also *smart-alec*. Unable to come up with anything, though - any twist or condensing - she starts thinking of something else. Here's something: Lucy, when in tunnels, always imagines the Metro-train is running flat - the tunnels just holes punched through something. But in reality, she could be going down and down, up and up, dolphining in a wavelength of travel. There weren't mountains around here, after all. These tunnels were burrowed, not stabled. In fact, now she is getting a bit noiac, antsy, vowing never to travel in this method, again. Because, for a moment, she can see no reason why the trains even need to go underground - why can't they just go, surface level, where they need to get? Then it strikes her that tunnels are piled on and twined around and intersecting other tunnels. Flats on flats, hilling and cross-stabbing each other. Who ever thought of such a dungeon way to get around? It seems greedy. Pathological. Only a madman would rather dig a hole to get where they could walk, overland, even if digging the hole got them there a bit faster. She is too conscious of what she would look like if the world were a cross-section, as though her torso were sliced in the process, as well.

Again: asleep. But not now - now awake, realizing again she was asleep. Lucy had been thinking the word *Pillock* before this latest doze. *Pillock*. Had been uncertain what the word meant or where she'd ever heard it. Fuzz had climbed in her eyes and she'd dreamt about a farmhouse and a wash-bin with what would be cooked for diner soaking in it. Then, now, she had woken. *Pillock* surviving the dream. She still doesn't know what it means. Lucy Jinx, the cat, seems to be trying to stand up, the top of the cloth carrier straining in a bulge, flattening, straining. Lucy scratches her finger over the mesh window and says in the direction of the train front 'We're almost there.' Then yawns enough that her body quivers and her knees go one-at-a-time up-and-down and then her feet stamp to the train floor of their own volition. Jesus. That seems an odd thing for a body to do just because it's tired! What biological function could all of that serve? But Lucy does not investigate that train of thought, so long - because her attention is drawn to the man there, who is working at an itch in his groin with a verve that certainly makes the matter borderline masturbation. How can that man be so blithely confident that he is not being judged *perverse*? He cannot be oblivious to what that must look like - well-dressed enough, face showing no signs of Mongol or anything. Perhaps he is a philosopher, so trained in the belief that a thing, if true, will be recognized for its truth he does not even consider alternative interpretations which might be leveled against him. He has an itch. He is scratching. What faith in tautology! *I have an itch, I am scratching - Well, it looks like you're jerking it - Having an itch and scratching it looks like jerking it, so it just looks like scratching an itch - which is what it is.* The lewd descriptor is the redundant restating, Lucy. You're such a groundling, muck-heading your dirty jibes at the wizened! By the way: he is still doing it. He is still doing it! Fair is fair, the matter is wholly questionable now. 'If he is erect' Lucy whispers in her head, aiming the comment at the cat in her lap 'is what defines this, now.' Eventually, yes, the physical world must be arbiter. The truth-as-idea can only go on for so long without needing to be reined in. That really looks like a man masturbating on a train, now.

Well, the train couldn't last forever. And now it is the grim street she'd better start finding beauty in, again. This area of town looks the same, but not like it had been waiting. The bottom-corner of an old toy-chest, tangles of soft hairy dust, pokey with specks of odd decals and bright plastics dots that once glimmered a doll's evening-to-the-castle-ball dress. That might be too fancy a way of putting it. Rounding the corner which makes Elliott's building technically in sight - it's that one, there - Lucy better paints the area, her return to it, as finding an old box of tea-bags in the cupboard you just instinctively know have been there too long to make tea with. Not tea you mean to enjoy, anyway. In her imagination, the drag of her luggage is getting more pronounced. In her imagination, kitty-Jinx is poised, ready to flee from any sudden onslaught. 'It's fine' she whispers, as though to the cat - and, to herself, she says there is still so much marijuana in her system and groggy from the train that she should not trust her impressions of anything. And that had been strategy. Getting high had been part of the plan. And check-listing off some of the things this return does not mean: Lucy does not need to get the *Deneven's Donuts* job back. No. Lucy doesn't need to work at *Stella Tom's*. No. Lucy doesn't need to drastically alter how she had been with Elliott. No. 'I'm just coming back, not saying I've metamorphosed.' Hard nod after this statement. The feeling she feels is nervous tension. Pot churning into thick melodrama. Lucy will be welcomed back, she knows that. It will not be dramatic, at all. Within a few hours, she will be drinking coffee in the kitchen, wet with Elliott's fuck, and feeling sleep in her eyes that has been building for decades. So: why aren't you walking, Lucy? No reason? Then start, again! 'That doesn't make sense as an argument' Lucy says, straying to the wall, here, and getting a smoke going. 'Am I not allowed to stop for a moment? To feel strange, smoke, get myself collected, then press on?' Is it the thought of taking Elliott to bed, tonight? 'No.' Is it the thought that Elliott might not want that, though still be glad you are back? 'No. No' Lucy repeats, then tells herself 'Shut up.' And snoots that Elliott'll damn well want it, anyway.

*Zilch's Dry Cleaning.* Last cigarette, Lucy. Or last two, at a stretch. She apologizes to kitty-Jinx, who she is thinking must need to use the litter-box. Elliott better have kept the litter-box! 'If not' Lucy dribbles out with an uninhaled mottle of cig 'then you can just go to town where you'd like. That's out deal.' And she knows the cat would shake hands if she offered it the chance. But: so what is the foot-dragging, Lucy? Elliott might have someone over. Well - she would be allowed that, eh? And you would deserve it, eh? 'It's still my apartment' smokes Lucy, crossing her arms and cool-girling her I-don't-care shoulders against the messy window of the shop. Elliott could come to the door, coitus interruptus. 'Maybe I'd like that' Lucy thinks. Maybe it'd give Lucy great pleasure to cause a sort of situation. To see Elliott make the weak decision of asking Lucy to go - brave-front for current tryst, chest puffing I'm-big-and-bad-now. Of course Elliott would give the quick-whisper 'What are you doing here?' And Lucy could just say 'I'll come back tomorrow.' And even play along, pretend Elliott has to forcefully eject her and now she'll never try to access the homestead, again! But maybe also, she thinks, Elliott would make the cuckoo decision of kicking her new lover out, no compunction about it. Tears or not, the bitch would be told where to go and no question! This arouses you, Lucy! But don't get ahead of yourself. Lucy adjusts her posture as though it will hide the fact she is Pavloving her panties at the thought of grabbing a hadn't-finished-Elliott and continuing on in the scents and tastes of the woman just vacated. Lucy. Lucy! 'What?' Focus. 'You focus!' Finish your cigarette and get up the stairs of that building! Don't expect Elliott to be with anyone! And don't let her not being with someone bring down the mood! Simple. Domestic. Happy. Mildly awkward. 'And remember' Lucy says, school-marming the air with her cigarette as ruler 'you are sorry, Lucy. You are sorry. And you have to remember to say so - and to mean it.' Yes. Lucy can do that. She feels she can do that. She is sorry. She is. And she wants to go back there. She wants. And by tomorrow, this will have already happened. So it makes the most sense to just get it done.

There likely had never been a time - actually - Lucy was not grindingly aware of her physical self. But climbing the stairs, cat-and-luggage laden, she fancies there had been. Brief and recent. She had not thought of her appearance, been satisfied with her interior and glitzed along, paparazzi free, any idea of her too self-centered to notice her. But now she is aware of herself. The size of every odor her pores leak and the temperature. How many veins show in her neck when she strains it. That dry patch under her eye for the past week. Her hair which, had she been masculine, would long ago have dithered out of her scalp. Her work-boot tits. The trolly-clatter in her hips as her legs stiff - a one-oar only row-boat, her motion a-side-at-a-time. Her tummy worst of all. That gut of hers looks exactly like the face of a senile old man spitting out his mashed peas and telling the nurse he's not hungry. Anything but her middle, she thinks. Even her dingle-berry nipples and her acne-raw left shoulder. If only her belly could be someone skittish enough no one could find it for looking rather than hung in the air like the sour of a garbage-disposal not run. Her feet are just things which skin has grayed on and toes have lost meaning. There is hair on the skin of her knee, thick as the moustache of the neighbor you always try to avoid. Her inner thighs now feel the same as her outer. No part of her could be called *creamy* yet each speck of her has a distinct thick of dairy. How has she been going around in this state? Her lips are lined like a comb someone left on a bus seat you have to move before sitting. And she can hear every motion her tongue makes, these days - as though in her mouth is a barrister with notepads and casebooks open, flipping through each for things to jot and to review things already jotted. My God! Elliott will want this? There is a kind of insanity in you, Lucy! 'But she'd had me before' Lucy tells herself, the first time already sounding the hundredth repeat of an increasingly weakening mantra. Look at your hands though, Jinx. Beautiful if one likes somber - beautiful like the smiles tried stoically the day after a house fire.

Lucy hasn't knocked, yet. It is almost midnight. She can hear the movement of Elliott in there. She knows exactly what the room looks like and exactly how it will smell, this time of night. The sound of one more breath, two more breaths - last one, last one - in her ears and she raps three times. Those are Elliott's feet, that sound of approach. Lucy knows she is being looked at through the peephole and just stands, knowing it. Nothing. And just to cut out the possibility that Elliott really doesn't know Lucy she is there, Lucy knows again, smiling. 'Elliott?' 'Who's that?' Lucy sighs and swallows and sets down the cat carrier, gently - straightens up and says 'It's Lucy.' 'Lucy?' 'Yes.' 'I know a lot of Lucys.' 'Since when?' 'Lucy who?' She can almost see Elliott actually playacting blindness, nervous hand near the door-chain, eyes unseeingly fliting as her brain tries to conjure up reasonable questions to ask to verify the identity of who it is at the door. 'Since when do you know more than one Lucy?' 'I said *Lucy who?*'

Elliott's voice sterns. So Lucy huffs out her nose, over-confidenting that she is about to be let in. 'Lucy Jinx.' 'Lucy *what?*' Rolling her eyes, a little louder - considering saying 'You know, I have a key and I need to piss - so alright?' - Lucy says 'Lucy Jinx.' '*Lucy Stinks?*' Elliott asks, curious. 'Yes' Lucy big sighs. 'Yes. *Lucy Stinks.*' 'Lucy does stink' Elliott agrees through the door, then says 'What the fuck do you want?' And without much to it, Lucy replies 'To live here.' 'To *what?*' 'To live here' Lucy four-year-olds, period between each word. '*To live here?*' Elliott confuses back, emphasis on *Here* and that word made long and triple-italic. 'I technically already do' Lucy brats, actually getting hissy. 'So open the door' Elliot says after a pause. 'I'm trying to be polite.' 'I'm actually not sure you are, Lucy.' 'What's that supposed to mean?' 'It's aggressive to knock and make me open the door.' 'What?' 'What, what?' 'That's stupid. That's not right, man.' 'You sure this is you being polite?' Lucy sticks out her tongue. 'I said I was *trying* to be polite. Pay attention. Pick out the important word in that statement.' 'Why should I let you in, Lucy Stinks? Why should I do that? You who have your own key and technically live here and generally fucking suck and are awful - why should I let you in?' So Lucy says 'Because I'm in love with you.' Nothing. 'I said I love you, Elliott.' Nothing. More nothing. 'I love you. That's not worth opening a door?' Nothing for a pause, then Elliot says 'I'm trying to do the math on that. Give me a sec.'

They are in the kitchen. Both Elliott and Lucy. Lucy has used the bathroom. Lucy Jinx, the cat, has been let out and they can hear him scratching the wall after having used the litter. Neither Lucy nor Elliott are much looking at each other. Lucy is exactly as previously described, while Elliott is sweatpants and this one tank top she has had forever that has three holes over the ribs at one side. Lucy has looked at those holes more than at Elliott. She wants to touch one, touch the skin after one. Wants to - very very very much. There will be a conversation, soon enough, because Lucy is here again, now. That has happened and it won't unhappen. Not tonight. Or soon. Lucy is betting the first words of the conversation will be Elliott's. She has narrowed the options down to 'Why do you love me?' or 'Is this real?' or 'You're not allowed to be lying about this, Lucy.' Or - now that she thinks about it - maybe Elliott will say 'Bringing the cat was a nice touch.' And even as Lucy thinks that, Elliott says 'When did you decide you love me?' Lucy claps, over-eager, and too-friendly-too-fast points both fingers Aha! at Elliott while saying 'I knew you would say that! Or I thought you would say *Why do you love me?* - but still!' Elliott, in monotone, how-drolls with her 'Okay, then: Why do you love me?' 'I can answer your actual question, El.' Sigh from Elliott, but they are looking at each other - mostly unbrokenly - now. 'Fine. What was my question? Oh: When did you decide you love me?' Lucy starts to speak, halts, holds up a hand with an apologetic squint - as if to say 'Just one teensy thing before I do?' - then says 'I'm supposed to be honest right now, right?' 'If you want, Loose.' Innocent eyes and 'I'm not saying that to fuck around - I mean: I'm being honest and that was my cute way of indicating it.' 'You're adorable. As always. Like a dollop of mustard, Lucy, just so cute. Answer the question.' 'I don't remember when. But a long time ago. Because I've been in love with you. And I got jealous and hated you and that's why I left. And I can't stand not being with you. Because it's stupid for me to say I don't love you when I know I do and can't even recall for how long.' Elliott keeps looking at Lucy. Keeps looking. Finally shakes her head in a slow sadness and mutters 'Oh Jesus, man - come on.'

The kiss was not resisted. Nor were Lucy fingers through the holes of the shirt. Nor was the those-holes-being-tugged-wider. Nor was the shirt being torn but not enough to be torn off. Nor was the viciously tugging the all torn-up shirt over Elliott's head and dragging her by the hair to the nearest wall where she was then slammed with her hands pinned back up above her as though the shirt had been tugged off, just there. Lucy feels Elliott's fingers all enter her - still pinned by pants and panties - and bites Elliott's cheek hard enough to mark it. Then - with both hands around Elliott's throat and trying not to react at all to the buck of Elliott's wrist driving hand up her in a blunted controlled slap of a lift - Lucy says 'You know I'm kind of disappointed you weren't fucking someone when I showed up.' Elliott is just opened mouth and the hand not in Lucy is clawing hard lines into the flesh around Lucy's waist. 'You would have kicked them out, right?' Then Elliott takes her hand out of Lucy and sloppy-fans fingers over Lucy's face, uses her hands to take Lucy's off of her throat, slaps Lucy once - hard - and bites an undefined amount of her breast through her shirt more than hard enough to make Lucy involuntarily squeal and push at Elliott's face. Elliott is harsh voiced, talking while - Lucy with chest to wall - crouched and tugging Lucy's pants and panties down to her ankles, clawing one half of Lucy's ass, the hand staying clamped there, suddenly pulled away, Elliot standing and mouth right at Lucy's ear saying 'You go here - right?' 'Right' Lucy begins saying - but even before the single syllable can get out is being tugged to face Elliott, fierce jostle of both shoulders, Elliott now clamping one hand around Lucy's mouth to mash up the lips, part them to show teeth, pressure enough that Lucy's eyes begin to tear up. 'You wanna know how much I missed you?' Lucy tries to nod - Elliott grips tighter. 'I fucking said: do you want to know how much I missed you?' Lucy tries to say something - knowing it won't sound like anything - and Elliott grips tighter, shakes Lucy's head back, forth, grips even tighter. 'You don't?' 'I do' Lucy growls - the words sounding IehOugh - tears streaming down her face, breathing impossible. 'You do?' Elliott has let go, is staring slaughter at Lucy's honestly trembling lips which manage a 'Yes.' 'Then down' Elliott says. And points. And says 'Down - all the way, Lucy. And I'm not fucking around here, pal.'

Later, Elliott is still laying - spread in the mess of her sweat on the forever-unwashed carpet - Lucy opening the refrigerator and drinking down the entire almost-full bottle of fruit-juice she blindly takes up. Certain Elliott is about to tell her to leave. Or that Elliott is going to sit on the sofa, turn on the television, and ignore Lucy until Lucy gives a timid 'Goodnight' and has to go in to bed alone. Sure of it. Liking it, hating it. When - instead - Elliott has sat up part way and says 'That was only a little of how I missed you, Lucy.' Elliott's voice? Soft, like pencil writing feels where you're in fourth grade. How Elliott looks when Lucy dares venture her eyes over there? Terrified, sated - vulnerable as a field of mowed grass, dandelions - and endless. Lucy figures she should respond, if even just to prompt whatever the rest of the statement is she sees Elliott about to give, but Elliott's words come without needing dialogue. 'So you can be arrogant and all. Because I'm too in love with you to pretend I just wanted to dehumanize you awhile.' Lucy does a shoulder droop, flirt-disappointment. 'Oh. I thought you just meant you'd fuck me some more, soon.' Elliott has lugged herself up, is full in the kitchen light - the only light on - now starts to say something but then gives Lucy a girlfriend shove. 'I didn't say you could drink my juice. You're an asshole, man.' Lucy just shrugs. 'Say the thing you were going to stay, instead - I didn't come back to hear you bitch like a cheapskate - I'll buy you more juice, you infant.' Elliott has hopped onto the counter, traces one of the many full cuts she had fingernailed into Lucy's blotchy wet body, Lucy wincing and Elliott then on-purpose-poking-harder with the edge of the nail of her big-toe. 'I was just going to let you know you can dream on. Never touching you again, Jinx.' And Lucy flutters her eyes in a yeah-yeah-yeah and asks if it's okay for her to microwave something or will that just earn her more bellyaching. 'Say something nice to me, Lucy' Elliott immediatelys, all posturing dropped - the demand hurt, actual, the exhaustion apparent in the curt of the tone. 'I could never talk enough to do that, Elliott. I'd need a throat as long as every Thursday in a month.' Pause. Elliott's face is blank, then perplexed. 'I honestly can't tell if that was nice.' So Lucy waits until their eyes hold awhile and says 'Okay. How about: You're the reason paintings dream they knew flesh?'


IT IS RATHER BEAUTIFUL. THERE is Lucy, chest to Elliott and back to the stiff of the wall - Lucy Jinx in that space, as though a favorite note in the page-margin, snuggly held in by the book being closed. And that is the cat, urinating in the litter-box at the room's far corner - that sound of rummaging through a large boxful of Christmas tinsel. Overhead is the sound of a middle-of-the-night cup being dropped on the hardwood of the apartment right above - and the thin sounds, also, of each larger fragment being picked up, tossed in a limp, empty garbage-bag, then a moment later the shish of broom bristling over and over the area of uncarpeted floor. And yes, Lucy feels content where she lays, chin a sharp to the skin of one of Elliott's shoulder bulbs, Elliott breathing like the click of a traffic-light changing all through the nights of an otherwise soundless winter. The scent of Elliott is something like potato bread, those small rolls Lucy puts sausage links in between. Or used to. Two, three-at-a-time. Heated, charred a bit, left to cool while she searched for something to watch on the television lest the relaxation of the consumption be lost to flickers of commercials, a cycle through channels of nothing-worth-stopping-on. Lucy's nose is starting to run, as it tends to after so much sex. Her head is lard from fatigue and no-need-to-think, thoughts mimicking the haze and fog of her limbs curled around Elliott's oven-warm body, asnooze. Something clicks to life in one of the walls, or the floor, or the ceiling - one of the areas surrounding her, framing she and Elliott in their conjoined position. That is the third time in-a-row Lucy has yawned so gaping, the third time she has worried it will have stirred Elliott, that Elliott will roll over and wonder why Lucy is awake. Answerless. Other than 'I just am.' Is everything alright? 'Of course' Lucy will say. And it's true. Another yawn. The unease of needing a piss but not wanting to get up. Oh such contours and textures to this moment in the dark - Lucy feels she is a detail on an out-of-date globe, a country she discovers by running finger over bumps and fine-print, a nation that no longer exists in an updated world.

Awake. From a silly dream. A calculator had not been functioning. Lucy had been shaking it, sound of rattlesnake or drawer full of spilt rice. Elliott is now coverless and on her back. What a youthful long of her there is! The dark maybe lengthens Elliott, even, but Lucy thinks she is also so lengthy, unaided - Elliott is just that long. Taller when flat to the ground. But so small-armed and trim-bodied right now that Lucy wants to test, roll to her back, lay full long and set shoulders to shoulders, see where feet end, where head gets to. She doesn't, she doesn't. Then awake. Awake. Dream of a box made of cardboard but with a glass front facing, Lucy worried the lizards she bought from the shop will spill their water bowl and this will soften the box floor and they will scratch through before she is all the way home with them. The shoes she recalls from the dream make her feel that she must have been dreaming she was seven. Shoes from an old photo she wishes she still knew where it was. Elliott has returned to back-facing Lucy. There is an odd warmth to the air like some conversation took place. Warmth and unease. That Lucy had said 'No' when asked something and the back-turn was a protest, something left off until morning to fully address. Lucy moves a bit closer and there goes Elliott's back, fitting to Lucy, asleeping its way backward in short jerks and breaths from Elliott, rather like talking. In Elliott's dream, something else narrative was happening. These sounds and this motion correspond to something else. Something Lucyless, maybe. Though - who knows? - perhaps Elliott dreams of Lucy. Or is now, anyway. Awake again. Awake. It can't have been long. Long enough. That unheated-soup feel to Lucy's vision, eyes sodium caked, film on a liquid left too long standing without coming to simmer. As soon as she tries, she cannot recall the dream at all. It had been of her finding what had seemed like a dead bird on the pavement, long cooked by city daylight. But when she had tried to lift it in her removed shirt to bury it someplace, all it was was feathers feathers - feathers and feathers and feathers. And a bit of fur. Fur like the cotton sometimes used in containers of medicine tablets. Tufts small and bean-grey, slimy to touch. She tries and tries to remember that but doesn't. And doesn't know she has hooked her arm in under Elliott's - loop, link, lock - Elliott again on her back, one ankle over that one of Lucy's, making Lucy aware of the socks she has on.

Room lit. Well into the morning. Lucy wakes and the bed is all hers, she at full splay, half-rolled across it. Let's look at Lucy a moment: she is booze nosed, dirty-dish breathed, eyes with a sting to their focusing like a far-too-cold hand plunged into water more than hot enough to scald. Let's listen to Lucy: faint imperfection to the flow of her breathing - an obstruction made by a ridge in the structure of her larynx, perhaps, or a swallowed fingernail that ages ago lodged down her gullet and her body absorbed but not all the way. Lucy's body in its current position is sensual, the contours of the top of a tooth. There is the toilet-air yellow of the room walls - or the kindest she will put it is *the nicotine stained forefinger-side yellow* of the room walls. Ah! A sound of Elliott, out there. Elliott who had not woken Lucy. Why had Elliott not woken Lucy? Could it be to microwave her up some breakfast - is that what Lucy hears going on? One of those always-hard biscuits with that circle patty of searing meat between it, that sausage-the-same-as-the-discount-brand-hamburgers? Lucy sits up and stretches, her legs luxuriating in the sensation, neglecting to let it have any effect. And there is the cat, squatting in the litter with its one eye on Lucy, wary, as though Lucy means to come lift it up, mid-evacuation. 'Do you live in the goddamn litter-box now, come to think of it?' Lucy puts to the cat. The cat just staring. Not even defecating, it seems. Waiting not be looked at. Or for a need. Positioned as it is because of an urgency that came and went without incident. Lucy lays back down. What is this feeling? Unnecessary. Lucy feels unnecessary. And likes the sensation. She's like the receipt still in the discarded bag or the memory of having been hungry after now being glutted to cramp. Unnecessary.

Elliot in the kitchen doing something requiring the sink to keep turning on, turning off - over again, turning on, turning off. Lucy feels like she is going to be able to skip school just from not waking up. Closes her eyes in case Elliott suddenly pops in. Feels Elliott at the door - where Elliott isn't - watching her sleep, watching her pretending - feels Elliot, who isn't there, must be wondering 'Is that sleep or pretending?'

Elliott can be found on the sofa - dressed in socks and panties and otherwise bare as a pulpit. Lucy roughs Elliott's hair and kisses her head-top, giving the eyeball to the program on the television before heading over to pour herself coffee. The Z-grade over-dub of fight sounds from what Elliott is so engaged in cuts through all of Lucy's preparations, even the opening of a new sleeve of saltine crackers and the crunch of a peanut-butter-sandwiched-two-of-them being popped in her mouth, entire, and dimwit-looking chewed. Lucy finally has to ask 'Just what in Hell are you watching?' when the ludicrously accented English voice-track has a character say 'Oh it stinks does it? Well, you're the one doing the smelling!' Elliott perks up, repeating this same line - in very, very accurate mimic of the dub-voice - over at Lucy, following her recitation with 'You've seen it?' 'No, Elliott. I haven't seen it.' Now Lucy lumps to place beside Elliott and watches the fight taking place on the screen. 'This is what you've been reduced to in my absence?' But Elliott will have none of Lucy's snark, just gives her a pointlessly lovey-dovey hug, lets go, and says 'This is *Shaolin Temple Against Lama*, you sophisticationless rump! Perhaps my favorite kung-fu movie of all!' On the screen, a man and another younger man are cooking a chicken over a fire when over to them walks a strange monk of some kind, eyebrows long hanging, beard the same. 'Wait - are we really watching this?' Lucy asks when Elliott, after a moment, has not averted her eyes from the screen and seems perfectly entertained. 'Yes, Lucy - yes, we are. I just told you. See' - Elliott points, as though doing so and making the statement she makes at the same time will sort everything out - 'that guy wants to be the best kung-fu fighter ever, but that crazy master is about a zillion times better than he is. Understand, so far?' 'Yes' says Lucy, devoid of expression up or down. 'But the crazy master won't take a pupil! So the kid - there - who is basically the master's lackey and who is friends with the main guy, convinces the main guy to steal the master's kung-fu. By attacking him over and over! Paying attention to how the master defends himself.' 'Cool' Lucy says. And when Lucy moves to stand, Elliott drapes her legs over her, stiffens them, and simply says 'Heel!' without even averting her gaze from the film.

The situation improves after Elliott gives Lucy a joint and restarts the movie from the beginning after they've both toked a few long-held-in drags. Now, in fact, Lucy is asking Elliott to explain things in as much detail as she feels like -

every last ounce of all that is going on. 'We're gonna watch a lot of kung-fu movies, Loose. Cause I figured out that's what your problem was, all along.' 'Okay!' Lucy enthuses, watching the main character do the splits in slow motion and then start to stand but then duck lower into the splits when his opponents tries to kick him in the head. 'Are they all like this?' Elliott scoffs at poor uneducated Lucy! '*All like this*!? Is she even serious!? This is *Shaolin Temple Against Lama*, Lucy! Don't be an idiot!' And here Elliot does her best to explain all about the Lamas being the enemy of the Shaolin, for some reason - how this is a thing, just a fact, no matter what movie. 'Like Ninjas and Samurai' Elliott you-sees 'or like Cowboys and Indians. Except, I guess, Lamas are always just bad. That's the difference. There's never a good Lama, as far as I can tell. They are just rotten, through-and-through! Not like how some Indians are good sometimes, you get me?' Elliott takes two longs drags. Lucy takes three, killing the joint. 'Why are they called Lamas?' 'Don't be racist' Elliott sneers 'or xenophobic. Or provincial-minded. Or whatever.' 'Did that question make me seem less than worldly?' 'It did. Why didn't you ask *Why are they called Shaolin*? You see?' Lucy does see, actually. Deeply apologizes. 'So: all the movies go together? About the Lamas?' Elliott just Gahs! and changes the subject a bit. She tells Lucy how her favorite sound in the world is the sound of a lot of people chasing each other down stairs in these old kung-fu flicks. The sound-effect that is dubbed in makes her tingle. 'Which?' Lucy says, leaning forward to intent her ears on the film - but Elliott says she didn't mean in this film, right now. 'In a lot of them, though. I'll let you know when it happens - though you'll probably just notice for yourself when it does.' Here, Elliott takes off Lucy's shirt and slapdashedly tucks it under the sofa. 'Sometimes when I'm fucking and I'm just right-on-the-verge-but-not-quite-getting-there I think of that sound and it finishes me off, Lucy. You'll love it. I promise.' Lucy takes off one of Elliot's socks. The other. Elliott lifts up her pelvis but Lucy just pats the panty-crotch and says 'Don't get ahead of yourself. You're not my boss.'

Awhile later: both in the kitchen, a burnt-but-still-edible pizza cooling on the counter - one both had forgotten was cooking even after the cook-timer had sounded, that sound treated as something they had just complained about and shut off - Elliott is telling Lucy this: 'If I had waited until I'd turned eighteen to seduce an older man I'd been attracted to forever - who knew I was, you know? who I knew was waiting just as much as me for me to get legal - I would make it such a point to say the dirtiest things imaginable, just so that right after I got him to say some things like that back I could say to him *Isn't it funny how if we had this conversation two hours ago it would have been illegal?*' 'So you mean you would just start seducing him the literal minute you turned eighteen?' Lucy asks, holding her palm over the pizza and frowning that it still seemed too hot. 'Or within the first two hours anyway, yeah. For that line to work. Obviously.' They agree that if they eat the pizza while it is as hot as it still is, it will be an altogether miserable experience. But they are in the tight spot that if they wait for it to cool, they will forget about it, entirely - and when they wander back into the kitchen later, it'll have gone off. Elliott says she - if on her own - would then microwave it because it would just get super soggy - which she liked - but figures Lucy is too much used to her silver-spoon to eat soggy pizza. 'We never should have cooked this pizza!' That is Lucy's conclusion. But Elliott finds this complete reversal of stance unappealing. 'You weren't complaining when it was cooking, Lucy. Jesus - you've got a sense of entitlement, don't you?' A pause enters. Lucy notices Elliott noticing the pause by way of giving her an insect-antennae type stare. 'What's going on?' Elliott asks. 'I'm not sure I can be high, forever - but I want to be. I was trying to come up with a plan.' 'Well, we don't even have another joint, Lucy - so I hate to bring that worse news in, as well.' 'Yeah' Lucy says, heart sinking. 'Yeah.' Elliott gives her a kiss and then a smack on the ass, doesn't seem perturbed when Lucy responds to neither.

But Lucy will have to go to work. Because this apartment does need to be paid for. As does food. And Lucy will need to get dressed, again. Sometime. And Lucy will need to leave these rooms. Ride on buses. Ride on trains. Lucy will need to answer telephones. Because life requires these things. Civilization has painted itself into a corner wherein there are no choices. The human-spirit will not let itself reverse - not knowingly, anyway. Things have come this far, the world runs in the matrix it has set up and will and will and will. Or worse: it will advance. Complicate more. No way it could ever just be Lucy, smoked up, Elliott in all-but-undress, kung-fu movies seeming pertinent, and no books to read, no thoughts to have, no people to say 'Hello' to or 'No' - and the world never bowing itself low to Lucy's lack of desire for there to be reason for anything. The time is fast approaching, in fact. Only so many more glimpses or long looks at Elliott before Elliott, herself, suggests they do something beyond jabber over burnt food in the kitchen or sofa-lounge or fuck. Yes, Lucy: the next fuck will be the last of these firsts and it will be followed by the first of many - at Elliott's prompt even - Hey-let's-go-do-something-or-anothers. Yes, Lucy will have to unpack proper. And Lucy will plug in her computer. And Lucy will have to keep herself from spending more than her paycheck on nonsense and momentary distractions, impulses that need scratching. Because if Lucy cannot control the spending she will need a second job, again. And that is no longer an option - she can tell. She'll have to keep the hotel and do the teaching thing - the whatever-that's-all-about. How was that meant to work, again? Was that still happening? Lucy will have to again have a reason not to kiss Elliott if she doesn't feel like it. A reason to not want to play darts out at some dive bar, not want to mingle with strangers-to-her who lurk half-her-age. Even though it is known and accepted, she will need a reason. All those silent reasons her posture will have to give. Explaining even when not asked to. Her silence an argument with silence, forever - her head a concussive bellow as thick as a whale freshly speared.

'Where do you work, now?' Elliott reemerges from the bedroom in sweatpants and a fitted t-shirt, flats with no socks. Lucy is still only in panties and by now the rise of the pot has altered to the sensation of knowing every bellicose tug of gravity to her flesh. She blinks, Elliott repeating the question. 'Sorry' Lucy preambles, trying to shake the resistance toward answering - managing, after a playact of touching her chest due to an off swallow 'At *The Elizabeth Bishop.*' 'Which means what?' 'It's a hotel. I work nights there, now.' Elliott nods. A small drizzle of follow-up questions. Type of hotel? Size? Exact hours? What kind of pay? How many nights a week? Any chance she might switch to days? 'I can't switch to days' Lucy says and stops short of explaining the situation at the school, opting for a still-telling-just-phrasing-it-specifically mention of how she 'might have another gig for days, starting soon'. 'And then you'll drop the hotel?' 'I might.' And sensing Elliott will point-blank about the day gig - no other direction Elliott could take - Lucy pivots the conversation to 'We need money, Elie.' 'Yes.' Yes, good Lucy. Important to have made that a personal address - and the use of an affectionate nickname should have done the trick! 'You know I work now, right?' Lucy oh-so-interested - making sure to mix in some flirt - says 'I did not know that. I knew you have red hair now and like to strong-arm me, but what is this new professional development?' Just Elliott works as a shift-supervisor at a bookstore is all. 'That's awesome!' says Lucy, knowing more and more she is twenty years - almost - older than Elliott and the one of them who is not currently dressed. Elliott is showingly proud, but keeps seeming-so to a subtext. 'A chance I might get an Assistant Manager slot, too. Just a chance.' 'And that pays well?' 'Yep' Elliott says. Then says 'Kinda needed it to' then says 'Yep' again. And Lucy says 'I promise I will eventually get dressed' and does a laugh enough for both of them. And the air in the room hasn't changed, Lucy - so stop thinking maybe it has. 'Why?' That was Elliott. 'What?' Elliott squints. 'Why?' 'Why what?' Elliott looks over her shoulder, the universal indicator that Lucy is acting strange. Elliott, with lowered brow, stage-whispers 'Why are you going to get dressed?' 'Oh' says Lucy, shaking her head in appearance of remembering that had been the question. Why is your head off, Lucy? 'I don't know, really.' She shrugs and Elliott facials 'Okay'. 'I just figured I'll have to one day, wanted to let people know that I know.'

'It's weird that men have penises, since stabbing is such a feminine thing -

don't you think?' That was Elliott, asking that. 'Think it's a feminine thing? Or that it's weird that men have penises?' That was Lucy. 'That it's feminine.' 'Stabbing?' 'Right.' 'I think there is nothing more feminine than stabbing - except maybe typos and approximate rhymes.' 'I think typos are feminine, definitely. But approximate rhymes are definitely masculine, I think.' 'Do you?' 'Penises and approximate rhymes seem like almost the same thing to me.' 'Then: as feminine as typos and sand in your socks.' 'That is definitely feminine. Yes.' 'What?' 'Sand in your socks.' 'I know. That's why I said it, El. I say things that are.' 'Do you think there will ever come a time when people forget what *Brimstone* means?' 'Is this entire conversation meant to remind me that I actually like you?' 'Yes. Is it working?' 'Actually, it is. And yes, I think there will come a time people forget what *Brimstone* means.' 'What do you think the first wrong thing is they'll think it means?' 'Elliott?' 'What?' 'I've already said *I love you*.' 'I know.' 'You can knock it off.' 'What?' 'Making me actually feel like I love you.' 'See, though? That's kind of what I actually want you to do.' 'You're supposed to think I already do.' 'You're supposed to not think I'm an idiot.' 'Am I supposed to not think that?' 'It'd be preferable. Lucy? Would you like to know what I think the first wrong thing they'll think *Brimstone* means is?' 'Is it going to ruin my day?' 'That is the aim.' 'Then I don't want to know.' 'I think they'll think it means *The length of time it takes blood to move faster when listening to violins from the cheap seats*.' 'Do you, indeed, think they'll think that?' 'That sounds like what *Brimstone* could mean, right?' 'Isn't that what *Brimstone* means?' 'Lucy?' 'Yes?' 'I wish you hadn't gotten dressed.' 'Sorry.' 'Lucy?' 'Yes?' 'I'm also glad that you did.' 'Elliott?' 'What?' 'Before we pursue that line of conversation: would you like to know what I think the first wrong thing people will think *Brimstone* means is?' 'Not as much as I'm glad you got dressed, again - but yes.' 'I think they'll think it means *The weight of a wet mitten when it works its way under a lover's shirt*.' 'That does sound about right. They sure called the wrong thing *Brimstone* didn't they, first time around?' 'Elliott?' 'What?'

Lucy and Elliott made it as far as the living-room carpet. Lucy's legs wound up - now - a quarter-way into the kitchen. Her heels move back-and-forth on the rough of the tile. 'Do you think we've ever washed the kitchen floor?' Elliott, Lucy can see, is playing the game of holding one eye shut, reaching toward the ceiling - and Lucy does the same, thinking it would be great to be one-eyed, forever, with everything always feeling at exactly arm's length. 'Did you ever wash it?' Lucy never had. Nor Elliott. And Lucy explains that she can tell how filthy it is just from her heels touching it. Her heels! Her calloused, Rumpelstiltskin old heels! Elliott wonders if it's dirty enough that they could catch and illness from it. 'Such as?' Lucy asks, moving the hand that was reached ceilingward now over her still garlic-warm crotch. '*Dyspepsia?*' But Lucy, tracing that still slick line of herself with middle-finger, does not believe *Dyspepsia* is an illness. 'What is *Dyspepsia*, then?' Well, Lucy thinks it is a state. 'Like *Misbegotten*. Like *Wanderlust*.' Elliott sits up and is working out an ache in her jaw, wubba wubba noises being made as though she were a puppet-show mask suddenly coming upon something unexpected, double-taking. And then Lucy is watching Elliot stand, tug in snips and pinches straight the panties Lucy never took all the way off of her - fresh torn, there, and soaked a nighttime shade of their yellow and turquoise. The apartment feels nighttime all the more as Lucy looks there - the amount of light everywhere an anachronism. '*The Incredible Kung-Fu Mission*' Elliott says, prodding Lucy's hand - thumb of which is now gently massaging her own clitoris - then prodding Lucy's thighs a bit more open. 'What are you saying?' Lucy sighs, removing her hand now to rest in the wide between her fallen-this-way and her fallen-that breasts. 'Is the next one we're watching.' And Lucy nods and nods, closing her eyes and wondering where she is. Still bright when she opens them - so she closes them, again. 'Is it supposed to be night out?' 'That's not up to me, Jinx' Elliott says from now-on-the-other-side-of-the-room-it-sounds-like. 'Elliott?' No answer. Lucy opens her eyes and props on her elbows. 'Elliott?' Droops back down, back flat. 'I need a cigarette' she calls out. And hears some response, but indistinct. So yells 'I mean now, El!' just to be certain.

*YOU ARE WIDE AS A sky without arms.* Lucy Jinx, pockets around her hands. The bus has been waited for and now the train has been waited for and now she is sitting in a seat with her eyes closed awhile, now opened - there is a man who looks the way cough syrup tastes right after coffee, man with glasses up-tilted to forehead and a crossword puzzle poked at like an unwelcome bird finding the last crumb after the feeding is done and the others have flown. *You're as friendless as tree bark's indifference to the veins of a fallen leaf.* Lucy Jinx, skin glued over thoughts. There is her notebook out, open over her knee like a badly drawn frown, each rush of words so imperative, pen pulled away hoping the mind will feel slaked but the mind doesn't feel slaked - there she is, observing the man and wanting to make him tragic but sniffing the menace of temper on him, how he's grown his beard just to seem larger when angry, to seem more pertinent when he hitches his belt a bit tauter under his gut and leans back into the next way he'll belittle someone. *You're only as long as a raindrop.* Lucy Jinx, who exists to warm coins in her hands for awhile. Why do you keep on writing and who is this for and what are you going to do with it and where are you going? That man, now she sees, has the flecks of a tissue over the chapped lips his beard overcoats - and knowing those lips are sore and how often his tongue will slither between them, hoping his spit will sink its moisture in roots, makes him seem all the more insulting, the smear left to the glass after an aquarium is drained. *Your cigarette is the sort of snowstorm kids wait for but that never comes.* Lucy Jinx, the Off-switch on a turntable. To work - is that it? - and then home - and then where? and then where? She ignores her inability to answer herself more than a step-at-a-time - eyes sticking, toddler-stubborn, to the page, to the words, no more of that man or of anyone. *I've seen your hands misspell their own name.* Lucy Jinx, the middle-most part of a corner. It is okay to feel comfortable. She just needs to grow accustomed and not forget that everyone else had to do the same - she looks at her words at her words at her words. *You are as honest about yourself as someone else's final symphony.* Lucy Jinx, copper paid for in hide. This is still allowed to be only the beginning. And even if not, you are allowed to begin as many times as you want - if it were the end, it would be only once and would always have already come.

Immediately in a better head - greeted with the shock of a different temperature - Lucy hurries along with the rest of the commuters just off this late train. Her head feels rather like a dishwasher drying its contents with long sighs of heat. No, Lucy, you don't regret anything. It's just you haven't slept since you last slept and that time was part of a larger situation - so you haven't slept since the sleep before that, which was fitful and anticipatory, really as much a part of the awake after it as anything after it was. So really: it's been a long time since you've rested! And look: now you're dutifully going to work! People call off shift for less than this - but not you, Lucy Jinx! This is a human being - you are, you're saying - who needs no congratulations for having caused herself a burden! Let the record reflect! Even since two sleeps previous - even counting the two sleeps since as sleep despite all of their ill execution of it - you have been put through something of the wringer, self-inflicted or not. Why can't we pity people who cause their own problems? Lucy truly would like to know! 'Considering that is an apt description of everyone' she even whispers now, so invested in proving her motely point. Or is pity to be reserved only for those who cause their own trouble and then also stub their toe? Get an illness - isn't that something as natural as anything else? Such vainglory, calling an illness an affront to the way it was supposed to go! But at the same time we call old-age peaceful. Isn't it just the slowest, burliest illness of all? We only pity the unique, is that it? Lucy is building up quite the steam-head here, wanting to know where was the origin of her subconscious insistence to tell herself 'It's your own fault' as though it makes it somehow more appropriate she should suffer. Is she allowed no mitigating circumstances? She's not a special addendum, like so many others? 'And anyway' she demands the court be reminded 'it is not as though actual bad things haven't happened to me, too!' She is only who she is because she is - same as anyone - so why should she be treated any different?

Still: it is a lot of laments to have, so she decides to go to a different coffee-shop than she would like to. No more of these Rozalijas and all. Those are all terrible ideas. Because now that Lucy Jinx has gone through all of the trouble of deciding this is the storm she will weather, she is also the sort that has much experience to draw on to know how to do it. Can I ask a question, Lucy? This will be her stewpot. What is a life, after all, if not a concentrated front against a specific battalion, a generator of certain casualties, a piling of advances and reversals that are quite arbitrary, then suddenly tallied up, then left in a page that will never be opened to again? Lucy, may I ask a question? What she means - as she orders coffee from this man who is exactly as substantive as his rented house's key and the receipt for the coat he still brags about - is that life is a ledger more than it is a series of poetical statements and, well, she needs to treat it as that. And her poetry is something else! Lucy, can I ask something? 'No' she says, disguising it as the response to this portly girl - look at her: the sort of person who can't shake the feeling her friends have secret low-class pet-names for her - when the girl asks 'Are you using this chair?' Now, admittedly, Lucy knows her vessel is leaky and that - things all considered - there are wiser places to entrench than this era of her life. It is tempting to say that 'The here-and-now will never be perfect' but it is also more difficult to say that when - if she were to catalogue backward - each here-and-now she has squandered seems increasingly more ideal - and if not Ideal, purely, at least Better-than-This. This is Lucy Jinx's final here-and-now. This is the finale of her. So leaky is fine. Sinking is fine. She'll bail water for as long as she feels like then laugh as she swabs the deck in the ever-deepening surplus of encroaching The End. 'Thank you' she says as she is handed her coffee. The name written on the cup is *Delia*. She almost asks 'Are you sure this is mine?' except odds are in favor of *Delia* being what she'd said her name was - and odds are that if this is not what she ordered it still was.

Question: Is it always so calming, walking to work? Answer: Actually, yes. There is something in the ritual of it that has always eased Lucy out. No matter the tempest she might be within - real, imagined, realimagined - the fact that her choice to ask for employment inside of some at-random building allows a sanctuary the rest of the world cannot get at her while she is durationed in is as close to magic as anything. There is something of the slow foot-by-foot to an altar, flanked by children and censors, in Lucy's approach to places she is employed. A *Hosanna-in-the-Highest* as she makes herself supplicant - yes, yes she admits to not being always the most conscientious or dutiful in her station, but nevertheless - to the tasks a work-shift litanies for her. Question: Is it the opposite feeling, walking out? As in to say: is it a gallows walk, back into the world? Answer: Not at all. In fact, much like breathing the world fresh-in after prayer - or even just the idle standing in pew listening to sermon and watching others head-down to receive the Host - there is a time-warp quality to exit. It is rather as though the aura of protection extends a few blocks and at least a half-hour on either side of a shift. Leaving always carries with it a long-enough dose of feeling-still-there or I-could-go-back - or even an I-could-use-this-brief-respite-to-stage-a-more-fitful-runaway-from-it-all - that the world re-surrounds like bathwater cooling while asleep. Suddenly, Lucy might be chilly - but the grogginess doesn't let her know the extent of it even awhile after that. Question: Is Lucy happiest with multiple jobs? And, if so, does she regret the fact that - at least until her *Teaching Thingie* starts - she only has the one? Answer: Oh yes, absolutely. The more jobs, the better - her dream would be to have a little room wherever she was employed and some sort of constant-On-Call position, so that even when she was interacting with people outside-of-work there would always be the understanding she was umbilicaled to inside-of-work and the lay of her loyalties would always be known. And yes, she regrets it. Any question containing the word *Regret* ought answer itself, barring it also containing the word *Don't*. Question: Does Lucy Jinx believe in God? Answer: Lucy Jinx prefers to think that the catfish and the barnacles were something's idea - and if that same thing also came up with the Ampulex compressa and Atropa belladonna then so much the better.

Gemma is working the desk as Lucy approaches. Gemma, who looks as elegant as a loose-fitted doorknob but who always has a sweet word for Lucy. Like now: 'Where do you get your pants, Lucy? You always have the best outfits!' See? Much can be overlooked when someone has found a way to be so innocuously obsequious. Gemma: a shadow at the bottom of a still lake that has learned how to blush. 'Gemma, you are so lovely. A shadow at the bottom of a still lake that has learned how to blush.' Gemma beams and asks Lucy to repeat this. So - big expansiveness of magnanimity - Lucy goes so far as to write it down - very neatly - and to title it *Gemma* and to sign and date it, to boot. Gemma's eyes rustle like alive leaves raked into an also-alive bag and her grin goes wide past rupture. 'Does the lake blush or does the shadow?' Lucy normally would have only the most selective words for the twerp who would ask such a question - but this is Gemma, after all, and so allowances are made. 'You know, Gemma, it's the lake. But it should be the shadow, as well. Hold on.' And Lucy - tut-tutting Gemma's 'Oh please no' and speaking assurances that no faux pas was made, but a welcomed poetic improvement, instead - writes on to another small slip of paper *You are so lovely. A shadow at the bottom of a still lake, the both having learned how to blush*. Title: *Gemma*. Signed and dated. 'There you go.' Gemma reads it again and Lucy prepares to be kindly to some further simpleton-critique, but all Gemma says is 'I love that we're both blushing.' And Gemma would love just that! Then: on to business. The evening shift had been slow. But there is a coming convention and people might start showing up in the wee hours. There is a whole separate pile of keys and Sign-In sheets made for that. And the folks can all go right in, even though their reservations technically are the same as any other and not dated until after one o'clock in the afternoon, tomorrow. 'Or *Today*, for you' Gemma, embarrassed, says to Lucy. But Lucy just winks and thumbs-up and 'I gotcha - it's actually good that you said it. I honestly find it hard to keep track of what day I'm in, most weeks.'

The coffee is prepped but not brewed. Oh heads could roll if Lucy wasn't planning on cleaving them middle-wise! Bloodshed. Lucy taps the button - how hard was that!? Jesus! - her teeth clenched in slammed over whiskey glasses. Meantime, Lucy finds her punch-card and listens to the old-fashioned mechanical of the stamp being stamped to today's date as approximately right as she can make the alignment. A lovely sound. A perfect work-sound. A machine older than anyone on the job, every chug and click of it resentful, condescending. She pictures it exclaiming 'There!' once it does its one function and then waiting for her back to be turned to mutter something obscene she knows she hasn't the guts to go to management with. Right now Lucy says 'You might be my favorite clock' and caresses the always humming-warm side of it, gives furtive glance over shoulder, then plants it a kiss. 'And I'm quite a catch' she whispers, conspiratorial. 'Just ask the coffee-pot - I'm the only one around here who turns her on.' Lucy, Lucy - why have you no Variety Show? 'But I don't need fame' Lucy could Roman-orator to her workplace. And then she would eloquent awhile about each and every mechanism she interacts with, filling their inanimate hearts with more heady import and sense of this-is-as-it-must-be than scholars being sent into Pyrrhic warfare. A flash of awareness of her sexy over-education. A flash of awareness of her French novelette persona. 'I'm like sour-cream naughty talking about a fruit-tart' she says - and as though in applause a big percolate hiss from the dribble-drip coffee resounds! There are worse things to be good at than lowly labor. Imagine being a gifted missionary! Tending to the dying in places where there is nothing to do but stay hopeful in the face of the agony of strangers' children! 'That would be a shit skill' Lucy slaps hand to the countertop in declaration thereof. Yes, a place like this hotel is the place for a Lucy Jinx. The clapboard of the employee area versus the off-brand opulence of the joint itself. Yes, off-brand - the trappings she now knows to be thick as cake icing, no more. 'I've seen up your skirt with your sweets all undouched, lady' Lucy says to the walls and the floors rising above her 'and I find that your truth need not be oversold. I love that I have discovered your secret is vanity and dishonesty is your solution. We'll get along, passionately.'

And why not watch kung-fu movies? Aided or unaided by herb! Lucy has a list going on some scratch paper and is doing her best not to monologue to the empty lobby under the over-loud *Contempo Jazz* station the public address is stuck to. And on this list she is jotting the things she is going to do, from now on. *New Lucy Things* the list is titled - this list, of course, subject to change, as she notes by the parenthetically jotted words *working title*. *Watch all the kung-fu movies there are* she writes. And why in Christ's not!? Watch them even when Elliott is not around - wind up more into it than her, introduce her to new wonders, widen the scope of it to infinity! She also quickly jots: *Red Dwarf* and then in parenthesis the explanatory note: *introduce Elliott to the series - Box set???* And right under this she hurriedly follows up with *And Rumpole Of The Bailey!!!!!* The note for this, set between two three-sets of asterisks *Imperative - promise her vicious fucks if she is not in to it to make her suffering better - but the bitch Will Watch!!!!* So far, the list could be gisted down to: *Watch various things with Elliott.* And even if that is all it turns out to be, there is nothing - nothing! - under Heaven the matter with that! Work a job. Have a steady lover, no shady stuff. Watch movies and outdated television. Lucy kind of wants to write *Get to know Elliott's lot* but can't quite bring herself to it, so instead writes *And listen to audio books.* Parenthesis: *from the library - always have a whole bunch around.* But Lucy could get to know those people Elliott knows - why not? And knows she'll have to, either way. Knows that as sure as she knows she has to answer this phone call and has to make the reservation for the caller according to the dictates she was trained under. 'I never promised anyone I was romantic' - Lucy almost said that to the caller and almost wrote it in the *Guest Request* portion of the reservation screen. She writes it on the list, circling it and drawing a line from the circle and writing the words *this not part of the list* after the line so that she'll be one-hundred-percent certain when she makes a clean copy.

Ah! *You are as wide as a swallow of bourbon.* She writes that. But then is disconsolate. *Wide. Wide as. As wide as.* Why does this sound distressingly familiar? Yes. Memory serves: she wrote that something else was wide. Earlier. She doesn't know what, so could take that for a sign of lack-of-importance - if not for the fact that she knows if she hadn't written this, just here, she'd have forgotten the phrase inside of the hour. So: notebook out as soon as she finishes printing the *Weekly Housekeeping Report* - why that is done on Tuesdays she will never know, but frankly quite likes the fact that it is. There's the rascal! *Wide as a sky without arms.* 'Shit' she seethes. The idea was for the past to be revealed as inferior, but that is quite a good line. The new thing seems knobby-kneed in comparison - or at least it does on the tear of paper upon which it is blue-inked. So she opens a file and types each out. *Wide as a swallow of bourbon. Wise as a sky without arms.* Lucy, is it important that the past bit be the worse of the two? 'Of course not, of course not.' In fact, she could fix it just so: *Thin as a swallow of bourbon. Lithe as a swallow of bourbon. Lanky as a swallow of bourbon. Articulate as a swallow of bourbon. Simian as a swallow of bourbon. Xenophobic as a swallow of bourbon. Paltry as a swallow of bourbon. Sickbed as a swallow of bourbon. All-at-once as a swallow of bourbon. Old-pain as a swallow of bourbon.* 'And so on and so on' she says, doing a bunch of dot-dot-dot dot-dot-dot on the next few lines down in the file. Then she notices the typo. *Wise as a sky without arms. Wise?* This puts a different complexion on the matter, because that is the best of all! I disagree, Lucy. 'Then you disagree!' Lucy fuck-it-all-right-out-louds. 'But *wide* and *sky* and *without arms* is pea-brained compared to *wise* and *sky* and *without arms.*' Oh - her vigor slackens. Or do you object because people will take *without arms* to mean *Without weapons* or *Peaceful?* Because you don't want to call the sky *Peaceful,* Lucy! 'Shit. No. No, no.' She corrects the typo immediately. People will comprehend the violence in the original, though? She wonders. She stares. *Wide as a sky without arms.* It will be understood, the implicit brutality? It will be understood, the cosmic lay of the truncation, the dismembered grandeur remaining of a thing lopped to less-than?

Sometime around three in the morning, Lucy steps out for a smoke. No sign of any conventioneers. Which makes it hard to enjoy the cigarette - surest thing you know they'll show up. But a second cigarette started, she is at her ease. By a third, she cannot help wondering if she has shown up to the correct job or is just loitering in a hotel lobby, gratis and dementia-headed, a sun-downing escapee from an elderly-ward. Back inside, all seems well. She has a Password for the computer, anyway - and a lot of the notes in the work-ledger are addressed to her. And her name is on the schedule. And - no - she does not tire of the game of verifying she is where she ought to be for quite some time. It is only when the familiar itch of horniness takes its full luxury in her thoughts that she cuts the thread, back to pondering 'Isn't there some way Lucy Jinx could view porn on the computer without being caught?' Or is the only solution, truly, analog? Back to days-gone-by, lugging mags around? None of the thrill of the hunt. Lucy Jinx, debonair wank-miner, reduced to an impotent magazine-shop pervert. Or she could buy mags from a sex-shop. It would not seem pervy, there. Though she has her doubts about that. 'Maybe not *pervy*' she says quietly 'but probably rather sad.' If you're in a sex-shop, you shouldn't need mags. That's what she'd judgmental on some poor punter, were she the shop clerk. But then: she's never been a clerk in such a place, so should not assume they would hire a person like her. Horniness subsides - or at least waits in the wings, a bit - while she tries to be honest with herself concerning how she would come off to a sex-shop clerk were she to go in to buy something - magazines, anything.

Nods, after ten minutes of wordless but intricate cogitation. Conclusion: they'd love her! They'd give her a cool nickname! Call her *Dame Jinx* or something along those lines. She would be looked upon for her wisdom, the assumption being that she is gracing the place with her presence. Yep. Lucy Jinx would make a sex-shop worker feel they were a rung or two higher than they'd been putting themselves down about. Spring in their step! Lucy Jinx would make price-gunning dildos seem something that helps out the upper-crust - the same as fixing potholes or keeping the lines on the road spic-and-span.

Something goes wrong with the printer. It claims *Paper Jam* but claims so despite the lack of evidence. The personality of this printer, it seems, is rather *Tractatus Logico-Philosophicus*. Except, Lucy points out, this machine has one-uped that slim tract - those seven propositions versus its one-and-one-only. *Paper Jam*. 'The word is everything that is the case.' *Paper Jam*. 'What is the case (a fact) is the existence of states of affairs.' *Paper Jam*. 'A logical picture of facts is a thought.' *Paper Jam*. 'A thought is a proposition with a sense.' *Paper Jam*. 'A proposition is a truth-function of elementary propositions. (An elementary proposition is a truth-function of itself.)' *Paper Jam*. 'The general form of a proposition is the general form of a truth-function.' *Paper Jam*. 'Whereof one cannot speak, therefor one must be silent.' *Paper Jam*. *Paper Jam*. *Paper Jam*. No matter how Lucy clevers this machine: *Paper Jam*, it states. Or maybe it is not the single statement *Paper Jam* but the infinite set *Paper Jam Paper Jam Paper Jam* - usque ad lassitudinem - each utterance not a repetition but a continuation only offered in response to new query or repeated same-query. Either way, she will be sad if she finally outwits it. The ghost of Wittgenstein is smoking pensively into Lucy's shoulder, ashing all over its own invisible shoes. Lucy stab-stab-stabs at the button which yields the result of a blip-toned shriek and the words *Load Paper* starting to scroll and scroll across the display screen. Which is progress and not-progress. What a microcosm of all human reason post-Descartes this machine is turning out to be! It is its own thesis, insistences, and then upending critique! Because Lucy can appreciate the deft drunkening the thing is making of causal reason, in toto. It seems - to the unaffiliated - the new remark is merely a louder reiteration of the same insistence that has been so patiently and repeatedly made before - but instead it might be a misguided *Eureka!* or a cat-calling set of theses nailed to a church door! *Load Paper* - sideways scroll forever. *Paper Jam* - offered imperturbably then vanishing until re-summoned. 'What do you mean, oracle? Jam the thing further? Or is it that you disagree, full stop? Do you propose I counter-intuit it - add paper when a glut of paper is said to be the cause? A curative poison? Or are you mocking mankind's folly!? We who try to fix the destructiveness of our thinking with further thought on our thoughts!? I'm writing this down, I promise!' Lucy says - and to not be called 'Liar' and lumped in with the rest of the heretics she does so, right there on the back of her hand. *Paper Jam. Load Paper.*


SO WHAT IS SUPPOSED TO happen now, Lucy? Your old rules will not be applicable to this new life? Or will they? Of course they will not - are you even trying to believe that they will? What is good for the hunter-gatherer, after all, is not what built the Library at Alexandria. 'It is what led to the Library at Alexandria, though' Lucy blows out as a fatigued leak of cigarette, not saying any of the words beyond the phffisssss of the blow - but in this case, that is how they are pronounced. Quick resolve: stop thinking about this. However: it is a psychological fact that when you wish not to think about something you set a subconscious program going that will make you check in on that thing to see that it is not being thought about and hence you will think about it more. 'That's silly' Lucy yawns, up-going the steps to the Metro platform. That would imply all there is to do is think about things and obviously some things are not thought about. Meh. Lucy sees the mistake in this thinking, but doesn't dwell on it. For all she knows, anyway, this is the program just checking in, keeping tabs. The routine has become aware of itself it has cycled-though so often. The eventual fate of the universe, isn't it? Every spec of it eventually gets to have been conscious for a little while? It's comforting to think so. All of existence just a slow-pulsing single thought, maybe - lighting up different universes as it passes through, the eventual demise of one just really the return to a waiting-state. When there is enough time, Time doesn't matter. If each bit only knows anything when it is lit up, it will fret through all of the confusion and coming oblivion, even knowing oblivion isn't oblivion - or, even if it is, *Oblivion* isn't what we mean when we say *Oblivion*. Or: even if it is what we mean, well, it shouldn't be. Lucy sees the coming train and starts counting down the twenty seconds she thinks it'll take for it to pull in. Turns her back and stubs her cigarette on the lip of this overfilled trash-bin. No train. Over there. Random, it has slowed to a halt. It sometimes does that. Should have seen that coming, Lucy. Hell, give Time enough time and every part becomes conscious-even-when-unconscious and the conscious parts are conscious but so long has passed that consciousness has taken on the properties of unconsciousness - so you should have guessed the train would play a trick just when you weren't thinking it would.

In the tunnel, Lucy has the distinct impression it has started to rain. And by *The Distinct Impression* let it be known what is meant is that when she exits the tunnel and it is not raining she feels disorientated. Let's examine that. It seems important. Exhibit *A:* Lucy Jinx on platform - it isn't raining and shows no sign of rain. Exhibit *B:* Lucy Jinx in a train, suddenly certain it is raining outside. Exhibit *C:* Lucy Jinx on the train, sees it isn't raining outside, is perturbed. Conclusion: Lucy Jinx is disquieted by things going as they are - by things being as they are. There was no reason - other than internal to Lucy Jinx - to have got it so firmly in mind it was raining - this was her concoction and it became, as one can see, even as she can herself reflect on, what was important to her. She didn't stop knowing it hadn't been raining. She just believed - for no reason - it had started. Why? She here posits that it must be because she knew it wasn't and for it to still not be would be a continuity she cannot accept. Ah, Lucy - the worst thing that ever happened to you was object permanence, wasn't it? But, why is that funny!? Yes - as a matter of fact that was the worst thing to ever happen to Lucy! That and the fact that different shaped containers seem to make the same amount of liquid appear more-or-less. The human mind is not meant to trust the world! It is a finely calibrated mechanism of I-know-not-to-believe-it. Lucy Jinx feels the new deal she is forging is forgetting her nature as *Person.* The last thing *Person* should believe is themselves. Doubt the world but always doubt yourself, most of all. Not even *Doubt* - Lucy shifts in her seat to emphasis. Such a weak word. *Doubt* is so dainty and polite. *Mistrust.* Skeptics *doubt.* Philosophers *question.* Poets *mistrust.* The declension declines in that direction. Are you choosing not be a Poet then, Lucy? Is that what worries you? Poets can't have full tummies and vow themselves to the same person, forever? 'Not' Lucy spits a reminder 'that she ever said *Forever.*' And anyway - you don't trust this life, you are just choosing it. Ah, weak tea, weak tea. You do trust it. You trust it to be incorrect. You trust yourself, now, because you know you are doing the wrong thing. No mystery if you make the choice. 'But then again' she sighs 'it was not raining and still isn't when there's no reason it should be - so left to its own devices, it seems the world can be trusted, as well.'

Being honest, Lucy isn't sure she thought any of that stuff. Look, here she is and has missed her stop. It doesn't happen often and so a ridiculous amount of frustration sets in. If this had happened on the way to work, she'd be in pieces. Yeah - she wasn't thinking any of that stuff. Rubbish. All this worry about *Oblivion* and *Trusting* and *Not Trusting.* A random-number-generator is also just a number-generator. Odds? They don't care what they are supposed to be. Does fifty-fifty think it is supposed to assert itself? What about thirty-seventy, then? Someone show Lucy - in the grand scope of all ungodly-sized creation - why it makes sense to say things balance, that given enough times a coin will flip Heads just as many times as Tails. Say roulette hit Red Three ten billion times in-a-row - which it could - and then hit Black Eight ten billion times in-a-row and then Green Double-Zero and then Red One and then Black Twenty-Six all ten billion times in-a-row - well, once the wheel had gone around three-hundred-sixty billion times, things would all balance out! Is that what we're saying here? Lucy is given - cruel example - the simple two options of going to the other side of the track and riding the train back the way she came until a point where she could have got off or of just walking the few extra miles. Oh - or getting a cab, of course! Ah - or begging a ride from this stranger. Ah - or this-or-that! Oh - or walking a bit and taking a cab a bit and getting a ride with this stranger a bit and then something else a bit. See? See!? What is it? Lucy has agency to decide which of those things happens, so odds don't enter into it? Say roulette, then, was governed by one person, at random, choosing which number won and announcing it aloud. Think that's any less random, after awhile? Once they've made twenty billion announcements think they'll have any idea if they have chosen This more-or-less often or in total than That? And if they make twenty billion more announcements, they'd doubt they'd make the same choices, exactly, they had the first twenty billion times - but they might well have done! Odds are they would! Ridiculous. Ridiculous. And now Lucy thinks she had thought all of that stuff, after all! She's sure of it! And look here: she crossed to the other side of the platform, waited a minute, then decided to walk, anyway. Already regrets it, as well.

Of course, this is all brand new to Lucy - the choice of being *content*. So it's bound to discombobulate her, awhile. It's a kind of exercise. Her brain is drenched in lactic acid right about now and her lungs feel made of latex with drying fingers inside pressing hard and rubbing along them. She goes into this fast-food place for breakfast. Hardly anyone there, she feels a bit bad when she chooses one of the three clerks at their stations over the two others - but what can she do about it? She wants to complain, quite frankly. 'What is this' she will demand of management 'some sort of intimidation? What's the trick? You have those three people stand there, so I have to stress at the knowledge I know I am being subtly judged on whom I select? The stress makes me feel bad and so I eat more? Think I deserve nothing more than to be lardy and judgmental!?' At her table, she chews on some waffle-fries and assesses the clerks. She chose the best one. She's certain of it. And she drinks from her coffee and thinks she should get chubby. More chubby, anyway - Lucy is kind of chubby, already. And she is so comfortable thinking about this that it sticks wrong down her craw when she deciphers what she should have done with those clerks. She should have laughed at the situation and let them chose which one would serve her! Any schoolkid should have sized that up, but Lucy's elderly mind couldn't even get out of the gate! Not that the game makes any sense, really. How are they so certain she didn't see through it and just pick one, out of spite, at random? Or that she specifically chose the one who was the most like her because 'Fuck them - who are they to conduct sociological experiments on her!?' Before she knows it, her sausage biscuits are concreting her gut and she hardly recalls the taste of them. The grease forms a seal between her cheek-lining and the coffee, the liquid swifting down to the chewed slop in her belly, a kid down on a slide on wax paper. Does Lucy's logic help her, though? That the experimenters are wrongheaded - sick-hearted, entirely beyond redemption - does that make their judgement cut less? 'But you know none of that is what actually happened, right Lucy?' she asks, hiding the vocalization with a napkin to her crumb-dirtied lips. 'The world is not like that. Not now. Not anymore.'

Concentrating, Lucy will show herself she can observe her surroundings without analysis or despair. Watch. There: she sees a man stopping short and clapping hands to his rear pockets, ire rising, clapping hands to his blazer pockets, seeming to calm down, then reaching hand into his interior blazer pocket, not liking what he finds, turning on his heel, almost knocking into that young couple who had even been giving him the wary approach since noting him stop from plenty afar. Good, Lucy. Keep going. There: that woman smokes a cigarette while her dog has a shit. The woman is accustomed to this and thinks the other people around are accustomed to it, too - and she is probably right. The dog kicks mulch from the area around the small tree - these trees all lining the curb for the next several city blocks - the mulch landing on slicks of oil in the unoccupied parking spot, there. But the woman would not have stopped the dog kicking this mulch up even if a car had been parked there. She is just that much a part of the ecosystem, just that much a part of the normal wear-and-tear a city vehicle can encounter. Still good, but Lucy will attempt to keep the editorializing out of the next observation. Which is this: a young chick sitting against the wall - at the bottom of the wall - feet wide apart and knees opened out, like she is a dot-to-dot of the letter $M$ - foot, knee, crotch, knee, foot. The chick sways her head and her wrists, which drape from the knees, flap as though barn doors caught unbolted in a storm. She points to that man passing, but it is clear that man does not know her and is irritated by the pointing. The pointing did have a trace of aggression to it - in Lucy's estimation - was more like it had been meant to call the guy out mockingly for having a look at her when - as far as Lucy could tell - whatever look there had been had been entirely incidental - the man would have looked at newspapers on the street just where the girl was had the newspaper rustled and the girl not been there. Excellent, Lucy. Odd that it was exhausting to do it, but excellent work! Next test: try to just walk and think nothing. Walk and think the lyrics to a song. Walk. Walk, like people do. Like people not like you. Like the people you are starting to be like.

All cut short. Comical. To explain: Lucy cannot fathom why the key won't work the door - nor why the door starts opening on its own and Curtis is standing there when it does. She laughs. 'What in Hell are you doing here?' she high-pitches with an over-friendly shove at his shoulder. Slight squint of wariness - obviously just at Lucy's affect, not at her merely being there - Curtis explains that he does still live in the apartment but was under the impression that Lucy no longer did. 'I don't' she laughs some more, asking if she can come in. Curtis ushers her, making certain to note that he did not mean she was not welcome if she was intent on coming back - 'In fact, Deb would be thrilled' he adds. 'I'm starting to get the impression I'm as much a visitor as you were' he explains 'and that your conversation was more interesting than my fornication.' Lucy lights a cigarette from the pack on the counter without asking and opens the refrigerator, taking out an apple-juice. 'I'm not coming back' she says on the gasp after a long drink. 'I wound up back here on accident. It's really quite a thing - but I am not going to worry, as it has a simple explanation.' Curtis nods, not pressing Lucy to explain. 'Is Deb here?' 'Deb is not here, no. She had to go to some appointment with a friend. I figure it's something personal and likely something built out of response to the systemic oppression of women, so I figured also it best not to ask. I feel guilty about things like that.' 'About the systemic oppression of women?' 'Yes. And things like it.' Curtis also lights a smoke, but out of a pack he has in his pockets. 'You're just used to coming here, is it? Don't have the muscle-memory for home, yet?' Lucy could not have put it better herself! 'And that's all' she adds. 'That is all. I have had a distracted morning and in my distraction moved according to an old pattern. A not-even-a-day-old pattern. That's all.' Curtis nods. 'I agree' he says. 'What else could it be?' she asks, rolling her eyes like 'Why would there ever be a question!?' 'Exactly' says Curtis. Odd silence. 'Can I take a nap here?' asks Lucy. Curtis shrugs 'Sure' - but he was just leaving, so if Lucy leaves before Deb gets home she should make sure to lock up.

The silent hum of an apartment that is not hers. Womb cover. On the bed - fully clothed - she stares at the ceiling which already seems unlooked-at-by-her for ages. The room without her few things, in fact, seems cavity. It seems the space left by something excised or prised or yanked from where it was lodged. Listen to your steady breathing, Lucy. Controlled breath in, the count of two-three, controlled breath out, the count of two-three. Still tense, though - thinking Curtis will have texted Deb and Deb will be calling and explanations will have to be explained. 'Or not *Have to*' Lucy says - and just saying that makes her lose the rhythm of breathing and thus makes her feel winded, though she has been prone for a half-hour. No, Deb would never ask for an explanation. And Deb would never even ask 'So, are you staying awhile?' That's how the evening will go, in fact. Lucy will be there when Deb gets back. They will hang around like nothing lives beyond the moments it's seen and only when it gets late and

Lucy shows signs of staying over will Deb finally ask if she intends on rooming in the apartment, again - even then, will only ask as an excuse to say that Lucy would be most welcome to. 'Would that be terrible?' Lucy asks the ceiling - and the ceiling tells her 'It would actually be better.' Ceiling are notoriously amoral, though - so Lucy closes her eyes and asks the gurgling hush of the inside of her eyelids. 'It would be good, Lucy. You should not have left.' Opens her eyes and asks the direction-of-the-ceiling, making certain to note in her thoughts this is what she is asking so that she knows what is answering. 'It might be, Lucy. But do you particularly need it not to be? Since when has that been the case?' This puts her off. So she sits up and undresses and crawls under the covers, first turning off the room lights and folding her clothes in the dark. Yes, Lucy knows this is not good. This is not good. But if she had made it back to her apartment - Elliott's apartment - it would be the same, she'd just be sleeping there is the only difference. She just needs sleep. And then when she wakes she will leave. Go home. Her apartment. Herself, again.

But five minutes later - her eyes maybe closed long enough to be called *Closed* before she scrambled from the bed - Lucy is dressed and berating herself down the apartment building stairs. She stole the pack of cigarettes on her way out - which she feels a bit bad about - smoking a second, already, making a turn in the direction of the Metro. And a new Pass purchased, through turnstiles, down escalator, pacing the platform-length, and nodding to people she passes who are pacing their own smaller circuits around benches or public-telephones, ducking her hand-with-cigarette behind her back each time she passes this father who seems exasperated with having to act so interested in the map that his kid is bubblingly excited about deciphering. 'Excuse me.' Lucy decides to pretend she did not hear, though that voice seemed aimed at her. 'Excuse me, miss?' Husky tone of a middle-aged woman. Lucy continues her walking, but now the voice raises and is following her. 'Miss, excuse me?' How are you going to play this, Lucy? 'You can't be smoking down here.' Lucy keeps walking. This woman will give up her pursuit. This will not reach fever-pitch. Lucy, you are allowed to make a transgression - this woman has no right to pound down on you, this way! But what in Hell is this? Her pursuer now overtakes her and - just as Lucy is inhaling a new drag - has cellphone pointed and is snapping her photo. 'You can ignore me, go ahead' the woman says. 'I will have you banned from this station. You should have just put out the cigarette.' Another photo snapped. Another photo snapped. This is just a test, Lucy. It's like a movie, you know? Steel yourself and this spectral-bitch will vanish. Lucy has reached the end of the platform again, turns to head back how she came. 'And don't even think about stepping that out on the ground. I'm warning you.' Don't make eye-contact, Lucy. This monster is not real - figment, nothing more than a sneeze from a dream that processed down the wrong tendril of your spine. The woman keeps following Lucy and the accusations and invectives just hurl and snowball and so now more people are watching and Lucy's cigarette is almost gone, anyway. There is the man. His kid. Their map. Lucy smiles as she passes - the kid smiles back, the man making his eyes quickly, expressionlessly avert.

Home. Home. It is a good idea. It is a good idea. Lucy plans to take a week off from work and not leave the apartment, fill it with scents of her unwashed body. Because she knows - corner-seated on the train, newspaper to her face as a clever disguise - that this - she, her life - still feels like running because it is running. It is running. But running toward. Chase. This is why she has always failed at being normal in the past. She has confused *Home* for *Peacefulness*. She has strived to remove herself from things instead of accepting her desire to writhe in the company of society. Typical of her wayfaring mind, she has romanticized things too much - confuted the *Wandering* with the *Wanderer*, forgot that the former is just motion and the latter is defined by the fact that they struggle to arrive. You cannot wander without struggle. But every time Lucy feels struggle, she flees. *Fleeing* isn't *wandering*. She has confused *driftwood* for *vessel*. Cross-witted Lucy wants to exist as the center-pages, where it seems no meaning has yet been found. But of course meaning is rife, there - the center-pages are the gut most full-up with nourishment, churning and aciding at meaning, that whole tantrum of weight only existing because something has been ingested and something will be excreted. Lucy, you only think you don't want to know what you mean. You only think that because you want to be clever. But be honest, Lucy! It's not even that you want to not know - because you already know - it's that you don't want others to. You want to be Immortal as only an unfinished book can be. Better still, to horror that further: an unfinished, unread book! You want to be the blank page outrunning the words! And the idea of somebody reading you - all of you - cover-to-cover? Jesus, Jinx - is that so abominable, so grey-hairing to contemplate? Be the page devouring the words, Lucy - you are not written-on but are swallowing them, hunting them, trapping them in you. That's what is happening! It's not them printing themselves to your skin - your vast blankness is a cage to confine words in, to display the specimens of your life. It is running. It is pursuit. The hunt. The acquisition. Home. Home. It is a good idea. It is a good idea.

Her phone buzzes with Elliott and she casuals her voice as she Hellos. Elliott seems to have not expected Lucy to answer, stammers, then asks 'How's it going?' 'Good. I'm fucking ridiculous. I was so beat from work I totally took the train to Deb's place. I'm about ten minutes away, now - just had some breakfast on the way.' Elliott thinks this is hilarious and says she will just have to redouble her efforts to make her pad the auto-pilot destination. 'I mean our place' Elliot quickly insists. 'I know what you mean, El. Aren't you at work?' 'I took the damn day off, Lucy.' 'Oh.' And after a pause, Elliott is laughing harder and says 'Well, since you asked: I took the day off because the woman I love has come back to me. Figured I'd make myself wholly available to her.' 'That's a really sweet thing to do, Elliott. Wow. You are demonstrably a better person than me, aren't you?' Now Lucy is laughing, as well - and Elliott has pivoted the subject to a dream she had. Some dream about finding an entire boxful of mice in the closet. 'Dead mice?' Lucy interjects when the matter does not quite seem clear. 'Neither alive nor dead. Just mice. Or I guess, by default, alive. I certainly didn't say *Dead mice* in the dream - and you'd think, especially in a dream, if it's a box of dead mice and I am telling you I found it in our closet I'd be explicit on that point. Dreams are usually pretty on-the-nose with shit like that, Loose.' In the dream, it is also explained, Lucy and Elliott decided - or just started doing it, there was no conversation - to put the mice in the pockets of all of the coats they had in the closet - 'It was a different closet than our real closet though, with about a hundred coats' - and then to stitch the pockets shut. 'Was it a bad dream?' Lucy asks. 'No, it wasn't.' It just seemed like something they would actually do, Elliott explains. She says she woke up honestly feeling more like she had remembered something than she had dreamt it. 'Do you ever feel that way? Does that even make sense?' Lucy says 'No' she never feels that way. But 'Yes' she says it makes sense. She says 'Yes, Elliott - that does make perfect sense to me.'

# .PART THREE.

# .I.

*HIS NAME IS LUCY JINX*. Lucy Jinx carved it on the stone herself and now the stone is there. This is on the side of the road, exactly where the two of them met. This exactly where the cat is now buried, a hole dug by Lucy, herself - she had paused to seem as though just smoking a cigarette the few times some cars passed by. How had Lucy carved the stone? Rather clumsily and with a screwdriver. And how is she certain this is the same spot, the spot where they collided? Truthfully, she cannot be entirely certain. She knows enough to remember about how many miles if was from the *Starlite Deluxe Hotel*. And this feels like the spot. It looks like the spot. Either way: the cat in interred and its rest will remain inviolate, so now this is the only place that matters. Lucy's hands are murky with the grave. Any dirt can be grave-dirtied, the world a ready-made stretch of places to bury. Ground should just be called *Graves*, she decides. Earth should just be called *Grave*. Soil: *Grave*. 'All the variants' she says with a dismissive wave of her hand, mouthing the smoke of this last drag all around. The chill night is doing its best to keep the air stationary. This night is trying to resemble a spine with fine posture to hide what a coiling, unkempt pile it is. To wit: a woman called Lucy Jinx just buried a cat called Lucy Jinx. Tell

606 / PABLO D'STAIR

that to someone and take odds on whether they deem it remotely ordinary or
above reproach. Such untoward things filth through this night, this dark, this
time that seems right for memories you want all for yourself or the ones you're
stuck with and stuck with alone, want them or no. What night ever isn't a mess
- yes - and so hence the only real reason for there to be daytime - the sun is the
moon's warm ablution. This must be the place, Lucy. Yes. Doesn't she recall
that exact building out in the field? 'Well no' she immediately frumps. She
remembers harrows of long flat and screaming and the smithereens of her vision
turned against her. This probably isn't the spot. And now it is. There is the
stone. Here is Lucy Jinx, noting to herself what bad shape she is in - the digging
has halved her, ready for bed. There it is. *His name is Lucy Jinx* - immortalized on
a stone no one knows no one but her is supposed to know of.

   Big old mouth, yawn crik-criking her jaw, Lucy is not quite ready to speak.
Another car goes by and she remains thankful that it, as like the others, did not
stop to see if she needed assistance. People are wise. It's only fictions who stop
to see what the shot is with women smoking near shouldered cars in the dead
waste of night. Movie deaths come from that. Or make-believe movie loves. So
help her Jesus, if any person who turned out to have children in the car with
them had pulled over to help her she would have brained them and called the
authorities to get the kids placed into more responsible care, toot suite. Each
drag of her smoke tastes a bit of her unwashed hands. Because of how noses
work. Science! It still disappoints her how taste and smell are not entirely
separate. Disappointed her since she was a wee little gal and first learned it.
Without smell you cannot taste. Without taste you cannot smell. She lost all
respect for both. 'Then why not just call them one thing?' she had asked the
teacher, expecting sagacity in return and instead getting - well, she doesn't
remember really - either 'I don't know' or some fa-la-la. Is it so important to
have five senses? That's how she had met Ginnifer. Ginnifer who agreed that her
parents had spelled her name wrong. This is Lucy, in a field after manual burial
- as with the ancient and languageless it must have been - hop-scotching
memories she long ago lost use for. 'Oh - this is the use!' She scoffs. Don't start
believing that chicanery again, Lucy. You could just as well remember the first
time you heard the term *Toejam*. Which you don't, by the way. Search as you
will, it is gone. Not the word, but the entry-wound of it. But it does put you in
mind of the worms crawling in, the worms crawling out, the worms playing
pinochle on your snout, eh? And - Holy smokes! - is that where you heard it
first? *They eat your eyes, they eat your nose, they eat the jam between your toes?* Unconvinced,
Lucy looks at exactly that cloud there and is pleased it resembles nothing, hardly
even a cloud. Might be true, that about *Toejam*, but still - first time you thought
of it or not, the term rounds nicely full-circle to now. So: Checkmate. Even

remembering something you'd forgot when you first learned ties well back to here at the head of a grave. 'Then again' Lucy sighs, discarding cigarette, ready to speak 'what doesn't seem reasonable on top of a dead cat?'

'I coulda written ya a fine speech, a real send off, Jinx - I could be orating a eulogy that I'd be able to charge folks to reprint in anthologies. But ah, Jinx, damnit, damn you - Jinx you woulda hated that. You'd have found it unseemly. A bore. You'd have yawned in that way you did which you pretended was so fucking original but really was just the way a cat yawns. I look around, Jinx, I see. You weren't the only cat, no matter how much you tried to tell me that. I humored you. Idiot. You really thought you had me fooled! Well - so my point is: I coulda done up a number for you, but you spoilt that yourself. Right outta the teat that was pinch-tart, so don't complain to me. What do I have to say about you, Lucy Jinx? My speech begins thus: *I will miss you.* I will be complimented for that, Jinx. The simplicity. For ages. *Look how she starts so simply with 'I miss you'! Ah* they will say. *Oh oh!* they will say. Morons, Jinx. Cooing over some speech I'm making up as I go, practically. The next line will be: *Really, I will miss you.* Rhythmic, that repetition, with the *Really* between - I'll say that word a perfect see-saw, Jinx, one *I-will-miss-you* to the next. *Ree. Lee. I will miss your one eye - which was my fault - and the way you would bug me for food when there already was food in the bowl because of your fuck-wittedness - and I will miss your tendency to vomit on things and to shit where I least wanted you to.* Those are the next lines. Of your eulogy, Lucy Jinx! Keep up, ya piss-ant cat! And then: *You were my cat and I took you around with me and often times I ignored you because, historically, cats prefer it that way. Other times though, my friend, I would insist you upon me and treat you as though - foolish, I know - you had the capacity for reason. You. You! Jinx - you, Lucy Jinx - who would lick the tin lid of a tuna can for an hour straight, if you had things your own way, never figuring out that is just your tongue that it tastes like by then!* 'Might as well eat your tongue' I'd say to you.' Remember that? Remember that, Lucy Jinx? I'd tell you *It just tastes like your tongue, by now. Might as well eat your tongue! It'd be less tinny, at least.* But maybe you liked tin, right? The fuck did I ever know, Jinx?'

Lucy in thought of 'How long are moments supposed to be?' Lucy putting on her seatbelt. Lucy in thought of 'How sad should something make you if it isn't making you sad?' Lucy turning up then down then up the radio - indecision not welcome, least of all tonight. Lucy in thought of 'Was that correct, how one is supposed to bury a cat?' Lucy depressing the car lighter because she's come to really dig the car lighter, has wasted her life in hardly ever using the thing. Lucy in thought of 'That was illegal - had I been caught, I'd be driving home with a ticket and a very dirty cat in a bag in my trunk!' Lucy watching the receding taillights of a car moving on past her, rekindling her argument that if it is moving away in front one should say the lights are *Preceding* away - only if the car had passed her in the other directly, hence going away behind her, ought the term be *Receding*. Lucy in thought of 'It was right to lay the cat not in a bag or not in a box' - she'd already domesticated it, she could at least let its passing remain unspoiled, unhumaned, un-ceremony-nothing-to-do-with-ited. Lucy lighting her smoke, the heater having lit the car wide with the overcooked damp of the tomb, this new crackle of tobacco coming across dog-wet and obnoxious, someone else's heat all over a chair you want to relax in. Lucy in thought of 'Did putting the rock there, with inscription, sully the naturalness' - concluding, correctly 'No no, cats don't care about rocks and were more than clever enough to do without the alphabet - have as much use for words as jawbones for corkscrews - felt feline-pity for bungler humans and their ungainly meal-wormy words.' Lucy putting the car in to Drive, wondering, really, what the other options are even for or if there is something odd about her because she never uses them - other, of course, than Reverse and Park. Lucy in thought of 'Is it okay to drive off, now - is it okay to ignore the worry I should not?' Lucy more than a mile away, in a minute - such is the marvel of the horseless-age and the industrial need to be somewhere-else. Lucy in thought of 'If I went back now - unless it were to claw the earth, to weep myself into botched soil and coat my throat with mulch-tanged mucus - it would be not only pointless but kind of pathetic.' Lucy seeing the sign for the hotel - still called the *Starlite Deluxe* but now with the icon of a major franchise worked into the prissy-pants neon sign. Lucy in thought of 'Well, should I go claw the earth, weep myself into botched soil - is that what people do, people other than me?'

Lucy, Lucy - she doesn't have a cat anymore and looks precisely like Act-five Scene-one of *Hamlet* and currently we find her making her way across a hotel parking lot. Previous to this, she had sat there in her car to enjoy singing along to a song, but that is more compulsion than courtesy. Even the cig she's been sucking had been flicked to cold anonymity unfinished. 'Unfinished, unfinished' she amuses herself with thinking 'is what happens when one has their citizenship to Finland revoked. *Un-Finnish-ed*' she says in a yuk-yuk tone of *Ya get it?* In a perfect world, her confidence from this quip would make her bold with the hotel management, tell them she would like to have her act booked, nightly, in the lounge. 'We have no lounge' they would say. 'In one of the meeting rooms, then.' 'We have no meeting rooms.' 'In that case, outside by the pool - weather permitting.' 'Then okay - but we cannot pay you.' 'Nevermind, then' Lucy would brusque and stern them how they ought to have cut to that chase off the bang! Automatic door automatics. Her odor mixes with the potpourri of lobby-still-wet-from-its-nightly-mopping. The young man at the desk seems chagrined - or, better word for him, *Timoroused* - at her approach. 'I'm dirty because I just buried my cat out on the road - several miles back, not on your property.' 'Shit.

Sorry.' 'There is nothing to be sorry about. I stayed in this hotel the night I first met him - my cat - and I shall stay here, now.' The lad does not how to be appropriate or that there is no way to be - which is to say this situation is elevated of a need for such trifles. 'We met when I ran him down with my car - nearly killed him - and I stayed in this hotel while he recuperated - and now I stay here after finally having finished him off. You see?' 'I do' the clerk good-natures, assuming that good-nature is called for, Lucy supposes. 'If at all possible, I would like the same room - not much has changed these seven, eight years' - though she notes many changes, in fact, or thinks she does - 'so I imagine it is still there.' 'I can check' and he, to prove this, is already tacking at keys, producing that sound only hotel-desk keyboards seem to produce. 'You might still be in our system' he says, eyes up to her 'should be' he adds, scratching the base of his head with his pen 'what is your name?' 'I am the poet, Lucy Jinx' Lucy says, turning her back on him to lean to the counter the way such a pronouncement of Self necessitates one had ought.

This is the room. Best described as? A lyric that Leonard Cohen would have scraped - sounded good for a second, then didn't. 'This isn't, though, how the room was laid out before, no?' Lucy's internal, calm-toned biographer asks. No. Totally different, in fact. 'But the description still fits?' the biographer follows up and then furthers 'Or you only meant that description to fit Now and not Then?' 'Both times, both times' Lucy says and lumps herself higgledy-piggledy on to the mattress and turns on the television. 'Is that what you did last time?' the biographer presses. 'It is' Lucy explains, though she does hasten to add that she is not trying to recreate that night and would never be able to. Biographer: 'It's just what you do when you first come into a hotel room - any hotel room?' Lucy: 'Yes. Because I am the same as anyone else.' This time, though, in the shower Lucy will be washing off scents of cold, disheveled side-road and perspiration, while last time it had been gore and snot and brain-scrambled fatigue. Last time, she had felt scabbied with guilt and a sense that she was the defloration of snow-not-yet-turned-crystal - while this time she is just kind of spacy and interested in the differences between Then and Now. Why in Hell is the room phone ringing? Had it in the past, she would have ignored it and watched it from behind a rock with spear, trembling and jaw shuddering, honest-to-God Cro-Magnon terror at the sight of the clang-a-lang-a-langing object - now she just tears the reciever up from off cradle and goes 'Hello, this is Lucy Jinx.' 'This is the front desk - sorry - when you have a moment could you pop back down to the desk?' 'Certainly - though may I know why, exactly?' 'It's probably my fault, but your card didn't go through - I think I did some things out of order.' 'But this cannot wait until tomorrow, you're leading me to believe, as your job could be at hazard if it turns out I've snookered the room overnight, feeless?' The clerk is so so sorry - he's actually seven *Sos* sorry if Lucy counted them right, tapping her finger to knee-top to each - but yes, it needs to be tended to, straight away. 'Word of advice then, my friend - for not all middle-of-the-night grave-diggers are as kind-blooded as I: next time, don't admit it might have been your fault! Make me - or whoever - think it was mine - or theirs.' He is grateful to her for understanding. He only sounds a little bit like he might have just - if he hadn't before - called the police on her.

Lucy, to the front desk clerk, once the matter with the bill had been settled: 'I was thinking earlier about smell. And it reminded how I once corrected a kid - a young kid - that steam can be seen because steam is something physical, but smells are not physical, cannot be seen. But I guess, if you're small enough, smells are physical objects. Think on it: if we shrink-ray you down and down, eventually a particle - that which a scent is composed of, a particle - rises on the haunches of its physicality and you are dwarfed by it! A single tenth-of-a-whiff of a sour candy, for example, would look big and flat as a mausoleum edifice! Admittedly, I tend to imagine particles - and therefore, if I kept getting smaller, each component particle-particle of a thing - as spherical, but that is just my upbringing. I didn't choose that - to see them that way. Societal, you know? Like I bet, nowadays, if someone born decades after me - if they think of particles, at all - would think of particles as *Glowing*. *Glowing* has become part of the societal unconscious for *miniscule*. I'd wager it has, at any rate. Me? No, my man - I see a particle as a solid, textureless, blot of object. With a distinct color! Though, I am bound to say, never with the color one would associate - when one is larger than the smell - with the smell. *Armpit Sweat*, a particle of it, would not be gym-towel grey, for example. It would be fuchsia, probably - but not fuchsia-like-a-rash-reminds-you-of, no, just clean fuchsia, like a sign for cold drinks might be. Mark society, young man - though doing so will not allow you to subvert it - and mark it with vigor and hawk claws. It's no accident that eighteen-year-olds think they should only picture other eighteen-year-olds having sex and sixty-year-olds other sixty-year-olds. Society! Taboos! But not just taboos - commonalities. Familiarity is just a softer touch of taboo, you know? Familiarity preps the way to greedily disown certain thoughts and actions. Look at me, for example - to you, I am *Taboo*. You to me? Utter *Familiarity*! There is nothing new about you, young man, except you came after me and so have references that haven't aged into vintage like mine. But I admit I am jealous of you - for all of my Otherness, I am jealous. And having admitted it, I can explain no further. Not just at your Youth or your Maleness or your Lack-of-anything-distinct. No. There are not terms cavernous enough for my jealousy. So we'll just leave it at this: I am. You have a good night.'

Good for Lucy! She has morphed into Johannes Nagel so absolutely none would suspect her of ever having been who she was. In the elevator, she rubs her hands around in her hands and then claps them. She is giddy with overlong emotion. But if she sorts it well, this will not crash, just coast her into sleep and then morning. The news is on when she enters the room. Tragedy! A large building in another country has been engulfed in flame! As buildings in other countries tend to engulf. Isn't that interesting? How Lucy thinks this is just run-of-the-mill? Not not-sad just run-of-the-mill. It isn't as though the news report is 'For the first time, a building in another country has caught fire!' It isn't 'First time anything bad happened someplace else - can you believe it?' Lucy's biographer is quick to her mark, Dictaphone out - old fashioned, reel-to-reel, and with a countless-pig-tailish cords attaching microphone to device and device-part to device-part - and asks 'Lucy, do you think it is easier - or less surprising - when a war is said to be happening elsewhere or when a war breaks out at home?' 'Elsewhere' Lucy says, the biographer unable to hide her surprise. 'At home, it doesn't seem like a war, even - every day you'd think *Is that really the right word? Is that really what we mean by that?* Because we cannot, by definition, remind ourselves of anything foreign.' The President himself - Lucy had voted for the bloke - is talking about the matter. The words 'Thoughts and Prayers.' Lucy likes that. He's such an orator! Like a pinball machine with impeccable manners! And glad she voted for him, Lucy undresses, down to undershirt and underpants, and flips through the directory to see about ordering a pizza. Will Lucy answer the door for pizza dressed like this? Yes. The President signs off, Lucy lowering the volume as commercials cue up. This directory. It takes guts, Lucy observes, to place an ad in it. Roulette. No idea what the other ads say. Look at this! Both places say *Best deal in town!!!* when one of them is so demonstrably the better deal than the other - even though it wasn't so on purpose - thus the other cannot help but come off a liar. Seven dollars difference between the two best, comparable deals! Lucy orders from the more expensive place so they don't have to feel bad. She is trying to come up with some clever way to tell them she picked them over the competitor when a prerecorded message comes on that they are closed for the night. Petulant teenager sigh, Lucy Jinx feels stood-up and walk-of-shames the other number in.

Dark except for the kids-firing-cap-guns of the television flicker, Lucy's thoughts dwindle to hyper-specifics which will dwindle to sleep. When could a memory be considered a *flashback* - how long since it happened before it gets that secondary-signifier? Is remembering the cat, Lucy Jinx, that ugly first night of each other now *flashback*? Or is it the dividing line - things before it now old enough to not be called *memory*, really? *Memory* is a thing that happened that is recalled as though a texture of the here-and-now. Is that right, Lucy? Versus, for example, a *Recollection* which is just the bringing to mind of a fact. 'I *recall* that

I went to school such-a-where, but I *recollect* something my teacher once said.' But to get caught up in the specifics - after thirty years - is to be in a *Flashback*. While a *Memory* is something immediately connected to the current narrative. 'Last year, that neighbor moved in - I *remember* it.' This works, because it ties - loosely, but directly - to the status of Now. What if you lived in the neighborhood for thirty-years and the same neighbor lived there? Just checking: Lucy are you asleep, yet? 'Nope. And to answer the question' Lucy out-louds, definite in her state-of-still-awake 'that might, at best, be a recollection - depending on the relationship with the neighbor - but is probably a flashback. Even if that neighbor, thirty years ago, did something that fundamentally changed you - say you witnessed them murder someone, just to be silly and late-night dramatic - after thirty years that's a Flashback. Important, no doubt - but more background definition.' The past is a broad-stroke and the older it gets the less need for the effect of the image. All of this fine thought, though, is dishearteningly interrupted by a leg spasm - the variety particularly bitter and long-clinging, Lucy lumbering around the room like an elephant practicing a choreographed speech-made-while-dying. The room is carbonated with the grey-blue yellow much-bluer black of the television and the shushing of Lucy's teethed-in breath and her shoulder rubbing to her one ear to scratch its itch while she uses the fingers of the hand of that same arm to rub an itch on the other ear. What a way to fall apart! Lucy had heard of middle-aged women her whole life, how things happened to them, but no one had even obliquely hinted at all this! She pours herself some tap-water and devours a room temperature slice of what's-left-of-the-pizza, the two tastes mixing together in her half-asleep mouth about as tenderly as bone-saw to loved-one.

She is awake now, pores leaking out pizzeria stale, skin feeling spongy as stiff crust that would be greasy-moist if chewed. Sweating. The dream had been about the cat. In the dream, she had been cutting off his whiskers. But she had only been six-years-old. And the cat could talk and had been begging 'No don't!' And she had been six-years-old and in her six-year-old cruelty had just mocked the broken English that was all the cat could manage, as though its plea was worth ignoring on that technicality. The cat hadn't reacted in pain. The whiskers had severed, not soft not hard - something between a snip sound of barber sheer and the snap of a single dry stick of spaghetti. 'Did it hurt?' she had asked - her grown-up voice, in the dream she now bodiless, the dream just an in-close of the cat like a documentary of it made ages ago. The cat had both eyes. It was busy licking ants off its claws. Its stub-whiskers seemed like roadside attractions and if one touched them they'd be porcupine, cactus, unforgiving little sumbitches. But now Lucy is awake. And something lingers from the dream like 'Don't be sure you're not still dreaming.' Terrors of arms in eelish coils under the bed, conspiring to slater her every inch with the feeling of arms-have-crawled-on-me. Lucy sits up and tries to let the television balm her. Volume up and the rhythms of a sitcom that still feels contemporary to her but is now old, wedged hard in syndication because nothing else has aged just to its ripeness. 'Poor little show - you were funny' Lucy says and she touches the television screen - in her imagination, only, in reality just dusting the air in front of her - like it is a single tear from a bashful kindergartner's cheek. 'We used to laugh' Lucy continues. And she can almost feel the feelinglessness of the image of those dull blades slicing the whisker-flesh. This is a feeling she hasn't felt since - well, how about that, Lucy! - she was probably six. Those old faceless nightmares she'd wake from. Those 'sleeps-that-feel-real' as she'd call them to her father and he would hug her and say 'I had those when I was young, too.' 'I had those when I was young, too' Lucy says now. Yes. Yes. This is what missing the cat will feel like. Yes. You knew it would be something. It would be this: the nightmare a six-year-old could only talk about by calling sleep real.

'*THIS MORNING'S SKY IS AN endless typo of crows*.' Good line. Lucy marks it. There on her dashboard, the little microphone she keeps - microcassette, none of the disaster of when she tried to do this with a digital do-dad. 'However' she explains to the recording 'I am changing it to this: *Today's sky was an endless typo of crows*.' Taps button, the thing goes off. This is not a poetical jaunt, keep in mind - that line was accidental. Brought on by observing the sky. Overturned milk gallon glug-glug-glug from it - this spilling of birds, peppershaker - sky-long and enough to blot bold the black of a treeline silhouette. Birds and birds and birds - whole birds of them, she thinks. Taps the button on: 'This isn't good for a poem, but I like the line - *Birds and birds and birds, whole birds of them*. Or maybe it is good for a poem. That's for time to mete out. Nevermind.' Tap off. And on Lucy's mind isn't the cat. That is a tar settled to her dreams, a new blockage in the contours of her brain - even here, passing by the spot with the marker, she just nods a brief Hello. Are we to judge Lucy? Think she is lacking? Think she, as compared to another, knows not how to grieve? Maybe. And an examination would find a cigarette in her mouth and her hair still soft with hotel conditioner and her teeth and the gums up under her lips still slightly gritty from toothpaste not brushed around enough, rinsed firm enough, spit gone enough. And an examination finds her happy and thinking how she should do all within her power to make it official that to heighten the degree of a curse-word one should up the first letter. *Bitch* is well and good, but rather than raising one's voice to show degree-of-venom just say *Citch*. And onward to *Ditch*. Skip the vowels, maybe. *Fitch. Gitch.* 'You Jucking Zitch!' she ha-has, just to give an example of how fun mixtures of core and modifier might work. Of course, there are tricky ones - but they are just the more fun, cards down. *Bhore* might seem, by default, to be a rather soft version of something - but really it would be five ticks up from its mildest form. Likewise, *Vhore* could seem one-step-backward from the basic but is really the thing pushed to its hilt! This technique, Lucy feels, should be easy enough to adopt, even by the shirt-sleeve illiterates - and those who treasure language should laud it the greatest victory since the apostrophe! That is where we find Lucy Jinx, this morning. Untroubled, headlong, word-cluttered mess.

Now, here is Lucy: miles away from hotel and cat-grave. Idling along with this stale plip of traffic until she can finagle her way into the sloping-to-form turning lane, get herself into the parking lot of this local franchise fast-food place called *Magpies*. Young Pastor Mitchell, as she calls him, is on shift - she can see this, plain as anyone could, from his parked car there, acned with sun-faded, lizard-scaled, and flaking bumper stickers for *Rancid, The Buzzcocks, Bikini Kill, The Loverboys, The Pawking Metahs.* She finishes out her smoke without the engine or radio running and wriggles with her no-matter-how-many-times-this-has-gone-fine-it-doesn't-matter-it-could-still-all-go-wrong nerves. Next: we discover Lucy seated at the table outside the restrooms, around the corner from the counter where she had purchased her sausage-muffin and coffee, store-length from the at-this-hour unpopulated *Playnet Kidz* area - done up like outer-space vehicles and escapades, Lucy appreciative of the whimsical addition of the alien-craft shaped letter *Y* in the signage - already having made proper held-stare and head-nod to Mitchell as he collected trays from the bins by the fountain drinks. Best not to overload him - dayshift and impromptu - Lucy settles on twenty-dollars-worth, folding the bill into the napkin she leaves at the ready. This procedure goes as thus: Mitchell makes his approach, as though toward the Men's Room, Lucy stands and sets the napkin-with-twenty on top of the trashcan, returns to her seat, Mitchell takes the napkin before he goes into the can and Lucy waits - waits, waits not very long - and out Mitchell comes, Lucy then standing, with tray, briefly lingering in front of Mitchell so he can drop the empty *Push-Pop* candy container on to her tray before going to bus her table, Lucy getting rid of her trash proper and simultaneously palming the *Push-Pop*, exiting right out that door. Now, whether everyone does the exact same dance with Young Pastor Mitchell or whether these steps are unique to Lucy, Lucy does not know. Nor does she know how many clients the delinquent has. Nor if he will grass on her to save his own skin when he is eventually, certainly, knicked. But she pulls out of the lot with a fine two nuggets of mellow-scented marijuana - and had even once been gifted an extra. 'Like a Loyalty Card perk' Mitchell had said, cryptically, that time, leaving Lucy with no idea how many transactions, exactly, it took to get the bonus, or if it was a one-time thing, or was his way of showing keenness on touring her interior. Now: Lucy drives with her skin the pickle taste of paranoia. She never feels better, after a buy, until she crosses the sign that says *Saulsbury Township* though the sign signifies nothing at all to do with her.

Ah. And here is home. Across the lot from, of all things, a *Hernando's Total*. It was the sight of this that had turned the final screw on Lucy's choice of abode - here she resides, in the well-weathered *Meadow Wind Eves* third floor up, room right at the top of the stairs, allowing her endless music from all hours' footsteps, smoker's coughs, laundry sighs, grocery-bag rustles, and cellphone chat excerpts - this well before she knew these neo-brand *Hernando's* shops to be diaper-rashed across the whole area. Indeed, even standard *Hernando's* would have sub-signs affixed, assuring all comers *Including Hernando's Total!* The difference between the two *Hernando's* being - Lucy had investigated thoroughly - that in a proper *Hernando's* the *Total* section was just the dimmer-lit, higher-priced, micro store - freezers and all - tucked to one corner - where the common shoppers would only venture by accident - while the *Total* store, standalone, was just a building the size of twice that area and with only two stunted-sized checkout lanes the lines of which were always snaked down the Produce aisle, around down the aisle with the high-reaching self-serve bins of various granolas and nuts-mixed-with-raisins, nuts-mixed-with-cranberry type things. Lucy shops there. She has a Points Card, in fact. No idea what the points accrue toward. Points maybe just meant to make her feel proud, as on printed receipts the number is always followed by three exclamation points and a *Way to Go, You!* Conspicuously absent, to her honest lament, is *Hernando's Highlights*. Poor Lucy - with her plagiarisms now resigned to obscurity - had a manager confirm they 'remembered that thing' but it had stopped 'being around' even before the *Totals* had spawned. Ah, well. And here, second-floor climbing to home, is the door behind which is That Woman. That Woman, That Woman - who is she? Lucy stares at the different-grey of this door, trying, as always, to perhaps by lucky glance get a staying impression as to 'Is it older-grey or newer-grey?' always feeling butterfly-flush when she thinks she might be observed staring, immediately hurrying along on her way. 'Lucy' says a man she knows is named Kyle - though she never feels she's remembering that right - as he approaches with two dogs who tug leash at Lucy as though she had given them a hand-job after class, once - Kyle tugs the leashes and the dogs heel, though flip-flop to this side of their faces and that go their tongues, these at perpetual, grinning pant - 'I was wondering if I could ask you a favor.' 'What's up?' 'I have a date' Kyle slowlys, familiarlies, dot-dot-dotting the end in a music of shucks-I'm-just-so-pathetic, Lucy picking up the melody with 'And it ain't to the point she knows you've got sucklings?' 'Thank you' Kyle says, knowing the tone is Lucy's assent. And as the dogs sniff her in passing he says 'Wednesday, six - overnight?' the last word said blessed-are-the-meek, Lucy fitting key to lock and over-her-shouldering 'Yeah yeah - happy whoring, man, I got yer back.'

Altar-like, this is the inside, immediate, of Lucy's apartment door: a mirror, small, not even enough to see her face in full within, and square, as well - a microscope slide of her which she looks at, lean-in-lean-out - and above this mirror, quite on purpose - high enough to have to crane neck proper ceilingward - is the framed *Cat Poem*, beneath-placarded *Never Forget*. True enough, Lucy does not always look up at the thing upon entry and exit - she hadn't forgot it is there, but it is not there beyond the ceremony of putting-it-there-seemed-important. As in to say: life having proceeded past Move-In date, most of her apartment - this symbolic gimmick included - is more-or-less haphazard, nothing beyond the result of having to share nothing and to share that with nobody - not space, food, air, or decorum. Shrug out of coat, Lucy. Over here goes sweater. And while you're at it, t-shirt. Bra left on the sofa-back and itching the slick underbreasts, Lucy enters the kitchen and flings shoes living-roomward, cracking cold-brittle toes in the moist of her socks. The apartment heat, this time of year, stays on enough to allow that the apartment feels always like being held in the glazed stare of a man at the end of a train-car moving his hands, peculiarly arhythmical, within his tight trouser pocket. Paper plates only, but set in the cupboard where real-world dishes might go. Even Styrofoam cups for the coffee - her kitchen reeks of the breakroom of a place you can't believe you applied for a job in! Mounds of notebooks there, and mounds there, and a few there. And as Lucy moves into her bedroom, flaps on the light, the wall is shown to be measled with poetry she has magic-markered around. No method to it. And the scribbles by the bed are in regular pen - a lot of times not read-backable when she wakes, always scratching the wall in the dark, not realizing how sometimes she's just dusting off the plaster, sometimes the pen is leaking, sometimes, quite beautifully, every third letter forms exquisite and perfectly legible, nothing of the in-between, a stutterers dyslexic alphabet written in substitution-code. It is clear that she eats - now completely nude, except old baggy lounge-shorts, and in her kitchen again - only these microwaveable meals - a discount brand she discovered at the gas station just outside her work, the town over - and drinks only coffee, water, and from-the-bottle tugs of wine, from time-to-time. Refrigerator top is graveyarded with old bottles, molds growing in their bases enough to make them seem moth-speckled. She opens a cabinet with her toes, coughs inelegantly, feeling her belly holiday-jelly, reaching across for a fork and a take-away packet of ketchup from in there.

Analog old answering-machine. Bought at a swap-meet in a town she drove through two years ago. She cannot look at it without remembering the pride of those parents watching their porky fourth-graders guzzle down neighbor-made pies for neighbor-donated prizes. That had been an education, eh Jinx? The elation when one of the plumpers raised hands like a tour-de-France champ and even people not actively spectating had burst uproariously into galvanized, hive-minded euphoria. Lucy would have bought the answering-machine, anyway, but even if she had not wanted the thing just the comic timing of her 'I'll take this' the instant the ruckus wore down would have necessitated the purchase. To complete the installation of the machine, Lucy had used somebody's *Long-Distance Funky Mix Tape* cassette - loving that, in brackets after *Long-Distance*, was the notation *5-7 km* - which she had purchased along with some old cassette of *Monty Python* she had not heard since her teenage days - and also the soundtracks to *Ghostbusters, Top Gun, Three Men and a Baby*, and a VHS copy of *Mr. Mom* had come home with her. More important: what sort of messages is Lucy Jinx finding on her machine today? 'Hi Lucy - Sylvia wants to do the last Friday, next month - but if you really, really, really insist we can leave it for the twenty-second. Or try to. I'm with you, but Sylvia draws more water, so you'll have to let me know. I know you don't care - but I want you there, if that makes a difference. Sorry. They suck and so I suck by dint of association. Hugs, high-fives, and call me.' That was one. Here is the next. 'Ms. Jinx, I just wanted to touch base since you didn't show up last week and haven't returned a call. Benefit of the doubt, always, but unless you get back to me today we'll have to take your resume out of circulation. I hope everything is okay - and if you have just been indisposed and unable to call, we can still get you in for training with *Hatfield Group*, if you want. I need to know, today. Office number is the same. Me, direct, is press *Five-five*.' Note: slight tingle up Lucy at so many uses of *five* at the end of messages. Technically, that is three utterances of *Five* between two messages and so vicious unluck - but she is softening the tremor by noting one of them was a *Fives* and the other two went together so really cannot count as two any more than *five fifty-five* could count as three-in-one-go. Next message: 'Oh you cursed goose, you! Looking forward to heckling you tonight' - here a staticy, broken-cartoon Bwahaha! - 'and I will spend the entire Reading trying to see your panty lines! Keep that in mind!' Grinning, Lucy corrects to the air, as the tape churns out the next message 'It's not a *Reading*, you dolt. I've told you nine times.'

Still patting elbows into her thick sides, playing with the sensation of freshly-shaved underarms - still-wet ribs in trickles to go with them - Lucy yawns and dials Mathilda, whose quirk of answering calls without any word of greeting Lucy has long grown accustomed to, right-ins with the business of 'Hey Math - got a sec to see if any e-mails came in? Just from that one broad, really - but let me know if anything is there. Including the Spam porn-invites, per usual.' 'But of course, you horse's mane, but of course.' Mathilda is not one for small-talk when having to perform a task, so Lucy sprinkles some of her fresh bud into the glass bowl she swiped from that backpack at that indie bookfair, wondering if she has time to take a hit while Mathilda's calcified computer kicks in to gear. Finally she just says 'Don't talk for a sec - I'm just taking a hit of this.' No answer, but there never is. Flicker-flick-lit. Thumb over hole. Thumb away and in suck - pins-and-needles, took in way too much heat - the count of twelve held and breathe out. 'I take it you have made another accomplishment' Mathilda chimes in now, Lucy picturing her puggishly little holier-than-thou. 'I take it I have an e-mail informing me that that Nobel to Coetzee was just a typographical mistake, after all?' 'Yes, yes' Mathilda indulges 'you have exactly that. But nothing from your broad.' 'Nothing from the broad!?' 'Sorry.' 'Shit, Times-Table, didn't I tell you about this broad?' 'You told me, Jinx-poo, you told me.' 'Jinxy-poo?' Lucy as-though-hardly-believing-her-ears. 'You're not as easy to do nicknames for!' 'I suppose that's true. Remember when I called you Multiplicative Property of Zero for a whole month?' 'Did you, Jinxy-poo? I don't remember that. Sounds like something someone as hilarious as you would do, though.' 'Lighten the fuck up, Base-six - and hold on, I'm taking another hit, that last one was the pits.' Mathilda silences and offers no glib commentary when this time Lucy exhales smooth and jumps right back into the chat. 'But didn't I tell you about that broad - *She's full of it* I said! Didn't I just say that very thing?' 'You told me never to trust broads, yes. Then started calling me thrice-per-day to see if she had e-mailed.' 'Well - has she?' 'Nope.' 'Exactly! Do you think I miswrote my e-mail? Or that she doesn't know what that *At* symbol means?' Mathilda does her time-to-get-off-the-phone good natured tone and says 'I'd never put anything past a broad.' 'Yeah fine' Lucy says 'I get the drift' and hangs up.

Let's keep in mind, though, that Lucy is very much to-the-matter-at-hand - when there is business needs tended to, she tends! As such, look: she hefts to her writing desk one of the three cardboard boxes in which are volumes of her collection *The Patron Saint of Choking To Death* which she, of course, sub-titled *poems by Lucy Jinx volume three*. This box is the lighter of the two, down to the sound of a cup scrapping the bottom. The three copies from it she tosses to the desk where they land with an effeminate smack. Mouse grey, matte-finish cover - darker at its corners, though only just subtly. Pea-soup green letters - the title all lowercase but larger than the sub-title, the sub-title all capital and three whole shades lighter, as though maybe not supposed to be there but an eraser didn't quite work. She adores this volume! But fish-dead, those three copies there, make her feel it vulnerable and she wishes she had reordered some copies of her other volumes of work to lay out wide on the table. Contra her position, of course, and contra the arrogant mystique of it all. As she always does, she opens the volume and grins at the misspelling bang-bang right there - *Table of Cotents*. Like each time, for a moment, it doesn't seem a mistake. Which is exactly how the mistake slipped through! The various commas and the one ridiculous stanza break in *The Sovereignty of Her Half-Penny Mouth* would not be noticed even if anyone read the things with a critical eye, so Lucy has conditioned herself to think of these as how those poems actually go. Unless she is ever interviewed by Bill Moyers - in that case, she will make charming hay of it, how scatterbrained she is and so impatient, has to see the printed volume as live-performance, something something something 'And anyway, it makes me seem mortal.' Oh how Bill Moyers will chuckle! '*Table of Cotents*' she scoffs. But it bugs her. She has lain extra-long in the bath trying to think up some clever way to make someone who points it out seem the fool. Like: didn't they notice such-and-such in such-and-such poem - say in *Dawns Who Mourn Horses* - that completely, cleverly justifies the front-matter misspelling, makes it a special wink to those in the know!? The best she has come up with, though, is to say 'It's how I spelled it in the first thing I wrote when I was six - and since this volume is based on dredging my youth, it seemed only right, even if only I ever know.' See here: Lucy repeating this aloud - lying to herself a lie she'll never need to tell anyway just to have told it.

Lucy decides to bring the entire box. Cover the table in front of her. An act of passive intimidation! Why she lets herself get caught up in any preparation at all is just for appearances with whichever store. And since this is a national chain and it seemed a real favor to get her a table - weekday evening, though it may be - and since they actually put up a few signs advertising she would be there - and its marked on the *Events Calendar* pegged on the corkboard by the toilets and in the *Newsletter* which they sometimes put into customer's bags - she ought to doll it up a bit. 'I'll even wear lipstick' she says - then, because she won't and doesn't want this to count as an unkept promise, immediately says 'I mean chap-stick - I just mean I won't have, you know, scabby lips or anything.' Opening the bedroom closet, she now manages to find the poster-on-canvas she once had made up for a shared table at a festival. Odd little relic. Just her face as though done in charcoal with highlights of beige. But it is kind of classy. Might as well bring it along. That is - come on, Lucy, think things through - if she can think of a way to mount it. As it is - look at the thing! - it doesn't even unroll all the way! Eyeballing it, she figures the cheap clip-frame to the reproduction poster for *Fitzcaraldo* she just has leaned to the wall outside the bathroom - usually, as it is now, mostly obscured by the high-piled soiled laundry - would work. Reality: she would have to trim it a bit. Frustration. Edge taken off by another toke from her bowl. Recentered: What? Having to use scissors a quick minute is enough to throw her off of a task? Think how splendid you'll look sitting there, Lucy! How confused-but-awed milling customers who don't even know how to spell *Poetry* will be by the sight of you sitting under your own larger-than-life portraiture, a poker spread of books with your name on them in front of you! In fact, Lucy, you should commission a new sign! On tin! And invest in a music stand or a tripod! 'Razzle dazzle and carnival-bark and whooping-cough or whatever' she says, scissors at the ready, not trusting herself in the slightest. Just as abruptly she figures 'Aw, fuck it.' What's she supposed to do? Look a right yutz there, pile of books and her picture, people in line to buy coffee and black-and-white cookies giving her the long eye and understanding to the micron how much she ought to be pitied?

Here is Lucy Jinx's shelf. The one shelf on the overall shelf - that is to say the one row of the shelf, but which she likes to call a Shelf-in-itself, knowing full well it is just a part-of-a-shelf - which she dedicates to her own offerings. The first two volumes of her collected poetry. *Volume One: An Affair in the Rickety Autumn.* *Volume Two: Salamander Debts.* Five copies of each - well, seven, counting the two copies each of the alternate-cover versions of the titles. And a hardcopy - only one in existence! - of the combined volume. *My Parisian Charlatan: Collected Verse.* Note: Lucy regrets that title. She likes the phrase, but it's such a minor, off little line in the overall unimportant poem that it's drawn from, not worth the titular spot, not by a length! *Grin is gaslight jilted / so spending one night as a whore / piles of fist over fist over fist-over-fist / you make good, my Parisian charlatan.* Added to which: collected volumes should always just be called *Collected Poems* no other title. Added to which: also, if she was going to call it after a line, she obviously should have gone with *The sour morning's broke paw.* Moving on: a collection of saddle-stiched, pulped paper, single poems. She had some help with layout from that chap - whatever his name was - but never distributed them as she had planned. Four different chapbooks, all made at the same time and given the appearance of a series. Covers are reproduction maps of various cities for the top two-thirds, then different solid colors for the bottom one-third, her name and the titles *Opal, Prune, Pickpocket*, and *Gallowsgirl*. One of those had won her a few fans - *Gallowsgirl* - but that had gone nowhere. Here are the three Anthologies she has something in - one of the trio some pure bunk from some charlatan small press counting on authors to purchase copies, one a contest win which she had to enter under another name because it was only open to residents of Georgia, one she is actually proud of and had even gone out-of-state to the publication party for. Also: the half-dozen print journals - each and every one either now defunct or else the only issue of them to ever come out. The folder, there, contains print-outs from the two-dozen online journals that have displayed her work - she refuses to call online work Published - and a photograph of when she, completely inexplicable, found a line she'd wrote graffitoed on the side of a newspaper machine: *Tell me your books, tongueless! Mire your soul in sewn spine!*

Why would someone be knocking on her door? And just now, as she guiltily takes a last little toke - too much for driving, Lucy, Jesus come on! Stiff as a spider that might not be dead she goes - still as something that might just be a shadow and your glasses aren't on. Again: someone knocks on her door. *Delivery man* her codgery mind is able to proffer, spit along with a bit of unchewed corn and burping spittle into the waiting hand of an underpaid nurse. '*Delivery man?*' she internally scoffs, doing her best to not giggle because it would high-note to a slap-pitched Haw! if she did. Explain how it would be a delivery man, nitwit! Knock. More insistent. Well, surely someone can smell her smoking up! Why they are only just now doing something about it is not a defense that will hold up in court. They could have the police on the way, right now. But wait, she reasons - yes, yes, you're right, Lucy - the police cannot break down the door because someone maybe smells pot! Not in this hemisphere, they can't! All she has to do is hide out in here until the scent is gone or until her high subsides and she's in the clear. Right? Oh God, this is the sort of problem a fifteen-year-old with a mildly bad upbringing has to deal with - a bit beneath the station of someone of the artistic stature of Lucy Jinx! 'Though, it's funny at the same time' she admits, and now is laying on the sofa, all bones tense with keep-the-hysterics-in, the laugher allowed no further than the very tip of her skin, massage roller feel of amusement exhausting her and willing her to burst. Well, whoever it was must be gone now. Or now. Or now. Definitely by now. Lucy opens the door and has a peek down the corridor. Not a thing. Nor a one. No note taped to the door or package left. And she strains to hear if maybe there are other doors being knocked on or shufflings on the stairs. There's always some part of the world nosing around her, is all. That is how she steels herself, re-chaining the door. And back to the sofa. Because she still has hours until she has to get on the road. The apartment silences around her - even the click of the unmoving dial-fashion clock above the stove seeming to be in extra socks and taking as-long-strides-as-possible to keep everything calm. This is what the very center of a tuft of dropped cotton must feel like. This is the life of the crumb that the ants overlooked.

*BB. WESTMORE BOOKS.* THERE IT is. Look upon it, ye mortals, and tremble! The needless gigantism of its façade - how many stories tall does it appear, three, four even? - plopped atop the no-bigger-than-anywhere-else interior - spacious-wide between shelves and boasting an entire section for blank journals, postcard, tote-bags, a café, and a magazine-wall taking up one whole store-length curve, a *Children's Books* section that has a community-theatre-stage-sized area of play-tables and seats that look like toadstools to encourage younglings imaginations or something. Thrill at it! Vast and seeming to suck wind from the expansive cracked-and-tar-stitched pavement of the parking lot. Camera pans around to reveal, equally monolith, the cold high front of *The Pet Store*, full quarter-mile of lot between the two Gargantuas. This patch of trees? What could the meaning of them be, other than keeping this place obscured from the prying eyes of the Interstate's on-and-off-ramp? Abandoned shopping carts - from *The Pet Store* - tipped in the postures of flood victims, ever-present scent of feces from squatters who maybe dwell there in the scraggle of trees, milkweed, and illegal dumping, nothing to pass their time with but peering and urinating, leaving cakes of waste to sully their own footprints with. Quite a place, this! The personality one associates with Art, certainly! Note also: those black windows? They seem to be a part of the bookstore, yes? And what of that blacked-out door - surely some secondary-entrance or exit, the backway out of the employee-only area in case of fire? No, no. Come the winter holidays - soon, soon in fact - and the truth will be revealed that this - which seems to suggest a wide girth to the bookstore - is really empty space, waiting to be chocked full with Halloween costumes or fake Christmas trees, cardboard turkeys and pilgrim-hats in shabby felt - anything that can be hucked for a few bucks to those who feel festivities must be frivolous to be worth the time. *BB. Westmore Books.* Lording over the world with back turned, aloof. The whole positioning of this place, on driving approach, is the epitome of standoffish - 'I don't need you, and if you come when you go I'll forget you, straight off.' No sign even, either on the road or affixed to the rear of the structure - which is all a driver can see - identifies it as habitable. The ass it sneers at the world - the paltry mall across the street, suffering death throes that more and more commuters ignore, getting the brunt of its scoffing - is sandy-brick in faded blue and red paint, two green doors and five dumpsters.

Lucy knows bookstores the way most recall people, from hip-high, looking up on their fifth or sixth birthdays. Moreso than libraries, even, though this is something she is loathe to admit. From bookstores her teeth were cut to literature. From bookstores and the sections of grocery-stores with magazines, stationary, Get-Well cards and gift-wrapping bric-a-brac. Draw a picture of her life? She'd draw what it feels like to stand in a bookstore aisle, leafing through something-at-random after straining her disappointed eyes an empty hour looking for something better - what it feels like to stand there, knowing she will not be disturbed, watching shoppers who, all of them, know better why they are there than she does why she. Those three prepubescent girls, for example?

Lucy knows they are not sitting, huddled to each other like tossed-aside backpacks, in the *Graphic Novel* section because they are driftwood, no idea what they want to be doing, aloosed into the roiling loiter that Lucy so often found herself in when a young girl - no, no, those girls came here to read *Graphic Novels*, do all the time, this is a treehouse, a closed closet, blanket overhead, their mixed warming breaths colored flashlight! Or that twenty-year-old, hair thick as a comb, looking far too T.S. Eliotted in his clean suit with aftershaved chin - that young-man-carbuncular-for-his-century, new kind of posturing, lonely frufru to him - that snappy lad is reading a biography of the current Pope with no irony and no honest heart of believer to him! Lucy sees. She knows. Interchangeably unique, the bookstore lot. The girl in specific-glasses and just-so-polka-dotted blouse, working the Music section, reading synopsis of everything she price-stickers so she can win later at trivia - Lucy knows her, a million times, each time, each girl, each Her, dissimilarly exactly the same. How about him? That guy? No longer even only-just-thirty in beard and over-obvious neck, prouder of how he jogs every day than of his PhD? Him? He has theories on all things political but has them only to conjure excuse to bring up his same favorite record to everyone at the party as though only just then recalling it. He carries the newest books around - see? like he already owns them, dustjacket-flaps used as bookmarks at random pages! - and has read every blurb on the covers nine times. And Lucy can see herself in all of them - where she touches, connects, overlaps. That one she once married and that one met someone she lied to and that one is her-in-four-years and that one her-in-twenty and the ones not-there-for-books are her hoping to be seen sneaking past unseen.

The man who she had arranged things with was squirrelish in behavior, seemed to have to stop every third sentence, look around, move a pace or two, touch at something, before continuing with his Hellos, giving her a pointless - Lucy and he remaining stationary, mind, he just gesticulating hither and nigh - tour of the store, and going over the timetable for her Event. Helpful though, the man - he has found a tablecloth to class up the semi-long table he'd unfolded the legs of himself, then finds a way to jury-rig up Lucy's framed portrait which he nods at as though duly impressed. Not the worst position-in-a-store she's ever been given, either. At least not just plopped at the front door where she would be confused for a volunteer gift-wrapper or some school kid's mom raising money for the coming spring's production of *Plaza Suite*. And not stuck back in the *Music and Movie* alcove, where people would make no bones about avoiding her, the static of their awkwardness as they grittingly browsed the *Criterion Collection* making her sweat and feel disenfranchised to the point of militarism. This time: smack middle of the store! Between the *Historical Non-Fiction* section - which should perhaps just be called *History* Lucy thinks, noting also this shares one shelf with the *Contemporary Biography* section and the first shelf - all hardcovers - of the *Literature* section. And a facing view, for Lucy, of the side of the Customer Service station, assuring her an endless few hours of hearing clerks good-naturedly pointing her out to people after answering their questions, polite obligation forcing these customers to turn their heads, smile, and suddenly remember they needed to use the restroom before doing anything else. Lucy likes the position. She feels like a booby-trap. Café patrons bussing their dishes will have to acknowledge they know there is a woman sitting at a table of books, too - she knows she might get some traffic from youngish girl's making their boyfriends come over with them because youngish girls always seem to do that when they have boyfriends in tow and are bored with the early evening, anything but back to the apartment after just having coffee, again, and a cookie, again, anything. 'May I have your attention *BB. Westmore* guests' comes a voice as though from everywhere. 'Already?' Lucy sighs, irritated at the earliness of the announcement - her phone shows she has half-hour still and was thinking to go out front for a smoke 'We are pleased to have in store with us tonight local poetess Lucy Jinx - available to sign copies of her work, upon request. Why not pop over and say *Hiya*? Just across from Guest Services.' Smile from the grandmotherly shopper just then passing by with two wooden puzzles and a bathtub-toy copy of *Everybody Poops*.

Here's the man again, but seeming sheepish. 'Sorry' he sheeps 'but they did explain how to do the sales? I'm not sure if you have the stickers.' Lucy has no idea. He will be right back, then. 'Not so complicated' he says on return - approaching from the complete opposite direction, startling her with his so-suddenly-there-at-her-shoulder. And it isn't. Complicated. At all. She is given a spool of generic barcode stickers. These are set to ring up at twelve dollars - this was prearranged, nothing to do with Lucy, just the way these things work 'per corporate' - and she can either sticker all of the books or just sticker as a customer takes one - 'Or' the man seems to suddenly discover 'you could sticker a small portion - say these - and direct interested customers to take those copies' - and the books are paid for at the regular cash-register. Yes yes - Christ in heaven this is abysmal to have to listen to! - Lucy will get three dollars for any copy sold - she wants no money, wants to sell none, but knows if she is caught giving the books away she'll be black-listed around town, has to all-but-giggle and display her appreciative-loins for the twenty-five percent cut. 'Also' the man puts down another, smaller roll of circle-stickers that announce *Signed by the Author* 'you can offer to sign and that'll bumps it up to fourteen dollars - you get the extra two, so five bucks a copy your way. But you have to put one of these on' he taps the sticker roll 'just so everyone is clear on that - so the cashiers know to add the mark-up to the sale.' 'Gotcha' Lucy gotchas, thumbs-up turning into an *OK* gesture. 'How's it going so far?' 'Fine. No takers yet, but some folks told me what they are getting their nieces for graduation.' This seems to confuse the man. 'Graduation from what?' 'I honestly didn't ask' Lucy says, conspiratorial, leaning forward to theatre-whisper 'Because they seemed kind of crazy and I didn't want there to be any incident, you know?' Oh ho, the man likes her wit well - but also, he points out, they could just be the types who shop early - or the nieces could have been in some preschool program, because those have 'graduations' - the man pronounces it funny so Lucy cottons to him using the term loosely - all the time. 'Though that depends on what they said they were getting as gifts, right?' 'Yep' Lucy agree 'I see what you mean.' 'What did they say they were getting?' Earnest bend to brow - think Lucy, think think, she playacts for the benefit of the home viewing audience who need their entertainments non-subtle - Lucy finally shrugs with a breath out as though having drained a pint at a single go 'I honestly don't remember.' The man nods, understanding. 'Then there's no way to know, is there?' 'No' Lucy tableaus 'none at all.'

Soon, Deliah shows up and asks 'How's the turn out?' 'It's like this, Del - I'm glad to be the one to break your naiveté, by the way - I thought I'd sold three copies - which just about flipped my lid! - but then this dude from the front counter brought them back over.' Lucy taps one-two-three the three copies. '*Since they were already signed*, the dude said. This lot is dicking me around, Del - me! And they're gonna be sorry when they're sitting in their houses and I blow them up, I can promise you that! The inside of an explosion feels like shit, man.' Deliah smiles the way most people who hang around with Lucy smile when Lucy answers their simple questions in the manner Lucy answers their simple questions, has a copy of Lucy's book open and face question-marked up. 'I thought you always write a bit of poetry when you sign - you give that up?' 'That's another thing!' Lucy explains - this joint is only bilking people an extra two bucks for her signature - so no way she's writing some poetry, too. 'Despite you tend to give your work away, gratis?' Deliah sets the book down, picks up another copy. 'I'm part of the economy here, my girl, and so have to do as the Romans do. Which is: shake people down.' Changing tone, Lucy wonders 'Say - would you man the fort a few minutes?' But this seems complicated to Deliah. 'All these books? Divided by Zero-people-interested? Crazy maths!' 'Yes, crazy maths' impatients Lucy, who already has her cigarettes out 'but just do it. You've got nowhere to be, right? If you did, why would you be here?' Except it seems Deliah really does have someplace to be - and a boyfriend out in the car awaiting her - so cannot be of service. 'It's five minutes, Del!' 'I told him I was just saying *Hi*, man. And now we've been talking all this time.' 'Who is he? The prince of fucking Siam? Late for the effing coronation? Say to him you happen to be a nice person and did me a solid - he's gonna bloody your lip for that or something? Come on, Deliah - grow a dick, here!' 'You take forever with your smoking, Lucy - and we have reservations, see?' It's all too much. Deliah brandishing her upper-classness and all, clubbing Lucy with Lucy's relative lowly station - 'Fine fine, then piss off. You couldn't bring him in to meet me? He got the plague or something? I'm not someone you introduce people to?' Deliah has been signing her own name to copies of Lucy's book while Lucy has been braying on, is now affixing *Signed by the Author* stickers to them all. 'You'd hate him' she says.

'I need to step out for some fresh air - meaning a cigarette' Lucy winks and touches her cigarette to the wrinkles of her wink, the mohawked girl now sentry at Guest Services nodding. 'So, can you just make sure none of the untrustworthy rabble you sell shit to steal my precious thingies, there?' 'No problem' is how the girl responded, Lucy already away at a whisk, raising her hand as she goes in a gesture of Thanks. She holds the door for a family - wonders if the husband noticed her giving a quick snake-tongue glance in at the wife's cleavage - then holds the second door for an old woman approaching, pushing one of those Walkers with wheels that never seem to properly turn. Lots of old people around here. What could they possibly read? An odd prejudice. Why do you say that? Lucy thinks it is a perfectly ordinary prejudice and says as much to herself. 'Who has ever heard of an old person sitting around reading? Buying a book for themself? To read!?' She is beginning to say some of this aloud - proper aloud - the long line of the lot ahead of her, nearest car twenty paces off, begging for some boisterous soliloquy. Maybe old-folk will sit with books in the library - just to keep from getting the bum's rush - but Lucy will be damned to Hell before she believes the elderly read! That woman - for just one example - would not even have been able to open the door to this bookshop on her own! Never mind the second door! It is positively insensible to believe she was here to buy a book which she would then read! To prove it - Lucy visualizes this little fantasy - Lucy will buy something for the woman and watch the woman vehemently insist how she doesn't want it. Like being strapped to a bedsore, it'd be, an indignity the old bat would refuse to suffer herself! 'I see through you' Lucy announces, stepping out her smoke. 'All of you' she addendums, lighting another - because why not? - and leaning back to the wall, using the scrag of the over-rough brick to work at this spot in her shoulder that has been murdering her for the past four days. Her eyes water in orgasm at the pinch of the rough stone being exactly the height for this task. Worth the whole endeavor of doing this book store trip - she knew all along there would be a reason. 'I'm such a clever girl' she all but cums, body shivering Oh-God-Jesuses at each first-painful-then-deep-bone-bruise-numb stab her wriggling induces.

Conversation Galante: 'How long have you been an author?' 'I'm a poet.' 'You write a lot of poetry?' 'It is all that I write.' 'I always wanted to be a poet.' 'That's the wrong way to go about it.' 'My teacher in fifth grade was a poet.' 'Never heard of her.' 'She did a lot of funny poems - for kids - educational - you know? - like interesting ways to see the alphabet.' 'What's her name - I've probably heard of her, after all, if that's what she did.' '*Mrs. Flatt* - two Ts - I don't remember her first name.' 'And she wrote poems, you say, about the alphabet?' 'Yeah - like an *S* would be a rope and an *O* would be a tire on it - like a rope-swing, a tire-swing.' 'That's very poetic - I see that image in my mind perfectly.' 'Oh yes, she was very good.' 'You don't get to be a fifth grade teacher without knowing your poetic stuff - that's well known, so I'm not surprised.' 'Who publishes this?' 'It's not published.' 'What do you mean?' 'It's just a book - I'm a poet.' 'So you just published it yourself - that's cool.' 'It's really not published - it's just a book.' 'Well, *printed*, I mean.' 'Oh - if that's important to you, sure.' 'My friend self-published his science-fiction novel.' 'Did he?' 'But I don't think he sells a lot of copies, you know?' 'What's his name?' 'I'm sure you haven't heard of him.' 'I have no doubt I've not heard of him - but what's his name?' 'Chester Goran.' 'Never heard of him.' 'Naw - he just self-publishes.' 'Tough biz, the science-fiction.' 'I think his stuff would work better as a movie - it's very visual, which makes it hard for a book - all that stuff zooming by.' 'It is hard to write *zooming*, I can vouch for that.' 'But if someone did a movie - if they did it right, real money and got someone good - these ideas he has would be amazing.' 'The *zooming*.' 'All of it - if they got the right person.' 'To direct, to star - what do you mean?' 'All of it.' 'Sure.' 'But no one would go for it - it's too big an idea - he has the screenplay all planned and everything, he told me about it.' 'Like Jodorosky's *Dune*, eh?' 'Yes! - it's so funny you say that - that's exactly how we always talk about it!' 'I could tell just from the few things you said, man.' 'It's just to that scale - if someone put the money there, maybe got the right people.' 'It wouldn't work with the wrong people?' 'That's so crazy you said that - *Jodorosky* - we say that all the time!' 'It's fun to say: *Jodorosky*.' 'I don't really read much poetry, I admit - is yours any good?' 'Yes.' 'Hey - confidence!' 'Just stating facts.' 'No, no - I getcha - that's great man, that's a great attitude.' 'Tell your friend to keep at it - have his elevator pitch ready - always!' 'I will - nice to meet you - and good luck!' 'You bet.'

A bit later: this nice woman - the closing supervisor - is perusing Lucy's book while Lucy is trying to figure out where she's heard this song that is playing over the store speakers. 'This is quite good.' The woman said that - *Sierra* the nametag reads - but kind of quietly and is still deeply invested in the opened pages, so Lucy does not reply. Five minutes - she likes Sierra because Sierra obviously has

an actual job to do and isn't doing it - then Lucy meets Sierra's eyes and says
'Which one did you read?' It takes a moment - because Sierra seems to still be
dealing with the effect of whichever it was - so Lucy uses the opportunity to say
'Nevermind' - that expression of Sierra's and Lucy's not knowing is better. But
what Sierra doesn't understand is why they didn't let Lucy do a reading - why
did they just give her a table in the middle of the week, not even on the night
when the *Poetry Collective* meets? *The Poetry Collective?* 'The Poetry Collective?' Lucy
grimaces baldly. But Sierra is on the same page, hip to the bullshit and all of it,
always. 'They're absolutely awful - but there are fifty of them and they always
make such a to-do about poetry. Who set this up for you? Clarke?' Lucy thinks
so, says she never pays much attention to boys, especially when they work at
bookstores. 'That's smart' Sierra says, but by this she seems to just mean that
Clarke is an imbecile and should not be in charge of Event scheduling. A
customer tries to abscond with Sierra, but Sierra gracefully pivots him off to the
Guest Services desk - a good move, but one Lucy sees is nothing to do with
Lucy, just that there is already a line at Guest Services and that sneak had been
trying to snooker himself around it. 'You're a good Manager or whatever you
are - dealt with that swine slick.' 'You like that?' Sierra suddenly smalls like a
kitten then back-to-buinesses: 'It must have been Clarke. It must have been dead
for you, tonight!' Lucy explains herself a little, so that Sierra will stop feeling
bad. And even while Lucy is looking for some clever reason to ever suggest
speaking again, Sierra says 'It's not really up to me to get you a reading, but I
do kind of a blog - I know, I know - for all kinds of artists and would love to
interview you or post some of your work.' Does the fact that Lucy wants to eat
Sierra's mouth - tear it off and swallow it unchewed - make it any more palatable
that the word *Blog* was just used? No. However: 'Yes' Lucy admits 'yes, I would
love that - you just tell me when.'

See? One can look at Life in all sorts of ways, Lucy - you see that, right? One
could see oneself being handed twelve dollars by a twenty-two-year-old part-
time cashier - could see this same cashier squinting at a receipt print-out then
adding two more dollars and speaking aloud 'Bringing the total to Fourteen' -
and could then see oneself signing a copy of the receipt the clerk just read from
and - well! - one could interpret all that in any infinite number of ways, couldn't
they? Does it represent anything, though? Really? Beyond the exact physical fact
of it? Ask the clerk, in confidence, what he thinks of it: it is all but guaranteed
he'd just find it odd. Why would someone - he'd means Lucy - go through all
the trouble? That must hardly cover the cost of gas, let alone the amount of
hours spent at the store! And it's true, what the clerk would think. So, Lucy -
how do you see it? Do you feel you have to justify it? Or do you go in the other
direction and overly deprecate? That'd be your style, eh? Make it all a Pyrrhic

Victory or something - some sort of contraption of tragedy-cum-triumphal - admit you come out behind but somehow find dignity in it - akin yourself to all the nameless dead in the wordless histories no one is even interested in, the lives upon which Life is built! Or else have a shrewd philosophy - misdirect those curious with some evidence that you must be more-than-you-seem. After all: Jackson Pollack was a drunk, eh? After all, Caravaggio was a murderer who then got murdered - or something, you admit you aren't sure of that, might be splicing in some story about Marlowe or Milton. Who is to say Lucy Jinx won't rise from the compost to marshal the fiefdom, gain posthumous immortality, interest accrued for the lifetime in which she was ignored? What do people make of this woman, Lucy Jinx? What do they who gobble pastry and speckle up table-tops with accidental coughs from iced coffee mis-swallowed think of the woman who is filling a modest cardboard box - it has the words *New England's Best Eggs* on the side, also note - with copies of the slim volumes of poetry she must have just worked her little-bity heart and soul into? What does she resemble, as she takes from its mounting a portrait of herself and totters the parking lot out to her shabby-shoed automobile? See, people? You see her? Lighting her smoke and leaning against her passenger door? That's Lucy Jinx! So, what about her?

Lucy had sat bundled into coat and was napping for the better part of an hour, the heater on more than overflowing, the radio the exact sound of an afterthought. Then - now, here - enough time has passed to reset the scene, so she exits the car and re-enters the shop. Quick glance for - what was her name? *Sherri*? Naw, *Sierra*! - Sierra shows Sierra nowhere to be seen. And already the table where Lucy had sat has been carted offstage and in the spot where it dwelt we find a table declaring *Hot Beach Reads for Teens* and another, sides pushed kissing to each other, touting itself *Winter Treats For The Book Lover In Your Life*. Lucy rubs her nose with her shoulder and takes one of the *Beach Reads* at random, intending to hide it behind an Almanac in some sort of impossible-to-decipher protest. But then she turns down the third *Literature* aisle and just leaves the book off wherever, coming to stand in front of *It*. *It*? *It*. Always. There *It* is. *It*. Did you expect *It* not to be there, Lucy? As you always expect *It* to not be there? Did you hope *It* would not be there, Lucy? That if whatever random bookstore you go into does not have *It* alphabetically in stock *It* doesn't exist? If *It*'s so much as in the Discount Bin then the world has cleaned its boot of *It*? 'Well tough shit, Jinx' Lucy says, breathing low and taking the front-most of the five facing copies - there are two spined copies on either side, too, just in case you also hadn't noticed. 'I'd noticed' Lucy hisses. *Chokethemgirls*. *Elliott Pine*. The powder-matte of the dustjacket. The sturdiness of it, so compact, just above mass-market size. The four-hundred-pages-thick. The uneven, ragged page edges - which, yes, Lucy, you hate, you hate those - threatening papercut, visually, but soft like the ridge of an infant's nose when thumb-tip caresses. The interior text-block - tight and seeming to come from pressed letters, not modern inkjets of any kind, letters that, if magnified, would seem shapeless, Rorschach dancing-men! The *for Amelia, who named me*. Enough! Goddamnit! Lucy shuts the fucker and puts it back. Then takes it back up. *Pine. Pine?* 'Really, Elliott?' And there - one shelf up, middle-set - is the origination of that namesake. *Amelia Pine - Magnets. Amelia Pine - The Books Father Forgot. Amelia Pine - The Misspelling Train. Pine. Elliott.* 'So what?' *Chokethemgirls.* 'So what?' Lucy walks off with the book in her hand. There is the door, Lucy. See what happens if you walk out. See what happens if you walk out with it. See what happens if you walk out without it. Go ahead. Go ahead.


THE PET STORE DOES NOT sell cats. 'Maybe a lizard?' The employee from the Fish Department is waved over and spends awhile explaining to Lucy about Lizards. Is that what they call it? The Fish Department? 'Would you say you work in The Fish Department?' Good laugh. 'Yes, actually - I've never thought about it, but it's funny to hear someone else say it: The Fish Department.' But Lucy doesn't actually want a lizard. Asks about turtles - but would feel too guilty owning a turtle, now that she's looking at one. 'Could a turtle possibly be happy as a pet?' she asks. 'Could a turtle feel fulfilled that way?' The Fish Department employee admits that Lucy asks very tricky questions. 'Most people who buy pets' he says 'just assume the pets are into it. Do you' he asks 'think a turtle can ever feel fulfilled?' It's a fair rebuttal. She tries to come up with a good response. Just because, after all, a turtle is turtling around out near a creek or something doesn't mean it thinks it has it made, that its heart isn't at rage. What do turtles want? They must want something. It's too ghastly to imagine a turtle as pointless. 'Can you imagine that?' she asks the Fish Department employee, point-blank. 'Imagine there is no point to a turtle! No teleological end! Do you believe in evolution?' 'Yes.' Then, Lucy paints this picture: 'Even evolutionarily: imagine a turtle is just the result of some string of curiosities, accidents - a complex lifeform that grew and altered and adapted - but never *because* of anything. It just changed over millennia as the result of other things evolving for various purposes, has none of its own. It's like some gunk, a turtle - always an offshoot, a discharge, overlooked and incidentally kicked into this patch and that patch, taking on new traits, surviving, but never was meant-to-be, in itself - the world's most evolved form of meaninglessness!' Again, the Fish Department employee has never thought about such things. So Lucy presses on: 'Think on it! Somewhere amongst survival-of-the-fittest and all there must be grooves, dents, rivulets, currents that seem incidental, just the results of larger struggles - areas of brackishness not even bottom-dwellers or carcass-snipes go poking into for sustenance - some blobbish dark-matter of the earliest pond-scum, a residue that was alive in some protoform, predating first-life, a thing that was alive just before the rush of what we now call Life but that got ignored as Life, ignored in the warring of survival, altogether! You get me?' Gee, he's still never thought of that, before. Well anyway, Lucy doesn't want a turtle. 'Sorry to bother you.' 'Not at all.'

Text query from Milos: *Have you ever heard of farting referred to as 'Freddy-ing' - not sure of the spelling.* The heating is at a passive-aggressive mutter, the windshield fogging, Lucy watching a *The Pet Store* employee on cigarette break being accosted by a woman - seems like a regular, but who knows about people who bring their animals around with them? - and her two dogs, the employee politely ducking the smoke behind her back, perpetual position of a succinct bow-to-royalty. Lucy texts back: *No. That's hilarious. I've heard Fluffing.* When the snow comes - and it will, nights have been getting orange-purple, dawns getting pink-orange - this season it is going to be unforgiving. She's only had to deal with the tail-end of a winter since her return and the complaint of the denizens of this burg had been 'It was so mild, I'm worried it will be like that forever - seasons are important' and other simpering chatter of that ilk. Lucy imagines herself in her apartment, calling off from work, concentric circle of herself under blanket-after-blanket-after-blanket, letting the rooms around her get frigid, giving her excuse to stay buried. Milos texts: *I've heard Fluffing, yea. I've heard Plutting, Frumping, and Egging. This old man said Freddying, just now. He was belching and Freddying something awful, he said.* Can you think of any other funny words for farting, Lucy? Or is the conversation dead-ending? To stall, she writes: *What old man?* But Milos - eerie-quick - zaps back *Just some old man, is all - what're you up to?* Yes, Lucy. Milos asks a good question. Lucy sets her phone on the passenger seat and puts the car in Reverse, not lifting her foot from the brake, though. Milos will assume she is just busy or else talking to someone else. And maybe, she thinks - car back in Park - she will call off from work, tomorrow. Maybe. The thought of it, just now, is akin to the scent of cabbage left untended down the disposal. Her phone vibrates - she just verifies it is Milos then ignores it - and out there the *The Pet Store* employee seems to glance in her direction. But is she? Is she glancing in Lucy's direction? What if you were to raise your hand, Lucy, in a friendly wave? Why not do it - why not see? Hand up. Wrist giving a swish-swish. The employee stiffens, shoulders tick and tock to place, a look given around - head hardly moving though - then a little wave back. Lucy puts car in Reverse, turns up the radio. Those are your eyes in the rearview, Lucy - that is you touching at your nose as though not noticing the employee's wave, this pantomime hopefully enough to confuse the poor sap they were wrong, you weren't waving. Lucy steals a glance - just eyeballs, head still averted - and can tell she is being looked at, is a curiosity as she arcs backward, pulls away.

How many copies of Elliott's novel has Lucy shoplifted, in total? Is there an end goal to this compulsion? Does it aid in the resolution of anything? Has she ever read the book? The thing of these questions is: they don't do any good. She feels entitled to the books. And books are easy to steal - they are designed that way! More so than most objects, right? They are made to immediately seem like they belong to whomever is holding them - no questions can really be asked. But then again, fine. 'Fine' she says, stuck for the third time at the same traffic-light - it only lets a handful go at-a-time, less if someone has to make a left-hand turn because they don't have their own arrow, gum everything behind them up while waiting for the cross-traffic to ebb - 'I've stolen a lot.' Every time she sees it in a store. And of course she has read it. Stove-coiled-metal is how she has read it, orange and over-hot in her concentration, simmering the book, over-boiling it until it sticks in hard clumps to the inside of her head. End goal? Nope. Resolution? Eventually she will either hate it or figure out how it is about her. How can it not seem about her? She had walked through rooms where it was being written, laid with feet touching the author's while it was being long-handed on loose-leaf - had bought the damned loose-leaf, on request, one night when she was already out and the message had come *Can you bring home paper? Lined paper? Like school kid paper? Pretty please, pretty?* Where has the trick entered Lucy's mind? Every page has no choice but to body-odor of her and she must be the pace and the sharp of most of the loping, long-structured sentences - that one that goes on for three pages entire, for example. It's you, Lucy. It's you. Steal it enough times, read it enough times, and you will see. Or: what else? Options? Throw this one out the window? Finally start your vindictive campaign of destruction! Obliterate! Kablooey! 'I don't want you to read it until it's done' she says in her most baby-bird Elliott. 'Not until it's done. I want you to be surprised.' And so now Lucy has stolen every one of her reads. It's done. And where is she? Where is Lucy? And what's the surprise? 'There is none' - she says this now, not mindful of what a recitation it is - 'there is no surprise. I'm, as always, on the outside of a book I belong in. I'm eyes on words that must be me I don't recognize.'

Here is Lucy remembering: Lucy had found, in the laundry room - nine years old? - a pair of chintzy binoculars and decided she would watch birds. Those plans luxuriantly endless which last an afternoon - the forevers of childhood, decades that can only concentrate enough to last for a long weekend. Wet field, morning chill, the clothes Lucy wore soaking and pimpling her front skin in a temporary splotch-pink that the day and a bath later on would cure. Wet clothes are irrelevant to children. Dirty hands or unwashed teeth, shoes that leave trails of sour mulch over carpet. Nothing and nothing, nothing and nothing. The binoculars could magnify no more than to make Over-there seem as though five paces nearer, but Lucy ignored the frustration and painstaked over the powerlines - post-to-post, post-to-post - until she was pointing the binoculars at lines so distant that even if she saw birds on them she'd seem no closer to the buggers than she actually was. Here, Lucy gave up. Pointed the binoculars skyward. Limply discarded them sideways. Knowing she would not pick them up ever again. Look - she remembers - look with a blink and not even a Gah! On her pant-knee was a partly crushed worm! Its middle a paste, its two heads - or two anuses - glueily moving in half pig-tail curlicues - one thing made two puppets trying to stand up without being tugged on. How long had Lucy watched the worm? She'd watched it until it'd died, she now thinks. Remember? Do you remember? At some point she had - so slowly, be careful, Lucy! so slowly - started to bend her knee so that she could sit up, get her chin almost to it, watch the creature, as though on a denim stage, performing an opera in mute. Was it dead, then? Was this a dream? Because she remembers seeing two holes - maws of whichever kind - opening black wide then closing wet-flesh grey, two dilating, undulating dots - and the middle-paste had a smell like the liquid left in the can after her mother had plopped some *Chef Boyardee* in a pot to give her when she whined she would eat nothing else. But had she seen a worm that close? The memory of stretched black, of tight-lipped grey outsizes the scale of her vision, as though a planet rising where a moon should, the sky lowering instead of the sun setting to equal nightfall. Had Lucy watched the worm die? Why would she remember the sight of seeing it when she'd first rolled over - that had certainly happened! - but then splice in an out-sized fantasy, a ham-fisted fable-death for the smooshed thing, after? But the more she thinks, the more unreal it becomes. And other memories seep over it, each seeming to contain some component of it. Her past is just a pile of things borrowed from things that came after it.

How did you wind up out here? Lucy is not exactly sure where this is, even. She thinks - maybe - that building over there is the auxiliary hospital - she had had to take Kyle's kid there for an emergency appendectomy when Kyle had been on some trip - but even still, this road so rear of it is peculiar. She pulls over to the shoulder, lights a smoke, and surveys. Signs indicating Lots of such-and-such amount of acres are for sale at "good" prices - the quotation marks around the word *Good* rather amusing. No numbers given. *Ten Acre Lots. Twenty Acre Lots. Lease or Sale. "Good" Prices.* Then a telephone number. Puckish, puckish, Lucy gives a call. The number has been disconnected. She redials - trying without the area code, also - but the recording insists: *the number you are trying to reach has been disconnected.* Other signs of apocalypse begin fungusing around now that the pall has been cast. Those hay bales? How long have they been there? They have to them the disuse of outer-shell after an arachnid has strawed out a beetle's insides. And that is a tool-shed - Jesus Lucy, where are you? - not an outhouse! It's just a rusted tin tool-shed, three hundred meters out into that empty expanse! Even the maybe-hospital seems sterile, a long standing puddle, nothing more. How much time would it take to see a human being if she stayed out this way? Here: a vision of her face to her car window's inside, a bison fogging and snotting the outside glass, slurping its tongue over the taste of its snorts where her face would be if it could get to her. Up there! Sad blink of light. The away of an airplane. Tiny and unmajestic - red blink, white blink, children disappointed it isn't a UFO, their combined imaginations not enough to make them even for a moment awe or wish they were flying there with it. 'You're just a dot that isn't even in outer-space' Lucy says. Her mind is so mired in the past, today. Remember you had said that, Lucy? To whom? To your mother? In a car? Driving somewhere? A road like this? Piano lessons coming up or being gone home from? 'It must be sad to be an airplane. Everyone looking at you knows you're just something that can't go to space.' This plane is gone. Lucy cannot stop looking at the blank where it was. Imagine, she thinks, if there were always so many clouds we'd never seen the sky. How smart would we be, then? How different would our art be, our music, our ambitions, our regrets?

Milos answers his phone mid-yawn, makes a jowl shaking noise, apologizes, re-begins with 'Well hi you - where'd you go?' Lucy, to be succinct, admits she had not been in the head to prattle with him before, but now she is in some quieter pocket of ennui - a happy pocket, she assures, taking her cues from Camus, always - so thought she would see if he had anything else of note to regale her with in regard to flatulence. 'I'm done with that, man. There was just an old man. Came into the pharmacy, needing something for his tummy - you know?' 'Sure - typical old man thing to do' says Lucy, shivering as she makes what she decides will be her last circle of chug-idling car before getting back inside with the heater. 'Where are you? You sound like you're an ungranted wish calling from the bottom of a well, baby - everything okay?' 'It's not that bad' Lucy says - yep, fuck it, back in the car, unguardedly shivering curse words as she does - 'I'm just, you know, a penny someone put in a payphone, stuck in a pile of nickels who won't talk to me. The usual.' Milos wants to know 'Who uses nickels to make phone calls?' 'The same people who try to use pennies sometimes, obviously.' She can see Milos nodding his slow-witted assent, hears him sniffle, hock phlegm, spit. Then he says 'Know what bugs me? That *nickel* is spelled *E L*. One of the few things that ever correctly is. But if you spell it wrong - *L E*, I'm saying - that looks right.' 'The word is an asshole' Lucy agrees. Then says '*Pennies* is a rotten word, too - because it seems like it should be an anagram for *Penises* but it never is. And that's not something you should seem like being without being. There's plenty of other ways to be spelled! Pick one that doesn't make you such a jerk!' But really, Milos asks, where is Lucy? Where? She is calling from the future. Long after he has forgotten her name. Then she decides - to complicate things - that everyone in the future is actually named Lucy - so no one forgets her name, but only in a way that is even worse than if they did. 'A very specifically heartbreaking place, the future' she says. 'Those who learn from the past are condemned not to repeat it' Milos sighs. Lucy smiles the scent of batter-just-now-finished-stirring. 'So where are you, really?' Milos asks - and she just asks where he is and says she'll meet him there if he'd like.

Lucy drives and in quick succession corrects both Dante and Dylan. This puts her in a good mood, changing cigarettes at a stoplight and deciding she will bring Milos a gift of some bourbon, but then will comically drop it on the sidewalk up to his front door, just so they have such a funny memory together. How did she improve Dante? Well: Dante says of Dame Fortune: *Her changes change her changes endlessly*. Lucy's edit: *Her changes change her changes for a little while, sometimes*. Seems like she's just being flip? Maybe. 'Until you really think about it' she says, tacking to the left as she sees the word *Liquor* on prominent display - not an uncommon sight at all, 'round these bends - the tint of the neon the distinct briny of a seafood restaurant's unwashed outside. 'Because no one wants a seafood restaurant to seem too clean' Lucy sages, pointing to the empty passenger seat as though she will get an argument, nodding curt and content when she doesn't. And how did she improve on Dylan? Well, Dylan sings: *I met the sons of Darkness and the sons of Light in the border towns of Despair*. Lucy's edit: *I met the sons of Doctors and the sons of Liars in the border towns of Despair*. This - this! - this is a vast improvement. So much so it's embarrassing she has to be the one to point it out! First of all, what an amazing thing to suggest how the words - and, indeed, the ideas of - *Doctor* and *Liar* are opposites! There's that! But then to use this seeming humanization - in contrast to Dylan - to actually make the notion of this border town more mythic is profound! Profound! Saying *Darkness* and *Light* - not to mention sons-of-the-things - is not only cliché, in itself, but such a lazy stretch toward something Larger-than-human. But to suggest our concepts, our identities - in abstrcto - given offspring, producing life beyond us, just brood of Word or Concept - to suggest that our own ideas beget creations - larger than our subservient creation of the ideas themselves - and that we must tend with these God-figures spawned from our offhand utterances is tremendous! Weren't you supposed to turn there, Lucy? Isn't that where you were going? 'Probably' she exclaims, and keeps driving. 'I probably was!' And while, for a moment, she was going to barrel ahead, regardless, now she wilts and slows and cautiously *U*-turns - because she does want to get the bourbon. Then - you didn't

see this coming, Lucy? - she just turns right around again because - Christ God!
- did you see those cave-dwellers milling in the lot? So flabby that even while
landlocked they have to worry about barnacles! How can a lower lip even get
that slovenly? Lucy shudders in contemplation of these thoughts and more as she
flees.

Better. God fearing strip-mall. Ordinary liquor store. Suburbanites putting
on airs of their best mock-sophistication to impress clerks with almost enough
community college credits to graduate, finally. Even Lucy kowtows to the
liquor store clerk. Same as with bartenders. You know about different types of
alcohol? Oh it makes all go weak-kneed and Lucy cannot exception herself from
that. You mean you've tasted all of these? You imbibe spirits as an intellectual
hobby? Wow! Lucy is practically a hooved-beast in comparison to someone who
claims to know the difference between *Belvedere* and *Grey Goose* and *Chopin*! 'Excuse
me?' The pot-bellied older clerk - who she suddenly realizes is not the owner,
distinct set to his eyes, terror of a first-week-on-the-jober - nods and asks, using
words in their quietest nibbles 'What can I help you with?' 'I don't see *Bulliet*
bourbon anywhere - surely you carry such rot-gut, yeah?' This man has no idea
what she just said. They hired a man who does not know the term *rot-gut*!? To
sell booze!? To rascals like Lucy Jinx!? 'What I mean to say, my man, is that
there is a brand of bourbon - this brand is called *Bulliet*, spelt *I E T* not *Bullet* like
I'm-gonna-shoot-ya, you follow? - and yet I do not see it in this store. My
instinct is that I must be wrong - that you've just hidden it somewhere too clever
for me to suss. Get me?' Lady-clerk, seeing poor-old-guy fop-sweating it up,
grace-notes over and asks 'Which were you looking for?' '*Bulliet*.' Now this
woman knows of where she speaks - that's the proper, shamefaced downturn of
eyes appropriate to saying 'We don't carry it. I have no idea why. Pietro never
orders it, for some reason.' 'Then Pietro - whatever that name's even supposed
to mean - is a delinquent. By which I don't mean something positive - as in
*someone who smokes cigarettes on the school playground after hours and leaves their corrupting*
*butts there for kiddos to find* - but rather a delinquent, like *someone who is always late with*
*the car payment, figuring his mom will have to take care of it 'cause she co-signed.* You tell
him I said that! You tell him I'm not even sure his name is *Pietro* and that if it
comes down to it I can make a pretty big racket if I feel I've been cornered.'
During this speech, the pot-bellied know-nothing was given a nod by the lady
how it was okay for him to go off and change his soiled nappies. The lady,
meantime, just lets Lucy finish and says 'Have you tried *Fighting Cock*?' Lucy
touches her nose, like just-between-us, and hush-voices 'Sure, I tried that' -
emphasis long-voweled on *Tried* - 'but - not to tell tales, man - I found something
better to do than that.'

Popular this evening, now Lucy finds Layla had texted. *Call me when you get a chance?* Starting the car, Lucy starts to dial, but then tosses the phone gently to passenger seat, and pulls out of the lot, inertia making a brief, pleasant crinkle-sound of the plastic bag around the brown paper-bag in which there is the bottle. Lucy has forgotten the brand, already. Yes, yes, she is a poorly played game of pinball, today - all spastic flaps, wrong lights going off. But why shouldn't I be!? I mean - sure - Lucy could diagnose the cause, but right now why not just see how many times around goes this spiral and let the return-to-work and extra-shift-picked-up-on-the-weekend tame her back into her stable? You buried your cat today, Lucy. 'I buried my cat, today!' And Milos is the best person to be with on a night such as this. True! He's the only one who will point out the ludicrousness of mourning something with claws that pukes out logs of its own hair! Right now, Lucy is under the impression that Milos understands everything. That he, due to the spoilt-brat life he has lived - being a good-for-nothing kept quarantined from any experience of consequence - knows things which normally only she knows. Or at the very least: he knows how to agree with her without raising her hackles. 'A feat in itself' she says, lifting a pretend glass to him. Though keep in mind, Lucy: you cannot get drunk tonight. Burying a cat does not stop the capitalist sprawl! You want your tea-cozies and to be promenaded and Jane Eyred and to skip vaingloriouser than any other stone over the smoothscape of high-waters? Well! You can't get drunk with lunkheads like Milos and quote movies all night like there's never enough head to keep stuffing with trifles! At a stoplight, Lucy happens to notice that there is an indication of another unread text-message. Also Layla. Pre-dating the other by just twenty minutes - when would that have been, then? while you had been fleeing the first liquor store? - it says *Hey, you around?* Tingle. Tingle - mark it Lucy - of that-is-not-like-Layla. Because it isn't. And those were the first words you said, Lucy - the first thought you thought - in the first moment seeing those words - all shapes, letters, colors, sounds - your thinking formed the simple quiet of *That's not like Layla*. Ignore it if you want. Ignore it, ignore it. Feel everything else rising back to smother it down, bubble-bath suds of your mind rising high over skin-dirty water and your submerged bulk. Ignore it. Ignore it. Ignore it.

Lucy Jinx has always wanted to say these roads are beautiful. These egregiously dangerous wends, road pavement abetting the natural curves of the earth in their snakish intents. The funk of old-rot next to new street-signs and of obsolete street-lights next to never-used wheelbarrows. And so on. And, in the daytime, maybe she can feel that way. Or in the twilight of overcast blocking a sun that is doing its best - maybe then, too. But as dusk comes on proper, as human light reveals that its hold over the pitch is feeble and sexless - the blink coming on and flatting everything while at the same time stretching it immense beyond the confines of gravity - Lucy just cannot grace it with the word. Does beauty have to be kind? Oh no. Does beauty have to be considerate, longing for touch? Oh no. But there has to be something distinguishable other than the mumbling, futile song of people trying to proclaim themselves part of it. Something other than the sky sort of red yellow green, or headlight, taillight, the unwiped mouth of streetlight in an otherwise uniform sneer of nature's closed lips. All the night - on these unknotted country roads - shows is people. People who are the liver-brown on the pure white of humanless blank. During the day, sure - in changing leafs or leafless limbs or verdant over-indulgence - these roads make it easy to ignore every aberration of fence-line or bumper-sticker, of chimney smoke or lawn-mower rotor, the greed of nature almost makes man's not-part-of-it-but-insisting-it-is kind of cute, adorable, like a kid dressed in robot pajamas growling at you and saying they're a dinosaur! But: at night. At night? Out here? It's ugly. Lucy cannot tell the roads from the people who built their huts along them. The whole area is ghastly, a rash hardening over an eye-white. Every window-light lets her know someone is blowing their nose. Every shush of car tire over pavement or gravel reminds her of the scent of some hands going from scratching the moist skin of where their belt ups into their under-gut into the salt of potato-chip bag. Why do you live out here, Milos? The sensation of knowing something will leap out in front of her at any moment - possum-small or bovine-immobile - the sensation of knowing the dark can see her and she can see it - but that it knows what she is doing and she has no idea what it is - saps her energy and pulls the sleeve of her enthusiasm the wrong way through. She drives faster. The way you dream faster when you want to wake up.

LUCY'S SHADOW, LEANING AND SHALLOW, she is imagining as overlong though at the moment it does not exist in the scab black of the paved driveway toward Milos'. Because - because! - there must be shades of light so subtle - as with anything - that human perception of them is irrelevant, yes? Shadows do not depend upon us. This is Science - the same as why we can take photos of ages away in to deep space - and nothing to do with Lucy being the sort who still identifies shadows as physical Things as opposed to just the shape of the brief obstruction of light. Get down in there, into the darkest spot imaginable, go teeny enough and every pipsqueak spec - even an impossibly miniscule mote of light - is a galaxy-wide star, flaring blindness and desert everywhere! Everywhere! Lucy has the bottle - unbagged - pressed under her coat arm, cannot lose the sensation it is slipping loose, tip-tapped a nudge with her each uneven step. Milos, never one to leave a porch light on. Milos, never one to even be waiting by the door, smoking. No - he will be inside, in the kitchen, drinking coffee or watching the last of whatever movie or show until she knocks. Lucy, if you were to get all the way to the door, not knock, not return whatever texts Milos might send - *You get lost? The Hell's keeping you? Hey - are you okay? Seriously, I'm worried* - he would yet never even open the front door, never peek out the blinds to see if maybe you had been victimized - by a strangler or some kid drunk on the philosophy of The Perfect Crime - dying, gasping, dead on his threshold. Keep in mind, these thoughts make Lucy grin. She has even slowed down to enjoy her thoughts of Milos before getting his company, both barrels. Oh the fact that Milos might even think to himself 'I bet Lucy's been throttled, there, in the sackcloth of my front yard' is pure sing-song to her. Milos, who could even bring himself to panic and fantasy tears and melodramatics 'She must have been killed even while I had been thinking that!' Milos - Milos is her kind of bloke. So she has a smoke, setting the bottle on the mailbox. Frog song - in this cold? are those frogs? - clots up the chill - and either a random door opening or else a distant cow groan icings the cake of her shivering moment of I'm-so-glad-I-came-here. *The endless complaints of crickets refusing to show faces*, she thinks. Write it down, Lucy. You won't remember. So she says it aloud and decides it will be the first - the very first! - thing she says to Milos, tonight. Prepares it like a speech worth a letter-grade in junior-high. *The endless complaints of crickets refusing to show faces, the dark edges of childhood evening ugly with them, ugly with them, ugly with those gripes*. That's what she will say. First thing.

Milos is in receipt of this bourbon, now. He holds it in front of him like some movie scene where one sword-fighter understatedly admires the blade and hilt of their opponent before battle. Then harumphs and complains that this means he will have to - such cotton-mouthed lioness disgust to his saying it - 'pour things' over and over all night. 'Thanks, Lucy, I mean really.' Clack clack go two plastic cups from the cupboard - one with a most-of-it-chipped-off illustration of *Cookie Monster* and *The Count*, mitts to giggling mouths, on it. 'You only need one of those' Lucy quicklys, just tossing her coat on to the hallway floor, as such things are done while at Milos'. 'And it wouldn't hurt you to admire my poetic greeting, either!' Snoot-sour mugged, Milos pours himself some drink and says her greeting was subpar and since no one else is cad enough to tell her so that task also falls to him. He swallows his shot, even the squishy gluck of his gorge up-downing the picture of a frown. 'Jesus, Milos - what's the matter with you, tonight? You look like you're pronounced wrong.' Milos bites the air, looking down at the new drink he's pouring. 'You're one to talk, man. You look like who a cobweb would take to the prom.' Lucy's question: Is Milos going to pout unless she agrees to drink. Lucy's second question: Is Milos going to continue to pout even if she agrees to drink because then there'll be nothing she can do about it and he's just that sort of smooth-operator? Milos answers: 'Don't test me' and 'You don't even know what my middle name is and yet you think you can speak so familiarly to me, eh?' The thing is, Lucy really does have to be at work in the morning. 'So, why not just move in with me?' Milos asks. 'And not have a job and just do things.' 'Like what? Like love you and dote?' 'Jinx, you can't dote worth a damn or you'd have caught something worth keeping with that honey jar of yours you just can't keep lidded - and you love me, already. I just mean: come live here and quit your job.' Lucy pours a decent amount into the *Cookie Monster* cup, clinks it to Milos' temporarily empty one - there on the counter - and says 'Name me one thing we would actually do and I'll do it, right now - you'll see - right now, tonight.' 'Lucy: we'll grown an apple orchard from scratch just to let it go to the worms.' She drinks. Winces at the heat of this brand - whatshername picked good - and watches Milos pouring some more. 'You drink too much' she pouts. 'You Lucy Jinx too much' he drinks.

The following speech is outdoors and Milos' - neither he nor Lucy are coated and they smoke their cigarettes like fruitlessly trying to pinch closed a gunshot wound - said in chatter-teeth matter-of-fact, even the louder parts half-muttered for cold and quite quiet. 'Here's something about Earth: Every minute, there's someone in an office building staring at a microwave. That's for starters. Second: that person - by the very fact that they are educated enough to hold whatever their job is - have food to eat, a steady - however meager - income. That person - even if ill that day but still well enough to be at work, even on antibiotic, Hell, especially on antibiotic! - is one among the five-percent of the most fortunate people on this planet. Humans - you know, Jinx? Us-es. One of the wealthiest, most literate, healthiest, most secure examples of our species. You might hate this bastard or this prima-donna - whatever they are - or you might think they are swell. They might house only the most vulgar and dreadful fantasy narratives within them - Hell, they may even commit atrocities that others make a living writing True Accounts of! - but - hear me, Lucy Jinx - if the world were dying and some alien race said *Let's* - going by what seems to be the contemporary rubric for quality, success, and worth - *save ten percent of this species and set it on a new planet* - that worker would be included! So would someone who called their own daughter *Some horseshit* when it took her more than a day to learn to tie her shoes! The Top Five-percent - modern standards - would include this person. You think I say this to scare you? You think I say this to be confrontational or to upset your mincing worldview - but no! I scare you - or try to, I do not know if you have an actual soul or are just a better hand than most at the playact - by saying that, statistically, there would be more philosophers, men and women of physic, more artists, more benevolent sorts, more Golden Hearts in this motley group than in the Top Five - even the Top Two - percent of any era previous to ours - and this, Lucy, judging by either our current, evolved standards or the standards contemporary to them. Rainstorms more, Lucy! More by the tragic mudslide! Pound-for-pound there are less people - per moment - standing and staring at lunch-in-a-box rotating in a microwave now than there were then - even taking in to account how they didn't have microwaves! The math is on my side! We need neither Socrates nor Jesus Christ nor Florence Nightingale these days - because we've got endless of them! One Kato the Elder in a room is *Wowie!* Three hundred is just a lot of well-worded Gentlemen listen-to-meing while nobody does and neither do they!'

That went on a bit longer. Lucy gifted it mild applause on reentry to the house. Milos asked her what she was clapping about and she said it was just a belated response to a piano recital she once saw, that now she feels guilty for waiting so long. Here is what Milos has on this wall: a bunch of paintings he bought from some children who set up an Art Show along a street he was once driving down looking for a *Pizza Hut*. Seventeen paintings, three charcoals, and - he has screwed a small plank to the wall to display this - a statue in Play-dough of what he was told was 'A goblin who hates food.' Normally, Lucy would find the act of buying and displaying such things hopelessly douchebag, hipster to a degree she would get acquitted for road raging about. Insert into the equation the fact that Milos had paid the kids - these were kids, at the oldest, eight-years-old - seventeen-hundred dollars and one would expect Lucy to disown Milos and to get quite Ludivico at the thought of him. So: why not? Why does Lucy - there she is, now - lean to him and even smack his ass when he turns his back on her for more drink? True, she had already liked him well before he explained about these paintings - but she fell for him even while he told her about the paintings, so that cannot be it. Head-over-headlong, she had. The reason is this: because he had not bought all of the paintings. Not bought all of the sculptures. The charcoals. And none of the several pieces done in acrylic-and-crayon. No. He had told two of the kids he simply did not care for their work. That they needed to improve upon their technique - their asymmetry was powerful, he granted them that much, but not powerful enough to be a financial asset. He'd told them the work, some of it, didn't even show promise. That he could not believe it had been part of the same showcase as - for example - one of the charcoals of some fish and a radio and moon-colored-peach. Then into his car and away! And when he told the story, this was the part he had tarted up - this was where the wind-up led. He did not hoot or cockcrow, did not what-a-little-devil-he-is - he just said that bit the most pridefully. And has no idea that Lucy liked him for it so much. Milos, now in the living-room and taking off his socks because he says they make his feet cramp up like defending-themselves-armadillos when they get cold, coughing into his elbow crook, telling Lucy once again that she'd look pretty if only she lost an eye. 'Put a coin there, if you do. But from some old, defunct currency. Something from one of those countries - you know? - that aren't countries, anymore.'

'If you come up with a really long word but it's easy to find a rhyme for it you kind of didn't do the job properly. *Immunosuppressant*. For example.' Lucy is under two blankets and her head on the sofa arm, listening to Milos but watching *Phantasm IV: Oblivion* on almost-mute, the television set to the floor near a few empty containers of kitty-litter. 'Yeah' she says. 'Also: scientists need to stop being allowed to named things after themselves. They say Science is supposed to be above such things. You know who I like? Modest people. People who know people far more important than they are have been forgotten about way before they ever had a chance to be.' 'Yeah' Lucy says, then says 'Did we ever take the French-fries out of the oven?' 'What?' Well Hell, Lucy - shed those blankets, get in there! And there the critters are - still on the cookie sheet and now room-temperature and crisp-yet-soggy with settled grease. She cannot eat them gluttonously enough to satisfy herself, even when she has trouble swallowing she keeps at it - and when she can't, she drinks a bourbon cup full of tap-water, mashing more fries down after it to aid it in clearing her pipe. Milos calls over 'You're missing an even more boring part than the last part, Jinx!' 'Wait' she sloppy-croaks 'pause it, rewind!' This sounds like Maiff, pdaudz unt reghingh. Milos knows what she means, though. Says 'Naw, it won't be boring enough for me, watching it again.' Hardest swallow of her life, then gaspingly 'Won't it be even more boring, sitting through it again?' 'You don't understand Jack about boring, Lucy. You and your mind. I'd explain it, but why bother. Like trying to teach a house-fire aplomb.' Lucy discovers Milos has Bogarted her blankets and stretched all along the sofa, besides - so just plops down on his legs and tells him how she's definitely gonna fart a lot, having just eaten exactly all of the French-fries. 'I look forward to it. Powder-burn me with one of your booming, dykey kabangs!' 'Why do you own this movie, Milos?' Milos owns all of the *Phantasm* movies. And thinks Lucy should, too. He'll sell her his, since she lacks ambition - or *volition* he says he's not certain which word is correct, if either - and will never track them down, herself. 'In the dark' Lucy says, Milos' eyes look 'like what we'd assume the inside of an unbitten raisin looks like - that which we think just because we've seen so many bitten.' 'My eyes look like tuning-forks lumped in with a bagful of horseshoes.' Lucy crosses her arms and slumps. 'Fuck you' she toddler-with-hurt-feelings. 'That's why I didn't leave you any fries.'

Is Lucy going to go to work, come morning? Hard to tell. At this point: nowhere near inebriated enough to count it out - she'll be able to drive home soon, even. Maybe just stay up the whole night. But here we find a Lucy Jinx sunk in the warm of a friend's house on a freezing night, skin sour feeling from too much food to soak up her swallowed booze. And what is it that would compel her away? Work? Some temp job? To stand sorting documents - or sit sorting documents - to lunch break with Samantha and Kurt, trading grievances concerning how if the job isn't going to make sense, anyway, at least it could be more absurd? This job? This job that teeters on the line between irrelevant and perfectly-sound-seeming? This will stir you, Lucy, from the warmth of fatuous intimacy and sluggish waking-up-whenever? Could it be that Lucy Jinx prefers her mundane to her pratfalling wordsmithing? Does something about handwritten timecards attract her, hold more of a grip on her heart's heart than silly-drunkenness and kebobbing words that have no business with each other into superficially delicious emptying mouths? This isn't a fair question. Lucy washes her face and dries it with the not-really-dry hand-towel, knowing full well it is not often laundered, changed, has touched endless indelicate parts and issuances of her dear, dear pal Milos. This isn't a fair question. Lucy has worked jobs and had friends and worked jobs and not had friends and worked jobs and poetried heaping bales of her choosey language out into life while she's done so. Lucy: has lived a life. Lucy: is not also at the beginning of another. Lucy: is not a cycle in repeat. Lucy: is new but not restarted. So, why does she have to make choices like this? What does Milos want her to do? He would say 'Nothing' or 'Whatever you want' - but she knows that, no matter what kind reason he might have for it, this still leaves her in the position of having to turn someone away, to stay or to go. Every damn minute of her life. So what if she likes her job? Is she not supposed to? So what if she could just as well sit with dullard Samantha while Samantha meticulouses each leaf of her fast-food salad as though there is something any worse to find about one than another? Sit and say nothing, at that! Lucy could do that! She could be just as well there and then come here - and could live just as long getting paychecks and worrying about rent and splinting her broken-arm self around with Miloses or his ilk than she could anything else whatsoever. She can go to work if she wants to! That isn't an excuse to godforake her!

Heave-ho are Lucy's leaky bones, now finding Milos just coming down the stairs. To Milos - he lighting a cigarette and, for whatever reason, squatting to arrange the two pairs of boots, three pairs of shoes, and one set of bedroom slippers lining the wall by the front door - she says 'Most conversations for me are like ponies growing up to be glue. People. They fail in nuance, you know? Everyone is a door that creaks so loud you think it'll open wider than it does. Noise, man. Changeless noise. I've had it up to here with it.' His task more than completed, Milos has been observing the alignment of footwear and now, still looking at it, clasps in one hand Lucy's shoulder - this feels rough even through her slight buzz - and exclaims 'Have you ever seen such a line of shoes!? I - sadly - feel that I've never been prouder.' Then - right to her - he says 'You think you're so clever, my love - but you have, all summed, the depth of the saucepan a neighbor who dislikes you might lend. You know the one I mean, sister! The one not as good as the others - that's what I'm driving at.' 'The one that holds the less sauce - that's what you're saying?' He pats her head and explains that he doesn't even know why she puts up with him. He claims to be lovesick and heartlorn and altogether disassociatively-unrequited - 'Your fault' he says 'and also: you're fault - the apostrophe the R the E' - and since that doesn't seem to be Lucy's intent, he cannot fathom her. 'You're the ship that's sunk the furthest down, Jinx.' Hip bump. Hip bump. Back into the kitchen. Lucy lights a cigarette with the coils of the stove. 'Milos - I won't be a victim. I will not suffer your grammar!' This is said apropos of nothing but Milos writes it down and tells her to put it in her pocket, she'll be glad she did, later. 'Know how many books I sold tonight?' 'How many?' 'Four. And I might be interviewed for a blog!' Milos rubbery quadruple-takes, grabs the sides of his head as though doing so is required to steady him. 'So I guess all of a sudden you forgot to tell me you're a millionaire!' 'I am. Famously. For being the only millionaire with less than three hundred dollars. Look me up. I'm in a book, somewhere.' Milos mentions, after drinking a bunch of chocolate milk - which Lucy cannot believe he is doing considering how much bourbon he's had - how he is offended that Lucy has given him Zero autographed copies of her books. 'I have one in the car!' Quick cut: Lucy, coatless, out the door, down the blackout driveway, into her frost-covered car - wondering why the interior light doesn't come on - then out of the car, into the trunk, books rummaged, one taken, Lucy inside, in kitchen, book on the counter. *'Autographed by the author!'* Milos yee-haws from a gobsmacked gander at the sticker! 'Aw, Lucy Jinx - you're so cool! You're like a stray cat getting drunk with a starver cat! That's how cool!'

Oh but Mother of God - what is that!!? Milos reacts more to Lucy's startle - flatting herself with a thud to the wall, not even moving a hand to her head-back where it struck - than to the sight of the arachnids, though he does take pronounced steps away from them, lifting both his feet high and - it seems deeply rooted, a nervous-tick response - dusts at his shoulders, turns his head to try to see his back, as though something might be lurking in the undercurves of his shoulders. The spiders are moving two-by-two. There are not Hells enough to explain this! Lucy demands to know what Milos has done - she must be caught up in some gypsy-curse payback he oughta be suffering through alone and is quite bitter about it - snarls at him 'What have you gotten me involved in!?' Each of the spiders is not quite a foot long, but might as well be three! The thing is - notice, look 'Look!' Lucy points - the damned monsters are gallivanting in pairs. 'Since when do spiders do this!? Or anything like this! Explain it to me, country boy.' 'It's maybe migratory behavior?' Milos offers, question mark the largest thing pronounced, arms cocked as though to punch the spiders should their paths change. 'Even if spiders migrate - they probably do, I'm not even going to dispute that - why are they doing it in your foyer!?' 'Good question, Lucy.' 'Nothing can move forward until this is answered. And you invited me to live with you!? I see it all now - oh fuck, Milos, this is the measure of you! What a narrow escape I've made!' Eight, ten, twelve spiders - nine-legged, they seem, and hairier than teddy bears - across the well-ashened hardwood and now they begin climbing the door to that closet. Milos waits for Lucy to catch his eyes to say 'It is alright with you that I'm going to kill them, right? That won't cause a rift between us?' Getting the impression this is a common happenstance, Lucy pictures kitchen-trash full of spiders on a weekly basis - corpse piles with a victim or two still living and mingled in the mound, mouthfuls of hair of dead brethren. Milos seems to pick up on this and punches her arm hard. 'I don't live in a Spider House!' he insists. 'To the contrary, Milos' she jabs at the crawling procession - in the name of all that is holy! now they continue from closet door to ceiling!? where are they off to!? - 'my own eyes, man!' 'I mean that I didn't know, before now, how I live in a Spider House' he mutters, crossing his arms. 'If I'd gone to bed with you or something those could be up our noses, by now!' 'I know, I'm sorry.' 'This is demonstrably why I can never love you, Milos - even you can see that, surely!' 'I know, I know' he increasingly defeateds. 'Look - I'm gonna kill them before they just crawl down the other wall and go back the way they came - because that'd be too much for me to grapple with right now, okay?'

Lucy Jinx doesn't argue with the 'Have another drink before you go' just to help her forget about how there are probably living creatures inside of her car by now, too - centipedes, ticks, God-only-knows-whats. Pretending their lives aren't ruined, Milos attempts to come up with a game they can play - 'A wordy kind of game' - in which they have a conversation but with the stipulation that each time a word is repeated they have to pronounce it differently than its previous utterance. No. This goes nowhere. They try again. The game doesn't work. It'd be a great game for people who could just do it without having to put in any work - some sort of savant could play with another sort of savant and those two would have a blast, no doubt about it. How many ways are there to pronounce *Pronounce*, even? Yes: the game has some unalterably strict limits they had not counted on. They also can't do anagrams. At all. 'Try to do one' Milos testily flicks Lucy's breast about. 'I did try!' 'Do an anagram of' he pouty-thinks - 'of *Yesterday night*.' Lucy thinks. 'I have nothing.' 'Shit.' They decide they aren't meant for smart games. 'I hate chess' Lucy snaps. 'Everyone hates chess except those few guys who are good at it - that's why they like it so much!' 'You have no real problems if you are playing chess for a living - and why in Hell do we ever ask these people their political opinions and stuff!? Like they'd know' Lucy snorts. And this is true. It's all true. It is! Fact: people who play chess at Grandmaster-level do not have superior manipulative skills wherein they can control every aspect of their life and the lives of those around them - let alone communities or civilizations! 'They are indolent dopes with phone bills' Lucy says. 'Just think, Milos - someone doesn't pay their phone bill and tries to elicit sympathy - and to get out of late fees! - because they were busy thinking about chess! That's happened! In our lifetime! And chess players would make horrible generals, too. And who cares that Napoleon liked *The Sorrows of Young Werther!?*' Lucy demands Milos answer for why this is important. 'You know what I mean?' she says, almost a shriek. 'You know what I mean? Who asked Napoleon about that - who was so insecure? Or what? What'd he - go around just mentioning this tidbit about himself to people?' She gives Milos a foreshortened jab to the belly which connects harder than she'd meant it to. But she doesn't relent - even as Milos laughs and recovers from the bad swallow the blow caused. 'You're worried about chess players! Putting that in my head! What about Napoleon!? What about his love of Goethe!? Think about it! Why do we even know this!? Why is there record of this!?' Milos tries to punch her in the tunny, back, but she blocks it and pretends to brain him with the empty bottle.

'You're not okay to drive.' 'I'm fine to drive.' This argument is outside. Milos' evidence: Lucy is standing with her coat draped over her arm instead of wearing it. Detail of scene: the car is thawing, talk-radio burbling into the dark, drowned by the exhaust which surrounds the thing like a loiterer. Here Lucy, overtop of Milos still protesting she stay: drops coat, claps, grabs Milos by shirt collar and announces 'A *loiter* of cats!' 'What?' 'Not a *conspiracy* - a *loiter!*' '*A loiter of cats*' he repeats, yawning into juddering jaw, teeth chatter, cigarette out-breath 'I gotcha.' 'Instead of a *conspiracy*' she says. 'What conspiracy?' 'A *conspiracy* of cats! Or a *treason!*' 'You mean like a *gaggle* - a *conspiracy* of cats?' 'Or a *treason*, I said - shit, you're bad at picking up on all the alsos of life.' Detail of scene: Lucy, in horror, remembering the events of earlier - the dark-now-exactly-black, the way too many insects to comprehend would look - takes up her coat and begins beating it furiously. 'A *loiter*, though! A *loiter!* A *loiter!*' '*A loiter of cats!*' Milos repeats, helping her beat the coat. 'Lucy - stay the night.' 'I have to work.' Bam - Bambam - Bambambam to the coat. 'Call off in the morning.' 'I can't.' 'You can't drive.' 'Why not?' 'You'll die, Lucy - and while that'd be sexy, in the abstract, I'd rather you not.' Bam. Bambam. Bambambam.

'How many of them do you think there are - migrating spiders, I mean?' 'More than the world has illiterates, Jinx. I don't want to think about it.' Lucy slings into coat, leans into car, wondering if she did not set the heat dials correctly, the windshield still thick with frost. 'You're not okay to drive' Milos is saying while she re-emerges and lights another smoke. 'I will call you when I get back. And I'll stop at a diner to eat something on the way.' 'Then call me from the diner!' Detail of scene: Lucy leans in and kisses Milos - wettish peck - and his fingertips touch to her hip a bit. And Lucy will not call him from the diner - but if he wants, he can come along. 'Why won't you call me from the diner?' 'You should get to know what it feels like to be certain that I'm dead, for awhile.' Wait. Was that a real expression on Milos' eyes or some combination of dark and drunk and cold and fatigue? Weird pause. What had Lucy even just said? She blinks. 'Did you want to come to the diner?' she tentatives. 'You really are invited.' Milos flicks his cigarette and says 'I wish there was barn over there and that would go it afire!' Lucy squints to see if she can still make out the smolder of the tip of the discard. 'I wish it made all the color orange in Milwaukee combust' she says, wiping wet nose with already-wet-from-wiping-wet-nose side of her hand.

STATELY, A KING-OF-ROCK-'N-ROLL'S HANG-BELLY, WE now find Lucy in her frequent corner booth, coffee in front of the gal, waiting on food. The fangs of outside carve obscene frost on the café windows while in here the dowdy scent of mop-water used more than it should have been - suds overcome by grime, the place not so much clean as its floors seem lapped at by some dog's fluorescent tongue. Lucy has her little recorder out, one of the earphones corded to her, the other dangled over the table-side, a scribbled line on her lap, thighs tight together. The shivers have passed but now the too-warm of just-thawed - that and the uncertainty of 'Is this warmth a coming fever - have I caught something or is it just the booze winding down and the late hour, these sniffles not virus-related, just the sort that grumble *Go to sleep?*' No paper. No napkins out or pens. Breathing more than she has to - it seems like some distinct denotation is needed of 'I'm tired and this is a bad idea, not having headed straight home.' The funny bit of it is: Lucy did not come in here instead of driving straight home - did not decide to skip sleep and to just dog-tired the next day at work - out of any sense of defiance or grit-toothed denial of her state - no no, Lucy knows she feel like sausage sicked-up with malt power, her entire skin a twist the way a mucous membrane feels when a nose has been blown too often - she just came in by rote, was parked and out of the car before she knew what was happening. And by the time she was to the café door - what? - was she supposed to turn around? Lucy Jinx: as autonomous as a coin return, as willful as the time between clicks of a turn-signal. Now, she wonders why the busboy is bringing her plate over - this man does not want to be working at a café this late, career-criminal arms and his coy look of Is-this-yours? so artificial she involuntarily touches her purse where it sits at her hip - but thanks him and asks if it wouldn't be too much bother to bring over another shaker of black pepper. 'This one is all out' she illustrates with a lift and a cha-cha-cha of it, gingerly held aloft from the table a half-inch. The busboy takes a pepper-shaker from the table beside him - the table is only knee high to him, Lucy notes, really calculating his height and much impressed - handing it with a smile that fails to contain the mock of Really? 'I wasn't sure I was allowed to do that' Lucy says, ticking too many sneezes of the stuff onto the cheese of her opened up roast-beef melt 'and I am the sort keen on the rule-of-law. I'm an active citizen' she emphasizes, pointing to her coffee and giving a look like 'Hop-to, my man - tarry not.'

Well, see that the cassette in the recorder is spooling 'round spooling 'round? Well, hear the faint burble of shush-shush-shush coming from the earphone is Lucy's lap? Well, note the tight, skeptical concentration on the lips and at the side of Lucy's eyes, her posture half-leaned-in, her toes pressing into the café floor so that her legs keep tensed, stuck in a still-frame of in-the-process-of-standing? What is it that Lucy is listening to? Have an eavesdrop: 'in that century when they did not number the days, hours, or years, in those decades when fires weren't counted and people died by the numberless and tombs were signed with chiseled chicken-scratch - this is just getting awfuler and awfuler as it goes, sorry.' For example, there's that. Then a scruff sound - like a crumpled sheet of paper would make if it were heavy enough to cause a thud when it fell. Then this - keep in mind, though, that while hard upon to Lucy's current hearing it could have been spoken inside the same hour, within five minutes of the previous utterance, or three days could have elapsed in between, what with Lucy only checking her tapes every week, two weeks - 'The fact that the first literate was an illiterate creeps me out, man. But backtrack all the merrier and discover literacy, itself, was the idea of an illiterate! The first person who wrote down a word was likely the least trustworthy person of all! When in Hell did it seem sound-minded to look back at history and say *You know what's missing? Writing this shit down.*' Lucy nods. She knows what she means. The vague disappointment of hearing her own ideas so inarticulately voiced by herself. No one would listen to her if they'd heard that. Lucy herself, here, hears all the flaws in that thought process. But she thought it. Yes, she did. And it is recorded for all posterity! Is she to be embarrassed? Hide the fact? Eloquent it up and rewrite a clean draft?

Dishonesty! 'Kind of proves my own shoddily expressed point' she thinks as other words pass and now the tape queues up 'There are her eyes, coins that have never flipped. Coins that can't flip. There are your eyes, coins never flipped' and the sound of a car horn and her saying 'The fucking fuck, man - what!?' then nothing but the faint sound of radio and then that crightighrick sound and then 'You don't have to tell me how long you loved me, it's exactly the number of bones left in my hand.'

Her waitress - Colette - comes over to check on her. 'There you are! What gives? I thought that roughneck had trussed you up and was running the place to keep suspicion to a minimum while he waited for his cohorts - turns out you were just avoiding me.' Colette reiterates - same old Colette, kindhearted smile and bosom moving like a snort to her chuckles - that she loves how Lucy talks. 'I love how you talk, Colette. How's your kiddo?' Colette said her boy was still getting in trouble at school - had an actual detention. 'They still do detention?' Lucy asks and Colette grows thoughtful, replying 'You know - that's kinda true. It seems sort of old-handed' - Lucy is stealing that phrase, *old-handed*, immediately asks for a pen and slyly commits the words to napkin - 'and with how things are - you know? - I wonder if kids even think of it as anything.' 'Did he?' Colette rolls her eyes so stingingly she might as well have spit. 'Naw, he adored it. They made the mistake of having him sit in some faculty-lounge or small office or something. Jesus. He wants detention every day, now.' 'They gave him a peek behind the veil!? Oh the fuckwits! I'd change him to another school - one where the administrators have the least bit of smarts.' Colette agrees, she agrees, she agrees. And Lucy presses on - since Colette likes how she talks, this is kind of in payment for the purloined phrase of a moment before - 'Children should never know that other things go on at schools. My life was sullied - irrevocably, yes, this is why I am unhinged and supping here now and relating this to you so feverishly - when I got the merest glimpse, through a half-open door, to the room behind the librarian's desk of my grade-school. It was too much! The brain shuts down! Something too arcane to make a mind of, you know? Like hearing a crab ask someone for a pencil but then hearing it talk bad about the person who lends it one. How do you explain that? You can't!' Oh well - a customer - Colette has to go away. Lucy takes the last bite of her meal. Ah! No, not a customer. Someone just asking a question and Colette comes right back, sits across from Lucy without any ceremony and sighs the exact timbre of a kitchen sponge being squeezed not enough to unload its damp. 'Everything okay?' 'I need a new job.' Pause. Then a second pause while Lucy pretends to drink coffee - shit, Lucy, Colette likely noticed your cup was empty while she'd been standing there! - and then a third while Lucy takes a napkin and pretends to have to blow her nose. 'Sorry' she says to Colette 'yeah, jobs are the worst.'

'It's - I really love this job. It's - where does he think I'm going to get the money for that? Sometimes I think - I don't know - there's nobody anywhere with any kind of balls. You know?' 'I know' Lucy tsks. Which sounded so false, Lucy - damn you. Colette, luckily, was too dejected to notice.

The bulb down in the toilet bowl does not seem feminine. No. The licey earmarks of male waste. Interesting: the main color of the turd - brown, standard - is no longer on the skin of it. Instead, we see its apple-flesh, pale-graphite like either a standardized test bubble only tentatively filled-in or else filled-in and then erased. Also of note: the grey-tone has a peach-fuzz to it - not exactly like hair, but rather the exact way Lucy had always imagined an enlarged germ would look, a microscope-viewed, single-dot-of-fungus. The brown - coming to it - is in a kind of hazy electron-cloud around the meat, this essence lasting about an inch, thinning in density as it moves off - uniformly diminishing in color, Lucy wants to add, both left and right in the exact same gradation of coffee to toffee to mint-tea - before the water is just water-colored, crisp to the circle edge of the surface. And there: down in the base, at the mouth of the drain, some of the coloration has fallen, sunk, and has an intensity, a sunset reddishness which even visually gives off the impression of a stabbing scent and a bitter taste, the same as does the over-bright of certain jungle frogs. Whichever woman this fell from is not an entity to be trifled with, that much is certain! Aggressively left, this specimen. Lucy staring and vaguely also looking around for other signs of extra-sully. Jesus. No. What a thought, Lucy! Colette? How could it be Colette's!? She seems the sort to follow protocol, if nothing else. Though - this must be granted - Colette seems quite disgruntled by life. A mound of her discard waiting to Hello some random person might be just the ticket - the powerless are often left to invent revenges abstract and somewhat ill thought-through. And now that this thought is in her head, there is something of Colette about it. Look. Look: Like a brain with no hemispheres caught in the cigarette-breath of a muddy boot, there stands the crap! Good-postured dump it is, the toilet bowl entire could be seen as a modern art of Colette's overworked, under-slept eyes, that grim-pink and vein-or-two that start to show past midnight. Ghastly. And profound! And Lucy left to flush it. But if it is Colette's, maybe she shouldn't. The gesture is wasted on Lucy - Lucy, a gal whose sensitivity has allowed her to sleuth the sadness of this refuse, the there's-nothing-in-the-world-I-am-anymore intonation of it. An epitaph. A living monument. If Lucy leaves the toilet now, the clot unflushed, Colette may enter, see it still there - all its bleary perfection - and know she has been understood. Maybe flush it herself, rejuvenated if only for a bit.

Kick to awhile later: Lucy with a new coffee and Colette - waitress-apron off, draped over that chair - sitting again at the same table as her. Apropos of her sense of guilty conscious, Lucy relates a story from her childhood - all of it true. The story takes place during, Lucy says, fifth-grade-might-have-been-fourth and concerns an assignment to make a papier mache puppet. A fair amount of class-time was devoted to the construction and once everyone had a puppet completed a series of little performances was to be given. The puppets were to be various characters out of American Tall Tales. That was the slant of the lesson plan: *Tall Tales*. 'I had *Pecos Bill*' Lucy says. But what Lucy had not had was patience or interest-in-making-a-puppet. So, instead of taking her time and painting the face one layer at-a-time, she spread wet paint on wet paint and the thing looked atrocious! Solution? Lucy Jinx decided to write what turned out to be a three-part, twenty-page script 'Reinventing the *Myth of Pecos Bill* as a semi-superhero sort of thing: *Pecos Bill Man*!' Yes, Colette was not hearing things: *Pecos Bill Man*, whose story was tragic: disfigured while trying to do something heroic - such as *Pecos Bill* was known for! - he is given new life by Death, Itself in order that he might wander the plains - or wherever *Pecos Bill* lived - and - she supposes, admitting this aspect of her plan is now hazy to recollect - right random wrongs or get revenge. 'Or something.' And the script called for a bunch of other characters. And Lucy had explained to her skeptical teacher that she would make all these other puppets before the week's end and that putting on the play 'wouldn't be much trouble at all.' Oh Lucy can still remember some of the dialogue between *Pecos Bill* - at that point dead but not yet empowered and revived - and Death - the puppet of which was going to be the easiest to construct, just a bunch of rags on a very haphazard spherical papier mache head. Not profound dialogue. No, no. Very meta stuff. A nod to the cheapness and obviously-shoddy production-values of the Death puppet. 'What's up with the rags, man - I thought Death had some boss clothes' would say *Pecos Bill*, not quite yet *Pecos Bill Man*. And Death, a resigned lilt to the single word delivered with stinging comic deadpan, would say 'Recession.' Yep. Lucy remembers and regales that all forward, longwinded, this coffee-shop, this night-early-morning. And Lucy's head swims with memories not quite touchable by exact images of just what that classroom had looked like, her puppet, how the teacher often kept only half of the overhead lights lit. 'And did you put on the play?' Colette eventually can be heard to ask. 'Of course not. No. That's the whole point of the goddamn story, man.'

And ah, the soporific of paying a bill and crossing an icicley parking lot to a car, knowing one is going to smoke and hating oneself for the need. Such is Lucy's cross-to-bear. The laceration of cold airless, she is surprise when the lighter lights and when the fire feels warm. Sigh. 'Which' she mutters, leaning to car-side 'ought to be spelled *Hhhh*. Obviously.' Not to keep dwelling on her own past, but she's said so for ages. Little-girl, she'd noted this flamboyantly incorrect word. *Sigh*. Odious word. 'Not just visually, but in pronunciation' she bulldozes aloud, not wanting to sound foolish. The fundamental mistake being that people think that *Sigh* is a word for the sound of a sigh when in reality *Hhhh* is a word, itself. That is: people say *Sigh* - though spelling it wrong - they don't just make a noise that needs to be dubbed with an indicator. 'We're idiots, though' she concludes. And proves it by mentioning that there is only one single correct way to spell *Idiot*. 'Any permutation of the letters should be correct' she brandishes the assertion out. 'Any!' *Idoti. Ditoi. Idtoi. Itodi. Iidot.* This way it always looks wrong and any person who insists 'No, this is the proper way to spell it, not that!' is actually being an idiot, playing their cards down how they've no sense of advanced grammatical stuff. 'Elect me!' Lucy implores the empty lot. 'Vote! Vote! I can fix it all!' But what is this? She steps out her smoke, proper past-frozen, and cannot make up her mind about 'Is that tire flat?' Does it look flat? Does it look like the other tires? Are they all flat? Oh God, the mongrel nature of this day will nag her until collapse! Kick. Kick-kick. Kick-kick-kick. Lucy Jinx has no idea what it feels like to kick a flat tire versus a robust one. Moreover: she believes tires are strong rubber - that to a human kick, there would be no demonstrable, felt difference. Now - when she drives - she knows it'll feel flat, the car maybe performing as it always has done but feeling warp-warbling. And she'll listen for oddnesses. Is that what going over a bump always sounds like? Is there more turning-sound from the passenger side wheel? And so on. Until infinity. She shuts herself in the car. And is victimized by her train of thought, immediately! Did the car sink a little in the direction of the suspected flat? Does it always feel like it wiggles a little to sit down? Oh goddamnit, goddamnit! Even not knowing things is too complex, these days.

This is the sort of road that wakes up very slowly. Still stuck in childhood head, Lucy reflects on this. Exactly, to the yawn, what driving-overnight-with-dad would feel like to an eleven-year-old - these roads look the part, down to the whiskers. Even the hinted coming of slow-bright - still dark, still dark - opens up over a road bereft of anything. No other cars. Or just the rare headlight off on a side road, going in another direction. As this residential patch is gone through, Lucy is haunt-songed by the fwump sound accompanying the sight of an idling pick-up truck - passenger-door open and exhaust scribbling the exact sound of radio-inside-vehicle-heard-from-outside - fwump fwump of some newspapers or telephone directories being dropped to porch pavement, unseen, by a driver who had parked, grabbed a stack, dashed into the cold night, desperate to hurry back. That's not happening, now. Just memory superimposing on sentinel house-fronts, cars, for the most part, garaged. In your neighborhood, Lucy, there were no garages. 'That's true, yes' she sniffs - sniffs, picks her nose a bit - sniffs, again. And fidgets to get her recorder out of her coat pocket. Gives it up - she had not listened to the end of the tape, anyway, so if she recorded this thought it would be at the loss of another. Fidgets again and sets the recorder back behind the steering wheel panel, near the button which resets the Trip-odometer, depressing Play while she does. And here Lucy's voice rambles - she strains to hear, hard against the wind now fingernail thick and insisting on being audible: 'anything else, too, either, whatever. Doesn't have to be. Okay: a wine bottle. Picture it. Very old. Hand-blown glass. Only bottle blown by that specific artisan - historical records prove that. So: rare bottle. The vintner spun the bottle herself, see? And the label? One-of-a-kind. Hand-inked. The adhesive that affixes it mixed from scratch - also by the vintner. And the same with the cork. First gouged, bulbous, from a whole board of cork - or however that works - then hand whittled - vintner - to the exact cork it is. You know what I mean? What about that bottle? I mean: so what? Knowing all of that and having the bottle in hand, isn't it like knowing nothing and having no bottle in hand? Since the knowledge has no value or purpose and the bottle is doing the one thing it was never meant to do - be had and kept and lorded over by you?' When had you said this, Lucy? And what does it mean? And how long have you been driving without looking at the road - here, drifted into the wrong lane, eyes squinted tight as the Ouch of a stubbed toe, as though being sightless will help you decipher this whatever-you're-saying, this whatever-you'd-said.

Your home, Lucy. You're home. A last check to the time on the car clock and a last yawn and a forcible heckling at yourself how you are not going inside to go to sleep. Work in a few hours. And all your idea. Glitch in you that will not allow the more sensible choice of 'Okay, just don't go in' all off now. Impossible for a Lucy Jinx. If you were going to do that, you ought to have stayed with Milos. You didn't stay with Milos. Therefore: you cannot call off from work. The guilt-addled syllogism struts unassailably sound! But suddenly: new trouble. All previous life seems a footnote. And let us explain how this went - because the world - its coming-for-her slink - did not do a thing to keep subtle. Over there, Lucy saw - or thought she saw - the red-blue flicker of police lights and got curious. They seemed to originate from way around the corner of the building, so over she went. This is the opposite direction of her apartment, of the stairwell that leads to her door. But on getting there: no lights. A trick of her tired mind? Train of thought and reluctance to go in and her no sleep cobbling a hallucination for her to investigate? Maybe. Until: so right there is a stairwell and she takes it instead of her usual - her usual which would have would her up right at her door, right at it smack-dab. Now: she comes toward her door having to first do this corridor and round this corner. And as she rounds that corner what does she see? There is someone standing at her front door! Someone obviously milling there and who even tries her door handle! All of this happened. In that fashion. This whole night has lead to it! That is a person. And they are still at her door. Lucy has ducked back around the corner, but has given strategic peeks. And so: now what? As she is pummeled by all of the circumstances which conspired to make this moment this moment - and as she is choked out at the horror of knowing, no two ways about it, she could theoretically be sleeping, unawares, in her apartment, right now, and this person would still be looming there, touching her doorknob - she has to make a decision of 'What now?' Walk over - see who it is, what they want? Stay hidden, try to glimpse where they go when they leave - if they leave! they are still there! why!!? - what car they drive, what direction they walk down the street? Make pursuit? Telephone the police, Lucy - should you do that? Why aren't you at Milos'? Or: why did you not come straight home instead of chatting with Colette in a diner? Why did Then lead to Now? How long has this Now been fomenting?

Okay - fine - locked, latched, chained, and sofa-pushed-in-front-of door. Lucy taps at her thermostat, still in her coat, and walks a circle, impatient to hear the click and the vibrating white-noise coming from vents at all corners. That had been a woman, right? Jesus - had that even really happened, Lucy? Look how tired you are and how much you're shivering! It could have been a man, though. The coat, the hood. Slight, sure, a slight man - but why insist it was a woman? What - you would rather it be a man!? And don't even try to pretend this is not directly connected to the knocking, earlier this very day! Or yesterday. Or whenever. 'Before the bookstore' Lucy says, as though exasperated with a student who says they have read the chapter but clearly have not or else are just worthless when it comes to comprehension. Anything else? Odd encounter? Why are you getting undressed!? A shower!? Warm up!? But yes - no, Lucy is right to listen to her reason, she is right - she had watched the car pull away. Loudmouth hot water fills the closed bathroom. Lucy gets shirt overhead, sniffs its underarms and her actuals. Probably, Lucy, you had shown up just right when the person had got to the door. Yes. Or else they'd been there, loiterer, but were not interested in breaking in? Lord, the too hot of even just mild-warm on her raw-with-cold skin is delicious, dementia grade joy - she feels senile with innocent bliss for the first few moments of contact, all thought driven briefly from her mind. They hadn't broken in. Fact. And if they were there specifically for Lucy, they'd have noted her car had not been present in the lot when they'd arrived. So: why not break in? Mouthful of almost scalding, odd how it feels cooler dribbling over her chin - why would the inside of her mouth make it milder and so quickly? And had they not noticed Lucy's car was there when they had left? It couldn't be. Because if so, then why not accost her at it - for they might think she was still in it - or go back and try the door, again? Oh Lucy - are you really just letting water shriek itself hoarse into the knots of your skull-base and shoulder-longs, feebly attempting to convince yourself they weren't there for you? 'Yes, actually. I am doing just that. And why not!?' Lucy can better explain why that woman - it was probably a man, Lucy - had nothing to do with her than why she - he - had any even fleeting connection - so why not be convincing herself of it? The truth. It's the truth. The truth is 'The Truth is a fine thing to be convinced of.'

But it isn't over, is it? Ever, is it? Dried and warm-apartmented, barricaded and lounge-clothed with clothes-for-work draped over dining-table chair, Lucy starts across the carpet of her living-room area and - the apartment all still in colors and tints of night due to the blinds being drawn and the dawn not yet burst - her toes come in contact with a small ball that rattles with a jiggling, buzzing sort of bellish sound as it moves along the wall, stopping against the metal of the floor vent with a slight sound of Tink. And finally: you're crying, Lucy. The worst time you ever could be, because it is for too many reasons. Lucy Jinx is dead, Lucy. These two days. Can it really only have been two days ago he died? You dug earth with your chapped hands and passed out after pizza in the *Starlite Delux* only within some forty-eight hours? 'Lucy' Lucy coo-cries and makes kissy sounds and then blats out the word 'Gah!' because now her head can't even just sponge thick with the emotion, finally arrived, which should have come already. Lucy Jinx is dead and in a hole on the side of the road where you killed him - yes yes, because that's what you did, Lucy, he's dead now, you killed him in slow-motion, a car crash years long and now dirt mottled, bug eaten-up, he's dead and it's you who killed him! Because look around: he's not here, Lucy - Lucy jinx is not here! He's dead and you stuffed him down a hole, finally - right where you'd killed him. Oh her - not just with this noise but it has to buzz also with everything else! Everything coming. Oh her - heartless, cavalier chatter with hotel clerk. And driving home and getting high and packing books up like nothing! And knocks at the door - again and again that you knew weren't nothing but you told yourself were! And Milos called and you weren't going to go but you did. And - yes, Lucy, that's the lurking, gibbonous leech-bellied thing of it, say it, that right there - that call from Layla, then, that call from Layla that didn't seem like her - it didn't seem like her! - and you ignored it and went on to Milos, regardless. And his 'Stay, stay, stay.' And your leaving. And stop in for food at the diner. And memories, soft, of the childhood-kind. And listening to your rambling blah blah. And thoughts of driving - a kid - perfect alone and infantile-safe. And police lights that weren't there. And a corridor you don't go down. And coming at your door from around a new corner, opposite-wise. And then someone there. Woman. Man. Womanman.

And you kick a toy ball. And now you call and Layla doesn't answer. And you text *Sorry - call me ok?* And have to have no idea will she or when. You might just be drinking a bit of juice, Lucy, and that might be a cigarette and you might be at home, an hour-and-a-half from going to work - but what else? You know? Oh you know. What else, eh? What else, all the time?

REMARKABLE, THE AFFINITY IN LUCY for being caught up in even the slightest traffic. And a wad of it, wet and mashed? There's hardly a thing she is more preferential toward. The world is thinking, admitting it is mortal, Lucy's place in it, while calculated, nevertheless only fixed so-much-in-advance at-a-time. Sure, sure - Lucy could think of traffic as just-as-much-a-part-of-what-happens as anything - after all, she sees sleep this way, she sees showers and loitering this way - but, as it happens, she does not. It's a feeling. Traffic. Traffic is a buffer - the guitar being strummed or the refrain being repeated extra times, fading out fading out fading out before the next song cues. Exception to this: obviously an event can happen in traffic - a realization, a telephone call - but, then again, this untraffics traffic. The same way we separate a moment-in-good-health from a moment-with-cancer - we don't call the latter a moment-of-good-health-in-which-there-is-also-cancer - no no - as the moment has now been revealed to be what it is. 'And likewise with showers and loitering' she mutters. Similarly, she adores - even venerates - time spent on the telephone when a receptionist is tacking through something on the computer or leafing through a manual. Or - this especially - the time within an argument - the more fitful the better - where the other party goes sea-at-threat silent, eyes glazing, spacing, unresponsive, twenty-seconds-of-drag-between-each-statement. She can tell the world is indecisive. She can tell the world is doing its darndest to think of something profound or hurtful. These are the spaces in life where Lucy knows, as fact, she is safe - out of life, away. Because it isn't ready yet. It is still becoming. Certainly, certainly, Lucy knows the logic: Well, since the table can be set, the pen stroked to paper quick-as-a-blink, the pause cannot really be trusted. That is: traffic can untraffic without ceremony or rumbling approach - now Not, now So - this is the method of life. So, Lucy - how can you love it, feel comfortable, say it cannot get you? It's the idea, though - this is Lucy's response - a faith. To be exact: what she loves is knowing there exists time when the churning of the world's decisions can be observed, where she knows that is what is going on. This leads to the unalterable truth that there are moments of safety. There are. And traffic - silence-in-an-argument, being put on hold at the dentist - are in the realm of this safety - are near to it. Nearer than sleep? Of course! Sleep is not sleep. The mind thinks about more while asleep that while awake! And the world gets away with murder wherever there isn't wide-awake noia to smack its hands when the world tries to get too up-the-skirt toward the cookie it's after! Traffic trumps sleep, all day long.

Now: Lucy's telephone. There in the passenger seat. It starts to vibrate. The traffic not moving - really not moving and hasn't for more than five minutes - Lucy, casual as can be, answers without even glancing to the number. Mathilde. Some general 'Good morning - Good morning' and all that lot of rubbish. Lucy watches the rear lights, red, of cars ahead of her - well past the bend, the road a discarded shoelace of nobody going nowhere. 'Is it raining where you are, yet?' asks Mathilde. Lucy glances skyward, shakes her head and - suspicious voice - says 'No' - pronounced slowly with ten Os - 'what do you mean? We're in the same place, aren't we?' What Mathilde means is exactly that! And Mathilda squeaks like clean window-glass in her fifth-grader enthusiasm as she says how it is pouring on her side of town, all of a sudden - and she had watched the rain approach, battalioning the pavement up her neighborhood while she was about to get out of her car, slam-clatter all over her as she got to her front door, under the awning where she could see the rain continuing on in the direction she knew Lucy lived. 'And I am watching the wormy progress of the cloud-cover, you know? It looks like the inside of a cupboard outside, here - just like that - but in the distance I still see it's sunny. I'm watching it get gobbled up, right?' 'Well, it's not raining here' Lucy shrugs, scratching her nose and adjusting at the dials of the heater a moment. 'And it better not, because it'll all freeze, Decimal Point! Think - you're supposed to be clever! Don't let simple weather phenomena make you dumb! The rain works like that, every time.' Mathilde, well acquainted with Lucy's bah-humbuggery, switches gears seamlessly into the matter at hand, which being this: Lucy has gotten some e-mails. 'From that broad' Mathilde says, as though unimportant 'for one' - Lucy cuts this teasing off with a simple 'Bullshit' and gets the revealing snort in response - 'and then this other from some woman who says she met you at a bookstore.' '*Sylvanna* or *Sylvia* or whatever?' '*Sierra*' Mathilde says, question mark letters, clearly reading the still open-in-front-of-her correspondence. 'What does she want?' 'Apparently you whiz-banged her and she wants to make sure you will still get together to have an interview. For her blog. Which - if I am to believe the link - is called *The Cheshire Twat*.' Amazing! Lucy has to tense her abs and force a fist into her thigh to keep from squealing she is so delighted by that! Composed, as though indifferent, she goes 'Blog, eh? You have it up? What's it seem like?' 'It seems like what all of them seem like. No finer description than that.' 'Only: it's called *The Cheshire Twat*?' 'Yes, Lucy - that's why I emphasized that to begin with it. It's exactly the same as them all, except for that.'

This is what Lucy means! She has to keep a better spirit about her, honestly! She is tired - and that is all that happened, earlier. That recurrent malfunction. And now it is revealed that it was not just maelstroms and papercuts in store for her, going forward, but all manner of tiddlywink fun. Yes. Lucy reminds herself, as the traffic picks up a little speed, that she will be - and is - fine. She is treed to a different species than the rest of the people she brushes up against. She is a sort. A type. A glance to her side proves it. See her? That driver - the one in the unwashed minivan with dents from horseplay and a scrape from a car-next-to-it-in-some-lot's door on the side of the side-mirror? Look at that woman's plump face, seemingly set like a paper plate on the over-brimmed top of a trash-bag filled past capacity. Lucy isn't like her! Glance the other way and we have those two! Two young men who live in full awareness of every of their numerous physical oddities and will never know the comfort of believing the words 'You look handsome, today.' The one with an old-fashioned hat, hoping this makes a difference - he'd be a heartthrob if space-time hadn't landed him in the backend of the wrong era! - and the other with an uncultivated beard of short-and-curlies giving the impression of the tangle 'round his loins, chin made the honest mistake of thinking his bulb-nose was his dick. Atrocious! They look like illustrations in an essay about the *modern malaise*, the world-given-up-on, the absurdity of having high ideals and such. Lucy has nothing in common with them! This is the reason for the world's odd fixation on her. This. Her. Who she is. And what. If she were whoever-it-is-in-the-car-in-front-of-her - someone individual as a roll of pennies and no moreso no less - then none of the machinations that are composed for her would be even limply considered. The world is mostly water and works hard to drown everything not like its others. 'Trillions of insects' she says 'but none of them really stand out! So no one bothers insects. They kind of eat each other or don't and that's about it. Five thousand kinds that all look the same except for this prickly-bit-by-the-wing-base or an antennae that wriggles the opposite way! And a zillion of each one of those! Lucy Jinx, however, is the only. She accidented into existence of her own haphazard will and now must be prodded at and then dismantled. 'Yep. The world wants me dead - because it's that or else admit it's my underling!'

And in celebration, she pulls in to this doughnut shop she has always wanted to pull in to, calling work from the lot, explaining to the receptionist who she is, that there was traffic, that she will be there as soon as she can. 'You're a temp?' the receptionist asks, likely ruffled by the expansiveness of Lucy's you-should-know-who-I-am tenor. 'Yes.' 'Did you call your Agency?' 'I was told that isn't necessary.' She can see the receptionist rolling her kindly, maternal eyes - twitch-twitch would be going her receptionist nose - while she says 'Oh I'm sure it's fine. I'll let them know. What is your name?' And now: doughnuts.

Two dozen. No - three! 'I'd like three dozen doughnuts, please. And - mind you - not just three dozen, but your finest three dozen!' The proprietor - this is obviously his place and that is probably his daughter Lucy can glimpse in the back area, there - has a big laugh, says 'They're all my finest - Oh every day, all day. Which would you like?' 'Sir' Lucy humbles 'I admit I have a sweet-tooth and can appreciate a doughnut when ingesting it - the same as the next man, the same as the next man! - but I am afflicted with a hatred of having to choose things. Therefore, I'm afraid this is going to have to be up to you. By which I mean: put thirty-six doughnuts into however many boxes or bags that requires and I will pay for them, sight unseen. Are you amenable to this?' Well Ha! the proprietor has never heard such a bit of speechifying and wishes to Christ his every customer could be Lucy Jinx! Of course he will choose the doughnuts! And the woman Lucy had seen in the back? She now lingers, just there, leaned to the refrigerator and has grinned herself hoarse during Lucy's displays. Closer inspection: wife, not daughter. The light hits the wrinkles and shows the lace-work of them - an alphabet of a face, it would feel the way a page would taste to lick letters from if that tasted the way it seems it should taste instead of just like paper. 'I want you to take these' the proprietor announces 'no charge, today.' But Lucy couldn't - dear God, now, that was not her intent! Wave of hand, the proprietor insists. Point-of-honor. If she eats them and deems them as good as he thinks they are - 'The Best!' he explains, plain-speak - he has no doubt he will see her every day and so more than make up the investment. 'But if they're as good as you say and you make me pay now, you'll have me anyway - plus the extra odd dollars! Think about that!' Lucy says with a smack to the counter and eye-contact on the wife who says to her husband 'I love how cleverly she talks herself out of a favor - now you have to let her pay' the proprietor laughing too hard to argue or to acquiesce.

Then the last ten minutes of driving to work. Lucy sees the squiddy approach of that rain Mathilde had mentioned. Over there. Or: not the progress. It seems to have settled on its expanse. What Lucy sees are the charcoal down-strokes of the downpours outer-reach. Above her, the sky is cloudless and it only seems shady because the sun must be way over there, subject to that muffled grey. A box of doughnuts left with reception - the woman, whose name Lucy maybe never learned and certainly never recalls, clapping in that disconcerting way semi-elderlies so often do, bouncing toddler-like in her seat, hands in short-short soundless claps, fast, positioned fingertips at chin-height in the fashion of standard prayer. Lucy is always troubled by such clapping - and as she is buzzed through the door into the corridors that lead to the offices she works in, she is trapped picturing some perversely stunted upbringing, some too-specific-to-imagine gone-wrongings of the receptionist's life as a little girl. Thoughts in the fashion of overexposed film-stock, people only portrayed from thighs down, no clear sense of narrative or focus, the vague sound of mom or dad coming through the door calling 'Hello?' along with the sound of a lawnmower. Now, Kurt calls to her from behind - must have just come out of the shared-among-offices Men's Room at the end of the hall - and catches up to her, saying he has to ask her opinion about something but she has to promise to not give her actual opinion but to really just say something nice and bolstering. 'Are you not even going to notice I have all of these doughnuts?' He blinks, opening the door for her, shakes his head and goes 'Those, you mean?' 'What do you need to ask me?' 'But, not here' indicates Kurt's face as Samantha is revealed to be at the photocopier - a winky-nod meaning 'Later today, though.' Lucy hisses to mean 'Yes, yes - run along' and tells Samantha 'I brought a lot of doughnuts and you can't have any because of that one time you said that thing I didn't agree with! Remember how I told you you'd rue the day? This is the day, baby. Get to rueing.' Frown-face goes Samantha with her always sotto voce voice accompanying 'Oh no' and her lack of quick-wit indicated by 'What did I disagree with? I probably agree, really. Was I joking?' Plops the boxes down and swats at Samantha's encroaching hand. 'But I wanna doughnut' she whines, reaching again and actually getting a smack to the top her hand. 'First: say you're sorry.' 'But I really am sorry! I'm sorry. I don't even remember.' 'Oh have your doughnut' Lucy says, starting to twist out of coat, Samantha removing the top part of the box, completely, and doing a sound like in a film when it's a joke about heavenly light illuminating the most unlikely of things.

While Lucy separates out all the Yellow folders - a technique she uses but which her co-workers haven't adopted, although it is clearly better for time and accuracy than how they handle their files - Kurt sidles over with the air of a tourist nervous about touching a stature but wanting a photo of doing so. 'What is it, man? I'll be nice.' 'The gist is this' Kurt sniffs, glances around 'you remember when that woman from corporate came in? Not our corporate, but this place's corporate?' 'Nobody ever came in from our corporate, Kurt - there's no distinction you needed to make, there.' 'That's true' he nods, more quietly, after honest consideration saying again 'that's true. Anyway - so you know who I mean?' Lucy just nods, now aligning the Blue folders with their appropriate Yellow - making Kurt stop talking for a moment when she remembers she has to skip one, because a file did not have a Blue and she doesn't want to screw up the order, then giving him a thumbs-up to continue, though he never really stopped, just started whispering even more quietly. 'I got a pretty big crush on her - for serious - even in just those few minutes - to the degree that I honestly - I'm serious - thought about her a bunch and wish I had said something.' 'No, you don't need to feel ashamed for jerking off' Lucy says in a seemingly disinterested way, now setting Red folders with their corresponding Blues and Yellows. Kurt chuckles, goes 'Well, okay, yeah - I won't - I did, I mean, but I won't feel guilty - I already don't.' 'Oh ye gods' Lucy says, overhung head 'I was just joking, man. Don't admit to any chick you've jerked off even once in your life - we like the fiction that only certain guys do that and that our true loves will be identifiable precisely because they don't. Just' she makes an impatient kind of shoving motion with her elbow, fingers wiggling 'get on with it.' 'Okay: I was on a dating website. And I came across her picture. Even before I verified - because everyone uses a codename on the site, you know? - I knew it was her. Even though she looked different. Like even better - but the same, like I knew her.' Lucy nods nods nods and affixes the sticky-grip to her index-finger, listening with eyes sarcastically wide. 'The thing is: I want to message her. But - one - I don't know if I should say I know who she is and - two - she knows what my job is but I kind of say I have different job on the site and - three - I don't want to change what I say on the site, in general, because that tends to work out fairly well, as far as getting people to message me.' This seems to be the end of what Kurt has to say. Lucy finishes going through the first Yellow, setting the three sheets she needed from it underneath. Then, opening the Blue file, she looks over and says 'She'll like that you lied. You're a temp-worker, Kurt. A temp-worker. Here. The fact that you're a liar is only a step up from that! Just send her a message. I promise she doesn't remember who you are, anyway. Hardly I even do.'

Sheltered by the fact that the rear door to the offices she works in opens right into the enclosure with the dumpster and compactor, Lucy lights a cigarette and can see that rain has stopped, feverish sunlight, still ashen cold, hiccoughing and shoehorning itself through any weak cloud-cover, as though in some delusional tizzy to save face for having been held up. Her cig smoke mixes with the treacly wafts from the compactor and this mixes with the umbrella scent of stale cardboard. Samantha taps Lucy's shoulder - which, Lucy knows, means Samantha had slowly approached down the corridor and stood looking at Lucy's back silently for at least two full minutes before working up the nerve to make this physical gesture - and Lucy, keeping to her resolution, just smiles, dead-set on making Samantha start a conversation, for once. Hopeless, though. Lucy gives up after the fourth time Samantha flicks the guardrail and giggles at the echoing Ding it causes. 'You need a cigarette?' 'Kinda' Samantha shrugs like a hug of her shoulders toward her chin. Lucy takes out her pack - while she does, noticing Samantha lightly touch her index-finger to a spot on her lip, look at this fingertip intently, seem to decide she does not know what the fingertip or the spot of saliva on it means, then wipe her hand, splat splat, front and back over her tummy - and says 'Sorry, it's a shit brand - but I was in the mood for something that tastes as much like glass and formaldehyde as possible.' Samantha mouths a cooed 'Thank you' catches up to what Lucy had said, uncertainly says 'I'm sure it'll be fine' turning the cylinder of the cig around a few tips before lipping it, lighting it, taking a long drag. 'Verdict?' Lucy says, wriggling her fingers for her lighter back after Samantha takes a second drag. And, with a blush, Samantha hands the lighter across while explaining she can't tell the difference between cigarette brands. 'That's okay' Lucy chains herself another smoke lit 'I still can't tell why everyone was so happy to learn the Earth was round, you know? Considering that's just the way it is and had been all along.' After a pause, Samantha ventures 'But some people were mad, right? In history?' Lucy goes thoughtful, wanting to encourage this unexpected contribution - and this gumption, as well - from Samantha, then says 'That's true. I guess I mean I don't get why people are still excited. I'd have thought they'd eventually have gotten sad because now they don't have anything else to prove it looks like.' Samantha nods. Actually smiles. Chuckles. Lucy nudges her, shoulder-with-shoulder, and she nudges back. 'You're funny, Lucy. I think you're funny.'

It's the same, this job. Endless. Elegant in its endlessness. A simplistic function. Like living the slow process of evolution but realizing along the way you're inside of a thing that ain't gonna sprout a different beak, ever. No permutations. No nuances. Not things someone who has worked the job two years knows that someone who has worked the job two weeks doesn't. No supervisor. Once-a-week the two or three people from the company's actual offices show up to replenish the files in the *To-Do* stacks and to cart off the sorted manila folders and the boxed-up Yellow, Blue, Red, but there is very little chit-chat between the two groups. Lucy has caught on that one of the men has a thing for Samantha - or at least likes to steal glances at her ass when he's able - but other than that they aren't even fun to dissect. This is a Wonder World for Lucy! It is what the word *Kindergarten* feels like to an adult. Cut-and-paste and glue-sticks! Paintings that will dry on clothes-pins and no one expects to resemble anything. Names written on papers by teachers. Sandboxes. Monkey bars. The days-of-the-week and the weather. Lucy could do her job neither better nor worse. No one re-checks the files. She knows they don't. If a manila folder is lacking one of the papers that should have come from Yellow, no one at the Main Office is going to go through Yellow - or even if they do, they just will, they won't care. Sticker shaped like an apple with the words *You're super!* That's what this job feels like, every second she spends in it. A cloak of mundanity the way mundanity should be - the way one would intellectualize it. No suffering. No progress. No longing. No summit. Just sameness always feeling the same always feeling the same - the samness never unsameing, the way it feels to feel the same never feeling anything but just the same as it did the last time it felt the same. No terror. No precipice. No down-comforters. No warm arms. This is exactly what a job should feel like and Lucy, while working, understands human blood should not be hot or cold but lukewarm, bathwater thick, flow with a trace of soap and a trace of grime from soaked skin. She even signs in and signs out on paper - no punch-clock! Timecards for the temp agency she prints right from the computer - there in the corner - always on the last of the week, just before leaving. One time the computer was down - so what did she do? Had Samantha white-out her paper and made two photocopies - problem solved! And then separate ways went until next week. Endless. The same. Beginingless. The same. It makes her loathe anyone saying they admire anything!

'Do you think it's bad that that fire-extinguisher says it hasn't been inspected in two years?' That was Samantha asking. The first impromptu question Samantha has ever asked - or at least the first chummy, standing-right-in-close and smiling, we're-in-this-together faced. Lucy's thoughts? One: Why was Samantha looking at the fire-extinguishers and reading their inspection tags? Two: It probably is bad. Three: Wouldn't it be marvelous if Samantha hadn't been looking at the fire-extinguishers, but really was having a mental collapse of some kind and literally meant the fire-extinguisher had said - as in spoken - to her that it hadn't been inspected in two years? 'We do work around a lot of paper, I mean' Samantha absently adds, whisking one of the necessary papers out of the Red folder Lucy is going through before Lucy gets a chance. 'You're an ace. I should pay you to do this for me.' 'Yeah yeah' Samantha very quietly says, hint of blush, and snapping-turtles another of the Red papers. 'Are you really worried about the fire-extinguisher?' 'Not unless there's a fire, I guess. There never has been, so far - so maybe that's why they don't inspect them very much.' Better and better - Samantha is Lucy's new favorite hobby! 'Where's Kurt, though?' it occurs to Lucy to ask. 'He had to go to the orthodontist.' Of course he did! And of course Samantha would say *Orthodontist* instead of merely *Somewhere* or *The doctor*. Because Samantha doesn't know what an orthodontist is, specifically - that's why it's so delightful! Prove it? Prove it!? Scrunch-faced Lucy: 'The fuck is an *orthodontist*? Kurt has cancer? Isn't that a cancer doctor?' Samantha - blink blink, waitaminute to her features - mounting concern says 'Is it? He never said what it was for, just he was going. I kind of pictured someone looking at his bunions or something.' Fight the giggles, Lucy - straight-face it. 'Does he have bunions?' 'I don't know' wide-eyed insists Samantha 'I just thought so because he said *Orthodontist*. But - maybe not.' And they spend the next few minutes planning out how they will delicately get to the bottom of it, upon Kurt's return. And then drift into Samantha's continual irritation that this place doesn't even have a vending machine 'Even though I always tell them how much money it'd make.' 'I'd buy something. Every day' Lucy says, tone of I-

664 / PABLO D'STAIR

agree. 'Me too!' Samantha beams. Then Samantha tells a story about how one building her boyfriend once worked in had a vending machine that even had sandwiches in it. 'That's nonsense' Lucy scoffs, opening a new Yellow. 'Sandwiches? Naw - you dated a maniac who told you his mad imaginings.' 'And salads and stuff. Even soup!'

The only gripe Lucy has with these offices is that, from the parking lot and from the corridor, they always seem they should be empty - Receptionist, Lucy, Samantha, Kurt - but every time she goes to use the toilet, someone else is in there. Always. She has not once been alone in the toilet within the confines of this office park. It has made her quite conscious of the fact that if she goes too long without the resetting isolation - the variety that only comes from alone-in-a-restroom - she feels a lack, a build-up, her thoughts become more bent on looking for companionship. Weird. If she had someone to tell, she'd tell them. She has told her imaginary biographer, because that is the only person she wouldn't have to spend twenty minutes explaining context and background information to before making her point. Even then, she did go into a lot of background. This time: both stalls are occupied and a woman - who looks the way one would personify a frowning toenail - is leaning to the counter between the two sinks, licking her thumb-tip and using the moisture to bit-by-bit erase something she had notated on the back of her hand. Note: this woman keeps licking and erasing even during the ten awkward seconds she holds silent eye-contact with Lucy. Now, turning her eyes down, the woman, as though paid to and not paid enough, gruffs 'Full house - so you can just wait with me.' 'I actually only came in to talk to myself while looking in the mirror' Lucy puts out there, over-solicitous, hack-comic posture of taking a stomp-step and opening her hands wide like Ta-da! Tough crowd. 'Where do you work?' Lucy hush-tones, leaning on the counter now too, feeling some wet soak in at the rump of her pants, imagining the other woman is sitting in a puddle, as well. Sigh as long as a derby-horse stride first, eventually the woman says 'For *Zing Entertainment*. Whoopie, right? *Zing!*' And Lucy stands awed by the performative vocal quality that allowed those six words to be the most rundown, wormwooded, and decrepit the language has to offer. More than ever, she needs to know what that woman has on her hand that won't seem to come off. Flush goes one toilet. And out of the stall comes a woman who has that bird-perched look of she will deny what she was just doing no matter how much the evidence has her to bang-to-rights - little strut of 'I'm not washing my hands, because I've obviously applied an antibacterial sanitizer and thus am lacing and rubbing my fingers like this.' That woman gone, the woman beside Lucy still does not move. 'Go ahead' Lucy hears, looking over from where she had admired the snooty woman's skirt as it had exited to find her companion making antsy head nudges indicating how Lucy should enter the vacated stall. 'Oh - you were here first, no worries' says Lucy. The woman shrugs, though. Explains 'I'm in no rush' licks thumb - rub rub rub - says 'Really, you should go ahead.'

LUCY JINX HAS ALWAYS ADMIRED the savvy of diners which open for business affixed to office parks and hotels. And this diner - which has the actual name *Cashdollar Diner* but despite this is referred to not as *Cashdollar's* or *The Cashdollar* or anything to emphasize the glory of that word, but just plebianly as *The Diner* by folks who work in the offices - had the double insightfulness to open plop in the middle of both sorts of places. Lucy is relating these thoughts to Samantha as they wait out the this-time-of-day traffic, always there to make it irritating to cross the road - which at all other hours is basically unused - also explaining that she had been looking to get a job at either the hotel or the diner when she happened to see an advertisement for the temp-agency that eventually got her working where the both of them now work. Samantha says she finds that spooky, but observes that it obviously doesn't really mean anything. Trucks and trucks and trucks and cars and cars and cars just come at such an unrelenting dribble that finally Lucy simply darts out - surprised she doesn't receive any honks, though she supposes there was no real danger - and then looks back at stranded Samantha, still toe-in-the-watering it at the opposite curb. So: what about Samantha, Lucy? What about her, what? She is a real pal, all of a sudden, and chatting - and now your adrenaline from that sprint has you smiling and clapping hands on both thighs trying to coax her to 'Run!' Plus: you asked her to have lunch with you? And look at Samantha - laughing and not moving, evolutionarily certain to starve to death, arms' length from the trough! 'Do you need me to play traffic cop!?' Lucy calls out. And Samantha gives Lucy a pouty-stern stamp-of-the-foot and - not running, just walking fast - finally braves the currents and arrives safe and sound. 'You were Shaft! That's how to do it, Sammy!' 'Who's Shaft?' Samantha asks. 'Nobody. Just some bad-mother-shut-your-mouth - you don't know who Shaft is?' Samantha gets out of this conversation by faux-impatiently pointing out to Lucy that now they are just standing there and 'Shouldn't we go - you know? - eat stuff?' Lucy I-suppose-sos and the two lock to step with Lucy saying how she still remembers the words to a piano song out of *Teaching Little Fingers To Play* called *Traffic Cop*. To Lucy's delight, Samantha starts singing it, straight away. '*Traffic go / Traffic Stop / All must heed / the traffic cop.*' And here Lucy joins in, as they approach the dingy door - Lucy noting there is an overturned hamburger and some mayonnaise smears all along the top of that newspaper dispenser, makes a wide berth of it - the two harmonizing 'When I'm grown / I shall be' - the last words said with decrescendo and dramatic baritone - 'Just - as - fine - a - cop - as - he.'

Boothed where - this is Lucy's feeling - Office-sorts are boothed - Lucy is certain this diner enforces some sort of tacit segregation policy, hotelers not meant to elbow-to-elbow with working stiffs - Lucy decides to see what will happen if she just let's Samantha take the lead on ordering. Why? Because this Samantha is morphing so totally before Lucy's eyes from being the Samantha who she has shared a work-space with for almost half-a-year into something as-yet-to-be-determined that it is a kind of entertainment to see how it proceeds without prompt. 'Have you had the pizza, here?' Lucy has not. 'Neither have I' frowns Samantha toward the face of her menu, a busboy tossing some straws onto their table without word, nod, or eye-contact as he passes 'but I want to - I hear it's good.' Lucy opens her straw - because she always opens straws immediately when they are wrapped and in front of her, has a hard time not opening Samantha's as well, just might in a moment, actually - and says 'I can't hear letter Ds - so to me you just suggested how word-on-the-street is that the pizza here is Goo.' Points for taking-this-non-sequitur-in-stride are awarded to Samantha, who just nods and says 'I've heard about people like you' in a half-distracted way, consternated kiss-lips still leering at her menu. 'Let's get a pizza, then. We can have an adventure.' There it is - Lucy has opened Samantha's straw, too! 'You're the boss' Lucy says, pushing the straw across, balling both wrappers together and hiding them behind the salt shaker. Points to Samantha for absolutely no reaction to that. Then: a waitress. Drink orders. And: 'We're ready.' And: pizza order. And: Lucy chiming up 'Can you not put a lot of sauce on it? I want to be reminded of the fact that tomatoes have something to do with my meal, as little as possible.' And: waitress No-probleming then heading off. 'I love sauce' Samantha says, but in a non-threatening way, just casually pointing out this defect for Lucy to know. 'This place should have jukeboxes' Lucy laments 'or well-thumbed joke-books on each table. All diners. Not just this one.' 'I've never been to a diner that had joke-books on the table.' Lucy hasn't either, but doesn't say so. And Samantha asks 'What song would you play if there was a jukebox?' 'Doin' The Butt by Experience Unlimited, obviously' Lucy scoffs, then - as though honestly affronted - jabs 'You probably don't even know what that is, do you?' Samantha just rolls her eyes. Points. High marks. One to keep some tabs on. 'You really don't like tomatoes?' 'I don't like anything that requires an E to be pluraled.' Which gets a blat of laughter - milk would be coming out of her nose had Samantha been taking a drink of the stuff. 'The alphabet has a lot to do with you, eh?' Samantha says, quickly, meekishly quieting down.

Prediction: Lucy will be invited somewhere by Samantha come the end of this meal - by the end of work, no question, but likely after the first piece of pizza is finished, at that pivoting segue-moment when all is causal and tossaway so people roll the dice. Reasoning: Now Samantha, adding pink-packaged sweetener and blue-packaged sweetener to her coffee, nudges nose in the direction of the diner counter and tonelessly states 'I have a thing for that guy' - and when Lucy looks, figuring it is the only regular looking guy at the counter whom Samantha is meaning, Samantha addendums 'Well, I had a thing for him, anyway.' Explanation of Reasoning: This is a sudden injection of not-exactly-small-talk, not-personal-intimation in just as harmless a way as singing *Traffic Cop* was or what have you - naming songs, things like that - and such injections, at this point in a first-meal-shared, are linked to the desire to be on familiar terms, a kind of insta-friending is achieved by mentioning some sort of unrequited romance - alternatives are to mention an ex being behind on child support or being irritated that a relative has been calling up, soliciting advice, out of the clear blue sky. Some Stray Observations: Lucy does not believe Samantha, at all - indicates this via the subtlety of saying 'What kind of thing did you have with him?' distinct emphasis on *Kind* - pronounced like *Kiiiind* - and *Thing* - pronounced as though lordishly affronted, gruff, face like observing a termite pulling up its pants after shitting on the floor - the trick being to replace the word *For* - as Samantha had used - with *With* - so that Samantha has to be caught between going with Lucy's seeming misinterpretation or making a correction to her original statement - the pause in which the choice is made all that is needed to mark the harmless falsehood. Current State of Things: Samantha chose to correct, saying 'No, no - I've never talked to him, I just see him here sometimes - or it might not even be the same guy, but I think that's him' - all of this covering the bases of the deceit, Lucy knows the drill - 'and it's probably some sort of conditioning, you know?' Note: Lucy knows, nods, gives another look over toward the counter and then changes the subject to 'What's the difference between the pink and the blue, there - and why do you use both? Just to seem like a goddamned serial-rapist or something?' Detail of Scene: that is the millionth time Samantha has glanced at the tattoo showing on Lucy's forearms - Lucy has caught Samantha looking at work, too - now that Lucy is out of coat and sleeves-rolled-up, but Lucy does not indicate she has noticed Samantha's glimpses, figures it will be brought up when they get together - 'If they get together' Lucy side-bars in her thoughts - as it is predicted they will, the invitation coming sometime during this meal.

So, Lucy is a poet? Each take a first bite of the pizza - both keen enough to let the pie, as a whole, stand for a few minutes before taking a portion, neither making any verbal note of this. Yes, Lucy says she is. The greatest living poet of this generation - by which she does not mean 'Her own generation' but rather the current generation - meaning she's better than the new crop. 'But people from your generation are better than you?' 'Yep' says Lucy, but explains she is okay with that - as long as she maintains her generation's overall superiority to the whippersnappers, she finds her ranking amongst her own quite irrelevant. 'I read poems in school sometimes, but I don't think I ever understood any of it.' And what did Samantha go to school for? Some sort of degree in something having to do with Psychology and then something else about a highly particularized sort of History that Lucy cannot help by point out 'Seems to have very little to do with anything actual, don't you think?' As it turns out, Samantha does agree with that. And tells about the moment - while reading some research on some trace elements or some-such-thing which indicated the Roman baths did nothing to keep the Romans sanitary - she decided she might be wasting her life by pursing the study. 'Because I couldn't think of a time anyone had ever once suggested the Roman baths had kept the Romans sanitary or healthy. I could remember the fact they had baths, but who ever said *Thus: the Romans were some squeaky-clean, clear-bill-of-health sorts*? It's obvious they weren't.' 'We need no germ come from the grave to tell us this' Lucy sombers. 'No. We don't. No, we don't' Samantha repeaters as though floating in Epsom salts. 'Are you a psychologist?' 'Kinda. Yeah.' 'Me, too.' 'Poets seem smart. But then, sometimes I got mad reading poetry because maybe they are just dumb.' This is fairest assessment of anything Lucy has ever heard! She thrills interior but exterior keeps the façade cucumber. 'Hey - do you like horror movies?' Lucy adores horror movies. 'As long as they are actually Horror - I don't like bullshit ones that try to be comedic or fun.' Yes, from facial expression it is evident Samantha agrees with Lucy. 'I saw they are playing *Texas Chainsaw* on the big screen at this midnight film-series. Everyone I know doesn't understand Horror, though.' Lucy will only go if Samantha can get the full question out. Fine: Lucy wants to go, so gives a bit of a prompt - 'I hear when it first played, people were so shocked they stood up and walked out, half-comatose, middle of the showing. Or that might have been another film - *The Entity* would have done that to me, for example.' 'You should come' - Samantha says, second slice of pizza to gob, bite taken. 'I hadn't heard that about *Texas Chainsaw* - but I could see that. Yeah.' Lucy takes up second slice. Chew chew. Chew chew. Drinks some coffee and coughs.

Is Samantha pretty? Lucy sighs where she is perched on the toilet seat. 'I don't know' she rubs her eyes, yawns 'who cares? Does she need to be?' But at the same time - does Lucy find Samantha attractive? Searching memory banks. The distraction of urine refusing to initiate gumming up the works of her thought process. What was the question? Gah! Fuck human bodies! What is Lucy's most fervent wish, these days? To once - just once, just to have the experience - wake up from a long sleep - she means an absurdly over-indulgent one, two days in a hotel, alone - without the waking being at all accompanied by the urgency to piss. Or shit. To be awake and to lay without some prickly-heat instantly getting her to feet, to chill, prodding her first steps to purpose. She hates how in the morning something that seems it should be too complex to be involuntary is, for all intents and purposes. No choice! No choice! She must have had her phone in her pant pocket, because she hears a muffled vibration near her ankles. And what had she been thinking about? Right. Samantha. Is she pretty? Lucy gets her phone out, crick-ricks her one shoulder, her other, decides 'Sure - she's fine looking, as far as it goes.' But then: all stop. Layla. Text-message. *Oh God - are you having an episode or something? What's up?* Dials immediately. 'Layla!' 'Lucy!' this Lucy said with a knowing groan of I-am-going-to-have-to-explain-something-to-deal-with-your-endless-make-believing-aren't-I? 'Is everything okay?' 'Lucy - oh God - why wouldn't everything be okay?' 'Is everything okay with you? There isn't something awful - you didn't die of some syndrome you never told me about or something?' And then just a string of long-suffering 'Oh Christs' from Layla and soon Lucy laughing. But then getting stern. 'You didn't sound like you in your messages! And you know what I mean!' 'I didn't sound' - pronounced *sss-ow-end* - 'like anything! Last thing I sent was a text!' 'You didn't seem like you, then! Whatever you texted' - right, Lucy, like you don't remember! - 'and so then I obviously figured you had to tell me you were dying - and then I never heard from you!' 'Lucy - this was all today.' 'It was yesterday!' But Layla meant it was 'within the last day.' And anyway, Layla shoves in before Lucy can get a head of nonsensical steam going 'I just wanted to talk with you because I was annoyed that Brigit won like fifty-thousand dollars!' 'Who's Brigit?' 'Some bitch who won fifty-thousand dollars - aren't you listening!?' The world has softened and loosed its tie, undone its top few buttons, little curve of white, oven-ham flesh showing and Lucy leans back, wincing a tad at the urine which still does nothing but sizzle and not fall. 'I feel like I'm pissing bubble-bath' she tells Layla who just says 'Are you pissing, right now?' with a degenerate solicitousness that brings to mind animated pigs salivating over other animated pigs they are boiling and adding apples to in animated pots over animated fires.

And Lucy shares the good news with Samantha: 'Oh - my friend isn't dead! I was so certain she was - and that I'd killed her through my lack of vigilance. You see, Samantha: it's very dangerous to know me - because I'm a marked-sort, I'm of the variety which Mother Nature was invented to snuff, no ceremony, meant to be scapegoat to every and anything. I'm sure you understand, you seem like you would. Because I'm cagey - a regular *Br'er Rabbit* - and I don't, for example, get into vans with serial murderers or go places people which are wont to blow up to prove political points. No - I am gifted in remaining statistically not-a-casualty. And so those close to me - I say this as warning as much as explanation-tied-to-celebration - are always at great hazard. The world, Samantha, is a coffee-swirl or a blood-stain-soaking-into-herringbone-blazer - some sort of mechanism mixing swirls and patterns, circling to close on me like the jaw of a clock-face. Collateral damage to this is: patterns emerge which can lay waste to those near to me. Miscalculations - you see? - on my part can cause something incidental - wanting to, I don't know, sleep in and so I miss an appointment which upsets me so I leave the house and miss a phone call or something, anything, it's hard to explain, it's felt in the guts, not blathered in the brainpan - which will afflict, severely, someone. My friend - her name is Layla - for example. She made the grave mistake of not seeming herself in a text-message she sent when I was in an odd frame-of-mind and in the middle of something. What happened? I decided to not respond to her, right away. But - this is the thing - I did note to myself I felt something bad was going on. Something bad - distinctly - it felt exactly the way you know someone in another room in a nightmare is also right behind you and already in front of you. Had I gotten back to her straight away - problem solved. Bad would be subverted - like resetting a time-loop. But since I didn't, it would have technically been allowable for the world - which, as I stated, but to reiterate, has aims against me, keeps me at caution - to do something as bad as what I thought to myself but ignored. Anyway. My point is that Layla is just fine and dandy. I talked to her in the toilet - on my phone, I mean - so I must have done something right which made the world think *No - don't kill Layla, keep her alive for now and think of something worse for later*. I don't know what good thing I did - but something. Just to keep you in the loop, you know? I tread a tricky life.'

Samantha decides - hesitant after Lucy insisted she wanted to pay for the whole meal - that she will take the pizza home with her. 'But only because you're making me.' 'I am making you' Lucy says, zipping coat, upping collar. 'I like microwaving pizza after it's been out all day. It gets soggy. I wish restaurants could sell it that way, but it's probably against the health laws of our democracy or something.' The expression *Health Laws* - for just a moment - sounds like an absurdity to Lucy. Then - now - on second thought, seems totally accurate and even banal. 'Hey - why do you work this job?' Lucy asks as they return out into the now paper-thin cold, wind like scissor cuts across perfectly dotted lines. Samantha doesn't know. She was surprised she stayed on, actually. She says 'I'm in good with the Agency - and they know I like to bounce around. I like to bounce around, a lot. This one just sort of stuck. I've been here' - shivering, pierced by wind-gust expression of thought - 'two years, almost! Most other places I stayed two months, tops. I mean - I've worked for the Agency almost eight years, now, all totaled. I just don't care.' The road is crossed with no trouble now that the mid-day commuter rush is finished. Lucy is in thought, trying to decipher how much of what - and how much of *How* - Samantha is saying is honest versus how much is based on cues from Lucy's meal-time rantings. Samantha is lighting a cigarette - not able to with the wind, no matter how she positions herself - now aided by Lucy standing in close and surrounding - Lucy's eyes turned down and chin nearly touching the top of Samantha's head as Samantha snuzzles in and cranes around her finally-lit cig. Lucy chains her own lit from Samantha's. 'That was a long lunch' Samantha says as the two loiter outside the entrance-door to finish smoking. 'It was' Lucy concurs. 'You think Kurt already left? Or is that his car? I never know which car is Kurt's. It's something so ordinary.' Lucy has nothing to say to this - watches her smoke thrashed and its bones picked by the brittle air, ghost-clawed at by ghosts. 'You know what Kurt told me the other day? That he has been divorced to the same woman twice! The one he's divorced from, now. But don't tell him I told you - I think I said it'd be something I wouldn't repeat. He was sad when he said it.' Is this a test? Lucy can't help but wonder. Is Kurt one to tell everyone something personal and ask not to have it related? And Samantha - recognizing how Kurt was telling Lucy something, earlier - is trying to ferret it out? Had Kurt mentioned to Samantha 'Don't tell anyone - well, I told Lucy already, but don't tell anyone else' and so now Samantha is bringing this other thing up to see how far along she and Lucy's new friendship has got? What's the best play here, Lucy? Or can you just relax? 'I'm freezing, man' Lucy says, tosses her stub away. 'You smokers are idiots - I'm going inside.'

Samantha either seems perfectly nice - the sort of person who just needs the right touch to bloom and once bloomed has unique trims in the way they view the world - or else seems like that sort of young girl who'd treat a foreign country like a Theme Park, keep telling French people they look French or point to sidewalks like research went in to recreating them just because such sidewalks are in Luxembourg - seems young like that, only a decade too old to seem young. Lucy can't decide. Samantha is either nuanceless as a bowl bought at the ninety-nine cent store or complex in the way basic math contains the sinews of the theories that we are all just holographic projections on the wall of the Seventh Dimension. Lucy can't decide. What Lucy needs is more information. These clothes Samantha is wearing today - or any clothes Lucy has seen Samantha in - are they just what she wears to work, or indicative of her actual persona, sense-of-self? If not relegated to *Cashdollar Café* where does Samantha eat? And what? Microwave-pizza-left-out - this is a detail Lucy can work with, but it is all too vague. And if Lucy had learned this not within the context of the sudden alteration in behavior patterns - had Samantha just shyly offered the information in one of her typical, nearly mute, nine lines back-and-forth, no more no less, conversations with Lucy - would it have had a whole different ring to it? It's not that Lucy cares what people eat and wear, it's more that she has to admit how today was an anomaly that hasn't proved itself not to be. What will Samantha be like to watch a film with? How harshly is Lucy supposed to grade her? On the one hand: Samantha is harmless and could fit snugly within the cast of a silent-film. But on the other hand: Samantha could be a slyly controlling sort, all imposture to lure those she is newly interested in into orbits meaningless except to watch for reaction. Wait. Do you feel manipulated by Samantha now, Lucy? No. Samantha - look - is just back to work. Yes, yes - Lucy knows that. But see! Samantha does not sort the files anywhere near as cleverly and efficiently as Lucy - and Samantha has been employed here two years! One file at-a-time? This is what Lucy means! Now it's going to be harder to hold her tongue about that! 'You're a trouble-maker' Lucy says, Samantha looking up. 'A trouble-maker - yes, you' Lucy says, affixing the sticky over her index-finger and laying out some Yellow folders. 'I just want you to know that I know what you're doing.' Samantha nods. Either thoughtlessly or having just won the hand-in-play.

Lucy is trying to seem as though she is not paying any attention to anything apart from the sorting out her documents, but in fact sees Kurt humbly whisper something to Layla along the lines of 'I didn't get enough to eat, can I have your pizza?' because Layla, after giving a snooty face probably accompanied by a tongue-cluck, graciously hands over the box and is quite clearly saying 'Oh stop, don't worry about it.' But why all the whispering? Lucy. Or has everyone always kind of whispered, at work? Lucy. Lucy! What? You do know you just called Samantha *Layla*, right? Had Lucy done that? She had. For how long? And now, on cue, there goes Lucy's phone and it can be all but guaranteed it is going to be Layla. *If I get a syndrome now - or die in even a general way - know I have told vengeful friends that you are to be held exclusively to blame. Asshole.* So Lucy texts back *In my thoughts, I have been calling my co-worker you.* Five minutes pass with no response. Lucy has gone through an entire folder without paying attention. There probably were necessary documents in there, Lucy - and while it is true you cannot possibly get in trouble for not going back to verify, you really ought to. Samantha leaves the room at Kurt's summoning. Which has some import. Had Kurt and Samantha been discussing Lucy? Discussing Samantha arranging to go to lunch with Lucy? Is that even what had technically happened? Who had invited who? But even if Lucy didn't do the inviting, had Samantha clever-girled it that way? 'Who's fucking in charge here!?' Lucy growls. And, again, reaches the end of the file and has not even paid any attention. Try again. Focus. Paper. Paper. Paper. Paper. Paper. When is the last time you wrote a poem, Lucy? It seems like it's been awhile. 'It was today!' Was it? You wrote it down? 'What do you mean - I write daily. Why are you asking this?' Paper. Paper. Paper. You didn't look, again! 'Yes, I did! There just wasn't anything there!' Don't you think Kyle and Samantha might be right outside, Lucy? Listening to you carrying on like this? You know: Object Permanence? 'I skipped Object Permanence class, so how would I know what you're yapping about!?' Paper. Paper. Paper. Paper. Paper. On until the end. Nothing. Are you sure? 'This is getting irksome! What do you mean *Are you sure?*' You didn't maybe get caught up with just going through the papers, not even look at them? Did you? Or did you just count them? Maybe you just went through, counting and not looking. How many were there? 'I don't know' Lucy whispers. But you have the number *seventy-four* in your head, right? Count them. 'Eighty-one.' But that's close - you might just have miscounted! And see: that time you weren't looking, either! 'I wasn't supposed to be! I was just counting! And it was your idea that I was!'

Samantha returns after almost an hour. Kurt does not. And right over to Lucy, Samantha flutter-steps. 'Hey buddy' she says in imitation of the way the phrase was once spoken by someone on a popular television show or in some movie. 'Did you eat Kurt?' Samantha nods and touches her nose, then moves the finger to her lips, hushingly. But really, it is explained, Kurt is in some sort of bad way and was trying to chum up to Samantha to plead his case about maybe room-mating with her for awhile. 'While he gets divorced, again?' Samantha smacks Lucy on the arm - quite hard, really, delightful - and casts anxious glances over her shoulder as though Kurt will prestidigitate and explain he is scandalized at having his confidence betrayed. 'So - are you going to let him?' A God-no! kind of play-shudder, Samantha goes on about she does know someone in the same apartment complex as her who would probably be keen on it. 'So - you know? - I try to be helpful.' 'You do know you sort the files in a pointlessly longwinded way, right?' Samantha blinks. 'What do you mean?' Lucy, stop. 'Well' - you can't even hide the haughty tsk, Lucy? come on! - 'why do you do it just one file at-a-time?' This question in grade-school tones of *Your dad works at the grocery-store, right?* mockery. 'How else would I do it?' Lucy indicates the spread in front of herself. 'Don't you see how I've been doing it? This is so much faster, man.' A pause. 'I can teach you. It's just' - Lucy grits teeth as though it's just oh-so-hard to bring herself to say this but - 'the way you do it is the dumb-person-way. But I don't think you're dumb.' Samantha guffaws. 'How long have you wanted to say this to me?' 'Since my first day or something - why do you think I do it this way? Seriously. You can get through it so much faster this way!' Samantha gives dubious once-overing to Lucy's spread, pointing and wiggling fingers as though taking measurements and building a mental ship-in-a-bottle. 'I don't think it winds up going any faster that way, Lucy' - did she say *Lucy* like *Loosey* like the first attempt at a nickname? - 'I think you might just be thinking it does.' A polite argument ensues. Lucy rests her case on the phrase: 'The Assembly-Line Method revolutionized modern production!' But Samantha is unmoved. 'We'll see. I think this is a John-Henry-was-a-steel-driving-man situation we have here. Let's put money to mouths, duel this out.' 'I don't need a duel, Sammy' - no reaction to that, either positive or negative - 'I have logic, math, and the fact that the Assembly-Line Method revolutionized modern production on my side!' And Samantha sighs like a kid scribbling out a perfectly fine drawing of a butterfly for some reason that will never be explained and drifts back to her station. Then after a moment says 'You do know I get paid the same as you, no matter what, right? That's where you can stick your assembly-line.' Lucy blinks. Blinks. Retortless. Samantha, Lucy knows, over there and all inwardly flushing triumphal.

WHY DRIVE HOME YET WHEN there are the remains of this early afternoon to roam the usual protractored circle in? The sky? What about it? Croupy, the wind - croupy, the sunlight - runny nose, the clouds. Out there, the weather, it's that barking seal cough and the slithering gravel upsuck of mucus from nostril cusp down throat-back - drip drip drip - down gut a tumult to tummy-ache. And Lucy is driving how she always drives. Postage-stamp of her current existence when not ready to shut in. Does she wish she were an agoraphobe? Sure. Kind of. Or something diagnosable. As it is, she is this: she knows that she will not get lost no matter which of these numerous roads she takes - that she will be able to find her way back from any directionless meander - but still tenses like how strong a kid thinks a pencil is at the thought of irrevocable wrong-turns, keeps to the round she has chalked out. And this round - what is it? Composed of the roads that lead to the few places she has normal occasion to go, linked together with the same stretch of connections. This: a jaunt through a well up-kept community of townhomes. Here: Lucy Jinx, pulling on to Highway *X*, which she will follow until the Exit for *Meal Road* - a good name for a road, though she was disappointed to learn it was dubbed for some local moneybags' previous-generation relation, Scott Meal or Carlton Meal or something, the *Meal Museum* disappointingly associated with the fella, as well - and *Meal Road* she drives as it becomes various other roads. She knows it all by sight. If she crashed, required assistance, she would be able to say where she was - yes ma'am she would, down to the nearest tree stump! Eventually her drive opens to *The Walcott Shops at Walcott* - creative to the last, eh? - where she will sometimes eat and sometimes shop for clothes. And then around the back of the shops, across a bridge that takes her through a brief industrial area - many things in these fields, rusted-out and reclaimed by prickers or ivy or mold, sometimes cockroaches, big as thumbs, in legion covering the street in stripes for her to plough through. This all coming her back out onto the Highway in the opposite direction, which she follows back out to her workplace before taking the proper Exit - *Marvin Drownding Avenue*, which she likes because she thinks it was named by a two-year-old watching their friend screaming for help as a riptide had at them - for home - sometimes doing an offshoot toward *Niice Plaza* or a different offshoot toward the abandoned shopping-center with the husk of a movie theatre and the husk of a gas station bold sentry, keeping the numerous overturned shopping carts and some discarded rubbish, which she always imagines to be a corpse-hid-in-plain-sight, in line.

Ah, Lucy Lucy. Now your brain feels lips-locked and lock-jawed and the recorder on the dash spins without your voice saying anything and your imaginary friends are in the backseat, pissy-hearted with body language of crossed arms. How shut down you have become - and all because you need healthier sleep habits! She chides herself and then explains to herself that chiding herself is no good because she isn't listening, anyway, tunes herself out so neatly she forgets which side of the dispute she is on. As she drives, what does she remember? Lucy remembers: being young enough that cold weather seemed a reason to go out, hands pocketed and ears muffed and borrowing extra scarves from whoever she was with. A pile of crusted, traffic-soot snow was something to be remarked upon, some statement made about it representing Beauty, maybe even a pal would take a snapshot to mark the occasion - Oh because Lucy, young Lucy, had so much to say that nobody else had ever or could! Remember when it was your place to enlighten the dopes, Jinx? The vulture sad-sacks who were living wrong and somehow not graced with your radiant above-it-all? This is what Lucy remembers. How she thought everyone was waiting for a mystery into their life, how if she said it hard enough that something could be cured by magic or forgotten about because she decided to do a little dance move and say 'Doesn't matter, let's go!' then - well! - that is how it would be! So easy to fix it all, Lucy remembers - she could see the seams of everything and had read ahead and knew how it all went. And she remembers Elliott's face, so puny in its I-think-I-ought-to-be-sad-about-this-so-I-am-acting-sad as Elliott said 'Lucy, I don't know' and 'I never meant to' while she was just waiting for Lucy to leave and - really really - wondering if Lucy would break something before she went. Every single thing replaceable in that damned apartment! No statement to make! Even the removal of herself didn't count, because that was the surgery-at-hand! Scalpel. Forceps. Nurse, my brow, my brow!! You wanted to be anesthetized? Shit, you should have said so - just try biting the bottom of yer lower teeth with the top of yer upper, there's a good girl! And: incision! And: remove! And:

cauterize! Lucy remembers all of this. And she remembers shoplifting youngster, when she would gladly have paid instead just had no way to get money. And remembers, not long later, paying for everything - would prefer to shoplift if she didn't have to worry about the results! Never the right age, Lucy - in fact, virtuoso at being the wrong one. Like now. When you were a kid, people as old as you are now would be talking about the wars they fought in when they were twenty-years younger than you are now! But don't think about that. Picture them young, those people. Not how they are, contemporary - spoon-fed food they are told the name of as though this means they chose it. Don't think of the type of clinical, bedpan-alone you will wind up - not even once-upon-a-time-war-hero, just Lucy Jinx.

Lucy has thought herself into a corner, so pulls in to park in this lot - outside a store identified as *VacuumsMops !!!* wondering why there is no space between the lit up first two words but there is a clear space between them, conjoined, and the exclamation point trio. And on this thought, nuzzles herself, head-top to window of locked door, and closes her eyes. Start slideshow: Lucy, teenaged, pushing in coin-return slots of public-telephones, curling her fingers ups, wriggling, padding all the cold surfaces she can touch. Next slide: Lucy, grade-school, watching, with her chin in one of the diamonds of a playground fence, two boys at the tree-line, grade-level below her, taking laugh-aloud whizzes out into the leaf piles, gathered brambles, and mulch, watching these boys, after, do long-jumps in the little pit used for that or for horseshoes in Gym class. Next slide: Lucy, mid-twenties, dressing as quickly as she can while whatever-his-name-was screamed at his ex-wife on the phone, Lucy with ears clogged and hearing the sound of her clunking feet-to-floor through pant-legs, feet-to-floor through shoes-put-on, head all the sound of a rattled drawerful of pebbles, index cards, and spilt soda glugging and hissing its froth bubbles, spittle on lips of cotton mouth. Next slide: Lucy, a-little-bit-later twenties, being given a free fancy-coffee at a bookstore café, this lad then sitting with her, the view through the huge café window of - first - some dumpster and - then - the vacant field of the Fair Grounds where - this lad was saying to her - he would sometimes roam after a car-show was done - or a carnival - and would find 'seventy, sometimes a hundred' dollars in loose bills or coins left laying around - all a lie, but she humored him and later didn't kiss him in his air-conditioned front seat. Next slide: Lucy, maybe five, crying in bed by herself, thinking how sad it is she had to die without getting to ever dream even the smallest dream - dignity in the suffering she was bearing, unknown, for all - this to the strains of Classical music she did not have names for yet and which played through static after even-toned announcer voices. Next slide: Lucy, high-school, listening with Scarlet to the tapes the two of them made, silly voices, improvised interviews with classmates, sketches as though radio call-in hosts, clips recorded from television. Next slide: Dorene. Next slide: Dorene. Next slide: Elliott, idiotic Elliott with her 'I want to touch your face so I know you don't hate me.' Next slide: 'But I do.' Next slide: 'Hate you.' Next slide: Refrigerator with papers affixed. Next slide: Lucy, kindergarten, watching Peter throw up, the teacher shooing 'Move move move!' to all the kids - 'Lucy, move, Lucy! Lucy!!' Lucy opens her eyes and can still feel how her arm changed with that teacher's yank.

Brand-newed, Lucy with leisure now parks outside *Hernando's Total*. Into the lot - employee cars, unmoved all, laced with frost and windshields pinning fliers-for-something - she feels like someone seeing their hands for the first time, post-gout. Even her joints popping seem congratulatory. Tonight, it will be Blush wine, she decides - and some microwave hamburgers. And writing! An orchestra of gaseous complaints her innards will be and she will write with pork-grease thick sweat coating forehead and leaking from roof of mouth, will sleep to be woken by Purgatorio urges to shit and will cramp over toilet issuing nothing but groans of how she should not have eaten things she knew would tide in revolt! The wine is easy to procure - cheap stuff, *Fox Street* - but then she remembers *Total* won't have the burgers she is after - those microwaveable, rubella looking patties, that artificial cheese which heats to white and cools to kind-of-seems-yellow-now - because *Total* is too head-in-the-past to admit to what the world has come to be. 'Fine' she states to nobody 'but note my objection.' She finds some high-grade ground beef and will just make her own damned hamburgers, then! But Oh how she will use cheap white-bread instead of a proper bun! 'Bread! Bread, do you hear!?' She will be damned to Hell if she will use a proper bun - and what is it with *Total* that all the buns they sell are sesame-seeded or seem to have raisin shavings embedded into the skin layer? She tells the check-out clerk 'For you own knowledge: the cheap microwave burgers you do not sell here - you know them? - well, the same meat is used in the patties of the cheap sausage patties. I have done tests. Visual and olfactory tests! The only difference - I tell you this just so you know - is a bit of flavor powder. That, and they bleach the sausage a bit more. What do you have to say about it?' The clerk happens to already know this - loves those burgers, he says, all burgers like that. 'You'll survive the coming purge, then - remember I said so when you do. I want it reported how *She was right about that!* when the new world rises. Promise me.' The clerk promises. But the clerk has to refuse the tip Lucy offers. So to save face she says 'That's for the best, really - I couldn't afford it, anyway. That's my rheumatism money! My rheumatism!' And properly baffled, the clerk is left. Lucy - you know you could have bought your cigarettes in there, right? Lucy refuses to buy cigarettes in *Total* because the clerks give her disdain - Oh yes! - and then they keep mum about it due to the hypocritical position they are forced into: health savvy but well hip to how money-makes-the-mare-to-go and that cigarettes attract the dollar bills like celebrity sightings. In that case - since you have to get cigs at the gas station, anyway - you do know you could get the burgers you want there, too? 'Shut up' Lucy says, grocery bag to passenger seat. 'Stop making sense - has it landed you on your feet, ever?'

In her apartment, she curtsies to *Never Forget* and, speaking broadly aloud as she moves to the kitchen, says to the framed thing 'I would flash you some tittie, too, but I'm still bundled up. Maybe later though' she adds after a pause and eating one of the caramels she forgot she still had this little baggie of next to the toaster. If she were the right sort of person, she would jump right in to cooking. Get it out of the way. But look: it's ten minutes later and she hasn't even taken off her coat yet - now laying on the sofa! - or her shoes. The shoes she is tapping the toes of together and looking at the television she would turn on if she hadn't left the remote-control over there. Tonight: maybe don't write. The thought is there. Tonight: just lounge, lay, do nothing, think nothing. You don't always have to be so profound - and you don't always have to strive to empty yourself. Sometimes, in fact, Lucy feels the compulsion to 'do anything but nothing' is unhealthy - that, at times, she is scraping the resin off from her skull curve, getting a result from it, sure, but at a cost. And anyway, she decides, people she greatly admires take breaks all the time! And not just to hang 'round with their pals! She is sure the most productive artist is lazy in their secret heart. That they take time to masturbate very gracelessly, to eat while watching documentaries about spree killers, enjoy arguing with lists of Top Ten this-or-thats in magazines and the like. Jesus, Lucy - is that the impression you have of normal life? Isn't that what normal life is, though? Why is that any less profound than Camus' summing up of modern man *He fornicated and read the newspapers?* Why is Lucy's slapdash derision any lesser than Albert's? It is enough she knows she is not normal. However she characterizes the rest of the world else, she knows she is estranged from it. 'Nope' she says, half-heartedly working at getting one shoe off with the other a moment before giving up 'there is no one else using their spare time to lay eskimoed on a sofa having a conversation like this. That, dear ladies, damned gents, is not what is going on in other apartments. Other televisions would be on! Other coats would be off! Other cooking would be cooking! I spend more time talking about doing things than doing things and spend more time talking about doing things than doing things than talking about doing things!' She struggles to ab-crunch herself upright, abandons the effort, rolls off the sofa and tries to motivate herself to get to paper and pen. This should be preserved for the ages, this statement! Lucy Jinx's rendition of The State of Modern Man! She rolls over on to her tummy. Tries to flop back over on to her back. Can see under the sofa. Doesn't remember when she would have dropped that many crackers or how that soda bottle got there, but sees them. Wants to get up. Doesn't. Closes her eyes.

That's better. The standard Lucy Jinx. Cigarette to-and-froming mouth in an arrhythmia, pantsless and in a t-shirt with a cartoon image of two alarm clocks on it, their eyes wide and scraggled with bloodshot, teeth set on rattle, laying in bed beside each other - one clock per tit, basically, the way this now-too-tight garment fits. While the burger meat starts its sizzle, she takes off her mushy socks and rubs her slick foot-bottoms over the kitchen tiles until they feel dry, scratches at her ankles - especially in the patch of her right one where the skin is a pickling of dozens of pimple-size scabs. Douses cigarette in an old, plump-with-sink-water, last bit of a sandwich, then lights another and adds seasoning to the meat before flipping. Over there? The television rolls out an episode of *Law and Order: Criminal Intent* but one she has seen more than eight times. And there? On the counter is a notebook opened to a blank page, an uncapped pen diagonal across the also-diagonal lay of the book. Big yawn. Poke through various cabinets. Bag of chips taken down - why do you always forget to buy French-fries, Lucy? those should be a staple-crop, by now - and she rummages out a handful, sets this pile on the counter, picks out two which she crunches while setting the remainder of the bag by the plate she will use for the finished burgers. No cheese, either! She moves some long-expired apples, a tube of she's-never-going-to-use-it dinner-roll dough, finds a single slice of wrapped American cheese and sets it on the counter. 'This is a fine how do you do, isn't it?' she pouts, jutting hip and one buttock - which she then scratches - waiting to give the burgers another flip after another seasoning. Finishes off those chips on the counter. Rubs at the spot where they were with the side of her hand. Another big yawn, this time followed by a 'Fucking Hell, sorry - stop yawning, man!' Anything to write yet? Naw. Adds more seasoning to the burgers. Flips them. But doesn't she have a bag of fries - even half-a-bag? 'No' the freezer tells her even before she opens it - but she opens it, anyway, and looks. The empty ice-cream sandwich boxes and the empty French-bread pizza boxes and the unfilled ice-cube trays blink at her like this peering at them broaches the agreement Lucy had made to let them sleep in another hour - all of them go 'What? There's no fries - we told you already!' and so she closes them back into their dark. Another big yawn. 'I told you not to do that, even just one minute ago. Are you just messing with me now or what?' Seasons the burger meat. Flips the things. Presses the spatula down and listens to the heightened cackle of the sizzling oil and fat.

*A word is worth one-thousandth of a picture.* She underlines this, chews the extra slice of bread she took, her burgers waiting for her at the sofa, now, the stuff to brew coffee all set out but just waiting there, still, while she stares at this phrase.

What's the matter? Nothing. You don't like it? I do. Then what? Oh I don't know. It's clever - don't you think? She sighs and supposes she does find it clever and that's why she wrote it. But Lucy is rather tired of *clever*. Of *glib*. Of *summation*. You don't believe in summation? 'No' she says flatly, starts in with the coffee prep. Her biographer holds out the recorder, at the ready, sipping some of the wine. And while her biographer waits, Lucy takes old coffee grounds to the trash, puts new filter in - eyeballing to the scoop of it ten spoonfuls of 'coffee powder' as she calls it - pours the dregs of the previous pot out, swishes tap water around in the pot, pours that out, fills the pot with tap water to the Ten line and sloppily dumps this into the machine before flapping its lid shut and jabbing the Brew button. 'Well?' asks her biographer, emphasizing with slight head-tick and intensity of focus that Lucy is being recorded and so far it's all dead air. 'Words are for moving away from sight, from pictures - words are a new Sense, one which does not require an organ' Lucy says - but then the wind goes out of her sails. 'Is that all?' the biographer asks, a little bit put out and not hiding it - after all, she could have the night off and be with family and friends but instead has lugged herself here, brought her equipment and everything. Lucy hangs her head, the first throat clearings of the heating coffee gruffing from off to her side. 'But as it turns out' Lucy starts, slow, faking a deliberateness she hopes will lead to something cogent 'language is a drift away from clarity. Words are a kind of mathematics - one needs two needs three, three is fifteen, fifteen leads to three more, each of which are one, each one of which, in fact, is four thousand, per. You know what I mean?' 'No.' Lucy moves from the kitchen in the direction of the front door, just absently dawdling her arms in some motion to match her inelegant word spilling. 'To give clarity, more words are needed. One word isn't clear. Two words makes it more clear. But now, each one of those two words needs another word to make each clear. But each time a word is added, it needs a word to make it clear - and, moreover, it never connects to the word it was trying to clarify to begin with, because it cannot clarify without first being clarified. Language is a generous yeast infection, man.' The biographer encourages Lucy to go on, so Lucy is bolstered. 'Okay' Lucy says. Nods. 'Okay.' Hears the coffee percolating and Detective Goran toying with a suspect while Eames and Carver sit idly by.

There are never enough books on her shelf. Lucy hates her shelf for never having enough - and always the wrong - books. Nuded for a shower but positioned right below the heating vent, she touches the spine of each volume, one-by-one, to be certain she is giving the shelf a fair shake. And realizes she owns a lot of books she doesn't even like! *The Declaration of Independence?* She takes this down, utter disbelief, even dismay. Maybe she has had it since high-school or it was used, ages ago, in University? But unlike nearly every other book she owns, it contains no underlines, highlights, or marginalia. A pocketbook of the *Declaration of Independence and the Bill of Rights*. Two documents she honestly has never read and now attempts to, for all of five seconds, before reshelving. *Rumpole* books. Those neat Collector's Editions of T.S.Eliot stuff she was gifted by a professor. *Star Trek* novels she stole with whatever-his-name-was, middle-school, mom out in the car waiting for them, none-the-wiser. *World Without End* one of them is called. And this one she takes up - somehow reminded of the Eliot but unable to think why. Had Eliot used that phrase - alluded to it? She opens the dingy *Trek* paperback, thinking it might open with the Eliot quote, but instead finds a handwritten inscription. *One day you'll be old, my girl, but you're my world, forever.* She blinks. Then, parenthetically, the inscription says *I have no idea if this sentiment fits with the book, hahaha.* Signed *Eliot.* Lucy stares. Blinks. Blinks. Somewhere - there, hear it? - is the shower running, a heat even moreso than the vent air to soothe you, massage you, Lucy. But you are just blinking at this book. Because - no no - it isn't good. This is not a good thing. *For thine is the kingdom.* 'Shit' she burbles and maybe is about to cry. *Life is very long.* Lucy blinks as though doing so will undo a command, keep a thought she knows is coming from being able to. *World without end, amen.* She carefully sets the book back. 'But his name was never Eliot' she says, sniffing, clearing her throat like she had just finished a daydream and was now responding to a shop-clerk. 'Eliot.' Eliot. 'Elliott.' Because the thing is: Lucy had never seen this inscription! From Eliot. Bug-eyed, seventh grade, brillo-haired Eliot. Eliot. 'None of this should be happening, though' she says 'and I'm not going to bother puzzling it out. Eliot's name is *Eliot*, Eliot's surname is *Eliot*, her name was *Elliott* with an extra *L* and an extra *T* like two Eliots collided together - I looked at the Eliot which made me want to pick up the *Trek* and then Eliot had wrote in it and' - here Lucy roughs her hair and menacingly goes Grarahgh! or some such sound before rubbing hands all over her face and declaring 'That doesn't even make sense as a thing!'

In the shower, she resolves to not write tonight. No. Definitively. And not to walk about muttering. *Law and Order* it will be. Though she is a bit wary of television. Likely it is booby-trapped with some connection that will ruin its function as salve. Then what? Just go to sleep? She will go to sleep - but to do so right away would be the wrong maneuver. Giving up. Hidey-holing it. The water reminds her that, these days, her body feels like a body stacked on top of a body, time and pressure geologically shifting the two forms into one. That or she feels like a melting ice-cream cone all over a fever-warmed toddler's hand. It's not very good, looking at herself. Or - that's not true! - it's not very good, others looking at her. Hmn. But even that's not it! *Touching.* The water is *touching.* Not *looking.* And reminding her how wary she is of touch. The water in its looklessness is bad enough - but can Lucy imagine fingertips, tongue-tips, teeth-tips, her flesh gripped and run over by tight hands? Of course she can imagine it - but does she imagine it happening to her, now? In this body? When it happens, doesn't she - automatic-switch - in her brain reconfigure the data processing to include an old image of herself? What a charming question, Lucy! What a delightfully disquieting existential conundrum you've hatched, here! Though - you must remember, Lucy - hadn't you said, just the moment before, this was not a night for thinking? The water reminds her of the feeling of give to her thighs, the weight of deflation, something once soft now hardened, then hardened so long it grew weak, gave up - her thighs are slumped shoulders or lips that can't stay pursed. Good try, Lucy - but you're still thinking about it, so just stare it down. Think of a recent time - go back even five years - and picture yourself entwined with a lover. Get an image. Yes yes, technically you never saw yourself - but you know what you're asking! What did you look like? Think. There is Elliott, Lucy, her hand to your throat and her other hand clawed at your ribs - and you're gripping her breasts as though to gouge from them pits: what do you look like? When do you look like? Ten years prior to that? Fifteen? Which you - from a mirror or photo - gets to live in all your best memories, proper or not? 'I told you, I'm not thinking tonight' Lucy says, shutting the water off and moving directly for her still-damp-from-that-morning and not-washed-in-two-weeks towel. She moves it over her and with it the scent of whatever is growing in it, this scent remaining to her hands until she soaps them in artificial coconut - which her hands will smell like for hours, ruining the enjoyment of at least her next few cigarettes, eyes tensing a headache with each approach of the filter-end for a suck.

It doesn't matter how nothing-to-doed with it feels: a thing is itself. And it doesn't matter how nothing-to-doed with she feels: Lucy Jinx is defined by being pierced by what's snared her. She now, clothed for eventual sleep, slips into her coat and thinks smoking out in the corridor will be the trick. Return from the freezing cold, pass out on the sofa, television mute, eventually groggily polliwog-shuffle to the bed, bury under comforter and - maybe - call off of work, tomorrow. 'And it's your fault' she soliloquys as she walks 'for making yourself so much to do with language. A ridiculous proximity you keep!' This is a very sound observation. She takes a moment to congratulate herself. Wow! It's been language all along, Lucy, that is out to get you. The world? 'Poo-poo the world' she says, dismissing it like some ear-wax unexpectedly found after a scratch. The world is a dog with a bitch and a leash. It's language! It's language which she'd walked into herself and never mistrusted the friendship of. Think on this! And like Bango! a memory that seems apt announces itself to fanfare. Hadn't someone once told her that early language patterns mimicked the physical nature of Hunter Culture? The formation of phrase-work - the building up, like the loping approach of a spear-holder, the spear flung as the sentence momentums, the import of a statement the skewering of the animal to be feted with? Lucy wandered into a thicket of language, a mobling of it and has gotten deeper since! And whenever language thinks she is doing something, reacting in some way away from it - in all of its forms - it reasserts itself through triggers. Language has laid her life out like intricate veins! But language has had her blame her woes on physicality. Two-faced and triple-tongued language! It took advantage of you, Lucy! Even now - proof positive - what are you doing out here? You said 'I'm not going to write - I'm not going to think - I'm not going to *Language*' basically and you made a plan to go to sleep, to off the words, the language centers, and resistance shook and now you're out here talking about it! Look at that graceful disemboweling it manages! You chose to walk back into its opium! 'But no' Lucy says. 'No!' She will undo this. She has to stop metastasizing umpteen words to everything. Everything is words? Everything is words!? Who said that!? There were things before words! Words have tricked us - and Lucy the most us of all! - in to thinking them component to reality. Lucy - you need to stop explaining. Lucy - you need to stop naming. It's all words. You need to unlanguage, unfetter yourself and just be. 'I'm not a word' Lucy Jinx says 'I'm a person.' But this doesn't sound right. *A person*? Isn't that a word - aren't people just words? You're Lucy Jinx! 'I'm not a word, not a person - I'm a *Lucy Jinx*!' she says - but oh! do you note, Lucy, despite yourself not wanting to note, that you are standing now just at that odd grey door, That Woman's door, as you boom this? - and then says it again. And Lucy Jinx is not a word - probably she's right. You were Lucy before you were words, right?

FROM ONE CORNER OF THE room to another to the other to another to the other to another to the other - by now she must have duplicated, duplicated, repeated, repeated, but it doesn't feel like it. Lucy has *Katydid* stuck in her head. Then *Caryatid. Caryatid. Pillars. Plyers. Ires. Plyers. Pillars. Caryatid. Katydid.* 'Why haven't you told me to leave yet?' She jolts because she thought he had left! 'Why are you even here? You should have left.' The table feels at nose-height - she will bang her teeth if she steps forward! But his weight is already on her shoulders and the trains-coming of the bathtub-tap spilling, drain not plugged so water just looping down curving pipe and away to join other water other water other water. Simple Goddamnits don't seem to do so - Hell, she has to - eventually Lucy starts punching him. But so ineffective! Her hands are buckets heaved, turned on their sides, forgotten to ever be filled. That's his breath! And she hears the rest of his rancor and the disc being changed in the player - all of those chug-chug-chugs, those mechanical not-wanting-to-budge sounds of the gadget her mother traded up for that day in that one year whenever it was, five CDs can be put in and chug-chug-chug. 'You can't breathe! You can't breathe, Lucy!' Lucy! 'Lucy, Lucy, Lucy.' How can he be talking? Don't you feel? One tongue up Lucy's one nostril, another up her other - and that tongue forked, ticking her with its plish-plash scissor motions like kids testing pool water with fingers when they aren't yet allowed to jump in - and his other tongue, the biggest of them, laying eggs into the sore it has burrowed in the skin at the top-most of her cleavage. At the same time, they are talking so calmly. 'You invited me in for the appliances and asked me to stay.' 'What? When did I?' She can remember. 'You remember.' He is sewing her spine to her left heel with dental floss! He is running his palm across the tight strings and she can feel the high-pitch of this skin parting in simple lines. 'Music staves! Music staves!' They are both laughing even as she is pushing as hard as she can - she promises! she promises she is, you have to believe her! - with both hand to get his face off of her, out of her - his nose is buried and its snuffling is making her clitoris tingle but not because she wants it to. Laughing at music staves - but he doesn't understand - and there is fire! 'Oh shit!' This stirs him. But he looks at her and they both need to hide - so now she is stuck in here and has to let him write on her leg because it's the only place they can see and they have to keep quiet but also have to say in pen *What?* and *What?* and *What?* And when she next looks at him, his jaw is an overturned patch in a field and - God! - all those worms are already dead!

In her life-long, Lucy has only woken this furiously on one other occasion. Here she is. Pacing the dark with broader circles than she should. Countdown to toe-stub? Feeling all of - all of that - it all over her and the presence all still in the dark. The dark is the worst just when waking. In the womb there must be nightmares! You wake and sleep, all bellied tight. A nightmare before you have context or even the right wrinkles across the lobes to move the images around. *Stagnant. Puddle as a child in a womb.* Terrified, she flaps up the light and her eyes shutter too much for her to think of opening them. Little kid reaction to light. Scream at the thought of sight! *Sightless eyes in the womb. Womb-fish.* She opens her notebook and writes *I'm stagnant - puddle as a child in the womb.* She writes *Eyes.* All of this half-blind. Wonders if it will be intelligible, legible, anything-at-allable. Wonders if anything will be. The dream-haunt is heavy, head aching her eyelids, making them want nothing but down. Her body, too. That beaten sense of night-terrors. That fake sense of 'It's over and if I sleep now it'll be fine.' She can't even force her eyes awake. Come on, Lucy! If you can't do it, no one can! - she hears this in tinny smacks of remembered television, overhead in some neighbor-child's living-room while those parents made her stay at the table until that cereal was gone. Force your eyes open. *Blind* she writes - *I remember that cereal.* *Alphabits.* Lucy had said to that mom '*Alphabits*? Mine don't look like letters - they're all just apostrophes.' And the joke had been taken for sass and the meal passed in terse silence. 'You may go watch your show' - that *You* so clearly shaped to mean just Patrick or Darin or whatever-his-name-was. '*You*' - this one said somewhat less sharp than the one for the mother's own boy but all the more cackling for it - 'may sit until you finish. Your mother should teach you' this mother had said, then long pause, then '*Hospitality*' like it was just that word being said, taught, introduced. 'I couldn't eat because you got mad.' Lucy tried to say it and couldn't. Are you still writing this, Lucy? I'm sure your eyes would be alright to open, now. And so they are! And - she is honestly impressed with herself - look at all of that you wrote without even it looking scribbled! Hell, your half-awake, terror-soaked-memory penmanship is better than your day-to-day! 'I've found my element' she says, shivering. Then adds this to the page. *I've found my element. Stagnant - puddle as a child in the womb.*

Luckily, there are microwavable sausage sandwiches. Which Lucy knows: this is the time for. Thud go four to the counter. Tug go Lucy's fingers through some over-thick plastic keeping the things two-by-two. Wrap go paper towels, one around each. Then another thud - this mixed with a clattering, echoish clang - of two being deposited in the microwave. Slam. Biep! Biep! Biep! Lucy types in how long to cook for and then the low-key hum and the every-now-and-again rattle-rattle-rattle of the glass base not set to its track perfectly, going uneven when its rotations reverse. Can't cook four-at-once, Lucy? The instructions on the box say you can. Except: Lucy has tried. Several times in her adult life. In several microwaves. Spread over almost a decade! Show her the proof, that's her motto - that box is all theory! 'Anything works on paper!' she had ejaculated in fury at these indicated instructions once, when the four sandwiches had seemed hot and cooked but each and every one's center was still ice-pellet to her bites down! Anyway - this dream needs to be out of her head, now. Almighty heaven, there must be horrors so much worse than this in life. Than a nightmare, Lucy? 'Yes, exactly' she says. Of course there are. In television shows, fathers - for example - have kids not even ten-years-old brutally, horrifically serial-killed and seem devastated - but in muted, supporting actor sorts of ways. They walk out of stations at episode ends, sometimes leaning to mothers, and life will go on, the program's primary cast looking on without expression or else downward, the audience reflecting 'Ah, I bet such-and-so is aligning this to their season-long arc thusly.' Meanwhile - in real life - think a dad ever gets over leaning that while his nine-year-old was burned to death and stabbed forty times by a neighbor, the neighbor kept laughing and telling the kid 'This was your dad's idea - he ain't coming - he gave you to me because you don't look right -

Oh he hates you - he gave me a whole list of things to do to you, so stop calling for him - he's at home laughing and trying on new shirts!'? Well? No - of course one doesn't get over that! You don't go to counseling - you eat a gun! The End! You don't cooly look at the killer and staunchly say 'You're a monster - this won't work, you belong in jail.' No, ma'am. You slit your wrists - and yesterday ain't soon enough to have done it! Beeeeeeeppppppppp! That microwave son-of-a-bitch sound of 'I'm duh-uuuuunnnnnnnnnnn-eh'! Gah! Lucy meant to catch it in the last two seconds, spare herself this elongated yarl. Biep. Biep. Biep. Low hum of the next two sandwiches around-and-arounding while she unnapkins the first two and gets them on a paper plate. 'Leave the napkin on and what happens?' she rhetoricals to the empty - entirely lit by this point, every single light! - apartment. 'That's right' she nods, kindergarten-teacher toned. 'The napkin fuses. Science. This is one of those secrets the atom has yielded! *Hiroshima, mon amour*, indeed.'

What Lucy doesn't understand about the plot of this Ashley Judd movie is: why doesn't Ashley Judd just take pictures of Bruce Greenwood and - whatever, Lucy can think of a million things! - hire a prostitute to sleep with him and to get a sample of his semen - or get a guy to cut him, walking down the street, to soak a towel in some of the blood to get that precious DNA evidence, then anonymously send this evidence to the police or a newspaper or something to prove the man she is accused of murdering is still alive!? That's what Lucy doesn't get! They could tell how old the blood-sample is. It wouldn't be a thing, by the end of the day. A triumph of common-sense! What is this movie called? It's gone to commercials and come back and still hasn't said! Calmer, Lucy figures Ashley Judd could just steal something with Bruce Greenwood's saliva on it - or finger-prints! Pay a private-eye to lift fresh fingerprints, run them through a database. 'Presto!' Lucy snaps 'I've fixed your life, Ashley Judd - de nada.' The private-eye wouldn't even need to know what's what - then Ashely Judd would have some verifiable evidence that Bruce Greenwood is her husband. The end of the movie. Now - now! - Lucy can hardly believe her fatigue-tombed eyes, but is Ashley Judd following a random kid around a cemetery in New Orleans!? 'This is how women get killed' Lucy seethes, imagining she would be, were other women present, preaching to the choir. 'They follow random children around cemeteries their husbands-who-framed-them-for-their-murder agree to meet them in. Every day' Lucy clucks. 'Stupid. Women are so dumb. Like you, Ashley Judd. This is why victim-blaming seems reasonable to so many people - they know people like you!' No one is sitting beside Lucy on that side. Or on that. Real. Imagined. Lucy is - in actual, demonstrable reality - sitting alone in her apartment, drinking straight from a three-liter bottle of *Ginger-Ale*, watching whatever this Ashley Judd movie is, while her stomach is in the early stages of cramps those sausage sandwiches always sick on her. And this isn't even the first time it has been like this. Not even the first time it has been this movie! Which is all the more annoying, as far as the title escaping her. She remembers seeing a John Travolta thriller - Vince Vaughn as the villain - in theaters on a date with some guy in her twenties and she can still remember the name of that picture! And most of the plot! For some reason. 'John Travolta' she says now, shaking her head in disappointment at him 'you really should have trusted your kid from the start'! Wait. She Hmns. Or hadn't he always trusted his kid? Anyway, she remembers something about a dock or a boathouse. Which is more than she actually recalls about this Judd film. Ashley Judd does kill Bruce Greenwood. Which is another thing she could have done, right from the get. Killed him - it'd be discovered, at time of death, who he was. Conviction overturned! 'I'm so much smarter than Ashley Judd' thinks Lucy Jinx. There is nobody in the room with her. Real or imagined.

See? This other dream of Lucy's is much better. And after all her fuss. After all of her thinking it hopeless. Right back in her bed, too - not even out on the sofa or some silly measure of protection-via-distance from scene-of-the-crime. This dream: Lucy Jinx is looking at violins in something like a store except not a store. There are clerks and people walking around asking prices, but it is distinctly not a store. An older man is answering her questions and is scratching the undercup of his belly, his dress shirt not actually tuckable because of this finger raking. Lucy, as it is a dream, is aware of his liver-spottedness and grey-scrags of belly hair - which would be the same consistency and shape as his pubes. His answers trail off into him lending Lucy some money before she has to climb a hill back to where she is parked, carnival sounds of the ocean behind her and before her. Her fatigue in the dream is livid. How it feels to swallow the milk she drinks is the way it feels to chew pudding one shouldn't have to and swallow it all in an unmelting whole. All kisses would taste like the pepper of dogs' tongues and the slick base like seafoam always tucked in up under their able-to-billow lips. All of the drivers on the roads have to turn at the same time and none of them will and so they snake along with Lucy and she knows the couple in that car - there - have forgot their canoe but doesn't know how to tell them. 'How can I tell you you've lost your canoe?' she asks them in a moment when they have all stopped and are sharing a sandwich, each wanting to wind up with the last bite. Only it is a backyard party, now. Fireworks. And Lucy was never invited! So walks down the sidewalk she thought was a neighborhood but leads her behind three automotive repair shops and a tattoo parlor and some abandoned office buildings she can still see chairs and telephone cords in some of the rooms of. 'Want to see this?' the guy with the cigarette she almost bumps into - though she had seen him coming - asks. Then her dream is awe and wonder at the loop-the-loops of a newspaper production contraption. She had no idea! It rollercoasters and rollercoasters, Lucy thinking it seems like a turtle trying to wend its way out of its shell! And she believes him when he tells her that turtles all have colonies of termites living in their bellies. 'Specific termites' the man says and goes to tap her shoulder to emphasis the humor, accidentally touches her breast. 'I don't mind' she says, but he won't stop apologizing. So it gets awkward. But they part on good terms. And wake! Wake up! The last image: a golf-ball somehow rolling the exact same circle again and again and again and again. The wind? Specific dips in the pavement? Lucy and a lot of pedestrians are watching, smiling the same smiles. She's awake, though. Hi, Lucy. Good morning.

Something about this knocking at her door is different than usual. Hard to say. Or her mood is lighter than it has been in some time. She doesn't even feel the need to not answer it dressed as she is. Let's have a peek out first, though. Policeman. Another knock as she is peeking, jolting her back, though the knocking is very courteous. 'Just one moment' she says 'I need to throw something on.' 'Take your time, ma'am.' You didn't need to say that, Lucy! Now you're giving John Law some fantasies - and boy will he be demoralized when only you open the door! Big sigh. These pants. This shirt. Peek. He's still there. That Hello? tone likely only ever given to police officers. She sees another police officer, back there. An odd atmosphere to the corridor. The air feels like sounds from too many people she can't see. One can tell. Lucy can tell. Has she been in all night? Yes. Well - she wants to exact - since *XY* hour, she's been in. In her room? Except for a brief time when she walked around, had a smoke. 'Around the neighborhood?' 'No' she says 'just' points past him, watches that other police officer, talking now to that neighbor 'around out there.' 'On this level?' 'No' she says. She had walked her level. The level above. Below. 'What time was this?' Is he suspicious that Lucy hasn't asked what this is about? Lucy is just doing what one ought to do when the police show up - answering the questions succinctly, promptly! These folks have hard work to do! 'Uh' Lucy stammers a moment. Says what time. 'It was' - here the officer says the time Lucy just said - 'you were out? You're certain?' 'Yes.' How can she be certain? She explains. It seems above board to the officer who seems eager to keep talking and to go tell someone he's - Lucy wonders what the lingo is - found a clue. Or something. 'Am I a clue?' Lucy asks, surprised at the apprehension in her tone. It should be fun to be a clue! Right now, it feels like being the victim of something. 'You might be' the officer says - but it doesn't seem he should have. He asks her to relate her movements. Had she seen anything? Had she noticed anyone? Not to be indelicate, but had she been on any medication? Drinking? Using any intoxicants or drugs of any kind? She expects him to say

'I'm not Vice, I don't care about that' like in the shows - except maybe he is Vice! How in Christ's should Lucy know what this is about? Is he going to come in? Where is her marijuana and stuff? Do people have to let cops in? Helpful people do! You're trying to be helpful, remember? 'Did you happen to notice - see, hear - anything amiss about the apartment directly beneath yours?'

This is the sight: the odd, other-grey door - That Woman's door - is opened and cordoned off with police-line. This is Lucy: vaguely recalling she had remarked to herself it was odd she had thought an exact thought exactly outside that door. Or something. *Do you mark it, Lucy?* The thought hangs like a buck-tooth, it coughs like ears clogged with chlorine water. Lucy doesn't feel caught up - despite hearing the word *Homicide* used and having to explain her timetable-of-last-night to a detective far less interesting than she figured a detective would be. And the tone is not so much of interest. No one cares that That Woman is dead. Lucy can tell. And can see a print of Caravaggio on the wall, there - common print, beneath it a reproduction of an old magazine cover in a silver frame. She has heard the woman's name was *Claire Seville*. She had not known that, she had said. No, she had not interacted with Claire beyond once or twice, maybe, and those times only incidentally. Saw her at *Hernando's* a few times. 'The store?' 'What?' 'The store?' 'Oh' - Lucy nods, she gets it - 'yes, across the street.' And for some reason - it will be explained at some point as nerves, processing, a mechanism - she goes on a bit about her old gig at *Hernando's Highlights*. The detective remembers it. So does this officer. 'Who wants an autograph, right?' Lucy doesn't say that, but one day she might say she did when retelling this all as a story. Eventually, she might say it without admitting it is a jokey add-on - she'll claim to have dealt with her detective-chat in a serio-comedic way. There must be disappointment from these lawmen that Lucy can't help them more. And Lucy must be consciously keeping from mentioning those knocks on her door and finding that man - she knows it was a man - outside her own door, just last night. Was that just last night? 'Oh my God - there was a man outside my door, just last night. Oh my God.' Well - this is intriguing! Popcorn for the detectives, eh? They want to get settled in for this! 'Oh my God.' And Lucy can't be sure, but she thinks the very same man had knocked on her door, earlier that day. 'Last night? Was it last night? The night previous?' She means the night previous, the night previous. Last night is when Claire had been killed - Lucy means the-night-before-last. 'You're sure?' Are you sure, Lucy? Or was it the night before the-night-before-last? 'Oh my God' she says - knows she is saying it a lot and feels she needs to explain 'I don't usually say *Oh my God* this much. Or act this way.' The detective smiles a bit. The officer, there, will tell that as a joke to his wife later. She can tell. The wife will make fun of Lucy. Lucy clenches her jaw.

A recent memory is the worst kind. A recent memory is still kind of being invented. There is no other way of putting it. Pieces haven't locked. Contexts haven't cooled down. Cookies not ready yet, that's the thing. A soda the furry head of which hasn't settled into surface sizzle. Lucy is saying it was a man, but then feels she needs to say how - because of the hood - she cannot truly say it was a man. But the policemen, detectives desire her impression and her impression is 'It was a man.' She tells them she made this observation to herself, several times. And she remembers this. And watching him walk away. Down the street she is now standing on when she says this. There's that street. Unfortunately, in the daylight it is not matching her memory and her imagination is lacking in giving it justifiable difference-due-to-nighttime tones. But it had been this street! Lucy, it looks different now because you hadn't been standing down here, that night - you'd been up there. Where you are pointing to, where you are indicating to this detective. Yet in Lucy's memory, she can clearly see the guy walking away from her vantage - her vantage now, down here - but along a dark street. So her brain is substituting - different guy's back, different dark street - she sees this so clearly. Likely something out of cinema! Therefore - she ought to be pointing this out to the detectives, making their job easier - it is not beyond reason that she might - though she doesn't think so - be re-splicing her memory of the man up at her door with the image of this other cobbled-memory man. See what she means? she might ask. She should point this out to whoever-is-caught-eventually's defense attorney - make their job easier. Lucy, you've read about eyewitness testimony - and this is what those articles mean! You've applesauce for brains, man! Applesauce-left-overnight-in-a-trickle-of-water-on-a-plate-in-the-sink for brains! Another thing? Lucy knows she didn't peek out her door when that knocking had happened - but yet here, front and center, azure-sky clarity - is an image of a hooded face - features just left-side of distinguishable - looking in through her own door at her. The lighting she is picturing doesn't even make sense! But since she just looked out at the policeman, it's easy to joint this memory to that. But - here and now - they keep asking questions and - sad as it may sound - Lucy not only wants to solve the case - this exact minute, by some offhand remark - but wants to stretch this out to make her calling off from work the most justifiable. It was the police. I saw something. Something. Something. 'You said the man was smoking?' Had you, Lucy? Are they trying to catch you out? Had the man been smoking? What is Lucy even saying!? Didn't someone else witness anything, last night? Someone real. You're asking Lucy Jinx what happened? Someone should explain to these fine sleuths that this is rather like asking a silkworm how best to polish a horseshoe.

Obviously, Lucy needs a cigarette. She can't smoke some dope on account of that's the last thing she needs: 'Couple more questions, Ms. Jinx. We think we can catch the guy if you just - oh Christ Jesus! Are you goddamn high! Let him go, boys! Land-o-lakes, Ms. Jinx - you've mucked this up, the royal court!' Disappointment all around. Lucy in the cuffs. O. Henry would be proud! Come to think of it - if Lucy has to give testimony or something there's going to have to be a drug test. Right? If she is some kind of a crucial thing - or even a non-crucial thing - any Public Defender worth his salt is gonna try to discredit her. And suppose this is one of them so-called Gentleman Murderers! In it for kicks - wealthy like Avarice, just waiting for the trail phase to begin - all part of the fun! More likely, though: it isn't that. But even a disgruntled lover could have a nest-egg or wealthy parents who will always believe in their babykins. How much of your life is this going to take up, Lucy? Was that it, those questions just here - and then maybe a touch of testimony? You said to them, point blank, you hadn't see the guy, proper - no way a conviction can be hung on your say so if that is your say so. No. Still not okay to smoke up - but this affair is probably all done. How far are defense attorneys allowed to go truffling into a witness' past? There has to be a limit! One doesn't sacrifice privacy because of one chance look to the side, some measly day. Vinegar-blood makes a few rotations through Lucy, her heart feels like a wet fist closed hard on a handful of tinsel. It's not that she is afraid of her splotches being shown around - it's just the fact that some specific people will know some specific things. People beyond those directly involved. And the fact that - say she were a crucial witness - the detectives and prosecutors would ignore her peccadillos in order to make their case - set certain elements of Lucy on one side just to make her seem not-subhuman to jurors while thinking her subhuman and then some among their own confidences - only gets her downer in the more defensive dumps. But calm down, Lucy. Just finish calling off work. Just finish your cigarette. Think about something else. Anything. Hell, think 'Last night, I slept less than five meters above a fresh corpse.' Think 'I had nightmare while a woman - That Woman, Claire - was killed, underneath me. I ate sausage sandwiches and stomachached in critique of Ashley Judd. Maybe while the woman - That Woman, Claire - was still alive, the killer gone. Maybe while the woman - That Woman, Claire - thought she would remain so. Maybe while 'Help!' was being Helped loud enough to be audible through the vent, were somebody named Lucy Jinx listening.' Obviously, Lucy needs another cigarette. She lays out five-in-a-row. Then adds another. Still needs to dial the phone. What's the word for this? There's a word. This is the word for when there should be a word but there isn't a word.

Lucy has an acute onset of the creeps. She can't shower. This is going to ruin her life! The police don't care about you, Lucy. Say the killer had been looming around - they return to the scene-of-the-crime, criminals do, and that's a fact,

Lucy has been a criminal and has done so, she can vouch! - and saw Lucy out there talking and pointing and going on and on like some kind of a crackerjack know-it-all little upstanding neighborhood-watcher! That's Lucy's goose cooked - and thank you all for coming! Lucy can't go out or stay in. Go out: she gets followed, done in the moment there is sufficient lack of surrounding pedestrians. Stay in: they killer will know she knows, wait to for her to go defenseless in her sleep, kick the door in, douse her in a bucket of gasoline, Zippo tossed, and beat feet - fifteen seconds, tops! Oh stop Lucy! You're not worth murdering! She texts Layla, straight off. *Am I worth murdering?* Two minutes of queasiness - bad move, Lucy - at the thought of Layla not getting back with her. Then: phone buzzes in her hand. *I'd murder you.* Grin. Melting-toffee tummy goes Lucy. *I meant: would it be worth it to the world at large. To kill me. Would anyone but you bother?* New cig lit and sack-of-bricks to sofa. The smoke stays in the air the way the tint of medicine overpowers the cherry of a throat lozenge - the rooms seem limited today, they seem to contain all they ever will. Cell walls. Tight. Another long draft out - Lucy can watch it thin and mix, the smoke, meld perfectly with the just not-quite-colorless she can see in the air. She texts: *I wish the air had a color. That's one thing you can take the air to task for, I say.* Right away a buzz, so this message nothing to do with the air comment. *No one would kill you, Lucy, even with someone else's ten foot pole. Me, though? I'd pull your lungs out through yer secret parts.* Unfortunately, Lucy does not feel witty enough to proceed in full banter, so instead - maybe can't stop herself - texts: *no joke: the woman who lives beneath me was murdered last night.* And now the air has equilibriumed with the smoke. The smoke has either dispersed itself around enough to have matched normal air-tone or Lucy's eyes have accustomed themselves to the now-everything's-smoke-colored so smoke-color seems invisible. Like walking in fog. Lucy has never understood fog. Why can you see yourself in fog? That seems like bad editing, if you ask her. Phone buzz. Layla asks: *did you kill her?* Lucy's skin all feels like it blinks while her eyes stay open. And even as she is typing *Do you already suspect me? Do you think they do, too?* her phone buzzes again. So Lucy cancels her message and Layla's - a connected statement to her last - appears and exactly says *Because you do tend to kill people, Lucy. That's very well known.*

# .II.

ARIEL LENTZ'S BELLY HUNG SUSPENDED, a ball kicked and too stubborn to up or down. Weightless and immense, the thing - a balloon with the drag of the ocean floor. Or so it seems to Lucy. Lucy watching it out of the corner of her eye while watching, also, Kayleigh draw outlines of things in ink and then haphazardly scratch color inside of and around these lines in colored-pencil. Or maybe not so haphazardly. Kayleigh insists it is 'her technique' - and Lucy can see this, but cannot rock the boat of Ariel's insistence it is the girl's inherent laziness displaying itself full-feather, not some precocious talent of messy precision. 'She's one of those kids' Ariel has explained 'who is under the impression that even if they did honestly have something of import to say there would be people willing to listen. A dangerous strain. I try to food-poison her, but so far she's been resilient.' This current picture is of a city-scape. A road clogged with the profiles of cars, trucks, big-rigs, vans. People are kind of scribbled circles on top of scribbled circles-stretched-long with single arcs going through center blob to make arms, to make legs - teensy abstractions, like a combination of *M* geese in flight and rudimentary storm clouds. Lucy sees people like this. She has often whispered to Kayleigh 'You draw people exactly the way they look.' 'What do you mean, Goosey?' 'I mean' - dramatic even-more-whispered whisper - 'when I look around, I see tiny scribble-blobs. All adults do. You see them already - you are advanced and will earn the presidency via a coup by the time you're thirty-one.' But Kayleigh, little skeptic of Lucy Jinx, shrugged on these occasion and said 'I just draw them like that because the picture is busy and they are little and they need to look like something. Cars don't look like that either' Kayleigh added, just in case Lucy was further lunaticed into other misguided perceptions. 'Yeah yeah' Lucy had retorted 'and not every building-top has a goddamn water-tower on it. You're right - your world is fucking crackers, Kayleigh' - Lucy always pronounces the second syllable of Kayleigh's name like some rubbish, like what the letters *Eigh* would be spoken like if one didn't know how to speak better. But Ariel's belly - expansive it goes, the size of how a dictionary will look in another twelve decades versus the single-sheet broadside it had started as. Ariel squinting at whatever e-mail she has composed. Tick. Tack. Tap tap tap. Correcting something or adding, slow motion, one extra word. Obviously Send now hit. Ariel leaning back and letting out a sigh like a mattress being deflated while a guest is asleep, a beach ball wheezing 'Sorry guys, I'm spent.' 'Ariel' Lucy calls across. 'If you're criticizing Kayleigh's bullcrap art again, I already agree. Have you seen all those water-towers? She's never even seen a water-tower! Schoolbooks seem to be producing exaggerating nitwits, these days.' 'I've seen a water-tower, mother' says Kayleigh - that *Moth-Her* pronunciation making Lucy melt like pudding to inedible. 'No you haven't, Kayleigh' Ariel long-sufferings. 'That's just one of those many, many wrong things that you think.'

Ariel just sighs when Lucy comes in with the laundry she has taken from the dryer, dumps the lot, and gets to it. The carpet is strewn with fluff from things the cat has sharpened its claws on, stickers, and pieces of toys Kayleigh has discarded - helmets, swords, lots of wheels off of those motorcycles she had been obsessed with all of last month, some of the bodies of wheel-less motorcycles too, and there there and there are the swordfish-shaped toothpicks from the packet Lucy had bought that time at the grocery-store, impossible to say 'No' to Kayleigh arguing 'I'd pick my teeth if I had colorful swordfish to do it with - I've never even been given the chance!' - and some of these thingies will, it never fails, wind up in the fabric of socks, skirts, hooded-sweatshirts, what have you. 'Stop living out your daydreams in my living-room' Ariel now snipes. 'I know you wanted to be a *Merry Maid* but that ship sailed. And you fold everything wrong and I just have to refold it later and each time I do I lose a little bit of respect for you and wonder if maybe you're where everything went wrong for me.' Lucy likes how when Ariel talks it is always, at heart, the same thing, just with a variant in the delivery. Oh sure - the content of the words wildly differs, nary a letter repeated, but it's the exact sing-song, like Ariel is a record that is too nervous to spin any way but exactly *Around*. And Lucy likes to pivot into unexpected revelations like 'I did want to be a *Merry Maid*. Or not a *Merry Maid*, but a housekeeper. For a hotel. And I'd never get hired.' 'And why do you think that is?' asks Ariel, long emphasis to last word. 'What do you think is the reason?' Long emphasis to last word and it somehow manages to kind of rhyme with *Is* - or to feel like it does, at any rate. 'I must have applied at twenty hotels. Never would they let me make a bed. Never would they let me empty a trashcan or replace soap. Let me tell you, Ari: that's a hard thing.' 'I bet.' 'It's a dismal head to live with - told you can't clear pubic-hair out of shower drain or fold the toilet-paper into a triangle to make the room's next occupant feel loved.' 'I bet.' 'And maybe you should ask yourself, El: Why do I associate with people who can't get hired as housekeepers at hotels? Maybe you should drink yourself in, regarding that - long and hard, El - before you think the fact that I fold your towels the wrong way is the root of your chucklehead life!' 'You're right, Lucy.' 'I know I am. But we're not friends again until you stop hurting my feelings for a whole week.' Ariel coughs and says that she saw her neighbor kill a spider that was on the rear window of his parked car. 'That kind of thing is just weird. Killing a spider when the spider is outside? It makes me wonder where I live, sometimes.'

Lucy Jinx so adores the mess of the counter in the bathroom. Observe: two empty tissue boxes - well, one has a dime and three pennies in it, for some reason - and three just-not-quite-completely-used-up rolls of toilet-paper, porcelain of basin splotched with a cinnamon of Ariel's powder-foundation and green streaks of toothpaste spit by Kayleigh, countertop butterscotch-messed with a curio of residues from set down toothbrushes - what is that? plaque? what makes that tin rust of red-brown? - over which one can find a used-up deodorant stick and another - completely different brand and scent - deodorant stick, some remains of the wrappers of Band-aids, a toenail clipper, three cheap razors used to the point the blades are fur-packed with stubble and would raise rash if swiped across skin - Lucy has seen, countless times now, Ariel use these on her underarms and in bird-peck quick whisk whisk whisk strokes to upper lips and jaw line, but has stopped calling her 'Ariel, *Wear-iel*' because the joke took too long to explain the first time and, besides, Ariel seemed genuinely sensitive to the fact that she is sprouting weird facial-hair growth with this pregnancy. What a perfect, disgusting countertop! Ariel tells Lucy all the time 'Use the one in my room.' And every time Lucy says 'Yuck - that's disgusting, man - I'm not going in there.' Every time. Every time, Lucy? More than once, anyway. Here is Lucy washing her hands and watching her reflection of hands washing, washing, round-and-rounding, and cleaning more than she ever does at any other sink.

Look: on the toilet-tank are three empty bubble-baths and someone had used - months ago - some bathtub crayon to draw a star and - what is it? a squid? - on the toilet side and this image has never been erased, has dried to a stiff like mummified lips. Lucy can hear Ariel having to snap at Kayleigh about the importance of gloves - 'I will downright refuse to let you warm your hands in hot water when you come in, but by all means go out without them!' - and can see the Oh-Jesus look Kyleigh can get - exactly like her mother's - stationary but evoking the eye-roll, a brief tightening of focus that brackets the world in sarcastic containment. What about your belly, Lucy? 'What about my belly?' she watches her face ask as though not asking itself. But she won't lift up her shirt. Not in the same home as the taut, always scentless-cream-scented strain of Ariel's. That curve. That size equal to the space left in the mouth of every letter *O* since the beginning of time. That infinite, unblemished can-you-be-sure-it-won't-tear that is Ariel's middle. No. Lucy's belly remains un-on-display. She scrapes at one of the hard-water stains on the mirror glass. That one. Just at the bridge of her reflection's nose. Scrape scrape. Scrape scrape. 'Just put the gloves on will ya, for Christ's! For Christ's, *K* - don't you imagine Christ would want - and be pleased by - you doing that one thing in this life!?' she hears from Ariel, whole speech pronounced family-friendly program tone of Sheesh. 'Everything with you is battlements, ain't it *K?*'

'Does it make me a bad mother that Kayleigh has never flown a kite? And that I distinctly don't want her to?' 'You don't like kites?' 'It's just something I don't want to have to say she's done. I don't want to be caught saying *My daughter was out flying a kite* only to have whomever I'm speaking to say *Oh was she now?* or to even look at me with an expression tantamount to that.' 'What is the question?' 'Does that make me a bad mother?' 'Oh - no. If you had a good - an honestly sound - reason for not wanting her to fly a kite I'd be worried - but as long as it's highly irrational, you seem golden.' 'I gave up trying to be rational when she wouldn't eat a fucking different-shaped French-fry. 'She gets it, you know? Life makes about that much sense.' 'Sure.' 'It's crinkled? Don't put it in your mouth. She's ahead of the game, if you ask me. Unless she doesn't eat waffle-fries.' 'She eats waffle-fries. But she calls them *Tennis-Fries.*' 'Why?' 'I don't fucking know, Lucy. You want to know about kids, there's ways to get one of your own. She calls them *Tennis-Fries* and I can either correct her or just think *Fuck it, that's yet another thing she's wrong about* and resign myself to that. And look at me? Do I seem to have a lot of free time?' 'Of course, I can kind of understand calling them *Tennis-Fries.*' 'Is that right?' 'Like the net.' 'In tennis?' 'Yeah.' 'She doesn't play tennis.' 'Are you sure? At school maybe?' 'To the extent she names a French-fry after it? How much goddamn tennis do you imagine they play at that school? Jesus, Lucy - I don't even know if it's worth arguing with you about which end is up, sometimes.' 'Waffle-fries don't look like waffles is all I'm saying. They look like a bunch of sharp sighs stitched together by a madman.' 'I'm not saying they look like waffles. She's never eaten a waffle, anyway. That I know of. Not eaten one with my blessing - that's a stone cold fact. I'm saying: I called them *Waffle-Fries*. Next time we were in visual proximity of some, she's calling them *Tennis-Fries*. In between *A* and *B* she got fucked up somehow and - well! - it's what happened - I'm cool with it.' 'She's Adam - naming the world anew.' 'Stop agreeing with everything my stupid daughter says, Lucy.' 'Sorry.' 'Fuck man, remember when you used to be my pal? When you used to just agree with any arbitrary thing I said? Go back to it being like that!' 'I'll try. You need to be more whimsical, though.' 'I'll try. Whimsy doesn't last long in the face of the naked absurd. It's very bourgeois, whimsy.' 'It is, I agree.' 'There you go! See? Back in the old swing! Doe-eyed, you follow my lead! This is how friendships endure!'

Leopold telephones and Ariel takes it upstairs. So Lucy is sitting next to Kayleigh watching *Gargoyles*. There is a bag of chips which Lucy - very self-consciously - is rapidly eating through. She has clocked her progress - four handfuls for every two chips the kid eats. 'Eat faster.' 'Eat what faster?' 'The chips!' 'You can have them all - I think my mom buys them for you.' The thing is, Lucy cannot press to get the full story, there. Is it true? Certainly Lucy would dig it were it true. What could be better than the chips even having been dubbed with some nickname: *Lucy Chips*. Maybe Kayleigh asks for them that way. Can I have some *Lucy Chips*? 'Why do these gargoyles fight crime?' 'They are compelled to. But I don't know by what.' 'I don't like this show.' 'Then why are we watching it?' Lucy is speaking with her mouth full, brushes from her shirt breast - she is leaned back, slothful posture of a teen - the spilling crumbs and sees a great deal of them freckling the sofa-arm on account of her doing so. 'I wanted to watch *Rescue Rangers*. I thought you were watching this.' 'I wanted to watch *Darkwing Duck*.' 'We don't have that.' 'I know - hence I thought you picked this, maybe because you thought it was close enough.' 'It's nothing like *Rescue Rangers* - you're weird.' 'So why are we watching it?' Eyes never drifting from the television, Kayleigh hands Lucy the remote, at the same time standing up - still staring at the screen - and saying 'I'm going to go draw some more.' 'Draw? Is that all you do?' 'Yeah. You can watch whatever.' 'Well gee, thanks. Hey - Leigh?' Kayleigh turns, Lucy shutting off the television, and approaches when Lucy bends finger one-two-three to solicit her over. 'What are we going to get your mom for her birthday?' Kayleigh shrugs, obviously having expected something more interesting from Lucy. 'Do you want to go out with me to pick something?' 'Can I get something, too?' 'For your mom? That's what I mean - we can pick together!' Kayleigh can't seem to believe she is having to explain

herself, baby-voices down to Lucy's level. 'No. Can I get something. For me.'
'Like what?' 'I'm just supposed to come with you for nothing?' 'It's to get your
fucking mom a present!' But Kayleigh will just draw her mom a damned picture
and write a little poem under it - her mom doesn't expect Kayleigh to go buy
something! What does Lucy think? That Ariel is a monster!? Sorry to break it to
the kid, but Lucy has to let on that 'Mommy' - she puts air quotes-around
the *Mommy* and mouths lips in the effect of a triple *W* to show her disdain - is
incredibly materialistic and probably only ever reads the poems Kayleigh writes
once and even that time hardly even. 'We could get her a gift certificate to
*Applebee's*. That's where her heart is at. Trust me.' And Kayleigh says she'll come
along but just so Lucy doesn't freak out. 'But can we do it later - I really am
going to go draw for awhile.'

Ariel is standing at her bedroom window. From behind - with the cold light
in through the just slightly fanned blades of the blinds, the room in twilight - she
seems semi-transparent, Lucy's vision kind of involuntarily doubling to attain
any amount of focus. If you backed up right now, Lucy, Ariel might not even
know you'd come up the stairs. Or can she tell you are here, looking at her?
How does sound travel in this house? Had she heard your ascent? Heard the
murmur of your downstairs chat with her daughter end off? Is that her position
of waiting for you, Lucy? To chat? To counsel? 'Do you know I'm standing back
here?' Ariel turns - the light still making her indistinct. 'I did not. What are you
doing back there?' Lucy shrugs, sways as though to begin backing up, but Ariel
beckons her over to sit on the lip of the bed. The thing to ask Ariel is 'Everything
alright?' but that is the not the sort of thing Lucy knows how to ask. Not to ask
Ariel. Instead: comb for clues, get a feeling. 'The problem is: figuring you out
is like transcribing the onomatopoeia of a garbage-disposal.' Ariel cocks her eye.
'What problem? Figuring me out, what?' 'What?' Lucy says. 'What?' Ariel says
back, tone of I'm-not-letting-this-drop-so-easy. 'No - I said *What?*' 'I know you
did - about what?' 'Is what you're asking me?' 'What are you trying to figure
out about me?' 'What do you mean?' 'You said that thing about garbage-
disposals.' 'Is that what you want to talk about, Ari? Something I said about
garbage-disposals?' Ariel gives up. Punches Lucy's arm and sighs a foreign
language into the expression 'Man oh man oh man - sometimes, right?' 'But
only sometimes sometimes.' Ariel agrees to the truth of that. Then asks 'Where
you working, these days?' 'Same place.' 'Oh really?' - Ariel is surprised,
physicals the expression of this 'the same assignment?' 'Yep.' Ariel will be
damned. 'And what's new?' 'I hear there's a war on.' 'A World War?' Lucy
thinks just one of the smaller kinds. 'It's hard to get into those big-time ones,
nowadays' Ariel says, then morphs this into a complaint about how she can't
even lay back on a bed properly, anymore. 'That seems to be the least of your

worries.' 'Does it?' 'Or it seems it should be.' 'What else should I worry about?'
'With a gut like that? I'd bet when you get out of a bath you realize the tub was
only like two inches full - that's gotta feel crumby, like you've been gyped.' 'It
does feel crumby. I do feel gyped. It does. I do. I get out of the bath and then it
hits me: that wasn't really a bath at all!' 'You must be filthy, all the time.' 'And
I have acne on my shoulders. And over my ribs. Rib-zits, Lucy. Think on that!'
'So stop complaining about not being able to lay down on the bed. You're much
worse off than that, you know? Remind yourself of what you haven't got -
hygiene, a least-bit-human-looking-body, skin that isn't some horseshit. Don't
settle, man - you have some problems, strut them a bit.'

Lucy has to insist on going to the store to pick up *Hamburger Helper* for Ariel,
forcing Ariel to sit on the sofa and to watch television. 'I have things to do.'
'No. You don't. You were going to drive to get fucking *Hamburger Helper*.' 'Yeah
mom' assists Kayleigh 'fucking *Hamburger Helper*, like Lucy here says.' 'You're
both right' relents Ariel. 'And meat, too. I'll need meat.' 'Oh we'll get you
meat, El. We know you like your meat.' 'And get - what's it called?' but Ariel
doesn't finish that sentence, just mutters something more-or-less like 'Fine, I'll
just watch TV then.' And after a beat, Lucy nods at Kayleigh to get her coat. 'I
don't need the car-seat anymore, Lucy.' Lucy gives the kids the up-and-down.
'Since when?' 'Since awhile.' 'That's not even a sentence.' 'You're not even a
sentence' Kayleigh says, moving to the seat next to the car-seat and belting
herself in. 'And since when do you even care about sentences?' Kayleigh
continues once Lucy has come around, sat to the driver's seat. 'What do you
mean?' Kayleigh says her mom tells her all the time that Lucy is a poet and that
Lucy has words in her head completely different than other people, that Lucy
can talk in ways other people don't get. Lucy nods. Kayleigh elaborates no
further. And then Lucy asks 'She says I don't use sentences?' 'She just says
you're beautiful. And since sentences aren't, I figured.' A lot to breakdown in
that. Lucy could either delve into any of the caverns of that utterance of
Kayleigh's or avoid all the pitfalls, turn up the radio, and drive. Well? Lucy opts
for, it seems, this: 'Sentences can be beautiful.' 'Not really.' 'What do you
know? You're a kid. And you haven't even been that all that long.' 'Name a
beautiful sentence.' 'I can name oodles.' 'Do it, then.' 'Well okay, I will.'
'Name one.' 'I will - just shut up a minute, fer crying out loud, and I'll getcha
yer sentence.' 'Then do it.' 'I am doing it.' 'Any decade now, man - not that
you can even do it, but if you are actually going to, I mean.' 'Oh - oh! - Oh I
can do it.' 'So I've heard.' 'You've heard right.' 'So I'm hearing.' 'You want
me to say a beautiful sentence or not?' 'I - personally - would like you to.' 'You
better pipe down then, because otherwise when am I supposed to? When you're
flapping your lip?' 'You're stalling, Aunt Lucy?' Waitaminute. 'Hold on -

sidebar - is that what your mom calls me? *Aunt Lucy?*' 'No.' 'Really?' Lucy is trying to watch Kayleigh's face in the rearview but also has to focus on the road - irritating. 'She just calls you *Lucy*. Or *Loose*. Or *On the loose, eek!* Or *Loose Change*. Or things like that. Or -' Lucy has to brake a bit due to the car I front of her slowing for no discernable reason. 'Or what?' 'Or what, what?' 'Were you saying?' In the rearview: Kayleigh's earnestly befuddled expression. 'Nevermind. Here's a sentence: *The glacial face of her, loud as the clap of a doorknock, got lost as it came, unrecognizable, someone else by the time it was her.* Pause. 'That's not a sentence.' 'Sure it is! A beautiful one.' 'It's beautiful. Sure. But it's not a sentence.' Lucy scoffs 'Whatever you say, man - I guess you would know, right? Being a third-grader and all.' 'I bet you can't even repeat what you just said. Sentences can be repeated - shit you say can't. I'm gonna trust my mom about you.'

Is Lucy staying for dinner? Kayleigh is asking. 'No, I'm not.' Why is Lucy buying dinner, then? Kayleigh is asking. 'I just do things - shoot first, ask questions later.' Then Lucy asks 'Is it you who likes *Hamburger Helper?*' And Kayleigh says 'I like it as much as several other things. Dad likes it.' So this trip is to buy *Hamburger Helper* for Leopold. Which shades it in a different complexion. Namely: did Leopold call Ariel to specifically ask for *Hamburger Helper* for dinner? What sort of thing is that for a grown man to do!? Briefly, Lucy doesn't care though - instead irritated by this old couple who are walking side-by-side and gumming up the flow of traffic down the aisle. Kayleigh seems to note Lucy's agitation, so Lucy feels ridiculous. Leans in to explain 'It had nothing to do with them being old. It's that they are walking side-by-side. I just want to go on record about that.' Kayleigh points out that Lucy should probably get toilet-paper, too. 'You need toilet-paper?' 'Me, personally? I don't think it's up to me, personally. To need it or not' - air quotes around *need* - 'you know? But - in our house - we do tend to shit and stuff, amongst the group of us.' Lucy involuntarily tenses as though she will have to bat off offended looks, playact scolding Kayleigh and her lowdown mouth for the benefit of society's peace-of-mind, but no one seems to have noticed. 'Do you? Well that's gross. But okay, if that's the case we'll get some.' Lucy randomly grabs a package of cookies and puts it in the cart, too, then snaps fingers at Kayleigh to hand it back to her, replaces it to on entirely incorrect shelf. 'I don't want those, anymore.' 'That was fickle of you.' 'Why do you even know the word *Fickle?*' 'Why wouldn't I?' 'What possible use could it be to you?' 'What use is it to anyone?' 'And isn't it kind of fancy?' Kayleigh seems confused by this. 'Does it strike you as fancy? Elmo says it.' 'The puppet?' Kayleigh seems about to argue this term, then shrugs 'Sure - *the puppet* - sure.' 'I just think you shouldn't say things like *Fickle*. As a kid. It throws me off.' Why isn't Lucy staying for dinner? Kayleigh is asking.

'I dunno.' 'You never stay for dinner' Kayleigh says. 'No?' Lucy grabs a large package of toilet-paper and sets it in the cart with Kayleigh. The child and the item fill nearly the entire space. Maybe it's weird that Lucy even put Kayleigh in there - though Kayleigh could have said something, in that case. 'You should let me know if you're too big to ride in the cart' Lucy says while they are in line, doing so in a playing-to-the-audience-of-other-line-waiters tone, like as though Kayleigh had prompted this as a response by some remark. 'I mean, if you don't want to.' What are you talking about, Lucy? Why are you saying this? Kayleigh, thankfully, knows better than to engage you at a time like this. Just reaches over and adds a candy-bar to the items on the conveyor belt, coughs into her limp fist.

The car ride home, Lucy tries to think of a way to vent off some steam by playfully suggesting to Kayleigh that they tell Ariel there was no *Hamburger Helper* so Leopold will just have to deal with it. But she cannot think of a way to do this without it seeming strange. Suspicious. Kayleigh is already clever in her noias, will see through it, catch the drift like a draft through thin bedsheets. But what would Leopold do? Get all pissy? Could such a miniscule thing hold sway over his state-of-mind? There is something uncomfortable in that. Bad enough he watches a different sport every season just to have a sport to watch, but to insists on *Hamburger Helper* and then raise stink at its absence - no, Lucy would not be able to hold her tongue about that! Kayleigh, though. She'd have to get Kayleigh on board to sell it to Ariel. If Kayleigh backed the play, it'd be no sweat. But Kayleigh is too much her own entity to just pick up and follow Lucy's in-the-moment-cues. Kid would need a briefing and then a debriefing, after! And it'd be a bridge too far, risking getting the little bugger thinking Lucy had something ill-blooded toward the father. Of course - it has to be admitted - Kayleigh might have sussed that out, solo, long ago, unbidden. Which could make a confirmation a sort of bonding exercise. It isn't a hateful thing to do, after all. Lucy could sell it as a prank - 'Wouldn't it be funny if' dot dot dot. Note: Lucy cannot help but know her actual hesitation might be in the form of Leopold-would-have-no-problem-with-it and then she would have to feel the dolt for this whole train of thought. 'Oh there wasn't?' Leopold might say. 'No worries. You wanna just order out?' Or: 'I can do a sandwich - Hell, I'll make some chicken, you guys go sit down.' Yep. Man might be hip to it! No. *Hamburger Helper* sounds just suspect enough it'd wise him to Something's-up and he'd go into defensive helpfulness mode. Wind up with bonus points. 'You have a green-light' Kayleigh says. Lucy plays her wandering mind off by turning around, as though nothing's nothing, to give a wink to the kid - not driving still - and says 'That's just a suggestion though, K. No one's behind me, so I thought *You know what? I'm in no rush.*' This seems to pass the feasibility test. The kid doesn't seem to feel her life is in danger. Appearances maintained. 'I have a red-light now, see?' 'But that's not a suggestion' Kayleigh says, both question and some trepidation in her voice. 'No no' Lucy says. 'Bad things are never just suggestions. You gotta always do what they say.' 'I don't think red-lights are bad.' 'No?' 'No.' Lucy allows that she sees Kayleigh's point. 'Did you want me to stay for dinner?' Kayleigh shrugs. Lucy shrugs back. The clock reminds her it is only one in the afternoon and just barely.

As soon as she and Kayleigh are inside, Lucy can hear that the shower is running upstairs. 'I think your mom isn't feeling so good, today.' Kayleigh listens, shakes her head, and explains how it's not that her mom is sick, it's just she has been getting really black backaches and bone headaches and so is in the shower a lot. *Black backaches? Bone headaches?* 'For the hot water' Lucy says, nodding. But Kayleigh emphatically shakes her head. 'My dad thinks that, too - but she told him: it's cold water. She says hot water makes it worse.' 'Your mom is standing in a cold shower, right now?' Kayleigh thinks so, takes the grocery bags from Lucy's idle hands and reminds her the toilet-paper is still in the car. Lucy heads up the stairs and finds that Ariel is undressed but not yet in the shower, just there - here - sitting at her desk chair, reading from a book. 'Hi' Lucy says, gently tapping at the door frame. Ariel looks up, then down, reading from the page *A frost of her / enough for one shiver / a warmth from her / as much as one glove.* Then sets the book down and sighs. 'My head is being a little bitch, right now.' 'Yer offspring tells me you stand in the cold water? Is that right?' 'Yeah. No. Not really. I say that so I can stay in there longer.' Lucy sits on the bed and lets out a long breath. 'I think I'm not supposed to ask, but is everything okay?' 'It's fine.' 'Okay.' Pause in which neither one of them move or breathe. Then Lucy leans even more awkwardly back to keep herself supported while she reaches her foot across and tip-taps the toe of her shoe against Ariel's knees, left-right right-left left-left right-right. The process of this winds her and soon she lays back, catching her breath. 'That was the most pathetic display of anything I've seen in a long time, Loose.' 'It's because I'm old. I'm supposed to ask my doctor if my heart is still healthy enough to do things like that. Commercials say.' 'How'd it go at the store?' 'Oh' - Lucy still in not recovered - 'pretty good. I only had to smack your kid, once - but then I threatened her enough she won't tell you about it, so my mind is at ease. I think my secret is safe, for now.' 'The ever-vigilant you, eh?' The shower is still running and Lucy listens to it a moment, wondering if it is set to Cold or if the hot water has just been going to waste. It sounds cold. It sounds like chill tile and a room you don't want to linger in. It sounds like a towel reached for with angry urgency. New tactic: Lucy sits up like someone else might and cuts to the chase as though someone else might - says 'Are you sure everything is okay?' But now what,

Lucy? Now what? Because like someone might to someone who asked something like how you just did - like someone who would ask it without asking it as though as someone who might - Ariel has let a beat down her breath, pulled on her ear a moment, absently flicked her protruding belly button, turned her head to that side and said 'No.'

HOW IS IT, LUCY? 'THIS is how it is. Time. Perception of it. All packed in less-than-all. Forever packed into a micron's finger-snap.' What is it Lucy means? 'When one is dying' she means. 'One is sick, dying. The mind, the processes, they reach a pace, a pitch, a state wherein a Sense of Immortality is produced. A feeling of this-goes-on-forever and of existing for so long the mind would crumble in contemplation of it if not for becoming so much more of what the mind is than what can be imagined at the most extravagant stretch before the moment of death!' Slow down, Lucy. We don't understand. 'Think of it like a dream, if you have to. The mind produces a dream - a sensation of life more resplendent in cartwheeling, free-associative, consciously clustering ideas than physical life, itself. In the last ten minutes of living - no matter what it might look like is physically happening - the human mind, the consciousness, starts a process of slowing down and creating. You untether from associating yourself with any sensations of life or body. You slip into this dream. And though you only live ten minutes more, the dream feels it lasts ten million years - thirty million, three hundred million, one billion, a length stretching past the point where doubling, trebling, exponentially multiplying a number means anything! You live forever. Everyone! In the space of the last ten seconds of life. The sensation becomes paradox. The infinity between any two inches of an atom seen at room size! Yet eventually, to anyone observing, those ten minute, ten seconds are over. They have passed. And only took as long as they were. But yet they never end, even in the finite scope of themselves. Because: finite examined is infinite. The finite never runs out of dimensions or permutations despite it not being the totality of everything! Do you see?' No one sees. No one sees, Lucy! 'Think of losing yourself in thought, as slowly and surely as every physical atom in your body is replaced throughout the course of your life. Only slower. More gradual. By the time you are no longer who-you-were you have been who-you-are twice as long! You see?' No. No one sees. 'You are you. Then every thought changes - paint-chip-by-paint-chip - replaced so incrementally, so minusculey by other paint-chips over such a stretch of time that the change, while absolute, is not an insult, is not even measurable. And this happens: all thought - all mental you, all consciousness - is washed over this way in the space of a physical moment - a blink. A reset and an elongation! Forever and forever! A box of unending! We die?' We die. 'We don't!' We don't? 'Our perceptions reach infinity while the perceptions of others do not - not in the same moment. An absolute isolation. The same way a place galaxies away is not *Here* though it could be brought here. The same way a wall could be replaced, brick-by-brick, and not be called *Another Wall* but *A Wall* - still just *That Wall*. Each new part was always part of the old parts - the process of change a part of the containment of never-changed!'

Why is Lucy's mind in this overdrive? She doesn't know, herself. From appearances, well just look: contently, even smiling, she drives her car in the direction away from Ariel's house. And look there, in the seat beside her: a drawing by Kayleigh and a cupcake in a little plastic baggie, beside. On the radio? An album she has not listened to for some time. *The Thrills. So Much For The City.* The easy gruff of the singer's voice *Oh how the sun sets on my boulevard* easy-going and somehow so desolate *but leaves such a shadow* oh so precise and yet lazy and bones-without-body *to fill*. She isn't even thinking about Ariel and what Ariel is going through. Perfect cordons have been set up! A quarantined mind! There is a gouge in the shape of a conversation and around it is swimming the sing-songy antiseptic of *So let's party, Dustin Hoffman* and the deadfalls and firewalls of *Those Hollywood kids, those Hollywood kids gotta pay*. It's only a happy-go-lucky o'clock of some kind and Lucy has a day set-to-full with activities! And no room for the thoughts in that exiled box. She is driving to see Mathilde. She is driving to see Young Pastor Mitchell. And then later she is driving for a dinner chat - to be interviewed as the glorious poetess she be! So who knows why she is in a caterwaul of philosophic jibber-jabber about *what dreams may come*. Here is what she knows of philosophy: we must picture Sisyphus as an absolute dickhead, totally deserving of what he got! That's the name of the game, as far as Lucy Jinx is concerned. *Bastards get got!* That is how she would set it down. If she ever caught Sisyphus happy? Well now, she'd wipe that damn grin of his face - and how! And anyway, she now thinks - the song on the CD changing - that is no punishment for intellectuals, anyway. We must picture Sisyphus as some dunerheaded yutz who would be so tortured by never accomplishing anything by way of pushing a rock? What - would the half-wit be satisfied if it got to the top and stayed there? This would be marked as a soul-stirring success? 'Moron' she says, and skips to the track she has had in mind. But why this track, Lucy? *Your love is like a city I visited.* Because it's groovy. *Your love is like a city that burned me good.* Because it was a track you ignored the first year - two years - of owing the album, then listened to and were blown away by. *Oh Las Vegas, I can only afford one weekend!* No other reason. And get that thinker thinking in a more pleasant-bending direction, Ms. Jinx - that is an order. Last day of the weekend. To the hilt to the hilt! Ariel has her own matters at hand, little thingie squirming in her belly - and besides, you don't even remember exactly what she said, right?

Though that is all well and good for this notion of A Peaceful Death - this white-picket-fence-demise, eh? Loved ones gathered and a physician serene, indicating when there is nothing more to be done than mill about seeming assortedly profound. Say, though, we're talking of a sudden demolition of self, entire? *Yucca flats! The A-bomb!* The body doesn't know to slow down, the mind to start a process of ever-after after-after. Unless Lucy now wishes to supernaturally posit the damn mind perceives itself out-of-time, forward and back, knows it is going to die, no matter what - fur prickled up in ways indicating it knows just then a pilot is pressing a trigger button, soundless above, and that canister falling is gonna Kaboom! it big time - game over! Does the idea of an explosion or a torturous death-by-fire - or a drive-by-shooting or a sudden aneurism or a television falling on one's head whilst at the same time one is suffering an epileptic fit - change this wonderful set-up Lucy has posited? That is to say: how sure is Lucy of her Everyone Is Immortal proposition? In some circumstances - even if it were true, what Lucy says, principally, most-of-the-time true - isn't it worked around? Isn't death just *death*. Death: the normal kind like we all figure we've got a handle on? And - if so - ought one to just lock oneself up, take great precautions to allow for the end to come in casual gait with gifts and transcendence? Lucy says: 'Not necessarily.' Lucy says: 'Think of the microscope.' Then: 'Think of the electron-microscope.' Now: 'Think of Time as even more miniaturely divisible than Matter.' Can Lucy clarify that? 'Say a hydrogen-bomb goes off' Lucy says 'or say one is being tortured and tortured and then - unbeknownst - a bullet is shoved through the brain, no shriving time allowed. To Time, this matters not!' Because Lucy's position is 'It only needs an *instant* - and whine though you might, there is nothing than doesn't need an *instant* in which to happen. And if there is an instant, Time will partial it to the point it expands to the horizons' arms' length! Every trace of your physical existence wiped out in a millisecond - so what? Once the mechanism of You is breached - once Death starts, in whatever form, once obliteration begins, fast or slow, square or round - the consciousness-safeguard clicks on and: immortality delivered!' There is always space and time for Forever in a Space-and-Time made of infinite infinities! In fact, Lucy finds it mock-worthy to call Death a thing when Death is a zillion things - and not always basically-the-same, not at all! Take even in the example she just off-the-cuffed: is death-by-slow-torture the same as incineration-by-a-hydrogen-bomb? Can we even say someone died in the latter case, if they were at flashpoint? The body isn't there - but it didn't *die* it *vaporized*! Very different than systems shutting down blah blah

blah. It was going full-tilt up to the moment it was nonexistent. Death? Is that *death*? This is where other words ought come in. This is why we know we don't know!

Again, Lucy, again - with respect and while all-gathered would like to commend you for these inquires and point out how, indeed, there is much good in them - why are you nattering yourself with this nevermind? Neither here nor there, of course - but speaking of neither-here-nor-there: you are neither where you were going or going anywhere else in particular, instead! Mind like a blind toy race-car, dragged backward to get wheels wound, let go and just any-which-waying into any which wall! Might as well take the upcoming left turn - though it is this bloody intersection - and get over to see Young Pastor Mitchell before backtracking - a considerable backtrack, now - to see Mathilde. This intersection. Would it kill them to install a left-turn arrow? And what about this curve of the lanes down the dip of this hill, at a wend? The approaching traffic, there? Impossible to tell if those drivers intend to stay straight or to turn, themselves! And - as always - Lucy finds herself the first car in a rapidly forming queue, the pressure clammying up her back and making her skull-base itch. For all the woman behind Lucy cares, Lucy should pull ahead and get creamed! The only thing keeping the driver behind Lucy from wishing exactly that is the selfish thought 'Then I'd be more delayed due to the accident!' That doesn't count as a compunction, though! The drivers back there suborn vehicular manslaughter! And Jesus God! Now this pedestrian is just gonna cross at the crosswalk, too!? Right just exactly when Lucy has time to turn? And so what should Lucy do - speed around to get out ahead of him - which she could easily do - or wait for him to take his idle time of it, as though he actually has a right to be walking there, as though that isn't just something people say about pedestrians but never mean to be taken seriously about? Wrong to think this has exactly to do with Lucy? Wrong? Fact: if she were third-in-queue, it wouldn't be her problem. She is first! But: if she were third, the man would still be crossing the walk - that is the point! In that scenario, his crossing the walk would have no impact on Lucy. Zero - none whatever! Light going yellow and only now does the guy get a decent jog going and - Sorry, sorry - his hands go up to some other driver who just has to make a right turn, coming in the opposite direction. Damn it! Not Lucy's fault. She grits teeth, but while also pretending she is imperturbably listening to the radio. She soundlessly does a pretend laugh, as though listening to a ribald observational-comic giving a stand-up routine. The driver behind her is applying lipstick. The driver further back, probably, is loading a shotgun. Green. Lucy ridiculously guns it and cuts in front of all on-coming before they know sniff about it! Eyes flit to rearview. None of the other cars in queue followed her. She cows. Hates that she has to slow down, already, at this light.

People can still see her. Sarcastic Way-to-gos are being sarcasticed at her, judgmental heads are being given curt, dismal shakes.

So where does this leave us? Returned to the question of Suicide? A question, Lucy, which you have never pondered. Oh and don't cite those paltry, chickenshit tantrums you had twenty years ago! That wasn't desire for suicide - that was just the guts of a Diva spilling themselves fatuously. Remember that whole long walk? Dosed on cough meds and good-old-Gregory's pain-killers sneaked from that never-used prescription of his - such a staunch, soldierly sort, Greg, always shunning the taking of pain meds, what a guy! - you had walked around that cold night, living away from home in the first nowhere you nobodied in, kitchen knife in your pocket, promising yourself you would use the next payphone, call Emergency Services, say you'd cut yourself - Oh God, you fantasized crying how you were so very sorry - and you would - remember? good Lord, Lucy, this is something you did! - wait until you heard the sirens before actually cutting, no real risk of going unsaved? Remember? Yes, yes, quite a laugh! The question of Suicide - is that what you are thinking about, now? Remember - back at that time - you were honestly worried the responders would know something was amiss when they saw how much blood there was, how much there wasn't? 'That isn't enough! No way she cut herself before the call. What kind of a trick is this!?' Remember your walking and arguing - as though after-the-fact - saying 'How could they know? They don't know how bad I cut myself! Maybe I cut myself some before and some after! I was distressed! They don't know!' The question of Suicide, Lucy? You mean to induce this la-la-land Eternal Life you are positing? Why not snuff it and cut to the endless chase? That is a fair question. Which you have answered. You will not kill yourself. Not because it has to do with the process - not some 'a certain amount of life has to be lived first' little rule or anything and not some 'question of morality' or what not - but because you won't. Since it will happen anyway - by which Lucy means the Eternal Life, as proposed - in fact it makes the most sense to continue living, as one lives, even in ghastly conditions, for as long as possible! How is that? Why is that? Because this physical life is - though limited - very unique. It will not come again. Eternity is in the realm of finitely-infinite consciousness. It is where the drain drags things, no matter - so by all means, before the plug's pulled, lust, dance, starve, suffer abuse and what have you! It's the only go 'round - and you'll forget it soon enough and live a billion million lifetimes past even a billion million lifetime past being able to remember it to begin with! You'll live so long you'll forget there ever being a thought having been had of not living! 'I mean' Lucy says 'it doesn't matter - sure, kill yourself and you get there, the same. But it isn't quicker or not quicker, in the end. All things considered, it takes as long to live as it takes to die.'

Sunday and Young Pastor Mitchell's car's not in the lot. Lucy lights a cigarette and wonders if he has just parked in another place, for some reason. Maybe his usual spot, there - as well as all the ones next to it - were blocked off when he had arrived, though now they are all wide open. Maybe there had been a Radio Event, a sweepstakes in full swing in the lot. Or a street-cleaner had been going. Rubbish, Lucy knows. She smokes slowly and grumpies her posture. The worst possibility is, of course, that dear Mitchell has been fired or otherwise found his goose cooked. Thoughts Lucy does her stoic-best not to entertain for myriad reasons, not the least of which would be her own video-image, more likely than not, at some point having been recorded in covert interaction with the lad. Thin - unlikely, very unlikely - though that prospect is on examination, Lucy does squirm a bit. 'Or he might just have the day off' Lucy says. Reasons? Doctor's appointment. Fucking some girlfriend who has new work hours, this having become the only available slot for such things. Death in the family. Weekend trip having been planned for months. He works a second job and got held over due to a no-showing colleague. All of these sound good but do nothing to moisturize the eczema-noia in spread. She wants to go inside. That's what Lucy wants to do. She wants to ask 'Isn't Mitchell at work, today?' She wants to do so with her mind full of 'Who cares that at least one, if not all, of his co-workers will know what I am for asking that question, know what I'm on about?' This is not something she wants to have to mark as *Uncertain*. 'Where I will get pot?' she hisses out with a drag, ridicules herself, interior. Why would she be asking after Mitchell? Just out of curiosity. Does she know Mitchell? Sure. From where? I'm sorry - why are you asking? 'That's good, that's good' she nods, feeling confident. Yes. Do it. Out of the car she goes. On approach to the door. Second thoughts. No! Inside. Looking around - no Mitchell - so taps the shoulder of this poor lug of a girl - first job and trying to convince herself she doesn't mind bussing tables and emptying trash. 'Do you know if Mitchell is working?' The girl has no idea who Mitchell is. Oh well. Pressing on - there is a Manager-sort, one can tell by the long sleeves and necktie under the apron - she raises a hand to get this older fellow's attention. 'I was wondering if Mitchell was at work today?' 'Mitchell?' 'Yes' she says, resolute, only now thinking 'Is that not his goddamn name!?' 'Mitchell DeWalt?' She opts for a direct 'Yes' with an 'obviously' head-nod, not knowing if the inflection he gave to the surname meant that more than one Mitchell was employed in the store. 'No' - shit, the guy is giving her the up-down - 'no, he's no longer with us. May I ask why you ask?' 'Of course, of course' she says, finger-to-chin as though surprised to have been given out-of-date information. 'I am with the *Youth League*. We have an invalid gentleman advertising payment to be wheeled around in his chair - two hours a day, eleven dollars per hour. Anyway, Mitchell was recommended as a lad who might like a hand in that. I was only sent to see if he would like first dibs. Inquiring on his behalf, you see - my name is Wedel-Jarlsburg.' Lucy bows and draws back, retreating while holding eye-contact, keeping her literary reference exact.

What about this? Isn't there *too early*? Say an infant dies, in utero - does it still receive this sprawling immortality? Of course. Why shouldn't it? How would that work? It would be without language - no sense even of the word *Identity*. What goes on for this not-yet-born? The umbilical mentality, the womb-hum on and on and on? First off: perhaps - and why not? Secondly, though: No. No. And this is why a limited mind has trouble with the limitless. Think on it: all of human life - in only a few thousand years - has invented and mutated and hacked and preened over Language and Idea and Sense-of-self - no single jot of which ever stuck as indelible and none has lasted, intact, long at all. Stretch that out now, ad infinitum. Do you know what would happen to the word *Carrot* in thirteen quadrillion years? To the concept of *Carrot*? My God - try to follow! It doesn't matter what knowledge the human mind and sensory processes have tiddliy-winked with In This Life - so to speak - once the next leg begins! An unborn is the same as a twelve-hundred-year-old man, as far as it goes for the sake of this which Lucy is preaching! Listen: first language, identity-as-person-and-word, goes - consciousness becomes just being things. All as thought. The thought of being everything. One thing at-a-time, all things at once. But then it gets bigger than that - because long after you run out of having been everything that there is to be on Earth - everything you could possibly know about - there are still infinite more things to be. Hell, you might not even be all the things on Earth. Or any of them! But be countless, endless other things, twining and interacting, abandoning and yeast-budding, linking and seeding and so on. Think, even in worm's-eye terms: what would it be like to be a human who has lived a thousand years, ten thousand, one million, one hundred million, ten trillion, ninety-four septillion? Even keeping the day-to-day perception version of Person, do you think you can fathom that? We're talking about Immortality, not just a three-day-weekend! Even if physically alive, as one is now alive - even if the body stayed youth-prime and all of those endlessly tedious and boring What Ifs all settled to Best Case Scenario - do you think you would be a halfpenny the same in three-hundred vigintillion years as you are, today? Think you'd recall this conversation? Lucy is talking about Time - all in an instant - on the scale of the damned cosmos and then some - Time past the notion of recollection or connectivity-of-moments! Imagine if - to put it easier, because it's what it becomes anyway - every second, so to speak, were thirty-nine Novemdecillion years long, but that only as much happened in a second-that-long as happens in a second-like-now - a second only one second long! Are you imagining that? Well: do you think one second would be concerned, by the time it terminates, with what happened in the previous second, might go on in the one subsequent? That one moment would plot its course on the other?

Wisely, Lucy decides she needs to stop driving, proper. She does not want to be in this state when she sees Mathilde, for example. And why are you even in this state-of-mind? Lucy is determined not to answer that question. Good. Every time she tries, she plummets back into this debate about Eternity. Good. Mind on other things. Step one? This text to Mathilde about how you are running late and are all apologies. Mathilde's response: *Lucy, I am just in the apartment where I live where I would be anyway like how I always am - you're here when you're here, man.* Lucy texts back *Good girl!* and Mathilde texts back the word *Sigh* and the word *Yep*. Whatever that means. 'You're so weird, Mathilde' Lucy tells the phone before putting it in her pocket and crossing the parking lot into this clothing store. An odd move. Clothing store. But, in truth, Lucy has phobias about going into stores where she feels she has no business and has discovered, over the decades, that clothing stores are immune to this. No one expects you to buy clothes! Whereas if she went into a store that sold kitchen supplies and said 'I'm just looking around' it would be grounds to get a dossier started on her, prep for eventual impeachment. First thing she notices, though: I'm too old to be in here. Exactly how she felt when she was a kid in a store that had no Kid's Section, only looking in the telescope backward so that the shore seems super far away. What Lucy does with this observation: actually relaxes. Purposefully lingers by a floor-worker long enough to be asked 'Can I help you find anything?' just to be able to have it on record 'Oh no - I'm just waiting for my daughter.' 'Is she trying on?' What a pesky question! 'No, no. She and her friends are still at the movies but will be here, after. I'm just the mom, you know?' Retail-worker nod and perfunctory 'Let me know if you need anything.' 'Thank you, sweetie.' Gawd. How pervy this all feels! Sweetie? Really, Lucy? And staring at the girl's ass, into the bargain? 'Shut up' she thinks - almost says - and now is self-conscious about the mannequins and about even just holding up any still-hangered shirts, pants, anything. Way out of this quagmire of awkwardness: if anyone noticed me giving that girl's ass a looksie, they would think I was giving it a motherly, disapproving tut-tut, hoping to innocent Saints that my daughter tends to herself more dearly. Do these clerks think your daughter is pretty, Lucy? Or do they think you have one of those daughters-who-shops-in-this-store-but-ain't-fooling-anyone? To judge from you, do you imagine they think you'd have cool, attractive offspring? There you are in the mirror. Have a look. Honest impression: your kid looks like what? But Lucy won't meet her own eyes because she can feel the weight of her face and how hard her reflection would seem to be looking back. Blushes a little bit. Looks at her phone and sends herself the text-message *Help*. Waits a minute. Buzz.

Presses button. *Help*. She tsks, as though disappointed, and leaves with a maternal infuriation porcupined to her.

But is this meant to be peaceful, Lucy? This indiscriminate foreverness? How certain are you you stop being Lucy? What if that never irons out? No amount of reinvention, no amount of countless hours achieves a loss of that deep down sense of *I'm-Lucy-Jinx*. You live forever, as Lucy Jinx - not as Lucy-Jinx-who-has-forgotten-she-is-Lucy-Jinx. Not Lucy Jinx, butterfly. Not Lucy Jinx, piece of a cup handle. Not Lucy Jinx, particle of stratosphere. Not Lucy Jinx, wet spot on lip from lemonade. Not Lucy Jinx, nebula haze. Not Lucy Jinx, comet tail. Not Lucy Jinx, bacteria frozen on Neptune. Not Lucy Jinx, smeared typewritten word *Orchid*. Not Lucy Jinx, sun flare. Not Lucy Jinx, vibration in vocal cords of walrus. Not Lucy Jinx, last atom moved by a particular chirp of a particular nightingale. And so on. Not to mention those ocean-depth, outer-space-distant, beyond-imagination's-cusp things you will be - but you'll be Lucy-Jinx-as-those. Like you were Lucy-Jinx-at-fourteen versus Lucy-Jinx-now or Lucy-Jinx-at-twenty versus Lucy-Jinx-ten-years-ago or Lucy-Jinx-at-two or Lucy-Jinx-at-three or Lucy-Jinx-wet-and-shivering or Lucy-Jinx-asleep-with-chickenpox-fever-flavored-mouth. Maybe there is a smear of you, in particular, to the consciousness that squeezes all-the-time-ever into a thimble and that smear stays on the consciousness, mucky and gelatin, no matter what. And Lucy, let us ask this next thing. What? What!? This life-after-death, so to speak, is all well and good - but what about after it? Or is that pocketed-off-eternity it? Well, fine. If so - does it not contain phases, in itself? Does it not have Ends and Beginnings? What do I mean? What do I mean!? So, Lucy: you say it goes from Physical Person, like I am now, to Consciousness, still in this physical world - do I, maybe, then go from Consciousness into Something-Past-Consciousness, all the while even still in this physical world? Or within the new-conscious-forever-realm? Is there a different Death to be tricky-dicked out of inside this Death? This Life, as we call it, maybe itself an already wriggled wriggle out of some other demise? Stop-gap in stop-gap in stop-gap in stop-gap in stop-gap. Buffering in a buffer in a buffer that's buffering? A line that we're pulling back from until it is revealed to be a single point, no height, width, breadth, duration? Come now, Lucy! You started this! How is it? Time. Perception-of-time. And what are you, Lucy, if not avoiding something and if not then eventually done in like you knew you would be? You want to perceive an eternity of eternities in which to try to get away, to put off the next with the next next and the next-next with the next next-next? I don't know about that, Lucy. All alone? Unbadgered by villains and false promises? What would chase you that long? What would? Nothing. An infinity of having escaped? Of nothing in pursuit? Is that Time? Is that Perception, Lucy? Why are you thinking this? What's set you off?

Lucy's cigarette seems to have reached an agreement with the heat from the vent. They feel connected. This smoke is rigorously enjoyable. She had asked Dorene - it must have been Dorene, right? - 'Do cigarettes warm you up?' This back before Lucy'd ever smoked one. When she just thought about that one she kept - she'd picked it up from out of a pack she'd found hid behind a cinderblock by the backdoor of a restaurant - hidden in her sock drawer for a year, two years, in a box in her sock drawer with coins and a photo of herself, age-of-two. 'Do cigarettes warm you up?' 'No. That's what liquor is for.' Dorene had said. And had been shivering. And Lucy had heard it as 'That's what licorice's for.' Confused. Intimidated. Puny. Wanting to stand closer. To stand closer. To share. Without letting on. Then not caring. Then having not cared. In the car, here, it feels like the inhales make her warm, the exhales warm her around. Not that this is the first time she has felt this or thought it or made these connections. But they are always welcome. Smoking a cigarette and it feeling the way her nine-year-old mind figured it would feel. And thinking about anything but Ariel and her boo-hooing. If it even was boo-hooing. Whatever it was. Lucy isn't even sure. Drags a smoke. Blows it out. Drags a smoke. Blows it out. The heater spills the sound of applause from the Conference Room two rooms over. One should measure the length of a cigarette in five increments based on the word *Smoke*. She hits Record on her tape recorder, settles back, and repeats herself before proceeding. 'One should measure the length of a cigarette in five increments based on the word *Smoke*. Depending how much is left, you get your designation. Reverse-order. Smoke just a fifth of a cig, you haven't had a *Smoke* just an *E*. Two-fifths is a *Ke*. Three-fifths an *Oke*. Four-fifths a *Moke*. And only when you've had it down to the stub or to the stained finger-betweens have you legitimately had a *Smoke*. This would help waitresses complain: 'God - I can't get five minutes!? I only had an Oke - I mean, Jesus!' And then, now, Lucy goes silent but let's the recorder keep recording. She smokes. Sometimes she says 'Yeah' or 'Yeah, you heard me' in a tone of voice like someone falling asleep in a movie while accidentally revealing a secret. Silence for some period she doesn't know. Between three and six minutes, probably. Not long. She opens the door and drops the remains of the cigarette on to the lot pavement as though needing to be sly, quickly putting the car in reverse and hitting the gas without even really giving a look around for the sake of basic safety. No harm done. No harm done. Though she does keep glancing at the rearview to be sure another meter's worth of driving doesn't reveal a sudden corpse. 'That'd be the last thing you need' she says to her reflected eyes. Wrinkle wrinkle. She looks like a gunfighter. She looks like shots fired.

*********

MATHILDE'S KITCHEN SINK, THE BASIN of it, gave off the look and smell of a schoolyard water-fountain. There are those chalky stains, overlapping in thickets of bolder white and fadeder grey. Ash on silver. Yes, like a water-fountain, the sink resembles the ashen palm of a grandmother robot. Lucy sips from her coffee, having just added a plink of cold water to it from the tap, this shushing up a brief froth of bubbles she rather wishes would stay always atop a coffee. Invent that then, Lucy. Some sort of bubbling-capsule should do it. 'Are you having a party or something?' she calls over to Mathilde who stands on a chair, taping some balloons to the corners of the archway from the bedroom area to the living-room. It seems rather than humor Lucy's fatuous line of questioning, Mathilde says 'I had the strangest dream, last night. I opened my freezer and a rattlesnake had given birth to dozens of babies inside of a vodka bottle.' Lucy strolls into the room - her coffee discarded, meanwhile-lit cigarette now going. 'And when you woke up your pillow was gone, right?' Again, a tactful ignoring of Lucy Jinx. 'The snake was shivering and hissing. Its tongue was frozen out of its mouth and looked breaded like a fish-stick. The babies were worm-like and didn't seem to be bothered by the alcohol they floated within, they just squirmed around like a fistful of fingers that are long enough to wrap around and twine like the fingers of two hands could, you know?' 'Your dreams don't seem to know a lot about how Mother Nature works. I don't know what that means, but I'm glad you're smarter than that in waking life.' Mathilde wonders aloud if she had given Lucy permission to smoke in her apartment. Lucy reads the banner *Congratulations Elise!* over the mantle, then notes the now-hung gauze streamers just inside the front door. 'Your guests have to enter through the tendrils of a kindergarten-classroom-octopus, it's like.' 'Elise had the children. The twins. Elise is the one you referred to as *That skinny fella who never seems like she has any arms.*' Lucy knows who Elise is and how she describes her, she snaps. A pause. Then, very excited, Lucy points out how this explains Mathilde's dream. Baby! Twins! Snakes! Weirdness! Vodka! Mathilde doesn't see it and Lucy realizes her defense of the position amounts to little more than repeating the words *Babies, plural* in this tone-of-voice or that. And by the way: why wasn't Lucy invited to the party? 'You call her *That skinny fella who never seems like she has any arms!*' 'That's a remarkable description! She should be proud I noticed her so particularly.' Which is all well and good - or so Mathilde, her-mind-on-other-things, sighs - but Elsie's boyfriend is also a poet Lucy had written something terrible about for some stupid Lit Journal, last year. 'Why do you throw parties for such questionable people, Square Root?' 'You know' Mathilde says, safety-pin in her lips while she is carefully messing with a table cloth, folding it to ready for a stab 'just to counterbalance the normalness and pleasantness of knowing you, Lucy.'

So Mathilde is on the phone. And laughing a lot. And didn't tell Lucy Lucy could have any pot, even though Lucy knows Mathilde keeps her pot and glass bowl in that hollowed-out book there, usually along with a few hundred dollars in petty cash. You should rob Mathilde, Lucy. Why? Just to see what that would be like! Yeah? Start a whole new chapter of your life - take the drugs, the dough, go on the run, see how long it lasts you! Starvation-diet and hoboing the tracks with the degenerates! Small-town love-affair with the soon-to-be-owner of a grain-mill. Until it all goes sour and you have to come back. Funny story to tell. All forgiven. What is Mathilde laughing about so much? Eavesdropping gives no clues. Damn Mathilde and her non-specific response patterns! Clearly just audience. Might as well be listening to a comedy concert played over the line for how little she is saying. Lucy slumps to the sofa and stares at the food-trays set out. Isn't this a fine sight? Mathilde's life is always so shocking. It reminds Lucy of her penchant to romanticize people. This party has all the potential energy of a back-to-school night, a fifth grade Sock-Hop sort of happening. All this work. And for what? Half-dozen of Mathilde's colleague-cum-friends from the school where she teachers will show up, loiter for few hours, eventually only one - maybe a couple, two technically, but really no different than one - staying on and a *DVD* will be started. 'All this work all this work all this work' Lucy says to the unturned-on television, as though the precocious brat in an amateur theatre piece scolding a dog in a bonnet. What in Christ's could be so funny!? Mathilde is begging the speaker to stop, pleading how it is going to make Mathilde urinate if she doesn't stop laughing. From the apartment above comes the sound like a chair or a table being moved from one spot to another was abruptly set down. Carpet thick thump. Lucy is staring at the ceiling, wondering if that happened exactly above her. If the floor had ben weaker, would Lucy have been done for? She stares and yawns and her eyes water and blur from staring and yawning. Mathilde laughs even while saying 'Goodbye.' Lucy hears Mathilde opening the freezer door, taking up a bag of ice and whapping it - smack! smack! smack! - against, Lucy knows, the edge of the lip of the kitchen counter. Smack! Smack! Sounds of bag being prodded, testing to see if the ice is differentiated enough. 'You should get a centrifuge for that ice' Lucy says in a whisper - but raspy, like she is pretending to yell. Mathilde walks by with a bowlful of ice and sets it on that table - there - and puts the soda from the six-pack into the ice. '*Raspy* should be spelled with an *H*' Lucy says. Mathilde hums something, then says she agrees. 'Actually, it should be spelled with two *H*s. *Hrhaspy*. Things should be spelled how it's the best way to say them. Simple rule to follow.'

This is it. Manilla Folder. Half-dozen sheets of paper. Lucy is disappointed, as she had been expecting a real substantive collection of documents. This isn't even enough that it justifies saying the word *Documents* in a cool Russian accent. Compound fragments. 'Dock-ooh-meants' Lucy accents. 'Dokumunts.' And Mathilde joins in, tries her hand with 'Doock-who-munts.' Anyway, it is really all Mathilde could find. She reiterates that she is not a sleuth or a hacker sort - that Lucy could have found the same information herself in five minutes if she would just get a computer. 'Speaking of which, did I get any e-mails?' Lucy lays the disappointing folder down on the kitchen counter, scratches her nose, the crease where it joints to her face. Mathilde vulgarly gestures that Lucy should just go check for herself, as long as she's over. But this would defeat the purpose of having Mathilde do all of this for her, so instead Lucy just decides to light another cigarette - 'I did mention she just had babies?' 'Are the babies going to be here?' 'No.' 'Exactly. Piss off.' - and to suggest that she stay over for the party but keep hidden in the bedroom until an hour in to festivities, at which point she will just sneak in and act like she has been there the entire time, insisting she had been, playing her part convincingly enough to make the guests doubt themselves. 'Because I'll have been able to have heard everything from the bedroom' Lucy explains when Mathilde just gives her a blank stare. 'I'll pay careful attention to everything everyone says, so that in the end I will seem like I was there and being attentive - but then I'll relate some things I will claim to have said to them and will say how they reacted in this or that way and they will have no choice but to go along with it. And they'll be haunted all night, after!' Mathilde considers this. Adds to the suggestion that she should make it her business to get everyone to talk disparagingly of Lucy, so that when all of a sudden Lucy is there, there will also be a sense of queasy unrest. How long has Lucy been here? Where did Lucy come from? Only now, quite mid-sentence, Mathilde says 'We're not actually going to, though' and drops the thread, entirely, telling Lucy she can smoke a little pot if she wants, but has to go into the bathroom and breathe through a make-shift filter composed of an empty toilet-paper roll stuffed with a scented dryer-sheet. 'I have to Art and Crafts that myself?' Mathilde is texting somebody, says 'What?' - types - 'Hold on' - types - 'Do you, ugh' - types - 'sorry - what? No! No, there's one already made. It's with the pot in the book.' Lucy feigns innocence with 'Oh right - that book! You still use that?' And Mathilde fetches it from the shelf, walks into the bedroom, exits sans the box, hands Lucy her file folder and says 'Have at. You can hang out here for another two hours, but then you gotta be gone. Deal?'

This is Claire. This is Claire Seville. Photograph-with-caption: *Claire Seville.* Eight pages total, containing the entire of what Lucy now knows of her. Minus a handful of caught-glimpses of the woman, of course - parking lot, stairs, just going in through her different-grey door. Only so few glimpses as that? Surely Lucy saw the woman - That Woman - more times than that? This photo - on newsprint - shows Claire either with short hair or hair styled so that when photographed from this angle it seems short, shows that distinct patch of freckles and skin coloration over one cheek, down under the neck - something like the remains of a label picked almost-all-the-way clean of a pop-bottle curve, something like nail polish chipped or the tarnish on some Thrift Store piece of lesser-grade silver. The photo accompanies the brief article explaining that Claire Seville was found dead. Treated as homicide. How can such words be real, used in alignment with actual people, honestly set down what whom did to whom? This other page? A print-out of the Staff page of *Arcturus Homes*. Much duller photo, but the beauty still resolute even in its Ink-Jet printered and pixilated rendition. *Claire Seville, finance officer*. Contact number. E-mail address. Lucy tries to determine from the header of the page - the logo of *Arcturus* - how it must have been to work there. Close-knit? No idea. Some co-worker or another every day celebrating something so that there is always a break-room cake, cut into squares more nicely than Lucy ever cuts squares of any cake she serves, dwindling supply of itself through the day, just a plastic knife with hardened frosting left by the time folks clock-out for home? Why would Claire Seville, though, be a part of this *Youth Soccer League*? Nowhere does it say she has children. Lucy pokes through some of the other pages - one a print-out of a Free Background Search listing *Aliases* - none - and *Previous Places Lived* - here and there - and any *Public Disclosures* like *Criminal Convictions, Bankruptcies* - none, one three-years-ago - and links to a few websites that must have been defunct by the time Mathilde finished her checking around because Lucy does not see any print-out of such sites. *Claire Seville*. Third row. One of only two women mixed in with other parents and the spillage of children knelt or sat cross-legged in front of them. *Youth Soccer*. This page just various captured photos Mathilde must have found - contextless, some very small, Lucy guessing no larger versions were available. Look at how she smiles, Claire Seville. Like the over-bright of sun reflecting in stabs off of an iced pond it is trying to melt. Those freckles tucking right under her chin, mossing over her lip - there - in a dribble like crumbs left on the floor if eating a cupcake while walking a circle in place. And this page? A profile from some community site for avid readers. *No Photo Available. Favorite Books*, nothing listed. *Books to Read*, Zero. *Books Rated*, Zero. *Friends With*, forty-two members. *Reviews Posted*, one - which is below, Lucy sees, but all it says is *Looking forward to reading this* - for some novel called *Like Being Killed* by Ellen Miller. A note from Mathilde - *kind of eerie, right?* circled with an arrow pointing to the title. *Member Since*, four years. And that book reviewed three-years-ago. This is Claire. This is Claire Seville.

Mathilde always has such terrific marijuana. It's practically a character trait. It allows Lucy to overlook how perfectly made is Mathilde's bed and how the lamp on the bedside table is clearly dusted, right along with everything else in the room. There is a full collection of ceramic turtles on the dresser. Those turtles are what Lucy is thinking about while she sits on the toilet and exhales through the cardboard cylinder scented of baby powder. They probably mean something, those turtles. All these little worlds that Lucy doesn't know about. Inhale. Count twenty. Exhale. Worlds and worlds. Which reminds her of how she does not understand how the discovery of eyelash-mites didn't stop the progress of humanity dead in its tracks. How microscopic things alive in your eyelashes - with legs! with mouths! with bellies and procreative urges! - is not seen through the aperture of 'It's like discovering magic is real' Lucy just doesn't fathom. How being able to see these things - to watch them, real-time, living, mating, sprawling in the up-and-down of flirtatious flut-flut-flut - doesn't change everything - in fact changes nothing! - is the true scope and extremity of the human's capacity for horrific disattachment! Lucy forgets to use the filter or to aim her exhalation toward the upsucking vent fan, instead watching a thin haze intersect with the patterns on the seemingly brand-new - but likely just well-kept - shower curtain pattern. Circles. Triangles. Thin rectangles connecting the two other shapes or else superimposing on them or else drifting behind them. Lucy sees faces. She sees shoulders. She see a desert of open mouths at night. 'Back to those microscopic bugs though' she says, taking what she promises will be her final hit 'we cannot minimize what they mean!' Imagine if one were to put on a set of magical - or highly scientific - glasses which allowed one to see, in the air around them - invisible-to-the-naked-eye - some creatures swimming about in the air, humping or dividing via fission over the heads of people in elevators and between the shoulders of commuters on trains. Why, it would alter one consciousness irrevocably! An invisible leech stuck to one's spine-base, seeming to suck some substance from skin cells our body neither misses nor our medical research has ever even identified!? Why yes, that would fuck with one, righteously! Try sleeping whilst knowing you have flatworms with catfish whiskers laying eggs in an invisible spittle around your tonsils! Yet any school kid can be shown images - moving video, even! - of eel-like monsters that fornicate and derive sustenance from the follicles that bat involuntarily twenty-nine thousand times every day - and nothing! Nothing!! They are not impacted by this sight, in any way! 'We don't bat an eyelash at the fact that there is animal life in the batting of our eyelashes! We discover, through our advancements, life we never would have imagined is currently living on top of, inside us - discover we are an ecosystem to creature after creature after creature and just ho-hum it. Like nothing! Well not me' says Lucy, lighting up - she promises - her last time. 'It freaks me out that I'm a patchwork-buffet for things more numerous on my body than humans are to this Earth!'

The floor of Mathilde's bedroom is like the coat-of-arms in some shag tapestry. Lucy is an almost letter *K* how she is curled, semi-fetal, just now, one her side, ignoring the pressure to the bulb of her hip. Her body mumbles numb shivers in waves from toes into the mush of her closed eyes. Bzzt. Bzzt. That is the sound and a sensation like being tickled when one's foot has lost circulation. Only: the felling is in her eyes. And what about Claire, Lucy? What did you think Mathilde would find for you? A mystery? A connection? Something that justified the fact that you even knew who she was though you didn't know at all who she was? Because, let's think Lucy: say you hadn't had an infatuation with the woman - come off it, you know that's what it was! - and had just heard that a woman was murdered in the apartment below you - well, you know you would react just the same as now! And say: you had never seen a man trying the handle of your apartment door. None of it. And then you'd learned of some murder had happened just the room beneath you. It would be the same! You'd react the same! You would have asked Mathilde to look up an article about the murder and then to look up information on the woman who'd died, convinced it had something to do with you by mere proximity! These same printed pages would have been tendered to you. This same moment of questioning arrived at - only you'd be asking 'What if I'd known her, even passingly?' and 'What if I had seen a man at my door, the day previous?' And you would have become attracted to the photos of a dead woman instead of becoming attracted to the glimpses of a woman soon-to-be-dead. All of the connective tissue you think exists only does so insomuch as you are insisting it so, Lucy Jinx. Did you expect a Public Notice for her funeral? Expect to attend and to discover a twin sister, an old acquaintance, see a book on a shelf that would remind you of some moment you shared with this or that person this or that time, note the type of handbag a mourner had and then see that handbag again in a shop window, go in for a look and then look out to see someone you'd seen before walking on the other side of the street and so have a puzzle to play with? Do you think things you just happen to look at have anything to do with you? Lucy luxuriates into a letter *X* then bends legs and weirds body into something like a lowercase *H* with a penchant toward being and uppercase *B*. Lucy Lucy, you are spectator and note-jotter! All of the things you've had to do with you've fled and now you are in a wilderness of unassociated looking! For so long. Claire? Claire Seville? You think she could have been you? Her killer could have burst through your door and killed you in panic at not finding her? Lucy dead and Claire alive knowing Lucy was meant to be Claire? At least in that context - the context of I-should-be-dead. Claire. What? You think she was meant to be you? She dead an impulsive accident, that man really out to get you? Lucy smiles and reminds herself she can't fall asleep. She hears Mathilde out there making something in a blender. Imitates the sound. Giggles. 'Claire Claire Claire.'

Lucy bows deep and thanks Mathilde kindly for her dutiful sleuthing and her sharing of 'some of those certain substances.' 'Oh yes, my *Grand Royal African Special Selection* is not to be missed' Mathilde gun-shot fingers at Lucy, Lucy's face a somersault of smile at how Mathilde was right on top of such an obscure reference. 'Isn't that the funniest movie ever made!?' 'It is one of them, yes.' And so here is Lucy and here is Mathilde doing - one sober and one highly-drugged-out - impersonations and recitations. 'He's taken a turn for the worst I'm afraid. Terribly ill. In fact he's so desperately ill ... that he's dead.' 'If we do something, he won't stop. So we do absolutely ... nothing.' 'Wait wait wait! How will he know we are doing nothing?' 'We'll announce it at a Press Conference!' 'But he'll never believe us!' 'On the other hand: if we announce that we're doing something, he may suspect we're lying ... and stop.' Both faces greasy with tears now, Lucy in a coughing fit, trying to keep the paper cup of water Mathilde has provided steady but dribbling on her shoes, the kitchen tiles, onto Mathilde's top. 'You can't even laugh without causing a damn ruckus, Jinx!' 'This is how we - meaning human-kind - are meant to laugh! You treasure elegance and decorum far too much. *Laughter* should be antonym to *Dignity*! I've always said so.' And - yeah yeah yeah - Lucy knows she has to go in a minute. And of course she is okay to drive. And if not, she will sit in her car until she is. 'Do you think I'm so without scruples that I'd run down innocents with a motor vehicle rather than lazing about doing nothing?' Mathilde shrugs. 'I'm sorry I smoked cigarettes and pot in your house' Mathilde. 'It's okay, Lucy. I knew it was going to happen the moment I said Hello to you when you asked me for five dollars.' That is how the two of you met, isn't it? 'That is how we met, isn't it!?' Lucy gushes and paws at Mathilde's arm and then pokes three of the still-showing wet spots on her blouse. 'Did you give me those five dollars?' Lucy whispers, faux-hoarse, comic-implication that she's winding up to beg more money. 'I did' Mathilde says, poking Lucy back - poke poke poke - poking her very randomly and laughing as the touch clearly aggravates Lucy but Lucy is trapped in a state where she can't actually get agitated just numbly confused until she bats at the air like she had stepped into a cloud of gnats. 'What did I use it for?' Lucy asks, composure re-attained. 'Knowing you? Something philanthropic.' 'Yes' Lucy nods 'like something to eat, you mean - or maybe I bought a magazine.' Yes, Lucy knows she has to go. But her feet are gluey and she kind of wants to ask Mathilde if she feels like laying down and going to sleep with her - but that would be absurd to do, right? 'I'll go in a minute' Lucy announces then coughs, then re-announces. Pause. 'Has it been a minute?' 'It has.' Suspicious, Lucy leans in. 'I don't think so' she whispers 'because if it has been, then why am I still here?'

Heavenly Father, no ma'am, Lucy will not be driving - that was three times she dropped her keys and likely a full ten minutes it took her to get into the car! Saints preserve us, she is freezing and sits without even turning the ignition for a moment, assuring invisible auditors that she is doing the civic thing and will just hang around, for awhile. 'The clever thing about me' Lucy says aloud 'and why I am such a high functioning drug-user, is that I always arrange it so that there is a lot of having-nothing-to-do between anything I happen to do.' Why is it so cold? 'Exactly' she says, turning on the car and fiddling with the heater knobs 'this is exactly what I mean. I'm not driving when I can't even remember to turn on the car!' Mystery: if the light there on the *AC* button is lit but she has the heat turned on does it make it colder than if that light is not lit? Investigation: presses button, hand to vent, counts to ten, presses button, hand to vent, counts to ten. 'That accomplished nothing' she says, petulantly leaning to the driver's door and trying to get her seatbelt on, the thing jamming. 'Really? Really!? Has it come to this!?' Lucy has a spate of laughter and, multiple times, does a playact of rending her garment in lament over her condition. 'Nothing to do about it now, though' she says. 'I can no more undo this than crow's feet or any of the unseemly signs of aging! This is just an elaborate wrinkle. A dark-spot blemish. Not getting too high to drive a car is just another wrinkle-cream to apply. Anti-aging! Hydrating! Rejuvenating nectars!' Lucy suddenly pipes down and pipsqueaks herself cowardly snuggled low. That group of teen girls passing her car gave a look in like they had never seen a zebra with that - all capitals *THAT* - many stripes before. She's just become a memory. Whoever the sensitive girl in that group was would think about That-shouting-old-woman-in-that-parking-lot for years to come. Probably tell her first boyfriend one day when he's treating her like rubbish and she wants desperately to cling, to have something to say, some moment of her life to insist the jerk into the loop of. 'Stop staring' Lucy says, with no conviction, watching the lank of the tall one, the Olive Oil wriggle to her away-from-Lucy forward sashay. Short boots. Khaki pants with rivets to the pockets over that now way-far-away ass. What? 'What?' What? 'What?' Lucy blinks, turns to the side as though to make eye-contact with who said *What?* 'You said *What?*' 'I said *What?*' 'You also said *I said What?*' 'I also said *You said what, I said what?*' 'You also said *I said What?*' She pauses. Not sure of the accuracy of that last statement. 'I'm not driving' she reminds those gathered. 'Civic. And that girl shouldn't be teenaged and beautiful if she doesn't want madwomen on drugs to give her ogles from parked cars! Let's not forget that!'

This is just a few minutes later. How bad has it gotten? Lucy - with heat blaring to the point it is hurting her eyes - is having an imaginary conversation with Claire Seville. Shall we listen? Let's listen. Lucy starts. 'Nature made a mistake with how mirrors work - it really missed a trick. Reflections should be retained in mirrors, Claire - not all-at-once and not fully, no no. But: if you were to stand at a mirror for, say, five minutes, the glass should have kind-of-like-a-stain-of-you, a fingerprint-smudge in the colors of you. Mirrors should have to be wiped, spritzed with special cleansers and cloth-buffed to get back to blank. Wouldn't that be the most gorgeous thing? Think of a mirror in a restaurant or a club, you know? By the end of the night, the mirror - and windows, too, I mean anything reflective - would be smeared with different thicknesses of hundreds of residues of thousands of images. Colors on colors, tangled and clotted and shading the shading of each other. After the chairs are put up for the night, someone takes a Windex bottle and has at it, making sure to work quickly so as not leave a trace of their own reflections even as they clean the larger mess. Oh Claire, I can see it now! The first swipe of the towel sloshing an autumn streak out of the commingled left-overs of wait-staff and lingering diners and steaks-at-sizzle and candle heat and all. Don't you think so?' But this ghostly Claire is no choir being preached to - this ghostly Claire scrunches face and crosses arms in a dismissive Harrumph. 'It would be terrible! Think about driving! Your rearview mirror would be worthless - your side mirrors. Why would we even have mirrors? And you don't even know how mirrors work!' 'I know how mirrors work, Claire' Lucy says, all attempts to keep composure, tone of mother passing dinner-roll to lout who has knocked up her daughter ten minutes after the announcement 'You're going to be a grandma' was made. 'I don't think you do' Lucy says on ghostly Claire's behalf. 'She doesn't' chimes in - unsolicited - Lucy's imaginary biographer. 'You look at them, you see yourself and the shit behind you - that's how a mirror works! I'm saying the reflection should - just a bit - linger.' 'It has to do with angles' says Claire. 'Incidence and reflectance' says the biographer. 'So what?' demands Lucy, tasting the words in her mouth as the windows now begin to cloud around her. 'Mirrors would always be reflecting something and so would always have a thick, permanent stain!' Claire can't seem to believe Lucy's utter ignorance on this matter! 'There would' Claire presses on 'be no mirrors.' 'Then mirrors shouldn't work like that! They should only sometimes reflect things. When you're using them!' Claire has her head turned away but Lucy knows what face she is making. And she notices now that the biographer has had the tape recorder running the whole while and so just gruffs down her nose and nibbles the skin around her thumb for a moment.

Little bit at-a-time, Lucy starts driving off. To prove to herself she is in control, first she just pulls out and then pulls into another parking space. Easy. So easy, she does it again. Like a rudimentary video game - that's what her life is, right now! She sets her teeth and selects what her next move will be. She will pull out, make a left at that traffic-light, and park in that lot over there, for a moment. That's a good test. And without a hitch it goes! Well done, Lucy. Question: Do you remember where you are supposed to be going, now? Answer: No. Shit. That information is at home. 'But' Lucy raises a finger to hush up anyone who is going to try to lambast her with this fact 'it isn't as though I don't have plenty of time, still. Going home, in fact, seems a better idea.' Question: Better idea than what? Answer: Than going. Question: Than going where? Answer, with exasperation: Jesus - to the interview! To the interview! Of course - comes a smack-to-the-forehead sounding sigh - that's where Lucy is going! 'And I just need to go home to get the directions to the place.' Interlude while Lucy listens to a song she likes, clapping softly and going 'Yay!' in a fangirl tee-hee when it ends, as though this is the first - rather than the millionth - time she has heard it. Now on the road. Good bit of driving. Head seems all clear. But she happens to see that a car marked *Security* is on the road next to her. Reminds her of police. She pulls in at the nearest place possible. And so here she is: in a church parking lot. And now she'd feel awkward leaving, being the only car there. Say a Priest or whoever lives in a church is inside, nervous peek through the stained glass, muttering his lines to himself, waiting to give her a benediction or some sacred thing like that - then this poor fellow will look out again and see she has scampered! 'Yeah' Lucy nods 'yeah that would be pretty bad.' Lucy decides Layla would be able to advise her in this situation and so sends off a text-message, squinting at the church-front as she does. Doesn't seem like anyone could be watching her, but who knows with churches. Last cigarette in the pack, she sparks it with the red coils of the car lighter. Phone vibrates in the seat. *Who's Claire?* Blink blink. Lucy taps up to her sent message. *Claire my love - I am high as a giraffe's scalp and accidentally pulled in to a church parking lot. Help! Do I have to go inside? I'm so confused, so confused. Counsel, pronto. Etc.* Blink blink. Phone vibrates. *You're taking too long to answer. My God! Have I been forsook? For this quote end-quote Claire!!!!????* Lucy types *No no - sorry - Claire's that woman I killed, remember? Church. Guilty conscience. Must be that sort of thinking. Raskolinkov or something. It's the beating of that hideous heart! And so on.* The car is hot and punctuation marked with a rumple of drifting smoke - it smells how the inside of Lucy's eyes sting. Phone vibrates. *You're mistaking me for the woman you killed now? Gosh, my Jinx, that's so sweet.*


LUCY IS STILL RATTLED BY the car that cut her off just before she turned into the parking lot of *Ondine's*. The two little kids - what we they, five, six? - had been goblinish in their sneers, middle-fingers raised, the father laying on the horn and - likely - belching out some denigration at her. What had it meant? It didn't mean anything, Lucy. And yet here Lucy is, wondering if she had been driving incorrectly. Putting the bad behavior of the children and the aggressiveness of the whole circumstance - the danger of it - to one side, Lucy wonders if she hadn't seen a signal or if the man had been patiently, pleadingly gesturing her that he needed something - what? to make a certain turn? what? what could justify it, Lucy? - and only when cornered, penned in, or thwarted by her lack of attention - her conceitedness and no-accounting, her failure to regard the needs of him, her fellow-traveler, human-as-her-and-the-next-man-or-woman - had he laid on the horn, swerved as he had. The anger. The assault in posture. All of it justified. Oh Lucy and her thoughts lumped in this spot like an ice floe, making her way to the door of the place, sniffing a bit, and overhearing someone emphatically telling the girl he is with 'I don't believe there will be snow - they always say it, but they just need to say something and it's winter so that's what they say.' *Ondine's*. Just one of those it's-always-the-case-isn't-it restaurants in a strip of some quaint, run-downish looking bit of downtown that you step inside of and turns out to be opulent, complex, and unlike any place you have ever dined before. When Lucy leaves, this interior will have re-stamped the exterior - even just glancing out at the street, through the panel of the door she has just closed, it seems a shelf restocked, bottles all turned the right way, labels completely readable and in some sort of poetic, by-size or by-vintage arrangement. Two levels, this place. No simple *Wait To Be Seated* sign posted, Lucy just milling, uncertain what is the ceremony. There is a bar - but there is one upstairs, too! What sort of mind-bend is that supposed to be? Can one just stroll to the upstairs bar, treat it like the downstairs? Or must one have excuse to be up there - that is the bar for the elite, not the grubbish likes of Lucy! None of the patrons in here seem the grubbish likes of Lucy. Her coat is an embarrassment - functionality is its bent, not fashion - she feels like a coal miner showing up at his estranged daughter's ballet recital without having gone home to freshen. But, Lucy - Sierra had said *Ondine's*. You had had Mathilde read it, spell it, the address as well, right off of that e-mail, last week. No dress code was mentioned. None of these facts are helping, though, correct as they may be. Lucy: a mess. She's a blotch, here, the first thick, runny footprint on the just mopped tile, signage ignored to *Please Step Around*. A coat-rack? For God's sake! Is she supposed to leave her coat there? A glance around. It seems so. What kind of place wants someone to do something like that?

Here's Sierra, anyway. And the first thing she does is give Lucy a hug - unexpected - and then go to her own hung coat to fish cigarettes out. 'I was hoping you would be late. I was early. Was just going to sneak a quick smoke. Join?' That Sierra has the speech pattern of a lazily drafted telegram endears her anew. 'Of course' Lucy of-courses and doesn't even have to move for her own just relinquished coat because a smoke is proffered to her with a grin. Outside.

Photonegative. *X*-Ray put up to the view-light backward, you can tell by reading the numbers at the bottom. 'Going into places makes me feel upside-down when I come out' Lucy says, leaning to Sierra's offered smoke. 'I know what you mean. I got us a table upstairs - but it's gonna be Hell to pay on my equilibrium when we leave. Fuck, you should see how discombobulated department store escalators make me.' Oh you like Sierra just fine, Lucy - see? This will be fun! This will be fun, Lucy! 'I hope this wasn't meant to be a fancy cigarette to impress me, Sierra. No matter the wind, I know not-a-hawk from any handsaw.' 'But do you at least like it?' 'I' - pause - 'note it' - she says in her best imitation-McGoohan. 'You seem to me the sort who holds off judgement on things.' 'Do I?' Lucy cannot contain the pop of incredulousness. Sierra rolls her eyes. 'Things-like-cigarettes, I should say. You probably just say things like *I am eating a piece of fruit* when you're having a banana over an apple, to Hell with specifics.' How does she know that? What makes her think that? 'What do you make of me?' Sierra asks, giving a glance to see how much of her smoke she has left. Lucy considers. Tell the truth? Why not, Lucy, go ahead. 'You seem like you work at a bookstore and had a boyfriend once who you hoped would cheat on you and then were annoyed when he did so because he immediately apologized and showed you the message he'd sent the other girl telling her it was a mistake and he was in love with you and had no intention of leaving or ever seeing the other girl, again.' 'I seem like that, eh?' 'You do. But amongst other things. I 'm not saying any of that happened - but it's what you seem like, regardless.' 'So you like losers?' Sierra's tone has become difficult to read because of Lucy's self-consciousness at her nose feeling it's growing puppy-snot wet. She opts to just play it back with 'You think that would make you a loser - something like that in your past?' 'That's just what I think, yeah.' Sierra flicks her cig thataway without even looking, the thing almost hitting the hump of faux-fur across the shoulders of that bundled up woman as she presses the button to unlock her car. 'Is this how you start all your interviews?' 'Interview hasn't started yet' Sierra says, holding the door. 'You don't smoke fast enough. I'm freezing. Inside. Cigarette's not even yours to begin with.'

Lucy is here told to order whatever she wants. 'No, no.' Lucy is here re-told to order whatever she wants. All very suspect. Why? Why suspect? You're right, Lucy blinks to say to herself, then starts perusing the menu in earnest. Order something you don't normally order, Lucy - this seems the best course of action, at first blush. Then, though - no, no don't do that. Because there are too many things that have a chance to go wrong. This seems the sort of place where everything served will be served with some declension of sauce on it - or else a soupçon of some sort of slaw - or another such damnable substance she will not know from a look is it cheese or butter or some sort of combination of the two. And that is not the sort of thing she has the guts or lack of decorum to ask for clarification on. Even the fact that the bread left on the table - which Sierra seems to be fornicating with - knife and butter and those to colored oils on plates into the business for some kicks Lucy can't even fathom the kink of - is several different varieties, no single piece normal-bread-color, is making her sit, shamed of her provincial upbringing. Those seeds all over that dark-brown piece, for example? Those are seeds added to the bread? Why? They won't taste like anything, right? But they seem a very particular sort of seed. And that crust seems to have dry oatmeal on it, jagging out in rufts like certain fungi up the legs of some tree's lower bark. Just order a steak. A burger. Order a pasta dish with chicken and - you can say it shyly - ask for it completely plain, citing something about your diet, something some physician said, something that runs in your familial *DNA*. Well, what condition? Maybe the waitress - who seems doctorial in her apron-wearing and exisiting-only-in-the-exact-moment-she-is-there-at-the-tableness - will have some recommendation. Say you'd rather not go into it, Lucy. Is giving you plain pasta with chicken such a goddamn difficult thing to do!? In a place like this!? 'You make it from scratch, right?' Lucy might have to say, on the offensive, defensive. 'Or do you just dump it, ready-set, out of a can, microwave on a Preset and charge forty bucks per sniff?' Steady, Lucy. Steady. 'I am ordering wine' Sierra mentions 'because I am something of a lush. Not that I will get drunk. Though I might.' Lucy nods but knows it was her turn to say something witty. Right now, she is too focused on the fact that she might have to seem like she knows the difference between types of potatoes - do all dishes come with them? That's what it says! She sees it in right there in black-and white! At the heading of each type of meal: *Served with russet, fingerling, Kennebec, LaRette, or Purple Majesty potatoes.* Lucy can feel beads of perspiration - globular, like hollow balls of earwax - lining up in her unshaved armpits, ready to trickle her ribs over. She sighs. Asks Sierra what she is getting. 'Just a steak. London Broil. But the flatiron here is superb.' 'Yes' Lucy nods 'okay. I was thinking to get the flatiron. Or' - she cribs a glance down - 'the chateaubriand.' 'That's good, too' Sierra nods. 'Yep.' 'Yep.' 'Well then' Lucy shrugs. 'One of those.'

But the wine is quite lovebird, really the ingratiating sort. Lucy's vision blurs as though the room were done in crayon and someone had tried to get rid of it with a pencil eraser. A wonderful sort of drunk, the kind that elevates - skeleton raised, skin sloshed off, brain hung from the base of the spine by some kind of umbilical. Sierra has a tape-recorder out, but so far has only been jotting notes in the small booklet she has at hand, not recorded a thing. Sierra's explanation: 'I don't have the guts to go full out and discard the first twenty minutes or so of the conversation the way some interviewers suggest. Only ever turn on the recorder once I know you've forgotten it's even there. I cheat. Take down impressions. But I drink, too. Anyway - you looked at the site, I'm sure.' 'Absolutely' Lucy says, waving-off gesture of I'm-surprised-you'd-even-think-to-mention-it. Lucy explains how she has taken to driving with a little recorder handy on her dashboard. 'Snippets of verse, if they come to me. Or that's what it was supposed to be for. Lately it's been rants or memories or things like that. It sometimes feels I'm all done with poetry. I sometimes feel like it's a villain I can no longer pretend isn't - I'm a victim who has run out of ways to explain my bruises to the good-meaning lady next door, you know?' Wait - Lucy saw that! - why had Sierra tried to be subtle in turning the recorder on, just then? Something doesn't feel on top of the table here, all of a sudden! 'What is your relationship to poetry? What introduced you to it?' 'I don't have a relationship with poetry. Or if I do, it's like someone-who-has-to-take-pills-to-piss-right's relationship with pissing. Isn't it just something everyone does?' Sierra takes a sip of wine, nose doing a thing that Lucy interprets as 'Do go on'. 'I don't trust poetry anymore, though. It's a con-artist. At first, you know, a confessional seems like a good idea. Awhile later? Blackmail! And it's a Lord-endorsed shake-down. We all know the score.' 'Your poetry blackmails you?' 'It doesn't have to. It just knows that it could. Or maybe that doesn't make sense. I don't know. If it comes to the point where a nonsensical string of description or an abstraction of an intricacy seems the most natural way to get at something, it's too late - you get me? I'd give up poetry if not for the fact that it's already bullied my immune system. The only thing keeping me alive is that the ailment ain't run its course. One of those situations, isn't it? There is a cure, but it's the kind that better come with an epitaph.' Sierra takes another drink. Clears her throat. 'Are you a fan of T.S. Eliot?' 'I'm a fan of how he thought that menstrual blood was the invention of a branch of the SS he felt was only out to get him. Other than that, he can pretty much suck my dick and find his own way out after, to be frank.'

Sierra wears a lot of rings. So many they seem to represent nothing. Which makes the wearing of a ring odd. No earrings, though. No necklace. Though, Lucy admits, with a dotting of moles just right across the chest where Sierra has a dotting of moles just right across the chest, why would she wear a necklace? Jesus, that is a sight! No bracelets. Lucy cuts in on Sierra's question to ask 'Do you wear toe-rings?' 'Toe-rings?' 'Right' Lucy says, glugs some wine and pours a bit more even though she still has plenty. 'I do not. But I sometimes where socks that are like foot gloves, you know? Little space for each toe.' 'Well, everyone does that sometimes' Lucy snorts. 'Anyway. Back to the questions.' The drink and the initial chatter did whatever trick they were meant to do, because Lucy is in the dark as to the methodology of this interview. It's a put-on, of course, this being a liaison for a personal blog and nothing more.

Rightfully, Lucy could be irritated at the in-depthness of it all. This is the sort of chat which could make one feel what they are saying matters, will be read, argued, commented on. Instead of merely wastreling until Kingdom-gone with all the other words out in cyberspace. Lucy wants to bring that up, but feels it would be indelicate. Bring up how humanity's greatest invention wasn't the Printing Press, but the Internet - because there is finally a vortex into which language can be flung, quarantined, an endless pit in which to shed the skin of every letter from every alphabet of every tongue. And then snap shut the door! And press the red button. Explode! Explode! 'The Printing Press was the worst mistake, ever' - 'Careful, Lucy - you're talking now' some part of her brain reminds her 'this is actually being said to Sierra, to the recorder, posterity has on its listening ears' - 'because it allowed Language a body it could exercise, muscularize, run amok with. It was a good job when an individual hand needed to shape each letter - that kept Language under the thumb of us, at least somewhat. A book was a singular entity and could only infect just so many. And no one by accident! Then those movable letters and it was like French-kissing wet leprosy! Every doorknob was perpetually just-a-moment-before-sneezed-on, from that point forward. Language got out of our heads in a way that could proliferate freely and accidentally. You've seen a hieroglyph?' Sierra says she has. 'You have any idea what it means? Of course not! They never would have made a Hieroglyph Printing Press - that's all I'm saying. I think the past understood the danger of Language. It's got us, now - we served ourselves up and it slasher-films us just for giggles. Don't you think so?' Sierra blinks, earnestly trying to come to a good answer. 'That Language is now a physical entity - a kind of lifeform with a specific body-type? That we brought about its genesis and have watched it evolve to a point of dominance?' 'Yeah' Lucy says, drinks, figures she probably was driving at something similar to that. 'The only thing as numerous as insects or bacteria on this planet is letters, man. And letters are both of those things, hybrided up into the ultimate killing, surviving device. Nothing but exoskeleton and brainpan!'

There are no restrooms upstairs, so Lucy slow-motions down the stairs, graceless, her feet under her when she reaches the bottom still accustomed to stepping down, her hip clicking odd as she moves in the direction of the kitchen, then in through one of the two doors marked *Ladies*. Shocking. Lucy looks around as though wrong-turned. For all the opulence outside, this toilet is no better than the one around in back of some gas station! She's surprised there isn't a still-full mop-bucket, headless stick leaned into it, right-triangling the gritty tile of the wall. Lucy notes the toilet looks clean, but still feels skeptical as she lowers herself onto it and her legs stay waiting-for-the-starting-gun tense while she tries to loosen up enough to void herself. The wine is coming into its second position, now. Weightier, a maturity that attracts the young crowd. Can you really be drunk on the hardly-two glasses you've drank, Lucy? 'But remember - I was on drugs earlier, too' she says. Taps the blackboard so the one student who didn't write that down does now. How can the sound of her urinating be this loud? How can it be echoing? Seriously, she wants to re-read the Feynman lecture on Auditory Physics, double-quick! It seems to her that sound from beneath her should be trapped, her ass over the seat-opening forming a tight enough seal to keep things at a muffle - or even just regular volume, she could accept that - not to give them an amplifier! But listen. That's her tinkling and spraying, hissy-fit of liquid, and the sound is as though someone imitating radio static with a traffic-cone held thin-side to their mouth. The sound doesn't even seem to be originating down there. It is omnipresent! Enough to make her believe a foley-artist is in the employ of this joint, micro-speakers lacing the room - as soon as sensors indicate water is being made, the artist plys his trade, overdubbing what he feels is the appropriate sound for the character he sees on a monitor. Lucy Jinx? She pisses like a five-year-old not lifting the damper pedal, it seems. Or like someone scraping ice off their car, loud enough to wake you two hours too early. Anyway. Done now. Straightened up. Mistrustful of the tap water - sniffs her finger, it seems fine - and cannot shake the feeling that the mirror is two-way. Or one-way, she thinks. Whichever term means someone on the other side can see in but all you see is your reflection. Two-way, then. That makes sense. No. One-way - one-way makes sense. 'Then what is a two-way mirror?' she asks the mirror, harshing her gaze on the tip of her reflected nose, then unfoucusing, as though her reflection were a specially printed image that would reveal something hidden if looked at just right. Mirrors should reflect back sound said at them, too. Another mirror-mistake! It's not proper how mirrors are so silent. It doesn't have to be room volume - it could be a murmur, even. And mirrors should vibrate a bit when reflecting. It's not appropriate how they just sit there. Doing nothing. Except allowing Lucy Jinx to stare at her nose, waiting for someone she knows is not there to respond to respond to whatever she asked.

'Did you ever have an ambition beyond being a poet?' 'I never had an ambition, including being a poet.' 'I admit, I find your evasiveness intriguing.' 'How am I being evasive?' 'Like that.' 'By asking directly about my evasiveness when we're talking about my evasiveness? That is the least evasive thing I could do!' 'But we weren't talking about your evasiveness.' 'We were - and still are - precisely that.' 'Only once you started being evasive, if you recall.' 'I recall you introducing the term *Evasiveness* - at which point I have done nothing but talk about it, so my point is doubled-down.' 'Do you recall what we were discussing before we started talking about evasiveness?' 'Before you started talking about evasiveness, you mean?' 'I thought you just said you were talking about it, too.' 'I am talking about it. However: I did not start-talking-about-it - only you did that - and then I responded and only then - in an entirely letter-of-the-law way - were we both talking about it.' 'You're doing it, again.' 'What - not being evasive?' 'Which makes me think I've hit on something, there.' 'Where?' 'Just before we veered down this trap-street.' 'I don't know what a trap-street is.' 'Down this blind-alley.' 'I don't really know what that is, either.' 'Down this rabbit-hole.' 'Of me being candorful?' 'Why do you think I thought you were being evasive?' 'How would I know?' 'I don't think you would know, I asked why you think.' 'I haven't given it a moment's thought.' 'Now, that is just dishonest.' 'Is that right?' 'It doesn't take long to sort out the fact that you, Lucy, are always thinking about something - if I bring it up, you have thought about it and are thinking about it, still.' 'What am I meant to be thinking about?' 'Analyze me: why would I think you were being evasive?' 'You're the sort who is used to there always being another bug under another rock - you never trust that there isn't something under the surface, then you peel the surface and call what was down there the surface, again, because that's what it is now, and on and on.' 'Depth, to me, is just a pile of surfaces?' 'Stack 'em like pancakes - probably that's your motto.' 'Isn't that just what depth is?' 'I think so.' 'So is what you just said your assessment of me - or your assessment of you?' 'We might have that in common.' 'We might not.' 'Well, that's how you seem, anyway - you didn't ask me to analyze me.' 'I think that's exactly what I did.' 'You're forgetting your question, then.' 'What was my question?' 'I don't recall - but it wasn't about this, because we've only just arrived at this point and you already asked the question, awhile ago.' 'Why don't you think poetry is an ambition?' 'For me?' 'Yes.' 'Because it does not require anything.' 'You think ambition requires something?' 'It requires being ambitious, if nothing else.' 'Like a primary color?' 'I don't buy into that - primary colors are made of something else, we're just are too lazy to figure out what.'

  Then Lucy - aided by another drink - tells the following, uninterrupted, certain her voice is carrying enough that she is serving as entertainment for at least the two nearest tables. 'I did crimes when I was young. At the time, I did the crimes and felt they meant something. It was a youthful conceit, maybe, but nonetheless it made my mind and body feel profoundly connected to some sort of Platonic Ideal. All sorts of math and philosophy made sense because I'd be out stealing some cheeseballs or dirty magazines or paperbacks or film for my camera or knit gloves - or whatever seemed to raise a physical response which felt emotional. There was The World. There was I-in-It. My mind conceived a notion. My body acted it out. Inner-workings went off and a feeling was produced. The feeling began as a physicality. The feeling continued until it became an emotional state. Then: my intellect processed the emotion and the cycle began anew. The first time I stole something and it seemed it was for a worldly-end - a day-to-day need or want rather than an emotional urge - is when something inside of me turned. I don't know how to say it. There was something comforting in feeling the world was Normal, I Aberrant. The world was Male, I Female. When the world turned out to be a woman like me and when it turned out the world was as absurd as my impulses were - that there was no Otherness to it, nothing but my own voice on and on for mile after mile after day after year - something at the very base of me dropped off. I lost a foundation. And since then, I think I have been unable to connect. I remember stealing money - not just here and there kid stuff, but stealing money proper. From work. And counting it as part of what would sustain my life. Allow me things. Theft was another job - or its end was the same as the end of an honest day's work. Someone - a friend I once had - said to me once, before the change - after I had laid out an elaborate plan to be able to steal ten-dollars-a-day - 'Why not just get a job - you'd earn that inside two hours, every day, and not to have to worry about consequences.' When I stole money-as-money for the first time, that made sense. The World made sense. All romance and personal invention was a lie! Liar. Liar. The world, I saw, was a waiting-game for each and every person to come around. Prodigal sons us all, right? My point is: I wish stealing felt like stealing used to feel. I wish I could surgery that part of my old mind into my new. My point? My point? I dunno. That I don't feel comfortable saying I write poetry for any reason. That writing it is about anything. Can't it just be a pocket-watch I stole to impress some chick by having a pocket-watch? To be excited that she thinks it's so fucking neat? That she'll always think I give a shit about it just because it was something I had the first time she met me? If she'd met me another day, it coulda been a bag-of-cookies or a corkscrew or an action-figure. But some girl will think of me every time they think of a pocket-watch just because I'd stole one the day I met her and was in the mood to show it off.'

Things shift, now. The tape-recorder is off. A good time has been had. The notepad is closed. Lucy is trying to insist on paying - but now without much gumption, as the bill is ridiculous, so Sierra better not suddenly renege. They are getting ready to go. But things shift. They shift on the statement from Sierra: 'I did a bit of research after reading your stuff, poked around. You knew Elliott Pine?' Things shift, now. Watch how they do. The air gets brittle, sharp-hard toffee, thin-crisp potato-chip lodged between this and that tooth. 'How did that come up?' Lucy asks, face pulled back into a scrunch like a bad high-school actor suggesting to the audience they are holding up a shoe that smells bad. Sierra says it was one of the first things she came across. She had entered Lucy Jinx's name into a Search Engine and an article about Elliott Pine was one of the first results.

'I adore Elliott Pine' Sierra says 'so it was quite a pleasant little extra.' Booby-trap talk! Play it clever, Lucy, don't tip your hand. 'I thought you said you said you learned I knew Elliott, though. You mean you were just asking - as it happens, I did know her, yes - but you were just asking because of that?' Nope. Sierra is quick to enthusiastically clarify. Sierra had been roundabout in the question for not wanting to come across as a gossip or a fangirl. 'You two were lovers?' Lucy rolls her eyes - which is lucky, because it has an impact on Sierra in the direction of shutting her up - without meaning to, shakes her face like a cartoon ending a daydream and says 'I mean, yes, we were. But that was years and years ago.' Had Elliott really talked about that in an interview? Had that been a point in some article? Anyway: now Sierra seems to not have land-legs. Things shift, things shift. A lot of 'So, I should have the piece up in a week - I work on these pretty hard, then I sit on them a few days - so don't worry if it goes two weeks and you maybe see a few other posts go up in the meantime' and a lot of 'This was really fun - I'm glad you came out, though I know it wasn't so glamourous' and a lot of 'Let me know if you are doing signings or readings - Oh and I'll get those people in touch with you, they've just been busy and I didn't want them to overlook something I sent.' Those kinds of things. Lucy puts on her coat exactly how one contemplates that maybe a piece of meat will still taste as good even though the faucet has run water on it and it has sat in the puddle for a minute or two. Yes. Lucy feels edible but wrong-flavored. She is something that an animal would lap up without thought but that nothing with intellect would consider still viable. They shake hands even though it is clear Sierra wanted to have a hug. Lucy wouldn't have cared. But Sierra just did that little thing like I-was-going-to-hug-you-but-oh-well-uh-instead-here's-a-handshake. And said 'Well' - a pronunciation to it like with a P added to the end - when shaking, awkward up-down, fingers let go just a half-speed too slow. 'Goodbye.' 'Thanks, again.'

Her car takes its time heating up, like its mulling something over to present in Moot-court. The radio is an endless commercial for seven minutes, no matter which station she goes to. Finally, some music starts on the classical station - but its one of those pieces Lucy doesn't think should have survived to modernity. All weakling woodwinds, the kinds that you go 'Hey, cool' about when someone plays but without any conviction. 'A piccolo? Hey, cool.' This is the sort of music Lucy used to grow uncertain of the world because of. Sure, it exists. Sure, someone somebody somewhere sometime decided to make historically important wrote it. But it sounds like nothing. It's a grown-up, canonized version of a kindergartener humming a melody before they quite get the concept. Is it meant to evoke anything? Lucy sees: tree branches. Lucy sees: a drawbridge, the wood of which looks like the phony wood of a theme park.

Lucy sees: a pile of dog-collars near a recycle bin in a backyard. But certainly the writer of the piece had not meant to evoke any of that. It goes on and on. And after eight minutes seems to stop, only to have the announcer come on and to explain that it was the First Movement of a larger piece they were not playing the totality of but which could be found at record shops and blah blah blah. Then the announcer lists the five people who had been performing - as well as a conductor - in a way suggesting he doesn't feel these six people should be ashamed of themselves. That is a far way to go for that! Art. Lucy can only hope she is the only human ear that ever heard this performance, outside the performers and whoever was working in the sound booth - and she hopes no one was, that one of the performers handled the mix, personally, after the fact. Yes, Lucy would die happy if, through some fluke, no one else was listening to the radio just then and the records had never sold - if this had been the one and only time that performance had seen life and only Lucy's deaf ears had caught it up! Now some piano music is on. Lots of valley deep lower chords are bulldozed uphill and then pecked at by bird-beak trills and gnawed on by the pizzicato tongues of wild deer. This is lustrous, like the mane of the world's least wild horse. Music that smells of the richness of home-care, warm as under the sheets while the lover you're curled to sweats out the break of a fever. Hand to forehead, Lucy wonders if it's safe to drive or if she should sleep for awhile. The heat has got itself together and in the bog of it she feels more intoxicated than she had. And tired. She hears crickcrickcrick and crickcrickcrick and crickcrickcrick no matter how many times she rolls her head shoulder-to-shoulder, droop-to-chest to droop-to-chest. Something with the meat didn't sit right, as well, and her belly quivers like eggs hatching jellyfish which land on sun-heated pavement, sizzle a moment, then pop. Her hands are clenched and her head feels the shape of a duckbill.


MOST DISCONCERTING, LUCY IS SLUNG, hands and knees, in an embrace of her toilet bowl, forehead to the warm of where she had just been sitting, vainly having thought this would have been a situation wherein regurgitation could be avoided. Her mind is set: she needs to vomit. Her body seems to agree, judging from the sour-fruit slick she feels, a sweat pinned under her skin, a nausea causing pin-prick headache in the dead center of her irises. Yet her gut, itself, seems to think it best to hold on to the slime - to pummel it, work at it, work at it - her belly seems pigheadedly set on 'This will digest, just give it some time!' There: a dry-heave. There: a handclap of another one, her ears unclogging, clogging back when she sniffles. What a person can be reduced to when some aspect of physicality won't cooperate! Her stomach acids are locked into a spiraling pattern, it feels she has swallowed a fistful of teeth and is waiting for diet cola to dissolve them. Desperate measures called for. Two fingers plumb her throat down and conductor up waves of reverse-engine peristalsis - but all this awards her is another belch and a cud-thick dangle of saliva that cools in a line over and under her chin-cleft. Again. Again. Acidic sweet. A scent of trash-can opened, baby diapers a week left inside. Her sides and shoulders are taking on that shrink-wrap feeling of cramp, crinkly and only able to bend if accompanied by crisp sharp snaps. Growl. Growl, goes Lucy. Growl! It is states-of-affairs like this that would get her torched as a witch in days gone by. And, Hell - were she witnessing this tumultuous exorcism of her meal, she could see herself lighting the first torch, waking the first neighbor, uttering the first 'We can't let this survive - we can't let this spread!' Oh Lucy. You're not a plague boil, you just aren't meant for food served to those who are your social betters. She goes into drastic maneuvers, forcing herself to stand, to tip-toe, to arch back, she makes fists and tenderizes her lower back - whap whap whap - then squeezes in, rotating wrists, the thought being to empty herself like the last of a flat tube of toothpaste you know there's still a brush's worth inside of if the wrinkled bastard can be mangled enough. Success? She sits and feels the rebellion waning, her bowels taking position for their last footwork of the show. Nothing. Bent over double and pinching her chin-sides with her knees. If only she knew Latin, she thinks - this seems like the sort of situation the language has been kept around for! Or there is likely a perfect phrase in Russian for it. That language of sounds more than letters, eh? How long will Lucy have to stay like this, graceless and in-half? That's the worst part. It feels like forever but she knows it'll not be. There is precedent. But the fact that it will end - exactly how she is trying to make it end - doesn't get her out of having to wait for that to have already happened. 'Thanks science' she giggles. 'Time Machine - any day now, thanks.'

This is the message: You need to write, Lucy! A whip has been cracked. Your attempts to avoid poetry have been found out and you are having the hard word put to you, no wriggle-room. You think you'll be able to sleep, instead? You think you can smoke up and watch a dirty movie and pass out, partially sated? Or what? Here you are: nude as a hooked halibut, embracing your pillow, bedsheet covering nothing but one foot while your sweat reeks a furry bristle from your spine-top to your ass-cleft, louse of your wafting in all directions like you've sprouted a tail from every blemish. You think it's going to let you pass out? No one is making any deals, Lucy Jinx! And Lucy gets it. She does. She should have cancelled that interview. She made the wrong choice, there. Her thinking had been: keep up appearances. Her thinking had been: not every writer writes every day. Her thinking had been: maintain the façade and feign blockage, act casual, just avoid writing anything down. But it's on to her. Yes. Got her dead-bang. 'And now' it says, all Leo McKern voiced 'my dear Ms. Jinx, you are going to play our game.' So here she goes: moving to the writing desk. The notebook left open, pen lightly aloft it. Another ploy, it knows. Leaving it out to make it seem at the ready! This treachery will not go unpunished. Oh the melodrama! Oh the Chorus and Choragus of it! Poor Lucy Jinx - forced by Language itself to write poetry. 'Aren't there enough poets for you?' she hisses, writes that down just to have written something. 'Aren't I allowed to stop?' What did she write? *Aren't there enough poets for you?* So now she writes *Oh there's more than enough - five times Nth - quite enough!* 'So what is it, then?' This feels like vendetta. This feels like having war medals stripped and then fed to the dogs she is instructed to slaughter and dine on. Write that. Write that! 'Write what?' she slathers, knowing, writing, but writes it with begrudging penmanship, purposefully hack-working the phrasing. *My war medals stripped, fed to the dogs I'm ordered 'You slaughter, you dine on!'* Look at it, Jinx - look at it! What about it? What about it - well, what's wrong with it? 'Who fucking cares?' she argues. Lucy Jinx, the flavor of a dry-heaved sore throat, arguing with herself about something no one will ever read. What a struggle, eh? Even she has to mock it - thinks this calls for alternate spelling. A *striggle* at best, eh? Let's not get a big head. What's wrong with the line? What can't it stay? 'Because' she burps '*War medals* and *dogs*? *Dogs of war*? It seems to be what it's not supposed to be!' So fix it. Lucy hangs her head. She turns on the desk lamp. Shadows in brown-orange and red-black are cast because of the gauze of the shade. *My paltry tattoos are tugged down, shat pants disdained.* Better. *Fed to the circling roaches I've orders to dine upon, vivant, entire.*

What have we here? Two pages of neatly recopied stanzas and Lucy would hardly know herself! Pacing the room, eating toast, snapping fingers, and poking a newly lit cigarette around. She hasn't even brushed her teeth and her body still has the dregs of sicking-up aches at each joint and stretch of long muscle. But this is how it feels! Junky girl! Back in the poison of your own element! Leaking the septic that had been urining the whites of your eyes and purpling the red of their bloodshots! Each drag of the cig brings a new partial phrase. A single word she knows she should toss down and build from. Drag: *overturned tin.* Drag: *oven grease.* Pacing in pretending-to-be-a-dancer circles, bantering *Down your shoulder I go, oven grease in my insistence, overturned tin you go, cat's gonna cut its tongue wide for nothing, tonight.* Shit. Good, good. Mad scramble scribble. New pages. Got that all? Read it back. Tweak, snip, prune, pat pat to check tailored fit, underline underline. New drag. Rest. Then drag: *candle wax.* Drag: *would be lost without her ticket stub.* She plumps her raw buttocks on the kitchen counter and opens a single-serve pack of diet brand cookies. Munching the tasteless mulch she splurts squishy *That daydream of her, oh it'd be lost without its ticket stub, she's stately as candlewax never made candlewax proper from flame*. Shrug. That one can go by the wayside. Then - no no! - she thunks to the kitchen tile, dutifully crosses, and without much enthusiasm slops that feed down. And on a re-read she likes it, well enough. She even recognizes who that's about. What was her name? Claudine? Gurgle of the just swallowed food, she burps, excuse-mes, and 'Was that her name?' And all in a harried splash, the memory is back. Not Claudine - Pauline. And why her? Why her? She had worked at that bookstore. Lucy had stopped in on her lunch-breaks to listen to albums for free and buy coffee. That long walk, that one time, and that ride home. The End. Pauline's doggy-bone son-of-a-bitch voice prattling on about her ambitions and what someone like she and Lucy could do for the world. Lucy too I-don't-care to bother pointing out 'You don't even know me.' Pauline, endlessly during those two get-togethers talking about that movie she had seen, the one wherein she had found herself and 'Oh you have to see it - you should come over, I'll cook!' And for some reason the word *Cumquat* is needed in the poem somewhere. Pauline and her cumquat heart and soul! Something. Lucy writes *Cumquat*. All capitals. And in parenthesis writes *Pauline*. Sneers. A shift of gas inside her relenting the shame of all that. How she'd gone home and crawled into bed with Gregory. Humped to his turned away back and said 'I love you, by the way' in the dark when there had been no need. And a luscious yawn here follows - and Lucy seems to have permission to sit. Point proved. She is cowed. She is heeled. And she can rest as the over-old sweat settles to a chill she'll need to bathe to get warm of.

Cut scene: Lucy with lungful of bubble-bath scent. Around her the popping of reduplicating bubbles, the soft patter of a drip from the shower-head hitting her raised-from-the-water left ankle. She is doodling around with the idea of seeing a therapist. A leitmotif of late. It's like she's waiting to learn how to properly forge the permission slip. What exact syntax will allow you to believe this is a perfectly allowable thing to do, Lucy? She's not sure. She's not sure. What she knows is that - current spike of noia abated - she is simply a person who needs some tinkering with. Nothing is out to get her and nothing controls her. There are people who make it their lives to sort into colors and shapes the way this-synapse synapses that-synapse and - yes! - Lucy could benefit from having a word with one of them. Is it she's hung up on who? Not someone younger than she is, because that is just outlandish. 'Likely against the Code of the Psychologist to begin with' she assures herself. One of those questions to trip people up before they are issued a license: *Do you think you can advise someone who has been around longer than you?* Kaput if you answer in the affirmative. And then again, she doesn't want someone with too many years on her. Listening to psychological logic from a grandmother seems ill-advised. And someone her own age - well, they'd have to prove they are better off! They'd have to prove they have something to offer other than something Lucy could just look up in a book, herself! The whole notion gets foggy. Lucy is probably at just the exact wrong age for therapy. A car that a fix-up would cost as much as a brand new one - therapists likely don't waste much time on her breed. She'd have a cover thrown over her and be told 'Stay in the garage.' And she can tell herself that. 'For free' she giggles. Blows at some suds and watches them airborne and disappear before retouching anywhere. She's past a point where change is possible. Change, now, is inorganic, a false word. She could say 'I want to change' but knows full well what she means is 'I wish I hadn't become this.' Too bad, Lucy, too bad. So dismantle and shelve yourself or else learn to embrace all of your ins-and-outs. Again: she can tell herself that! And if that is going to be the advice, why bother? *Just keep doing what you do but be okay with it.* 'Thanks, doc' she scoffs, blowing at the wet skin of her knee not quite hard enough to feel any change to its temperature. You should buy a pipe that blows bubbles, Lucy! You should take it out in public with you and be just that cool! Dress in art-teacher purple! Wrap your sandwiches in newspaper and feed pigeons chewing-gum! She opens her eyes, jolted by whoever was touching her. The slant of the bathroom is off and her nose is running a little bit. The water still warm, though. How long could she have passed out for? A washcloth is draped over her breasts and she doesn't remember putting it there. Feels her eyes closing. Feels the air bubbles trapped under the small of her back wriggling free, tickling her ribs like kitten paws chasing at millipedes.

How does it make Lucy feel, knowing she has decades left to live? Shall we ask her? Let her towel off, first. Let her brush her teeth and relax. Let her slip into the first panties she takes from the unfolded clean laundry, still in the basket, and then take three, four, five full minutes to choose which of several t-shirts she wants to wear, too. Now? Well, let's let her smile as she reads over what she wrote, there. Let her have one cigarette in peace and quiet, the nighttime normalized, tomorrow readying itself in the same way as always. Let's time this just right. We want to ask just about here. When she is thinking about saying something to Samantha - saying 'Hello' - when she is wondering if Samantha will be wearing those slouch-boots, again. 'Where did you get those boots?' Lucy thinks. And so how does it make Lucy feel to know she has decades left to live? Because this storyline she is in now? It isn't the end of anything. This next week? These next five months? These next eight years? Eighteen? Is today going to be a memory, come then? Does that scare you or comfort you, Lucy? Does it make you want to give up or to press on? Isn't it true that everything you plan only ever has the next few months taken into account? That you treat every decision like it is the last sentence is a novel the point of which is not to think 'What happens afterward?' about but 'What does that sentence mean, retroactive through what came before?' Death won't come like a book, will it Lucy? It won't just be the first and last stanza of a poem to be kicked back-and-forth between. How many things that you planned for and even did - because you have accomplished things, Lucy! you have! - went anywhere near along the lines of how you intended them? Years of things. Decades, even. Little things, full in themselves, that become speckles of light in a slug trail slicked down a storm-door front. And you have decades more of that! Lucy at fifty. At fifty-five. At sixty. At seventy-four. It isn't up to you! And those years won't lack detail - they won't lack event. They will have nuances and intricacies the necessities for which haven't even occurred yet! If only you could suddenly be eighty and think 'Wow, it's like I was never anything else!' But when has that ever happened? Is it happening now? Are you thinking 'I'm forty-whatever and it's like I just blinked at twenty-two and now I'm here' big gaping blank between *A* and *B*? Doesn't that drain you, Jinx? To know you will know every minute and every hour inside every minute and every day inside every hour of every minute from this day until that? And so many of those moments will be spent remembering previous moments - and moments to come, further on, will be spent remembering moments when you remembered previous moments! A stack of remembering remembering! Will you remember this? Sitting here? Do you remember what you were thinking to ask Samantha? Boots? Her boots? Will you remember remembering how you remembered remembering to remember to ask her about her boots like how you pretended you would?

Lucy Jinx. Kitchen. Deciding to cook sausage-links. Sandwich them between white-bread. Is this wise? She feels so. Why does she feel so? Hadn't she just been vice-gripped in limbo-regurgitation? But now look at her! Lighter-than-air and needing her own groove back. Which means her own food within her belly. Never should have agreed to meet that Sierra at that svelte restaurant - should have insisted on some pudgy little coffee-shop. But anyway: that is all smoothed over. She has made good. Let's explain: It wasn't a mistake to arrange the meeting - that part is in keeping with being a Poet. It wasn't a mistake to show up and go on in Lucy's usual, unpredictable way - haranguing in thoughtless composition some poor broad who just wants to make friends by hobby-farming indie-poets and short-story writers or whatever. Because that is in keeping with being a Poet. What was a mistake - and the only mistake! - was to have been telling herself the whole time it was all a deception. She has now returned home, written poetry, reset the game-table and all is good. Lucy is allowed to wring her hands and woe-is-me her state all she wants - she just isn't allowed to betray it. This new food will sit well. This new food will sate her, reward, purr her knotted shoulders into melted chocolate staining her lip-creases. And look - everyone, everything, look - she realizes she was swatted on hand-backs and has learnt her lesson. Good-little-Lucy will continue ahead. She is all of a letter, herself - part of the disease - and her job is to twirl and make replicant, replicate the replicant, dip herself in her ink and press down the letter *Lucy Jinx Lucy Jinx Lucy Jinx* - and when she sees it fade she needs to re-dip and find another, new, unsullied spot and muss it up good! You can't resign being a disease! That was her mistake. Some sort of denial phase. As though her condition has to do with her will, is a reflection of her core. Nope. Poetry is something that afflicted her - and it has lain waste her until she became it and now she is it, trying to find new healthy cells to weigh plump with sick. A simple life. She is a germ turning over sausages, quarter-rotations at-a-time, watching the grease sprinkle the counter-top, dull-orange oven light caught in it, winking a shimmer like crust on unthawed car windshields. People forget when they wish for immortality that immortality isn't so impossible. Many things are immortal. In effect, you are wishing to be one-of-those, not something unique. Self-birthing with fission. Two starfish then four then eight - then all of them might as well have come from just one. There is one Starfish. There is one Poem. It is a disease so incurable it has transcended to the strata of Element. 'Light is an accomplished bacteria' Lucy hums to herself, turning the sausage, yawning, adjusting the fit of her underwear which has grown too tight in the month since she bought it.

When had this message from Ariel come in? While Lucy had been bathing. *Hey Jucy Linx, I hope I didn't freak you out with all that earlier. You seemed freaked out. And I meant to wish you luck with your thang tonight. Don't hate me, I'm just that last cracker in the pack, right, the one that is always broken. Crumbs in a corner. Just send me a word to let me know we're all cool, will ya?* Involuntary go Lucy's fingers - but she slows, stops, erases without reading. A delicate touch, here. The thing to do is to call, yes? Sending even a lengthy text would seem to be reinforcing a distance, when the communique-at-hand is best translated to *Promise me there is no new distance.* Though, consider: Ariel did not attempt to call first. The text is not a follow-up to a clear attempt at some verbal touch-base. This could be deciphered as *I well know there is no distance, please just shoot me a simple 'Don't be an idiot back' nothing-is-nothing, so I get that you get me.* In which case, a call could show a lack of understanding of the subtle currents that stir the silt through the vein of the friendship. *The friendship,* Lucy? Is that what you said? And then - taking the previous observation as correct - there is the matter of striking the exactly appropriate dismissive, snarky, all-is-well tone. To even seem to be giving the message from Ariel a consideration at face-value - i.e. to write too long a text, even too long a text on an entirely unrelated subject - would be catastrophic and would, indeed, lead to a discontinuity. The next time Lucy and Ariel spoke, face-to-face, the texts would stand as needing to be addressed even before the two of them could verbally go into whatever needed to be gone into - and thus would the reality of the lack of making a voice-call in response to Ariel's text here be made into an animal with aims all its own to tame out. So: that means a call would be best. Except it should be a call not-exactly-on-another-subject but to just touch voices, brushing aside any need to talk. Like what? To say 'My phone is out of battery - didn't want to risk a text not going through and not knowing if you got it. Sorry - I'll charge up and call you. Bye!' Except why not just call with the phone plugged in, charging? Or: call to say 'Hey, did you get my text? Sorry if that was in bad taste.' Subterfuge. Indicate something is the matter with the phone - say a joke was sent back, text-wise, ten minutes went by, just checking up. Though that is kind of thin, the cover-up rather apparent. And the urgency to take a pulse. Could it be it's best not to get back, at all? Wait out the night and then *What is this nonsense? I go to sleep and you unspool? Give it a rest, Ari - I'll see you tonight, yeah?* Except all of this is discounting the fact that Ariel probably is actually worried. And Lucy - well, Lucy, come on - you have been acting strangely. So maybe just text to say *Call?* There's the word, Lucy. *Call?*

'No, it's fine. Leopold is out with the barnacle - I'm more than free.' 'I don't want to Bogart your alone time.' 'Lucy, you are my alone time. Where are you? How did it go?' 'What?' 'Didn't you have some interview, tonight?' 'But the thing is, El: I told you about that a long time ago and didn't bring it up once, today - do you go around remembering shit I say? That's a form of stalking, when you really give it a squint.' 'You did bring it up today!' 'Don't fuck with my head, my fine feathered friend - you don't know what you're in for.' 'You told me - you said it was gonna be a drag, but you thought she was cute and was named after a crayon you liked.' 'A crayon I like?' '*Sienna?*' 'But her name is *Sierra!*' 'Then what were you talking about?' 'What are you talking about?' 'You said *She's called Sienna. Like that kind of crayon I like. Not as light as raw umber* you said.' 'I've never said *Raw Umber* in my life! I don't even know what that means - what kind of head-fuckery are you do-dadding on me, you louse?' 'I'm just lashing out in jealously.' 'Jealous of whom?' 'Sierra! And yes, I knew her proper name, all this while - I said that whole crayon thing just to unfoot you, get you on the low ground to lop off your pretty head at the larynx!' 'Don't be jealous of Sierra, you fool! She's a blogger who overcompensates by paying for interviewees' steaks.' 'She paid for your steak?' 'But it made me throw up, later. Or anyway, I didn't throw up but I thought I ought to have. My body forgets that sometimes it's supposed to do things, not just clutch over in imprecise agony.' 'I hear you, there. Do you know how many pimples I have, now? And on my thighs!' 'I could come count them.' 'It's awful. I know I'm supposed to think it's beautiful and all, but I trust you to remind me it's repugnant.' 'I don't envy you it, if that's what you mean. Hey - isn't it nighttime? Where did he take the kiddo?' 'Oh he's an over-reactor. Took her to an Urgent Care Clinic on account of she stubbed her toe really bad and it looked like there was, as he put it, *a bleed underneath of the nail*.' 'What is he, a Medicine Man? And why is your kid stubbing her toe like some commoner?' 'Oh Lucy - she is a commoner! My only hope is that she is smart enough to want nothing more than to marry Gaston, you know? I'm keeping her away from any book that doesn't have the word *bosom* in the first chapter.' 'You should bind her feet, it'll make her more of a commodity.' 'Sell her to an Easterner, eh? I hadn't thought of that, but it might be just the ticket.' 'And her foot is already fucked, right? Just let nature run its course!' 'Lucy?' 'Yes, dahling?' 'You don't really have a crush on that raw umber girl, right?' 'Well, just to make you jealous, only.' 'But you kind of regret making me jealous, right - that I've been sitting around stewing in my feelings all hurt?' 'Yeah.' 'Okay.' 'You okay, El?' 'Jesus, Lucy, I don't know. Probably. Lucy?' 'Yeah?' 'Read me a poem, would ya?'

And so another hour passes. And when we find Lucy next, she is in the dark of her bedroom, back-splayed and ceiling-staring. A middle-aged teenage girl. Heartful of rockabilly lyrics, headful of the homework she's left undone. Yawns like some tiger from a documentary, real show-off about it, smacks her lips and rolls over, rolls back. She sleepwalks a cigarette and clicks through the channels awhile, can smell the pasty perspiration that gathers in the creases of her nose when she scratches at an itch and gives the fingertip a quick whiff. These women in these Infomercials - they want nothing more than hair to please their husbands! They aren't satiric, the feelings are likely genuine. Paid shills are not necessary, no. *Gladys L.* sincerely likes the fact that she can be brought to her hubby's work functions without having to feel that she's bringing him down. *Before Photo. After.* A shocking difference, Lucy agrees. Channel change. Channel change. The News tells her an old man died from exposure while waiting for a bus. It warns how those with elderly loved ones ought to be sure they are dressing their memaws and poppops such-and-such appropriate ways for the elements. Inherent in that statement: someone didn't love this dead man enough. A wide shot of the cold bus station, man-on-the-street interviews with Calvin and Lois and Rochelle, all of who say 'It's heartbreaking' and how they sometimes see people not dressed proper for the cold and 'Hey, wow' now they really know they need to be more aware of it. Change channel. Change channel. Change channel. Television off. Sizzle blink of darkness and quiet. New smoke. Lucy says to her biographer, who must be taking further notes for the chapter on Lucy's atrocious sleep habits 'I was talking about Time Travel before, right? Bet it would screw over copyright-law, pretty bad. Patents. Imagine having to give Whosit from ancient-wherever royalties for the bloody Inclined Plane! The

Pulley? Having to pay out royalties on the Gospels, you know? People wouldn't be leaving the things for free in fleabag hotels, I'll tell you that!' Her biographer chuckles and says she had never thought of that. 'People back-in-time would be way greedy - especially when they see their ideas caught on! We'd rue the day we ever had a Past, man.' Lucy moves to the kitchen, runs the faucet to douse the stub of her smoke. Her biographer doesn't follow, doesn't watch Lucy poke her head in the freezer, stare at the box of ice-cream sandwiches, using all of her concentration to magic at least one left instead of none. She considers having a pull of the vodka, but shuts the freezer and goes to knees at the refrigerator instead, digging around for the last of the string-cheese and eating it too quickly to enjoy. Back to the bedroom and splayed to the bed. Ceiling-staring. Pressing her belly out skyward, keeping her back flat, tensing her abs to make things taut. Then long breath out and collapses, innards agurgle, writhes a bit, rolls to her belly, one leg flopped out wide as though there was a lower back to lay it around, waiting.

Lucy dreams of Ariel, now. In this very room. But another day. It is a dream that is smeared, painted and effaced and restored as it goes. At one point, Ariel is having Lucy poke her finger through a hole in the t-shirt over her belly and when Lucy does it does not so much seem pregnant but engorged and waterlogged, a thick latex over wet sand and metal objects. But then at one point, Lucy and Ariel are playing a game where Ariel dips her fingers in wine, holds the fingers over her now naked belly, and when a droplet falls and cascades, Lucy is to trace the path it flows with magic marker, Ariel's belly electric in soft green, blue, purple, orange, yellow zigzags. Except at the same time, it seems that Lucy's belly is pulsing with child and Ariel is hovering around, fretting over not having a warm enough sweater for Lucy to borrow. 'They all seem fine, they all seem fine.' And Ariel is the one trying them on, not Lucy. Pulling them over her then instantly re-nuded body, pulling them over, pulling them over - way over there on the other side of the apartment, talking in the direction of the opposite wall. And Lucy knows there is someone at the window - she can just tell! She knows Ariel is not telling her about them because it will mean something has to change. The dream is one of avoiding eye-contact with this interloper, of knowing he'll start mouthing moans and scratching at the window glass, tapping the pane with his only-three-teeth in his salivating gums. He'll point to Lucy like to say 'She's seen me, she's seen me' and Ariel will know. And also none of that is happening and Ariel is showing Lucy that if they turn off the light and aim a flashlight just right, shadows like an Ultrasound of the baby can be cast on the wall. 'They aren't accurate, but this is the best way to see her.' Ariel whispered that right up to Lucy's ear and Lucy woke - at first expecting to find Ariel's face pillowed in front of her, but then clenching her eyes down and refusing to open them, nothing but the presence of that gibbering drooler, that face at the window in the air of the bedroom. Awake, Lucy thinks of Ariel while she knows the man is holding his finger just an eyelash-thick away from the tip of her eyelid, quiver to the digit, at any moment his skin could touch hers and so she thinks of Ariel and wants to slip back into the dream. And she does. Ariel submerged in a bathtub to the half-belly. But odd. As though standing. As though the tub goes deeper down than the floor Lucy stands on, twice Ariel's height. And when Ariel raises from the water, the bottom half of her belly doesn't appear. Just Ariel's top-to-middle, nothing, then privates, unshaved to the extent they seem like caveman's loin-cloth, then legs downward, normal-at-first but joining into just one leg as thick as both before the single foot. And the floor is topsoil. Ariel having to hold out her arms like keeping balance on a curb while Lucy shouts friendly jeers to topple her - to make them both roll together laughing.

THE TRAFFIC, THESE CORN-FED ROADS, the lanes sniggering from two into one so morosely, the drivers not seeming to catch on until too-late-to-not-make-it-difficult - so that if seen from overhead the line of cars would be bent all weirdo, some art-project cat-whisker shaped out of a straightened staple, an uncurled paperclip. For some reason, Lucy has *Glengarry* stuck in her head, this morning. Since the shower. She depresses the button on her recorder and spouts 'Baby, I can't make a dollar on these deadbeat leads - and you're killing my ass on the street!' Shuts the recorder off. Scoots her car forward a half-inch, re-reading the sticker of who the driver there supported for President more than a decade ago. 'Loser' she fuck-yous with a wink. Hits play, rewinds through a squeak, and lets go just at 'make a dollar on these deadbeat leads - and you're killing my ass on the street.' Click. You should be an actress, Lucy. Tread those boards and hit those marks like a deadbolt! And now this situation: can the woman whose face Lucy can make out very clearly when she glances to her rearview mirror make Lucy out? Are they looking at each other? Does the woman know Lucy is looking at her? Somewhere lurks in Lucy's mind some idea that if one can see the eyes of someone else's reflection then that person can see them right back. Incidence. Reflectance. But take this situation: that woman is back there. Her face appears large to Lucy in the mirror - almost normal face size. To the woman, though? If she were to be able to see Lucy it would be in Lucy's own rearview - same as where Lucy sees herself and the woman - and the distance would make it rather cumbersome for the woman to make Lucy out with any detail. Technically, sure, they woman could 'See Lucy in the reflection.' Could she, however, make out where Lucy was looking? Unlikely. Yet it does seem they are looking at each other. If Lucy were to smile, this woman would smile back. If Lucy were to mouth words, the woman would get coy faced, eyebrows raise, mouth back 'Say that again?' or 'What?' And Lucy can make her out just as well in her side mirror - from where it seems, also, the woman is looking directly at her, their eyes sharing connection. No chance, though, that the woman can tell from there that Lucy is looking at her - and it's not as though Lucy is looking at her in both mirrors at once! One then the other - back-and-forth - this or that. How could the woman possibly know the exact moment Lucy is going to change connection points, have eyes readily waiting to greet? And there's this: Lucy cannot make out the face of the driver ahead of her in that driver's rearview. Or side mirror. Though, to be fair, Lucy does not know if that driver can see her, either - so that's not much to go on. Lucy, you think everyone is looking at you and no one would want you to be looking back. 'That's true, Lucy.' Beat. 'Baby, I can't make a dollar on these deadbeat leads.'

Like a comma technically correct but not really needed, Lucy turns into the office-park lot and snugs to the space she prefers. Note: Lucy has not had one sip yet of the coffee she so imperatively had to stop at the gas station for. And the candy-bar is still on the passenger seat. Note: Lucy is wearing her ratty sneakers with duct-tape holding on the bottom of the left one, the right one with a classic hole-straight-through-the-center-bottom. Precious objects. Dug out from a trashbag full of shoes she never wears anymore in her closet. Out there? That is a man called Edwin. She knows him, vaguely. Nice enough. Though a bit too quick to assume people care about proper lawnmower maintenance. Lucy had been waylaid by him for an hour simply because she'd politely said 'That's really interesting' to something he'd said about blade-oiling. Edwin is shaped like the drooped beak of a seagull held sideways, lips-side-up. Tall but center-bulbed. Lucy has remarked to herself how often the man seems to be checking the tuck of his shirt, re-stuffing this or that bit of it down his waistband, some endless noia, a woodpecker irritation, discomfort he never seems to be without. And what does Lucy think of this? Lucy, here, smoking a cigarette to put off going in to work for cigarette minutes. She likes it. Nods as she thinks so. And likes, most of all, that it is a problem Edwin seems disinclined to solve. Buy more tailored clothes? Different sized shirts? Sweater or sweater-vest on top or blazer or something? It doesn't seem any of these methods occurred to Edwin - or if they did, he never once tried to institute them. A man most comfortable with this little nuisance to keep him company, follow him on his appointed rounds. If not that, then something else. Edwin. A wiser culture would worship you by now! The inside of Lucy's mouth tastes sour like overcooked coffee from the previous night and teeth not washed. But she had brushed and used gargled-blue mint, so what gives? Some mild form of reflux, a candy-coating of her mouth with stomach bile, acidic and aftertaste vague. She tried for the billionth time to test her breath by huffing out into her curved palm - to the same end as always. She doesn't smell much of anything. Which either means her breath smells fine and always has every time she's tried this out, that this method of testing does not work, that she is doing the test improperly, or that she does not know what to be smelling for. Her breath feels bad, anyway. So she says it 'Feels like it smells bad.' But maybe that's not accurate. Questions this morning - questions. Lucy is the kid every second grade teacher likes at first but soon doesn't, despite what they say. Frowns. Now: the thought that sometimes she can smell when her shoes are mildewed from rainy streets suggests to her her sense of smell is well calibrated, top shelf. Can she smell what her shoes smell like, now? Nose in direction of feet. In goes air. Is that her feet? What is she smelling?

Samantha says 'Oh thank God it's just you.' Who else would it be? 'Why do you say that, Sammy - who else would it be?' Well: it seems that Kurt is not going to be in for a few days and Samantha had been told some new guy was going to come in, today. 'Yuck' says Lucy. And Samantha agrees by sticking out her tongue and making a hacking sound. 'I'm hoping he doesn't show - it's better, now you're here - but still.' 'If he does show up, let's pretend he's invisible and that we can't hear him. See how long it takes him to disintegrate mentally. See how long it takes before he does obnoxious-little-brother things to catch us out, make us have to admit he is there. Oh yes, we'll elder-brother the life out of this intruder!' But Samantha worries 'He might report us.' 'Report us!?' ejaculates Lucy. 'Could you imagine the poor boy lasting a day, after that? First day on, calling in to complain that two veteran workers are inexplicably treating him as though ether? What in Hell would that sound like to Trisha or whomever at the Home Office? He's screwed either way, Sam - we have all the power here. Because we're in relative-good-standing and no one has any reason to think we'd all of a sudden behave so radically - we can do it and rest assured we'll come out in a sympathetic light. Especially if we lie and say *He came in and seemed a bit off - then said he needed to use the toilet and never came back*. We're believable, Sam - we're believable. We're women working sorting files - what percentage would the Home Office think is in it for us to badger some poor new hump?' Samantha had been scratching a spot on her forearm with increasing agitation while Lucy went on, but now it is too much. 'Why are you doing that? What are you trying to prove?' Samantha is sorry. 'It's some kind of bug bite.' Or she didn't rinse some soap off properly. 'It's driving me insane, frankly. It's making me hate arms, in a general way.' Lucy notices for the first time how much hair Samantha has on her arms. It goes in three shades, starting at the wrist. Black like a not-quite-black-dog to start, then a blonde for most of the way toward the elbow, and finally dusting off in a kind of gingerbread brown. 'What?' Lucy blushes. 'What?' 'Nothing' Lucy says. 'Sorry. My mind is all over the place.' Lucy watches Samantha giving her arm the once over, twisting it, looking there, there, there. Does she really not right away assume it was the hair Lucy was looking at? Look, here - look. Samantha seems to think it has something to do with the rough ash of her elbow, is circular-rubbing the elephant hide of the point as though she could uncrumple the roadmap of it smooth. Lucy has walked past Samantha on the pretense of grabbing another few files. She now stops right behind her, leans in and says 'It's not your elbow. I like the hair on your arm but didn't like being caught looking.' Samantha kicks her heel up, striking Lucy harder than she meant to - probably - and so Lucy makes a point to not let on that it hurt, just chuckles and says 'Really mature. Violence. That's your style, eh?'

They work in silence, awhile. Lucy likes the sounds of the work. Shishes and thwips and phit and snap and little thunks of whole folders set there - hughs and fripipip of large piles of paper being flipped through, sniffles from Lucy, more-constant-than-she-realizes throat clears from Samantha - little words like 'Ke-hey' the sound of these subdued coughing utterances - and lacquering it all, the hummed out air from the vents overhead. Also - Samantha has remarked how strange this is, too, in prior conversations with Kurt and with Lucy - sometimes the sound of a car door closing or a toilet flushing someplace. How do those sounds get into this room? Samantha now goes 'So you read things, right?' A rotten question that Lucy hates. All of her responses sound terrible, especially if she is just honest. So this time she goes with a noncommittal 'I did, once-upon-a-time - I did.' And Samantha doesn't delve, as her question seems to have been nothing but a rhetorical lead-in to her asking 'So is there an actual answer to that riddle *When is a raven like a writing desk?*' Lucy thought it was *How is a raven like a writing desk?* Pauses. Look on her face like she's trying to recall the answer to the riddle, not the wording. *How. When. How. When. How. When.* Suddenly Samantha goes 'Or it's *Why is a raven like a writing desk?* - yes? *Why?* Right?' But Lucy likes *When* most of all - and so says so. 'What do you mean?' 'Of the three options.' Samantha wants to know - as this is how Lucy put it - all about her preference for *When.* So Lucy explains. 'Doesn't he give an answer?' 'Just some nonsense.' 'That's right' Lucy nods 'that's right.' They agree there isn't an answer, then mock the Riddle-of-the-Sphinx as really kind of simple for being so important. 'But it was a long time ago' Lucy decides to say, going easy on the ancients 'so we have to keep that in mind. Riddles were still new, in general, and they took everything so literally, back then. Those old languages, you know? Not a lot of room for fun and games.' Still, Samantha and Lucy do not let the

*Walks-on-three-legs* explanation go - that is just silly. 'Not everyone walks with a cane in their old age. I don't care how long ago it was.' They also try to remember if there is a bit about *One leg*. Because that would seem more elegant. 'It's fucking clunky, man. And it's not like the Sphinx didn't have plenty time on its hands to come up with something a little more structurally smooth.' 'Back to Carroll, though - it's kind of dick-headed coming up with a riddle there isn't an answer for. Why is that an accomplishment?' 'Truth' says Lucy 'it's basically just not coming up with a riddle.' 'I'm so clever' Samantha says in some weird British voice she must think is what Lewis Carroll sounded like 'look at this riddle I didn't come up with. No one will ever figure it out - ho ho ho!' They both turn their heads as though someone is there. Stare at the empty door-frame. Stare. Give each other a sly look. Then keep staring.

'Are we waiting for the new guy? Is that why we haven't left for lunch?' Lucy mulls that over. 'Baby, I can't make a living on these deadbeat leads - and you're killing my ass on the street!' And, duck-to-water, Samantha ins with 'Well, I'm sorry you aren't happy here.' Oh glorious day! Lucy's tummy does a dorky hip-hop-hooray and she claps like an infantile preteen before continuing with 'Well, that's very cute. But you're running this office like a bunch of bullshit. You're on an override - and you make money, we make money.' Samantha: 'I'd like you to make more money.' Lucy: 'Then get me a better lead and don't waste my time. A sales conference?' Samantha: 'The strategy comes from downtown.' And now both of them, in unison: 'Oh the strategy? *The strategy*? Well I think I'll pass.' Oh a jolly good, back-slapping laugh is had. Lucy woke up with that movie on her mind, she says, and Samantha hadn't thought about it in forever but now wants to watch it. 'Right now!' she whines. Anyway: are they waiting for the new guy? 'Are the obliged to? What I mean' Lucy says 'is this: Samantha - were you told it was, in any way, your responsibility to show any new guy anything? Are you even qualified to do so? You're just some ditz in a *Ross Dress-for-Less* pair of slacks, aren't you?' She is, she says - that is what she is. 'I wouldn't trust me with a new guy.' Why does Samantha even think there is a new guy supposed to show up? Does she see Lucy's point? The more time and effort put to this question, the more absurd it seems! 'They said so, last week.' 'Who said?' 'Kurt.' 'Kurt? And did Kurt know he wouldn't be here, today?' 'The new guy?' 'No. Kurt.' 'Did Kurt know Kurt wouldn't be here, you mean?' 'No' Lucy says, not caring if Samantha is playing the same game 'did Kurt know that he wouldn't be the new guy?' 'Kurt's not the new guy?' 'Well, is he? You talked to him.' 'I talked to the new guy.' 'Kurt?' 'About Kurt.' 'You talked about Kurt?' 'Right.' 'To the new guy?' 'No - I talked to the new guy about Kurt.' 'Who isn't the new guy.' 'Kurt isn't?' 'He can't be if the new guy is unless he is also the new guy.' 'Logical' Samantha agrees 'logical. So: why aren't we going to lunch?'

Lucy does a heavy-handed stage-gesture of 'Search me, man' and Samantha is already getting her coat. In the corridor, Samantha tells Lucy 'You're fun' and Lucy says 'Thank you' and both of them have cigarettes ready by the time they are to the Exit door. There is a new woman at reception who gives them a friendly enough kind of once over, but Lucy gets the feeling they had better not light up, inside. So out in front they huddle to each other and flick lighters, both quickly bird-beaking into the measly flame before it is doused by this wind with its sound of the fabric of a shirt being tugged overhead.

They each tell a thing about each other while waiting for Lucy's coffee to be brought, waiting for Samantha's mint tea. Lucy tells this: 'I first decided to try French-dip sandwiches because this cool bloke in high-school talked about getting one at *Arby's* - he talked about the Au Jus and that sounded fancy to me, dipping the sandwich in something, you know? And even when I'd order it at *Arby's*, I felt like it was fancy. Because when you're a kid you have no sense of the world, you're kind of like a crayon trying to figure out how to be the texture of dry daubed acrylic.' Samantha tells this: 'I never once made one of those models of the Solar System for school - not successfully. I did my best, one time. Went to the Craft Store at the last minute and bought wire and Styrofoam balls. It seemed like it would be easy. I learned a lot about my limitations, that day.' They both order French-dips and Samantha asks for something called Smothered Waffle-Fries. 'But they aren't really smothered' Samantha says a few minutes later, breaking in on a totally different conversation topic. 'It's melted cheese and bacon crumbles, you know? But the fries are more-or-less just lightly drizzled. *Smothered* is a misnomer.' Lucy is grateful for the explanation. And the Devil spake of - here are the fries, themselves! Delicious. But Lucy agrees with Samantha's argument, lifting out three fries in-a-row without any trace of cheese or bacon to be found upon them. How about the sandwiches? Not very good. And the Au Jus kind of tastes like grease and sink water. 'How are we going to handle this?' Lucy asks, figuring that Samantha will catch her drift without need for elaboration. Samantha wonders aloud - the question put out generally rather than directly to Lucy - 'Couldn't we be the sort to actually complain and ask that alternative food be brought us?' But no - no - no, no, Lucy does not have the stomach for this. Reason? 'Well, if we weren't in here every day, who cares? But we are. And don't want them to know we're critical of anything.' 'Why not?' Samantha asks. Lucy just makes pathetic eyes, evoking someone who just needs the status quo and would gladly send a generation of youngsters into battle to die for it. Samantha thumbs-up and says she will be right back. Lucy eats the only fry she can find that is even kind-of-smothered. And here is Samantha, returned with two boxes. 'I said we were summoned back to the office early and couldn't bear to leave the food.' 'Brilliant' Lucy beams. And she really feels it is. Left to her own devices, she'd have been stymied! Would have just sat out the hour and made some see-through excuse about a medication she was on upsetting her stomach - but that would have left Samantha's untouched food yet unexplained! 'Did you already pay, too?' 'Yep' Samantha chirps. You're safe, Lucy. 'You're like a sensitive foster-mom or something - working so hard to show that you understand me!' And Samantha chucks Lucy's chin in a *Yer alright, kiddo* kind of way - also whispering 'I do need you to leave the tip though, freak.'

'Do these count as dates?' That's Samantha asking - the two of them safely out of sight-line of the *Cashdollar*, dumping their boxed sandwiches in this rubbish-bin. 'Our lunches?' Samantha lights a cigarette, then - after a quick pip and exhale - says 'Yeah. Are they dates?' Lucy occupies herself with fishing out her own cigarettes and - to keep an air of levity to the proceedings, in case she suddenly decides to clam up - gives Samantha the very clear once over, stem-to-stern. Samantha does none of the cliché striking-a-pose or acting flirtatiously put upon. Samantha just slouches and smokes, nodding when Lucy says 'Not technically, no. Not technically.' Samantha wants to ask Lucy on a date, then. 'What kind of a date?' Why doesn't Lucy come over to Samantha's apartment for dinner, for example. 'Except' Lucy says - quick to point out this does not mean she is trying to squirrel out of the date - she hates it when chicks want to cook her a meal, because that means she'll have to feel uncomfortable when she doesn't want to eat it but has to to seem nice. 'I'm not very into food, is all I mean. I think it's a waste of food.' But Samantha had had no intention of cooking. 'Oh no?' 'Nope.' Samantha had intended to get Lucy over, order a pizza or something, and then ply her with drugs or whatever it took to get her seduceable. 'Which kinds of drugs?' 'The Roman Polanski kind - I don't remember what they're called. All very classical, you know? None of these thuggish modern swills.' Lucy thinks this all sounds like a swinging fine time, but does have a few more questions. 'When is this supposed to happen?' *Whenever*, according to Samantha. Follow-up, then: 'Does that actually mean *Whenever*?' - like does it mean Lucy could say 'Sure' but that it'd have to wait two weeks and that'll just be the end of discussion, no prying or arm-twisting to see her in private before the fortnight agreed on? 'That's what it means.' Next question, then: since Samantha isn't cooking, could they do it at Lucy's apartment, instead? 'Sure.' And that's actually all of her questions, Lucy realizes, so she sighs and goes 'Fine, then I guess so. But let me also point out - that means tomorrow's lunch and stuff still isn't a date.' Samantha gets it. Dates don't start until after the first date. 'Whenever that is' Lucy leans in to emphasize, dotting her cigarette a flick to drive home the matter. 'Is it two weeks, though?' Samantha asks, adding in that she is 'Not pressing for earlier' just didn't know if that had just been a 'For example kind of timeline or what.'

'It'll be less than two weeks - but I am not in the habit of being more specific than that. So, you know, deal with it. Or whatever.' 'I'll deal with it or whatever, then' says Samantha. And that there is the face of a woman Lucy knows she can and should kiss but also just can't and so doesn't.

There is a new guy! 'Hello' the new guy says, standing up from the chair he had been seated in. 'You're like a surprise party you forgot to invite anyone else to' Lucy says, unable to help laughing at the Jack-in-the-box way the fellow had sprung standing, his over-toothed smile and hand so obviously wanting to dart out to be shook. 'I'm sorry I'm late' he says, and explains he had a medical appointment that ran long. 'It's no problem' Lucy says, since they had been planning, earlier, to ignore him when he did show up, anyway. 'Not because of anything personal' she adds, to soften what could be perceived as a blow 'not at all! Hell, we don't even know you. We just wanted to experiment on you, psychologically. Because how often do dweebs like us get a chance to wield authority, you know?' The man does not respond, but seems to take this in stride. Samantha comes to his rescue and says 'You can ignore her since she's my subordinate, anyway. What's your name?' His name is Eugene. 'Is it?' 'Yes' he nods, face now set to suspicious, expecting the question is a wind-up. But Samantha just nods and asks if he has a second name? 'Like a last-name?' Lucy is busying herself with a new set of files, figuring it best to just let Samantha field this person. Anyway, Lucy needs to suss out what she's going to do about this whole having-a-date-with-Samantha thing. She'd like to just let it squeak by, not give it to triage, but that would not be advisable, she knows. She should call Ariel - put off tonight until tomorrow - just spring it on Samantha at end of shift 'Okay, see you tonight' and then if Samantha can't make it say 'Oh too bad - it was now or never.' Or not put it off with Ariel - no - that isn't a coin on the table. Maybe tell Milos that she can't come by, tomorrow night. He wouldn't care. But then, he wouldn't care if Lucy didn't show up without explanation, either - or would care only insofar as it gave him something to be a priss to her about for a few minutes. 'Lucy' Samantha cuts into Lucy's thoughts by saying 'have you seen the box with the' - she wriggles her fingers, then rubs index and thumb-tip together - 'the, you know' - she tap tap taps index and thumb-tip hard, almost enough it sounds like a clap - 'finger things?' Lucy turns to where the box always is, behind her hearing Samantha exasperate 'I already looked there, man, or else I wouldn't be asking!' Lucy doesn't even respond, just feels herself warm in the loins when Samantha mocks to Eugene 'I didn't train her, by the way. I just want that on record.' Eugene does the nervous 'Oh come on' sort of chuckle that new guys do when the old-hats do their bickering. And Lucy sees the box of *Stick-E Finger-Z* there on the bottom most slat of that shelf - the slat which serves no real purpose, has Lucy ever once got anything off that slat?

how did those things get there? - but keeps the discovery to herself and returns to her sorting - slow and unlooking - while she hears Samantha moving around, poking through things, foreshortening her statements to Eugene with blows of huff out and 'Well, if we can ever find the damn things!'

Lucy waits her turn for one of the stalls to free up, then sits down without undoing her pants. The woman who vacated seems to have a lot to do out there at the sink. The faucet is run, shut off, run, shut off. A purse is set to the counter and clanking sounds of rummaging. Clicks of compact opening, silence of whatever being applied, click of lipstick opening, silence of arc and arc and lips in and mwah-mouth. More rummaging and then a tish sound of something being spayed - then more rummaging and another sound like that. Faucet run, shut off. Paper towels used, coughed in to - Lucy can tell, it'd muffled the cough - and nose blown and faucet run and shut off and paper towel used. Click click clack clack heels moving to the best look-at-myself posture - Lucy knows the woman is touching hair, pinching fabric of shirt here or there due to some frayed string or the odd bit of fuzz or long piece of hair found over forearm sleeve or a shoulder. Lucy just sits. Listening. And only when she hears this woman leave does she realize the wait was pointless, because there is a high pitched whistle of a very forced bit of air out the bowels of whoever is in the stall next to her. Yes - presto! - all of a sudden Lucy is aware of every oink and grunt the woman there makes. The only sounds in the room, they are amplified until they seem thoughts in Lucy's own head. This must be what it feels like to go mad, she supposes - a head that is full with someone else's toilet noises, no control, no control. The picture in Lucy's mind: an older woman. This older woman: thin as a hospital gown and flimsy as a field mouse's paw - skin hotdog pink and eyes hotdog brown. Every push of mess out of this woman would feel dry, like she shits torn up biscuits of shredded wheat and pisses only the brine left after cooking a lobster. Lucy feels odd, suddenly, just being in the bathroom to sit, expecting to have privacy, a stage to gather her thoughts. She stands up and makes an elaborate amount of noise to give the impression she has to pull up her pants and get her shirt tucked back in and all then makes the dynamite blast of the flush. And she washes her hands - thoroughly, soaps them up twice - to give the still-seated woman the best impression of her. And a pace or two down the corridor - you didn't see this one coming, really? - wouldn't you know that Lucy realizes she does need to urinate! So? What are the chances that the woman saw her? None. No way. And even if so: what does it matter? This is a judgmental old crone, all of a sudden? Likely to spread slanders about how some woman - 'I think her name is Lucy' - used the toilet two times? Is that so unforgivable? 'Of course not' Lucy staunchlys. Of course aware how the real problem is that if the woman does know it is her and this time hears her using the toilet, the woman will realize how last time she hadn't and rightfully be unnerved by the knowledge.

Where's Eugene gone? 'Where's Eugene?' 'I fired him.' Lucy gives a look of 'But, really?' All it turns out is that Eugene got a call he needed to take and asked would it be alright to go out to his car. 'When was this?' Samantha goes Uh-mouthed, does a kind of hand-jive gesture, snaps her fingers and one-fist-in-to-one-palm says 'Minute or two ago - why?' And almost synchronous with the *Why?* Lucy kisses Samantha and says 'I probably meant to do that before.' 'Okay' Samantha says. They kiss again. Lucy feels rather like she is shaking hands with a pickpocket after receiving an apology. It's an odd feeling. She says 'Sorry' and Samantha looks confused. 'Sorry for what?' 'I'm being weird today and kissing you and stuff.' 'You are being weird. And you are kissing me. And you are and stuff. But please don't say *Sorry*. It makes me feel like you don't want to be weird, kissing, or stuff but are some compulsive who nonetheless has just done all three.' 'You just need to get that I'm not the same as most other people and I thought the best way to get that across would be to kiss you while Eugene was in his car making a phone call and then apologizing for it and then saying this.' Samantha kisses Lucy again and then doesn't say anything, just keeps sorting the Blue file she has opened. Lucy notes that Samantha is still not sorting via the method she has now explained three or four times. But that's okay. Lucy gets to sorting herself, chewing on her lip, wishing she'd bit Samantha's. But now Eugene is back and is explaining the content of his phone call in far more detail than is required. And Lucy can tell that Samantha is listening intently, showing interest - just the same as Lucy is - because Samantha's mind is on the kiss and on Lucy being weird and on wanting to know when they will be in Lucy's apartment. Lucy watches Eugene sorting a file - that must be Samantha's sticky-finger thing he is wearing - and then glances at Samantha, sorting with just her fingers unaided. She sighs. Sorts through a Yellow. A Blue. Another Blue. Looks up and Eugene is whispering a question to Samantha about 'Is this one of the things we need?' Samantha matter-of-factly saying 'No' Eugene nodding but explaining why he thought it was as though he needs to justify his existence, prove that he will catch on, that he does deserve his chance here in the big-leagues. What are you doing, Lucy? I don't know. Just working. Just working. 'Do you smoke, Eugene?' she hears herself asking. Eugene says that he used to, but gave it up when his brother got sick. 'Not with cancer or anything - but it still seemed like I should do something to be healthier.' You don't think that makes you come off as kind of a dick? *Look at me - I can make choices before it's too late!*' No - Lucy doesn't say that. Samantha would like it, but Eugene is too new. 'Well, I do smoke. I'm going to smoke, now.' Yeah yeah - Eugene doesn't have a problem with smokers, like he says, he was a smoker until just this year. And

Lucy is eyeing Samantha, willing her to understand this is a come-with-me cigarette not an I-need-a-moment-to-myself one. Look at me Samantha. This is a come-kiss-me-again cigarette. Get it. Just get it. Come on.

YOU HAVE TO THINK ABOUT it, Lucy. 'No. No, I don't.' Does that seem logical? You are just going to keep an area around a particular five-minute span of memory cordoned off, your own curious nose waved away when you come sniffing? 'How many five-minutes have I forgotten in forty-odd years? How many years have I even lived out of how many years I've even lived?' Squirm squirm, Lucy - but you feel yourself, like the block that's shaved in thin curls to violin, becoming nearer and nearer the shape of having to think about it. 'It was just Ariel in a room.' How many rooms, how many with Ariel? 'Not many.' Exactly! Exactly - so why is something so miniscule something that has to be so reduced? You slavishly remember things embarrassingly lager, excruciatingly more time-consuming and on to those you throw more girth - the thing and the remembrance and the analysis and the reframing and the on and the on and the on. 'So it's too much, already! Why let this thing plump - gaseous and roadkill, crawled away by the insects that larvae it, sweet smell, then stink, and then sweet, and then washed by the ozone of rainfall and the antifreeze lace of car leaks?' Hiding behind words? 'I'm not hiding anywhere. Fine - fine - fine!' Well? 'I've changed my mind.' You don't think it meant something - Ariel in that room, child-bellied and nude and diminished to her chair and holding your eye-contact while she said words she figured she'd be slapped for? 'That's over-dramatizing. And her nudity is irrelevant - she's often nude for me.' She's often nude for you, Lucy? Her daughter at play downstairs or in the front yard, lingering alone - Ariel has stripped and been waiting for you *often*? What did she say? What did she say that you don't want to think about? 'She won't say it, again - so it doesn't matter.' And you're okay with that? 'It's her decision. Ariel isn't in need of a diaper change - she is a grown woman and has eons to choose what she chooses and can swap out this life for that, same as anyone!' Anyone but you, Lucy? 'I can as well. I don't have to be this! Lucy Jinx! Lucy Jinx! How many times was I not this, before coming here? How many Heres have I been that aren't There - how many Heres have I left that become There? I'm just the same.' What did she say? Reading to you from a poem she thought was about her that wasn't about her, really, but that you let her keep thinking was - what did she say? 'She thinks all my poems are about her!' Because you told her that. 'I never told her that - it's never what I meant.' Or are all your poems about her? 'I have been many things instead of Lucy Jinx!' Have you? 'Now a cloud, now a claw, now a rap-sheet, and now an iron-peg-in-a-wall, reasonless.' Is that for her? 'She said *I'm leaving Leopold*! And she looked at me!! And she just looked! And I didn't make a sound. Like a kid who has wet the bed and thinks she needs to fall asleep to hide from it.'

That was a good line. Lucy does her bad habit of neglecting to check the mirror, turning her head to look backward as she already begins maneuvering the car. Once again, good fortune finds the road nearly deserted. But one day that'll be it for you, girl. One day, you'll become infamous in the memories of the family of some number-was-up motorist. 'Well, I'm just a part of Fate' Lucy says, too-fasting the curve and the speed-hump of the entryway to this shopping plaza. Commerce, stately and new - or at least newish - three full stories tall! A boat in dry-dock, this place! Restaurants and a carousel and a band-shell with some amateur group of middle-aged dads covering classic tunes most of the shoppers only know from being used in new advertisement - a *Burlington Coat Factory* and a store that sells top-shelf wine next to a clothing store that sells only things black or else white and a statuesque patchwork store that is part-grocery-part-electronics-part-toy-store-part-clothier. Lucy finds a place on the middle level of the garage to tuck her car in and sits. Wishes for something to write with, but settles for the recorder. Too much on this tape. She's speaking into an already discarded document. If she ever even does play this back it will be so far removed from the import of these lines she won't note them. 'Anyway' she says, hitting Record. 'Anyway. Something like: *sometimes you're a cloud, sometimes you're a claw*. Something else. I think I said' - but she trails off, just gazes at that car - that one, parking there - and at that one, which it seems the exiting driver of only now realized had bikes in the rack atop, is laughing to his also-getting-out companion how goddamn lucky they were that the things weren't scraped off by the low ceilings of the structure. Stop. Tosses the recorder. It lands hard and opens up, but the cassette in no danger of falling so she pays it no mind. A soundtrack over the garage speakers mingles with the soundtrack of the street down below - speakers down there, strategic on light-posts, in the trees lining the path from the cosmetics-shop-slash-stylists to the bookstore to probably other places - and all of this under the freezing rain of shoppers' voices and shuffles and cars passing, hating each crosswalk they come to, each 'Sorry sorry' raised hand of each mommy or young couple who indulge their right to stroll at leisure and thus halt progress - to cross in front of lulling motor vehicles at a few hop-steps then a normal slow mosey. *No Smoking* placards everywhere. Taking no chances. The walls are paranoid with thinking they won't be respected. A security guard golf-carts along, four sizes too large for the vehicle, for his uniform, for his own self-esteem, no matter how many trivia games he works

754 / PABLO D'STAIR

so hard to always nearly win of a Wednesday night out at the pub with the other men who were kids with him and never left the neighborhood or came back. Stop judging people, Lucy. 'You stop judging people, Lucy.'

Stop everything. Nothing stops, but everything does. Lucy flats to the nearest wall surface - an awkward shaped curve, *Coming Soon something-or-other* says words on images she is too close to see, vinyl to the insides of the eat-off-of-clean windows. To Lucy it stops. All stops. And she dials Mathilde, ordering her to be able to pick up the phone right away despite how the text came in forty minutes ago. 'Hello?' 'The fuck do you mean she called?' 'What?' 'I said: *the fuck do you mean she called?* The broad called?' 'Oh - yes. She did.' 'How did she call? I don't even understand.' A pause, then Mathilde goes 'Oh fuck - wait, did I say *call*? Sorry.' Is Mathilde playing Lucy for a tune, here? 'Mathilde' Lucy rattle-snakes. But Mathilde is explaining how 'I didn't mean *call*. She *wrote* - she *e-mailed*. Did I really say *call* - hold on, I don't think I did.' And Lucy says something, but obviously Mathilde has moved her phone from her ear to check and a moment later is back on with 'I said *wrote*! I said *wrote*!' 'But this is the broad who you mean by that - The Broad like I mean when I say *the broad* - not some mix up?' Mathilde is now - Lucy can see it all like a run-of-the-mill-bit-of-thriller-cinema - leaning to squint at some words on the computer - in the film she would be eating Chinese take-away or gingerly painting her toenails for nuance to the supporting role she would be, sense of textured reality - and question marks 'Leanne F. Fenkke?' If Mathilde is exacting some sort of revenge by lying about this Lucy will have Mathilde know that while Lucy may go to prison for the crime of incinerating her, she will still be incinerated and have to go through the ordeal of that and then be dead - so should keep that in mind! 'Do you want me to print the letter?' '*Letter!?*' 'Well' Mathilde says '*Letter* is overstating it, but it is a substantive piece of correspondence.' 'The gist, you heartless number-bot! The gist!' Mathilde clears her throat and just says 'She'd love you to give her a call.' Recites a number which Lucy - and Mathilde must know this! - could not possibly have been able to just jot down, ready-set-go. 'Why call her?' 'To discuss the possibility of putting out your collection.' 'Is that what the letter says?' 'Well, *Letter* is overstating it' - yeah yeah, Lucy doesn't care - 'but that language is used.' 'In conjunction with *would love it if you would call?*' '*Please call when you can, I would love to talk about putting your collection out there.*' 'Out? Or *out there?*' '*Out there*' Mathilde sighingly verifies. 'She would *love to talk about it?* Or she would *love to do it?*' 'To do what?' 'Put the collection out!' Mathilde re-reads the verbatim and Lucy does care but doesn't but does. 'What's the number? Nevermind! Hey - can you print it?' It's already printed and Lucy can come over, anytime. 'I will just have to do that, soon - can you leave your door unlocked?' Mathilde tells Lucy to take a walk with that, reminding her, though, that the spare will be where the spare always is. 'You're welcome' Mathilde says. 'Yep - yes, you're welcome' Lucy says back and has hung up and her heart feels like an arm that can't find the right way through the sleeve.

There is a long stretch of bike-path - Lucy probably shouldn't be smoking, but is - Lucy decides to walk along - she does her best to bow and slip her smoke behind her back if young children toddle or training-wheel by - that rounds a lake before a large building off a ways from the shop area but still to do with it. A Sporting Complex, Lucy sees, smoking and strolling and kicking at cold mulch, wondering why so many geese are still in the water which is partially ice, just there at the edges. Ugly, the look of the water. Up against the mulch, frozen and foot-stepped and chipped at by do-nothings' boot-heels - it looks curdled, off-milk with something like coffee or dark grape soda poured in. What are the geese thinking? But Lucy stops pondering. That complex. Where is it ringing a bell from? She continues along the path and lies about her current cigarette being her last to some young guy who asks for one off her then regrets it when she sees he was with a cute girl with whom the plan was likely to share the smoke with. Well, they should grow up, Lucy decides, letting herself off the hook deftly, still glancing back, away, back, away, back at the signage for the complex. One more curve and she'll be to it. Salt of poorly-cooked seafood from the restaurant at the base of the place. The long, high wall is even-paced with movie posters, so a theatre must be in there, too. Aha! And Laser-tag, an ad done up in mock of a film about Laser-tag, the photo cheap, though, which is a shame because why not actually make it look cinematic? What'd that take - two more minutes of work? Claire. Claire! Lucy lights a smoke, restaurant patrons aheming her, she making a conscious effort to behave as though she is oblivious. Keeps moving. Claire. This is the name of the joint where Claire was pictured, volunteer coaching or whatever it was! Really? She flicks her cigarette in the direction of a goose-honk, hoping the fowl was savvy enough to nip it before it hit the water, could glissando the semi-frozen lake and blow taut-east the windsocks of passerbys' minds. Definitely. Really. This place. And just inside the door she can practically smell where the photo was taken. Though it wouldn't have been here - probably in one of the areas that payment is required to enter. Youth Soccer was it? Youth something. Youth. At an Information kiosk, she asks if there is possibly another branch of this facility - a place with the same name. 'No, no - this is us' the jolly retiree says. 'And this is where, like, soccer moms and stuff, they do their thing?' 'Oh soccer and flag-football and basketball and hockey and field hockey and tennis and racquetball' - the guy hard pronounces the $Q$, like it is three $Q$s and an $R$ or two $Q$s and a $KH$, what a terrific accent or speech impediment or what have you! 'And there's no other place called this?' 'Nope.' Did he know a woman called Claire Seville? '*Seville?*'

She is kept in suspense, the man glazing, long pause, then seeming to come out of it and opens a laminated ledger. 'What name was it? *Seville?*' 'Yeah' Lucy says, bored with this fella but indentured to this conversation. Head shake, she thanks him very much for his time.

Through a window still in the public area, Lucy watches - as best as she can make out - four different groups practicing soccer. She breaks up the groups by age, but mixing seems to go on amongst groups, as well. Who knows how this works! Grade-schoolers to high-schoolers, she guesses. So hard to tell. Tree-barked as Lucy has become - hundred-ring-trunked were she stumped and counted - distinguishing between gradations of Young People is impossible. Once, Lucy would have figured those ones there - ones she now thinks must not be yet thirteen - were grown-ups with whole scopes of vocabulary she didn't have yet - or had but did not know how to use appropriately, her early-maturity, as teachers had liked to phrase and praise it, stolen from books and film-reviews and photography magazines she would sneak glances through while her mother grocery shopped, always hoping to see nudes, even if the images were too composed or too not-meant-to-be-erotic to be erotic. Funny. Funny how now the teenagers - sixteen - and their nimbleness and seemingly defined physicality which is actually anything but still seem older than her. She could have had them at their age, lived their age again - and almost again - and be herself, now, with them as her kids only with them twice their current age! Did Claire have a kid? Wouldn't Mathilde's information have shown that? Maybe. Maybe not. How hard had Mathilde worked on this investigation? Perhaps one of the kids in that one photo was Claire's, different surname due to a split with the progenitor! 'Lucy?' Come on! Lucy - how old are you? Okay - you have committed yourself to you are Lucy and whoever said the name was right to think that's you. Who is this kid now, though? And why is he saying your name? Claire's? Don't be a simpleton. 'Lucy?' That incredulous, semi-insulted, don't-know-if-I-should-be-excited-or-am-even-allowed-to-talk-to-you face only a - what is he, something-teen? - teenager can slapdash up. 'Is that you? What are you doing here? Lucy' - the kid pauses - 'Jinx?' Flynn. Flynn! 'Flynn' she says, third-times-the-charm, played off the abortive first tries as a wrong swallow and now coughs tentatively to justify that move. 'Hey' he says, now nodding. 'You got a kid in here?' Flynn didn't cock his head toward the soccer area, just kind of lifted his chin generally, so Lucy turns and glances around, all air shirking to the length from her shoulder to her shoulder, going from colorless to a kind of auburn-blotched-with-green like a lightbulb burnt out in a room left pitch black. 'No, no' she is saying. 'I had a friend who mentioned this place, I just happened to be' - she points, disoriented out of knowing is it in the correct direction - 'over at the bookstore and so thought I'd stroll by.' Flynn catches sight of someone to that side - Lucy doesn't look - and then just sniffs, touches his nose 'Cool' and gives a wave like he was asking for a high-five then just as quickly changed his mind. And trot he goes, canter canter, to that girl who is trying to reach around the book-bag she is wearing to get something out of it, something she - now both their backs to Lucy - brandishes like a surprise - or the revelation of an explosive it's too late to undetonate - to Flynn.

What Lucy is thinking is the same old fatalism - causality tick and because-of-tick tock - that she always thinks of. Exhibit *A*: well, that stretches far back, but to just put it in a throwing-up-one's-hands place let's call it *Ariel*. Exhibit *A*, detailed: Lucy the runaway, halted in the supposedly temporary place of this dithering burg, needs something to eat and while eating sees the ad placed for *Hernando's Highlights* - Lucy looks into the job - bang! Ariel! Lucy-needs-a-place-to-stay is Exhibit *B*. Exhibit *B*, detailed: all of that stuff - the mother, Natalie, the child, Flynn. Exhibit *B*, detailed, more: oh God, all of that stuff. Exhibit *A* leads to Exhibit *B* and is within it, all at once. Is it. Exhibit *B* is Exhibit *A*. And *C*? And *D*? *E F G*? Well, Lucy's mind does the quick run-through - all of that stuff - and then fleeing and then away and then Elliott - and then Ariel. And all the other stuff. Trying with Elliott - 'You should publish! You should try, Lucy! Oh oh' Elliott had said - and so, Lucy, you did. And then puff-of-smoke went Elliott. And then you had to come back, eh Lucy? Because: Ariel. So here you are: back. And: Ariel. And then this woman - That Woman, Claire. And the man at your door. And murder most foul, as with the best it is! And why had that broad needed to get back to you? Today!? While you were in a fit of thought about That Woman - Claire - and Layla - come on, what two things could have less to do, one with the other!? And then a headful of Ariel, brood-bellied - and that thing she said to you and that you just couldn't cut out! But that broad called. Because Elliott said 'Try to publish' and you did try and didn't stop - because fuck Elliot, as gone as she is! And so here you are: you stop in this shopping-center and wander a daydream. And where do you end up? The soccer joint from the photo of a dead woman: Claire. Because of course it is here, where you stop, because of that broad and Elliott, because of Ariel, and because of running away because of the mother because of Ariel! Because you ran and then there was Ariel while you were running and where you ran and where you ran to and where you run around. Claire, the dead woman - and you turn around and Flynn! And then you are going to go to see Ariel, tonight. All in a lump! All in a goiter that has grown goiters its own in the shapes of the fingers of a new hand! 'Well' Lucy thinks 'life doesn't work that way!' Except it obviously does! How can so many things be so much at-once while being so untouching while being so far removed and ages between? That's how it went, though. Not just one thing. Not even just two. And piles more if she goes looking. The world roaring in its sleep and bad-dreaming Lucy around. No one to shake it awake - she's dreamnt and associated and things that have nothing to do with each other become each other's exact context. This just isn't how the world works, Lucy, it's all just a funny coincidence! The harder you look, the harder everything always is. This is just the only thing you ever insist on seeing.

When did Lucy light the smoke? Sometime. Those guys there appreciate it. The girl glances to the sign, the other girl whispers to that one boy. If Lucy's doing it, why can't they? Admire her and worship at her wake, kids - that's Lucy's advice! She walks the corkscrew of the lower-level of the lot to the center, feeling herself being perused like a book bought and sold just for the cover. Milling traffic, fathers and sons, lonely blokes on their days-off from shit-jobs they blame on who they helped get elected or didn't stop the election of or something - to them, Lucy is a comment to make, a sniff to sniffle, a sprinkle not good enough to eat like the others because it fell on the table so noses must be turned up, lips smacked on the residue of previously slurped sugar. She rounds the row where her car is and here has to stop. As would anyone. Why? Look!! That's a goose inside of a car! A goose. A car. The first question, obviously, is 'How could this have happened?' As in to say: Could this goose be in this car somehow accidentally? Well? Lucy is stumped. She even works up the nerve to try the doors, but they are locked fast. Might be a good thing, Lucy. Why? Because why did you assume this goose was trapped? The goose isn't even looking at Lucy while she cups hands to glance through glass, watches it. The goose, on a longshot, could belong to someone - but who travels with a loose goose in their car!? She cannot help but chuckle, tugging one of the door handles a bit harder. Evidence of a towel, a box, a resting spot of some kind? Negative. Goose-toys or goose-food? No. Does it look hurt? Even if so, who leaves an injured goose around while they go shopping? Another possibility is that whoever owns this car is some dunderhead who has stolen this goose. Big frat-boy laughs all around - tricked the fowl from the lake or some other place. And then just leaves it in the car? A wild, pilfered goose? Trusting it not to shit up a riot, molt, piss, and ravage the vehicle's interior with beak stabs or whatever? It's a nice car, this car! And Lucy stops herself from walking away before she really even starts. She is incapable - evidenced by she isn't - of walking away from a goose in a car without some sense of understanding its context. It's freezing cold. Isn't she within her rights to smash this car window, same as if that goose were a newborn or an invalid? Are you honestly going to do that, Lucy? Never before in your life have you broken a window, yet now you will to get a goose out of a car? And then what? Shoo it away? Call the authorities? From where she is to her car, the goose-car is in eyeshot, so she hups it over, sits inside, gets her heater cooking. The goose hadn't honked once, had it? No. Had its beak been tied? Lucy doesn't think so. She thinks she saw it open its mouth a few times, nibble at its side feathers. Why didn't it honk? Or struggle? Why is that goose okay with being there in that car?

The radio talks about a crisis of ground soil. The way this crisis intersects with the woebegone denizens of some flood-pelted town. Lucy smokes slowly, trying to be a conservationist so she doesn't run out of cigs before her vigil ends. And the radio talks about bottled water technically being worth more than new cars in the town, but nobody is selling it. And others are boiling pots of the stuff that has risen to drown them, the commentator pointing out they are foolish because doing so will not make the water any less poisoned than it is. Those people don't even know about the soil issue - the soil now within the water - they only know about the flood and the loss of emergency services, let alone trips to the store. Here's the tickle, though: something in this 'interesting situation' - Lucy names it, such - that's going on elsewhere while she's here, watching a car for the owners to return - this interesting situation being described over the airwaves relaxes old Lucy Jinx down. It's a list of choices. That's all. Not a painted-in corner. All of the occasions which have coalesced here today? For Lucy, they amount to a fair-copied list of what Lucy has to choose from - all in her mind, all at once, to be seen in relief and contrast and in couples and in singles and in links-to-each-other. It's just a rendering of all of the choices she can still make on a day she needs to make one. All of the paths she can choose to walk. In fact, she admits, it's like an act of Grace, this trolly-crash day - because now that she has the exact trails to focus on she knows she won't just blind off into the brush. Before this, she would have thought running was an option - to another Unknown, another Start Again, Same Start, New Start, doesn't matter if it's Again. Just choose, Lucy girl! Just pick! Ariel? Alone writing? Elliot - or a substitute of that, whoever, Samantha - fought to gain back? The mother, Natalie, who must be around? Interesting, eh? Other things, too - but why not just pick one of the main roads? This is the snaked fork of your last turning, Lucy, all your energy left is enough to coast you kindly down one of these avenues to its natural terminus, but only if it's only one. Lucy is grinning and watching the car, her thoughts gas-swelling with indifference and ready to leave. 'You're a representative-goose-in-a-car' Lucy says with a clap and a courteous doff of her forehead down. 'If I stay here' she continues 'it means that figuring-out-gooses-in-cars - pondering whatever crumb I find in the sheets - is my lot. My life will be no better than yours, goose-in-a-car. I'll be but a thing that stabs my head into earth of any temperature or variety, automatic, hoping to find a mouthful of worm to get me to the next field I stab until feted, except displaced to a car in a parking garage!' She puts her car in reverse. Promises to write the goose a verse - or immortalize it in some fashion, at least. 'My aim is away from you, goose - the breach the breach, from whence I came to whence I return, the definition no different now than was then!'

Even if she - that *She* being *the mother*, in this case - were to look for Lucy, Lucy doesn't have a way to be found. Twisting, how that isn't comforting. It means Lucy's done good - computerless and a telephone no one except her choice few know the contact of, even her lease is under someone else's name. Lucy's job wouldn't have her listed on any website. Oh. Wait. Pea-brained, she changes lanes to the slower traffic but wishes she hadn't but stays. Wait. There's the books! The signings! Those are a trail. But honestly, if Lucy doesn't do any more of those she could not be found that way. That's not a way to find Lucy Jinx. It isn't as though in all this time she's been back - back - the mother has come across her. Accidentally - sure - Lucy could be stumbled-upon - that is not the same as Found. And keep it in mind: the mother is not looking for you, Lucy. True. Yet this truth doesn't keep Lucy from being hyperaware of every car - isn't that what the mother had driven, only newer, maybe a newer model of the same? isn't that the mother's hair from behind, what her profile would look like now? - and every driver. Is sighting Lucy something Flynn would bring up to his mom? He had hardly made a shebang out of seeing her. How mild a memory Lucy must be by now to the child. To the mother? Even if Flynn told, it isn't for certain the mother'd go looking. Maybe she'd look to know which side of the street was the opposite and so therefore the one to walk down! Maybe she's back with the father or the father has the kid, all alone. Lucy says that aloud, because it needs to be someplace-elsed. That will be the case, going by the indications. If Lucy decides to 'Pick the mother' it'll turn out the mother is back with the father and Flynn - simply because, at this exact time, Ariel is deciding to not be with Leopold. And because that is obvious, it becomes the thinner-air-to-breathe sign that the mother would not want to find Lucy. But, sake of argument: what if the mother looked and found you, Lucy? That's the bother. It's not what the mother does, it's what Lucy chooses. And Lucy has a feeling everything is waiting for her choice to be named before starting the next player-piano jingle. In goes Lucy's coin and out of the juke blares the tune. The songs are all pre-recorded. Choice does not rule out Predestiny! You just choose your Predestiny! Maybe a few times, like now, you get to choose a change of performer, style, instrument - but once it is going the song goes till it's done. You never pick the last go 'round - the last go 'round is determined wholly by how many coins you had at the start. You get to exist longer than the music plays, remember each song - the order is irrelevant. Rearrange thoughts of First and Last and Second and Seventh enough times and everything has been everything and soon you don't know if you only picked what you picked first because you hadn't seen what you picked second before it or if you'd picked what you'd picked third because you'd seen it first and recalled it only after choosing the second.

Into her recorder, Lucy makes this speech: 'Well, you've lived yourself up into a box, Jinx. A new womb, maybe as loud as the old. Who says you, unbirthed, didn't have to go through as many hem-haws and permutations, then after some fundamental shift, no longer breathing through someone else's lungs and so no time to remember the struggles that came with, were birthed. No - don't get me wrong, Posterity don't mishear me! - I, Lucy Jinx, do not believe I was alive before I was born. When I was a cluster of microscopic stuff and even when I started smoothing to shape - it wasn't until birth that I was. Don't let's wring hands over when is the exact moment. Listen to me: there was a time Before and there was The Time and there is the time that came After. I've already talked about this at the other end - Death, I am referring to, for those in the far seats who might not have heard over the ocean of other Lucy-goers crinkling their candy-wrappers, squeaking their straws through the lid-holes of their soft-drinks - and it's the same at the first end. Birth. The moment just before being a person, alive - before being Lucy or whoever - can be divided forever and then, quicker than it takes to even divide it longhand once, it is passed. But there was a moment, whenever, before me and so there was a moment just before before me - on and on, down to the tiniest imaginable sliver of duration. I happen to think it happened somewhere in the birth canal, my becoming - likely after my eyes were out in the hospital air - but that's just me, just my personal slant. And I was birthed! Then I lived! And I've lived myself into a box. Are you listening? The more you pay attention, the less choices you have! Wandering in a desert make sense because there is only one thing to do! Same as being chained in a tall tower or lost on a dingy no one much feels like rescuing you from. Too busy mourning the loss of the ship to much think of survivors. Come on! The boat goes down, all hands dead, then we find five that aren't - that's gonna change how we feel inside? If anything - we're human - it'll bug us, show us the universe cares not for absolutes or symmetries while meantime all of the people we praise-to-Heaven say it must deal only in those things! *There's spirals everywhere* that man said? We call him brilliant! Look at this painting, this sea-shell - everywhere, the spirals in a ratio like this! Me? Fuck, fellas - I got the goods. You're the one drawing the spirals and it ain't hard to make 'em fit if that's all you want 'em to do! I've scribbled in library books with crayons, myself, and I can easily scribble on the world just the same! That's nature! We picked what we admire then tell enough people and they think there was no first person that just made it up and we've all slipped lock-step, since. If some Ruler somewhere hated Symmetry and had had enough slaves and a large enough army - well! - to this day we'd abhor it, some artist pointing to spirals every-which-where or no! You know what is in more places than Symmetry? Lack of it! Examples of that everywhere! Way more instances than of perfection. Nobody makes a big deal of it, though. See that there? Formless, ugly. And that too and that too! Amazing how nature does that, eh! Amazing how there's infinite examples in every aspect of existence of things that seem ill fitting and to go with nothing. Sometimes a cloud, sometimes a claw! An abyss is only something if you pay it mind, man.'

LUCY JINX COULD STEAL MATHILDE'S mail. Any time. But she doesn't. This is a point of pride and maturity for Lucy. Has she stolen mail? Yes. She did it all the time when she was a young woman working in a hotel. Who could resist - especially if it was handwritten correspondence, personal? But had Lucy ever stolen the mail of someone she knew personally, considered a friend? 'Well yes, of course' thinks Lucy. And has the defense that she assumes and respects how people must have done the same to her. Friends. What is a friend if not someone who has read some of your personal correspondence that you haven't? The point of being a friend is to transgress in just such a fashion then keep mum about it. Oh so much the better friend if you know something important your friend does not know but longs to, if you contain a secret that would be altering to them and keep it well buried. Lucy has this in mind while she uses Mathilde's mail key to retrieve Mathilde's apartment key. The apartment key is in a small envelope at the back of the mailbox, behind a sheet of crumpled paper. 'Defenses, defenses' Lucy mumbles and cannot help but love Mathilde a little! This ruse - and for whom? For someone who happens to break into the mailbox? Who would be breaking in to commit theft but who would not bother to see - if the rest of the box was empty, especially - what's on that crumpled sheet of paper and - Hello! - find a key? This is a very specific person to defend against and simultaneously a person who needs absolutely not be defended against. And the key to the door, Lucy re-questions: Why not just under-the-mat it? She speaks to the empty apartment as though to Mathilde: 'Dig it, man - you get a piece of paper, tape it over the key to the mat bottom. No way it can accidentally be found! Make the sheet of paper look like a label or something - it's just as fancy as the mailbox ruse. Who goes looking under random mats, anyhow?' Well though, Lucy - think about that question. 'Yes, yes, yeah yeah' she sighs. That man at her door. Maybe Claire hid a spare key, is that it? It or not, what's notable is that you are thinking this, here, now, Lucy. 'More so than were I to think it somewhere else, sometime else?' Yes. Lucy has walked to the computer, expecting the print-out to be waiting there. She stands looking at the powered-off machine a full minute before registering 'It's not there, though' blinking, looking around as though this were Mars and the fact it looks like Earth makes matters haltingly befuddling. Not on the kitchen counter, either. Nor tacked to the fridge. A right menace, this! Hadn't Mathilde even said it was already printed? Blank-spot where that memory might be. Had Mathilde forgotten? Or printed it but left with it, too? You don't think it was that crumpled up sheet in the mailbox, do you? 'No' Lucy says, taking a bite out of one of the cookies she finds on a plate on the television table. 'If so, what was the point of leaving the key, as well?'

Where did it turn out to be? On the bed! What kind of thinking is this? Lucy nearly called Mathilde just to be antagonistic, but then decided to lay down and read the thing over and over, over and over, over and over and over and over instead. Why had the broad written now, after all this time? When had Lucy met her? Half-a-year-ago? Not so much. Four months say - so even still! How many times had Lucy upped herself, downed, revved herself, rattled? Countless. Countless. Why is Lucy questioning it? Why doing everything to rob this correspondence of potency? Because: Lucy Jinx. But even so, she cannot help feeling warmth course her and each word enters her eye with the force of a balloon pop. The letter isn't an offer, no, but even in Lucy's disdainful instant self-abnegation she cannot make this sound less than promising. Nothing in this correspondence is kiss-off or indication she should vamoose from herself her dream. But: why now? Lucy conjures an image of the broad: at that joint-reading, Lucy had somehow gotten roped in to buying her a drink and chatting casual before she even announced who she was - Lucy shifting from certain she was being picked-up on to certain she wasn't to uncertain if she could believe her luck or let herself think something of the card being handed her, of the copy of her book she was penning her contact information on to the title page of. The next week a giddy blur of she'd won, she'd won! All of it paid off and on her own terms and the victory of Adam and all!! The second week thinking 'Of course it wouldn't be the first week you'd hear back, the first week doesn't count - this second week is the first week, for all practical purposes.' The third week the first twang of 'If not by now, why ever?' Yet not until the month mark - not even four weeks, she'd held out thirty-one whole days, yes she had! - did the ache of it-all-dying start. How had she convinced herself she'd cursed it, exactly? Because: she hadn't written to Layla to braggadocio herself in a grandiose spew of I've-done-it-I've-done-it! - that indicated she must have known to be cautious. And the only reason to be cautious was because she'd known it was too good to be true. Yet if she had just run with it, stunk the wide world with her farts, the momentum would have gone pandemic and a response would have come. *I love it* the broad would have written. *Yes, publishing in May - this doesn't need a revision, not a touch*! Chewing the circle of wrinkles of bent knuckle, Lucy reads this e-mail again and now cannot even make it sound bad if she thinks the words in a tone suggesting disingenuousness. Don't let yourself get excited yet, Lucy. Not again. Answer your question. Say this was a go-ahead letter - *We want it. We want you* - why now? Why would it be now? She winces - pulls hand from her mouth. 'You bit me!' she says, looking at the freckle of skin dented deep enough to draw blood, wound in the shape of a tooth texture. 'I bit me' she gums, wound-in-mouth, picturing the skin around the puncture going white to her lips' taut suckle.

Had Lucy drifted off? Her eyes feel like they haven't closed, but here she is opening them. Mathilde's bed. Curled to her side, but non-committal. She feels groggy in that way of having started a fantasy but fallen asleep unmasturbated. The letter is set on the opposite side of the bed, folded in half now, which she does not recall doing to it. Shoulder and neck share the same soreness, a muscle pulled spanning them, her massaging doing nothing to help. It feels like the curve of a plastic coat hanger is lodged up her, just next to where the spine meets the base of her skull-bulb. Yawns like a fallen tree, one that is longer on the ground than one had reckoned it would be. The kitchen clock, if it is to be trusted, assures her 'You were only asleep - if at all - for less than fifteen minutes.' And she stuffs letter in coat pocket, remembers to leave the key on the counter and to lock the front door from inside - tests it four times to be sure - then, yawning the fifth in a seemingly-never-to-end string of the things, she scratches her ear all the way out of the lobby, into the cold. What pests, these little naps. The sunlight now seems off and her mind is convinced it is a weekend. Why does a smidgen of sleep have such repercussions!? These sensations are hard to rid herself of, condition how she will spend the next bit of time. For example? For example: she knows she is off to see Ariel, but kind of wants to go home - a feeling of 'Every place is going to be crowed, just wait until a weekday.' Madness. Lunatic. Harmless? You say *harmless*, Lucy? Then explain why you are even walking in this direction when you are certainly parked over there! Lucy tugs at her ear some more, fingernails pinching, kneading, pinching harder, pulling the pinch down. Fact: Lucy had slept plenty. Fact: there is nothing illicit in her system. But there has been a lot of shifting about. Earlier. Then a bit later. 'And now Now' she says. How many minds can one be in the span of four hours? Should she be pacing her pulse? Should she be finding a drugstore to get her blood-pressure taken for free? No fever - or so she thinks. Hand to forehead, hand feels warm - not hot, just warm - which someone when she was young told her meant she was feverless. 'If you touch your own head and feel cold, that's a problem' this person had said. 'Or if you touch it and feel heat, almost-cool-over-burner heat - that means a fever, too. But your hand feeling neither hot nor cold and you're fine.' So trusting Lucy once was, she obviously took this to heart and now finds it one of those automatic programs within her. Another thing you believe, Lucy. Another mark of lackadaisical concentration winding up with a thought that is not yours and which you don't know how to shake. Who had said it? Where had this idea that's not her own got its heels in, stationed where she has no choice to believe it even while she doubts she does?

*Please bring junk food. No. Never mind the Please. The junk food is compulsory.* Yes, a whammy has been put on Lucy's shoulder, she massages and massages while the car idles, unable to stop, awkward text with one hand back *Whch mnnr of juk ood?* She doesn't even want to know how many misspelling she's atrocioused into those five words. Reply almost instantaneous - this message could have been sent, standalone, though it does fit as a response. *What I'm saying is: burger or chicken sandwiches and curly-fries and that kind of thing.* Phones buzzes. New message. *I just told you!* And preadolescent wit, Lucy texts back *You already told me what? What do you want? Sweet? Salty?* And Jesus, is this shoulder thing going to become a matter for her primary care physician to look in to? The pain is now spreading inside the shape of her bra straps, the skin feeling pickled or dehydrated, jerky, space ice-cream. *I'm going to overlook the fact that you're mucking me around, Jinxy - get me fast-food. If you don't, there won't be enough generations left in mankind for the curse I'll lay on your line to run out!* 'My shoulder, Ariel' Lucy says - to anyone listening, she'd sound genuine in her anger, her interrogation tone - 'don't you even care!?' She moves to get the car going, notes she will need to get gas. Which is fortuitous, as she can get some ibuprofen, some acetaminophen, as well. Grease, yellow-cheesed gas station burgers, buns either slightly stale or preposterously soft, bacon that's chewy like thin cuts of rubber doorstop. *I'm getting gas station food* Lucy writes to Ariel. Reverses the car. But waits at the turning out from the lot two minutes to give Ariel time to send some further word. *That's fine - burgers or pizza though - if you mean chips or candy, you're obviously as illiterate as I admit now I have long suspected you of being.* And to this Lucy texts *I serve at the pleasure of the president.* Tosses phone to passenger seat. Foot begins to down pedal when phone buzzes. Message: *What's up?* Foot off pedal, deep press to the bruise-green streak that at one point was her shoulder. *The fuck do you mean 'What's up?' I'm getting you your goddamn gas station pizza or whatever.* Glance to rearview shows one two three cars heading her way so she has to pull on to the road, new message coming through while she drives. And the next traffic-lights - two, three, four - turn green even as she slows approaching their red, so it isn't until five or six minutes later she can check the meanwhile-has-vibrated-again phone. Taps to bring up the latest message. *This is why I love you.* Now brings up the message from before last. *Gas station food? Who?*

*What? Lucy - who are you confusing me with now? Oh - oh God no! Shock Horror! Have you struck again?* She pulls into the gas station, here, a parking spot instead of the pump - don't forget to pump, though Lucy, you do need gas - laughing quietly as she texts Layla back *I have. And I'll kill again. Your life is now done in tones of Argento! I am an up close of an eye and a flashback of a high-heel!*

Lucy eats three doughnuts while she waits for the food to be prepared. Then - as always - her number is called and she is just allowed to take the bag without showing her receipt to prove the order is hers. Everywhere, this phenomena. Nothing troubling, just something she's noticed. She eats two more doughnuts in the car before moving it to the pumps for a fill and eats the last doughnut standing with the nozzle in the tank set to automatic, un-doughnuted hand now knuckling in oblongs at the progress of this cramp into her ribs. The rest of the drive is spent boisterously singing along to *Blue Moon* by *The Marcels*, *Come Right Back* by *The Honeycombs*, *Psychotic Reaction* by *The Count Five* and *Chicka Boom, Don't You Just Love It* by *Daddy Dewdrop* - which she hasn't heard in a decade-and-change, glorioused to her core that she still knows seventy-percent of the lyrics! The late afternoon has probably shifted to the early evening, people imperceptibly altered from thinking what they are going to do later-on to what they have to do tomorrow. Lucy in song. This happening and Lucy just singing. The car is comforter-thick with the scents of the cheap food through the brown paper bag, Lucy's mouth watering even while her stomach regrets having eaten the doughnuts. That Playdough-thick shit is forming down in her, the kind that will stay camped down there for a day-and-a-half, poking her with gas swells, reminding her of her mistake. An allergy must have developed to doughnut-bread, because this nonsense did not plague her youth, her twenties, her thirties. It's the same with how even a bite or two of a candy-bar makes her aware of her mouth, now, breath congealing and glue forming at the roof and in the spaces between lower-lip-back and front teeth. 'Just add an earache in, why don't you?' she demands of the Gods 'why not just cause numbness in my extremities or an over-awareness of my throat pulse?' The Gods aren't answering, though. Lucy can't blame them. It's probably been so long since they've been believed in that having words aimed directly at them is too delectable a thing to not ignore. And now it seems there is a party somewhere right by Ariel's house, the sides of the road lousy with cars - yep, balloons adorning the mailbox of that house - and no spot in the cul-du-sac lot, either. Here is Lucy, having to park four-minutes-walk away, her agitation making her shiver more than she needs to. Do the colors of those balloons suggest a baby-shower? A birthday-party? What event could have summoned enough strangers to clog this whole development? And are they shoved in that modest townhome, clown-caresque? Lucy hears no evidence that they are out in any yard - besides which, the weather seems to inform against that being a viability. Those clouds are a coming rain, an overnight freeze. Grass in the morning will be brittle, tense as a regretted kiss.

'Where's the kid?' Ariel cocks an eyebrow, indicates her nose down. 'Not that kid - the one that's already been actualized.' Ariel says she's all done with that one, snatches the bag from Lucy and is rummaging through it at the kitchen counter while Lucy removes her coat and drapes it over one of the dining-room chairs. 'You don't know this, being fallow, Lucy - being salted-Earth and all - but children only last between two and seven years. But I'll put up with your questions, betray though they do your lack of a nuanced understanding of femininity.' Lucy Socrateses 'So how did we get here?' Mouthful 'What's that supposed to mean?' Lucy reaches for one of the fries - one of the spring-looking curlies - but Ariel smacks her bicep so she retreats, palms up in apology. 'Get your own food!' 'This isn't my food?' Gob-smecking 'Ha!' and through not enough chews to make the swallow pleasant Ariel mocks 'Because you paid for it? Look at the world, dope - you think things belong to the people who pay for them? Welcome to the concept of Economy, baby - welcome to being the low-man, okay?' Ariel pointy-faces due to how she sucks soda through the straw so greedily, child-table manners 'Ah!' after her swallow, winded and rubbing the skin around her unborn. 'In answer to your question, Lucy, logic is enough: either you were never a child or you're still less-than-seven. That's where you came from. Refute either proposition if you want, but you'd be arguing against your own extant state. And any schoolgirl knows the oldest philosophical trick in the book is to point out *If you're arguing it must mean you exist.* People who say *Prove it* to that don't get what *Prove it* means or when to use the words defensively.' There's something in Ariel's ravenous consumption of the third burger - by the kitchen clock, not ten minutes have elapsed since the bag top was spread - and the house void of Kayliegh-noise that uneases Lucy. Has something gone down, already - Leopold ousted and he's took the kid with? Would Ariel be okay with that? 'So what are we doing, tonight?' Ariel maws, then stabs straw-back exactly in the space of pre-tight-puckered lips, its color going from white-with-blue-stripe to tartar-stain-brown-with-blue-stripe. 'I was thinking to just watch you eat. I bought you a trough, but it's still being engraved.' Ariel thinks this is a terrific gift and goes on awhile about how she gets why animals just eat grass and hay, says that if she were living in the same conditions as them those things would look delicious, too. 'It's important to think what it must be like for animals and to insist it must be awesome. Nobody like the idea of an animal having a glum time of it. Don't you agree?' Lucy says she does. Something to Ariel's mile-a-minute is just a shade left-of-normal, though. 'But really - what are we going to do?' Ariel crumples a napkin and then dabs her lips with it, palms it to make it tight and then juts it at Lucy, it hitting her nose.

They sit and play Hangman for the next hour. One word Lucy chooses is *Contradistinction*. Ariel eventually gets it, but several additional, purely vivisectionist parts of the titular stick-figure have to be added, before. One of the words Ariel chooses is *Limpid*. Lucy gets that without so much as the circle of a head being jotted. Ariel declares Lucy a Permanent Cheater because of this. Note: Lucy at no point yet has shared the news about the broad getting in touch or the possibility of her book being published, hep. Why? Well: Lucy is in a cautious frame-of-mind - half-friend, half-detective - doing her best to seem an identityless object for Ariel to play with until ready to address whatever reality there might be. Another word Lucy chose was *Ribbit,* which Ariel gets but declares 'Not a word!' with further demand that Lucy explain 'Just what she is driving at here, cheating both on the offense and on the guard?' 'If it's not a word, how come I know how to spell it?' Ariel scoffs the sound of a faucet hitting a ceramic plate. 'You know how to spell you too, Lucy - are you a word?' Another word Ariel chooses is *Dinosaurus*, which Lucy gently explains is honestly not a word, but has no retort that can stand up to scrutiny when Ariel says 'You got it right - why are you making a thing out of it, now?' Note: Lucy hasn't said a thing about her haunted day, the jimble-jamble of coincidental circumstances, her idea of being at the point of choosing her final avenue, Ariel herself being one of the possibles. Why? Well: what kind of ridiculous question is that!? Another word Lucy chooses is *Spectral*. Ariel gets this one and decides it is worth one thousand extra points, laughing at Lucy's bad luck for choosing a word like that and not being clever enough about it to keep Ariel from guessing. 'There's little chance of you winning now, Jinx - do the math and we'd have to play at least a thousand more words, which I'll straight up tell you: we ain't gonna.' 'What if I get a word worth one thousand points?' Scandalized, aghasted, Ariel horror-faces 'What word!? I already got *Spectacle* - what word are you thinking of other than that that's worth a thousand points?' 'It was *Spectral!*' 'Was it?' Lucy points to the paper as evidence. 'I figured you just couldn't spell. In that case, it's worth two thousand points! And now I suppose you think you're gonna find two other one-thousand-point-words to catch me up? Good luck, man.' Here, Ariel has to use the toilet. And opts for the one upstairs. Lucy pokes through the cabinets for something to eat, finally just taking a toaster pastry she finds in a Ziploc bag, the thing stale, tiring her jaw and somewhat unaligning it with her chewing. 'You know what I've gotten good at?' Ariel asks - rather in the tenor of a royal announcement - and seemingly assumes - correctly - Lucy knows the question is rhetorical, presses right on to saying 'Going to the bathroom. There's really more to it than people like you think - you probably, for example, still do it in the workmanlike way of the Everyman. Not me. Like I say, I've gotten plum dandy at it.'

The next thing is Lucy and Ariel laying on the floor of the living-room. Ariel plays with a nude doll - nude except for the one shoe Ariel takes off and on and on and off of it - walking it over her tummy, holding it by the hair, dangling it upside-down by the ankles. 'I find that I feel we went to school together, you know? That I've know you since girlhood. But I haven't.' Lucy has her feet up, legs bent at the knees, on the sofa, purposefully laid down on a hard rubber ball and is wriggling to work the thing into certain spots of her still tortured body - moans in pleasure awhile when a good spot beneath her shoulder blade is got to, dumb luck. 'What do you feel like we did together, in childhood?' But Ariel doesn't have a particular memory, it's just a feeling. 'You're some kind of glitch, Lucy, and always have been. You're kind of insufferable in that way. Hey - did you know I thought you were an idiot for about the first week I actually knew you?' Lucy laughs, the ball now worthlessly wound up in the small of her back, she too lazy to reach her arms, currently angel-spread, underneath to get it. 'Why the fuck did you think that?' 'You don't remember how many times you spilled your coffee?' Until this moment, no - no, not at all - but as soon as Ariel says this, sharp cinderblock corner, images and memories fungus up everywhere in Lucy's thoughts. 'I do! But wait - that happened privately! I was just at my desk, I never bothered you with it - and you never bothered to help clean it up!' But why should Ariel have done that? 'You spilled it three times, one day! I didn't even understand it! The odds of seeing someone do that in life? I can't calculate something like that! But I know it's rare. I know the fact that I saw it ruined my chances of ever winning the lottery and protected me from being killed by a Great White shark - no way someone could have two rarities of that caliber in one lifetime.' 'Glad to be of service.' 'Maybe I would have liked to have won the lottery! I'm not thanking you, man. Jesus, you're so full of yourself.' Here is Lucy pointing out that if a Great White had eaten her, though, then Ariel wouldn't be around, full stop. Ariel counters with 'But if I'd been eaten by a Great White, at least while I was I could've thought 'It was this or the Powerball' and died thinking I'd come that close to having it all!' 'Have it your way, Ariel - I'm wondering why we're even friends, at this point.' Ariel explains it's like one of those movies - she made a deal with someone to befriend the loser, the little ugly duckling with the braces and pocket-protector. 'What do you get out of it?' 'I get plenty' Ariel cryptics 'don't you worry about that. You just enjoy feeling accepted like you've always wanted - I can take of myself.'

'Will you stay here, tonight?' Lucy was lighting a cigarette, the back door opened, wrapped in a blanket, in her haste to answer breathing in wrong and coughing, unable to reply. 'If I order a pizza or something, will you?' Cough-

cough, cough-cough. Lucy gasps out, between islands of hacking 'You don't' cough cough 'have' cough cough 'to order food.' Cough. 'Then I won't - but you'll stay?' Of course Lucy will stay. And now is where she decides to just ask 'What's wrong, El? Where's the kiddo and whatshisname?' Ariel moves her fingers over her belly, pinching the fabric in little tugs, exact hand gesture of pulling petals from she-loves-me-nots and - no more joviality to her voice, sunk down the worm's gullet at the wishing-well bottom, now - fairly pleads 'Can the deal be you just stay and we, in particular, don't talk about any of that? Just tonight we don't?' Lucy finds her throat constricted and while she struggles to swallow and get voice reentered, Ariel says 'We can if you want, but I'd rather just even sit here and both shut up if you just stay around, can we?' 'Yes' Lucy gets out - fifth try of the word, nodding with the first four tries to be sure Ariel knows the answer - 'yes, of course.' 'Except: how about we do talk, because nothing is more boring than you not talking.' 'That is boring. I mean - El - it just is.' 'I know it is. Even in the space between words, it's like I have to pop trucker-pills, dig?' 'I'll try to keep talking.' Listen. Listen to that tone, now. Do you hear it? You do. And now silence lapses in and Ariel kicks at a child's sock just there on the floor, Lucy watching it lift in the air, flop down in an inverse shape from how it had been slumped before the kick. 'Hey, Ariel?' Ariel answers by sighing and looking about to cry. 'Oh stop - hey Ariel?' 'What?' 'What did the policeman say to his belly-button?' Ariel - Lucy huffing that she does so - takes a moment to try to formulate a guess, finally says 'I don't know.' 'You're under a vest.' 'He was wearing a vest?' 'Or this specific officer didn't know what he was talking about, yeah. There's a few interpretations. Hey, Ariel?' Drama-queen sigh of is-this-what-it-has-come-to then 'Yes, Lucy?' 'Why shouldn't you write with a broken pencil?' Ariel clicks her eyes up, smiles, starts to answer so Lucy blusters out 'Because it's pointless!' Ariel growling 'I was going to say that!' 'You're not supposed to say anything! Hey, Ariel!?' 'What!?' 'What word is always spelled wrong in the dictionary!!?' 'I don't know, what!!?' '*Wrong*!!!! Hey, Ariel!!!!?' 'What!!!!?' 'What's the difference between Ignorance and Apathy!!!!!!?' 'No idea, what!!!!!?' 'I don't know and I don't care!!!!!! Hey, Ariel!!!!!!!?' 'What, Lucy!!!!!!!?' And on and on that goes. It becomes a coughing fit. It becomes a laughing fit. It becomes a coughing fit again and they start shoving each other then punching each other's arms when their voices can get no louder. Both are panting. Back on the floor is Lucy, a shapeless pile on the sofa is Ariel. Five minutes and they remain breathless. Ten. Lucy sniffling and running her handback over her nose again and again and again and again.

'I don't think the heater is on' Lucy whispers, still on the floor, the random Made-for-TV movie that Ariel put on winding into its last act. Ariel whispers

'Is that why I'm cold?' 'I think so.' Lucy is sitting on the floor, back propped to sofa face, Ariel now laid out in full. 'I bet you fifty dollars that the husband isn't actually the killer' Ariel propositions, flicking Lucy's ear, but not enough it stings - Lucy pretending it does, though, to stave off being flicked harder, then getting flicked harder, anyway. And after Fuck-is-it-with-youing, Lucy says she doesn't have fifty dollars. 'But you might, one day. This will be like a Fairy Tale wager, you follow?' 'Okay' Lucy says, but addendums that Ariel has to say who she thinks is behind it all. 'The brother.' 'And why - you have to say why?' Ariel flicks Lucy again, twice in-a-row, then is about to again, but Lucy grabs her wrist and Indian-burns it viciously. Shrieking, Ariel explains in no uncertain terms how out-of-line that was of Lucy, Lucy trying to get at the wrist again for another go. 'I'll kick you out!' 'If you try, I'll leave.' Ariel droops, moves as though to say something, slacks arms, sits back down and mumbles 'Okay, nevermind' resignedly, wrist extended, bracing herself. Lucy Indian-burns her wrist again, even harder, Ariel then cradling the thing as though it was a long-lost sister reunited just in time for a death bed vigil. 'I don't even remember what we were betting on anymore, so bets off.' 'Oh you bet the husband isn't behind it all - stop being such a wussy.' '*Wussy* isn't even a word, so it's not something I can be.' 'It's a word.' 'You're a word.' Lucy says 'Pretend I have a microphone and an amplifier and I am sighing into the microphone with my lips right against it and the amplifier is up too loud - that's how I feel like sighing in response to your retort, there.' 'So why don't you then?' 'Imagine it, again - because I want to do it, again, to that.' Silence. And who was behind it all? The therapist! What is the meaning of that? They hadn't seen enough of the movie to understand this at all, so it seems brilliant. 'Most things, though' Lucy sages 'seem more brilliant if you take away the context.' 'But this seems really brilliant' Ariel snaps her fingers at the screen, the therapist brandishing a gun, holding it to the woman's head and backing out of the room with her while the husband makes dimwitted You'll-never-get-away-with-thises, the wife apologizing and calling herself a fool. 'She kind of is a fool, though.' Ariel and Lucy don't see why the husband's bothering. 'It's the perfect excuse - the goddamned therapist killed her or kidnapped her or whatever! He's free and clear!' And in the film is the sound of a car pulling away down a gravel drive, the husband wheeling around from where he was told to stay put to bug-eye out the window, slamming the glass and calling out 'Janet! Janet! Janet!' Then a commercial for feminine-itch cream. Ariel says 'That's fucking gross, man.' Lucy says 'They shouldn't put cute girls in a commercial like that.' 'Hmm' Ariel says. 'You don't agree?' And groggy-drenched, Ariel half-voices 'I wasn't watching, just listening - the picture in my head of the bitch was ghastly.'

**********

LUCY'S SLEEP IS EASY, THE way salt's taste just stays on the lips. Her waking every five minutes with a head feeling asleep for hours is easy, as well, like those same lips split and unhealing. Lucy, except for in-the-exact-moment - a moment which only is as long as it is and then obliterated, a true, segmented off, non-overlapping piece of life - is not aware that she is waking so much. By morning, no no, she won't have this idea that she'd slept fitfully. To the contrary. The memories of subterranean slumber, of warmth the weight of being tied in a sack, will be the thing. Not that she will sleep the entire night. Because Ariel is not. Up three times inside two hours - Lucy not aware it's three times or two hours, but stirring each time and sleep-voiced croaking 'Hey, you good?' or 'Everything okay?' or 'Need something?' - Ariel apologizes to Lucy and touches her shoulder or hip through the blanket and tells her 'I didn't mean to wake you, I'll be right back.' Lucy - she thinks to stay awake - is under the impression she listens to Ariel turning up the bathroom fan, clicking the door shut, clicking the door locked - but Lucy is not aware of these things. Not at all. It goes from 'You good?' to 'Sorry, be right back' to Lucy suddenly finding her eyes opening, syrupy flutter, the etched form of Ariel arced to allow Lucy to curl back around. Skin blurring to skin. Heft of breathing and humid of bodies under the sheets curled and twined as though extra limbs or other hair for fingers to tangle in, strands to tickle at nose, cause still-asleep touches to faces or hard-in sniffs, snorts. Here and there Lucy wonders, when waking, if she hears something in the house - and there is a tremor over how this sleeping arrangement had not been discussed and 'What would it seem like if Leopold came in to find it, if Kayleigh needed to climb into bed with mom?' Lucy, she was not told 'Leopold will not be home.' Lucy, she was not told 'This is okay, get into bed with me.' Ariel's undressing had been sluggish and moaned over, especially getting off her socks - which she ten minutes later wanted back on, Lucy helping her in to them - and Lucy had removed her own pants, then her shirt, her under-things, mild conversation accompanying, and had slipped to the bed when, already drifting, Ariel had palmed the mattress beside her pat pat, turned to offer her still-nude back. Sometimes, Lucy's arm is asleep, pinned under some aspect of Ariel. Sometimes, Lucy's arm is asleep, draped and reaching around Ariel's belly. Sometimes, Lucy shifts to be more on her back, just shoulder and arm-side and poke of hip-tip tracing the body beside her. And sometimes, she has arm laced under Ariel's and hand near Ariel's neck, rested over the plush steam-heat of cleavage and collar-bone skin. Lucy and Ariel sleep like this, three-bodied. Lucy and Ariel wake like this, three-bodied. Then drift, then wake, drift, wake, a kind of ebbtide of two or three hours.

'I'll make you the fucking sandwich - God, you're dumb' Lucy grumble-grins, sitting up, keeping Ariel from going, holding Ariel's wrist tight until Ariel relents into 'Fine, but hurry up.' 'Are there special instructions?' 'Just make me a sandwich, Lucy - don't be a headache. I'll start to think I made a mistake about you all along.' 'Meat? Peanut-butter? Lettuce? How should I know what you want on a sandwich!?' Ariel, Lucy thinks, might not even eat - look how she is already, sheetless, turning back more on her side and incoherently jibing Lucy for offering if Lucy had no intention of doing it. Well: so here is Lucy, up from the bed. Ariel klaxons a snore. Does Lucy get dressed? She should, it seems. Then she can slip out or whatever upon returning. Or - hey, look - Ariel has a robe right there in that pile by the desk chair. How does it go? Lucy inking through the dark, down the stairs with hand-to-the-wall and hip-to-railing, eyes burning with not-ready-to-be-opening and the still bottled fizz of a headache. And how will it be if Leopold comes in? Or if he has already and is downstairs on the sofa or sitting at the dining table? How will it be if Kayleigh has been home and hears what she thinks might be mommy and blinks into the now dimly lit kitchen to find a nude Lucy, laying thin-sliced ham onto slices of somewhat toasted generic bread? What does this house feel like? Lucy feels familiar. She cuts some rectangles from a block of Colby-Jack, then cuts these strips in to small cubes, sprinkles them over the meat, lays another slice of ham on top and microwaves the lot for fifteen seconds, surprised at the sound of sizzle when she removes the plate. Now she wants a sandwich, herself! And note: Lucy has never made this exact sandwich, before. This concoction occurred to her out of pressure, out of knowing the food was not for her, the need to not show up with working-stiff *PB* and *J*. Lucy wants to seem intricate, even in making a sandwich Ariel will eat and not recall having eaten - maybe, foggy, will, weeks later, the sensation of a dream, look at her bed and think 'Did I eat there, one night? When?' Lucy finds potato-chips, too, and garnishes the plate - lamenting she had not thought to put some of these in to the sandwich - grabs a bottled water - already open, side-lain, lowest shelf in the fridge - and returns up the stairs. Ariel is sitting up, lamp on, puffy-eyeing a book. 'What are you doing?' 'Waiting for you.' 'I thought you were sleeping.' Ariel shrugs while making gimmie-gimmie motions, already asking 'Why did you only make one?' while taking her first bite. 'Is it good?' Lucy asks, two minutes later, Ariel crunching chips with the penultimate sandwich bite. 'Dunno, probably' Ariel answers, swallowing with a painful squish sound, forcing an unchewed amount of the meat, cheese, bread, chips down her with a long draw of water.

The headache-tablets Lucy finds in the bathroom cabinet are the same brand and shape she normally takes, but tinted a different, milder color. These: a pink-near-to-tan. Her usual: a red-near-to-brown. And on these tablets, the name of the medicine printed on the coating is underlined. She doesn't think that's how it is on the pills she has at home. While she urinates, she massages her stiff neck and opens her jaw in awkward faces, hoping enough of this will get it to stop clicking. Meh - her breath is such a street urchin - Ariel is the pregnant one, but Lucy feels she has a child growing in her mouth for the stink. Mouthwash. Mouthwash. She'll use some before getting back into bed. Ariel, whose breath does not stink. Ariel, who the whole house is scented of, no way to distinguish her different. Blegh, Lucy thinks of herself - the veins on the back of her hands spongy, the skin discardable, cheap Halloween costume, last-minute, to be worn once for a function no one wants to attend. What else? The coming lurk of menopause. Lucy can whiff it on her, every spot her skin has age. All her body - eye-wets to slick of toe-betweens - membraned with a mild reek, as though, nude, she rolled on a countertop unwiped after poultry chopped and mingling leaks from cut carrots and peppers. Sigh. She used to only be aware of her own odor after a jog, a fever, a wanton lay. Now? It's all the time. The rattle of a part that doesn't work. She is fragrant of slipping-past-viable. A screech of a blossom, that's Lucy. A tap at the door and Ariel's 'Are you actually using it in there?' Lucy stands, flushes, opens the door and says 'Some host you are!' 'I don't want to have to go downstairs, man, and I know you like to just diddle about in the can - excuse me.' Ariel wriggles past and sits, Lucy taking the mouthwash up from the sink-top, only on hearing the spray realizing Ariel had not shut the door. 'Not a shy girl, eh?' Lucy says, uncapping the bottle, Ariel telling her 'Hush it, you - or it's the back o' me hand!' Lucy opens the tap and swishes more vigorously than usual. No no - she doesn't care about hearing Ariel, it isn't that. Maybe it is. She doesn't know how to be. She wants a hug, but the kind she thinks has to be asked for and - swishes louder - what are the words for that - swishes louder, cheeks straining - what are the words? Spits. 'Did you swig that right out of the bottle?' Ariel asks, sound of her also rubbing a just lightly blown nose with toilet-paper. 'No' Lucy lies, reasonless 'I poured it in the cap. Like a regular person.' 'Okay' Ariel says, nose blowing. 'Because otherwise: you're gross.' Lucy here pulls up one side of her lip and uses fingers to inside-out the thing, looks at her gums, looks at her lip's reverse-pink. What were you expecting to see, Lucy? She doesn't answer. Taps at one of her teeth, the enamel around the edges seeming kind of transparent. 'Can you make me another sandwich, for real?' Ariel asks, flushing instead of waiting for an answer.

 Don't you have questions, Lucy? Doesn't Lucy have questions? Shouldn't there be questions, an evening, a night like this one? Questions like these, maybe? Does she even wonder if she has questions? If she should? If there just are questions, even if she does not want to directly associate with them? How come, Lucy, you aren't questioning your somewhat automatic go-along with all that is happening? How come you don't remark that you haven't given any of your words tonight a thought, any of your thoughts a thought? Can you recall, as you so usually can, verbatim any one thing you and Ariel have said to each other, tonight? And what about the morning? Are you going to just to ask how it is meant to go? Or what is the plan? You'll just keep doing as you're told? Though you aren't told anything, are you? How come that isn't bothering you? These are choices you have been making - originating your own time spent, doing what you see fit - wouldn't you say? This isn't Ariel's idea, in other words? Why aren't you nervous, fingernails chewed to scabs, at the idea that Ariel will be assuming Ariel is doing what you, Lucy, want? That you are being seen as the instigator, the navigator, the vessel itself? Shouldn't you worry? Even if just to dismiss the concerns, ought you not to be having them? Does it give you no pause to think that you might leave in the morning, causal as that, because you will be thinking that is what Ariel wants - because she is not stopping you - but in truth Ariel is just watching you go, thinking it is what you want and that she has no voice in it? You want her to know she has a voice, yes? And - be honest with yourself Lucy, okay - would you not prefer her to have the leadership voice, the proclaiming orator, the only voice? Don't you have questions? Like: what does it mean that you are here and making her middle-of-the-night sandwiches, sexlessly naked in her bed? Where is Leopold - isn't that a question? Where is Kayleigh - isn't that? No? Yes? No? Well? If Yes - why aren't you asking it? If No - why aren't you ravishing in disquiet at your non-utterances? Would you rather start with a simple question? Just to get the hang of it? Do you want to try: Do you like this night? Too difficult? How about: Do you want to stay here? That is, too? How about: Do you care that you don't know Ariel and that what you do know makes no sense to you and seems as far from how you think of her as imaginable? You don't think that's true!? Oh Lucy - you can admit, can you not, that the way you think of Ariel, how you feel, has never once matched up with the evidenced actuality of the woman? Okay? Okay? Don't you want to know what that means? You see that's different than other people you've known - and see they seem like they are when you think about them? Don't you have questions? Like: Is tonight really how Ariel is? Like: Ariel seems like how you think she is, tonight - but is she, is she, is she?

'I think about ghosts, a lot'. What? 'What?' What is this now? 'Since when?' Lucy asks. 'Since I've been pregnant' - only here Ariel makes a quick puff sound to announce her edit - 'well, more since I've been pregnant, but since I lived in this house.' 'You think there are ghosts in this house?' Ariel pinches Lucy's arm, Lucy - it really hurt - snatching the sandwich plate and bag of chips away from Ariel in retaliation. 'I need to eat that!' Lucy demands apology - 'And make it eloquent' she hisses. 'But, I'm not sorry!' 'Then you will starve' hard-heads Lucy as though this is an outcome her hand has been forced on, much to her own regret. 'Fine - I'm sorry you aren't cool enough to like being pinched.'

Lucy gives the food back, but does mumble something about how that 'Wasn't very eloquent.' 'Can we talk about my actual problem, now? Do you have the decency to let us do that?' 'The ghosts?' Lucy says, after head-scratch pantomime of What-were-we-talking-about? This earns her another pinch, one she does not try at all to defend against or out-of-the-way from. 'I'm not saying there are ghosts - just I'm thinking about them more and more.' 'It might be, though' Lucy pauses for effect, acts as though the rest of the statement pains her to have to say 'that you are thinking about them more because there are ghosts here. Maybe your senses and all pick up on it more, what with being in the family way.' This is what Ariel has been thinking! 'Exactly!' Ariel is so different - it was like this with Kayleigh too, she hastens - when pregnant, that maybe she has tapped into another realm! 'Do pregnant people have a sense of ghosts?' 'I think we might. Why not?' 'What kind of ghosts?' This baffles Ariel and she just chews and stares a full minute before, still chewing, making sounds, in mostly vowel approximations, of 'What in Hell does that even mean?' 'What does it mean!? What does it mean?' snoots Lucy. 'Are they ghosts of people - people who have died - or are they like ghost-ghosts.' 'Ghosts are dead people!' 'That's what I'm asking. But in some cultures they are just spirits - entities - not of people.' 'I'm in this culture, Lucy, the one we're sitting in' - Ariel dots her fingers variously to indicate the full of the room. 'Like the Ghost of Christmases Past, right? That wasn't a person.' 'It also wasn't a ghost, Lucy - that's a character in a story. I'm talking about real ghosts!' 'But' - Lucy leans in, stealing a chip, waiting for Ariel's nod of approval before actually eating it - 'are there real ghosts?' Ariel has had enough, says 'That's what I'm exactly asking. But nevermind. Let's talk about something else.' 'No no no - fine fine fine' - Lucy apologizes and will stay on topic. 'What have you been thinking about ghosts?' 'Just: What's the point of them? Even if they told somebody something they saw, no one really would trust a ghost, right?' Lucy ponders this, has another chip - without permission, but it doesn't seem Ariel notices. 'I don't know, honestly. That's a good question.' 'It's what I'm worried about.' Ariel makes a clicking-suck sound, trying to work something out from between or off of a tooth. 'You see what I mean? I'd just like to know what in Hell would their point be?'

Lucy buses Ariel's plate back down to the kitchen and brings up a fresh bottle of water - though it is one-quarter empty, Lucy doesn't find any full ones - along with four chocolate-chip cookies - Ariel had asked for 'Two, just two, one or two' - two of which she sets on the bed stand, Ariel gloopily looking at her book again, two of which she keeps with her, munching a bite off the first. Ariel puts down her book and eats a cookie, too. That is the only sound. Lucy aware of churnings down in her, stomach pre-objecting to this ingestion for whatever reason, gasses building up and leaning pressure to this spot of her, that spot of her. Lucy does not talk. Ariel does not talk. Lucy finishes both of her cookies and realizes that it is the main room light which is on, not just Ariel's lamp, so starts to stand up. Why the pause? Had she expected Ariel would ask 'Where are you going?' and that she was to deliver reply still from the bed? Anyway - flap - down go the lights, the room blue-dark and soundtracked with Ariel's crunching her final cookie, soundtracked with that and the it-seems-too-many noises of Lucy getting back on the mattress, under the sheet. She is scratched a bit by Ariel's untended toenails, but does not react at all - their heavy shins then jockeying for whose will be crossed over-top, whose will be crossed under-bottom. Ariel's on top. Until she changes her mind. Sqwegg sound of Ariel's last swallow, squish squash of her having a drink, after. Then, hardly any force, Ariel having shifted - it must not be so comfortable due to her heft - Lucy feels Ariel's wet-cold lips on hers, part around hers, feels her tongue touching the still chew-pasted tongue of Ariel. Three seconds. And then, wordless still, they take their time and find laying position, each facing, foreheads a bit touched. Another kiss or two, just a handful. Not long or short, substantive but not hungry. The cold of Ariel's mouth warms and the dry of Lucy's dries more - it is like receipt paper soaking up a spit cherry-pit, the kissing as it feels to Lucy. This is how Lucy first kissed Ariel, it occurs to her. Officially. That is what happened. This is, both of them, currently wide awake. Unless one was swapped out in the dark. Maybe Ariel isn't Ariel. Maybe Lucy isn't Lucy. Lucy Jinx thinks like this after her half-dozen kisses - laying silent in the passing next five or six, ten or twelve minutes, Lucy thinks 'Maybe I am the one who was switched and so Ariel doesn't know she didn't kiss me - or maybe Ariel knows I was switched and that's the whole reason she did, but maybe Ariel thinks I don't know that I was, that it was safe because of that, that is was something.' Yep. Lucy Jinx thinks that. Dark covering her too-elsewhere-to-smile features, Ariel's breathing shallowing, deepening, see-sawing to clearly asleep, dreaming. Lucy giggles at the twitch of Ariel - maybe she's dreaming of falling, maybe she's dreaming like dogs dream that they're running.

How about Lucy? Does she dream? Of course she does. Many things. Here are some. She dreams: a bright room, a store, but she doesn't know which - all items in wicker baskets, wicker shelves, a store seen from her height at maybe six-years-old, bright the way stores were bright to her childhood eyes. She dreams: sounds of animal tails wagging, just through that door, and she is trying to inch closer, the sound louder, like, in the dream, as though if she could lean to the door she would know exactly which animals, see them, even be able to pet them, though still outside - inside, outside, the same in the dream if she can get past the crawling to the door. She dreams: light has weight, now, and must be negotiated through with effort, her arms are burdens, drooped ropes, after exercise flimsy - the light is like pudding or fitting between the tight space between the end of a fence and a brick wall, her movement is measured, gun-shy, Lucy like with each step she will strike her head-top to a beam. She dreams: Ariel, but not Ariel - Ariel like someone in a classroom with her and they have to figure out things from a sheet of paper that doesn't match the image of the sheet of paper blown up by the projector, cast over the wall and the chalkboard of the room front - 'The lights are on more, then' one voice is saying, Lucy feeling more and more compelled to say the same, but nervous, knows she will be mocked if she does. Lucy dreams: a camera breaks and because of it the photos she is looking at are like leaky watercolor - her hands hurt as though gripping chlorine, her hands ache like the feeling she is a match-head that strikes lit but pops extinguished in a blink, the analog equivalent of a blown fuse, the bright blue of a lightbulb fritzing off as soon as the switch is moved. Lucy dreams: milky territory, drifts of fog in clean lines amongst otherwise fogless air, the sky brightening to dawn with all the appearance of water gritty with orangish medicine powder - a fake looking sky, not paper or drywall, more like tin with something growing on it, the clouds in the exact shapes of subway grates. Lucy dreams: not a word, she can't get a word out, everyone else in the room talking and some obnoxious girl is nervous-tick laughing at everything everyone says, no matter how banal, sleepy-laughter, four-in-the-morning and not used to going to bed past ten kind of chuckling, restating the words it is laughing at and sighing 'Oh man' after the laughter dims, each time. Lucy dreams: her bones are skin-thick and her skin bone-thick - she is trapped in a suffocation of herself and knows something is wrong, that her shell should not weigh her down, her insides should not be weaker than her out. And she wakes silent, globby mouthed, but in her head had been calling out 'Help!' until she lost track of how long, old woman placation, retirement-home floor-tile, bathroom disinfectant air the only thing answering her.

They wake up like a malfunctioning percolation. 'Hi' Lucy says and 'Good morning' Ariel says at the same time. The sun does not seem to be up though the room is bright enough it might be - just with clouds glued in front of it. Where did Ariel get that scratch on the side of her nose? Lucy touches it while Ariel looks at her with an expression like 'What?' 'There's a scratch on your nose.' Ariel touches her face, piano trilling her second and third finger to move Lucy's hand away, intakes a sharp breath up her nose and whisper below 'My God - I am hideous! The curse was real!' Lucy doesn't ask which curse - figures this line is a direct reference to something while also entertaining the possibility it might be an off-the-cuff invention in the style of supposed-to-seem-like-a-line-from-something. 'Thank you for all of those sandwiches.' 'You're

welcome.' 'They weren't the best sandwiches of all time, though.' 'I'm sorry.'
'But they were good.' 'I'm glad.' 'Just not as much as some other things.' 'I can
see that.' 'But I don't want you to think I'm some grateful-less pig.' 'I
wouldn't.' 'Well - Lucy, come on - we both know you would, but it warms my
heart to know you don't.' In the next silence, Lucy senses a stiffness to Ariel -
or to the air around her - gets an impression that Ariel's ears are straining toward
the outdoors. 'Do I have to go?' Ariel yawns, bends her knee so that it presses
Lucy's thigh. 'Not yet. But maybe get dressed.' And no need to be told again -
and not with an air of rush or apology or 'Oh no' - Lucy gathers her clothing
and reassembles herself in it. Ariel watches. What's that look of Ariel's? Lucy
feels she must seem like a shadow being seen when it doesn't know it's even
there, yet. She doesn't say 'What?' though or in any way address or
acknowledge the gaze Ariel gazes. And now sits to the bed and on go her socks.
And she wants to kiss Ariel, again - it'd be easy, lean in, even if just on the cheek
or the head or the shoulder - but certainly doesn't. 'Did we watch the end of
that movie?' Lucy tries to remember. Decides 'No - we stopped.' 'Yeah' Ariel
says. 'After the gun-guy was driving away with the wife.' 'Yeah' says Ariel, then
she says 'I think I dreamed we watched it. My brain must label that a Regret,
trying to correct the mistake - that's what dreams are, I heard science say.' 'How
did it end in your dream?' But Ariel can't explain because it got weird, the way
dreams do, and it seemed to have nothing to do with anything by the end. 'Do
you have work today?' 'Yes. How about you?' 'No no' Ariel is off all week, she
took the week, has a doctor's note and all. 'But everything's okay?' Lucy has to
ask when Ariel takes her hand with closed eyes. 'What do you mean? With the
doctor?' Ariel moves her head - seems like a nod, but due to how she is laying
it's hard to tell. Ariel lets go of Lucy's hand to use both to cover her face,
sneezing a shotgun sound. 'Stop sneezing' Lucy scolds 'Jesus Christ, already.'
And 'Sorry' mumbles Ariel.

Up there, the shower is running. Lucy, as requested, is preparing some tea.
She is eating some mini-marshmallows she finds a bag of, too. More than she
should be, maybe. If they are there for a purpose, then certainly. She tries to say
'Last few' but again and again it is not the last few at all. Enough time to get
home? To change and all, freshen up? The clock says it shouldn't be a problem.
And you can't call out, Lucy? No. No, Lucy needs to work. And she - why is
she anxious about this thought - wants to see Samantha. She gets her cigs from
her coat on the dining-room chair and goes to the back door. Unlit, dangling
smoke. Opens the door and lights up. What a splotchy-faced cold this is - gah!
- how miserly, she thinks, though this feels quite the cliché word for the cold.
Little droplets of wind sneak away some breaths of her smoke, magpie them off
someplace, while other smoke frog-tongues her face even if she feels she has

blown it out hard enough it should be deep right-field, easy. Something about the morning. Out there, it feels like some busybody is up to things not really required to open the shop but they won't hear 'No' about it and complain even though they are bringing the vexation down on themself. Half-done smoke tossed, door shut, and the shiver she has is deep-boned, so cold she feel semi-transformed to a fish. Upstairs runs the shower. Lucy does not know what to do with the tea - bring it up, wait down here? If Ariel doesn't finish soon - this is another thing - won't Lucy have to take off? 'You will - if you want to get home.' Regard Lucy's clothes: she could re-wear them. Someone might notice? Samantha? So what? Of course Lucy gets what she is thinking - but she can just tell Samantha something. 'I was over with a friend - I didn't get back in time to change, really.' That sounds phony. Or maybe not. To Lucy it sounds that way, because it is phony. And since she knows it is, she has to admit 'Well, how can you be in any position to know what it would come across like to someone not in the know?' Lucy has some more marshmallows and drinks some microwave-warmed coffee from the leftover cold in the pot. Her mouth squirms around, a snail tensing, rearing, posturing itself a serpent. The shower continues and continues and continues. Ten minutes pass and it has to come down to it. Lucy makes the cup of tea and heads up the stairs, leaves cup on the desk and pokes nose into the steam of the bathroom, knocks on the door, the wall, but Ariel might not hear through the shower curtain, through the hiss covering her face. 'Ariel?' Waits a moment. 'El?' Wiggles the curtain. 'Lucy?' 'Hey, El' - but Ariel, distress voiced, talks over Lucy 'Shit, just a second - don't go yet, I'm sorry!' The shower goes off. 'It's okay, I brought the tea' - and again, overtop, Ariel says 'Wait wait wait' forced tone of joviality 'I'll be right out, I'm sorry.'

Ariel pulls up the kitchen blinds while Lucy is getting her seatbelt on - neither wave, they just watch, and Lucy playacts some busier-than-she-is this-and-that, volume-switch and heating-dials and all. And backward drift and arc and a last side-glance - she can't even see Ariel with it - Lucy then just makes her way out of the neighborhood, careful to not seem slow-going or lingering or anything other than the normal she feels she has tacitly contracted to be. Not Normal-for-Lucy, but Normal in the sense of like-a-person-not-Lucy-would-be. Normal. And she manages. Even in her head she is mild-mannered, this drive, just coasting. It's all very much like the middle stretch of a long trip home after stopping for lunch. Her mind knows not to really think, her body knows to not be particularly alert nor overly unaware. The radio, between songs, warns of harsh weather but names counties and areas she does not know much about, certainly not specifically how close they are. Sometimes she hears these names and pictures distant cow-towns, tucked-away in mountains, every house with a mailbox a mile from front door. Then other times, she'll catch glimpse of a sign and think that sign means 'Oh this - right here - is one of those towns - I'm in another town, just like that!' The sun through the clouds is like the voice of some overloud bumpkin, speaking-volume always a bellow, a kid that needed to scream for mommy's milk, was given it only to pacify, never to nourish. Yes, Lucy, that's good. But she doesn't turn on the tape recorder. She doesn't do any of that. She drives like she is just sitting and she paints a buck-toothed satire of the sun over this town - fat-woman dressing in lingerie behind a dainty cubicle wall. What else about this voice of the sun? It announces everything as complaint and as though everyone agrees, intimately, and repeats its argument like people will laugh if they just hear it some half-dozen more times. Harried and pork-skinned and diner-pie mouthed, the sun over this town is the scent of a mothball stained into the fibres of a raincoat pocket. You sure you don't want the recorder on, Lucy? 'I'm sure' she says, yawning and wondering if the old take-away coffee there in the cup holder is poison or potable. More road and more road - some work-commuter pulled over, hazard-lights winking, explaining themselves to a motorcycle patrolman. Why did Lucy notice this? Because she caught eye-contact with the man and does not like that he must now think that she slowed down to gawk. 'I am not a gawker, by nature' she explains as though to the Grand Jury. 'I only gander, from time-to-time - as was the case, here.' And Lucy eases her car in to her usual spot, shuts off the engine and sits. Lucy? She sits. Lucy? Lucy? 'Yes' she asks, eyes closed, head that way over like lopped off. Are you going inside? 'To get ready for work?' she asks. Is that it? And did she really not think once of last night? Did she not have a thought? Did she really drive from There to Here as though nothing had happened? Did something happen like nothing had happened? Did something happen, but only the once and now nothing? 'Yes' she says. And then repeats 'yes' and 'yes-yes' and 'yes-yes-yes.' To go to work, yes.

THE SHOWER WHICH WAS SUPPOSED to be short has now gone on long, Lucy giving futile, incremental turns - here - to the knobs, as though even one more spit of hot water will be spat against the getting-cold lukewarm she has wasted the previous heat with shivering under, pining. 'The privilege, though' she says, wishing she could skip brushing teeth 'of having a job it doesn't matter if you're late for.' Not that - deodorant on, out of order, that usually done last, shirt tugged out of the way, rolled in and under through head hole - Lucy ever would have thought herself the sort to take advantage of an opportunity like that. There is record, she knows, of her, at this very job, being irritated sometimes when it comes to pass that Kurt shows up late, then leaves early, saying he will come back in, later. That might be jealousy, though - because she knows Kurt worked all that freedom out with the Home Office and, really, her own flexibility cannot so contort. 'If Samantha were my enemy' she says, hating every microscopic body-strain needed to manipulate her socks on - 'I would not even have this current luxury, most likely.' Temp jobs - Lucy has a history - are often staffed with people who would make good extras in films about intergalactic lowlifes, barflies in some dive on one of the moons of Neptune, bed-bug sorts who think they have it all together and are in the position to throw their weight around, hold others to the strictures of handbooks none of them really read. Yes. Lucy has been on the receiving end of such Stanford Prison Experiment role-playing. Remember that guy who would brag about screwing the two women who had mothered his offspring out of their child-support, but who would, at the same time, report asinine things like Dress Code Violations - colored socks, non-professional footwear, visible tattoos - or would grass on people out who took three half-hour breaks - or one half-hour, two twenty-minutes, or a forty-minute and one other thirty-minute - instead of the allotted half-hour and two fifteens? Sure, Lucy remembers. The guy who got fired for cussing out a client. The one who would lob business advice at the young hires who were also taking classes, badger them out of studying, make it so they didn't even bother to bring backpacks because they were green and thought he had authority. Dressed full, now, yes, Lucy recalls that man. But what of him, she wants to know? And why does she remember him? How many of her school-teachers does she recall? A few? But every detail of - she even knows his name was Harold! - her former co-worker Harold is pristine marble in her mind's eye. And she has a feeling time won't dilute him. Her brain sorts him into the keepsie-pile and Mrs. Whomever - fourth grade, sixth, junior-high - who for all Lucy knows bent over backward and would have wanted nothing more than a connection, who maybe remembered Lucy even now, well, she is piss in the sea! 'The world is just like that, Mrs. Peaks' Lucy sighs, not using a teacher's name she does recall but some cobbled-up a-teacher-was-probably-called-that one. 'Get close in, you see it's shirt shoulders aren't just flaked in dandruff, it's dandruff, itself, down to its scalp-paste bones, man.'

So Lucy heats a toaster pastry. The gesture is an odd experiment in symbolism and she feels it will not cause any real waves but nevertheless will have observable results. Never in her life - or only enough times to be wholly negligible, not since childhood - has she done this. Her thing? Break the pastry into pieces, dunk them in milk. Sometimes not dunk them. Now: she will heat, not dunk - in fact, will drink coffee as the accompaniment. She figures: last night happened. She figures: I've come home, had a shower. She figures: if I think I will treat things as though last night didn't happen, suggest so by maintaining my same patterns and all, I will be made to pay Hell, no doubt, for the choice. She figures: if I do something distinctly different, it may be enough to show I have embraced last night. She figures: I then can go on, no conscious decision other, just how my day will take me and not have to face a reckoning. Sounds sound, Lucy. A fist of a noise, the pastries are upped from the toaster. Hot to the touch - too hot to bite - but she must not let them cool because that will deficit the potency of the difference she is forcing. Wonderful! The taste is spread and adheres to her mouth, her throat down, like it is a spore-sticky perfume mossing her, filling her with some other animal's breath! What was she saying? Now too busy wolfing down to think - Oh sweet heaven! the coffee redoubles the delight! - she knows she wanted to further some sentiment or another, but cannot think of which. Ah yes: she must not make further little alterations - just this pastry as sacrifice - otherwise hazards the Fates thinking she has found a way to cheapskate upheaval. That is: a bunch of little tweaks do not amount to a change - logic and percentages aside. That is: she must show she knows herself sucklingly dependent on grace and whim, not come off an upstart who thinks she has gamed matters. The Powers-in-Charge, they don't much care for fair-and-proper - regulations are determined by caprice and whether a headache is going on, a spouse was rude, a television show concluded in a way that was satisfying. And Lucy appreciates that. She is not one to wonder why an omniscient God, for example, would get upset if Its creation did not love It. Why it might be vengeful, hurtful, petty. Omnipotence does not discount such things - it would amplify all! Were Lucy omnipotent, she'd see to it the Universe would quake at her holding a grudge - especially over a misunderstanding where she was in the wrong! The cosmos and any peoples she created would know damn well to live with teeth grit, waiting for a slap they didn't deserve. A father killing a son because the father sired the son makes no sense, a mother killing a son because she birthed it makes more - the two working in concert, counterintuitively, make the least sense of all - but a God killing a whole Created Race because He ex nihiloed them and now they seem pesky or not up to snuff makes perfect sense. Perfect sense! She writes down: *If you believe in God and believe in fair you don't understand one of the words, the other, or either.*

That thought carries with her into her commute. She blathers into her recorder about it until a song she likes comes on the radio. Which song? *Stop All The Dancing* by *The Hollies*. And - good streak! - after it comes *Do You Wanna Dance?* by *Bobby Freeman*, *Two Silhouettes on the Shade* by *The Rays*, *Ode To Billy Joe* by *Bobby Gentry* and *I Know a Place* by *Petula Clark*. She belts this last one, especially - overtly gyrating for kicks and pounding the steering wheel to freak out the squares. When a commercial comes, she is winded and - inexplicably, it feels, though maybe there is good reason - she has the song *The Night They Drove Old Dixie*

*Down* in her head. 'Not by *The Band!*' she shrieks. 'Fuck *The Band! Joan Baez*, you stooges!' She bangs the roof above her like a fifties speed-freak who doesn't know a damn thing about poetry but decided to grow a beard and hang 'round. Radio down. She sings and sings. And her imagination figures all of these things in the song happened. That was the goddamn world! Will be again! *And all the bells were ringing!* Who cares? Build temples for alters and crates for the dogs! *And all the people were singing!* Who cares? This will be so far under-hill eventually - this time, this place - it won't even be the soil things are buried in - no! - so many centuries of new soil will on top of it! *They went na na nana na na - nah nah nah nah nah!* The recorder isn't going, but she wishes it was. Don't do it now, Lucy! *You can't raise the cane back up when it's in the feed* - man, listen to your singing! And these tapes - aren't they feeble? And your poetry? What gives, what for? Here's what's what: no more of consequence than who won the playoffs, who bought the sofa you wanted, why there was a sale on sponges last week but this week not. What poetry that has survived should have? Why? So someone can read it? So a sliver of humanity can say *This is what the bulk of us die for!*? 'Yes, by Jupiter - I must elevate this from my tenured chair!' Lucy Jinx hates the world and its layout, its architecture is like some sandstorm that swallowed her village. Why does she participate? Because she was born into it? Because words termited her heart and leak through the slushing blood that whirligigs her veins? Lucy thinks she is the charlatan's twin-sister, the one whose job is just to appear at the other end of the room and bow, to strut the length, lift up the cape from where her sister faked vanishing so that her sister can slip back up and resume the routine. Lucy is culpable in the bizarre justification for the suffering of nameless billions. The world dies so a cabal of effetes can dribble crocodile tears and recommend each other's books! The slaves die and they don't even get the satisfaction of having built pyramids! The poetry they result in is not tongued by them! Their sweat means words, unsweatedly set down, can be pondered in silence under trees by girls who think being lonely is both beautiful and profound!

Anyhow, Lucy also stops and buys some doughnuts for Kurt and Samantha. She does this sometimes and, thus, her fabled likeability! She uses the drive-thru, which she still finds absurd for a doughnut-shop to have, and leaves some coins in the transparent Charity-Box bolted to the lip of the cashier window. The usual wondering about 'Who collects that money?' If it isn't a representative from the charity who comes around, is instead just someone who works in the shop, then obviously it's either all stolen or most of it is. Hell, if it's someone from the charity, same deal - it's all absconded with, proper crooked! What are they, required to videotape their entire trip, real time, no pauses for funny business? Of course not! They could never justify the cost of doing that - justify not using the money it would take to make sure the money donated all makes it in instead of giving the money it takes to ensure that to charity! Good point, Lucy. You've made it before, but good point. So what percent of donated money into these boxes is swiped? Ten? Fifteen? Thirty? What is the dollar amount on that? Per day: say there are twenty boxes for the charity in an area, thirty dollars put in each one, total. Lucy slows to do the math, the radio volume back up, chewing the doughnut she cannot wait until work to devour. Six hundred dollars a day! Ten percent is sixty a day. Now, that's just this area. Say there are a hundred areas with that type of box. Six thousand dollars, then! At least. In a year, that's over two million dollars stolen from charity! In this area alone, it's twenty-two thousand or so. That's what Lucy makes, working her job, annually! Add in even a pittance for the person who drives around - even if they made ten dollars a day for that, which they clearly make more than - and that's basically twenty-six thousand dollars! For stealing from charity! Lucy should write a pamphlet full of vehement, inflammatory anger to combat this, except all it would do is get whoever isn't already stealing from charity to start stealing from charity. She points out, further, that if there were ten charities in the country working in the same way - just asking for pocket-change, ten-percent of which is grifted - then over twenty-million dollars a year - just like that! - vanishes out car windows. 'Sure' she says, patient with the traffic at the intersection caused always by the idiot timing of this traffic signal 'the charity does things - but the fact that everyone working there knows each other are thieves and that they could be doing more is overall a demoralizing thing.' And being demoralized, well, that would weigh on someone. Which would likely make them steal more. Every once in awhile, no doubt, they make a point to sting-operation someone, but they all know they just do that to the low-man-on-the-pole or as a power-play of some kind. Charity: so politely cut-throat. The ugliest bug of all, living under the dead belly of the other bugs. A bug to the bugs! 'Yes' sigh 'goes to show ya. It's the same as it ever was. The world just spins while it rounds while it hurtles while it dies.'

Opinion: excellent drive in to work! No extra effort made to have thoughts just go the way thoughts go. Lucy just really did drive into work like any other day. She parked her car. She's here. In a funk? Negative. A fog? Negative, A tunnel? Negative? Feel delicate, like a harsh breeze would crack your egg, Lucy? Nope. She feels good. Not too good. Not euphoric or new. And not dismissive of what transpired with Ariel. This is how a person does things. They live as they were constructed to. Acknowledge. Go on. Kurt groans at the sight of the doughnuts, complaining that his paunch needs not grow more sugar-based, Lucy twisting the knife by lifting the lid of the dozen-box to show a full line-of-four of Kurt's most favored variety. 'I'll find a way to make you suffer for this, but thank you' he says, lifting one of the treats out, setting it on an unneeded bit of scrap paper, sucking his thumb and his third finger where they got icing and sticky on them. Where's Samantha? 'Where's Samantha?' 'She is running late. And the new guy won't be in.' 'Why not?' 'They didn't say.' Wait. 'Wait! Lucy says. 'Why are you here?' Kurt stares, chewing unhurriedly, swallowing in a way that is probably normal but seems dramatic because Lucy is staring and waiting. 'Why wouldn't I be here?' Hadn't Samantha said Kurt would be gone for a few days? Are you sure, Lucy? She feels sure. 'Samantha said you would be gone for a few days.' This is news to Kurt. 'You weren't here, yesterday' Lucy says, jabbing a finger in his direction like unmasking a killer, Kurt shrugging and confessing he wasn't. 'So what got Samantha under that impression?' 'We will ask her, together' Kurt dismissives, taking another doughnut bite. And that kind of has to be the end of that. Except for the feeling like Kurt shouldn't be here. And the queasy, un-get-away-fromable tang the sensation gives to each swallow. Don't backslide, Lucy. If you start reading into this, you'll find something. Yes: Samantha had said what she had said. But: in a casual way. She'd obviously thought it, but this may have been for any number of reasons. Kurt might even have said so and just not remember. What? Well, he might have said something like 'I might not be here for a few days' offhand, before he knew he only needed to be gone for one - said this to Samantha, Lucy means - and by the time things had changed, a day passed, his memory of that moment - saying that to Samantha, Lucy means - was gone. He might even be remembering it, even now, and just have his mind proper on other matter, not think it worth bringing up. What were you out for yesterday? Just ask, Lucy. It's easy. Hey - what were you out for, yesterday? Go on. Ask. Ask! 'Kurt?' He looks up from a text he is sending? She says 'I'm sorry I got you the doughnuts, I should show more respect.' He smiles. Pats his tummy and mouths something like 'It's fine' or 'Bless you' or 'Too late'. Some two words. Lucy looks down. Decides it's good she didn't ask. That was restraint. She'll get recognition for that. She passed a test, negotiated an obstacle. Proved herself. Opens her eyes, sighs, and goes to get some files.

A cigarette looking down into the empty compactor. Not that it is ever *Empty* in the technical sense. There is always at least something down in it - and the splotches of leakage, the stains and pulpy paper of stuff made wasp-nest looking with it - but here we still call it *empty*. A grammarphile would be so put off! They would point out 'It's the wrong word!' And the argument 'We all know what is being said' would get nowhere. Those are the true lost souls, see Lucy? Those are who language overpowers and bullies. Zombies to the Religion of Contemporary Usage - and their guilty pleasures are that they like certain phrases or usages from olden times, though they know it is no longer proper to use them. They would not say *Improper* though - and this is where Lucy has tripped them up, before. Cigarette in. Cigarette out. Remembering her younger-self. Remembering the feeling of triumph in stitching up their self-assuredness, these people who feel protectorate of language, temple-slaves to its rich-man-behind-a-curtain holiness. Lucy had said - and speeches aloud now - 'Language doesn't change, it becomes wrong. It isn't okay to spell how we used to spell, syntax how we used to syntax, structure how we used to structure. If you, today, spelled a word how it used to be spelled, defined it how it used to be defined, you aren't any more right than someone just utilizing the word outside-of-current-rules, outright. It's just wrong. If you are some scholar of old-languages, you are a scholar of incorrect-spelling, of incorrect-speech. You are studying discard, stool-samples of tongues! And so, now, knowing the rules is knowing what-will-become-wrong. The same way this sandwich' - Lucy was eating a sandwich at the time of this glorious tale - 'will be shit once I eat it. I am eating shit. All of your rules are wrong precisely because now they aren't. They don't alter, they are just digested and shat. Correcting people's mistakes is like swallowing and expecting it to pop out your lower half the same as it popped in.' Yes, those grammar-lovers had had to stop. Never had she felt better. Except when she explained the term *contronym* - though she had used the more-fun-word *autoantonym* - to someone complaining about *Literally* meaning *Figuratively*. That was only a few years ago, though. One of Elliott's friends. Not even a few years. That was pretty recent. '*Cleave* and *cleave* is more confusing - not to mention *Sanction* and *Sanction*' she'd said. They had tried to argue. Failed. Two weeks later, Lucy first heard the name Pine. *Professor Pine*. And now Lucy tosses her cigarette down into the empty compactor. It smolders, the smoke scrambling up from it like in a hurry, like it knows where it has fallen and fears the anguish of being flattened. 'You're safe, cigarette. You lived a rich, full life and are dying with dignity.' You only think of a cigarette as alive while lit, Lucy? The pack is the womb? 'No - the pack is oblivion. A cigarette's life is fire and diminishing, like the molten that cooled to a planet.'

'Samantha's still not in?' 'Neither is the new guy' points out Kurt. Insinuation in his tone. Lucy plays along to keep from having to not. They decide, quickly, that they two have already married and Samantha is in the family way. 'What's the new guy's name?' asks Kurt. But how is Lucy supposed to remember that? Hadn't she worked with him all day? 'Only one day! It can take a long time to learn someone's name! Does Kurt know the name of every person he only spent one shift of work with? Exactly!' Point conceded, Lucy moves on. Sort of. She dwells long enough to say 'It isn't like I had to say his name, a lot. I don't say your name, a lot.' Kurt agrees with this, too. They decide names are passé and try to come up with something else to use that wouldn't just be - as Kurt here puts it - 'another name for *Name*.' 'Hieroglyphs?' 'Why didn't those catch on?'

Kurt wonders. Lucy surmises: 'People don't want to sit around having to interpret stuff. Words give the easy illusion of smarts and the ease that any common dolt needs.' But Kurt - laughing first and saying 'Agreed' - explains that he meant 'Why hadn't they caught-back-on - with artists, say?' Like painters? Is that what he means? But - and he's correct, Lucy likes Kurt now - Kurt says that hieroglyphs weren't paintings, they were writing. The people who did them were writers. Same as - they both feel racist and ignorant mentioning - Chinese characters. 'Yes, we in the West' Lucy candids 'consider those *paintings*, but that must seem crazy to the writers writing them.' 'They must be like' - Kurt seems to want to use a caricatured accent but doesn't, admittedly things sounding the stranger for it - 'What? Do they consider writing the word *The* or *Cat* or *I went to the boathouse* the same as painting? Because that's all that we're doing, too, really.' Lucy goes whole-hog and says 'We overpraise their letter writing - very ignorantly - because we're - and we know it - too lazy and dickish to learn their alphabet.' Yes, Lucy could think of nothing worse than being a Chinese writer and having to listen to blowhard Westerners think they spent ages perfecting the strokes of writing *The building is green.* 'As though all their writers are old, beared, long-eyelashed hermits in caves.' 'That it takes them forever to say *It's raining.*' 'The worst must be listening to us go *And see? The way they write it looks like rain! You can see it!*' Kurt claps he agrees so much. 'If someone said that about me writing *Eggplant* they'd be fucking committed! Though, in a way, the word *Egg* does look like an egg.' 'It's evocative of it, yes.' 'But the word *Tupperware* or *Lamp* or *Dice* don't look like those.' 'True - well *Lamp* kind of does, but still - you are correct.' 'Not to mention things like *Sour* or *Dismal* or *Yellowish*' Lucy adds. '*Yellowish* looks like what *Yellowish* looks like. Especially if you write it in yellow!' Now Lucy laughs. 'It's true! If I wrote *Yellowish* in yellow, I wouldn't even be certain when I looked that it was quite yellow!'

'There's Samantha!' 'Here I am.' 'There she is!' 'I am here.' 'We missed you!' 'That warms me.' 'We've been bonding' Kurt says, hand motion between himself and Lucy. 'It's true' Lucy says, as though such things are distasteful to admit. 'I thought you had already bonded' Samantha says, putting her purse down, her coat on top of it on the floor. 'No' Kurt says. 'No. This was new. Otherwise, why would we have? That's the sort of thing you don't have to do again, once you've done it.' 'I see' says Samantha - Lucy picking up on something, but not knowing how to change speeds - 'I stand corrected.' 'You really missed a show - I don't think we can replicate it' Kurt says, his phone sounding, indicting a message he leans to read after tapping his screen. 'Lucy?' mouths Samantha and she dot dots her head like 'Will you come with me?' Lucy does the international sign for *Cigarette*, her brow doing its bit to give it the interrogatory tilt. Samantha shakes head, again dot dots and Lucy just puts down her in-progress sorting and follows her. 'We'll be back, new friend' says Lucy and Kurt gives a thumbs-up without raising his eyes from what he is texting. Samantha is already several paces down the hall. Lucy catches up, is about to say something when it becomes clear that Samantha is tractor-beamed on the bathroom. In they go. And - how about that! - the place is empty. Technically - Lucy is deflated to admit it - it's not actually empty, because Samantha is there. Oh well. 'What's going on?' she asks. And Samantha pauses, lets out a breath, then says 'Can I ask you something, very bluntly?' Eyes wide like a many *U*ed many *M*ed *U*m Lucy says 'Certainly.' 'And you'll just answer me?' Rolodex of 'What could I have done to upset Samantha?' Lucy can come up with nothing other than the absurd 'Does she know I kissed Ariel and slept nude with her last night?' 'I'll answer. What's up?' But it seems Samantha cannot bring herself to ask whatever it is. Which is a relief, but insufferable. Is Lucy supposed to coax the hard word out of her own interrogator, leaning in to say 'Don't you want to ask me how I knew the victim?' Is she supposed to show concern and hold Samantha's hand through this, though she has no idea what it is? 'What do you want to ask me?' There we go, Samantha takes a shy orators posture, sucks in air, hand up to ready the outlet of words - Lucy poised to listen, all ears - but it fizzles and goes no place. 'Is everything okay?' That's as much prompting as Lucy feels obligated - last chance for Samantha to speak, then Lucy's any reaction is termed Fair Game. 'No. Nevermind.' Sudden change of expression and vocal cadence, Samantha now says 'Hey - do you just wanna come over, tonight? We'll do something? I could use someone to hang out with.' And Lucy says she'd adore coming over, leaves it at that. But kind of feels she had been tricked. The whole build up a feint to get Lucy feeling she had to say 'Yes' even if it meant canceling other plans.

Next time Lucy checks her phone, there are four texts waiting. Firstly, Mathilde tells her that *That broad wrote, again* and Lucy might want to give Mathilde a call, immediately *for some very good news*. Or Mathilde *thinks it is good news* Mathilde writes *Anyway, the e-mail seemed very, very positive*. Then a message telling her she can pay her bill Online now, if she wants - this message comes up from time-to-time, she wonders if she is charged for it. And then two messages from a number she doesn't recognize. *Sorry it's been so long. I honestly did mean to get back, before. Let's catch up, if you're able* and then, a bit later from the time stamp, *Oh and you can also try this number or my email*. And an email address Lucy also doesn't recognize is given. 'Lucy?' She looks up. At Samantha, who evidently had been talking. 'What - sorry, what?' 'Where's the new guy?' She looks to where Kurt was, but Kurt isn't there. Had Samantha been waiting for Kurt to leave to ask? Why hadn't she asked Kurt? 'Hey! Come to think of it' Lucy cuts in with 'why did you think Kurt was going to be gone for a few days?' Confusion sits on Samantha's features. 'Yesterday. You said so.' 'Did I?' Samantha asks, stage-version of the question, exaggerated face to make sure those in the cheap seats can make out everything. 'Yes!' Lucy is not going to relent from this. 'Yes, you did! Are you trying to drive me crazy? Is this a game to you? My psyche is fragile, Sammy-girl - fragile! I am the sort for whom it all hinges on things like this. So if you have something up your sleeve, play it and have done. I'm not to be trifled into a loon, for your chuckles - derangement of my sense-of-self and history! No! Do you truly not remember saying it - I charge you, tell me!' No - Samantha doesn't remember. 'But are you just saying that because you're so amused at how I talk when I'm at my damned wits end! I warrant, I am amusing - I speak in a way such it is understandable you would want it to go on, elongated - but this is beyond such fun-and-games. Did you know, I'm asking, that Kurt would be back today?' 'Sure.' 'You did?' 'Or, I know as much as I knew he'd be here, any day. I assumed so.' 'This is vexing then, my friend - this is a real pile of hokum! Or harem-scarem. If you say things, you should remember them! I shouldn't have to tell you you said something like *Kurt will be out for a few days*.' 'I don't think I said that!' 'So you think I'm crazy, then? That I'd invent such a banal thing as that, mesmerize myself into a staunch belief of it, and now am insisting it on you?' 'Yes' Samantha says. 'I think you fucking Manchurian Candidated yourself, to be honest. I bet you do, all the time.' Lucy is pleased that Samantha thinks this - and more pleased at the use of the term *Manchurian Candidated*, however loose a fit it is to what Samantha was actually driving at.

Because: no one should have Lucy's current telephone number. Lucy - right now - is in her car, smoking, and has just dialed the phone and someone picked up right away and said 'Lucy!' This is why she is reiterating. Because: no one should have this number! No one she doesn't recognize. And she doesn't recognize this voice. It said 'Lucy!' though. And Lucy is barring the insane coincidence that a random person called her random number for some random other specific-Lucy. Lucy's move, then? She plays it like this: 'Who is this?' real sit-com silly, pal-joshing-another-pal who is calling up in some crazy situation, audience having a big laugh as the calling friend gesticulates and spittles 'Knock it off, I'm in a bind!' and so on. 'It's Bianca - sorry, new number. I just found my old phone and got your number back. So sorry.' Yep - this is not checking out. *Bianca?* What is this supposed to mean? She has never - never ever - met anyone named *Bianca* - certainly not since she has had this phone, and one-hundred-thousand percent did not give this number to anyone with that name. So Lucy keeps up her act. Sit-com pals, she ons-with-the-joke, goaded on by the pal's protests 'And I gave you this number?' Bianca - or whoever this is, Lucy cannot verify the name - laughs like an acquaintance in on the joke and says 'This is Lucy Jinx, right? I can't imagine there's more than one of you - that would be a bit much for the world, eh?' Fine, Lucy can badminton this all day. She alters tactics to pretending she is an impersonator and that Bianca is just a friend of the person who's life she has taken over, the only acquaintance who was overlooked in the planning stages. 'It would be, yes. Unless I have a doppleganger also named me. With a number similar enough you misdialed it. We have to keep all possibilities open.' Why did you say that, Lucy? Now you're thinking about it. This isn't some looney you-really-did-give-out-your-number situation and it certainly isn't a you-have-a-twin-out-there-you-never-knew-about situation. Then: what is it!? Well, Lucy, you don't know. But this person knows you and you don't know them and they got your phone number and are pretending you gave it to them! That is the reality! That is dangerously bad. Bianca has said something Lucy didn't catch and now she acts as though her attention was taken from the call and she was barred from hearing - 'Bianca, I'm sorry. I'm at work, now. I thought they'd leave me alone if I stepped out, but I gotta get in there.' Bianca understands. Asks 'Can I give you a call, later?' 'Of course! Yes. Sorry I have to run.' 'And we've gotta grab coffee, okay? On me, I insist.' 'Absolutely' says Lucy and then sputters how sorry she is, really has to go, sorry sorry and hangs up. Lucy Jinx: cigarette almost out, giving it suck taps back-to-life. And here's what will happen next: the cigarette will be finished, Lucy will go back to work, and on will go the day as though never once has it gone on any other way.

# .III.

LUCY JINX LIKES TO THINK of the sea as sentient and being punished for something. She enjoys imagining the lap of the tide as excruciating, an endless sort of tug-and-release, skin being pinched, arm yanked, hair plucked, over and over, over and over, the extreme end of any bit of the body never at rest, the recipient of agitation it cannot get used to. And the creatures, currents, the warmths, colds - all of this criss-crossing and clotting, tumoring its insides - none of it is welcome, all an affliction, a plague made of crabs and anemone, boils in grape-clusters of starfish and reef, living pustules that breed and egg and hatch and school inside of the sea's head - its thoughts, its eyes, its lungs, nothing, no part of it, not the most inward notion is unlived in by encroacher, the deeper down the more monstrous, the devils in its belly or its heart blinking in pitch-black, mindlessly numb and pressed down by its weight but circling and devouring each other, tremor of gnashing jaw and squirming ink, tentacle and upset silt-bed always, always, always regaling the sea out of its desperate, countless yelps for alone. No creature is more self-aware than the sea and none more stricken. Not to Lucy. No mind is more lacerated, no spirit more horrendoused than the endless frothing and screaming 'Murder-me!-Murder-me!-Anything!-End-it!' soul of the brine-strangled ocean. And what does Lucy like to think it is being punished for? Something it deserves? Something it doesn't? Does she think of the sea as a victim or instead as a prisoner deserving no pity - its very essence poisoned as over time no ounce of it is itself, all that it is is divided into millions and billions and trillions of other things that yet it still is? Lucy feels it is being censored for something simple. Something that anciently would have warranted such a disciplining, all would agree, but that nowadays seems absurd and only understood in Mythological reasoning. She thinks the sea is being punished for being a bad sister - unkind and aloof, not what a sibling should be. Through no quirk of bad upbringing - no, Lucy does not allow the sea any outs - but through choice, deliberate and flying-in-the-face of its own well-taught morals. The sea knew Right and then decided that it also knew Better - knew Better wasn't better but was what it was going to be. And, Oh the sea had a fine life before it was caught and dragged down for its comeuppance - yes it did, yes it did. But the sea is lost, now - those memories, it cannot access them any more than a woman being burned on a spit, punctured and skin peeling, eyes sizzling to blindness, would be able to retreat to thoughts of her favorite friend from youth, the touch of her father's hand to her forehead at night, to remembrances of the one she loved beyond all and could laugh beyond reason with over the slightest observation for succor. Lucy Jinx can go on and on when she needs, detailing the specific machinations that rend the sea, eviscerate it, keep it a throat with a lung half-squeezed up it, perpetually nearly-choked, nearly-ended, never time for anything but gasping-automatic that just won't end. It has forgotten its transgression. It has forgotten anything but being pain. Yes, the sea is a sentient, miserable ache, a wail that only knows its ludicrous horror, too screaming to even see the air above it - and if it did see the sky it would only think 'That's another part of me that is part of this anguish.'

Lucy Jinx doesn't go into all of that with Simon, her neighbor Evan's little boy. She doesn't upend his young mind with a bestiary of how each pang is suffered by the water ships sail in. No. But she does tell him all of this like a Fairy Tale while he eats his microwaved pasta and asks for one of her stories. Lucy eats too, but just a sandwich of peanut-butter with some potato-chips added - which Simon calls gross but which Lucy can tell he will try one day and love. 'Why is it punished so bad for being a terrible sister? Don't its sisters forgive it? Aren't they kind of just as bad, after awhile, for knowing how much it is suffering? Shouldn't they be punished, too?' Lucy rather loves Simon and has sometimes daydreamed of a kidnap. This would only go on two weeks before she gets caught - and Simon would never know anything amiss, just think it was a crazy long road trip, hotels and mini-golf, restaurants and toys. 'That isn't how punishment works' Lucy says 'not pure punishment. This is original, man - this is the way punishment was in the very beginning, when things were absolute, before everything whined and whined and parsed every idea into offshoots and subcategories. There was Time, you see Simon - but Time didn't mean what it means now.' 'What did Time mean?' Simon asks, adding more Parmesan Cheese to his meal. 'Time just meant Existing. You either did or didn't. You were in Time or you weren't, capital *W Weren't*. Not like now. Where we say time even affects the unreal, time even has something to do with pretend. This was before Pretend, Simon - Pretend is practically new-fangled compared to how long ago I'm talking about.' 'You're talking about a time when there weren't people like us or animals are - when seas and things were people.' 'Exactly' Lucy says on another swallow. 'I mean, it wouldn't make sense, nowadays, for example, to cut out someone's tongue for telling a lie. Lies are fine. We expect them. But it makes perfect sense - and you would have been an idiot not to - back when we were just wandering, hunter-gathering, tent-living, never certain even what the weather would be. Think of it, Simon! Suddenly there is a blizzard and no one has ever even heard of snow! This is what you're dealing with. Then someone starts lying, into the bargain? Jesus, what would you do?' Simon agrees. 'Cut out the tongue. Or kill them.' But Lucy here has to correct. 'This was before Death was a punishment - before people were convinced of that. Death is nothing compared to having to still pick fruit without a tongue and to watch people come to forgive you and befriend you again, but nothing in your mouth will ever grow back your voice.' Simon chews, think-face. Swallows. Says 'That would fucking suck.' 'It would, Simon. It would truly fucking suck.' Then, to answer his questions, Lucy says that 'Yes, the sea's sister forgave her. And the sea's sister got in trouble her own - unrelated, way later on. But that has nothing to do with the Fate of the Sea. Forgiving doesn't mean punishment isn't deserved.'

While Simon does his homework, Lucy smokes out on the terrace. Evan has a flowerpot stuffed inches-high with cigarette remains, pulped and rained on, frozen and thawed - it almost seems like an art project by this point and she idly wonders if Evan has grown attached to it, if it will be hard for him to eventually discard. Maybe it will be nothing. Not a thought given to it - not while it amassed the cigs, not when it comes time to dump out or throw away in its ceramic-entire. Is it ceramic? Lucy gives it a kick. Thus concludes her extensive investigation of the matter. She decrees 'It is ceramic' notarizing the proof by giving the thing another tap with shoe-tip. Simon raps on the glass behind her, she turns and smiles to his shy wave. 'What's up?' 'What does *Inordinate* mean?' She wants to know why he's asking - she explains she will tell him, but is curious, all this to buy her time to try to figure out if she can actually define the word. It seems it is one of Simon's vocabulary words and he is to use it in a sentence, but the print-out the school gave him is wonky and he cannot read the provided definition off of it. 'You don't have a Dictionary?' Simon gives her a look like 'Have you met my dad?' and so she changes her question to 'Can't you look it up on the computer?' 'Touché' his face says. And he says, in no negative way 'I can do that, yeah' starting to go. Lucy stops him. She didn't mean that she was suggesting it, just wondered if he had considered it. '*Inordinate* means something is not justified.' 'What does that mean?' 'That it is not excusable. You know? Well' - Lucy has explained badly - 'first it means like *Too much, excessive amount, unwieldy.*' 'I don't know what *unwieldy* means.' 'It means *hard to wield, to control - due to excess. Inordinate* means *Exorbitant* or' - she searches for the expression - '*out of proportion to other things - way too big, considering.*' 'Considering what?' 'The thing - the whatever.' Simon nods in a confused way and says 'It means *big? Too big?*' Lucy gestures 'Sure' but then says 'But in the sense of *unjustifiable.*' Lightbulb, Simon takes a breath, checks his thought, and says 'The sea's punishment was *inordinate.*' Lucy claps - 'Exactly.' But then goes 'Well, no - because the sea deserved it. Better to say: *The sea's punishment seems inordinate, by today's standard.*' 'Okay' Simon nods, understanding. 'Or better - try this - the sentence should be: *The sea's punishment was not inordinate, though some people, who would be incorrect, hold that it is.*' 'Okay' Simon nods. 'And back in time it meant something else. The word.' Simon is puzzled again. 'It has' - he squints, looking for a word - 'multiple definitions?' 'No - only one. The other definition isn't the definition anymore - it just used to be.' 'What was it?' Lucy can't recall. 'But it had one' she explains. Simon turns, but turns back. 'What's up?' He says 'I just don't want you to be sad if you look at my homework and see I didn't use the sentence you just said. It was a great sentence - I liked it and I get it - but no one knows what you're talking about - about the sea - so I need to write something else.' Lucy nods, shoos him on his way.

These - infrequent as they are - nights where Lucy does a spot of babysitting are treasured. The kid aside - she babysits for a few other neighbors whose kids are not as delightful as Simon - there is just something to the way her mind can shut down, exist in a place to the side of its normalcy, a relaxation she never attains, elsewhere. Not even in sleep. Lucy is not susceptible to her normal barrage of doubts and paranoias in idle moments - such as now, Simon running his own bath and generally tending to himself, Lucy just laying on the sofa - she is simply idle. Lucy thinks about how she feels about a list she read in a magazine. Nothing to it. She thinks about making herself a French-bread pizza, later - again, nothing to it. Here? A memory of answering the phone once as a teenager, it being a wrong number and the caller upset at her, making demands of what number it had reached and how could that mistake have been made and why would someone have given out a residential number when the caller had asked

796 / PABLO D'STAIR

for whatever the name of the business the caller had said was. Yes - incredibly, this does not work Lucy up or make her think about anything. It could be the combination of her mind on her duties - however slight they may be - and being in rooms not her own that cools her out - just enough responsibility that she has to forget herself. Or it could be something else. In any event, she is glad for it and doesn't look forward to Evan's return. Maybe he will call and say 'Can you do an all-nighter?' as he has done on occasion, promising her double extra-pay which she turns down with mention of how she will just be sleeping on the sofa, anyway, so the money is nothing to worry over. Simon is singing as the water fills the tub. Lucy should probably check to make sure the tub isn't overflowing. 'Meh, he won't let that happen' she says and looks at her socks with her toes moving inside of them, closes her eyes and thinks 'I will just sleep for five minutes.' And - closed eyes - she is a soup-scented fog, the humidity of a flavor seeping through a wall. Lucy might be meant to exist as sentry in the homes of other people. She ought to have been a nanny. Or maybe the caretaker for an invalid. She could relax into that and would like the intricacies of how complicated it would be to keep another human clean, fed, comfortable, healthy, versus how simple it is to live well herself. Or maybe just fascinating to note how she could - not being an invalid - live unclean, hardly fed, not-exactly-comfortable, and think little of it. To someone who cannot stand for themselves, who cannot rise to get a cup from the cupboard, being a bit dirty on top must feel like failure. She opens her eyes, still hears Simon singing and the water running. How long had she drifted for? Less than five seconds? A brief trickle of she should check to make sure Simon hasn't drown, but then - exactly, Lucy - she hears him, singing like a dope, out-of-tune and repeating words in obnoxious-kid-trying-to-big-his-voice-to-baritone. 'So unless he can sing while he's drowned, you can just stay put' Lucy says, eyes closing. A wave of shiver through her. Her eyes open. The apartment is silent.

Lucy, don't you feel bad? A little. You usually read him something, have a chat while leaned in his doorframe, he doing all he can to stay awake and keep you engaged. I know. Why didn't he wake you, do you think? Maybe he tried. Do you think he did? Maybe. You don't think he went to bed upset, do you? No, no. Lucy imagines the kid thought he was doing a mature thing, helping her out. He liked that you fell asleep rather than reading to him, talking? He liked the novelty of it, yes. Ah - but if it kept happening, he would come to resent it? Yes - this one time, though, it felt special to him to just let me doze, snore away, to let me know he can take care of himself and that he wants me to be comfortable. How sweet. Isn't it? Lucy eats some mini-pretzels and pours the last of the coffee from the overheated bottom of the pot, decides she will open the tube of cookie-dough in the fridge and have a few spoonfuls. Like Evan will care. Even if Evan planned to actually make the cookies - how likely is that? - what does it matter if just a little dab or two is gone? Lucy, do you think Simon thinks you and Evan are intimate with each other? It wouldn't surprise me - but then, it wouldn't surprise me if not, either. Because the kid seems to like having you around - you mark the rapport, do you not? Kids dig me. Do they? They've always seemed to. And Lucy nods at this, taking a moment to make sure there is a large enough Ziploc bag to put the cookie-dough tube in when she is done. Finding one, she then opens the fridge, cuts the tip off the dough-tube with a steak knife - this she just rinses, vaguely, wipes with a hand towel and puts back in the block she had pulled it from - and scoops an amount of the dough up with a gouge of her index and third finger. The taste satisfies, but she decides she will leave the stuff out so it warms a bit, is mushier. The cold of the chips she enjoys, as is, but the soft brown of the dough, itself, is not pliable enough yet - too much of a bite to the chewing she has to perform. And a missed message from Evan on her phone asking how things are going. From just about when she would have been passing out. No follow-ups though, which is gratifying. Nice to know one is trusted, eh Lucy? She yawns and does some elaborate stretching around, slouches into her coat and heads back to the terrace for a smoke. The night is warmer than the evening was. For a moment, she thinks she must be running a fever. But no - see there? - some of the ice at the base of the cigarette pot - it was hard, crusted earlier - now is melted, a trickling puddle. She congratulates herself on not only her keen detective work, but her body's natural aptitude for gauging temperature. A car alarm is going off somewhere, mocking-bird of it, modern cicada. Lucy triangles a foot to the wall, can see back in the apartment, leans forward her weight in bounces, stretching out her calve or whatever this particular stretch - one she remembers learning in junior high, never forgetting - stretches.

Here's Evan now, less drunk or high than she had expected him. And an earlier night of it, she must say. Jibes him a little bit for this punctual return and laughs at his typical vulgar assessments of barfly womankind. 'You'd think they'd think that they don't have other places to be or options of any real value - to the contrary, they seem irrationally self-possessed and able to point out my shortcomings!' 'Fuck em' Lucy says and then gives a narrative of how things went with Simon. 'I thank you again, Ms. Jinx, for your help in my trying to pretend I'm still young.' 'Not a problem at all' she says, tucking her payment in her rear pocket and explaining about the cookie-dough. 'Cookie-dough?' She opens the fridge and Evan seems shocked. 'That was clever of me to buy - I must have known, someplace deep inside, that I like to eat it.' Then Evan stamps his feet, snapping his fingers, and whisper curses about something. 'You did Simon's homework with him?' She says 'Yes' then admits Simon basically did it himself. 'But yeah' she finishes 'Simon did his homework.' 'Did he happen to mention the poster project he has due?' Lucy sucks on lower-lip and shakes her head, eyes titled up in pretend of honestly-thinking-about-the-matter, as though it is one with subtleties and some hairiness to sort through. 'That's fine' Evan beat sighs. 'That's fine - it's due tomorrow and I forgot about it. Damn bag with the poster-board is in my bedroom so I never think about it.' 'Sorry, man' Lucy offers, now eager to go - not that she dislikes Evan, but she doesn't like to linger too long, give the idea they are bosom friends or anything. No. Lucy likes to play the role of older, very-mature-and-together person: a trusty neighbor, grandmotherly, not the sort to feel on equal footing with. 'I'll stay up and do it, I guess' Evan says, shrugging like a television commercial then drooping his arms. 'You're a good dad' Lucy says 'and it'll give you someplace to direct that pent up turmoil in your loins.' Evan seems embarrassed, which makes Lucy happy on two fronts - first, because she would not expect her comment to have raised such a reaction, and second, because it indicates to her that Evan was not, in the slightest degree, thinking he might try it on with her. Or else he's embarrassed because that's exactly what he was thinking, she points out to herself, waving in through the closing door at him, but it matters little. 'Wait' - the door opens and he leans out, beckoning her to come closer like he has to tell a secret - 'Could I ask you another favor with Simon? I'll pay, of course.' Lucy flops hands like 'Sure, man - name it.' 'I'm starting a new job and I need someone to either drive him to school or wait for the bus with him - I know he could do it himself, but I'm just not ready for that. Around here, you know?' Why Evan, Lucy cannot help but be endeared by your honestly. 'Sure - you mean like every day?' Evan squirms, kid-needing-to-potty, finally puffing cheeks and saying - long out-breath after - 'Yes, kind - well, yes. Yes.' She chuckles - did you just touch his shoulder, Lucy? brush his shoulder after giving it a squeeze? - and says 'It's not a problem. When's the bus?'

And here is Lucy's door - but Lucy is not going through it. Why ever not? She looks over her shoulder and takes out a smoke, lights it, tests at the locked knob, playacts angrily attempting to tug it turned. Long exhale, the smoke fracturing into separate streams off the grey paint. A memory of Elliott comes unbidden. Unwelcomed, just now. Elliott had been writing some story about a woman - a woman in a harried mind - thinking she was being followed by a customer from some delicatessen, a woman who was trying to get her key out, her apartment door unlocked, to get inside as fast as she could. Lucy had called the scene 'A bit too television, yeah?' and they had discussed whether this entire scene had any place of origin within Elliott or whether it was, no matter how it fit with the story, just a regurgitation of a type of scenario she had only ever seen on television, in movies. And - from that - was the whole piece a possibility Elliott only considered based on seeing flimsy fantasy? 'Would you ever think to write a scene like this if you hadn't read a scene like this, seen a scene like this, elsewhere?' That had been Lucy's argument. And Lucy had pointed out that all of the details were borrowed - cold hands, difficulty fitting key to lock under pressure - keys dropping, for Christ's! - lifted, no bones, from unreality. And so Lucy suggested that Elliott, if she was going to write the scene, at least test out what it would be like - at least inject something personal, something that would translate to the page as genuine rather than - albeit well-worded - more-or-less hackneyed and been-done-to-death word-tinkery. So they had both tried it. And it had been a blast - the story forgotten, it became a challenge, a race of sorts, each trying to beat the other's best time. Exacting conditions reset with each attempt. Hands five-minutes-under-cold-faucet. Thick wallet and jumble of receipts in pocket with keys. Grocery bags or backpack weighted, just so. Walking briskly the corridor seven times to simulate being winded from hurrying all the way from the Deli, feeling pursued. A very revealing exercise! First of all, it was not very difficult to get the keys to the door and inside - even adding in an extra bit of time to their total to account for the impossible-to-reproduce X-factor of genuine fright - and second of all, little happenstances gave Elliott better ideas for the story. See how each time some of the receipts fell out? Well, in the circumstance, one wouldn't think twice about that - just receipts. But say - something they had found in Lucy's inside coat pocket is what prompted this - one receipt was for a new prescription at such and such pharmacy, adorned with medication name, various personals, insurance carrier name, primary care provider name, any number of little ways a pursuer could set up devious, long-planned-out traps! Lucy blinks at her smoke hitting the doorknob where her hand is again and she does not want to go inside. What had the story been called? It had been published someplace. Or it had won some bartlekind of prize - maybe not published, but earned money or an in with some person of merit. Lucy lets go of her door. She takes the stub of her smoke and smushes it to the knob as though her key, twisting it and twisting it, trying to make it screw-shaped, trying to make it hump itself down in like some cockroach that would find itself pinned and unable to reverse out of the vice-grip.

A car in the opposite lane flashes lights and gives a little cough of a horn honk as Lucy passes. Yes, Lucy - your headlights aren't on. And less than a minute later, Lucy passes a waiting police car, thing tightened into place, ready to spring out and fill quota with late night tipsies. What luck that the other driver had warned her! She instinctively slows her driving now and squirms where she sits, suddenly her shirt not seeming to fit right, like it goes over her shoulders wrong and so does not cover her whole lower-back - car fabric feels like it's right against her skin though in reality her shirt is fine and, even if not, her skin would be touching her coat fabric, not the bare seat. Would Lucy ever think to warn somebody about a waiting cop? She doesn't think so. And also isn't sure how that person did that light flashing thing. They had not turned their lights off and on, off and on, instead had managed to wink them brighter, normal, brighter. She doesn't want to try now - no - but wants to remember to once she parks someplace. And had the driver been warning her about the cop? Or just reminding her, cop or no, that she needed to be driving more conscientiously? Again: would Lucy ever flash lights or honk horn at another driver to alert them to their mistake? No. No, she wouldn't. She can distinctly recall seeing drivers without headlights, thinking to herself 'That's gonna get them in trouble or kill somebody or something' but no action taken to alter their state was made. The closest Lucy has come? She sometimes has picked up something someone dropped, handed it back to them. But even there - only sometimes. Other times, she has watched someone drop something she figured was even important to them and had just noted the event, moved on. And why isn't the radio on!? Rectified. And this road, that road, this road, that road. She says 'Yee-haw' randomly then starts driving slower and taking turns that add time to the journey. Lucy has had cars flash lights at her before - she goes so far as to assert that she would never be allowed to drive far without her lights on without someone alerting her to it. Anything. People seem drawn into her business, fascinated the way one might be to overhear native speakers of a language one is only just learning - move in closer, strain the ear, is that what they said? is that? is that? But Lucy, for herself, she takes all pains not to get involved in the life of anyone she sees - would feel terrible about it, on top! Flash her lights at someone? No way! They'd just be annoyed even if they realized she'd been a help! This is why Lucy hates it when traffic has built up and between her and the car in front of her there is the mouth of an intersection. Is she required to stay on the other side - even if there is a traffic-light that is going to change? - because she never does. But everyone else - she has noted this - they all do. 'They all do' she hisses. 'Everyone but me.'

Lucy parks out on the street, not feeling she got in close enough to the curb. Little matter, as the car is chugging away still and she is either going to drive away home or pull in to her actual destination. The mothballed orange of the streetlights - this neighborhood has a tone to it of a photo found in the bottom of a shoebox in a closet, someone unfamiliar but standing-next-to-you and smiling. The moisture in the air is a powdering of matte, everything she sees having the false depth of a photograph's flat. Why did Lucy come out here? She smokes and plays the part of not-belonging so well - she is certain she will be accosted by a dog walker, that some neighborhood-watcher is scuttling in the oily dark of out-in-the-grass-where-she-can't-see, binoculars and notepad, taking her plate numbers to report to whatever authority that is reportable to. Do you think the mother still lives here? Over there? Are you even sure that is the exact court to turn at? Well, of course Lucy is sure! This was her home. It was. It was her home. But why did she come here, tonight, if she hasn't come here before? What gears are turning, what clock-cog is finally being grabbed by another to produce some every-once-in-awhile phenomena to the face? Lucy Jinx is so mechanical - there must just be some simple, physically describable prompt to this decision. At the same time: why is she stopped on the street, then? Why not go park in your old spot, as was intended? But that's so silly! Why is Lucy stalling? Is that really a question!? Precisely because she is so much a mechanism - parking on the street is just what a Lucy with no will of her own would do! Are we to believe that being contemplative, nervy, that being a timorous little pity-me-pity-me is some indication of free will? 'Am I going to park in my space or am I going to leave?' Lucy has asked that right into the air, right into a new cigarette. She is as much in suspense as anyone - because the fact is that being so automatic does not require her mind to know a thing. She's a carnival target, conveyor-belt-duck or mannequin-head-in-clown-wig-and-glasses. She just watches herself from a point of remove and gives commentary. 'Prove me wrong' she says. 'Go over.' Go over? How does that prove you wrong? 'Drive away, then!' Drive away? How does that prove you wrong? What drew you here? 'Who cares' she says. Jesus Christ, she is tired of wanting to figure herself out. No answer means anything. If knowing why you did what you did - why you do what you do, why you'll do what you'll do - could reserve anything once it has been done there would be a point in asking, in knowing. Otherwise? Lucy knows she is comfortable, sitting and smoking and waiting. No more questions, no more answers that once obtained merely reveal that an answer is less than a question. Am I going over there? 'Yes. Yes.' Did I choose to? 'Who fucking cares.' And that's not a question. Statement: Who fucking cares.

*Coffinous.* Lucy remembers the word. Those windows. How often she parked just here, looking at them. *Coffinous.* She had called the windows, the house-front that. Had there been a swell of congratulations through her at the invention of the word? Had it even gone into a poem? *Coffinous. Coffinous?* Had she ever written it down? Maybe in a notebook, the moment it had occurred to her? That was in the days before her recorder. Which here she clicks on and says '*Coffinous. Coffinous. C. Off. In. Ous. Kun. Hoff. Hin. Us. Cough. In. Us. Coffinous.*' The brick all looks just the same - but why wouldn't it? The doused windows look douse-windowed. But why wouldn't they? And this is where you lived, Lucy - remember that? 'Obviously I remember that' she says after a pause, then silence, then aware of the churning of the microcassette on record. Clicks the thing off and - she could not make it up, she could not - in just that same instant the kitchen window lights up. Now, how could that be? And why? That was like the button did that! Stopped the tape and upped the light! A choreography! This whole night a player-piano and everything leading to it a pause before the tune being struck. The blinds are up. She can see the fridge. She can see the counter. She can see things stuck to the fridge. Is the mother about to step in to frame? Is that where this film is going? Lucy feels a flurry of gnats in her stomach and herself tingle in exactly one tremor of arousal before her skin goes wet-sand and her breath flexes, widening her throat with the strain of it. No. No. No. That isn't the mother. A woman, yes. Decidedly younger than the mother. Or maybe not. Younger, yes - but not decidedly. Thin, but the glow of kitchen around her Rubenesque - sweatpants and a tank-top, hair in a dishevel of recently asleep or else trying to be. Who is that supposed to be? Pouring a drink from the faucet and eating a slice of bread. Who is this? Lucy's whole chest feels like a drip down her nostril-back and she is gripping the steering wheel, uncertain why she is staring, terrified that after another bite the woman will drift out for frame, the light go off, stage struck, nothing to do but sit and watch the empty theatre. But the woman doesn't go anywhere. And she is talking. To who? To who!? Turns her back to get something from the cabinet on tip-toe - glimpse of tattoo which must cover that entire back, cloak it utterly - and lowers down, turning back, mid-laughter. 'Who are you supposed to be?' Lucy says. Do you want to leave the car, Lucy? Maybe if you went to the window you could see who else is there. Angle your look, you might see who it is - they could be right there at the kitchen table. It must be the mother - look! The same break in the blinds of the other window! Look! It must be - because if there were new tenants, wouldn't those blinds have been replaced? The woman is wearing slippers, ballerinas her leg, bent up enough she can scratch her left thigh with the heel of the right slipper - precise, muscular motion, exactly where the itch is it soothes. The mouth talks and talks and talks, diaspora of soundless open and closes, laughs - another another another. Goddamn it! Lucy wants to leave but she won't. You mean she can't - you mean you can't, right Lucy? But she means she won't. And who the fuck is that woman supposed to be? Here's what Lucy says. She says 'Who are you supposed to be? Are you supposed to be me, now?'


'REMEMBER, MY LUCY, IT ALWAYS will take more people to build a pyramid than to be buried in one.' So says Milos, rash-pink eyed and daintily lifting two French-fries at once, mawing them whole. They two are the only two in this diner - *The Moremont West* - and the three people on staff are paying them little mind now that the food has been served. Lucy - poking her thawed-rather-than-cooked tasting burger patty - gives a glance to the staff, far end of the dining floor, all in one booth, two of them rolling silverware in to napkins, one of them animatedly relating whatever it is he is reading off the screen of his gadget. Here, another burst of laughter-applause from the lot, the sound muted by travel and lost in the midst of the music from public-address speakers, overloaded tones of, currently *And no one's getting fat except Mama Cass*. 'You think about Pyramids too much, Milos.' 'That's impossible - I could think until Now becomes Then and it would never be enough! Pyramids are the perfection of what we do. As people. We enslave. We paint. We entomb. And that they are plop in the middle of a desert' - Milos does a gesture of kissing his fingers and blowing the affection skyward - 'is so keen an understanding of our state, what more could one ask?' 'I don't like pyramids. I've told you. Triangular things bug me.' Milos, though still having plenty of his own, takes some of Lucy's fries, explaining he likes the long ones that are soggy at a pinch in the middle. 'I don't know about this burger, my friend' Lucy sighs 'but I doubt our illustrious staff could be trusted to redo it with much sense of duty were I to ask.' 'Your first mistake was asking someone to make a hamburger at two-in-the-morning. Your second mistake was paying money for them to do it.' But Lucy hasn't paid for it, yet. Could she ditch the bill? Look again at that motely lot over there - what would they care? Other than, of course, that vicious line of 'Where's my tip?' But isn't Lucy - or anyone - to extrapolate from their entire disassociation from customer-service over there that they consider any tip not to be? What do you care, Lucy? Run away and let them grumble! It's not like you'd have eaten the food. 'Milos, we're going to dine-and-dash.' He nods, eating more of her fries. 'So be prepared.' 'We'll need a plan.' 'I don't think that requires much of a plan, merely the will to sink so low. Which, as we both know, we have in spades.' 'Are you really not going to eat that burger?' 'Do you want it?' 'Are you really not going to eat it?' 'Do you want it?' Lucy agains, little brat antagonism. 'Are you really not going to eat it?' 'Do you want it?' Milos harumphs and leans back, declaring he is going to spoil Lucy's plan by - first - paying for the food and - then - letting the air out of her car tires so she cannot escape. 'Shouldn't you' - she yawns, goes Gahr! - 'shouldn't you let the air out of my tires first?' Milos answers by taking her burger and having a mouthful, putting it back to her plate. 'It's fine! It's delicious, actually. Eat!' Lucy crosses her arms and tells him he will never understand her. Lifts the top bun, looks at the patty, the cheese, replaces the bun and then takes one of Milos' fries.

'So: what is going on?' Milos wants to know. And Lucy is not ready to tell, though likely it's why she asked him here. Or maybe she asked him here because she knew he would show up. Maybe she asked him here not to talk about anything actual, but in case something popped and she needed to, without offering context, rage and demagogue about tonight, her life, this, that - just Gatling-gun out some frustration to an ear interested in nothing but listening, agreeing, furthering, indulging. You don't want to answer, Lucy? Isn't Milos a friend? Look at him: lacquered in his unwashed face and clothes he must have thrown on whilst blinking irritably in the pitch-dark, cozy and stable as a prop cigar. Isn't he a friend - nothing to sense or mistrust in his questioning? Tell him. 'I don't know what's going on' Lucy says. She says she thinks she has finally squeezed through a passageway, erupted from the pinhole aperture of a hole that was cavernous on the other side when she started and that now she simply is run down, her body with too much space to exist. 'You're nothing if not complex' Milos calmly assesses, Lucy warmed by the fact that this is all he says, does not call her out on the rambling nothingness of her less-than-half-attempted explanation. When Lucy doesn't so much as say 'Hmn' for a full minute though, Milos sniffles to indicate she is either to go on or he will have to begin making oblique, leading statements with an air suggesting he is not actually interrogating her. 'My problem is this, Milos: I will never be a significant female character because I would never work a Sex-Chat line in a complex and symbolically empowering way. I'd just do it on account of my being downtrod and a slut, you know?' 'That's a hard thing, Lucy - it's like a riddle from *The Bible*.' 'It is like a riddle from *The Bible*! That's the best explanation for me - you've hit it on the nose, man.' Milos finishes his coffee, looks disdainfully into the empty cup, gives a gander around, abandons hope, and says 'The bloke who wrote the *Book of Revelations*, he didn't make good on that title, did he? I don't turn to my Holy books for irony, I turn to them for family planning and advice on what I ought render to Caesar and what I oughtn't.' 'I'm the same way' Lucy soberly exhales. Talk to him, Lucy! He'll play your games for decades, but you can also talk to him. 'Milos?' Good - now tell him something when he says, as he now is 'Yes?' 'Where do you think it went wrong?' 'What?' 'For me - where?' He pauses, gauging, and she likes how he does. 'You just want me to guess?' She does. But the way he's looking, he won't answer the question. He rubs his eyes and offers offhand 'Something tonight, something happened - and you think it all comes down to that, right?' 'Right' she admits, which is surprising. 'But I want you to guess what it was, really.' So Milos takes the pose of a proposition-gambler, then the pose of a guy in a sitcom trying to look cool, then the pose of a boss about to offer his secretary a raise but only because he is flirting and both wants her to know it and not know. 'Lucy' he says 'it went wrong the moment you pretended you weren't sure you were in love with who you were sure you were. How many times that's happened by now, knowing you, I'm at a loss to guesstimate.' Lucy. Lucy? Lucy! How long have you been staring over there, silent? 'You're either not right at all or exactly.' 'Same as anything, eh?' Milos smiles.

Drift goes the conversation to other things. Each one delved into with enthusiasm and as though the discussion will be hours long even if it only winds up clocking five minutes. They can talk, Lucy and Milos, with the specific excitement a third-grader has about doing a book-report or a geography project before they actually have to start the work. So: later on Lucy is meeting with the broad and Milos' congratulations are too many pages to bind so he loose-leafs them in the air and they rain down like binoculared confetti, a total trick-photography of Hurrah! seeming to bury the two under freefalling rapture. No! Milos doesn't want to be in the *Acknowledgements* - either a full *Dedication* or nothing! 'What sort of lout puts an *Acknowledgements* section in a poetry book!?' he what-in-God's-names. 'A poet owes nothing to anyone but neglect!' Milos is right. And Lucy concedes she is playing it just right by teasing it out with this so-called Bianca in text-form until her memory is jogged. Milos well understands her noiac mind: how she, for awhile, had been thinking that the caller is no one named Bianca, at all, and is only carrying on the charade because of how bizarre, to them, it is that Lucy is agreeing she knows someone named Bianca, talking as though nothing is amiss. 'Because: why would I do that - from their perspective - right? They would be compelled to continue the gag just to see how nuts I am!' 'But by now, they would have dropped it' Milos says. 'Yes. Exactly.' Because Lucy, one time, admitted to not knowing what Bianca was talking about - even as Bianca seemed perplexed, borderline put-off, and fed detail after detail to get Lucy on the right track - and kept up the line to the bitter end. Surely Bianca would have changed her tune, pulled off the mask, then, were she disguised! Milos says Lucy should admit to Bianca she has no idea who she is, next time - but Lucy admits to finding it all rather comfortable. 'It's nice not knowing who I'm talking to or about but believing they know me. Hard to explain.' But Milos says he gets it and Lucy knows he does. He's jealous, actually. Jealous of Lucy's stature - someone so luminous her existence inspires complete strangers to seek her out in some ecstasy of false-connection. 'What if it is some odd condition this woman Bianca has?' They talk about the movie *Birth*, awhile - then this drifts in to each recapping to each other episodes of *The Twilight Zone* and old radio programs like *X Minus One* and *Suspense*, episodes they both know about, have described to each other before, enjoy hearing each other's renderings of even more than the programs, actual. Then they talk about O.Henry, but neither can remember what the guy's deal in *Gift of the Magi* was. 'She cut off her hair for something, right?' 'Right.' But what - they jointly wonder - but what? Lucy has been thinking about getting rid of her hair and

Milos says if she does, so will he. 'You'd look terrible with no hair' she cautions, but he coos that she would look edible. That's the fourth time Milos tries to drink something from his empty cup. Tilting it all the way back. Lucy tells him something sweet and he tells her '*Syringe* rhymes with *Orange* if you say them the way people say them.' '*You drip just like an orange / then I suck you up my syringe* - and so on' Lucy says, yawning, wanting more coffee, too.

They make curlicues of the parking lot, ignoring the shivering, though Milos does, a few times, mention his ear hurts. This has to be most worthless strip-mall Lucy has ever seen - and a two-story ordeal, too! They go up the stairs at the center of the lower stretch - expecting to be accosted by junkies at the pivot - just so Lucy can tug on the door of the Rare Coin store. 'Rare coins' she scoffs, tugging - tugging tugging - the door. And Milos gets a cigarette lit and tsk-tsks, then wondering aloud why the shops on the top level of this place just get generic signage - *Rare Coins, Travel, Insurance, Lamps, Hunan* - while the stores on the bottom level get proper brand name signs. The Rare Coins shop, they see, is called *Douglass Armory*. The Travel agency is called *Equestrian Tours and Destinations LLC.* They see nothing particular about the Insurance, but the Lamps is actually called *St. Lucia* which makes Lucy happy. 'This Hunan place really is just called *Hunan*, though' points out Milos. And the mounted menu, slightly crooked and ordinary-taped to the inside of the left-side door does, indeed, say '"*Hunan*"'. 'What do double-quotation-marks mean?' Milos shrugs his Dunno, murmurs a sound, cigarette tight in closed lips, hands down to his pockets as he goes to toes to stave off a shiver. 'These kinds of places' Lucy says - now they are going back down the stairs - 'I always wanted to get a job in one when I was a teenager. But they were never hiring. And now that I have age on me I want a job in one even more! It seems like the employees hired would work there forever yet always feel they are certain to be fired next week. How many lamps can that place sell? How long can a worker's will to show up and do whatever they do last?' Milos says he always wanted to work at a mattress store, but when he once had an interview at one and they asked him questions particularly having to do with mattresses it freaked him out. 'It was out of my league - they weren't fucking around! Mattresses ain't like hocking paint, man - you gotta know your shit.' Milos definitely states that there is no worse job that could exist than the job of mixing and selling house paint. And he holds that position firmly until Lucy points out there are stores that sell tires and stores that sell sheet-music. 'Oh dear Lord, you're right! Sheet music. What could feel more like doing nothing?' 'I once needed a music book and when the person in the store not only told me they had it but took me right over to where it was I felt a swell of pity such as I pitied myself even more!' 'But could sheet music be worse than selling flutes? There is a job that simply couldn't be rewarding, spiritually!' Milos, playing the part of a husband-and-father: 'Did you get Patricia her flute, today?' Lucy, playing the part of wife-and-mother: 'Oh yes. We went to the shop and she picked out a flute. The fellow there was so helpful.' Milos: 'He didn't commit suicide there and then, did he?' Lucy: 'No, no. Not there and then. He just answered all of our questions, really sold us on the idea that there were specific flute-centric considerations to be made.'

Here is Lucy Jinx's logic: she doesn't mention Ariel or the mother, she doesn't mention Layla. Thus? Those must be the people she actually is in love with. She does mention Elliott and she does mention Samantha, amongst other assorted-names she plucks from history-recent and history-quite-aged. Therefore? Those must be the people she does not actually love. They are sitting interior Milos' car - the heater so hot it seems perturbed by them, like they have done it offense and it is being mean-spirited - and they are sharing the energy-drink Lucy found on the passenger seat, something it seems Milos forgot that he had. On the radio: *R. Kelly - Remix to Ignition*. Then on the radio: *Smashmouth - Walking on the Sun*. Then on the radio: *Semi-Sonic - Closing Time*. Lucy could sing along to all of those, but keeps that in her head. Actually - look - Lucy does mention the mother - but in an underhanded way, deceitful in the admission, calling her 'This one woman, Natalie, I knew like ten years ago.' Milos has not before heard the name *Natalie* so Lucy feels free in toying with time, space, and detail. Anyway, she says she bumped into Natalie's kid, who is now all but grown. She exaggerates Flynn's age to eighteen and tells about how she once flirted with a kid not much older than that, but claims she did so 'in her forties' - all stories, it seems, being unconsciously shifted out-of-time and post her departure, post her collision with the cat, Lucy Jinx. But before she can go into her thoughts on Natalie, she veers into thoughts on the cat. A part of her life is bookended, she says, by her nearly killing it and it dying, it being buried right where she nearly killed it. She doesn't know why she is saying this - this is new material, it might not even be accurate or stay in the final draft, she thinks, but does not shut off - but cannot help keeping on, Milos lighting a smoke and handing it to her, she taking it and lacing it into her speech-patterns without any conscious beat of recalibration. 'I think the time between those two nights on that road has nothing to do with me. It was like being told that the next four years of my life, while real, are de facto imaginary. And so now I am back. Like no time has passed.' She stops. Milos is trying to get at a subtext. 'But' he slowly tentatives 'Elliott is on one side of the line, Samantha on the other?' 'No. No' Lucy says. No. She is not going to lie that much. Not to Milos. She tells him, truthfully, that is not it. Lies just enough to say 'Not that, but something. Something about Before and After. And the length of time in-between. How a second can contain much more, you know? Like those years were just a very up-close, very detailed duration of the one second between car-crash and burial, between Lucy Jinx being living and Lucy Jinx being dead.' Shit. Nope - he's on to you, Lucy, Milos has got wind that there is evasiveness. Milos doesn't pry, just goes quiet until the next song starts, turns it up, tells her 'Maybe your problem is you approach love too meticulously. It's really mostly something not to look at, too much. Like wallpaper. Like the legs of a piano. Like the color of the numbers on a clock face.' 'Yeah' Lucy says. 'Yeah, you're right. I notice too much to appreciate things like clocks.'

They drive together, separate cars, as far as the gargantuan *Gas SenStation!!* standing silently while Milos fills his car and then going in to poke around at snacks and get new smokes. Lucy has to use the toilet and Milos says he does too, but they find the Men's Room is closed. Lucy gentlemans the Ladies' Room door open and head tilts him in. Red faced, he enters, then nervous voiced, needing-something-to-say prattles how weird it is that he has never been in a ladies' toilet in all his years on Earth. Lucy quickly makes a round of the room, pleased it is empty, and asks him 'Well, what do you think?' Milos gushes, at a loss, pointing to the tile, the sinks, the mirrors, the stalls. 'This is a Women's Restroom! Why the Hell do you all get it so posh? You know what a Men's Room is?' - Lucy makes a disgusted face, vigorous No of her head shaking 'Why would I know that?' lips in a militant snarl - 'it's nothing but a wicker-basket full of shredded newspaper and a few tins of breath-mints you aren't sure were provided by the establishment or just someone left them there on the floor! Oh Lucy' - he spins - 'why do you need all this?' 'Do you have any idea how complicated it is for a woman to piss? Our goods are like one of those backpacks with buttons on everything instead of zippers - we have to refold like origami and the dotted-lines are always hard to see! You don't even get it - you know, like when you buy a cheap toy thinking *What's the difference?* and the arms fall off right away? That's it - pissing - every damn time - and those arms just won't snap back on! Shit, Milos, going to the bathroom as a chick is like trying to win an argument with a misprinted copy of the *Qur'an*!' Well, strike Milos down - he never knew! He thought - here he is leaning over a toilet bowl and giving an impressed nod - it was fun and games, all day long - but if it's as Lucy says, then they deserve all the luxury the world affords them. Milos refuses to leave the room until she is done - because if he is spotted exiting alone it'll be a life of water-torture for him. 'That's good torture!' Lucy says, talking loud to project through stall door and across to where Milos is bobbing up-and-down by the sink. 'It is good torture' he agrees. 'Everyone laughed when the guy first suggested it, but boy do they feel dumb about that, now!' Flush. Wash hands. Now: in the pastry aisle. Lucy bumps her hips to his and tells him he can stop being so nervous. 'They are looking at us because they think we fucked in there, man - just act like we fucked, they won't bother us.' So Milos hang-dogs his head and droops his lip, pack-mules and obediently drags behind Lucy, taking the items she arbitrarily picks up just for the sake of the game. 'I'll be in the car' she says, leaving Milos at the counter to pay, slapping his ass, and shouting at him 'And don't forget the cigarettes - my brand, not your horse-shits, okay?' She can just picture Milos continuing his part. His mouth, his eyes. A tremble to his hand as he pays. The game is done by the time he exits, though. Lucy is just at her car, waiting. Milos strolls over, gives her her bag, and says he wants a call tomorrow, after her thing.

And so: further on than five-thirty, no sign of sunrise, and the usually-too-much-traffic at all of the traffic-lights, turning out from all of the side roads. Cars driving with windows too fogged for drivers to see, some vehicles armadilloed in only limply chipped-at crustings of ice, exhaust pipes nervous-ticking in huge gasps or flits in all directions at once, smoke grey and black, blue and almost-perfectly-white. She wants to gripe about traffic but finds it too lovely, right now. The illusion that this coughing leakage from don't-wanna-go commuter-cars is what slowly raises the temperature, gas for the spark of the pilot-light of the sun to grumble-flame the day through, then blip dead, night just attention wandering and fires untended. Mixing images, mixing poetics, tired, tired, Lucy knows what she means. And love? *Love?* She needs love like she needs a seventeenth verse of *Yankee Doodle Dandy*! She needs it like she needs the knowledge that the song has sixteen verses! Why is this all even a consideration to Lucy? This woman or that, this person, that, this house, that - isn't she surpassed of such things? Lucy is meant to be a Poet, is meant to be in a realm outside - and unneeding - of humanity. She should write about Heavens, about life-transcending-all! But Lucy, you never write about that. You never even try to drift out of the gravity of your bodily sensations, the things your own eyes have witnessed. You stifled creativity in favor of observation. You relate the avenues of abortive thoughts and times you looked out windows rather than summoning orchestras of considerations beyond this flesh, beyond this skull, beyond the breaths that string together like garments waiting on racks to be bought. Love love love! Lucy hates it all. She might as well love Milos - and she does and why can't she!? Does she imagine him pining away for her right now, flummoxing his heart about how 'I merely have to be her friend and not her everything'? He comes when she calls and she loves him far less than someone who doesn't. The distance - it's needed. She can bear his mind being on everything-on-Earth-except-her until the moment she remembers he exists - and even if he didn't come when called, she'd name it No-big-deal. But these others? But these others, these others? But these others, these others, these others? Others. Others others others. Then this anger passes and she just wants to be under a blanket on her sofa. She just wants to wake up, having left the heater on too high, throat concrete sharp, neck in pain from stiff sofa-arm bending it like a tube-rolled dollar-bill pressed in half. Then this want for abnegation passes and she listens to the sound of her turn-signal and easy, mirthful joy settles on her. Someone chose that sound. No, Lucy, it was not just the sound that happened when the device was assembled and switched on - that specific sound was aimed for and attained. Someone wanted the sound of *Turning* to be just so. And different people wanted different sounds, studied engineering, assembly, the desire for this Click-Click-Click versus that Klt-Klt-Klt versus that Tsh-Tsh-Tsh versus that Ki-Cluk-Ci-Cluk-Ki-Cluk-Ci-Cluk versus that echoing, rubbery Tlouk-Tlouk-Tlouk were strained over and tested and focus-grouped and consensus-formed and auteurs-fighting-consensus and all of the history of the human heart into the thing! The wonders that are important, the songs of ages ago? All of it! Important! 'We're human as the sound of a click' Lucy says. Wants to write it down. Wants to remember it the last five minutes of the drive and slather it in the color of her pen on her paper. *We're human as the sound of a click.*

Why is this old woman only wearing shorts and slippers, a baggy t-shirt, to take out her trash? The dame must be seventy-eight, eighty-years-old! Her veins grow out of her leg-backs like fresh bulbs of potato eyes, her neck hangs with the appearance of a candle that melted onto a melted candle. And what is she doing, now? Wriggling fingers and bent over posture, kissy face - and certainly kissy sounds, kissy voice - trying to coax an animal - over to her? Lucy has the motor off and already feels the temperature dropping so that she pre-shivers, skin tense for coming complaint. That woman must be senile. Or has lost so much sensation that temperature makes no superficial difference. No - senile. The temperature thing wouldn't explain the outfit. The mingling of lack of health-mindedness and sense of modesty suggests faculties out-of-control! If Lucy asks this woman later about going out to the trash this morning, would she even remember she'd done so? Is that woman's life such that, with no intervention, she could do nothing but ferry trash from her house to the dumpster, her house to the dumpster, her house to the dumpster, until her body keels over from starvation and atrophy? Oh come on now! The woman is going to her hands and knees, arse upticked, pavement - and around the dumpster who knows what else, glass bits, flecks of spilt every-old-thing - digging into her knee and shin flesh, her palms and elbows and forearms. Is she trying to reach under to get her hands on a hiss-spitting stray? Is she shushing it as though it just needs to be calmed, ignoring its low-motor growl sound, ears retracted, body coiled to sharp out its claws in slices that could tear the woman's feeble old skin like used tissue would be by pressing fingers blowing snot into in one time too many? Okay. Okay. Now Lucy sees the woman give it up, just stay there on her knees and dust her hands, wipe them on the dumpster side - classy, smart, definitely round the bend, this biddy! - then on her thighs - Lucy imagines those browned with blue bruises, something like uneaten bananas left out and the circles of new mold on bread. Lucy honks. She honks long. The woman doesn't react - now has her hands to her hips and is rolling her head around, clucking her shoulders out while she does, rotating hips like hula-hooping. Lucy honks again - long - only stopping when she sees a window light - there - come on. This old woman, Lucy - this is one of those things you see you are supposed to do something about other than looking at. Okay? She sighs. Honks again. Again. Someone at that window, now - Lucy sinks where she sits, feeling eyes all over. Who told this wretch to live so long? Who is Lucy to say what she is seeing is anything more to call *sad* than a Katydid wilting? Wanting to live is wanting moments like this - wanting to experience life on your knees at a dumpster, stray cat just refusing to come! Why isn't it beautiful, Lucy? Why isn't it the same as a garden that once grew and now dies for the winter? Look at the woman, now - see? She is standing up and pulling the elastic of her shorts, looking down into the fabric gap at her crotch. Still. Still. There she is - letting go of the waistband, it snapping back to her. And now she is sneezing into her hand and wiping her hand on her lower back. It's just like watching a tree leak syrup. It's just like watching a cloudless sky cloud or a cloudful sky blank.

Just in case you were wondering, Lucy: here is Why. You're following this old woman, remembering spooky stories from childhood, yes? Songs from grade-school? Ghastly illustrations in folklore anthologies? You're wondering: Tonight, why did I go out? You watched Simon and said 'Goodnight' to Evan and then you went out - you just didn't want to be home. Oh - at the door you had thought about Elliott and then had driven out to where you had lived, back-in-time. Why? You remember thinking *Why?* don't you? And you had seen that other woman in the mother's house and had got yourself in your tizzy and summoned Milos and dinered and parking-lotted - remember? Remember wondering *Why?* Why not just have gone to bed? Why not? Then you had parked - just now - and noticed that woman. Oh - oh! - you remember that, too? Well: if you had parked at any other time, if you had gone to sleep, not gone out - if any other pattern had happened, any other choice, any other events - you would not have been there just then, just here, just now, following that woman from the dumpster up stairs and down corridor. Would you? No. And why? Why are you following her? Because you saw her. And just got to wondering. And because you saw her, you decided to follow her. Why? To see if she was okay - had you thought that? To make sure she got home safe, didn't die of exposure while making Alzheimer-loops of the apartment's outsides? All good theories.

But: here is Why. Did you think it was going to be left a quaint thing to ponder? A rhetorical? No, no Lucy Jinx. The night was to see her and that's why you saw her: *Cause* ventured you out into that cold, pointless, made-up-as-you-went night. Champion, you loitered until the appointed time and now here is your answer. Lucy stands, yes, actually horrified. And feeling porridge-brained for not seeing this one coming. You've stood in this same spot, one story above, watching down at a door, just there. Even now Lucy stands, having watched, and her mind stalls with suspense and questions, as though keeping words away, photo uncaptioned will keep the final stroke from the clock. In through that different-grey door - just below yours - the old woman had gone, nattering to herself and barking something over the balcony, there, before pushing the door - which hadn't even been closed all the way, let alone locked! - opening it and closing it with herself, behind. There's the woman's - That Woman, Claire's - replacement. Her ghost, might as well be, yeah? That's what you find when you go looking for someone who used to be someplace. You find out what's there now! This old woman: saggy shorts and poison-sumac veined! Or that young woman: ballet-poised and tattoo-backed! The ghost of Claire. The ghost of you. You want to know what you're thinking, Lucy Jinx? Well: you're thinking those words. And Lucy feels her foot cramped as though being screwed to the floor, final spasm of 'Move now or this is just where you stay!!!' Lucy walks. She walks toward the different-grey door and knows, if she tried it, it wouldn't be locked. She knows the old-woman-thing in there would welcome her, serve her food, would believe she was anyone she said she was, any relation. She knows if she said her name it would say it back, chipper voice, so-glad-to-see-her again.

And now your door, Lucy. Plain grey. Same as always. What happens if you go through it? Lucy feels cored, but the door feels safe. It feels she is allowed to go inside, a boot wet and heavy from foot, permitted to stain the wood of the floor, thump the wall when tossed with a yawn. Maybe she should not go in, though. An act of resistance - stay out. You're already dressed. Stay out until it is time to meet the broad for lunch. Except maybe that is the idea - twice-shy you of returning home so that this device wends on and on and on, grinding you down, meeting the broad with your mind dulled and brain wrinkled like cold fingertips. Go in, get some rest. You do things backward, now: nightmare awake, safe-and-sound sleeping. If you wake up, you'll be powerful and can convince yourself - warming in fine scented soap under tooth-sharp streams of shower - that it had been a dream, this - let the sensations of memory fog like the mirror glass, shake yourself up with restful lungs to a day nothing like that bleak night. Live long enough and memory is a dreamscape. Live in the same location your memories took place in and it only serves to reason the dream becomes physical and confused for waking life, reality - you smear up the two, you know? So: go in? 'Go in' Lucy says. Bloody fucking Hell, though, why did she have to touch the knob without taking her key out only to find the door unlocked!? Like the timer in a kids' game had buzz-rattled, all the pieces flotsam around and she recoils, laughter trapped by a hiccough of startle in her throat, becoming a wrong swallow, becoming a cough. It is plausible you would not have thought to have locked your door. You had just been going to watch Simon. This is Lucy's thinking. Under those circumstances, you might have left with a different jaunt and less caution than when actually venturing out someplace. Maybe. Maybe. Go in? 'Yes' she says. Because hadn't you unlocked the door when you left Simon? When you had left Evan's apartment you had been coming back here and something had changed your mind. Yes, yes. You had unlocked the door. See, Lucy? You had been thinking about something and unlocked the door. About Elliott. Which kind of doesn't bode well - no - but nevermind that, for now. You had thought about that game of pretending you were chased, getting key from pocket - remember? 'I remember' she says. And Lucy had unlocked the door, thinking that - right? That's why it is unlocked. No other reason. She takes the knob, turns it, presses forward. Her rooms glare at her and at the same time barely flutter - something between the struggling lid of a sleeping dog and the up-rippling lip of one baring teeth. Lucy enters and closes the door behind her. The new trick is: What to do now? Out of her coat, weakling shouldered and not bothering to let it anything but slosh to her feet. Did she lock the door behind her? Should she check or just trust that she did? She checks. It's locked. Which, of course, she doesn't remember doing. For all it amounts to, Lucy might as well have apparitioned herself in here. For all it matters, Lucy is an eye ticking side-to-side, deranged into thinking its walking through what it is only thinking about.

LEANNE IS NOT A GOOD name for the broad - 'or for anyone' thinks Lucy Jinx 'it's kind of a placeholder name' - but in some ways it fits the broad's appearance. Squat, like half-of-the-bottom-half of one person, half-of-the-top-half of another with a head that seems more a neck and a dome shaped out of carefully pinched up clay from the solid mold of torso, meticulous and in just such a manner as to make it impossible to tell it is all one piece unless standing extremely in-close. Glasses have a thickness more like they are meant to keep drafts out than to aid with vision. Shirt the sort a television detective wears when the weather does not call for long-sleeves, fabric stoic and refusing to wrinkle so finding odd, asymmetrical places to bend in deep shadows, marker-stroke thick. Leanne's forearm is tattooed, but Lucy cannot make out what it is - so there is a sense of an illustration half-colored-in then abandoned to her, someone careful with the pencil and trace-over ink, but regretting they decided against black-and-white after the first side-to-side of light, tentative crayon. Not straight-to-business - and Lucy is being well-behaved, because this is real business, this woman is legitimate, accomplished, has the power to make others so, not just some three-penny-simp who has spare time and some dilettante interest in 'Art' heavy quotation marks, but would settle for Friends triple-capital F but said with a mimbly sad sotto voce - Leanne takes a good while to select a drink, asking questions of the server - questions more specific than Lucy has ever heard, regarding amounts of ice and olives and stuff - and then wants to move tables to get out of a draft Lucy does not notice but doesn't say she doesn't notice. How is this going to go? Where is your gregarious bent, Lucy Jinx, where is your three-mile-a-minute freeform? What does this broad think of you - Lucy thinks, only now, only too late, of how long ago and how briefly it truly was that they met - based on what you had behaved like, previous? What had you behaved like, previous? No, no - don't beat yourself up! You aren't going mute, you are volleying and handling the casual patter and the broad seems to take delight - or to, at least, not find it not-to-be-expected - that you are in a waiting-state while she gets settled. Every moment though, a crisp of impatience, a shrimp of self-sabotaging 'Why not just scuttle the mission and Woman-overboard! now?' Lucy, you should have the upper hand - Leanne has invited you and the e-mails were solicitous! Lucy, you have every right to feel like a veterinarian impatient for a dog to stop making circles and just lay down so you can stick it - annoyed with the animal's owner for being there, insisting you not handle the mongrel with force, not lay it where it ought to lay without regard to its autonomy. Leanne apologizes for the fourth time, lays her napkin on her lap, and undoes some of the buttons of that gorgeous leather carry-bag she has though does not yet take anything out. To Lucy Leanne says 'Thank you for seeing me - you're a bit of a recluse, it seems?' 'Haha' Lucy hahas - but figures she is now considered On and has to field the question - it was a question - with aplomb, comedy, hoping to hit a note something-like-honest.

First test - obviously a test - Leanne goes: 'Unorthodox, but I start every discussion with a Potential like you in this way - I call you Potentials and it's best you don't find offense in that since I hold all the cards and am fathomless in my lack-of-concern for your comfort - I want you to tell me something you have been thinking about, of late, that won't remind me of my own life. Can you do that?' Well, Lucy says, she can certainly endeavor to try. For the record, this is Lucy Jinx's response to that salvo: 'I was thinking, just a few days ago and then again today - a few days ago because I realized not only hadn't I vacuumed my apartment but I wasn't going to, and today when I noted I had stuck to that resolution and the older thought process jogged - that outer-space gets on my nerves. Think of it this way, I thought: if our planet was the size of, say, a taste-bud in a goat's mouth - I assume they have taste-buds - we would not care about space exploration. Space would still be there, but our thoughts would not trend toward it, even suggests its existence. All of our aesthetic would differ, but only superficially: Religions would be the identical, sense of scientific experimentation, history would have gone quite the same route, but our renditions of the sky would be of whatever the upper part of a goat's palate would look like from the microbial distance of the specific lay of a taste-bud. We'd know of other taste-buds, but not know if they are populated. Our exploration - with the same vigor as that concerning Mars and Neptune or wherever - would be up a nostril passage, down the gullet, taking samples like moon-rocks of nasal-drip or membrane. We'd discover veins and cram our Mythologies into them, we'd discover capillaries larger than our capillaries - planet-sized capillaries, you know? Elements of us in large! And we'd spend decades exploring the first tooth we landed on and do films about what lurks in the caves beneath a gum line! Electromagnetism would be the equivalent of us marking the durations of the goat - we don't know it's a goat, of course - chewing cud or a can or of else of wafts clambering up from bowels we have not yet even begun to theorize! We'd maybe - maybe - with advanced theoretical math come up with the idea of the underside-of-a-follicle, but the notion of it having to do with Hair - really, how preposterous! - would only be explained in mathematical scrawl meaning nothing to nearly one-hundred-percent of us. On and on, on and on - human history and heart and progress without the faintest notion of atmosphere or starlight or high-tide or nor'easters. Except: I'm saying our planet-on-the-taste-bud would have those, itself - don't misunderstand. The taste-bud is us - our planet - as like now. What I mean is: there would exist no sense that those same things are to be found outside of the goat we are part of - and in scale perfectly comparable to on our bud, except larger than we could ever compute! We'd have clouds, but the notion that there were clouds in the sky that the goat is looking at - that big! - it would never occur to us! A cloud in the sky of the sky! Poppycock! Even with numbers being endless we wouldn't get there. I was thinking: all of that would change nothing - it would change nothing about my life - so what, ever, does change anything? Change is just a notion someone thought up that every discovery since has kind of shown to be not-so-clever - even doltish - you know?'

Leanne is eating some sort of pasta-and-crusted-meat which looks exquisite. Lucy? Lucy played it safe and got pasta-with-chicken. Now Leanne has her notebook and some other files out - all of this looks weather beaten - but Lucy

- perhaps defense mechanism - just tries to come up with a reasonable way to ask for a bite of that crusted-meat. 'You have odd publishing credits' Leanne abrupts and Lucy, not missing a blink, agrees, shrugging, saying 'I have not given much thought to the serious pursuit of poetry.' Why is this? 'I stubbornly stuck to the notion that I would upend the system by becoming an underground sensation, find my immortality in a Biopic wherein I am portrayed to the level of award-garnering by a woman who would go on to be known as the Actress of Her Generation. I would be her big break, don't you see? A relative-unknown playing a complete-unknown! And thus would my work be unearthed and thumb-tacked to dormitory walls and used to impress people. That was my trajectory, I thought. My obscurity would weather away - very surely if very molasses - over decades, until quoting me was not even expected but cliché!' Is Leanne finding this charming? Lucy - why aren't you answering straight? Fun fact: Lucy Jinx is desperate for some kind of deal - here, now, today, today! - something she can go around and tell people and cockcrow and chest-jut over, because she knows if this lunch ends vaguely the dream is over and done, over and done. Fun fact: Lucy Jinx is a coward, incapable of helping herself. Fun fact: Lucy Jinx is Lucy Jinx and likely will always be but sees this broad as her last Maybe Not. Leanne says - still, though, is she charmed? - 'I am proposing to throw a bit of a wrench in that - though stardom and Tinsel-town is not something I can promise.' Lucy just chuckles - eloquence be damned, she downright snorts and repeats the words 'Tinsel-town.' 'Yes' Leanne chuckles too, seeming caught off guard by Lucy's - or maybe not so much - 'but' - Leanne wipes her nose with her wrist, says 'Excuse me' Lucy nodding like 'No worries' - 'but I can promise you a run for being in-the-thick.' 'What does that mean?' Good, Lucy! Direct! Fuck Leanne and her vagaries! 'It means I want to publish your work and am positioned to do so - though not necessarily the manuscript you submitted.' Blink, blink. 'Or rather - some of that, with additional pieces and other work. A new volume.' Blink, blink. '*New volume?*' Leanne explains the desire would be to - something in line with Lucy's daydreams - unearth Lucy as a poet who has been continually and vigorously at work outside of the normal scope and to present a cross-section of her work culled from throughout her entire timeline. 'A compendium of sorts.' Lucy is certain something somewhere is licking its lips - that Lucy will make a fine, fat slaughter. Or: this probably isn't happening - this, right here, right now. 'I'd be amenable to that' Lucy lawyers. Where is her fine garble-tongue, her towering babble? *Amenable* did you say, Lucy? Too late now, you said it! But anyway, it doesn't seem to strike Leanne as odd. 'Good. I'm thrilled.' Had Leanne reckoned on there being a fight? A resistance? Is she disappointed there wasn't? Why is Leanne just eating now, returning to her food like she suddenly remembered she needs nourishment, chewing each new piece before her previous swallow has really flushed down? What just happened, Lucy? What did you say? What did you do?

Sitting to the toilet, Lucy catches herself up to the scene. Last night. Last night. She had slept, after. Woke in a panic, remember? Woke thinking this meeting had been missed. One of those nightmares that was a nightmare of what she had just seen - gone through - that night, some hiccoughing remix of it, her subconscious noodling in details of other stuff that must have been on her mind. Remember? Lucy had pinballed through a rough shower, corkscrewed her apartment around drinking coffee and then started to drive without letting her windshield unfog - dangerous to everyone, unable to get herself calm. 'Now I'm here' she says, pants down, knees spread with panties trampolined between them, no need to be in a toilet and so acting seven-year-old nonchalant with herself. Lucy's breathing seems normal. That conversation? Leanne? Lucy, you acquitted yourself admirably! Nothing signed yet, but that will be what's in those folders. And you know it. Lucy: right before your coming into the toilet here, Leanne - the broad - had been listing off poems you had self-published in fucking chapbooks and printed out only eleven copies of! Are you here? Is this real? While it still seems to you there is a deep-end to go off, you might have gone off a shallower one - one deep in its own right, nevertheless. Can you trace last night to here? Because take that facts - you printed eleven, count them, eleven of that chapbook! That poem. About Dorene. Why would the broad, Leanne, have that, have heard of it? Can you prove this is what is going on now - before you flush, having not shat, not pissed, before you get up to leave, to return - can you prove Leanne and the restaurant will still be out there and that you were paying attention and not dunderheading yourself, now nervously breaking down and assembling a not-quite-right-jigsaw out of glass that will never be a window again? Last night. Old woman. Claire. Unlocked door. Apartment. Passed out. Panic. Shower. Dressing. Car - dangerous drive. Actually got here, early. At the bar. Broad came in. Sat down. Chit-chat. Drinks - questions. New table. Goat tongue. Poems. Compendium. Leanne said 'I especially, personally, want to include *her timbre was in itself restless*'. 'Excuse me, please' - and Lucy to the Ladies' Room. 'Yes' Lucy says. 'And you have to leave, now. This is longer than you should be in here.' Leave before you have to make an excuse about how long you were gone. You don't want to say the 'pasta disagreed with me' or some lie about a medication you are on for a viral infection. 'Don't fuck yourself, Jinx' Lucy says, remembering a time Dorene had said 'Don't fuck yourself, Jinx' at the same time Lucy had said 'Don't fuck yourself' without her surname and they had laughed because it had meant that Lucy needed to not talk until Dorene said her name again. Oh they had rolled, they had died from the laugh of it! And Lucy now is arranging herself back in

her pants right, staying quiet, as though still waiting for Dorene to say 'Lucy.'
But goddamnit, right? Goddamnit all! Dorene isn't supposed to be on Lucy's
mind, today! Where had Leanne got that chapbook? And why did it need to be
mentioned, so particularly? What kind of poking around and unearthing had
been done? What the fuck is Leanne playing at? Why isn't this straightforward?
Why is it both everything Lucy has ever wanted and the thing that is going to
make her furiously scramble away, swinging her arms as though everywhere
foes, everywhere foes!?

   Countdown to it? From Ten? Ten nine eight - no? Better from Five? Five - no?
Better from Three? Three two one - from Ten, then? Ten nine eight seven - or
just go with the one from Three? Then: Zero. Leanne, it seems - this is the
reveal, unbidden - had been impressed with Lucy's work since first they'd met,
but had set it aside for some time - hence the period of lapse, of waiting for
contact that, for Lucy, had become certainty contact would not come, the
period wherein 'Anything from the board?' had become a wry leitmotif in
calling Mathilde about e-mail updates. What had brought Lucy back to mind,
for Leanne? Well, it seems one of Leanne's colleagues - 'Not quite a friend'
Leanne admits, though they get on famously when they wind up around each
other - is the Agent of the novelist Amelia Pine. Aside: do we need to mention
to you, Lucy, that your feet don't feel there anymore? And Leanne happened to
be chatting to Amelia's Agent, Pauline, about another artist Leanne is working
with - an artist, Leanne says with a kind of noncomittal gesture, who is 'Fine,
but not my cuppa, it turns out' - whom Leanne thought Pauline might be
interested in. Leanne had coyly joked that she would gladly trade the new talent
for a crack at Amelia's rumored first work of theatre, and in reply Pauline had
laughed, said 'Nice try' or some vulgar equivalent, then offhand had said
something about how Amelia's protégé was the one to look out for as far as
being a voice in the Stage scene. 'Elliott Pine - who it seems you might know'
Leanne says, like a swimmer turning head sideways for breath before cutting on
through the pool length. And attached to that aside was Pauline's mention that
Elliott Pine had just been the cover-feature of *Interview Burlesque*. 'No' Lucy says
when asked, Lucy had not been aware. 'Well' Leanne beams 'you should make
yourself aware. Because who' - 'oh who, oh who' Leanne is now in primly-
amused-kindergarten-teacher-voice saying - 'should be mentioned at some
length in the interview but a poet called *Lucy Jinx*?' Nothing's nothing, Lucy does
a mock-up of mock-astonishment and leans over, whispering a cutting-in 'Hey
- my name is *Lucy Jinx*!' which Leanne thinks is hilarious and touches Lucy's hand
about and says 'You certainly are. And the same Lucy Jinx whose book was still
on my desk!' - Leanne makes a halting gesture, sighs - 'well, I won't lie, had
been moved to my floor-pile. But that still is My Desk!' - Lucy nodding, nodding

Sure sure, Sure sure - 'And who I had' - Leanne points, emphasizing this-bit-is-true - 'been meaning to look into, again. And now: the adventures of a real, honest to goodness mole-woman!' *Mole woman?* Lucy doesn't ask, but is not sure it means what it obviously seems to mean - or rather, wonders if it is actually a specific term-of-art in the Publishing World, not just something Leanne likes to say. Leanne continues 'So I took some time to sniff out your old burrows, to see if you were as you had been painted and - quite frankly - my excitement grew in exponents. A regular Professor Seagull you are, Lucy Jinx - except not a liar, right?' Who is *Professor Seagull*? Pathetically, Lucy pictures the movie version of *Clue* and not even *Professor Plum* - she thinks about Tim Curry doing the frenetic reveal in the film's final scenes. But Lucy nods 'No. I'm no liar, not me.' 'And I have to contact you through a mirror e-mail set-up - and you show up for lunch and talk about goat tongues! Imagine my delight.' 'I am imagining it' Lucy says. 'I am.' And if this were a movie and the movie was set in the Old West and Lucy a woman using seduction to get at the villain she would - right now, under the table - be pulling her single-shot snub from her stocking, trying to cock it in silence.

Has Lucy ever worked with an editor before? And Leanne hopes the question is not indelicate. Answering the second part first, game-show-wise, Lucy does not find the question at all indelicate and - 'No, no' - Lucy has never worked with an editor before. 'But then, I have never had occasion.' 'I suppose' Leanne was driving at 'the question is whether it is something that would queer a deal for you.' 'It would not queer a deal, nope.' Would Leanne be editing? No, not Leanne. She has a very trusted, very dear friend in mind for that task - this is a trap, Lucy! oh fuck, you don't want to hear whatever name this broad is about to hock up! - and with whom, in fact, in a presumptuous way, she had already shared some of Lucy's work - 'It's out there for public consumption, after all' Leanne adds - and has this editor's notes for Lucy to review to see how Lucy rapports with this editor's style. Lucy will likely not meet the editor, in person - 'Why?' Lucy doesn't ask, but if she did it would be knife to the you'd-better-answerer's throat - at least not for some time. 'It's one of the reasons I thought of him - quite the recluse and quite the l'art pour l'art minded gentleman.' Lucy, you must have had a look on your face! 'No, I don't mind working with a man, at all. I am enthusiastically curious as to what this all even means, in fact - and hope I'm not a wet-blanket to it all!' Lucy shrugs, says she 'Just writes' and shrugs again. Well, Leanne wants to be clear that she is not looking to rework, reboot, diamond-up anything Lucy's written out-and-out, but - yes - there is a sense of 'Let's do this overview, this volume, rather as though this editor's voice had been in the mix since the get-go. Which, I know, might not be palatable' - why is Leanne so anxious, now? And why is this editor just being referred to a *This* or *The Editor?* - 'but considering where we are, I hope it doesn't go too anti-your-bent.' 'My bent can hardly be antied' Lucy says 'whatever bent, indeed, I may have.' *May I ask who this editor is?* Lucy still doesn't ask. Lucy stares at the folder which contains her work - edited, her work, touched, her work, readied for presentation if she feels it is still hers enough. That other folder must contain something to sign. That will be the indicator that the con is on, the fix in, everyone wearing a wire - if Lucy does not need to sign anything today, she will tear down her shanty-town and hobo it out of this orbit, toot suite. Leanne has been talking and Lucy listening, replying - now Leanne is on about some anecdote concerning her own youthful desire to write and her early rejection from somebody famous who later she went on to represent. 'I never told him he'd ruined me. Because, in the end, I blame no one but myself. I was too easily made to bow, Lucy' Leanne candors, out of the clear blue sky 'and something in your words strikes me that you would not even know a head could do that, let alone a knee. Sometimes, the value of standing can be forgotten when you see how sore backs can become. Collapse seems terrifying, laying down just comfy - you know?' Lucy finds emotion in her throat and knows something Leanne does not, something she keeps tented in her silence and hopes she doesn't betray by her nod and however her lips wound up shaped when they tightened and shifted as she swallowed.

So: is that what you want, Lucy? That is your name. Letter *L* - the corner of a map. Letter *U* - an unwound treble clef. Letter *C* - your drinking cup overturned, on purpose, on accident. Letter *Y* both two earlier forked roads coming to the same cul-du-sac. Letter *J* - leg stiff, foot in mid-spasming curl for relief. Letter *I* - a throat straight down into the descent down a well. Letter *N* - a fall and a struggle to stand and a fall, if this way, standing and falling and standing, if that. Letter *X* - the nightmarish, impossible tangle of a serene endless loop. Your signature, Lucy. That is Lucy Jinx's signature. Or rather: it is her printed name on the line beneath the scrawl - that letterless, shapeless, affectless scratch of her identity. The world is real and your name is signed to it, accepting. Of course, lawyers could undo this - this is not anything binding and no monies save a paltry advance, them-to-you, for a mere consideration is promised - but the paper bears official names - Leanne's and some other person who pre-signed, and, in typed-letters, the identity of the publishing house, address, various still-to-be-undersigned parties. Leanne's pen is still in Lucy's hand. The moment passes more like the purchase of a firecracker and it into a generic plastic bag than the rat-tat-tat sparks irritating neighbors at all hours, the whining out-of-tune ascent and then soft clay Boom! of bright yellow, bright green, ordinary white. So what Lucy cannot do is go convincing herself that all of this was mere fiddle-faddle, idle-talk to get her worked up then shrunk past how small she remembered herself being. And it is something she has always wanted - however much rhetoric she may rhetoric or how many times she will deride those who have also achieved it and who she feels more worthy than. The entire space of her insides has doubled, the entire scope of her outside one-thousand-folded. While Leanne is putting some papers away - Lucy has signed a copy of this document, however it was explained to her, for herself, as well, even less fanfare to the repeat of her name in double - Lucy drinks the last of the coffee she has and tells herself she feels waves of alcohol humiding up from her belly to the inside of her forehead, that she is not hearing properly. Dining forks sound the rubber of door-stoppers. That cough over there? The shift of someone flipping a telephone directory, lumps-at-a-time, to get nearer their destination letter. The waiter seems too up close and soundtracked from a broken mic on the opposite wall. Should you be doing this, Lucy? Have you thought about any of this? Two hours ago - three? more? - you weren't even going to come here! And a month ago you didn't know this was a Here you could go! Lucy folds up her paper, nervous she shouldn't - perhaps it had delicacy, like a too-softed, too-creased dollar bill, now wouldn't be accepted by a vending-machine or a coin-changer. Ask for a folder? Only touch it with napkins? Where's it gonna go? Onto Lucy's desk? Onto Lucy's fridge? She pretend sips from her empty coffee and smiles when Leanne addresses her and the smile must have seemed appropriate because Leanne seems to be laughing like it was apt, turned again to her business and silently - not really, but to Lucy - sneezing four times in-a-row, Lucy, increasingly laughter-based, saying 'Bless you' each time except for the final where she says 'Good God, what've you got? The plague?'

'I don't smoke, no, but please - I'd rather like if you do' Leanne says. Lucy already slapping her fresh pack into her palm. This is out in front of the restaurant. The day has gone the overcast the bright of a fever four days strong and the bed no longer restful. 'You look like you'd smoke' Lucy ventures, bully-girl. Leanne used to smoke - oh yes, quite thorough she had been with it, too - but gave it up in support of a friend. 'But please - smoke' she insists, Lucy doing so with maybe a slight suggestion she had been thinking about not, though she had not been thinking about not. 'If you would like - there is no requirement and I've no intention of impinging on however it is you live - but if you would like, there is a reading I would very much like you to attend.' 'If you'd like, I'm there' Lucy unthinkings, blowing smoke pretty much straight down Leanne, not apologizing because Leanne seems to pay it no mind. 'If you give me that bag of yours, in fact, I'll go wherever you say - where on Earth did you get such an item?' It was a prop in some film Lucy has never heard of, apparently, and un-part-with-able - the word pronounced with just those exact breaks, the last *Able* said *Ibble* - even in exchange for the spiked heads of all Leanne's dearest foes! Lucy will have to watch the movie. Leanne recommends it, but says 'Don't expect the bag to play a part of much prominence.' 'I expect the bag to be the central character! Or at least the McGuffin! Which, by the way, should be spelt with two Gs and no C.' No argument from Leanne, Leanne insists, and claims to think it's time for a shake-up in general concerning how things are spelt. Going just with Orwell's Newspeak, Leanne feels it a shame it got a bad reputation just because that world around it was so dystopian. 'Dystopias aren't de facto full of bad ideas' Lucy seconds. 'Look at our history - pretty much everything we're proud of came out of a dystopia!' The details of the reading are exchanged and Lucy has a feeling that - seeing as she recognized two of the seven names mentioned - she should be even more nervous than she suddenly is. Those other five names? Likely important folks. Lucy is relieved Leanne will put it all in an e-mail and send it to 'your cohort'. 'Or I could put it in the regular post, if you'd like. Do you corresponded by letter, still?' 'I don't correspond' Lucy sighs 'I've never corresponded with anything.' Tipping nose to acknowledge the joke with only the brevity such a joke warrants, Leanne anecdotes how she still carries on ink-and-pen correspondence with a few people, but the intersecting of her old age and the ease of technology will sort that out, sooner or later. 'Or you'll die - and either way, no more letters, eh?' Boisterous goes Leanne's laughter and apparently Lucy reminds her of her daughter. 'She's an asshole, too' Leanne means 'and a rather talented poet in her own right' though a shade too traditional for Leanne's heart to burst with pride over. 'You have children?' 'No. I have too much time for that' Lucy says 'never was able to get too busy to have them, you dig?' 'I know just what you mean. Well, it is a peculiar thing - to know you are proud but kind of itch to be prouder. I'm sorry if I'm admitting too much.' 'There's never too much to admit.' Leanne nods. 'That's not what I said, but I agree.' 'What did you say?' 'I said I might be admitting too much, not that there ever is a bereft of things to reveal.'

Fifth time Lucy has puffed cheeks and gone phooougghhhhhh since she sat to her car. This time she manages to keep the exhale going for thirty whole seconds! Doesn't breathe in after. As empty as no more canvas on the roll. Her windshield is little-kid-freckled now with the early fall of rain, shadows cast in grey-bordering-on-white. One of the compact discs on the passenger seat has caught a glint of light in such a way as to cause an incision of over-bright on the ceiling. Lucy thinks it is the color of an infant's first scream if the child is born with something the matter with it. Dramatic that, Lucy - what's going on? But Lucy doesn't mean this in a grim way - it is just too peculiar a color of light to do anything but find a harsh description for. Light shouldn't be colored, anyway. The world shouldn't be colored. Seeing color should be revealed by medical science to be entirely a defect. That is Lucy's new wish! The genome is mapped and the 'Hello, what's this!' discovery is that if *X Y* or *Z* was recoded so that the defect of perceiving color was undone - well! - cancer would be impossible, as would be Asperger's, albinism, malaria, and the human lifespan would, baseline, increase half-a-decade! Initially, Lucy was going to say the thing it would be reveal is that 'We would be immortal!' but that is too obvious an idea to argue out of or argue into. She adds - in the fabulist bent - that if the defect is corrected in one person, it trickles down into everyone - she doesn't clever a description of why this would be - just so it cannot be an optional element of life. Nope. We would all have to choose - together. Let our precious colors die and take our chances, or monochrome the world and help out a bunch of us but not all of us. Phoooouuuggggghhhhhhh. The car battery is on, so there is radio - but the engine is not on, so there's no heat. Would that sentence work: *The car battery is on, there is radio, but the engine is not on, there's no heat?* 'I think so' Lucy's biographer chimes in. 'What happens next?' Lucy asks her. But the biographer says 'That's not how biographies work. I write it after it's done. Ask me in a week and I can tell you. Pretend I'm not available until then if that keeps things romantic - that I only got to your e-mail, last week, after you know anyway, but it'll seem like I would've been able to've told you.' 'How do biographies work?' 'Well' the biographer says 'I only write it down afterward, like I said.' 'But when I die, you die.' 'So you won't have a biography for that part.' Phooouuugggghhhhh. 'I should write your biography' Lucy bickers, an aside the biographer either doesn't hear or finds it more entertaining to act as though she did not hear. And Lucy is looking at her unfolded publishing agreement. And Lucy is thinking about the rain that is harder, now. And Lucy is listening to the song on the radio, one she doesn't know but is digging. And Lucy's biographer has scampered. No. There she is. Outside. Loitering and small-talking with someone else Lucy imagines for her. 'This could be important' she bitters 'me in the car, here. You could be missing the very key moment!' Phoouuugggghhhhh.

Ideas for book covers go through her mind. Scenarios of having an affair with the woman who translates the volume into French. A little domestic scene of her in her old age being visited by - she supposes someone else's - grandkids and they having no idea they will grow up to study *Mammy Jinx* - why not? why not call herself that? she doesn't have time to work up much gumption for an original nickname, this is just a brief idle while she is driving and driving, soon to be cut off by other thoughts - one of them guaranteed to grow up to hate her work and to dunce-wittedly mock it to her high-school comrades on the strength that 'Well, she was practically my grandparent - I know her pretty well, I know what I'm saying is legit.' More thoughts of book covers. They had better give her input on that! Then an idea of one of those editions that have replicas of the originals included - or at least one of those editions where the main page is the Official Text, the other page a printed copy of what the Early-text read like so that folks could ponder and turn-your-head-and-cough the minutest little change to their heart's content. See? See? Lucy doesn't want to get ahead of herself! But, even modestly, she'll be interviewed on the radio once - this Agent? this Press? Oh at least once they'll get her on the radio! Not fancy radio though, probably. Or maybe! Why not! Fancy-pants Public-Radio - Lucy will be able to drive and hear how well or how shabbily they edited her into the segment-lengths. She will, in her life - at least once, now - be in front of an auditorium - be modest, Lucy - half-full of admirers! Or at least half of the half-full crowd will be her admirers, the other half of the half-full just interested parties who are there for nonspecific reasons. A few will have been dragged along by whoever it is they are hoping to get in the pants of. Lucy will make some joshing remarks about that very thing in her opening statements! Laughter. Blushes. Some people tensing for this reason, some people for that. What will you call the book, Lucy? 'If they give me a choice?' she says, deciding to make the same loop she just made once more, still some time before she has to be where she said she'd next be. Yes, if they give you a choice. Oh she doesn't care! She wants to get high! She wants to fuck! She wants to be in a city on another continent! She wants to have done all of this twenty years ago! She will never be called a wunderkind - though she was a wunderkind. 'I wus a wunder kund' she says. 'I wud a wunderful wund er kund. I wunder wud Lucy a wunderful wunderkund.' And so on and so on. She turns in to this drive-thru, but changes her mind once she's trapped in the line with no way to maneuver out. The speaker outside of her closed window repeatedly asks for her. Why isn't there a way to peel out of this fucking line!? 'Sorry' she says to the kid at the window 'I didn't mean to pull in.' 'You weren't the roast beef and the cinnamon sticks?' 'I wasn't, no.' The kid looks stricken, like Order has fumbled the world! 'What I'm saying is: I didn't order anything - I just got trapped in the line.' Nope. The kid does not follow. Flash of panic when he notices Lucy is pulling ahead because the car in front of her has made room. And soon: Lucy back on the road. A moon that briefly imagined it would still be the moon if it wasn't in orbit.


LUCY, POLITE DISTANCE, HEALTHY DISTANCE, sips at her cigarette and watches Ariel spread peanut-butter on a cracker, sandwich it with a different variety of cracker - the bottom one circular and orange-toned, the top a crisp square, white - then mouth the entire thing in and get chewing. This is underneath the wood pillared plaster-roof of the picnic area of the city park.

The drizzle is thicking into a not unsubstantial rain and Kayliegh is out that way, galoshing around, umbrella used as some kind of musket, it seems. 'Isn't it cold and raining - as far as letting a kid come to the park to play, I mean?' asks Lucy. Ariel swallows, already almost done with her next cracker, and says she's never thought about it before. 'I'm fairly certain it puts you into the not-murder-but-manslaughter category of being a fit parent.' Ariel parries that 'Doesn't Lucy remember being a kid and thinking the rain and the cold were terrific and even preferable places to be in?' 'I suppose' supposes Lucy, watching Kayleigh go to knees, take aim with purple umbrella-gun, simulate the kickback of the shot she takes, squinting as though watching to see if she hit some target, far off. 'Who do you suppose she is shooting at?' Lucy thinks, yawns, then asks. 'She's been reading some book in school. My guess? She's shooting at whomever the people in that book are shooting at. I don't know the content of this book, mind you, so that might be distressing if delved in to. All I know is one day she had no idea what a gun even was, next day anything she happened to pick up would be pretended into a firearm. And she's always shooting to kill.' Lucy says she can see that, steps out the remains of her cigarette and joins Ariel where Ariel is sat. Kayleigh, all of a sudden, stops what she is doing long enough to look over at Lucy and Ariel, raise her arm high in a soggy noddle waggle-wave, clearly saying something though whatever it is is lost in the muffling wall of distance and rain. Lucy gives a wave back, Ariel shooting a thumbs-up and yelling 'Very cool, man!' as she spreads another cracker with peanut-butter. Triple-decker sandwich this time, orange-white-orange. Or does that make it a double-decker? *Triple* Lucy thinks. 'Why isn't there school today?' Ariel shrugs in a dismissive way, holier-than-thouing Lucy into obedient silence. So Lucy focuses on how much her wrist is hurting. A possible old-person malady? Every time it rains? No - the pain has been there, off-and-on, all week. On, now. Because she had been gripping the steering wheel of the car so tightly, teeth grinding as the weather got more officially bad. Ariel wants to know if Lucy thinks a pizza place would deliver a pizza to them, here. 'I don't see why not.' But they can't come up with which pizza place is nearby and, besides, then they'd have to look up the number and who wants to do things like that? 'I'll drive and pick something up' Lucy imagines herself saying but doesn't say. Ariel hastily rolls the packaging back around the remaining crackers in each sleeve, returning the both to the duffle-bag full of whatever-it's-full-of. 'I need to stop eating crackers. I think they're making me pregnant.' Lucy chuckles, looks at the skin of Ariel's' legs through the hole in the denim, leans in and pecks a kiss to Ariel's heavy-coated shoulder.

'I always knew you'd get something like that!' Ariel enthuses when Lucy explains about the deal she signed. 'So I'm not going to leap up-and-down or anything, but I am going to start being more sniveling and solicitous - because my assumption is that this means you are loaded, now.' Lucy does explain she gets an advance, even if nothing goes through. That was on what she'd signed. A retainer sort of thing. 'Then, on principle, you should do all you can to make the deal not stick! That would mean you'd gotten money for nothing, man! That's hard to do.' 'True.' It's a good point. The longer it goes on, the less the deal will seem to be worth from a purely financial standpoint. This is the most successful Lucy will ever be - the pinnacle of her fiscal achievements as an artist. If she gets the book out, by then - even if she gets four times this retainer - it will seem a paltry little honorarium was all she'd got for decades of poetical struggle. 'How much is it per word, though?' Lucy consoles aloud. 'Poets have that over normal writers. Not many words in some poems, so the rate will be pretty premium if I just only look at it through that prism.' Kayleigh is not in sight, but Ariel insists the kid is 'Just drowning in the water that is sure to have treacherously collected at the base of those rock piles, over there. Or that's my best guess.' Then Ariel snaps back to the subject of the book. She forces Lucy to dish dish dish, to braggart and get big-headed, queasy on her own self-given praise. They debate the idea of having an editor, but conclude 'What could it hurt, since everyone who reads something is just editing it, anyway?' True. No one reads what is written, how it was written, in a sensible order or manner or concentrates on just the right part for long enough or whatever. In fact, the more a reader tries to convince their nerdy-little-self that they are painstakingly only considering the words of the poet - as the poet wrote them, how the poet must have intended - the more the reader is not, is revealing themself to be a simp! Reading carelessly is the best way - and editing is just the slow-motion equivalent of that. 'Too much attention' Lucy summarizes 'is as careless and offhand as a glance or two and assuming you got the idea of the parts you didn't read from the parts that you did.' Yep. Growl growl to the notion of some purist thinking there was anything pure! A poet shouldn't even know if their work is edited because they should not have had time enough to memorize it with certainty before never looking at it again, moving on! Editors should be the most worthless, workless things under Heaven! An editor should be able to do nothing-at-all, an artist none-the-wiser. An editor who edits should be seen as a real hump by his or her peers, a genuine what-a-sucker. There's Kayleigh, anyway. Still alive, for the moment. Summiting the middle-heighted one of the three piles, lifting, with struggle, what, from the distance of Lucy, seems to be a cinder block and hoisting it overboard the side of the hill, it disappearing due to the trick perspective of lowest-hill seeming on a tilted rise from Lucy's vantage.

Kayleigh's first complaint is how cold it is and her second is that she can't use the slide because it's wet. 'I thought you were smarter than this' Lucy remarks and Kayleigh says 'I never told you to think that. Even the tunnels are full of water! How can that be!? They're supposed to be tunnels!' 'Ah, her first existential crisis' Ariel says, linking her fingers in Lucy's hand as Kayleigh goes over there and kicks the undersides of swings again and again, water inelegantly jolted into spattering handfuls of every-direction drops. Lucy is holding the now open umbrella that had ten minutes earlier been Kayleigh's gun. Ariel is putting her hand in Lucy's back pocket, having a tough time of it, grumbling 'What's the matter with your body - I'm trying to be able to grab your ass, here!' Lucy has a picture in her mind of some kind of animal stuck in the cut of her pocket, this transitioning to an image of a chicken-egg hatching on the rotating glass of a microwave tray. Ariel removes her hand, dusts them both, heavy breathing 'Screw it. Your ass is too big, Lucy. I didn't know that about you until now and so I gotta rethink a whole bunch of things. Nothing to worry about, I assure you, just cosmetic concerns. But you're kind of gross, now.' 'Or you mean I've been gross awhile and now it's dawned on you?' Ariel hisses and steps away from Lucy as though a scene in a film where a traitor is revealed. 'You mean you've been like this, awhile? Oh God. It's like discovering you have hyperdontia or something. You don't have hyperdontia, do you?' Ariel actually seems to be regarding Lucy's - now, for the joke, on-purposedly closed shut, lips pinching down colorless - mouth and inches closer, poking Lucy cheeks with fake-quivering index-finger then squeezing with thumb-tip and third finger-tip both cheeks at once. 'Open your mouth - I feel like you actually are tricking me, now.' Lucy opens wide. Ariel kisses her, goofy, rolling tongue the full scope of Lucy's hollow. 'You're missing a tooth!' Ariel declares. But Lucy is taken aback, scrunches features and says 'No, I'm not.' 'Open your mouth, again.' Lucy does. Ariel repeats her kiss-probe. 'You're missing a tooth, Lucy. Sorry to break it to you.' 'I'm not missing a tooth, Ariel. You just don't know how to kiss thoroughly.' Kayleigh charges over to ask if something she has found is slugs or just a bunch of wet leaves. Holding a grudge over it - Lucy can tell - with each step into the sploshy-grass and then pure mud and then sploshy-grass, Ariel follows her daughter and Lucy umbrellas them both as best she can - herself getting pelted unprotected. Ariel would have said something had Kayleigh seen the kissing, of course. This is what Lucy is thinking. Kayleigh had been distant and occupied during all that. Or Ariel wouldn't have done it, of course. Of course, Lucy. Right? Right. And - Jesus! - it is slugs! Ariel says 'No, it's not' but then kind of gags and backs away. In a divot of mulch, underneath a patch of several trees, there is a pustuling mound of slugs, over-and-under, in-and-out of the squeeze of each other. 'It looks like a brain a cat started to eat but then threw up' Kayleigh observes as Ariel insists they all walk away. Lucy flicks the back of Kayleigh's head, Kayleigh all teeth and then kid-face wrinkled from too much smile when Lucy say's 'God, you're the motherfucking best.'

Lucy had moved off - this back under the picnic area, Kayleigh eating some sort of make-shift lunch comprised of Ariel's leftovers - to smoke without feeling infectious, but Ariel comes over and leans to the same pillar, their shoulders touching a bit. 'I'm going to have to stop smoking if you don't waddle off, El - I couldn't stand being your go-to excuse for what's wrong with your second born.' Ariel does a speech about how much shit is in the air they are breathing - car exhaust and soot from boots and body odor and cooking chemicals and on and on and on - finishing by saying 'It's not like I'm giving birth to a butterfly, here. People start as people and stay that way.' 'I think this is to-the-side of what I'm saying' Lucy says with her next, still shy-girl, drag. 'My point being: whoever it is inside me better just get used to things. I'll be a good parent, but I can't go around doing shit about wrangling the air cleaner. I leave that to my elected officials, man.' 'That is why we elect them' Lucy concedes. Lucy should probably ask a direct question about something. About Leopold or something. Or else return to the subject of her book deal, which already seems real in that lusterless way real things are. 'You don't think Kayleigh saw us kissing, do you?' is what she settles on. And said right-in-front-with-it, not only not caring if it shows how she feels uneasy about the possibility, but showing she is uneasy about the possibility being the point. For a moment, Lucy sees a snarky - and likely quite witty, it's almost a shame she doesn't get to hear whatever it would have been - reply about to be proffered, but then Ariel softens, scratches her ear, and says she honestly doesn't think so, but will keep a better eye on. 'It's fine' Lucy says - cigarette nearly down enough to hear the skin pinching its heat - 'I just don't want to freak her out.' But Ariel tells Lucy not to say 'It's fine' because Ariel knows it must be weird and all the more since, as she here says 'What in Hell am I even doing?' Yes. Exactly. The radio-turned-up-way-way-way-to-loud of Lucy's next breath keeps her from saying anything, but yes - yes yes - exactly. What is Ariel even doing? Thrilled to know Ariel doesn't know, offended Ariel doesn't know, dizzy with joyous sick-to-her-stomach and not sure if things are going to turn Southbound, Lucy flicks away the dregs of her cigarette. 'I don't mean don't kiss me, though - that's not what I mean. It's not like you've even ever done it very much.' Kayleigh has a bit of a coughing fit and Lucy goes over to attended to her, having touched Ariel's side to keep her still when Ariel, at first, had started over. 'Are you choking?' Kayleigh says 'No' between rough sounding coughs. 'You just don't know how to eat, is that what it is?' 'I just' - cough cough - 'don't' - cough cough, cough cough - 'know how to' - cough - 'eat' - cough cough says Kayleigh. Lucy opens a new juice-box, dug out from the duffle, inserts the straw and holds the thing while Kayleigh sucks most of the contents, her one little hand massaging the teensiest circle on the skin of her little girl throat.

The kid all settled - Lucy knows it's silly to check, considering Kayleigh's age, but she does tug at the seatbelt connection - Lucy comes around and takes the driver's seat, giving Ariel the You-okay? face Ariel's bemoaning aura more than warrants. Then Lucy carefully backs out of her space - pointless, the only car in the lot - and slowly makes her way over the speed-humps. And during this, Ariel tells Kayleigh 'You need to tell Ms. Jinxy-poop how proud you are of her.' 'What am I proud of her for? Checking my seatbelt or something?' Ariel starts to turn, but decides not to - spends a moment adjusting the positioning of the mirror on the flapped down visor to see if she can get Kayleigh in sight, giving up on this, too - and just uses a general voice of announcement 'Because she is getting a book published. Of her beautiful poems! Don't you know anything? I thought I never stopped talking about Loose-goosey.' Kind of a comical under-her-breath Kayleigh says 'Well, you never do stop talking about her.' 'And I never mentioned the fact that she's publishing a whole book of poetry?' 'Congratulations' Kaleigh says, long sigh of it - con-graaaa-gew-laaaayyyy-tchins - but not because, Lucy feels, the sentiment isn't genuine, just on the strength that she was being prodded into speaking by her mom. 'Tell you mom to stop talking about me, okay?' 'Lucy says stop talking about her, mom.' 'Tell Lucy *Nobody asked you*. No? Fine. Tell her' - Ariel Ums and Uhs - 'tell her I only will if she gives you fifteen dollars.' Kayleigh leans in, as close as she can manage 'My mom says she'll stop talking about you if you pay me fifteen dollars.' Lucy says she will when they stop for lunch. 'Really?' 'Yep.' Triumphant at something she didn't even know she was attempting, Kayleigh gives the update to Ariel who does hammed-up theatrics of shocked-at-having-her-scheme-thwarted, then asks 'Where are we going for actual lunch? Are we just going home?' 'No' Kayleigh whines and 'No' Lucy curts - though for entirely different and many many reasons. 'Let's go someplace that she can run around, then - and we can just sit.' 'I was just running around for hours or whatever amount of time that was!' Ariel scoffs, clucking her tongue, breathing our harshly. 'Kayleigh, no your weren't. You need to stop lying about things. You know who lies about things? Orphans. In orphanages. For starters. Think who people might confuse you for!' 'You two are both weird.' 'We are' Ariel mumbles, eyes drifting like already two-thirds asleep. Silence for a moment. Then Lucy, realizing Ariel is down for some kind of count, goes normal tone and asks Kayleigh 'Where do you really want to go to eat?' Well, Kayleigh does want to go someplace she can run around - or at last play video games - but that doesn't mean her mother was right. 'Nothing means your mother is right. I've known her for longer than you've been alive - guess how many times she's ever been right?' 'Zero?' 'That's

830 / PABLO D'STAIR

exactly correct' Lucy says, turn signal going on 'Zero. Mathematically - statistically - even if she had been right one hundred times, all the times she's been wrong still amounts it to Zero.' And Kayleigh names the place to go for lunch. And when Kayleigh asks 'Can I use some quarters for games?' Lucy reminds her of the fifteen dollars.

The pizza is delivered by a teenager who scarcely makes eye-contact - not rudely avoiding doing so, rather in a manner suggesting he thinks that is how pizza should be served in a place like this, out of respect - in Kayleigh's absence, Lucy taking a slice and tearing a bit off immediately despite the burning this abuses her mouth with. 'Can I talk about Leo, for a minute?' Ariel says, stirring her ice around in her soda with the pink-and-green crazy-straw she chose. 'Of course' says Lucy, ridiculous over her second scalding bite, then attempting to swallow the irritant whole as quickly as possible - gasping and readying her soft drink - 'you can always talk about anything you want.' Drink down, Ariel doesn't really want to talk about it - that is Ariel's thing. 'Because - you know? - there's Kayleigh and all.' Lucy is resisting another bite - it's hard for her to stop eating once she starts, a plague of hers since forever - and Lucy is nodding. 'And there's the fact that he has no idea - I mean no fucking idea, Loose - about anything about us.' Relief, confusion, terror. Terror, confusion, relief. Confusion, relief, terror. Terror, relief, confusion. Again. Again. Mixed order, same order. All while Ariel goes on. Ariel tries to articulate this. This. This. Ariel does not get very far. 'All he knows is I left him and I don't want to be with him. And - is this crazy? I don't think it makes any sense - I don't want him to think it's because of you, even though it is. Not because he'll care why and not that I'll care that he knows why, particularly, except that *Why* is *You*. I just. Don't want him to.' The thing is, to Lucy, this - none of it, none of it - matters. If Ariel wants to keep things secret, Lucy will keep things secret. It is gossamer. It is nothingness' threadbare. Lucy's knees tighten, hurting her stomach around the over-hot food her intestines are flattening, acids working at - why does there have to be any talk like this? 'That's fine' she says, but it sounds incorrect, the placement of the words odd. 'So I think: hey, then why not just live with him. Because otherwise he'll know. Maybe I want him to think I'm back with Annette or Joseph or that I'm just alone - but no, no. It's just I don't want him to know about you. That it's because of you. And it doesn't make any sense.' 'It makes perfect sense' Lucy says, real specialized pronunciation, real why-can't-you-see-that tone when, truth being blunt, it makes no sense to her, either - the strain of panic-reasoning Ariel must be within the throes of is foreign-body to Lucy, inaccessible. 'What does Kayleigh think is going on?' Lucy asks. 'Kayleigh didn't see us' Ariel immediates, referencing the park, and to this Lucy overtops 'What I meant was: about you and Leopold.' 'Oh. Oh. Oh oh oh' goes Ariel, stalltacticing. 'She doesn't know we're broken up. Leo's swell and Kayleigh just thinks some stuff is different with job schedules. However it goes, we'll keep her in the dark until the cows are roosting, as they say.' Big sigh. Lucy mirror-reciprocates. 'You made my life really stupid and hard, Lucy Jinx - you made my life as frustrating as not having a fly swatter, man.'

Kayleigh wants to know what a *Cornhusker* is. 'Why?' 'Can you just tell me? 'A *cornhusker*' Lucy Hmns while Ariel passes Kayleigh the shaker of Parmesan Cheese and says 'Yeah, Lucy, we're asking you: what is it?' 'You know what corn is?' 'Yes' Kayleigh smacks the bottom of the shaker again, again, again. 'You know what a husk is?' Slap slap slap. 'You know corn has a husk?' 'No.' 'Well, it does. So now that you know that, can you figure it out?' Kayleigh nods, taking a bite of the adorned pizza slice. 'Then what's a *polecat*.' 'A cat that lives up - or upon - a pole.' 'Someone told me it was a skunk.' 'Does that make sense to you, Kayleigh?' Kayleigh is out of soda, so chews a piece of ice. 'I don't know.' 'Why call a skunk a *polecat*? What does it have to do with a skunk? You think the words *Pole* and *Cat* would be brought together simply to obliquely - in an almost absurd way - reference a skunk, rather than to just mean, easy-as-pie, *a cat who lives up a pole*?' Kayleigh chews more ice, giving Lucy a look of sincere scrutiny as though suddenly able to see the blood in motion behind the skin of her face. 'You've heard the expression' asks Lucy 'that *nature will always take the easiest route?*' 'No.' 'Well, let me be the one to tell you, then - and this is a time-honored thing, what I'm repeating here: *Nature always takes the easiest route*. Gravity. Tides. Whatever. Predator-and-prey. All really beginner ideas not needing much nuance to be executed. Words are just nature - always simple, direct, mean what they say. Especially in cases like *Polecat*. Imagine the word needed to survive a night outdoors in the winter - think it'd manage it, meaning *skunk*, that it'd last long?' What Kayleigh wants to know then is 'Do words die?' 'All the time!' 'How?' 'We kill them.' 'So if *Polecat* is around, it's alive, then.' Frankly no longer at all certain what they are talking about - even more not giving a damn - Lucy cautions 'Not of necessity. Say I killed that man - him, there - right?' Kayleigh looks over, Lucy snapping her to attention - 'Or any man' she adds 'it doesn't have to be him.' 'Okay.' 'His body wouldn't just disappear, right? It takes awhile to rot. Even if it's buried. And even then it's still there. *Polecat* doesn't mean *skunk*, though - is my main thesis here. I'll be goddamned if it does!' Ariel continues being preoccupied with her phone, ignoring Kayleigh's many glances toward her. 'So: consider your question answered.' Kayleigh eats. Lucy eats. Silence while Ariel types what must be two dozen messages in quick succession to someone, then Ariel - snapping to - takes another slice of the pizza and inquires how everything turned out. 'What?' 'About *polecats*. What do they do?' 'Was that dad?' Kayleigh asks and Ariel nods.

'He's gonna pick you up in like two hours.' 'Is he coming here?' 'No, no' Ariel gives a quick knee-touch to Lucy, under table - knee-side to knee-side, only, both hands on the tabletop. 'We're gonna meet him at his place after Lucy leaves.' Another knee-bump. Lucy bumps back, uncertain what is coded in these touches. 'And we have to remember to give him the medicine for your ear thing, okay?' 'Well, I won't remember' Kayleigh bickers, but cute-bickers 'you remember. Jesus, mom - I think sometimes you're the wrong page in a book, man.'

Again, Lucy is driving. Kayleigh has found a filth-ridden book on the car floor and is reading it, pure concentration and silence - Lucy knows the feeling, young girl, mouth drying, lips chapping, from that shallow, airless way breathing goes when a book is placed in front of it. Ariel is saying 'Lucy Jinx, I want you to keep in mind that Tragedy is just Comedy that isn't very funny, and Comedy is just really very poorly written Tragedy. That's it.' 'Thanks, Ari.' Then another pause. Lucy trying to make out in the rearview what book it is Kayleigh has, daydreaming up that somehow it'd be a book she, herself, had read at that age. Unlikely. 'Can you stay over tonight?' And Lucy has to say 'Absolutely' and has to say it without letting on that she kind of is already thinking how she'll be able to get out of it to instead see how it goes with Samantha as she is slated to see. 'When can you come over?' Fuck - right into it! Lucy's brain stops up, a drain still draining but a washcloth acting as slowing agent - Lucy can only think to zap back 'What time is Leopold picking up Kayleigh?' Should Ariel be talking like this? What if Kayleigh hears and offhand mentions to Leopold how Lucy was going to be over tonight - or whatever innocent way a kid would say something like that - no idea how loaded it'll sound. 'Well, he'll be out with Kayleigh in about an hour from now. I didn't know if you had plans for the first part of the evening - do you?' 'Kind of' Lucy says, but her hope that this will be sufficient to say withering in time-lapse, three-years-in-four-seconds, leaving her to think on her feet, Ariel's unspoken follow up of 'What plans?' looming and sharp as the afternoon through the thicking cloud-cover. 'Of course!' she blurts it - so obvious - and wishes she'd sounded less surprised, but Ariel doesn't seem to notice. She says 'I really wanted to go through the first notes from this editor - get a feel for what it's going to be like with the poem book, you know?' And goodness me, goodness me, Ariel touches Lucy's arm with 'Oh shit' and 'I'm an idiot, yes yes - you don't even have to come over if you don't want.' Lucy. Lucy? Lucy!! Oh Jesus, too late! Now Lucy has said 'Of course I'll come over' and she even names a specific hour, happening to be the same hour she is supposed to be meeting Samantha. 'I'll make dinner' Ariel states. 'You'll do nothing of the fucking sort. I have other plans for you.' Do you, Lucy? What is this - is there some hidden wisdom which all gathered are missing? And ought you be talking like this around Kayleigh, while that subject is generally on? Do you really think Kayleigh isn't hanging on every word of the conversation between you are her mother - the book, by now, a prop she has read the same two pages of to death? 'I look forward to that, but I'm still going to cook. I have meat in the fridge that'll go bad if it waits. Just burgers. I'll do fries, too - those ones I make from scratch.' To which Lucy says 'Awesome' though she has never had fries Ariel has made from scratch - that is not a reference Lucy understands, that is something Ariel has done with someone else enough times it can be shorthanded and left so unelaborate.

Ariel slouches along behind Kayleigh to the front door of the house, Lucy just watching and turning up the radio. Then there is nothing to do. But leave. Which, look: Lucy is doing. What does she look like while she does? Someone confused as to 'Is this today or yesterday?' Someone who does not know if Time is like this now because of her age or because of her situation. Maybe any situation just feels like this at $X$ point in life. A processing mechanism reshapes the world into conundrum where it once-upon-a-time would have been graceful, the slipping of a coin across an iced-over pond. Take music, Lucy thinks. She has music playing that she likes very much. But does she like it how she did when first she heard it, decades ago? No. Not remotely, in fact. And not just to say the excitement has faded - dulled in appropriate decay corresponding to passage-of-time, the discoloring of old paperback pages, the potency lost of herbs. It is more than that! Lucy has distance from the words. See, listen: Jack White is saying *How you gonna get the money? Send papers to an empty home?* And listen: Jack White is *saying How you gonna get the money? No one there to answer the phone?* And Lucy feels the words are young, juvenile, no weight or ideals to them. Things to say. The spendthrift of cool-combination over abstractly-thin drums and guitar. But when she first heard it? Oh it was whiz-bang! It had seemed all so pertinent! It had seemed scathing to her thoughts not to have known it always - and if someone did not hear it, find each nook and rivulet and crick and cram of it profound and delicious she would doubt things about them that ought not be doubted! Now? She can see, understand, totally get someone just listening to the song and being unmoved, saying 'It's cool' and liking some other thing more. Something before or after it in time. What Lucy is thinking is: maybe some shift happened and she thinks now of everything - physiologically - in a way that is foreign feeling only because it is the first time it is going on. Give it another few years, this will all seem normal. Elderly. Everything must seem normal to the elderly. This is likely Lucy's last great confusion - so it follows well it would be disconcerting everywhere, a rash sprouted overnight made all the more awful for vanishing, wholly, in the hour it takes to get to a doctor's appointment, show up at the office, undress. Lucy? Where are you even going?

Home for awhile? Then where? At this traffic-light, she checks her phone like
it's a fortune cookie on a first date that happened impromptu, just bumping into
the object of one's desire on a middle-of-the-night street, this joint the only
place open. Or better: like a number you know is lucky 'cause it won someone
else a pile of happiness, but you know will do nothing for you. No message. No
guidance. Her bones all bristle their back-hair and her stomach issues threats out
toward the extremities - an awful feeling of knowing she will have cramp when
she stands, cramp without precipitating cause or course toward relief, an
affliction of the body being the body until it can go back to being ignored and
hardly part of things.

  You live in too many imaginary worlds. What if this is this, what if this is this?
This seems so cleverly like something it isn't and something it doesn't seem like.
The ring of words struck off teeth - or the mind rendering interior, noiseless,
sensations of what words sound like struck off teeth - can be mesmeric to the
point of replacing all honesty. Lucy Jinx: not the sort to describe things how
they are or what they are. Any old convoluted amalgamation of phrase, the least
organic the better, instead! It makes more sense for her to call - there's someone
- that milling man at the crosswalk 'a loose door on a mailbox only the neighbor
ever opens' than just to say 'A guy there.' But the phrase is devoid of humanity.
All of Lucy's phrases are! Reality is easy to describe, but Lucy wants it to be
thrilling, award-winning. Be honest, Lucy: Do you ever have so much as a five
minute conversation - one concerning rote, perfunctory matters, even - with
just some someone-or-some-other without your hoping they will admire your
voice, your word choices, your presentation of mother-tongue? Lucy Jinx: she
says 'What time is it?' and expects the person there not to answer but to say
'The way you say *Time*! Holy cripes, my friend! It makes me contemplate the
very placeholder nature of the term - of any term!' And how many hours a day
does Lucy spend talking to pretend folks? Being honest? Let's say six hours. Even
if she spent twelve talking to actual people, that is a ludicrous amount of time
spent talking to whifts - yes, the comparison makes her tremble. Can Lucy Jinx
not spend one single day - even one awake for only twelve hours, let's make it
easy - without feeling she is blundering with Daedalus in some labyrinth or lying
to some Cyclops about her name? Lucy Jinx: your name will not be synonymous
with *Compass* after your death. Lucy Jinx: you will not evoke, by mere mention,
thoughts of the struggle only primordial protolife must have known! Even when
you are direct, you are direct to avoid the fact that in that moment you feel you
ought to be indirect. Do you ever, ever do - not even what you want, that's a
stuffy-nose word *Want* - something that you think? Do you do what you Think
or only what you Do? Can you identify what you are going to do - not what is
going to happen, but what 'Lucy Jinx is going to do' - before it comes to pass?

Or is your life a sweeping up of the bottle that's broken because you decided to emphasize a phrase with a swing of an arm, no looking around, words pouring out of you and even blathering over wrists hurt from the impact and smash? The world is exactly what a television light looks like and a low volume from it sounds like if you passed out with it playing without meaning to and don't want to stand yet and don't want to drift back off. Lucy - what can you do? Lucy: do something. Lucy, decide where you are driving this car of yours. Now! 'Fine' she says - and it's the most earnest *Fine* she has said in ages. The car shifting into this lane - looks over her shoulder, never one to trust mirrors - then into this lane, then this. You aren't 'Seeing what is going to happen.' You are 'Going there.' You are 'Doing this.' This isn't 'Happening to you' Lucy. You are *Doing This*. Now.

SO ARE YOU GETTING OUT, Lucy? Lucy is thinking: a chair isn't a chair until the person making it sits in it - all of the actions leading up to its being are irrelevant if there isn't that spark of existence. An unused chair, she furthers, is only an abstract postulate, not a thing. Like atoms are only what each one is until they are combined and even when they combine if they don't cohere, in the sense of become-one-function - having a function - they are still just individuals. Grass is not grass until it breathes, for example. A mountain not a mountain until it prevents air or water from these crops, allows it to those. So - this is Lucy's question - if the first time the maker goes to sit down the chair collapses, was it ever a chair? Is Collapsing something a chair can do? Sure. But only after it is a chair. But if it was the solitary action associated with the Perhapsed Chair, does that mean 'The one thing the chair did was collapse' or does it mean 'The one thing the chair did was fail to be a chair?' And, by that thinking, that those actions that led to a chair being made also led to a chair not-being-made. Lucy? What? Are you going over there? Lucy is thinking: it is a mistake to confuse something being Smart with something being True. As in: it is not Smart to say water is drinkable - even to say 'Some water is and some water isn't' - despite it being True. But it can be very Smart to suggest why 'That lot must suffer for this' or why 'The value of a dollar can fluctuate.' Just for two examples. We should not admire the Truth - so thinks Lucy. It is like praising eyes for sometimes being open and sometimes being closed, when that is just the definition of Eyes. So are you going to the door? Lucy? Lucy!? What? Are you going to the door? Lucy is thinking: One thing Lucy knows is that when someone says they are 'Looking for the Pawn Shop' they tend to mean they are 'Going to the Liquor Store.' Anecdotal? Nevertheless: accurate. And that they might go to the grocery-store, instead, or to pick up their kids' prescriptions doesn't alter their intent. As an aside, Lucy adds - *Liquor* should be spelled differently. Spelling it with the *Quor* makes the word look like the name of a medication. The visual seduction toward solace and healthful physique those letters cast a spell of should be outlawed under some sort of governmental authority. The last bastion, Lucy thinks, of pretending getting drunk was a way to see visions of a life beyond this one, that drunkards dancing were summoning magic borrowed from forgotten gods, that the blather your cousin might spout before vomiting on his shoes after pissing behind a car were sage just because they came from an old man who spent his life in a tent! A word can convince you of anything. Language is the Great Placebo. Exactly why the word *Placebo* does not look like anything - you'd never in a thousand lifetimes guess what that means from those letters. Are you going, Lucy? Yes. When? Now. Then go. I'm going. She's going. Lucy Jinx is.

This is a door Lucy knows. She doesn't know it. She never knew it. This was her door. How comfortable coming in it became, once. Yes? No. Had it? These steps to it. This length from car to door. Had she ever even considered it that way? No. Car to room. Car to sofa. The door used to be quite irrelevant. Then, slowly, not so. Then, more than slowly, not so. Then: absolute. Now something - right here - Lucy Jinx only has rights to the-other-side-of. Yet, the-other-side to her is the inside, yes? 'If we are being that way' she says, clammy with about to pull the storm-door open to knock - hoping, hoping, hoping that none of the cars parked in front are actually correspondent to the house, that no one is home - 'then fine: I only have rights to' - she pauses, word-poor - 'rights to' - what is the opposite of *Other*? - 'rights to the' - she is destitute of ways to explain - 'rights to my side.' This is the most portentous thing, ever. Eh? Why run out of words just as hand touched cold faux-gold handle and spittle-thin reflection on glass hardly bothering to exhibit its properties beyond I'm-a-clear-solid - why have this moment where you are robbed of the one thing you are never without, Lucy? 'Turn back' the lack-of-words is saying. Or? Or - she has the glass storm-door held in place with her shoulder - or this is the first step out of the shackle, the first foreign of 'My momentum is not being stopped.' This is head-above-water, no longer lungs pounding out their last scribble before suffocating on what they cannot expel. What is the opposite of *Other*? Do you actually want to know, Lucy? Is it so important? 'There is no opposite of *Other*' she says and figures some lame-brained philosopher someplace - or some sociologist - came to the same conclusion but done up in holiday trappings that make it seem pertinent, profound. Lucy just stands, slight rattle to joint and spring of the storm-door's frame from the little wind that is now pressing the not tightly held open glass. Of course there is an opposite to *Other*. It is. It is. It is. *Same*? Other side. Same side. *Other*. *Same*. Sigh. Mystery solved. Happy now? Lucy is happy now and feels torched, still warm, enough that if one didn't see what was there before they might think the heat was growing and the ground was about to burst skyward in flame. Meanwhile, reality has it, Lucy is a heat that only ever existed burnt down - surface thin, irrelevant air above it, temperature its own - and below it the intricacies of thick and packed Earth, mostly cold, mostly cold enough that it might as well all be. What are you talking about, Lucy? What if you had been seen walking up and she knows you are here? 'She'd think I left a letter or something, I guess' Lucy sighs. 'Or she'd remember what I'm like. And this would all make sense.' And she'd be right there, nose twitched in 'Is she going to knock?' And would wait a full half-hour before opening the door to see 'Is Lucy still there?' Absolutely certain 'Of course Lucy is still there' when Lucy is still there like, obviously, she always would be.

In the quick pronunciation - the immediate - of the word *Lucy* - not the name, the word - it is clear, two things. One - of lesser importance - being that Flynn made no mention of seeing her - whether because Flynn no longer lives here, Flynn had other things on Flynn's mind, or Unknowable Reason *Y* or *Z* - and Two, that Lucy should not have come here. 'Hi.' 'Hi.' 'Come in' and the mother steps back, broom gesturing Lucy over the threshold, pointing to where boots and shoes are piled as though to say 'Pile your shoes there, too.' The house smells of winter dander, a cold humidity, a funk of staleness from over and over deciding 'There's no reason to clean that, vacuum that' all of those putting-it-offs that closed, warm rooms in winter breed. The living-room - just a glance that way - has likely been rearranged several times, now isn't mirrored or cubisted, just some concoction of new furniture, arrangements, lamps glowing brown in the shut blinds of the place, the built-in corner book-shelf now home to file papers, photographs, only the top shelf anything to do with books - and those not arranged across, but into squat stacks like they were set there temporarily and then the realization there was no use for them anywhere, no use for there, so the two went together well. But that was the length of three or four seconds, seeing that. Lucy has not taken off her shoes and the mother - don't be shy about it now - is giving her an embrace, skin juddering with fabric to Lucy's skin and fabric with warm laughter of childish 'Holy cow - what are you doing here!?' Not that the mother asks that. She just laughs and repeats 'Lucy' again and, removing from Lucy's - maybe the mother didn't notice - unreturned embrace now whisks to the kitchen and says 'I only have cold coffee, will cold coffee do?' Disorienting. Goddamn it. How did Lucy get inside? She's like that bug on a hand-towel spotted just before you use it, making you relieved but also wondering 'How many times have I not noticed similar bugs?' 'I love cold coffee. Sock it to me, right?' *Sock it to me* did you say, Lucy? 'Shut up' she says aloud, the mother - offering cold cup - giving her the crooked eye and Lucy just saying 'I still talk to myself, I was saying something snarky and needed to take myself to task for it.' 'Of course you were - of course you did' says the mother, who, let's be clear, has likely gone mad due to - this must only be Act One of the play Lucy has stumbled into, opening night, hoping to glean her lines from context clues - some past tragedy that will not be revealed for some time. Harold Pinter nervously chews on his Playbill in the back, lips still stinging of head-cold and nicotine and withering under self-doubt of 'Why would I think somebody would want to watch this shit?' What is Lucy supposed to say, now? How long a pause should she take before assuming it's officially up to the mother to salvage the scene? But even as she worries, the mother says 'Shit - should I microwave that for you?' Lucy goes 'Yeah, actually I just figured you'd lost all sense of decorum and I didn't want to point out your bad manners - but if you're offering.' The mother takes Lucy's extended cup, flaps open microwave door, and hits one button twice, the thing vrrrring to life. 'My mind is elsewhere' the mother says with a back-stepping forgive-me bow - 'just calculating how much you owe me in back rent, you know?'

Lucy has never eaten the Silica Gel in one of the packs that come in the pocket of the coats or are stuffed in the slots of the wallets - but how her head feels now is how it would have felt had she. She imagined a body's worth of moisture loudly slurped into the spongy space of just one of those little balls, the result a still-dry spec that would taste of salt-lick and resonate with a sound like ears ringing for three miles around. See there? The mother is nodding to Lucy saying 'I actually bumped into Flynn at the' - Lucy waves her hand - 'sports complex a few weeks ago and then got so busy with shit - but I had a day, finally, so here I am.' How is the mother reacting? She is reacting like this: 'Yes' - leaned, Lucy knows, with the edge of the countertop cutting a straight-line divot at her mid-ass - 'he said that. He said he thought you were meeting one of the groups and he would have talked but' - she touches Lucy's elbow, a brush but also a press - 'he has a' - this whispered - 'girlfriend and I don't think he can focus on more things than one.' 'Boys are dumb' Lucy nods and the mother agrees. 'They are' they mother says and goes on about how Flynn used to be smart until he got old enough to choose his own music to listen to. 'Now he's pitiful.' 'At least she's cute, though.' 'But she is in the *Junior League of Washington* or something and so Flynn thinks he needs to learn about political what-nots. Shit, Lucy - you can imagine the hilarious outtakes reel my life has become?' 'Is it okay if I smoke?' Lucy decides to say, making it clear she is not going to offer direct commentary on the Life and Times of Flynn. 'Of course. Share?' Does she no longer smoke, Lucy wonders - why not have her own pack? 'You're the one with the house' Lucy says - her banter is on automatic, no idea why she is being personable when all signs point to Get-the-Hell-out-now - 'so it terrifies me your having to beg off me. I live in an apartment that probably used to be a storage-unit and probably will be a cautionary tale to those just moving into the area by the time I move out.' What? That might be the least sensible thing Lucy has ever said - and plus, she's locked into grinning like a dog that figures all shit tastes as good as its own. The mother says she has plenty of cigarettes - in fact had meant she was going to share some with Lucy - but now that she's reminded of Lucy's presumptuous cuntingness she's glad that wasn't clear. And she lights the smoke Lucy offered. 'You never noticed my presumptuousness' Lucy sneers, lighting her own. 'You thought I was a shy little hatchling!' The laughter the mother cannot contain is as intricate and alarming as a diagnosis that begins with the words with 'Are you familiar with' and then a word which you immediately know means the only answer you can give is 'No' and the physician, well, they knew that but had to start somewhere. Some moments pass like that. Laughter subsides. Stage light reset. Audience given time to glance to Programs to see *Scene: Same room, later* so they are not under the impression that whatever is said next is said linearly.

'How long have you been in town? Or did you ever leave?' 'I left - Oh Christ yes, I left. Things were burnt to the ground gregariously and without ceremony. I left in the Biblical use the word, if there is one.' 'Sounds about right.' 'I've been back awhile, though. Just doing my usual brand of counter-intuitive lifestyle choices and working jobs that are called Temporary but that which I hold longer than any position I was ever hired on at salary for.' 'And still writing? I saw a book by you at a café once - they said you had done a reading when I brandished the thing and demanded they explain it, you know?' 'Which café?' 'Oh I don't know.' 'Downtownish?' 'This was long ago. I'd ask you to sign it if I'd bought it.' 'I'd stalwartly refuse. In order to make you think that's the sort of thing that has proper channels to go through and an intern with a rubber stamp is to handle. But, yes, I am still writing. More and more. Or not so much. But doing more and more with it.' 'Terrific.' 'Moving up in the world.' 'Terrific.' 'And how about you? Are you still doing whatever thing is was that you did that I was never entirely clear what it was and so now admit I cannot remember what you ever even told me it was?' 'What's the question? I'm kidding - yes. Well, no - why did I say *Yes*? - no, no I am not still doing that. I am doing something else.' 'Which you are going to not tell me about.' 'Right.' 'Bitch.' 'Right.' 'What do you do?' 'You'll lose respect for me.' 'Have you met me? I haven't much right to lose respect for folks.' 'It doesn't strike me that stops you.' 'Touché.' 'I work in a plant.' 'I am picturing a hibiscus with a cottage door on it and you making cookies the secret ingredient of which is *Embiggining Powder*. Also - you are animated and rosy-cheeked and there are pervy undertones to the way you wipe your brow after applying the icing to the center of each shortbread sandwich.' 'On the nose.' 'I'm thinking of the right thing?' 'That I am employed in a cartoon advertisement for *Keebler*? Yes. Except I don't know what a hibiscus is. I work in an apple-tree stump.' 'I thought you were a girl - how do you not know what a hibiscus is?' 'What's a hibiscus?' 'Honestly, you got me, there - though I never claimed much to be a girl - I admit when I picture that word I think of a kind of cracker that always suggests being served with cheese and I always think *Oh yeah, that's something people do, cheese-and-crackers.*' 'I work at a shop - a human cog, assembling cosmetics kits.' 'That sounds awesome, actually.' 'It's like working in a deft satire. Punchy. Oh very punchy. The ironic aspects of my working hours have been awarded the Pulitzer more times than horses have been awarded anything, all put together.' 'Do they pay you in make-up kits?' 'They pay me in intriguing amounts of dollar bills, actually. Very inventive portions of money.' 'Only one job, though? You trying to show off or something?' 'I'm sorry - how many do you work?' 'I only work one. I meant trying to show off like trying to prove you're on the same level as me. It's impressive. I'm impressive.' 'You are, Lucy.' 'I am Lucy.' 'Yes, you are Lucy. You are Lucy.'

Lucy feels she won that conversation, but it might have been the sort of thing where neither were really doing anything but playing a holding action. Lucy does have to leave. No idea, now that it's happened, how she'd thought this would go, but that it has gone on this long is peculiar and now must be addressed. Blah blah, Lucy some-salvos of 'I'm going to have to head out.' And the mother says 'How about you call me or just stop by, again?' And though Lucy would adore there being some tone in this she could sniff out and scream 'Desperation!' at, it seems like it's just a casual invitation. All a trick. All a trick. Except now the mother - Lucy having said 'Let's have drinks this weekend' and the mother replying 'Sound perfect' handing across a scribbled telephone number and quipping how Lucy is the only bar-slut she knows who does house-calls for pick-up - is saying 'It's so great seeing you - and I'm glad you came back' just matter-of-factly, nothing left to be parnoaicly intuited. 'I wasn't sure I was going to come by here, today. I never did, before. I wasn't sure I would, ever.' The mother nods, crosses her arms, but just wrapping them to cause that stretching crack of her shoulders, then arms dropping slack to her side, and asks 'Why not?' Lucy sits to the stairs, slowly getting one foot into one shoe. 'I didn't think it'd be very welcome.' No response. But in the sound of that no-response and the slight bobbing of grey shadow over peach, unlit stairwell wall Lucy knows the mother has tilted her head in a question. 'What a dreadful state-of-affairs these shoelaces are!' Lucy says, now both feet in both shoes. And, yes, the shoelaces are of horror-shoes, like snakes who tried to shed skin but got stuck in themselves halfway, knots made of part of other knots, backbone of the things such a thin thread Lucy thinks if she tugs them tight they will snap. And the mother just calls them 'the ugliest shoelaces since that one famous pair' voice instructing Lucy to now change the subject, please. So, Lucy is looking up. And has just said 'I didn't think you would ever want to see me again.' The mother leans to the bit of wall to the - if facing the front door - right of the bathroom door, tucks her hands in the small of her back, rolls at some soreness in the blades of her shoulders or something and finally sighs. 'Why would you have ever thought that?' 'I dunno' Lucy says, unable to keep eye-contact, wanting that to be the end, Lucy some schmuck kid the principal knows they were wrong about the potential in, about to head home for the last time before expulsion. The mother says nothing. Says nothing. Leans there. Lucy out of excuses not to be standing, so she stands. This close to the mother. As close as she is comfortable being. Has to repeat 'I dunno' to keep from her head caving in like a skin of fruit sticking its chest out to make up for its mealy insides finally being lifted and squeezed by hungry fingers. 'I hope you didn't really think that.' 'I really thought it' Lucy now kittenishly shrugs, then makes some kind of lip popping noise she has no recollection of ever having made before. And the mother says 'I don't want you to be alarmed, but I am going to kiss you - not that I think you could stop me now even if it's the last thing you want.' 'What's that supposed to mean?' Lucy says after a long beat in which she still hasn't been kissed. 'That you're a weakling, right now.' Lucy still hasn't been kissed. 'Well?' 'Well, what?' Lucy still hasn't been kissed and stamps her foot - or not stamps, shifts it and breathes down her nose the sort of huff that tends to accompany a stomp. 'Okay' the mother says 'but you come here.'

Odds of That Didn't Just Happen? Calculate. Unknown. Consider this, though: Lucy is now in her car and already has the radio turned on. Interesting. Also into the algorithm: why can't Lucy remember if she ever slept with the mother, before? She had. She hadn't. One time - up in the room she rented. Right? More than one time? A few times, there toward the end? Or no? No - that had all been unconsummated upon Lucy's departure, hence it was so, you know, difficult. Wrong! It had been difficult because you had consummated, physically, and then just flipped out over whatever-it-was. What was it? 'Fuck' Lucy says. Returning to the point: what are the odds? Lucy can recite little of all of it verbatim. And she thinks this is the taste of lip-gloss on her mouth, but it could also be just dry lips she has recently licked. Does there exist any chance that that did not happen? Start there. There's always a chance! There isn't always a statistical chance, though. True. In this case: is there a statistical chance that Lucy has been asleep, that she didn't go to the door, that the mother didn't answer, that all hadn't been more-or-less nothing like Lucy had ever even feverishly cobbled a daydream of - that she hadn't just kissed the mother? No. 'I mean' she says, turning on her recorder 'No. Just no. No: there isn't a chance.'

And she turns the recorder off. Then, to feel cinematic, she reverses the tape a bit and presses Play. She hears the last bit of something she must have said whenever last using the tape - parked, raining, difficult to hear herself - which goes 'mildly, I can't think of anything easier to do than to get a countess to fall in love with you for no reason. What could be simpler than that? If you have to put real effort in to impressing a countess, that should be an excuse to apply for disability. Countesses are such sad sacks - man, they must get sick-and-tired of themselves.' Now the sound of the recording going off. Recording starting. 'No. Just no. No, there isn't a chance.' Click. That proves it! The recording had a chance to say anything back - to not have anything recorded at all past that rubbish about the Countess - but instead it just mocking-birded. So congratulations or something are in order! Lucy is backing out of the neighborhood. Lucy is at a traffic-light, wondering why her head feels so unburdened. That's the ripple - she feels light, effervescent. Not good. She doesn't feel happy. She feels immaterial. Her head flushed of things like an ear scoured of wax by precision-aimed rinse. That's what it probably feels like to just do something. Except, counterpoint: that was not the sort of thing someone means when they say 'Just do something.' This is why the dreamy feeling. This is why the still distant-drums insistence that no one was home or that Lucy is still home, herself. She's just having a dream that will only end when she dreams she lays back down and in the dream dreams a different dream she can wake up and only remember. Lucy isn't sure where she's driving. The clock says something. Home. Why? To get changed? Why? Samantha. She speaks that. 'Samantha.' And the sound is a coin dropped on a train platform - way over there - the person who dropped it not picking it up yet still milling there, meaning she couldn't go pick it up, either. That would still be stealing. Or it would be weird, anyway. It would involve eye-contact and something communicated. And coins aren't generally worth that.

A gas station for some more cigarettes. Lucy buys four packs under the ruse that she works at some nearby offices and is gophering for everyone who has to work late. The speech seems unneeded, but at the same time it was fun to give. Rattle-rattle - get the spray-can of her head firing straight, again. Palm slaps and car lighter, windows unopened, and heater blares - she wonders how deep-seeded the rank of this car is. And the water around her finding buoyancy and temperate equilibrium, her thoughts begin floating face down how they are accustomed. Didn't take long. Which is good. Lucy must be on the defensive. Isn't it odd - isn't it? - that the mother didn't bring up anything of feeling betrayed or seeming dazzled by Lucy's appearance or of there being even the chintziest bit of discombobulation to the sudden appearance? This isn't being paranoid! It isn't! Christ's sake - what? Is Lucy supposed to not reflect on the world around her? Take at face-value everything? There are words for that that are never used except pejoratively and - thanks very much - Lucy would like to side-step at least one turd in this lifetime! Thinking is not Overthinking. If everything the mother said is to be taken at face-value - can I interrupt, Lucy? - does it not seem just a tad off - Lucy, please may I just clarify one point? - that she would be so instantaneously welcoming, back to old patter, kissing her? Lucy? What!? Quickly: did you like how the mother was - do you like what just happened? Yes. Noted. And moving along, Lucy proffers this alternative: that the mother was aware - perhaps for some time, maybe that was why she mentioned that damned coffee-shop book! - that Lucy was living in the area, again. Or maybe as recently as Flynn mentioning it - which, come on, he did, you know he did, she said he did! - so the mother had been processing 'How would I feel about seeing Lucy Jinx, again?' and has been reflecting on 'How long ago it all was' and had concluded that 'The past is long distant, and if Lucy was around I just want to try again.' 'That' Lucy blats out with uninhaled blue of smoke in hot-boxed grey and whiter-grey of smoke - the whiter-grey the more apparent, it should be noted, the grey the more faded - 'would make sense.' And it would even make sense that the mother would have played it that way - as though light, casual. If it was planned, rehearsed, fantasied-out-in-advance - well that was exactly something one could expect! But: the alternative? Has she been living in that house for seven, eight years, pining after her old tenant? Has she not moved on, relegated Lucy to 'That once happened, for awhile'? The mother doesn't feel here-and-now for Lucy - and Lucy was prodded in to this all. If someone just showed up - a decade removed - who had spurned Lucy's affection and fled without word, Lucy might say 'How are you?' but would not basically propose in the kitchenette after twenty minutes chit-chat! 'She doesn't make fucking sense!' Lucy says, honking her horn, which startles that young couple - the guy still not sure, thirty seconds later, it hadn't been directed at him, Lucy can tell by that final glance over the top of his car. 'She doesn't make sense and is up to something.' Like you would be? 'Like I would be.' Lucy clucks her tongue in the saliva under her tongue until it has bubbled a mouthful.

Driving, a yawn pops her jaw and her jaw now clicks with any movement. Doctor Lucy prescribes: the shower she was going to take anyway and some cough-syrup, just to confuse her body. No pot? Lucy is conserving. Seems like a good night to be out-of-body, one could argue. And there would be acceptable politics to such an argument. But: Lucy is conserving. Now, more than ever. Figures maybe she should check in on the Mitchell situation or else take up Evan on his offer to source her. Not much time to think about it, though, before Lucy is struck in her bumper at a traffic-light. Bites the inside of her mouth, the pinch of this causing a pop and a deep whirr to begin in her ears - makes her hyperaware of the base of her skull being bone, it feels ball-and-socket though she sort of thinks anatomy doesn't have it that way. The driver behind - Oh Lord! - is already getting out of their car, hands up in 'So sorry, so sorry' giving a glance down at what Lucy figures must be something shattered. 'Fuck!' The light is green and the cars ahead moving, the cars behind snaking past the crasher's probably-on hazard-lights. Muffled 'I am so sorry.' 'It's fine' Lucy says through the window. 'It was totally my fault.' 'I know' she says, avoiding eye-contact the way she would with a home-invader, hoping this would give her an argument for being spared while the others were executed. This bastard - he already has his insurance information out! And the police will show up - this prick has called this in like one of the authors of the *Constitution* would have! You'll have to roll down your window, Lucy. He's not going to let you out of this. 'It's really fine - I can get one of my cousins to fix this, don't even worry.' 'You don't need to do that' he such-a-good-guys 'I was distracted - you could be hurt, it's my responsibility.' 'Oh life isn't a Chinese proverb' Lucy good-natures 'and I really need to get someplace. I don't care about this sort of thing - because of my Stoic upbringing.' That smile - yep - means the accident has already been called in and an officer is going to take down the particulars so this Samaritan can get his proper punishment under Law and God and everyone. 'My name is Lucy Jinx' Lucy Jinx says, final argument tenor 'and I am a poet and I absolve you of everything. Just describe me as somebody else and say I fled the scene. No one here will contradict your eyewitness testimony. I promise you: this will never be spoken of again and nothing negative will befall anyone.' And Lucy is about to peel out, but the light has gone red. At the next opportunity, though. Fuck! No. This man will not play along. If she flees, that's probably a crime according to some wrong-headed notion of Due Process or something! 'You do know you're inconveniencing me, right? I want you to think, sir. What if I was rushing to attend to my lover at their hospice bed? What if I had to be getting my kid from Daycare!? I should fucking charge you with elaborate kidnapping, because that's what you are doing - using loopholes in the law to get away with it!! It's perverse, man - you're sick in the head! Crashing into women then using hardly-veiled-threats of *If you try to leave you'll be the one in trouble for fleeing the scene*? Damn you, sir!! I am not the usual trifle or cooze, do you grok that!!?' Never has Lucy seen a man's eyes lifting to see an approaching patrol car with more relief kilned to them.

Lucy smokes three cigarettes before the whole ordeal is over with. The man introduces himself - Vince - and gives what seems a heartfelt apology for causing so much trouble. Lucy humors him listing off his reasons - some complex backstory, might as well be regaling her with how he wound up with a superpower - and says she doesn't apologize for her outburst, at all, but nonetheless is glad he is being so stolid about it. She even chuckles when he ventures 'So, this wouldn't be the time to ask you out for a drink?' and just says 'Naw.' The damage to the car is bad. Shattered glass, large dent. The sort of thing she hopes maybe Layla will convince her not to fix - just pocket the money coming her way from insurance. The wind is out of her sails now and she feels cramps of guilt over her upcoming evening. Hand to her shoulders - yes, that's an injury - she finally starts driving, again. But with radio turned all the way down - clicked off. And daybreak gone in her head. The only thought she has is for sleep. She purposefully does not take the road toward her apartment, instead pulls into this oddly placed, generic brand *Hair Stylist* - entering the premises dubiously, asking all three of the people there jointly 'Are you open?' None answer with any enthusiasm and only one steps to the till to start up a transaction, asking her what she's after. 'Do you have time to color it?' The stylist seems confused. 'Do I have time? Or are you asking - what?' 'I don't know when you close.' 'Oh' the stylist expansively says, pronounced like the key on a computer is stuck, head-roll to accompany, then becoming nicer, like a switch has been flicked. 'Absolutely. What color are you after?' 'Just lighter. No. Darker. Dark red.' '*Dark red*?' 'Yes. Dark. Like if black ink was red like it ought to be.' 'I can do that' the stylists says with perfunctory confidence. 'And how short would you like it?' 'Short. Like it's only just technically hair. But, you know, so that the color still works.' The stylist thinks and Lucy finishes jotting her text to Samantha, explaining how she will be late but will be all the more worth it. 'How long will this take?' Lucy asks just to have a detail to add to the text - really, the time doesn't matter now that she is committed. Jaw still disagreeing with her and a dense variety of sorenesses hardening her shoulder, Lucy is asked to wait just a moment while the stylist steps to the back. One of the other two - watching the corner television on mute with closed-captions - takes a moment to say 'Short hair is where it's at, man. I think I'm gonna do mine short.' Lucy nods, but is offput. Too distinct an image in her mind of how many crumbs this woman lets litter her shirt-tits, shirt-belly, when watching a movie past midnight, blearily snacking - the sort of person who makes Phew sounds and says 'Excuse me' after they belch, even when all alone in a room. The remaining person seems to notice, asks Lucy 'Something the matter?' This drawing another look from the television-watcher. 'Nothing's wrong.' Television-watcher says 'Don't worry. Hair is always nerve wracking - but Lily is the best.' If *Half-hearted* felt half-hearted, it would speak in exactly the tone that woman just did. If that woman were a piece of film Lucy had to Foley, the only sound would be an overloud crunch of wet chewing.

**********

'I'VE NEVER WANTED A SPLIT-LIP more in my life' is the first thing Lucy tells Samantha - Samantha standing from her seat as though startled into abject terror or reverent awe by the sight of Lucy. 'So if you want to punch me, right now - wanna just punch my fruit-skin little lips right into my teeth sharps - I will be yours forever.' 'Tempting' Samantha says, slow-motion - teee-emmmppp-ppptttttt-eeennnn-nnng - now a more playful appraisal being given to Lucy's entire appearance. A sliver of self-consciousness squeaks from Lucy, outwardly manifesting in a 'What?' And Samantha explains she just doesn't want to be missing any other shocking alterations. 'It gives you a whole different line. Like a more decadent version of my favorite two-door coupe or something.' 'I'm the sort of girl you don't mind reeks of cigarette, eh?' 'You do reek of cigarette.' And they kiss, standing at the table of this bookstore café that should properly be called a café-bookstore. 'And this is a date, right?' 'It is.' Lucy might - at one point later in life, depending on the breaks - admit to Samantha how tempted she was to - right of the bat, right after this kiss - say something along the lines of 'Full disclosure: you aren't the first woman I kissed today, though you are the first one I planned for.' Now, she does not. A real political-animal, Lucy Jinx! The bread is buttered on this side, the bread is also folded in half. She might - quick addition - also add on that she is not quite sure if she'd kissed Samantha, before. For a moment, it's all a blank and what she remembers is this one time she had been planning to sleep with a woman, but the woman had gotten drunk - Lucy still spending the night in the hotel with her, but asleep on the room sofa, uncertain of what the woman was called. What was the woman called? No idea. Lost in the undulating city-breeze of history. Back to the scene: they are sitting down and a barista is placing a muffin that Samantha ordered in front of Lucy, Samantha not correcting the moment, Lucy deciding not to seem as baffled as she is. 'I think that chick is trying to tell me something coded - walking right up, giving me a muffin.' Hard pronunciation to first-syllable of the last word there for the wink-wink. This the point where the 'I ordered that' is explained. Lucy is a loopy mess of Indie film continuity freeform. 'Hey, Samantha?' 'What's that, Lucy?' 'Guess what I did today?' 'What?' 'Signed a contract to publish a compendium of my verse spanning a decade or so. What did you do? Regular chump things, I bet! Gas bill, electric bill? I just wanted you to know that the things I do when you can't see me are nowhere near as mousey and anonymous as the things you do when I can't see you. You're free to like me more for my accomplishment and less for my cretinously vain candor - which evens us back out to where we were, I think. Agreed?' Samantha tells Lucy she is more impressed that Lucy was able to keep track of that whole sentence while also having to be the one saying it than of any publishing contract she could have managed to procure. 'You'd be a blast to transcribe, I bet.' 'I'd be a blast to just about anything, Samantha. I got a hair-cut, too. And bought a bunch of cigarettes. And was in a car accident. Et cetera. We should order wine, but this place probably is too groundling to know what that is, eh?'

If one knows how lovely a line in a song you've never heard can sound when heard for the first time with just a quarter-headful of alcohol in you, sitting warm and silent in the back seat of a car while the driver soberly navigates and the whoever-it-is in the passenger seat is nodded out-cold, greasing window glass with their night-out slick forehead, then one could know how lovely Samantha seems to Lucy, right now. This is how Samantha dresses - checkered pants, clashing patterned shirt under male-cut blazer with the crest of some private school or secret club or something on the breast, a hole at the shoulder patched over with copious scotch-tape. Boots, abbreviated cut, that show some bare, unshaved ankle when legs-cross or when feet are looked down at while just simply sitting. Face with no make-up and a blemish unhidden on the crease of skin where jaw meets ear. Samantha cannot take credit for the tape on the blazer, which Lucy scoffs her for. 'You have to learn how to take credit - for things you don't do, especially! I read that in a book on business or a book on war in feudal Japan or something like that. Or just a book about medicine in the Civil War. The point being, I have it on written authority. Taking credit for the ideas of others is what separates the actual innovators from the charlatans - in that the charlatans, as history tells us even in many dead languages, always finish well out ahead! Don't you want to be a winner, Samantha? Don't you want to triumph?' 'I do' Samantha says, smile and shifting-in-the-seat early signs of 'If Lucy quit talking now, these checkered pants are easily get-intoable.' 'Then lie to me, man. I'll always know when you are - don't think you'll get the dupe of me. The important thing isn't to trick me, you know - it's that you let me see you know how to pick the right things to lie about. And if you don't know how to do that, then it's best you lie about everything! Because I'll assume you're covering all the bases to be on the safe side. If you say something true, it's easy enough to tell - because it'll be more boring than everything else. And that way I can - at the same time I'm being deceived - gauge how honest you are, underneath. That's the part I'll fall in love with, Samantha. The underneath. The surface is surface, so one ought make it bluster and braggadocio - Hell, make it full out masturbatory zest! - because if you put your truest-self on the surface I'll have to assume what's underneath is a rubbish-tip. This is good advice I'm giving you, Samantha! I must like you if I've already used the word *Love*!' Samantha says 'You make me dizzy, Lucy.' 'Is that true?' 'It is - but I deceptively made it seem complimentary.' 'That's very artful' thinks Lucy, who thought she had already bulldozed this gal fruit-roll-up flat. She decides to award Samantha a contented smile and a lean back. She compliments Samantha on being so different outside-of-work than at. Someone taps on the window glass and Samantha is the only of the two who looks up - startled, then beaming, then waving, then laughing, then attention-back-to-Lucy with 'Sorry.' 'Because you know people? Yes - admittedly when I thought you were a recluse shoe-bomber you had more allure, but there's no shame in having pals, I guess.'

The worst thing Samantha can admit - the rule being 'Actually try, because if it's not bad, I'm leaving' - is this: 'I have, on several occasions, started erotic pen-pal relationships with death-row inmates.' Lucy is about to stand when Samantha calls her an impatient bitch and scolds her to sit down. 'As I was saying: I have had pornographically vivid pen-pal correspondence with death-row inmates and ended each with a letter - just a few days before their slated execution - telling them I had been screwing with them, entirely - that me and some pals were just taking the Mickey out of them - and include in the final letter specific mockery of several of the inmate-in-question's dirty phrasings. Because I want to be as close to the last thing they are thinking about when their veins are chilled with poison - or whatever, some were gassed and stuff - as I possibly can. And I have gotten off to the fantasy of them having as their very last thought *Fuck you, whore!* or something. In my direction, you know?' Lucy remains seated. Impressed. Suspicious. Gauging whether it is, in fact, Lucy herself who is having the Mickey taken. 'Is that true?' 'I'll show you. I have all the letters in a box. I make copies of all of mine, too.' 'What might impress me more would be if you do, indeed, have all those letters, but they are all fabricated just to say this to women you date.' 'I'm not quite that interesting' says Samantha 'sorry.' Lucy is sorry, too - but admits it is enough to have survived to the next round of the game. And a little tinge of nervousness over Samantha playing the game, hard, back at Lucy. What would Lucy choose if she were called out to answer the same challenge she had just posed? There is no short supply of ne'er-do-welling, but Samantha's was such a queer pepper Lucy would feel compelled to compete not only for Passing but for points awarding Most Exotic as well. Thankfully, Samantha seems more relieved to have gotten through than desirous to rock the boat. Wise. Because Samantha, if Lucy had to play a hand, would have to play another and Lucy doubts someone who gets their jollies dicking around with dead-men-walking really has much actual dismal to unbury. Lucy's worst job? 'I worked as a cashier at a truck-stop - a monstrous, sprawling fucking truck-stop place! - a kind of everything-all-in-one: restaurants and gas and rooms-by-the-hour-or-night and shops. Just the most wretched place imaginable. I couldn't stand it. Behind the counter - I am not saying this to sound topical or alarmist - there was a binder with photocopies of blank *Incident Report* sheets, each one broken up by categories - specific questions, you know? And one was a *Rape Report*.' Samantha skepticals. Lucy holds up a hand. 'Best part of it? When taking down the information about this sort of thing, you had to get two names and they were categorized *Rapist* and *Alleged Rapee*.' 'That division - the term *Rapee* aside - seems unsettlingly askance.' Lucy nods, thumbs-up gesture. 'I leafed through a binder of past reports this one night - for a chuckle, you know? Someone called Dona Ty was a recurrent *Alleged Rapee* - different *Rapist* every time.' Samantha has that look like perhaps it is time to start indicating she is responding more to the graveness of this story than the gallows-humor. To let her off easy, Lucy gives another one-moment gesture and asks 'You want the kicker? The moment I quit is when I noticed that Dona Ty was also the second-shift supervisor. A well-oiled machine - paper-work filed and all, you know?' And what was Samantha's worst job? Lucy queries, voice all girl-scouts. 'I hated this one summer where I worked at *Mrs. Field's Cookies*. I didn't even get a discount.'

After a little bit, things settle into a banal groove and Lucy feels genuinely content. She looks at Samantha the way a leopard might look at the horizon-line when it is made distinct by the sun lowering to cast distance as lean silhouette. Lucy tells the story about the car accident, but they mostly wonder if Lucy's defining what the guy did as *Kidnapping* is technically accurate. They both think so. Lucy's freedom-of-movement was taken from her, against her will, so the fact that the guy was using the traffic, the traffic-light, the Rules of Insurance, and the approach of law enforcement as kind of underhanded replacement for his own bodily heft or a bolted door should make little difference. 'Wanna go egg his house or something?' 'I want you to write a letter to him on death-row, man. And my highest compliment, Samantha, is that I'd rather watch a documentary about you than fuck you - so take that to the bank, man, and laugh yourself silly the whole time you're in line, you hear?' They exit the premises - Samantha's heavy coat is not as shockingly impressive as the rest of her ensemble, but is pretty cool, like something an old woman would accidentally have in her closet and a granddaughter might steal - and smoke up and down the front of a nearby grocery-store. Lucy wants coins for the Space Ship ride, but Samantha doesn't think Lucy can fit on it without the thing breaking. 'Just give me the coins! I didn't ask for an editorial.' Samantha forks over fifty-cents. Lucy promptly tosses the quarters into the parking lot and they hear two solid Tinks of cars being struck. 'Calling me fat costs you fifty-cents and the possible damage of private property.' 'You are kind of fat! And anyway, had I not called you fat it still would have cost me fifty-cents and the possibility of damage to public property - you'd have smooshed this space-ship flat like a *Super Mario* mushroom!' Points to Samantha. Lucy is in a real pickle of erotic desire, here. 'You wanna smoke pot and play *Super Mario Brothers*?' Samantha would enjoy this more than she knows how to express, but her Nintendo is on the blink. 'Which' she clarifies 'is to say: I don't have one.' They decide to go into this clothing store to get warm and to see if there is anyone worth ogling. 'The best thing about both of us doing it is that it won't seem like ogling.' Samantha approves, again, of Lucy-logic - but the place is a dead-end when it comes to subject matter. They compensate by Lucy trying on some blazers and Samantha some fashion-print flats. The blazers all make Lucy feel like someone who dresses too nice for a job they are actually not any good at. Samantha buys some patterned stockings, which Lucy cites as further evidence of her being a twat-tease. 'Do you know how often you complain about things, Lucy?' 'I've noticed it since being around you, yes.' Oh haha - aren't you two the cutest couple, Lucy, aren't you just a delightfully comic romp! 'If you complain about one more thing, I'm gonna punish you by becoming clingy - by becoming downright needy. And I'm not joking - I will and it'll suck to be you. You see the bottom-of-the-sea? Know how hard it'd be for a fish to move a shipwreck? That's how much I'll be all up your ass, man.'

Lucy detours to the privacy of a single occupancy toilet to regroup. The problem: doesn't Samantha seem different? The problem: not different in the way that is acceptable, reasonable - yes, this is her outside-of-work, yes yes, Lucy has now known her awhile and they've been paling around and flirtatious for some time, yes yes yes, it is called getting-to-know-someone and many people go from shy to bold. The problem is: doesn't Samantha seem an awful lot like the mother? Who seems an awful lot like, say, Elliott? Who seems much like Ariel? Conversationally. Rhythmically. It is the close proximity of Ariel to the mother to Samantha that has brought this out - otherwise, the buffers Lucy keeps in place, the cigarette filters between lips and various human contact, would have kept the sensation separate. They still would have felt the same, but just in the way that they feel Good. What do you mean? Lucy means: no, not that I am going nuts or think I am dreaming, but rather something else, altogether. Lucy thinks that, perhaps, she has a mechanism in her own psychology that is convincing herself of a Sameness - a way-conversations-go, something that takes in raw-data and jiggers it into processed-memory of wit and dirty-talk and intimacies and randoms all in a palatable way. So, to sum up: Samantha might be very different than she seems? Yes. And, moreover, Samantha - or anyone - might not be compatible - might not be even remotely so! - just input feeds subject to the quirk of Lucy's processing, a mind that makes All Women the Same Woman, is instinctively designed to always convince her she has what she wants no matter what she may actually have. Exactly! May I offer a counterpoint? 'Certainly' Lucy says, sighing post-defecation 'please do.' Lucy sniffles, waiting for the thoughts to process. You might just have a Type. Hmn. And be sensitive to that Type, no matter how it first presents. Hmn.

Samantha is not like the mother who is not like Elliott who is not like Ariel - or any of the bit-players being left off the main Cast-listing, a group that is numerous, we must admit - except that they eventually reveal as Lucy's-Type. Hmn. Think of yourself, Lucy - you wind up Lucy with all who you meet, but you don't begin the same way with any of them. You have started various courtships as shy-girl, terrified, pig-headed, extravagant - and then have wound up just being You once the initial asserting winds down to non-essential. Lucy strains a tad more feces from her, coughs from the effort. May I say something else? 'If you must.' Carrying on three-simultaneous, erotically-charged relationships - with satellite thoughts for more on the side - might just be running your poor heart hamster-wheel! 'I don't have a poor heart. The main thesis, I agree with, but my heart has deep pockets - no one knows the murk it bores down to.' But yes, Lucy gets it - she might just be overwhelmed. Thinking about the mother makes her think about Ariel and the book makes her think about Elliott and that makes her think about Ariel and other things jutted into the bargain - murdered neighbors and Layla and old-chapbooks-about-Dorene and things. 'Let's not discount that my mind might be lying to me, though' she says as she flushes, depressing the lever, film-noir, with her foot. 'We never forget that' she waits until she is at the mirror to say. And she focuses hard on her reflection so it is crisp when she says this. 'We never forget that.' And lets her eyes make the reflection blurry when she replies 'Good. Good. I think that that's wise.'

Déjà vu. Samantha says 'You know, I almost didn't bother to try being friends with you.' Lucy says: 'Why's that? I mean, that's a good instinct, largely - but why?' Samantha says: 'You did tell me you figured I probably didn't have a soul.' Lucy remembers having had this conversation, before - not about saying Samantha probably didn't have a soul - that she has no recollection of - but Lucy remembers, kind of, Samantha telling her how Lucy had said that, once, and how Samantha had almost decided not to befriend her. 'Is your soul particularly important to you?' 'This is the thing' explains Samantha 'on reflection it turned out not.' 'Do you know why I said that?' Lucy is more involved in trying to recall the conversation Samantha is referencing than she is on keeping up the spice of the current banter. 'Because you're awful and lack decorum, I suppose.' But Lucy meant: specifically. 'Something like I just said *St. Anthony* by *Belle and Sebastien* is not my favorite song.' 'Oh' Lucy says 'well, then I kind of had a point, right? Is that what you mean? You realized I had a point?' Holding her own - Samantha has turned out to be quite the whipper-snapper - Samantha just rolls her eyes and goes 'No, you don't have a point. I just realized it's kind of immaterial to get upset by something some dame working a temp-job says about souls when said dame doesn't even believe there are souls to begin with. I just recognized your weakness and found you piteous but was still interested in spending a couple of hours downtown with you, right?' Lucy pops a laugh, caught off guard, and says she finds applied-logic in her defense the sexiest thing in the world. Samantha does a doffing her cap gesture and points out they have wandered in the most ridiculous direction possible from their car, are currently standing outside of industrial buildings and a Medical Supply store with prosthetic legs on display in the windows and three mannequin-heads on display to showcase a variety of eyepatches. 'Then again' Samantha adds, regretting she didn't start with the joke 'I figure we walked out here because this where you do most of your shopping, right?' 'Just need to pick up some of the necessities. Milk, eggs' says Lucy 'catheters, splints.' 'And that's just to serve breakfast to houseguests, right?' They fall into wondering about the fact that such a shop even has a window display. 'What sort of clauses in what sort of contracts necessitate this? Do the parties involved have no idea that this shop is located down this odd backroad - that no one could arrive to it by accident?' 'We did' Samantha observes. But Lucy ignores that, nose-to-glass and focused on the eyepatches. 'They aren't even different!' Samantha, like Lucy, goes to her haunches and gets close enough to the glass that their breathing, off-sync, keeps the pane fogged like the blinking of an out-of-order traffic-signal. 'That one has some different stitching' Samantha says, snapping like she has solved some puzzle on a children's placemat at some diner. Lucy nods, but insists the other two are exactly the same. 'This place seems shady. That's all I'm saying. If I had to come here, I'd feel my doctors were neglecting my care.' Samantha slips her hand into Lucy's back pocket, both still knelt, and says 'What about this selection of surgical masks and gloves?' Lucy looks, Samantha removing hand from back pocket, slipping it down into the pants, outside of Lucy's panties, tensing it back to the same grip it had held. 'They're nice' Lucy says. 'But I'm more in the mood for a neck-brace.' 'A neck-brace?' Samantha says, slacking grip, lifting hand slightly, finger-tips in through the tight-pinched elastic of panties now, down no further. 'Or a crutch' says Lucy. 'Do you think they sell crutches?'

Let's take a moment to discuss this night: overcast coming in now, brightening things by distributing the blotted moonlight and sopping up - or so it feels - the streetlamps from underneath where Lucy and Samantha quite shiver. Starting with that, how silly it is to think the ground affects the night sky, yet we think the ground affects the night sky! The clouds, don't they seem close? Not childish, not like one eye can be closed and a reach can be given and fingers will come back sticky from sugar - but still close, as though it would take less than an airplane to reach them. The night shrinks the world when cloudy, makes each person aware of the shuttered storefront that is their realm. Clouds like this, they finite the cosmos, make the stars honestly - when they appear through a crack - seem specifically to have to do with our sky. Our sky, nights show us, is just clouds. The far-reaches beyond? Nothing to do with us! Not ours. Not ours. And closer in: let's discuss the cast of different shades of streetlamps, orange taking on and distributing the cast of green neon from the *SaveMoreRT* - Lucy notes to herself that might be the best sign she has ever seen, especially for its scurvy-gilled lime-tone, fritizing a bzttt as she passes under and her skin is flushed of all blemish - or the red from *Calzones To Gooooo!* - this is a paradise of signs! this rink-a-dink shopping-center she would avoid from the main road like an open sore! - the blue blink and white blink of this bank advertising *Free Checking* and *something indistinguishable something indistinguishable Credit*. Somehow, the pavement takes all this light in without seeming changed - glances down are glances of the reality without the trappings of man-made, glances side-to-side a flurry of Crayola-fogs and shadows clacking off angularly and waifly through. At what age did Lucy start hurrying through the night to her vehicle or to her home? At what age did Interior seem to take the place of loitering-no-place? Is this as much pretend, this comfort, for Samantha? This is looking around at the penned-in Earth, bound by vastness beyond, this is side-glances caught up in cough-into-hand colors that distract for seeming real - but give it an hour, give it back-to-the-car and any kiss or 'Let's go to my place' and will it be eyes down to pavement, to gravity, to where they stand and want to get warm from and remember? 'Is this a memory?' Lucy asks. Samantha just says 'Yes.' 'This already happened?' 'Yes' Samantha says again. 'Then why are we here?' Samantha shoves Lucy and tells her 'My friend, there is more to life than thinking cool things. Can I tell you something?' 'You may' Lucy says, snooty with her grammar she cares nothing for, really. 'I don't care if this is a memory or if I remember it. Do you know how I can't even name all of the places on a map? If I am going to be worried about something, it's going to be that more than why I am walking with you.' Sweet, that. But let's get back to the night. Lucy and Samantha crest a parking lot hill and the shop-front-long banner for the Rules of Layaway for items - a thing the shop offers - is presented as though a declaration that each customer has won top marks and should come in for their crowns! Racks of clothes are left out, all overnight. And someone is washing the outside window of the *Hunan Impressive*, meticulous and grid-like in their application of the squeegee. Samantha waves like she knows the man and he says 'Hello' like maybe Samantha actually does.

They mill in front of their both parked cars, only Lucy smoking and Samantha's car already chugging. Lucy says that Samantha's comment about maps really struck a nerve and she needs to spend some time letting it make her feel bad. 'It made me realize: I'm the sort who trusts anything. I could go into my bank tomorrow and they hand me anything and tell me *That's just what money looks like these days* - well, not only would I take their word, be alright with it, but I'd seek no independent verification other than waiting to see if people won't let me buy things.' 'You're a chump.' 'I am a chump' Lucy says, spraying smoke like a dropped hose and pointing at Samantha's chest with the cig like she is emphatically dotting a *J* on a chalkboard. Further evidence? Lucy used a lot of Check Cashing joints in her life. They tell her 'We take *X Y* or *Z* percent of your money, each time.' 'And all I say is *Okay*. And do the leg-work of explaining to myself: *Just pretend your job pays you fifteen dollars less than it does.* I' she points at herself 'tell myself' *My Self* pronounced as two words, two pats to her chest 'that. But if they told me that, you know what I'd do?' Samantha wiggles fingers for a smoke - Lucy is glad, Samantha has caught on they will be here awhile still - and says 'Just tell them *That's right* but glower about it on your drive home?' Lucy lights a new smoke and passes it to Samantha, saying 'Yes' with the slight edit that 'it would be a *walk home*, not a *drive.*' Samantha smokes kind of funny. She places her cigarette right into her lip corner, the crease, like someone with a wired-shut jaw being served dinner. She doesn't so much seem to inhale as to swallow - Lucy swears she sees and hears the glu-glug of gorge up and down - and she lets an inordinate amount of the smoke out down her nose, like there is something different about the inside of her head than most people's, the smoke just channeled to the nostrils by air currents based on screwy digestions. Or something. 'What are you thinking about?' Lucy blinks. Admits all she had just been thinking. 'What are you thinking about?' Well, now Samantha is thinking about how self-conscious she has become and wishing she could find something to mock about Lucy's smoking technique! 'I wasn't mocking you!' 'I didn't say you were mocking me, I said what you were thinking makes me want to mock you.' Samantha makes belittling snap-snap gestures like *Pay-attention-dummy.* 'There's more to the world than you, Lucy Jinx.' But Lucy maintains that she isn't so sure about that. And if she has to, she has science to cite which, while not backing her one-hundred-percent as being the only extant thing, at least puts all other considerations in to question. 'You mean to tell me' Samantha seems genuinely surprised by this 'that of all the things there are to trust, you trust Science? Mathematics?' 'What isn't to trust? It's a whole branch of human thought built on proving in more and more complex ways that everything is utter rubbish! I'd vote that in to office, any day.' Lucy shares the few math facts she knows - how the folks building the pyramids were able to make sure the base was level and about that thing about the guy in the bath finding out the density of gold. Lucy asks if it's true that those standing rocks at Stonehenge were really just rocks already in the ground that those clever little Druids dug down around. They kiss. They kiss. Samantha tells Lucy to get in her idiot car.

There: Samantha's taillights. Above - there - now we see the moon, grousey old potbelly of it. The clouds are parting like over-dramatic fingers revealing amateur-applied stage make-up to a quarter-filled house, last night of the show closing early. The radio plays *Duke of Earl* and Lucy sings along. And cannot help thinking what would happen if she just stopped following Samantha - just didn't make this right turn, for example. How would life go? Would Samantha notice? Sure. Would she - what? - pull over and wait, try to raise Lucy on the phone? Yes. Likely. But what if Lucy didn't answer? Or go in to work ever again? What if Lucy went out of her way to have the last moment between the two of them be that look they had shared, Samantha mouthing 'Follow me?' fingers dot-doting in the direction of the main road, Lucy giving her an 'Aye-aye, Captain' salute? Speaking of phones, Lucy feels hers go off in her pocket. Or she thinks so. Yep, it is ringing. Wrangling it out, she finds it is Samantha calling. 'Hello?' 'I need to pull in at the bank to deposit something. I forgot. Just so you know when I do that that's why I'm doing it.' Lucy just says 'Okay' but finds this call weird. Like Samantha had an insight Lucy was thinking of scampering, needed to assert herself backwards, keep the cord taut. Obviously, Lucy was just following and would have added one to one to get two when they pulled in at a bank how Samantha needed said bank. This bank. Lucy is tempted to keep driving, just to have Samantha call her and go to Samantha 'Oh! That's right! Bank! I wondered what you were doing - now I see what you meant!' Instead, she idles in line and tries to see if she can tell what Samantha's pin-number is just from watching. Not at all. Not at all. But if she were really trying to find out, she'd set up better surveillance than this. Phone buzzes, again - this time just a text. Layla. *What are you doing? What if I told you I was in jail? What if I told you there were bees in my house, if I had a house? What if told you I wanted to narrate a dance I was doing? Explain yourself!* To which Lucy, obviously, texts back *I'm right behind you.* And that to which Layla obviously texts back *Liar. I just looked.* To which Lucy, obviously, texts back *I meant when you're facing the way you're facing now - sorry, I thought you understood that without it being spelt out explicit.* Layla: *I haven't turned! I just looked over my shoulder!* Lucy: *It's not surprising you didn't see me then - you have to give a good look, man, or am I not worth the time. You should see what I'm wearing. It's unbelievable.* Now an extended car honk and Lucy looking up to find the air in front of her car vacant. Blink. Another honk. Out ahead. Samantha's car lulling at the turn out of the lot, Lucy's phone buzzing with an incoming call. 'Sorry - I think I had a mini-stroke or something, I'm coming I'm coming.' Samantha laughs and hangs up in the middle of doing so. Lucy takes a moment to wipe at her eye with her shoulder top and to yawn, shoving her phone back down in her pocket. And there: Samantha's taillights.

And now Lucy: following behind Samantha to the elevator. Beside Samantha in the elevator. Behind Samantha is this corridor. Behind Samantha in through the door. Samantha doesn't want to sound presumptuous, but would Lucy mind if she makes herself something to eat before the night continues. And without waiting for an answer - Lucy sluggishly getting out of coat, shoes, stretching her back in the trace of a lackadaisical *ampersand* - Samantha flips on a kitchen light and lifts a pot from where it had been overturned on a towel, filling it with tap water, setting it on the stove and turning this and that kind of dial. So, this is where Samantha lives. 'So, this is where you live.' There is a *Henry: Portrait of a Serial Killer* poster, there - a nice one. There is a *Driller Killer* poster, there - gorgeous, not anything official, it must have been fan-made. And there is a *Man Bites Dog* poster, there. And on the table a bunch of issues of *Captain American* and the *Submariner* from - if Lucy were to venture a guess - almost twenty-five years ago. What else? *Bikini Kill* framed album art. A blown up image of Nick Cave from the video for *Stagger Lee*. Some old nude watercolors by probably-someone-important. And painted on that wall - hard to see, but Lucy knows the words so doesn't have to really be able to read them - a quotation from Remedios Varo: *On second thought, I think I am more crazy than my goat*. Lucy joins Samantha in the kitchen, Samantha poking at raviolis and stirring a sauce in a separate pan. 'You give yourself the tour?' 'Some of it. Did you write that on the wall?' 'No. The person who lived here before. She died.' Lucy figures this is a joke - or rather doesn't care - and starts opening cabinets randomly, explaining she is looking for hidden cameras. 'Cameras come later. They shalln't be hidden. I do wet-plate photography, is all I mean, and might ask you to just hang around while I set up a still-life.' 'Why do you work where you work?' Samantha gives Lucy an aggressive pinch in the flab of her hip, Lucy smacking Samantha's wrist with some actual anger. 'What the fuck, man?' Lucy laughs, but aggravation toning the laugh tentative. Samantha apologies, says she really didn't mean to get that much skin. 'I'm joking about the cameras, too. And yes, I painted that on the wall. There's a bunch of quotes on the wall. I went through a phase or something. See all the shit on my walls, in fact? I bought it all over the course of one week, like two years ago! Before that, there was nothing in this apartment except for the same stuff I'd been lugging around since junior-college. I even had an aquarium in here for awhile - no fish in it - but I started creeping even myself out with that. I think, somewhere' - Samantha sighs, sticks a ravioli, lifts it, pokes it with her finger, drops it back in water - 'I came under the impression I was too normal and needed to compensate. I'm not the cleverest or most socially apt, so ordering things over the computer seemed the best proposition. I own a lot of comic-books, too - but I have no idea what most of them are. I bought, sight unseen, a lot of the inventory from some shop going out-of-business. Boxes of that shit in a closet and more in storage, downstairs!' Lucy kisses Samantha's neck, just to feel things have gotten back to equilibrium, and asks if she has any pain-reliever tablets. A drawer is opened. Lucy swallows some pills. Jokes 'See how much I trust you?' and Samantha joshes back 'See how much you don't?'


IN LUCY'S DREAM, SHE IS saying to a woman she knew long ago - a woman named Juliet - 'It's funny, because I'm not drunk - I know I'm not, I remember I'm not - but my arms feel really really really like I am.' And the woman, Juliet, is peeling gauze from off of a painting, Lucy feeling patient about that, watching in the sort of mildly interested way one watches someone they care a great deal about doing something they are indifferent to, themselves. The gauze drops to the floor, crisp as old chicken bones. The paint globbed to the peelings is adhesive, sticky in the fashion of bubble-gum stepped on, and a dog gives some strands of it a sniff. Focus shifts: up-close of the dog's wet nostrils, the snout-skin looks luggage-leather solid, the slick is more like the glaze of a stale doughnut and - as in the dream Lucy suspected! - the fuzzy look is the result of groupings of ants cluttered and feeding on the animal. 'There! Do you see?' An old man is nuzzled close and now they are both looking at the up-close of the nose - the dog in a glass case, a circle of magnifying lenses showing the vermin devouring it while it is snuffling and this-way-and-thating, in and out of the scope of the viewer. They complain how the dog won't sit still, that this is always the way with such things! 'Animals are never easy' Lucy says and in the dream she is rolling the chair she was in to the far corner of the room, then with awkward sitting-steps making her way back over. Two dogs. Three. But small. The size of porcupines. The size of ceramic porcupines. And the weight. They are statuettes bought for gardens. They are stale from sunlight hardening the once slick green moss that ponds had coated them with. Lucy watches the water surface litter with lily-pads, an adventurous fungus of them, so many she thinks she could walk right over the pond surface, reach the food waiting and the water-fountain on the other side. But then the dream is from underside the carpet of floating growth. Claustrophobia and sounds like in the hollow of a steel-drum. This changing to Lucy with ear pressed to a wet wall, listening to the silverware-drawer sharp sound of an old television screeching pornography. Lucy is in the room. It is empty, abandoned and unwashed feeling, the way dust at windows in a movie you never learn the title of made years ago feels. Lucy should not be there. The food in the dish belongs to the man who owns the place and he is sick in bed upstairs! She knows it and so mutes the volume of the television. Grotesque! A tongue entirely covered in tiny-ball piercings is being sucked by a man with three missing teeth! For some reason, in the dream, Lucy is not appalled enough to turn away. Her mind seems to jam on the image, in fact. All sounds go tuning-fork-struck and this louder and louder and the feeling of the dream is suffocating - as though the world is a broken foot that cannot be removed from a shoe it has been burnt inside of, flesh melded with fabric and pain the exact words of the only song left. How long does the dream keep going? It might be a sound - is a sound - that sounds exactly like twenty-nine years. Things are hard to tell. Then she wakes.

Samantha has her eyes open, but only just barely - drapes her arm over Lucy's chest but then rolls to the other side upon realizing Lucy is standing up. 'Don't make breakfast - I'm making you breakfast' half-asleeps Samantha. Lucy assures her she has no intention of making breakfast. Bleary, Lucy makes her way to the bathroom, closes herself in, and sinks to the blunt of the toilet seat, surprised she doesn't pass out, full on. The inside of Lucy's mouth seems waterlogged - it seems a pocket inside-outed, wet from the laundry, and her breath taste like she vaguely recalls it did when she once chewed a dollar bill up and tried to swallow it. Whenever that was. Middle-school. Now? Now: Lucy is making herself stand up. Nope. She is not going to go to sleep on the bathroom floor! 'Why would I?' she yawns, and meanwhile has fit her image to the mirror in front of her rather as though getting fresh sheets arranged around a typewriter roll, snap of the first keys testing the ribbon's ink smack smack smack. When her eyes adjust to the light, she can make out very easily several dense bruisers around the curve of her neck. She drinks some tap-water, testing a proper swallow - some difficulty, but not too much. She coughs and it is mildly sore throat. The marks are kind of magnificent. The result of a two-handed grip, carried away in the pitch-black, Lucy's legs bent, tense, and her lower torso bucking like a mousetrap. The gradient of purple against the toothpaste-peach of Lucy's flesh makes her feel like an artwork, a sheet water-colored on either expertly or accidentally-well by some child. Lucy's presses the bruises. No pain. No sensation. No whitening and then re-purpling of the color. If there were a way to tattoo this exact pigmentation, she would consider it. Wounds the always-stain-seeming of birthmarks. Some other less intriguing evidence of fingers raked and teeth applied adorn her. Nothing as interesting as the result of the choke-out. Lucy had never felt her head swim so much. Had never felt her eyes strain and seem to carbonate from the pressure at their roots. It was like seeing the sound of a gasp that couldn't issue so needed another sense to render itself. The words on the mirror read *Not for all the tea in China - not if I could sing like a bird - not for all North Carolina* and Lucy Jinx is tempted to add the rest of the lyric as she lets the tune fill her head and she curls her toes, cracking them again and again until curling them is silent. Back into the bedroom, Samantha is snoring at a sluggish lilt, completely unearthed from the covers and entirely goose pimpled to the touch. Lucy's body shivers as it finds a fit and Samantha's body does not react at all, the curve of her no more welcoming than the lowermost of a ship's bobbing hull. Lucy pulls covers over both of them. Just as she drifts off, though, Samantha, asleep, suddenly tugs the comforter from both of them and rolls over, back turned to Lucy, foot of one bent leg kind of hard pressing down as it sleeps upon one of Lucy's shins.

Quite suddenly: a very bright room, music from a stereo outside of the door, and Samantha setting a plate with some potato-chips and an egg-and-bacon sandwich on Lucy's nude belly. 'I overslept.' Samantha is dressed and showered, air scented with her applied perfume. Lucy glue-mouths a 'What time is it?' Samantha only saying 'Later than we meant it to be - but you wore me out. And I'm just lazy. I've got to get going though, either way.' Lucy chews a chip and also notices coffee on the bedside table on top of an issue of a comic-book called *Megaton Man*. 'Where are you going?' 'I have to help my cousin pick out a dress for a job interview. You can tell that that's what I actually have to do too, just on the strength of why else would I say so?' 'To trick me, all the more?' Samantha concedes this point, but Lucy assures her she believes her and to ignore her first-waking-moments' paranoia. 'It's like my version of morning-wood, you see?' 'I see.' Samantha kisses her on the nose. 'I am going to trust you not to let any of my prisoners out when you snoop around and find them, okay?' 'Okay' Lucy says through a mouthful of bread and egg, no bacon. 'And I shouldn't call the police, either?' Samantha says 'I'd appreciate it if you didn't' - *Appreciate* pronounced *Ape-Pree-She-hate* - 'but I don't make it my business to go bossing other people around.' Lucy nods and swallows, assuming Samantha noticed and took it as a response. 'I really am sorry to split like this' Samantha calls from the kitchen. 'It's fine' Lucy calls back, hurrying a sip of coffee down to answer without too much of a pause. Samantha at the bedroom door, shoulder-bag and yawning, puts on a sweet tone and says 'I had a swell time, last night - even though you turned out to be kind of creepy.' 'I had a jolly time, too' Lucy retorts 'even though you're a little bit dull for my taste.' 'I won't show you all my vacation-slides next time.' 'I won't tell you so many ghost-stories or, you know, insert-whatever-you-meant-by-creepy there - I'm not really awake, sorry.' And then Samantha is gone, proper. The radio is still playing from outside the bedroom. The sounds of someone walking in the apartment above become omnipresent. Had Samantha told her what time it is? Looks around. No clock. No - there is a clock, but it is unplugged. Another bite finishes the sandwich, this bite only half-chewed and forced downward by swallowed coffee. A yawn that pops her ears. Then, she pads to the kitchen, feeling thudding bounces of her chilly skin as she does, and finds it is not nearly as late as she was fearing. That is: if she trusted the clock. The time does seem to sync with what it feels like from the sunlight glowing the room apple-meat white, though, so Lucy takes it as correct and stretches out on the sofa, hugging a pillow to her chest and working another one carefully on top of her feet. The usual game of telling herself she will sleep just five more minutes. Not even sleep. Just lay for five minutes. Just lay for five minutes. Now waking. Now knowing more than five minutes have passed, fully awake, thinking about nothing. She is more fatigued than she feels in warranted. Starts to have tricks of memory, her body convincing her it threw up at some point during the night. Her mind feels like a faded stamp that a tilt side-to-side keeps convincing her she can read - she can read, she can read it if it stays moving and she looks at it just the right amount of hardly.

Something is wrong with the shower. The water sounds like voices in another room that just won't shut up. A spoilt silence. Bloated, ugly voices. Laughter both false and angry. Lucy does her best to shake the feeling. She lathers herself fully, taking time to move palm - or fingers, at least - over every piece of her, but the usually hermetically sealed sensation of showering is unattainable, for some reason. The water seems to be reaching her through puncture holes - unexpected, leaking in, a sensation of the world deflating around her accompanying it all. Laughter laughter. Laughs pronounced instead of laughed. The mirth of people who have nothing to them except their sour bellies and reasons they shouldn't exist. What's the matter with you, Lucy? She gives her face a light slap - splish-splish - wanting sincerely to snap out of this funk. At the same time as it agitates her, though, she cannot just shut off the water. The heat of it soothes her and makes her feel elsewhere. What it's like? Like a curtain that needs to stay closed because she's crying and doesn't want the audience to know. But you aren't crying Lucy, you're just listening! That is the trouble. Her ears are straining. It is worse for her not being able to hear what is being said! It would be so much more bearable to just hear what the loudmouths are yuking it up over, to sit bitterly tearing down their odious humors inside her own thoughts. Why can't the voices be drowned out, entirely - and how can just a scrap of something be worse than a glut of it? Because - understand - it truly is like Lucy is listening! As though there are voices there. No, no, Lucy doesn't think she is hearing real people - the particular sound of this water against this tile in this bathroom just hits the same pitch that her brain interprets as voices through a room-wall or from up on a roof while she is sitting in a chair on the front porch. Nothing she can do! Her instincts react to the glitch and no amount of reasoning or analysis can undo that! And so when she does shut off the water, she feels spent - which could just be the physical wringer she went through last night filing its report, but it feels more internal, the way only sound can exhaust.

Another problem, see? Lucy actually has plenty of energy and almost is too bouncy to dress properly. Each article of clothing goes on with five minutes of pacing and free-roaming talking-to-herself in between. Another cup of coffee and a peanut-butter sandwich. A cigarette and a feeling of the rest of the day opening like a phonebook in a hotel room just to idle a free moment away, no one to call. Here, Lucy touches fingertips to forehead, pulls them away as though expecting to find out the evidences of a wound. Nothing. Except the fingertips seem pruned from dehydration. A telephone rings and rings and rings. Lucy finds herself eagerly waiting to listen to whatever Samantha's answering-machine message will be, but when the ringing stops there is just nothing. Or not nothing. There is the persistent sound of footfalls above her. The radio. And now trash-trucks outside, bansheeing away in through whichever window Samantha has left open.

What could be going on? What is all of this a sign of? Lucy, if she had to put a term to it, would say that she feels *Normal*. She feels this must be what it feels like to be not-Lucy-Jinx - just some dullard, just some one of those people she sees all the time and cannot fathom. But why does she feel this way? It's offensive! She collapses to Samantha's bed and stares at the ceiling as though enduring small-talk and conversations with co-workers about overtime and inconsequential matters they are all lying about having heard from assistant managers are 'the plans from Corporate.' This must be what a car-wash employee feels like who does nothing but wonder who will win whatever ballgame is being played while they work. This must be what it would feel like if being infected by smallpox was a sentence stuck in your head - the words for it, the words for it - Lucy is convulsing in an infection of ordinary language. No one to help her. An aneurysm of banality, she flops to the floor like spilt gelatin from a plastic spoon. Oh God. You always knew it would happen one day, Lucy, and this is that day. Eventually, the bottom would fall out and your thoughts would no longer be able to maintain, whatever forces were helping you stay aloft would defunct or lose interest in you - or realize, more likely, they had no idea they had been helping you, your previous lack of descent had only been on account of an oversight - the end coming instantly, all of those words you were lost in now a thicket burst through and after that thicket just an expanse of blank, of the same green here as there, exactly the same warmth, exactly the same cold, a world long and preordained, a life like an experiment done in Science class to prove there can be something everyone is already looking at so knows well there can be. How about it, Lucy? That night with Samantha you are no longer even articulate enough to recall was your final night as someone possessed of grandiloquence - and from this point forward you live and breathe the way a catalog is printed and circulated by being placed on shop-counters!

What's that? What's that? Of course you don't know what you mean! That's the entire worm of this terror, Lucy - this panic-attack is reminding you that that will be your horror! Not even clever enough to notate, to jot down what it is you are in scared shitless thrall to! The panic of the masses! The depression of someone who has never even spelled the word ennui, malaise - the unnamable not because it can't be named but because no one around is intelligent enough to remember the alphabet! This is the feeling of being a stain that no longer has a smell. A residue-of-a-residue, that last shadow, barely there, that cannot quite be scrubbed away, chipped gone with the point of a knife, so is just resigned to be, ignored, considered part of how-things-are-now. What is the opposite of *Cherished*? Lucy Jinx, you are now. This is a taste of what it will be like to fall out of favor with language, to choose another mistress, to leap from the heat in the pan where you sizzle! Lucy splays out on the bed and this-sides-and-that-sides and tangles herself in the used sheets and brandishes herself around to be rid of them. Then - a cold breath - she is calm. She is calm. And just lays. Staring. Or not. Eyes open, anyway. Doing nothing. Was that asleep? Awake? Both? Neither? Language returns to her like a post-nasal drip.

Messages from Layla. Five of them. Lucy mumbles some curse-words and opens each up, feeling lousier than she needs to. Layla had a good attitude about Lucy dropping off from the conversation, so abruptly. Of course. But Lucy dashes off an apology, nevertheless, fully blowhard confessional of what naughty business she had got up to - because that is the surest way to earn Layla's forgiveness. And the phone, she keeps it in her hand as she makes her way to the elevator and down it, out through the lobby door, and tries to get her bearings as to where she may have parked. Phone vibrates, but it is Samantha. *You wouldn't still happen to be in my apartment would you?* Lucy waits until she has a cigarette going and has held the door open for a young man helping an elderly woman with a walker before typing back *I could be. I'm having a smoke at my car. What's up?* The air seems particularly pagan, just now. Lucy is at a loss to say why, but it does. Or not *pagan* - she doesn't mean *pagan*. The air seems that if it had always been like this people never would have advanced past worshipping plants, moved on to animals, moved on to things shaped like giant people and then on to forms humanoid but incorporating abstract ideas. Samantha writes *Nevermind. It's not important.* And this Lucy finds kind of irritating. So writes back *Oh for Christ's, just tell me what you need. I can head back up.* And hitting Send, Lucy realizes she actually cannot. No key. Unless she hadn't locked the door. Had she? 'Shit' she says and steps out her smoke, hurrying through the door into a stab of the elevator-summon button. *No, really. I needed you to do something inside. If you already left, it's no good.* Lucy clomps the corridor length and is breathless when she finds the door, indeed, is unlocked. No help to anyone, Lucy, no help to anyone. You can't well tell Samantha you had left her door open! Why not? Well, you can if you say *It's funny, I just realized I hadn't locked your door and was heading back up*. 'But I don't want to do that' Lucy says, very harried, wringing the words like a sponge coiled harshly so it would dry in one twist. But Samantha is doing her mind reading business again. *Or were you not able to lock the door?* Samantha should be a goddamn politician, phrasing the question like that! *No, I locked the door. I just realized you're right, I can't get it. Sorry man, I'm worthless*. And back at the elevator, it occurs to Lucy she's still not sure if she locked the door! Samantha: *It's no worries*. And Lucy cannot help laughing aloud, as though someone is watching her and she wants to visually and aurally confirm she finds herself absurd. Nope. Door is still unlocked. Mother of God, Lucy should be kept out of public circulation! She tests the finally-locked door several times, hardly trusting herself to be able to.

And the drive home is radioless and no more messages from Layla come in. There is the distant smoke of what Lucy imagines to be a barn-fire, neighbors in a line passing bucket person-to-person - from the creek-water dipped into to the splash, hiss of this effort accomplishing nothing. And at one traffic-light are the languid sounds of a band playing music in a parking lot, the morning doing nothing to grace the cymbals and trombones with any sort of contained acoustical precision, just a music of split thumb-tacks being pushed to a pile carefully by bottom edge of palm, picked up a-few-at-a-time and plink plink plink dropped back into their container. Somewhere near to her side of town Lucy tenses a bit, fearing some further consequence of the shattered backend of her car, a ticket she could be burdened with - but then she recalls she has the report of the accident in the glovebox, so no one could hold her at fault for any regulatory infraction this morning! *This afternoon* her car-clock reminds her. 'This afternoon' she says. Time, time. It moves in pace with the blood or the boredom. Lucy hits Record and repeats that. 'Time moves in time with the blood or the boredom.' Clicks the recorder off. *In time?* Or *In pace? To pace?* Well, anyway, it's no good. Because blood moves faster when one is bored. Everyone knows that. There might never be a time that the blood is more furious in its curling flow. Like a hyperactivity leading to a paralysis! Speed gets so fast it outpaces itself! The world could seize on its own momentum! 'You should be recording all of this' Lucy chastens herself. Not that you'd ever play it back. Which is a shame. You're a wise woman. 'I am a wise woman' Lucy says, gritting her teeth when the car in front of her decides not to drive through the light at the yellow. The fact that boredom is a hyperactivity, though? That is true! Lucy has remarked, even in thought, the same heavy feeling of standstill when her thoughts race as when she cannot manage to find one. A tick more, in fact, when her mind is a blank! Things so hyped to a tizzy they discorporate a little bit. '*Sandstill*' Lucy says. 'The word ought to be *sandstill*. That is evocative. *Standstill* is so lifeless and without musicality - it brings nothing to mind except idleness. *Sandstill* is beyond that. The gnawing refusal to move and the fact that even a rapacious sandstorm, all that motion, does nothing to change the overall definition of a desert! Not only is the sand *Still* - as in the sand is not moving - the sand is sand *Still* - as in no amount of motion or flux can alter it into anything but what it always has been. It is *sand, still*. And it is *sand, still*.' Leave Lucy in charge of everything and complexity reaches children's-rhyme level! She smacks the wheel and makes a gnashing growl to assert her authority. 'I am the motherless tongue!' she exclaims. And there. There! That should be the title of her compendium! *The motherless tongue: poems by Lucy Jinx.* Road underneath. 'I am the motherless tongue, poetry, Lucy Jinx!' Road underneath her. Lucy is hurrying home.

She had left the heater on, it seems - had she set it to eighty degrees? - and the apartment is doused in the scents of the dishwasher having run. Tip tip tip, she downs the temperature and leaves her coat on the floor. Her shoes on the floor. Cigarette. Maybe it doesn't smell like the dishwasher. Maybe that's something from one of the apartments surrounding. She can't even smell it, now. Maybe a waft of some scent in from outside, last minute. Lucy has removed her socks and fallen face first onto the sofa, feeling around on the floor for the remote control. There's no need for that, Lucy. 'Yes, I know.' And the rat under the sofa swipes at her, cutting the flesh of the webbing between thumb and forefinger. She opens her eyes. Body startles. Foot in a spasm of cold, as though her toes are trying to unscrew themselves, teeth biting them, jaw twisting to get the damn things going, sweat on the brow for the effort. Spills over on to her back. The ceiling is there. Patterns of shadows like a gravel walkway shaped like the mouth of a screaming child. And out the throat rolls a wet banner, painting the brick wall in a slobberish silver, everyone coming out from work to tug at the objects, sparkling, that seem caught inside of it, all of them insisting 'They're diamonds! They're diamonds!' Lucy not so sure, lurking back, enduring spun around distrustful eyes, everyone certain she will use the knife in her hand to stab them when they have unstuck their fortunes, hid them under their coats and tried to hurry off. 'I won't' Lucy says, but doesn't see why she has to drop the blade. 'You're a liar!' the little girl screeches and the screech goes so high that the sun leaks a cascade of wasps that land in new shadows, filling in the blank spots of these women who are all disappearing. Awake again, Lucy snaps up, lifts herself from the sofa and shakes her face around, bulbous and long, her arms soggy, slick, wet rubber tentacles. She starts the oven and takes a pizza out of its packaging, leaving it to thaw on the stovetop, certain this will keep her from slurping down into sleep again. But not so. She is foolish enough to sit on the sofa - and back tilt goes her head and all around her are people fitting themselves against each other, closer and closer, a school-teacher reminding her it was all her smart idea so she needs to just watch what she's done! The beepbeepbeep!! of the oven-temperature being reached wakes her, but she can't quite muster the necessary energy to stand. Her shoulders are tight, seem stuck to together like the hastily scribbled lines of a doctor's signature. Or like a stamp being stamped three times in not-quite-the-same place because each time a certain part just doesn't quite show up on the paper. What? What!!? Lucy jolts and begins coughing and her neck won't move from where it is turned sideways now on the arm of the sofa, her foot against the wall, arm underneath her and tingling asleep, the numb in pulses painful and calligraphic in their precision.

'Ariel! Oh thank God you called! I think I have the sleeping sickness!' 'That's actually what I was calling you about. So you do have it? Good. Okay, bye.' Lucy opens the oven door to see how the pizza is coming along, not trusting it to cook proper from having been so thawed out when she stuck it in at the temperature appropriate to it starting out frozen. 'Any chance you want to come over?' 'I thought I was coming over. Wasn't I? I was planning to, I think.' Ariel makes a big sound of thinking about it, but in the end is fairly certain they had no plans to meet today. 'No?' 'Nope. Are you supposed to meet someone else and just spliced me in there because I'm the classier option?' Lucy sidesteps this by explaining her pizza situation and that she was only half-joking about the sleeping sickness. 'But you've never been any good at sleeping' Ariel offers. 'How would you know if I've ever been any good at sleeping?' 'You used to tell me.' And Lucy kind of remembers. Yes. She would. She'd narrated, several times back in the *Hernando's Highlights* days - told Ariel about getting caught in piles of unsettling dreams. 'Why do you want me to come over?' 'Because I'm in love with you and long for you by my side. Is that all of a sudden something to fault me for?' 'It's just that - not at all - now you have me worried I have an actual obligation. Today. Or that I'd promised my time to another.' Ariel non-sequiturs that she had been typing an e-mail and has misspelled *Today* as *Oday* and then the computer had offered her the correction *o'day* and when she selected it and looked up a minute later *o'day* was marked incorrect. 'What happened next?' Lucy peeks at the pizza, which seems to be cooking everywhere but in its dead-center. 'I saw what options it had for me, now - and it was just *Oday*, without the apostrophe. Which is what I wrote to start! My point being: did you know none of those are words?' 'Except *Today*, you mean?' 'Well, I'm not sure I can even trust that!' Lucy suddenly just blurts out 'I love you!!!' and Ariel drops her tone to a register suggesting suspicion. 'Nothing is going on! I just do love you.' And Lucy agrees to come over and Ariel says 'Great' and hangs up. The pizza is a lost cause. Still edible, but it has a chalky sort of flavor, very much like something in it might have turned unhealthy in the period of time it was just a doughy, luke-warming thing on the stovetop. What was Lucy going to do today - *o'day Oday* - if not see Ariel? And is it a good sign, how much she had assumed she'd see Ariel? Hadn't she just kissed the mother and fucked Samantha last night? Aren't those exactly the sorts of things she shouldn't be doing? This seems to be a recurrent conversation, so she does her best to ignore it, focusing instead on how proud she is of herself for not having fallen asleep, again.

Bianca! Lucy - you had agreed to meet with Bianca! Which is an obvious thing to not remember, since you don't believe there even really is any Bianca - but that is what you had said you'd be thrilled to do. And you are remembering it now with basically exactly enough time to get to the restaurant you had agreed on. Simple solution? Call Ariel up, apologize, say you will come over but it will have to be a little bit later on. 'Because I'm meeting Bianca' Lucy says aloud, as though in explanation to the woman she loves, over the phone. 'Oh don't be that way! I just need to see who Bianca is. I half-suspect she's you, just dicking me about!' In all seriousness though, Lucy: are you going to flake-out on Bianca? 'Don't say *flake-out!*' What if you do know Bianca? Aren't you interested in that intriguing possibility? 'Not especially, no' Lucy is able to say with all candor. See? Lucy has finally become tired of all of this! This is a goddamned toothache of a situation! Lucy isn't going to go see Bianca, no, and finds it unfair that she has to define a situation in her life by Going-To or Not-Going-To this basically imaginary intruder. It isn't fair. Because now Bianca - who might not be real - will be in Lucy's head all day and will, in fact, gain in power and presence and reality, in a sense, for being shunned and treated as figment! Other plan? Tell Ariel you just have to make a quick stop, drive to the restaurant where Bianca will be meeting you, and see if you can recognize anybody you see there. That's not a bad idea. 'That's not a bad idea' Lucy says. 'But I'm still not going to do it. Oh I have a reason' she snaps, before she can even nag herself with 'Jesus, Lucy - why in Hell not?' *'Why in Hell not?* Because I won't recognize anyone - I won't - but then - I know me - I will convince myself and convince myself - after the fact - that I did, on second thought, recognize someone! And my mind will come to forget what anyone I actually saw looked like and will conjure up an appearance for Bianca and I'll have inadvertently given her more life, more power! I will end up crafting her and birthing her - full-grown and historically intact - out of my pure will to ignore her! I am a bad fabulist novel from Portugal or something. I am sick-and-tired of me!' Lucy is slamming her purse to the counter, opening it, checking she has her cigarettes, checking she has her car keys. Then she just sulks on the counter and eats the last little snip of peperoni that was left behind on the cookie-sheet. 'I've picked Ariel. I pick Ariel' Lucy says, but then adds on 'I am just saying that to see what it would sound like.' Then she thinks 'But obviously, I mean, I picked Ariel - I pick Ariel, right?' This is like a nightmare she once had about a genie that would grant wishes even if you only thought them and so went granting all sorts of things just because the words *I wish* were thought while she was still thinking what to add after. Then - here we go! - she comes up with the following convolution and is satisfied. She will tell Bianca she was there! She'll not back down from the assertion and say she waited for two hours and even had them see if someone named *Bianca* had shown up and they told her 'No'. 'So - I don't know what could have happened' Lucy baffles to her empty apartment 'but, I mean, I was there.'

A MAN OPENS THE DOOR. And he looks like this. Object. Glasses on object. Pleasant enough smile under a mouth afflicted around with hair. A sweater - green-with-grey-stripes or grey-with-thick-green-stripes. End description. Now: the man is saying 'Hi'. And he is looking at Lucy not like she doesn't belong here just like she has never been here, before. 'Well, hello' she says. Anything else, Lucy? Thankfully, the man does not note the pause because he is turning around and calling 'What?' up the stairs and reacting as though listening, now - but Lucy cannot hear what, even as a garble, the man is listening to. Suddenly: 'You're here for Ariel?' 'I'm Lucy' Lucy extends a hand forward to say but the man is again turning, laughing, saying loudly in the direction of the stairs 'I'm talking to someone at the door.' Not angry-loud. Humorful-loud. The man speaks as though he is the only one not missing something. 'Come in' he says to Lucy and backs away to give her some space. Then Ariel is padding, hair wet and barefoot, down the stairs. 'I asked who it was - Hi Lucy, sorry, I meant to be ready.' The man has peeled off from the conversation in the direction of the kitchen and Ariel's face goes ashen with apology, imperative wrinkles to eye-sides, to brow, nose so tense it might swallow itself. Ariel mouths something Lucy doesn't catch - this happening quickly - then, in a voice not matching her features. says 'I told Leo you were coming over - I don't know why he interrogated you at the door.' The last of that sentence was said loud and aimed to bend around the corner to where Leopold - I mean, Lucy knew that's who it was, but now it is confirmed - could be heard crunching on some carrots or something. 'He didn't interrogate me' Lucy goes, matching the casualness of Ariel and trying to exude There's-nothing-to-worry-about and Should-I-leave? at the same time 'he just exercised the appropriate amount of caution when a questionable character shows up, unsolicited.' 'For all I knew she was hiding pamphlets somewhere, trying to get my guard down before wheeling-and-dealing me some Sunday School, you know?' That was Leopold. And Lucy laughs, still doing variant facial expressions at Ariel, saying around the

868 / PABLO D'STAIR

corner to Leopold - and also generally to include everyone - 'Exactly. It's your fault, if anything, Ariel. You can't just spring me on people and make them answer the door for you, on top.' Leopold shuffles into the space where Lucy and Ariel stand, Ariel not moving close to him at all, he giving a smile to her belly, an attempted smile to her face - which Ariel seems to know how to time glances-away-from perfectly to genuinely seem to just-have-missed - and says 'It's he who should apologize, because it is his presence that is aberrant.' 'I'm Leopold, by the way' he nods. 'She knows who you are, Lee - this is Lucy goddamned Jinx.' 'Is it?' Leopold asks, playful awe. 'It's actually *Goddamn Lucy Jinx*, but she's close enough' very awkwardly jollys Lucy, Leopold moving to the living-room, out through the back door and lighting a cigarette. Now - in earnest - Lucy - facing with back to where Leopold was until now - goes 'Should I not be here? Are you having one of those domestic squabbles I hear so much about in the Self-Help aisle?' Ariel just scoffs a Fuck-you and says 'Go smoke with him while I blow-dry my hair, okay? And try to not seem like you seem, if you can manage.'

So, what does Lucy do? 'I'm a poet.' Ah! Lucy is the Lucy that worked with Ariel, back in the day. Is this supposed to be a known quantity? Why hadn't Ariel briefed her? 'Yes.' That is where Lucy and Ariel had met. 'Oh interesting.' The impression Leopold had always been under was that they'd known each other prior to that. 'Is there *prior to that*?' Lucy quips. Then - because she's aware of all the ways that could be misread if one were of a paranoid bent - she riffs instantly to 'When you get to be as old as I am, my good man, you have to kind of pick a starting-point and go from there. Life, you get me? Too much to keep track of if you count the older bits. And the early work is so amateur, anyway.' So Lucy only turned Pro after meeting Ariel? Careful, Lucy - this seems a little bit large for small-talk. 'Ariel has nothing to do with it - she was just a technical component of that period.' For example: during the same era, Lucy realized how much she liked a particular brand of cheese-curl and almost killed a cat - Ariel amounts to a bean in a hill of them, truth be told. Which is fair enough, to Leopold. Lucy tries 'Where's your daughter?' as it might betray something - her voice - to ask after Kayleigh by name. And Leopold says 'The Sheriff is over at my place - I just had to take care of a few things, here. I'll be out of your guy's space - just having a smoke.' So Lucy goes into a Hey-I'm-new-here stance, breathes a drag of her cig down over her chin saying 'It's your space, I thought - certainly don't feel you're getting the bum's rush from me.' Pause. Fuck. 'The Sheriff, eh?' Peshawing, as though there is no story in it, Leopold says that Kayleigh is going through a Western Phase. 'Cattle rustlers. Civil War stuff. The Sons of Liberty and all.' Lucy thinks that last one is the Revolutionary War, but also doesn't care to dwell on what is obviously a glissando away from the subject she wants away from. However: if Lucy is as much a foreign-body to this as she is playing at, she should not be aware of the moving-along-now nature of the remark so she doubles down with 'Johnny Tremaine got his hand all stuck together with silver or something?' 'Something like that' I-don't-cares Leopold. 'My daughter just likes anything with muskets or those pistols you have to load with a stick, right?' 'Who doesn't?' prims Lucy. 'Now - is Johnny Tremaine the same guy as in that song *When Johnny Comes Marching Home*?' But Leopold seems to have seen through something - or, anyway, can no longer keep his thoughts from some matter obviously more pressing - and begs Lucy's pardon, grinding his smoke out on the brick wall, heading back into the house and up the stairs. You should leave, Lucy. Yes, Lucy knows this. But she lights a new cigarette and thinks going would only makes matters worse. She - to be egalitarian - allows that the vibe of bristling-at-her she got an under-taste of off of Leopold could just have to do with her being here, at all, nothing to do with any thoughts of her relationship to Ariel. Except, in the same moment she thinks the word *Relationship* she hears, from the window above her - the one she takes pains not to look up at - the first muffled sounds of Ariel's raised voice, then silence, meaning either Ariel had made a shush face to Leopold or - Lucy's stomach curdles - Leopold had tensed eyes to 'Settle down' in Ariel's direction and Ariel had complied.

Lucy is old-hat at things like this, of course. No, she doesn't stay outside - because that would signify to Ariel and Leopold, when they come down the stairs, that she, without question, knew they had been at each other. Same as she doesn't turn on the television or get too comfortable at the kitchen table or some such innocent-seeming activity - as those would suggest too much a familiarity, an intimacy with the home that, also, would show she had a bead on what was going on and, worse, would indicate she had a territorial stake. Lucy Jinx adopts the air of someone who has been in the house, but still kind of hasn't - hands clasped museum-patron behind her back, bouncing knuckles on the top of her buttock, the top fist of the one clap-clapping into the curved palm of the other - and she looks at things on the mantle, at the books on the shelves, really commits to the part, doing her best to tune out the floorboard creaks or voices she catches certain letter collisions of. *Shs. Cks. Huhs.* That is the creak of a bed being sat to. That is the sound of something several papers thick being swatted to a desk. That last thing, well, it might have just been Lucy's imagination, though. It all might be. Widening and thinning of air in pipes. Leaning and loosening of window panes. The house is hollow and set on stilts and everything sounds like everything else. Hell, they could be laughing up there! They could be making love! Lucy is the scent of fire-elsewhere drifted here, she must remember. Any resonance to the walls except the dullness of normalcy is on account of her. This is the effect Lucy has on walls, the effect Lucy has on stairs, the effect Lucy has on ceilings, the effect Lucy has on cabinets, the effect Lucy has on faucets, the effect Lucy has on knobs that have fallen off things and are set on the shelf to maybe one day be put back on the whatever but probably not. She tosses this knob up - the one she was looking at as that train-of-thought ended - and tosses it up and tosses it up and - looking around - puts together a different two-and-two. Is this house laid out exactly like the mother's house had been? Was. Still is. *Like the mother's house is*' Lucy blinks until the words are screwed tighter to the point the driver strains and then is repelled with a jerk at the application of too much torque. This built-in shelf in the corner is the same. The living-room entry, the glass sliding-door, the bathroom, there, the dining area and kitchen. No, no - it's just as similar as any house is to another. There are a finite variety of ways to arrange living quarters. And Lucy had only just been in the mother's house and it had a similar vibrating stillness, the same as the mouth of a grave she has no right to be looking down. And, being truthful, she'd felt Samantha's apartment had been like someone else's. That everything is. This is the symptom of going backward - of aging to a wall and having to grow older, still, but only able to so by drifting back through the space you'd advanced.

Now. There. There! You heard that? It was definitely a laugh - that was laugh, with no question! Going right along with the sound of the bedroom doorknob turning and the more audible voice of Leopold, who was at the top of the stair heading down, saying 'I'll have Henrietta give them a call - they should have that.' It was laugh. Sounded just like Ariel and Leopold, right? Maybe. Leopold's feet thud thud thud down the stairs - the speed and heavy of someone who has lived someplace a very long time distorts the only almost-heard sound from before that door opening and maybe overtop of whatever Ariel had said in reply about Henrietta. 'Hi, Dory' says Leopold, gently winded as he gets to the tile of the main floor, flashes a causal grin, and moves back around to the kitchen where Lucy hears a drawer opened and rummaged through, mixed rattles of pens tapping each other, tapping bottles of medication-tablets, mushing against papers, plastic being compressed and the drawer not closing right due to a cardboard box, only finally banging shut when given a forceful shove. Leopold again, smiling, letting out a sigh and saying 'I really will be out of your way - you know how she likes to talk, right?' Lucy laughs like the expected segue she is in this more-or-less monologue of Leopold's, then is taken off guard when he directly says to her 'I wanted to thank you for helping her out, you know? I know it's a hard time for her and she never seemed to have many friends.' Does Ariel know he's saying this? Lucy's brain is the sound of unwrapped cellophane. 'I'm happy to help her' Lucy's mouth goes, unbidden and regretted, a phrase that seems to please Leopold, as his face appears to unconsciously soften, betray weakness. Leopold now says 'I just mean, I'd be here more if she'd let me - but I know she won't and I'm worried.' Lucy's brain is the sound of dry spaghetti strands in a fistful being bent-to-broken and the titter of many sharps of it landing on the floor while others land in the simmering water they're meant for. 'I understand you might want to tell Ariel' Leopold sighs, holding the eye-contact Lucy doesn't hold back and just can't think where else to move to 'but could I, between us, give you my number and just' he closes his eyes, looks down like he is about to say 'Nevermind' closes his eyes again, looks up - directly at Lucy - and finishes - or restarts - or anyway - says 'Would it be alright if I asked you to let me know how she's doing? Or I can call you. Just sometimes. Because I don't get much but the company-line from Ariel - and I understand that.' Lucy is the equivalent of a field no one knows where it is. She maybe said something, because now Leopold has said 'Which makes sense and I get that. I'm just worried.' And - a business-card? - he hands Lucy a business-card, finger gesture she should note there is handwritten information on the back of, as well. Now Leopold has busied himself around just a bit, puts some things in the tote-bag he has, taps at his shirt pocket where he keeps - Lucy sees - his cigarette pack, and nods at her to indicate he is on his way. As he passes - why? - Lucy touches his arm and says 'I won't tell her you asked.' And he says 'Thanks.' And Lucy smiles - why? - and says 'But I don't think I'll be able to call you.' And he says 'Thanks' again. And goes.

'Ariel?' Lucy knocks on the almost-closed bedroom door. 'Ariel?' Lucy slowly presses the door open. 'Ariel?' The size of Ariel, shaded - the window has a dark blue blanket affixed over it, bright day coming through this other window by the bathroom sink area before the door to the bathroom, itself - is rising and falling without pride of symmetry. There is a bath towel in a harsh tangle in and around Ariel's ankles. A whistle, low-pitched, like a scream underwater recorded and played back at almost no volume on a television heard in the next room. Lucy sits, slow to the point she feels ridiculous, taps two fingers on the bulb of Ariel's hips, noting how the denim of her pants seems loose, the garment not closed up at all. 'Everything okay?' Absolute lack of answer. And the world reduces to the squeeze of the room walls the way the rest of a Hospice house is irrelevant except for the length of one person's breaths from that one person's lips. 'Ariel?' There is every chance she is actually asleep. Unsettled thoughts of 'Did he fucking do something to her?' muddy up Lucy's thinking, make her want to get to her car, leave, never come back, but she swallows and listens and thinks: Ariel really is just asleep. But she had been talking - yes? - not ten minutes ago. Not that ten minutes is an impossibility as far as lengths-of-time-it-might-take-to-fall-asleep. Or: had Leopold been talking, leaving the room - Ariel a long time unresponsive - but he just talking to be sure that she'd heard what he'd said, knew what he was doing? Ariel, impressive in density as her piled body is, now gives off a fragility the same as an elderly woman's wrist might, a child's elbow, one never certain if it is safe to squeeze her, to lift them, to guide her, to swing them around if they ask. Or: had Leopold upset Ariel - had he hurt her? - and then playacted all of that whatever-it-had-been-down-there just to give off a false-trail - the desperate invention of a criminal, feeling amazed that they had not been stopped? 'You're making me a little bit worried' Lucy sing-songs and puts her chin on the shirt-sleeve of Ariel's ceiling-most bicep - the last word especially melodioused like *Whir-heed*. Lucy kisses the fabric. 'Hey.' Gives it a little nibble and feels her head gummy, the underside of someplace it was foolish to reach around in. 'Ariel?' Now a whisper. Ariel's eyes are open and she is looking at the wall. Cold feels hot and Lucy's breath feels like a serpent stuck coiled in a space too tight to even tense against, serpent like just-readied ship-rope, perfect circle, not even gale-winds will un-round it. So what does Lucy Jinx do, here? She lays and wants to leave. And then wants to be nowhere but here, forever. Wants to somehow give off a color and sleekness that the world would know to never approach. She is lain beside Ariel and her nose is pointlessly mashed in the shirt of Ariel's shoulder-centers, one arm peculiarly angled so that her fingers can rake in striking-claw-closings Ariel's hair at the base of the skull. The room? The room smells like waking with a fever and not opening your eyes. The room? The room is a sea with a bottom but a sea with no top.

It's later - not much - and also suddenly and Lucy reacts with heavy, resistant waking to Ariel standing up and sliding her feet over the side of the bed. 'I need to get something to eat, I think - sorry.' Lucy sits up. Ariel touches her face and tries - not hard, but enough there is effort on Lucy's part to resist doing so - to push at her shoulder, get her to lay back down. 'I can get you something. Do you want a sandwich?' Ariel sniffs, rubs at her nose with the side of her thumb - Lucy can all but hear the numb juddering this would sound like in behind Ariel's eyes - eventually laughing and going 'Your famous sandwiches - those were awesome - but no no. I have to just have something and take some pills.' Lucy is now sitting, feet draped off over bed-lip and one on top of one of Ariel's, their shoulder's heavy to each other, center-sheets of a ream of paper together. 'Is Leopold gone?' 'Yep. He left awhile ago.' Ariel makes as sound of assent, sighs, asks if he seemed 'Okay' and then - before Lucy can do anything but ready her face to give a noncommittal reply - says 'He's fucking annoying, isn't he? Do you know how long he's had that sweater? Do you think he wore it today, on purpose? I swear he thinks I have fucking early-onset - whatever - dementia and he's a fucking Memory-Facility.' Ariel leans her head toward Lucy and

Lucy, noting this, leans her head toward Ariel so that they touch. 'Hey, Lucy?' 'What's that?' There is a long pause and somewhere outside is the sound of car doors closing, the deeper bellow of a trunk being pushed shut, a dog barking a single yap and being told 'Quincy!' three echoing hand claps. Silence. And more silence. Ariel says 'Oh I don't know. Sorry. I thought I would come up with something to say. I guess I'm not witty, right now. Can I take a knee from being witty - you'll still hang out?' Lucy figures it best to answer just by taking Ariel's hand and, fingers twined, lightly squeezing out the melody of a song - see if Ariel figures out she's supposed to guess which. Of course Ariel figures out she's supposed to guess which! Ariel just guesses wrong and gets a disdainful snort of 'No! Come on!' from Lucy who then says 'Starting again' and starts the squeeze-song, anew. 'I don't know' Ariel confesses after - the timing seems right - picking up on the fact Lucy has rounded back on the beginning. 'Well, you can't have your medicine or whatever until you guess.' 'But I might die if I don't have my medicine.' 'Then, you'll die. But it will be because you failed to guess the song, not because you didn't take your medicine.' 'That's murder!' Ariel tries to say louder, but her voice abrupts into a cough sound, a throat clear, an inaudible excuse, another throat clear, a normal volume 'Excuse me.' And then Ariel says 'I said: *That's murder!*' Lucy is squeezing the song, harder. 'It's not murder if the cause-of-death is *Ignorance*.' 'It is if you use my ignorance as a murder-weapon. You're like that truck driver in that one movie. Only not using his truck. Using my ignorance.' Lucy fesses up. 'Yes' she says, squeezing bully-hard now the tune 'yes, I am just like that.'

When it is clear that Ariel - swallowing some pills without water - has no idea what she wants to eat - the refrigerator door has been opened half-a-dozen times, the freezer door likewise, all the cabinets gone into and rummaged around, again, again - Lucy tells her to just sit down. 'But I'm hungry.' 'I'm making you some of these chicken strips, then' Lucy it's-finals, grabbing the bag, which was really just the first thing her hand came in contact with. 'But I don't want chicken strips.' 'All very intriguing, El - but nobody around here said you did want them. I am making them for you. You will eat them. And for dessert' - the freezer is still open, so Lucy gives a squint - 'you can have two of these frozen strudel things.' 'Two?' Ariel says, the closest to perky she has sounded since the bedroom. 'Sure.' 'Can I have those, first?' 'No.' 'Why not!?' Ariel smacks her thigh and Lucy hears her rubbing it, after, and whispering 'Ow, fuck.' 'Because you're a small child and it's about time I treated you like one.' But Ariel reminds Lucy she is highly educated. 'So's every kid.' Ariel reminds Lucy she single-handedly came up with the word *Visigoths* for the Visigoths. Lucy asks her how long she plans to rest on those laurels - also taps the oven to preheat, opens it to verify there is nothing already inside, lets it shut with a bang.

'Do you know what they called the Visigoths before I came around?' 'What?' Lucy says, kind of humping her shoulders and giving an impatient foot-tap.' Exactly!' Ariel rolls her neck and the popopopop is audible. 'That's what I do! I name things and make people forget what came before!' To which Lucy, in a 'Well dear' kind of haughty tells her 'You thought up one name for one group of people and they aren't even around, anymore. So be proud of that forever if you want, but it makes you seem desperate. Like your too-much lip-stick and how short you wear your skirt.' Ariel - Lucy knows the game - makes noises as though sniping something under her breath, the noises actually just nonsense, though, Lucy telling her 'If I were a guy, I'd fart at you to show you how dumb you sound.' 'I wish I was a boy so I could do that sometimes' opines Ariel, putting her chin to her chest but - honestly - seeming to do so in good humor. 'I really don't want chicken strips.' 'I really said *Too bad.*' 'I mean, seriously, I won't eat them.' 'Then I'll eat them.' 'You can't eat my food!' 'Then no one will eat them.' 'Then fuck you, man. You waste chicken! You're a waste of chicken, Lucy!' 'You're the waste of chicken' Lucy gives Ariel's shin a kick and then makes an obnoxious, dullard-voice moan, in the same voice saying 'I'm Ariel. I don't eat chicken.' 'Well, I don't eat chicken' Ariel little-brats, trilling her fingers on her belly. 'Leopold didn't give you his fucking card, did he?' Lucy, who was looking for a cup for coffee that didn't seem still dirty glances back over her shoulder. 'He did.' Ariel says the word 'Jesus' but inserts a lot of excess Ghk sounds and ends it with a squirty-raspberry noise. 'You're the one who keeps having his babies' Lucy blithe-spirits, running a finger around this one cup, finding the stain is set-in enough it shouldn't matter, is basically clean. 'This isn't his baby' Ariel startles. *His* pronounced just very loud *Is.* 'The Hell do you take me for, Jinx?'

Lucy is perfectly content with the patter between she and Ariel falling back to its paces - lock-stepping it goes, the universe of no more consequence than a crossword mistake, already erased and corrected. She might - at another time, in another headspace - take stock of how much she is letting herself giggle at the innuendos Ariel makes out of all the words in a television commercial or at Ariel's DeNiro impersonation - 'You know what he called you? He called you *a little piece of chicken*, you know that?' - as she devours her tenth of the strips she'd asked Lucy to heat up the rest of the bag of. Lucy might - at another time - wonder at how eagerly she accepts kisses, unwashed mouthfuls, and how long she resists wincing and saying 'Stop it!' to Ariel grabbing her hair, tightening grip on it - tightening, tightening, looking Lucy in the eyes like she would skin her alive just for kicks. But now: Lucy is breezily at ease, questions nothing in how she acts, nothing in how Ariel reacts, the entire first portion of this trip to hang out drying down to nothing, nothing, nothing again. 'You're going to put some of the poems about me in your book, right?' Lucy takes a bite of chicken - Ariel has not averted her gaze from the television, the movie back on, something Lucy has seen before and recalls enjoying but, on this viewing, realizes she remembers absolutely nothing about. 'I might.' 'You should. I do love you. And you wouldn't be a Poet if not for me. And you're a bitch. And this chicken tastes bad. And so on.' Lucy dismissively pouts that the chicken tastes fine and then demands to know the name of the movie. 'It's called *Suture*' Ariel sighs. 'That's right' Lucy nods, another bite of chicken. 'And they are twins even though the one actor is black and other one white and they look nothing like each other, right?' 'You're as good as a chorus, cousin' Ariel mock, slapping Lucy's chicken out of her hand. 'Promise me there's poems in there about me!' 'I shouldn't have to promise that.' 'I agree.' Lucy squints. 'Don't play clever word-games with me.' 'Which clever word-game?' 'That you agree I shouldn't have to promise - by which you, twisted mind that you have, mean I should just promise, not have to promise - I should already have promised.' 'Well - you should have already promised!' Lucy pointedly stands, bends to pick up the slapped chicken from where it landed, luxuriouses a bite and chews in a grotesque of erotic-throes, then says 'Recite one line I ever wrote for you and I promise I'll put in every poem I ever wrote for you.' Ariel assassin-eyes and low-growls. 'You can't do it?' Lucy taunts and is about to taunt further, really jab into Ariel, when Ariel goes: '*I wanted other continents, but never this many / I wanted fewer tides, but never so none.*' Lucy - this is true - does not recall the line so has to put on an affect of being unmoved. Ariel stares, blank-faced. 'Do one more - that was a lucky guess. For all I know anyone would say that, just randomly.' Ariel sneezes, sloppily wipes her face with whole palm flat and Gahs the word 'Fine.' Then takes a breath. And says '*You're a day that's the coat I never borrowed and I'm a pocket of the day you never were.*'

   Returning from the bathroom - Lucy didn't hear a flush, is just about to point out this possible oversight - Ariel tells Lucy that she needs to call her mother and it's going to suck and she hates to do it but she needs to ask Lucy to leave while she does. And - pistol-start - stammering how 'It's not a problem' Lucy stands and asks 'Is everything okay with your mom?' 'Not really' Ariel says, shivers like a compass-needle settling on North 'and I get you're going to ask if you should just hang around - but you shouldn't.' Lucy has shoes on, already, stands from the stairs and lifts her coat back over herself. 'Nor should I come back, later?' 'That's up to me.' Ariel makes first a gesture like cracking a whip and then a gesture like tugging a choke collar. 'Beck-and-call, Jinxy, beck-and-call.' See? Now Ariel is kissing Lucy long and meltingly, open-mouthed and hand up her shirt, clawing the flesh over her ribs. See? Now Ariel has stopped and is going on about how it should really be her mother making the call to her but that is never how things fall out, eh? 'I guess not.' 'Do you have a mother, Lucy?' Blink. That was Ariel asking, actually. 'I think I do. Don't I?' Ariel makes her face go confused, wide-eyed, staring in back-pedal at a madwoman. 'Don't you? You're supposed to.' 'Oh then I do' Lucy says. 'You should give her a call. I hate my mother. Do you hate your mother?' Lucy almost says 'Yes' for comaradish reciprocity, but at the last minute says 'No. I don't. I just nothing my mother.' And Ariel, now, is somber and nodding, touches Lucy's shoulder and tells her 'I'm not a bastard for making you leave all of a sudden and hating the chicken you made and all?' 'Not for that, no.' 'I love you.' 'I love you too, Ariel.' Lucy leans in, kisses Ariel's unresponsive mouth, biting the lips gently and tugging the lower one long as she steps back. Ariel lifts shoulders big, sinks them little, and when Lucy turns to go tugs the back of her coat and says 'I said: *I love you.*' 'I said *I love you.*' 'But you're supposed to say you know I love you - that's the thing.' Lucy steps forward and takes Ariel's chin in her fingers, then pushes up so that Ariel's lips plop open like a stepped on cardboard box and says 'I know that you love me. And I know how much.' For an instant, Ariel's eyes tear, get that glassy heat of saline, but settle back to limpid as Lucy lets go of her face and steps back. Behind Lucy's back closes the door. To her pockets for cigarettes go her hands. The sky is somewhere between daylight and the purple of evening with sore-throat of coming snow, infection pink at the horizon-line out that way where there's a pencil line of highway and a pastel smear of tree, branches empty and stern as a concrete-stair's corner. You could just go for a walk, Lucy. You don't need to drive away. You could just amble around - there are stores within walking distance, even a place where you could have a drink - and then come back, see how Ariel is doing. Yes. Yes. 'Yes.' Lucy says, opening the door to her car. But to do that she would have to not be unwilling to admit that she doesn't really know Ariel well enough to know how she is - staying, going, coming back, anywhere, anyhowing.

Do you recall, Lucy - you likely don't - how in grade-school you once wrote a letter to a poet and in the letter you recommend a lot of words she could have rhymed her words with better? 'I do' Lucy says, the road empty and fitful, not allowing her to take any turn-off, just stretching her onward and onward, lost in her thoughts and her need to be Transit, be Nowhere Yet, and long enough driving to seem Nowhere-Just-Before, either. But do you remember any of the words? Any of your replacements? Do you recall the poet's name? Your teacher's name? Do you recall your hair-length? Do you remember if your fingers were chunky and squat or had they lengthened to the thin they are now? 'How thin are my hands, now?' Lucy questions, acting affronted, gripping the steering-wheel to seem threatening, like she had better watch what she says - or else! Your fingers are thin as the veins of the poet whose name you've forgotten.

She turns on the recorder, drifting lanes - then, once the recorder is going, she doesn't want to speak. But let it record. Let it take in the line you don't want to say. If you play this bit back, you'll likely know just what you're listening to, the words will leap forward. Or even if all you hear is silence - that is the same as the words, as you don't want to say them, right? And by this, what Lucy is trying to get at is: Does a word count as a word as soon as it is thought? Without physicality in the form of ink - or vibration, even - does it have to be called a *word*? But - groan - she doesn't care. She's thought about this before. Lucy, you've thought about everything you've thought about before! So what? So what!? The radio does nothing to help her and her mind feels like it is going to pummel her again if she can't find a distraction. She wants to believe she is being led someplace, roaded someplace, that she will suddenly take a turn and realize - Shock! Horror! - that it is someplace associated to some thought she has been thinking. Some thought. Some thought. She wants to be a tug to the stitch-wire, be a moment jointed to another moment without having to try. Oh but this time the road isn't going anyplace, Lucy. This time if you don't stop you just aren't stopping - you're not being corralled or foreshortened, you're not being duped or ensnared. Do you feel that, Lucy? Everything letting go of everything's grip? All stories can move to conclusions without you, now. Do you recall, Lucy - you likely don't - how in grade-school you once waited in the bathroom and shoved the first girl who came in hard to the wall and stood over her and tea-kettle screamed 'Get off of me!' into her face and then ran back to your classroom as fast as you could? 'I do' Lucy says, the road erroneous and ripe, allowing her to take any turn-off - there it goes, marooning her onward and onward, clogged in her attentions and her need to be forced, be someplace, anyplace at all as long as it feels at once like she's never been there and like she's never been gone. Why didn't that girl ever tell on you, Lucy? Why didn't they ever come looking for you?


LUCY GETS IT. ABOUT GOD - Lucy gets it. Why's it so baffling to others? 'Dunno' Lucy dunnos. Those questions that come up: omnipotent this, omniscient that, then how could blah blah let such or so happen to innocent blah blah seems callous or jealous blah blah - and how can you call $X$ a *Miracle* when at the same time $Y$ flood-waters or $Z$ blood-borne pathogen pillages in the veins of blah blah? 'Isn't it obvious?' Lucy bemoans to the ignorance of all sundry. God wants to be talented. Talented! God wants to have a skill, something to gauge Himself against. And so come these infinities of cosmos and microscopic avenues and collisions He blindfolds Himself to willfully - and so then He moves in attempts to prevent any sadness, any mishap, anything unjust. Oh what a skilled hand He desires - balanced, deft, not automatic, devoid-of-aspect. That child is dying of malaria - could not God stop it? These molecules are not bonding with those - so children are born without eyes, limbs, souls - could He not intervene? But Time has been created and things happen within it - He is bound to this for the challenge, the pursuit of having all things go perfectly, nothing falling to shambles. And inside of Time - which he welded His creation to and so too affixes its judgement of Him - there is only so much time. And He wants to be talented enough to stop the mutation of germs over here from rampaging the livestock - but perhaps his attention slips and billions of pin-balling isolations go leading to a car-crash killing a family-of-five He didn't even see coming, wasn't quick enough! He'll get better, He'll get better! Perfection - God must believe it is attainable, not just an unavoidable, irrevocable component of Him and unquestioned. Genocide? Oh - He thought if He had this young-woman witness a single act of kindness it would blossom her to a state where the genocide would have been prevented long before it started - but then He was busy inspiring someone how to mix new pigments out of some leaves He once invented and - Whammo!! - this girl's best friend had stomachache and so her attention was taken and she left the café early, kindness unseen, and three-and-a-half million were eradicated, decades later, from her lack of voice - no way to stop that ball once it was going, He just had to watch it hit the gutter, miss all ten pins! And Lucy gets it - this Godly desire. And she gets the roiling anger and the disdain and the seething-at-pissants who screw Him up, keep Him from being perfect in the eyes of His creation. Slam a fist on the table, ever? Or scream at your child? Of course! And yet God shouldn't do that? Well - fuck! - he should be talented enough not to, but talent must be developed - and He cannot develop! What a sad state. A flawless-being. What a stupid idea He must think of Himself - an existence that, logically, indicates there is no need for anything else to exist. What kind of fate is this but a spoilt one? What kind of torment - ought it not to lead to the invention of Torment itself? Want to be near to God - to know why you are in His image? - then suffer! Imagine - Lucy gets it - being a voice so loud but so alone that a bellow would have to travel the expanse of Eternity just to hit a wall and return as the echo proving there is nothing there but a shriek and then that shriek quieter, whimpering from the distance and loneliness. Those who celebrate miracles, Lucy likes them - they are kind to the lowliest thing: the Creator with nothing to show for Itself but Its flophouse of product and Its empty hands needing to be most-times too slow in order to give It something to hope for that's more than Itself. Oh God - who can only be talented in lack, in mediocrity, in failing. Oh Lucy - she gets it.

In the meantime, Lucy returns to her table at this - she hadn't paid attention to which - fast-food joint, sitting and regarding: there is a chicken-sandwich, with bacon, with cheese - fact undeniable, fret though some contrarian might. 'Lucy' Lucy hears after the cliché sound of Psst actually pronounced *Pissed* like as though for humor. Over her shoulder turns Lucy. 'Well, well - if it isn't Young Pastor Mitchell - last I heard they had you strung up and you were only thirty into the fifty lashes been allotted.' He takes a seat, grease grinning and exactly the same as he always looked, unchanged as an animated character. 'You work here, now?' Lucy gestures, mouth full of chew, to indicate her nonchalance at how Mitchell is sitting and helping himself to some of her fries. 'I do not, but ply my trade, other, without the trappings of hum-drum commerce. And to be blunt, my client list is somewhat wanting - I saw you and am a deep believer in Fate and also in being a forward-leaning pest.' Lucy takes some fries on purpose to have her fingers touch his - dominance, dominance, he knows to wait while she takes hers, his fingers hovering aloft until she has selected the curly with most rounds around - chews sloppy, mouth open, to say 'You're a desperate little bottom-feeder now, is it?' 'Tis' he doffs his brow 'tis.' And so a paranoiac playact coats Lucy, eyes tick-tock-tick-tocking and her words 'Pretending I know what you mean - because I don't, you know? - I say that I have always had an interest in Book-of-the-Month Clubs, but, as they say, do not trust people with my home address no matter how many books I get for a penny.' But Mitchell digs, he digs - or so he says - and, in fact, this is a radical set-up that does away with any human interaction. 'I am intrigued, in a rhetorical way, by this - by which I mean that I find humans to be untrustworthy sots, the less of them the better.' And Mitchell has taken a napkin and, keeping the banter all bantery, writes down and spins this napkin to present *Do you know what a dead-drop is?* Lucy takes the napkin and deposits it in the half-full of her coffee, saying, as though non-sequitur and to someone off to one side 'Something you learned from a television show, I take it, if you watch the same shows as me.' Mitchell - clever, which is why Lucy had marked him, a good game player - has another napkin and on it writes, while speaking entirely on subjects dissociative *You say where. Here and now. I check daily. If ever you pay and something isn't there within twenty-four, never shall our twain again meet.* And Mitchell - hardly giving Lucy time to read - to-pieces this napkin and deposits the shreds in her cup, by himself. Lucy has to have a moment to think, so they talk about their mutual hatred of *3-D* movies - to Lucy, the greatest strength of cinema is that it makes you believe that life can be rich and full in only two dimensions - and Mitchell watches some pudgy employee squirt and wipe down a recently vacated table, laughing aloud at the wretched state of his own past - 'I used to do that' he moans jovially 'Oh can you imagine it? Me!?' Lucy has written down *Cashdollar Diner. Ladies Room Trash. Wednesday. Bi-Weekly. Starting Wednesday Next.* She flashcards it long enough to get a nod and into the squish of pulpy coffee it is seeped. 'What's your favorite number?' Mitchell asks, eye-cocking, voice warbled as though he is asking the question embarrassingly and for the Nth time. 'I like several numbers that fall between one hundred and two hundred - I'm fickle about numbers, they're like letters that forgot to sound like anything, you know?'

And another thing - Lucy, upset tummy, turning her car back on, having had to sit around five minutes after Mitchell left just to feel clear of all gravity of it - imagine how vast our scope would be if the world were large and mishappen, not smoothed to a uniform round. If life were such a hill-up in one direction there was no such thing as Horizon Line, such a hill-down and then - way in the distance - a sudden spike-up or coiling-back-in-on-itself, the other side returning to slope down so massive that up-crops and down-crops would keep the eye, from any vantage, obstructed from ever finding a focal-point to say 'What happens after that?' regarding. 'Knowledge' Lucy sighs to the passing motorists 'limits us into its idiot mitts.' Because - she unalouds this whole thing, just on automatic, the route she knows well enough to ignore as she takes it - as soon as we learn about the horizon we stop thinking 'What would life be if there wasn't one?' Knowledge of how this planet is and how we move on it afflicts our Art, our Science, our Theology, our very lust for one another. How unoriginal we all not only become but want to become. Even our zest for originality - 'Those few who have it!' she does a stamped-foot voice of this right out in a bang - is reduced to just wanting to be somewhat unakin to other things around us. Original with all the components of unoriginality! 'We're terrified' - yes, Lucy has her recorder on now, the traffic at halt, is trying her best to not gesticulate and to keep her mouth movements semi-invisible to those at her left, at her right - 'that our words won't be understood, that our plans will seem confusing, that we won't link to the link in the chain nearest us. When did Originality become a trick-of-the-trade for being Accepted - and when did other people who happen to be alive at the same time as you become attractive, become necessary - why did we set ourselves up so simpleton to have to either befriend the here-and-now or be forgotten forever? Oh can't everyone see it? Can't they!? Can't they!? How this moment tries to own all before and all after - Black-Hole of desire for this-moment to contain all-moments! And the discovery of the horizon was the start of it all! The proto-limit! We've let a shape dictate us! A goddamned shape!' Lucy is shouting, thinks she is in a right tizzy enough she ought not be hurtling a missile down the freeway, even at the ten-feet-per-second it is currently clocking. 'The telescope - it screwed us!' Lucy would have been on the committee who wanted it banned. 'Knowledge is dangerous - because it limits us, it defines us, and makes our desire be to contradict the aberrant, makes dutiful-acceptance into a point-of-pride, a Sanctity!' Lucy is sweating at the underarms, itch-raised flesh through hair stubble, a real manifesto of perspiration she feels soured and desperate because of. Her head is a light in a house that is probably empty but that you aren't allowed to enter in order to douse. What's wrong, Lucy? 'Nothing's wrong!' She is a closet door that comes open enough that a face could be concealed when you know that one isn't - a reminder, in safety, of the fact that danger could be anywhere, safety only some places. Nothing is balancing in Lucy. Her breath sounds like only letters *F*s that are all trying to get through a turnstile at the same time, deforming into a mash of what sounds like the letters *E H* and *K* all in a smush. The traffic isn't moving. But Lucy Jinx is.

Where has she parked? Some Outlet Mall. In her car, she watches - way over there - some employees turn on colored lights outside of a restaurant made to look well-worn, been-there-forevered - and to Lucy Jinx all the world seems like is restaurants and roads. Something has to be done. Her cigarette tastes like a throat not coughing anymore that has been coughing non-stop of two days. Lucy? 'Yes?' She sounds small, a little-girl dressed as a kitten pretending to sleep. Are you feeling okay? She is not. This is not a normal kind of thing. Here: she checks her heartrate, for one moment not finding it, then it is all of a sudden there and she has no idea what her heartrate is supposed to feel like. Hasn't she taken for granted her whole life her physiology - the rate at which she blinks, the lack of taste to her saliva, how sometimes she can smell the inside of her nose, what temperature at which she begins to feel warm, cold, when her feet cramp, when they don't, how often her stomach gurgles, when she hiccoughs from her throat or from her middle - and isn't she, now, like the first line of a map she is trying to fake? How fast is her heart supposed to beat? Are her eyes supposed to look that way? In the rearview mirror: there she is. But looking is a mistake! Watch this: beep-bop-boop Lucy resets back into thoughts about God and can't stop them. That's her point, after all! 'We - people - we, people - we admire and pride ourselves on eyes, on legs, on bodies, on all manner of things not our own! God? Maybe He takes some glee in seeing us cockproud and chest-strutting because He gave us those things. But we - people - we, people - we can say *This was given us* and feel special for it. Not God! No - no sir, no ma'am' Lucy says holding the tape-recorder to her mouth - 'nope, He gave Himself all of it, gave Himself the power to invent everything - it must strike Him sometimes how He can't be proud of His eyes, proud of His legs, proud of His stature, proud of His All-encompassing. Don't you see!?' she see-saws and ebbtides in the car, honestly feeling that her rocking is moving it a bit, which seems patently impossible. 'I'm sorry for anyone who can't be proud of what they have because they can't feel special for having been given it!' Oh Lucy cries

- a bubble of mucus goes plip out her nose and she shudders into a sob like a five-year old who has been told he lost a game he doesn't even yet know how to play and yet wants to be best at. 'No one feels special when they comfort themself - and no one writes a letter to themself to be read later and believes what it says when it says *You need to know you are wonderful*. We - people - we, people! Just a bunch of old notes God wrote to Himself, wanting to pretend were from Others - from other Hims, other anyones - now just a pointless concentric circle of His trying to be given something that isn't given to Him by something He's given everything to!' Pause. 'Lucy, Lucy, Lucy' says Lucy, and then that she needs to calm down. But at the same time another kink in her mind is saying: You need to let this out, let it pass.

Sandwich-shop - all stale smell of standing onions and standing bell-peppers, smell of toaster-ovens warming bread for over an hour. Lucy is just in the realm that can be considered composed and, stopping briefly on her way to the restroom - there it is, down that narrow, billboarded corridor - at the sight of the portly, smiling man snapping on his thin, transparent gloves, says - arm all the way out to the side, wrist rotating her hand in an endless and-so-on-and-so-on-and-so-on sort of propeller - 'Please start making me the largest sort of sandwich with' - she can't find the words - 'with chicken and bacon - with just chicken and bacon - and, please, toast it, then put some cold cheese on after - cheddar or whatever cheese, surprise me - I'll pay for it when I'm' and she lets her motion, headlong, toward the toilet door serve as whatever the last word or several words would have been. Single occupancy, she thumbs the lock shut and unjackets and peels her shirt over her head and unsnaps bra and her skin prickles and feels dry from a rash that the mirror is not equipped, it seems, to reflect. Dry-heaves over the sink. Side-eyes the toilet bowl, but doesn't want to go to her knees. A rectangle of her very loose tummy - here, the sink-lip flirts with it. And dry-heave and dry-heave and then one loud enough to make her cover her mouth with her hand like the door is about to be burst through. Logic: this is all the result of some poisonous food! Logic: maybe the chicken sandwich!! Uncertainty: hadn't she eaten a lot, today? Uncertainty: had she? Logic: this is a result of an insult to her bodily processes, cells in her are functioning properly to fight of encroachers - this is what this is supposed to feel like with all that business at war inside her, she should be glad! She spits and the blop is discolored and heavy and has bubbles only on one side - like the eyes of a spider just stepped on. Her hair is sensitive to the touch. That is further evidence of this being illness and nothing more - that, since girlhood, has been a sure sign of a body at combat with the elements. Her glands? They feel not only unswollen but curiously vacant. Are glands ever supposed to feel concave? She pats her neck like aftershave, like a tailor figuring out belly-hang and how it will affect thigh-fit. Some shivers. More spit - this not wanting to form a ball, just a line over her chin like it has something to say if she would just listen a minute. Oh Lucy - what a mess of you! Nude to the waist! And you know that poor sandwich-maker out there is probably not at work on your food prep, is waiting to see what you act like when you come out. He'll have an excuse ready - the scene plays in Lucy like it's a story someone told her last week. 'I hadn't asked if you wanted Turkey-bacon or the spiced-chicken - I'm sorry.' Very clever. 'Clever little sandwich-maker!' Lucy spits, but has to admire the guile, that his thoughts would be toward the good of the shop before the whim of a flummoxed customer like Lucy, loony-binning an order before bounding to the shitter to thunder out belches like frogs might croak as hands squeezed their damned eyes out!

Lucy's eyes first fall to the poster for an amateur production of *A Delicate Balance* - that is, her eyes find this when she tries to find a spot on the glass-covered bulletin-board with something dark posted, mirror-making - and then, beside this, to some advertisements for massages. Perhaps, she's thinking - wanting a few moments more to occupy her before going to pay for that sandwich she had ordered - a massage would do the trick, chase out the devils that have rooted in the twines of her muscles. The last bastion for Witch-Doctoring - massage, acupuncture, acupressure, meditation. Then she sees some advertisements posted for motorcycles - poorly photographed, the things look neglected and sketchy, backdropped by cluttered garages - and some for cars, one for a boat. Then - this is the important part - she gets to wondering 'How do these get posted?' and 'Why do some have tabs with phone numbers if they are behind glass?' deciding to test and discovering - oh ho! - the glass opens upward in large panels. Important - why? Because: on scooting down to find a spot where it'd be easier to lift the full panel up - just because, of course - she has moved to the spot where her eyes see a card for one *Sue Ellen Fist* - terrific name - a therapist. Now: in fact, there are many cards for therapists and analysts and counselors in this area of the board, but - beyond the swell name - what singles out Sue Ellen Fist is Lucy - squinting, confused - thinking 'Isn't that my telephone number?' She mouths the numbers, already having removed the card - its stock thick, pleasant as she fingers it, holds it at the extreme of its rectangle-tips in a press of thumb and third finger. She's certain it is her phone number, even after she deciphers that it is off by one digit - the last of it three-three-four, the last of hers three-eight-four. In a sense, not even a digit off, just the closure of two loops off! A poor ink-ribbon, a key not struck hard enough, the number would be the same! Well, so what? Did you want a therapist, Lucy? She puts the card in her rear pant pocket - she doesn't tend to do this with cards - and dully says 'Yes' she might, barely aloud. And the circumstances of her arrival here are not lost on her. And in case she was ready to stop believing in balderdash currenting her around to where it wanted her, she has that recent run-in with Young Pastor Mitchell, wherein the fellow had just had to explain he was a - what was it? - 'deep believer in Fate.' Lucy can choose to ignore this, but it - regardless - cannot be ignored. Her sandwich is ready and the man who prepared it needs to know if she would like the chips that come free with such a purchase - that is, if she also wants a drink, he clarifies, then further clarifies he mean *The Meal* - or else does she want the three cookies. 'Well, which kind of chips do you mean?' He gestures to the rack behind her, filled with nothing appealing. And the cookies look hardly any better, but so that she does not cause any turmoil she says 'Give me two of the peanut-butter, then, and one of the fudge - unless they all three need to be the same, in which case three of the fudge.' Maybe the man smiles because, like Lucy, he is realizing that her statement has a kind of backwardness to it - but more likely it's just at the overprim way she is speaking, as though Lordship to coachman when it should be more like flies on one cheek of a horse's ass to those on the other.

She listens to a radio interview with a politician while she eats - halfway through the sandwich fidgeting to worm the therapist's card out of her pocket, setting it there on the dash - rather admiring how the man has probably convinced himself that one can still be taken as charming and off-the-cuff when repeating the same anecdote for the eight-hundredth time. It's well studied, the tone of voice, the precision of the delivery. This is what a homespun pause sounds like. This is the appropriate length of time to hold out the word *Very* - veeeeerrrrryyyyyy - and this is the time to trail off, humble-pie, as though not even seeing much merit in saying the words one time let alone this time. More work goes into this fellow's idea of normalcy than Lucy's concoction of the bizarre, to turns-of-phrase meant to be all her own. A dawdled over, excruciated banal-tone - like fifty words other than *And Then But Whenever* and *I* have been tried in the place of those words and crucibled down to this story's residue, the most elemental, the most Everyman. When the politician is done, Lucy misses him. Supposes he would have her vote if she ever had much use for voting. And there? Those people seem shy on entering the Outlet store that sells only ladies' underthings, the man girding himself to act all-business when the girl would rather him be wolfish, sincere. 'You're in a shop' Lucy swallows 'that is strewn to the brim with unmentionables - mention them! Idiot' she swallows again, and then just lets out a truck-braking sound of dismissive scoff. Men. 'Men!' she says. And the radio is playing a commercial for a funeral-parlor that seems to be over-selling itself. Two testimonials? They really must be the best in town! It's practically lucky how your loved one has passed - otherwise you never would have felt so well cared for and understood!

Lucy envies those mourners and hopes that they got paid and did multiple takes of their speeches. A little more this, a little less that. 'You said *Comfortable* - could you maybe tweak that to *At Ease*. Or maybe *At Ease* is too without humanity, considering - how about you say you felt *Understood*, you felt *Welcomed*?' Lucy? When's the last time you thought about dying? 'Eh' she shrugs and crinkles the wrapper of the sandwich up, shoving it with other wrappers into the container space on the side of the driver's door. 'Eh. Death.' Lucy knows hers won't be a surprise - this is one of her troubles. Most people, they figures there is a chance they will die from an accident, never see it coming - but Lucy is painfully aware hers shall be well announced, trumpeted by heralds months - even years - out in front. In truth, she has passed the date she had once superstitioned would be her last - but that was a long time ago, now, a youthful trifle, she doesn't even know what she had been thinking. 'Young women' she sighs 'always think death is nearby - the inverse of young men.' Now: five minutes of silence. Or of radio-not-listened-to. That kid, there, eyeing that oil-smear on the parking lot's black and saying something to his father? Lucy points her fingers - rattattat - and she guns the father down, leaving the kid's question unanswered, in her bones feeling that violence is the best favor. And her eyes close while nausea gallops a dressage course her belly around.

'Thank you for calling. This is Sue Ellen Fist, PhD. I am in session or otherwise unavailable. At this time, I am accepting new clients. At the tone, please leave a brief message and I will call back when next I am able. If this is an emergency, please dial nine-one-one. Thank you.' Then a mechanical voice 'Begin your message after the tone.' A long wait. A quick Beep - more a Bp. Lucy says: 'Hi. I suppose I would like to have a call back about perhaps starting treatment. I don't know. However that works. I think we should meet and we can see if I'm any kind of match or even if you think there might be some merit in talking - I don't know, it's not like a toothache, what do I know, what context? I think that - well that, that, that - I think that my head has stopped being entirely - or not *stopped being* - that something in me - you understand what I mean? do a lot of your people sound like me? - has stopped being the way it feels like it used to be. I'm sorry. The machine said *brief message* but I wanted - I'm stalling - you to have context, to understand, right? Even the way I found your card - I'm paranoid - I think I'm paranoid that if I tell you about that then you won't believe me or else think that that is part of my problem - so nevermind. It isn't. I just want to be able to think. I want to be able to think a thought. In the singular. I want a word to have an end. You see? None of mine do. But that must be a mistake. Words end - they all do - and I think I have somehow gotten underneath of a context, underneath of a way that things are supposed to work. I want to be able - sorry, I'm sorry - to think about - well, pick something, anything -

886 / PABLO D'STAIR

even this phone call! Though *this phone call* isn't the best example, because that is an odd thing to have to describe while I'm doing it. *Why do you want therapy?* I want a word to end. And to then - after a beat - go on to another word. To begin and end, both. I think there might be a condition or something - like a finger has smeared the charcoal of a drawing all across a canvas, it all touching it all but the image still discernable. Which would be cool - I'm saying - if that was Art and that was an artist's idea - but I think I'm talking about how I see things, so don't misunderstand me. Not literally a painting or a charcoal. I sometimes wonder, right after I listen to someone talk, if I think so quickly I have altered their words, you see? Does that make any sense? Like I am a calculator that can do long-division without having to do each bit, able to give the answer in less time than it would take someone to pronounce it - so someone could say - well, whatever, someone could tell me a story that ends in a question - and I might be out so far away that while my answer makes sense to them it shouldn't. Are we talking? I don't think I talk. People and people and people - I feel like part of me is disguising myself and that everyone is tricked and likely in some kind of danger. Which might be a trigger-word - I don't mean like I'd hurt someone! I mean people might be infected by what I say. Because it sounds so right. How much bacteria does it take to make a piece of unheated meat dangerous? I am right on the borderline - my intentions are so close to not-my-intentions that nourishment is only separated by poison by like a single dot of germ - a germ with its toe over the line, halfway out of the photograph, you know?' The sound of a mechanical voice says 'Thank you.' Lucy pushes her tongue around in the lip over her two top front teeth.

Noticing she has left her turn -signal on - though she did turn, had it not been sharp enough to count, doesn't this click-click usually end automatically? - she decides to keep it on and warily watches her side mirrors and rearview for signs the choice is confounding any of her fellow travelers. But traffic is not dense enough, no one much seems to care. Likely they think - if anything - Lucy is a harmless old ditty, enjoying her last jaunt before the authorities deem her unfit. 'At least she's not hurting anyone' people will think of Lucy Jinx 'let her keep repeating *I'm-turning-left I'm-turning-left I'm-turning-left* if it gives her a sense of accomplishment. Ignore her. No need to embarrass the gal.' 'Or the fellow' Lucy says 'they might think I'm an old fellow.' The mystery of Bianca finds space in the recently vacated city-square of her mind, stretches out and loiters itself around like it's the glances of fifteen pedestrians, one at-a-time, at the same sound of something breaking. Why isn't there a message from Bianca? That is the thing that starts occupying Lucy. She isn't alarmed, exactly, just curious enough to wonder if it signifies anything. Is Bianca through with it, no longer interested in reconnecting? Is whoever it was that was pretending to be Bianca just done with the joke of pretending there is a Bianca to begin with? Or is Bianca just mad - had Lucy hurt her feelings? If Lucy wasn't driving, frankly, she would, here and now, go through her phone and verify there are messages from Bianca at all and that they aren't originated from Lucy's own number or something. She would accost a stranger, place a call to this alleged Bianca, and when Bianca picked up Lucy would talk for a moment, pose a question, then hand the phone over to the random citizen she was waylaying and say 'Repeat to me what she's saying!' That would out the ghost, the little quiver in Lucy's brain that was hallucinating this Bianca! She'd have to test twice, though, because the first person might take pity on Lucy when they realize no one is on the other line and spin some nonsense, off-the-cuff something and credit it to Bianca - they'd have overheard Lucy's conversation, is Lucy's point, so could approximate, if they were kind-hearted enough, something that might, they'd hope, pass for understandable-to-Lucy. Better still: Lucy could start the conversation in private and then just suddenly spring herself upon someone, say to Bianca 'Just a sec' and then to the passer-by 'Can you understand this person - I just underwent a Procedure, can you tell me what she's saying?' Only then, of course, if they said no one was talking it might be because in the brief interval Bianca got confused, said 'Hello? Lucy?' a few times and hung up. Or else the phone just could have disconnected. It's hard to prove someone exists - whether they do or not - if one only has a telephone to do it with. Lucy notices the left-turn blinker is off. Which of course it is! She took a left turn to get on to this current road. The cramping up of night is full of repetition, is a sky she thinks she has seen a bunch of times, the one that will do anything to linger, a night that has lied and cheated to have itself again hang overhead, triumphant and guilty, sweating but sure now that it's there it is safe until morning, at least.

Absolutely nothing to note in Lucy Jinx's walk to her apartment, this time. The parking space she likes, it wasn't there, but one near enough to be the same was and she parked without - even in her mind - noting where she was parking. A song was near enough to the end that she felt done with it, so not even the grumble of 'For everything that does seem to sync up in life, why couldn't this?' Even her train-of-thought stayed right on that subject while she opened the car door and zipped her coat up a tiny bit more - also, her thoughts about not having gloves anymore were mild, even particularless - and started to walk toward the first of the stairs up. She thinks about fade-outs in songs, wonders when that became the standard, if it would ever go away, if it was now merely copycatted out of nostalgia or if those with musical minds understood something maybe she, not possessed of one, did not and so always decided to fade-out a song of their own volition, regardless of how many times others had done so before. Up up up, pivot, up up up and Lucy runs across no one and doesn't get the feeling anyone is looking at her and hears no sounds that don't seem to belong or smell any smells that give her so much as a pause worth a sniffle. It is as though Lucy is a bowl cleaned to be dirtied with the mixing of something, now just waiting in an empty room with the towel that had dried the last beads of water from it neatly folded and patted and, itself, drying beside her. Not that Lucy thinks she is that - she just is that, thinking or no. If anything, maybe, Lucy has a sensation to her like she would sometimes have when considering opening a jar that wasn't hers. Maybe that sensation is over her shoulders and somehow flavoring the outside-edges of her thoughts. Maybe kind of an image of this old jar with a large cork stopping its mouth up that she always wanted to look inside of but never did. Remark, of course, remark that this thought being there - if it is - this image - if it is - would not be intrusive or carry with it anything. Lucy is not noting this Empty. That is the point. The point of Lucy Jinx is she, if she were interested, could honestly be observing herself in a several-minutes-long buffer between This and That - because there was This and, sure as certain, That is almost here - but she doesn't seem interested. Automaton? No, no. She's Lucy - she's thinking, she is seeing her door but - please understand the difference - just seeing her door and none of the affixations she has dreadfuled it with. Even in over the threshold, lunk-shouldering the weight of it open and letting it close hard, Lucy is in a serenity she might like to have a look at, is water her diddling finger will eventually ripple, pointlessly, just to watch her reflection disappear and reformulate, maybe the same, maybe different. Lucy Jinx, coffee. Lucy Jinx, removing her shoes and her pants. Lucy Jinx, cigarette while she chooses what to drink from the refrigerator. And Lucy Jinx, lighting a cigarette and yawning and listening to the can-pop sound of a cough, smoke splaying, into her hand back, cigarette tip, just then, close enough to her cheek that had she coughed harder, needed her hand to move faster to cover the cough, she would have been singed.

BEFORE SHE KNOWS IT - OR not so much, exactly when she knows it, a bunch of blank and then a laborious all-of-a-sudden - Lucy has written some things on the page. Amongst them? For example, she observes that this line is written: *I know you, but you mean me the way Tom Waits doesn't mean Mule, the way Dante doesn't mean Paradiso, the way Cordelia doesn't mean Lear.* Hover go her penless fingers, scanning the dry ink there like the name on a list corresponding to the number on a gravestone - thinking thinking if she wants to add in another thing, something that sounds more like *Mule* than *Lear* sounds like *Mule*. It's tricky. Rhyme, it isn't Lucy Jinx's thing, but she admits the pitch in her head, the melody of this line is a rhyming, rhythmic inevitability, how it should be - so ought she not, she thinks, make that official? Or - just a possibility - isn't not making-it-official the point of such a thing? That line, Lucy Jinx will leave alone. Image: Lucy Jinx, leaving that line alone. Here is another line - it is circled off to the side and sloppy handed, rather like it was said in a drool too imperative to be articulate: *the empty book's a library, my thoughtless mind what flames it Alexandria*. But - 'Hmn' Lucy hmns 'Hmn hmn' she hmn-hmns - but she is very self-conscious, now reading it, how the lust in the line will be lost, the coming destruction that unrequitedness will lead to. See that? She is walking a circle around the notebook - or is pacing alongside the kitchen counter where it lays. See that? See that? The limits of other minds, the thoughts of folks set outside of the pit of her experience trouble her. The fire seeks to engulf the library at Alexandria out of lust - lust traumatized to love, a mouth that there isn't flesh enough to bite or enough without-someone to ever scope the size of its longing. Should she write that down? More of an explanation isn't it, Lucy? There were some good lines in this. Point of pride: Lucy's explanations of her poems are poems! People should line up to hear her ramble, they might actually get close to the pulled tooth, the icicle jabbed in the exposed gum that is her true mind. What's the line? *The empty book*? What's that? Well, she is - not Lucy, but the person who is voicing this. Who is? 'Shut up' Lucy snarls and crosses the line out. And she dreams - in big faded technicolor - of the futility of the buckets passed hand-to-hand to outrace the lust of the fire that read every word it burnt, cackling to Heaven how it was the only one - the only one the only one! - laughter so hot that eventually all people just backed away, rent garments and lament, the flame reading black-grey skyward in the force of merciless throttle, in a readership that would douse only with the very last punctuation it eyed. Another line - Lucy glugs some coffee and her foot tenses to a spasm she steps down on, the tile of the kitchen leeching her heat into a headache - another line. *There's a prudish Rasputin in your walking away, and a bitter Oblomov in your calling me Stay*. Lucy presses her foot harder, crosses out *Oblomov* - thinks, thinks - writes it again, crosses it out with the rest of the line, scribbles and underlines *a kind of Agnes Gray in your screaming me Go*.

Then Lucy amuses herself with cigarette tangents about how she would name her daughter *Pneumonia*. Pneumonia Jinx. Her daughter would be statuesque, thick as the sides of a shelf, would have the cold weight and intensity of a clay-bed underneath four feet of stagnant creek. Briefly, she considers *Pandemonium Jinx*, but when she writes the both words on the back of her wrist - not entirely certain of either spelling, but certain enough - there really is no visual competition. *Pneumonia*. Lucy licks the word *Pandemonium* until it is thin enough to be dabbed off with her fingertips under the gauze of her t-shirt. Cigarette hurts her eyes with its squawking while she undertakes this erasure - almost down to the stub burning, a bit, her lips which still smart from their split. Back of hand tests for blood and she is disappointed when there isn't any. Layla and she had used to speak of having a child - Layla wanting to name the kid this or that silly thing, always so jokingly - the conversation turning to which of them would build up enough will to impregnate the other through the thrust of three fingers and other such vulgar old hahas and tee-hees. And Lucy almost now - almost - texts Layla *Our daughter will be named Pneumonia Jinx* before stopping herself to consider it for the length of a shot of room-temperature bourbon. The bourbon hits bottom almost before she hears the sound of the swallow and it car-exhausts the inside of her eyes, head burning like someone thinking that frostbite needs warmth. Why is Lucy crying? Why is the thought of Layla making her cry? Just a moment ago, Lucy, you seemed so damned giddy - and it's not like you've been drinking, really - and there are four pages - at least - of some of the best poetry you've written in ages there in that book on the countertop. That's your hand, Lucy. That's your happy! Anyway, it passes - the crying - and now Lucy is laughing, snorts of she needs to blow her nose but doesn't quite feel like it, just dabs at the wet sneaking out past the shadow of her nostril's berth. She does write the message to Layla - and then another message of addendum saying *And you're the one who will be carrying our little Pneumonia, my dear, I've let my figure go to shambles far enough to suit your kinky pleasures, now you get your turn in the barrel bwaha bwaha*. Then - here, now - Lucy Jinx turns the open notebook to the first page, which she always - ever since she is cognizant of first owning a notebook of any variety - leaves blank and then to the second page - which she always leaves blank as well - and on the third she writes *Pneumonia Jinx* and on the fourth she writes *a poem for Layla, my only, my perfectly always away*. Flip flip flip flip flip to another blank page. But it's not time to write, yet. She shadow-boxes thoughts, shoulders swooning as though crooners call to them in all languages from all sides. Lucy Jinx: in her elements - in love with abstraction, herself, alone, an apartment, nobody to Lord over her words but her words and her dizzy-brained, drunkening tired! She pours one more little glass - modest, be modest Lucy, there is work and normal life to be tended to come morning - and says 'Firstly, when one has to pour a little when one wants to pour a lot one should say they are *Pouting* a drink, not *pouring* one. And second' - she lifts the glass as though it means a point at the poem - 'that is for you Layla - it is what I give you, from my always-the-same-too-many-miles away.' Cheers goes Lucy and swallow goes Lucy and smiles.

Some kind of despicable creeps get the better of Lucy when she becomes conscious of how she is standing in an apartment only lit by the small light above the sink. Eyes as loud as subway cars seem to be hidden in the flat of the dark, in the tricks of murk-on-murk that her memory tells her have shape and space for thing to go hidden. Kitchen light on. Living-room light on - ridiculous how Lucy only has one of the three bulbs in the overhead fixture a working one, she even bought three whole packs of bulbs, on discount, and they just stay on top of the washer-dryer, rattling with each rinse cycle, heat cycle, likely shook out of functionality by now! - and then turns on the television, volume negligible, and the two room-lamps. Finger-snap blues the second of the lamps, zapped out-of-service as soon as its knob is ticked around, the glaze of sick green-purple floating in its place, impenetrable and always first immediately where Lucy is trying to focus then drifting left-upward when she holds the gaze. Bedroom light on, bedside light on - futile, she pulls the string that would turn on the closet bulb if she'd ever bothered to put one in there. On goes the bathroom light, on goes the bathroom fan and - cold cold, in case she wants it hot, actually, after a bit - on goes the shower. Is that everything? No place left for any unwelcomed witnesses or Peeping Tom's to be pretended? The coast seems clear. Odd sounds unaccounted for, though. The room suddenly as complicated a machine as a sleeping lover - shuffles, noises, breaths, creaks, gurgles, sounding in every moment from somewhere, louder for the more one might lay suppressing giggles and trying not to hear. Lucy is giggling now at what must be a neighbor's door shutting harder than they'd meant, secretive chuckle like overhearing a belch she won't mention that endears her to a lovebird and makes her next kiss with them seem yucky with cute, adolescent amour. So is the paranoia over? She roams and waits until her thoughts stop exploring the questions. The most ridiculous scenes of horror films from her youth rivulet down from her brain-top to the point of the spine that sends images out. And not just from films. Some cheap paperback novel on sale at the grocery-store entitled *Hell-o-ween* - a description of some shapeless, massive, dark form rising up from a path to kill! How primordial her fear of that is! And the memory mixed with the long walk to Dorene's second house - she calls it Dorene's second house, the second place she'd known Dorene to live - just to sneak a five minute conversation before not seeing each other for the weekend for whatever reason they sometimes couldn't. And ghost stories. The same ones told again and again, no variant, because how quickly it was discovered that variant - detail, elaboration, any tweak - ruined the perpetual-same shiver just the simplest collection of words would never fail to provoke. The way she pictured the backseat of the car, driver at safety, still not seeing the person the truck driver claims is hid there. The moment of everything collapsing and Safe seeming possibly the actual snare. The way she pictured the honestly-nothing that accompanied those footfalls in the upstairs room, the honestly-nothing rushing down the stairs and out into the snow. Now? Now she stands, grinning, and those footsteps could be right beside her - could be hers - and she would welcome them. Perhaps her ideal evolution would be that: Lucy Jinx, the sound of a footstep of someone who isn't actually there.

This is a more delicate line though. She moves to the sofa, muting the television completely - after watching the punchline to a joke in a sitcom she doesn't know the name of, unreactive but amused at how they had the audience guffaw uproariously - and keeping a cigarette unlit, a paper plate of buttered toast warm-enough-to-notice on her bare, side-turned knee. *Lean like a grace-note / not practiced / there and explained / no idea the sound / instructed / ignored / another time grace-note / another time taught / but never, but never / oh the small of the shadow you stand in.* She hisses in a sympathetic way, because this is too personal. There isn't explanation for it. To understand her reaction to it, she has to pretend it is something someone else wrote - maybe if she were still teaching her poetry, right? maybe if one of those students had brought it to her, maybe she is pretending it's that - and something she is unable to explain beyond just eyes soft-insisting 'You must never change a word of that line.' Lucy - this needs to be noted - doesn't think of those students often. She has stopped even - for the most part - noting in her meta-analytical way how she doesn't. But this line pulls them to mind. Because it sounds like them. Like her when she was them. Like her when she was them, which she never was. No Lucy Jinx for Lucy Jinx - no voice to hear the perfection of her run-of-the-mill quivering at life from her young woman's head! No Lucy to not teach Lucy a grace-note - no Lucy to explain to Lucy what music was, but more to express the unneededness of ever playing a note. No Lucy to tell Lucy she need never accomplish anything, need never compete or reveal herself to be worthy of adoration, of elevation. 'Worthy' there had never been a Lucy to tell Lucy 'has nothing to do with act, nothing to do with accomplishment or fact.' No Lucy to just look at Lucy so Lucy would have been looked at by someone who really looked even if Lucy had not known that is what Lucy had been doing. Now: Lucy writes *I never got to be the grace-note left grace / I was learned and became essential / a tinker no longer at loiter outside / but an essential to be played / to be played / correct.* But Lucy Lucy Lucy - you're drifting into explanation, again. What would you tell your students, eh? Think of the line just as the line - saying that other thing, it isn't needed, it just tells people something they should be forced to confront they don't know! Isn't that what you'd tell the students, Lucy? What you'd tell Lucy if you could tell Lucy anything? 'Don't show them what isn't theirs - show them how goddamned nothing is! And least of all You! Every word you say you rob them the chance of!' Yes, Lucy - that is what you'd say. And if they ever come looking, they'll find you a language stillborn and have to stare at the dead literatures of you! *Stare at the dead literatures of me / Stare at the stillborn of the words I plucked dead from the soil up first / I'm the death of this tongue / I'm the death of the tongue you'll never know absent.* Lucy puts a box around that. Doesn't know. She is the face of a student who doesn't know. Who wants to please Lucy, but who wants to love their words, too.

Another shift in mood. She doesn't want this notebook. She should be looking at the edits from the editor that whatshername gave her. Why aren't you doing that, Lucy? Is this all you are capable of? Wearing yourself down - you must know you are in a shitty head, do you not remember just a few hours ago, let alone all day, let alone yesterday, for Chirssake? - and then thoughts bubbling off into anything but something of relevance. What? What!? *Isn't it as important?* did you say? Lucy, come on! Isn't it as important to sit around and scribble a poem - not even in your senses! - that you will never transcribe, work on, read, as important to just let the engine chug itself silent - which is all you are doing, just winding down until the machine stops for the night - as it is to be having a volume of your collected verse prepared? Your life's work - out of the sweet blue, a compendium of your history-in-verse, rendered clean, official and forever! Is it just as important to arbitrary some other words on to some arbitrary other page? Lucy, be honest with yourself! When did you ever believe in that idea? You started calling it Purity only because you thought it was all you would ever have - admit it, there isn't any shame or harm in doing so! Or what are you going to do? Burn down your chances in order to look unrelenting to an imaginary voice in your imaginary goddamned head? No one is holding you to your weaknesses and fear, Lucy - and everyone understands them. Oh God, Lucy! What? What!? You think people believed you? You think anyone ever didn't see through your brilliantly nuanced talk of trying to 'invert Humility for Arrogance, Arrogance for Humility - Prestige for Cold-Water-Flat-Anonymity and vice versa'? You never even fooled yourself! You never sought out company merely because you knew your façade would not stand ten minutes scrutiny. You weren't outside it all, Lucy - you just refused to approach! As apart as the inside of a vacuum shop from the inside of the florist across the way - nothing to do with one another, not one the proof of the other's falseness, the one the reveal of the other's legitimacy. Are you going to pace your apartment, pace the world, pace from pointless-new-lover to pointless-old-lover to pointless-never-lover to pointless-remembered-lover - pace forever instead of just embracing your poetry, the only thing you ever wanted? Lucy: abandon this poem, now!! Why? Lucy: burn the fucking notebook!!! Don't just abandon it, don't just not-continue - please, Lucy, please destroy the words you wrote!!! 'Why are you saying this?' Lucy demands of the apartment, newly cigaretted and putting on the rhetorical voice of 'I agree, I agree - but explain to me why you think so' - emphatic, all capital-letter, italicized *YOU*. Don't you feel it, Lucy? 'Feel what?' That you need to stop. That this poem on this day at this time - it is a mistake.

This day was a mistake. Lucy: you can make mistakes. And you can admit it. And you are allowed to say what you really want. 'Why are you saying this?' Lucy asks again, exhale, now pointedly, trying honestly to hide her alarm. But the other voice goes silent. And plop flip flip flip goes the notebook back on the kitchen counter. And sniff and drag, puff, knuckle crack, pen up goes Lucy.

About here, though, Lucy does step outside of the apartment - repulsed by her decision as soon as the cold scours her face, makes her feel made of a tin, a sign with the letters sun-bleached and frost-faded off of it. She makes sure about the door being locked, though, and just grits to walking awhile. It's like the one year when she convinced herself to get in shape by swimming - the agony of the first push off from the wall after every lap, the resigned misery to the fact that being out-of-breath doesn't mean anything has been accomplished, at all. The pants she didn't want to put on seem to raise an allergic reaction - she has to stop to rake her fingernails up and down her legs, skin which seems powder sharp, dandruff-scales of some reptile, rough touch to a toad hardened by lack of wetland. It has been a five minute loop of the level of her own apartment and not a word offered in thought, but she wishes she would just go back inside. Yet no. No, no. She has to wait, now, for a new wind to take her. To go in now will be to weakling into her comforter or to up the thermostat and lay blanketless on the sofa, deceptioning herself that not covering up means she does not intend to pass out. Lucy knows all of her tricks. And she knows if she decided to try to stay awake it's because whatever-it-is-isn't-done-with-her isn't done with her - to resist it would be to invite catastrophe. If she was at the mercy of any creature that could be hid from, well, she would have long ago found herself a hole and died there rather than risk her neck. But Lucy's only hope is to be caught - jaw-clutched, head-shook-side-to-sided - to have it revealed that her predator only had the desire for her to play dead and would reward her by letting her do just that, forever. Thrash. Thrash. Drop her. Ignore her. Thrash. Thrash. Drop her. Ignore her. She needs to be a good play-pretend carcass - more dead than a real victim for her very performativeness! Lucy needs to impress the loping thing that follows and waits to pounce, really bring it to salivating, mauling applause by how much she can tease out the details, the nuance of death by so desperately wanting to live. Now? She has gone down to the ground-floor, just stood in front of a drink machine and read the names off of every push-button. Pressed each button to see the words *Insert Coins* or *Selection Empty Try Again* appear on the display screen. One scrolling word, letter-by-letter, across at-a-time. *Insert. Coins. Selection. Empty. Try. Again.* And then? Back up to her floor and really hoping she would feel a bound in her legs at the sight of her door, an upsurge of words or activity or destination that would allow her warmth. She tries to say 'If you fall asleep, you won't even remember this' - in fact, she does say this and even knows it is true. But then feels tense and guilty. Remembering it is not herself she needs to fool.

Another ten minutes and it is fear that gets her back in through the door - maybe a trick she pulled maybe not, but fear, either way, fear does it - fear that maybe this endless cold walk is a way to keep herself from finishing the poem, of getting her weak and willing to destroy it like she had been telling herself to do. Her skin aches from the heat against her eyes, steam-blurred with fatigue, when she removes coat, pants, back down to her t-shirt, panties, one sock on and one off. This is where you live, Lucy! This is where you live! She does a kind of countdown of how long she is going to let herself still consider herself cold - one more circuit of the apartment, one more time running hot water into her hands, through her hair, one more time looking at her electric tea-kettle and thinking to get some water to a simmer. Finally, she reads this line: *the morning is owed to the littered floor, the evening is owed to the dogs that don't need it.* Doesn't that seem like the last line? 'You're just telling yourself that' she says. But she counts how many pages she has filled. Obviously, were she to write this thing out fair it would not be so many pages - though, on the other hand, some pages are thick with scrawls all over, maybe contain more than full-pages-worth, spacing considered - but even still, it is a considerable work. What is it even about? How do you know you aren't just trying to coax yourself, again, into stopping? But - logic, here, logic to prevail! - it could be that the walk was needed to palate cleanse, re-center her thoughts, let her see the poem as a Finished Object and so nothing that she could bear the destruction of. That is what it is now. An accomplishment! Look at this line: *when we were both sea-bottoms, things bred only enough to be open mouths, not enough to scream.* No memory of writing that, eh Lucy? Not that she doesn't recognize some of the lines as she flips - now - through the twenty covered sheets. But this is some forgotten, never-thought, not-to-be-remembered verse. Is it done? You should copy it, Lucy. But no - this notion sits ill. To do that would actually be diminishing. This has another purpose. It doesn't go to anyone. It's for Layla, isn't it? Yes - pay attention, pay attention to what you're thinking, Lucy - it is, but it will be sent to her otherwise, not in this form, Layla will understand this - Lucy, Lucy, listen, mark yourself, mark yourself! - regardless of it being sent, copied, it just needed to be done. The words just outed and to-paged. What is sent to Layla is something here but not this. And another line: *wind gave a penny and snow gave a cent, tree gave five dollars, tenth avenue spent.* What's that supposed to mean? Lucy shurgs. She likes it. Circles it, even though nothing about it seems to fit her usual reasons - however many and varied those are - to circle something. But she likes it circled. Draws legs on the circle and antennae on top. Signs her name to the doodle and dates it - but not with the proper date, at all. A yawn signifies she is through. And she does not doubt it any longer. A drain at the core of her inside has its chain tugged and the beginning of the gurgling that will end in the final sucked gasp of her empty begins.

The scent of the bubble-bath gives her a headache. She regrets lowering herself into the water, already. The entire soak seems to raise a fever, toxins released from the relaxation as through a brutal massage, hands applied to her after being wetted in an oil derived of the drained insides of wasps. But the sensation of the room air to any wet bit of skin keeps her pent to her place. Rocking slightly so that the surface water laps up her neck, up her raised knees, drifting heat away from the one, returning it to the other, the soothing repetitiveness and strength of a cat's tongue cleaning its kitten. Lucy is making sounds of breathing much like snoring - but eyes are wide open, ear focuses on the crackle of the bubbles shimmering slowly to nothing but sullied skin on water. If she falls asleep, she will wake to misery. Either the water will have turned against her, she'll rise from it already stiff with shuddering chills, or she will still be warm but so clumsy from half-awake that on standing she will not have the presence of mind to towel before assailed, abruptly, by the standing temperature of the bathroom air. She won't drift off and she won't think. Lucy Jinx is in a kind of imbecile womb. This should be a cause for alarm - were a loved-one present, even just a decently-liked person spending the night, they would liken Lucy's state to some mild catatonia or maybe even the signs of a mini-stroke. Lucy Jinx, that is, appears decidedly the worse for wear. Look how one eyelid is more open than the other, the more-closed one with a kind of flutter to it, moving, not exactly blinking, the way a horse's skin does to shoo off biting insects. That isn't proper seeming - that would be a symptom a doctor would notice to help aid in a difficult diagnosis! Or how about how she will take three or four seemingly even, seemingly perfectly measured, breaths in through her nose - is she numbly counting? timing them? she must be, they seem precisely trimmed to the size of each other - then suddenly a gasp in through her mouth as though no breathing at all had be going on during the span of time those three or four nose breaths were took. Okay - Lucy has stood. The cascade of water off of her girth is a bit overdone - the sloshing noise is rather ostentatious and it makes the entire room seem disheveled, left inside-out - but Lucy is up and has a towel around her and shuts the bathroom light off, knowing the tub is still full. Who cares? She scoops her cigarettes up from the sofa-arm and closes herself in the bedroom, giving a wink to what she can see of herself in the thin rectangle of mirror that is stood, slanting, to the wall over by the laundry pile. 'So - that is what's left of you, Lucy' she sighs, but at the same time smiles because it must be admitted that there is quite a bit of Lucy, there. Her belly gets a juddery clap and she wriggles her index-finger and then her little-finger into the round of her belly button, expecting to find something crusty there, but instead touching nothing out of the ordinary, everything smooth, Golden-ratioed. Another clap to belly. It hurts. Lucy Jinx lays back.

Simple query: Does Lucy have to go to work tomorrow? She doesn't have to - as in to say: she is scheduled, but could call off - but thinks she should. Likely it is just her fatigue thinking - but to skip work, tomorrow, on the heels of today would seem a length down toward never-going-in-again. And Lucy needs to work. Simple query: Why does Lucy need to work? She hasn't run out of places she could mooch, that's for sure. Or not even mooch. The mother, for example, would likely let Lucy live with her, no charge, just for the promise of never ever going away, again. And adding in that Lucy is so-hard-at-working on her poetry compendium - her legitimate, wildly important, real deal - well, the mother would insist that she stay! Samantha would let her move in, no question. Milos would pay her to stay! Simple query: So why doesn't Lucy just stay with any one of those people? Because she has tried staying and it did not work. Is that really it, Lucy? 'Why wouldn't it be?' Well, when Lucy tried she had painted herself into awful corners: landmines in all directions and the necessity of shit-jobs - and more than one, at that! - of being in proximity to situations at a time she could not control herself. Lucy, it should be noted, is only referring to her time with Elliott - to the time in-and-around her being with Elliott. Now, though, Lucy would be under no such strain and would, bald-faced, put on no airs how she was interested in being a contributing member, financially, of anything. Say the mother or Samantha - Milos even - so much as hinted that 'Maybe you should kick in a bit, Lucy - even just for groceries' Lucy would then defensively throw on guilt-trip baiting talk, chastise herself, and say she had better move on with her life, that it is correct to point out she is giving nothing to earn her stay - so on, so on, so on - until she seems so pathetic she would never be sent packing! Simple query: And, moreover, if one person kicked her out, Lucy could say with another, right? Yes - there is that, too. Lucy could flit friend-to-friend, wearing out welcomes with the lot. 'Or I could just go live with Layla, right?' she simple-queries. But she yawns and shakes her head. 'That would last the least time of all' she alouds and laughs, getting the covers up around her as best as she is able. Entirely, her body swims in an instant paste of not-going-to-wake-for-twelve-hours-easy. It will still be another fifteen, twenty minutes before she is out, but there is no more fight toward awake, toward even shutting off the lights. Lucy is abandoned of Lucy - the start of a husk waiting for the new body to creak through, leave it behind, seeming a solid whole, itself, until close inspection shows the fissure where newness escaped. 'Oh that'd be nice' Lucy mutters - no idea, none at all, of the words - 'to be the empty crust of myself, to be the stiff, crisp skin left behind while the other one chirps and flutters for a mate.' Lucy would trade all sense of nearness to another living thing to be just the outline of her old physicality, her young dimensions with nothing inside of them.

What does Lucy dream? This night. This night she dreams one thing over and over, over and over, over and over. She dreams the image of the surface-glass of a flashlight. A long, lingering, ten-minute view of it - menacingly in-close, her dreamed eyes hurting from the stay of the white-yellow straight into them. She dreams this image like it is the only thing there is to dream. The only thing ever dreamed. She dreams it in a calm and familiar way - the way something that lived a billion years in sight of something else that lived a billion years must feel on the last day it will see this other thing. She dreams it like there would be no difference it dying, going black or her dying, going black. It is certainly glass, though, and certainly the light is artificially generated by stored electricity. Nothing living in the light. A captured, phantasmal light. She dreams it and dreams it - getting no more used to it or less, no more aware she is dreaming well into the dream than right at the start. It is the most peaceful dream she has ever experienced - or so she would think if she manages to recall it - these the most peaceful passing minutes in her entire life. And she does not inspect the light or the glass, does not try to squint to make out more-or-less of the bulb down in there, the centered light of which is widened by the circle of the round surface. Lucy dreams this as though she will dream it, again. Each minute of the dream contains the dream in a thousand copies over - or might just as well. It could be, of course, that it is a single ten minute image of the flashlight - perhaps the real memory, even, of a time a young Lucy maybe had looked at a flashlight so long. Or maybe it is an extended, oversized version of a memory of looking at a flashlight for just a split second, that split second devoided of time, even the ten-minute duration not a duration just an arbitrary distinction from the part of her brain still functional enough in sleep to need artificial constructs - or if not need, at least to apply them. No lift or sink to it, not inside or outside. The dream does not become a description of the image or a dwelling on the image or an alternative angle of it, even by a centimeter. Just a lens of a flashlight. The flashlight on. Lucy Jinx asleep and dreaming millennia of it, all other thought ousted from whatever place it would normally be. Lucy is trash-compactored by this dream, is snow-plowed into a high wall by it. Lucy is everything-she-was-made-into-a-single-notion and that notion seems to be glass - not heated, she also knows the glass would be cool to the touch, no sensation of it so much as luke-warming her nose or her cheeks which are as near to it as are her reacting eyes. This is what Lucy dreams this night - all night - for as long as she is able. It is a dream with no ambition and no humility. Lucy Jinx's mind offers her up - why? - this night - why? - a rendition of peace - why? - that she will already lose

- why? - as she wakes. As she wakes - is it night? - and in the moment she blinks, the room still dark - how dark? how wide did she open her eyes? - the image, the dream is gone - and in its place is the thought of the sharp front of a boat, dry-landed, still wet, salt-tasting air around, nausea in all the sailor's eyes and all of them faking youthful abandon and bodiless grace.

# .IIII.

MATHILDE HAD LEFT THE MISSHAPEN, folded-around, weather-beaten envelope under her apartment doormat - the green sticker, barcoded, all peppered with some sort of tarry gunk, some of the manila torn at the corners, a stuffing like asbestos leaking, spooring into where the corridor bulbs caught the flickering, nearly still-standing-in-mid-air gathering of dust - dirt from cold shoes, boots, flecks of tissues brought up to sneezing mouths. Lucy could have had this delivered to her own apartment, but in a way felt bad about not giving Mathilde anything so exciting do be involved with for awhile - just the drudgery of informing Lucy when the broad or the editor or whomever was in touch, taking Lucy's dictation and always chortling in mockery of Lucy's half-hearted 'I can pay you for all of this, really.' A mysterious package - or rather a package Lucy refused to explain - must have been an oasis of intrigue! Otherwise, what was Mathilde's life? A boyfriend and having to see about an extension on student loan payments? Always some headache with a brother-in-law - which, as far as headaches go, seems the most absurd sort of all. 'Keep your family to yourself' that is what Lucy would tell whatever rat tried to cramp her up with woes of artificially-jointed familia. Yes, Mathilde could use someone like Lucy! And, no,

Lucy has not done anything but pick up the package, look at Mathilde's name as the recipient, and then stop looking at the package without changing the position in which it was held. Why the devil this is a moment to draw out - well, it should be admitted there are reasons - why the devil it is not just perfunctory for Lucy, as it would be for anyone else - even with the self-centered curiosity taken into account - there really is no saying. The short of it: Lucy cares. The long of it: Lucy is afraid of what she is going to read in the pages of the magazine inside of the envelope. So this slow peeling away of gauze, this slow unbandaging of a wound which, sure, she knows is healed but that the exposure of healed-flesh to elements could allow a re-wounding of, infected and septic, maybe, this time. So - it's a magazine, Lucy. 'You know it's a magazine.' Which magazine? 'You know which magazine!' That exclamation point isn't a jab, mind - no anger or distance - Lucy is just screwing with her own impatience. Like with many moments anticipated what is more anticipated is the moment being passed - and much much more anticipated is the moment being missed, not acted on. Regrets, they last so much longer than fulfillment. Want to die in the blink of an eye? The orgasm. Want to live forever? Then hold your tongue and think about it from another room in another state, never having told it your name. Lucy? 'Yes?' Which magazine? 'But that will be revealed, all in good time' Lucy greatest-show-on-earths, suddenly sashaying like a broom plucked from resting and immediately over-applied to a floor too dusty for dry-bristles to much affect. 'All in good time, monsieurs et mademoiselles - and not in these environs! This is corridor, after all, and a place of buffer - a wall to keep out all of East Germany!' Lucy knows better than to mix the moment of reaction with the place where she is supposed to be hidden. 'Come with me' Lucy thinks to herself, finger, in her mind, poor cartoon animation coiling 'Come, come - follow, follow' the frame swirling to color and reshaping to the next scene.

So what about this magazine? It's called *Charactor Acter*. A periodical about the theatre? Indeed. Interview-based, primarily, with reviews and excerpts and the lot. On the cover of this issue? In bold, some play on words, something tongue-in-cheek - perhaps? - or the actual title of a play Lucy has never heard of, something modern. *How Do You Solve A Problem Like Malaria?* Lucy hopes it is a title. The image is striking, a photograph - as many photographs of theatre-in-progress are - from an elevated vantage and, at first, Lucy thinks it is a black-and-white photo with little touch-ups of color, then comes to realize - no, not at all! wow! cool! - that is the costuming and make-up! Underneath the bold letters - blood orange - it says *Responses by Edwin DeWitt, Ramsey R.H. Jillet, Suzane Pond, and Cashmine Craw*. None of this means anything to Lucy. Those are likely important names. Were now back-in-time, Lucy a young woman, she would know these folks well, from anthologies and long researched volumes of analysis, striving to come off as though she knew them well enough she would be missed from their tables each night, missed from some of their boudoirs. But does this title, these people, this photo of swell theatering have a thing to do with Lucy? No. But: she dwells on the cover - its heavy stock and matte finish, soft powder like her fingers should smudge bits of the image wherever she puts them next. It's another world, one that does its rounds and to which a Lucy Jinx is irrelevant. One of countless countless-such-worlds, another gear turning another clock the time displayed on is ponderous and far removed from Lucy and her personally used tick-tock. Other print on the cover - different shades of orange for article titles, same shade of mint-blue for contributor names - have equally little to do with Lucy. Only here - look, look - on the *Table of Contents* page do we find our raison d'etre. Why, it is a faux-candid photograph of one Elliott Pine, mid-phony laugh - or the laugh might be real, but not a laugh based on anything but stimuli from an obvious photo session. And on the photograph is a little bit of letter and number that goes *pg. fifty-nine*. That's right, no digits used - the abbreviation for *page* then the number all written out in letters. Zip over to the down-scroll of Contents and we see the name *Elliott Pine*. And we see the announcement of *First-time playwright talks out her tour de force debut, her first loves (literal and carnal) and why she refuses to ever know how she got here*. Lucy crinkle-mouths at that, but admits it's cool how it sounds like one of those stupid magazine teasers would sound. Oh and also to mention - bold print, above all that - it says *The Altogether Another Florence Dredge*. Lucy lays odds that is the name of Elliott's whizz-bang play, then 'Oh ya reckons?' to herself and sniffs and wonders why her windshield-wipers are on though it is sunny and the engine isn't even turned over, just the battery, the car around her still struck through with a long winded beeeeeeeppppppppp of key-in-ignition-unturned. Fine. She gets the car going, right away the heater demanding cold air into her face, she working at the dial so that the heat is drifted up the windshield, unfogging it up almost all at once. What's on page fifty-nine? Generic, full-page photo of Elliott Pine - legs crossed like a fella, too cool to care, on a chair, bare stage, a coil of microphone at her feet, a rose, a bunch of discarded paper, and a pair of lacy panties over one foot.

On another subject - Lucy has the magazine tossed on to the passenger seat, where it atops some CDs and a glove she really wishes she knew where other one of was and some envelopes she meant to mail about a week ago but by now what does it matter - Lucy has other things, plentiful, to do today. Just for example? She has to go to work! Isn't she mortal? Doesn't Lucy Jinx, like all those sad deaths of kings we sit upon the ground and tell sad stories of, live with bread et cetera? And, if so, doesn't she need employment to earn the dirty funny-paper to keep her as she is accustomed? Well, sure. Sure! She's no Elliott Pine, after all - Big-Chief Wigwam of the Metropolitan Theatre Swing Circuit or the

Appellate Court of *Dramatis Persona* or whatever! No - if one were to trace Lucy's noble dust, might they not find it stopping her own bunghole!? Plenty to do and never enough time - work and she has to go to lunch and errands to run and then to meet this and that person and all of the multitude of involvements there. And - hey! - knowing Lucy, a bunch of random fluff will jam the circuits and she'll have to endure and overcome that mess, as well. Truth be told, Lucy got up extra early to venture to Mathilde's for this magazine - is on her way to her gainful employ even as she says she is. To herself. 'As I'm the only one here' she puts the pin on it, just to be thorough. Right now, Lucy has to change to this lane. And in a minute, she has to take *Exit Forty B*. That is a thing, in and of itself. No one on the acropolis, for all their high talk, in their wildest imaginations would have foreseen Lucy having to take *Exit Forty B*! And never could they have conjured she had to do so to only then have to keep left to remain on *Pellet Road* and then - well, she doesn't know the name of the next few roads, whichever and whichever - arrive at work! Built a democracy, did they? Well, that's what we say now - but, technically, they were the first people to not-build-a-democracy. 'Which is to say: it was corrupt' Lucy growls 'and based on enslavement and classism and not to mention other deplorable attitudes they were not even clever enough to have known they were displaying!' Lucy's feeling? Her feeling is simple: When we realize people did shitty things in the past we should deride them. Learn from the past? Ha! Do that and we learn to give a pass to modern despots and Mengeles! Simple lesson - we should destitute that stuff from Human History - efface it! The shyster who first convinced someone the way to keep an atrocity from happening again was to keep careful records of said atrocity and study them fervently probably made a pretty penny - but is that something to admire? History has a percentage in being repeated, after all. 'People overlook that! People overlook that!' Lucy says twice to make sure it is well understood. Now, maybe someone who is as Wayne Manor stately as - Oh I dunno - Elliott Pine - just for example - might think that history isn't a virus bent on self-replication the same as anything and will go to history to find the advice 'Remember history' and not think twice about it - think someone said it fucking tomorrow! - but a lowly little turtle called Mack-called-Lucy-Jinx knows what history is up to and thinks the cure for all of it is amnesia! 'It might happen again, still? That's your point?' Lucy scoffs. 'What kind of a point is that?' Let it happen again - at least this time it isn't everyone's obvious fault, it's just the way it went - what history is supposed to be, a time stretching forever devoid of human input! 'If that's okay with her majesty Elliott Pine, that is' Lucy under-her-breaths.

'Ignore me' Lucy thinks to herself. 'Just ignore me.' She eats the breakfast she got from the drive-thru in the parking lot of the not-yet-grand-openinged *Percy*

*Shoe Outlet*. She recalls avoiding some lover called Violet - was it Violet? maybe not - in a shopping-center like this. All the time - staying on extra shifts without pay, anything - just hiding out and smoking cigarettes back in the area behind the shops, that thin line of forest separating the suburban row-houses and elementary-school from the ruckus of commerce. But she can't quite timeline it. She knows she lost her cool, screeching into one of her first cellphones - coiling around, semi-circles then off balance sideways stepping - unpacking all of the reasons she hated whatever her name had been - Violet? - and how, despite it, Violet had had no call to have aired Lucy's laundry - she'd used a better colloquialism - all around. Even here, stomach wishing it didn't have to be receptacle to these hardly-chewed chicken-biscuit sandwiches, Lucy works herself up in to quite a froth, the memory not even full, only the core of its rapture left. Violet - or whomever - had acquired the intimacy of Lucy's life, her circle of acquaintances, and had weaponized them. It hadn't mattered - it never would have, to any of them, whoever they were, whoever Lucy had once known, whenever this had been - they had more than happily peeled let's-call-her-Violet from their card decks, unneeding her for any future hand or parlor trick and had heartily rallied around Lucy, cursing Violet-or-whatever and Pariahing her soundly. But Violet-we'll-call-her had gotten to Lucy - gotten to Lucy as though a priori - one of the first to consciously see how it was the mere fact that Lucy knew even her dear friends - or whatever they were, whoever they were - knew her business was a sour enough poison, a sturdy enough tree to noose Lucy's cowardly, deserter neck from! Make no mistake - she doesn't know when it was, but the words *Decades, plural, ago* most certainly apply - decades ago though it may have been from Lucy, here sitting - ignoring her current day with thoughts of this one she can't place - the memory, even the faint flicker of it one-fiftieth whole, rises her hackles, lowers her to defensive haunches, makes her dismal and wanting her bones to unfold into sacks to bury herself in. Shame never goes far, because it never needs to and no one ever wants it to. Shame is kept close where it can do as little harm as possible. Bad enough there still exist people who know some of Lucy's old predilections - some of her very candid statements or desires - but imagine the shame itself being unburdened from Lucy to loom and lurk, to snigger from bushes and, itself, be a freeform possibility, not just a diamond-tight scab in the lining of Lucy's charred privacy. 'Ignore me, ignore me' Lucy says, drinking coffee finally settled enough to not be stinging and knowing she will need to stop for breath freshening chewing-gum. How this grease coats her mouth so quickly she doesn't know! And how it makes her teeth scrape over each other - slick seeming and dry as impossible-to-rid-from-hands sand - is a riddle of science she knows will never be brought to illumination. Her coffee doesn't taste like coffee

- it tastes like she wishes she hadn't eaten what she had just eaten. All she tastes is it being kept from penetrating to the flesh of tongue or her cheek, its weight less than the grease, just glissandoing down her gullet where it is likely surrounded - a liquid centerpiece as though a termite queen - protectored in a swirl and pulse around it, around it, around it of recent-chewed muck.

According to the interview with Elliott Pine, this: 'Lucy Jinx. If anyone. No - not *if anyone* - I'll start again. Lucy Jinx. Who was she? She was - and I have no doubt still is - a split-atom splitting a hair, every breath, halving each syllable until everyone in the world is too tired to care.' The interview - questions from Interviewer in italics - indicates there was *Laughter* at this point - this word *Laughter* like a stage-direction inside of parenthesis. *Laughter* from the Interviewer. And *Laughter* from Elliott Pine. Elliott Pine's line ending: open parenthesis *laughter* close parenthesis. Interviewer's line starting: open parenthesis *laughter* close parenthesis. Asked to elaborate? According to the interview with Elliot Pine, this: 'She was a poet. We were lovers. I loved her. Above anything I ever adored. The way you can only love the poison you know will curdle you the fastest, I suppose. And I say this knowing full well my wife is in earshot' - more parenthetical *laughter* - 'but she knows, she knows. She was a poet and she was sublime and she made every word I could conceive of - and anyone I read, anywhere - seem so impossibly small, empty-pocketed and just mothballed, aching with obsolescence.' The Interviewer - *laughter* is not noted, so maybe this was asked solemnly, voice quieting due to some shift in Elliott Pine's face - asks - and this gets a whole line in the magazine, mind you - 'You admired her?' According to the interview with Elliott Pine, this: 'There aren't enough letters in *admire* - I don't know what I did. When I want to terrify myself, I think of Lucy. Not of my time with her - that I can't even say what it does to me - I think about her poems. And I think about how she would read every word I wrote and must have had nothing but derision for it.' In parenthesis *laughter*. 'And of course' says the interviewer 'that is famously how you met your wife.' 'Oh famously' says Elliott Pine, according to the interview with Elliott Pine. 'Lucy wrote that fucking story. It's haunting. And served me up to my own betrayal of her and the rest is history.' *Laughter*. Why isn't that one in parenthesis? Did Elliott say *Laughter*? And did the magazine just italicize it because of - what? - how Elliott had said it? Anyway, the interviewer is smitten with the fact that Elliott Pine 'pays such reverence to an unknown poet.' And to this, according to the interview with Elliott Pine, Elliott Pine says: 'Lucy wouldn't even have a name if she could help it. I think she is the purest not only for saying that - well, she never said it - but for thinking it, feeling it - I know she did - not just in some *Woe is me* or *Such is life* way, but because she tormentedly did everything she could to get out of the contract of identity.' 'The Contract of

Identity' the Interviewer, it seems, felt it apt to interject 'being front-and-center - the, shall we shall, *Paranoia* or the *Disquiet* of your play?' And according to the interview with Elliott Pine 'Yes' Elliott Pine 'would say so - Yes' Elliott Pine 'supposes.' No further mention of Lucy. Unless Lucy is this *Florence Drudge*, but it doesn't sound like it. Pages on goes the interview - Lucy not reading, just scanning for her name, mention of her, something else. Continued in the rear pages - but no Lucy there, either. The magazine closed. Lucy: either snarling or just not making any face and that is how her face looks while she is thinking whatever this is.

Lucy Jinx's Interview with Elliott Pine. Starring Lucy Jinx as Lucy Jinx and Elliot Pine. 'What the Hell are you talking about?' 'In the interview?' 'No, Elliott, in anywhere! Since when did you - what do you say? - *admire me*?' 'I always admired you, Lucy - you know that, come on!' 'And don't give me credit for writing your stupid story - do you know how dumb that makes me seem to anyone of my caliber?' 'Well, I don't mix with people of your caliber, do I?' 'No, sweet-tart, you don't. And what - is this how you flirt with your darling wife? Don't use my name in an interview to flirt with your dribble-bib wife!' 'Don't tell me how to flirt with my dribble-bib wife - she doesn't enter into it, I use you for everything.' 'Yes - shitty stories, stupid wives who write books-in-their-fourteenth-printing that have been translated into dozens of languages!' 'Don't be jealous of her, Lucy.' 'I'm not. I'm jealous of you! For being clever enough to Tom Ripley your way into the world of *Letters of Note*.' 'That's kind of petty, man.' 'I didn't say it wasn't. Yes, El, congratulations on recognizing what I was doing there - you identified a petty statement as petty, how do you do it!? Your acumen, El! No wonder your play is so giving its regards to goddamned Broadway and being remembered to Herald cock-sucking Square!' 'Don't try to make theatre jokes, Loose - you're shit at it.' 'You're right - I'll leave the theatre jokes to you.' 'OOh good one. And you're welcome, by the way.' 'I'm welcome?' 'Yes - p.s. You're welcome.' 'What am I welcome for - or to or whatever the case may be - what are you on about?' 'For giving you your introduction - you are now going to be on a shelf in the same store as me! You have been identified and plucked!' 'I haven't gone through with anything, yet - and I don't owe you one damned thing, El!' 'I mentioned you in a premiere literary periodical and gushed about you for two-thirds-of-a-page! You don't think that has exactly everything to do with why you have a contract signed? The broad even told you it did, man! Now you get the picture, eh?' 'You think the broad is going to stake her reputation on you mentioned me is a fruity Stage journal!?' 'Yes.' 'Then you're an actual simp and I feel kind of bamboozled for sometimes missing you.' 'You never miss me - you hadn't thought about me until the broad brought me up.' 'Fuck you, man - you know that isn't true.'

'You thought about me the same way you vaguely remember having made homemade peanut-butter in kindergarten.' 'I do remember that! Fondly - yes.' 'Or the way you remember seeing a straw on the floor of a restaurant once - by the jukebox, at *Pizza Hut* - that exact straw.' 'What are you bitter about?' 'I'm not bitter. I basically announced in a magazine I'm in love with you!' 'What are you going to do about it? What's your plan, El? Gonna stalk my launch-party or something? Bump into me at some conference somewhere and pretend you don't have a wedding ring on?' 'You wouldn't want me to pretend that - the ring'd be your favorite part!' 'You've grown a sense of self-flattery - I'm so glad.' 'Just say *Thank you*.' 'No.' 'Just say *Thank you* Lucy!' 'No.' 'Fine. I'd expect little else from you.' 'I'd expect little else from you than expecting little else from me.' 'Just tell me one thing, okay?' 'No.' 'Lucy!' 'No!' 'Goddamnit, you're a child.'

Lucy should not be Lucy. She should be some lout-legged, heft-stomached fella who could - morning, middle-of-the-day, whenever - be expected to lunge his gut up over some bar-counter and scratch at the rash around his navel through his three-days worn shirt fabric, just say 'Give me something' to get the bartender to pour and the sort who the bartender would feel obligated to laugh shotgun at if Lucy - this bloat-fella - said so much as 'What about it - right? - 'nother fucking day!' This is the consensus of Lucy with Lucy. And how she still has more than an hour until she needs to be at work is beyond her! She tried to reason out how she must have tricked herself, must already be late - how there must be high-level sorts right now debating her, the ones she has ingratiated herself to at the same time coming to her staunch defense and assuring the others, who bridges she's burnt, that Lucy would never be late if there wasn't an urgent reason, rallying this to be the truth in the grim of the other's I-don't-know-about-that's. Isn't this what makes you comfortable though, Jinx? The freedom to come and go like you are another disposable entity, each day? Work at nine at ten at eleven, don't work at all - you're chunder and discharge as far the world goes, you are muck that is scraped from the bottom of the pond that someone found clever use for but only if manipulated by heat and science, just so! Annoyed at the cliché of the thought, Lucy says 'I'm what - a grain of sand?' But no - come on, Lucy - you aren't a grain of sand. You are far more than that! Lucy: you are a whole two-inches-deep of an entire two miles of shoreline of sand! Does that make you feel better? You're more than infinitesimal, it just so happens that you're multitudes more of something that just doesn't matter. 'Droll' Lucy sighs 'droll.' And she drives right past the place where she works, under the bridge at the base of the hill, up the next wend of the hill, around the roundabout, stops at the traffic-light, goes through the traffic-light, stops at the next, goes through it, keeps moving because she is turning left and that is what the sign says to do if one is turning left - she doesn't trust it, tenses for a coming collision and feels sinister looks from the other drivers, annoyed at her for following the letter-of-the-law so absurdly - then over this speed-hump, that speed-hump, and is in the parking lot of *Tower Bay Mall*, outside of a *Boscovs*, car still idling, and the radio whispering a song so low all she hears is the chh-chh-chh of occasional cymbal-drum smacked or evenly-struck. She picks up the magazine - good natured - and gawks at the cover price, wondering if the people who think it's worth almost sixteen-dollars-per-issue are greedy or if they truly regret the price but find it's the only way to ensure the quality of material and production that an adoring audience has gotten used to. Lucy tears out one of the up-close photographs of Elliott, folds it into a square that would unfold into a larger square with four square quadrants creased to it and she tucks this into a slit of her wallet. She also takes out a five-years-outdated Insurance Card and bends it back-and-forth until it snaps. Nods. Important stuff. Jobs well done.

The ceiling of this department store - not *Boscovs*, it might be *Lord and Taylor* - is mirrors interrupted by panels of purple or some terrible green. This is horror. And nowhere Lucy stops does she seem to be underneath, directly, a reflection of her looking up. Moreover - her criticisms are many - the mirror-panels seem to be not squares, but three rectangle-strips laid to make an approximate square, the fit of them not seamless so that what they do reflect comes off as broken, repeated, stuck in the middle of some sort of fit, like the ceiling is trying to wake up from something but just cannot, just cannot. Poor ceiling. Except for the fact that it seems nasty-hearted. Yes. Lucy can tell things about ceilings, she imagines telling all who pass as they stop to listen, fingers to chins. This ceiling wants to agitate all who pass under it, unsettle them out of feeling permanent, whole, entire - there is an epilepsy to its stillness and its waiting pool of reflections that do not add up to image. What? 'What!?' Lucy actually whisper shouts with full jut of arm out in defense of the imagined argument. 'Do I think I am just projecting on to this ceiling?' Projecting what!? That last shout was in her head, only, and she now settles into some semblance of Lucy-Jinx-is-a-person-like-any-other-just-in-this-shop-to-see-about-something, pleased to see the Jewelry counter approaching. And - Ah! - the sinister reason that wretched ceiling caught her eye! The Jewelry department is the ceiling-in-miniature! The shimmer of these cheap, likely-not-actual doo-dads is not the way film and television, descriptions in novels-of-old, lead one to believe *Precious* should look. This looks like candy in a grandmother's jar, playthings the neighbors have that make them always eye yours much more, with greed. The jewels with some sort of color seem poorly painted, models that dad wasn't there to help with, trinkets sold in a shop about to close, the illustrations in a book in the Remainder Bin of a drugstore. The diamonds on the rings Lucy is looking at - intently, choosing -

seem no more glamorous than the false bronze of the connective parts of the glass display-case - indeed, the reflections of the white-cheap lights, bought in bulk, caught from overhead in semi-reflection - Lucy's lean-over shadowing them out - seem rather as beautiful as any long string of pearls for retail. Add in the green felt of case bottoms, the purple felt, the reddish table cloths, the print-shop tones of the display signs - wherein rings, flat and photographed, seem heavier and more permanent than the trifles held up by clerks who could care less for you to pretend to care more about - and the chintzy fray, hobgoblinesque dinner-coat of the place reaches its miniature precision of reflecting the rippling Hell overhead! That's a lot of angst, Lucy! Holy cow! See these other shoppers - see that woman who is too shy to look at the mannequins in the mannequin unmentionables? see that fellow not the least bit bashful of the same, but who averts his eyes after taking a drink of the bulges at center-focus in the images on discount packages of boxer briefs, checking glimpses just-to-be-sure, tightening his abs after, touching his undernose with his thumb? - do you think they find this place such a deathbed? 'No, probably not' Lucy says, crouched, pretending to be deciding between that ring and that ring and that ring, liking the roaming, nonchalant way the woman working the counter was able to seem right there yet miles away, poised-to-clutch and hum-bugly disinterested in Lucy, all at once.

Lucy Jinx says to the clerk - she clocks her at fifty-four and never having had a thought of marriage except one something like the sound of condensed soup poured in a cylinder from the can - 'You know what I've always thought is this: I've thought that a necklace is more of a sign of possession, so shouldn't that be what's used for engagements? A ring on a flimsy finger - so breakable and replaceable - doesn't much amount to Ever After. Snap a neck? Well, that proves you belonged to someone - you'll know it as it splinters.' The clerk smiles at Lucy - that smile of 'I guess you are someone else I should have been friends with in a youth I don't have now but never got to be' and admits she had never thought of it. 'Though' the clerk says - Lucy bracing in readiness the politest That's-interesting-too expression of lower lip out over upper - 'I imagine the hands are the parts that touch - of people - necks don't touch. I was going to say bracelet - but wrists don't touch either.' Okay, Lucy gives an actual nod. Adorn the part that touches - sure - not so much about possession - yes yes - she allows this - though does have to point out that history stands pretty staunch in saying marriage is about possession and cracking eggs for unnecessary omelets. The clerk agrees 'Yes, it's terrible' and makes some political-minded statements and goes on how if she got married she'd get a tattoo or buy a book she'd always wanted but that was too expensive without an excuse like wedlock. Lucy likes this clerk, this clerk who now says 'But at the same time - as awful as the most slim-pricked brute is - they probably think romantic things, even if those romantic things are only enacted as slavery.' Points to the clerk. This suddenly seems dangerous. Lucy mentions how once she was married. In Lucy's view, vows should be accompanied by joint, voluntary disfiguration. 'And not' Lucy Jinx raises admonishing finger 'in the way like some peoples of the world do thing - not decoratively. I mean: the idea is *Let's throw acid on each other's best bits to prove this, shall we?*' The clerk, it seems, could not agree more - and next time it appears on the ballot she promises she'll back the proposition! 'More subtly' the clerk says now 'maybe anklets should become the fashion. Nothing drives home the actual truth of a marriage more than two people with matching ankles everywhere they go.' Lucy is leaning and the clerk is leaning and between them is a current of shared mockery-of-it-all such that Lucy wonders if she will be looked down on for finally making a purchase. It's such a treachery, moments like these! Women and their always-working-at-Jewelry-counter ways. Why couldn't this clerk be a man - even horny in his indifference for any customer, hoping the way he said 'How can I help you?' butterflied long fields of afternoon delight in the thoughts of some biddy like Lucy Jinx? Why just this woman - Justine, poorly-printeds her nametag - why just this sad-but-wanting-to-be-happy Justine? All sad people want to be happy don't they, Lucy? 'None of them I've ever met' Lucy says, grinning at the codedness and the perplexed I-want-to-know on the clerk's face. 'I admit: I have to buy two rings. I don't want you to think less of me. I promise you: they mean something quite complex - something complex so that it can only be called *erroneous*.' 'It is my job to sell you things' the clerk riddles back. Lucy - to see what would happen - flicks the clerk's hand-back. What happened? This was middle-school, again, and this was a crumpled sheet of paper found in an old backpack almost thirty years later, as well.

Two of the exact same ring. Lucy - she also bought a pair of toothpaste-blue gloves - walks back to her car sighing how 'That was supposed to be my drugs money.' And the parking lot is gumming up with milling exhaust and drivers annoyed at the speed of shoppers to-and-from cars and stores, the stop-motion circulation of commerce Lucy finds uglier than roadkill. Closed inside her vehicle, Lucy checks the time on her phone, not wanting to alert anyone looking for a spot that she is leaving. A few minutes more to herself. She tries on one ring. She tries on the other. She tries on both. By this point, she wonders which came from which box, if there is any conceivable way to sleuth it out, any forensic way to discern - from just the on-hand evidence in this automobile - which-from-which. Can she make herself more fond of one? Left hand? Right hand? A mother's love tendriling a selection of this twin more than that twin? One is always prima, yes? A mother knows. You came first. You came second.

Choices are made and bonds are struck and only a fool aims to fight them. Left hand. Right hand. If Lucy said 'Right hand' dropped both rings, would she ever know, again? The noia of the mother of twins - of triplets! Lord, Lucy hopes there was something olfactory to help, otherwise the situation seems untenable! She boxes both rings back - one to this coat pocket, one to that. She removes the tags from her gloves and licks and massages at the little snag in the soft leather this tug-away of plastic caused. The gloves fit to her hand so quietly. *The night with you, quiet as the fit of a glove.* Lucy clicks her recorder on - a bit awkward in this thicker blue skin - and says 'You're night fallen, quiet as the fit of a glove.' Lets it record. Lets it record. Turns it off. Then starts the car. And the view in front of her - with the gloves griping the wheel as part of it - renews the world the way fresh prescription lenses alter everything. Suddenly trees don't just have leaves, those leaves have bones! And everywhere one steps are signs of mortality! Lucy gets those holy men who live with arms elevated until they atrophy - she digs that, knows why it's an accomplishment. Lucy could see herself - whether she wants to or not - kind of worshipping a person who went thirty years without trimming their toenails, who treated them with oils to preserves them, who venerated humanity in keratin curls. There would be nothing so miserable as ones toenails being asundered after decades - even after just a year it would be a permanent trauma! Holy Lucy Jinx: she will wear her gloves, never once removing them, for the next forty years! Can't help but laughing how, of necessity, that means her fingernails will grow for exactly as long, untrimmed, too. 'Unless' she says 'they wind up bursting through the leather.' In that case, Lucy might as well trim them. She wonders if her heart would tell her 'That counts as having taken off the gloves, though, them bursting at the fingernails.' 'Oh probably Lucy' Lucy sighs, but then, sighing again, says 'But Lucy, you're always too hard on yourself.' And she holds a hand, fingers spread, in front of her face, like blocking a light shone in a beam right at the dead center of her eyes. Turns open the hand, turns closed the hand to fist. Clenches the fist hard and straining - plays as though that strain is what was propelling the vehicle onward.

SAYS SAMANTHA TO LUCY 'WAS the Tally-Man a slave like the others?' And says Lucy back to Samantha 'Eh?' '*The Tally-Man.*' 'Who' Lucy has to scratch what feels like a developing blemish on her left cheek 'tallies the bananas - is this of whom you speak?' 'Yes. I'm wondering whether he was also a slave.' But Lucy doesn't know what Samantha means by *also*. Well, what Samantha means by *also* is that 'Weren't they slaves - slaves of the banana plantation?' Lucy snorts, but then thinks. 'I don't think there were banana plantations.' But, as Samantha deftly points out 'Anything can be a plantation - what it depends on is if you build a sort of house that functions as a headquarters there.' Cutting to it, though, Lucy doesn't think any of them were slaves. 'They got paid.' 'Where does it say that? In the song, I mean' Samantha says she means 'where does it say they get paid?' Lucy runs what she can remember of the song through her head. 'I'm thinking of some other slave song.' 'So they were slaves!' 'Or' Lucy staves Samantha's sematic enthusiasm 'I am thinking of another song that was a slave song and perhaps is therefore unrelated to this song.' 'Which song?' '*Pay Me My Money Down.*' 'Oh right.' 'Or *Every Time I Jump Up, I Not Jim Crow.*' 'Right' Samantha nods. Lucy nods. 'I think the Tally-Man was not like the others, though. He was management, not labor.' 'What I mean is: was he white?' 'I have no idea' Lucy shrugs and Kurt just continues to sort his files as though none of this conversation is even happening. So Samantha then says to Lucy 'Has there ever been a horror movie based on the Tally-Man? Has he been used in a conceptually terrifying way?' Lucy points out that Samantha is the one who is supposed to know about movies. But Samantha presses on. So Lucy says 'A movie set on a banana plantation wherein the Tally-Man kills banana workers or something?' 'Or just one of those atmospheric ones - where he represents some kind of, I don't know, psyche or conflict-in-the-human-heart. A revenge-from-beyond-the-grave.' Lucy says she can see the poster with the worst tagline of all time, even now: *The Tally Man: Daylight come and me wanna go home!* Blood-shaped letters! A face screaming! And the poster designed to look as though claws have torn though it! There should be a movie! Lucy and Samantha agree. 'Shouldn't there be a movie, Kurt?' asks Lucy. 'In my mind, there is already a movie. I assure you. I see the exact picture you have painted.' 'And a bunch of lesser sequels' Samantha let's-not-forgets. 'Yes' Lucy nods. And Samantha says 'And they probably once failed to make a loosely-associated television series out of it.' 'Yes' Lucy nods. But Kurt seems distressed by how much he is, honestly, able to see this movie playing in his mind's eye. 'Is what you see a cross between *White Zombie, The Screaming Skull,* and the poster for that terrible remake of *Carnival of Souls?*' 'Yes!' bellows Kurt as though the rug has been pulled out from under his soul. 'Oh God - that is exactly the film I have in my head!' 'Very grainy coloured, right? Coloration something between *Scream Bloody Murder* and *Mountaintop Motel Massacre,* eh?' 'You're a fucking head-fucker!' wails Kurt, grabbing his temples in non-mock anguish. 'That's the song *The Ramones* should have done' Lucy cuts in with. '*Mountaintop Motel Massacre?*' Samantha says, nodding vigorously. 'Oh yeah - those dimwits missed a trick there. Pedestrian tastes, man.' 'But they *used to make a living, man, picking the banana* - so full-circle, right?' Lucy blushes with pure wishing she had seen this connection before Samantha had.

Lucy finds what must be a week-old, disused French-fry on the office carpet from when Kurt had won a raffle at some pizzeria-slash-sandwich-shop and had to claim the prize, immediately, so had ordered Avarice amounts of lunch into the office which Lucy, Samantha, he, and the newest new-person had eaten - the newest new-person, whose name Lucy doesn't even recall ever bothering to learn, quitting over that weekend - and lobs it at Kurt, he - in a move that got applause from both Samantha and Lucy, despite it meant she failed in her attack - seeming not to notice until, at the very last second, springing into action and slapping it out of the way, a precision-smack that dinged it off of the out-of-service lamp on the shelf, over there. 'I found that very masculine, Kurt - that was a good moment for you!' Kurt bows, but now seems overly on guard, a game of hand-slap with confidence waning, so some of Lucy's respect for him drains. She doesn't know about Samantha. Samantha seems to have other things on her mind. The rumor is that they are all going to get two dollar pay-rises because some other client bought out the contract from the Temp Agency and struck a far more lucrative deal with whoever is actually in charge of what they are all doing. All of which confuses Lucy even more regarding how her job works. Why she gets money for this, to begin with, is beyond her. The promise of more for this kind of work doesn't comfort her, honestly - it makes the whole set-up seem pasteboard, it'll fall apart neatly at the earliest vibration. Kurt - it's kind of cute, the naiveté - has already jotted out how much it will improve his finances. His plan? He will act like he is getting paid exactly the same as before, because that is already more than enough for his existence, somehow. 'So two-extra-dollars-per-hour is sixteen-dollars-extra-per-day which is eighty-extra-dollars-per-week which is three-hundred-twenty-extra-dollars-per-month which - with taxes outed from - is just about two-hundred-eighty-extra-dollars-per-month which - over a year - is more than three thousand dollars!' Kurt has explained, like a *Pater Noster qui es in caelis* sort of thing. Lucy hopes it will last. She hopes that that three thousand buys all the indulgences it takes Kurt to get through them Pearly Gates! For herself? The creeps. Whenever the pay-rise is mentioned, whenever it is met with enthusiasm. She has lived a fairly long live, Lucy Jinx has, and worked a fair amount of jobs whose existence had no tangible purpose. Never does she remember one working out swimmingly for a someone-or-another like Kurt. She is just pointing this out. Though, Lucy - did you pay much attention? 'Still' she says to Samantha, without context, and Samantha - somehow already old-hat at Lucy-is-moving-on-from-something-she-just-thought - says 'Absolutely, Lucy, absolutely'. Kurt makes *Absolucy* Lucy's new nickname, either because of or in spite of the groans he gets when he - falsetto-voiced to mock Samantha's lub-dub attitude - first voices the expression as a jibe. 'If we all got a small apartment together for a year - just a one bedroom - cordoned it off so we each had space, shared every meal for one year - we would have been able to save almost all of our pay! But we won't' Lucy says, clapping Kurt and Samantha - who aren't paying any attention - to attention 'and do you know why? Because of greed, is why. We're greedy. Think where we could be if we weren't us, guys. Think of anyone else' - she jabs a finger at Kurt, at Samantha as though telling them 'Yep, that person - the one you're thinking of' - 'think of them. Yes! You could be that person if you only weren't you. Individuality doesn't seem so precious all of a sudden, yeah?'

Suddenly coughing in disappointment with herself, cigarette dropping from her grip - she trying to bend without going to knees to pick it up, still coughing, failing, going to knees, picking it up, at last - Lucy makes gestures around at the area she and Samantha are smoking in - the usual spot - and Samantha watches the display with a face like one reserves for a great-aunt's senility. 'This place! This place!' Lucy goes 'Agrah!' and pretends to kick the wall harder than she would ever dare. 'I should have used this place!' 'For what?' Yes, Lucy - you have to catch Samantha up. 'Sorry' Lucy composes herself 'let me get you up to speed, here: I am contracted into a clever plan wherein I pay for drugs and someone leaves the drugs in an anonymous place after I leave the money in the same place. It just struck me how back here' - Lucy gestures giddily and feverish - 'would have been far better than the spot I picked.' Note: while Lucy says this, her mind already has settled with the jury on the fact that there is no way she would have been able to explain what and where *this place* is during her sneaky-Pete conversation with Mitchell that day. Note on this note: While she thinks this, she also realizes she could easily have slipped a piece of paper in with a payment, explaining the matter. Meantime, Samantha is affronted that Lucy didn't come to her for drugs. 'I can get you pools full of drugs, man - what drugs are you on?' But Lucy just smokes a joint here and there, nothing exotic - 'No prescription junk' she adds, as there was an oddness is the way Samantha had said the word *Drugs*, suggesting absconded samples off pharmaceutical reps or something. 'Let me get you your pot, Jinx - where are you getting your pot?' 'Narc!' Lucy says, backing away as though bustling up her prairie-skirt in aghast. So Samantha drops the matter - though not before mentioning how much better her pot probably is than Lucy's and driving the nail in with a solemn vow to not share her pot with Lucy, under any circumstances. 'Nana boo-boo, eh?' Lucy pouts 'my head is stuck in doo-doo?' 'Your head is stuck in doo-doo, Lucy. I am officially on the skits with you.' Silence. Five minutes. Another smoke. Lucy then remembering she is at work and et cetera. 'Can we be lovers, again?' 'No' Samantha says, dart throwing her cig butt at Lucy with the clear aim of using her to start a tragic forest fire. 'How about now?' 'No.' 'How about now?' 'No.'

'How about in five minutes from now?' 'Fuck, you're so lazy! You're just asking that so you don't have to ask but once every five minutes.' Lucy admits it, lights another cigarette just to assert herself, her tongue a grimace at every inhale no matter what her face is. 'If I had things my way' non-sequiturs Lucy 'anytime a typo resulted in the word *Hat* it would have to stay *Hat*. I think little nuances to language like that will keep people interested in having one. We don't game-show enough things. It's not so much Clever that we need, it's hard-and-fast rules that are actually interesting. I could care less about the proper use of a Christ forsaken semi-colon, but I'd be a grammar-bitch if it meant I could say *Don't change that to 'What'! You said 'Hat'! 'Hat' it must remain! It's the English language, man, there are rules!*' Samantha decides this is funny, but says that is off-the-record and her written statement will reflect a more ambivalent political opinion seeing how she needs to worry about the upcoming caucus. Lucy bites her lower lip, nudges her shoulder and says '*Up Cumming*.' Samantha rolls her eyes. '*Cock ass*' says Lucy. Samantha opens the door to leave. 'It's understandable to worry about!'

They have a conversation - Lucy and Samantha do - about making Kurt really self-conscious about the fact that they are just quietly listening to him take a private phone call, right there, where they are all three working. 'Or we should keep asking him questions, pretend he's our supervisor.' 'Or we should get out our phones and keep calling him, so that annoying beeps interrupt him and make who he is talking to very uncomfortable - more and more so when he has to keep insisting *No no, I don't need to answer it, it's nobody*.' The second plan was Samantha's and Lucy calls 'No-fair!' because it sounds more like it should have been her plan. And soon they are having to congratulate Kurt for staying the course. 'Was it just your mom or something?' 'Nope.' 'Was it a contractor or a doctor?' 'No.' Lucy and Samantha shrug, perusing the line of questioning no further, drawing the 'Oh fuck you both' from Kurt they had been in tacit tandem working toward. 'I am kind of your supervisor, anyway. If you bother to look at the bulletin-board.' Lucy, straight up, doesn't know what bulletin-board Kurt even means. When he points - there! - she says 'Oh!' but admits she had no idea that was functional. 'Did you know?' she asks Samantha, who nods 'Yes'm'. 'That bulletin-board says you' - Lucy makes a dubious motion of indicating Kurt's presence - 'are technically-in-charge?' Only now Kurt seemingly has to bring up something actual - namely: 'You honestly never look at the board?' Not seeing why she should not admit it, Lucy says 'I never have, no, not once.' 'How are you sorting the files?' And Lucy shows him. And he Oh-Gods and Samantha just keeps working, shaking her head as though at a cartoon in a local newspaper not funny enough to be funny but not not-funny enough to complain about or not acknowledge was read. 'There have' it is explained 'been new sorting regulations for almost a fucking month!' 'Really?' 'Yes!' 'Samantha: has there been a new way to sort for almost a month?' 'According to the board there sure has' Samantha confirms. 'Well that's a fine how-do-you-do isn't it, Kurt?' Kurt seriously-are-you-fucking-with-me faces at Lucy who I'm-just-a-girl-in-a-classic-Hollywood-film giggle shrugs. 'And anyway - some boss you are! - shouldn't you have noticed?' But Kurt won't have it. And it's not even he's mad at Lucy, it's 'Why hasn't anybody called us out on this?' Samantha tells Kurt he puts an undue amount of faith in the workings of this place. But - and it's probably true, Lucy sees his point - the mistake likely hasn't been a thing just because the transition to new management is coming - 'The two dollar raise' he says, like this will get enthusiastic Whoos! and Yee-haws! 'Lucy, you better learn the new system.' 'Or you can both go back to the old way - we take down whatever paper was posted there - see what I'm driving at? - and we blame the old management for never telling us! All in it together!' 'Except she and I have a month's worth of doing it right!' 'Then it'll just seem like you two decided to give up on that and slacked back into line with me - we're still all together. Hell, I might even come out ahead, there. Seem like a trendsetter! I'm the minority, here' Lucy philosophically sounds 'and like Tribal Art and things I need to be protected for my singularity.' Now: is Lucy not at all worried about losing her job? Now: is Lucy very worried about losing her job? Now: is Lucy going to change? Now: is Lucy going to be stubborn, just to juke Fate? 'Hey, Kurt - if I gave you half my paycheck, would you do all my work, too?' Kurt looks at her, but then looks like he's honestly thinking about it.

Very quickly - Samantha is weird about flirting in corridors even though there is little chance anyone could come upon them suddenly enough they wouldn't have ample time to get composed even from a truly compromising position - Samantha hikes up her skirt to show off her patterned stockings. They are green and greener and a green-approaching-chalk-dust of almost no color at all. The skirt that swishes back to cover and back to slip-slap motion is beige and textured like linen only it isn't linen, is far stiffer to the touch than the breathing of its shadow-crinkling sway would suggest. Also: Samantha has three pins along the shoulders of this old jacket she has been wearing the past few days. A much more Samantha-sort-of-thing to wear to work than Samantha used to wear to work - not that it spends much of the work day upon her, but still. The buttons? Lucy hasn't checked. Samantha is either disappointed at that or hasn't given it a thought. And suddenly Lucy is telling a story about how she and Layla often liked to buy packs of Magnum Ultra Large condoms together - the Economy-Size boxes, which they would so wittily call the Family-Size Packs - taking the things to the counter and splitting the cost between them just to see the commotion in the face of some new-hire teenage boy. 'It was funnier to do than it sounds' Lucy points out, then says 'we should try it. Or something like it.' Then, thinking the walk across the parking lot is getting awkward, says 'What are the buttons on your coat?' Samantha either pretends not to even remember they were there - let alone what they were - or really just hasn't thought about them in ages - no, she's pretending, she'd see them and have some thought, however minor, every time she put on the coat, she's obviously toying around for some reason. 'That's Richard Hell. Tony Coca-Cola. Jorgen Leth. And that's former vice-president Schuyler Colfax. Richard Feynman. And' - she seems honestly unsure of the last - 'Oh that's Don Lapree - the *Makin' Money Guy.*' Lucy remembers that guy! 'Holy shit' she Holy-shits 'I remember Don Lapree!' '*All you gotta do*' Samantha starts her impersonation and Lucy pipes right in on top '*Is place tiny classified ads*' and then they are both laughing. 'I never even understood what it was he did with those ads!' 'He made money!' 'Yeah, he did! He funded the movie *Undercover Angel!*' And now it is Samantha's turn to burst into a clamour of explosive remembrance and unabashed joy. They try to remember every last little bit they can about the longer *Makin' Money* commercial, the one with the entire featurette for that movie. 'Do you own that movie?' - they are about to cross the street, Lucy passionately clutching Samantha's arm - 'Do you own that movie, Sam? In the name of Christ I compel you to answer me!!' 'Naw, naw' Samantha doesn't. Samantha, in fact, doesn't think it ever got made. 'I'd buy it in a heartbeat if I ever saw it on sale, though. Hell, if I ever strike it rich I'll fund the damned thing myself - film one copy of it on an old-fashioned, shoulder-mounted camcorder, the kind you load a full *VHS* tape into. And I'll pay off the cast and crew to never mention its existence and will watch it every day for the rest of my life - alone, without you, Lucy! Don't tempt me, man.' Between the two of them, all the way to the *Cashdollar,* they half-talk half-unintelligible through the concoction of a comedy-sketch depicting Don Lapree's ploy to bang the model he had star in the movie. They are laughing so hard by the time they are to the diner they both forget to go in and forget to smoke, just loiter, simmering down, silencing, eventually realizing how cold they are and going in.

Samantha is looking at what Lucy is doing now with a kind of anthropological curiosity. Observe: Lucy taking Samantha's hand. Observe: Lucy bending - with some difficulty, as Samantha is not understanding her role and thus incidental resistance is offered - to coils all of Samantha's fingers, save for her fourth. Observe: Lucy letting go, slowly, of Samantha's hand, dotting the air around it so that Samantha understands to keep it there, elevated over the booth center. 'Close your eyes.' 'It's not much of a magic trick when it involves the phrase *Close your eyes.*' But Samantha closes her eyes after Lucy makes her face into the outline of the letters *Shut up.* And unobserved goes Lucy's hand to her coat pocket. And unobserved on to Lucy's finger goes the first of the two cheapskate rings. And unobserved goes Lucy's other hand to her other coat pocket. And unobserved is that second box opened and that second ring taken out. Samantha opens her eyes as Lucy is fitting the thing over her extended finger, bending her elbow and rubbing her bicep immediately after Lucy's hand moved away, only then - after a cough, too - holding her hand out to look at what she was betrinketed with. It also takes Samantha a moment - and it takes an 'Ahem' the word pronounced practically phonetically, from Lucy - to look up at Lucy's raised hand, palm facing Samanthaward, blinking before taking in the same ring. 'Is that the same ring? You got me the same ring as you wear?' 'Since when do I wear a ring?' 'You don't wear a ring?' Samantha is looking at her ring again, picking at it like there is lint in its zipper. 'It's hard to be romantic with someone who is unobservant.' 'I'd imagine so' Samantha says after consideration, laying her palm to table, flat, cocking head to take in the ring from arbitrary tilts. 'Where did you get this ring?' 'Why?' Samantha looks up. 'Is that an unromantic question?' 'Probably' Lucy supposes, has no idea. 'Pretend it's an heirloom.' 'Are you the heir to something?' 'Pretend I am.' 'Okay.' 'Is that making you like me?' 'Yes.' The waitress shows up and gleefully announced how hot the smothered curly-fries are and that she will be right back with some little plates and 'Do you guys need refills?' 'Naw' Lucy says. Samantha quickly straws up some more of her soda - as though to not seem deceptive - and goes 'Yes, please.' '*Sprite?*' '*Ginger Ale.*' The waitress was already shaking her head in regret, snapping her finger, and says '*Ginger Ale*' her *Ginger* falling on Samantha's *Ale*. 'And you're sure you don't want more coffee?' Lucy is sure. Samantha has taken the most smothered fry, eaten it too quickly, and is trying her best to ease her mouth by chewing on an ice-cube. As she does, she somewhat says 'Does this mean I'm your girlfriend? Or are we just a superhero team, now? Or is this a disguise for a caper you're about to outline?' 'All of those' Lucy says, as though put-off and blows bubbles into her coffee, this causing far more of a spray than she would have imagined, her face immediately feeling speckled and the napkin she runs over it coming away brown as the last toilet wipe before thinking 'Well, that's good enough.' 'Am I the leader of the caper?' 'Did you buy the rings?' Samantha deflates, snatches up a few more fries and mutters 'Oh' nibbles the ends of three fries at once 'I guess I see what you mean, yeah.'

Lucy has no intention of moving in with Samantha. She makes this abundantly clear to herself while she is washing her hands in the restroom. In fact, she has to remember that it's probably for the best that Samantha is taking the whole ring business - there is a ring on your finger, Lucy, and you and only you put it there - with such aplomby nonchalance. Not that Samantha's reaction-in-the-moment can be trusted. Evidence is bountiful! Bountiful! 'First' Lucy explains 'it has to be taken into account that Samantha is no garden-variety dolt. Samantha - no, no dolt - has not gone through life unobserving - and so any sign that she is bemused or just taking it-as-it-comes is actually a sign of stratagem!' Look how Samantha has morphed, even from when Lucy first worked with her. But Lucy is wise. Lucy keeps every gleaned-gesture and experienced-scenario in her pocket like miserly coins to be brushed as though the manes of show-ponies when it comes time to get at what someone in her orbit is trying to take her for. Samantha is never shy-girl, always game-player. Samantha is shapeshifter and time-bidder, sonaring out the exact shape and trajectory of Lucy before approaching to even loose visual range. Now: Samantha just offers vague banter about having a ring put on her finger? 'No.' Lucy is a quick-wit and great in the bonus-round, babe! Samantha is back to intake-mode, collecting data sets to Florence Nightingale odds and death-rates from - and from those to haughtily proffer what it all means. Which means Lucy has thrown Samantha for a loop. But when a con-job is thrown for a loop it means they are de facto under the impression they might be being conned, themselves. A trickster never believes they are in proper possession of the bauble they've coveted, so therefore Samantha is - Lucy can see it no other way! - out at the table - right now - looking at the ring while she has a free chance and is trying to delicately peel off the applique decals of Lucy's intentions from it. What are Lucy's intentions? Or has she none? 'Why should I play fair' Lucy riddle-me-thises her reflection. 'Am I supposed to know why I did something and that be why I did it?' There isn't a law or even a sound theory in place in support of that! Samantha can figure Lucy out, save Lucy the time and effort. Lucy will take the findings as Gospel - as Galileo, man - and then will decide what to do. 'So that was your plan, Lucy?' It's Lucy's reflection asking, raising a hand to draw Lucy's attention back just as she was turning to go. 'What do you care?' 'I don't' the flat-glass-Lucy flat-glasses, shrugging with an extra-humped *W* brow. 'Then why are you asking?' 'That's what Lucy does.' 'You're not Lucy.' 'You're not Lucy.' 'I'm not Lucy?' Lucy touches her chest saying and is annoyed at the kindergarteness of her reflection touching its chest and saying the same thing right on top of her. 'Fucking mature' Lucy curl-lips, then sits to sink counter, her back to the mirror, crossing her arms, figuring it's time to go. The ring has no weight when she takes it off. It has not left any mark on her hand yet, even. She wonders if it would be fun to pocket it, now, see if Samantha even notices. Notice Samantha noticing. Wonder at what Samantha notices when she notices. Wonder at whether Samantha is being Samantha in the reaction or lack thereof - or is she is just being waiting-to-see-is-Lucy-being-Lucy.

Neither Lucy nor Samantha much want to go back to work. And this is a dangerous energy for Lucy. The job is starting to lose cohesion - to the ether and to the ether more it stagers, its roots not sunk deep enough that Lucy believes she would even give it a thought were she to leave. Not even sure would she give notice or contact the agency for another assignment. The coming illusion of a two-dollar raise, the early ozone scent of coming shifts that will unbelly the animal, anyway. And Lucy has prised something out from the place: Samantha. Even if this were the last moment she ever saw Samantha, here over empty plates and a check - that one there, not even looked at, one that Lucy will not pay because she knows Samantha will, especially right now. So what good is it, this job? Jobs, places, apartments, cafes, shops, areas-where-one-loiters are good as incubators for some particular moment, some nugget to be prospectored, but then to dwell further is to Cargo Cult one's very essence. It's easy. Arithmetical. Practically alphabetical - or reverse-alphabetical, perhaps, a countdown of letters to Zero. Will Lucy be working this job in five years? No. *ZYX*. Will Lucy be working this job in four years? Is that even a question!? *WVU*. Will Lucy be working this job in three years? All signs point to 'No'. *TSR*. Will Lucy be working this job in two years? See how Samantha smiles, there, and a new thought Lucy is not asking after is evident in the set of wrinkles-in-blue-skin around her eyes? That's the answer. Nope. *QPO*. Will Lucy be working at this job - sorting files for no reason, parking in the same spot, coming to the *Cashdollar*, joking with Kurt and Samantha and whoever else - in one year? You get the trend? Exactly. *NML*. Eight months. Not likely. *KJI*. Five? Not even five - and once that is evident, things break down far more easily, no real interpretation needed, the rest of the countdown just for show. *HGF*. Three months. Lucy can't do it. *EDC*. Next month? Look at Lucy, look at her! *B*. Tomorrow? Maybe - maybe tomorrow, maybe to the end of the week. *A*. Tomorrow? She is shaking her head. Zero. 'Do you like this job, Sam?' 'No.' 'Then why do you work it?' 'Because I frittered my life away on penny-whistles and such, didn't pay attention in dissection class, never made a friend.' 'This is where people like you end up, eh?' 'It is one of the places.' 'Where's another?' 'It might be the only one, really.' 'Will you be working here in a year?' 'I might.' 'Why? I won't.' 'Where will you be working?' 'I'll be famous by then, I think.' Samantha nods. It's frightening. Lucy thinks Samantha believes there is chance Lucy might get famous. Quickly to note: Lucy wants no one to confuse that with a sentiment of Lucy thinking that Samantha believes Lucy believes it, right now. No. But Lucy thinks Samantha believes that Lucy will be in a place she hasn't been before within a year, in two, in five. Does Samantha not understand time? Does she not understand? What does this woman think of Lucy Jinx and how has she missed the blatant facts of things? How can you be - 'How old are you, Samantha?' 'Thirty-nine' - thirty-nine and still believe things will happen if those things hadn't started to happen, before? 'I'm not Saul' Lucy says.

Samantha nods. 'Of Tarsus' Lucy says, wanting to be double sure the nod was registering the import of the statement. 'I know who Saul is.' Lucy huffs, looks around like somebody should be bringing her something and is dallying. 'There's a lot of Sauls, Sam' she now sighs, sulking. 'I know that. And I figured you're none of them. But I know about the one from Tarsus.' 'Yeah?' Lucy blinks, down-pitted but trying to hold-her-breath her way back to surface level. 'Yep. And I know you're not him - don't worry.'

There's Kurt, harried and tugging at the back of his hair, making appalled sounds and not even noticing that Lucy and Samantha are standing behind him. Lucy feels the suspense of 'Should we not make any move or sound, not risk startling him?' But Samantha says 'Kurt?' in a concerned-roommate way, Kurt turning to face them without any indication of shock at their presence or embarrassment of being found out in his present state. 'Everything okay, buddy?' Samantha says, Kurt now back-peddling to where Lucy has just moved forward from. Crane of her neck, she see a file on the floor, face down, a few loose papers from it - there there and there - in a splash caused by the gravity and currents of the fall. 'Is that file haunted?' Lucy says, deadpan and halfway worried he'll say 'Yes.' 'Is it *Zuul*?' Samantha demands Lucy not joke about *Zuul*! Then, Lucy hears Samantha smack Kurt's arm and admonish him to 'Tell Lucy it isn't *Zuul*, goddamnit - everyone stop talking about *Zuul*!' 'It's not *Zuul*' Kurt eases-everyone's-mind-on 'but I caution you not to go near that file and I think we should burn this building down, immediately.' Lucy, for one, is not going near the file. She can feel the air in the room turning cotton, backs up in the same fashion, at the same speed as did Kurt, needing no sight of whatever he sighted, just his word it is *The Unnamable*. It's magic, the dark energy, here, now. Maybe Kurt didn't see anything, either. Maybe there was another man or woman in the room, looking at the downed folder when Kurt had come in, some time back, Kurt just following that stranger's lead, that stranger now having made tracks. Next, Kurt will go. Then, Samantha. Then, someone new will show up. Then, Lucy will go. And two other new people will show up, the stranger who came in before Lucy left leaving. The world will become this. A record skipping while an image blink-blink-blinks, all of it the equivalent to the last rounds of a tornado down a bathtub drain, somehow never thinning enough to give off that final glug of suction. Blink. No one is talking or moving. Existence has stopped. And it was so easy! Just come into a room at the right time and escape! Everyone is free to go, free to go, free to go!! Until Kurt says 'Obviously, this must be an isolated thing - it's never happened before, obviously - but I will have a great amount of difficulty working this job, from now on.' 'Well, what is it?' Samantha says, bored nine-year-old-who-does-too-much-homework sounding. 'Look and you'll see.' 'How profound' Samantha says, wink-at-Lucy voiced but Lucy is just looking at her own feet. And soon enough Samantha has turned the file over and has gone 'Oh gah fuck!!' toe-hopping back from it and batting invisible cobwebs from all around her, spinning in place and - suddenly - hugging Lucy's arm hard. Lucy braves a look - her turn, it seems - but from a distance-off enough to be spared the shock-horror. Three millipedes or centipedes - the thick kind like in nature documentaries, flattened, the hardened residues of their juices long stenciled and scabbed to the sheet of paper beneath them - are dead, there, gargantuan even more than they likely actually are for their coiledness and distinct-from-each-other's coloration. The rippling, undulating personality of each's individual horror has lived on past death. 'Why are those there?' she hears Samantha ask. And Lucy looks at her, pity in her eyes. Pity. Pity in her eyes for Samantha. And she says 'Oh Samantha. They were always gonna wind up somewhere, right?'

 Together, the file is - by way of push-broom Lucy was brave enough to steal from the unlocked supply closet in the Ladies' Room - ushered down the corridor and outside and then - by means of a long rectangle of cardboard, part of a broken-down, razored-to-component-panels box found alongside the control panel for the compactor - chucked into the appropriate dumpster. Kurt feels, it seems, obliged to say 'Under normal circumstances, I would not just discard a file like that.' 'Because it's illegal?' Lucy asks. 'For one' Kurt says. 'And could cost you your job?' 'For another.' 'And the company this contract?' 'Third, yes, three - yes yes.' 'Not to mention' Samantha chimes in 'how we can now blackmail you, mister Supervisor.' But Kurt waves this threat off, telling Samantha that girls don't blackmail about stuff like that. 'And besides - what would be in it for you?' Lucy wants an answer to this question, too, but Samantha seems not so interested in coming up with something witty to say. Agreed, agreed, agreed - very much a 'Rest, rest perturbed spirit' kind of moment - they, after agreeing, just file back into the office and stand there. 'They were already dead, right?' Lucy asks. Kurt confirms this. 'All-in-all, though, that is the more horrific thing.' But - bright little cloud in the wrong sky - Lucy says 'At least that means they didn't come from here. As in to say: we, as an office, are not infested by millipedes or whatever they were. Or, anyway - we aren't, as far as we know.' Kurt says 'That's true' and maybe the sound of his belief is what does it - but something does it, even if not that - and now Lucy is saying: 'Or not, actually. I guess those files came for someplace and maybe other files have come from that same place, too. Maybe there is no telling if, at some point, a living, vital, giant millipede made it on to the premises - or even, say, a squished one that wasn't quite dead, and it, a millipede, has some sort of slow-motion metabolism and, while in the file, tucked away, finished giving birth to its innumerable offspring. They could be hatching intentions on us, even now! We might be where they want to incubate, Kurt - what do they care about our particular hopes or dreams? Do you have hopes or dreams, Kurt? Maybe that gives off a scent they like, you know? We can only speculate! But really, they might be able to lay eggs without even being felt, piercing some small flake of epidermis. Think on it! Small enough that they get in the sides of your shoes - you think it's just your toes sweating in your socks or something, an itch, while meantime it's slow-cooking larvae that attack your lymph-nodes and eventually cause early onset dementia! Like really-early onset. Like tomorrow. How old are you, Kurt? Well - however old you are, that might be the best age for them - brewing in a skin of froth in your stomach acids or on the surface of your bladder, becoming a rash you'll never feel because nature doesn't put nerves inside of you like it does outside. Oh Kurt. Oh Kurt - you're done for, man! Fuck, I'm so sorry.' This whole time Kurt has just been staring at the floor where the file was. And Samantha has inched closer and closer to Lucy. Right now, she has a hand in Lucy's back pocket. Right now, she has a scent of leaned over hair inside Lucy nostrils.

LUCY JINX LEAVES THE OFFICE, herself, after Kurt - Samantha having had to head out an hour-and-a-half previous. There is a feeling of shirking something, but she cannot tell what. And as she opens the door and steps outside, the warmer-than-she-had-expected-considering-a-few-hours-before gives her the feeling of a glass overturned she was sure something was going to spill from - curse-word already hissed in reference to - the glass revealed to have been empty, the anger remaining, regardless. Or something like that. 'I feel like something' she says, air of an old-time film actress lighting a cigarette like it is on one of those long black holders. Oh Lucy feels thin as the film over a cataract eye, vaporous, she feels as though a keyhole to which nobody bothered to affix the mechanism which could actually lock. Lucy always feel like something, so it's no surprise she does now. 'But what about other people?' she cannot help but wonder. What about other people? She wants to give an example, but no one is around to single out for scrutiny so settles on an approximation - what about people like whoever owns that car, way on the other end of the lot? If pressed, how often would that person say they don't feel like anything? What do you feel like, right now? 'Meh.' What do you feel like, right now? 'Oh I dunno.' What do you feel like, right now? 'Nothing, man, you know?' What do you feel like, right now? 'What do you mean?' Much of life must be spent without simile, metaphor, imagistic-alignment - and this makes for a cold and dreadful apartness Lucy instinctively seeks to spare herself from. Well, Lucy feels like something! And even if she didn't, she'd stand up for herself by claiming to! She has the dignity to falsify herself. Leave a record - enough years pass and honesty becomes irrelevant. Think a lawmaker in Qullasuyu is really sweating that someone might, this very minute, be sniffing out that they coerced the favor of someone to ply their opinion on whatever type legal system there was back then? 'Rubbish to that' exhales Lucy, not having moved a step toward her car. And if not that, think some Johnny Whosit just farting around in Chimor would even bat an eye if someone called him out on the fact he said he felt like the sound of a crow heard by another crow who mistook the sound for a rockfall? 'How the fuck would you know if I felt that way or not?' Johnny Whosit would say, eternally adolescent and thumbing snot from his nose onto the interrogator's shoe. 'Who'd you ask? You believe them? Fossil records? Parchment?' Hell - Johnny, just to be contrarian, would say 'Yeah, I didn't feel that way at all - you got me' and the interrogator would go home and realize the ineptitude of history and human experience itself, look at his doctorate and wither a little in the testicle area! What are you talking about, Lucy? She is staring at that parked car, still. Way over there. And if she could see further on, she supposes, she would see Sarepta and she would see Cagliari and she would see Soluntum. She is looking as though she just trained her new telescope on the light bearing down on her, but as though she were sturdy-footed at bedroom window on a planet galaxies and galaxies away. She could see her here, today, in ten million years, somewhere else. That's a fact. And it doesn't seem like it should be. Why would it take someone ten million years to be able to see her just standing here? Because of light? All her secrets, willy-nilly, spilled out for a Universe to perv over whether she wants it to or not! Every blink or chuckle or ass-scratch a scientific amazement of image-capture! Every secret kept would be revealed to another civilization so far away how could they understand us at all?

Now all that was very interesting. But getting back to it, here we are: Lucy Jinx, car, driving, windshield-wipers on in a punk-rock way, middle-finger to rainless sky she sees the belly-drag of at the horizon-line. Samantha had given her a kiss without asking, Kurt still in the room. Even if Kurt hadn't been looking, that's the sort of thing one notices just by proximity. Kurt may have zapped sight of the matching rings, too. Such things can happen. But Kurt had not said anything to Lucy. 'But' Lucy Lucys 'Kurt knows Samantha much better than he knows me and would likely wait until he had an opportunity to ask her about the matter, otherwise he might feel prying.' Samantha was gorgeous, today - the accidental bend to the corner of a book cover, regretted at first but soon the thing that makes the book instantly yours to your eyes. Aw, what a delight - Lucy Jinx, the romantic! Match that up with a bouquet and serenade Samantha with hipster ukulele tunes, why don't you, Jinx? But Samantha is swell

- the pop of a bubble, the surprise to the tongue of I-didn't-realize-this-was-seasoned. Do better? Lucy takes the next left, last minute, cringing apologies for a risky maneuver that her gut tightened to apple-seed over. Do better? She shakes her head, refocusing. 'Well' Lucy right-out-louds 'they say one can season meat with gunpowder. Samantha is meat seasoned with gunpowder. What is this taste? *Gunpowder*, Samantha could say.' And she would, that's fine, then - Lucy feels they have really gotten to know each other during this car ride, just now. But to business: she lifts the sheet of paper from the passenger seat where she wrote the address of the restaurant down, notes the next two turns she has to watch for - one in ten miles, the other hard upon that, just a decimal-point from it - sinking into her seat like the dubbed in back-beat of a bubblegum oldie. Samantha's teeth are cobblestone grey, Lucy thinks, cobblestone winter-boot-walked-on grey. 'That's fine, that's fine.' Samantha is the stick of a label on a bottle of overpriced wine, she is the danger of an electrical outlet to curious fingers without a mother who cares. 'Yes, yes, yes - that's Samantha.' But let us be clear - Lucy demands the world be clear on this point, not think it can be twaddled up like everyone's scent on the towel all are too lazy to launder - that Lucy doesn't care a scar-tissue for Samantha! That Samantha is *X* or *L*, is *A* or *R*, is short or round or square or tall are just facts! Lucy has a penchant for identifying things! A poet's love for naming! 'We weren't given language to be goddamn mockingbirds' says Lucy, eruditely 'if that was all language was for there would only be mockingbirds - that seems plain as yesterday, right?' So: this is how language is used - in a spill as enthusiastic for that over there are for the thing nearest one's heart. Lucy is as principled in her application of language as she is ambivalent about her feelings toward Samantha. Samantha - a being, let's say, an object, let's grant - is, as such, deserving of the detailing slather of language as much as any other. She is to be identified, rendered, as scoured into the myth of personal-past, personal-future as anything else. Is that the turn? Lucy anxiously brings up the paper to her hands on the wheel - terrible trait of Lucy's, if while driving she looks left the car then goes left, or right, or wherever, she is surprised it doesn't go backward when she checks the rearview, but safeguards beyond her prevent that - and sees 'No, not the road.' Not anything like the name of the road. And she's only gone four miles when she knows she has to go ten. Sighs. Samantha is the sigh you give again to be funny but also because you still need to sigh.

This will be the first time Lucy does this. Will Lucy do it? Over there: the restaurant. It is a restaurant called *Table Dote* - a play-on-words that doesn't quite, to Lucy's accounting, hold much water. Putting that on one side, though. Lucy, it must be noted, is parked way over here. In a moment, she will drive closer to park in a normal spot. She might even park just next to the mother's car, which

- she sees it - is just there. Lucy is not late - she would be only just on time, now. The mother showed up less than five minutes ago. Lucy watched her walk - in a denim skirt and sun-glasses raised up over her head-curve and a tote-bag that looked weather-worn and laden down with something. Here is what it looks like when Lucy removes her new ring. Exactly like that. Did you see? Then allow Lucy to repeat the moment. The ring on. Watch. That is what it looked like when she took it off. So: where does it go now? It goes in this zippered compartment of Lucy's wallet. The outline doesn't even press through the shark-white leather. The ring is thin like a business card or a receipt kept for no earthly reason. Lucy Jinx's knuckles have cracked. And that is Lucy's least favorite use of the silent K. And she has a big heart as far as silent Ks go. Either pronounce it hard - this is obviously how the word should be uttered - or leave the word to visually seem its meat-head self. *Nuckle*. 'Or, in fact' she says, pulling ahead slowly, but not quite ready to arrive yet so swinging a loop of the shop backs 'if you're not going to say the first K leave off the second.' *Nucle*. The word seems to be purposefully belittling Ks - one not said, the other the remove of which wouldn't be noticed. 'So many mistakes in language' she pretends she is telling the mother, first thing when she sits down with her. 'A C can sound like a K? Lazy. No letter should be able to sound like another. There should be no obvious obsolescence to the alphabet!' The mother agrees and there is lasciviousness in the agreement, licentiousness. Lucy imagines the agreement. Another way of telegraphing lust. Longing. Lonely-for-you and I-hate-you-for-being-here-to-not-hate, again. All of a sudden, though, this thought: none of this needs to happen! Lucy - you don't have to be Lucy! Lucy! This is your one chance for clarity! You've taken off that snaggletoothed ring - now you can drive away, but make a success of it like you didn't before! Your flee will not be interrupted. The ballast is shed. Go. Go like they would say in an over-romantization of the Beat Generation - go, Lucy, go, man, go go go go go! Go like the word is said so many times - written so many times and with such ferocity - in succession that sometimes it is *go* and sometimes *gog* and sometimes *og* and sometimes *ogo* and sometimes *ggogoog* and sometimes *goo* and sometimes *gg*. 'This is your last chance' probably Lucy says, but already is rounding the corner like making a proper approach and playacting a 'Hey! It's the mother's car!' and pulling in next to it, faker-faker glance to the side as though expecting to catch the mother out, adorable-and-vulnerable, testing her chap-stick in the rearview or a compact, wishing away a crag of acne or something, a spot that assures her she's her.

'So, it turns out Nevada means *snow covered* - did you know that?' Lucy gives a quick kiss to the mother, then sits down, breathing like she has just removed a scarf, a hat, two gloves, and is setting the lot in the booth snuggly beside here.

'Is that right? Well, that's stupid. And here I was - on the drive over - just thinking about how stupid language sometimes is. Albeit, I was thinking about it in a much more interesting way' - the mother nods and says 'Of course' in the shape of another kiss quick-pecked while Lucy goes on - 'but it doesn't change the fact that that's a very unapt name.' 'It could have been to cause trouble.' 'Like someone was pissed off at someone?' Lucy vaguelys, opening her menu but not reading it, continuing with her voice blocked and the mother's face blocked 'Like someone said *Oh I bet if I call this place 'snow covered' that little prick'll come a runnin' - and won't he be surprised*!' - Lucy pronounced this *sir-prized* - 'and did some sort of jiggity laugh afterward, eh?' 'Just like that' the mother patientlys 'you put it perfectly. The soul of wit you are not, I know, but you put it well.' 'Wit has no soul and things are funnier the more you say them. Ask anyone. If they disagree, ask yourself *Yeah, but how funny do they seem?* You'll figure it out.' Then Lucy snub-noses 'You look beautiful and I am bound to say so.' 'Blush' says the mother and gives Lucy the finger - the finger is Band-aided which makes the gesture all the more seedy - 'you'll make me go misty.' 'How is the old Flynniss Book of World Records?' The mother groans and hangs her head shakingly at that one, but gives the low-down on Flynn and some recent trouble he had due to his puckish nature and lack of moral grounding. 'He always seemed so upstanding to me, your kid - as though *mild* was the only temperature he ever figured a *mannered* could be.' 'He's a punk. Because of influences like Thought and Literature. He's been stealing and bragging about it and getting caught.' 'Not a good trio.' 'Exactly.' 'So straighten him out!' Lucy does a slap motion from where she sits and a Whip-shah! sound. 'Tell him: kid, the first two things are fine, but then you'll wanna knock it off.' 'I try to tell him, but he thinks it's in vogue to be caught with one's dick in one's hand or wherever one puts a dick. Eventually he'll, you know, passeth into dust though so I might as well let him steal things.' 'It's true. Scripture backs you.' 'Scripture does back me. Lucy - you look good, too.' But Lucy wants to know what the mother means by *Too*. 'I look good and you look good.' 'What?' The mother explains again, more detailed. Lucy corrects 'I said you looked *beautiful* not *good*.' 'Oh. Then you look good, by yourself. The opposite of *too*.' '*Too* doesn't have an opposite, you just don't say it.' The waitress is sorry to interrupt, but can she take drink orders or are they ready? 'Do you serve champagne, here?' the mother asks. 'No. We have wine.' 'I'll have coffee, then.' The waitress smiles, kind of - Lucy can read faces, she may have mentioned - not sure if that was supposed to be taken as 'And by *Coffee* I mean *Tell-me-about-the-wine*' - and then asks Lucy 'And you?' 'Do they call soda something stupid, around here? Like how some places called sprinkles *Jimmies*.' 'We call them *Jimmies* around here' the waitress laughs, biting her lip like she knows she and her environs are the butt of every upper crusters joke. 'Then I guess I'll have a *pop*' Lucy says, but then quickly goes 'just coffee, actually. Real coffee, by the way - I'm pretty sure that bitch, there, meant *wine*.'

A dissection: Lucy is not the least bit deceptive or game-playing in her saying the mother is beautiful. Meaning: she does not mean it in-a-general-way. Returning to the dissection: Lucy has found herself daydreaming about the mother - increasingly - finds the mother alluring in bounds more than she ever remembers from the past, the attraction some new flow of water, now over-ground when it used to just be under. Noting: she does not mean she thinks she had been unaware or ignoring of her previous attraction or its depth - this woman has frying-panned Lucy's noggin' proper from way back, not a word otherwise - it is just that the past pales to the present. Side question: Does Lucy truly believe that the past pales to the present? Question about side-question: Why are we asking - does it seem particularly unlike Lucy to think something like that? Response to this: No, no - the question was earnest and surfacely presented. Then here is the answer to the side-question: Right now, Lucy does think the past pales to the present - and before it has to be asked, by 'Right now' Lucy does not just mean in-reference-to-the-mother but means her life philosophy is to short-change the past at the expenses of impressing the present with some overpriced trifle. Returning to the dissection: thoughts and words have been trying to form about the mother. Request for elaboration: What does that look like, physically? Response to request for elaboration: Like this - imagine some scribble scrabble, a sturdy mess of a pen in an almost hair-ball knot on paper, and then imagine, over time, somehow, being able to unstrangle it like an actual knot, like it becomes a strand, then many strands, and these strands can be sorted and, when set individually, each has curled or bent to the shape of some letter and these letters, if arranged right, will spell something - and not just one word, maybe a lot of words, maybe pages, there is no way to know and so it will take a long time to sort out. Further question: Does Lucy have an idea what words they might be - or even if not 'an idea' does Lucy have 'a feeling' of what words she hopes the words will be? Response to further question: No. Returning to dissection: Lucy might be brewing a fiasco by letting herself say things like 'You look beautiful' to the mother when she thinks the mother looks beautiful - especially how she said it. Detail of a-few-moments-ago: Lucy said 'You look beautiful' and her eyes tightened along with her jaw to stave off heat from boorishly stuffing her chest - she said 'You look beautiful' the way other people do when they not only mean it but want it to mean something, to connect, want there to be soil for the words, the words to be more than pronunciations and assent-that-I-heard-you from the recipient they were aimed toward. Another dissection: Lucy wants to ask about the three

Band-aids on the mother's hands, but won't - and this is because if she starts asking things like that she'll never stop asking things like that and the world will become a broken pencil and a broken paper and a broken set of ideas. A request for clarification: What does that mean? Response to request for clarification: Lucy cannot bring herself to say, but figures the answer is probably what she thinks anyone looking would think it is.

Prefacing it, of course, with the mention that 'this isn't a booby-trap' the mother asks Lucy if Lucy might be interested in house-sitting for a week or two. 'Or at least looking after the cats' the mother addendums. 'Which cats?' The mother finishes her second glass of wine. 'My cats.' 'Since when do you have cats?' 'You say *since when* a lot' the mother sighs, treating the comment like it is a condemnation of modernity. 'That isn't an excuse not to answer my question, though.' The mother has had three cats for the last two years. 'And I had cats, before!' What does she mean *before*? 'What do you mean *before*?' Anyway, the mother has three cats and they have irritatingly cutesy names and the mother will be out of the country and Lucy can stay at the house if she feels like doing something decent with her life, for once, and can feed the cats. 'You can even eat some of the cat-food too, Lucy - and use the litter-box. I'll turn off all the Nanny-cams.' 'No, you won't' Lucy flirts, but knows she is flirting to have to avoid giving an answer. Wise to this, the mother says 'You aren't going to do it, eh?' Is that a trick? It could have been a trick! As Lucy is immediately saying 'I'll do it, asshole - just because it takes me ten seconds to decide I've thought about it enough doesn't give you a right to presume' it could have been a trick! That would have been the desired result of a trick - right, Lucy? 'Maybe I'll overfeed the cats and they'll get that kind of whitish, ashy look - the same houseplants when they get too much water.' 'Try it. You don't have the guts.' 'Or maybe I'll only feed two of them and the third will have to learn that's the way it goes.' The mother, it should be pointed out, is - with foot removed from shoe - caressing the outside of Lucy's pant-leg over Lucy's shin. No - you're right, Lucy - it isn't the most erotic touch, but the fact of it not being the most erotic touch is the thing that controls you. It's a touch and is one enough to clearly not be accidental so it counts as all touches everywhere - and all touches that could have been had time never started and if things could slouch backward, forever, without finding a first. 'What are you thinking about?' The mother's brow ups, the question one of actual, imperative need-to-know. 'About a cat I once had.' 'Which?' 'Some cat. Named *Lucy Jinx*.' 'Is that where you got your name?' the mother says, not making fun, non-committal toned to see if Lucy feels like being drawn out and to give her the chance to sarcasm if she doesn't. 'I think so. I had the name already, but that's where I got it from, I think.' Now Lucy wants to know what the look that - just there - crossed the mother's face was. 'What look?' It was a smile and lips parting with - if one had an ear to them - an audible tear-of-saliva-sheet sound, but since one is far away - or far enough away - with no sound at all. 'I was thinking about how we used to watch *Star Trek*. But I didn't want to tell you because you don't seem to like memories.' 'I don't?' The mother gives a you-must-be-joking pull back of her head. Then says 'No, Lucy. No, you don't.' Lucy nods. Nods and nods. Says she'll watch the cats, sure, and will wear some of the mother's clothes and things, too.

Soon enough, the mother is sorry about having to cut it so short today, but she has started to attend a Yoga class and doesn't want to lose her steam with it. Lucy, for kicks, pretends never to have heard of Yoga, thus forcing the mother into the absurd and unenviable position of having to explain, reasonably, what exactly it is. Needless to say, Lucy's end of the pursuant conversation contains a lot of Oh-yeahs, Is-that-rights, and What-exactly-do-you-mean-bys. 'Are you going to be able to stop by, tonight?' The mother is calculating the tip - or, more likely, is staring at the paper bill and trying to figure out what amount she can leave without having to calculate that won't make her feel either guilty or self-swindled - and Lucy puts her hands in her pockets, rocks back-and-forth - heel-to-toe, flat, toe-to-heel, flat - blows out a long breath in imitation of actually having to consider, then says how she thinks so 'but it will certainly be late.' And in the same moment, it occurs to Lucy that the chase might as well be cut to - she had not acted on it when the cat-sitting came up, but this obvious second opening makes it impossible to not ask - at least, not without that seeming the choice and her current avowed stance is to not make the retreating choice but the headlong. So here is Lucy Jinx - with a sigh because, after all, she is Lucy Jinx - saying 'Natalie, why not just give me a key so that it doesn't matter how late it is if it's late - you know what I mean?' The mother holds a finger up as though to hold off addressing that a moment, asks 'Did she say to pay up front or do you think it's okay to leave this? - *this* being the cash for the meal, none of it contributed by Lucy - and Lucy just shrugs and says 'Money' and 'What do they care - they gonna arrest you for doing it wrong?' No, there wasn't suspense. The mother has an extra key on her - on her key-ring, it turns out - and likely has had it for a good long while, nothing at all to do with Lucy being back in the area. 'You do know this means there is no excuse - when you say *It'll be late* I will nonetheless expect you.' 'If you expect me, you'd better - you know? - expect me' Lucy says, hoping her clumsiness in not finding an innuendo will serve as one. They briefly discuss the mechanics of Flynn's presence - or, rather, Lucy brings it up to have the brought-up peshawed by 'Flynn's used to all sorts of strange women in and out at all hours.' And the mother also adds that, by the way, sometimes Flynn's young lady-friend stays over and sleeps on the couch. 'Or I hope she sleeps on the couch - she at least starts the night on the couch and is back there by morning, which, in thinking about it, shows how cleverly my kid can ploy me, probably. My point being - if you come in, know that the warm body downstairs cannot just be ransacked without, so to speak, verifying it first.' 'I'm sure that supine line is more than nubile enough to alert me a wrong tree's being barked up, Natalie - I haven't gone senile and you hardly look youthful, even in the dark.' The mother elbows Lucy as-if-on-accident and they exit the restaurant, Lucy kind of wanting to whine that the elbow - just where it hit - actually did hurt, but figures she had better keep up a show of strength, not betray her hand over such an immaterial complaint.

The question becoming: is there a strategy at play in any of this? Because: Lucy Jinx is back in her car and the engine is idling and the restaurant she just ate in is closing up its outdoor sections officially for the day, even shooing away the worker from the neighboring franchise Tax Specialist who is smoking under one of the grey-skied umbrellas. And while Lucy is in her car, she is - for the first time, proper - putting back on the ring which is twin to the ring worn by Samantha. Though there was the following consideration: Should Lucy only put it on when about to be directly in the company of Samantha? It is a puzzler, that. Though not even a skilled paranoiac such as Lucy would imagine how somebody - whoever, she can't think who exactly - who would be put-off will suddenly come upon her and be shocked by the ring being 'round her digit, despite the fact that, frankly, Lucy had not considered living with it seeming she was betrothed - or even associated - with anyone else whilst drifting about in the general population. Does Lucy drift around in the general population? What does she mean? Going to the store? Going to get gas? Going out for fast-food? Lucy is not much of a mingler - she is more of particular-situationer. All the more to the question then, though: should she condition herself into always costuming up prior to each time leaving the home, going from point-to-point - for example work-to-early-dinner, early-dinner-to-Ariel's, now. Why is the ring on, to begin with, if Ariel's is where Lucy is going? 'To get used to taking it off' Lucy decides. And she also hooks the mother's key on her key-ring, as sharply as a fish biting the bated lure and feeling its eye dislodged forward from behind and under. Ring: Samantha. Key: the mother. Ariel: needs no object. Has Lucy's life really reduced to a formula and a way-it's-played? What does she mean *Has it really*? The question is *Why had she never done this, before?* Lucy knows for a fact she cannot count on other people to have roles, let alone maintain them - they are all the motion of water while she is the propeller chopping the surface of the stream with her rounding, unseen, unknown. People only come alive when she needs them to and how. People like Samantha. People like the mother. People like all kinds of people. Like Ariel? People are the result of Lucy's motion. People like Ariel, Lucy? Lucy-People have no volition any more than a plant does - not leaning toward the sun because it particularly cares not to suicide, but just because that's what the green-things between its cell-walls tell it to do, a part of it it thinks is a part of it that is really something else driving it, turning it, using its brainless stem as a straw. Lucy? What? How does Ariel fit in? 'Ariel doesn't fit in' Lucy says, car in reverse and already at the traffic-light and already turning right and already at the next traffic-light and looking at the window displays of the odd foreign-run gas station and wondering why they are so proud to sell ice that they have a banner, cartoon decorated, saying *We Sell Ice!!!!!* while she turns right again and hates the wends of this road and the left-out of soccer balls and hula-hoops or snow-men or lawn-mower shavings that make her feel obliged to remember there actually is a chance one of the people who lives in one of these houses could die because of her drift in attention. 'Ariel doesn't fit in' Lucy continues 'any more than three pieces fit into a broken toe or a drowning fits into a lung.'

Like always, the early moon keeps to its outskirts, semi-transparent as though with its back turned, the sun there but not insisting itself relevant. In her younger days, Lucy would compare the early moon to all manner of things and repeat them boastfully to whoever would listen. Creaks of disillusionment at how no matter what she said it seemed so wonderful, so perfect, so exactly-what-the-early-moon-was. The early moon can't be everything. It can't even be two things. Lucy wanted her observations to be correct, mangles of language so ungainly they could only be miracles. But enthusiasm in strings and strings, this person to this person - or this person forty-nine times - made her seem flailing, compliments all taking on tones of the word *Tomorrow* in a retirement home. The early moon is as wordless as the pain of a bird hatching to no mother. The early moon is as wordless as the inside of a sack that turns around and is still the inside of a sack. The early moon is as wordless as a cigarette dipped in ink. Blah blah blah. Blah blah blah. Lucy has a special place in Hell for the moon when it creeps out in daylight to mock her, where it announces to children the night is always there and it's just a matter of color that determines when and what and when and what and when and what. The early moon is a bully that can't just belong to black like it should. And it has to show itself thin as the last dreg of milk that can't quite be tilted to cover the cup bottom and then show itself luminous as the lover you wish you'd killed when you could've. It flaunts its imperfections, the early moon, craggy as the thigh of the one whore you ever paid for and just as beautiful. It hangs, missing pieces, and it doesn't even hang - it rests in the corner of a curve and it doesn't rise as much as it makes the world lean down to it, the nightfall a bent knee and a bowed head so humbled it thinks the only view in the world is the skin of its own chest. And any old memory of her frustration with the early moon leads to a new one - Lucy feels exactly the way History must, beholden to people not imaginative enough to admit that something gets to be last. 'Why are we all so greedy? Why can't there be a last day? Hell' - no, Lucy hasn't turned on her recorder, she is just fuming at the feint of moon, there, always in eye-line, there, always in eye-line - 'we as a collective of creatures have invented philosophies and sciences just to prove there will not be an end even after us - as though History will just be our urban-sprawl, forevering into the darkness, all of the cosmos just the first day there wasn't us, the second day there wasn't us, the third day there wasn't us, the fourth day there wasn't us, the fifth day there wasn't us - good Christ, we expect Endless to be expressed in our increments! Oh in our greed we invent Eternity just to be absent from it!' But all Lucy ever wanted to do was to name the early moon exactly right. Her voice and her life is a gloom of knowing she'll never have the words. If the moon didn't rise, Lucy could be quiet. If the day would just be strong enough to be longer, to shun the lives it supports, to makes itself a statement, self-contained. 'Pathetic' Lucy mutters, as though the day doesn't even deserve her voice, today 'if that's what you are, we never should even have named you.'

Other times, Lucy thinks what a profound birthing it would be to realize all she has ever been is a train-of-thought that got well away from someone. She would look down and see herself turning to something like salt, flaking, bit-by-bit uncoupling and reconstituting, the eager concentration on her dwindling, the very idea of gravity that holds her together no more than part of the notion she is the drift of - and now that idea is over and thus she becomes a focus on what some mouth she's nothing to do with is saying, a thought that will only exist until a conversation being boringed through comes to an end. Wouldn't it be Holy, that? Wouldn't it be the very reason anything ever wants to be anything? Lucy Jinx: a great idea that was had and was lost. A notion that would have revolutionized an art-form or made someone feel not alone. Lucy Jinx: the coming of a word that never came. Just rotten luck, Lucy, just a perfection that got waylaid and sideswiped by something more immediate. It's a boisterous dream, big as the bottom chords of a piano struck with extra notes so numerous the chords are not identifiable. Lucy Jinx: the idea Faustus would sell his grease-palmed soul for. Lucy Jinx: the revenge that would actually quench the revenged! But Lucy Jinx, she is never to be - drive a car as she might. Look here: it is Lucy Jinx, driving a car, and it looks much the same as it always has - everyone has seen it at least once and even if not, well, Lucy Jinx driving a car is hardly different to the eye than any number of others doing the same thing. Sometimes, Lucy Jinx pictures the Universe as a long pile of words waiting to be spoken - unaware of time so no need for patience, unaware of physicality, so no need for stature or shape. And when Lucy imagines all of existence to be nothing more than this - eyes and all else just the organ that words are to be pressed through - she thinks of herself as the one - the one the one the one the one the one!!!!!!! - and the only word never thought of. She invents a scream of on-and-on and a babbling, unending loquaciousness so vast there aren't numbers to denote the first number of it and in all of that there is no space for anything not to be there except her. Except *Lucy Jinx*! Nobody and nothing says *Lucy Jinx*! She is the only word there isn't language for - no no, there is language for her, she is simply the single, perfected word that language fails to elicit. A woman in a car? A woman with a ring on her finger only to be removed from her finger? A woman with some poems to edit and some cats to feed and some people to lie to and only one person she cares to ever have waiting for her, only one place she ever wants to arrive to? Sure, Lucy Jinx is that. But she's only that. To her, though - to Lucy Jinx - she is the one thing all of her bringing chests of language up into her will never accomplish - she is the one word which isn't even there to find. And here, look: Lucy Jinx, calm. Calm as a carpet. Drab as an unput-on sock. Lucy Jinx trapped as Lucy Jinx. Lucy Jinx, failing. Lucy Jinx, failed - yes, failed, because here she is.


KAYLEIGH EXPLAINS TO LUCY 'WHEN cats die, they don't bother being ghosts because they have been being ghosts, already.' Lucy nods in a more polite showing of her lustful appreciation for the child's comment than her inappropriate heart is feeling and, to seem doily-fringe casual, asks 'So what does happen to a cat when it dies? 'Nothing, for awhile - then when it feels like it a baby is born.' 'Cats just come back as cats' Lucy says, liking this, her mind throwing up a slideshow of living-cat-ghost-cat becoming living-cat-ghost-cat, but Kayleigh gets a startled look that shuts Lucy's film-projector down. 'Not kitten, Lucy' - Kayleigh always just calls Lucy *Lucy* - 'I didn't say *kitten*.' 'No, you didn't say *kitten*' Lucy hangdogs 'you certainly didn't - explain to me, for I am old and my brain sometimes backfires.' The breakdown is this: A cat lives - we take for granted it is also a ghost when it feels like it - 'Cats aren't people' is how Kayleigh sums this up - and then a cat dies and then it - 'there is kind of' Kayleigh says when trying to make it clear to simpleton-Jinx 'no difference between living and dying for a cat' - waits around until it feels like coming back - 'and since it was already a cat it becomes a person and that is how babies are originated' Kayleigh says, the word pronounced a curious mix of the words *Orange* and *Refrigerated*. 'But why do cats want to be people?' Lucy questions with Mrs. Yuck-face, tongue out and twisted like a cheese curl. 'So they get to have cats.' Obviously, Lucy - obviously, you silly half-witted twat. Some other observations are, for example, this: cats who have come back as people - 'By now, every person is just someone who was once a cat - except for bad people' says Kayleigh, though she then throws in the caveat 'Unless they are really bad - those worst people are probably just cats being cats' - always name the cats they have the same name they had as cats. 'I see' Lucy nods, still smiling from the *those worst people are just cats being cats* remark. 'Will there eventually be a last cat - will cats run out and then there will only be people?' Lucy must not much understand cats, Kayleigh sighs, but apologizes immediately and says 'I mean, you are a cat - I get it - so you must understand something about them - but you might not be the smartest cat out of every cat there is, you know?' 'I know' Lucy says and drinks a sip of her coffee. Kayleigh holds up what she has been drawing and coloring - a yellow colored-pencil makes the main lines and a green pencil did most of the fill in, some pink for details and Lucy hasn't a clue what it is. 'Is it a Totem-Pole?' Lucy ventures, having held the paper and having handed it back. Kayleigh doesn't know what a Totem-Pole is. 'It's kind of a pole' Lucy explains, sipping more of her coffee. Kayleigh sarcastics 'You don't say!' and asks Lucy if she ever watches television. 'I do. Do you?' 'I do, too. Have you ever seen *Josie and the Pussycats*?' 'Yes' Lucy nods, enthusing. 'I haven't - but my mom talks about it all the time and taught me the song. My mom is very weird and sometimes I think she was the very first cat.' Lucy thinks this too, but doesn't mention how she does, just asks what Kayleigh means. 'Because nothing she ever says makes sense. She must be the first. You make more sense than her, even.' 'What cat am I?' Lucy wants to know. Kayleigh says 'You're the one hundred-nineteenth.'

Lucy is not as good at cutting as she wishes she was, but she is better than Kayleigh at pasting. 'I'm better than you at pasting.' 'You're an old woman' Kayleigh says and Lucy haughties 'Exactly, I'm glad we understand each other.' 'Kids are the future.' 'Who told you that - a teacher?' 'Yes. And I saw it on a show.' 'Did the show and the teacher bother to point out that kids are also the very distant past?' Kayleigh doesn't seem to like the sound of this, is - Lucy notes it - sniffing out the pitfalls of continuing the conversation, so Lucy - she'll have her cigarette in a moment - swoops in to her advantage and hammers the coffin shut with 'And you know who the present is? Old women. And by the time the future comes no one will care, anyway. The future never seems futuristic - it's all a sham, Kayleigh. It'd seem futuristic to someone from the past - sure! - but there were times in the past where no one had come up with the idea of a chamber-pot yet, so we shouldn't be very proud of wowing those old timers exactly, now should we?' Kayleigh wants to know what a chamber-pot is. 'It's a pot that people kept under their bed to go to the bathroom in.' 'That's kind of a good idea, though' Kayleigh has to point out, though her tone of voice is admitting of Lucy's primary argument. 'I didn't say it wasn't, kiddo - it's a fucking terrific idea. But you know what they did, after? Just dumped the stuff out the window! Why? Because people can only be smart about things one-at-a-time.' 'I want to live until people think of a better idea than a toilet.' 'Man' Lucy high-fives 'so do I. I'll tell you though, I've been waiting for that and it might be beyond us. People are so stuck on the idea of toilets they even put one on the goddamned space shuttle, Kay - and do you know how hard it is to make that goddamned toilet work? Someone had to go to college for almost as long as you've been alive just to be qualified to do that! That's one smart person. But you know what never even occurred to them?' 'To do something other than a toilet' Kayleigh says, dejected and no longer seeing the days ahead as Utopic. 'I'm going to go have a cigarette' Lucy says, standing, working her thumb-knuckle out from within the trap of the child-sized scissor grips. 'I think those kill you.' 'Name me something that make you live, I'll do that instead' Lucy says as she strides to the back door. Glass open. Screen open. Still visible of daylight-just-about-to-cease casting some sound from the trees over there that were it warmer would be insects but in the cold is just chill and shivering branches and dead piles of leaves. The cigarette no longer satisfies as it once did. It has lost universality, rotted from Icon to Object - each one different, now, twenty-in-a-pack instead of a pack just being the most convenient way to sell people part of a Platonic Ideal. Everything, though, was once larger than it was. Even as things grow they are components of enormity shedding itself, the dribble of unnoticed crumbs even broom-bristles don't bother with, figure are nothing to do with them. Looking up, Lucy sees up. If she waits awhile, she'll see down. Her exhale is eraser-clap but seems brick-red clay-motes from a discarded shoe.

Finally, Ariel shows up and sets the bags with the food down, complaining 'How complicated are tacos? They seem easy - but I guess I'm not legitimately worldly so I held my tongue.' Kayleigh says Lucy already let her have a sandwich and some cinnamon applesauce. 'Liar' Ariel ahas 'We don't own cinnamon applesauce! Oh Kayleigh, you Kay-lie!' Kayleigh, patient as a wrinkle, explains that Lucy sprinkles cinnamon into regular applesauce. 'Because Lucy does things like that - they occur to her.' 'Is *Occur* one of your so-called vocabulary words?' Ariel asks, busy setting Lucy's food on a napkin at the spot of the table Lucy supposes she is meant to sit at, Ariel's own food staying in the bag. 'No - I learned *occur* from you! It was all you said for almost a week.' Some sort of secret laughter passes between mother and child, Lucy fishing car-key out of Ariel's coat pocket, Ariel grabbing her wrist and warning her 'I drained the tank - you'll never escape that way.' A magician's gesture to the table, Lucy says 'Drinks' and then says 'Idiot' and then says 'Kayleigh, tell your mother she's an idiot' and Kayleigh says she would but doesn't want to have to hear the word *Occur*, again. More laughter and a chuck of hand-to-face - super-slow-motion fake-punch, Ariel-to-Kayleigh - Lucy out the door and to Ariel's parked car. The lot seems strange. Lucy's head tries for poetry and the words *It seems a fingernail dulled by trying to dull the edge of a coin* ping to place - but since she can't really explain this doesn't imagine the description is apt. The sound of ice rotating in the cups she takes up, the cups also seeming not to weigh enough somehow, giving Lucy the feeling the soda will taste flat or be the dregs from the dispenser before the flavor-bag should have been changed. Back inside, dramatic extra-shiver for her own amusement and maybe to seem - Lucy doesn't know - kid-friendly in a more normalized way to Kayleigh or something, Lucy puts the drinks down and sits, opening straws and inserting them one two, sip from each, both containers seeming to contain the same thing. 'Did you get something different from me?' Kayleigh asks 'Me?' 'Yes, you' Lucy sticks-out-her-tongue-with-her-voice 'did you?' 'I don't remember. Hey - if a tongue didn't have taste-buds, would it still be a tongue?' 'I think so' Lucy says, watching Ariel there staring down into the kitchen trash, a tart-purple gilled look and tapping the heft of her belly on one side in a kind of Morse-code. 'How much different would a tongue have to be - how many pieces would it have to lose - to not be a tongue?' 'It's just the color' Lucy says, trying to catch Ariel's eye as Ariel finally lifts her foot from the lever that had been holding the trash open, fusses with her hair, turns her back and opens a cabinet, seemingly at random. 'I don't believe you' Kayleigh says in a way that shows this is a decisive choice, then says 'I'll leave you two weirdos to your weirdo food - I'm going upstairs.' Kayleigh is heard by Lucy to take the stairs two-at-a-time, breathing hard at the landing, the railing creaking under the strain of her needing to tug on it to continue taking the stairs two-at-a-time after the bend to the top. Now: Ariel is looking at Lucy. 'I think I can't eat tacos.' 'Are you okay?' Ariel's face is like she is trying to hear a phone conversation she shouldn't through a wall - then it goes blank, she coughs, and says 'I'm going to try, I'm going to try. Tacos might be a little complicated, right now.'

When Lucy looks at Ariel's belly, she pictures within it some one of those old models of an atom - a cluster of wood balls for a nucleus, the sort of models that were never in any of her classrooms as a child but were always in the educational films they would watch. The insides of Ariel's womb are painted in cracking-butterscotch tones, would be wet to the touch, would keep staining napkins no matter how many times, how many napkins, you ran over them or with what force - a finger touch to the interior limits of Ariel would turn whole fingers into oil pastels and the rest of one's life would be spent dwindling, dwindling, nothing left but a stub and maybe the last fleck of a wrapper that nobody bothered to all-the-way peel. There is something human, though, in the stable, cordoned-off wood model. It seems, in fact, that if one were to keep leaning in closer the scale would change, all trick perspective, the thing not tiny just far away, really immense, dwarfing and tapering like a trap for an abstract tiger. Sometimes Lucy wants to ask Ariel if she might just stare at the skin - she will avoid looking, however, when Ariel is applying some sort of sour smelling, medicinal butter-rub, thinking she would seem too much of an opportunist, her longing to eyeball the taut and impossible-tight of the bulb just despicable, just too gauche for words. She wonders if there is a sound of ticking, microscopically, that accompanies it all - if there is that whisker-twitch sound like a perfectly calibrated watch held a micron from the ear. Before thinking about Ariel's baby as a wooden model-nucleus, Lucy always imagined the sound of the microscopic to be nothing but screams the memories of which hatched from the minds of sleeping William Blakes, things to be thought only in poetry really just the sound of electrons being nowhere-and-everywhere, suddenly having to be just-there because someone decided to look. Ariel's face, these last weeks, has aged peculiarly, like clay untouched on a wheel spinning 'round. Older, but older like a step-to-the-side isn't a step-to-the-other-side. She wrote on Ariel's belly once *to your child, who is older than saltwater* and three weeks later it was still there, Ariel tracing it every night in red. Except - or Lucy dreamed this - the *Y* had been left to fade - not vanish, for fear of giving the game away, but fallen into neglect as though as example to any other ill-belonging letters that might transgress their way in. 'How old is saltwater?' Kayleigh had asked on one occasion and on that occasion Lucy had just flicked Kayleigh lightly on the cheek and said 'Don't go reading bellies, they are like diaries' and Kayleigh had said 'That's why I read it' to which Lucy smiled and at which Kayleigh seemed satisfied not to have an answer, understood the statement wasn't a riddle, just a truth. Ah, dibble-dabble romance all in Lucy's head! One day and then another day - time-the-cork that stops time-an-empty-bottle from spilling. Which brings us to the present moment and to Ariel knowing Lucy has had a thought and asking 'What?' Lucy explains. Ariel understands. 'If an empty bottle spills, nothing comes out - and that is the very worst thing to make a mess with everywhere, right?' And Lucy cups her hands over her mouth and extremes her face as though screaming across a void 'I love you' but whispering it so that what Ariel hears is exactly what she would were Lucy a void away instead of less than the length of a barely-stretched leg.

Ariel speaks first. Lucy speaks second. Ariel speaks third. Lucy speaks fourth. Ariel speaks fifth. Lucy speaks sixth. It's almost alarming how badminton their dialogues are! Lucy bets they both secretly think they are each doing the other's voice. She'd deny it - Ariel, she thinks, would deny it. If they interrogated each other, it would be as unoverlapping as a glove's outside and in. 'If I had to move to another country, I'd move to the smallest country that still had telephones and places at least far enough away to be driven to.' 'You would have every country to choose from.' 'Then I'd move to a country that decided postal service was a bad idea, really something they decided to jail people for.' 'In that case, you're not describing any country.' 'Then I'd move to a country that matches the population number of birds to the amount of currency printed each year and every time a bird is found dead, the finder - as a noble tradition - takes a bill out of their pocket and burns it, there and then.' 'Again: then you'd have no country to move to, El.' 'Well, what kind of country would you move to?' 'I'd move to a country where they venerate plagiarists, where perfect imitation is seen as improvement, in fact - where an original is an accident and a duplicate is an achievement necessitating the destruction of the genuine.' 'Is there a country like that?' 'I don't know anything about countries, El - you tell me.' They decide to forget about countries, Ariel instead demanding Lucy give a speech that will convince her that Plurals are always bad. 'Plurals are the worst idea ever thought of' - Lucy needed little prompting, the entire time she speaks she wonders if she's said this, verbatim, before and Ariel is just taking the elaborate piss out of her - 'and I'd damn the person to Hell who lazied them up and plague-of-boils plague-of-slain-first-borned them on us. Think of a new word? This is a *Clock* - fine. These are *Clocks* - no! More-than-one-clock is a thing in itself! And three-clocks is another thing! And four-clocks another! Plurals are one of the primordial lies, the early mistakes from when the brain hadn't formed enough divides to account for the infinite. Ariel - fuck the whole notion of Plural! I say that while even admitting it is pathogenically a part of me - it is laced to my marrow and I cannot even love without it being in plural. Still: if I could excise it from me and with it every part it touched, if I could scrape the stale of Plural from wherever it has curdled and rust-hardened I would - damn it all, I would! - and I'd just be whatever deformity of me was left.' She pauses. 'I can't tell if this is making you hate Plurals.' 'It's making me adore Plurals, you fucking bitch! You never do anything I ask you to - it's like you hate me, on purpose.' Ariel talks. Lucy talks. Ariel talks. Lucy talks. Ariel talks. Lucy talks. Kayleigh asks from upstairs 'Mom, can I take a bath?' 'Do you know how to run one?' 'It's a bath - yes - I just pour it there, it isn't exactly going to outsmart me.' 'Okay then - but I don't take kindly to your tone.' 'Is Lucy still here?' 'Yes.' 'Lucy?' 'Yes, Kay?' 'Can you tell my mom to shut up?' 'Do I ever tell her anything else?' Ariel yawns and touches the side of her jaw like she's either lost teeth or sprouted a handful of new ones. Lucy leans forward, concerned. Ariel says 'Bodies are stupid. Make a speech. Make me hate bodies, okay?'

'So, we're not sure if it's going to be I'm going to stay in the house and he's going to move out somewhere and I'm in the house with Kayleigh mostly - or if I'm going to move out somewhere and he's going to be in the house most of the time with Kayleigh - or if Kayleigh will stay with him, most of the time, when he moves out - because he might get a larger place, kind of far off - or if she'll stay with more when he moves out - because he'll be kind of farther off in a bigger place - which might make better sense, as far as Kayleigh is concerned - I don't know, what do you think I should do?' This speech, while it could be said fast - even breathlessly - and felt like it had been said fast - sometimes words connected to one another, especially as the need to take a breath would have been approached - it actually was almost drawled, kind of like coming up with a tune one thinks is more formed than it is and forgetting the tune partway through then finding an ending and assuming it was for the same tune and feeling satisfied, but only vaguely. More to the point: in all honesty, is this something Lucy has the remotest interest in discussing? Can she be honest about her feelings? Can she say to Ariel 'Don't ask me what to do about your husband and your kid, man - I don't want to talk about that, I'm not your friend on those counts.' Is that the truth? Or does Lucy just to have to tightrope, undecided and uncommitted whether or not she is advocating for Ariel or advocating for Kayleigh or advocating that to do the one is to do the other? Or does Lucy have it in her to saloon-door - back-forth, back-forth, quicker or slower or coming-to-a-halt depending on the speed of Ariel's entrances or exits with whichever mood, whichever stance? Well, having to say something, Lucy says 'When would this be?' And Ariel makes a complaint about Leopold leaving all timelines up to her. 'He's the one who could get his job and get his house. I mean, I guess I could, Loose, but I do currently have an offspring, interior. Then, he insists we should wait - and if I agree it's like I'm not allowed to even discuss it, generally, until the baby is born. But why not? Can't I want to take the interim to make a decision? Should I really be deciding things all post-partum and likely thinking very little of myself due to chemical combinations that are difficult to predict - I read that in a book and it happened when I was pregnant, before.' 'Is it his idea, in general, to leave - or to split - or is it your idea?' Ariel coughs, fake - coughs fake fake fake - and after she is done stalling in this way says 'I forget. Probably mine. What do you think I should do?' But Oh goddamn it with Ariel and her codes! Or maybe - be honest, Lucy - if Lucy wasn't so scattered right now, spinning so many plates, this would be the simplest thing to consider. And to Ariel that is what Lucy is trying to posture: not spinning plates, unburdened, there for her, there. It's so obvious even that it doesn't matter what Lucy says, here - as long as it isn't another question. But in the sucked-thumb wrinkles of Lucy's brain all there are are questions and they all are jabs and voodoo needles. Never has she felt the stab so much of the tip necessary for letters - it's like a dry-spot always at the top of her throat that every swallow to moisten slips over.

Kayleigh - not pajamaed but t-shirt-and-underweared - announces her presence to Ariel with 'Shit, mom! We didn't get that book again, can we?' This is something Lucy hears through the bathroom door while she urinates. Hears Ariel groan as though drunken and say 'First: why aren't you asleep? And second: what is the point of books, all the time?' Kayleigh now is promising she will stay up to read it if Ariel will just go get it 'Because this is technically, literally, and symbolically the last day, mom - I kind of need to read the book by tomorrow. I will stay awake, I promise - it's long, but I don't want to not read it.' Lucy tries not make any sound, holding in the urine that is finally ready to loose, tries to breathe only slow-motion and only through her nose and only through one nostril. Why? She can feel the lean of Ariel, listening listening for her. Knows that the comments to Kayleigh are also kind of aimed for Lucy to overhear, process, Jack-in-the-box out of the toilet door on the sound of the flush being depressed and join in the flow of conversation like nothing. But Lucy's only plan is to go get Kayleigh whatever book it is - and this is likely not a very motherly plan. See? Ariel is saying 'I can write you a note Kay 'kay? I can explain to the teachers that it is all my fault and such things - you won't be faulted and we can get the book tomorrow and I'm sure you'll get extra time to read it even if Mrs. Dixon has to give you a separate assignment.' Now Kayleigh sounds more like a kid than usual - Lucy can see her own childhood face, see how she would repeat her own whining in the mirror after whining it to mark the cascades of her misery, see how shadows fell on a distraught, blemishless seven-year-old, twelve-year-old, acne-lumped fifteen-year-old jaw-line. 'I don't want extra time or another assignment - and I don't want to say it's your fault. I just want to read it, actually. They'll say I don't have to! And then - even if I do - it won't be how I wanted to.' Ariel says 'Kayleigh, look' but Kayleigh counters with 'Mom' and Lucy hears her own voice, ages ago, saying 'Dad' and thinks of books and extra paper and poster-board and *VHS* tapes that were never retrieved, a blank journal she never got and so she drew her cartoons on the back of fliers she stole from neighbors' mailboxes and stapled with her mom's stapler in secret. And she is peeing, now. And the overhead fan, through a door, never covers that sound, amplifies it for dulling it, enough and exactly the right decibel surviving the din to register in any nearby ear. 'The library isn't even open, dude - I'm sorry. I am honestly sorry, Kayfka, I am - but there is no way we could even get it if we wanted to. Pretend you slept and this is tomorrow and it is too late, already - because it is and as much as that sucks doesn't change how it sucks.' 'What about the bookstore?' Kayleigh asked that, Lucy was thinking the same thing. 'Kayleigh.' 'It's not that late - you sometimes go to the bookstore this late.' 'When does Ariel go to the bookstore this late?' Lucy arbitrarily wonders, but then returns to listening. 'We don't even know if they have the book. It's kind of a weird book, right? Isn't it optional, too - why did they not provide you a copy?' 'Oh Ariel, stop it' says Lucy to herself, dabbing herself with a folded over length of toilet-paper. Good for Kayleigh, Kayleigh says 'How about a last deal - then we can do it your way and I'll agree.' 'Kayleigh, come on.' 'No, mom - mom, mom - no mom: call the bookstore. If they don't have it, I'll forget it and will think this is even how it was supposed to happen. I can deal with things if they're supposed to happen.' 'I can deal with things if they're supposed to happen' smiles Lucy. 'I can deal with things if they're supposed to happen' each word individuated semi-mock-astonishes Ariel. 'Okay, then. Jesus. Fine. Can you get my phone from my purse?'

The temperature has made itself kittenish, any heat and light - if anywhere - is close in to the walls, underneath things, inseparable from the shadows, and not worth crawling around kissy-sounding for. Ariel is shaking her head as Lucy blows smoke and tells Lucy to - on principle - just drive around the block, come back, and say the bookstore lied. 'I can't say a bookstore lied.' 'Plenty of bookstores lie!' Ariel fist-brandishes 'I'm sure they've lied to you personally, man! Tell me square you find bookstores truthful - at your age! - tell me that and I'll leave you alone.' 'Bookstores are hideous liars - but I can't tell a kid that. Kids are supposed to believe all kinds of falsehoods, otherwise why not reopen the mills and the workhouses?' Ariel's position is staunchly that if Lucy is doing this, she is not only wearing a Dunce-cap the whole time, but she is footing the bill for the book out of her own pocket. 'I'll foot the bill. I'm made of money, Ariel. I'm not some lowly sort like you whose only upward mobility is to tiptoes to get the crock-pot from the top shelf, you know?' Ariel pins Lucy to the wall with her bellied-child and tries to lean in far enough to kiss her. Then she gives up - for comedy mostly - and says 'I wish it was still when they said it was okay to smoke when having a kid. Life's such a pain when they figure things out!' 'Doctors?' 'Anyone. Those doctors are killjoys, though. When did they ever figure out anything good?' Lucy explains that nowadays toothpaste is allowed to taste like phony-watermelon or bubblegum, but - and it's a fair rebuttal - Ariel doesn't believe it's correct to say doctors thought of that, it was more likely profiteers and ad executives, who are - another fair point - always coming up with wildly fun ideas. 'And by the way' Ariel says, sighing as Lucy steps out her smoke-stub and reopens the screen door 'what is the difference between a friar and a monk? I think history is confusing enough without that differentiation. *Friar* is just an old word for *Monk*, right?' 'What do you mean *an old word*?' Lucy asks, going to the kitchen drawer where she knows Ariel always keeps either mints or chewing-gum - chewing-gum, this time, some kind of cherry-mint flavor, her breath in thin around it like when sucking a lozenge. '*Monk* is the updated word - or the word that won out. My point is: there's no such thing as a *Friar* anymore - why keep the word around, eh? Retroactively, we should just translate everything forward to *Monk*.' Lucy, zipping her coat and first telling Ariel she's stealing Ariel's gloves even though they aren't as nice as Lucy's own gloves explains very patiently to Ariel that 'There is probably at least one friar, someplace - and until they have tracked him down and killed him they have to keep the word around. Otherwise, who are they supposed to say they are hunting and killing - and why?' The logic of this is whisky-barrel solid, nothing in or out, so Ariel gives a low bow and says 'You really are too nice to my kid, considering she's not yours.' 'I'm not nice to your kid, Ari, I'm just a dick to you. Make sure she doesn't fall asleep.' And Kayleigh says - from clearly having been listening to everything, seated out of sight in the dark at the top stair - 'Of course I'm not going to sleep.' 'You better not' Ariel seethes and then says 'and you better tell the teacher you read the book three weeks ago - that you read it three times three weeks ago! There's better things than honesty, you know?'

So: now it's on the way to the bookstore and the radio is screeching *Buzzcocks* Lucy isn't listening to because they are like womb-warmth by now, something only vital if she feels like paying attention, something nourishing and not needing notice. Her memory? Lucy's? Lucy Jinx's memory? Well: a long time ago she knew of a radio station that seemed to play random tracks off of comedy albums. *Monty Python. Cheech and Chong. The Jerky Boys*. On and on. And late at night on television - this is where this thought goes - she used to watch some program called *The New Red Green* but when she was too young and too disinterested about particulars to really get an idea what it was. Same as how she watched those black-and-white *Sherlock Holmes* episodes which are now so fretfully boring to her. At the time? She loved every hissy recorded warble of what-did-he-say audio. And this book that Kayleigh needs? A bit advanced for Kayleigh's grade-level - even smart as a sin as Kayleigh may be - is it not? *The Endless Steppe*? Hadn't Lucy read that in a much later grade? Or had she just gone to a fish-tackle grade-school, been some bumpkin mishap who everyone figured only needed to learn so much, just somewhat-more-than-nothing, enough that some appearances had been kept up? Yet: is Kayleigh truly reading this? Is that even the book Lucy is thinking of? It's fucking impossible. Nevermind how Kayleigh speaks like a gifted propagandist, that trait is just so much mimicry of her odd parentage - or at least her quirk of a mother, Lucy doesn't know Leopold from a give-a-damn - this cannot be the right book and there is no way that Kayleigh is going to be allowed to pull an all-nighter to get through it. Lucy? Lucy? 'What?' Speaking of Sherlock Holmes: didn't you stay up on the sofa and read through the entire *Sign of the Four* the entire *Casebook*, didn't you discover Robert Louis Stevenson's penny dreadful and H.G. Wells' insistence that as we can move about in three dimensions - but better down than up, more safely side-to-side than down - then why not in four, when you were about Kaleigh's age? No. Older. 'I was older.

I was older.' And yes, this is true. It checks out. That was closer in to middle-school. But then again, you'd never heard of Aesop until fifth grade, either! Second grade you'd watched that film based off of Ray Bradbury, though - and third grade you'd been given *The Martian Chronicles* and thought them a bore but loved the teacher for trying. Is that your life? Are those your memories? Are those scenes from some film? Don't you remember how you lied when you were a kid and a teen and a young woman and how you never stopped lying? 'What does this have to do with Kayleigh?' Lucy's more sensible angels butt in. And the air cools. And the fury of headache returns to *Johnny wants to fucky always and always / he's got the energy / he will amaze* and Lucy decides to scream the refrain just to drown herself out. Just to drown herself out. Just to drive to get this book and be done with tonight - at least this part. Then she shuts the radio off and thinks there is a weird sound from the wheel. And then thinks - because of this sound - how it feels like the car is driving uneven. So she turns the radio back on and tries to remember something else from her past, something she can't argue with, something that time hasn't sort of made false.

Now why exactly has Lucy Jinx turned in to this shopping-center? This is not where the bookstore she needs to go to is. This is not where any bookstore is. This is not - she scans the storefronts - even where anything she has ever gone to is. A genuine veer. She even verifies the time by both the car-clock and her telephone. No blackout. Nothing dramatic. So what triggered her to pull over and park? She is parked. There is an employee of the grocery-store - the name of which she only vaguely recognizes, a sort she has never shopped inside of - gathering up a few stray carts, pausing to take a drag off his cigarette and to check the message that just came through on his phone - stopping to shiver and to look around as though getting caught out not doing his job would cost him his job - now back to it, sluggish and almost like in a state that would justify a doctor's appointment. Nope. No. Lucy can glean no reason for her decision - or lack thereof - to be here. But surely there must be something, however subtle. Surely she could look around and from the ample landmarks and colors and shop names and positioning-of-buildings and whatnot she could come up with a reason her unconscious drew her here. As simple as she's been here but forgot? Naw. She has never ventured down this way at all, really - not in the past, not in the present. What had she been listening to? What had she been thinking about? Well, what does it matter, Lucy? Really - what does it matter? It doesn't. And yet. And yet. And yet. She does not want to leave without having poked around, turned over a rock or two, gotten a whiff of something. It would be easier if she had by now - it's only been two minutes, she has just re-checked both clocks - been reminded of something, but no luck. Let's say there had been public-telephones there there and there - exactly where, years ago when there were public-telephones everywhere public-telephones would have been stationed - then would this place remind her of something? A long shivering talk feeding coins down the cold gullet of the device, hearing the glug and the voice she was laughing with continuing three minutes, five, fifteen at-a-time? Further back? Does she need to go further back? Remember when you saw that man steal that woman's purse? While your dad was inside the store getting a refund for that item the clerk had accidentally rung twice? Why is Lucy thinking so much of her dad, tonight? And why isn't she leaving now that it's been four minutes, say five - even call it ten to kick yourself along, Lucy - and no sense of connection has formed? Or are you stuck? Quicksand of no association. Will you be sequestered here unduly, forever - no more Ariel or Kayleigh, no more Samantha or Natalie, no more Elliott or anyone or anyone or you? Lucy Jinx honks her horn and it seems bashful compared to the radio she now has way turned up. She turns down the radio and presses the horn, again. It is still quiet, but she doesn't feel certain she is pressing it as ballsily this time. Oh Lucy must have been nowhere before, felt nowhere before, she reasons. That must be the feeling. She must have spent ages in expressionless corners of corridors and crossed over places she never even regarded. She has been nowhere and now recognizes it. It's here. 'Hi.' And now she can move on.


BOOKSTORE. AGAIN. AH, LANGUAGE, THE leg you don't have to stand on is long! Language is the sinking spider and history the strand that paces its sink. Lucy, despite Kayleigh, is not in a hurry to purchase the book and to leave. See here? Lucy is even ignoring the five-minutes-ago text from Ariel explaining that Kayleigh had broken her resolve down and *is even now eating a piece of cake!!* so Lucy had better hurry. See here? Lucy is also ignoring this most current text saying *If you died en route to get a book for my daughter I'll actually just wind up loving you more.* Language is the worst technology, so corrosive and vain it invents words to describe its own plagueward progress. Why *technology*? Oh it all came from words! Every mechanical failing and toggle-of-switch to make-better! From protolanguages came it, came it! When the lifeform of Concept oozed itself out of the leakage of tissue the world was made temporary far more than just the burning out of a star could ever make it. There is nothing destructive there is not language for first - language harbingering, language, in fact, falling over itself in such a hurry to be the first word that named the hard-upon doom! What does Lucy Jinx see when she looks in this shop? Why, she sees a lackadaisical slaughterhouse! She sees a poison so sure of its pang it stickers itself at discount and she sees swallowers of the arsenic not even particularly caring for the words - just what they say, what they cost, how they make them feel. A word is no different than any other pet, any other creature that won't near a doorstep but you know is moving right out there, two inches from sight! You don't cage a nightingale because of what it is about - no! - or leave a milk-dish out for a stray because of what the stray means. Words used words to trick those who know language out of seeing word's life and their swamp stretching presence. But imagine language gone - never-wasing - never having got the first shape of itself off tongue, off esophagus, out of smack-of-hand. Oh book! Book? Book, so hilarious! All language ever needed was the sound of a foot on the ground or a breath breathed at one speed and then another at another. Life - the most powerful Life - birthed out of muscles learning to stretch and organs fumbling to fornicate when they didn't even know how to mix into growth. Bookstore again and again and again. Lucy Jinx is honestly here, half-hour from closing, to buy a book for a child who is supposed to be asleep and should have either read it already or shrugged it off and not bothered. So indicted is Lucy she offered to come out here. So predator and in-the-pocket of her own tongue is she she will douse the kiddo with gasoline, call it *Perfume,* light the match to alight her and call that *Read this.* There is no salvation for Lucy Jinx. Where she ought have sense she has the word *Sense,* where she ought have mind she has the word *Mind,* where she ought have empathy she has the word *Empathy*, where she ought know better she has the words *Where she ought know better she has the words 'Where she ought know better'.* Lucy has ignored a third text that says *I meant it about you being dead - but seriously, Loose, get a book to this kid before I Medea her, man.* Lucy smiles. She texts back *O what will she do, a soul bitten into with wrong?*

Her phone isn't good enough, her recorder isn't good enough - Lucy smacks on the overhead dome-light and bends around fish-blind hands scampering for a pen. Here's one! Here's one! And she uses the title page she tears out of the now purchased *The Endless Steppe* - why would Kayleigh need an entirely superfluous cover page? - and look at this: on that page isn't Lucy writing the following line? Just look - she is - horrendously rushed and stifling a sneeze she can't stifle - has to sneeze at fifth word and then growl and rub face and then continue. *You're so much a cat you forgot to know me.* Underline underline underline. Bravo! Lucy claims. Bravo! Lucy emblazons. Bravo! Lucy *Apassionatas!* Lucy doesn't even mind that she seems to be writing a lot lately about cats and the moon. It may be if she ever bothers to read what her editor said in their edits that that is what her editor will have said. *Dear Lucy, you write a lot about cats and the moon - let's change some of that.* How much of Lucy's life is a pile of the words *Cat* and *Moon*? What else? What else is she a self-replicating strand of? Likely there is much. But for now, as though it is imperatively destined, she recalls the yearling Kayleigh and to the yearling Kayleigh points, here, her car. Choose a sentence from *Finnegans Wake* to be and Lucy's choice would be this: *Lord, heap miseries upon us yet entwine our arts with laughters low*. No! Wrong - Lucy, you do forget yourself! Start over - still driving toward Kayleigh as though now suddenly possessed of a heart that beats - start over, Lucy, start over. Starting over: Choose a sentence from *Finnegans Wake* to be and Lucy's choice would be this: *Thus the unfacts, did we possess them, are too imprecisely few to warrant our certitude*. Better. Still likely wrong, but better. You know what Kayleigh is: just a set of eyes that have not eyed Joyce or not eyed Pound or not eyed Stein or not eyed Highsmith or ears that have not pricked to radio low playing *The Hollies* singing *Look Through Any Window*. What a lament for youth Lucy has become! What does youth have to look forward to? Suicide - age is just youth suiciding! Pipsqueak old Tommy Sterns Eliot - as often he is - is wrong and obvious and pedestrian and pale-boy not-as-smarty-pants-as-he-reckons. 'It is youth that is an island that is surround by death! Endless death: pre-birth at the one side and boring old growing to old-age death-death and then the eternal of nothing on the other.' How long does youth last? How long for Kayleigh or anyone of her ilk? *The Endless Steppe* is just some pages of words, intractable, hyperaware, and insidiously vicious in their robbing Kayleigh of the time she is young and empty and nowhere and no one. Lucy drives like she knows the way but she doesn't. Lucy is unclogging and becoming what a clog unclogs to. Lucy will deliver the pestilence to the firstborns and will wink at the old-maids who were spared for being the generation too boring to bother with damning for show. Lucy! Lucy! Are you saying this into your recorder? No no, you have quite forgot yourself! You have become a pillar of salt that will not remember anything it thought about. You will become a labyrinth that forgot to have a middle or a way out or to be a labyrinth at all! She slams on the brakes and it all seems familiar. She puts on her hazard-lights - this might be the first time she has ever hit that button - and on the same paper as that other line she has now written *You're a lie, not a riddle - just a square that says it's a square when it's not, posh hair you have, posh coat supporting you - you're Euripides without my translation*.

The radio is loud and at this traffic-light Lucy feels blaring, herself. Kids in that car. Not kids. Young men and women. They have plans they are keeping secret from each other. Maybe Lucy is right, after all. She grins at the guy who is looking at her, her hope to either make him uncomfortable, in love, or to rise ridicule from the collection of teenagers in the halted car with him at herself. Maybe Lucy is right to have constituted her life of secrets. Why should age lead to certainty by Free Will? 'If anything, anything else' Lucy sings to the tune of whatever this song is, the left-turn green arrow lighting before Lucy's straight going green-circle and so off that young lot of men goes, Lucy left with more things never to know the result of. Why can't life just be a series of moving around thinking? Why can't life just be a series of physicality that amounts to the blank it eventually decomposes to? Was it a poet - it probably was, Lucy - who first decided to celebrate decay? Was it a poet who first decided to snake-oil science that all things just unconsititue and reconstitute, that the infinite is a bunch of finite crumbs taking different shapes depending on this or that relation to each other? Why can't Lucy's life just be this question? Which? Which!? Pay attention! Lucy asserts that Poets invented Science just because that was the only way to say one last thing - the question is why did they do it? Greed? Gluttony? Grace? Charity? Why can't Lucy's life just be asking and answering and asking and answering and asking and answering? Every crumb in her meat wants this, claims it, and yet she has done anything but it, anything save seal herself in the same question and ask it and answer it until she has become bored so many times with answers that she becomes excited again with questions. Think about this: Lucy is almost back to Ariel's house. How much time has passed between leaving and coming? How much and how is it measured? If we contain ourselves to Earth-and-just-Lucy we'd say half-an-hour, forty-minutes, round up to an hour, max. If we confine ourselves all-inclusively to Earth - well! - a lot more than that has happened and so to relate it all would take time longer than the occurrence - and the explanation is what Time really amounts to! Venture from Earth? You see? Don't you see? But suddenly: Lucy mocks herself in cartoonish caricature of stoner-comedy films. 'Deep, man - that's so wild, man - you should run for president, man - you should free the slaves again only this time for real!' What if Lucy came in the door and handed Kayleigh this damned book in this state she's in - it would color the child's life until the end! What would Ariel think of a rabid-eyed Lucy, mouth as mushy as a chewed tissue, sing-songing away about all of this and returning in shattered ceramic from just a simple errand of book retrieval? Lucy, Lucy - you're just an animal, lick yourself clean. Have you forgotten how to be an appearance? How could you, when it's all you've ever been!? Did you finally evolve, choose just this moment to go from pupa to wingspan, from translucent segmentation and writhe to color meant to seem a face to keep away all who would devour you? Lucy, calm down. Lucy? 'What?' Lucy - calm down.

Kayleigh doesn't look tired. 'Kayleigh, I got your book. Remember that when I am nothing but a grave you never visit, okay?' But Kayleigh is a child in a child's world and yanks the book like some loose-tooth from Lucy's grip-as-a-gum and pounds up the stairs even while Lucy asks Ariel 'Is she really going to read it, right now?' 'What am I Lucy, a tea-leaf? How would I know?' Lucy sits down at the kitchen table and picks up a random piece of mail and reads the return-address aloud. Ariel keeps stirring something at the stove. 'What are you making?' 'Noodles. Do you want some?' 'Are they sophisticated noodles - is there tradition behind them?' 'Fuck you, man' Ariel says and yawns and - even though the yawn didn't garble the statement - repeats the words 'Fuck you, man' and says 'I bet you never even had to register someone for kindergarten or have to make a Well-Child visit or talk about *Desitin* like that's just something you would have talked about anyway.' 'I haven't' Lucy admit. And then they talk, while Ariel stirs, about a movie they once wrote fake-reviews for and phony-interviews concerning and which they have, in the almost-decade interim, both seen and quite enjoyed. What Lucy liked best was the fact that the cinematographer didn't care if things went out of focus. What Ariel liked the most was that the soundtrack used the entirety of every song. 'Which one of us was the other's boss?' Lucy asks, knowing the answer but curious to see what way Ariel will turn the question into a cudgel. 'You were my boss. You had that great plan to sail the ship underwater and it worked!' 'You blame me for the demise of *Hernando's Highlights*?' 'I blame you for everything except how terrific *The Velvet Underground* is, Lucy - and it's high time you know that.' Then Ariel explains how, despite Lucy's kissing up, Lucy doesn't get to have any of the noodles. 'It's a mug's game, knowing you, Ari - it's Chinatown.' Lucy watches Ariel mix a packet of beef-flavoring and a packet of chicken-flavoring around in the steaming brain of noodles and something in her once vital ovaries ticks like the color of an old advertisement for bubble-bath. 'Ariel?' 'Yes, Lucy Jinx?' 'How did we first meet?' 'We never did first meet. We skipped that part. Like with *Return of the Living Dead*, it's better if you just pop in partway through, so we did things after that fashion.' 'And it worked out?' 'You ever seen that movie?' 'I have.' 'Then: you know.' And finally - just entirely sick of it - Lucy Jinx stands and crosses to Ariel and comes at her sideways and kisses her mouth for three minutes and in those three minutes there is nothing but the awareness of the kiss and the no-idea-what-it-feels-like-because-truly-who-gives-a-goddamn? Then breathing. And proximity. And color. And scents that don't belong there. And then Ariel bites Lucy's cheek and Lucy hopes it leaves a mark but she doubts it. 'Yes' Ariel says. 'What do you mean?' 'To your question.' Lucy isn't sure if this is a game and her instincts fail. Then breathing and silence and breathing and Lucy returns to her seat and Ariel adds some taco-flavoring to the noodles and Lucy returns to the sound of her making a grossed-out gag and then laughing at Ariel saying something witty in retort. 'Ariel?' 'Yes?' 'You should be the name of a month.' 'Why?' 'Because there should be something to say between October and November and you seem like it should be you.' Ariel nods, blowing on a first forkful of noodles that seems to be alive-but-not-quite-aware-it's-alive, an odd motion like how moss must be surprised when it sees that it has spread.

    To leave, Lucy first has to dwindle and seem as though she is not leaving - and seem as though this is home and where-she-comes-back-to not just where-she-leaves-home-to-at-times. One could question here: then why the resistance to involving her opinion in the eventual living situation of Ariel, of Kayleigh, of Leopold? Why the reticent tongue, so recalcitrant Lucy's resolve to seem out of it? One analysis: Lucy reverts to a state of childish waiting. Maybe because of Kayleigh, a proxy to Lucy - why else are so often thoughts of Lucy's own kid-years sprouting forth, weeds so much grander in height than grass? Another analysis: Lucy is having to exert extra-effort to treat Ariel as on the same tier as the other people she knows, cannot afford to have a predetermined desire, cannot make the mistake of working against several possibilities for one - or against a certainty, even, because isn't that how Lucy sometimes feels? Tonight, the 'I love you' and 'I love you' are traded without thought and without snark or theatric, tonight the parting is not treated as anything indicative of adhesive losing bond. Tonight is Lucy not turning to see how Ariel - but knowing it is so - is watching from the open door until she gets in her car and tonight is Lucy not staring at the lighted window-blinds knowing Ariel is looking at their insides but not even parting a slat for a peek. Just because of the extra effort for the book. Lucy knows she served the function she not only is supposed to serve but wants to. She grins, thinking of Ariel as having masterminded the thing - maybe Kayleigh tucked in cahoots with her, both of them now peeling off make-up like in a film about a long-con, feet up on ottomans, cigars, and calls from whoever they are working for and who is thrilled at their Robin Hood double-cross! Lucy is driving in precisely no direction. Lucy should not be leaving, but she is. Or: Lucy should be staying, but she isn't. Lucy is a wind questioning whether it belongs on the desert, high-pitched and strong-armed, bird-throated and canine in its resolve. Lucy is a binding too tight, creaking then cracking and pages coming loose, pages kept pinned then by owner between the pages that have not yet fallen away. Yes. Yes. Lucy is that. The preservation, in spirit, of a book that knows it will never be read, just kept. Yet how light she is - the joy before fainting, the moment when waking with a fever feels like waking to tremendous good news, stomach on tent-hooks with knowing a Hooray! is about to cannonade. Lucy thinks back on Ariel's most recent 'I love you' looking for the flavor of the mouth in the image of it, wondering if there was some sore in the cheek by her back teeth, some tooth that felt loose she was always slightly worried will have to be replaced - thinking about every bite she takes, every time she absently tongues her tongue around while daydreaming. Lucy romps with the thought of the words and she tries to recall did she hit the proper return pitch, show the understanding of bubble-gum harmony right. Had Lucy been the correct Lucy tonight - and how could she make certain, if so, to be the correct Lucy, again? How can Lucy stop feeling every moment is the last moment and the one to sum up with? How can Lucy feel confident she will get it all again - like she always gets it all again - but this time this thing and next time this thing, again?

Then: she is waiting her turn in a drive-thru line - she has ordered, she is waiting her turn to advance to the pay window. But she is still next to the speaker-device where customers order. Window down. It's been twenty second. The goldfish memory of the device forgets her. Through the glass - she's never sure if car windows are glass or are they plastic? - she hears the voice thanking her for choosing the establishment and can the voice take her order. Pause. 'Hello?' Pause. This same process repeats twenty seconds later. And again just as she is finally pulling up enough to be past the thing, the car behind her not quite near enough to be to it - look, that driver is leaning out his window and yelling how he wants three double-cheeseburgers and some manner of fish-sandwich. And Lucy turns up the radio, not to be subjected to another word of this. A little like dancing drunk, soon Lucy is parked in the lot, head back-titled, reaching into her bag on the passenger-seat for fries and chicken-strips, eyes shut, the idea that she is just snacking on a few but soon the entire meal is finished and she is bloated wide with enough scentless flatulence to last the next two days entire. The coffee tastes hideous over the grease of her teeth - teeth which seem melting without ever having frozen and just partway through their melt - feel gummy the way a popsicle sometimes will if left in the freezer too long, glob of its syrup over an oddly tasteless frozen core. So: is Lucy in her ring or not? Not. Is she supposed to put it on or not? Not. Yes. She nods. Trying to turn her tiredness into a game of pretending to be intoxicated. The unfortunate truth is: she is fiercely aware of what she is doing and regrets eating that food. Shame, shame how Lucy knows that it is too late - even were she to purge she would still feel bloated, full up, even heavier, really, for the effort of scraping what went down back mouthward and out. Something about metabolism: it knows it has eaten and will feel the way that feels now, regardless - this is a principle thing. Has Lucy ever felt hungry after vomiting? Nope. Not even after violent illness. Hunger, as any pamphlet will tell you, has nothing to do with how much food has been ingested but exactly what and how the body bubbles because of it. Chew and swallow a fingernail, you'll feel more distended than if you eat a whole steak! Lucy knows it. Everyone does. She breathes the letters *SH* in the mash of sounding like a whistle and sounding like a hard shush, lets the sound pirouette a long while before silencing. Then: a coughing fit which makes her start sweating. Then: more coffee and deciding against a cigarette. That bit? The decision against the cigarette? She already regrets it as she makes her way down the first bit of road, every traffic-signal taunting her by not making her stop and knowing she does not remotely enough trust her ability to steer, retrieve pack, light up, and not wreck. 'Vehicular homicide, vehicular homicide' she says with an odd swish of guilt, apologizes as though a victim's family were sitting beside her and refusing to see anything punk-rock about the words as a song lyric, anything interesting about them as a point in a story. Some things happen to you, they lose their value as abstracts. Tragedies, if one is not careful, deaden the instinct for Art.

The only thing factual is that Leonard Cohen has it right: never found anything beautiful not to complain about. Even in comparison to the fact of Lucy, car-parked and staring at the windows, unlit, of the mother's house, what she thinks about Cohen is the more definable thing. How Lucy has it is: the man's dissatisfaction has produced clear lines that are physical, while the dubious meaning of Lucy being in this car - in this place, on this night, at this stage - has kind of been spit-on-sleeved at and is showing less signs of being actual, more of being merely some stain that resembles a shadow of something which no light will alter. Listening to a song, at times, the song has more concert cruciality that occupying a place. The biological reason for a brain is so that the body can have something ignoring it. 'Fair is fair, fair is fair' Lucy mutters and likes how her lips and the pace of her exhaling makes the smoke seem barber-snipped into the individual sizes and shapes of the words. Skin could have to think about what it does, blinking eyes, the squeeze and release of peristalsis - who says it makes more evolutionary sense that the body automate it? Lucy does not buy the argument. One would be more apt to survive the more parts of oneself one had to consciously command - and if consciousness could be spread out to toes and elbows and creases in love-handle flesh and hair-all-up-in-nostrils then it would be harder to damage. A thought could originate and just be ignored or - and this is better - the subconscious avenued around the body instead of kept back-burnered in the single engine that runs the whole show. How does putting everything crucial in one place that can be severed in so many places make survival-sense? The very fact that science can make the body keep bodying when the brain dies but can't make the brain brain one single more thing if the body kaputs is the hard proof anyone should need to take another long look at the finch's beak and think 'Maybe we're getting a little bit ahead of ourselves, here.' Off goes Leonard - now he's just moaning for the sake of sounding pornographic. A quiet car except for someone laughing - maybe into a telephone, maybe just to themselves - as they - though unseen - pass by somewhere back in that direction. Be sure, Lucy Jinx - be sure, be sure. Of what? Does going in here close out the day how you want it? This is the better move than back to neutral-ground, home-base? But yes - her resolve returns. Otherwise, her entire life is a tourist trip, conversations with the owner of the bed-and-breakfast as though they don't have a bottom-line with an eye glued to it in every place they could think to adhesive. And remember, Lucy - it might be just this time, only. And it might be twenty more times. And if it is twenty times more than that, even, it won't have questions in front of it - you'll just have chosen this as the place you go to at night. Some nights? No. All. The air in the neighborhood seems new, like the fence around a demolished shopfront. The walk to the front door is a zipper that's broken and which convinces you a coat doesn't need to be zipped to keep warm. Lucy's key in a lock is turned like a spot rubbed from a countertop with a wet twist of one corner of a wet enough still from before to not be rewetted hand towel.

Coat slung to the sofa back. The living-room a mess. Blanket and pillow there, but no evidence of recent use. Some sort of toys and loose sheets of paper splayed about over by the tri-level cat scratcher. Or at least Lucy thinks that's what all of that is in the bit of light glimpsing its way in from the backyard bulb left on and nudging through the winks in the slats of the lazy-drawn blinds. Now barefooted - regretting it, her soles resting tense on the tile and keeping their backs raised to the hard contact, semi-spasmed, as though she is walking with square blocks roped to her - Lucy yawns and her stomach is tight from another sensation of suddenly needing to defecate only to take a half-step further to have the sensation relieve. *Nausea* is another word that should have a rotational spelling. Any way but the right way. *Naseua. Nusaea. Anesua.* The word should feel like the word, should look like the word, looking at the word should make you feel the word - it all should commingle in a loogie of some kind, really repellant and hard to read without feeling the philosophical seasick the physical sensation always rises. And Lucy yawns another time, also quietly opening - in only of the stove-light she has switched on, too brown and reflecting off the pale-salmon appliances to really make things visible-objects, they seem easier to discern in the full blink - a package of cookies and taking three out, dividing the sandwiches of them and eating each half in two bites which might as well be one as she has a whole in her mouth by the time she swallows. Then, Lucy has her back turned and then hears a gasp and an 'Oh fuck' behind her and turns to see some slip of a thing, inconsequential as a neighbor's drapes, back-pedaling and holding one hand to flat chest - nipples tauted through sleep-shirt from recent use, no doubt. 'Hi' Lucy says, gritting teeth in an embarrassed sort of 'Dude, I really am sorry' expression. The girl is holding up her hands, though, like trying not to guffaw. She eventually sniffles and rubs her face as though washing it roughly and says 'Are you a burglar?' 'I'm just Lucy' Lucy whispers. The girl nods, wide-eyed. And Lucy is doing her best not to be over-elaborate in her taking in physical details. Even in the dark, though, the overall flush to the girl - shock aside - is unmistakable of orgasm, like the scents of a barn just five minutes after rain. 'Do you live here?' the girl asks - really doing so super a job of being caught on the sneak-back-down from Flynn that Lucy wants to commend her. 'I'm just with

Natalie' Lucy shrugs 'I just got in.' Then, Lucy does a pointing in the air between she and the girl - like paint-brushing in a rhythm of one-two one-two - and then puts her fingers to her lips with a wink. So accepting, the girl accepts, starts to turn - the panties are not even perfectly resituated, Lucy wonders if they even exactly came off - but quickly turns to say 'That does mean this is our secret?' 'I'm your alibi' Lucy nods 'as of my crawling into bed with Nat, you were sawing logs in a hardly ladylike slumber - I'll even joke about it so she believes me, you know?' Then - like it was silly to have forgotten - the girl extends a hand which Lucy shakes - rubbery whup-whup - lets go and says 'I'm Aimee, so you know. This is probably the sort of moment a first name basis is good for, right?'

'Nerd. Nerd.' Lucy pokes the mother's nose the fourth time. 'What if I was a murderer? Nerd.' The mother starts waking, bats away Lucy's hand at the next nose-tapped 'Nerd.' 'What?' 'You're a nerd.' 'That isn't something I have to be awake to know - why are you waking me up, Lucy?' 'Wasn't I supposed to?' The mother humphs her back to Lucy and makes further battings over her shoulder, only connecting with herself in limp finger drags. 'I don't care. I'm asleep.' 'You don't smell good when you're asleep' Lucy half-climbs on her 'at all.' 'Why are you here?' 'I just wanted to let you know I'm taking a shower.' 'No. You're not taking a shower, you're just being a pest. Go take a shower if that's what's so important to you.' 'Fine. Hey' - the mother doesn't respond - 'Hey' - the mother doesn't respond - 'Hey!' The mother rolls over and smacks Lucy's arm then rolls back over and casually says 'What?' 'You're a nerd' Lucy says, even as she rubs the honestly hurting arm where the mother whapped it, putting on an air of giggles, seemingly nonplussed by it all. As a last gesture of her authority, Lucy yanks the pillow out from under the mother's head and then limply drop its on top, the mother already lashing out and growling 'Piece of ice, you are a brat!' Lucy blinks and does an unobserved face of 'Whaaaa?' pretending its harder to stifle her laugh than it is. 'What did you say, just there?' 'I said you're a brat - a bully. Kids have to have assemblies at school because there are people like you - cautionary assemblies.' 'Did you say *Piece of ice?*' 'Yes.' 'Why? Is that a colloquialism from Squaresville or Dweebtown or Wallflower Boulevard or somewhere?' The mother props up on her elbows and says 'Some of us are creative. And though we do like the general sound of the Lord's name taken in vain, we'd sooner rather than later avoid a lake of hogfat heated to boil, you know?' '*Piece of Ice* is your *Jesus Christ?*' 'Yes.' '*Piece of Ice?*' 'Or *Pizza Slice.*' 'Aha.' 'Or *Pete's so nice.*' 'Do they all start with *P*s?' 'Most of them. *Just us mice!* You've never heard of these?' 'Nobody has heard of these, nerd.' The mother slumps and re-turns her back on Lucy and tells her to 'Go fiddle-stick' herself in the shower and them come to bed. 'I'm going to paddywhack myself' Lucy garbles right in the mother's ear, but the mother does not turn violent or even move. So Lucy hurt-feelings 'I thought you were nice, man - I thought you were cool. Now I feel like a medicinal-grade chump.' No response. 'I'm taking a shower then' Lucy announces in a loud voice as she pulls her shirt over her head, this rise in volume earning a Cobra-quick sit up and belly pinch from the mother who armadillos herself back to curled over, obviously taut with waiting-for-retaliation. Lucy finishes undressing while standing up and takes a peek outside at her parked car and the dumpster and discovers there are flurries of snow. Even as she looks - weird, in the fifteen second she looks! - they stop. In her opinion, the weather should be like that. It leaves too many things unknown. There could be intense rainfall localized to a single three-foot radius in the middle of a desert at any time - three-tons falling in a given day! - but no one would know, ever - it could always happen in the midst of a sandstorm, whole phenomena we'd never think to measure! Unimportant, Lucy supposes while realizing she's thrown all her clothing in the mother's laundry pile but shouldn't have because she'll need to wear it all again, in a few hours.

What is the purpose of water? Of this water? To cleanse? Says who? Says Lucy? Where'd she get that idea? It came from somewhere - or did she generate it? It just doesn't seem organic to her - is that something her mind, any mind, would come up with? It's taught. It's passed down. Water to cleanse, to clear, water to purify. But is this so? Lucy could lay semantics of *rinse* versus *wash* versus *whatsoever*, but her point is that there was someone, whoever - wherever - who first said there was a purpose to water - but why do we assume, in the face of all evidence other, that water's goal, its end, is to be used as an agent of purity? We said so? People? One of us first, then the rest? We claim dominion over water? Over our very essence we claim the role of denoter? And why do we hold to the ancient misconception 'Water cleans' when in most cases it does anything but!? We have improved? Improved upon water? We have boiled from and strained from and centrifuged from and found microscopic ways to sap from this substance its substance and lay claim to superioring - and by this to say subordinating - water!? Lucy sees the gall in this, sees the furious gibber of mad fiends going large strides too far! Wars against weather! Planting flags of Claim in the bellies of sharks! Have we gone so derange-mouthed as to turn water into a carcass, a trophy we choose the display of? We look at the vast ocean as a mistake, as an unfortunate 'Ah, yet none to drink yet none to drink!' Well, you shouldn't be on the sea! What good did it do you to begin with, your exploration!? And we look at ourselves dying and blame water for containing life that doesn't care if ours continues! And we say the things that water supports are our pestilence - Purity! - the things that water harbors are what we rage against and will extinct! This is the sound of the showerhead going silent, the creak of the knobs turning it passive, the sound of Lucy dripping from all round angles of her flesh to the it-doesn't-seem-too-often-if-ever scrubbed once-white of the tile where she stands. And, out there, Lucy knows the mother is sleeping. The sound of Lucy showering is immediately something she's not unaccustomed to. Maybe. Or maybe it is crocodile-sleep, in there. How would Lucy ever be able to tell? What indicates genuine slumber? Lucy is in no position to answer. In a way: is Lucy awake, right now? In a way: doesn't it always seem a reasonable choice to Lucy to decide that something has been a dream, a delusion, a concoction? So many things are. Impressions. Places. Opinions. Name any time in any life that any of those things stay the same? Even germs want change, even the most ra-ta-tat virus wants to advance, has ambition, has plans beyond 'Let's keep this the same and keep me the same.' 'We don't spawn because we want immortality' Lucy says in the steam of the unopened door. 'We spawn because we want to draw a line and to say *Everything before here is dead - I have made what's alive and where it's come to, things previous are going to have to be content with being reworked to my whimsy or rotting with it, same difference.*' Lucy Jinx is a Poet. And she pens the codex to everything. If anything, her words will live on. And every time they are read they are the laughter of a victimizer! They live on - and the first thing they shed was the person. Lucy Jinx? Lucy Jinx. Those are words. Two of them. Attach them to poetry, they are the first words people won't care if are forgotten. Who wrote that? Unknown. That wrote itself.

SOMETIME, FAST ASLEEP, LUCY'S LEFT arm was *sonnez les matines sonnez les matines* and sometime, maybe drifting awake a snort, the mother's lower back was *oh wither oh wither oh wither so high?* And at one point, snored to wet-spotted pillow, Lucy's elbow was *Portrait of Dr. Gachet* while in the same moment, ceiling faced, mouth unhinged, the mother's mole third up from her left hip-middle was *La Mort Du Papillon De Nuit*. Sometime else, well, Lucy, just at the out-of-place part of her hair - just right there and just then - was *put him in the cabin with the captain's daughter put him in the cabin with the captain's daughter early in the morning* while perhaps ten minutes after that, in the same time there was the off-putting sound of swallowing phlegm that collects heavy while slumberers do slumberings, the mother's shadow cast into her shirt from the side curve of this or that nipple was *and nothing strange a single hurt color and an arrangement*. Lucy Jinx might have dreamt a little and it was *The Gashlycrumb Tinies* and the mother might have dreamt ten-percent less and it could have been *whose epitaph is for o for o the hobby horse is forgot*. There are many things Lucy's sighs could have been, still counting as sighs though asleep themselves: *There's No Such Thing As A Dragon* and

*The Year at Maple Hill Farm* and *on Blueberry Hill where I found you*. Could it be that the mother's motion at the change in pace - what is this unregulation in sleep - of breathing here and there, here and there, over the course of six hours denoted *gonna walk on down the street just like Bulldog Drummond* or *Inspector Javert, conscience is a higher law*? It could be so believed that three inches from the rough of the always bending hinge of her heel, Lucy Jinx is *something hesitated in the sky when I met you* or *Nacer de Nuevo*. No one was there to see, of course, and both were sound asleep, but if one imagines someone there to see - or imagines at least one or the other awake - it could be imagined that the mother's freckle that is halfway engulfed in the up-line of her nostril is *Miss Mary Mack Mack Mack all dressed in black black black* and that - if one were to continue imagining as previously stated - then a certain shadow, not cast but rather lazily drooped, in the contour of Lucy Jinx's spine was, to a *T*, Luigi Alamanni, in a whisper as he wrote, writing *Vaucluse, ye hills and glades and shady vale*. Many things in sleep, many things - a belief of Lucy's and of many others - courses of her which are never awake, just live in her waking thoughts, revealing their forms not really not really, like this: the pad of the middle joint of her third finger itches for a full eighteen minutes but goes unscratched just as though it is *the town looked on in silence as little Willy, carrying Searchlight, walked the last ten feet and across the finish line*. And perhaps, it can be thought - Lucy might think it - the mother is much the same, if not the same, and that sometime while they slept - and maybe at a point where the mother's skin somewhere was raised to that weak, damped paper of perspiration from other warming skin touching to it - the mother was *Sana Sana Culito de Rana, si no sanas hoy sanaras manana*.

All well and good - but now both Lucy Jinx and the mother are awake. They just wake, are awake, beside each other. Hardly a sound passes unheard by Lucy - she assumes there are some things she doesn't hear, does not want to overstate matters in her thoughts - and neither of them shift or drape-to or address each other. It's a serenity. And Lucy also not wanting to move because it will jar from her more the rising urge that she has to pee - what an undignified way that would be to end this kind of first-moment-like-this. Is it that, Lucy? Is this a kind of first-moment? It does feel like one - the way she feels present and planning to already be running away, remembering intently as she blots at forgetting. To break her growing unease - is it unease? at what? - Lucy says 'It's funny how people think showing, in cinema, a brief but wide-angle shot of devastation or something does the same as expressing that devastation in words. The opposite is true. I think it's because some people assume visuals are more powerful than words while, really, words can express so much with so few. It takes a lot of pictures to express what just a handful of words can cause the mind to silently elaborate into images forever - forever.' The mother coughs, says 'Did you hear me cough?' and Lucy giggles and says she 'heard it, but not exactly' so the mother coughs again and then says 'Give me an example.' Lucy Jinx then says this - hands gestured above both she and the mother to set a blank space to fill: 'This is a play - blank stage, two characters walk on, become brightly lit, emphasizing how much nothing-else there is to see. Minor-image, the minorest manageable. The first person says, as though carrying on from some previous talking we were not privy to *You speak as though there are still houses here* and makes a gesture around at the pitch. Then the second person says back *You speak as though there never were any*. We see it all. We see it all.' Lucy sees it all. She sees it all. The mother is breathing and Lucy thinks she sees it all, the same. The mother must see it all, the same. 'In a film they would maybe show a wide-shot of the bombed-out village or what have you - or the very-aged-ruins or even just a long expanse of nothing. It doesn't express near enough! Not near enough nothing! And even if the same words - the dialogue I just did, those words - were spoken after this image and amongst other images of the town's remains around them, they would lose their impact, the words. Words are meant for the sightless. I think they were thought up in the soup, you know? They are so much earlier than eyes - no one looked around and named things, the very word for *Sight* came before it, paved the way for it to be recognized. Nothing is named by being looked at - or after - words live in our blind-brains, they are the pulping of the fingertips of our blood as it chatters about. You know?' The mother tells Lucy to do some more of the play, yawning, and says 'I was actually digging it. I mean, I agree too, with what you're saying - but more important: what do they say next?' Lucy says 'There is a pause and then the second man speaks again and he says *It's the same as how you drink water like there will never be more*. And the first man laughs and says *And you?* And the second man says *I drink it as though I ran out months ago!* It's the difference. It's the difference.'

Why has Lucy stayed in bed though the mother is up and pulling on more clothes? Of course, the first reason is that the mother - perhaps - needs to see Flynn off - and Aimee, too - perhaps needs to see to it he remembers something - or there may be a ritual of breakfast together in the morning after nights Aimee stays over or what have you. But the second reason is more the reason - Lucy is, at this moment, saying 'Oh I'll be up in a sec' when the mother smiles from the door and says 'You can get some more sleep if you don't have to be anywhere' - and that reason is this: a few minutes ago, in all of that talking, Lucy had very nearly called the mother *Ariel*. Technically, she had. Technically. The thought had formed with the word - the name - attached to it and the feeling was 'I am speaking with Ariel' - in fact, in that moment, it felt as though the entire conversation had been with Ariel. But this feeling is not an accurate portrait, overall, of how Lucy feels, on reflection - it is just that Lucy had managed to not say the name - or any name - had just made the statement at a - to the mother, at least - unnoticeably slowed pace. So what? So what? So what? Are we supposed to pretend all of a sudden that this means something? People likely say the wrong names all the time - and even hear the wrong names without noticing when people are talking to them! How many wrong names has Lucy been called? No - this isn't helping. No - this isn't giving Lucy any less the creeps. What does she fear? The mother saying *Who's Ariel?* Naw. Lucy overwhelmingly thinks the mother must assume and keep mum on all manner of thoughts and opinions she harbors about Lucy. It would be unthinkable otherwise. Added to which, any number of simplistic pivots get Lucy out of that. 'Did I say *Ariel?* She's a friend - I was thinking I have to meet her, later.' Or: 'That's funny - probably because I talked to her about this same thing once - I must have been remembering.' Or just whatever. Whatever. Lucy hears some laughter downstairs and excruciatingly shifts around until she is sitting in a phlegmy spill over the bedside, her feet at half-cramp, flags stiff from frozen-rain, doing their best to give, regardless, some semblance of a flowing to the will of the wind. Ariel's name is the same kind of danger as the ring Lucy gave to - she slows in her thoughts, part-joking, squinting her eyes, making sure she has the name right - Samantha. The ring is just for Samantha. Ariel's name is just for Ariel. 'Life is made of moving parts' Lucy stands, sits right away, reminding herself. And to the sink moves Lucy, like a tooth ripe to fall out, her body a jiggle as though a deposit held to firm ground by just a strand or two of tissue that is weakening under even the minor dissolvent weight of saliva. Water to her face. And she uses the mother's toothbrush and then dries it very thoroughly on a hand-towel, paranoid and testing the dryness after a minute, grinning in the direction of the cord to the blow-dryer - the blow-dryer itself must be on the floor between the small bureau and the sink-side, likely sprinkled in the same beige foundation that inch-thicks all surfaces and closed-containers and pouches of toiletries. Lucy uses some floss, as a joke, because when else has she ever and so what could the point be to doing it one time? Lucy opens the medicine cabinet, selects one of the pill-bottles at random and dry swallows two of whatever is inside. There she is, after. Flat as a mirror with no one looking in it, she imagines, is how flat she looks when she looks.

Lucy does her bowing reintroduction to the mother Barnum-and-Bailying her to Flynn when she reaches the bottom stair. And Flynn reacts as though this is the first time he has seen Lucy since forever ago. A wink in that. The same as the wink in Flynn's introduction of Aimee and Aimee's saying 'Hi' as though not having the slightest clue there was any such thing as a Lucy Jinx before that every moment of handshake - Lucy cannot help but laughing when, only just now, she wonders how clean, exactly, had Aimee's hand been when she'd shook it just hours previous. But Lucy - mostly to not ruin the comradery between she and Aimee, the last thing she'd want is to make the kid think she was blowing the gaff - pivots the laugh directly at the mother and accuses the mother of using her in a regular Von Trapp Family way. 'Am I supposed to do a choreographed little routine and sleepy-pie up the stairs backward now?' Aimee seems to get the reference and Flynn gives her an eye like 'Oh do explain - I want to know as well!' the two of them kiss-mouthy at either side of the far end of the table now, whispers the size of sneezing whiskers. And now, Lucy standing shoulder-to-shoulder with the mother, the mother whispers 'That's the girl I mentioned - the sofa-dweller.' 'I noted her as I came in, yes. Good you had warned me because from the snorting sounds of her I would have assumed she was your little wart-hog self, awaiting me.' The mother does a tsk-hiss sound and makes a joke how she is offended that Lucy would think so little of her snoring. 'I'm not some punk kid' the mother announces to the room, bringing a plate of microwaved bacon and putting it on the table with a cartoonish gesture of backing away before dogs combatively violent for it. The mother, though, had palmed a piece for herself which she breaks in half and hands one half to Lucy - the taste not pleasant at all when mixed with the remaining granules of toothpaste which Lucy, in her hurry, really didn't get off her back-teeth so well. 'Is this a school day?' Lucy asks, glancing at the microwave clock which shows the word *Pause* and the oven-clock which shows the word *Reset*. 'And what in Hell kind of way do you bastards keep time in this house?' Aimee finds this uproarious and does an unnecessary covering-her-mouth 'Oh-my-God' and Flynn laughs overtop 'You know I told my mom how many bad words I learned from you in our brief tenure together, Lucy.' 'Don't call Lucy *Lucy* - call her *Auntie Jinx* or something to make her feel on precarious ground.' '*Auntie*' Flynn says in what must be supposed to be some certain accent or impersonation 'taught me to curse like a sailor when I was knee-high to a newt, you know?' Aimee must know what this means, the voice, because - though she also slaps at Flynn's arm to show her solidarity with Lucy - she laughs in a burst that only getting a specific in-joke can suckle forth. 'It is a school day, yes' the mother says 'but these two ride the short-bus and so can linger a bit longer than most - the county doesn't like to burden its needier youths with obligations like waking up and stuff.' 'What do you do, Lucy?' Aimee asks, still chewing even though she just swallowed a mouthful of milk before speaking - 'What must that taste like?' Lucy thinks, holding back an expression of primeval horror. 'I'm a Poet and an all-around Big-Shot, young lady' Lucy says 'I just go around being what everyone else can't match up to. Don't worry' she adds on, dismissive hands with fingers moving like sprinkling fairy-dust 'you'll never be asked to measure up to the likes of me - just keep soldiering on as you do.'

Lucy announces she will do the dishes and bumps her hips to the mother's hips, telling her 'Shoo shoo, go shower or whatever - you gotta work at the mausoleum or whatever it is, right?' But the mother doesn't want Lucy doing the dishes - 'Or anything else that will make you seem like some sort of indentured servant' the mother says, giving Lucy a kiss and then breaking from the jokey-tone to a straight 'Thank you for actually coming over.' Lucy keeps to the har-har though, opting to riff how it wasn't ever any question as she has been living out of her car for weeks. 'Which isn't so bad' she adds 'but try doing that while also running your Private Eye business out of the back seat! Clients, they start to notice the laundry piling up - there's only so many places to put it and only so many places for them to awkwardly look around to while I tell them what I've found out about their stray wives or whatever.' 'Your life sounds pretty shaggy-dog' the mother nods 'but I still don't want you doing the dishes. Seriously.' 'Well, with you in your condition I'm going to, as I've already said.' Shit. Shit! Blip. Blip. The world shakes and makes a sound like a flimsy sheet of aluminum being waved. 'What condition?' the mother says, voice showing she is on the defensive for whatever underhanded little snipe Lucy is going to lambast. 'Being gaga - having me back in your life - don't pretend, Natalie - ah, don't pretend. I could make you do your own dishes or anything, now - I have so much power!' Did that work? Did it? Seems to have. The mother just rolls her eyes a gloopy well-aren't-you-hilarious and says 'Just don't actually start the dishwasher or anything. *A* - there aren't enough dishes and *B* - we don't have any detergent and *C* - I'll be in the shower because you got you smell all over me - stay on your side, tomorrow night.' Lucy chuckles - over-jovial, mostly because she doesn't want the moment to have to extend - and listens to the mother as she ascends the stairs saying 'Or whenever you next slink in - tomorrow, whenever' and then some others words Lucy doesn't hear. Of course: Lucy doesn't want to do the dishes. She actually kind of really doesn't want to. And audibly growls when she see she will have to empty the washer first. So why did you offer? 'I didn't offer, you offered' Lucy contrarians. Well, why did I offer? 'Why did you offer!?' Lucy jabs. I didn't offer, you offered! 'Why would I do that!?' Why would I? 'One of us did - and I think we both deserve some kind of an explanation.' And so on and so on, the task of emptying the washer not taking much time with this distraction and - look there! - it is already stocked up with the new dirties - job well done, hands dusted and all. Now this is Lucy Jinx: standing in the mother's kitchen in the clothes Lucy Jinx wore all day yesterday, waiting for the mother to finish her shower and to come back downstairs so she can say 'Goodbye' before simply leaving. Not that that was discussed. 'It's not like' she points out expertly 'I said *Hello* when I showed up, exactly.' Eh. No, she did - you did, Lucy - she realizes - poked the mother awake and all. Fuck.

962 / PABLO D'STAIR

'I'm always so bloody courteous' she says in her best Basil Fawlty. Then she does it in the same tone Jack Lucas delivered the 'Forgive me' line in *The Fisher King*: 'I'm so bloody courteous' she says - *So* pronounced *Soooooooo* and *Courteous* pronounced *Curt-he-Us*.

The living-room floor fits Lucy's back. The sounds from the floor above, the shower on-offing, the faucet on-offing, stresses to carpet and the boards beneath on the other side of the ceiling groaning - that was a towel and that was a drawer opened, shutted, that is the faucet, again - and now the would-be-horrendously-loud-up-there-down-here-it-is-pipe-whisper whir of the hair-dryer drying hair - it is all a kind of auditory stop-motion, Lucy hears it in hiccoughing tick-tick-tick progressions, the illusion of fluidity, the reality of photographs can never be stilled so and tapped through to have grace. For a chuckle, Lucy does a motion like making a snow-angel, feels this is just what someone would expect of a character called Lucy Jinx in a film about Lucy Jinx - one of those cinematic moments that have no corollary in real life, one of those things which if you ever saw someone doing them would feel magical but disquieting, give you second thoughts in spades, but that when seen in a dark apartment on digitized celluloid you smile at and sigh internally and think to yourself 'Exactly, yes - I knew someone like that' or 'I would love someone like that.' Now Lucy lays, spread *X*, like she'd done a belly flop, the carpet the air behind her, the blank space above her the fist of the water connecting. How long until the mother will come down? Is she even thinking Lucy is still there? As though in a restroom, Lucy coughs to indicate her presence, not wanting the new arrival to be too boisterous in their voiding. Then: she has propped up and wonders if this is what it would feel like for a cork to be bottle-necked or if it's what it would be like for a cork to feel itself pierced, twined to the gut by a corkscrew, and tugged from its comfort. What about corks? Lucy has never considered whether they feel a bottle is home or a bottle a prison-term. But it must be one or the other! 'Just look at a cork' Lucy says as though her beginning to speak aloud will hurry the mother down the stairs, make her feel summoned 'are we to think of them as indifferent?' But what does Lucy know about a cork? What does she know about a bottle? What does she know about the tug of a toothy corkscrew? Where did this swell of arrogant know-it-all come from? Was it inborn? Did Lucy have a choice? Why can't she lower herself to the humility of not assuming she knows the soul and mythology of every inanimate thing? Because isn't it true that if she believes any of these nonsenses she spews - in a nutshell, if she believes dead objects aren't really so, but are as conscious and alive as the burp of her heart - then she must also admit she has no reason to claim any in-depth knowledge of them. She has never looked in to things, never researched! Lucy just uses the physical world to throw her bloated, wordy weight around in! And if she knows that a cork, for example, has no thought, no mind, no soul - well then why in the name of God does Lucy spend so much time thinking about such things and talking about such things? Is she talking about something else? Her life a series of always-the-wrong-word, leading to some Wonderland scrapple of Creation Myths and End of Days? 'What do I know about you, ceiling?' Lucy asks and hears, through the ceiling, a toilet flush she attributes to it, knowing she shouldn't but can't act on how she shouldn't - same as she never can.

What do you think the chances are that I'm insane? Lucy looks at the mother. She almost says 'What do you think the chances are that I'm insane?' The mother notices the almost question. Lucy says 'Do you see a therapist?' The mother nods, but with eyes set like 'Now you tell me why you're asking.' 'What's that like?' According to the mother it is like such-and-such. 'But, I mean - that's good?' The mother gives an eloquent version of what could have more simply been stated 'Yes, it's good.' Lucy sucks in on her lower-lip, curling it and compressing the curl until painful. 'Do you want to see a therapist?' 'What?' Lucy had heard the question and her 'What?' is not a playact that she hadn't - no - her 'What?' is a comical 'What?' as in 'What!? What could ever have given you that idea?' Also note: the mother is gathering her things to head out the door, it is Lucy doing the lingering around as though she will stay - and she knows if she loiters she will just be left. There is a key is Lucy's pocket. There is a key to this house, again. Time doesn't know a thing about time - about increments' beginnings or ends! We - people - we say time separates things from each other - but Time doesn't see it that way. What a misunderstanding! The mother is gazing at Lucy, who must be showing signs of this epiphany or something. 'We make big mistakes about all kinds of things.' The mother - bag now shoulder-slung-at-hip with momentum to exit but holding the pose, all motion kept potential energied, building, building - nods and even though Lucy knows the mother is thinking that Lucy's comment touched back on what the mother must think is a genuine chat about therapy and therapists - what an awful chat that would be! - Lucy continues - let the mother think what she wants, same as anyone! 'Time, for instance.' 'Time?' the mother asks, going so far as to move to the open door of the hallway bathroom and to stand there, checking her already several-times-checked appearance. 'Yes, Time. Someone tells us what it is, we go with that. Since we're little or whatever. And we are kind of told how - all the way back - people measured it or kept track of it - but that is faulty to say! Do you see what I mean?' The mother doesn't really and takes a posture of relaxing to the wall, maybe her last five minutes of not having to actually hurry out the door. 'You can build a sun-dial, for example, to keep track of how many times the sun comes up and how long shadows get or whatever, without thinking about it in terms of Time. You can scratch things on a wall - sun sun sun sun moon moon moon moon - and just be keeping track of how many times you saw those things. If I drive along and count - you know? - lampposts, I am not thinking in terms of Time!' The mother is certain she understands all of this but - no, no! - this is all just the preamble, let Lucy set her mind at ease on that count. 'So then, someone comes up with Increments and Measures and all the tickity-tockety that we pass along and that is what we call Time - duration, measure - and then we say what Time does and how it interacts with us, but that is all our invention! You see? Someone made that up the same way someone made anything up. But what if that's not what Time is?' The mother is looking and looking and has to go. 'Penicillin both always was penicillin and not - last thing I'm saying, sorry, last thing. It always was just exactly what it is - but now that we have a use for it we say it Is That Use and decide how to use it, according to that. Same thing with Time.' 'Same thing with time' the mother says and smiles - stupid flirty smile, Lucy's not flirting, she's flying! - and Lucy goes 'Exactly, but yeah' - apology hands - 'you have to go - and I'm leaving soon.' 'Take your time' the mother says and 'Oh man' Lucy is allowed to snarl - but the mother is allowed to laugh not knowing the snarl's a proper snarl not a smooch.

Now what? The house is the exact shape of that thing never picked up from the corner you don't quite look at enough to know what it is until one day, quite on accident, you do and are surprised. Are you satisfied with that, Lucy? Is that the description of the house? To whom it may concern: Lucy is just fine with it all. And this is a hollow spot in a creek-bed where Lucy could hide - an odd pocket of air formed out of a lucky falling of rocks that stays dry and noisy of the womb for the flow of cold and writhing with life and death in the currents around it. Lucy just paces the living-room and sits at the piano and arthritises her fingers, gouts them into what she hopes are the claws that somehow her mind has retained memory enough of to sound like Rachmaninoff when she weighs them down to the keys. Why, that is nothing at all like Rachmaninoff! That was hardly even a sound - if there were justice it would be crossed from the list of what deserves such a designation. What about this? What about this? Lucy knows the keys were around here and that her hands were something like this - she could just go through all the permutations imaginable and eventually hit it! That must be possible! This? This? This? 'Bah' she grarhs and does a very weak and very slow trill. Then she does a faster one - thumb and third finger - but even it is not very fast. What is the point of a piano if one cannot just play it without education or memory? If someone invented an instrument that anyone could just play - an instrument one could intuit melody from - that would be progress! Pianos and cellos and steel-drums - steel drums! Jesus, those somehow get to count as music! explain that to Lucy, please! - are all so counterintuitive the inventors of them ought be ashamed! Surely, the keys did not need to be arranged in octaves, little eight-sets one after the other. It's just strings and hammers! Make the notes arranged in some more elegant way and odds would be that striking here and here and here, randomly, would produce a fine and interesting tune - dumb-luck would count for so much! As it is, the very structure and cleanness only invites dissection and then working-in-confines - no sense of sprightliness, Hell even improvisation is learned! That's what bugs Lucy - she applauds at herself. 'Even improvisation is learned!' She stands and repeats it several times over and is done with this house. But in reality, she just moves to the sofa - then to her coat for cigarettes then back to the sofa - and lights up and crosses foot-over-foot like that's where they've always been supposed to go, puzzle complete. Not even a hideaway - the smoke is the color of chalkboard slate underneath erased chalk - this house could be Home. It was, once before - or had been just about to have been, anyway. Now the smoke is the color of an ivory button down at the bottom of an unlighted drawer. No one will ever come to make Lucy leave. No one would ever question her being here. Never. Not that - now the smoke is the color of the lighter shadows in the bends of a crumpled letter, discarded - Lucy had not had her share of places she could have been, stayed, and never been shooed from. 'Daffodil bulbs instead of eyes' she T.S. Eliots, grinning smoke that is the color of a grin covered in dribbled smoke.

The last straw is her starting to drift off - this gets Lucy to her feet, into coat, out the door, within two minutes, rushed and rather irate. Did she leave the cigarette stub in a cup on the floor? 'So what?' she hisses. Should she have aired out the house? 'Oh no' she fans herself, Southern Belle 'whatever shall I do?' And now in the confines of the car - it is a lovely morning, also, and the sound, distant, of the ball that man is throwing striking the ground before his dog is upon it and trotting it back is quite lovely, like what a heartbeat is trying for but cannot quite pronounce - Lucy's mood shoe-shines, quite neatly. All-in-all, yesterday and this morning - so Today, so far - have to be considered a great success! If Lucy had bothered to have planned any of it it would have gone according to plan, no way to say otherwise - no way to say otherwise! So it is with a smugness like wiping hands on thighs after pouring a mix from box into a bowl to be stirred that Lucy backs out of her parking spot and turns out onto the road. The radio has one woman interviewing another about the evolution of some particular mental-illness - moving from Taboo, to Theory, to Treatable-with-a-pill. The tone seems triumphant, but Lucy is not so sure. That a clump of something swallowed could alter the entire presentation of a person doesn't make a person seem all that complicated. If Lucy were a cynic, she'd say 'It's no different than saying I invented a way to bash in your head and it's called *this candlestick*' but that seems a bit adolescent - and surely making a pill to treat whatever this pill is treating is a bit more complex than bludgeoning! 'But will it seem complex in two hundred years?' That should be the interviewer's next question. Lucy figures the interviewer knows it too, but just isn't bothering - and because of this, Lucy imagines the interviewer thinks little of the interviewee and so Lucy thinks little of the interviewee. But it doesn't matter, because in a line of traffic backed up by this traffic-light set to blink-yellow, Lucy decides she will spend the entire day in edits of her poems. And while thinking that - exactly then, a practical tango with the thought! - the telephone vibrates in her coat pocket and - scootching forward another car-length - Lucy sees it is a text-message from Milos. *Though I can well imagine how indispensable a quantity you are - is there any way you can beg off work to come over here? I have a bit of a problem and need to speak to someone who is morally ambiguous and not likely to want to hear both sides of a story.* A polite honk behind her, Lucy tosses the phone to the passenger seat - it slips over the front, onto the floor, and while she moves to get it another not-quite-as-polite honk and she mea-culpa-mea-culpas a wave at her windshield - while making eye-contact with the windshield of the car behind her in the rearview - and moves forward two car-lengths, sighing. Her turn through the intersection, Lucy forgets to take the turn and now has to go straight all the way until the next shopping-center because she is too uncertain in her ability to do a tight three-point turn on this narrow road and too timid - or frankly terrified! - to pull into one of these Podunk driveways just to maneuver a one-eighty. Look! Look there! Someone bought a hand-crafted sign that says *Trespassers will be Gator'd* - in stone with moss on it, the letters chiseled and painted in what likely was once blood red and now is kind of bloody-nose brown.

And onward to home or onward to Milos - she still could go either way. And thought into thought and thought into thought. This is what most of life amounts to and it's probably too late to do much about it. By the time one is ninety-nine, there's little point curing them of cancer - at least let them go by what defined them! Naw. Lucy finds that thought unsophisticated. Everything is cancer by the time you're ninety-nine, anyway. The air, your bones, the fit of the shoes around your feet that probably aren't really shoes anymore just cloth you call shoes because at that point you call things whatever you want! Lucy, in a way - she sees a horse running a circle in a fenced-in yard, no person there to see it but her, no point to the activity, but it is still running by the time she passes out of sight of it - is very envious of people who live to be one-hundred-and-four or nine or one-hundred-fifteen. What a state of knowing you-are-relevant-to-no-one you must enter into! A realm of self-understanding and ultimate inside-outing of reference. Any college student knows the history you lived through better than you! You have nothing to add but a largely ignored footnote! That part of History is finished. That part you remember doesn't need a memory, anymore. Words have gulped it. 'Hell, we don't even pay attention to old film footage, really' Lucy says 'we look at it but it never seems to prove anything. We watch images captured by early film and always kind of doubt them - they seem a put-on, a picture of something that just couldn't be exactly how it looks, plus what was a camera doing there anyway?' Milos. Fine. Milos, then. This is where on the road she must decide and she picks Milos. Where are her poems gonna go? No place. Even if she burned her every copy, now, they are preserved places she will never know about. Here is what Lucy Jinx does know, however: *Yesterday* should be a shorter-pronounced word than *Today* and so should *Tomorrow* be. Self-evident why, so she doesn't bother to explain. Whomsoever decided that *Today* - the endless-state - should be a shorter-said word either didn't understand Words or Today! Lucy shivers and discovers her air-conditioning is on. But she doesn't change it, just gives the orange-lit button a look of disapproval, the absent-minded knob turned in to the blue stenciled-arc instead of the red just seeming deserving of pity. The brightness of the day gives everything the quality of walking past parked cars after a swim, eyes green-licked and chlorine scented, skin feeling drowned but still having to function. Stuck now behind a mail-truck - the female carrier giving a Howdy-do! nod as she walks the path mailbox to mailbox - Lucy hesitant-but-eventually turns into the oncoming lane to go around. And a wave, again, from the carrier as she passes, which Lucy grins bent-paperclip in return to, grin sticking and the inside of her cheek by her back teeth feeling canker-sore. There must have been civilizations that decided against fire. They must have left the planet already, shaking their heads at the dimwits who ruined themselves with warmth and cooked meat! 'Wisdom is shivering' thinks Lucy while shivering and eventually speaks out 'bodies incubating genius bacilli that are cooked off, boiled to the skins, eradicated as temperatures rise - and what ones do survive soon enough starve for not having bellies full of uncooked flesh, the germs and viral parasites within it the gazelle they stalk to broil and char, dehydrate and preserve, and the mud they sanitize for use in mortar-and-bricking their civilizations. Comfort makes us want to stay. Only freezing will ever flee us.'

'LET ME ASK YOU, MILOS' - Milos is wearing a suit, red blazer and green pants, bone-yellow shirt and a tie of black that looks like a raven coughed it up and lost track of it on its sleeve - 'when did it get heavy, life? For me - I don't care about you' Lucy Jinx asides, separate dialogue to it - 'for me, when did life get so heavy? Can't I just flap my arms and have it away, like a song lyric or a guitar chord? Do you see how simple those make things? And we hiccough our applause! As though they have summed up life when really they just avoided saying almost one-hundred-percent of life! Chomped out one tasty mouthful to swallow and we applaud the ignoring-the-rest we allow ourselves.' Preeminent in his slouch, Milos smacks cigarette package to his palm more than he probably needs to before taking one out and Lucy eyes him the hard-line, not sure is he making a joke of her talk about applause or just absent-minded and enjoying the stare-down which now he sticks his tongue out at, toddler-shy. 'Or like in a book' Lucy continues, beginning as a mumble, shaking her head though, stopping, because Lucy no longer sees herself as a book. Well, wait. Well, wait. Let's not go that far, Lucy. Or if she does see herself as a book it is as one read and the details of forgotten - the voice of it, the flow, the way it was alive when it was still unread being pawed at, revealed. 'The sort of book I am' she snaps- and to snap-snaps at Milos and he - thinking it is what she was meaning, she supposes - tosses her a cigarette and then a lighter when she catches the cigarette and - as long as she has it - snaps-snaps at him again for the matches which she prefers to use for lighting 'is the sort on a grumbly little shelf, squat and not-quite-in-a-corner, untouched in a waiting-room, the sort mixed in with Word Finds and infant puzzles, the kind come there to that shelf from being bought from a weather-beaten bin on discount - the kind not even chosen, simply lifted with whichever others and brought along as a lot, mildew scented pages someone will inhale and sigh because of, misremembering the actual way a spread book is supposed to be breathed in in nostalgia - or else just not knowing the correct scent, a book only pantomime-admired by pretenders!' 'Your question is *When did it get like this?*' 'Yes!' Milos shrugs and kicks the boot that is in the middle of the entryway, not hard enough it causes much clatter when it hits the umbrella-stand that isn't so much an umbrella-stand as a thing without any umbrellas ever once having been in it, something stuffed with mismatched gloves, stiff-from-filth scarves, and a pair of tennis-shoes Lucy remembers the night Milos threw up on, outside. 'You know how I remember life, Lucy Jinx?' 'You only remember it? I envy you!' 'I am enviable.' 'How do you remember life, Milos?' 'I reduce everything down to one memory of my own life I know no one else will recall but which I marked and which to this day I can still be raised to a tumult about.' 'From childhood?' Lucy wants to know for verification, for a hint at how to do with life whatever Milos is talking about, because at this moment - despite all the ominous of why she has been invited over - he seems light as an insect falling from a tree, a living object which height and falling don't affect, which will land on the ground as just another place it belongs - the opposite of Lucy falling out of a tree. Milos nods emphatically and seems just about to tell her something when his phone rings and he grabs it, growling, saying 'You see what I mean!?'

So what is going on with Milos? Well, first and foremost - and he admitted as much almost as soon as Lucy arrived, very donkey-browed and tiptoe about it, like he knew summoning her was a trick he'd pulled - it is nothing that Lucy's amorality will enter into, nothing that, in fact, will require action on her part outside of being the muse to Milos' tantrumic ranting. It is a family situation. Something to do with his younger brother making a cock-up of himself and then having to tap in to some funds which were set aside for their mother's elder-care. It all sounds awful, really. And it sounds like the last thing Lucy Jinx is particularly set to proffer comments on. Again: which is why she was summoned. Milos is the only vaudevillian to whom Lucy could ever be considered the I'm-not-Rappaport and that is how the conversation goes for the rest of the night, really: straight-man Jinx, uproarious violence outpouring from Milos in the form of an almost tap-dance mixed with moments heavy like he was suddenly slapped by an overturned bucket of water, stiff-shivering and rickety-walking off stage with exactly the dripping wet and aghast look of ungodly indignity a cat would have if so splashed and standing on hind leg in front of a room of knee-slapping gawkers. For example, Milos says: 'My mother doesn't even have real knees - how can you swindle someone without even real knees! Goddamnit, you know I used to look at fucking baseball cards with this little grifter - and I even had to comfort him when he thought his first orgasm meant he'd broken something and didn't know if he should tell our dad to make a doctor's appointment! She doesn't have knees, Lucy! That doesn't get less expensive as you deteriorate - I can promise you that! My own brother doesn't respect my mom has to consider in her budget how goddamn expensive it is not to have actual bones!' Lucy appreciates Milos' delivery of all of these lines - and she knows he brought her here to appreciate the humor in his anguish, the comedic-chops of an anger he would cut off a limb to unburden himself of. So Lucy laughs and asks if he wants her to get her recorder from the car so they can make a kind of documentary of this all. 'You'll think it's funny too, one day Milos. You'll die, too - and you'll kind of be pissed off that your mom's death is funnier than yours will be, but it'll also amuse you that you were the one giving the best performance.' 'You ever hated everyone, Lucy?' She nods and says 'Yes' very honestly. But, we have to be careful: Lucy, though she heard him, assumed he meant 'You ever hated anyone?' in the singular or the, at worst, contained plural - and she wonders if he now is assuming, though she agreed fast, that he has said 'You ever hated anyone?' too. And she is sure they both wonder if they need to mention how, even though they weren't responding to what they heard, if they were responding to that they would have said the same thing - so what is the point? The raucous ravings are laced with facts. Lucy especially likes how Milos explains the phrase *Coronary atherosclerosis due to lipid rich plaque.* He explains it like a pamphlet which can break it down to three illustrations that are softly drawn to seem fruit-snack succulent, colored almost to invite a tongue to give the cheap paper a lick. 'Do you know our blood is basically sand - it's just moving quick enough to not be, Lucy? If you heated our blood enough, man, it would be glass.'

Which is not to say that they do not make plans. Murder plans. The sort of murder plans that radio-shows from decades previous were built around. The sort that buttressed literature and cinema up in to something people figured they needed to pay attention to. Perfect Murders. Most plans involve making it seem like an accident or a simple-crime-taking-a-tragic-turn. This is the most obvious starting point for both of them, as they are convinced that statistically eighty-percent of deaths are, in fact, murders and that the big joke is how people in the Arts and in Politics - and in a few other positions-of-stature - perpetuate the myth that 'Murder happens relatively little' while of course saying that 'this little is a lot' meaning 'relative to how much worse it could be' none-the-wiser that the reality is it's even worse than worse-than-that and isn't doing them anything but favors they're in the dark about by its being so. Milos has it as thus, streamlined for minds less linguistically elastic: 'If people knew how often murder happened and how easy it was they would stop finding anything wrong with it - and if they stop finding anything wrong with it they would stop finding anything interesting about it and a lot of money would stop going to a lot of coffers, man.' Lucy seconds this motion. It's shocking how easily the two of them could get away with it, too! Provided nothing happened accidental to get them red-handed, it breaks down like this: Lucy does it or Milos does it and each serve as the other's alibi. After that, it's just frosting and little decoratives put on tippy-top the thing. Milos' brother lives in another state. So one or the other of he or Lucy drive out that way and lay in wait with a blunt object or a sharp object and splat or sluice-open the shyster bastard, then, quick-as-a-wink, start driving back. What details? It all depends. Knives aren't rare. They buy one and wait awhile and wait until the brother is unobserved and filet him. It doesn't take long. They start laughing, mocking this reaction in the human mind to always assume there will be pesky-eyed witness or some simple way they will be caught out. 'Oh the fantasies not-wanting-to-actually-kill can concoct' laughs Lucy. Milos could even show up at his brother's apartment unannounced, be let in, kill him in the first minute, then just hang around awhile before he leaves. There is nothing hard about this. Or: Milos could stay the night, unlock the door to let Lucy in while the brother sleeps, Lucy does the wet-work, and that'll make it seem like the killer had no idea Milos was even in the house! Since Milos didn't do the crime, there will be no forensics tying him to it! They will have all the time in the world to make it look like something deeply personal - or else just seem Byzantine in its monstrous, random, unspecific specifics! Lucy elaborates that Milos could actually rent a motel room for two nights, stay the first night in it, then tell the brother he is going to crash at the brother's place the second night, then leave when the brother passes out, letting Lucy in, then Lucy will wait until Milos is back at the motel to do the killing so his alibi is solid and then will wait until Milos comes back over, finding the door unlocked, at which point Lucy will slip out and Milos will find the corpse and Lucy will do whatever - something unspecified - before going back home. 'It's not like anyone is going to suspect me' Milos says. 'Especially if we wait until after my mother dies - penniless and hoodwinked by her second-born. If we do this in three years, it's not even a trick, man!' Lucy likes the sound of it. She's bloodthirsty, she says. She says she wishes she had a pickpocket brother to murder, too. Family seem like the easiest to kill.

But this little oasis of life-about-a-brother's-murder isn't without its lines of paint chipping to patterns, chinks in exactly the shape of the veins and sinews that tint Lucy under the façade of her skin and those invisible tendrils which are the even truer network of fissures that exist as part of someone even when limbs and flesh are removed. Here is someone named Lucy Jinx in a bathroom at Milos' house and the facts stand twofold. One: an insect, a centipede of some kind - soft, light, legs sniffling the basin the ways hairs on a fluffy cat's tail would brush the wall or a wood floor would move, the thing is a miniature fluffy-cat-tail given agency - is being flushed, without ceremony, down the sink drain by an endless torrent of the tap Lucy opens - and she is uneasy with each second the bug is somehow managing to chug-chug those legs to keep from the gravity-gulp of the water sucking it out to sea or at least to the disintegrating tangle in a drain clog someplace miles away and underground. Two: this same person is staring at her face and coming to terms, teeth-bitten, with why they have come to this house, at all. Lucy. Lucy. Lucy. She came here to avoid her poetry. But why? Why would she want to avoid her poetry? She cannot deny it, now aired - but why oh why would she have intents on avoiding her poetry? And Lucy could have avoided her poetry, anyway - she has been for a long while, in every feint and entanglement she can imagine. If she had gone home, she would have avoided it, still - her future, her past words suddenly rumbling up from the earth to be a hill above her, mudsliding down to efface her, bury her at the bottom of, as deep as they were buried, before. Lucy - Lucy Jinx - she came here to avoid asking 'Why?' Some instinct tells her she can rabbit herself this way and that, elegantly - as though certain of talon and catch-claws in all nooks and open skies are lurking - and by always being someplace or doing something will box-out asking 'Why?' Lucy Jinx came here to avoid 'Why?' And now it has found her! It has her! It is asking her Itself and she is asking It It. And her breathing in the mirror is kin to this stupid don't-let-me-drown-don't-let-me-drown fuzzy

warble of legs with hardly a brain to process the desire for life - Lucy is tensing
her hands to the basin-lip as she tries to flesh herself dead and out of the clutches
of things, her thoughts, and pivots hopeless against the worm-certain eventual-
grave, open-air or well-tended, no matter. Ah! Mistake, Lucy. Mistake Number
One: She, in a lurch, shuts off the tap and would likely even cradle the insect,
now, and let it trill through her one nostril and out the other in a sheer jubilation
of forgiveness if not for the fact that it is the shutting off of the water which
finally disappears the thing! Slloooooopppppp - she can almost hear the pig-
hearted chuckle in the zgrhtghkk belch-gurgle of the water down-piping and
taking the critter off with it. Shit! Mistake Number Two: Lucy looks up to see
her two eyes, just after. They are looking out and all they know is 'Why.' Worse
than asking, they know knowing. Her poetry is 'Why.' It always has been. And
she has a mountain of it behind her and a mountain of it before her. 'Why' is
poetry. 'Why' is her. 'Why' is words, all of them fit into a perfect slim-volume
disguise. The most unstable center of the most stable center. Lucy killed the
insect and sees herself not asking 'Why?' but answering 'Why' - and the idea of
hiding, of deceit, is once again cored from her heart like something not quite
the shape anything or anyone wanted and so was merely sniffed once and then
tossed in the pile with the rest of the scraps to one side.

Skinflint, the afternoon moves on. And Lucy can tell its eyes are on the
pockets of everyone, looking for signs of thickness, of wealth tucked or beating
inside. Afternoons are the most groundling part of the day, keeping distant and
Lording it over everyone but not willing to invest in a thing, to mean anything
- not two nickels to rub together between every afternoon in a year, they horde
all of the riches that morning and evening - that especially middle-of-the-night -
drunkenly spend on Thank-yous and unmeaning hugs around waists from people
just met and who won't be remembered, who will be remembered far too
much. 'Are you thinking about how much you hate my brother?' Milos eyes
Lucy, shifty, his tone-of-voice showing the exhaustion that will lend him the
coming sense of forgiveness, of familia concert which, by this time, he likely
values over loyalty. 'Naw' Lucy says 'I am making keen analysis of you. I have
you dead-bang and there's no more for you to say - Zero-sum game.' 'Hit the
bricks pal and beat it, because you are going out!' Milos guffaws in his most
gravelly intense Alec Baldwin and then yawns and, fanning motion at himself,
says 'Timba, his arms open - tell me more about myself.' 'You're through being
done with your brother.' 'Yeah' Milos slumps, the weight to him of nothing-
else-in-this-bottle-either-how'd-that-happen. 'You probably don't even love
you mother, Milos- you've never mentioned her before.' 'I mention her
proportional to how many genuine body-parts she has left. Fake teeth, too. And
a nose-job, which I count as losing the nose.' Lucy red-flags that bit on the

grounds of Medical Science. But Milos fumes and says 'Knees are more scientific than noses - so are you saying we still count those!?' Lucy pivots: 'Bunko Science, I mean - the science of wonder and fancy! Replacing knees with brass or whatever, that is all well and good, though rather utilitarian. Changing a nose we don't like? That's what put a fucking man on the moon!' 'Good point' Milos has to award 'you sometimes see things in a way that makes me want to dress like The Emperor, man. I always thought the moral of that story was: *Little kids need to shut about things they don't understand*. Little kids shouldn't even come with mouths! We should be able to shove porridge in their ears until after they've at least been to middle-school or can demonstrate a working knowledge of using irony to ease the pains of this modern life!' Milos keeps on his gripe about the story, though, insisting how it is implied that the tailors were scientists and really had made the most delicate thread - thread so precious and fine it truly was invisible to the naked eye. 'That's astonishing!' Milos demands of the wider world. 'Think about the computer machines of today! A computer that can fit in a droplet of water!? A robot that can be injected into a cell!? Ask some little kid to take a peek and they'll say what? They'll say *It's just a drop of water* or *I don't see any robot, whaddaya mean?*' Lucy is smiling much more than she needs be - maybe because she had thought all this herself, once - almost verbatim - decades ago and had clucked much the same speech. 'Are we gonna write Fables about asshole who think radio-waves aren't real cause they can't see 'em? What moon will that land us on, eh? The moon of the motherfucking Stone-Age is what moon!' Maybe Lucy is smiling to stave off the fear that she thinks she may have even said that bit - all of it - that these thoughts of Milos' word out like her thoughts once did. 'Cave-men' she'd probably said. Maybe she'd said something about '*Through the courtesy of Fred's two feet* - that's where it'll get us.' Well, she had, actually. But for now, she listens to Milos and just thinks 'Maybe she had.'

A hug at the car-side and a sing-a-song-of-sixpence of 'Let's have one more smoke - or two more - before you go - and I'm sorry I took up your whole afternoon.' Lucy forces Milos to smoke one of her smokes and tells him 'You didn't waste my afternoon. Or anyway, if you did my afternoon was asking for it - did you see how my afternoon was dressed?' Milos laughs, over-pronounced-mumble, to compensate for his busyness getting his third failed match to fail, readying his fourth, and then he, also muffled from cig being tight-liped, says 'Isn't that always true?' in the overly-chummy way of someone who doesn't care what you just said and is repeating an expression from a movie they like but don't often get the chance to say. Describe Milos? Why? Describe Lucy? Why? They are the first album either of them bought - the actual first album, not just the first one they remember and so hold a special place for. And Milos tries to describe a certain type of cookie he'd once had, wanting to know if Lucy had ever had the same kind, but for all of his efforts he comes up with nothing but 'They had a very unique taste and I only ever ate them once or twice' so Lucy has to admit 'No, I don't know anything about those cookies, Milos.' And to her, Milos looks like the leaf the caterpillar was already filled up before getting to and so had not taken a bite of, the leaf watching with anguish the butterfly un-chrysalising, knowing it is the leaf that is no part of that wingspan, no part of those colors, that flight. 'What are you going to be up to now that you've cured me of my bad shoe?' Milos winks, Lucy having to roll her eyes at the bizarre in-joke timing, knowing just what Milos means by his finger-twiddle and the over-jaunty cock of his head. 'Why did you have to remind me of that fucking play!' Milos laughs, gunshot-under-the-table proud, claps his hand and does strangling gestures in the air two feet from Lucy in triumph. 'Now you'll have Thoreau in your head all night! Take that, Lucy Jinx! Take that!' 'You'd think he was the first and only person to live by a lake, not pay his taxes, and get bailed out of jail after one night by his fancy-pants philosopher friend! Well, Milos - I know loads of people who've done that' and, in unison, making the same umpire-calling-a-runner-safe-at-the-plate gesture, wide as firecrackers, both Lucy and Milos say 'Loads!' booming voiced and gargantuanly elongated. New joke-voice, Lucy says she actually now reads that play as a comedy in which Thoreau is a rakish con-man who guilefully succeeds in making his friend pay his taxes for him. 'That does make it a funny play' Milos nods his second smoke to life while he mutters. But then they fall into mocking the maudlin scene wherein, as Lucy puts it 'The dumb girl is all *Maybe God made your brother kill himself shaving to give you pain so you can*' - Lucy adds an extra set of ellipses, one then two then three sets, between *So* and *You* and *Can* and Milos joins in, with a face of ghastly lovelorn and tenth-grader profound-thought - '*transcend it*.' They both take a solemn beat, nodding as though agreeing with someone who'd just explained literally everything, first try. 'Know what I'd do if some bitch told me my God killed my brother to give me something to transcend?' Lucy shoulder-bullies. 'Marry her?' Milos replies, hands indicating the word *Obviously*. 'Other than marrying her - and other than coitusing her, too!' 'Other than coitusing her? Oh' - Milos Winne-the-Poohs some think think think then admits those really were his only guesses. And Lucy lights her third smoke and points toward the random bit of forest just there and says 'After this one, I'm leaving.'

'Before I go, I need your opinion on something.' Milos spreads his arms, bareknuckle knockout strut, Lucy taking a karate pose and making a karate sound before continuing. 'The situation is this: you or me - someone, anyone - is down a well or a pit and it starts raining.' 'Got it' Milos sobers. 'The question is: why is this a problem?' Lucy presses on over the about-to-speak 'Well' in Milos' expression 'I get that the worry is you would drown. I get that. The question: Why would you drown? Scientifically - in the realm of physics - why would not the pit or the well filling up be the best thing, the thing that would get you out?' 'Because you would float' Milos now rolls his hands he's-on-the-same-pageing. 'If I just stand in an empty community-pool and they start filling that pool would I be worried I'd drown?' Milos doesn't think so, a look of alarm akin to being told he's been eating endangered-rhino disguised as chicken-strips his whole life. 'Wait a minute' he declares, spinning in his spot, going hunch-backed and stomping, one fist in to cupped palm, then reverse-roled other fist, other palm splat! Milos says: 'If you were down a pit the best way to get out would be to fill it with water!' 'Or a well' Lucy says, yeah-yeah-yeah in a kind of belly sticking out bump bump bump. 'In a pool, as soon as it got a little deep, you could just lay back and float on the surface! Why not in a pit or a well? Jesus, Jinx! You've done it! Holy smokes - this is like something I think school kids in certain places will be forbidden from studying due to small-mindedness in a generation or so!' And they mutually agree that even if you had to tread water, alternating between that and floating a bit - even in an upright float position - there should be no bother. 'Mankind has leapt out of your throat, Lucy! So many dull documentaries will dramatize this moment, one day! Why in Hell is that always depicted as a situation to worry about?' They do - Lucy and Milos - know that if is was in a closed area it'd be bad - but films, television, they seem to always have people panic when they are in a hole that starts filling. 'Are we missing something?' Milos thunders, pacing up-and-down as though the sky is a scribbled-past-legibility slate-board, classrooms wide. 'At the very least, this ruins the suspense of that scene in *Apocalypto*!' Lucy cheers. 'Plus I have eradicated the trope, generally.' 'But I think it's more than that! Think about when people used to be afraid of getting sick at the hospital and then someone just said 'Wash your hands!' and the world changed like the scent of bread from warm-to-burnt - extreme, irrevocable! This is a fear that is now gone! Gone, Jinx. I'm not afraid of it, anymore. And soon no one will be!' Okay. Okay, then. Lucy is satisfied. The whole day seems to glow the way glowing looks in older cinema where colors could get that bright. The warmth is warmth despite the cold, the melting that is always a part of the icicle. 'I knew I invited you over here for a reason, Lucy.' 'Scratch the *Drown your brother in a well* plan!' 'And that was our best plan, except for all the others!' They hug and Lucy slings a moment to Milos like a bag everything probably would fall out of if slung so offhand. She hangs, slung, and lets her weight go, Milos grunting at the heft of her, the claw that's him gripping the bent flesh of her bent into itself's side.

Now, sometimes things just have to be. Nothing to them. Objects they are and objects in relation, but even that only incidentally. Lucy feels the sweat beading out through the single pore at exactly the tip of each one of her vertebrae pressing out her back-skin, the simultaneous soak of it into her shirt fabric, shivering from it in the car heater to the thought she has no idea how long it has been since anything has just been something. Let's do it now, Lucy. This is the view out the windshield as you drive. This is what it looks like when you have to check the side-mirror and the side-mirror is lit in the functional-rhythm of the turn-signal, mutely, the daylight not oppressive enough to stop it. No! That's just the side-mirror! That is just the glove-compartment! That is just a grain-silo - or something, it's something farm or silo related - and that is just a sign indicating a School Zone begins there! Lucy feels her ears warming. They are just warm ears. But - no no - even that isn't what she wants. And she calms and mellows into it. Gas station. Woman at gas pump, smile-waving in through her car window. To kids? To dog? To a camera she has set up? Lucy! And that is a truck, brown, and that a truck, bigger than the brown one and red. And the road has crags in it, but though they are unique they are not individuated - you see a lot of them or you aren't looking, you never see the road a single spot at-a-time, a glint or loose rock or line of tire rubber. You're pushing it, Lucy. Just the road. And more of the road. The road is more of the road and less of the road. Lucy! That is a mail-box. And that is a frozen-yogurt shop still boasting its Grand Opening for what must be almost a month, the banner dingy and not even comfortable still being there, knowing the looks it is getting, that its allure has worn off and no one believes it is so casual as that. Just a banner. And shrubs that are dead, at least for now. Plants that get to wink between living and dying, that turn to skeletons when they sleep - a power people would kill for! Lucy has a headful of picturing winter-long sleep, skin going taut, sallow, crisping, powdering like fallen leaves, the hard roots of bones eventually just left until season-change kicked in, cell cores and flesh grown back and blossomed hair and eyes, nipples and loose bellies, the bloom of humanity waking, smelling unwashed as the first day of Spring! But that is just a dog-dish. And that is just a front door. And that is just a tennis court, unused - no, just a tennis court! - and that is just a thatch of trees and that is just the back steps to a restaurant and that is the sun, too bright and soaking out the traffic-lights, and that is Lucy's hand coming toward her face to cover her sneeze and that is a woman with a limp and that is just that and that is just that and that is just that. Not every glance is a narrative. Nothing is lost if it goes uncommented on. 'Worth it or not, Socrates, the unobserved life is lived and lived and lived and lived and the more one observes it, anyway, the less one wonders why it should be.' Don't, Lucy. Keep them away. But she breaks. Words don't need to be observed. They have grinned past needed to be noted.

During the wait at the drive-thru window, Lucy asks this young girl 'Don't you ever wish you were selling cartoon hamburgers?' 'What do you mean?'

'That the hamburgers you sell were exactly like in a cartoon - looked and tasted just how they did in a cartoon.' There's a smile, the first crack to the glaze of this girl's eyes in hours, Lucy'll bet. And so the girl riffs. 'And they could be eaten in two big bites, like that? And swallowed with a bump going glug?' Oh yes! Oh yes! Lucy is the one smiling, now! 'Hamburgers seem heavy and light at the same time, when animated, bulbous and puff-of-smoke!' The girl laughs and says 'Now I'm depressed, man - thanks a lot!' Lucy hears another clerk - a boy - say 'You're depressed?' in a co-worker snark that is always a flirt and Lucy seethes a moment at a kid trying to distract a kid, then melts when it doesn't work and the girl-clerk - lidding Lucy's drink which had been finished filling, awhile - says to the boy 'I'm not talking to you' turns her head to Lucy, handing drink and straw, and says 'I'm talking to you.' And she adds 'I always wish I had a cartoon Boss who just always had the day's profits in a pile on his desk.' 'And he'd be kissing armsfuls anytime someone came in?' 'Yes!' the girl says 'Yes!' 'And he would never notice the knock on the door so he'd be caught off-guard, every time! And pick up the downfaced photo of his wife, each time!' The girl accepts a bag from the worker who has gathered Lucy's items and Lucy tries to steal a glimpse at this girl's name-tag, but the girl doesn't have one, just polo-shirt with the company insignia - the sort of clerk who pinned her name-tag to a sweater or a coat, one day, and just never remembers to switch it back to the uniform-shirt. Then Lucy takes the bag and says 'Thank you' to the girl's 'There you go - have a good day.' Drive away. Drive way. Go park in another lot and eat this swill. Or just drive and listen to the generic news report about events in a state you couldn't point to on a map. So here is Lucy: eating with a napkin pointlessly draped over knee - she never once sets anything down on it - in the parking lot of a building that is a *Credit Union* an *Ophthalmologist*, and a *Foreign Service Mission Annex*, whatever that could possibly mean. Lucy has images in mind, but they are mostly of crappy meeting-rooms lined in fully erect poles with flags dripping from the ends like after-cum. 'Beautiful' she says 'beautiful way to think of the grimy masculinity of a flag! No wonder women sew them - what a clever bit of satire that is! Good for us' Lucy swallow-says, that bite particularly poorly chewed and she pays for it with hiccoughing three times, painfully, hiccoughing more when she tries to ease her gullet with a sip of the soda. Is this Root Beer? Had she ordered Root Beer? Wait - is it Root Beer? She cannot determine by taste, so sniffs. The sizzle is soft, milky, the always half-flat of Root Beer, every-other kiss of carbonation sharp, the rest of them balloons deflated enough to be round, still, but clearly down-hanging. Lucy feels like she is thinking the word *Down* a lot. *Down. Down.* She feels her thoughts are full of a trend of the word *Down*. The word is cat-calling her, showing her it can be anywhere her thoughts go! And now this decision: does she leave the bag of remains in her car, down on the floor of the passenger seat? Does she leave the car, walk down to that trash bin? Does she open the door, leave the stuff down on the lot face, drive away? Can she do the third without the noia of some ophthalmologist bursting out that door she can't see anything but the reflection of herself parked in, shouting 'Hey! Hey!' lifting the rubbish and frantically waving her to slow down?

This close to home, the afternoon with Milos seems decades ago. But then, what doesn't? Lucy turns up the radio, selecting music, and fakes some enthusiasm and a speech about how she is just going to shrug off all nonsense and make a rule that all decisions will be fast-paced and lively and irregardless of who reacts to them or how. When there is no desire, specifically - her reasoning goes - it is best to settle on an aesthetic and trust to it. She will have the energy of this old-time pop song - bip and boop or bip and beep and bop - through conversations and moods, always keeping her actuality behind the door at her back. And on her deathbed, fine, it can all burst forth! And her last moments can be whiplashing regrets and apologies too fast for her metabolism to process! 'This all sounds great!' Lucy says to start her new choice off with a bang. Yes, of course you're right, Lucy - you have tried such plans before and, like all things, you have to move from place-to-place and they get left behind on accident and then new enthusiasm has to be throttled out of thin air. But this is good, for now. First order of business: just go in and edit some poetry to goddamn shambles if need be! Embrace every advice from the editor, but remove exactly one word from any line he suggests alterations to! The word she gut-reaction-thinks readers will notice least, anyway! Isn't it better to do it at random? 'Sure, yeah' she tippiddy-tippiddys on the steering column, eyeing the apartment driveway - just there - past the blinking arrow cautioning her of roadwork that never seems to be happening. When things aren't expected, it's a trap to try to interfere in their unfolding. It's like thinking about Nature and also thinking yourself part of it! No! Observers, of necessity, remove themselves. Think of the world as though you aren't there. Footprints are myths, invisible to anyone but the one who left them - Nature doesn't even recognize mankind - only we see the oil spills, only we see the roadkill! 'Whatever that means' Lucy shrugs, cavalier and Hollywood-icon, knowing teen kids will imitate her poorly for decades to come. 'Whatever that means' they'll say - and after awhile will add on 'Man' to the end or 'I'm sayin' to the end, something, the phrase slowly bastardizing until someone can have a conversation starting with 'That isn't what she actually said, you know?' 'The line is just *Whatever that means, man*' Lucy says, already forgetting - wary of these fifth grade aged kids who are idling, waiting for her to pass, it seems, while also seeming like they are trying to get her attention - the *man* was not initially there.

She watches them gaggle across the street in her rearview, then - as she takes her last turn - sees them crab scrambling up the steps of that apartment front. Here is your parking spot, Lucy. Resignedly you come? Eagerly? Matter-of-factly? Wondering if today counts as part of yesterday, still - if tomorrow will count as part of this? Lucy spits at her dashboard and the smeck disgustingly suctions to the gas gauge. Is her saliva that color? She spits in her palm. Lord in Heaven! This spit seems to be exactly why someone decided it was a good idea there be such a thing as a doctor! It must be just colored from the food she had eaten. This can't be what the new flowing spit looks like. Lucy lets her mouth fill, afresh, until saliva overtops her lower lip and suddenlys down over her chin to the waiting palm she doesn't even watch, yet. The dibble she looks at in the mirror, the line over her chin, is properly water colored. She swallows, sucking as much of this strand back in as she can. The pool in her hand is murky. It seems chlorinated. Something about that thought, parked here. *Chlorine.* Something makes her ask 'Why did I use that word, exactly?'

THERE WAS, IT COULD BE said, some initial foot-dragging and some angst aimed at the entire endeavor, but now Lucy Jinx considers the notations - which aren't invasive and aren't so numerous as it had felt when first burdened with a pile of her old poetry, commentaried marginally in ink and sometimes containing detailed descriptions of what the commentaries meant, these descriptions amounting to *The commentaries are just some thoughts I had* - kind of like propositions she is free to play with. In truth: how long has it been since Lucy read this stuff, wrote this stuff? Forever. Does she recognize it? Yes and no. There is an undeniable lope to it all that is her - she recognizes the underneath, the quirk, the altitude and tilt of it - but the specifics, naw. This line? She knows it's hers, but just because, in reading it, she gets it and cannot explain what she gets: *hey my sinful lemon-lime / hey my dollar and my dime / mouth you wide and square your collar / box your wine and scale my daughter.* That is Lucy Jinx. No one else would have written that. And if someone else had written that, Lucy would look at the words and feel repelled in the way poetry always tends to repel her. What she gets has nothing to do with the words - it is the squirms of some kind of breath memory, muscles in wrists and fingers recalling some microscopic tensions, there is an odor the lines bring to the mind of the inside of her nose, one that Lucy had not even noted beyond it was there, let her nose deal with it. Now: what of this line? Does it have commentary or call for edit? Not in the way Lucy had been thinking - and this is illustrative of what she is discovering from her editor - but yes. There is a small scrap of paper with another line from another later poem copied on it - along with notation of which poem and which page the poem and this bit in particular of it can be found on in the manuscript - and the note suggests this other line could be paired, seems to oddly belong. In whole, the note says *This just strikes me - and of course your continuity is puzzling and something I have not got much of a handle on other than the few dates I have come across, but those are of publications and might not reflect composition - but would not this line couple to this one, here, quite well? In fact, I wonder if these poems are sisters - or at least cousins - and it might be interesting to, if not conjoin them, at least set them nearer each other than currently. Just a thought.* Lucy loves this thought! Here is the other line: *for her and all her praytelling / there aren't statues enough / nor paltry enough / no clothes unworn enough / no corpses unwormed.* Why does this editor-man think this line goes with this other? What a profound and delightful mysterioso! Lucy darts between the two, alouding them and doing them first in this order then in that. Flip flap flap flip she finds the full poem of the *Praytelling* line and sets it on the ground - she is belly and groin hard to carpet, cold cup of meant-to-be-hot-but-not-even-sipped-once-yet tea in that blue cup, there, her elbows aching at points, her forearms, too - and starts playing games of mix-and-match. Why not!? *Sophomore is her earringed tooth / show her what's what, credenza, legato, Palmetto, Achoo / I have cups that could undo her / bare the Knave of Clubs flush, it's poetry the same as any Knave Spade Diamond Heart Player Pimp.*

   Her shoulders now itching from the floor, Lucy lays on her back, crosses ankle-over-ankle, and stares at the vent just above her, willing herself to feel more of the heat from it. Her thoughts bloat with a desire to recall where these poems came from. When they came from, more. Don't the two things go together? Don't the two things go together!? 'What a sot question' Lucy gruffs, gurgling a not-quite-burp and swallowing a squish, then breathing out as though rude but, really, the breath hardly seems registered let alone distasteful. She knows where. And who. Well, she knows the idea-of-who. This line had been written while staying for a few months - it would have been longer, a few months is just what it turned out to have been, Lucy thinks, because of something she doesn't recall - with that girl. *I've never seen fields or learned to fold to corners proper corner / I've never wished for snow once / or wanted the weather that came / or tired of seeing you go.* Lucy sees in front of her the ceiling but also - Oh she can damn taste it! - that odd, garageish room, that basement place, how she was certain the old wood was hollow-rot, birth-saced with spiders. The horror of what must lurk in the piled paint cans! How she had slowly backed up while the girl had prised them open with the screwdriver - not the right color, not the right color - hammered them back closed. Oh Lucy had been expecting fortune-cookie sized grey-with-brown-striped nameless insects to belch out from being so long entombed with each other - spawning and devouring each other, spawning and devouring each other - until one can was the color they had been looking for and Lucy had already begged off to use the toilet, a last glance backward as she upped the stair when the girl had sneezed. So what was the girl's name? When was it? Where? A city, the outskirts. Had Lucy been in school? Why had she taken to renting rooms - she remembers the flag and the building she always thought was a market, the building which turned out to be a Post Office and remembers the time she had driven to mail a letter but gone to the market instead. Insides-out of playful confusions! A time when that would have been a delight! The poem was not to do with that time. That's just when she wrote it. The poem was acid-rain, trying-to-be-subtextual, about a man named Jakkob - a fellow the only redeeming thing about, it turned out, was the second *K* in his name. *Hardly a hurricane, maybe sacked sugar / bones you have and trim those toes / I see you dream in needlepoint and watch you sweat / stale butter.* 'Oh!' Lucy Ohs - then this must have been after University! It must have been even after her experience of one night in jail! Isn't that where the phrase *sweat butter* had occurred to her? That doorknob-shaped woman vomiting into the trash-bin by the telephones? The crack of her ass! Hadn't the smell - like mildew in too long worn shoe-soles - emanated all the way to where Lucy sat, recalling her first handcuffs? Then - Lucy coughs from being too near the carpet too long, tries to sit, but her abdomen won't tense enough, sighs, coughs, sighs, coughs - it must have been before she did the long drive with Benjamin and that girl from that band. Had Lucy really rented a room during that interim? Because other than that, it would have been years later and Gregory would have happened - happened already the second time. Lucy sneezes, head rising, head clunking down, harder than she'd meant. The girl had been called something. 'We were never lovers' Lucy says like explaining - and Lucy says 'I know' like someone else already knowing that.

Lucy does take some affront - no, not affront, she is being combative, likely just on principle now, coffee surging and clotting up her sense of forward momentum, this is the agitation of holding a spot when she knows she ought to be concentrating but can't - to the following note: *I think you like the word 'vestibule'.* Then there is a smiley face. *And I wonder if it is a kind of tick - I've counted it and highlighted it green throughout the manuscript - and between it and 'mezzanine' there are nearly sixty instances.* The note goes on in some blather, but the meat is this mathematic. Well, so what? As it stands: Lucy adores the word *Mezzanine* and would rape the word *Vestibule* if she could ever catch it alone and off guard! Highlighted it green, though - he sure did, this editor! There and there. There and there. There. There. There. *High you carouse, vestibule / through, knees like wicker / smell grandmother / your throat sore your lozenge cough Hollyhock Hollyhock.* Well, is there supposed to be another word to use? *Vestibule!* Or this: *I listen to you as much as a coat-hook awaits anything / in between your words I vestibule / I cart around these hatpins.* Again - Lucy puts the challenge to anyone, straight - what else should she say? Are there going to be dissertations written discrediting Lucy for a vestibule fetish? Added to which: these poems are spread out over years! Decades even. Ah - *Mezzanine. This May's the Opera's mezzanine / This March hadn't already come.* 'That's true' Lucy says, drinking more coffee and lighting a cigarette for kicks on the stove-burner, wets of her eyes stinging so that she growls as she pivots away, leaving the coils orange-glowing. 'And moreover' she continues, face normalizing and breath steadying to in-and-out rhythm, making enough space for lungfuls of tense smoke 'this is the first *Mezzanine* I see.' She flips flips flips. *Vestibule. Vestibule. Vestibule.* Was the editor just being wry? Maybe subtly hinting she should swap out *Mezzanine* for *Vestibule* in a few cases. Gah! Or is this what the louse means? Lucy brandishes the page like proof she has paid an overdue fine. Spinning in place she wants to be reading, but due to the kitchen lighting has to stop, staying as stationary as she can manage - rocking heel-toe-heel-toe in staccato thunks, though - to recite *'Your teeth chew mezzanine your heart chews mezzanine your claws teeth mezzanine your mezzanine atriums your mezzanine awfuls at me atrocious old heartfuls of youth.'* Is he really counting those all - she counts three four five - five instances of the word!? Oh shucks, Lucy - he never would have meant you're to do anything else with these ones. 'They are highlighted green!' It's all a comical dandy, now! Oh of course her editor will have idiosyncrasies, but this is tantamount to justifying committal! She loses interest in justifying her *Vestibules*. It was likely meant to be chummy, the editor was probably nervous about the whole thing so went over-the-top. It isn't, Lucy, as though you are being social with the bloke. You've never even seen the man! So a picture forms of a widower who's home has been robbed and the only keepsake remaining of a cancer-died wife is a particular black scrape along a wall to a light-switch - the man will never forget it. And this poor widower - hermit with chest a nightly juddering mausoleum and a ritual of saying 'Goodnight' to the empty - just hoped his smile would be felt through his *Vestibule* comments and his green highlighter. 'There's a reason he chose green, Lucy' Lucy sighs and concedes to. It's a friendly color. Green is the color of timid 'Please-smile, because I'll never see her again and think she would.'

Dissociated, Lucy recalls another girl - a lover - and recalls exactly where and when and under-which-circumstances and for how long - and recalls the taste of sugared-milk-after-cereal-for-lunch off her tongue, off her chin, in dribbles down her navel, lapped from her foot like a kitten would off a princess'. Alyssa. Where had you vanished to, Alyssa? And why? Tall as a leaf-stem is thin. Freckles in Xerox - copies of copies of copies - and a voice that seemed to always be reaching to strike out to catch a flipped coin. Where had Alyssa gone? How many years had it been since Lucy had thought of her? That car crash they'd watched out the window and spectatored until she had said to Alyssa 'Are we doing this instead of the movie?' and how that had become the thing Alyssa had always said to her, ever after - even when it didn't make sense. 'Is this what we're doing instead of the movie?' How many recesses must there be in the fold of your memory, Lucy, if Alyssa could have been tucked someplace, a page between pages watered wet and fused - or a sheet folded and closed in a volume because it was the volume always carried around at one point, the volume reshelveved without thinking to shake loose its secrets, first. They had bought a broken violin and never fixed it and eventually sold it at a Yard Sale, high-fived each other for finally getting rid of it, then had bought cheap hamburgers from some weird stand only open on Thursdays with the spoils. Lucy had gotten a job with Alyssa, they had worked the same shift - just hanging up clothes and hanging up clothes - and Alyssa would get so disgruntled that some days they would walk home as though they had been berating each other for hours, the fumes of battle on them from Alyssa's silent anguish at having to right-side-out shirt-arms or pile dresses with deodorant whisks on them separately from those unblemished, aching each time, as though fearing an admonishing slap from a supervisor even though the messes had nothing to do with her. Lucy bites her lip and smokes and looks at the framed *Cat Poem* and blows smoke at it and mumbles 'Alyssa Alyssa Alyssa, where did you go?' And those checkered pants Lucy had just randomly said she had picked out specifically and Alyssa had trusted her implicitly from that point on though Lucy had no idea why those pants fit so well - that odd square-pattern of front buttons, that extra-lengthening to her already armchair-sleek ass curve, making the entire lower-half of her seem like a spill of thoughts you were caught having and could not stop blushing about. If this drunk electric wasn't bristling Lucy with very-nearly-hugging-herself-giggling she might be horrified how it seems Alyssa had been erased. Or misplaced. Or dispossessed from her. Alyssa: a Diaspora girl of Lucy's memory. And of course, underneath, Lucy is disquieted by the not-only-disappearance-but-reemergence of this Alyssa. Alyssa, who had worked as a hostess for three weeks at that restaurant-bar and who had received better tips because she spoke German and so many Germans came in there because of the Embassy. Alyssa, who told Lucy *There's no German word for you* when Lucy had asked *What's the German word for Jinx, what's Jinx in German?'* Germanic - Lucy would always say *Germanic* and then it would always wend around to repeating the line from Albee about how being from Crete would make you a Cretin. They both swore they remembered Richard Burton doing the line - chuckling exactly how he would chuckle when portraying George - and every time they re-watched the movie were furious to have it proven again that that particular line wasn't filmed. 'Why did you tell me it was, Lucy!' And Alyssa would vicious-whip Lucy with a pillow or couch cushion and Lucy would laugh even if the zipper of one of those damned cushions got her, left a scratch she would hiss 'Fuck' about as soon as Alyssa went to put something in the oven like she always was doing mid-movie. 'I hate you now' Alyssa would say whenever she'd come back after an Albee accusation. 'I hate you now even more than I hated you now, before.'

But this line, here - this whole poem! - Oh Lucy doesn't know, it might even be a trick, something from another manuscript slipped in to test her, some flimflam poet, maybe - hey! maybe the editor trying to slip in one of his own pieces, maybe this guy has a kick for such things and Lucy seems a ripe target due to her bizarre flamboyance! - or else maybe it's here to make sure she's not the sort willing to compromise or do something shady just for the promise of a few bucks. This poem is all perfectly formed, like a duck bill - each word fits where it ought, same as the way the dust on the top of a lightbulb blackens just so. Oh it leaves a real scrum in her mouth to recite, like half-tasteless spearmint she has to chew after someone else started the stick. Yep. Yep. This can't have been Lucy! Even her spittle doesn't form right, pool or swallow at proper time-signature when speaking the words - she never would have chosen this phrasing out. *A lamp for limping by / a crutch to poke at cripples.* 'Dah dah dah-dah-dah-duh' she snaps fingers to 'dah dah dah-dah-dah dah-duh.' And it gets worse! *Whiplash, horseless / home burnt, gold fish / give me the weight of the teeth in your skull.* This is meaningless! What does the editor have to say? Nothing much! Why didn't the editor-flag this as out-of-place? She checks and this seems to be something that originally appeared in a zine called *Collide-o-Scope*. Never heard of it. A wave of nauseous relief! Lucy had never published in something called that. Never! And she looks at the date - as researched, Lucy supposes, by the broad who put this collection together - and there is no way in the name of Christ-in-Heaven Lucy wrote this, not during that time period! Phew. 'Phew' she articulates, as though alphabeting each letter individual. It makes it more bearable to read, though. *Glimpses of all of the underthings unbought / borrowing shoes to go trod in.* She laughs at the abysmalness - the abyss, really, the vertigo forever-down - of how truly unpoetic this nonsense is. Half-a-mind to keep it! Except - why would it be in the manuscript and with Lucy's name on it? The broad seemed to have done her research meticulously - and this isn't just a page in-slipped from some other project. The source-line: *Collide-o-Scope*, the issue, the date, where to even find it online. Lucy whirls to look it up as though there would be a computer in her bedroom, but there is no computer in her bedroom - she is discombobulated by this, the expectation had been so genuine, as had the expectation of another bedroom and the wall now in front of her feels it should be the wall behind her. Memory Lane is upending her, tonight! But why did she glimpse that old bedroom? Which? Had she written this balderdash verse? 'Shit' she glowers 'shit shit shit.' But there is an easy enough way to deal with this mystery, Lucy. 'Is there?' Think. 'What?' I said think! 'Mathilde' Lucy nod-nods, fingers wriggling, drumming her bicep-side. Also: it's not the middle-of-the-night, Lucy. 'Did I say it was?' You're thinking it, Lucy. She supposes she is. Is glad for the correction. It isn't even that late - evening, she confirms, it's evening. Likely the best time to catch Mathilde, so she tries to just call but only gets voicemail. So: quickly she types, squinting at the Source-line as she does *Top state imperative - look up this poem at this website and tell me who actually wrote it.* See, Lucy, even this title - *Lollipop number eight* - that isn't you! 'Well' Lucy drawls - no, the title is fine, she'd call something that, she actually likes the title. Precisely she types in the web-address to give Mathilde all avenues and sends the missive off. Dust dust dust go hands hands hand and hands-to-thigh-fronts. That's settled. Lucy opens the freezer for vodka.

High pitched memories and low groans, the weeble sounds of coins being scraped in sink bottoms after plunking through the surfaces flush with sink brims. How can a memory of walking a path you walked only once seem like that path had been walked many times? How deep, Lucy. 'It's not a deep question' she says with a snarl, implying her interrogator is being a putz 'I'm talking quite literally.' Down goes a second three-sheets-of-paper thin tipple of vodka. Lucy is referring to the memory of a night from her adolescence wherein she had been depressed, or at least in a bad mood - 'Depressed' she finger-points to emphasize 'Oh it was depression and you know why' - and so she had walked far from her house and wound up passing through what she, at the time, thought of as series of affluent neighborhoods and then through a long field to a large pile of bulldozed earth which she climbed to the top of and then descended with great difficulty, becoming snot-rag filthy, and then crossed a road - much much further from her house than she had realized - and passed through a kind of brambled, wooded-path, back behind a series of office buildings, and on which path she stepped - the things collapsing - right down through the ribs of a perfectly cleaned, wholly full skeleton of a deer. Well, that's why you remember! You stared at an almost-polished skeleton you had just demolished a part of - that is going to stick in your mind, Lucy! But Lucy doesn't question why she remembers - she knows why she remembers the image of the bones, of her foot inside them, the air of that night, the streetlights clogging the empty road and making it seem toothlessly perverse before and after her jaunt through the woods, the taste of the grease of the microwave hamburger she had eaten, not wanting to really, before she had headed out in her mire-souled state. All of that is enameled on her brain. That will never go anywhere. The question is: Why does she have image-after-image - all weather, all lights of day - of her walking the path - alone or with companion - as though it was a regular thing, frequent as her daily jaunts to the store for shoplifting and loitering or as the path home from school or the weight of herself up the stairs to her first favorite chair in her first ever library? Even the fact that she thinks of it so often - and finds it referenced in poem after poem after poem, today - doesn't explain these false memories. Different ages. Different people. Even if she thinks 'Oh you've spliced it with the walks in the woods you took when you were fifth grade age, tucking your dirty magazines under rotten limbs of fallen trees' this can't be the thing - because she has every memory of those woods, those paths, those people, pristine, nothing like the deer-skeletoned path. She isn't making a mistake. There are unreal parts of her that are real. Hasn't she let memories of this path - not the time of the skeleton, even - dictate her moods at times? Haven't thoughts of Miranda or Charles, lighting her a joint or teaching her an elaborate high-five, from time-to-time had her desiring to contact them? Or are these extended memories false, too? Lucy, Lucy - you'll wind up as false as a poem if you keep down this path! 'Lucy, Lucy' Lucy says back 'I'm false as a poem, already - I'm a liar like the pen to the ink, the ink to the ink left behind it!' Full swallow of full shot of vodka. Only when emptied is the plastic cup raised 'To your health, skeleton deer - to the health of your ribs I unribbed you of!'

Another sticking-point - yes, Lucy is drunk-editing, but she has already given the speech defending it and so let's move on - she is having with this editor is these notes on this line in this poem. It's a fun sticking-point - Lucy is seasick with enjoyment at this whole process now, wants this book swatted out in one night even though she'll wait a week, two weeks, before sending any pages off and then send them in batches so she seems conscientious - she admits to those listening - her imagined biographer listlessly doing made-believe dishes over there, unmanned tape-recorder whirring reel-to-reel on the countertop, microphone propped on that cookbook Lucy found in the drawer when she had first moved in - but a sticking-point, nevertheless. *Not my place to question, I just wonder: is this line meant to be so angry? There seems to be little anger else, if any, in this verse and this line really vacuums everything to it - colors the water, so to speak - until the river seems to be blood when it is really not, I don't think.* What a hedged-bet way of putting it, first of all - 'First of all, first of all!' Lucy by-Neptunes! - but isn't that a profound overstep for an editor? If this bloke thinks that the river is not-blood-but-seems-like-it, why wouldn't that be assumed to be the point of the work? What? 'What!?' Lucy seethes over at her biographer and dares her to repeat the remark. 'Or it could just show a real insight - it could just be a keen understanding, Lucy.' 'You just stick to the biographying! You just tend to that, okay!?' Lucy's pretend biography holds up hands 'Alright-alright' knowing that was coming and goes back to whatever background pantomime she's up to. Lucy's mouth is the flavor of stomach cramp, though, because her biographer has a point. It wasn't the point to make a serene-river out to be or into a plague-river. No. It just wasn't. Though that is really cool! Not that Lucy agrees the line does it. 'But who am I to say? Isn't that the point of this? Sigh' she sighs, French-accented. Then sighs German-accented. Then sighs in the way a sigh went prior to considered tongues. Is it okay to proceed? Tell the editor 'That was the point, sir! Yes. I appreciate the question - but that was the point.' Or - since it wasn't the point - should Lucy give the honest response: 'I don't know what you mean.' Because: she shouldn't say the editor is making this point with any measure of enthusiasm - nope, she re-reads, confirming the comment is not enthusiasm, but bald-faced critique! - so she'd seem contrarian or dense or - the horror! - disappointing if she said 'That's the point' in reply. She reads the poem without the line. Maybe it doesn't belong there. 'And it isn't' she now lights a smoke - it lights funny so she starts another one, fresh - 'as though I have never removed a line from a poem - I do that all day long!' She consults the chapbook on her shelf - she has a copy of this one - and reads the piece in there. She'd published it that way, though, not just had it in some notebook. Is it relevant that she doesn't know why the line struck her bad? Maybe it is just meant to seem out-of-place. *You're flawless, a water bowl / your flawless water left standing undrunk with / your flawless lack of gullet to down / you're a closed mouth / waterless / already perfect in your already drown.* It has nothing to do with the rest of the piece. That's true. Nothing. Nothing! Who is that line about? 'It's not about anyone' Lucy says, that poem wasn't directed at anyone and she knows it. It's a real mystery. It's just some formless, inarticulate insult that is trying to seem proud of itself. An insult by some sad-sack with no one to insult, some poor girl bullied by abandonment - no - abandoned by abandonment, even - no, no - just alone, not left alone, not asided. Just nothing. 'This line's just some gal's just nothing and bad poetry' Lucy piles it on 'trying to belong where she doesn't.'

Mathilde's text back begins with an apology for the lag - funny, because Lucy grinned to herself 'Service with a smile' when her phone vibrated and she saw who it was - explaining how the *Collide-O-Scope* journal - or whatever it was - no longer had a website - 'Of course it doesn't' Lucy wizeneds as she reads - and though it is referenced around a lot, it took some time to track down the poem. Blah blah blah, the message concludes *the poem was written by someone called Bianca Doormouth, credited to Collide-O-Scope with all the other info you provided, listed on her CV or whatever. So you owe me ten bucks and all - I'll put it on your growing national deficit.* Lucy read past - but moreso did not read past - the word *Doormouth*. And when the phone vibrates in her hand again, she reads and does not read the message *I know you cannot get links, but I can snap a photo of the dame, if you want, and send it, let me now.* Lucy writes *Surely, please do* but only kind of - and then, afterthought, sends a message *Yes, ten dollars, put in on the debt, yes.* And by the time the phone vibrates - now, there - a third time - with what must be the photo and maybe a further comment or two from Mathilde - Lucy is too busy pacing to the far wall and putting her back to it and wondering if the look on her face matches the look on the face she feels is buried in her innards, just then. Bianca. Doormouth. Bianca Doormouth. The voice, the manner - the everything! - from those text conversations and the chats - until she had decided not to go meet Bianca at the restaurant that day - now lock-step so easily, parade formation, yes yes, exactly. There isn't a word for how Lucy feels just now, but if there was she feels certain it would begin with an *R* contain at least one *K* and an *Ough* somewhere in it. 'Something' she says 'something.' She is careening. The vodka helps her careen. 'Why did I not know who Bianca was?' Lucy asks, squeaky student-at-the-back-of-the-room, really wanting to know. Bianca. Hey, Lucy? Why had I not recognized Bianca - or I guess I did, halfway - I had some sense it was someone, didn't I? Hey, Lucy? Didn't I? Lucy? 'What!? What!?' Want to see a trick? But Lucy doesn't even let the thought complete itself, scrambles to the phone as though getting there in time will do anything to change the fact that she had erased the messages and the Call Log - everything, several times over - since back then - since back then not meeting Bianca. Just one of Lucy's ticks - she clears her Call Log and Message Log when she is waiting in line or after she has sent a message if she sends one while on the toilet. But you can get the Call Log, no doubt, Lucy - these were calls, they are recorded someplace. 'What? Are you on my side now?' Just think - even if you have to get every number from that period-of-time, it won't take long to find the right one. 'But this is just cruelty! Why are you saying this?' she says, but it feels like she shrieks and - what accidental drama - when she picks up the plastic cup, thinking it empty, it is vodka-filled and the kitchen is splashed, sink-to-oven-clock-to-side-of-fridge, and she hears a bit of it thud to the carpet. 'You know it came up *Unknown Number*! Or I would have looked up the number, before!' Is that true, Lucy? 'What?' I said: *Is that true?* 'Shut up!' Or don't you remember. Lucy types to Mathilde, feeling like the inside of a nose when it still tastes full and plump from crying but tears have stopped: *Find Bianca Doormouth.*

Stop-motion. Collage. Slide-show. Begin! Bianca Doormouth twitches and overlaps and side-to-side-to-side-to-sides across the surfaces of Lucy Jinx's apartment. Question: How had Bianca found Lucy's number? Hadn't she said Lucy had given it to her? Hadn't they talked about things and none of those things had seemed quite right, jarred reality from Lucy's forgetful? Scene: Bianca had an amazing talent for replacing letters in words with *X*s and for pronounces them, appropriately, without any forethought. A parlor-trick which dazzled Lucy, who would increasingly try to catch Bianca out wrong - as though one mistake after a thousand successes would prove the thing a sham-show. Lucy says 'Replace all the *T*s *D*s and *H*s' and then Bianca says 'In what?' and Lucy says

- no idea if there are *Ts Ds* or *Hs* or in what number - '*He went to the corner and there found dented plates of steel from Lord knew what and it alarmed him, the sun sharp to his eyes off the things in a glint*' and then Bianca - the memorization of the sentence itself was impressive, let alone the switch switch switch - said '*Xe wenx xx xxe cxrner and xxere fxund xenxex plaxes xf sxeel frxm Lxrx knew wxax anx ix alarmex xim, xxe sun sxarp xx xis eyex xff xxe xxings in a glinx.*' And Bianca always pronounced *X* like *X* ought be pronounced, like *Cgh* or maybe *Cughgh* no slow-motion in her progression, like this was a normal thing to do. Lucy would record it and play it back. Would write the sentence and then rewrite it with *X*s. All of these things Lucy did to check took twice as long to do as Bianca to spit out the substitutions. Question: How could you forget this - because Lucy had not thought of this until now - and how could the name Bianca not just bring that - even that alone! - sharply to mind? More important question: had Lucy's odd certainty that Bianca was a game or a ploy been some spiral in her brain-bottom recalling her, doing its best to make sure Bianca wasn't forgotten, entire? Since not showing up at the restaurant, Lucy, have you thought of Bianca, again? 'No.' No? Lucy is desperate to say 'No' to that questioning No but 'Yes' she has to say 'Yes!' The depraved act of forgetting! The last scream of recalled-Bianca saying 'Be suspicious, keep the game going, don't forget me, don't let me actually vanish!' Calm down: because Mathilde will write back and then you can pour this all out on Bianca and it will be well and - Lucy pivots, hand claps, and the silence in the room is seven bricks dense. And what? 'What?' And what about Bianca, Lucy? 'What do you mean?' You've remembered her? 'Yes.' So what? And it is a fair question, Lucy knows it is. She recalls how they once blanketed themselves under the clothes they had removed from some boxes when their bed was just a mattress and they were too shagged out to bother with opening any of the other boxes for sheets or comforters. She remembers Bianca bleeding into the sink from that slice to her hand - that impossibly sharp cup-shard alligatoring her - Lucy on the phone to an ambulance and Bianca saying, after probably ten minutes bleeding 'I can't feel my hand and I think I should be applying pressure, right?' And there was less color than no-color in Bianca's lips, then - and Lucy felt bad for wanting to kiss them because of that.

This is just distraction, but Lucy - it seems - once wrote this: *sometimes mouths are only letter S / I could taste your shoulders, they could not taste my teeth / sometimes mouths are only letter R / Wednesday everywhere, Waters in pyramids on Ozymandias' Mars*. She's skipped to the last stanza of the last poem in the manuscript. Relatively recent. *What's it about?* That isn't her asking, that is the note from the editor. The stanza is circled. The poem, entire, is only that stanza and four other small couplings of lines. Apparently, for example, the editor understands *Grim are the veil bearers / rakes are the rakes through the sand*. Lucy has, she explains to her imagined biographer

- who is dunking cookies and leaning to the counter, way over there, listening, hand over her mouth as though to minimize the effects of the crunching on the recording - stopped so much thinking about her poems and these lines are a kind of style built of free-association and abortive-meter. 'Oh fuck, man' she suddenly tone-changes 'I don't think about it and I rush and get bored until something is on the page and kablam! - you know? Who cares?' Another glance down to her phone, tapping a button to light the screen. No reply from Mathilde. No Bianca. No answer to what that might matter. It feels like it's eighteen-hours-past-midnight but not yet the next day - and Lucy finds the still present sense of liveliness to the sky out the window ludicrous, even a kind of libel against her. No, she can't really hear anything - but the things she can see just look still-functional, the hour hasn't come when cars on roads seem encroaching and parking lots with people crossing them seem like small caves in bellies of large whales that swallowed them. Another glance to the phone. 'Why do you write poetry?' the imaginary biographer asks, furthering 'I don't think we have ever really addressed that, you and I. Why did you start? Do you recall?' 'I was kid' Lucy begins a well-known recitation of a few stories about her almost-pre-memory days - this irks her now though, because why does she still have these memories!? Oh you likely don't, Lucy - you merely remember the stories from telling the stories and the pictures from making them up and remembering them each time you tell the story you remember having told. Anyway: this is not what the imaginary biographer means, she means 'Not as a kid' - 'who don't make choices' the biographer adds somehow on top of herself - 'but as a grown woman: why did you start to write poetry?' Lucy begins Part Two of Speech with: 'Well, when I was an adolescent, especially in high-school, I would' but the biographer - aggressive gal of herself, tonight - groans and says 'I meant: as a woman!' 'What do you mean *meant: as a woman*?' 'Are you saying, for posterity, you did something as a woman because you did it as a kid and then as a teenager?' 'I did it because I couldn't think of anything else to do! And anyway' Lucy moves to continue. But stops. Writes *Dunno* under the editor's question, then puts a smiley face, knowing he will - if he ever sees this response - think she found the question cute and was cuteing him back, will think that she was relieved to be done with the volume, was being cryptic, was being poetical-coy. Glance to the phone. Nope. No nothing. 'Who is Bianca?' the biographer asks, late-to-the-party voice, tilt up to the *Who* and long - 'Whhhooooooo' - then the *is Bianca* and question-mark fast, all together - 'isBianca?' - as though the biographer is sure she should know already and feels dumb for having to ask. 'I think I loved her' Lucy says and looks up. At the kitchen. The empty kitchen. 'I think I'm sure I loved her, quite a lot.'

*********

LIKE A THEATRE PIECE: LUCY Jinx, scene, diner counter - well, *Diner* in the sense of Family Restaurant shaped like a diner, but Lucy sits at the counter so it seems shoe-bottom working-class, she feels dive-skinned and screw-the-bossman. Characters: Lucy Jinx, mid-forties - Waitress, mid-fifties, always positioned as though leaning on the counter, even when not. Waitress finishes with other customer - the audience would see this as pantomime, Waitress interacting with thin air, would hear only Waitress' side of the commonalities of 'Goodbye' et cetera. Waitress: 'Alright, Hank - you tell Gladys *Hello*. Well, you two will make up and it'll be straight come the weekend. You too, Hank. Goodnight.' Lucy Jinx has made a circle of her spoon in her empty coffee and Waitress takes up a fresh pot, pouring. Waitress: 'You know what you look like?' Lucy: 'What's it I look like?' Waitress: 'One of those thingamajigs - you know them?' Lucy: 'I seem like a thingamajig, is it?' Waitress: 'If you don't mind my saying so. Lucy: 'Not at all. Hey - let me ask you - no, nevermind.' Waitress: 'Ask away.' Lucy: 'No. Nevermind.' And Waitress Okay-shoulders and there is the sound of a telephone ringing and Waitress goes around the corner, from where the audience and Lucy - Lucy reacting - hear occasional peals of laughter. Note: Lucy's reaction to each peal, once each peal has subsided, is a sigh, increasing in volume and length. Pause. Waitress reenters and Lucy - to indicate time has passed - makes a circle of her spoon in her cup and Waitress grabs the illusion of the fresh pot from before and pours. Waitress: 'What do you seem like?' Lucy: 'What do I seem like?' Waitress: 'I'm asking.' Lucy: 'You, you mean, are asking me?' Pause in which Waitress says nothing. Lucy, continuing: 'That's some flagrant unorthodoxy. You tell me what I seem like, you don't ask me.' Waitress: 'You'd be the one to know.' Lucy: 'What I seem? What I seem - seem - seem like? No. How would I know that? I'm too close. I am a dot in my own pointillist actuality.' Waitress sighs in the exact way that Lucy sighed, before. They have - the script would note - a sighing contest, something they, as performers, would either wing each time the scene is performed or else would have worked out, meticulously, the particulars of in advance, do them the same-to-the-sniffle each curtain-up. Lucy: 'What's it like working in a Diner?' Waitress: 'You ever found what you were looking for in the bottom of a shoebox?' Lucy: 'From time-to-time - not lately, but yes.' Waitress: 'It feels like that. Which is to say: complex.' Like a teenager, suddenly, Waitress hops up on countertop, sliding her legs to dangle over the side where Lucy is sitting - bounce bounce bounce go the legs. Waitress, continuing, bubblegum-voiced: 'Because what you found is at the bottom of something, but it's still what you were looking for. You've scraped the bottom of the barrel, so to speak - which is generally, to go from cliché, meant to be bad - but the thing you were looking for - which makes you happy - is there.'

Lucy: 'What were you looking for?' Waitress: 'My Social Security Card - I needed it for a loan. What about you?' Lucy: 'I was looking for a photograph of Dorene.' Waitress: 'And you found that was what was there when the barrel-bottom was scraped?' Lucy: 'The box-bottom - your metaphors are forced. And anyway - how did she wind up there?' Waitress: 'I guess you put her there.' Waitress plops down from counter, folds on the floor a moment, stands, and walks to the stage limit, pauses, turns around and comes in, taking the seat next to Lucy's, both of them facing forward, Lucy making a circle in her empty cup with her spoon.

  The reality of Lucy Jinx is: she is in a booth by the window and she can hardly even see the counter area which had been to-the-brimmed with people all watching something on the television - a sporting event or something, Lucy has already scoffingly determined, though for romance's sake she at least makes it a boxing match or a dog race - faces all laced in the same wet that will wind up left across their plate-fronts and bowl-bottoms, reused and reused tissues in a kind of traffic-jam metronome of honks. The reality of Lucy Jinx is: the waitress in the scene she had imagined up isn't even one of the waitresses in this place - here are still these last groaning swing-shift staff members and the pre-deflowered-evening-to-mid-overnighters procrastinating in postures as they actually start their work, early. There: a young-girl peer-pressured into the affect of wrong-turn-after-wrong-turn-resentment at herself for still not needing prescriptions - three-of-them-a-day - like her elder colleagues - poor slip not even sure why she feels a malaise to her, as etched and exhausting to stab at as the half-mawed French-fry left in some ketchup smeared in syrup - pressed on by three plates above it - for hours before being washed. The reality of Lucy Jinx is: hardly a word has been said except 'Coffee' and how she might order something in a bit but wants to see if her friend is able to make it out to meet her, first. That was where the theatre-thoughts got started. Lucy deceiving people who technically don't meet the criteria to necessitate deceit. You didn't fool the hostess into thinking a friend might be meeting you, Lucy - the hostess just believed you. Deceit is complex and involves effort - this is how one knows the difference and why it can be so trying when one is accused of it from some chagrined party. 'You lied to me!' Lucy envisions someone telling her - or remembers, Lucy, you might just be remembering someone telling you, yelling you that - and she envisions herself saying 'No, I just told you something - there is a difference.' There is. Her very soul - trapdoor shaped as it is - knows that there is. Deceit, of necessity, requires an understanding of the game-table, the rules - only children think that saying 'I really found a magic-lantern and used the magic to be able to do a perfect jump-kick' is the same thing as Dishonesty. Even Dishonesty isn't the same as deceit! Deceit is not Dishonesty - it is not the inverse or undoing of Honesty - it is an active march forward with reality, the exact same as Honesty is. 'Deceit is Honesty that brushes up against someone being upset.' Lucy tells the young staff member this. Or thinks she should, anyway. She wants to tell that girl: 'And even call it *lies* if you want - lie to people, lie to people, lie to as many people as you possibly can, because you cannot imagine the grave you have dug if you tell person after person the truth! Oh a ponderous grave - the mountains are the only parts left that haven't been dug all the way down of the first honest woman starting to dig!' Let Lucy tell you this, young lady! 'And even those mountains started out Jupiter tall - the world has been dug down to its miniscule by Honesty.' The waitress - a real one - re-approaches Lucy and Lucy orders some sort of meal she won't eat and the waitress doesn't mention how there might have been another person showing up. If this is even the waitress Lucy told that to. The reality of Lucy Jinx is: waiting for a food order and not talking about things to people.

But wait - everything, wait, Lucy, wait! This is not what things have come to. The facts of the case are: Lucy is still a bit vodkaed - even if only in the sense of the aftermath - and is just tired again after marathon editing and the pitfalls of memory, in all senses of the word. Meaning? Meaning: this is not a reflection of what Lucy is, at the moment. What Lucy is at the moment is a result of several other moments - fact - and should not be seen as representative. Lucy tells herself this. So - she is out and eating randomly some randomwhere? 'Good for me' she could say. Here is the string of things she did to get here - being here does not diminish those things! Lucy is no nihilist - Christ God, she is as far from nihilism as one can get! So much Everything exists for Lucy there isn't room for even a fleck of Nothing! Remember, Lucy? To you, Infinity is so crammed through with fullness it couldn't so much as tighten its belt or uncrane its neck! If you had gone to that therapist, that therapist would have rightfully pointed out that this state-of-mind is the result of your refusal to sleep! This is what you do instead of sleeping, Lucy, so these mindsets should be given all the hard advantages of dreams, merely. You are dreaming. You are dreaming despair. Dreaming words. Ah. Ah! Ah!! That is it! Lucy almost hoots, almost claps her hands hard like the chalk-dust of a finished equation would confetti the air and manna-from-Heaven her - almost rubs her hands praying-mantisingly self-satisfied, big pile of coins made out of roast-beef the table long out from her poised belly, knife and fork ready and napkin-bib a left-open wallet! She should be asleep. Sleep has been heisted from her! Because dreams - those dreams that used to get all over her - those were images, those were not words. But this - this, now, this, here, this - is all words and words, a dreamscape of letters and punctuation - pictures, sure, but things seen only for raw material, reduced to their descriptions and then con-man feinted into descriptions of other things.

One cannot live as all letters! One cannot sleep when one has to say and spell or - misspell, even! - every single word of every single aspect of the floatsam the mind needs in order to reset. Sleep is supposed to be the brain getting a scrub down, visual cortexes or something being stimulated and randomly lighting lights to things that will be forgotten. Words come in when waking, when trying to remember things not seen. But Lucy is now a kitten that's just a sack full of worms in a yeasting bloat - Lucy is a pen that never stops spelling letters even when no one is holding it. Hey! Terrific! Lucy takes another bite of this dismally breaded chicken and tastes mostly the smell of the soaped hands that touched it to position it on her plate. So you've found out your problem, Lucy: You should sleep instead of sitting around thinking! Profundo! Molto profundo! So go get some sleep. 'I will.' You will? 'I will go get some sleep' Lucy says as she napkins her lips, the very act making the words seem hidden away - but from what? The words know you said them - all you've done is hide the shape of your mouth from anyone who might have seen. Is this sleep really, though? What does it feel like? Lucy is chewing and not sure what she means, anymore.

When Lucy's one friend had had her first child - or when the child was gestating within the friend - the friend had been reading books about what to expect from the newborn. And one of the friend's greatest fears was - as she had put it - 'The child will confused night for day.' A ridiculous way to put the matter, as children cannot confuse anything for anything, but Lucy knew what the friend meant. And Lucy has become that infant, now, and thinks on that friend, glad to find her not nameless but instead to find her named Trista. Trista. Lucy remembers you. Even though Lucy has confused night for day, she remembers you, Trista. The question is: could Lucy actively efface you? Or is Lucy without that sort of agency over herself? The situation is this: Lucy only remembers you because she is in a diner and is convinced that words have shanghaied her ability to sleep and dream properly and so this kicked her into a state of worry about fatigue, about 'What will I be like tomorrow?' which reminded her of 'The night not being used properly for sleep' which - there you were, Trista! - plucked your observation of worrying about your sleep cycle reversing due to being in the family way. If not for all of these things converging, Trista was on the way out. That seems almost certain. How long will this remembrance of Trista endure? Does Lucy now, for example, remember Trista better than she remembers someone she talked to a few minutes ago? In one sense, Yes: Trista is fresher feeling to Lucy than any of the people in this restaurant. In another sense, No: Trista is vaguer than, say, Mathilde or Samantha. Though: that is only because Lucy has thought of them more often, more recently - or been exposed to them, which isn't the same as thinking about them. And in that sense, Who knows: it would need years to pass - a decade, perhaps - of not seeing Samantha and not seeing Mathilde to see how they compare. And at that time, still, if Lucy could remember so much as a cracker-crumb of Trista it would mean she has a stronger recollection of Trista. Whose name - shit! - is *Krista* and - as it so happen - is actually *Kiersten*! 'Well this is a fine how-do-you-do' Lucy pleasantries to the waitress, who is just then asking Lucy if she wants more coffee. 'What is?' 'I have an old friend who is named Kiersten and I have been calling her Trista!' The waitress sympathy-faces and asks 'Not in an e-mail, though, right?' Blink. 'Not in an e-mail' Lucy reassures the waitress, who breathes a sharp exhale of camaraderie. 'I called someone the wrong name all the way through an e-mail - I don't even know why I used his name so many times - and it didn't end well.' 'Or why you didn't use his name so many times' Lucy says with a nod, all of this a substitute for 'Thanks' at the refilled coffee she then moves to sip, the waitress laughing to demonstrate, definitively, that Lucy's comment is the funniest thing she has ever heard. Then the waitress opinions to Lucy that 'Your friend will forgive you - old friends have to forgive you.' But Lucy isn't so sure about that. 'Old friends shouldn't be trusted - they're the ones who can basically do anything they want, you know?' 'Truth' the waitress says, in a way suggesting this is the way the word was said in some film - haven't you heard it said like this, like-in-a-film, before Lucy? - 'but anyway: I ended up marrying the guy who I called the wrong thing.' This baffles Lucy. 'And then divorced him, right?' Again, the waitress rolls like a dog in-its-old-hardened-shit-in-the-grass at Lucy's comment. 'I'm working on that part' the waitress says, peeling off to tend to some other-tabled man raising his hand 'I guess he does sound pretty pathetic, out loud.'

Here's a thing: Did Lucy really forget Bianca? Yes. But: Did she really remember Bianca? If this is a sleeping state, don't these thoughts count as gossamer only, flimsy as stage-boulders? This is a dream of having forgotten Bianca. For the dream to work, Bianca has to be remembered. And this is the process of thinking that only fast-asleep can maintain. If Lucy woke up - were this literally her asleep - she would have a greasy feeling, her mouth as though she'd been gag-bound by cat hair, limbs ill-working and eyes unwilling to differentiate depth, would seaksick her way to the sink for a gargle and a splashed face and a dirty towel roughed over the skin hiding the shape of her skull - and then she would look square at the mirror and say 'Bianca - I remember Bianca!' If this were real sleep. If Lucy were waking. It would be joyous, delight invading like car-alarms her thoughts! And she would wakingly be pelted with all the niches and nuances of her remembrances of Bianca and just think 'That's why that name was so familiar!' The logic flags, here. Lucy pays for her food as the logic flags. That would only be true if Lucy remembered Bianca in a dream out-from-nowhere. But Bianca had texted. Had called. They'd spoken. It had been no dream. Bianca, Bianca. Lucy wonders: Couldn't it just be a mistaken name thing? Is she recalling someone else now? Replacing the name for Bianca due to the Bianca mystery and then the Bianca poet? Except it was the *Doormouth* which had struck Lucy so. Though maybe it could have been Somebody-else Doormouth? But the photograph, the photograph! Yes. The photograph. Lucy cannot deny facts, even in dreams. You really forgot Bianca. You really remember her, now. So why is that bad? 'It's too late to go remembering things that are forgotten!' Lucy says, slamming her hands into her pockets and walking, head bent bullet-forward, passing through the parking lot and only vaguely eyeing it like somehow her car got there without her. She wants to be driving! Slamming her door, not her hands in her pockets! It's no good remembering things, anymore - there isn't enough time for it! Lucy is angry at Bianca for making herself known, again. And how had her damned poetry gotten into Lucy's manuscript! Why is this the continual way Lucy's life works? It has happened again and again and again - and again and again and again - and she is tired of it. She is the odor of the dry-heaves of circumstance - no, worse! - she is the taste of the next swallow after the final dry-heave of circumstance! Lucy has fallen into a pit of bones and dissolving flesh of all the words people decided not to use - the words which have fallen forgotten - she is wading on the bottom of a corpse-river of the language of everything she has forgotten. She only remembers words about Bianca. She only remembers corpses about Bianca. She only remembers remembering Bianca - she doesn't remember her! Look at you, Lucy: do you even have a body, anymore? You're a headless dream! You're a paper without a top or bottom, just a tear no one can agree on the right-side-up-of - not triangle, circle, or square, just scrap. 'Half-of-a-word of every word, that's me' Lucy says and imaginaries kicking a can she could have actually kicked. There is a fence beside her she kind of wants to lean against. Instead, she walks faster to be past it, to be past its allure. Lucy is tired of everything owning her, of nothing owing her - she feels like a light that's been on in the same room for ages and that will have to stay on just showing the same things it shows.

Now: Lucy has brought this all on herself - if anything, indeed, has been brought. Lucy is an educated woman, after all. Lucy is a highly educated, very gifted woman. Anyplace Lucy has wound up, she has chosen to wind. Sadly, this makes her current waking-night-terrors all the more potent. There was a point, demarcated someplace, when Lucy's rather insulting desires and fantasies were charming, then - later - there was maybe an acceptable window wherein she was caught in the current of them - a bit depressed, perhaps, and in this depression it was excusable she would have proceeded along, even self-destructively - but now look at her! Look at Lucy! All of her chances weren't ages ago - she knows this is true - and yet here she rages against the fact that she has chances still!

What is Lucy thinking about? Right now? What is Lucy - pretending herself having to walk everywhere and no chance to but be penniless with no soul else, wondering where she is, pretending herself anonymous and in some kind of unique-to-the-dispossessed despair - thinking? She is thinking - thinking every word of it: 'And such is the danger, such is the price of senseless love - of senseless affection, anyway, if not love.' This is what Lucy Jinx is thinking! And - regard, regard! - she is moving herself to emotion with it! More? Hands fisted to the size of coffee beans with their tautness down pockets, she is thinking: 'I never chose anything sensible, least of all where to place my heart, my desires. Anything that stimulated any socket of me, I jousted at and then was jostled from and then jested for and - Jesus - I don't even think I love any of the people I loved and who say they loved or love me! I could point out the poor structure of the grammars of their, as they think it, reciprocal desire, show them how they conned themselves into believing my deck was unshuffled and that more than one card repeated and repeated.' Poor Lucy, eh? Poor, poor Lucy. But it goes on! Here she is thinking - the pit of her stomach a rubber-band pulled to and held at the point of snap - that it isn't her fault. That it isn't her fault! What has been her simple desire? To be left alone, to do her thing, course her track, live in a saltine-cracker room with a few books to warm her lap and a hallway with a toilet at the end of it, the door with a working lock - nothing else! Everything Lucy needs, she has. Well educated? She didn't want that! She just did that because it presented itself and there were people she didn't want to see and others she didn't want to make sad and places she - just a kid, just scared - wanted to pretend she already belonged. And then she wound up belonging there and having to pretend the specific desire was genuine, not just the escape. Lucy has only ever wanted to escape. And she never has. She's learned to run, but not to outrun. Lucy Jinx is no more free than the sidewalk her toes scrape on, every fourth or fifth step - she is no more free than dew chilling the air. But she must be trapped, she must have been crookeded to this, because she ain't a dimwit - no one would say that of Lucy, icy and mock-destitute in her coat, here - and to wind up everywhere she wished she hadn't with her head full of distrust is something that must have been stuffed down her like goose-feathers.

Blink-of-an-eye, more-or-less, as they say, and it's over. Lucy has worked her way out of it. Aloft she goes on her cigarette, her whole body the glee of a child at tiptoe! How did she accomplish this? Through a conversation with some stately woman she conjured up, some voice attached to a vague fixture of angles and geometries she obviously felt ripe to respond to, to place trust in. The conversation - spoken while walking the same block three times like some church in Dublin where the dead could be summoned by such an arounding - had started 'Lucy, what's the matter with people is they fear recurrence.' 'I totally agree!' The stately woman made Lucy immediately calm, though still her thoughts were distempered. The conversation moved on and came to 'When is the last time you thought of your body, Lucy?' 'Never.' 'Not never, Lucy - I want you to think.' And so Lucy thought - or took a pause like she'd thought - and Lucy said 'I really don't remember.' 'How many times have you pinged and ponged back-and-forth and always felt like you were wrenching yourself out of thoughts of your flesh?' Lucy said 'All the time!' She called that thing 'Youth.' She called it 'The prison she used to think life was' or 'the underside of an unused bar of soap left dropped on that prison's floor.' 'Again and again, again and again - not just once' Lucy said 'not just twice or even too many times to count - but more than that!' 'How many times have you started your life? Where did your life start? But aren't there memories before that? You always start where you remember and it is always a tumult and it goes on and on, it repeats and repeats. And now it's just repeating, Lucy.' 'Yes.' This may be vague talk, but to Lucy there is deeper subtext - she understands the undertows of it and intuits the eddies and the sudden colds, the unneeded lukewarms. 'Everyone else will ball their life into one moment - one encounter with the void, one moment they will say defined them - and have no energy else to go on. That is weakness, Lucy - that is the flesh and the throat of a coward! That is resignation and death! You repeat, Lucy, because you refuse to be defined, Lucy, you repeat, Lucy, because you refuse to say *That is the moment that made me*! There are no reversals for you! There is only head-over-heels and yourself! No moment made you, Lucy! You haven't been made! There aren't enough absurds to make you - and certainly no one word, click of tongue, wring of circumstance, is enough to tether you and keep you as goldfish or cockatoo!' 'I'm not a cockatoo!' Lucy revolted into the night, now festive as a pair of flip-flops, everywhere-at-once like sand in the wood of a shipwreck. The stately woman told Lucy to think of how hard it is to stay undefined, to be a thought, to be an idea that can't trust it knows itself - a stack of ideas that have to rather believe that they are necessitated by body, symbiotic, not whole, not nothing to do with any tug of any lust or any tears in any lungs! 'Think what it means to have the strength to not let what happened to you define you, Lucy - to not let anything have given you a name, language you, made you the vocabulary of the gallows! Think of the resolve in you that has kept you from being! Lucy: the woman who refused to be - the thing, the thing, Lucy, the thing that will be remain unbound forever, overcome its desperate desire to have been!' 'I'm no cockatoo' Lucy had repeated and the car-crash of that cigarette to that brick-wall had orange-then-blue-smoldered how it agreed.

Now Lucy remembers: she doesn't have to be a philosophy. The point of her isn't to be proven correct, to add up. Now Lucy remembers: she isn't a story and doesn't need this instance of her life to gel with that, doesn't need events to circulate like a set amount of water stirred in a bowl, a set amount of silt stirred up into different, but altogether the same, murkinesses, this time resettling slow, this time resettling fast. Now Lucy remembers: there is nothing to her - her beginning, same as anyone's, was set in motion well before there was Time, and her end, as much as it goes, is to be decided deeply past her but will likely be ignored. Now Lucy remembers: her lavish encircling of language, now she remembers her squirrel-cheeked arms aching to the bones with all they could carry - even a slim volume in a back-pocket enough to grind her under monolith foot! Now Lucy remembers: the peace of abandoning Self to the irreversible evolution of being bodiless, gutless - lungless but wordful! Now Lucy remembers: Language will live on in its proper habitat, with only the plant and animal life left on Earth. Now Lucy remembers: human beings won't lose their tongues, won't fall out with languages, languages will wrest themselves from their slavery and live without needing the crippled hanger-on of voice or eyes or cognition. Now Lucy remembers: Words will be littered long past when humankind reads books - they will live the way fungus lives and will be so multiple as to never need more examples of them. Now Lucy remembers: people can be utter bladders for language, anuses just spreading the words everywhere, messing the world with the unwieldly, untamed ravages of babbling jungles that will never be traversed. That, or people - Poets, Poets like Lucy - can be servants to the immortality of language, build its temples, shape the very face of its life, participate, be useful. Now Lucy remembers: nothing will make humankind immortal - even writing itself down, listing every name, everything - no, that was just a carrot words dangled to make feeble-minded bodies do the work of being a surface for them to lichen, a stone-face to moss, a water to speck with their unpotableness. Now Lucy remembers: some future race, some other intelligence, might reconstruct a skeleton, but will treasure a Rosetta Stone more than a mass grave - it is only the language that matters, only the language which has evolved in this other species' heads, using its space-crafts and its venturing the cosmos to eventually fill the almighty void with just words that are not said. Now Lucy remembers: words are Godheads! Words invented God! God is a word words made to spread words and everything needs to be expressed in words! Words are the bloody monsters of old and the final teeth waiting to be stuck in at the universe's final clenched jaw! Now Lucy remembers: the feel of unrusting, of fatigue, and a sense of vertigo-just-above-the-precipice when reading too long into the night, willing to burn eye-sockets to malt-dust, willing to breathe thinner and thinner rather than stand for a sip of water, willing to contort - press pillow or object into herself - rather than leave the scope of her brain filling with words for the toilet. Now Lucy remembers: language itself marked her! Language let her say she'd marked herself! It let her say she'd found fertile soil in her and shoveled her full of coal, her sore throat aburn with needing to sing, her fingers ready to thrash out new iterations of that which she had choked on while feeding off! Now Lucy remembers: now Lucy remembers! Now Lucy remembers: Lucy has remembered before! And the terror is that of being left empty, of feeling abandoned! An anger at not doing her duty, of settling for flesh, for humanity - for death over duty over starvation over indecipherableness! Now Lucy remembers what language has told her: A minute only takes a minute but takes so much more than a minute! Think of proportions! Think of the statistical breakdown of your time! You should pack as much in to every minute you can - even if just filling incidental air-pockets with horror, eh? Now, Lucy. Now. Lucy.

A dog-walker - eye-whites poison-ivied, not in the mood at all, it doesn't seem, no socks and in dress shoes, large coat around pajamas - asks her for a cigarette and she obliges, almost greedily. 'Could you call a strawberry *auburn*?' Blink. 'Which is it?' Lucy asks, the man Never-minding and 'Thanks for the smoke' but she Now-hold-on-there-son gestures 'Let's back up - I just didn't hear you' she says. 'The color of a strawberry' he says, piddle of smoke out like it is a shelled pistachio sucked of salt 'could you call it *auburn*? And be correct about it' he hastens to add, snorting phlegm as he takes another drag and not bashfuls about spitting it in the opposite direction of where the dog is snuffing the curb. 'I don't think you'd be right. I am sad to feel that way, though.' 'Well how about' the man waves off his resignation about how Lucy is likely right about the auburn matter 'could you call a strawberry's red *cherry*?' What a delightful query! Lucy doesn't even mind the rising cold-stink of feces from the audibly panting dog, wheezes like it's dog-asleep from the beast, as well. 'I guess you'd be looked at sidelong, but I would say you could say that. Strawberries aren't distinctly *red*, as compared to cherries. And apples - the red ones at least, whatever those are called - are certainly *cherry-red*.' That seems to be what the man was looking for, he insomniac applauds - no, not insomniac, he was wrenched from natural sleep, his ache is against the roister, not against his own chemistry - and points out at the empty road with both pointed indexes - leash in one hand, limp, cigarette in other, tight - as though a crowd of people were there to finally go 'Oh we get what you mean!' and to let him rooster like Peter Pan over himself, awhile. 'They are called *Red Deliciouses*' he says when he finally remembers he had ought to still be addressing Lucy. Lucy had realized this, of course, and was in that moment thinking about how apples shouldn't get to be so bossy in their names. 'What do apples have to prove, anyway?' Lucy says this without explaining her whole train-of-thought, but the man snorts, knowingly.

'We're quite the vainglorious lot' he says then, smecking his mouth like an unexpected taste or a cobweb got in. 'We're the jet-set of braggardry.' 'We are the jet-set of braggardry' Lucy silently agrees and then - why not? - vocally echoes 'We are the jet-set of braggardry!' and off-the-cuffs how 'We couldn't even leave *Brag* off our *Humble.*' And the man then takes his turn to repeat her, expansive voice '*We couldn't even leave Brag off our Humble,* no' - he smiles, long breath out, chuckles - 'no indeed, we could not even manage that. Remember being a kid - did you ever race cars?' Lucy is shaking her head, but even while she does the man says 'I don't mean soapbox derby racers - I mean just running along the sidewalk when a car is coming down the road.' Ah. So Lucy switches to a nod of assent. 'Worst day of my life, ever, was when I realized that the few strides I felt myself ahead of the car it was really just the car overtaking me. I'd never had the lead.' 'Then you have, indeed, lived an awful life - that doesn't ever occur to most kids, they just stop doing it or never really expected to be faster.' There comes the sound of the dog - the brute is likely pissing on its own shit - the sound something like the braking of a Big-Rig in miniature.

The final wend of her way home, Lucy is thinking of the man's nod - his last nod before she made her abrupt 'Goodbye' - the man enveloped in his own thoughts, not like they were a cocoon fresh-spun or a hermit-crab shell, but more like a roach had crawled into the husk of a cicada to warm from a chill. The man had smiled *Glumly.* But Lucy would rather the word be *Glummy.* 'A *glummy* smile had the man' she says, without likely realizing she is doing a mimic snort-spit to the brick, there. And here is Lucy's parked car. 'Be parked then' she snarls 'like some ne'er-do-well group of teenagers trolling the late night and just freaking out poor workers stuck home-commuting after their shit shifts!' *Ne'er-do-well*: that is one of the most exquisite uses of apostrophe Lucy can think of - reason enough for the invasive little teeth to exist, to have mutated past their need to distinguish possessive, evolving even past contraction, there. Lucy's phone buzzes in her pocket and she is about to reach for it, but decides to up the stairs first. Then stops short. A sound of lighter and then the sound of a can - that sound of thin aluminum - being set down and then of a sniffle and a light cough - all of which could only be happening right outside of her door. Lucy halted. Lucy in halt. *Lucyhalt.* Her veins are making too much noise and her insides scrunching into too many funny faces, trying to squeeze out the increasingly labored breath of her ascending. She manages back down the landing and trots to the other end of the lot, feeling whoever-had-coughed's head floating behind her as though a stalking Macbeth's dagger. 'This is worst apartment ever - it's like a toothache with a headache with an ear that itches' Lucy bastards as she goes up the far stairs, wondering what her plan is. What is so fascinating about the outside of her door!? What is so fascinating about Lucy she invites the very abstract of *Lurk* to loiter wherever she goes? 'I'm my own fucking poltergeist' she thinks as her phone in her pocket vibrates and she startles enough to hiccough. Who is texting her? Layla. Lucy stares at the name a moment before even opening the text. And when she opens it, all she sees is her name as a question. *Lucy?* The word seems quiet - a peek around a corner with lips pursed, knees tense, and ears pricked. Lucy looks at her name, still. And it's as though the word of her is repeated, Layla poking around for her, needy. *Lucy? Lucy?* Wait - is Layla outside Lucy's apartment? Is Layla peeking down the stairs, having thought that would be Lucy coming back up? Lucy doesn't want to get ahead of herself, but does hurry to the corner to give a look around - the déjà vu a taint to the hopefulness, but not so much - and her gingerly peek singes her to recoil. Not an unpleasant recoil, she just fears deeply she may have been seen. Ariel. She doesn't double-check - that was Ariel, is Ariel, leaning against her front door. Ariel is leaning against her door as Lucy returns to descend the secondary-stairs and to make her way back around to a normal approach home. A silly thing to do? Yes. What would Ariel care? And Lucy, you could just say you had come from the other side of the street - Ariel doesn't know what you've been doing or your typical habits. 'What? Should I go back?' Lucy scoffs herself, quickly typing a reply to Layla, grinning with an easy flirt while she does *Ah, my Lay lady wanting to lay me - booty call appreciated, my midnight-blue, but alas you have been usurped, my pot-bellied love-bird awaits.* And for kicks she adds *XXX* - on purpose all-capital - then types a semi-colon wink and the dog-howl grin of a close-parenthesis.

ARIEL'S MOUTH TASTED LIKE POPSICLE-STICK, water-fountain, and the snail thick grease of too-warm soda five minutes after a swallow - the creaking slick of her teeth tap-danced Lucy's and scraped her dishtowel-dry tongue for the first clumsily-into-the-room moments, inside with Lucy's back on to the closed door, the hiss of the Shut-ups the Hi-Lucys the hiss of the I-said-shut-ups. Ariel - Ariel! - Lucy thinks, must have woken and come here, her limp shirt releasing from her body overhead and the tepid-there of undeodoranted underarms haloing the air the two were stuck in while Lucy's fingertips scratched down over Ariel's perspiration streaked ribs, her acne-bumped hip flesh being peel from the sweatpants which seemed to evaporate and then to splash the floor rather than fall, this lump tippy-tap-tippy-tap stepped out of while, with sweat-toned fingers, Lucy's grips the now-found Ariel's hair and is fisted inside of it. Lucy Jinx and Ariel Lentz are hands over bodies, bovine-over-saltlick palms wanting to feel, to taste the walls on the other end of the room or the carpet beneath. Then a moment of pause and Ariel - denuded entire except for panties still ankleting left leg - holds Lucy firmly, until Lucy relents in her writhe to move on, the two of them mid-room and slightly swaying, Ariel at first kindergarten-kissing Lucy's nose, then just holding forehead to forehead - a twist to her body to manage it with girth-belly - this touch becoming a tap becoming a series of metronome head-butts, each a bit harder until Lucy instinctively breathes the word 'Okay' and lets Ariel take her by the hand and pad her through the dark. 'Are you trying to go to the bedroom - or do you need to throw up?' Lucy whisper-jokes and is rewarded by Ariel giving her arm a whip-tug, Lucy stubbing her toe on some there-piled books but Ariel just laughing and calling her drunk. 'I'm not drunk' Lucy says, the light flipping on in the bedroom slashing her eyes while Ariel's hands proceed with thuggishly undoing her button-fly - Ariel pants and odd-swallows the breaths of the questions 'You're not? You're not drunk? You're not drunk, Lucy?' while Lucy - huffs of petulant protest, but moving hips thus and thus to help Ariel peel her pants the way down - says 'No, I'm not drunk - what are you, just coming here to slander me?' Lucy stiffens at Ariel's two fingers entering her fully, parting her unmoistend slit, Ariel saying 'Well, I think you're drunk' removing her fingers and very slave-driver shoving Lucy in the direction of her unmade bed. 'You're mean, Ariel' Lucy says, but figures - since her shirt was being pulled up and Ariel made no retort - that Ariel did not hear and so she switches tracks to 'You can't count on me not to play rough because of the kid - it's not even born yet so it won't remember a thing.' And honestly, Lucy shows no concern in the placement of her weight or where she claws or bites or presses, does not react to the sometimes sharper hush sounds or Ahs from Ariel with any mindfulness of the child-at-womb. For all Lucy cares, Ariel could have wineglasses inside of her being splintered, powder-sharded, roughing into the lining of stomach and inside-wet of skin, the fierce tight of the bulge deflating to feel like a sharp, heavy beanbag, the rough in the nose of Dorene's old stuffed giraffe. Ariel - it should be marked Lucy, the moment it happened - wrest from where she was obedient and turns Lucy to belly, forearm holding Lucy's neck to place and Ariel's mouth close - tongue touching ear - to Lucy while saying - though Lucy can hear more the grind of Ariel's long hair to her own short - 'Only think about me - only think about me, okay Lucy?' Lucy's mouth too pillow-stuffed to even Mmph the word *Yes*.

To Lucy, the room is overcooking the wet of perspiration and Ariel is over her chest, her chin traced in yes-that-left-marks all along her. She splays on the carpet, the fibres at her back not helping, puddles of drip becoming pineapple-prickers in the small of her back and to the tip and curve of her shoulders. Ariel is up on the bed, having just Ughed the comforter and sheets over there, knocking down the unlit desk lamp which she'd said 'That will still work because it wasn't on when it fell, the bulb is fine' about. Lucy feels like a rash in the microwave, but cannot muster the desire or effort to actually stand. 'I wish babies would be better off if we smoked cigarettes, you know? That seems like it's just to bother people, how things didn't go that way.' Lucy concurs. 'If it was proven that drinking water was harmful to babies, they'd tell us not to. Is all I'm saying. About that.' Lucy concurs. 'Do you want to go outside and I'll watch you smoke from a court-appointment distance?' Lucy says that will be fine - but in a minute or two, she is too busy trying to figure out what specific charges she is going to press. Briefest chuckle, Ariel blithely turns to random matters, her talking laced with yawns and with trying, Lucy guesses, to get some strands of her own or Lucy's hair out of her mouth. 'There is an office complex I drive past every day called the *Huckster Business Park*.' 'No there isn't.' 'Oh but there is. And I can beat that, my pet - want me to beat that?' 'I am weak at the knees about you beating things, Ari - proceed.' 'I kid you not on this, I tell you no tale - *Huckster Office Park* is on *Shyster Boulevard*.' 'Caught you! You said *Huckster Business Park*!' 'Oh - well, it's *Office Park*, I think. Fuck, man - stop being a gadfly.' 'And next you'll tell me it's located in the *Shuck-and-Jive District*.' 'It is located in the *Shuck-and-Jive District*! You can get to *Shyster* from turning left on *Flim Street* or, if you're coming in from the South, on *Flam Parkway*.' Lucy is pondering a funny name to suggest for another business in this locality, when Ariel curtly prods 'Are you done feeling all honey-dewy, down there on your stupid floor - don't you want to smoke?' 'I'm well past being honey-dewy, yes - I'm kind of in the stage between Bargaining and Regret.' 'That isn't even how those stages work!' Ariel pouts, with locomotive effort getting her legs over the bed side, untrimmed toenail scratching Lucy's wrist. 'You're a goblin, El - and I hope you know that! Sensual as a case of shingles!' 'A case of *roofing shingles*? Or a case of *the shingles*?' Ariel asks, emphasis on the *The*, seeming confused, to judge by her face, why none of her garments are in grabbing proximity. 'Either, you know? Take your pick.' 'I pick the ones on the house, then. I once saw them, up close, and they looked kind of delicious. Where are my clothes?' 'I left them in the front room for burglars. Quite the walk-of-shame awaits you, dumpling.' Ariel scratching Lucy with her toenail again, this time quite on purpose. 'They're like corn-chips with one bite out of them, man - knock it off!' 'Don't mock my body, Lucy, or I'll compare your complexion to something obscure from the Produce Department and I know that'll get you because it'll seem so specific.' 'You actually cut me!' Lucy complains, gravely over-exaggerating her horror at the few pinheads of blood the latest toe-assault drew - admittedly the wound caused only because Lucy's skin there had been dry for ages and now was weakened and porous with afterglow. 'If you live, call me - if not, just know I thought you were a swell chick, okay?'

'So - what brings you out at this most peculiar hour?' Lucy asks - no idea of the actual time - from the balcony railing, her view down the stairs to her landing if she wasn't fixated on Ariel - Ariel there, filling the frame of the door, unlit apartment behind her, shirted but nothing beyond. 'To visit you my Lord, no other occasion.' 'Beggar that I am, I am even poor in thanks' replies Lucy, in her fatigue not certain if she has just spliced two scenes, then certain she got it right, then immediately uncertain again. 'Is it your own inclining? Is it a free visitation? Come, deal justly with me - come, come - nay? - speak!' Ariel deflects having to keep up with the dib-dab recitation by observing how Lucy hardly needs any physicality beyond a crook-of-a-mouth and a smoke. 'You're very flattering, cheri - but I'd like to think you'd miss at least another thing or two.' 'Actually, I don't even need it to be you, just a cigarette. I'm waiting for you to finish and to come kiss me, again. You mean very little to me other than I knew I could count on you to be poisoning yourself - being honest, that's all that brought me.' 'How long were you here, waiting?' Lucy scratches her nose and pivots to - her ears unclogging though she hadn't known they had clogged, and she wishes they would go back to as they had been because she can hear some annoying sound like a rusted gate from below, now, intrusive like the bite of a chipped tooth. 'A long time, Lucy. And it's hurtful of you to mention.' 'Why no call?' 'Because I'm a spontaneous woman and thought to spring upon you, unawares - and because then I was just pissed, because your car was here and I thought you were being deranged or something, hiding under your sofa to avoid me.' 'Very rational thing to suspect.' 'I thought it so.' But Lucy means it and pipes up to say so, furthering 'Especially tonight.' 'Why oh why is that?' 'I believe I have been having what the peasant-folk call a Nervous Breakdown.' Ariel seems unimpressed, even bored, and says 'I meant what was unusual, Jinxy - what was *unusual* about tonight?' 'I decided that Language isn't my enemy, after all - that I was right all along about it being the World, as a murky, dimensionless entity, that is out to get me - and it is precisely because I am in Language's employ.' Now Ariel perks up, noticeably, gives a thumbs-up and says 'That's exciting, right?' 'It is exciting, Ariel. Though it puts those I love in grave danger.' And here Lucy is surprised that Ariel does not go with obvious scripting - like a sarcastic 'Then I'm safe' or a self-aggrandizing 'Should I turn States Witness, relocate?' - but instead, with some vehemence, body tensing like all of her is the stamp of a foot, just seethes 'Fuck people you love!' Lucy smiles, grin-chuckles while letting out a last long drag, turns her back to flick the cigarette stub out into the over-the-balcony-blink, then, subservient, asks Ariel 'Do you require another?' 'Yes - please and thank you' Ariel says 'get your mouth all yucky and ashtray - you know, so it taste like the rest of you.' Flick flick flick goes lighter like har-dee-har and Lucy says she doesn't believe that Ariel hasn't snuck a smoke while stomach-ached. 'I haven't! I'm a tremendous mom! A blog once wanted to interview me just to ask me *How do you do it?* They wanted to make it so other moms have an Icon to look up to who isn't hopelessly outdated.' 'Did you do the interview?' 'No. But the reason was political and I'd rather not go into it because I think you vote too much along party-lines to be of much use to me in things.' And Ariel makes a hush sign of finger to lip then a scoot-scoot motion meaning Lucy needs to just shut up and smoke.

And when Lucy adds another quick tilt of vodka, Ariel demands a few more kisses, which come off more like a cotton-swab being smeared across a microscope-slide, Lucy sighing as though irritated until it goes on long enough she can't hold back giggling and gives Ariel a shove, forcefully, which hardly budges her. And then Lucy rolls her head around her neck, hearing bubble-wrap cracking, rubs at the top-bulb of her spine, saying 'I am actually going to have to literally sleep soon, dear Ari - you, of course, are welcome to stay or to show yourself to the door in your own good time.' 'I want to live here' Ariel says, nothing comic about it and not even really connected-as-reply to Lucy's statement, just a long-waiting statement outing at the easiest opportunity. 'I want to live here. Can I live here? And you live here, too.' Lucy knows her face is doing the eye-widening, mouth-opening Um she most wants to avoid in this moment, but Ariel seems to not notice and says 'I'm in love with you. I am in love with you. And I'm tired of everything. And I want this to be my home - can this be my home?' 'Yes' Lucy says, but doesn't like the speed, the frog-tongue of the word, it sound like an inarticulate Eyaye! when someone is about to do something that might injure them though most likely won't - opening a champagne-cork pointed at their chin or bringing a razor across a package toward navel instead of away. Again, Ariel pays no mind, though seems to have heard the 'Yes' because now is nodding and nodding and looking that way like she has some reason she doesn't want to show the emotion on her face to Lucy, all of a sudden. 'Is it' Lucy manages to get through without, she feels, any prodding pauses 'just going to be you?' Ariel, back to herself and Lucy-facing, says 'Just me. And I won't be here all the time, no' - quick sniff, but not like in response to emotions, just like runny-nose from all of the earlier tumbling around - 'I just want to come here at the end of every day. At least. I want this to be where I come when I come home.' Ariel's tone has gotten somewhat breezy, so Lucy ventures more specifically to inquire about Kayleigh and Leopold and things - having it explained how they are still living in the other house and Ariel will be there, still more-or-less all the time. 'But I don't want that to be where I am.' 'I don't want that to be where you are, either' says Lucy, returning to a worry of coming on too thick, the words maple or molasses, the words many-times bottom-slapped ketchup finally plating with a shrugging plop. 'I'll give you a key' Lucy says, then repeats 'I'll give you a key' and goes through the kitchen drawer to find a duplicate - in that moment, such a swirl of tired and shagged-out and no idea what is what, wondering if she had given the mother the key or had the mother given her a key to that house - which she holds up, flourished, coin-out-from-behind-of-an-ear. 'You're sure I'm not being a bully, right?' Ariel asks, taking the key, pretending to drop it between her cleavage, then putting it back on the counter because there is nowhere else, really, it can go, just then. 'I might have to buy a bigger bed and some kind of a wading pool for you - but other than that I don't see the problem.' Ariel's eyes are searching for something. And Lucy knows exactly what. For the lies they know Lucy is telling through omitting what all she is. But Ariel's eyes seem satisfied to just know those lies are there, that Lucy cannot so blank out to actually convince her she has nothing to hide.

By this point, Ariel has asked if it would be alright to stand in the shower awhile, alone - and Lucy has said 'Of course' it was alright and that if Lucy is asleep when Ariel finds her to either wake her or not, but to get in the bed. So: what is Lucy doing? A bit more vodka. Why? To dull the rising hornets of thought. What do the hornets sound like? They sound like too many sentences where Lucy wants none. Lucy just wants silence until morning. Morning: where she can navigate all of this awake, not asleep - where her mind will be hers and not at the whimsy of merely the mindless parts of itself. Second drink done, she returns the bottle to the freezer and - hey! - she finds her phone in her coat pocket, wondering what Layla's reply message had been, hoping for a snort. Nothing. She feels like a gnat has dragged an eyelash into her left tear-duct and rubs, worthlessly, sweat addled fingers over it, lifting lid and trying to pincer, almost feeling nauseous from thoughts of how much grime must be under her nails along with how much pleasure. There is Lucy's last message. And there is Layla's *Lucy?* which continues to seem church-mouse brunette and the echo of last week still roaming the darkened apartment rooms. 'Your Lucy is a ghost' Lucy says to the phone, thinking to type the words, but then doesn't. Check the front door, Lucy. Good. Locked. Have to be paranoid for more than one, now. This would be the worst night to be murdered. 'Common courtesy' Lucy mumbles, cricking her jaw side-to-side 'common courtesy - white knight and do unto and all.' The water of Ariel's shower, it has to be said, sounds like an argument next door, but, in fairness, this can likely be blamed on the rise of the new alcohol, the anguish of Lucy's brain having likely just gotten back to functionality and so moaning 'Jesus, more of this, now?' But Lucy has little sympathy for her brain! 'If the ledgers were lain on the same table and given the same scrutinous audit, who do you think comes out the debtor, eh? You or me, brain?' Lucy says, giving her forehead a poke and pretending in there her brain is nebbishly gathering papers to its chest and ducking backward with Quit-it-quit-it nervousness and flush-cheeks. Lucy questions, honestly, where she expects to sleep, right now. It wasn't a joke about needing a bigger bed - even if Lucy rodented herself to the wall, flatwormed there, Ariel would be slightly over-ledge. Would she? 'How did my bed get so small?' Lucy, like some old cartoon, puts her hands to the outmost parts of her hips, stiffens them, locks elbows, and brings the measurement out in front of her like carrying an invisible globe. She carefully teeters to face the bed and sets the hands down - yikes, they cover quite an expanse, do they not!? Erase erase erase, her mind goes. She stands back and puts one hand to foregut - should she put it to crotch-face, instead, as her gut could smoosh in? - and other hand to the longest reach of her ass, drifts the measurement sideways, positions this in front of her - doubting she has maintained things with fidelity - and sets it down as though, truly, she were going to sleep with her chest flat to the wall, scrunched in like the just-one-more-book crammed to an overfull shelf. 'This is shameful!' she thinks, even when she shortens the measurement. A toilet flush, but the shower still going - there, the sound of Ariel's body re-obstructing the hiss-flow - Lucy sits down and wants to sleep. 'How did my bed get so small?' she repeats, working thumb-knuckle around in her right nostril to no purpose. 'How did everything so everything?'

Lucy and Ariel share a shoulder, just here - Ariel's shower-wet skin having suctioned at downslope of bicep to Lucy's still-sticky-with-all-of-it. Both are on the edge of the bed, it confirmed that comfort is not in the cards for a sleep together. 'How were we able to, before?' 'Which time?' 'Any of the times.' 'I have a gigantic-person-sized bed back at the house, the other time was in the hotel - wasn't that a tight fit, as well?' Between them, they honestly don't remember. They settle on 'Probably' and Lucy says she will sleep on the floor. 'Why don't you bring the sofa in here?' 'The sofa won't fit in here, man - and what am I gonna do, bring it in myself?' 'I can't do things like that on account of I'm pregnant' Ariel says as though admitting her greatest regret at a job-interview. 'On account of you're pregnant - sheesh. Just don't be a pest - I'll sleep on the floor. We can get a new bed, tomorrow.' 'You can afford a new bed?' Can you, Lucy? 'Can't you afford a new bed?' Lucy faux-snipes. 'I'm pregnant, I can't afford things.' 'Cheapskate. You're just a pregnant old pawnbroker and I'll have you brought up on charges of usury! Or I'll just ax off your head as well as the head of whoever else is in the apartment.' Ariel cracks her toes on the carpet and repeats the word *Usury*. And then Lucy repeats '*Usury. Usury. Usury.*' '*Usury Jinx*' says Ariel, nudging Lucy who nudges back without repeating the name, not certain of the reference. 'Is everything okay, Ariel?' 'Everything is fine, Lucy. And I will go into details, even though I know you'd silently pout for years while letting me not and then hold it against me in a kind of Inferno resentment - but I think, from how you describe yourself now and how I feel, it might best be left until we have a single wit left between us.' 'Charlatan' Lucy says, nudging Ariel. 'Flint-heart' Ariel says, nudging back. The two of them, Lucy thinks, are both leaking floor-ward, in the same pace someone once told Lucy that glass, being a liquid, is flowing. 'Does glass really flow?' 'Lucy, don't be demented right now - what in the name of St. Martha could that possibly mean?' 'Someone told me about how glass is a liquid.' 'Who? Who told you that? Someone? *Someone*? That could be a lot of people! Are we talking Someone as in, say, Lucretius? Or are we saying Someone as though to say *A person on the bus with a plastic bag filled with empty cat-food cans*?' 'I don't remember who.' 'Glass isn't a liquid, Lucy. Wanna know how I know?' 'How do you know, Ariel?' 'Look at it. Give it a tap. If you still think it's a liquid, I mean, I'll still live with you but I'm never gonna give you Power-of-Attorney or use you as a beta-reader or anything.' 'Do we have to get a crib, too? Or has that been debunked as a bad idea?' 'Well, I have a crib. I'll bring it here.' Lucy nods, hoping that Ariel doesn't need anything further as she, frankly, had regretted - or at least found herself inwardly wincing at - the question once it was asked. After a pause, Lucy says she always thought having Power-of-Attorney over someone would be awesome. 'It sounds like something no one should ever actually have, but then someone else decided *Eh, let people have it sometimes, it'll be a hoot*!' 'I said you can't have it over me.' 'I don't want it over you. What would I make you do?' Ariel nudges Lucy, hard. Lucy nudges her back, nowhere near as hard. At the same time, Ariel taps the callused pad of her big-toe one-two-three-four one-two-three-four on Lucy's itching, veinous foot-top.

Lucy is sofaed, trying not to make a sound or to fall asleep until she feels certain Ariel is zonked - at which time the plan is to maybe crack the front door a bit for a smoke. Why? 'Why what?' Don't you go to sleep, Lucy? 'It doesn't feel like time to sleep, Lucy.' And her weird-headed sureness that this is her new method of dreaming is nothing to do with this sensation of it-isn't-the-time-for-that - the feeling is independent. Why is there an Ariel Lentz in your apartment, Lucy? Why did you let her in? And why did you tell her she can stay? 'Evidently, that is something I desire.' Something you *desire*!? 'At the very least, it is now something I have agreed to. Stop harassing me. You're already keeping me up, so why are you trying to tell me to go to sleep!? I demand some consistency, please!' Are you going to go buy a bed tomorrow? Is that your true and honest plan? 'Maybe not tomorrow.' Because you have work, right? Lucy, though, had not actually thought of that. It is a fitting reason not to go out to make furniture purchases - though, thinking on it, the images of obtaining a bed had an evening-errand feel to them. 'And beds need to be delivered' Lucy thinks. And she also thinks she just means 'Mattresses need to be delivered' as she is fairly certain the frame of her current bed can be readjusted to format out for any size mattress. And you know how to do that? 'Didn't I do it with this one?' No, Lucy - this bed came with this apartment. As did this sofa on which you lay. But Lucy doesn't think this could possibly be true. Does Ariel expect you to not work? Does she think you have the ability to finance the both of you? Does she think you are interested in supporting her and the child she is currently one-and-the-same with but soon will very much be postpartumed of? 'I'm sure Leopold has to pay for the kid - or wants to, he seemed a good guy.' I thought Ariel said it wasn't Leopold's kid? Lucy has sat up and blames everything wrong with her mechanics on the vodka. She wants to piss, but knows she will also have to shit and currently is too fearful that Ariel, being pregnant, will have to use the can immediately afterward and will be waiting out the door, entering into the fresh wave-lines of Lucy's just-then flushed stink. Lucy wants that cigarette, but Ariel would hear the door open. She wonders if she could smoke through the keyhole. *The keyhole*!? 'Why not?' Lucy! 'What?' Open the damned window! That window or that window or that window! Yes, Lucy's inner romance had convinced her she had no windows, but - just look! - she has several. And in a comically slow, excruciatingly quiet way, Lucy moves a chair toward the window, undoes one lock, waits three minutes - though is sure the unlatching was silent - undoes the other lock and goes back to the sofa where she pretends to be asleep, then goes and inches the window open in a series of two dozen countdown-of-fifteen-between-each tugs, tiptoes to her bedroom door and counts thirty snores from Ariel, then lights up and shivers while she miserably inhales, exhales. Lucy recalls - while she waves at over-evident wisps of smoke causaling their way into the room no matter how she might feel about it - that she has some sort of scented spray - why do you have that, Lucy? - but it is probably worse for pregnant women than nicotine fumes. She burns a hole through the screen and plugs the stub through it, closing the window quickly, but not locking it. Surely, the scents through her pores are more caustic than had she even smoked over Ariel's sleeping body - Lucy half-thought the word *Corpse*, but laughed even as it was thought so it doesn't count as an odd sentiment, just a blip - and surely all the rough-and-tumble from earlier would be the scapegoat for any damage to wombed-goods tonight may have resulted in.

So: if Lucy was asleep, then what is this? It seems Lucy is dreaming. Dreaming she is in a room with two clawfoot bathtubs and one seems to be filled with either a lot of pubic-hair sizzling like bubble-bath suds or else a rickety pile of

Daddy Long-Legs tick-tocking in tugs free from each other, stuck to each other, free from each other, stuck to each other. What is the other tub filled with? In the dream, Lucy seems to be wearing only socks and mittens and in this second tub is scrubbing a mint-blue residue from the sides, irritatingly aware of her own nudity, her raised backside - not concerned that she is being observed but over how it is vulnerable for something to drip on, something sharp like burs from a cold, grass-coated field to affix to like Velcro or over-dry cotton. The blue down the tub-side seems to come away in layers and as things go on it seems that a painting might be being revealed - but the sounds from the first tub grow more menacing and now, through a door, Lucy can see that whoever lives in the house has returned and are out there and will likely see her removed uniform hanging off of the doorknob. In the dream, it is another place - but the same time - and Lucy is trying to rinse chalk off her hands at a hallway water-fountain before anyone can come by to see that she hasn't left. The exact feeling of she had been told what is physically in each glass display she passes. And it becomes cruelly evident how she will not be able to exit, because there is only one way out and everyone lives just in the windows out there - no way no one will see her and, anyway, she can't lock the door behind her! So what is this? If she was dreaming awake, what is all of this? Will this count as Awake? This incongruous imagery with the counterfeit feeling of logic and connectivity, causality this-to-this-to-this-to-this? Is Lucy thinking about this while she dreams? Has she even drifted to another state? See? There is an awareness of herself on the sofa, yet far too small, she seems far too small - like a child who recently threw up water and saltine crackers and the still-pleasant cherry-sharp of medication she was not given more of because the bottle was empty, her mother will get more in the morning. Had Lucy woken up, in this moment? This moment where she finds herself tittering and thinking of *The Mouse And The Motorcycle* and *Temp-Quit* - and why would that be on her mind? Had Ariel said that? Had Ariel called her a cat-skinner and then apologized and said she'd meant something else, something with significance to Philosophy or World Religion? 'Even still, why would you call me that?' 'It means something respectable. It means something respectable, now' Lucy is dreaming she is burbling in apology to - Lucy, it turns out, being the one who had used the epithet and someone else is slamming already out the door, Lucy's shoulders shaking like vibrating train windows and her teeth all seeming filed down. 'If she even once lets her guard down and chooses wrong, they will be wedged up like unfallen testicles! It's hilarious!' The old woman in the seat next to her goes 'Ewwewewew' and gnashes her own gums and the doctor tells Lucy 'I've changed my mind' and closes the door. But is this supposed to be sleep? Is Lucy supposed to be awake, now? This feels like awake. Like breathing. But there are too many hands on her legs and not enough skin to cover the marks on her back. Lucy? 'Lucy?' she hears. Lucy? 'Lucy?' she hears. She juggernauts herself asleep - she is able to sound like the final moment of paint drying, the final moment before it is finished.

Sunlight in dirty-spade shovelfuls. The room is chill with the sound of trash-trucks and is scented with air in from - Lucy confirms - every open window. First she shoots up, feeling the hangover, but not so bad - this is more the sour-swamp-stomach variety, she will be flatulent and her nose will seem warm for hours, but not too much lethargy. Lucy seems alert enough. Vodka never skewers her uncorkingly. Her arms are tapping the sofa beside her and then she hocks up phlegm, standing, moving quick to the kitchen sink to spit out the blob, rinsing it unregarded with full faucet and sponge - which needs to be changed, Lucy, my God! - all around the basin perimeter, squeezed, fingers sniffed, tart stab of overuse. 'Ariel?' Lucy asks around behind her, but - no, you must have been wrong, Lucy - does not hear anything. She opens the fridge and drinks the contents of an apple-juice down, stifling a belch, putting the empty back from where she'd lifted it, closing the door. 'Ari?' Lucy finds the bedroom empty - the bed not made, but it is evident someone other than her slept in it from the position the pillow is left in, the sheet having come up from the mattress' corner and not yet re-arounded. The bathroom has faded evidence of having been used - final condensation on mirror, droplets along the inside of the transparent shower-curtain, the floor-mat still depressed from where it was recently wet-footed. 'So what time is it, anyway?' Lucy asks out to the empty apartment, in general, attitude to the words as like she is the only one with guts enough to pose the question to the collective mind of all gathered. To the kitchen she goes. In the kitchen she is. And it is, indeed, far later than she had thought. Here is a phone with no messages, but beside it - how did you not see that before, Lucy? - is a sheet of paper - the back of a flier advertising deals on fried-chicken from a fast-food joint that is partnered with a nearby car-wash - and on this is a note, with illustrations, in Ariel's hand. Or Lucy assumes it's Ariel's hand, but feels justified in doing so - explains this all to the person who isn't standing right there with her, just then. *I tried to wake you. But, alack alack, I could not. I have to go to a doctor's appointment or two and then I have K all evening, but I will be back. You can pop over if you're not doing whatever. I really did, by the by, try to wake you, but it looked like you had mutated and you were highly unresponsive so I cut my losses. See below. I love you. Voraciously yours, Uncle Screwtape.* And so we can see that the illustration is referencing Lucy - clearly labeled, but within quotation-marks and triple question-marked - and that Lucy in the illustration is Lucy in the mutated state that kept Ariel from rousting her. According to the drawing, Lucy had violently muscular arms and her loins had sprouted Medusa sharp tentacles - it seems she may have had spikes on her head, but that might also be disheveled hair or a crown of some kind. In a sharp-shock, jagged-action voice word-bubble, Ariel included one of Lovecraft's intonations of the Elder Gods and there is also an asterisk which leads to another, beside which is very tiny-printed scribble Lucy cannot read except for that one of the words, all capitals, seems to be *Poop*. Giving up, Lucy magnets it to the refrigerator, turns on the stove, but then realizes the effort to boil water is a bridge too far, just at the moment, so shuts the stove off and closes her eyes hard - over and over - until they stop crackling each time.

The scent proves something to Lucy. The scent in her bed. How quickly she becomes accustomed to it. How foreign it is, at first - the still slightly damp of the sheets too, how this dissipates, permeates her skin until she is a cloud composed of it, it just rain previously fallen, returned - and then how imbued of her, what she seems to scent out now, herself. All of this convinces Lucy of reality and that a decision was made. There is - let this be noted - no moment where she thinks to herself a decision has been made, rather there is a moment where she knows it is past the time a decision was made - the decision is effective and she just a turn of its screw, but a turn made of buttermilk and screw as soft as spilt talcum. Lucy is laughing. Lucy is laughing in a voice she hardly recognizes. Her head is unburdened, like a black, leather-rough stove-pot discarded for leaking. The sound is unbidden and doesn't seem to be going anywhere, like a flight of birds just wanting to hear the great sound of tumultuous, innumerable flappings. Her laughter alights back to her, swings on the perch in her chest-center. And now Lucy sits up and begins surveying the room. All kids play, all dollhouse, figuring a bigger bed will fit thusly and the table can go there and the lamp over there. Lucy pictures herself - maybe even computer lit, why not!? - in the corner, there, while Ariel reads or breastfeeds, hears the future sound of herself tacking away, music on headphones soft enough in her ears that she'll hear in case she is summoned or Ariel wants to share another 'You know what?' It seems, really, Ariel just meant she wants this to be a place she comes, a place where she nests down, at night. But still, Lucy roams around and tries to figure out how new furnishings, brought by Ariel, might be incorporated and where other clothing might be hung. Not that Lucy's closets are tight packed - and most of the clothes she has in them don't fit, anyway, can be skedaddled. Here she is back in the bedroom and she opens the closet and looks at the trashbags in which she believes she has old cotton dresses she had been undecided on parting with. Tugs the bag out. And looks down at the litter-tray. A light goes out inside of her - only noted by the sound of the new lights drowning her insides in overblown white like fresh bathroom bulbs, orange like streetlights in winter at three-in-the-morning, brown like how lampshades protect books from full yellow when read before sleep - at the sight, a light that seemed to have remained on until that exact moment. The litter-tray. It had been emptied into a bag, but is still crusted and scab-clumped in places along bottom, at sides. The towel from beneath it just limp-folded, still full with granules and by now petrified and lighter-than-air morsels of discard. The scoop, jagged tear to its handle - spot of Lucy's dried blood like something spilt to a stovetop and cooked to a scorch-mark too quickly to wipe. And tufts of hair. Tufts of hair, dander-laced, showing clear-as-oatmeal flecks of the always irritated skin beneath coat. Lucy lets go the weight of her unneeded dresses and the bag shrugs the same as the folds of her side-flesh as it and they take on fallen postures. Lucy makes a kissy sound - kissy sound kissy sound - feels a distinct, single spot of spittle on her lip's pucker, rubs fast her index-finger across thumb over and over, over and over, friction building. 'You didn't even know how to meow' she says to the closet. 'That's the sort of cat you were, Lucy Jinx - you were a failure I failed.' Lucy is staring. Lucy is staring. Lucy is boiling to get rid of the tray but just staring. 'You didn't even know how to meow. Even though I told you. Even though I fucking spelled it in cat-food, that time!'

# .V.

ON DAYS LIKE THIS, LUCY Jinx opens her best yawns, bored as the clergy. Measuring afternoons as car-trips-filled-with-other-people's-groceries. She has become a literal symbol - she lives the way she has always seen herself, destitute as uneaten corn littered to birds-waiting, yet purposeful as the flip of an Ace. The company vehicle, she knows, gleams around her, the skeleton sleek and every day washed, buffed, secured under tarp - as she has always desired for herself - the skin and the bones of it one and the same, peach-orange paint with rust-fierce letters accented to wingtips, as though every feature of humanity was only given one way to display - hair, throat, blush, pupil, scratched-calves, toenail bases, fingers white with wrinkles from water and cold. Company car. Lucy jets it like a spaceship in an old movie about the future that overshot ambition by forevers! Could this be when Lucy has felt most blissful? No, likely not. But it is, anyway, when Lucy feels blissful! Because of this job? Or this job because of other circumstances? Everything seems a marvel - an apple which never lacks peel, torn to the core but still red-gleaming, green-gleaming, lacquered well past seeming natural. Transcend! If angels were reality, would they seem natural to regard? If a book-flat, crotch-faced, slumbering beast were to yank itself out from the murk of the sea-bottom and come to slake its hunger on the works of man, would we think it looks natural, merely because we now know it exists? Nothing seems natural except - Lucy daresays - when it first seems unreal. *Natural* is another sense of *Accustomed* which is a declension of *Forgotten* which is the definition of *Unreal*. Or something. She doesn't care. And the radio *Pretty Ballerinas* by *The Circle* and a few minutes ago it *The El Dorado*sed some *Bim Bam Boom*. Perhaps it is just the tinted-windows, windows which even if not tinted have the protection of letters and images of crisp cabbage and a two-liter of soda and a box of store-brand cookies and whatever else - prescription bottles, wine, magazines - printed magically over them as over everything else which make Lucy comfortable - this less like driving but more how a goose must feel, unselfconsciousing its neck bent to nibble an itch, flapping wings before leaving black-and-whites of acrylic shit behind to indicate it took flight there. Lucy's most righteous place is ferrying groceries, over and over - a mechanism, someone who so many people have come to count on, people who Lucy did not even know existed before, let alone had already passed the 'Why don't we try' phase into the 'This is expanding, boys - this is taking off wheeeee'! Why? Oh because Lucy finds it endless and teeming with mundanity - so much of anything is a jungle's worth of exploration - a million miles of the same sort of tree, no variety at all, would not be something to exactly get excited by, but it would certainly never be anything to ignore. She sees herself as an Aguirre, Fitzcaraldoing her way deeper and deeper into a wilderness that will yield no treasure. She is Magellan, coming all the way back around for the umpteenth time, having tried every angle, reporting to his financiers, all gathered, how the final jot of the planet's surface has been skimmed and, well, there's a lot of water, but nothing but port and return-to-port to show for it. 'Death, the most discovered country to whose bourne all travels return, glaze-eyes the will and makes us rather bear those ills we have and are dimly aware of than fly toward others we know every goddamn thing there is to know about!' Death is the most boring item imaginable, Lucy thinks, and hence it is feared. 'We say in death we will know everything' she pontificates, seeing the turn for the apartment houses she will spend the next twenty minutes wandering floors of 'to remind ourselves how awful, insipid, nothing-but-a-repeat it all is. If you don't know everything before you've died, you haven't been paying attention - if you've been paying attention enough, then you've died.'

Mr. Nathaniel Myrtle. Every inventory sheet is a story. Mrs. Linda Ciinnoo - that's a real name and, well, that real name needs *Flonaze, Tampax*, three *Canada Dry Ginger Ales*, nail-clippers, shredded Parmesan cheese, and a package of mini-baguettes. She is almost a children's book, this woman. In fact - see, Mr. Myrtle has a large order, six-bags-worth, a normal-haul - what makes Mrs. Ciinnoo so worthy of being fabled to wee ones is that she uses the *Hernando's GrocerEaze Service* to only get a single bag - not even a bagful! - of items. Somewhere - Lucy sees where, in apartment *Four HJ*, which as an address, itself, is a kind of giggling clapping hands, fingertips only, just under chin - there is a woman who selected with such specificity these items and who took the computer-time to order them brought. A queen! A hermit queen! She is a regular St. Francis - who would have utilized this service, don't even worry about that! - Lucy thinks, loading Mr. Myrtle's goods into the push cart, dividers between each bag, divider down the middle, two stacks-of-three. Should Lucy take Mrs. Ciinnoo's bag, pile it on top of the cart, deliver it on her way down? Quick math indicates 'Meh, naw' get it with the other two medium loads. Who cares about the name? It doesn't scream Urgency!! Lucy closes the refrigeration-unit door, locks it, taps in a wrong code to prove it is locked, then shuts the rear, unswung open door, pressing the button that makes the car bristle three beeps - it too is locked, this means - making her way, then, through the driest parts of the lot she can find, the melt of this peculiar late snow treacherousing deep puddles Lucy's junkie shoes could not handle so much as a wet sneeze from, let alone a dip-in. This rear door seems familiar - maybe Lucy has been here, her first training drive or something - even the way it seems locked until she pushes a little harder and the swinging door slurps opened, rubber flaps clanging bitchily as the doors shut back and she is nodded at by a janitor. In a film, that janitor and that nod would spell trouble! That janitor might be an early role played by someone who becomes famous, later. The quiet of her footfalls to the basement elevator seems celluloid and tinny, the television on next-door showing a movie a decade old, old man asleep in front of it. Yep. That's her footsteps. The things one learns, Lucy! Never too old, no matter how cynical one may get. *Hernando's GrocerEaze* only delivers to apartment complexes with rear doors like this. A mystery. Why? They deliver to houses, Old Age Homes, to apartments above shops, to hotels, to motels - but only to apartment complexes with entrances set up for deliveries like this. It must be purposeful. It couldn't just be no one ever thought of it - to deliver to other apartment complexes via front doors. Lucy might revolutionize the business by clearing an Ahem and going 'Boss, sir, er, um - what if delivered to all types of apartment buildings?' Then again, she sighs, breathing in ascending scent of elevator-shut, that's likely what happened with the atom. 'What're those?' 'Atoms.' 'Cool.' Centuries later: 'Ever thought about fucking about with them?' 'The atoms?' 'Yeah.' Oddly, it was discovered, no - 'No' - no one had ever thought of that! Another yawn. Lucy is a crackling fine vintage - the oldest, moldiest barrels of malaise. And she thinks: 'That's because we used to have respect for things. We used to have manners.' It all went wrong when the first mathematician gave in and said 'What do you mean

*How do you say it?* Say what? What do you mean *That?* You don't *say it*, that just *is it*. Why do we have to call it something? Fine! Uh. *One.* That's *One.* Spell it? You spell it, I don't care!' No bing! to this elevator. Just everything stops for longer than it seems it should and the doors cardboard open like they are just pretending, stagehands late-for-their-break at either side, sighing. The light in the hall is the color of the carpet, the color of the carpet is the light in the hall.

But skipping a bit, here we find Lucy at the door of Mrs. Ciinnoo. And what does Mrs. Ciinnoo look like? Younger, perhaps, than Lucy had imagined, though presenting in exactly that way wherein age is hard to pin down - could be old-looking-twenty-three, could be young-looking-forty-one. An artificiality to the skin which does not seem make-up paced and a peculiar allocation of physical dimensions - something off enough to be noticeable, irk the overall, a thing Lucy notices always in women who seem to frequent Arts and Craft stores - a forehead too long, chin pinched in too small, a kind of extra turn to the back when the waist is lamppost thin and could be taken in both hands enough that fingers could slightly entwine after aroudning. The voice is that scratchy-throat type where one never knows if the person with it is sick or sarcastic and the manner shrinking exactly the opposite of the words to her dialogue would suggest. Lucy smells plant-life and oil-paint, Lucy sees torn stone-grey jeans over probably-ashen knees, Lucy can hear a radio discussing theatre or politics or financials - or all three at once - and there is a distinct sound of either a fountain or an aquarium, somewhere in the apartment, there. Small-talk isn't required on the job, but Lucy feels too much a foreign delivery-driver if she doesn't say something. She cannot remark on the contents of the order - though it is known she must have verified, partakers of this service likely think she even filled the bags herself - and so she always goes with: broad and friendly. 'Are you an artist?' Mrs. Ciinnoo is signing her name and mousey Excuse-meing a cough into her small, replica-statue hands and she brightens at the question. 'I am. Do I look that much a mess?' Lucy laughs because Mrs. Ciinnoo laughs, but it's the kind of laugh Lucy prefers to avoid, because deprecation like that - except when amongst friends - comes off as weak, and weakness is hardly something to converse with, even for two minutes. 'You do. You look just like a paintbrush, actually, so I assumed you were painter. The way people start to look like their pets, you know?' Oh what a delight, what a delight Lucy Jinx is - glad-hander like in the olden-days! Oh how Mrs. Ciinnoo is loving the peculiar way how Lucy tells it. 'I am a painter. Do I really look like a paintbrush?' Lucy give points to the woman for not taking it as an insult - see, Lucy, there must be some self-esteem there - as it seems, to Lucy, there are more ways to see the comparison as a disparagement than a laud, and says 'You do. Added into it: I knew a painter who wore pants just like that - I almost think you stole her pants, really - so especially starting from that bias, yes.' And what does Mrs. Ciinnoo paint? Mrs. Ciinnoo paints city-scenes, mostly, and does commissions of just about anything - but mostly people's pets or their spouses. Lucy wants to press on that *their spouses* - why had that been so particularly pronounced? - but has taken her tip - Mrs. Ciinnoo tipped her well and Lucy, taking the money, also remarks to herself how it's likely Mrs. Ciinnoo's mouth that makes her seem off, one of those can-lid mouths, seems all the way across, head-opening-like-a-trash-can-lid sort of person - and so just says 'I have always admired painters. I used to think I'd be one, but no - I just delivery groceries and read a lot of debunked philosophy from Spain in the seventeen-hundreds.' See? Now Lucy is sick of Mrs. Ciinnoo - there was no need to laugh so hard at that last remark, Lucy herself doesn't even know what it means! You're trying too hard, Mrs. Ciinnoo - far far too much effort, my dear. It becomes the causal advertisement it was always going to becomes - Mrs. Ciinnoo shows her paintings in such-and-such quote-gallery-endquote and is at *Worchester Mall* the seventeenth of each month for the *Art Mart* festivities. 'I will have to check that out' Lucy Jinx Lucy-Jinxes. She hears the door to Mrs. Ciinnoo's room close behind her far too long after she has been walking the corridor, can tell in the soft click the woman had hoped for even a cursory glance back.

What is it about these assessments of folks like Mrs. Ciinnoo? Lucy makes the same things, in micro, of the people associated with her several other deliveries in the building and then takes to the road to do a few town-house deliveries before swinging back to load up, again. Lucy has a regiment, now, of allowing herself to find - she even seeks out - small allures, hourly if possible, to indulge in, delve into, and then walk away from without further thought. See? See? She isn't dwelling on Mrs. Ciinnoo or any of those others - the faces of people from yesterday and yesterday and yesterday are a blend, a blur that blurs enough to become an erasure - she isn't certain her speaking will lead her to contact Mrs. Ciinnoo or vice versa - indeed, quite the opposite! This is Lucy building up an immune system. This is Lucy correcting a past miscalculation. Lucy needs this job of momentum and of face-to-face-to-face of particular-to-particular-to-particular of detail-to-detail-to-detail and should never have taken the sorts of employments she had in past - hotels and filing and in one office with one somebody-else all day, restaurants, book-stores, doughnut-shop, places where casts-of-characters met and grew and blended. People like Mrs. Ciinnoo are given her to kitty-cat paw and then kitty-cat lose interest in. Even if they recur - she has recurrent customers - it's just because they do and her roll does not deepen beyond 'Here you go' small-talk and 'Have a good day.' This builds up a reflex in Lucy for shedding, not clinging - and the theory is that this will extend to the more-already-entrenched parts of her life. Hypothesis: Lucy dwelt too long in places and grew attached more than the people there grew attached to her. Hypothesis: those who did grow attached to her did so in direct response to Lucy's intruding herself on them - that is, had Lucy gone, she would not have been sought. Supporting evidence: a long list of names of people Lucy misses who have not sought her out. Contra-evidence to this support: a shorter list of people who have sought her out and the uncertainty about whether there way have been more. Further contra-evidence: Bianca, whom Mathilde had not been able to find hide-nor-hair of. Detail of this further contra-evidence: Lucy has taken steps to make herself untraceable to some, therefore a reasonable amount of those on the list of folks who have not sought her have to be disincluded. Sub-theory lacking support: Had Mathilde tried hard to find Bianca, or had Mathilde gotten sick of it? Because, after all, Lucy did not want Bianca found so is not pressing the matter and this might have been assumed by Lucy's lack of follow-up - Mathilde, obviously, very used to tenacious 'Any news?' when Lucy had begged out her services for sleuthing on other matters. 'What are we talking about?' Lucy asks the windshield in front of her. 'We are talking about how I am useding myself to being able to interact and uninteract. I am building up a skill-set I lack, removing myself from the influence of physical humanity.' 'Noted' Lucy has the windshield say in a gruff, puppet-creature voice, something between a head-cold and boredom to its tone. Lucy see herself as a twig in a river now, as something caught in an endless flow of anonymous hyper-specifics, nothing more than being able to glance a glimpse at anything. It's like that experiment she once read about. Subjects are shown a photograph and told to memorize it, to draw it, then they are shown a slightly different photograph of the same person or scene, told to memorize it like as though they would draw it, again, and then are shown a series of rapidly-flashing-past images of thoroughly different looking people or scenes whisk-whisk-whisk-whisk-whisk and then told to draw the person or scene they had drawn before and looked at twice. 'Is it ever the same?' Lucy asks, as though having the experiment explained for the first time. 'Well' she says, scientist-voiced 'that's what's so interesting. Concentration' Lucy scientists 'active remembrance, choice, randomness, result.'

Even parking with the fleet - back at the store, as here we find Lucy doing so - she manages, or has managed these few weeks, not to get to know any of the other drivers who seem to have no interest in getting to know her. Funny. It's funny. Lucy still manages to see herself as girlish, wallflowering and no-wonder-these-grown-people-don't-try-to-approach her, but Lucy knows the reality is far from that. Lucy: older woman, driving a grocery delivery car. The young people who pull bagged-orders from The Line-Up and arrange them according to the delivery-address-order in the refrigeration-unit back of the cars would never mistake her for one of their peers nor seek out her counsel concerning their contemporary issues. Lucy is hardly more than their mother, she supposes, and does nothing to indicate otherwise. She is a question mark to them and were she to say 'I am a Poet' or some other such utterance none of them would - even if poet's themselves, young and naïve and unknowing of reality outside of recently graduated from high-schools, two-year junior colleges - mark the title as having the meaning they - young and bold - affix to it. She has drifted out of the sphere where she is romantic to youth - she is past the threshold where youthful ideas find themselves romantic. 'You were the same way, Lucy - the same way' she says in her mind's voice, signing the sheet indicating she confirms the loaded groceries and is ready to drive out. Live in a cold-water flat? Sure, but not past the age of fifty - at least not without having refused the Nobel Prize and chosen obscurity and trips to whatever whores you can afford on Public Assistance! Lucy is like the fifty-five-year-old in a punk-rock band who still plays and doesn't seem to know that old-revolution is the same as never-touched-floatsam. Here goes Lucy, again - into the wind, a handful of grain, a predictive superstition in someone's half-made-up faith. She lights a cigarette, despite policy, because no one has ever faulted her and everyone likely smokes in the cars. She keeps the windows open a bit, true - no more Rebel-Rebel in her - and will spritz the parfum she keeps in her bag before heading back - but there is a defiance, there is a defiance if only the least thin of superficially so. Is Lucy content? Look at her. She looks content doesn't she? Is she content in her mind, though - her heart? Ah - well is that what determines contentedness? Is she not still cancered if her heart is light and she accepts death as inevitable and each individual death a work of Art, not to be argued with, liked, or disliked? Lucy is content as the flung arrow piecing its victim. Lucy is content as the drought which clears man and animal from its sight. Lucy is content because that is the purpose of choice. And Lucy has chosen and does not need to choose again. Fact: this job pays better than her previous job and the history of *Hernando's* suggests she can exist in her function until retirement, no worry of rugs out from underneath her. Yes: a forty-plus year old woman grins at seeing her paycheck directly from a company after those few years of temp-work drift. She even reads the bulletin-board and has signed a few of the large *Congratulations Jenni!* or *We'll Miss You, Mr. Figes!!!* that are posted, grade-school poster-board projects, neatly laminated at the *Home and Office Shop* at the other side of the lot. Lucy has eaten mouthfuls of cake leftover from celebrations and poured froth fizzy store-brand soda over slush melted ice in paper cups dozens of times already - dozens of times! - before leaving to the last crumbs of traffic and the new route home that has become as old as the previous one in much less the time. Lucy has wondered what life is. Life is what it becomes. 'The past isn't life, now is it?'

1022 / PABLO D'STAIR

she says. 'The past is the very complexion of death, all of its contents in the state they'll remain.'

A first! The wonderful thing about new jobs, these first. Lucy feels like a surgeon, thinking on her feet, not expecting the brain she is about to incision to have toenails. She presses the doorbell a third time and waits the allotment of time she thinks sensible before pressing it a fourth. Protocol. Protocol which she has not memorized, but has the gist of. *Hernando's* - they are big and caring - prefers not to take the groceries back, but they cannot just leave them there due to perishables and what have you - prescription medications sometimes included, as is the case, here. The policy for the Subscriber - you have to subscribe to the service or else pay an additional, silly amount per-single-order - is that if the groceries go back, the card is refunded, but a black-mark is added to the account. The black-mark can be erased if the Subscriber signs in and gives an appropriate excuse, but to have the black-mark erased also adds a surcharge to the monthly bill. Why? Lucy gets it. That's work! People have to do that! And the excuses are almost certainly always deceits. Processing the refunds is time, not to mention the gas used for the trip out and blah blah blah. Aren't all of those things covered in the cost of subscribing? No, which is the brilliant cut-throat part! Subscribing is free - it just requires a credit-card or bank account - and these little charges are why. A few of them and any sign-up price is more than made up! Fascinating, Lucy - but what is the protocol here? Lucy is doing it: calling the number on the receipt - which goes to voicemail, of course - and saying to the beep 'This is Lucy with *Hernando's GrocerEaze*. I am at the front door with your delivery, the time is' - she verifies, says it - 'and I have not received any response. I will swing back by, soon, after making deliveries in the surrounding area. Please do give me a call in the interim. Also, please be aware that if you are not present when I return, an additional charge will be taken from your credit-card when the grocery-fees are refunded. Thank you.' Weasel-speak, that last bit, but Lucy rather likes having to say it. Additional charge? Additional to the charge for the black-mark removal, which - are you remembering this right, Lucy? - is charged automatically after thirty days or something even if the black-mark hasn't been argued. How much does *Hernando's* wind up making from these fees? Enough to make it worthwhile, of course. More than enough. Lucy is paid well, as far as things go, and the tips, which are not required, make her actually paid handsomely. But do you have to swing back by, Lucy? Or do you only have to if you get the call? 'Shit' she mutters, because there might have been trickier language she was supposed to use there, too. She presses the doorbell, again. And wonders - but even as she does, she sees why not - why *Hernando's* doesn't just leave the groceries and charge for them, minus prescriptions - let perishables perish! Or better: take the groceries back and charge for them, say they were left and shrug 'They must have been stolen' resell them later. 'One investigative report would queer that up, quick' Lucy mugs for the imagined hidden-camera, posh and professional as she makes her way back to her car. And here she is driving, about to move ahead to the next customer, when it strikes her 'You just used your own phone, not the delivery-phone to leave that message, Lucy!' Hard brakes, not even out of the spot. Retrieves the dialed number from her phone, dials it into the delivery-phone and thinks. Okay. Try it - even if it isn't to script, it seems legally savvier. Beep: 'This is Lucy with *Hernando's GrocerEaze*. I was just at your front door with your delivery, the time is' - she verifies, says it - 'and I did not receive any response. I left another message, accidentally, from my personal phone and apologize for the repeat. If I receive a call in the interim I will swing back by after making deliveries in the surrounding area. Also, please be aware that if you do call but are not present when I return, an additional charge will be taken from your credit-card when the grocery-fees are refunded. Thank you.' That good? 'I don't even remember what I said' Lucy sighs. A crick of tension in her shoulders. Noia of 'There is some way this can be used against me.' Symbolic - these groceries are something remaining with her, after it was supposed to be disposed. Lucy's mind recalling it is Lucy's mind. Nothing is ever simple. No door is ever locked enough.

Long artful still-shot: Lucy Jinx, deliveries done, sitting sideways out the front seat of the car, watching the still bricks of the side of that elementary-school - she could not park closer to the delivery address, as regulations do not allow *Hernando's* drivers to *act like pizza-delivery drivers* and just pull to a halt in the road - not inhaling, letting unsmoked smoke ooze in upward cream, mostly warming her left cheek, a few times overing her eyes. She checks both phones and the customer - Mrs. Doris Mealy - has not called back. The excitement of the job-first has been overtaken by the fear and trembling of the Lucy-first: what is Lucy - as a Lucy, not as an employee of *Hernando's* - going to do about this situation? Is she as boxed-in as she seems? The very idea of coming up with an outside-of-the-regulations plan seems the laboratory model of Wrong Move - yet the regulations themselves have marked this as something that will linger. And the defect is Lucy's: why are you still excited about First-things? That's like giving the opponent a place to set a lure. The very fact that Lucy was happy and is now agitated drives home the permanence of all of these particulars. A name to remember - an address - something has gotten into her shoe, into her throat, into her lungs - or into wherever is most troubling. A different color ink in her diary. Something. No one should overstate: Lucy is not losing it. She has not had really a hiccough in weeks and that should sound like a Tall Tale, considering. *Babe the Blue Ox. Johnny Appleseed.* All of it. She will drive back, of course, because she believes it is in the regulations, but would do so even if she didn't believe that. Which gives her the chance to try something clever. Leave the groceries with a neighbor? Maybe this was all a ploy to meet that neighbor! Leave them on the sidewalk? Would she be fired for that? Hurl the bags away, Lucy - they are infected! You've been smoked out - cleverest cockroach you may be, but nothing stops the spread of deadly chemicals! 'The damage is done' Lucy thinks, stubbing out the smoke 'and that might be the worst part.' She is a mouse with a broken neck just sprung down on it, lamenting the fact it is still capable of hunger. 'If only not that' Lucy-mouse thinks 'if only not that' gurgle-gurgle dead. What she is trying to do here is to find a way to minimize this mood. To find other examples in the last several weeks to which it is comparable. Lucy is price-comparing her angsts, holding coupons to coincidences and seeing if That-and-That-together equals This. Nothing. So she bargains: this was going to happen, sooner or later, so if she gets on with it she will be rewarded by learning that in her new protective life-flow coincidences are just coincidences. Sure, Lucy. But this feels too precursor. Do you know Doris Mealy? Does she know someone you know or knew? All sorts of half-way skeletons dance in the baubles of Lucy's strained vision, her clenched teeth their clatter-clatter feet. This is hilarious! Lucy - you've culled your life down to only hiding from about a half-dozen people at most, but now are convinced a whole army-of-the-dead are actively pincer-movementing your encampment, any old person from any old history mounting stead and watching you from just there where the horizon goes too dark to make out. 'Please' we find Lucy saying, trying to keep it song-and-dance. 'Please. Come on. Just let this not be anything and I'll do whatever you want.' She tries to pick something that would be a good deal, a promise to give shape to her 'Please' something to anchor its feet, staple the paper to the windy tabletop. 'I promise, okay.' She sighs like the last words of the credits slipping past the top of the screen in the movie-house. 'Please.'

'Oh my goodness' - the accent is unforgivable to the language it speaks - 'thank you so much for coming back. I couldn't call you. I fell asleep. Thank you so much.' Lucy is aw-shucksing how it was no bother, it is her job, explaining how she left two messages as well and all that. 'My phone isn't working' - the woman, fossilized, breath like an inside-out pocket, cradles one hand in the other at the height of the drooped bulge in her night-shirt - 'and I have just been knocked out with this sick.' Lucy is empathy-browed and cannot find a reason to say 'No' when the unsarcophagused thing that is this woman motions her in with the bags, around through the scent of endless lozenges and wet left from cat-food tins by the score. 'It's nothing to apologize for, at all.' Relief is what Lucy feels, she is taking in details from objects and the particulars of the brine-tan of the woman's liver-spotted arms hungrily, overloading herself with this to

forget by the time her shift is all done. 'It was the prescription I needed, dear -
is the prescription in there? Oh I haven't had my voice for two days, but its back
a little now.' The voice? The sound of an already cracked egg cracking again,
shattering to children's fingertips - tap tap tap crack crack crack - poking it until
it yields no further crunch. 'Is the prescription in there, dear?' the woman asks
again, followed by a cough which is something like a frog-croak, a tire over a
gravel drive, and a torn page from an aged-to-blue-edged paperback being
roughly balled inside a clammy fist. 'Oh I do believe it is' Lucy daughter-voices,
duty-nurse voices, diaper-changer voices 'let me just get this stuff away and it'll
be there.' Some bristle - but not aimed at Lucy personally - the woman is venting
that 'They better have remembered it. All they have to do is fill up grocery bags!
If they can't do a prescription too, I could have stayed with the service. I used
to be with the service' she tells Lucy - poking Lucy for attention - likely not
aware that her decrepit fingers give the poke the sensation of being prodded by
a damp stick. 'The service, eh?' Look in that cabinet, Lucy! You are putting
away a bin of raisins and there are one, two, three identical bins in there, as well
as two three four of the six-packs of individual boxes and next to those are three
piles of generic birthday candles - though in thinking about those, Lucy wonders
if the total number of candles equals the woman's age, maybe that isn't as odd
as it seems at first blush. 'The service never missed a delivery. And they could
call the doctor, too. I have to call the doctor, now.' Pause. 'I said I have to call
the doctor, now' the woman repeats, Lucy putting milk in the fridge next to
five cartons of orange juice - all full, Lucy knows this from having to move them
each over a tap to make room for these two half-gallons - and responding 'The
pharmacy can't call the doctor?' only knowing to say this because she has had
almost this same conversation with a few other old people she has delivered to
since taking the job. 'Well, they used to be able to!' - cough cough goes the
woman, a squeeze-box that doesn't work and is discarded with a shrug at a Yard
Sale - 'But now my doctor tells me I have to call and the girl at the doctor says
it's all for my protection. I say: I've been getting my scripts at *Hernando's* for
longer than she's been alive! This girl is so young. Is she telling me, I ask, that
*Hernando's* is going to start robbing me or giving me medication I don't need like
some poisoners!?' Lucy hesitates between a 'You never know' chuckle to show
rapport and a 'What a stupid thing to have said to you!' to seem like I've-been-
there-myself. The woman's eyes are the same color as her false teeth. Both are
the same color as the not-as-white tile closest to the drain in a janitor's closet.

What's this in your hand, Lucy? 'What?' There is something. 'It's the receipt
from that woman - who cares?' No, no - this isn't a receipt, Lucy. Look! 'Why?'
But of course Lucy already is looking, eyes watering as she takes a glance at the
time on the car clock, waffling about whether to have another smoke. *Atovaquone.*

*Pneumocystis pneumonia. Doris Prescott Mealy.* Lucy? Lucy? 'Yes' she says, stuffing the paper into her pant pocket while she wriggles to get her smokes out of her other pocket. And the outbreath of the first drag here is miraculous! Everything is going your way, Lucy! You are what they mean by *In the name of the father, the son, and the Holy Ghost* and always remember that! How much shift is left? She'll do another swing out, but knows that the well-oiled machine that is the loading-bay will have her schedule and give her just one location with multiple deliveries - likely one of the Halfway Houses where she just delivers everything at the back door and the staff deal with the distributions. Those lots are lawned with cigarette stubs, many of them soaked by rain and then sun-stiffed to odd angles of anguish - a real Hellscape, nothing natural about it, Lucy always has the impression the things weren't so much smoked as had their throats slit and pockets picked while out strolling, tried to crawl away, hopeless, eventually expired, and had themselves picked at by rodents until they all look naturally used. Or maybe a Soup Kitchen. Anyway: a single-order kind of place. Though what day is it? Thursday? There probably won't be another load - they always let her go home early Thursdays because they have to overstaff the evening shift. *Always?* You say it like you've been here a lifetime, Lucy. 'I have been here a lifetime' Lucy says, failing again to find the lever that will make the seat recline though she knows there is one. '*Atovaquone*' she says. She Al Pacinos '*At-oh-va-quone*, hey?' Then, like a dialogue in a foreign language '*At? Oh va! Quone!*' Or else - different accents, a dialogue - '*At oh!*' '*Va?*' '*Quone.*' The second dialogue was said to mean '*Hey you!*' '*Me?*' '*Sorry*' - the *Sorry* in a sheepish voice indicative of '*No, not you.*' 'Other languages are easy to write' Lucy says, letting her eyes drift shut, the pretend of a small gathering of readers listening to an interviewer who sometimes lets them interject questions of their own. 'Once you have one language, you just think *Well, what would I say in that language and then spell everything different*. It's not complicated, language - it's just a question of who you know, really.' What do you mean? - Lucy is drifting - one of the audience asks her. 'I don't correct people who make mistakes in English very often, right? And I know people who speak French don't correct each other - and when someone who learned it as a second language hears something and thinks it's a mistake they are never sure, they let it slide, because they don't want to be interrogated too hard about their understanding of participles and the like.' The snout is close enough to her she can count the droplets of perspiration and breathes the mucus-salt humidity. Lucy jolts. Her neck is stiff from being awhile corkscrewed around, head-top-to-window. Curse words as she massages her neck-shoulder and can't get feeling proper one bit. Only two minutes have passed, going by the car clock. Her cigarette must be somewhere, but where? She opens the car door and it drops to the pavement, cold. So she recloses the door and cannot get her eyes to stay wide - they're like toilets in the neighboring apartment that won't stop hissing. What was the dream? What was that? 'It was a nose that smelt like it was snorting out after breathing in something that had already died' thinks Lucy. Her eyes stick. And when they open they sound like miniature loose drawer handles, jiggling when pulled, rattling tiny when shut.

As Lucy pulls into the company-car lot, she notes the commotion - or not commotion, just a lot of people milling - around one of the company-cars - this specific one not in a space. Extra squirt of the parfum and spritz to her wrist-underside - on which she rubs the other wrist-underside - and she slowly makes her way over to see. One of the drivers is boisterously relating the events that led to the vehicle's hood being dented, windshield cracked, and speckles of blood - like dampened pinches of cinnamon flicked this way and that way - all over the place. Lucy doesn't want to listen once she hears that there had been a flatbed truck in front of the driver, two young women in back holding steady a cage in which some half-dozen or ten rabbits must have been inside of and then a weird bump or something caused them to lose control and the cage took flight, smashing the car, rabbiting carcasses everywhere. From the way the driver is touching his hands repeatedly to his face, Lucy cannot help but think, on impact, some of the blood must have shattered through the windshield to his skin and she buries her face in the air in front of her and gets to the desk where she hands the keys to Lucille. 'What are they talking about over there?' 'Nothing' Lucy says, then doesn't want to feel like a dope so says 'Some driver hit an animal or something, I dunno.' 'Jesus' says Lucille, kind of a laugh, but sad - defensive - like she thinks she is supposed to laugh to fit in or otherwise wouldn't even hint at doing so 'where was he delivering to, I wonder? Or do they need to start issuing deer licenses, again? I see them in my back yard, all the time - my kids and I watch them.' And perhaps sensing the thorns growing in Lucy, Lucille touches her forearm and says 'Not to kill them - we think they're beautiful. In the fog, you know?' Lucy knows - or so she claims - and heads to the door that leads to the stockroom, through the stockroom to the door that exits into *Hernando's* over by the sushi-counter which never seems manned. 'Hi, Lucy' says a man she knows is named Carlton as he slouches by, pushing a palette loaded up with replenishments for the Paper Plate, Plastic Fork, Tupperware aisle. Why does he know your name, Lucy? Why do you let him say 'Hello'? Who cares, though, really. Lucy just makes her round and selects her jumbo packet of fruit snacks and her canned coffee, pays at Customer Service to be given her discount and exits the place without further ado. There is no percentage in loitering around after work. If she hadn't habited herself into these coffees and snacks, she'd never set foot in the place - not in the actual store. Or if she wasn't lazy, she knows, is the real reason. Paranoid and lazy are an odd mix, eh Lucy?

Won't park in the back because that makes it too obvious she works here, so she parks in the front lot - over by the bank, but still on the grocery-store property - but she is too lazy to walk all the way around the store at shift-start - and doubly so at shift-end - so has to go through the store, through the store. 'Everything is calculus' Lucy says, eyeing her reflection like she expects her face to be bandaged or still healing from stiches. Her yawn, here, throttles chills out of her, makes the spine of her feel eelish, wanting to be free from a jar. 'Hi, Lucy' she says to the reflection, which is semi-transparent and composed mostly of the color of the sky and the graphite striations of the cloud-cover over her shoulder and above. 'Hi' she makes her reflection say back. She touches her hand to the reflection's hand, makes her fingertips a claw while it does the same with its. 'I assume I'm smiling' she pretends the reflection is telling her 'and I assume you think you are, too - because that's what I'm doing.' About as certain as you can be, I suppose - trusting in eyesight and glass.

IT'S TREMENDOUS HOW GEOGRAPHY CAN change inside of geography when reasons are mustered to make a space only-as-large-as-it-always-had-been smaller because one wants to hide without concealing, one wants to change without altering. A tweak of time, a tweak of space, and the same exact circumstance - the same exact actions, the same exact place - can overlay something hardly an eyesight away. Over there? When over here used to be the stomping grounds, over there wasn't even thought about. Over here? Now that this is the place, over there is just as foreign as any undiscovered summit. Lucy - here - indicating what this all has to do with, parks her car behind the discount mattress-store next to the bookstore, finishes listening to her song. That - there, see it? - enclosure with a dumpster is where Young Pastor Mitchell now secrets her stash, as obviously the former spot won't do under Lucy's new-life regime. All it took? Lucy included a typewritten note - never touched by ungloved hand, library computered and printed - indicating that, from now on, this place is where her money would be found - Thursdays not Wednesdays, every other, still - and so this is the place that she *needed to have her books delivered*. Young Pastor Mitchell wrote back with the first delivery - that one only plastic-baggied and taped to the rear dumpster's left underside - explaining how, in future, what he would do would be to put *the books* in a mini *Frosted-Flakes* box, which he would scrunch up and tape to the structure because he did not trust the plain baggie. All so very perfectly cute and not a need for any of it! And say the condition of the dumpster changed between Lucy dropping money and Mitchell picking-up-stroke-dropping off? They'd each always check all four corners of each dumpster. Simple. Paranoia surrounding drug-drops never lasts so long. For all Lucy knows, five other people use this same dumpster for the same thing - and some other things, scores worse! - but none of them would ever know it because all they care about it their little disguise, their little take. And Lucy likes the *Frosted Flakes* box - this is the first time she has received her goodies this way, delighted it is literally *Frosted Flakes* - she can picture Mitchell pausing with a *Lucky Charms* box or a *Honeycomb* box thinking 'Weeeelllllll, naw - I did say *Frosted Flakes* and it's best to keep things unmanned-machine-precise in matters so country as this.' This lump seems like more than the Young Pastor should have left. Though Lucy always thinks that. Perhaps a result of the week - usually she is dry before a fresh pick-up - perhaps because she believes all are in love with her and attempt to curry favor with excesses just kiss enough to be noticed. If the police came down? If lights in multicolor surrounded Lucy and upped her jig? If some incidental happened on the drive away - a fender-bender, say - and she was too shook up to notice the goods had slipped from her pocket to police view? Honestly? Honestly: something inside of her desires this. Where is the trial in her life? She'd only been in a courtroom, once, and that over a dispute with a plumber - and even that courtroom had been more like being in a back office at a *Holiday Inn* for the second phase of a job-interview, knowing from the stale of the manager's tie you won't get a call back because nobody will. She watches two young men crack from the bookstore's rear employee-door and snap snap into their cigarettes and their pugilist up-and-downs of whatever they were taking about - grand philosophies, upcoming readings, films that they saw, or trips they intended to take with young women who wouldn't fall in love with them so nearly as slavishly as they would, morning after, bare-footed, shivering by the microwave, bloat themselves to believe. Those are who would have been young-Lucy's friends. Those are who would have been young-Lucy's bedmates. Those are smiles she would have memories of the way one knows a plate from the detergent spots, one knows a fever from a pillow's cool.

Another theory about Lucy's new job? Transit has become incidental to her. A real loss to the shoreline, that - the hive has been gutted, the tree-stump that it was has been out-by-the-rooted, Queen, slaves, and all! Even here - anyone could see - Lucy is driving to Mathilde, but the drive is flash-card, definition of something she'll never say, memorized for a grade, and then stuck inside noggin because Lucy's too tight to empty. She goes from place-to-place still, but it now seems she goes same-place to same-place - the mathematic of non-terminating non-repeating has reached a da capo, the endlessness of a round pattern is gone. She is the piano when every combination has been played in melodies every length long. Lucy is Plunk. Lucy Plink. She is sideways-hand Plangggggggg. So: the job? The job is a concentration of transit, a pocket-universe, a Science

Fiction. She has had to literally make an empty room move, her imagination no longer functioning, it is a bump on the head that has smoothed to just a head. Let's not go so far, Lucy - listen to this thought, this is lively! On paper - on paper, you see? Words that won't stop often indicate a mind that already has, an experience whose limit is reached. When there is nothing left to do but write words on a page you know the corner's been painted and you're not in it, anymore. But, Lucy - but but but - you aren't writing. You are just thinking! No tape-recorder, sure, no imaginary biographer, sure, no delusions of grandeur or of persecution - maybe a bit of the latter, but that's par-for-the-course - and you are still thinking. Thinking of how it used to feel endless to drive a car to Mathilde's and now it seems like driving a car to Mathilde's, contained! 'Pin a rose on my Slow Joe Crows nose' Lucy says - remarkable, she's already here! - as she pulls up the parking brake and pops out of the car, patting the baggie in the tight fit of corduroy on her ass. Even up the stairs, it's no event. This might be what it's like to know you have lost your last eyelash, the Hospice nurse not even concerned! 'Not that you don't still have your eyelashes' Lucy corrects the possible misimpression to herself, catching her breath after the upward exertion, wanting to seem even-keeled when she knocks 'just you lost one - one of many - see it on your fingertip and know *Well, that's not going to happen again, today*. And you know what *Today* means in that sentence' Lucy intones as finale with ominous flourish, knock-knocking Mathilde's door-front and pretending she is a Freshman who will have to pretend for the whole date - and for the next several months - that she has kissed someone, before now. Mathilde doesn't answer right away because that has become her habit. Lucy would claim herself a bit feeding-hand, but what has she ever offered Mathilde but strife and a sense of being ill-worn? 'Mathilde, what have I ever offered you but strife and a sense of being ill-worn?' Lucy asks when the door does open. 'You used to give me not very funny nicknames' Mathilde unenthuses 'but then you stopped - and that is gift enough, Lucy, a treasure untold.' 'Didn't I once call you *Base Six*?' 'Once?' 'Or *Cube-root-of-seven*?' 'No no, that's a new one - wheeee' Mathilde does her finger like a poorly working whirligig, pointing Lucy a path to the kitchen around a lot of laundry and newspapers laid out on the floor. 'I can't even guess what you're up to, Math' Lucy says, elbows to kitchen counter, surveying the room. 'And please don't guess, okay? Let me think I've out clairvoyanced the Oracle, shown it lands beyond the gaze of the Empire.' Lucy will allow this, but doesn't promise not to judgmentally theorize in her own free time. 'That's my leisure time, Math, and leisure is not bound by social decorum or it wouldn't be so profitable and easy to commoditize.' 'Sure, Lucy - and you have a package and your e-mails are over there.' 'Business business' Lucy huffies 'I know what you aren't getting for Christmas, anymore. Whatever I would have grabbed at the last minute. Chew on that.' There is Mathilde's best I-put-up-with-you cute face. Lucy likes Mathilde more, every time.

'Doesn't you job do drug tests? You do drive a car, right?' Lucy feels bloodless with betrayal and goes muscleless at the jaw to show this. 'Why would you say something like that? Are you some kind of wet-blanket salesman?' Mathilde has the giggles and so nods in a Hell-yes-I-am! manner. 'I think I'll turn you in, Lucy. What would you do about it? Haunt me?' 'No. I'd skip a generation - two generations - haunt your granddaughter and she'd never know why!' 'Wow' Mathilde admits 'that is actually a good thing to threat.' 'I'm like a rain-cloud that knows exactly how dark to be to make people drive recklessly without having to actually give up any rain.' 'You are!' Mathilde high-fives Lucy and tries to grab some of the unboxed manuscript, but Lucy is quick enough to defend it. 'I can't believe someone finds you noteworthy, Lucy. You are evidence of what is wrong with things.' 'You hate me for being undeservedly better than you? How hum-drum, Ten's Place - you're talentless even at jealousy.' Mathilde sticks out her tongue and asks, in that way only someone sharing a bowl packed for the fifth time with marijuana can - forehead semi-sweating from just how many times a lighted flame has been relatively close to it inside of ten minutes, nose sniffling from exhaustion at the odd patterns of inhalation, exhalation, as like walking slightly-faster-than-normal on a treadmill - 'But really: why did they decide to publish this? I'm proud of you - et cetera - it's you just never talk about it, so you seem like an asshole.' 'What do you mean?' 'I'd be bragging, Lucy - I have ambitions and if I butterfly-netted one I'd talk in the pitch of a fart for the rest of my life and who would be man enough to stop me!?' Lucy, pot-headed, almost meeks and honests some humility, but instead is reminded of the plot of *The Brain That Wouldn't Die*. 'You remember that, Cosine?' 'Sure.' 'Remember that thing in the closet?' 'I remember.' 'That's why. That's why I don't brag.' 'Because you are a monster made out of grotesque errors while attempting transplantations on kidnap victims?' 'Because this book is the result of every one of my failures and I should have kept it locked in the closet!' 'Isn't that monster the hero, in the end?' 'You're drunk! I mean - Yes. In a way - Yes. All monsters are heroes in that they reveal how man is the monster which, in turn, reveals how the monsters are monsters and men are men so, in essence, maybe monsters aren't as bad as not-monsters, if you follow it through. But I just meant: stop changing the metaphor!' Mathilde found that uproarious and upturns the bowl, apologetically repacks it in a posture of seemingly-about-to-fall-over the whole time. 'You know what the true goal of a poet is?' 'What? What, Lucy Jinx - what oh what is the true goal of a poet?' 'To beat words! To sit there and want to express and by doing so discover the thing there are no words for - then to resist the urge to lash and cut and brutalize and pillow-talk and everything-and-anything words until you think you have somehow found a way to say the unsayable - then to walk away from the paper! To walk away with nothing having come to you but the desire for something to come having deserted! That is what poetry is! And the stuff that we read is the architecture of failure, a skeleton made out of chips from the mausoleum cement!' 'Oh - I thought it was to write cool stuff like *Hey Diddle Diddle the cat had a fiddle the cow jumped*' - Lucy interrupts with a barked Eurkea! of 'What!? What - what!? What!?' 'You sound like an owl who got the word wrong!' Mathilde convulses with saying and does her impression, as best she can while busy being doubled-over 'What! What what!' Even Lucy finds it funny, but fights through the mirth to say 'Say that, again!' Mathilde recovers, sobers enough to perlexedly say '*Hey Diddle Diddle the Cat had a fiddle the*' - 'Yes! The cat *Had* a fiddle - *Had*!? Haaaaadddddd!?' Lucy seems on the pivot-point of epilepsy trying to explain how she always thought the verse was '*Hey Diddle Diddle, the cat And - And! And! - the cat And the fiddle*!' 'Have I altered everything, for you?' Mathilde says, shamefaced. Lucy grins and guffaws - amused, though quite wary-hearted - 'What else have I missed!?'

This bathroom. Hidey hole. Lucy chuckling at the possible dirty recriminations of that term, considering, when all she had meant was how, face it, over the years and decades of life-to-date the purpose of the toilet to her - and of whatever space it is surrounding the thing - has differentiated itself severely from the need to physiologically void. Now - is she in a state, right now? No. She is romantically in sway with the marijuana and that stuff always gives her a waterlogged butterfly head, wings going flit flit then suddenly dragged-down from the soak, then whup whup whup her slats beat the air and give her a lift and then flit flit flit, drag. As thoughts stretch like parallel-lines to the imaginary point-of-intersection they also lose cohesion or meaning and Lucy has no concern to track them, anymore. To wit: hadn't she been remarking something interesting about these toothpaste blots, hardened like grandmother's joints on the basin - something about them being like the sound of a sea-bottom, that when shadows pass it seems like faces are moaning then going stern? Well? Sure, probably, don't ask Lucy - maybe she had been thinking that, so what!? She has lowered pants, panties, sat, giggled, stood, thought up a treatise of some kind - or not a *treatise*, what is the word, what is the word!? - about what could be understood of someone's psychology and political beliefs just from a thorough examination of their education level, relative job-satisfaction, and how long they let the bathroom trash go unchanged. *Thesis! Dissertation*! Yes - mark her - mark Lucy, Lucy! There is something in that, try not to forget it - but if you do happen to forget it, well, forget it! But then Lucy thinks how strange it is that when certain rolls of toilet-paper - not these, here in Mathilde's place, but the ones in the toilet at a certain place she one worked - had cardboard rounds big enough to insert an entire hand through, they were never on mounts, and when one would unwend from them a length to wipe, it would sound like the bushes-distant chirping of crickets! Oh Lucy wishes she could be in a large bathroom - highway rest-stop in length, airport in length - and everyone in every stall could be loosing paper to wipe the entire time while she checks her appearance at the mirror, a kind of bucolic, antiseptic modernity, a new Mother Nature built from the need to keep anuses tidy! A train could be going by outside, Mathilde could be franticly hiding behind some fixture with hands clasped to her ears, screaming, and Lucy wouldn't know a thing about it, right now. Is that her? Is that you, Lucy? Look how warrior-brave that vein under your eye-bottom is! What a champion! Think of the microscopic building-up of platelets and the like in there! Lucy thinks of the insides of her veins as posh, furry, dainty as the slip of a child's fingers over the weep of a willow! Is that how your teeth look, Lucy? Look at them from this angle, down around the backyards of the ones in front. Coffee did that! And nicotine! But coffee and nicotine knew to keep it tucked back there. Is the underside of your tongue supposed to be this color? Are your taste buds supposed to seem as pronounced as the nostrils of warthogs? Lucy picks up a can of shaving cream and wonders how long Mathilde has had it. It is restless with dust, the can - Lucy wonders if it could still spew foam, wonders if the inventor of the foam-spew device would be sad if it turned out No. Mathilde must use that on - what - her legs? Her legs? Down here? *Down here*, Lucy - what do you mean by that? This apartment is only one floor high. There isn't another bathroom, Lucy - where do you think you are, right now? The majority of Mathilde's nudity likely happens in this closed space. Beautiful to think of that! Oh what a sport nature has come to! 'We are that animal which is only naked when locked away, we contemporary women' says Lucy. And she thinks of Mathilde at shower, at soak, at shit, at sigh, at sour-head from too much or too little wine or from sleeping too long. Tonight, Lucy is going to shower clothed, she proclaims! And knows that she won't - oh she won't even remember the thought. But right now, how much she wishes she would makes up for the fact that she'll never.

'Lucy, can you give me some advice?' 'Of course!' 'Is this the stupidest mistake I'm ever going to make?' 'Is what?' 'Asking you for advice.' 'Are you asking me for advice about being advised by me?' 'How would you advise me, if so?' 'It depends on how I'd advise you, I guess - I'd have to know that, first.' 'Say you advised me not to take your advice.' 'Did I give a compelling reason?' 'In a way.' '*In a way*!? What was lacking?' 'You seemed to be waiting to get advice from you - it seemed half-hearted.' 'I give good advice, though, so it makes sense why I'd hesitate.' 'That's fair.' 'I mean, it's why you're coming to me for advice, isn't it?' 'Why?' 'Because I give such good advice!' 'I don't know if you do - I was asking your advice on whether I should be wary of being advised by you!' 'Wait - did you ask it like that? That's rather loading the deck, isn't it?' 'How should I have asked it, instead?' 'Are you asking me?' 'I'm asking you if I should ask you.' 'No.' 'But since I already did, can you answer?' 'You shouldn't take my advice.' 'Even that advice?' 'Especially that advice!' 'Even that advice?' 'No, not that advice.' 'You're not helping.' 'I didn't say I was going to - at most, I said I'd advise you and I'm not even sure if I've committed to that.' 'I have a serious situation to discuss!' 'I'll bet.' 'What if I told you I had done something illegal?' 'I'd say *Did you, actually?*' 'And what if I said *Yes, I did*.' 'Then I'd say *How illegal?*' 'Say I said *Illegal enough that I'm thinking of turning myself in?*' 'Then I'd say *Are you sure I'm the one you want advice from?*' 'I'd say *I'm not sure, but I figured you might be the best one for it*.' 'What did you do, Calculus?' 'I think I should turn myself in.' 'Are you going to get caught - what type of illegal are we talking about?' 'Jail-time illegal.' 'For you - or you were conspirator in something that would send others to jail, but not you?' 'For me.' 'I'm getting the feeling this is rather a serious question.' 'It's not.' 'It's not?' 'No - have I ever done anything illegal?' 'How the fuck would I know!' 'I haven't. I'm just stressed. You know stress?' 'I have heard of stress - it is what people poorer than me and in not as fine health have, yes?' 'I stole some money.' 'Did you - wait - is this the illegal thing?' 'I told you there isn't an illegal thing!' 'You also, in essence and immediately afterward, told be you stole money or did something - did you say you stole money?' 'But not in an illegal way - just from someone.' 'I need to see you in my chambers! What jibber-jabber is that?' 'I just had an opportunity and stole some money - not like I robbed, you know?' 'I see - it was just there and you took it?' 'Yes. I am not talking about the other thing, which was a joke - the thing I was talking about before.' 'That was a joke?' 'Yes.' 'Why did you steal money? Was it existential?' 'I was stressed about my health and my bills, Lucy.' 'It feels like you're trying to ply me with drugs, lower my inhibitions, and then make me feel guilty about something here!' 'I just want you to be proud of me, Lucy - I need someone to have my back!' 'I have your back.' 'You think stealing is cool, right - to get over stress and stuff?' 'Absolutely - clink, clink - I toast to that.' 'Clink - okay, yes, toast, yes, clink. If I hadn't been stressed, I wouldn't have taken it - you know?' 'Bet that makes you wish you were stressed more often, eh?' 'Exactly! Only stressed about stuff that will solve itself - you know? - so I don't need to spend the money I steal to solve the stress.' 'That seems underhanded. I bet some indigenous ethnic group is to blame for that.' 'I'll see you - whenever - later, okay?' 'Yes. Fine. I'm the one whose been trying to go!' 'So go!' 'Fine!' 'Jesus!'

It's like groceries, lugging these files and the package to the car. And when had this rain fallen? Everything smells like a sink without the disposal-switch having been hit all night long, the sweet waft of decay making the grime lip-smacking, saliva speeding up from the cheeks, greedy-greedy. Lucy has to wriggle around to get her keys from her pocket with the files on top of the box and the box balanced and pinned on her outshot hip, because she never trusts cardboard to be thick enough to not let contents get ruined if set in the puddles on car-tops, hoods, trunk-covers. Lucy, it might have been easier to have opened the trunk, put everything in there. 'Maybe.' Well, *maybe* all you want, Lucy - but you also could have squatted, gone to your haunches, set the box and files to your thigh-tops, table-made, got key to the door of the trunk or the driver's door without acrobatics. But where had this wise idea been, five minutes ago? That's what Lucy would like Lucy to tell her! Like most things that would have made a difference, it arrived when it couldn't. Cliché. Ghastly cliché. As ghastly cliché as the phrase *Ghastly cliché*. Lucy begins chewing gum, now, and spritzes liberally with one of the fragrances she keeps in the glove box - entirely different from the scent she spritzes in the work vehicle - and she sits in the sizzling settle of the wet as though she is a bite-mark inside of a headache. Then, like the second crack of a soda can being opened, Lucy remembers an earlier excitement and moves the file-folder from the passenger seat to her lap and flops it open. There it is splayed - the same as a frog cadaver returned to the third-day-in-a-row in Biology class - and she pokes around until she finds the e-mail she thinks she recognizes. Not that one. Not this one, either? 'Shit' she says, sniffling - hard sniffling, not enough to keep the growing form of a thin droplet of snot from weighting the in-loop of her nostril - wipes her hand-back across nose and then doesn't wipe that anyplace before continuing to tweezer through the papers, reading now more than she scans. Aha! Lucy had been remembering the bit she wanted as italicized and inset - different margins - when it is really just quoted off inside a thick, unbroken paragraph. *And yes* the broad's message reads before what Lucy wants is got to *it's not completed, I know, but still thought you might be pleased at an early response from one of the few readers I've let have a look.* Lucy almost doesn't want to read what she has just dug to, again, but of course she does. *Imagine finding a raw-nerve inside a raw-nerve and splitting it, atomic ash of shred sensation outpouring and irradiating the surroundings. That is the best way I can describe my reaction to the journey through what we must imagine is the mind of Lucy Jinx. And I say we must Imagine, because this is poetry of a mind palpably uncertain it is a mind and recalcitrantly opposed to belonging to its namesake. Almost a shame to have this work published, because it reminds one how there exist currents our feet have never dangled in, haunted chills and heated fathoms around us of which we might never be witting.* Lucy is a little bit hyperventilating, a sensation rather as though a lot of people are peering in over her shoulder and are reading faster than she is, getting to each sentence-end before her, their Hmns or chuckles or clucks or tsks or what-have-you-noises informing, against her will, her impression of the tone of the praise. The blurb. It is praise. It is praise, Lucy, yes, obviously! Are you toiling to convince yourself otherwise? It is praise, Lucy - from Priscilla O'Parke. Who has read your book. From Priscilla O'Parke! Who read the book or else committed herself so much to claiming she has as to commit to those sentiments, there, burden her name with them like anchor-shaped tombstones, fish-eaten rope dangling upward from them, the wreck oceans away and plundered for bones and relics. What does that mean, Lucy? That thought is incomprehensible, even for you! 'Shut up' she says, hating to her spleen the way her throat is stiffened in strangle. 'Shut up' a hiss, a cat sneeze 'shut up!'

And by this point, we have Lucy roaming the block awhile - because she has decided this is something she can do. This is something people do. Just stroll and roam and enjoy headfuls of spy-game bought drugs and the icicly joy of Ego ballooning to pop, the invisible insides of it rising still, shed of their pimple-skin. This is something Lucy can do, now - she can roam, hands out of pockets and unburied from her shoulders-at-hunch or her tight steps hurrying to get herself done with the roaming, her breaths rushing to have herself inside, waiting, inside, waiting, inside, waiting - waiting, which was once a kind of journey all its own but had lost its wanderlust, become more of a fixture than even the tables and chairs which at least could be brought together, individuated, stacked upside-down on each other come closing time. Remember, Lucy? Don't you remember? These streets and how they were once lengthed, just for you? Walls bidden to attention by your legs or your feeling like experiencing rough to the tips and the pads of your passing-by fingers - bricks there, each one, to sentinel your mittens, give them just the right tugs, same as your coats or your sweaters or your slacks? Remember how you could have been one of these ones you see, youthing their legs around - words no more permanent than butterscotch, excitements so rude and overwhelming that all would be forgiven, and I-loves-yous would be waited for, given, took, returned, loved loved loved? Remember when that was a drug-store you would have gone into just for a bottled water you'd later discard, having slept on the train and then being home, no longer needing? Or when that was a machine where you'd take out the cash that you shouldn't have, preparing the arguments to back up the excuses you were deciding not to offer, anyway, instead resigning to your best-breathed insistence that 'It will be dealt with or it won't'? Remember when streets like this told you secrets about life and you told streets like this better things still? And when you had jokes you'd invented yourself and could grifter-deck better jokes you had overheard - your mood always beer cold, your wits always sharp as food eaten too much at a rush to let cool? Remember how you could have spent all night into morning on balderdash humming, how yours were those eyes that never feel more solid or shrunk than when the dawn actually brightens and you know rest was ignored, discarded, wasted on absolutely nothing at all? Remember how you'd go meet work or the person you'd been avoiding, so weak as to feel beaten, so beaten as to feel corpse, but to feel corpse like the bones that masses make pilgrimage to awe at? What? What!? What do you mean? What do you mean, Lucy? That's not memory - that's fantasy! Even the words you use cannot bother efforting enough to hide the deception! *Remember when you could have?* You mean *Remember how you didn't*! *Remember you weren't*! *Remember you never*! *Remember you couldn't*! *Remember these streets*? You mean *Imagine them*! Imagine them as they always were and you were not - not once, not even barely! Did you do those things, Lucy? Are you counting ten minutes of life inside any two-year-period the defining moments of you? Or an hour? Twelve hours, if all of your jaunts are lain side-to-side? 'Hello, Street - do you remember Lucy? Remember Lucy from way back, Street?' The Street would hardly recall you from yesterday without looking you up in the Index! 'Oh bah!' Lucy Bahs. 'Bah!' Lucy Bahs, again, louder. 'There was plenty of me in loiter and linger and licentious we-shouldn't-but-we-are-about-to-but-we-are-but-we-did on these streets - or any street, The Street! - these never-flat grounds underfoot of life when most lived! There are memories - real ones - of being unhidden and burning myself like a mound of scented wood for the glee of drunks dancing!' Lucy Jinx had been that fragrance many times! To this block and that block! And she wonders if she has walked a total of ten minutes before she comes to the car again, closes herself in the door, into the still like-it-had-just-be-made cheap of the department-store perfume she'd squeezed out in twik-twik-twik squeaks.

The turn signal ahead, there, on the mirror and at the bumper of that car is one of these dastardly sorts Lucy simply cannot abide! See how fast it goes? The sound of too much exercise, the sound of an elevator not coming when summoned, impatient, knee jiggling, hands down pockets with breath down nose in a display and a sound-effect for those around. Lucy does her best Gary Oldman and says 'This is the sound of his agitation!' What should a turn-signal be? Steady. Penny-pinching. A-half-sandwich-will-do-and-is-even-more-satisfying-really. It is a sinewy aggression to let the signal have more speed - and though it might be tempting to think it accidental, there is nothing in the world less accidental than the overkill stab of left left left left left left left Lucy is seeing. See? She has tensed up! Evidenced by her letting her breath go when the turn is complete and the signal goes off. It had been screw-drivering her, gotten further under her skin than even she had surmised. Someone did that to you, Lucy. To everyone, in a sense, but specifically to you! Did no one on the Production Staff say 'Why is the light going so fast?' Or was it a priori to the car being built? A scientific-study commissioned, some proof based on Control Group versus Variable that 'It makes more sense to have blinkers blink faster.' A committee signed off on it! The government! 'Anyway, it doesn't matter' Lucy shrugs it off now that it's gone. She is a tulip no longer reaching for sunlight - at ease at ease - not some weed which just keeps sprinting its growth on through midnight, the dawn coming and meaning nothing to it but what the night coming again will mean, then. Three long sighs in-a-row. Lucy tries to test her faculties. What is the test she came up with? Recite, aloud, *The Raven* without repeating anything once or using silly or over dramatic voice. Why *The Raven*? Because it is the single easiest thing to memorize on Earth! Lucy has had it memorized since third grade - no - since fifth grade! She hasn't even looked at it in print, actually, outside of some dozen times since then - or, realistically, maybe fifty - and a lot of those times she didn't read it, entire, maybe just wanted a quote spaced out proper or to check on the order of a few random words. *Let me see then what thereat it is - Though thy crest be shorn and shaven, thou, said I, are sure no craven - Plutonian.* Gah! What a word! *The night's Plutonian shore.* And to use it more than once! Gah! It's the least poetic phrase imaginable! Why in Hell does it repeat? 'Quaff!' Lucy exclaims. 'Quaff! Quuuaaaafffffffff!!!' First of all - don't be a prick, Lucy! - Lucy does realize Lucy is failing Lucy's test. And second of all - yes! - Lucy said she knows she is failing Lucy's test! Maybe it's the poem's fault, though! A fair thought. What shall we do? *Gerontion*? Shall we do *The Weight of Oranges*? 'I'm as random as a bird' Lucy says 'I am as clockwork as a leech!' Lucy's mind is un-made-up. The first thought was 'Clockwork as a kitten' - but that is too obvious - then 'clockwork as a crab' - except those actually seem clockwork - then 'clockwork as a squid' - but squids just aren't very poetic - then she - all of this in an instant, too quick to wince - had blurtedly settled on *Leech*. But are leeches clockwork? Are they particularly not? 'I am as clockwork as a leech!' Saying it louder doesn't help. But maybe saying it even louder will. 'I'm as clockwork as a leech!! I'm Clockwork As A Leech!!! I'm A Clock Work Lee Cha!!!!!' Lucy fails and fails her test - and betters and betters the fail to the exuberant applause of the blokes who quote Beckett to mean quite the wrong thing. 'When I was child, I had a beautiful violin' Lucy Armin Muhler-Stahlls. 'And do you know - do you know what he did to it?' Then she Geoffrey Rushes, timid grown-man made a defiant little-boy, finally 'No, daddy. What did he do to it?'

Coffee-cupped and anonymous-loted, Lucy is listening to whoever this is - she once knew, she thinks - sing about meeting the ghost of Steven Foster at the Hotel Paradise. She could begin a poem *I am a word if every paragraph is a fortress.* She could also scratch her eye. She could also lose an adult tooth - or at least make one loose. 'I could do it all' she says, raising her coffee-cup and sulking. But she thinks her head is clearing, because now it confuses her why just thinking that stuff about weeds growing would have put such notions in her head of driving on a dark country road that she, for a moment while driving, had thought she had been doing just that when it is still perfectly daylight and it is still perfectly suburban-shopping-center all surrounding her. Lucy, Lucy - she wears a fit like a forehead, her book is as creased as her brow. 'My book is as creased as my brow.' She wishes, sincerely, someone else had said that so she could admire it fully without seeming grotesque. If it ended here, now, Lucy Jinx, you would feel justified in thinking 'How had it come to this?' How is this where you had wound up? Not taking the posture that there is anything the matter with her, Lucy just means 'How did it progress from whence to hence?' Does everything follow a set of causal progression except for her life? Or do most lives so rouletteize? Has she wrought this? Through what - impoliteness? Through what - having a desire and then another? She is dandruffesque in her affections, maybe - they are part of her, but the part to be rough-brushed away. Is she suffering some Hell-tax for that? And where does this over-exaggeration come from? Why is she unsettled even by how she is unsettled? She is a goddamned *D* that can't keep from tracing itself the same as an *O* - she is a *D* that's an *O* with a limp! But her head is clearing. There is, on the radio now, an advertisement for a mattress and furniture store and she recognizes it from years ago - not the ad, in particular, the content is specific to an event this upcoming Sunday, it is the jingle she recognizes, not updated, the same recording on a cassette tape in a box with a ballpoint pen spine labeled *Commercial*. An episode? 'What?' I said *Do you think you are having an episode right now, Lucy?* 'I'm just high. And have been at work.' That is the wash Lucy puts on it, gives the surface a quick puff and a satisfied nod. Yep. 'What do you mean? Repeat that!' Fine, Lucy: *You don't think the drugs are just a way to pull leaves over the buried parachute of you-are-having-an-episode?* 'I don't know what kind of episode you could mean' Lucy insists, then hugs her arms tightly to herself and her armpits feel distinctly more than four decades old. That skin, the stubble over it - it has breathed liquid through artificial repression for forty-plus years! It's just a thing, the armpit, that has been on this Earth that long and this is absurd! 'If an armpit is around for forty-plus years, why is a sea-turtle living to four hundred so impressive? Shouldn't a slug have a lifespan of fifteen years?' They might, Lucy - you don't know about slugs. 'No. No' she admits it. But her head is clearing. She has watched those people work together to fit the box with the unassembled desk - or whatever that is - into the back of their car, watched them decide how it's fine the trunk can't close. 'It's fine' she thumbs-up to their turned, pleased-with-their-ingenuity backs. And now Lucy Young-Mister-Grace's 'You've all done very well!' and there is in her heart the prompted laughter of British live-audience. But her head is clearing.

She doesn't know what she could have meant by *Episode*. She stares at what's left of the sun off in Heaven and squints, trying and trying, trying to focus to see to its heart, to the single cold spot it surrounds.

Shock-cut to her parked outside her apartment, the building trying to lo-and-behold itself with some sense of majesty - or at least to present with the power of a middle-school administrator - but coming across more like an unfolded packing-box from the store which, when shoved three dimensional, is discovered to not be the correct size. There is much of the world best described as the under-breath of a cuss-word, there is much the world only agreeing with an unexpected burp can sum up. Though, to take proper pulse, Lucy's mood has bettered - she is the last lift of the tea-bag from the hot, red-browned water, now a scent and a steam and a readiness to exist. Real life, now! And real life is nothing but a choice. Choice! And Lucy has more than been-around-enough to understand that a choice doesn't just get made - nope - all of the addendum and implications and future applications of choice are agreed to or else one best just admit to a choiceless existence, an existence wherein a choice would be meaningless. In a matter of five days, it seems, Lucy has come to reject and loathe such home-spuns as 'Life is a choice - but you have to keep choosing it, you have to re-embrace it, again and again.' Illogical. Slap-happy. If you say you have chosen, then choose and be stalwart about it! There are worse things in this world than it turning out you made the wrong choice. Lucy balms herself with the science-fiction truth of it, thus: say humankind does yeast-spread throughout galaxies, assures its existence post-globe and all - the surest thing is how, in five thousand years, there will no more be mourned victims of this current time and place than we mourn, now, those wrongfully savaged by Denisovans! If people meant anything by saying Ethics and Understanding - well! - Archeology would be a study of Justice, seeking out the stories of all those murdered, pre-society, making sure we understood the loss to this planet of each and every one of them - the potential, the ramifications of Ig or Urgh not having been around! Imagine how different the world would be if there hadn't been a dawn's-light murder of that slumbering group in Tertiary Period Siberia, if those sophisticated wood tools hadn't coldcocked her or him! The deaths of the first great philosophers, those might as well have been! The massacre of the Birth-of-Science! The prolongation of the period prior the discovery of fire was due to a primitive sense of being made cuckold, heart inventing premeditation when a rock-wall large enough to hide behind was found and a lure could be made of false-animal rustle when that woman-robbing-bastard was at casual hunt! This is a long way to go to make Lucy's point that a choice is a choice and - no matter the moral consequences - if one has faith in the existence of the future, at all, one has faith in the quality of Forgotten coming to everyone, everything, and every concept.

Just as there existed a time when nobody thought about charging money to mail a letter or the treatment for uterine cancer, there will come a time when nobody thinks about those things, again - and if they were brought up, they'd be dismissed out of hand! Let this always be said for Lucy: she has faith the future will exist. Always. It is the only thing there is any certainty of. An intuition of what will happen next week is often more provable and more substantive than the memory of what happened a week ago - at least until it dwindles to that. The past is watching the taut chest of History sag. The further back, the more Spina Bifida goes the wring of what came before. The moment someone told Lucy she could not actually dig to China and that someone on the other side of the planet wasn't upside-down while she was right-side up is the moment they told her 'There is a lie in every explanation - you can talk your way out of your eyes after seeing your way out of your instincts, every time.' History is the flavor you never tasted, but no one will challenge you when you say that you have. The future is the fire cooking what everyone smells, hungers for, and keeps to themselves.

LUCY IN THE DOOR, IT closes as though automatic or afterthought - just now she was entering through it and right now she is over here and it's closed. Ariel is eating a popsicle at the kitchen counter and evidence of others recently eaten - manila-brown bones and white slick-crinkled skin - liter the area surrounding, a stray spine in the sink with still one hunk of decaying green flesh, cold and leaking, atop it. 'What was the name of that one old-time philosopher' Ariel asked, munch sounds like old shoes through pebbled plant-beds 'the one who just was pretty sub-par at the whole thing?' Lucy take takes a popsicle from the freezer herself, shivering and immediately aware of her neck-ache, plops to standing beside Ariel, giving her belly a snarl, and says 'You mean *Mediocrates?*' Ariel nods deep, slurping a suck from the purple she has. 'Yes! That's been bothering me, all day.' Then, Ariel changes to a dismissive, scandalized demeanor 'I can't believe you work for them, Lucy! How can you work for those jackals!' 'You like bread and baby makes three, bunny - the piper don't pipe for his health, I'll tell you that.' 'Collaborator. And don't use me as your excuse, either.' 'You think I like it? You think it gives me pleasure to coal the mines and shine the boss-man's cane-tip?' 'You're a scab, Jinx - I can't believe you did it. Haven't you ever seen *Billy Elliott* or any of those other movies pertinent to how bad it is to be a scab? He hangs himself, Lucy! The clown! The clown hangs himself!' Lucy agrees she is complicit in many of the ills of the world, but then offers a narration of history which, in the end, seems to justify her, so Ariel is left without a corner to stuff with her retreat. 'What does *Egress* mean? It means *leaving*, right?' 'It does' Lucy says, her pop worn-soft enough she starts biting rather than sucking. 'That's what I thought. What word sounds more like itself than *Egress*?' '*Caterwaul.*' 'I mean what actual word.' 'Oh.' They kiss and Ariel gripes about reflux and Lucy asks if she had tried the old gypsy-remedies they had heard about. 'I gotta wait for the head to shrink more before I can boil it with three leaves of lettuce - and I don't think that was even the thing, come to think of it. That's for mind-control, right?' 'Depends on the gypsies' Lucy says, last bite, turns the stick and frowns that there isn't a joke printed on it, leaves it in the sink. 'We have a trashcan, you smarm.' 'I know. Which my taxes paid for, never forget that. You're teated to me, Ari - *teated.*' They kiss again and Lucy rubs her shirted belly on Ariel's only partway camisole-covered hump. 'How was work, really?' 'It was fine.' 'What's in that box?' 'Oh more shit about my book. They like sending boxes. That and some print-outs from Mathilde.' 'How's she?' 'She's having some sort of nervous collapse, clothes all in piles on her living-room floor - and every place, really.' 'I think I might buy a computer.' 'With what money?' Lucy narrows her eyes. Ariel fakes being caught out - gasp! - puts her hands to her little mouth. 'Your mouth is little, my bonbon.' 'I think it stopped growing in third grade when I fell off the slide.' 'I thought you were pushed off that slide!' 'I never even told you a story about a slide!' 'I didn't say you told me, I said I always thought you had.' They kiss and Ariel peels away, looking at the arrangement of magnets on the refrigerator. 'Do you think the Crisis Intervention Hotline is mad it doesn't have a cool number like the police?' 'I think it's more worried that it's called something no one is ever likely to call because it just never seems like that's the right number. *Crisis?*' Lucy character acts. '*Hmn. It's not like there's a flood or anything - better just call the cops.*' '*Sigh*' Ariel picks up the scene, but Lucy knows it is from the point-of-view of the Crisis Hotline worker '*hear a tornado's coming, how many idiots you bet're gonna start calling?*' Lucy picks up the scene, caller-voice '*A tornado*' - pronounced *tor-nay-der* - '*is comin! Ya gots ta intervene!*'

Ariel thinks they should paint the walls and get a big, huggable chair. 'What are we supposed to paint with?' 'It'll be a project - we'll make our own brushes and find things to crush into pigment. We can bond while we do it.' Lucy taps the spatula on first the grilled-cheese sandwich she has going on the pan on the left burner then on the one she has going on the right burner, flipping that one then flipping the first one. 'Did you ever get a call back about what to do about the rash on your foot?' 'They said it'll go away.' 'If what?' Ariel shrugs and turns the page of the newspaper she is reading, briefly recounts what she just read about a bank closing nearby, then says 'Just that it will.' 'Who did you call? An actual physician?' 'I don't like' Ariel overtops, finger wagging at Lucy but the gesture meant for the party she is discussing 'how the place calls itself *Gilead Creek*. That makes me begrudge them everything they tell me.' 'Did they tell you to ignore a rash? I'm pretty sure from a medical course I once took that that is one of the main things a doctor isn't supposed to say.' 'When did you take a medical course?' Lucy lady-of-the-courts about how she has pursued, obtained, and left-to-rot-and-ruin an education which had many facets. Then, Ariel tells a story about how once there were some people she knew - this she edits, aggrieved at having to do so, as though physical exertion is involved, to *'Some people I knew of* - who made a big fire one night when out camping and when they woke up and came out of their tents they were all grabbing their faces and looking around - desperate and horrified - for reflective surfaces, soon discovering their skin and eyes and mouths and inside-of-mouths and necks and scalps and ears were just termite with poison ivy. 'Gah' Lucy says. And Ariel can't imagine it. 'Not having seen yourself, moaning droolily in anguish - then seeing your pal doing the same and getting a peeper-full of what they look like in the moment you are seeing their disfigurement, they getting a load of yours and recoiling at the realization they now understand what they didn't a moment ago!' 'The wood was covered with poison ivy?' 'Or there was enough mixed in that the fire just airborned it and they breathed it in and drank-beer it in and it was terrible.' 'The horror' Lucy concedes 'is without easy corollary.' Here: Lucy is trying to think of some story to say that will be equally grotesque. Here: Lucy is dropping the attempt. 'I like how things that happen in life have no moral.' Lucy likes this too. 'Though' Lucy adds 'it would be cool if the last thing you see before you die - no matter how you die - is just blackness with the word *Moral,* a colon, then some glib platitude written out, floating in the void.' Ariel is excited by the prospect, but Lucy reminds her that the chances of it happening are nil. 'But any moral would sound cynical, with that timing' Ariel then says, now like she feels maligned. 'Morals are always cynical - name one moral that you don't think of in a snarky voice. *If at first you don't succeed, try, try again?* What's really the difference between that moral and bad advice?' Lucy moves the two sandwiches next to the pile of sour-cream-and-onion ruffle chips on the large green plate, clicks off the stove dials. *'Don't bite the hand that feeds you'* she says. Ariel calmly waits, reading, for her plate to be brought, musing 'Oh come on - you fucking know the hand's just asking for it - like it wouldn't get off on that.' 'What's happening in the news?' 'Some kind of war, someplace else' Ariel says, setting the paper down, mouthing a chip as she says 'but I haven't figured out between whom - or don't know the name of the place, anyway, which amounts to the same.' 'I hope we win' Lucy says, kicking Ariel's shin. 'We will' Ariel says, quiet petulance like she's being nag-nag-nagged.

Lucy nixes the first three sets of baby-clothes Ariel pulls out of the bag - how do they make the bag look leathery? it's just paper, Lucy touches it to be sure - saying that they won't photograph well. 'In twenty years, you'll want whatever the kid is wearing in its earliest photos to seem obscenely archaic, to make one question *Did I actually buy that?* These ones you bought just look cute and normal.' Ariel puts them in a pile, but doesn't offer her verdict, so Lucy does not yet know if that is the discard pile, the keepers, or if this whole thing has become more a 'Look what I got, Lucy - no need to comment' type affair. 'Doesn't that bag look like real leather?' Ariel kind of droops, as though she has just realized this is damnation, giving Lucy the piteous glare of post-doomsday. 'Amazing, right?' Ariel blinks the words dry. 'You do know how they do that, right Lucy? They just take a picture of leather and then print it on the bag.' 'But usually that doesn't look real - maybe it's the thickness of the bag, but I'm bound to say this one seems genuinely leather from where I'm sitting.' Choosing another few outfits and laying them out like dolls on the carpet - dolls absent the dolls - Ariel suggest Lucy would make an excellent person who is fooled by magic tricks in Ancient Egypt or something. 'It's sad' Ariel yawns for the fifth consecutive breath - says 'Excuse me' which she only did with two of the other yawns - 'that if you think back, the tricks magicians did to fool Pharaohs probably aren't even that good. Compared to even basic modern illusions, I mean.' Lucy likes the outfit with the pinstriped pants more than the one with the itty-bitty-corduroy, but admits if the shirts switched out she might switch her opinion, right along. 'Remember when Jesus got mad at the Pharisees?' Lucy switches the shirt-pant combination, nods, says she's better with kids than Ariel, immediately after pointing out 'Pharoahs and Pharisees are not the same thing.' 'I hope you're telling yourself that' Ariel says, pausing to bite the tag off of a set of three mini-size pairs of socks 'because I never said they were and you might come off presumptuous and ignorant for suggesting I did. Jesus' Ariel spits the tag out, licks the back of her hand, wipes it in her hair 'never even met a Pharaoh. Fun Fact.' 'That is fun' Lucy says, touching the bag again, scratching the side of her nose-bridge very hard, face slick with a grease she worries about the scent off from when Ariel will move close, later. Both of them await the day that babies will evolve into being born with socks. And then they further await the even later time when babies born with socks don't shed the socks after three years - when the socks become a permanent fixture of anatomy. An orange baby-shirt with a brown elephant on it. A purple baby-shirt with a lime green giraffe. A charcoal grey baby-shirt with three alligators in-a-row, mouths open, word bubbles above each with the same musical note in them - one note's stick zig-zag, the others' sticks straight. 'I want a tattoo of that, man.' Ariel leans in closer, nods giddy, says that shirt cost ten dollars more than the others, it was in a specialty-shop window. 'One pays for quality.' 'One does' Ariel designated-driver nods 'one does.' 'Will the kid even be small enough to wear all of these things one time - small enough for long enough, I mean?' 'I'm thinking if we put into our accounting the vomit and shit and stuff, then probably. The meconium, you know?' 'I don't know' Lucy says, as though she has never heard of anything more ridiculous suggested, ever 'why would I know about that?' 'Hey, Lucy?' 'What?' '*Birth canal.*' Lucy makes her face Grargh. She can picture the person who coined that term. Nobody loved them. They'd never seen birth. They'd never seen a canal. 'Hey, Lucy?' Lucy covers her ears. She picks up one of the outfits and chucks it across the room, Ariel just shrugging, Lucy hanging her head, groaning herself up to retrieve it.

'Wait - what in Hell is this!?' Ariel stomps - back at the kitchen counter the both of them - brandishing a sheet of paper! 'Priscilla O'Parke read your book!?' Lucy plays it cool. 'That's the way my life is now, man - Priscilla is just a person, you know?' Ariel razor seethes her accusation, not able to keep the note of genuine question out of it 'You didn't meet Priscilla O'Parke.' Lucy folds her hand - no, no she didn't - but - yes! - Priscilla O'Parke read the book! Ariel doesn't listen to whatever Lucy is saying while Ariel reads - and seems to read and read and re-read and re-read - then re-reads the part of the e-mail with the O'Parke blurb. Then suddenly, Ariel snapping-turtle looks up 'I love Priscilla O'Parke!' 'I know that' I-knows Lucy 'it's one of your actual redeeming traits.' 'I love Priscilla O'Parke!!' 'I know.' Ariel is practical misbegotten with hatred at Lucy for this, which she claims counts as a sincere and principleless betrayal. 'It's like corporate greed, Lucy - you're like a stockholder who's capable of anything!' 'Priscilla O'Parke loves me because she is a corporate shill.' 'Mutter mutter' goes Ariel, Lucy knowing she is trying to decide between having to side with Priscilla's opinion of Lucy, now, or else saying how Lucy, in fact, is Priscilla's leisure-class overlord. 'Are you going to get to meet her?' Lucy fakes a guffaw to let Ariel know how she knows this diversionary dodge is a diversionary dodge and it's only working because Lucy is letting it. 'Probably.' 'Honestly?' 'Honestly probably, yes - I have no idea, really.' 'They'd better let you!' And they share details of their times in University, woodcarving their eyes over O'Parke's lines and being astonished by the first time professors said what would turn out to be rather glib and often-told interpretations of stanza or anecdote. Ariel takes five minutes and describes in flourishing, polished-brass detail, the grime of her first copy of O'Parke's *Porcelain's Plagues* and the absurd illustration on its cover she still could not fathom - Lucy cementing an image in her mind of the volume exactly, but certainly an image that would never resemble the real thing. If there was a real thing. And Lucy admits she once tore a page out of a magazine because it had something by O'Parke written on it that she hadn't read, before. 'And I even had money, then - I coulda bought that magazine!' 'You're an anarchist bonfire, Lucy! What poem was it?' 'It was prose, actually - it was a small piece of prose about a time she had to change her pants in the back of a halfway-full cinema.' 'What!?' Ariel has never heard tell of this and her hands roll like an about-to-break-down conveyor belt - more more more more more - and Lucy is sure she recites the story verbatim as O'Parke had written it but cannot remember the name of the magazine. 'I was just killing time waiting for' - she voluntarily pretends an involuntarily crick in her neck, says 'Ow' rubs it, the redirection almost enough to make her forget what she was still technically just pretending to forget - 'which is likely why I decided to steal it, you know? The suddenness! The it-being-there - her-being-there - she!' 'She!' Ariel exclaims in the same tone, that way O'Parke is recorded in that grainy old-basement ages ago reading, her voice under shifts and statics of milling crowd, some whispers and random conversation just as audible as her recitation and some of these asides even transcribed. 'Remember that?' Lucy asks and Ariel - of course she does! - does indeed remember, thought the whole of that book about O'Parke was a bit much but would forever adore the author for taking the time to transcribe that asinine chit and that insipid chat. 'If you get to meet her, do I get to come?' 'If I get to meet her, I'll be kind of more focused on do I get to come, Ari - but you can tag along, anyway, if you can drag yerself away from wet-nursing or whatever it is you'll spend all your previous time doing, now.'

What time is your thing, in the morning? What time is your appointment, tomorrow? When do you have to do that doctor thing - is that in the morning, right? Lucy, just ask. Any of those. But you know the answer, already - right? Yes. You do. Do you need to get up particularly early, tomorrow? Do you want me to sleep out here so we don't just slug-cuddle and oversleep - it is tomorrow you have an appointment this week, right? You don't need to be that complex, Lucy. But you have no reason to ask? You want to! Wanting isn't a reason? And - no - you're right Lucy, you don't want to ask - you want to go. Why not? Why not say 'Ari, is it - you know? - alright if I come along, tomorrow?' or 'Hey - El, hey - I'll just drive you, in the morning - I just kinda want to be part of it - whatever, I know it might be weird with me there too, but I can drive you, we can even go early so I drop you off before they get there or anything.' What rules, Lucy? Yes, there isn't any reason you need to be there. No, you're right, nothing is going to happen - and no one said you were worried about anything and - of course not! - Ariel isn't taking it the wrong way how you are about this. True: she asked for it to be this way. The first day. True, as well: that was the first day and you never asked again, Lucy, you didn't - and things can change after days and things might have been said on days for reasons precise-to-it-being-the-first-day or the fifth-day or the whichsoever-day - but she put it forward. Ariel did. You two played a hand-clap, thigh-tap, finger-snap game while having the conversation, admitted how you could not have jump roped - let alone Double-Dutched! - even if you wanted to because you'd never learned how. It was delightfully happy - yes, Lucy. An agreement. Well - Lucy, come on - it doesn't go as far as to say revisiting the arrangement - just asking, friendly, this once - nullifies the joy or connection of that memory. And what is it a memory of, Lucy? You agreeing to something you'd rather not, right? Egg-footing the room out of fear Ariel was going to change her mind, was going to not change her mind. This is a madness you didn't inflict and so it's okay to question, no one will eject you out the rear door - door with no knob on the outside, flat surface painted to look like the brick which surrounds. No, your answers to the little dearling questions Ariel is asking - bowl of ice-cream goose-pimpling her protuberance while she lays on the sofa, legs over you, eyes on the television - do not sound to Ariel like the questions in your head. Yes, you are allowed to touch her anywhere and anytime, there are no clicking heels of the Sergeant-at-Arms to prick ears for, be ready to dash away, empty breathed, hoping not to pass out from the lungless sprint. Sofas? Yes, you've been on many. With people, yes. Just ask the question, Lucy. Any of them! All of them! Yes - if you want the truth - it is wormwood of you to think for one minute it is her place to invite. Did you? Did you let her come here? You hadn't been begging her, eh? In the way you are shy as the hair a cat leaves in the corner it hides in, you aren't the little piece even hunger-bravery can't bring with it to the bowl? Ariel - would it be that bad if I came with you? Love, I think I want to come - in the morning - even if it is trouble. Hey, Ariel? Can you even get that out, Lucy? Even just the prompt - yes, you then can ask something unrelated, something about this movie, this commercial, this movie, this commercial that you have watched while moving empty bowl to carpet, warming taut not-quite-round-with the hands you've been sitting on waiting for the time you're required to do so - can you even get out just the prompt? Hey, Ariel? Hey. Hey, Ariel? No, Lucy? No? No.

The first few times the following happened, it was a conundrum for Lucy: Ariel talks with Kayleigh on the phone for awhile, a little bit with Leopold, and sometimes with someone else - Lucy has yet to ask who - and Lucy will think to use the opportunity to step outside to smoke, but knows this could seem like purposefully not wanting to hear the conversation, Ariel's side of it. Meaning: that Lucy is hurt by it, unsettled. The truth: Lucy very much likes listening to it, but fears it might make Ariel feel self-conscious, a houseguest - and this thought is acrid, the mind's eye showing Ariel behind a closed bedroom door, voice kept controlled volume, even measuring her phrases as though imagining each and every one is heard, dissected, will be required to have conversational footnotes when finished. Like a secret. Self-analysis from Lucy Jinx: Lucy would feel that way were she Ariel and so Lucy is projecting - Lucy would lower her voice and hide, therefore anyone would. In the history of things, though, she knows herself hard-pressed to find any example of other people who think like she thinks, motivate how she motivates, live life like a well-tempered lurk. Now it has happened every night for weeks and the moment the call comes in there is a tacit shrug and Lucy gives a smile and some gesture which directly translates 'I'm gonna go puff puff puff' and Ariel thumbs-up to it and no longer even lightly - not that she anything lightly, but Lucy means *In spirit* - drifts toward the bedroom, already beginning to speak - always answering as though it is Kayleigh who dialed, though most of the time it is Leopold who then - after an Ariel-warm laugh - puts the daughter on as Lucy hears suction of door close behind her and feels the length of outside against her face. Another change: Lucy no longer moves from the door - trepidations of Ariel-might-see-me-through-the-key-hole-and-think-I'm listening, as she had done the first week - just mills right outside it - or if she strolls that way or lingers at the top of the down-step, the bottom of the up-step, she does so without assigning the movement gravity. Lucy is coming to define herself by differences. Lucy is coming to see herself as I-am-now-specifics-of-what-I-used-to-not-be. It could be drawn as a slow-motion of tropical-storm force pulling up planks from a boardwalk, or time-lapse photography of a mosaic floor, this bit, that bit tooth-rooted out over time until eventually the thing is thought of as used-to-be-a-mosaic-floor. Lucy used to be a mosaic floor. She used to be a boardwalk. Now, she is a floor which once had mosaic on top of it. Now, she is a place where there used to be boards. Another truth: this is coming to be one of her favorite times of a day. And not in some subversive, she is given pause by the thought way. It feels - dare you say, Lucy? - intimate. It feels like it is a favorite part of Ariel's day too, and that it holds cohesion by neither saying so, each assuming. Did Ariel used to be a mosaic floor? How does Lucy think of other people? Does she assign them more-or-less history than she does herself? Lucy thinks of herself as a secondhand book stuffed with as many Post-it notes, receipts, ticket stubs, paper scraps, folded electricity bills, business cards, glossy brochures for someplace-she-never-went-and-can't-exactly-remember-the-meaning-of as there are pages - all books should grow old, become secondhand, become secondhand-stuffed. And does Lucy allow that other people's lives are as complex as her own? Ariel, for example. A perfect example. Isn't Ariel all the more complex than Lucy? If so: why does Ariel seem so simple, so streamlined, so organic? Something like the exact tip of a record-player needle, that's Ariel. She is something predictable that touched something that spins and one never knows what it might sound like. This also: Lucy has started going in after finishing the cigarette, straight away. Like now, Ariel's voice laughing and talking in that automatic to-my-kid sing it songs.

Ariel - cripple-hobbled to the wall, insisting on putting on her own socks - asks 'Did you know there's still Social Studies? Did you know there's still Guam?' 'They haven't gotten bored with that?' Lucy says, having stopped on her way into the bathroom, continuing once the question is done, looking under the sink for her razors. 'I'd think, considering, they must be more into it now than ever! Do you think the people there know that's where they are?' Where are Lucy's razors? 'Where are my razors?' Lucy loudmouths, still looking under the sink, peeking up over the toothpaste-bristle wet, brown-smeared counter. 'In the kitchen drawer' Ariel answers, addenduming 'which I only tell you because I felt there was a pre-condition unspokenly understood that you won't ask me why I had them or why they wound up there.' Ariel is still village-idioting away with her sock attempt. 'Why did you have them? Why did they wind up there?' 'I needed to cut through the shrink-wrap on something and thought of it while I was in the bathroom so grabbed the whole pack of your razors because it wasn't open and only thought how I could have waited until I was in the kitchen to choose a kitchen-based cutting tool, there, once I was already in the kitchen, at which point it seemed nitwit to not use the razors I'd brought all that way, so I opened the pack and used one and then - what? - was I supposed to walk all the way back to your depressing bathroom when there was a perfectly fine drawer, right there?' For revenge, Lucy watches - intently, arms crossed - Ariel continue to fail with her sock. 'Your feet, themselves, look pregnant.' 'Don't try to distract me - and stop sidestepping my question about Guam!' The Ariel-watch boring now, Lucy yawns to the sofa, sits, directing her sentences back over her head by speaking a bit louder and doing a little motion like pulling a lawnmower cord with the very tip of her nose every few words, head to the side, palsy, internal creaks to where her neck meets her skull by the ears. 'I guess they know they're in Guam. Probably there's a lot of signage there to remind them.' But what Ariel means is: 'Do the denizens of Guam know how Guam is viewed in the eyes of the majority of the world - as it to say: that most human beings do not know the name of the place were they to observe its physicality, let alone that any of the individual citizens of the place, personally, are there, concretely.' Ariel furthers: 'While people may concoct myriad images in their minds of America or Japan or the USSR, at least there is some accuracy just from passing association. But anyone who hasn't been to Guam and pictures Guam is - de facto - not picturing anything having to do at all with Guam - even if the images are accurate it's because Guam, incidentally, looks like someplace else and, generally, places can only look so many ways.' Lucy pictures a thatched roof and bicycles roughly dismounted and left against a pile of long weeded weeds waiting for pickup, bulbs of roots and soil, brick-large in softballs at their bases, mangled, bark-peeled sticks, and some other things mixed in making the pile seem uncomfortable, forbidden, sometimes scratching the bicycle paint. Lucy realizes she knows the words *Thatched Roof* but has never seen one - or, if she has, doesn't know which one of the roofs she's seen was one and thinks the roof she is picturing isn't so thatched at all, the building suddenly looking something like a movie Wigwam and a television Headhunter Shaman's hut. 'Being a historian in Guam must not take long.' 'No' Lucy concedes, believing this is likely true. 'Or else it must get demoralizing to realize how little of the study of History is the study of Guam.' 'Yep' Lucy yeps 'some places have history the way other places have parts of town people always think *Why did they put offices here?* about whenever they drive past.' 'Can you help me with these socks or are you truly this much of an asshole?' Pause. Lucy swivels to address Ariel directly 'I'm this much of an asshole.'

The conditions of Ariel's bath-before-bed are cultish in their need to be specific. There needs to be a bowl of *Honey Nut Cheerios* on the floor outside the tub, the thermostat in the apartment needs to be turned to *Cool* with the fan on - because it makes a different sort of vibration in the walls, a soothinger hum than the heat or just the fan alone - the lights need to be off, the door propped open the exact thickness of Ariel's copy of *Malone Dies*, a radio needs to be set to an oldies station called *W-WAP Sixty-Three* which, it often mentions, specializes in 'Doo-wap and Feel-Good Soul' and which plays forty-percent commercials per hour - Lucy has estimated - most all of them for local joints, and the volume needs to be set at exactly *fourteen-point-seven* by the digital read-out - this radio is a change from the first three days before Ariel's remembered to bring it over, on those days the dishwasher needed to be running - and Lucy, preferably, is to be in the bedroom doing whatever she does, able to hear the sound of Ariel rapping on the bathroom wall if Ariel needs something because Ariel says she gets nauseas if she tries to talk when she's in the water and it's dark. Lucy tends to these set-ups while Ariel undresses and runs her own water, but does not do so in a fervent or catechismish way - more like fitting new pillowcases to pillows, stacking towels so the most will fit on a shelf, capping syrup so that a gunk doesn't build up, slowly ooze over the bottle sides until one hardly wants to touch the thing. Tonight, Lucy in belly laid on bedroom floor, re-reading O'Parkes praise and a few other of the e-mails which are more business in tone. It seems a rendering of the cover - the possible-cover - will be forthcoming. Lucy gets no say in the design and fidgets when she sees that *One of several photographs will probably be used and designed around*. Photographs of Lucy? Is that what this means? But Lucy had not been asked to provide any photos and cannot think which they might have pulled from the few she has memory of putting online.

And would they design a book with just an image clipped from the internet? Wouldn't Lucy own rights to those and have to be asked? Maybe you will be asked, Lucy - don't get conclusiony. 'True' she says. But then thinks 'Wait.' Then thinks 'No, wait.' Photographs would be of her, she would have to approve - but the book is about her, so why would the publishing team think she would disapprove? Did they get photos from Elliott? Did Elliott choose what might well be considered the definitive-image of Lucy Jinx - oh your famous modesty, Lucy, it never ceases, eh? - the way Lucy sees Mina Loy always in profile and oddly warrior-brave or sees Chantal Ackerman always with hand to her face, cigarette in it, posed posed posed until that is just the pose that is her naturally? There exists a simple solution in that Lucy could just ask where the photo came from. And if it is from Elliott, then Lucy might politely - without mentioning why - say 'If I have any say - could my photo be left off?' Would it matter if you liked the photo Elliott chose, Lucy? 'It would not' Lucy children's-book-petulants 'it would not matter if I liked the photo Elliott chose.' Is it supposed to be Lucy's way of being forced to say 'Thank you'? Will it be Elliott smiling to herself that she knows Lucy would have to approve the photo and so would have approved of how Elliott chooses Lucy is to be seen? The e-mail is a cryptogram. The e-mail is a rock that may or may not be an arrowhead and there's only people around whose opinions are less-than-definitive so you just leave it be. 'Who needs an arrowhead, an old arrowhead?' Lucy thinks. And look how her lip is, now - a bridge half-collapsed and other half upped-too-high while she eyes other e-mails she doesn't read.

'Would you want a son or a daughter?' Ariel asks Lucy, rubbing the mint-lotion, after on her belly, up-and down her arms to get her hands dry of, eyes closed, then coiling hands around Lucy's wrist to try to get the dregs off. 'A son' Lucy says to say something with no idea what. 'Why?' Lucy can't think of anything, though. Just fatigue, Lucy - you're just tired. 'I really haven't thought about it' she says, even though part of her thinks 'You shouldn't have said that and certainly not in that tone and most definitely not at this time of night.' 'I've thought about having a son' Ariel said. 'I've thought about having twins too, though.' 'Twin sons?' 'My dream is to be Tatooine, you know? Seemed like the best way.' Lucy doesn't give Ariel the pleasure of admitting she thinks that is kind of a clever thing to say, but since Lucy can't come up with anything spontaneous, now she feels like her silence is beginning to alter the mood. 'Do you need me to sleep out on the sofa - in case we don't wake up, you know, in case we sleep in?' Ariel doesn't answer. After a moment a sound like a snore. So Lucy lays quiet on her back. Minutes. Minutes. Snoring, that kind like right at the spot where the hole from the nose into the throat is. Then 'Oh Jesus, Lucy - I'm not really sleeping - did that actually fool you?' 'It did!' Lucy laughs. 'That was a fake snore?' 'I was creatively suggesting how bored I was by your comment.' 'That was a fake snore - bullshit! Fake snore like that, again.' There she goes! Ariel does it! Lucy tries to imitate and falls way short of the mark. 'How did you get so good at fake snoring?' 'I listen to people when they sleep - it's like that story Richard Feynman tells about remembering the way Aeschylus wrote down the sound a frog makes, you know?' 'Oh yeah.' Lucy does know. She hasn't thought of Aeschylus in ages. 'Too bad about the space-shuttle, huh?' Ariel asks. 'Too bad about the atomic-bomb' Lucy adds. Ariel - now honestly seeming drowsy or else showing off even more impressive acting chops - explains how she has come to not mind the bomb so much. 'You wouldn't be saying that if I had one and I was going to drop it on all of your stuff - then you'd be homeless and even if something survived it'd have fallout all over it and that stuff doesn't come off.' 'Insult to injury' Ariel, admits 'I'd have to watch the surviving piece be destroyed for my own protection.' 'I destroyed it all for your own protection!' 'I know you did, I know you did.' It must be fakery, this yawn voice - this too articulate, too getting full thoughts out lullaby-high-pitch Ariel is speaking in. 'I think you're just bamboozling me with sleepiness, right now - I bet you're gonna stay up all night just to be mule-brained.' But Ariel promises she really is just passing out. 'If I had a son' Lucy says 'I would name him *Dario Lamberto Jinx.*' 'Not *Dario Mario*? Or *Dario Lucio*?' Lucy gives an impassioned defense of Lamberto Bava, here, in which Ariel starts snoring, again, exactly as she had before. 'The thing about being clever is it isn't clever when you keep being clever after people know how clever it is, Ari.' Snore. Snore. 'Ari.' Snore. 'Ariel!' Snore. Bump bump. 'Ariel!' Mrmph sounding 'What?' pronounced *Wherat?* 'I know you aren't asleep.' 'I am asleep!' 'I think not, senora fake snora - unless you sound exactly like you really sound when you pretend.' 'Leave me alone, Lucy. I don't go waking you up.' And Ariel Lou Reeds how Lucy shouldn't treat other people that way, to which Lucy scoffs and again won't admit that she likes this wit well. Instead: 'Do we have to leave the light on? If I move will it wake you up?' 'Yes. If you move it will wake me up. Yes. We keep the light on. Now' Ariel Bella Lugosis '*do as I command*! Go to sleep!'

The fragrance of Ariel's greasepaint perspiration through the gauze of the lotion as Ariel sleeps reaches a tone where it is just exactly what Lucy always figured plastic Easter-grass would smell like if mowed. Lucy's own drifting is hardly enough to even be called intermingled with her awake. The pressure and urgency in her to both urinate and defecate has now built enough that it serves as fulcrum and lever for her to prop up without ceremony, leave the disused doorknob of Ariel there, unperterbed in the cold polish of its slumber. Remember that. Why? Lucy thinks it unwise to poke the hive of poetry now, so on-the-heels of this venture of letting her past-self be aired. 'Let the haunt of pressures past roam the moors awhile until the coming Lucy becomes the spectral glint the caught-out traveler fears, so accustomed becomed they to the murk-weight of the bog cloudy expanse. Or something' says Lucy, overhead vent-fan on, door locked, only the secondary-light associated with the fan illuminating her. Lucy is exactly an unwalked-on London street - that is exactly what she is! Lucy is a current that flirts with a dousing rod but then giggles and currents away. Yes, Lucy does want to smoke. 'Thank you for asking, by the way' she says and then says 'Oh you're quite welcome Lucy, we are pretty addicted.' Has there been a night yet where Lucy hasn't awaked to smoke? No. And has Ariel ever noticed? No. And this is a problem for the mind of Lucy Jinx - let us wager and see the wager pay off. Indeed, so observe: if Ariel had caught her - is that the word, Lucy? - on the first night or the second night, well - one - it would have been out of the way and - two - it would have seemed like 'Hey, I just am used to smoking at night so that's what I'm doing - be right back.' But now it's at this point, so if Lucy was caught - *caught?* - it would still be the first time, for Ariel, with implications of I've-slept-through-all-the-other-times. So what? So Ariel might feel bad. She might pride herself on how sweetly Lucy sleeps beside her and how immediate the deep restfulness is. Ariel might wonder 'Why didn't you mention this before?' Because Lucy being found out and then Ariel hearing Lucy say 'Oh I smoke every night' has an air of secretiveness, an air of 'I'm acting like this is nothing to think twice about but that just reinforces I've thought about it, prior, and decided against wording it.' I mean, Lucy is almost embarrassed by the simple psychology she is displaying - but, anyway, lights up and breathes out the window. Lose the feeling, Lucy. Lose it. Before it grows elephantine, Lucy - just lose it. Ariel is not hunting you. Ariel is not hunting you. Ariel is not the world, not just some disguise, not just something that doesn't seem like spelling but then will be lousy and worm-gutted with *LMNOP* and all - no, Lucy, Ariel won't give birth to a bawling Thesaurus or a Dead Sea Scroll or a *Mwindo Epic*, okay? Stop the thought. Smoke the thought. Ariel is not trying to catch you, piece-by-piece. Is not absorbing you. Ariel is not flypaper and you are not a spider that got too close, not even understanding this death wasn't even aiming for you, was, in fact, quite specifically not. There you go, Lucy. There is goes. The thought. The cigarette is its shape. The window is its path to shoo shoo. Goodbye thought. Goodbye deranged Lucy-needs-to-be-tucked-in-goodnighted. All that Lucy wants in her is sundry nicotine-remains and lapsing memories and Ariel always perplexingly saying exactly the thing Lucy never would. Goodbye. Hello. Goodbye. Hello. Yet still she feels something weak in her heart, like this is the one time the hand is going to shudder before the clot goes, before an odd chill passes which the brain flounders at trying to verbalize and suddenly the world pool-bottoms and she'll hear voices all saying 'Lucy Lucy Lucy' exactly in the shape of hands roughing the surface, offering grabs to hands too deep to clutch them.

NO DREAMS. BUT A DREAM about a department-store. No dreams. But a dream about a floor, dirty and looking worse in the dim light, pieces of scotch-tape on the tile, long soaked in - it seems, at times, people tried to fingernail them up, the light catches them and makes it seem there are more than there are. No dreams. But a dream in which someone in the geometry of a celebrity she cannot quite name is saying 'There's something that goes wrong with every theory - eyes aren't actually glass, I mean, so everything you're saying just doesn't work.' No dreams. But a dream of trying to scrub the word *Lancelot* from a wall, froth taking the color of the paint, scrubbing to bubbles and filth, buckets of water thinning it away, somehow the letters stained so that they can have pigment cleansed and yet never diminish - black turning brown it is scrubbed so much, chocolate-milk foam warming and glopping to coffee-cake mud. No dreams. But a dream about a hallway and rhinoceroses behind glass, stationary as though false, stationary in perhaps the way such animals actually are. No dreams. But a dream in which the only direction wind can blow is skyward, every breeze of any speed emanates from the ground like the world is the netted surface of a speaker, wind with the soft thud of tennis balls on glass pumping in beats easy to dance to, the clouds taking on strange properties but somehow no different than the clouds have always been. No dreams. But a dream about a line of taxis. No dreams. But a dream about the crinkle of a book into a bag, from a hand into a hand. No dreams. But a dream about a friend saying 'Fog can be scooped in a jar, the jar heated on a flame and brought to boil, meat can be put into broil in the fog, but the lid has to be opened every few minutes, new fog brought in, new flame struck - it's complicated.' No dreams. But a dream about hopscotch with not enough boxes and boxes unevenly sized and the pathway the boxes lead is off crooked, like it is all a slug suffering salt. No dreams. But a dream about an escalator, a hand touching something sticky on the rubber rail, a mind wondering 'Is this rubber or is this polystyrene?' No dreams. But a dream about the sound in the distance of gallop and of knowing what the gallop pertains to, having associations with the clip of it, both frightening and comforting, at once. No dreams. But a dream of a yellow segmented jump-rope, some of the links cracked, the only thing available to use as a belt but the belt won't tie - and anyway, there is a sticker on the thing which spells jump-rope *Jump Roap* and there is no one around to laugh with. No dreams. But a dream of snowfall. No dreams. But a dream about licorice too hard to snap with downward teeth. No

dreams. But a dream of the warmth of distant fire being enough to warm the
eyes looking at it - this warmth enough to spread, a smear at-a-time, with
fingers, hands slathering bodies out of their shivers, everyone freely undressing
once they see Lucy do it and the nudities eventually sizzle and perspire and think
that something in the world has anewed itself, now, and the bodies press
together to preserve the heat, to make new heat, and like a match-head the
bodies are a fire in pin-point that Lucy watches from a distance and smears over
her face and lathers her body with, undressing while others watch and do
likewise and rejoice and coalesce and burst into flame which Lucy sees in the
distance and realizes warms her eyes enough she can spread the warmth in
smears - the speed of this sequence more and more without control or respect
and the feeling of 'Everything has gone too far - everything has gone too far!'
No dreams.

  The first thing Lucy says to Ariel's face - some rasp of intense dryness to
Ariel's attempted 'G'mornin' - is 'Light is just a thing that is asleep right now
and when it wakes up oh boy are we gonna be in for a shock, you know?' Ariel
clears her throat and asks the time. Ariel had told Lucy they wouldn't oversleep
and she begins the awkward and lazy back-and-forth semi-roll that will dislodge
her from the bed she so obviously doesn't want to leave. And there goes Ariel,
struggling with herself, from the room, flapping the wall switch outside the
bedroom and hack coughing and spitting into the toilet on her way into the
bathroom, tug to the turn of the shower-tap and sharp rustle and plastic snap,
straight-still-wrinkled, of the shower curtain, and then some more gravel-wet
hocks. Lucy has the option of she can go back to sleep. She has the option of
even if she wakes up, hearing Ariel dress, she doesn't have to let on that she has.
But dutiful goes she, instead - deep rubbing the fabric of her shirt underarm,
stopping here here and here to rub rough bulb of heel over side-shin of opposite
leg, no relief to the dry itch - to the kitchen. And Lucy suffers herself through
the trudge of filling the coffee-pot with tap-water after emptying the dregs,
pouring this into the maker-top, diaper pinching the overnight-still-damp filter
and its grounds, this to the trash, and - the worst part of all! - new filtering the
basket and counting out the endless eleven spoonfuls she always does, always
making the fifth and the final one over-large to balance out, she figures, any
spoonful she may have shortchanged. Investment idea: learn to use the set-timer
and get the coffee ready at night. Wake to the aroma - like a caught-out ghost in
the rooms having to allow itself to be drunk down for its trespass and inability
to slink away with the cock-crow. Lucy doesn't even note what she thinks of
her belly anymore - these scratches are irrelevant, ignored - she no longer
wonders if her shoulders look like the bottom part of a very full sack. Yes, Ariel
is beautiful. God yes. God yes. And always has been. And Lucy had never heard

of the quality of shadow a person like that could cast to a pasteboard apartment wall. God yes, she is lovely. And that her voice has become a falsetto slowed down past being identifiable as such and her delivery of words has become labored like she has dug through the pile and knows none are adequate so just selects them based on 'Eh' is a delicious that could cause fits were Lucy fit-prone. Does this change the fact that a kitchen, making coffee, is an awful place to be when one could be sleeping? No. Does it change the fact that the shower sound is serving as a kind of countdown, forcing Lucy to feel she needs to be more awake than she ever honestly is? No. But Christ God, Ariel is lovely. Her forearms are like an overflown riverbank and her neck's left side is like the memory evoked from a water-faded ticket stub in a pair of pants packed away ages ago, after a wash. Lucy would not name anything more beautiful than Ariel, even if she could. She has principles like already thrust daggers on this, ideas that have already stabbed their promises home. The first reluctant falling of coffee to pot, the liquid plopping as though it has had its will broken, science reminding it how physical properties go thus: solid, liquid, gas, coffee like plasma, like magnetic fields, like dark-anti-matter or the physical weight of atomic-time. That was Ariel sneezing, heard overtop of the subdued shower hiss. And again. Ariel is like the sound of the uneven wheel on the cart that brought library books to the schoolroom those weeks that the library was closed for repairs and Lucy was not even old enough to need two fists to count.

Ariel asks: 'Have you ever had to use a second trash-bag to wrap around a trashcan just because the thing got so overfilled - the garbage compacted down, you know? - and then you have to flip the trashcan over and kind of negotiate the wriggling it in little humps, not sure if the plan will even work - because why would an overfilled bag, turned upside down, fit in a bag the same size of it - and worry that the mess will be not only your fault but worse than it would have been because you won't feel smart while you're standing in garbage?' 'Yes' says Lucy 'why?' This, it seems, is what Ariel claims it feels like to choose an outfit at this point in her pregnancy, especially because she is getting a lot of acne along her shoulders. 'What does that have to do with it?' 'That feels like that greasy sort of gritty stuff that you can see through a white trashbag and smell, so it feels like you're touching it even when you aren't - only I am touching it. It is, in fact, growing on me.' Lucy gives a thoughtful pause and claims to understand. 'Except: You didn't have acne on your shoulders, last night.' 'What were you perving on my shoulders for - is that what you do?' 'It is what I do. They looked like porcelain washed by a beautiful well-paid paid-maiden, scrubbed gently with buttermilk and silk-scarves.' Ariel gives Lucy a brief explanation of physiology - which Lucy isn't so sure the veracity of - then Lucy asks to see the pimples. 'They aren't pimples. It's more like eczema.' 'At least they're like something that's a cool word.' Agreed, mutually, to is that more words should do 'The *C* and then *Z* thing.' 'Do you want me to come?' Lucy doesn't ask while she, to be a pest, picks at some lint on the side of the pants Ariel has finally selected. 'Are they not pristine enough? I'm going to a place that is okay calling itself a *Gyne Clinic* so I don't know how many photogs will be lining the shrubbery.' Lucy cringes. Ariel waits a moment, then - as though on to another subject - feints 'Shit - Lucy?' getting Lucy to offhand say 'What?' and then Ariel springs the trap '*Obsto-Gyne.*' 'Gah!' is Lucy's only response - that and saying 'I'll poor your coffee, grossy.' Ariel is probably sticking out her tongue in some kind of fatuous way to denote triumph, which only makes Lucy wish she wasn't so lame-brained, at the moment, so unable to summon quick-wit. Coffee poured and - to be even more sweet-leaf - Lucy cuts in twain an English muffin and depresses the pieces down the toaster-throat with a mock violence, saying 'Die die!' Remember to take those out, early, Lucy - because Ariel does not like them honestly toasted and the auto-setting still overshoots it. Sproing! Not done enough. Keshuck! Count twenty. Sproing! Not done enough. Keshuck! County to forty, but lose confidence at twenty and Sproing! 'Whatever' Lucy hisses, putting the things directly to the countertop and before she goes to the fridge for a stick of butter to rub over the things - the end of this cream-yellow caked in crumbs from its use already since being unpeeled - she calls across the apartment 'You are really a prissy bitch, Ari, with all of your needs!' Ariel's retort just sounds like 'Wrahwrahwrah' so Lucy figures that must be what she'd sounded like too, so it is a bit of a startle when, full five minutes later, Ariel, entering the kitchen and taking up the buttered muffin says 'That left you speechless?' 'Wait - you heard what I said?' 'That I'm a prissy bitch?' 'Yeah.' 'Yes - you didn't hear me?' 'No.' If Ariel were a portrait in a gallery she would be titled *Skepticism with muffin in mouth.* 'I didn't!' So Ariel rolls her eyes, somewhere between disappointed and convinced. 'Are you going to eat that?' Lucy looks to the other muffin-part Ariel is pointing at. 'No. Because I love you - that's the whole reason there's two there.' Ariel takes it and gives it a long tear, having to push some overhang into her mouth with a finger as though Dear-me-how-uncouth-of-me and nods a nod like she's winking but thought of the nod first.

How things have gotten: Ariel doesn't seem to possess the apartment yet, in her absence. Her things around suggest, still, the limp of half-unpacking in a hotel for a vacation that is longer than a few days but not quite a week. The first thing Lucy does, still, once alone is smoke - and she has gotten so that she doesn't wait twenty minutes and send some seemingly cute Hi-hi message as a way of depth-charging sonar to verify Ariel really is gone. Right to the cigarette and with a tone of reclamation to her strides. Silence and alone is not something so easily parted with and more time has been spent roaming this short place than has been spent sharing it. Shuffing skin, huffing it out in long breaths of cigarette she knows she won't have to bat out, time will dissipate the carcinogens by the time there is real need for them to be gone. So, not so much has changed. A mantra of Lucy's, that - like it is a relief instead of a shrill whistle heard from a distance but knowing the train is getting closer and soon will be bullying thoughts out of one's ears with its rambunctious clatter. Not so much has changed. Not so much has changed. Lucy, in fact, spends less time in other company now than before. And there was always a chance - in any era she can think of - that her nights would end with the either someone else there or at least the feeling of someone else there. The change is subtextual - Lucy knows the person will be there. But the change is also, she has to point out, that she wants the person there. When has that ever been? It's an honest question. Isn't her time with Ariel a different caliber wound than her time with anyone else - isn't the welcome she feels of it unique? But stop - stop, Lucy! How will this end? You'll find some obscure reference to your past somewhere and think 'Oh - that's just like with Ariel! I wanted that, too! Ariel is not unique!' and from this trend all the way to 'Ariel needs to be made rid of - Ariel is repetitious and reverse-order.' But Lucy - you are reverse-order! The hill-climb becomes the hill-descent and the destination of both is the same. 'What?' Lucy snarks 'Death?' But she knows that is pure, elementary-school avoidance - obnoxious how she cannot make herself keep to her line of thought. She starts the shower and undresses, each garment an accidentally bumped and torn-open-on-a-hinge scab - or else an adhesive-bandage slowly pulled like birds pecking dropped rice, thinking enough tiny quick pains will amount to less than one sudden-pulled Ouch. Is that noticed? How Lucy doesn't even look at herself in the mirror? Is it noticed how Lucy hardly even looks at herself in the outrageously curved image of her leaning over toward the tap to adjust the water to lukewarm for entry? In case not: Lucy avoided looking at herself. It started as an idea of seeing if she could go a week - just one full week - without any idea of her appearance but when - due to rear-views and door0reflections and all - this obviouslyed itself impossible, Lucy decided 'I won't look at myself when I'm at home.' For a week. The water is orange-warmth on her thighs, it is green-warmth on her chest, and purple-warmth to her face as her eyes close and she steps into the stream, air of someone first dunking head under a pool just to get the smooth flat of their hair over with. Lucy has taken to - along with her refusal to regard herself at home - thinking of herself as a painting, slithers of all of her multicolors snaking down her flesh to the basin floor, gulping fast and greedily through the drain to the sewer to the sea. She thinks of looking down to see colors she doesn't recognize what parts of her are they from and it dawning on her those are the individual colors mixed, now separated, which make her tones - she will decipher her underneath while her outer-face is cleansed away. She dreams of looking to the mirror and seeing blank. Seeing something to write on. Seeing something that isn't the hard work of brushes with minds she is foreigner to.

There's her phone - but how did it get on the floor under here? Not that Lucy bothers much putting effort into the answers to such questions, just takes the phone up and walks it to the sofa with thoughts of splurging on fast-food for lunch. Tapping some button at random to see the time, Lucy finds a message waiting, gut issuing its annoyance with a very squishy shift of interior gases. Samantha has sent a message. Do we want to play a guessing game as to what in the world it could be? Samantha is aiming to find you out, Lucy - she's sounding you, likely just wants to nab something with a new scent for the hounds. This is all in jest, though. Honestly, Lucy is a little bit surprised it has taken so long - her sigh, right now, more demonstrative of a lament that Samantha didn't just not bother, because there was an allure and a dignified power in that. So look at the message and see, Jinx, look and see, just get it out of the way. But, no. Watch. Resistant Lucy, the new flavor of heroin, she just erases it unread but then - coincidence of course, but admittedly shaking - no sooner does the phone-graphic of *Message Deleted* end than the device vibrates, vibrates, vibrates three messages from Samantha in-a-row, Hydra-exact in their replicative properties. Lucy drops the phone and stands, but finds there are only so many places to go and she'll need her phone, eventually, for any of them but here. Fine. The second message picks up from the first - now erased - one, and says *or like you once said, even better*. The third message - to be a jerk - picks up an entirely different thread - or so it seems - starting with *Anyway, or not - hey!* - and says *Anyway, or not - hey! There are two, or three maybe, paychecks sitting around for you that Kurt and I haven't reported. No, we weren't punching hours for ynk.* And then the final message is just an Erratum that says *for you.* If it's a ploy, it's a clever ploy. Lucy gives top-marks for creativity and guile. Two paychecks might make sense - why would there be three, though? Perhaps there are just three envelopes and only two of them are clearly paychecks and this was just Ariel's shorthand - Samantha's, Lucy means, Samantha's shorthand - of denoting that. You know how you could find out, Lucy? 'Yeah yeah' she says, Moneybag valves in her heart pumping harder than the Be-Careful ones, and is already typing *I think I missed the first message - Like I once said, what?* Send. Immediate vibration - too immediate to be a response. And - fuck! - of course the message indicates any contact was unnecessary but now Lucy has popped her head out from the warren! *I'm not at work, today, but Kurt just has them in an envelope and if he's not there the new girl knows that you're probably coming in and doesn't know what the* - the phone vibrates a new message before Lucy finishes, though she got enough of the gist she just presses on with the new message. *Oh hey! I guess you weren't murdered - that makes writing to you so much less sexy. Frown face frown face frown face. How are you, man?* Was that a chuckle, Lucy? Sure, it was a chuckle. And now Lucy is typing back *How do you know this is Lucy? It might just be someone who wants money.* The response comes: *Ooo, touché. Is that who this is?* And Lucy write *If it is, you wanna grab coffee?* And Samantha - Lucy concedes the point to her - *Well I sure as Hell don't if it's not.* Now. Now, again. Now: how long are you going to stare at the phone waiting for a response? The words change their tinge. They begin to form the face one reserves for pointing toward a laughingstock. But, anyway - enough blinks happen and Lucy's thoughts turn to calculation. To worry how the third envelope might be an official note explaining not to cash the paychecks due their having been issued in error. Maybe Samantha knows that. Maybe Samantha is having her victory lap.

At any rate, unseasonable warmth and humidity spots the day - banana bruise, soft as the final press of a thumb to an otherwise hard peach now discarded. Lucy keeps the coat because the weather is not a thing that has shown itself to be exclusive - and also there is something about being dressed, no logical fault of her own, in ill-fit of the world. Surely there will be others like Lucy, maybe even some with umbrellas - a thought only based on Lucy's twinge when indoors that it likely would be raining or have recently rained or the sky at least gesturing threats of it, but a thought she feels others must have had, too. Lucy is at step and out, a wrong snap to an otherwise in-sync metronome that nevertheless seems to go with the melody if not to be full-blown the point. From this distance, her car behaves with her as an illusion might, the sun making it almost vicious to observe for the light in canine teeth off from it - also carrying the sense of recent rain, as Lucy always observes such harsh reflectance, most, after a downpour. None of the other cars much follow suite - they seem actually sunbaked, codgery, too long on the porch, tanned-past-a-crisp even though tan had never been intended. Still nothing from Samantha? Still nothing from Samantha. Seatbelt on and still nothing. Lucy pulls out and feels foreboding tension in her forehead, in the veins drying in her eyes enough that the left one is watering - which Lucy rubs at, knowing rubbing will only turn matters worse. It's going to turn out the checks are no good. Or they will be some kind of stubs, just Void things - two cycles through a pay-cycle coming out all Zeros, yet some policy or glitchy-thing about the computer record-system that prints checks two times past when an employee was deleted from Active. Because, isn't that the thing? Lucy isn't marked Inactive - she actually quit, proper and politely, and so there is no need to think the Agency doesn't have her on Standby. Yes. Lucy is certain that is it. The third letter will be Official Notice of End of Assignment or something. Though why the checks are showing up at her work rather than in her mailbox is odd. She wonders if there is trouble with her address in the file or something - has she ever gotten anything sent to her apartment? No. No, Lucy certainly hasn't. And the way she is being summoned - by Samantha - no no! This has bad moons and tea-leaves that even a layman can see indicate an exsanguination or choking on mouthfuls of gnats and attempted-to-be-upchucked-but-blocked-by-these-same-gnats hot bile. The roads seem to have no opinion. The roads function the same as they always do - perfectly understandable how they are such ready symbols for so many things, roads. Get the checks, cash them, have done with it. Whose gonna track her down to collect when the error is spotted - the world's most hardline gumshoe, an accountant whose job is on the line and will French-novel-desperation to keep it together for the sake of his pride, even though he knows his wife is leaving him for another man? Wowee, Lucy's blood is up about this! Who knew she was such the truffle-hog capitalist, gets the sniff and goes juggernauting toward that thin Yankee dime! True, Lucy - it isn't peanuts. And true - life does cost currency and now there will be considerations you know you will take the brunt of. The road is so willing to let Lucy move on - the colors are flowers all lining up Bingo for her - that she cannot help but be rightfully bothered. Ambulances aren't this lucky even when blaring the road clean! She feels Kafka-hands under each elbow - yes! - she feels the skipped-to-the-end of an unfinished thing bearing down. It's good money, though. No, it's not that. It's the idea of taking something that doesn't belong to her. It's the idea of still being herself.

There is a Parking Lot Sale of some kind - Lucy doesn't get it - people dressed in running-clothes with numbers all stapled to them and booths selling various Arts and Crafts and food-vendor-trucks and carts and kiosks from various local-establishments competing with likewise things from various national-chains. Oh - there, see Lucy? - it's something to do with the hotel. Balloons and an unreadable-from-this-angle banner, over there. Fine. And Lucy winds up parked way behind one of the offices owned by computer-chip makers - or whatever these are, that's what she has always thought *IllChip* was, the company which seems to own this entire side of the business-park - least used - to go by the piled-up old boxes in the loading area and the look of not-opened-in-months to the glass of the rear door, sun showing thicks and thins of the long built-up soot which has been streaked by rainfall and snowfall unevenly and then laced with fresh grime which now simmers - buildings, by three dumpers filled with the bottoms of rolling swivel chairs and purple, cracked, circular, plastic disks. Is there a way to wend to the doors of your offices - former offices - without having to weave through the crowd of whoever-those-people-are, Lucy? What if - she thinks - she were to cut along this grass path, round this building in front? It seems quiet from where she is standing, but the overall din - both distant and near - is so aluminum it is hard to tell if anything is accurate. The whole world is a melody played by bending a saw while sawing it as though a violin. 'Hell with it' Lucy says, imitation of some line from some movie - which? - and now feeling all the more Gouldian in her too many layers. She approaches the unflattering shorts that somehow make even muscular, gorgeously fit-thighs seem sexless, their only purpose to run, sweat, and breed yeast-infections at the crevice of where their tops meet. 'Running' Lucy reiterates - a favorite line of her fans - 'is something that never seems sexual and which no one seems attractive while doing. At least not when dressed for it' she whispers - politician finger up - not wanting to go on the record wrong but wanting to say something to sound momentarily fearless. Yes, yes fitness folks - give Lucy a look and wonder what is the matter with her. They are all inventing you maladies, Lucy! Healthy people do that, you know? They don't think in terms of Faithful and Unfaithful, Crooked or Corrupt versus Saintly and Above-Reproach - no, no - but instead just in terms of Healthy and What-do-you-think-that-person's-condition-is and they confer about which exercises would help with the proper vitamins supplementing amongst themselves for hours? Might as well tart it up, Lucy, take the kind smiles of women who are so proud to have water bottles and bent brimmed ball-caps and stories about how they 'once didn't stop at fifteen miles' but went ahead and wet themselves as they pressed on, who are bedecked in their most heroic shirts from previous-length runs, take the looks of almost being offered e-mail addresses or fliers for Community Outreach and play into them. Lucy wishes she looked like she was just porridge standing on the shoulders of cake batter, wrapped in a coat and a wig to pass for an adult to buy booze. What does she look like? Well, she looks like something. She looks like the opposite of the over-the-hip and between-shoulder rashes these people all look like to her. 'Only the ill will survive' she wants to turn as she gets to the door she is after and brandish at the crowd in a cornered-cat yarl. But actually, the reflective door shows she doesn't look bad. All those smiles might just have been all those smiles. The air-conditioning assails her and the receptionist looks up - Lucy has never laid eyes on this man - and she just does an Ariel 'G'mornin' and moves for the door - hears the Thump of it unlocking from the button the man pressed - says generally 'Thank you' and hears a laryngitis 'You have a good day' and a chuckled ahem ahem hack-cough ahem.

Observe: Kurt greets her with 'Holy smokes, skinny!' - Lucy has taken her coat off while striding the corridor, despite the fact the temperature in the offices is making her shiver, likely kind of a rote thing, the removal, because it's stupid, all totaled, since she's just getting the envelops, no intention of staying - and this is not the sort of remark Kurt has ever once made toward her, before. 'You look like a goddamn pistol-shot - what have you been doing?' He moves to give her a hug - which, though this has never happened from Kurt is not off-

LUCY JINX / 1063

putting - and she pats his back with her embrace, just laughing and calling him 'So odd.' He - indicating with the words 'I'm serious' that he's serious - reiterates how terrific she looks and as he moves to retrieve the not-yet-asked-for-envelopes he questions her as to why exactly she left, very good naturedly. 'I'm famous, now Kurt - I actually do things.' 'Oh - your book! Has that happened already?' Lucy shrugs that it's happening and supposes this is the drift Samantha has been giving, maybe also lacing it in as an excuse as to why their relationship dissolved. What has Samantha said about that? And, speaking of Samantha, why is Kurt saying 'So you finally decided to come out - Samantha said she's left you like ten messages, we figured you'd gone the way of all flesh.' Had Samantha said that? Well, no time to ask, because Kurt is holding the not-the-same-as-the-other-two envelope up, Lucy having taken the two obvious paychecks, explaining 'This one just came in' - he Ums and he says, rhetorically 'Well, was it then?' before snapping envelope in the air with a quick loose-tight of his wrist - 'yeah, it was just yesterday. No idea' he shrugs, ready to hand it over but standing-by while Lucy opens the first of the checks, sighing at the labyrinths of bends and perforation tears necessary to accomplish this. 'What's the verdict?' asks Kurt and also says 'Samantha almost brought them to you when you kept not being able to make it.' 'Yes' Lucy does find that odd, but puts it on one side as - holy shit! - she sees her full pay, dated past her last week, right there, still valid, just money for her to robber-baron! 'Bam!' she says, forcing the check in a thrust at Kurt's face so that he has to snatch it as though otherwise he risks a nose-break and already is - less carefully - opening the second. Look, Lucy - another one! For the following week! And - she is falling over herself now, this is the best thing that has ever happened to her! - she suddenly thinks to ask, because of the date on the second check 'These have just been coming in on payday?' - yes, Lucy, maybe they will just keep coming, everyone needs to just keep silent, not mention to anyone hep when they show up! But - even as Kurt says it 'Oh well' goes Lucy's heart, a downbeat despite this huge windfall - Kurt says 'Well, until yesterday. This one came' he now tenders it 'and it was payday yesterday, so the jig must be up. And Jesus you look feline unholy, Lucy - sorry to keep saying so.' 'Hmn?' goes Lucy 'Oh. I already said you're odd - I get it, Kurt, you wanna jump my bones. Who doesn't?' And this is the strangest most beautiful sight Lucy's eyes have ever seen! A check! She holds it out to Kurt - indicating how he can just cut it out with the practical jokery and everyone can leap out and take the last drop of piss out of her - and demands 'Is this real?' Kurt leans in. His eyes indicate the emphasized final word in his thundered 'What the fuck!? Why do you have a check for three thousand dollars!?' Kurt refuses to relinquish it when she snatches for it. Why do you have a check for three thousand dollars, actually,

Lucy? 'Why do I have a check for three thousand dollars?' Kurt holds up a One-second gesture, as he is reading the sheet of paper the check is attached to the bottom of. 'Your Health Plan or something - never took a sick-day. I don't know. It's been accumulating since you've been with the Agency.' Kurt seems rubbery with jealousy and finally reliquishes the paper across. Lucy reads what he read. Lucy's eyes are stacks of questions boring back to her brainpan.

'I thought Ariel said there was a new girl working here?' Kurt pivots from the file he is sorting - Lucy is slung the wrong way around a chair, just licking her chops at the three checks she shuffles leap-frog over each other like a child might his three favorite trading-cards - and says 'Who said what?' 'Ariel said' - Lucy! - 'or - sorry - there's a new girl - Ariel or something - working here?' '*Ariel*?' 'Samantha said - is the new girl not called *Ariel*?' Kurt has to think. 'There's two new girls. One is definitely *Isabel*. The other is *Glynis*, I think - something weird, maybe *Ariel*.' Lucy does her most award-winning work on the line '*Glynis* - maybe Sam said that - but I thought she said *Ariel*.' 'It's a weirdo name, anyway' Kurt says 'but Glynis - or whoever she's actually called - is terrific. Better than you ever were' he says, not without vindictive drippings. 'She's not here today' he adds, back-to-work voice. 'Just me. I am sorting the treasure today. I am in search of the blood-diamond or whatever. Glynis said something like that - I mean Isabel did - something funny - I don't know if it was about blood-diamonds.' 'No' Lucy absentlys - four-hundred-three dollars sixty-four cents - 'blood-diamonds are not known for their yuks' - another four-hundred-three dollars sixty-four cents - 'though, who knows? People gotta find a way to laugh, right? It's what separates Man from Beast, makes us so much more dangerous' - three-thousand-seventeen-dollars eight-two cents - 'our ability to laugh.' 'Laughing makes us dangerous?' Lucy gives Kurt a glare until he looks at her, then changes her tone to scholarly. 'Kurt: Are we the most dangerous species on this paltry planet?' 'Yes' he says, looking like he might object - make some remark about venomous insects or something - but obviously he comes to his senses and realizes Lucy would just point out how they don't seem - these venomous insects - to be making inroads toward stopping mankind's spread and that mankind could easily eradicate them, wholesale, along with everything else - and Lucy says 'Yes. And Kurt: are we the only species that laughs?' Kurt is grudging in saying he supposes so. And Lucy settles the matter with a shrug. 'Comedy is a weapon, Kurt - you ever heard that?' 'I've heard that.' 'You think people were just saying that to be wrong, or what?' Kurt thought so, yes, he admits 'Kind of - or that they meant it in a sort of term-of-art way.' 'How many of the worst things have a laugh-track accompanying them, are justified and balmed through with laughter? I'll spare you the brainwork - a lot.' Kurt says maybe Lucy is forgetting there are different kinds of laughs and that they all aren't based on humor. 'Aren't they, Kurt?' Four-hundred-three dollars sixty-four cents. 'Aren't they, actually?' Four-hundred-three dollars sixty-four cents. 'You don't think someone laughing maniacally at a revenge or in the aftermath of an eye-rattling cum thinks it's pretty fucking hilarious?' 'Well' Kurt punily tries not to back down. But Lucy pounces 'Do you laugh when you don't think something is funny, Kurt? Have you ever?' 'Fine. You're right.' 'And that's why I don't work here anymore and you do, Kurt. I'm famous. I'm flush!' She smacks the checks. 'And you might be wise to start shining my shoes - maybe you'll get some of the droppings, you know?' Kurt croupier hand-wash-signals and then, faking the suddenness of his remembering to say so says 'Oh! Are you coming to Samantha's thing?' 'I might' Lucy says, never one to miss a beat or seem off-step. 'Why?' - Lucy stands up, thinking this is as good a cue to split as any and these checks should be cashed double-lickity-split if she wants to not have this good fortune ulcer on her - 'Are you?' 'I was thinking to. But it's mostly people she knows, so I hoped you might be there - lifeboat, you know?' 'Sure, Kurt - you can ride my coattails at Ariel's thing' - Lucy! - 'at Samantha's thing - Gah!' says Lucy, flit-flitting her tongue like banging reception from a radio-signal - 'I meant is Glynis or Ariel-or-whoever going to be there?' Kurt doesn't know about Glynis - 'It is Glynis' he says 'I was just being nice before, I have no idea who Ariel is - but Isabel won't. Or else I wouldn't have asked you, believe me.' 'I believe you' Lucy says, slipping on her coat. 'Yeah' she furthers, pocketing checks to inside breast-pocket 'I have no idea who Ariel is, either.'

So, there we go: Samantha becomes a tad more interesting. There is some machination here and Lucy - she gives credit where it should be given, as a rule of thumb - cannot say that she sleuths it. Point A: Samantha chose this day to send a message about the checks. Point B: If Kurt is to be trusted - which, come on, Kurt is to be - Samantha, from when the first check came in, had been pretending contact with Lucy to have control. Point Maybe-C: Could be, Samantha was just going to destroy the first check or was still making up a plan when the second came in - at any rate, Samantha was up to something for weeks. Point D: Samantha, in retrospect, was a bit more solicitous than necessary in her texts - even before taking the aloofly distanced glib stance she had in the final salvo - her writing meant to get Lucy's attention - oh Lucy knows if she hadn't have replied right away Samantha would have kept writing with details, oh Lucy knows she just would have! Point Likely-E: Samantha must have either known Kurt would mention Her Thing or else told him to - whatever the thing, the get-together, was to entail. But all that just to get Lucy to go someplace? It's irksome that this couldn't be it. Samantha would be capable of a plan, but this was a lot to have happen - all on a particular day - and a lot of control to relinquish to the Fates if any precision was needed. 'Not' Lucy reminds herself - lighting her second smoke, leaned to her parked car, watching an airplane overhead, the kind that is audible, which she always imagines are the out-of-date ones - 'that I care.' Lucy is four-thousand dollars the richer, for all intents and purposes, and that is all there is to it. 'So, Samantha: good try with whatever it was - but no cigar!' You tell her, Lucy! The cigarette goes bad tasting, the sunlight and warm weather running everything's melody. The car on and the radio going, the air-conditioning going as loud. To more important questions - her phone buzzes - what should she spend the money on? Not a message, just a warning of *Battery at twenty-percent* - Lucy had meant to charge this last night but hadn't. Again: more important - what should she spend the money on? Just get the cash-in-hand, Lucy - worry about it later! 'Yes.' And don't use the bank! 'Why not?' What if the company catches it out and has some way to stop payment or rescind or something, after the fact? 'Good point, Lucy' Lucy says. Check Cashing joints - they don't care. It'll be their problem, anyway. The money settles on her like a fever, pointless and center-faced, cold slick down her back. A smile like touching something unexpectedly sharp makes her hiccough, the hiccough making her laugh, the laugh coming out a snort which makes her laugh, that one coming out with a hiccough so it sounds like a clown horn, this making her breathing heavy, the next hiccough making her sneeze. Okay? All done? Caught in all kinds of tides, eh Lucy? Driftwood to your own expressions and whimsical diaphragm. A few minutes later, turning down this road. A few minutes later, taking this turn at this intersection and up onto the Highway ramp, right into a finger-splint of traffic. 'The cost of greed, Jinxy' she says. And a panic-flare, she notes the gas-gauge and You've-got-to-be-fucking-with-mes! Discomfort like sepsis fills her as cars pull in snuggly at her rear and her sides. 'Okay' she says 'okay okay.' And ahead of her strain unmoving cars that have given up. Lucy wriggles in her seat like a half-crushed firefly and grips the wheel, her hand-bones connected to her despair. Do you see nothing, Lucy? What do you even pay attention to anymore!? Her phone buzzes and she snatches it, just for something to do. No message. Just another warning of *Battery at twenty percent*. 'You said that already' she sighs, and then says to the still traffic and another glance at the gas-gauge which confirms the stick below the line and the yellow-light on 'You all said that already, too - everything's already been said!'


THE PRISTINE, POISON-TANG TO THE scent of gasoline - never so sweet as here-and-now - Lucy feels she should be baptized in it and set aglow with Bic-flick the Holy Spirit! All stress leaks from her skin. She is the bottom of a store-bought cup of coffee left too long in the beverage holder, lifted and revealing the puddle beneath. Her sense of importunate invincibility rises and she is accepting - mark that, Lucy, mark that - that this is how life goes after a choice. One wars and one triumphs and one accepts - mark that, Lucy, mark that - how, in battle, no one knows where a mortar will hit, despite the whistle and despite the aim of best intentions targeting but - mark that, Lucy, mark it - this goes the same for both sides. Removing the nozzle from her car, replacing it to the pump, pressing a button declining printed-receipt, Lucy feels she is tired after swinging away through a fiendish battery from her opponent - or at least from this or that of its soldiers - feels she has survived sniper-fire with hand-to-hand combat. How will you celebrate, Lucy, as your eye swells to the shape of your felled opponents boxing-mitt? How will you celebrate, as your lip bleeds freely your heartbeat out in a slake over the pulsating skin of your breast? Because to fight a war is not just to live, eh, but to wildly indulge! Lucy, you have the means to strut cockfight-victorious for awhile, to bring the prize home to your lover and watch her plump-feather and purr and claw at the turf of you, howl at your moon. 'I snatch victory from the jaws of Death' - mark that, Lucy, mark that - 'and I have chosen my prize and will so bejewel her!' And in such a state of accolading chants and folk-hero songs being made of her, Lucy pulls off onto the road and she thinks she remembers - most certainly you do, Lucy - where the nearest Check Cashing joint is. What was that sound, Lucy? Oh nothing but your phone, eh? Mark this Lucy: Lucy thinks 'Shall I press my luck or head home?' The phone or the money becomes her Lady or her Tiger - either destination is just exactly the same length of driving away. Do you mark how this is a decision, Lucy? How you are thinking about this and in which terms? Do you mark this, here and when you are making this a specific point-of-choice? Maybe Lucy does and maybe not. The thing is that the money is not a certainty - the checks could have been voided. But not the three thousand dollars, Lucy! That one was not a mistake, but a legitimate amount you are owed! True. But what is the other thing? Do you want to be out without a phone, Lucy? What? Best get the money now, right? You're already out, after all. A retreat at just this moment could give an opening for a backstab. How would it feel, Lucy, if you went home first, went out later, only to learn the company had just - how you would learn this, never mind, but just saying for argument - in that interim canceled the two checks and if you had gone out a few hours earlier you would have had the cash in your pocket? Could you imagine anything - are you marking this question, Lucy? - that would make you feel worse, stupider? 'No' Lucy answers. And - mark it - the phone buzzes and this time Lucy sees *Battery at fifteen percent*. 'No' she repeats. The only way to survive now, the only way to negotiate what Lucy considers the steps into the end-path of her life - Lucy, mark it - is to actively consider and actively accept. 'This is profound' she says 'and this is proper. And' - why do you say this, Lucy? - 'I go forward with my eyes open and my chest bared, waiting to be wounded - for my desires are righteous and my choice' Lucy says, turning out from the lot 'is the one I will admit to with pride, come Hell come Heaven come Void!'

Such glitzy bravado zips the car ride along, the radio playing songs unlistened to, the tires beasting in rolls as precise as equations can make round go round and as lighter-than-air - Lucy drives, the perfect harmony of the concrete and abstract concepts of Circle. The day seems now the glaze of a doughnut, the pristine smooth of the yogurt wrapping a raisin. Lucy's head drifts to ways she will break the windfall to Ariel - she is holding back from calling, as she does not want to hex things by counting her coins before they are minted - and is oscillating between wanting Ariel to be involved in discussions of how the money will be spent, wanting to have laid out some bit of travel, or wanting to be the domestic budget-balancer, letting Ariel know she can relax as far as things go with money, at least for a short little while. No, Lucy has never been one for reality! The thought of Ariel's offspring still unsprung does not keep images of travel from filling the tight of her mind, cream pressing its way through her cake - she even gives Ariel Ariel's current dimensions, as though this exact moment she chose is the shape of things to come, always - the future a retaining of the present, just aging, superficial differencing, until done. Anyway: Lucy feels a bounce like she hasn't felt since youth and recalls a time she spent months saving up about two hundred dollars, hoarded it from every little place she could think, and then presented it - the fulfillment of a vague promise - to a girl in her class, pressing the money to palm and answering 'Yes' when she had been asked 'Wait - are you serious?' and 'Yes' when she had been asked 'Are you sure?' What had that girl's name been? The question is idling the twined-wire of Lucy's brain - not bothersome, pure entertainment - as she dismounts her car and enters the Check Cashing joint - far more immaculate an establishment than she's used to, a sofa she has no need for and coffee brewed and cheap pastries out next to the soda-machine - no line to wait in and is immediately greeted 'Why hiya there - and how may I help you, today?' 'Sheryl!' Lucy says and laughs at the 'Okay' and the odd smirk from the young man on station, then patting the air with her hands, explaining 'I had been trying to remember somebody's name - from ages ago. *Sheryl*, it turned out to be.' '*Sheryl*' the clerk repeats, Lucy blinking before remembering she needs to hand over the checks. And how does this go? Observe: the checks handed across, identification, Lucy explaining she isn't a member and 'No, thank you' to joining, though she'd get less taken out from each check. Observe: the tiktiktik of calculator buttons then the thkthkthk of computer keys, all of her information entered, the numbers from the checks reentered between fifteen, twenty glances from the screen-to-the-checks from the checks-to-the-screen from the clerk. 'And do you want cash? Or to have it on a prepaid card?' 'I'm not a member' Lucy mentions as though the clerk will go 'Oh right' but the clerk smiles and says 'I know - but there's still the option. Some people just like having it on a card, though I think it's kind of dumb.' 'Why?' Good explanation about cash machine fees - counterpoint that 'It lets you shop online.' Just cash for Lucy, thanks anyway. And the clerk will be right back. And in whups overhead slat the ceiling fans around. And the low-energy buzz of the fluorescent lights and the chug of something starting or stopping in the vending-machine's bowels. Lucy pictures the clerk just burning the checks in the back room, returning as though he's never seen Lucy before and saying 'Well hiya there, and how may I help you, today?' Absurdity would go from there. The door opens behind her and she thinks of the coming bag-over-her-face of a kidnap - how none who enter here ever will leave, then almost bellows a Grendel of laughter at the sight of a nearly miniature old woman, bent semi-colon shaped with time and arthritis, coughing a smile and Bless-meing a sneeze. And on the turn-around, Lucy faces the shish shish shish of money counted and recounted and recounted as the clerk comes from the back room and twenty-forty-sixty-eighty One twenty-forty-sixty-eighty Two twenty-forty-sixty-eighty Three twenty-forty-sixty-eighty Four twenty-forty-sixty-eightys out four-hundred-eighty dollars then ten-fifteen-sixteens another amount before starting the fifty One fifty Two fifty Three fifty Fouring and upward the other three thousand.

So: let's allow Lucy a victory cigarette. Let's allow her the make-believe of triumph. Reality? If the checks are discovered by the company, Lucy will likely be in actual trouble for cashing them - as, obviously, she knew she could not have earned that pay. She cobbles some schoolkid excuse, even laughing about how she will say 'Since there was the three-grand for the accumulated sick-time and all' she figured the other checks must have been overlooked pay. Something. Blah blah blah. Her phone buzzes - but this time it buzzes and buzzes to indicate a call so Lucy picks it up. 'Layla!' Battery-bar in the corner ablink. 'Layla!' Lucy booms 'I admit my phone is about to die - but my God do I have a triumph to tell you, my girl, how I am an unstoppable, cutthroat, money machine! Can I call you back in twenty minutes?' Lucy has just enough time to be thinking 'It's odd how Layla called rather than texted' while she finishes her greeting and Layla says 'Lucy?' Or somebody does - somebody says the word *Lucy*. 'Hi, sorry. Who is this?' 'Is this Lucy?' 'This is Lucy - I thought' - but Lucy shuts off because she hears talk on the other line, the phone moved away from the speaker, something like 'I have Lucy, here - I have her, okay.' Pause. Pause. Lucy says 'Hello?' to the sound of a cough or something much like the sound of a cough if a cough were what was coughing. 'Lucy?' asks a voice with about the tone of a mushroom growing on the one penny down a wishing well otherwise surrounded by dimes. 'Layla?' And the voice - it is irreducibly small, the center of the final wrung twist that could be made to an atom's very center, nothing left to drip out - seems to laugh and go as jolly-tone as it is capable of going and says 'Oh God, Lucy - I was so worried. Hi, Lucy.' 'Layla?' There isn't description for the way Lucy's shoulders feel. There isn't description for the way Lucy's tongue feels. There isn't description for the way Lucy's forehead feels. Lucy has escaped, it seems, all language for a moment and her head throbs with emptiness, desperate to be distracted by anything. 'Lay - hey, are you okay?' 'I'm sorry I haven't called, Jinx - I kind of haven't been much awake.' But those words are too small sounding to be words - escapees from tongue, breath that by will dons a cloak of meaning to slip past the guards that cage it just breath. Lucy's phone beeps and the next few sounds of Layla are drowned. 'Lay - Lay my phone is about to' - note how something like instinct kicks in, Lucy, how you say 'Cut out' instead of what you were going to say. Why? Why, eh? What do you know, Lucy? You do see how you already know, don't you? You do see that, eh? - 'My phone is gonna cut out. Are you okay? I can call you right back, okay?' Layla laughs and goes 'Eh, it's always some goddamn thing with you, right? Lucy, I just really wanted to talk to you for just a minute' - another voice is speaking and it makes Layla pause - 'oh Lucy, shit - I don't want to tell you and I'm sorry it's the only thing I have to call about but, hey, it's all that's going on with me.' 'Layla' - fuck! - 'Layla' - just shut up! - 'Layla' - Lucy is already shaking - 'Layla' - why isn't she talking? 'Hey, Lucy - don't be Lucy for a second and I just need to tell you. I'm dying. I think is the word for it.' And was that a chuckle, a sound-effect like a Gak? 'Doggone went and got myself the sniffles, but good.' 'Layla - shut the fuck up, okay? Fuck, man - you are seriously going to ruin my drive home - my battery is dying and I'll be in fucking suspense till I get to my charger' - yes, Layla is talking underneath this, but Lucy presses on - 'and so just knock it off.' 'Just talk to me a few minutes, Lucy.' What's a voice with no sound? It sounds like a scream. It sounds like a goddamn sepulcher having its tail stepped on, fang-bearing a shriek.

In one sense, we could praise Lucy for going quiet, seeming calm, having a few minutes of the following conversation. We could think this meant she had accepted something, had set all aside, found a way to live in the interior of a moment - albeit the worst one imaginable - to rein the unbidden melee of her throbbing thoughts and bloodless mind. Except for even she hears in the stillness of her car interior the glacial cracks to existence that eventually she will selfishly try to repair with all the tanglebush nonsense she can throat at it. Layla starts. 'Don't worry about your phone - I'm kind of passing out and I might not wake up.' 'Layla, I want you to be joking - are you hurt?' 'Naw, Jinx - I just got sick and it got worse by trying to get it better, allergic reaction and all. Same old fucking song.' 'Sick how, Lay? You're in the hospital?' 'You wanna story, Loose? Come on, let me just say something to you.' 'No - I want a fucking story. If you're dying so much, I would like a story.' *'Once upon a time there was pneumonia in my both lungs and I drank some powder and my body went bang and I'm done for - the end.* Pretty good, right?' 'Except for the last bit. Layla - I am flying out to you. I am coming out there.' 'I don't - shut up. For a minute. I dying right now, it's not a vacation to plan.' 'What do you mean, *right now?*' Beep goes the phone. 'What?' Lucy asks, because she caught only a stray syllable of Layla. 'I mean they didn't think I'd even wake up and I can tell I'm drifting.' A voice from somewhere else in Layla's room. 'Oh it's all so stupid. Listen a minute, because there's a last thing I want to say, especially if you're phone is whatever. Such a modern death, right?' 'Layla - I'll go in here, buy a phone, let me call you right back.' 'There isn't calling me right back - you are the worst friend in the world, right now' - laughter and sickness and coughing and death - 'there isn't calling me back, Lucy. Lucy. Lucy?' 'What, yes, what - I'm here. Are you - Lay - Lay, come on - Lay.' 'I love you, Lucy.' 'I love you, too. You don't need to die to drop me a kiss about that.' 'Oh sure I do. Or anyway, I am. I fucking love you and I miss you and I wish you were here and, frankly, I also wish you were dying, if it comes to that.' 'I am dying!' Lucy promises, wiping absently the back of her hand across her mouth. 'Okay? So, that's fine. I am.' 'Are you? What are you dying of?' 'You're going to not trust me right when you're dying?' 'Eh' Lucy hears Layla say, then something is obscured by a beep, then hears Layla coughing then hears Layla say 'Fuck man - you got another call you gotta take or something? You got someone better than me, that it?' 'Oh everyone is calling me to die today, idiot - I was on break from it when you called with all your dramatics.' Coughing. Coughing. Coughing. 'Yes yes' Layla in her almost-voice manages. 'Yes, I am the dramatic one, we've both always said.' 'You're in the hospital?' 'No, Lucy - I'm at *The Party Mart* and I'm buying *Thomas the Tank Engine* plates for a party, tonight - you wanna come?' 'Yes.' 'Too bad.' Coughing. Coughing. Coughing. 'Lucy, it honestly is important to me for you to know that I love you.' 'I love you.' 'And I think if you were a color I'd scribble all of you myself.' 'Okay.' 'Yep. The only picture in your color would be my scribble-scrabble - Lucy, I wouldn't even try.' 'You don't need to. I love that picture.' 'I don't even know if anyone likes that color. I like it, though.' 'I like it, too.' 'Arrogant - yes, do you? Well, I just thought I'd tell you before I'm dead that you'd make a great' and there is a beep and a desperate Lucy asking 'Make a great what? Sorry, my phone!' and a sighing Layla saying *'Crayon,* Lucy - *a great crayon,* keep up.'

*Ten percent.* Lucy agrees to let Layla just speak and sits, folded forward, finger holding down tab of her unphoned ear to block out all outward sound, dot-dot-dotting the volume button on her phone-side well past it could be doing anything. Layla says: 'It might be good about your phone, right? I didn't have time to write much of a speech and don't know how much ad-libbing I'm up for. What I was thinking I wanted to tell you was I was scared shitless that time we stole those raincoats and I spent the next two weeks thinking about sneaking mine back into the shop. I was so glad - don't hate me, man, you don't get it - when I needed money to move, this once, and I sold that fucking coat with a bunch of other coats at this shop that paid for clothes by the pound. Bear with me - this is my big story, okay? And I know you're a real bitch about time-limits - it's like an argument before the Supreme Court with you. Anyway: it was also very very anguishing to sell the coat. I never could have done it if it had to be sold on its own - only because it could just be thrown in a bag and weighed could I do it. That day we stole the coats I realized you were the person I loved more than anyone in the world, man - that you were the best thing and I could never hope to tell you how terribly lovely you were. And the day I sold the coat - this all sounds rehearsed, sorry, it is kinda, but I'm drifty, it took them awhile to understand I wanted to call you, that you're a real person, they thought you were fake or something - is the day I decided that I was right that I loved you. And I didn't need the coat. Or something. This sounds dumb now that I'm saying it. Anyway - I'm saying *anyway* a lot, shit, don't let that be my final word, okay? - I just figured there was no way you would ever know that story if I hadn't told you because you kept your raincoat and always brought it up and stuff. Why did we steal those? It was my idea, I know, but just because I figured you'd think I was something you'd like and I kinda wanted to be that and didn't think that I was. I remember everything about that shop and nothing about that raincoat except I didn't want it and was glad to get rid of it and I loved you. I hope you don't mind. Saying things, sometimes, is the wrong thing to do. Maybe you really had another moment in mind you thought was the one where I realized I loved you and so I'm queering that all up. Too bad. I'm dying so you can be polite. Was that the same day? The same day we saw that old man with the shit running down his legs at the pet-food store? I know we were in those coats - but that would be a lot for the same day. Oh fuck, Jinx - you'd die so much better than me. Did I just say the words *Old man with shit running down his leg at the pet-food store* in my dying I-love-you speech to you? Leave it to Layla! I hated your guts about Gregory, you know that? You know I once read a book about poison to poison him but then I read another book about a poisoner going to jail and it made me feel bad, like I shouldn't. I hated you so much then - but it didn't matter. It didn't matter it didn't matter. You would die with much more eloquence and without mentioning anyone you hate - with or without it directly connecting to me - I know I know. But I never understood you, Lucy. I never ever did. Now you talk. You talk, Lucy. But just say something all Lucy. I don't want you to say anything about right now. I might fall asleep and I really just want to hear you saying something Lucyish, will you do that?'

*Seven percent.* So what can Lucy do? What can Lucy say? How much can be crammed into however long her voice can go until she realizes it is going, one way or another, but Layla not hearing? Let's see, Lucy, let's see. Lucy says: 'I was thinking, the other day, about whether or not words are In a page or On a page. If you follow me. Are words In a page or On a page? By which I mean: if they are On it - if the page is a surface the words truffle atop - that is quite one way of looking at them, of understanding - or trying to understand - how they themselves might understand themselves. Space is how we understand ourselves - our positionality, or angularity inside a fixed set of dimensions. Words being On the page, for example, makes them exposed and - moreso - makes the surface a finite, concrete thing. The page is a surface - no choice - and the words are on it how we are on land or whatever. It exacts the dimensions of the letters - they are actual sizes, they are insects this long and that wide. But if the words are In a page, our understanding - and their understanding of us - might be galactically different, Lay, galactically! I look at a word on a page it is In - well, how far down is it, you know? It could be miles! It could be oh! fathoms deep down there! So I can never be sure of its size - a word's, its individual letters - first of all, and I can never be certain at what distance I am seeing it from. And the space itself, the page - let's just picture a white page, right? - we have to wonder: since we see no difference between the spot the word inhabits and any spot around, well is that the bottom or just a plank - equally-invisibly white to the rest of the world - it has landed on, petrified to? Is it the crest of a hill? Or the ledge just to one side of a further drop, you know? Picture two words, side-by-side, and they seem the same size - but maybe one is one-thousand feet more down an abyss than the other, but also one-thousand times - or however many times - larger, so that from our vantage-point they seem almost the same size. Like stars, Lay - like stars, for example! We see one or two, they might have such distance between them as it would boggle us, but they seem, to our naked eyes, the same-sized crisp pinpricks, the same cold, immovable light. Because don't get me started on motion, Lay! Words on the page? See for yourself - grab a book, Lay, look and see! - are they moving? Maybe the way glass moves, right? Maybe the way a stationary thing is technically moving because science says so, somewhere, but not how we mean. If the words are On the page they are in our realm, they are equal to our physicality or anything else we can prod and gauge - but if they are stars away, Layla, then our eyes are Hubble telescopes - you know? - and the things may be zipping along at speeds so ungodly we have to fucking invent numbers to clock them - invent numbers to know the speed of still words on a page, Layla! Think of that! There aren't numbers enough we can make out of one-through-ten to do the trick. And the white - what is it? It doesn't have to be ground! If words are In the page they are in a cosmos, they are celestial, they are in an electron-cloud, they are Heisenbergian, Schrodingerian! How do we know there actually is a letter *K*? What if, spatially, it is some odd, outer-space confluence of an I moving this way and a *V* moving that way? Like an eclipse! Or a planet revealed when hopelessly immense orbits kind of unalign? I know what you're thinking, Lay - I know you - you're thinking *What? All Ks? Pish-posh!* Open your mind, Layla - goddamn it, why not!? Everything makes a difference! A lowercase *B* could be a lowercase *L* passing a lowercase *0* - or wedged, permanent, deep nebular glacial, Lay! You know what I mean - right?'

*Three percent.* Lucy panics, now, but is allowed - how can she not be allowed!? 'Listen to me, listen to me - can't they just have you stay alive? - go to sleep and I will fly out - what hospital are you in, where are you?' Layla is silent. 'Fuck - are you still on the phone! Fuck! Weren't you even listening!?' The flimsiest kind of cardboard chuckle, inhuman - no scent, no pulse to it - and then a voice that can't be Layla's 'I heard you. Are you still talking about letters?' 'Now I'm saying *What hospital are you in?*' 'I drifted off, sorry.' 'I don't care - I'm coming to you - be dead for all I care - fine, dandy, you do that! - but I am coming to you so you be all the dead you want.' 'I will thanks' kind-of says Layla who again says 'Lucy, I think I fell asleep a little - but I really like what you were saying. That was good. Are you just making it up?' 'Which part?' Silence. 'Which part?' Silence. 'Layla?' 'Mmn?' 'Which part?' 'I don't' - some kind of sound, irreproducible - 'what?' 'Part of what? Of what I was saying - what part!?' Lucy is just yelling now, pleading like a liar child, cancerous to have the other kids blamed. Saying 'What, man?' 'Lucy, sorry - I fell asleep.' 'Okay.' 'I think - I don't stay awake a lot. It's why I didn't' - the longest drawling sound Lucy has ever heard then - 'uh, you know?' 'It's why you didn't what?' 'Oh. Call. Or write. I kind of. Awhile ago. I. There were. Everything it all is a long and it happens. I was dreaming, though, I think - you know about it? You know?' 'About dreaming?' 'I was listening, I think, or I might have been dreaming?' 'About what?' Nothing nothing nothing. Is the line dead - no, there is a beep! - nothing nothing nothing. 'Layla - what were you dreaming about?' Another voice talking and Lucy just - fire-hydrant bursting full into and out from her chest - demands 'No! No! No! No!' then quiets and 'Lay, Lay, Lay, Lay, Lay what are you dreaming about?' 'Are you still Lucy?' 'I'm still Lucy!' That mirthless, lifeless chuckle. 'I mean *Are you still there?* Of course you're Lucy - just listen to you.' 'I'm here - you said you were dreaming.' 'I was dreaming you were talking but I don't remember what you said.' 'What do I ever say?' The chuckle - it is the wet left at the drain-face after the tub is empty but slick enough you'd slip on. 'There's other times, you know?' 'Other times what, Lay?' No response. 'I agree, Lay, I mean - yeah, you've always said that - but what other things? Hey - name one or two.' 'I don't know what you were saying - that's the only thing I remember.' A beep - was it a double beep? Lucy struggles against moving the phone to see how much time she has because doing so means Zero, no miracles ever come from looking in doubt. 'What did I say, Layla?' 'I love you, Lucy - can you hold on a second?' 'Layla - sure - Layla.' A muffle sound. Then a beep. Then the sound of a phone on a bedsheet or with a hand covering it - or just a phone breathing out the still of a room, maybe digitizing some atmosphere, some peripheral machine sounds, hospital haze. 'Layla?' Lucy's chest compresses to exactly the size of an overlarge cashew - why that, why does she know that, who knows, but she knows - and it is dry like one and has a residue of neglect and of salt added to it outside of its nature. 'Layla.' 'Lucy?' 'Lay - hey I just want to say' - but Lucy is cut off, silences herself enough that her bones feel lashed and left to bleed out, strains to hear Layla saying 'I'm just going to go to sleep and I don't want to talk and be weird but I told them to let you keep talking - can you just keep talking?' Another odd shushing, dog-sniffing-microphone muffle, then 'I just need to ask this person a sec and then I' - a sound fills Lucy's ear of a ding-ding-ding-dong jingle as Layla cuts out and that is what Lucy never knew saying Goodbye to Layla would sound like.

If Lucy were an outside party looking in, she might hesitate at calling the minute that passed in abject silence a *Minute* - the word might trouble her, it might seem either indelicately shortshrift as an expression or laboriously overstating the thing - but nonetheless, the rational part of her would admit that for the next minute, connection severed, Lucy sat with a blank phone to her ear doing nothing. Then there was a period - it would still look like nothing had happened were Lucy an outside party watching - where some mechanism in her brain kicked in, like the sound of a fan from an adjacent room, of her thinking 'How am I supposed to keep talking, now?' And sometime during this - what could be termed Second Silence - she said 'Okay. Okay.' And then she said a series of words. She said 'Layla.' And she said 'Okay okay' - but like one word *okayokay* but pronounced, because she was stuffy, like *Oakyoaky*. She said 'I.' And she said 'Hello?' And she said 'Hi?' right after that, like someone touching tea they were sure was going to be hot, found it wasn't hot, then dipped finger in a bit longer, disappointed at how lukewarm it was - which is to say it took her longer to say 'Hi' than 'Hello' despite the syllable difference. Then - Lucy still has the phone to her ear - she reboots and, rubbing harshly at her ear, makes some sounds like Grah and Weahgha and shakes her face and goes 'Talking - keep talking - yeah, of course - that's fine - of course, okay.' She pauses. 'Do you want me to talk about the same thing?' Pause. 'Do you want - or it doesn't matter? - you said it didn't matter?' In front of her, objects lose focus, cohesion, refocus, solidify. 'I mean *Page* in the Platonic sense - I think Words exist, you know, on a page, on a thing-like-a-page, and we have - we have paper, right, paper-paper and parchment and all - but we have it in imitation of the realm where the Words exist.' But no - no, Lucy doesn't think this and so apologies. 'No - I mean, not really. I don't. Sometimes. What I say. Layla. I don't know. What did I even say? What did I even say? What did I even just say to you, Jesus - I mean you asked me to just say something - to just say - and so I said but I don't know - right? - I don't even know what I said - you were the only one listening.' Very on purpose and with drama Lucy balls her fist and assaults her thigh - a viciousness, a real desire to do damage - then, just as abruptly, stops and grits her teeth and tightens her abdomen as though to ball over around the wound. 'I wanted to say something else! I wanted to say what I wanted to say, Layla!' But then, for some indeterminate amount of time, it is too much for Lucy - too much - and the only thing in her head is the highest pitch of a pitch rising high like a piano-key servicing as the sound of a pin falling in cinema, the sound hollow as an empty theatre would make it, the theatre roofless, the sky cloudless and grim. 'But not really' Lucy corrects 'no - I feel on the spot now, like I'm trying to make it make sense about what I said, but I think it didn't make sense and now I'm trying to just justify it because I could at least sound smart while you die. Lay?' Beseeching. 'Lay - Lay, wait. Wait, hold on a second. Fuck!' Lucy smashes the phone from her ear to the radio panel, pretends it ricochets hard enough to force her hand back into her nose, but really just forces her hand back into her nose and then smashes the phone some more, mostly just hurting the tips of her fingers wrapped a little around it. Something hits her windshield, but she doesn't look up. Something again, and she does. No. Not the windshield. The roof. A third time. She tenses waiting for a fourth - for tsunami, for tentacle, for the lungs to be wrenched from her, leaving her body intact, Lucy nothing more than a tablecloth trick.

To the clerk - who coughs after he smiles like the smile caused it and in whose expression Lucy knows she looks like someone who was crying and is glad because it is making him listen how she wants him to be - she says 'Do you have a cellphone or a phone I can call long-distance on?' 'Is everything okay?' A customer - old biddy - gives Lucy a look and obviously wants the clerk to ring her and the clerk says 'Just a second, okay?' very earnestly, holding Lucy's gaze until she nods. Even as he rings the old woman - to the old woman's guttural horror - the clerk addresses Lucy. 'You say it's long-distance?' 'It's overseas.

Yes.' The old woman says 'The sign says three of those for three dollars.' 'What?' asks the clerk, looking down at the *Almond Joy*. Huff - like having to re-explain symptoms because the first nurse forgot to note things on the chart - the crone says, enunciating like cobra stabs in a switchblade fight 'There is a sign. It says three for three dollars. Of the candies.' Lucy can't help but look where the old woman is twitching her nose, but the twitch is just emblematic, it is not in the direction of anything but the store's front window - Lucy's car way over there, still parked where it was, the three balloons on the brick pillar outside the Florist next to the Check Cashing joint limply slung toward the freckled-with-tobacco-spit sidewalk cement. All Lucy is doing is watching. This is all that exists. 'You want two more?' the clerk well-hides his growl inside a putty of customer service 'this was the only one out there?' this second question said with a lean over the counter to at least indicate - if not grab two more himself - that other candy-bars are right at the old woman's knee-high. 'No' the woman says, as if for the twentieth time instead of the first 'I would like to pay one dollar for this one, but it has rung up' - emphatic click-click to those two words, volume raised - 'as one twenty-nine.' The clerk gets her drift and is apologetic - and Lucy sees the wires of his muscles straining with pressure not to bite, sees the need in him to get back to addressing her, the hatred of having to not help her, the horror that she will walk away - and explains how the discount only applies if three candy-bars are bought. Well, the old woman doesn't want three candy-bars, she only wants one. 'So, it's just a trick to get more money?' she disparages, disgusted, the clerk in her eyes nothing more than an anthropomorphized rubbish-strew brothel-floor, still sticky from business and the soap mixed with the too little water in the mop bucket. Lucy sees the clerk losing his tether to her, now eager to mix it up with his foe. 'I think it's more true to say it is a particular deal that does not suit all parties - like the fifty-cents off pepperoni pizza wouldn't help someone who wants cheese, or the buy-one-get-one free burgers are a wash for a vegetarian.' The clerk smiles at Lucy, like his winding up this old cunt will be just the medicine she needs, his abominable way of flirting, of telling her 'Hey, smile - let me take care of it.' 'Well, congratulate your bosses on the twenty-nine cents and the loss of my business.' The clerk moves to speak but is silenced by the woman's blurt of 'Ridiculous - I work right over there and come here every day, you'd think it's worth thirty cents.' The clerk isn't cowed, just sees his chance to be rid of her. Transaction tendered. In violence leaves the woman, the soft rustle of plastic-bag her final say - that and the overhead electronic ping-pong of a synthesized bell while the automatic doors spread for her. The clerk is looking at you, Lucy. Lucy? 'Ma'am?' Lucy! 'I'm sorry' she says 'nevermind.'

Lucy Jinx. Cigarette. Lucy Jinx smokes, numb as saltpeter. That is her third drag. That is her fourth. Lucy smokes, numb as a shower-floor. The sound in her head is what it would be like to squeeze a brain were a brain made of paper filled with crickets who have been crushed past the point where they can rub legs to chirp but are living enough to writhe. It would take twenty minutes, thirty minutes to drive home. So why aren't you driving? Isn't she already dead? But Lucy is just smoking, not knowing if Layla is already dead and is uncertain that rushing home to plug in her phone is the thing that Lucy or anyone should do. Smoking is an easy thing. Lucy Jinx. Cigarette. Numb as the length of a lake. Thinking that Layla had to realize Lucy was gone - no no no no no - Layla had to realize there was no more voice - no no no no no no no - Layla had to say something in that moment and had to end the call, hand the phone to a nurse - impossible, impossible. Lucy Jinx smokes, numb as the tread of a tank. Her brain is wetted paper with crickets inside, crickets in a stale mass of cracked, spilled, and uncooked eggs. She does not know Layla's number. The only thing for it is plugging her phone in, at home - but home is not here, not here where Lucy went. Exactly not where she went. Exactly not. Where she went was here and here she is and here she has her Judas pennies in her Doubting Thomas pockets. But couldn't Layla still be alive? Waiting? Are we just saying Layla is dead, now? That it is impossible to call her? 'Shut up!!!!' That was aloud. That was aloud and Lucy is just standing outside, not even a pace back in the direction of her car. That father, holding hands with the child in that lot over there, both of them look at her and walk on and Lucy sees the building they are walking into is called *Early Shubert's Music* and so those books under the kid's arms must be music. 'So what?' she snarls. 'So play music, who cares?' Lucy Jinx. Cigarette. Numb as the bottommost coal in the stove. Is someone begrudging Lucy her grief? Why shouldn't she stand here smoking? Because Layla might be there waiting for Lucy, picturing Lucy - in some death-addled-delirium, Layla might be picturing this - rushing to the nearest phone or else home to retrieve the number from the guts of her telephone to give one last 'I love you' or 'See ya, so long.' Lucy Jinx smokes, numb as the twitch of a dreaming dog. 'I said *shut up*' Lucy says, based on no prompt or goad from herself, no belittling remark at how she should be conducting herself different. What is the point of a moment like this? What is the sense in any one thing over another, right now? Is this feeling vast or minuscule, is it orange or peach, is it chlorine or Clorox, is it piecemeal or mealworm, is it over or to-one-side? Lucy's ear aches like the first mouthing of a hatchling, hungry for vomit to dribble from mother's mouth to its belly. Lucy's hands have to them a quality like the severe bleed of an animal claw trimmed too far down. Lucy Jinx. Cigarette. Numb as an amputee's brother. She pats for cigarettes, remembers she left them on the ground, but puts hand in her pocket, a moment, at the touch of paper, the sensation of curiosity like the citrus of a wound being cauterized. A last tap of her cigarette - just the stub, her lip heating like a bug bite - she discards it and looks at the paper, expecting a bit of some poem. *Hernando's Rx.* A sequence of numbers. *Linda Ciinnoo. Atovaquone.* A date. All well and good, but Lucy - of course she does, look at her - focuses, like duck-net dragging her, on the next line down. *Drink directly from packet or pour the medication into a dosing spoon or cup daily for treatment of pneumonia.* Recoil. Reset. Typewriter slap. *Hernado's Rx.* A sequence of numbers. *Linda Ciinnoo. Atovaquone.* A date. Lucy Jinx looking, numb as a recited alphabet. Lucy Jinx - expecting a bit of some poem, of course.

WHAT DOES MAKE SOMETHING FEEL like something? A basic question of will and reality, Lucy thinks, an atomic precept of identity. 'Let us dispense' she decides 'with the notion that so quirks the rationality of these many many others, this notion that feeling - what causes it - either comes from external or from internal.' But Lucy - does it not need to come from one or the other? Lucy offers this as response: 'It is not as easy as emotions being response-to-stimuli - plants aching toward sunlight and such dither - and it is not as easy as saying that it is some form of personal perception with regard to each stimuli having to do with personal mood and bearing at whichsoever time - such random superficials aren't what determine or govern things.' Things aren't Humanist or Stoical or whatever rubbish - is that what you're saying, Lucy? '*Emotion* is another word for *choice*' Lucy wizens 'but caution! We don't choose an emotion like a plum from a pile, a preference from a list of availabilities - no, not so simple a thing as a Gimmie-that over a Gimmie-this as some may slip the slope up with, bifurcating a thing, portioning it and calling the pieces wholes, themselves, trying to figure out how the slices relate to each other!' Can you be more specific, Lucy? 'Imagine a skull cleaved in cross-section slivers, a few inches put between each - do we say to each other *How does this eighth-skull correspond to that eighth-skull?* as though each eighth-skull is a natural entity, complete-in-itself, ignoring the full skull we know has been eighthed?' Of course not. 'Exactly!' We are only dealing with one skull, moved around, and no moved-bit has dominance. 'A mirror isn't a bunch of shards and shards are not a bunch of mirrors - simple as that.' Well - what of it, Lucy? What of it? 'Lucy' Lucy posits 'is in a state wherein it seems she should be feeling a thing called Grief. And so Lucy is feeling Grief, regardless of wanting to or not. Her physicality is feeling it like temperature - if it so happens three-degrees only cools her two-degrees but would cool someone else four, what can she do about that - shiver more?' No, that would be silly - we're with you, Lucy - so let's dispense with physicality

- worthless little doodad it is - and get to the - what? - psychological, spiritual-state of feeling. 'At some point, Lucy's mind calibrated Lucy or Lucy calibrated Lucy's mind - but this is all one and the same. Lucy was calibrated by language, let's say, at some point what she verbally is - wordily is, linguistically is - took hold.' And Grief is just an arrangement of her language within that? 'Emotions are stubbed-toes while words are the reality of plasma. Lucy is feeling grief exactly how her language dictates. She feels grief exactly as language says *There is a door over there and she walks to it* in accordance to language's architectures and rules.' To make sure we understand you, Lucy: a choice was made that this is the language and this how it works - a craft was put into that, then history invented Here and There and history invented She and Door and the language expressed those things according to its chosen dictates? 'A fool - yes - thinks that language had no choice but to say it thus! There is There, Here is Here, there is He, here is Door - therefore language must say the thing it says, it is simply looking and relating its sight. Yes, a fool thinks that! A language made all choices in advance - in its glory, its horror, its pride, it's impossible-to-escape - and so time and space are crumbs and curtsies! Sequence means nothing to language, as language is what defines all things, most of all what came before it to lead to its being!' Lucy feels grief the way language says Grief? 'No more, no less. Lucy has become the relief sighed by language when it was set and knew it needed do nothing else but consume.' Lucy consumes? 'Lucy is the shadow that covers every bit of light even as light thinks it causes shadow.' Ah, understood. 'I grieve for Layla' says Lucy. 'And Lucy is Grief for Layla and now there is the word *LucyisgriefforLayla*.' And now Lucy has said so. And there, from this time forward, exist only other things to say. Lucy is winged in language and as still as a bone in a yard, full as *wax* is unsaid *candle*.

But what ho, Lucy - crawling back to sniff at the crotch of language, nuzzle your snout up there from your forehead to its rear? Has there been some backroom reconciliation, a friend-on-her-death-bed conversion? Or are you just scared? Scared. Scared. Of course Lucy is scared - it screeds through her veins, the fear. She is the poet, Lucy Jinx! Avoiding fear is not something she was born to. As for language? As for reconciliation? When a wrist aches and then doesn't, has there been reconciliation? When the marathon has run, do we say the body revolted with each hiss of gastric acid, with each breath that tasted sea-salted mucus and chalk? We say the body obeyed! The body which viciously cramped and the body which allowed itself to be dehydrated and reduced to a single imperative keeping the pace. Did the body cower through the marathon? Did the body pull up the bedcovers to its toddler little chin as it made the ascent up the peak? Was it some piss-pants I-want-my-mommy that allowed the body to contort into spirals and land to the water clean, to smack to mat without bounce or lost footing after macabre contortions it has misshapen aspects of itself for in gymnastic? Perhaps! Perhaps! And well, if so even, what prompted it to do so - language! Do we think there are not words which make necessary, which make meaningful, every crisp of musculature, every gloved fist to the bag, every accidental shin shatter? When the athlete in anguish has destroyed themselves, do they dare blame Athletics? Do they dare blame the words, the meanings, the principles? No! They, at most, blame nothing and, at best, the limitations of wordless physicality, the tongueless torque of muscle over bone leading to rupture and to paralysis. And while in the throes, while in the unimaginable-by-some torments of exertion, do the athletes curse the words that brought them there, do they revolt and wish they had never heard *Perfection*, never heard *Champion*, never heard *Transcendence* - things that they had only heard, bodiless - ethereal bodiless words that they matched to pictures and then matched themselves to the same hoping to transmute into? Never so! Well: she is the poet, Lucy Jinx! She has no physicality to rail against so she does lash out at language - her only body - at the physical of it which is just her own flotsamy bone-bag. And just like the decathletes prods themselves on with lauds and ramshackles of abuse - with words - as they disgust themselves with the possible limitations of their limbs and their underneath, well so goes Lucy Jinx. With words! With words she attacks language! With words she lashes insult to her feebleness when she feels her poetry is flagging, her will to press on is gone slack, with triumphs in lungfuls and with despair in rent-breast she whips herself on. To go on! She despairs to go on! And it is all in service of language! She has not reconciled, but always has been - body and language, the mound that the current of consciousness streams through and reveals itself in touchable, malleable shapes for her to rearrange. Lucy is and has always been a pronunciation birthing itself - a thing that needs to be said and needs to stand white-haired with infeasible terror at the other words she will stand beside. So call Lucy scared - call her language a hidey-hole and she a runaway, a deserter, something mutinous to humanity - and she will take it. Lure her back with the body of a dead friend - tell her 'Abandon your essence for that!' Why not say 'Leave the side of your ailing lover to go bury a lobster?' or 'Allow grasshoppers into the hospital and watch children waiting in illness while these insect's green eyes and being surgeried just to go flit in some cornfield!' Why should Lucy invent regret, remorse - why should she convince herself of the shattering of the world? None of those ideas are hers! None of those should she have to live any more than an avalanche should have a conscience and keep itself starved for the sake of those who have decided to dwell within its mouth-reach! No! Even a rockfall has to eat! It's inhumane to say otherwise. She is the poet, Lucy Jinx!

Well - anyway - this has all been seen before. Where is Lucy, anyway? Where have fine speeches gotten her - literally, look out the window, shall we? Oh Lucy is just in that state where she is convinced she is in the present-moment, that she's caught up to the front lean of light spilling the edge of the universe - but she hasn't, she isn't. This is the past as much as anything - Lucy knows it, anyone who knows Lucy knows she knows it - let's let Lucy have her speeches and we'll have a look. These are roads, same as before. Lucy sees them, too - she makes all the proper turns even though she, at this point, is not in mind of a destination. Patiently she is at a traffic-light, just here. She, while her mind riffs on song lyrics and spins them into gold - chucklingly knowing how she knows Rumpelstiltskin's name - notices that couple having a fight out in public, both on display and not. We see them sawing arms and we know the shapes of their raised voices, the colors of their profanity and of their derision, the exact way a shoulder leans to feint I'm-about-to-step-away when it is just positioning for the turn-back - but they are outdoors and know not a word can be made out, a kind of do-it-yourself room wall, a cobbler's whimsy of seclusion made out of thin air, exhaust, window-glass, radio, and conversations caught up in while waiting out traffic. See? Lucy is not so outside of things as she claims - look how she is fascinated and so not only lowers the radio volume but lowers the window. And what does she hear? Not a thing. See? Don't we all see? For all of her razzly-dazzly speeches and philosophicals, Lucy doesn't even begin to understand herself! She is just putting the window back up with a sigh and trying to sink back into the exact same excitement for *On a chain devouring the light / there's a kid going insane over her man / insane over her man / insane over her!* But - ah - she can't do it. So starts the track over, again. Then starts it over again once she is not stationary anymore, this time singing along. Where is she? This is the road that leads, if she goes long enough, to the Post Office, a lumbering, prone body of a building, daunting, and the parking lot for school buses behind it - there must be a hundred, she's thought, though how could there possibly be? And if she were to drive further, there would just be fields with mile-long walks to front porches - there is, in fact, a roundabout way she could get to Milos' from the very road she is currently on if such is her inclining - and into those fields she might drive her car, act a real car-crash, claim a blackout and baffle a medic who is called to her aid. 'Well' Lucy masculine-voices 'there is nothing wrong with your vitals, you seem fine - so maybe just drive home and get some rest.' Like always, see? What does that thought have to do with anything Lucy is going on about? What does it have to do with Layla? What does it have to do with the money in her pocket? Are we really going to be fooled by some length of time, some words in response to a surprise, and by where Lucy is with regard to the end of her life that she has changed? Come now. At this point, change, newness, is flippancy, a spit in the face to the throes of the past! 'Do you take me for a bastard?' Lucy says, shoulders dittying to the song. 'Do you take me for one who would cast all experience away for one new flirtation in my final days?' No, Lucy - no one takes you for that. 'Well, good. One has to be loyal to what has happened.' Yes, Lucy. 'One has to be a solider for the inarguable.' Yes, yes.

Stall tactics stall tactics, Lucy's mind will try anything - she is practically medicinal. As it so happens, she now cannot remember - this occurring to her with, as it often does, a vocalized 'Shit!' - whether or not she is meant to be at work today. This is a direct outcropping of her current noia, of course - she feels lured out of her home with the promise of money only to learn she has lost her job! Lucy Jinx starring in *The Con of the Magi*. But - naw - she wouldn't have planned to go to the appointment with Ariel if she had been scheduled for work. Though - yes, yes - she had not honestly planned to do that, at all. Leading to: Ariel hadn't brought it up because maybe Ariel knew Lucy had work and so to last minute the invite - passionate and intimacy-building as it might be - would run the risk of coming off selfish - which, while Ariel is it, is something Ariel likes to avoid being in ways she feels she can easily avoid. The point being: Lucy has pulled over and gotten out of the car to pace around it in a cigarette oblong, the way she might on some long-distance drive, to force herself focused on 'But do I actually have to be at work?' What clues can Lucy grab to find out? Where can she squirm in her memory to get a good solid kick? 'What am I reduced to?' she asks the cloud-cover, as bald-spot as it is, comb-over streaks of white failing to ever fully blot the blue scalp beneath them. 'Is this how I am to exist? Derelict? Is a disease, even now, mudding my thoughts beyond repair? Peh' she smoke puffs - the sky can do nothing, it has trouble enough maintaining just laying there, bedsores of sunrise and sunset as day turns from its side to night turns from its side to day. 'Fine' she says and pulls her phone from her pocket because the only thing for it is to call - give some flim-flammy 'I was wondering if next week's schedule is up, Terry' - and 'Oh I'm' conspiratorial voice 'not supposed to be on route right now, am I?' 'Oh yeah' Lucy says when the screen won't light up to her holding down the word *End* 'my phone doesn't work.' And addressing her suddenly reappeared imaginary biographer she points with a sitcom wink and says 'Or otherwise Layla wouldn't be dead, eh?' The biographer, it seems, doesn't feel like influencing this moment, doesn't even shrug, just acts like she's toying with some dials on her reel-to-reel. 'This is how wealth goes' Lucy commands in the direction of the figment, the figment cartoonishly blundering to get things rolling and microphone pointed - the few cars passing by this cow-pokey offshoot road not finding the sight of Lucy, clearly giving a speech to nobody-actually-there, the least bit strange, as she is cleverly disguising it as a telephone call, making all of her motions jovial - 'Say I have enough money to pay for the next ten months of my rent, in advance -

well, my neighbor, who works the same job as me at the same rate and pays the same rent - will become bile-eyed at me because I seem to be growing richer than him - he pays his rent each month, you see? - and when, in ten months, I can again pay the next ten months in advance and seem to be retaining my whole paycheck while he scrapes meal-to-meal, month-to-month, couponing and actually keeping track of how much is in his change-jar, he will start to see me in shades of blood-tint! But it seems it's all an illusion - he is doing as well as me! I have ten-months-worth of money while he just has the leftover of one month, after ten, but it balances because then I have to spend all ten-months-worth and restart from Zero! *It's a put-on*, he thinks - and he feels better. Until I have enough of him and at the end of ten months drive way and rent some other apartment. That is wealth' Lucy nods. 'That is all.' And she flicks her cigarette aside like a sweaty handkerchief to an adoring fan in the third row. Her stomach upturns and her vision goes soup-yellow and she vomits all along the hood of her car.

Who's this? Flimsy man, mustache old-tooth-brown and skin all mustache-grey. This is the kindly soul who happened to crest that hill - there - just as Lucy projectiled. Multiple times. That is his truck - there - its hazards blinking, parked in the thin shoulder on the opposite side of the road. That's who he is. And he happens to have - yes - a plastic gallon-jug filled with water and is using it to splash at the crude covering Lucy's car while she sips from the thermos lid of some coffee she asked for when he had unscrewed the thing to offer her water. Of course the man is now wiping down the car - 'They're just dog towels' he is saying, grandpa old singsong, answering questions no one asked, loving the melody of his helpful old country-lane daydream. 'What kind of dogs?' Lucy asks because she can't say nothing while the guy is lifting high the legs of her windshield wipers and wetting parts of a new towel to give them specific strokes, length-to-length. 'All kinds - I'm a breeder' he says 'got all kinds from all over.' 'It's jolly of you to stop' Lucy continues - she chooses phrases like 'Jolly of you' not only to match her prejudice of what she figures will sound normal to this type of person, but also to hide her identity, colloquialisms like a hat-brim turned down and a collar up. 'Oh you bet, you bet, you bet' he repeitititouses 'my gal just got over the bug and some of my nieces got it with the goop in the eyes and everything - I might get on some moxy myself.' Yes Lucy, he probably does mean *Amoxicillin* - and yes, his wife probably schedules annual *Mommygrams* - that is just the area of planet Earth you've decided to live in. 'I think my boyfriend - well, fiancé - gave it to me. The docs said it might not be the bug, but it's something squirmy, you know?' Lucy - what are you doing, man? But the old-timer doesn't mind, he even picks up the verbiage and blithely goes his own hopalong trail with it. 'Oh sure - the boy down the shops, he got the squirms and the aches and all - said he had a fever wouldn't break without surgery, you know that's bad.' The old man is now cleaning her windshield, itself - doing a thorough job of it - which Lucy ought to stop him from, but figures she has been meaning to do that for awhile and never thinks to at the gas station. 'You know those few dogs they always have outside the Pentecostal after services, nicing up on everyone?' Lucy does a thinking face and says 'The Boxers?' Lucy! This guy is washing your car - come on, now! Well, that's why I'm talking to him! 'Boxers? Oh' the man spits, but nothing to do with being upset by the question, just spits on the windshield which Lucy guesses is fine - it was a real hocked loogie - as he is washing it, after all 'not Boxers, no. The Sheepdogs, the Sheepdogs.' 'Yeah' Lucy duhs 'I'm sorry - at the Pentecostal, yeah - why was I thinking Boxers?' But the old man says that Boxers are good dogs, repeats 'Boxers are good dogs' mixes it up with mentioning he's 'known some real nice Boxers, real nice Boxers.' 'Those Sheepdogs - yours?' 'Well, I raised 'em - Sheepdogs, all the time, bitch 'em, pup 'em, send 'em off. They love those dogs - I say one time how someone put them in the newsletter and another time put the picture of them on a coffee-mug like you can.' 'Those're some famous dogs' says Lucy, now wondering if it is advisable to actually be drinking this coffee, the old man giving all the door windows a good wipe-down, then tossing the last of the water from the gallon onto the hood. She gulps the last of the coffee down - it actually does taste good, better than most coffee, but she refrains from asking why that might be - as the guy gives the all-but-some-meaningless-amount-left-in-there gallon a shake, a shrug, and a discard to the rocks at his feet. 'Hey - you need to let me pay you' she says as he gives her a smile 'you didn't need to do any of that.' He won't hear a bit of that and now gives a wave at the next car that passes - though the driver doesn't even seem to note him - and limp-steps his overalled way back to his truck, giving a honk as he aways.

Precision is an abyss - if not The Abyss - a deadfall lain and forgotten about, the mawing pit filled with infinite, forever-falling prey, too distant from each other to know how more than one person flails, screaming, floundering arms and making hands to atrophied claws in all directions as though 'There must be a wall, here - there must be a round to this well - I was on the surface, the surface cannot be just a wafer-thin crust cordoning off a hopelessly wide freefall beneath it!' Precision - the search for it - is a jaw that can bite down forever - always another detail, another angle, another ripple, something smaller the amassing of which redefines something bigger, the majesty of which packages the miniscule in different groupings which, in turn, lead one to realize the broader whole is even more broad and by this time the first focused bit, the attempt at precision, has ballooned to dwarf the original mass while at the same time viraling microscopic out in all directions - and the same is true for each of the bits, large begins on a small-scale within small-scale defining the large ad infinitum. Try to understand something, to give it meaning, definition - try even to affix a memory in sequence, to understand the flow of your own life! - might as well try to rhyme *Brussel Spouts* with *Conestoga*, eh Lucy, eh? The best you can do is convince yourself you have. Language is lesions forming while we sleep along the skin of our animal mind's raked fingernails. But language is a defense - counterintuitive as it may seem - because it wars against our animal desire for precise. What does a dog want, you know? Lucy, you know? What does a dog want? Precision. The same with a mule or a lioness or a hippo or a sperm whale or a barnacle. And so homeostasis is formed - precision, all of life clinging to replicate its station of sameness which, invariably, will lead to the wreckage of all. Leave if to language-bereft nature - well! - all we'd have left is a universe where there exists one pond the length of a puddle with one toad croaking on one mossy stone, flies hatching out of a growth on its left leg to keep it fed, it letting enough live to mate with each other, to burrow their eggs in, to hatch to keep it fed. Precision! The demise of the universe! So words come along and can ceaselessly bloom, predator-to-themselves, carrion and vulture all-in-one, an evolutionary quirk of looking for the most exact while spilling waste water of inexactness everywhere! There's never just one word - try nine-thousand-eleven! No closer, much further. So narrow it down back to one and watch each one muscularly fission itself into ten-times-one times ten-times-one-thousand! Parasitic, it needs to keep its host alive. Puppeteering, it needs to both define, instill, and create Doubt of Hope. Why didn't the first philosophers say something tethering - think about it, think about it - why didn't they suggest 'Plow our fields, birth our young, get along?' Language knew that fury is needed - and malcontent - the vocabulary of life, that people are just mechanisms, jumbled mechanics to set a whirling pattern of 'Try to be precise' going, occupying flesh with itself, teasing it with a chance of ever lasting as long as a sentence. Nothing survives by loving itself! Nothing survives by longing for others to! That is why we have language that says we do - so we don't actually have to! We have a place to set aside the algorithmic anomalies that would rightfully lead us to accept our place on the Food Chain - you think kelp has ambition, you think gnats aspire to understand gnats? The only thing that keeps us from acceptance is the word *Acceptance*, the only thing that keeps us living is the word *Death* - that is what can be avoided even while we dig the grave of our mother while our daughter watches us picturing herself digging ours.

Like Alkazang! it is revealed that Lucy is in a franchise bookstore, roaming the rather large Photography section. All that rubbish she was thinking? It is safe to assume she does not recall a word of it. If asked to answer 'What did you think, three minutes ago - how about before that, how about before that, and how did it start?' she'd just demure and say 'Look at this photo' her boredom a closed bedroom door that, yes, your lover just doesn't feel like opening, right then. The final thought stays on a dribbling record skip, the final thought being *Passion is not uncomplication*. She nods along to this and observe: photo of train, photo of another train, photo of train, photo of another train, photo of another train, photo of people building a train, photo of another train. As though being pinned with a ribbon depends on it, Lucy flips all the way to the end of the book, the trains going from spot-grainy black-and-white and seeming heroic - even absurd - in their grandiosity, to mute color, to gloss color, to practically a brochure for the damned Metro! A flipbook of things becoming less imperative while becoming more necessary, things becoming so relevant we'd do anything to be rid of them! Now observe: a photo of a rioter being clubbed, a photo of an eroticized foreign woman, a photo of a hummingbird, in close, a city café, a clamour of people over there as a bank fails - Lucy admits, well she has to, that this is one amazing photo and she cannot help but think it a sham! What these photos have in common is that they were all done by photographers from the same Agency and they all won awards. As good a way to sort History as any, Lucy supposes, bloated with tut-tut-tut ready to fart her profundity into an op-ed. What a slithering foul mood Lucy Jinx represents! She moves from Photography to books of Paintings, thinking to shun the classical painters but then diving in. It's interesting to Lucy how, for example, she always thinks Ruben's paintings are wrongfully considered realistic until she looks at them, again. Down to the skin-tone, they are dynamite. Dynamite! And she is certain Ruben would be flattered to hear her say so - it'd just make his day! Then she remembers what angers her is that his name is attached to the types of bodies he painted - like how a botanist gets to name a type of bloom. He didn't think up anything. He just executed. Lucy - I thought you liked the work? 'I love the work' Lucy thinks 'but Ruben didn't invent the way he depicts the bodies of these women - and this odious little essay explaining he was the *Original lover of the Reubenesque woman* is both insipid, asinine, and oddly wrong-headed.' 'Oh thank you massa' Lucy says aloud, wishing she could be stood in the same room as *Venus-at-Mirror* - the first woman she ever essayed herself over - or could be coiled in the waves under *Marie de Medici Landing at Marseilles* - which is exactly where, if he had a brain instead of rock-candy in his skull, Ruben would have painted Marie, herself, as that is where she, Lucy knows, would have painted herself! Closes the book. 'Passion is not uncomplication' she reminds herself - nothing to do with Ruben - and wanders to the Fiction aisle rather hoping to find Elliott but finding no Elliott for sale. Fingersnap - wrong surname! - tries again for the redubbed Elliott, but still nothing. To the restroom, just to wash her face. A woman in the stall leafs through something she likely should not have brought in, sniffles, seems to be taking measured pauses between exertions of voiding - maybe on medical orders - the grunting pronounced. You look interesting, Lucy. Admittedly, yes - you look not yourself, but not so much you'd be mistaken for anyone else. 'If I was a mirror, I'd be a liar - though the same is not true in reverse' she whispers. You want to write that, don't you? 'No.' Yes, Lucy - you do. 'No, Lucy - I don't.'

Bagel, borrowed pen, three fliers for a Kindergarten Story-Time to litter the backs of. Here is a line: *reptilian and hourglass laden / the avenues end in their mayhem / the mayhem they end in their mayflies.* Here is another: *cup your hands to the pretend window / pretend you are looking out at what you are standing in.* Here is another: *thrifty as cotton / you loved me / a bus ticket length.* To the window at her side is announced rain in some droplets that manage, by wind, to get the five feet from the end of the awning to the glass. Impressive. This is the sort of rain that falls like Xerox. *This is the sort of rain that falls like Xerox* Lucy writes - and there is her pen-tip poised to elaborate, to tack on a secondary. But she resists. All the editing, if it has accomplished one thing, has revealed to her the crinkle of this technical, the vein of its seam through all of her work, growing like sumac in pythons. That's good. She writes that. *The vein of your seam is all through me, now, growing like sumac in pythons.* No more! Do you see the automatic of your wrist, Lucy? How it ker-chinks to place and the pen is almost junkie to add in something that dah dah dah dah dwindles, dwindles more, building into a final faucet drop? Read back the bit, there. *'This is the sort of rain that falls like Xerox.'* You even say it in the tone of preamble - or think it - you have a melody in your head to fit phonetics to and you really need to disentangle yourself from the habit. Forcibly ugly, she reshapes the words physically - yes yes, just to disgust herself, but she needs to be a little rough, this is a kind of purging, she knows - and it goes *This / is the kind / of rain that falls / like Xerox.* See? You read it different. 'Thank you, *Poetry one-oh-one*' she subvocalizes 'and I suppose you'll tell me why?' You only love shapes. 'Bullshit' she argues. You only love forms and aesthetics. 'Fiddlesticks' she says 'stuff and nonsense.' Even now, though, she admits some creeper of plotting to either discard this line or else add to it - or, if anything, to make it a single standout, asymmetrical, off-rhythm bit in an otherwise Lucy-tuned poem she'll scape up. Over-exaggerating? Well sure, sure. Lucy has written all kinds of verse - that is demonstrably true! - but even she admits, from all that editing, how there is a proto-nugget, so to speak, a jingle she can recall back to adolescence, if not earlier. Tack on, elongate, elaborate into reverse, make end-point so far from start-point they lose relation to each other over the curve of the horizon between them. There is nothing wrong with this, Lucy - that is not the proposition here. 'There isn't a proposition here' Lucy says, then covers the flier she has been writing on with a new flier and writes. Here is a line: *we loathe mornings in umpteens / we calculate how many breaths / we've just snored*. Here is a line: *the weight of your suitcase is turpentine / the line of your dress is a boxcutter dulled*. Here is a line: *when we remember a minor key / we remember a dream / when we remember a major key / we remember a thought*. Eh - that bit is terrible, Lucy. Yeah, yeah - she's already scratching it out. It seems true, but it's twaddle as poetry. A fly has landed on the lip of her coffee - the lid on the table, droplets of fop-sweat permanent freckles to the overturned valley of it. Lucy flicks the air a few inches from the fly and it doesn't move. She makes her finger - oh Jesus Lucy, you can't even hold your hand without shudder, why don't you go home!? - a solid point and slow-motions it toward the fly. Tick-tock goes the pest's legs at its face. Someone told her every time a fly lands it poops. Closer in weebles her fingertip goes. Someone told her every time a fly lands it throws up. Closer. It doesn't even pay her mind. A blind fly? Closer she gets, now kind of half-giggling, half freaking herself out, as though this is the moment she will learn she is a ghost, old-fashioned double-exposure special-effect she will pass right through the thing, prove herself a blur, an eye out-of-focus. Tap. She pulls back. The fly remains on the lid. Now - well! - come on, that couldn't have happened! A little faster she moves the finger in until - poke! Tick-tock go its legs. It's probably pooping - it's probably throwing up. Tap. Poke. Lucy scoots her chair back, a bit. Something unnatural in this.

So everything is back to normal. Lucy tidies up her papers - the usual circles and underlines, a few more deletions by way of cross-hatchy strike-throughs, never enough to totally obliterate the ability to read back the words, but enough it will be well known to History 'I decided against that' - and folds them to her coat pocket and will likely never look at them, again. Here: Lucy Jinx buses her dishes. And here: Lucy Jinx wipes down her table while a helpful employee says 'You don't need to do that' to which she says 'Oh it's fine - I made a mess' - though honestly, Lucy, you didn't. The pleasure of a cigarette in the somewhat cat-urine smell of the rain - pinch smelling, her eyes feel tense, like they are avoiding near-to-them needles. Lucy puts it this way: say she just hadn't gotten the call? Wouldn't it have been terrible for Layla to have had to leave a message? Oh Lucy stage-shudders - what an existential night-sweat that would have been! Though, knowing Layla, she would have done the decent thing and just not have left a message - because Christ, wouldn't that have been rude! No - Lucy snorts - not nearly as romantic as a letter. 'From what I have put together' she says, careful to keep faced to the wall now that she is being audible 'a letter was out of the question. It's lucky Layla woke up at all! And, truly, is there a more fitting goodbye for us? How should we have ended it? *You hang up - No, you hang up - No, you hang up - No, you hang up* - waiting like brats in silence? *Layla! - Lucy! - You said you were hanging up - You said you were hanging up - Well, I am - Hope you do - You'll get your wish - So I keep hearing - If you so insist - It's nothing to do with me - You keep telling yourself that - I thought you were hanging up?* That's not Lucy's style - that's not Layla's style. This can all be summed up in a tearjerker, inspirational essay, you know? *We Died As We Lived* I guess is how Lucy would call the piece. 'It's an image of a murther done in Vienna - Gonzago is the Duke's name, his wife Baptista' she antic-disposition-but-not-reallys, a kindly that-is-that to the shimmy she gives her hips, it just amounting to her turning around and deciding to smoke another. In essence, Lucy died just as much as Layla as far as Layla is concerned. Probably. 'Or something like that.' Lucy flick flicks, turns wall-faced, flick flicks again, lights quick, exhales, turns to face the lot. Lucy wonders if she had been meant to be Layla's last call. Maybe there would have been another. Maybe in her delirium or whatever - Lord knows what dope they might have had her on and how greedy she had been pressing the button for more - Layla had thought 'I need to make a few calls' and started with Lucy and the whole Last-call tenor was just meant to be Last-call-with-you natured and she would have had similar calls with a bunch of other people if she hadn't keeled over. Maybe Layla is on the phone with people, right now! It's not like it's up to her when she's dying! Lucy's thoughts are getting manic, again - she knows it from her fist and the curls of her toes and the rising need for relief from her stiffened legs. She is avoiding thinking something. She is avoiding wondering 'If I suddenly died, would Layla have been my last call?' And suddenly she is thinking it. And suddenly she knows 'That seems unlikely.' And suddenly she seems ungodly monstrous. There is a tick drowned with the blood it had supped where her soul ought to be! The blood in its bulge has cooled, muddied, grown flaky at its outside - its outside still in the crisp-husked membrane of the bloodsucker's back - and hardened to a lightness like petrified turd.

'But why should Lucy have to be profound and magnanimous, right now?' is what Lucy wants to know. It isn't her that is dying! There is no need to soften her tone to a purr for the quote-books. 'I'm still alive, so being Saintly is not in the cards, from Go.' You need someone to talk to, Lucy. 'Yes' she nods. 'Yes.' You should go to see Milos. But maybe not Milos. You need to get out of your head - you're the only one there and you aren't very good company, chatterbox though you are. This motion is passed. And Lucy pulls out of the parking lot, ready to implement. A therapist would come in handy, about now! 'Yep' Lucy nods, but they don't usually do walk-ins, she doesn't think. But this proves why she needs to get a third-party into things. She misses the old man who washed up her vomit, for Chissake! She wishes she had said a few more things to the café employee who had told her not to bother with the table! The rain has grown bellyache, whatever the sky ate is coming out liquid when it should have been solid and columnar in a pile. Lucy has the wipers going frantic, they even stutter as they arc. See? If Layla had died much later, Lucy, you wouldn't have been pacing around when you burst your gravy, you might have done it right here on the dashboard. 'Good point' Lucy says, not bothering with this intersection because it is always torture, nevermind with the rain and the idiocy such weather raises in people's urgency to get-home-get-home-now-my-God-water!! She drives about a mile up, turns in at a small set of shops just to turn out to take the well-measured intersection turn back in the direction she had just been coming from because from that angle the intersection she hated is just a straight line - red, green, wait - not some starved Gladiatorial winner-take-all. The roads become easygoing by a few minutes on. The rain realizes no one is listening so goes back to the corner to strengthen its rhetoric, come up with some soft-sell for next time. Sure, it dangles some last of itself, but all for show - no more than a dog leaves a scent on the sofa. Rain comprehends language, quite frankly, it behaves by it, serenely, even though it can't voice it correct - rain is palsy-hand trying calligraphy, an infant trying an aria. Language, language - you deserve it, Lucy, it suits you to the ribs, it flatters you to the chin-bottom, you know? Pitied? Some would so say, now wouldn't they? Language should be pitied, but Lucy won't pity it. Why not? It is always so terrified - listen to it, Lucy, look! Have you ever seen something so desperate not to be alone? It's no wonder languages sound as they do - all teeth and blind-eyes, all claws and fingers numbed from clinging. Well, no - Lucy won't pity the terrified. The terrified expand and never have to sleep! And terrified-language, in its cowardly sprawl, consumed Lucy with everyone else, pity and all. Language didn't leave so much as a word behind for anyone to offer it. It begs in the same terms which could be given it as alms. Too famished to not starve it invents the word *Potbelly*. Oh Lucy, get out of your head! Lucy rocks as she drives the same way a child in a crib thinks will cure a stomachache before it learns better how a wail will. She turns off the radio and feels faces pressed to the windows, feels the car is uneasily held in the arms of the people there - some making Vroom noises, some Putt-putt-putt and some just giggling at the trick they are playing. It's all Lucy's special damnation. To think she knows what is there but be too proud to look, to invent wet-leprosy and feel the splash of a sneeze on her back and think the cure is to look even straighter ahead.

LUCY DOES HER BEST PANTOMIME of being surprised at finding herself wound up here. Here - here of all places? Why I'm simply flabbergasted, what a curiosity! It looks like she's trying to shake coins out of her toes while her shirt is biting at her shoulders, nibbling in needlepoint like a kitten's knead, unaware of what claws are. Maybe it's a studied impersonation of a ghost - it couldn't be an unconscious one, not so jiggery like that - or maybe it is just trying to get her keys out of her pocket and discovering that her fingers are refusing to not be halfwits. There is a sweet drift like throw-up - she doesn't mean that in a grim way, it is just a fact - from the dumpsters and it must have rained over here - or there must be sprinklers, now, out in the field - because the recent mowed grass adds a sour-lime cut with the sink-stale-cinnamon of worm-writhed soil. Not that Lucy didn't know she'd come back here. Oh Lucy, you knew and you know that you knew. You could have whisked yourself rid of the key, anytime. By now, you could have even lingered on it for weeks, returned it by post, dispatched with it with or without any ceremony you might imagine. After all, where is Samantha's ring, eh Lucy? Left in the coin-return of a vending-machine with the remains from the dollar you broke on the *Butterfinger Bar* you left down in the trough - some lucky duck, what a haul, eh? sweets and loose-change and a dazzling little bauble! Why, you even left it outside of that dance class, didn't you? You drove into that lot on purpose just to make it the best odds some young wraith would find it, giggles and body still aching from first-position, headache from hair over-bunned. Oh of course you're not arguing, Lucy. It would have taken something like this to orchestrate the use of the key - yes, you're right. All agree - see, look at the auditorium, the dark rustles with the nods-of-heads and quick looks at person-next-to-thems, hard-nods and rabbit-nods of there can be no doubt now that the proof is presented - that you would have kept that key on you until something abusive made it useable. And it's a fair question - 'What does it mean?' - and one which, Lucy, you may figure out later on. It does - it does feel like home. Her car - her car is not in the lot. Do you slow because you think you might come unexpected upon Flynn and whatshername - what is her name, what in Hell are people's names!? - making the beast with two backs - what is her name!? Lucy, you met her the once, only - why would you remember? Are they in there, quietly fondling? Would they continue if you came home and they saw it was just you, you gave them a wink, a kind of conspiratorial 'I'll distract her' - meaning the mother - 'when she comes in, go your ways.' Home? 'So to speak' Lucy smiles. Smiles? Ah Lucy Jinx, who can be summed up as such: she knows she will wind up places but knows not what she'll do once she's there. *Josyln*. The name sticks in Lucy's head. *Paisley*. But, no. It was more commonplace. But only *Paisley* and *Joslyn* stick in Lucy's head. Is it as simple as: something will happen when you go through the door - yes, it could be that, yes? - that it will mean a thing that cannot be unmeant. This is where you came after, Lucy. You haven't gone anywhere, before now - and over a threshold means this is where you have come. You left your cigarettes in the car on purpose, eh? Here goes Lucy, taking the retreat that she carved. Here is her hand on a cold door. There is her, looking at the pack fondled in beige-amber cabin light, in syrup-deep shadows. Here is Lucy, touching the already-there ache in her lower back from holding her bent posture even this long.

What's different? The bathroom light is a series of uncomplimentary angles and overlapping shadows of shadows tilt some of these lines almost seasick - triangles, squares, $X$s, and stripes with portions of the shape of Lucy's head done in segmentations softly white the otherwise pepper black downstairs. What is different, really? Lucy sniffs, then she pushes up into the underside of her chin with her shoulder-top and uses the force to pinch her tongue between front teeth enough to cause the blurry between just-enough and pain. What is different is what is the same. Even in the dark, it is Lucy's long dormant accustomedness - not hosed away by her few visits and the more than a half-decade - with reaching her hand to the piano-top and touching for the back of the sofa with her foot that jogs it all. The sofa is rearranged. Rearranged, purist. Return-arranged. This is how the room used to be. And this must have happened in the last two - no - the last week and three-quarters. She plops down on the folded, not-been-washed-in-awhile therefore crumb-sharp and flattened-of-downy blanket, the give of the unfamiliar sofa cushions under her making her body feel seesaw. Someone might toss the question from the back of the room to the front: 'Is Lucy making anything of this up?' Someone else might try to speak louder, raising their cap to show Press credential and be a bit more leading: 'Today of all days, Ms. Jinx - whaddya say about it?' Lucy Jinx's handler might begin stepping toward her microphone as the uproar of follow-up questions becomes cacophonous, Lucy giving a genial, smiling wave and whispering something to a confidante and the handler would be raising hands like settle-down settle-down and tell everyone 'Thank you for coming, but inside voices, please' this causing a laugh from seasoned Vets in the back-row who have memories too long to need pad or pen. Voila! Lucy Jinx lays how once she laid and crosses her feet how once they'd crossed and - blow me down! - it's the same mirror, though different knick-knackery and spined books, on the mantle, and sheets of paper are clothes-clipped to clothesline in front of the fireplace which is now grated in wrought-iron and glass. Well! And at just that moment the blinds - these are different, cloth now - Lucy can see if she arches back her body and neck light up like stovetops and the illusory nighttime is lost, not completely imploding the time-warp, but the quick fade-back-to-twilight now seems textbook magician's trick, every shadow cast by the bathroom more the fault of how many blinds are drawn than anything else. Next moment? A cat lands on Lucy - full potato sack of it - and so alone did she think she was Lucy honestly shrieks, springs into sitting up, feels her flesh torn in several places and the clattering-clatter like kitchen stirrings of the animal freeing itself of her, hitting the carpet, scrambling the tile and thudding the stairs going up. Cue the asthmatic wind outside and the little-girl hiccoughs of high-pitched lighting in flicker-flicks not even mature enough to thunder. Now standing - Jesus, the cat stripped her hand around, too, that blood is flowing! - Lucy cannot help but open the piano jaw and back-teeth some ominous, uneven trills. The tap-water sings falsetto across the deepest of the wounds, sings citrus on the two thinner, and - though there is no real way she can tell - Lucy feels she can hear the distinct trickle caused by the mix of the thinned blood and the driblets of just-water dribletting the stainless-steel basin. The light over the sink is on in its hogwash green, its muddy-boot white, so the blood that would be pink looks like queer orange. Without much thought, she reaches wounded hand for garbage-disposal and the cerement-burst din of a spoon down there rings like a wooden fire-bell, Lucy's quick second flap to the switch, she knows, littering her soft blood all manner of places, like the juice off from under the lids of a cat-food tin when the last twist to the top is made full.

Lucy heads upstairs with the strawberry eclair, her one foot - both feet only in socks - stepping in something wet she'd rather not think about. That old totter - she's used to it from pet ownership - of one regular foot, one foot that is nothing-but-a-heel - and that heel dainty and mortally phobic of full weight bearing down on it - gets her all the way into the bathroom she imagines is exclusively Flynn's. Deciding to have some suspense, Lucy does not tap the moist sock with her finger to give the finger a whiff, put rather peels, very carefully, one handed - the unéclaired mitt - the sock off while she eats, leaves it on the toilet seat - while she dissolves nearly an entire third of the remaining eclair in hot tap-water then discards the stick in the overflowed bin - before taking it back up, inhaling. Yes. Urine. And hatpin-masculine in variety - wow, what pungency! So she peels off her other sock, into the mother's room she goes, lobbing the both underhand into the empty hamper she sees, going to where she remembers the panty-and-socks drawer residing, next to the master-sink. Cavity there - carpet, a coat-hanger, some cardboarded tags with plastic bits abandoned sans care after plucked off of new garments. No dresser. But there was a dresser just last time you were here, Lucy - the same dresser as years ago. 'Yeah?' Yeah! Look there, Lucy hyperactive-gumshoe insists - even points as she notices, all the dialogue in her head - look, you can see the impression where it was picked up from! True. And the carpet is an obvious shade cleaner. Lucy's best guess is the dresser will be in the closet - but the dresser is not in the closet and now things are so off the rails she starts to worry she's in the wrong goddamned house! Where does the mother keep her clothes, now? Dart-to-there, dart-to-there, dart-to-there, dart Lucy's eyes. The small bedside table has a top drawer and a bottom, but Lucy knows right well the contents of those.

'Where the fuck are all your clothes?' Lucy laughs aloud as an ask, happening to see her hand is bleeding quite unabashedly, again. A good gauze of toilet-paper, she curls her fist around it, tries to concentrate on keeping the grip honest and thorough. The sensation of about-to-step-on-something-sharp - because that seems to be next in the scheme of things - drapes Lucy, tingling like the residual of something recently crawling and, at a startle, batted off, the spot it had been then roughly and insistently patted at. And she crosses the corridor, surprised to see the room that had been hers and had then become Flynn's has the door slightly open while the opposite door is closed, flush. Vacancy. Chill and ozone of a window open. Hangman of the cat-has-pissed-in-here-sometime-recently-too, this odor thinned by the fresh air but spread like the last scrape of marmalade around due to the newest wet dribbling the carpet near the vent-grate from the again falling rain. In the closet, accordioned open, is the mother's dresser. On it, a clock blinking two twenty-three and a hammer and three screws. What else? One of the knobs to one of the drawers. One of the dresser claws is there on the carpet, its proper spot now occupied by a hardcover cookbook or something. There is a scrap of paper on the ground. Lucy crouches to haunches to examine it, honestly expecting it to be something she wrote long ago, but the penciled handwriting is not hers and none of the full words can be made out. One line has *ough* writ on it, the line below, bigger print, just says *fer*. She puts it in her back pocket, then strains herself standing, the hand flatting her gravity-downed buttock, the room seeming to echo with the bubble-wrap of her joints as she normalizes her posture. Top-drawer is socks and panties. The panties she stares at a moment - she sees a book under them, she's certain, in the corner is a book - then snatches a pair of grey socks with some colored stripes and moves back to the lit toilet to put them on.

'Flynn?' Lucy tippy-taps the door. 'Whatshername?' Tippy-tap. 'Flynn?' A little louder. The knob she gives a jiggle and it is locked - but from her tenure living here she knows this is the sort of lock where if you press in with your thumb and twist wrist it comes right open. 'Hey, Flynnisota - it's Lucy' Lucy nostaligas with a smile, the already turned-on corridor light more than enough to show the room an empty assortment of in-shambles. Thought: wouldn't it be nuts if it turned out the family had been kidnapped a few days ago and you are lurking in a not yet discovered crime-scene, Lucy? 'Sure would' she eyebrow-raises. Or hey - hey hey! - if you go to sleep here and are woken by long flashlights on the front door come morning, a neighbor finally suspicious and the authorities called? But Lucy is too busy snooping to much bother with nonsense like that. Glibly, she says 'I'm sure that would be a riot, yeah - solitary-confinement for me, please.' Flynn is quite the artist, it seems. Or maybe the girlfriend is. None of the abstract watercolor things are signed legibly and the nudes - is that the girlfriend? - could be self-portraiture or could be, she supposes, just not of anyone specific. She opens a desk drawer and finds a coiled bag of Doritos - full-size bag, so assumes that's where he keeps his pot or whatever he hides hid, though she still feels around to the drawer-back in case the bag is just a diversion, something to make the drawer seem a catchall for junk - coins, paperclips, a few random trading-cards or something, an old harmonica - but she alights on nothing of merit. His closet doesn't seem worth the thorough bother it would be to look through, though she does lift the replica handgun she sees on top of the dresser next to a baby-picture of he and the mother and also a ceramic piggy-bank with a cigarette taped to its mouth. Is it a replica? A pellet-gun? 'The murder weapon' the it-might-be-a-kidnap voice chimes in, reminding her she has contaminated the scene with her blood a bit too, so she might as well use the opportunity to fake her own death, into the bargain. She levels the barrel at the globe over there - she can tell just from what she can make out of the colors throughout Europe that it is woefully out-of-date. And she closes one eye. Lucy! Click. Jesus - don't pull a trigger! 'Like this?' Click click click. She does her best to replace the firearm exactly where she found it, tells herself 'Chill out, mom, I'm just playing - goddamn, right?' She figures under the mattress she would find the obvious pornography stash, but - not far off - just finds a few - multiple varieties and, curiously, multiple sizes - condoms as well as - she rolls her eyes at the workings of the adolescent mind - some empty wrappers of used ones. She is surprised to find a dresser drawer full of cassette-tapes - red-lettered spines, the proper cassettes inside, even - and logic tells her these must be hiding something, but for all of her supposed intelligence she cannot even come up with a fantastical what-it-might-be. Not enough light to look under the bed, but she does do a reach underneath the dresser and knocks out a box to an old computer-game. Floppy-disk old. Two-eighty-six processor old. *The Hound Of Shadow*. Lucy lifts the box and when she turns it feels weight - too much - and a muffled shift of said weight. Inside, two coverless porn mags - mostly girl-girl - and a blue plastic *VHS* tape titled *The Perfect Brat*. She leafs through one of the mags, reading some of the copy-text accompanied to some of the images. *Jasmine says to Jordan* this narration goes '*This is just to see if the settee can stand up to the hot sex.*' Carefully replaces the box where she found it - or vaguely slides it back down there, anyway - and straightening up she sees the calendar on the wall is from almost two decades ago, the date *March seventeenth* circled, in the box for that day a scribbled lightning-bolt exclamation-point. Where did the things in this room come from?

Question: is Lucy comfortable leaving the upstairs lights on whilst preparing *Ramen* noodles in the kitchen in the dark? Answer: she has the bathroom light in the entryway on, she has the light over the sink. So that nullifies that. And besides, her shadows - her shadows down here, they run the gamut from looking anemic, like spilt grape-juice, to thick enough to bulge like veins at temples in rage. The longer the mother doesn't return, though, the more convinced Lucy is getting that she some time ago back-lapsed into hallucination. The oddity of this house, for example? It should be troubling her more than it is. She has the surest tang to her gut right now - a real nausea - that were she to go back upstairs she would find rooms reversed, wallpaper altered, she would find a doll in an inch of water in Flynn's bathtub, headless with tutu pulled up toward its shoulders, wrong directioned like an umbrella inside-outed. Question: isn't keeping things dark - treacle colored shadows with crème-coffee brown accents - adding to the sense of disorientation? Answer: What's your point? There was a time Lucy was coming here to get out of her head, to be in company - she'd intuited she needed that - like how sometimes one gets a craving for olives because one is lacking some mineral - and this is where her intuition told her to find it. Yet here we find her: thinking goblins are afoot, deviling the furniture and cat-piss around through the ceiling above her - yet here we fine her: cooking cheap noodles in the dark. Question: are you going to leave, Lucy, if the mother doesn't get home soon? Answer: I'll give her awhile, still - where else would she be, later? Lucy moves to the window, parts the blinds hardly a Bible-page, eyelashes right up to the space but - nope - the mother is not parked there, so Lucy raises the blinds with her fingers a *V* and cranes her neck side-to-side, able to make out exactly Zero more of the lot than she could, previously. Flavor powder - beef flavoring, the mother doesn't have chicken flavor, which in itself is downright bizarre, these must be Flynn's - added and pot poured to overlarge plastic bowl, a few Saltine crackers crumbled to make the dish more of a paste, Lucy leaves her meal to cool and takes the cigarettes from her coat, laid on the dining table, not even flung over the chair. Yes - yes - this is all rather odd. Lucy and this place. This is all kind of *Tales Not For The Timid*. The glass backdoor opens, but the screen-door is jammed - though anyway, Lucy decides to smoke out the front door, instead, because the front porch is covered and the backyard is not. She winces at the sweetener scent of sick-up, again - in fact, this odor is more pummeling now that the rain is falling, full on - though by a drag or two is accustomed, begins to breathe proper, deep. There weren't those houses off that way, before - the streetlamps lit up, now, one back-porch still dangling decorative lights from some holiday, every third bulb seeming out, or so Lucy assumes because otherwise that is a deliriously odd way to arrange lights on a cord. There on the walkway is the plastic-bag covered Telephone Directory she'd passed on the way in - she cannot quite tell but could know for certain if she turned on the front light - but it seems the pages are soaked and warped, the plastic with a flaw to its defenses. Lucy imagines, three-months-from-now, that same Directory in that same bag there, sun-parched, faded, plastic long since shredded and in imperceptible bit-by-bit wandered away. Lucy sees herself smoking her, three-months-from-now. But all in the same thought, those three-months-from-now seem ages ago, that Directory another driftwood thing which has wound up in this evening she had better have someone confirm is not utterly figmentary. She smokes. Staring. It looks midnight, smells three-in-the-morning, but cannot but be six-thirty in the evening, at the latest.

A door closes out in the lot behind Lucy. Lucy, you're awake! She jolts and her throat is a scab. The car is having the boot put to it by the two-fisting rainfall - and that wasn't a door closing, Lucy, that is the thunder. Wait. 'Wait' Lucy says, shaking the images of where she had just been, finding her books on the shelf in the living-room corner - finding *Her New Sister's Best Friend* finding *Claudette, the Bashful Girl*, squinting in the poorly scrubbed lighting of the lamp, its bulb coated grey. 'Peculiar' Lucy had thought, peculiar coated grey the tone of a mold-spot on a skeleton - squinting to read the inscriptions in the books from Dorene to her which turned out to - she noticed the signature - be from her to Dorene in young-woman penmanship. But how could there be inscriptions in these - they were bought secondhand? And did Ariel really put them on the living-room bookshelf? Wait. Did the mother? 'Wait' - Lucy does another on purpose jolt, looks through the cascading warp of the bilious window, the water out sideways from it seems a finger-joint thick. Lucy shivers and instinctively reaches for the keys which are not in the ignition, unearths them from her coat pocket and here comes the radio to life and the windshield wipers laboring - here comes everything! Oh this is most discourteous of her mind to herself - she has seldom felt more at a divide! And if the car-clock is correct, she has been parked here all of twenty minutes - short twenty, short fifteen, or maybe not, but the afternoon is a swamp of the color of day, the wind rocks her car like it's an apple overboard from a leisure cruise. See the windows, Lucy? The kitchen windows? 'So - what of them?' They're lit. And so they are. And Lucy says to herself, mottle-mouthed 'Did I leave them on when I left?' even as the crumbs reconstitute to the cake of 'No, Lucy - you never went in.' That was meant to be sleep? That was none-of-it-real? Lucy wriggles her feet in her shoes thinking 'Socks' and even then makes effort to verify, by a twist and an attempt to lift her pant-cuff for a look, that the socks are her own and not the ones purloined, just now, from the mother. So: did Lucy not go in there, at all? Or did she go in awhile then leave? Did she, perhaps, go in and just fall asleep on the sofa when she had lain back? Her head won't unclog - thoughts sickly rattle, grumbly, gravely, constant like the slush of pool water is stuck inside of them. She pinches her nose and blows out hard, hoping for a pop and that warm feeling like a dribbling leak, the tingle at her lobes. The right-hand window-blind is more than halfway open and she sees the refrigerator and much of the countertop - the handle of the broom - leaning there. And now is alert enough to find it intriguing how the tone of the dream had been so doubtful, how she had assumed hallucination - a dream had thought it was seeing things. She congratulates herself for being so astute. Gregh-hrmgh and cucgh-cugh sounds as Lucy Jinx does wake-up movements, not wanting to clear her shed snake-skin throat full on. Looks to the drinks in her cup holder, wondering if either are remotely safe to take a swig from, collecting spit but too impatient to wait for it to amass a full swallow, forcing blank gullet up and down, blank gullet up and down. She turns down the radio and the presence of the weather seems to pack into the car, rambunctious, teenager, everyone talking at once and with different ideas about where to go next. She stares at the lit house, again. Looks to the cars at both sides - neither the mother's - and yawns. While she does so, for those few seconds, the individuated tattooings of rain becoming harmonized, volume-downed sounds of a patient audience applauding an old woman being helped to a podium.

Supposing this counts as as much of a lull in the rain as there is likely to be, Lucy gets her coat draped overhead, steels herself, and dashes out, foot down into the river-run puddling of wobbly curved lot soaking both feet, her door not closing proper - metallic clank of it shutting on the seatbelt clip - having her stand there, creek-bedded, cursing, reclosing the thing and then - her stride all wrong and her breathing off - continuing at a saunter to the house's front awning. Slips arms back through coat arms, wags first this foot then that, giving the doorbell a touch, not hearing anything, so giving it a harder touch - ah, there's the flimsy ding-dinnnggg - and finally snorting up a good phlegmy wallop she asides to the bubbling mulch, there, some of this stringing a solid wisp over her chin. Wiping up, she knocks. The idea is to give Flynn and his lady-friend all opportunities to decent themselves, if need be. Finally, she rummages her key to the lock and pushes into the house, immediately setting her shoes by the other loosely-lined footwear she sees, removing her socks and tensing against the cramps the tile induces. 'Hello?' she asks, clumsy voiced, now setting her coat over the dining-table chair. She asks for Flynn by name, for the mother by *Natalie* - she pours herself tap-water and slakes her thirst. What's different? Nothing. Nothing is different. You sure, Lucy? 'Yeah' she alouds 'are you sure? You asleep, again? I'd rather not have to keep doing this.' Cigarettes on the counter and cup soggy with compost-remains of dozens of stubs for a moment makes Lucy think she should go ahead and light up, interior, but then it seems odd - the cup is by the sink, this might have been the outside depository brought in for a clean. The stale waft from it - mucusy chocolate, bitter watermelon, and plate of rotten-soft pears - is a grease throughout the downstairs, so Lucy empties the sludge into the sink, forcing it down the drain with a wetted, soaped sponge, turns the disposal, pouring more of the lemon-lime green cleanser down with it, scrubbing the cup itself. She has to spot-check some cutlery - a plate, a pan, and a cup - to make certain the dishes in the machine are clean, puts them away - the mother has changed where everything goes, it's so organized 'She must be having a crisis-of-midlife or something, good Christ' thinks Lucy - and places the single malt-blue cup on the upper rack, slaps the device shut. What next? She takes suggestions from cabinets and appliances, but they more-or-less tell her to go with her gut - though the one fridge-magnet tells her 'Just smoke, already - what, do you fear some sort of eternal banishment?' - and her gut suggests making a sandwich out of the wheat bread - not the mother's usual - some of the thin-sliced ham, the baggie of thick-sliced pepperoni, and peeling a string-cheese enough to layer it across the top like a paper-shreddered slice. Never has her throat seemed more satisfied to ingest and the bulk of the hardly-chewed swallows anchor Lucy down, her thoughts becoming more immediate - a real change, this thirty-seconds to the following, rather like a week has passed. She makes another sandwich, same configuration, superstitiously hoping it will double-up the curativeness - it doesn't go that far, but seems to bolster it - a solid second, shorter wall, if not an angled pillar of reinforcement to the primary battlement. 'You might as well do the cigarette, now' the twist to the bread-bag says, its voice a whispered aside like it doesn't want anybody to know it has an opinion, being it's such a prideful little piece of waxy wire. Is this the mother's new brand? The box looks like it should contain matte-finish after-dinner mints and the filters being speckled bronze don't do much to make these things seem of-the-people. 'If there were such a thing' Lucy thinks - lighting up with a sniff - 'these would be what prescription-cigarettes would look like.' Yes. Lucy feels she is smoking a pill to stave off sepsis.

It is a bit off-putting - but it's also just a book on a shelf - that is Lucy confronting this. Elliott Pine. *Chokethemgirls*. Lots of people have the book - look, Lucy even finger-taps the fact that it was *Prescott Book Club Selection*, adding at a dismissive mumble 'Whatever that is and why ever it is stamped on a book cover - grasping for straws, I suppose, the world is competitive' - and it's not like she is finding it spread open on the mother's bedside table, every other page dog-eared, a loose-leaf containing some naughty bits like an uneven tongue out the otherwise flush of the rectangle end, opposite the spine. No sooner is this thought - along with the thought that the mother could well have gone to bed with the book at some point, maybe after finishing it she put it particularly on this more-public-downstairs-shelf as a kind of showoff piece, though the books beside it, for several across, nil this consideration and remind Lucy how the mother was not world-renown for her literary acumen - than Lucy opens the book and finds highlighting and underlines - a pestilence of them, the highlighter and pens both even change color after the halfway-mark! An almost allergic reaction - anaphylaxis! - until Lucy notes the sticker-gunned price on the corner of *one ninety-nine*, proving the object was bought Used and - yes yes yes - in pencil on the inside cover a lot of notations show that clearly a student used this for a paper of some kind. Relief at coincidence. Hatred of Elliot. Pity for this poor student, putting their faith in this voodoo snake-charmer mumbo jumbo. Lucy! 'Oh shut up' she says. And to close off the coming assault of she-has-never-even-read-the-thing, Lucy turns to a page at random and reads what is highlighted. *'The tress, felled' the man pointed out to her 'we start to call them Long instead of Tall.' 'Nothing could be more obvious or less profound' the girl says, sipping the soupy water with a prim nod. The man gives an expansive gesture, indicating the forest itself and the glow behind it, by extension the glut of the gambling-town there, and says 'Soon enough, I plan to make everything tall long - I plan to sideways the dimensions to tame this bastard pride.'* Lucy is snarling, but not giving the thing an opportunity really, just flea-flitting to another page, looking for no context. The writing is fine, but so banal. Tree. Long. Tall. Man. Talking to a girl. 'Ooh' she flounces. Next: *Under the snowdrift, Ana knew there would thaw the evidence of it all. She wished for frigid insects. She wished for evolution to make delicacy of frozen carrion for beetles who never come out in the warmth. Ana wished for the inverse of everything - everything but the act she feared the warmth would bring life - sulfurous, rot gutted, mummified skin life - to.* What about that, Lucy? Lucy? Lucy Jinx reads a note in the margin. *Timid vainglory, the same as 'the asphalt scene'.* Lucy flips to the last page just to check the number. The book ends on an outfaced, even-numbered page - and on the facing odd is Elliott's photo done in black-and-white. Unposed but posed. Artificial but exactly her. Bent finger like a French-girl pretending to be unimpressed. Lucy turns back to the first page, leaning to the wall, crossing one ankle in front of the other, her legs shaped like an upside down Four or a spade about to start digging. *There is never enough nightfall, but plenty of night. Barb first thought that in second grade. She feels she should be able to say it now, here, to boast it. But to say so, here, might alter these fine folks' opinion of her. She might come off as too-big-for-britches. Oh they might even say to her face 'So this isn't adult profundity, this is childish random.' She might argue there isn't much difference. But, of course, Barb would like the money. And these people, though their girth might not suggest it, are the delicate purse-strings she wants to tug on. Open the lips of the treasure bag.*

Teenager angular, diagonalling the bed, Lucy Jinx with hands behind her head, elbows pretending they're mirrored, large triangle elephant ears. The mother's computer over there is really whirring. Lucy touched the keyboard when she first entered and it was hot - not a scald or anything, not fire-hazard - almost enough to make her shut the thing down. A dog barking outside and hands clapping - how crystalline the sound of it - leads Lucy to believe the rain has stopped and she meanders her thinking into how well she could do, by now, without eyesight. If she had someone to maybe wheel her around every once in awhile - someone she could trust to get the right things from the grocery-store - she wouldn't be at all averse to the life of a cave-fish shut-in. Nature only gives sight to things it thinks need it, after all. Sometimes, conditions change. 'People evolve ahead of the curve' Lucy thinks, thumbs-upping the air above her - and maybe one day there will be a corrective mechanism that allows unneeded senses to shut down, one that then kicks them out of dormancy if, all of a sudden, they are needed again. 'I'd be so good at Nature, if I got a vote.' Of course you would, Lucy, yes. Then, all at once, she sits up, gets to belly, leans way over the side of the bed - just decides to fall all the way to the floor, a gentle, controlled flop, because the bed is higher than she'd expected, the lean over its lip hotly uncomfortable - and peers under the bed, expecting an animal. The mother did say there were cats, right? The dream sensation of her wounded hand prickles, her mind asserting its oil-painting-of-events over the bulky, hardened acrylic of reality. Lucy now inspects her uncut hand, doing her best to convince herself she sees even the faintest trace of upset - lines a tad pinker, indicative of touch-up, of pencil-erasure. A look out the window - yes it has stopped raining, see? those three youths are smoking cigarettes at the dumpster, one of them lifting a leg high to bring it down on the wheel of a discarded, sideways-leaned child's bicycle - verifies the mother's car has not returned, and - having run out of things to do other than loiter - Lucy begins undressing for a shower. 'The idea is to seem like you understand you are welcome here, right?' she has her nude reflection ask her. 'Is it?' she asks, the reflection imitating, she supposes, the scrunch to her question. Her reflection quick-shakes its head - Holy-moly like - and point-blanks her 'No - I'm saying: that is what you are acting like. But I thought you were just coming here to talk!' 'To have someone to talk to' Lucy corrects, even as the reflection already rolls its eyes in mock like to say 'Oh blah blah blah - you know what I mean. Anyway: what does showering have to do with it?' 'But water passes the time' Lucy says - just in her thoughts - slipping out of panties, lifting her folded shirt from off of her folded pants on the mother's desktop, setting panties on pants, laying shirt back down over them. A sniff to the mother's towel gives off the ripe of overuse, so Lucy tosses it to the corner-piled laundry - there - and gets another from the hall closet. Flynn's door is a bit open, so she really hopes he hasn't just been playing possum. 'Flynn?' Don't call to him, Lucy - what would that look like if, say, he had had headphones on, prior, has only just taken them off, hops to the door and finds you boogy-man nude in the hall!? 'Hey' she ignores herself 'Flynn?' And she presses his door in, open, flipping on the light, for a moment startled that there might actually be someone there - though it is obviously just a poster of Charlotte Gainsborough which then rather makes Lucy disappointed at the emptiness of the bed. She closes the light, returns the door to an approximate attitude of how she found it, chooses her towel, and closes the master-bedroom door behind her, locking it by habit, chuckling, unlocking it, and leaving it open a sliver.

So: Lucy had heard something. 'Yes?' she says, moving her face from the still-so-delectable hot stream in her face. Another knock on the closed door, again her name muffled by the steam and the overhead fan chugging. 'Lucy?' She moves the shower-curtain enough to curl her face around, keeping her nudity censored - why, Lucy? you know who it is - 'Hi, I'll be right out - you can come in.' The mother opens the door shyly, also just pecking her face in, raising a hand high, then slinking back like she is cat who has been clapped at. 'Sorry.' 'It's fine' Lucy says, running hand over face, thumb-knuckling one eye. 'Sorry - I'll be right out.' 'Take your time, take you time' says the mother, now opening the door a bit more and giving a solicitous, R-rated leer, like trying to rubber her neck to get a reach around the curtain. Lucy flashes - or maybe doesn't - one breast for a blink, the mother fanning herself ooh-la-la then saying 'I just wanted to be absolutely sure it was you, you know?' 'As opposed to anyone else who might be using your shower?' 'Well yes, precisely. It's a gall-dern Central Station 'round here sometime, Jinxy - I thought the hobos found a new back door or something.' 'Just me' wink-faces Lucy and the mother says she will be downstairs eating fast-food and can save Lucy some, if Lucy so desires. 'How much food did you order?' 'I'll give you - you know? - like a bite of my hamburger or something, a pinch of fries - they have sea-salt, in case you didn't know.' 'Fantastic' Lucy says, then explains she already raided the fridge. 'And I put away the dishes' she says, but regrets how eager it sounded, something inside her shifts to 'Be quiet, what are you doing?' and she goes 'Okay - eat eat! Stop letting cold air in, you louse.' The mother exits, a soft clunk of the door gently closed, and Lucy tombs herself back behind the sweet-tart purple of vinyl curtain. She refills her palm with the almond soap, really massages in the exfoliates all over her, shifting her belly bulk and manhandling the give of her arm-flesh, her leg-flesh, with more gumption than she tends to, like to get forever into to crevices she has never thought of before, her skin now a series over overlaps upon overlaps, an organ like the intestines which, if unwrapped properly, could stretch the length of the Atlantic and back. The scrubbing becomes more manic, to the point her palm forces up into the rise of her nose and she hears a thud like a crunch - the sound like snatching a fishnet sack of marbles from someone would feel like in a palm - this shutting her down, utterly. When she unshuts her eyes, she expects there to be blood in alcoholic vomits all over the tub-bottom, all over her feet, coursing in outside-veins the flat through her cleavage and building in the unevens near her belly button.

Nothing like that. Just the tub and a sensation like she had been coldcocked - as though a step-parent had had enough of her and lashed out, is now standing there, hoping she doesn't start crying, a parental-figure tense with irateness, having to waver between further-threat and deal-making. She shuts off the water. And stands. She towels herself off - her habit, nothing new - before stepping out of the tub, working her feet as dry as she can get them, one-at-a-timing them onto the dingy mat - this set closer the toilet than the shower - a high-pitched squawk as the weight shifts from her second foot on the slick porcelain into the air where she holds it, roughs towel around it, sets it down as though fearing it will land with heft on broken glass. And into the bedroom - the mother has left the door open so she assumes Flynn has not also returned - the towel left on the toilet seat, she sits to the end of the bed, three-fingering a touch to her nose, her wrist tense, as though not trusting the fingers keep from suddenly attacking, again.


THE MOTHER IS SMOKING, EARNING a hairy-eyeball off Lucy and an 'Are you trying to kill the kid? Don't you listen to Surgeon Generals?' But Flynn is spending the night with his ladylove elsewhere, for the first time. 'And you fell for that?' 'Sweet Jesus, Lucy - you think I want to lay abed at night knowing it's going on in my very home?' 'Kinda' Lucy says, giving a saunter toward the smokes the mother holds the pack of out, Lucy rubbing her hands and pudgy-boy licking her lips in smecks and Ah-mmn-well-mmn-heehee-well-mmns, real pervert-like. A minute later she has one lit and they are sitting, the mother in one of the dining chairs - it away from the table, out-angled - Lucy on a small stool she is not the least bit comfortable upon. 'I was worried you changed the lock.' 'That'd be a right twat of me, eh?' 'I'd just roll with it, you know? *If they treat you that way, Lucy, then they're not really your friends* I'd tell myself.' 'Am I plural, now?' 'Everyone's plural - how garrulously non-progressive of you.' The mother doesn't know what *Garrulously* means. Neither does Lucy. *Garru-Lucy* is the mother's new pet-name for Lucy, it is promptly decreed, and they blow smoke into the same part of the air, Lucy joking 'Clink' the mother picking up, not missing a trick 'Clink' as well. 'I fell asleep in my car' Lucy says, thumbing back over her shoulder, earning herself a thumb jammed against the wall and a sympathyless chortle from the mother 'when I first got here and I had the weirdest dream about your house being full of cat-piss - some of which I stepped in - and Flynn had a gun I shot at a globe.' Lucy decides that makes the dream sound really cool, so she keeps the other details on ice. 'Why did you shoot the globe?' 'Only I didn't actually' Lucy says, a quick lean forward and steady hand in the air, as though soothing the mother's nervy knees as they restlessly jitter in vibrato. 'They say dreams symbolize things. I think it means I hate globes. And it's right. Shooting a globe is a great symbol for that.' 'Flynn hates guns' the mother says, seeming almost distracted by the trail of her upward-diagonally from corner-mouth blown smoke, watching it as though it were a small moth she planned to kill with a hand-clap. 'My dreams don't know Flynn personally, you know? They haven't looked through his stuff. In my dream, my dreams did - or this dream, anyway - but retrospect and browsing through some issues of *Psychology Today* would probably indicate that it was mostly my own old room or something, really.' 'What was he hiding, in there?' Lucy explains the whole part of the dream about Flynn's room - then adds in the part about being naked and knocking on his door, just to get a taste of will that seem like something that really might have happened - in the opinion of the mother as listener - or just another flitter of dreamland - and the mother shakes her head in the shape of 'Oh I fucking knew it - that kid!' A moment of perfect silence except for the mechanics of cigarette passes, the sink makes a gurgle like it just can't wait any longer, and the mother takes off her shoes. 'Where did you get those?' Lucy points. 'At some shoe-store - no - at a store that had nothing to do with shoes, actually, but there they were.' And before Lucy can give another formless retort the mother asks 'What did you eat? Really, I can fix you something - you don't exactly look emaciated, but you also look somehow malnourished.' 'I'm always somehow malnourished' Lucy replies, for a moment trying to stand up in cue with the mother doing so, finding the effort too much, so disguising the motion as a wriggle of torso stretch, elbows apoint. 'How about some sort of pasta. And I'll melt butter on it. And shake in some kind of prepackaged three-spice seasoning?' 'Sounds like a hot ticket' nods Lucy, holding her cig now between fourth and fifth fingers of the hand that usually doesn't hold cigs while she uses the index and third finger of the hand that usually does to scratch hard the side of the thumb of the hand that usually doesn't but right now is.

What has Lucy been up to? Well, did Lucy tell the mother about her job at *Hernando's GrocerEaze*? She hadn't!? Oh - does the mother know a few people who use the service? Say! - maybe Lucy has brought them their things. Yes, Lucy agrees it is a kind of an absurd concept, but the popularity must be growing because *Hernando's* has invested in seven more vehicles and is extending operations to their twenty-four hour seven-days-a-week stores. 'And *Hernando's* - you know? - does not make bad decisions' says Lucy 'they are successful as plague-boils, those stores.' Oh - certainly Lucy is in concert with the mother's feelings on the point that - yes - the overnight-shift is to service, exactly, the needs of the Rapist and Murderer demographic - it is the delivery drivers, themselves, who are being sold and, yes indeedy, Lucy bets that Hernando himself picks up some pretty snazzy subsidies on that! No - *subsidies* may not be the correct word, that's true, Lucy and the mother see eye-to-eye on that. What is implied, though, Lucy explains, slowing it down and raising her voice like she's trying to pull a quick-change con on an opioid addled foreigner, is that Hernando is getting his back scratched by fiends. 'Yes, like *The Midnight Meat Train* - exactly!' Lucy applauds - quick flit of Samantha, who showed her that wretched film before far less wretched things went down, spreading like musk through her eyes - but is sure that if the two of them - Lucy and the mother - put their heads together they could come up with a better movie than that to compare matters to. One of Hernando's kids is in prison, now!? Why hasn't Lucy heard about that? Oh yes yes, spot on - the mother deftly points out that it wouldn't be in the Newsletter, *Hernando's* being a well-known den of censorship and Gilliamesque loosey-goosey. 'I used to be that Gilliamesque loosey-goosey' Lucy says, as though hurt by the mother's callousness - not in associating her to something low-brow, but in failing to acknowledge her tenure as a pretend Cinema and Cultural critic. 'You really don't remember that?' 'I do now that you're talking about it - was I supposed to read that stuff?' Anyway, Lucy sheds the mother some light on the inner-workings of a set-up like *GrocerEaze*, pointing out that the hiring process seemed rigorous when Lucy went through it, in that it took three different interviews before she was abruptly hired and then started, exactly then - 'They merely walked me to the Punch-In clock and it was like *Here - you, random person - show her the ropes* - all very Third World militia' - but then Lucy got a snootful of who else was on staff and it plundered her of any grease-dribble of self-respect she may have retained as a person. The mother tells a story about how a delivery-driver flagrantly stole the condoms a friend had ordered - the friend caught the driver red-handed, because the driver just smoked a cigarette in the company-car and had the things in his pocket when this friend stormed out to discuss his receipt. 'How did that end?' 'About how you'd think.' 'Wait - *Hernando's* told the friend the driver was terminated!?' Lucy hates to tell tales, but on the strength of the description the mother here gives, it sounds like that was Vincente - who, by the way, Lucy could well imagine would steal condoms, yes - and so this friend of the mother's got swindled of something more precious that prophylactics! 'Justice! Yes, *Justice! The truth*! He traded the truth for a dick's length of latex.' 'Here, have another smoke - this pasta isn't getting soft, there's something wrong with the water or something.' Lucy doesn't mind if she does - about the smoke - suggests - about the pasta - the problem might be all the butter the mother put in the pot. But the mother is already adding more water, convinced this is the more *Heloise* thing to do. 'Can I have a lighter?' asks Lucy, but instead tosses the cig to the mother in response to her Gimmie rub-rub of the fingers of one hand, the toss landing short, the mother calling Lucy a pussy as she bends to pick it up, to which Lucy says 'I'm going to write a ballad about you' as the mother moves the pasta pot, lights the smoke on the burner, winces in pain from too much heat in her eye, the lit cigarette - quite on purpose - flung to the far side of the room, landing on an ant-trap by the window, right there. Lucy blinks at this. The mother, attention back to the pasta pot, says through a yawn 'You can write your ballad after you fetch, okay?'

No, Lucy never does much ask about the mother. Even here, Lucy doesn't. The two have moved to relax, watching television while Lucy takes her time eating. Their chat is some trenchant commentary on the way commercials are made Now versus how they were made Then and there is a sense that Lucy is idling a connect-the-dots or retracing the loops in a Word Search. There's something to the way the mother speaks which doesn't let Lucy free from the malingering sense of dream the house still excretes - every word from the mother, while Lucy could not predict them, is not a surprise, seems known, like whale-song is recognized immediately and sounds exactly like how you'd think it would even if you'd never thought about it sounding like anything. Picture a physical object inside of Lucy's mind, just here - maybe something like a bent penny spinning down in a throat instead of a diaphragm, the in-breaths and out-breaths still possible, but irrevocably metallic. The mother isn't touching Lucy or behaving solicitously and - if an honest analysis of anything is to be proffered, here - the mother is not asking Lucy much really, either. 'You know whut show I started watching?' the mother says - at this moment or some other physically exactly-just-like-it but miles away. 'Which?' Lucy asks, as though proving the point - what is the difference between one moment and the next, there? Slightly different vibrations in vocal-chords, less than two feet apart, thirty letters instead of five? Add up a column of Differences, one of Exactly-the-Sames, and guess which one weighs a phone-book and which weighs the White Cliffs of Dover! *In The Heat Of The Night.* Lucy is fascinated! 'With Carroll O'Conner?' 'Yep.' 'Why?' The mother shrugs. She says it always came on after another show she watched - but which she won't name because of Lucy's persistently my-shit-don't-stink look-at-my-fancy-pantism - and now, sure, the mother admits it, she kind of finds it comforting, she feels very at home in that world. 'I loved the show *Wise Guy*' Lucy says and the mother explains that very few people don't like the show *Wise Guy* so if Lucy thought she had discovered a cheaper way to refine ore or something, there, she's better off keeping back home on the farm. The mother still hasn't touched Lucy and hardly has glanced at her. One could wonder: What are these two watching? One could wonder: Is there something unspoken going on between them? One could wonder: If so, unspoken to what end - is there tension or slack, is there comfort or spilt-milk? To wit: Lucy is thinking all of those things. However: Lucy does

not so much think the mother is, too. Regard, as Lucy does, the mother's actual
focus on the flicker-trick of human form, the audio-mix trying to make music
seem natural to a man narrowly avoiding being swiped by the corner of a passing
car. Regard, as Lucy does, the unknowing-she's-up-to-it of how long the
mother has been scratching the red-marbled dry skin of her ankle-bulb with the
sock temporarily set around her heel-base. Isn't that a little bit loud for someone
to be doing while complexing about how their silence might be perceived, their
physical body in space? Now: Lucy is wondering if she could just kiss the
mother's mouth. It is right there. It doesn't seem like the long-game is being
played just to prove Lucy the patsy, sucker's hand, and send her packing with a
smack of the bum's-rush to her backside, too boot. The mother doesn't even
notice Lucy is so fixedly taking her stock, Lucy chewing her noodles as quietly
as she can, doesn't see the way Lucy has had a piece of hair in her mouth for the
last seven bites but is chewing around it, or pinching it just proper when she
swallows so it doesn't swallow down, too - nothing worse than swallowing hair,
Lucy staunchly believes it is the source of wicked, banshee-loud stomach-cramps
- keeping the hair to herself as there is no way she is going to draw attention her
way due to the multiple takes it will require to pinch it from her mouth, so
recently sweaty from mastication - no, never, not Lucy, not here.

A little while later, Lucy says 'A very dear friend of mine died today' and she
continues on while the mother - just a brief flutter-of-face like to smile before
seeming to get-it how this is not a wind up - says overtop of Lucy - but quietly,
respectful to let Lucy keep talking - 'Just a' leaving off the abbreviation *Sec* while
she leans forward from the sofa to get the remote-control from the television-
stand, draining the green-line of volume down, then, after thirty more seconds
of listening to Lucy - eyes full on Lucy, who is, however, watching the silent
image of whatever it is on the screen - shutting off the power, Lucy's eyes not
averted, maybe keen enough to see her reflection in the pot-kettle mirror of the
screen, hazy as it is with finger streaks. Lucy is to the part where she is explaining
'My phone was dying and it was like a kind of cartoon - you know? - everything
choppy, seeming to flow, but to flow in abrupt lines - how like dances in
animation, even when smooth, show all the imprecisions that wrists make when
penciling and painting. Do you know what I mean?' The mother is silent, then
comes to realizes Lucy is actually waiting for a response, manages 'Sure - like
in *Beauty and the Beast* or something' Lucy snapping 'Yeah-yeah, yes - exactly' with
ant-leggy fingers on tumbleweed hands, weather-cock wristing into 'Or some
movie like that - like *Pocahontas* or some of those - yes - or how cats walk in *Oliver
and Company* or whatnot, sure.' The mother nods. And again. Lucy saying 'I'm
sorry' in the chirp-tone of a meek sneeze, then saying 'I suppose it's better,
though - right? We got cut off and all. She was in and out - she was kind of

delirious I think, she might not remember the call - well, she doesn't remember anything, by now - and it's better that way, you follow?' The mother - and Lucy, you see it now, you appreciate it - sits immobile, neither concern nor empathy in her face, just a stiff wall to lean against, to drum fingers in whatever melodies Lucy needs to pretend to hear on. 'It's not natural, how people die so in contact with each other. Overall. The way, historically, most people die - well, they don't get anything like being with or near each other. Life was just snatched. It would have been more historically human for Layla never to have woken up, to never have called me. We chit-chatted - we just gabbed - it wasn't any kind of proper Goodbye, at least - we didn't reduce life to that, like something you Fare-thee-well at the end of or think this-is-how-this-part-goes - am I making sense? We have this idea of Prehistory and Tribal Life - it was everyone lives to be an Elder and dies surrounded by Ceremony and the brightest colors the civilization knows how to make out of whatever hoist on flags and such, powder smoke, firecrackers - Old might have been Thirty or whatever, it might have been Layla's age, but it was Old - that's what we think it was like. But that isn't memory - it's make-believe. The fact of it is that the majority of human beings - you can think about this, Natalie, you know? - the majority - if you count them all up - died ages away from each other - most never learned, specifically, their acquaintances, even dearly loved ones, were dead. They just assumed. Pioneers and hunter-gathers and soldiers and pilgrims - just children going out to learn to play in the forest - oh I mean a long time ago, not like now. The common-death is Away and Sudden and maybe not noted except by *That person is gone, now*. Layla almost was that. Such a modern little cellular-phone-way she died. It's almost disgusting. It's almost disgusting, Natalie - the way I sat there and let her die on the telephone. Or I would have. The only thing that kept her death Ancient was a phone-battery - was a battery, you know? - that's what gave her the anonymous dignity Life is supposed to end with. I'm glad, really. I don't want Layla to dwindle off while I blather distractions, my digital-voice becoming incoherent while she specters - Jesus, Natalie, right? That would make Life soup - and Life isn't supposed to be Soup, do you think? Layla deserved to die as alone as the first aneurism. She should have been the first person ever to die - everyone else just pedestrian imitation of her.'

A few things that are true - no one, really, is recording these truths except Lucy, but, as she is thinking them, they are true, nevertheless. One: Lucy is dissatisfied with what she just said. The order - she uses that exact word *Order* - seems like a meandering bean-field - she can't think of a better term than *bean-field,* loads those words with derision - and if she could have she would have taken time to polish that, to make it have meant something. Egregious terms in there - she can't remember it really, but none of that sounded very good. It was supposed to be the solo, not the plucks in the tuning-pit! Two: the mother did not understand a word of it. No. Lucy knows, on a technical level, communication was not achieved. She didn't even keep it a narrative other than 'Some broad called *Layla* snuffed it - boo-hoo'. How is the mother going to get the point about the telephone? What was that rubbish about Modernity and the Ancient World? Yep, that could have been said a lot better. Three: the mother is only being quiet now because she knows Lucy fumbled the ball, there. It's Lucy's fault that the most the mother could say is 'Jesus, Lucy - I'm sorry' or - as she is saying, after five or ten or whatever minutes, maybe thirty, have passed - 'Are you okay, Lucy?' What else is she supposed to say? She's likely bursting with corrections. *Soup?* What was that about? Or how about: *So, in a sense, it was the most-Modern element of Layla's death which tethered it to Antiquity - but doesn't that mean Antiquity and the Contemporary World are one and the same?* Oh - Four: Lucy thinks that, so the dichotomy is false - the mother is thinking that, her hand pats are the-dichotomy-is-false. 'I'm fine. It was just a surprise' Lucy starts patting the mother's hands, now cognizant of the fact she didn't cry during any of her ramblings, either. 'Do you think I should have cried?' The mother blinks, her mouth a bent rubber-band saying 'Dunno.' 'I mean, not when she died - I think I might have done, then - I mean now, while I was telling you.' 'I don't think you should have anything, Lucy - this seems like you just kind of be.' 'I wanted to go someplace to talk. I drove around all day. And I was way jammed in my head. You know how in back of your eyes it seems hollow, like there's miles of air between your eye-back and the front-most lean of your brain?' The mother waits, says 'Yes' but Lucy, immediately after, changes the subject to 'I'm not allowed to really not-be-sad, right?' '*Allowed?*' 'You would be sad if someone died. If equivalent-to-you Layla died - like if Flynn or something died and your phone wasn't charged up and you said whatever you were saying and he was saying something to someone else and the line cut out, right?' The mother nods. Lucy waits. The mother says 'I would be very sad.' And see - see! see see see!!! - the mother is almost crying even at the phantom-sting of it! Lucy stands up and says 'Hey, let's have another cigarette for awhile and then maybe I have to go. I thought Flynn's girlfriend lived here?' The mother stands, too, and Lucy - perceptive one, Lucy, but she lets it slide even though she tenses, bristles in her sinews 'Don't you fucking bring it up, anymore!' - notes the hesitant sway to her following to the kitchen, knows that, while Lucy is lighting her smoke, the mother is back there, trying to decide how to proceed. Invalid-old-Lucy, Old-Memaw-Lucy, needing to have the menu read to her, reminded how much she likes corn. Lucy lights another cigarette, meaning to bring it to the mother, but doesn't move. Not until she feels the mother touch her shoulder. She can feel the worry in the hand, but it's worry about how Lucy might be spring-loaded, might mousetrap around, froth-mouthed, and shove - it isn't worry based on wanting to comfort. Lucy realizes she's still holding both smokes and smoking neither. The mother takes them. Stands there. Puff off one. Puff off other. Puff off one. Puff off other. Touch to Lucy's cheek. Puff off one. Puff off other. Until Lucy opens her mouth, naked-bird desperate, and the mother gently sets filter at her lower lip, waits patiently for Lucy to bring her jaw up in a grip of it.

Now Lucy - right here - with more of a flounce about her composure, affect entirely summed up thus: she looks as though she has just whipped a scarf around her neck and flirtingly said 'Harumph and good day to you.' Now Lucy - right here - after a casual laugh at the mother's anecdote about a tow-truck driver flirting with her exactly how a spree-killer in a television show might, is leaned to the counter, very tip of her elbow there sharp - she looks like a cracked plate balanced on top of a teacup with another teacup on top of it with a fork balanced on that. She says to the mother, bringing the tone down to sober - but face meant to give off 'I'm saying this, but no more melodrama - let's agree' - 'I think I need to give you back your key.' 'Why's that?' the mother says - it could be remarked that this back-and-forth comes off as a hybrid of a conversation between Therapist and Client, a lawyer talking to a prisoner through plate-glass, and a school-teacher comforting a child who just threw up on the picture she was proud of, waiting on the building steps for dad to show up. 'I want to be honest. I am in love with someone else. And we're living together, now. She's having a kid - well, she's been doing that for awhile - and I'm all but certain it's meant to be our kid, you know?' The mother pours more coffee - Lucy with hand on dagger-blade of herself, ready for distinct upslash at the slightest twitch of passive-aggression - and says quite plainly 'But you've always been in love with another women, since I've known you.' So unflavoured-yogurt is this said, in fact, that Lucy, just-caught-out-but-not-being-punished, goes shrug and 'Well, yeah.' What is that smile on the mother's face? It looks like the words some previous asterisk lead to. Is Lucy in her back-pages? *Notes and Errata and Alternates*? 'Do you know I'm in love with you, Natalie?' Note: Lucy says this - this note not a judgement - exactly like a diner would say, pointing to their check 'No, I did order the cutlet, just not the onion-thing - but I did order the cutlet' because the diner earnestly wants the server to understand the problem and not overcompensate in their desire to refund the credit-card for the whole meal. The mother says 'Yes.' 'I still am. But I' - this sounds kind of mean-spirited to Lucy, saying it anyway, obviously - 'I didn't pick you. I guess I'm in love with her more - or first, or whichever.' Lucy would be more comfortable, by now, if this were going worse - or if the mother had taken on that meditative tone, that I'm-pretending-I'm-well-while-prepping-belladonna-and-while-I'm-stealing-your-hairbrush-for-gypsies. 'You're living with her, now?' Wait.

'Wait. Can I ask you: Are you in love with me?' 'Yes, Lucy - I am in love with you. But that's no reason to return the key.' All tension breaks and it is laughter - maybe the first breath of Albee-free laughter Lucy can recall in recent history, pure and at nothing funny or comforting, distinct-in-itself. 'You know you can still be my friend, right?' Lucy says she does not know that. She does not think so. Lucy says she is under the impression she is an equivalent Void and to befriend her is to wear a null 'round one's shoulders. 'I'd like you to keep the key.' 'I'd like to keep the key.' 'Then keep it.' 'Then I'll keep it, then.' The mother lights a cigarette without offering one to Lucy - either oversight, symbol, or nursing tactic - Lucy now chuckling like she's complimented someone's bracelet but not thought of what to say about the painting their hands are still daubed with the effort of. 'This is where I came to not be by myself.' The mother nods and to Lucy looks a bit like a sandcastle several days old glanced at in passing by children too down-shore from it to muster the eagerness to poke it, to give it a kick. 'What's that?' the mother asks on a tip-tap of ash to an envelope she pulls from a pile. 'I was thinking you look like a disused sandcastle. I know what I mean. But you probably don't.' 'No' the mother says, sniffing a touch to her nose 'but I imagine you're probably right.'

There's no sensation to it, exactly the same as there isn't sensation when a film showing in a theatre reveals that a major splice has happened, midsentence jumps to already-going soundtrack of altogether separate scene, obvious the continuity is affected but - just at the split of one-image-to-next - impossible to determine the extent - could be five seconds, could be an entire reel went unwatched, the viewer will only know next time or learn in conversation with a friend, weeks after. No sensation to what? Hyperventilate, Lucy is sitting on the stairs, now, and we pick up mid-fit: 'before that though. Way before it. And I thought to myself she was dying. A weird parking lot. But this time was different. Oh - my mind was everywhere else! But it can't be just ignored - listen to me, listen. Layla texted me right then, you see? Right then! I was walking home and my head was clear and she texted me. *Lucy?* She texted me *Lucy?* in the middle-of-the-night. And I would have answered. But Ariel was there. I didn't know it was Ariel. She was outside my apartment. And - see, see! - earlier - weeks earlier! - the person below me, they got murdered and - oh it was terrible! - and now a ghost lives there, now the woman the dead woman would have aged to lives there or something. But: I saw the killer outside my door! And I think they knocked, once before. This has always happened. You don't understand. You don't even fathom how much I'm followed. And - oh listen - I started to think it was Language. That I was wrong - that it wasn't the World, it was just Language! I tried to stop, see? But then I couldn't stop. I don't think it's Language - it was always the World tricking me into thinking that it was

Language when it was always the World - I was always right, it just wore me down into doubt. And Layla said *Lucy?* - or she texted - and I told her like a joke, like *Haha No time for you, girl, my true love awaits* - because I was so happy Ariel was there! I was happy! And I think that was Layla, the last thing she said, maybe, before she fell asleep, you know? Like *Help.* Like *Help, help, Lucy!* Like *Lucy? Lucy, are you there?* Like *Lucy, what's happening to me?* But you see - when I was supposed to be editing my book, I couldn't stop writing a poem. And it was for Layla - this is before she wrote to me but after I thought she was going to text me to tell me to call her and when I called her she'd tell me that she was dying - and it was called *Pneumonia.* I said *Let's call our daughter 'Pneumonia'!* And I dunno what else I wrote - that Layla was the one who should be pregnant, you know what I mean? I don't remember. And then I just didn't think about Layla until that *Lucy?* and then not again at all because I was with Ariel. And anyway - Layla is someplace else and her life is different and there's always a different thing. I killed her, is what I'm getting at. The World gave me warnings and I didn't pay attention to any of them. I just wasn't paying attention to anything! I told the World I'd decided and it started trying to show me. Showing me it could erase. Showing me the shambles I'd be tattered to. It showed me! It was even nice about it. Making me remember someone I had forgotten in order to show me what it could do, the number it could pull on me. And it even gave me a warning to remind me of Layla - but it didn't remind me of Layla. It didn't. This woman. And her medicine. I bet you - I fucking bet you, I bet you! - it's what Layla was allergic to. And then it made her call me. To show me. To show me. To show me what I'd done and what I do. And it won't hurt Ariel - it will hurt people like you and erase people like you! The World. All that will be left is words. The last words about Layla are titled *Pneumonia* and are supposed to be because it's funny how we'd call our daughter that. It's a perfect line! If you look at it - it's a perfect, straight line. But I stopped looking. I chose! And that means not looking. What if it kills you? You see what I mean? It needs things to take from me. It might hurt you. So I should give you your key - that's what I meant. I don't care that I love Ariel - that's nothing to do with your key. If you love me, Natalie, you love Tetanus - or no, nothing like that, nothing so easy! - if you love me you love *Cueutfeldt-Jakon Disease, Fatal Familial Insomnia, Granulomatous amoebic encephalitis* or something - like *Naegleria fowleri* or whatever you want!' And needless to say, oh so needless to say: this speech goes on. Lucy is still talking.

Probably Lucy is the one who started kissing the mother. And the kissing is very soft and has been going on for five minutes, swaying like a slow-dance at junior-prom. Two kids who have never danced before and seem to think that something - in their arms just so and their totter around - has been accomplished. It's Lucy who breaks off the kiss - too harsh, she just stops kissing

- and now she does a heave-ho-heave-ho of unneeded doctor's office breaths, the last one out in a sigh. Then what? Look there: Lucy does a very monkey-man kind of flimsy-legged tap-dance, shakes her head and, while scratching behind her left ear like the hind-leg of a dog, says 'I'm really sorry - I think I'm just not over my friend dying, you know?' There isn't anything to be sorry for and the mother points this out. Lucy points out 'It's a good job how Flynn isn't home, right?' and the mother agrees, though says Flynn would probably just think it's interesting - 'He's always thought you were a queer little customer, you know?' 'He's a good kid.' 'He is that.' The mother wants Lucy to stay over, but isn't calculating in her saying so, very postcard-with-advertisement-on-it about the whole matter. 'Is the woman you're with at home?' 'Probably' Lucy says, glad for the excuse, though not stopping, now saying 'She had an appointment today and I figure has been trying to get a hold of me but - as I may have mentioned - my phone stopped working. Did I tell you I knew Layla was going to tell me she was dying before she said it?' 'You had mentioned that' the mother says 'You said she sounded like what an eggshell in the rubbish-bin would sound like to the nearest piece of trash to it when the bag is lifted and the drawstrings pulled taut to be tied, right?' 'Oh right - so I did mention it.' 'Yeah.' 'I should probably get home.' But the mother offers Lucy her phone and suggests calling Ariel, suggests just explaining that she is okay and will be home in the morning. 'I could do that' Lucy admits, because Lucy is the honest lark of the songbird and she doesn't go around being false-grinned or false stiff-lips at times like these. 'I don't really feel like going home. I wanted to come here, I guess. I could have seen Milos, you know?' The mother isn't even there while Lucy says this, but rather has gone into the kitchen - Lucy, herself, on the piano bench, scraping her thumb nail rickityrickityrickity over the gaps between white keys - and so Lucy's words, which are facing carpetward and would be strained to catch even from there, to the mother do not exist. 'I say - yeah - I feel like staying - I decided to come here instead of X or Y other place' Lucy brings the mother up-to-speed about as the mother comes in with the phone. 'You know Ariel's number?' Surprisingly, Lucy does. And the mother says, sensing Lucy's imperceptible-about-to-say-it and cutting it off 'I know - you don't know your dead friend's number - I know, it was the emptiest your head had ever felt, like a worm realizing it had dug so far down it could never dig back up, the ground down there, in fact, nothing but a strata of other worms who had all done the same thing.' Lucy does a finger-snap-turned-into-a-thumbs-up, then holds her palm out for the mother to give a high-five. 'You're an above-average mocking-bird, Natalie - don't let anyone tell you otherwise. That likely wasn't verbatim - what you just said, there - but most people would have just said *Yes, I know* or *You told me* or something.' The mother says she will give Lucy privacy by way of taking a shower. Lucy does an admonishing point and forebodes 'No monkey business out of you - putting images in my head.' The mother takes the first step of the stairs up and Lucy goes 'Oh hey!' - the mother stopping to listen - 'I don't think that people in ancient Rome would think technology is magic, you know - like how people say that?' The mother gives a dot-dot-dot think-face, then 'Yeah, I agree.' 'Obviously they'd catch on pretty quick. They were smart.' The mother heads up the stairs saying 'You do have a point there' and Lucy looks down at the phone.

'Ariel, hi!' 'Lucy Jinx! As I live and breathe and leaf through this copy of *Entertainment Magazine* that showed up in our mail, for some reason.' 'That's happened before!' Swell.' 'Last time it went on for almost ten issues before they caught on.' 'Where are you, my pet?' 'God - I am so sorry. Have you been trying to call me?' 'Indeed. I answered this call despite the fact that I didn't recognize the number because I figured I'd have to start my whole scheme over with someone new, anyway - it being you makes this far less afflictive to contemplate.' 'I have had quite a day, which I here briefly summarize - do you have something to write this down with?' 'Yep.' 'Are you lying?' 'Nope.' 'Are you lying about that?' 'Nope.' 'Are you lying about that?' 'Yes.' 'By *that* do you still understand what I mean?' 'Nope.' 'Okay.' 'You don't want to know if I'm lying about that?' 'Not actually, no, Ari - no, I don't. Even if you did write it down, you'd probably use the wrong end of the pencil, it'd turn out.' 'Your day, you were saying.' 'First - you know my old job?' 'I guess.' 'I scammed over three thousand dollars out of them - cash money, currently in my pocket! Unless I get robbed before tomorrow which - now that I've said that - I most certainly will.' 'So all that to say: you didn't get any money today.' 'Exactly.' 'Fascinating.' 'So: I was out doing that and my phone was dying, but right before it did my friend - that's where I am, by the way - called me and had an emergency - or more like a tragedy - and so I had to come over and have been tending to that and just now thought to call.' 'That's fine. Like I said - I got a free magazine.' 'Oh shit - I'm sorry! - how did it go today?' 'It went like it does - all well in the netherness of my belly.' 'And Kayleigh and Leopold were good? They must be about sick of having to put up with all these appointments of yours.' 'Oh Leo wasn't there. Kayleigh was great. She wants to be a doctor when she grows up, I think.' 'Nice. I guess I meant - not Leo - *the father was happy* - pleased-as-punch or whatever pleased-men are like.' 'I was trying to wend around to saying *Obsto-Gyne*, Lucy!' 'Gah! Oh - about Kayleigh?' 'Yes.' 'Sorry.' 'Sheesh - you think Kayleigh wants to be a doctor? She doesn't want to spell *doctor* even if she gets to abbreviate it! Why do they abbreviate it to *D R* anyway? It sounds like *Der* - meaning *Der*, you know? Like *der der der* - like how a dumb person hums that when they walk or open a jar, is what I'm driving at, there.' 'I get it, El, I get it. If it was *D C* though, that wouldn't be much better.' 'Like it takes so long to spell *doctor*. Jesus, doctors are lazy!' 'Why do they give medicines such long names if they're just going to call them Icons at the end of it all? Like anyone is gonna check.' 'Botanists are the same way. Who do they think they're impressing?' 'Naturalists all around have inferiority complexes, I think - there is nowhere Latin is less necessary than classifying a new type of tree-fungus.' 'So is your friend okay?' 'She's fine. She's a mess. I'm staying over, though. One of her best friends just died. Called her from the hospital, today - like in-the-process-of-dying, you dig?' 'Holy shit. Yeah, stay with your friend. Shit, man - tell her I'm sorry but make it sound like that isn't a stupid thing to say, like I'm not just saying it in an offhand way even though I'm still reading a magazine a little while I'm saying it.' 'I'll strike that very tone.' 'I appreciate it. Seriously, though - shit.' 'Shit, indeed. And her kid is shacked up with his girlfriend, like on their first overnight, so it's best not to leave her with thoughts of her dead friend and her son getting his rocks off into some chick, you follow?' 'Loud and clear.' 'I'm really sorry I didn't call.' 'Well, you phone died.' 'It did.' 'And then your friend and all. If you'd called, I'd probably think you were kind of a fiend.' 'I am kind of a fiend.' 'But I mean I'd think you were for that reason, too.'

Lucy has been watching television for twenty minutes before the mother comes down, pajama dressed - or night-clothes dressed, let's say - giving a wave like 'Is the coast clear?' 'Is this the same movie that was on before?' 'When?' The mother is at the sofa-back, touching the very tip of the bump at the bottom of Lucy's neck. 'When we were talking, before.' The mother leans forward, says she thinks so, then comes around and sits, immediately upon easing into relaxation saying 'Shit - I wanted to make some tea.' 'You can go make some tea.' 'But now I'm sitting. So. Obstacles.' '*Obstacles*' Lucy repeats, then wants to know what the movie is about. 'I think she's a nanny with a deadly secret.' 'Based on what?' 'Based on the fact that I happen to know that the movie, in actual fact, is called *Nanny: Deadly Secrets.*' Here's what Lucy points out: The mother assumes too much. 'The nanny could be the hero of the piece. The nanny could discover the deadly secrets of others. The nanny and others could be the heroes and they are all caught in some outsider's web of deadly secrets. Et cetera ad infinitum.' 'But look at her' the mother counterpoints 'she obviously is the one with a deadly secret.' 'Touché.' They watch for awhile and the mother lays out, calves over Lucy's lap, Lucy grabbing the mother's big-toe for about five minutes in a way she hopes is obnoxious but that seems to rise no reaction, either way - gives up with a frump in her heart. 'It would be better - my opinion, anyway - if the nanny didn't have a deadly secret, at all!' 'It would' the mother agrees. 'Maybe that will be the twist - discovering who has the deadlier secret.

It is plural - the title, you know? Titularly, we are clued into the fact that we are to expect - nay, are owed - more than one secret and that - see the descriptor - the secrets must need be deadly.' And from here, Lucy cannot help put riff philosophic that she and the mother have no way of knowing, now. 'If we only observe one secret - from this-point to the end-of-the-film - how are we to know that there wasn't at least one prior - also deadly - secret, perhaps in a pre-credit sequence or one even simply alluded to, subtextually, in an earlier act?' 'This world is crackers, Lucy - and that is why alcohol invented us.' Lucy likes this. She has a picture of a timeline in which, yes, the chemical reaction of yeast - or whatever causes alcohol - caused alcohol while humanity wasn't even a twinkle in the lascivious eye of the primordial slop - that it was a reaction of this alcohol across the membraneous jism of the Earth that slip-slapped these certain sub-molecular whatnots over here to over there and early bacteria got distracted from something by getting sot-headed, some of it more easygoing, some of it more aggressive, and on and on and on until the first Zap! of what lead to the first thing that lead to Lucy and the mother sitting on the couch. 'I'd love to be an Archeologist if it didn't take so long to just find a bone, you know?' 'Sure' the mother says. 'Anyway, it seems like people should be embarrassed when they find a fossil - after all, those things have been laying around for the longest, right?' Have you told that joke before, Lucy? Maybe. Though it isn't a joke - not to Lucy. 'Coming across the ruins of an Ancient City shouldn't count as a discovery. If anything, you'd be wise not to mention it - save everyone some face.' Lucy? Lucy? What? You aren't saying that to anyone. Lucy grabs the mother's big-toe, this time pinching with fingernails, this time the mother wriggling the toes like an overweight rabbit might try to sniff sniff its nose, get too exhausted, try to hop, but just instead seem like it sighed. 'That's two deadly secrets' the mother points out. There's the mother's finger, pointing at the screen. Lucy blinks at the images - some action in its aftermath, the scene dissolving from the nanny's close-up to a busy highway at peak traffic, the pater familias telling the mater he'll be home, that there is some kind of accident on the bridge. 'I wasn't paying attention - I didn't see it.' 'Well, fuck Lucy, then you'll just have to take my word - that counts as two.'


WHAT IS SUPPOSED TO HAPPEN, Lucy? Are you supposed to go to sleep, now? All of the arrangements are set for it and you have a body that requires it, yes? There is little else, little else. How to consider this? Try: beside you a woman is shaped like a chewed nectarine, beside you is a jaw you could break without worry of retribution. Or try: there are hallfuls of darkness leading to carfuls of stale air you can let out and new air in you can cool. What are these?

Poems? Are these attempts at describing the world? Why is your head on this pillow and your body the stiffness of the potential spring of a cartoon plank that a cartoon chin-uped scoundrel might walk? Why are you down to your skivvies and have your eyes closed when they could be contemplating the ceiling while you do a countdown until you are forgetting you are doing a countdown until you start to do a countdown until you forget you are doing a countdown and then the crumpled brochure of your dreamscape being pawed at and smoothed as though pawing and smoothing can make the pock-jagged texture they crumple recreate the smooth of the unnatural gloss before it was touched? Some people - Lucy might know this, right now - are slumbered even before they hit the pillow - not like they faint, but the basic processes of awake-brain shut down even while the rote still stay going. Oh yes. Computers have modeled it! Oh yes. You can do the home-version: try to remember not what you did right before you went to sleep, but for the ten minutes of lead-up! Is that right? Is that right? But really: is it? Really is it? Ah - but you're cheating, Lucy! You're thinking to yourself 'But I, Lucy Jinx, always remember laying in bed, and I always remember, yes yes yes, what I did before I climbed in.' But then you lay awake! You sit there thinking! You always take more than ten minutes to fall asleep! Hmn. There is no pivot out of that - no - philosophy is useless against a good solid fact. Are you incapable of imagining a life unlike your own? Are you at the same time incapable of living a life like your own? 'What kind of life live I, then - is it is it?' A life like that, Lucy Jinx - you can't even straight ask yourself what it is! Anyway, Lucy can pivot from that: She thought we were talking about sleep, here! She is steadfast in her disbelief that even if someone falls asleep the instant they go prone to their mattress and that if, say, they had fed the cat in the last ten minutes of consciousness prior and, say, written a note and, say, read a piece of newspaper - or any sort of thing, the sort of things people do - that they would not remember it. Shit! Except, even now, Lucy thinks she does believe that - watch it swirl more and more certain. That someone wakes up thinking 'Did I feed the cat?' That someone wakes up thinking 'What's this note, did I write that?' That someone wakes up and is surprised by something they read in the newspaper - or else kind of vaguely recalls seeing something like it on television or hearing somebody talk of it, once. 'It's all a cross between sleep and awake, anyway!' Sure, Lucy, sure. Take the easy road and lay in this bed, beside a woman shaped like a medicine cabinet, a loose knob and a mirror with rust coating the silver you look at thinking glass is silver-colored. Sleep here, next to a woman who is shaped like the hairbrush on the floor. There is a kind of chittering to the silence, right now. The night moves like a vest being unbuttoned or else the strap of a stolen shoulder-bag being loosed to make it feel as though it will appear to store-detectives you already owned it, awhile. Lucy Jinx has managed to open her eyes. And she sees the ceiling. She's old enough she could have been the first person to ever have seen this ceiling. But she's too old to have ever been a child laying looking up at it.

Lucy Jinx dreams - and at least this dream has the tone of a dream. One part of it is: through some trick of perspective, things in the distance really can be plucked and pulled close - 'Look' says a man who Lucy doesn't turn around to see, but who seems to have lived nearby this shore all his life, is horrible and inviting - exactly the same and exactly invisible - behind Lucy's back because of this 'look - if you grab the plate just here and you lift it, it makes the other part slip over this way.' Holy Hell! The man is right! All the things, keeping just as miniature as distance made them, are now physically in the air just in front of her, having hit the metal ring of the wobbly aluminum and atomized like the scent an old woman sprays to smell old. Lucy, in the dream, sees her hand pass right through this boat and she becomes distrustful - and through this pea-sized airplane and through this flock of migrating large geese. 'Tell me why this is and we should tell everybody, tell me why this is and we should tell everybody, tell me why this is and we should tell everybody' Lucy's dream loses track of how long this repetition repeats, seems to curtain it off into a single unit, some kind of lie-people-tell, a lie like how the game of Go has more moves than there are atoms in the universe - which, in this part of the dream, Lucy decries and debunks and dissembles and denounces and diatribes against, slap-slapping at the nails of its ignorance until she pulls her hand too much back while coughing and rip comes off the fingernail like the tail off a cat tugged to fiercely. Lucy woke up at that point, but it didn't register. The mother said something to her and she said something back, but it is lost in the flurry of shifting the covers and arguing in grunts at the length of herself. Then this other dream - awake is what separates dreams, you wouldn't call them different if they had continuity, we wouldn't call such a portion of us not-us if it picked up where it left-off, as awake seems to do - begins and Lucy is putting price-tags on gloves and laughing with these men who are putting price-tags on gloves and one of the men has a single strand of hair pierced through his tongue which Lucy cannot help focusing on. The subject? How soon it will be till the singer is elected. That weak sense, so often in dreams, of having to fake everything, pretend the minutia of your own observations, pull them together like the last pieces of dough after all the cookie-cutters have been used, rerolled and reflattened, one more stick - Circle - one more stab - Star - one more puncture - Christmas Tree - one more excising - Candy Cane, tapering Snow Man, a Square with a bump on the top to frost in the shape of a bow! Lucy doesn't know who the singer is or how to vote or where to put these very crumbly sealed-envelopes after they are handed to her wrapped in a napkin - the only thing down the hall is a children's portable training-toilet and Lucy sees other votes down in there. So she runs! Goddamn it! The other woman has fingers too long and Lucy's back starts to be cornrowed! She is a cartoon gopher burrowed and knuckled in their image! She has eight long tapeworms growing bones under her skin, enough that the skin isn't enough to keep opaque, is translucent, is stretched so hard it becomes the grey-purple-puke-sheen of the worms, all of their divisions ribbing and sharpening, like Lucy has too many spines about to sprout too many wings! And yet another part of her dream. And yet another part. The mother wakes her, again. And Lucy and the mother kiss, but neither will remember. Lucy will remember the touch of the mother's feet, though - toe-tip edging out of a hole in a sock - will remember it and the way she dreamed it exactly as big as her mouth and as hard as a chipped tooth.

'You can't sleep?' 'No. I can't get any sleep.' The mother sits all the way up, seems to have to do a lot to position herself comfortably. Maybe a minute of slippery and then suddenly-sharp rummage sounds before 'Is everything okay?' 'I'm fine' Lucy says, as though addressing a cornflake she knows is sunk under the milk but she can't find with her spoon. 'I think I'm just going to be up, for awhile. I'm sorry.' 'You don't have to say *Sorry*, Lucy - I don't think I can be awake too, though.' Lucy can only manage to respond with a chuckling noise and the most shopworn, formless think of 'Was that rude?' she maybe has ever thunk. The mother scratches the back of Lucy's neck and it feels good - Lucy says so - and she positions herself for more, sensations to her skin fountain-water to cold stone beneath smelting-hot cloudless summer. 'Can I use your computer, awhile - I'll take it downstairs?' 'Sure - absolutely, Lucy. Hey' - the mother's voice sounds concerned, but more personally - 'you aren't leaving, are you?' 'No.' 'I'm tired. But I want to see you before I have to get to work, in the morning.' 'Yeah' Lucy says 'I might wind up sleeping on the sofa, I guess, because it kind of reminds me of you, a lot.' 'That's the coolest thing you've ever said about me.' 'Which?' Lucy had drifted. 'That I'm sofa-like.' 'Well' - Lucy inserts a quick 'Thank you' dipping forward a cluck to indicate the scratching should cease - 'you are. It's one of the more memorable and attractive things about you. You're exotically *Sears* cataloguesque.' As she stands, Lucy thinks *When I rust, it'll be like a battle-ax not a key left in a knob and forgotten about* - wonders if she'll remember to write that down. *Key in a knob. Battle-ax.* 'Meh, it's already gone.' 'What is?' the mother says, already laid back down, but to her back - Lucy is alert enough to cotton to how the mother is waiting to make sure Lucy is able to manage the computer okay before she passes back out - and obviously watching Lucy in the dark, making Lucy's near-nudity, to Lucy, feel more like she is a burn-victim who light wouldn't be good for. 'Something I was going to write, I thought. About something - maybe, or not - I don't even remember, anymore.' *Lie. Liar. Lucy.* The declension. Denying it to someone cements the line with her signature finger-traced in it when no one was looking, the line is a whole city-block Lucy feels the name of her on the ground of is proof that she owns. *When I rust it'll be battle-ax, not a key left in knob and forgotten about.* Oh - she has added improvements, of course. She even smiles and knows she made a sound of amusement the mother doesn't react to, the mother, by now, maybe knowing that Lucy is lying, maybe thinking whatever she wrote was about her - and, gee Lucy, you know, maybe it was. 'Do I need the cord?' Wrong again, Lucy, the mother has to wake up to answer! 'Lucy - are you okay?' 'Sorry, go back to sleep - I thought you were just over there staring at me.' 'What time is it? I can't even see you.' 'It's the same time - go to sleep - and if you weren't sleeping, I bet you could be.' Well, the mother explains that she's sleeping and Lucy just takes the computer, sans cord, leaving the room without another word. You want to go into Flynn's room, eh Lucy? Into your room - into that room, right there? Her thighs seem to make wheezes like corduroy as she descends the stairs. The railing sounds like a bite seeing if it is stern enough to splinter a lamb-bone. There's something about a house in the dark that makes Lucy think it would get boring to be able to walk through thin air. Imagine the skyscape to loiter in. Imagine how it would soon enough be about the same as the square-footage of a living-room - or not even a entire living-room, how it would get, over time, to be the same as sitting in a chair in the dark, too busy talking about something in your head to bother with standing. Oh - the sky would be the worst place for hands down to pockets, it would be the worst place for legs that think bouncing will keep heads fresh and vigorous.

Lucy's face is a blue lung in the computer light. She feels stenciled. And after arbitrarily checking the weather and reading some lengthy reviews of television series she's never heard of - then looking up a few old series to see how many episodes were in them - she feels like the rope has har-har-hared over the side of the boat because the knot was tied but not around anything like an anchor. 'What now?' Lucy ponders into the limp of her hand-back hurting her wrist under the weight of her grocery-bag spilled head, cheek pressing down. A few moments ago - or anyway, upstairs, while she lay awake before sitting up and the mother noticing - Lucy had planned to look up old names, get the bearings on where people had wound up, like screaming a light on to catch the roaches you know clamber the pantry, at night. Now? Not a single name interests her. Or - she doesn't think this, but feels an excuse is partially necessitated - perhaps she is defending them. That's a romantic idea! She has figured out the trick of the horror-killer she is - the plucky way to out maneuver the monster in order to give the film a closure amounting to 'What is real isn't real and we just showed you some of it - ta-da!' If Lucy doesn't know where people are, what they are called anymore, then the people are safe - that's the idea, right? She can know the names - well, that likely at least marks them, some tendril is fault-lining if not in their direction at least in the direction the tendril hopes might just happen to be theirs - but as long as the whereabouts are unknown-to-Lucy they are unknown-to-the-Poltergeist that gibberingly dogs her every sigh. Yet she can't help herself. And she types the name *Dorene*. Dorene what? *Dorene Crumbling* she types, though that isn't the name. Images fill the screen of all manner of people and all manner of things. Lucy - you do know her surname, right? *Sampsonelle*. Lucy types it - but after *Crumbling* and including *Crumbling* and so many of the same images pop up with a whole line at the top of the page of *Paintings by the artist Lisette Sampsonelle Truncart*. Tack. Tack. Tack. Glorious works! Glorious! But enough of that. *Crumbling* goes backspacing away and Lucy strikes Tap! And now the computer shoots daydreams of all the wrong faces - and, for some reason, the diagram of the proper way to perform a Heimlich maneuver on oneself over the back of a chair if choking to death all alone. Lucy opens that image and scours the page to figure out why *Dorene Sampsonelle* is associated with it. A woman called that didn't draw it - clearly the image is copyrighted and used with the permission of *Carlo Davies*, from a textbook called *Keeping Safe, ninth edition*. Perhaps in these comments? *You have to be the loneliest fucker imaginable to need to know how to do this! Keeping Safe: for losers.* Lucy smiles. The next comment is *You've never eaten by yourself? Really?* And the first-commenter responds *I'm not a loser ... so no.* And another commenter says - mark that, Lucy, this was said more than seventeen months later - *Are you actually trolling safety diagrams?* So - not a very satisfying investigation. Lucy then scrolls through cascading screen down down down down of all manner of faces. Sometimes she clicks and sees the picture isn't even of anyone named *Dorene* or *Sampsonelle*. Sometimes she sees that there are links to elaborate Fantasy Art which all more-or-less looks the same - a lot of floating islands, thick undergrowth, boats made half out of wood and half out of what seem to be old alarm-clocks. Erase goes the History. And then - to look like she wasn't trying to hide anything - Lucy pulls up this or that site. This or that site. She is watching a Nick Cave music video with the volume down. 'Yes' she thinks. And her eyes feel like the cold hand inside of a mitten holding an oven-warmed muffin. 'Crybaby' she calls herself without conviction while the night around her does lazy curlicues, a kid's hand getting bored coloring in a circle with side-to-side lines.

About now, Lucy is jostled and she can tell - this time she opens her eyes and sits up with her stomach paused half-somersault - this is at least the third time, only a few minutes between each. 'Shit, Lucy, I'm so sorry - hey, there's no breakfast, I so overslept.' 'You overslept?' Lucy takes three seconds to diagnoses: this has no impact on her. 'What? For what?' 'For work.' 'You're a terrible person. Did you say there's no breakfast?' The mother is zipping the side of a boot, seems to hurting her finger in doing so but seems also to decide against sucking on the pinched bit just when she was about to, going to the knee of the now-booted leg and lifting the knee of the unbooted. 'I can't be late, today.' 'Yeah yeah yeah' Lucy menaces, giving a proud-of-herself stretch as she manages to stand up without losing her balance at all. 'I'm sure the place would just shut down without you - Natalie is all that stands between a functional pet-food store and Chernobyl!' - another yawn and the yawned words 'Or whatever you do' and then the non-yawned words 'Or, you know, whatever it is you said you did when I wasn't listening.' The mother gives Lucy a quick kiss, which Lucy kisses back quickly, and Lucy lets the mother's moving off that way trace her fingers over the turning away shoulder, the bicep, the elbow. 'You can stay as long as you want. Flynn won't be back until, well, eventually, I guess.' But Lucy will be leaving too, she explains, wanting that officially on record. 'I might take a shower first, though.' 'Have at. Plenty of hot water, because I scarcely defunked.' 'What in Hell were you sleeping about so much, anyway?' And the mother sings the lyrics to some song about having migraines-worth of heartache and broken-shoulders worth of blues. Lucy has never heard the song. She's kind of jealous of it, but holds her peace on that. They agree that they will get together sometime soon - and as soon as Lucy grows up, the mother would love to meet *Mrs. Jinx* - whatever her name honestly is. 'Her name's Ariel' Lucy says and the mother, in her rush, seems surprised - so much so she pauses, stares, head cocks, then blinks instead of saying something. 'Or when you two have the kid.' 'Or then' Lucy says. The mother says she really must be running. Runs. Ran. Lucy can hear the sound of a car door closing. She tenses like as though the house door will open and something will have been forgotten and quips shared and maybe another, more lasting 'Goodbye' - but instead there is just silence. Window-blinds spread. Parking-space empty. Lucy's car there. Look left. Now, look right. Floor, ceiling, thermostat, knob to that closet door, other kind of knob to the toilet door. And Lucy - what a piqued look, as though she is not her own doing - livid as centuries-old sculpture, she looks smooth the way ancient pottery looks like hard-sugar so delicate one bite would powder the rest, sound of a crunch like a building collapse must sound to an albatross passing. And she has to settle for her own cigarettes, too. The injustice of it all! Then: Lucy Jinx just standing there - the last pin, the one left in the cushion, the one not needed to pin anything. Always best to have an extra. She'll wind up in a desk-drawer, she'll wind up used when there's no thumb-tacks left. Lucy Jinx will hold something to place, trying with stiff neck to train her eyes straight enough down to see what is written on the flat surface of it. Oh Lucy - she'd go so blind as a pin! But then, she'd go blind as basically anything, wouldn't she? Wouldn't you, Lucy? She grabs this pen, here, and writes on the upper side of her left forearm: *the first cat died from asking Why? the rest of them from asking Why did the first one ask Why?* Right away she hates it. Words - they keep failing her, they've lost all their helium, they've flattened their fizz. Lick. Lick. Lick. She scrubs herself clean as the feathers of a talony gamecock.

Necrotic go mornings in daisy-chains along, this one no different. The world is a dog-legged steeplechase, a limerick as long as a horse in the face. Lucy Jinx wants nice leather driving-gloves, the ones that Italians always figured murderers would giallo in. She wants her radio to be playing something other than *Who's going to steal the rowboats from the lifeguard station?* and second voicing half-overtop *We will we will we will will* but cannot help lower-lip biting singalong *Who'll type manifestos at my summer job?* And as she waits at the first red-light toward home - proper Home, she supposes, and, at least in this instance of saying so, does not seem begrudging - the radio asks *Who's going to build my bomb!? Who's going to build my bomb!?* and if Lucy is lucky, with the lyrics passing pass her last thoughts of Layla - thoughts of a past bunched with winter coats and wakening irritated at car-alarms and seething at fat neighbors singing in the shower out the open windows of those apartments where Lucy would get so feeble in her misery she would throw away books and Layla would go dumpster-dive them back to the shelves, not mentioning it for another week, claiming 'The Tooth-Fairy's Cousin must have brought those back, curious, curious' or whatever such drivel. 'What did I lose then, Layla?' 'You don't have to lose anything - she just brings back books idiots throw away when they're feeling like pissantly sons-of-guns - frankly, she doesn't approve of her cousin's oral fetish at all, she's just her cousin.' Lucy would call Layla tit-sagging illogical and Layla would remind Lucy 'The only reason I even like you is because of that one joke.' 'Which joke?' Lucy remembered, of course, but liked to have Layla retell it. They had walked a corridor at a shit job and someone had left a binder of work papers on the floor by the water-fountain outside of the Ladies' Room and Lucy had, very mater-of-factly and not trying to call attention to it - she'd only known Layla three days, by then - said 'Someone got zap-gunned - we need to watch out around here, it looks like.' Logic - anyway, now Lucy hobbyhorses along - is about as reliable as Chinese Checkers. Logic is the equivalent of writing a scholarly critique of the philosophical leanings present in the assigned-for-class short-fiction of tenth-graders - the world makes itself up as it goes along and since we see patterns we think we've found Reason, found Order. Patterns are not Order. There are so many ways that one scribbles their wrist, eventually the doodles become rote and they don't suddenly grow foliage in the shape of Gertrude Stein! Patterns are the world exhausting its creativity but thinking the umpteenth-time it's said 'The butler, he done it!' they are still being surprising and the umpteenth-time times the Nth-degree they say 'Ah, I had it happen that way because the trope is so avoided it has become fresh, again' they think that something old and disused is honestly New and not just old and disused. Everything becomes a pattern - all mathematics proves is The Infinite got bored and just kept going, the worst sort of date but the one you wind up waking the morning next to, ashamed of yourself. Why'd you bet on Red? It just kept winning! Why did you bet on Black? It was bound to win sometime! Stand around roulette long enough and you'll become richer than compost - it's not the odds that grind you out, it's just that you only have so much money in the bank. 'Yep' Lucy says - why has she taken this road? - 'if we take into account the big wins, the world around, versus the big and small loses combined, Roulette proves out to be the real loser' - oh yeah, it has paid out more than it has raked it, Lucy will bet on that. If wheels were treated like horses, we'd have green-black-red glue enough to wallpaper all Mother Russia - those wheels think it's funny how the ones who pauper themselves spinning them are also damn right their round-around can be beat.

It's mostly a matter of keeping things fact-based: had Lucy been called, suddenly, to deal with the needs of a friend who was creakingly depressed at the sudden loss of their own dear friend - a friend inconsolable to the point that a night needed to be spent with them - it would not wash so well that this friend then had to rush right out the door for work, first blink in the morning. That's for one thing. A whole separate story of 'I had to try to convince her to call out from work, but there was something or some other thing' some skin of some teeth or a thread being just barely clung on to, the company would roil bumper-cars down the drain if this friend did not show up, an appointment or a bladdity-blah. You'd seem callous for not insisting, Lucy! 'Lucy - what are you doing home so early?' That is what Ariel would, most rightfully, ask. This way, making the story simply seem true - to be brief, Lucy would say she stayed until another friend or some relative showed up to more-or-less take over suicide-watch duties - Lucy could walk in and deliver protestations of exhaustion, wave the matter off with an 'Ugh' and full-tilt ahead to asking Ariel about things to assuage this growing, ulcerous guilt. *Guilt*, you say? 'Yes, I feel guilty' Lucy's very posture as she drives says. About Ariel? 'Sure, why not' - and then thought goes no further than that because - well it repeated a bunch of times, she supposes - by the time it had the slightest chance to do so, here is Lucy, pulling in for the bite to eat which will consume the time naturally she will, only if asked, say was consumed in dour, sad-chuckle looks and memories that started happy but ended sad and asides made that went nowhere, dangling attempts at mirth and bolster of her mourning pal. It would not be untrue to comment:

Lucy is starting to believe her new version of things. It would not be untrue to say, not with full certainty but some: I believe Lucy will never go visit the mother, again. But oh - yes she will, yes she will. She just needs to get back to a pattern. She needs this all to have been months ago - until then, it seems lifetimes away - or at least lifetimes on the table-across-the-way, the one she isn't eating at, the one with plates already cleared. The setting? A strip-mall sandwich-shop that - now she is inside - is doing its best to seem a legitimate Diner. Example of a prop? This sign says *Have A Seat At The Counter Or We'll Be Right With You.* Sounds a tad like a threat - and she is smiling when the hostess walks up, so she points this out. 'That is funny' the hostess says. 'It's almost as though little thought went into that sign.' 'It does almost seem so' says Lucy 'it does.' The hostess gives her a widening then narrowing glance, seeming to slow in her retrieval of a menu. What is it? Lucy puts the question all smiles 'We haven't met, have we?' The hostess shapes her eyes 'Eh?' But then, now, for the first time, gives Lucy a scan over, clearly not thinking so, and not having thought so just before, either. 'You were looking at me.' 'Did you want a table?' The hostess points to the sign. You're the one not with it here Lucy - you're the one the merry-go-round merry-go-rounding! 'I will sit at the counter.' The waitress good humoredly walks a few steps with Lucy in that direction, then slows, like letting go training-wheels, and Lucy, shamefaced, continues all the way to the stool at the far end and turns over the coffee-cup waiting there on a napkin - after, let us note, a pause, because she is not certain whether this is a used cup or the way this particular shoppe indicates unoccupied space, a physical colloquial of 'Please, sit down.' 'Be right with you' Lucy hears. By the time her head turns, no one she sees seems to have specifically been the speaker. She's left imagining a hidden pre-recording. She's left doubting it happened. She's left assuming she assumes it was said because she assumes it must always be.

With derision, Lucy: 'I don't see how a restaurant can sell fruit. How much did you charge that guy for that apple?' Setting Lucy Jinx's coffee down, immediate conspiratorial voice, with lips moving as little as possible, this server, Sarah: 'I agree.' Then, immediately on the heels of that, this server Sarah, normal waitress-voice-laugh, as though everyone is free to hear and join in, this restaurant built for a Studio Audience: 'Oh we get those apples from a local orchard, so it's worth every red cent! What can I get you - or is it just coffee?' Cheek-to-fist propped-up-on-elbow, wedged-to-counter, Lucy: 'Not fruit. I will maybe have an omelet. Are we allowed to eat those at the counter - is that counter-appropriate food?' Stern, hard-as-broken-glass, I've-seen-it-all, veteran slouch, Sarah: 'Did you bring your own drool-bib? Otherwise we charge extra.' Lucy, eyes practically kissy-mouth: 'As much as you would for an apple?' Sarah, ginger-snapping in semi-apology for breaking scene, but-this-is-important: 'I'd like fruit more if they made it taste like Popsicles.' Sidenote: everything about that statement uncoils yearn-stoned anguish in Lucy, her head leaden aflutter, mouth dry with what's-the-best-word-for-here? Then - scrambling to make sure this keeps the server's attention, because she intuits that brief flit-glance - there, that that-wayish one! - was well-worn code for *I'll be right there, just finishing up with this bore who I am only talking with because I am paid to*, Lucy: 'I won't trust Science at all until they make spoons that can reflect things the way that things look - why's that so hard to do?' Staging Suggestions, in prose, to the director: *it should be suggested, in the immediate way that Sarah drops posture - arms crossed with each hand gripping around the inside-crease of elbow, forearms entirely flat to the counter, heavy, like sunbathing walruses, chin hovering close enough to Lucy's still steaming coffee - that her glasses, the left lens especially, fog somewhat - that Lucy's words struck some sort of mesmeric zazz - Meanwhile: Lucy - which should seem out-of-character - should instead of aloofing her stance - this all at the same time - sit up straighter and turn sideways in her seat, the suggestion of the movements almost like these-are-old-friends, as like Lucy is about to give a hard shove and a 'Fuck you'*. Then: Some few minutes have passed. More customers, but Sarah ignores them as she, unneeded, checks on Lucy's coffee, again. 'I could always have more.' 'You know what I don't vote for?' 'Senators?' 'Yes - obviously - but also I don't vote for Comptrollers.' 'Not very civic of you.' 'I don't think that sort of thing calls for a vote - democracy can run amock if we let it.' 'I tend to not vote for dweebs or anyone who comes off as churlish.' And this pit-patter would go on, but this new customer - who actually is churlish - says - as though he was asked - 'Coffee and the Special, the Egg Special' finishing with his telephone and smoothing his withering face with his hands in a way as though he's just narrowly avoided frostbite. Note from the Director to the Cinematographer: *we need to find a way - not overt, not just cut-shot and then face-reaction - to show that Lucy is assuming that the Francis Bacon book on top of the display-case for doughnuts belongs to Sarah - we need to let the absences of Sarah - who does not return, ever again - kind of build-up - that is: the question we suggest in Lucy needs to become ours!* Then: This new waitress - long-legged but spread-torsoed, almost seeming hump-backed because of it - brings over a coffee-pot and fills up John Churlish's cup, pointing at the just-freshed, fish-egg-black of Lucy's and asking 'Any more for you, hon?' regardless. 'I think Sarah was getting it' Lucy Jinx says, testing the waters. 'Not your order, hon - just coffee. You good?' 'Aces' says Lucy, chipper in the exact measure to express her grub colored sigh, this new waitress Quasimodoing off and with a Tsk that sounds like the swish of an elephant's tail, taking Francis Bacon from the counter and dundering 'Tell someone to not leave their school stuff out please, thank you - thank you' - the second *Thank you* louder, the *Someone* the literal word *Someone* that all the mispronunciation and hatred in the world cannot make Lucy certain meant *Sarah*.

Why would Lucy be sitting out in her car waiting to see if she can catch Sarah leaving or smoking a cigarette or something? First - the sad truth is Lucy walked all the way around the building, posturing a causal reason to do so, hoping to find Sarah there, but learned how there must be a corridor separating establishments in front from those in back because a whole different set of store-facades is all she found. Second - is Lucy supposed to ask after Sarah, to tug the tied-apron of some other staff member and begin an oblique interrogatory? This question has answered itself. When - quite all of a sudden - those two men who are talking there - one in the outfitting of a farmer with an over-groomed beard and a motorcycle helmet in his hand, the other who looks exactly like a high-school History-of-Government teacher everyone learns three-years later has married the mother of a girl who left the school mid-Marking-Period - become agitated into faces of raised voice, threats of violence. Threats? Lucy - there is no sound reaching her from the lot at all, her car interior is a Novocained lip - giggles 'Oh my God' as she watches the slick-bearded-farmer whack the left-out-too-long-blueberry teacher bang in the nose with the helmet, fleeing with a surprising grace, the muted Vroom of his motorcycle - from Lucy's vantage as innocuous as a phone ringing three cubicles over - seeming almost instantaneous. And there he is - there he goes! Already out at the traffic-light, squeezing into the space between cars and curb - now up on the curb, cutting the corner of the grass, thunk-thunking to the road as the traffic approaching slows down, Lucy assuming with honks and a collection of spittooning invectives and sputtering growls not on the ball enough to work out their spelling into *Fuck!* fast enough. Amazing! Lucy, though, sinks low in her seat, noting the wounded man - bleeding impressively, unabashedly, shirt-up and exposing a malt-colored belly brilloed with silver-beige hair - now wringing some blood from the fabric of his shirt, is having a look around. For three minutes, it feels as though she is only aware of the sound Thrssssheeeee she is making and that she is testing how slowly she can move her lower teeth close to her upper, how steady she can make the rise, annoyed how it seems to ascend at premeasured ticks, terrible thought of feeling manufactured. 'Excuse me' - muffled but quite abrasive the voice - and turning her head Lucy finds there is the man and his blood has slightly misted to her window, he backing up as though in apology, already, for that. Lucy aghasts and - this is unconscious, practically involuntary - pulls on her seatbelt and - people do strange things - opens the glove-compartment then closes it and presses the volume button on the radio. The man, freely bleeding, holds up peace-talk hands and from afars 'I didn't mean to startle you - did you witness that? Did you witness that?' 'Did I witness what?' Lucy just mouths, making no sound - Lucy, is this really the time for head-games? - the man holding bloodstained hand to his ear, universal sign of

'What-what!?' Yelling face, still silent, Lucy does a cramped-in shrug gesture, her wrists touching - hands spread like shadow-puppeting a tree or what have you - and pretends to say 'I said *Witness what?*' and adds - or doesn't but seems to - 'Are you okay?' The man signs with scissor-fingers to mean 'I am walking over, now' so Lucy starts her engine and lowers the power-windows just enough to let in a bullying of all the sounds outside, including the man - what an awful voice, like a sneeze buck-shot with crumbs and steak sauce - saying 'Did you see that man hit me?' 'Somebody hit you!?' 'You didn't see him? Just now?' The man is pointing the way the motorcyclist zoomed to his freedom. 'I'm sorry' says Lucy. 'You were sitting right there!' - but the man waves her off in a tantrum before she can bother herself with getting upset at the fact that his tone suggested accusation not question-mark and what right does he have! 'Yeah' she says, shutting her window, suction of her silence returned 'you go into that Supplement Store - you go ask them!'

Lucy thinks it would be best to pick up something for Ariel, but is resistant to actually doing so because even as she commits to the turn lane - you're boxed in Lucy, live with it - her stomach tightens hard and the taste of bile slithering over a lollipop globe coats her insides. Like a little grubby mitt has a got a fist-pinch of her underskin and is trying to pull it into the narrow aperture of a rusty storm grate. That wannabe Diner! Yet Lucy, for whatever reason - yes, yes, she knows the reason - cannot bring herself to cast a curse in too harsh a heart at the place. 'It's all your own fault' she says - stopped again at the red-light due to - isn't it always the case? - some chucklehead twerp not noticing that it was time to get hopping - so why didn't you honk Lucy!? 'I don't need to do everything. I have a stomachache - that's what I'm doing, right now.' A gurgle-pop-belch, the flavor of a lemon pulled from water that had speckled throughout it the thin spread of scratched around ketchup - though not all of the scent - seems to expel from her, but Lucy is unable to force a burp further, seems to swallow a solid remainder, a breath thick as left-over gruel. She weaves the parking lot oddly, mostly because some dumb pedestrians decided to stop to let her pass instead of thanking her for obeying the sovereignty of the stripes on the almost-white asphalt and it seemed like another lot of them - a family weighing, between them, another family-and-a-half on top of themselves, easily - were readying to do the same. So she comes to the drive-thru of the doughnut-shop screwy, reverses her car to make a better approach, and hears the crunch of a lurking glass bottle. Is Lucy making anything of this up? Is she threading a tapestriac needle and getting ready to embroider some snug connectivity? No. Honestly no, no she is not - this is just what is happening. She even has to note the spots of blood on her window as she prepares to lower it, how they seem pliant though stiff, like the spatter to a bathroom-mirror of toothpaste or mouthwash, those orphans of the swish of head side-to-side, the whip of head-up after head-down to spit. She over-consults the menu, trying this squirm and that against the suctioning cramp that now seems to radiate exactly from in back of her kidney - how did you determine this, Lucy, do you even really know what and where your kidney is? - as though there is a bulb there sprouting untrimmed toenails, calcium leaking snarls of heat like a steak on the grill. 'Can you tell me if you have any peanut-butter filled ones?' The speaker coughs back 'Peanut-butter crème?' 'Sure' Lucy, gripes, actually unbuttoning her pant front now and lowering the things with hip flounders, her half-ass exposed into the crumby sharp feel of the seat under her. What do you mean 'Lord-knows-the-last-time it was vacuumed!'? Lucy, you've never once vacuumed this car! 'How much are they?' This much, it seems. 'How many do you have?' Lucy enunciates with her eyes closed. It seems they have three. 'I'll take those three. And do you have strawberry icing with - you know? - the chocolate drizzle?' 'The *Sweet Zinger?*' In a struggle through grit-teeth Lucy goes 'Sure' then growls out 'And just give me three of those and any six with sprinkles to end out the dozen, alright?' Maybe you're being dramatic, Lucy? 'I'm not being dramatic' she sneers, too corkscrewed to speak further, sweat from all parts of her that could properly be designated *Crevasses* - and her scalp under her hair feels wrong, exactly the moist of a sock pulled on that you know from your fourth toe through a hole in it isn't yours. Lucy bites down briefly on the ribbed stiff of the steering wheel as the voice tells her her total is exactly some amount. Orange box in the passenger seat beside her, she parks and just screams. Shock cut! Bumper-car thud! And all at once, the feeling is past. She feels silken, feels like refrigerated butter. Like she has bled a rash out her pores, her skin feels hamburger marbled as though she's been too long in a hot shower - but it also feels like the inside of an over-exercised throat, pulling down ice-water too fast and unceasingly. Oh suddenly she feels like the taste of her tongue to a tongue that has just spit out a fresh stick of wintergreen.

HERE WE FIND - IN STACCATO, up-down reveal, rather like seeing from hardly afloat something approaching on sea-face, each bob under-surface, to-surface and so on making the incremental announcement - Ariel shuffling at loiter in front of Lucy's apartment door, giving a timid wave 'Hi' and pointing at the box Lucy - meager and out-of-breath - balances, look of happy-but-alarmed, happy-but-perplexed to her nose-wrinkles and side-scrunching lips. 'You know you do live here - you are Ariel, right?' Ariel just wants to know 'What's in that box?' 'Doughnuts. But not for skeevy, mincing little loiterers -

and I count two of you, here, so nothing, neither way.' 'Droll and all, yes yes' but Ariel takes the box, at first thinking she can balance it on her pregnancy like a decorative table, then goes - Lucy just laughing - to her knees and snaps through the two pieces of Scotch-tape holding the box-top to bottom. 'How long have you been here?' Lucy asks while Ariel voraciouses one of the sprinkled doughnuts - chocolate-cake, chocolate icing, sprinkles so hot pink they look like Serratia marcescens. 'I just got here, ten minutes ago' Lucy translates from Ariel's gob-full mangle of the sentiment - this while she live-bird crouches down and licks thumb-tip to wipe at a smear of chocolate on Ariel's cheek. 'Gross' - pronounced *Graouwerse* in Mouthfulease - says Ariel, batting the gesture away, Lucy dousing crumbs from Ariel's almost triangle-stiff rotund before straightening to a stand, going to tiptoes, the last wince of that fierce stomachache easing gaseously in a squish down her taut and leaned belly. So: why isn't Ariel inside? Ariel forgot her key. 'Trouble' Lucy announces, as though to stage-left 'due to the amount of murder and all that has happened in this part of town.' 'I forgot my whole purse, is how' Ariel explains. 'Then how did you drive here?' 'I didn't.' Blink blink. 'You forgot your purse - at your appointment?' 'That was yesterday!' Ariel says, now more daintily selecting a second confection - 'and you don't need to worry, you freak - I know where it is and I'll get it later, I figured you could give me a ride.' Lucy is about to press for some details - yes, true to Lucy, more out of further teasing tete-a-tete than due to curiosity regarding the genuine happenstance - but doesn't seem to be able to find her own keys. 'What?' Ariel trepidates, overstuffed concern in the shape of her cheeks bloat with mashed frosting and glazed bread. Nope - Lucy does not have her keys! 'But I just drove here' she explains, Ariel's expression ready for the punchline, Lucy patting herself up-and-down, over-and-over, as though there is a either a pocket she had discovered by accident, earlier, or else as though her current pockets had properties and recesses she was not giving them credit for. Ariel - old hat - dismisses Lucy as 'Weird' and keeps eating, scratching at her hair with unconscious aggression and stickiness, strands of it coming away on her digits she then rub-rub-rubs on her pant-thighs. Left Lucy looks. Right Lucy looks. 'You really don't have your keys?' Ariel resembles a squirrel with other squirrels stuffed in it, holding a doughnut with two hands, slowing her chew and eyes widening like some snap-of-twig predator approaches or a cough from someone smoking a cig on their back porch has been overheard. 'Me? I'll be right back' says Lucy, turning while brandishing the epithet 'Scavenger - lice-ridden scavenger!' on Ariel, who is scratching her head again - behind the fit of her ear - Lucy's last view of her showing her disappointed by the state of her fingernail, using one nail to try to unjam some pasty residue out from under another. Through Lucy's head goes: my car tire is going to be flat, the doors will be locked with the key still in the ignition - I will go up to use Ariel's phone which she won't have and find that her water has broken. Degree of certainty? 'Well' she says 'thirty-percent, if I'm being fair' but this prediction is predicated on the fact that she held off making it until seeing the keys through the windshield, right there - see? - on the dash and feeling the clunk of the handle allowing the door to be out-swung.

According to Ariel - or according to Ariel's doctor, according to Ariel - Ariel has had a broken toe for quite some time. 'The middle one, at that!' which she feels would be the easiest toe to notice is broken. It makes Ariel feel, Ariel explains 'that not a lot is known about toes.' 'What do you mean?' Lucy wonders into a sip of new-brewed coffee. 'Toes' Ariel elucidates 'are the sort of things when one takes it for granted that everything is known about and so - because of this - one thinks one knows about those things, themselves.' Lucy nods. '*Societal osmosis*' Ariel snaps her fingers 'genetically passed on' Ariel finger snaps 'the same as we know how to, say, get jealous of people and so stick it to them where they live!' Lucy summarizes: Ariel Lentz believes knowledge of toes is something just gleaned from living daily-life. 'Street smarts' nods Ariel. And Ariel presses on about how it makes sense to think so, but moreover says 'How is it fair that stubbing a toe hurts like a motherfucker' - adding in, a different tone-of-voice, candid 'Don't you always think *I've broken my toe* when it is stubbed, but you never have anything even remotely like broken your toe?' before continuing her thread - 'but then you go ahead and break your toe and it doesn't even register!?' 'You have ill-evolved' Lucy offhands and says 'A quick climb through your Family Tree could find the backwoodsy culprit, no doubt - some great-aunt who decided to slum it and got stuck there, I'd wager.' The thing is: the toe had been broken a long time - 'Like a long long time' Ariel emphasizes with plentiful *O*s crafted in to pearl strings - and kind of broke even more, as it went. 'How long are we talking, here?' 'Since, basically, I met you. Do you remember breaking my toe? Have I had the wrong impression of you, all this while?' That depends, Lucy sagely observes, on what impression it is Ariel has had. Pointing out: 'I have never asked what you thought of me, you know? I'm just keen to all comers.' 'So I've heard' winky-winks Ariel and starts removing her shoe. 'I don't want to see your Christ-loving toe, Ari! I imagine it looks exactly like the rest of you, but a toe.' 'Oh just look at it' Ariel insists, also noting - 'See? See!?' - how she is just tugging off her sock with no bother. It is interesting that the toe doesn't look broken now that Lucy is looking at it - the two of them sit on the sofa and Lucy takes the whole foot in her lap, trading it between hands like she's trying to figure out, unaided, how to go about scaling a fish and what bit, specifically, she is supposed to eat. 'It doesn't hurt?' Ariel tells Lucy 'Grab it.' 'No.' 'It feels like the - whatever those are - beads inside of a bag.' 'Beans?' 'Whatever they are - like big pieces of rice.' 'And it doesn't hurt?' And after a through-a-few-times cycling of such banter and hesitations and coaxings, Lucy finally squeezes the toe and moves her fingers around on either side of it like she is sign-languaging 'You owe me more money' the feeling exactly as Ariel had described, at first making Lucy queasy and wanting to pull away, but then just feeling relaxing, kind of pleasant. 'Actually, let's keep your toe this way - that really doesn't hurt?' Ariel claims not to feel a thing! Lucy is curious as to when, honestly, it was broken - wonders if any of her own toes are broken since there is no telling when was the last time she was X-rayed. 'Do you ever go to the doctor, Lucy?' 'Meh' Lucy says. 'I would if I thought there was something in it for me.' 'Do you even have a doctor?' It's a fair question, Lucy suddenly feeling very adolescent. 'I'll get a doctor, El - you've convinced me. If only to look at my toes.' What else is that in Ariel's face? What is that second thing? 'What?' Lucy asks. 'What, what?' 'You're thinking something.' So Ariel tells Lucy that Lucy makes strange noises when she sleeps. 'What noises?' 'It sounds like something is humming inside of you.' 'The fuck is that supposed to mean!?' 'You just sound like you hum. I don't think bodies are supposed to do that. Mine doesn't.' Lucy quips something about 'Oh! If you're considering your body the Model Exhibit then blah blah blah' but something she hopes is more clever than that, standing and patting Ariel's calve, saying 'Be right back, stay there.'

But here is Lucy's body. Growths? Lurking areas within that have closed off or otherwise ceased functioning? You would be able to tell wouldn't you, Lucy? This series of moles, here, beside your left breast - you recognizes them, no? Those are your moles, the ones to the left-side of your breast. How many? Don't count, now! Say, first. Okay, then: guess. It goes without saying the fact that you have to guess indicates you have never counted - which does not bode well - but go ahead and guess. Now. One two three four five six seven eight nine ten eleven. 'Eleven' Lucy says, as though the point was just to come up with Eleven. But you'd guessed Eight! 'That was' - Lucy points out as though the more important thing in this study is just to be True in whatever statements she makes - 'just a guess, though - it turns out there's eleven. Moving on to this whitish flesh here' Lucy says. Then Lucy kicks in: No! No! Not *moving on*! 'What?' It isn't alarming to you how you don't know how many moles are beside your left breast? 'Why would it be!?' How can you ask that, Lucy!? 'I've never paid attention before - fine, there's eleven. Yippie-de-doo! I'll make a note of that and count on a bi-monthly basis - that's likely more than a doctor would tell me to do, so I come out ahead.' But you have noticed the moles before, Lucy - you know you have. 'Sure' Lucy admits this, no resistance. 'They're beautiful.' She loves that detailing of moles there, figures its why so many lovers prefer her left

1134 / PABLO D'STAIR

breast - or why she enjoys it more, anyway, figures there is extra hunger to the pleasuring of that one on these lovers' behalf. 'I am an unequivocal work of fine art!' You've never counted them. 'I've never counted the wrinkles on the brow of *Judith Beheading Holofernes*, either, it's no less a great painting - what, should I realize she's got a touch of the croup?' You're not a painting, Lucy. 'Well, if asked I couldn't say how many letters there are in *Miss Macintosh, My Darling* - and I've even read it!' You aren't a book, either. 'Anyway - moving on to this whitish bit of flesh here: some skin is probably just like that.' And the fact that this skin is dry? 'I'll moisturize.' And on goes Lucy's denuded, contortionist slide-show, her every nuance declared pristine, her ever blemish rhetoriced into an extension of the Natural Beauty of Age. A doctor would agree: You are beautiful - strikingly so. 'So why would I need to go to one, then?' Say you were ill, Lucy - are those moles haloed? 'Again with the moles!' Lucy demands, now troubled by why she has picked them, is singling them out, is brayingly demanding they be paid attention to. 'I have other things to worry about.' What was that thing in the car, just now? 'Who knows?' Who knows! Lucy is talking to the mirror now, putting her shirt back on, but not her bra. And sabertoothed, she is bent and stepping into and pulling up panties, giving herself a Greyback stare, insisting dominance, proclaiming 'Don't take it out on me, you monster. Medical conclusion: one person can walk around on a broken toe and not be bothered - bang goes the Science of Medicine! If we discovered planetary orbits could just change, willy-nilly, we wouldn't be so hot on Galileo anymore, now would we? Maybe we'd say, in new History books: *He was someone we thought was right until we learned he was totally wrong.*' And a cough into a hand and a few phantom-punches toward her phantom-punching reflection, Lucy decides her little episode has passed and reminds herself of the phrase 'It only just happened yesterday - it's not like it's been even a week' thus coercing her reflection into softening its eyes, its brow, and granting 'That is true.' 'It is.' 'You're right.' 'Let's see how it goes.' Flush goes the toilet. Run goes the faucet. Lucy decides she could do with some mouthwash, so really does that. Run goes the faucet again and - to be nice - Lucy takes out a new roll of toilet-paper from under the sink, sets it on the counter, even unsticks the start of it and tears off a bit so it is all set for coming applications.

'Would you mind it horrendously if I took a bath, for awhile?' 'I find it bloody disquieting that you specifically chose the word *Horrendously*, there. I am to infer that were I to find it anything less than that qualifier you would not even think my counsel was needed? Is that how things work between us, my bloat-bellied Sneech? As long as I would not find *horrendousness* in what you do you just do it, untroubled?' 'If it helps, it is kind of a step up from *Blood-curdlingly*, which used to be my metric.' 'Would I mind it *blood-curdlingly* if you took a bath, for awhile?'

'That is how I would have asked before, yes.' 'You've never asked anything that way.' 'Don't read too much into that, though - just let's stick with the present, the past is a grave we can easily leave raked-down, eh?' 'How recent was this upgrade?' 'Again, Lucy, again - what did I just say about the past?' 'I thought I wasn't supposed to talk about the past?' 'I'm glad you still have a sharp wit and an endless need to make a simple Yes-or-No question into a short-story you would likely just spend an hour deriding if you ever read.' 'It's more like a bad essay in *Rolling Stone*, I think - you know how I hate the political ones, the ones that young people write?' 'No - no, no, what? - you don't like political articles in *Rolling Stone* - you, Lucy Jinx, don't like those - the ones young people write, specifically!? - why haven't I ever heard about that!?' 'Are you going to do as poor a job raising your this-or-that as the maids clearly did raising you?' 'I'm not even gonna raise the scamp! Lucy, I did this whole thing just to start lactating - do you know how much a wet-nurse can earn? Freelance? I get me some rich benefactor thinks if she keeps her boobies taut until fifty-five she'll get on the cover of *Time Magazine*? This is all for profit, baby - this bun-in-the-oven is bread-on-the-bakery-shelf, pre-ordered and waiting to ship!' 'That's probably actually really a good idea, Ari - if I looked into that would you do it? For us, I mean. We could keep your kid, but feed it formula or goat's milk - like cults, we can do whatever cults do! Babies in cults always survive - they usually wind up in leadership roles, too.' 'I think it's more complicated in the Digital Age. People just sell their milk online - I read that somewhere. In *Rolling Stone*, maybe. Rich people do it that same way due to knowing someone who got a grant for a Start-Up. I don't like the thought of selling my milk to bidders in cyberspace.' 'What do you care?' 'What if they use it to get some sick-in-the-head jollies! Lucy - I don't mean to alarm you, but anything wet can be repurposed as lubricant. The only way I could trust I am actually nourishing a kid is to have it at suckle - you know? - feel its weight in the crook of my elbow.' 'You were born in the wrong Age, Ariel Lentz.' 'Tell me about it! Jesus, I would have been great when all there was to do was wander the desert or wait for the Barbarians to figure out they could come around the other side. You though, my love, were born in the wrong Era, certainly.' 'I know.' 'It's the Printing-Press, I think - you should have predated it. Abbots should have illuminated your work without thinking there was an easier way.' 'I'd have been the first one to burn Guttenberg at the stake. The first headline in the first newspaper his dismal machine chugged would have read *Read All About It: Here's Why You'd Better Not Read This*.' 'So: can I take a bath for awhile?' 'Was I stopping you?' 'You weren't exactly aiding me in the process.' 'You expect me to run it for you?' 'You expect me not to expect you to run it for me? Have you forgotten your place since whenever the last time I saw you was?' 'No, ma'am.' 'No, *mistress*!' 'No, mistress.' 'Chop chop,

you wench - and put in the oatmeal stuff or it's the cat o'nine tails! And not on
your tuckus - on your jelly-roll front-side this time.'

To say a stain came over the room? No - one could not say a *stain*. No - nor a
kind of current to the air, some sort of parceled-out chill amidst a heater-unit
humidity - no, not even suggesting a draft would be true. It was under an
ordinary ceiling and between perfectly ordinary walls and atop perfectly
ordinary floor that Lucy Jinx - happening to think to call in to her job, where
most likely she was supposed to be today, wasn't she? - decided to now finally
plug in her phone for a charge. Nothing was on her mind while she pouted at
going to the bedroom, seeing the outlet blank before recalling it was plugged in
by the toaster - and nothing was on her mind, of consequence or otherwise,
when she plugged it in and turned off the coffee-pot switch, deciding to pour
herself the last of the pot. Really - and this, in retrospect, is odd, at least in
certain senses, because she might have been curious, it would have made sense
to be - it was an automatic gesture that led her to hold down the Send button
and to wait for the thing to activate rather than let it charge, inactive, until it
read *Battery Full*. Ghost-story it may be, in a way, but nonetheless also hum-
drummily the-way-things-just-are that Lucy had poured her coffee, that two
minutes had passed since the phone's screen went lit and she read the time and
all off of it - and maybe more than two, the coffee moving slosh-booted down
in her doughnut-filled insides, her mind wondering if it would be fine to cram
one more sweet down or if that would be the one that took things from Bad to
Untenable - before - look, there it goes! - the phone vibrated, over and over,
too quickly to indicate Incoming Call - this is rather a barrage of text-messages.
Fourteen of them, in total. Lucy - note it, note it - did not have a sinister sour
down in the pit of her, she didn't think anything other than 'Maybe I was
supposed to be at work' and this she thought wistfully - or *laughingly* or *musingly*
or *coquettishly* - and was still grinning with her la-di-da word choosing when she
lifted the device, put her finger to it and saw - the display showing the
information from the last of the messages - the name *Layla*. Oh now - even now
- Lucy did not go ashen - her complexion, if anything, rosed to Rosacea,
brightened to lily-white-buttercup-yellow in tincture mixed. What would, in
reflection, turn out to be the oddest memory shot through her head: Lucy Jinx,
living in some anonymous apartment - always dark in there, like the inside of a
portable-office on a construction-site seems it would be - had had her door
knocked on and a man she had never seen had said 'You have a cat, right?' to
which Lucy, who had at that time had a cat, had said 'Yes' and the man had said
'I think your cat is trapped out here, it seems hurt or something' - but no, Lucy's
cat, was there where it had been, on the countertop, and as she said 'No, my cat
is right here' the man had described another cat Lucy had thought was a stray

and had named *Gaugamela* - a cat she sometimes left food out for or told her roommate to when Lucy would have to work late or would stay over with whoever her lover had at that time been - and Lucy remembered exclaiming 'That's *Gaugamela*!' and, with paramedic imperative, had grabbed her wool-cap and run out the apartment, stocking-footed to help get the kitty out from under the wooden baseboard on which a Cable-box or something was situated. That memory. Which made her smile, but did not make her think something bad. It made her think humor. It made her think 'Layla!' It made her think 'This was a joke, all along - and you're a bitch and I'll fucking end you for this!' Strange. Strange. But, see? Not so strange. Because the Time and Date stamp showed today. Broad goes her smile. And the time-stamp shows - no, Lucy does not think it odd - *Received* at *Just now*. 'The fucking timing' she thinks - this is Lucy Jinx thinking, her phone in her hand, its plug to the wall - 'that is that most insane thing ever, that timing.'

The first text reads: *I'm thinking about glue a lot, I'm thinking about paper a lot, I'm thinking about the taste of both, each other, togethered.* Lucy Jinx is a face trying to blink fast enough to clear itself room to see. There is something, now. *Cauldornous.* Lucy feels *cauldronous*. There is a heat to exterior bringing her interior from middle-point out to a sharp. Is this poetry? Lucy understands it and hears it in Layla's voice. But her eyes - Lucy's - are tearing - her throat is not constricting, there is none of that, she isn't sidelong or becoming shaped like a spilt-over bin, just her eyes watering to the point it is agitating. She sniffs as she sets her phone down and roughs at her both eyes, eight-fingered, but the sniffs are like snorting in sand, scabbing, flat. The second text says: *hey - that train didn't have windows. Recall? That train didn't have windows or memory, you said.* Who said? Lucy had not said this. Had she? Her memory is a frantic trill movement through of paper-turns, the pages directory-thin, being torn as she goes, some of them, the phrase always seeming to be at the start of a chapter then, no, the end then, no, in an upper-paragraph then, no, a bottom one, then - it's in dialogue, it's in dialogue, somewhere between quotes! - then, no no, it's just prose, it is part of a description, right, right? The third text reads: *what about Holidays?* Just that. 'Is Layla texting me a poem?' thinks Lucy. Lucy starts typing a response - *Is this a poem?* - then her ears start to ring at the thought 'Layla can't write you back - you're asking the loose-dirt on the packed-dirt on a box in the ground if this is a poem.' *Durt* Lucy types into the phone. *It should be spelled Durt, Layla* she types then erases. But these messages just came in, right? Layla recovering. Layla out-of-surgery - Layla just had been under sedation or something, had not meant she wasn't coming back, she was just only worried! See the fourth reads: *We held hands about as convincingly as you could picture grapes on an empty grape bunch, hey, didn't we? That first time, that second time, maybe the third?* And the fifth reads: *there's not enough* coins in this river! And the sixth reads: *I don't think there's sound enough to drown because some things have to be loud we are safe we are safe.* And the seventh reads: *Don't look behind you.* And like it's a joke - breaking from her now half-circle pace, hawk-in-flight, shoulder-humped aching, her side-to-side since she cannot around-and-around march over with the phone in her hand - Lucy looks behind her and expects almost a 'Boo!' or then the next text to read *Bwahaha* or else *I said 'Don't look behind you.'* This is reading, though, Lucy, this is not conversation. The eighth reads: *find someone to tell, but then don't tell, I never did and I certainly won't.* And the ninth reads: *I think every bed was made to hide sleep and misused.* And the eleventh reads: *There aren't as many colors as there are Uppercases, there are only as many as lowercase, eh?* There's the feeling, Lucy, there it is girl - there it is rising your spine high like Valkyrie, there it is, silent lungful of everything that you'll never say wanting a sound - and so what, Lucy, so what, you get that this is really the end, don't you girl? These were just sent, though! Lucy sees it! *Received - Just now!* Ten minutes ago or whatever! That is today and that is the time! And the twelfth says: *Do you know how lowly it is, the last thing that is known for the first time? People think about exactly what you fear.* 'Wait.' Lucy says that. 'Waitaminute.' And she reads the thirteenth - which says: *I have wrinkles as wide as the miles you'd have to climb* - and sees these were all sent yesterday. These were all sent while she smoked or drove, cigarette or eyes out a window or hands on a wheel or a song in her ears she might have been forced to think things about, the same things she always thought things about. 'Wait a minute' she says 'no, hey - wait a minute, Layla' - and it's to Layla Lucy is speaking and Lucy opens the fourteenth and says 'Hey - wait a minute' even while she reads: *Lucy. Oh petty Lucy. I hope your last moment is one you don't have to live.*

Sometimes, Lucy Jinx is the same physicality as anyone, blasphemer it may make her to her. Observe: Lucy crinkling like bubbled bath-water on the floor of the living-room after having tried to sit to the sofa and found it made her feel dizzy. She is as long as the sofa - though, right now, is side bent - when stretched out tallest - never truly thinks of herself that way, or indeed about the sofa in any dimensions but its height. Observe: Lucy leaks mucus thicker than her scalp inside her palm wrapped around brine-thick mouth breathing and making suction sounds that someone would make fun of her by saying *Hee-haw hee-haw!* regarding. Observe: Lucy scratches the top of one foot through the sock-heel of the other foot through the sock of the scratched foot and this makes her uncomfortable enough to finally perch on the sofa, though almost drooled from the bulb of the lip-like cushion's plump front. What does she do about the snot? To the kitchen, where she uses dish-soap to lather her hands, feeling them simultaneously go dry-wood and yet feel slippery no matter how long she rinses. The unnatural scent of the washed skin she now breathes - and it mangles in nicely with the drift of her unscented underarms. Lucy is soft grinding when she moves her neck and her stomach seems to pulse in exact contra-her-heart, each organ takes a different beat and somehow are able to maintain a balance. Then she forgets that she has a body, at all - feels she has covered over the evidences of it the same as a how a cat buries its voiding in sand or wraps fabric around it when the litter-box seems too crowded to conceal. Layla died yesterday, of course. Lucy, you can call to confirm. Or are you going to refuse that - refuse who? refuse yourself, Lucy? come on! - are you going to try to hold on to the idea that Layla just went into surgery, has another week-and-a-half before kaput? Admit it, Lucy. Admit it. If she was nearly dead, you'd prefer her to have gone through it already to the finish. Admit your endless shivering heart! Admit that you are glad that call got cut off - oh you couldn't have bore it, Jinx! Oh you never would have lasted! Blind panic - it's about as close to human as you can get. Confusion and doubt and then having your choice plucked from you! No? *No*, you say? Look here, Lucy Jinx, you are really the living end! Would you have wanted to fly across to her, to have sat with her, held her hand for it all - could you have faced the moment of knowing her body had been taken from the house and you needed to board your flight back? Because, Lucy, that is what people do. Horror-show, ain't it? Just admit that you're glad that it's over and it needed be nothing to do with you. No? Admit you're so flattered to have had the starring-role! You're Lucy Jinx, then - well, aren't you? You are the last person that old Layla called and even when you were taken from her, as a vice she spilled her last letters from finger to you. 'No.' No? 'No.' No? 'No.' No? 'No.' No? 'No.' No? It's just you here, Lucy - and you're both stating and asking, so I think everyone watching knows what it is they've observed. Confess. Confess it, do succor for your soul. You have found words that have nothing to do with you now - words that you caused that have nothing to do with you and that you don't understand. The gift of a dying friend is a fourteen-high pile of language, the tape-recorder got her death rattle, maybe, but it was the Poet got the phrasing. Go confess, Lucy. Go be who you are. Go take what you've earned. Go name what you've caused. Go steal what you've been given. You like the sound of that last line? Of course you do, Jinx. You have dug the ground, after all, now go put the bones the last place they belong.

*Pneumonia Jinx*, it says here. Then - here - *a poem for Layla*. Does Lucy read back what she wrote? Sure - a bit - she reads more of the things - here - markings indicate she'd decided against, though - if for nothing else than to remind herself that those decisions were correct. 'The decision' she reasons 'is primarily aesthetic and only secondarily principle-centered.' Does Lucy insert these lines of Layla's - they have so been dubbed, she will never say of them otherwise - throughout the poem as writ? Or perhaps even use each as a pace - the opening-line followed by some of her stuff? Or do sections which open with Layla and end with Layla with maybe some Layla between? Absolutely, Lucy will write no more lines, herself. So she can take a moment to mathematic this all out - perhaps a nice balance will be presented in the numbers and then it is just the making of some sort of lock-and-key model, the whole thing a lock-and-key model, a simple enzymatic reaction. Lucy makes an offhand count of stanzas and stand-alone lines, writes the details on the reverse-side of the blank page she winds up open to - which brings her quite gracefully into her consideration of Principle. Inasmuch as Lucy Jinx started this poem when she was supposed to be editing her collection for the first time - and inasmuch as Lucy Jinx forcibly made herself stop and resisted returning to it - it so would follow that these lines of Layla's have grounds to lay claim that they, on principle, are all of a single Section and, in fact, belong rightly as the finale, to be given that grace and dignity, that defining power of Ending. And not to overlook, by-the-by, that Layla - rest her soul - is dead! That seems to clinch the position of the deceased on placement - no more ongoing a position can be held than the tomb. Doesn't it somehow seem more fraudulent, though, to finish off this last poem - not ever, but it will be last of the current collection, Lucy will walk coals in Hell to hook-or-crook the no-two-ways-about-that of that - with an entire run of verse that is purloined, coins robbed from the eyes of the resiliently slumbering, as they say? Or does that seem more honest? What Lucy is hoping is that her mind will convince her while she argues that Aesthetic is best served by Principle - Principle, Aesthetic - and so, of course, no decision will need to be made. Alternately - see? Lucy isn't exactly doing anything but staring - she is hoping she will just say 'I don't care' and do one as though the choice is no more hers than the coming upon the words was. It is - as ought to have been expected, of course - only the act that will so determine - and it does so, just here. Having to open each message and tap and then re-tap the *OK* button on her phone to keep the screen bright enough to transcribe, Lucy writes out the phrases - in exactly the order sent - and now has them to reckon with in the scrags of her own hand. Now that you've written them, Lucy - now that they read in your voice - they seem kind of less like a branch and some leaves which could scatter and more like a trunk still there after its branches have been struck off. If ever there were words more columnesque, more elegant ruins, well, Lucy does not know of them. Attached they will remain and affixed to the page as the last breaths they are. Except what to do with this last one? With this one that Lucy has not written out, she means. *Oh petty Lucy.* A weaker sort might think Layla had meant *pretty.* But Lucy is not such a namby-pamby - no ma'am, she is not. And no, it was not a pet-name, not something that Layla had lovingly butterfly-kissed throughout conversations, a repurposed word to mean anything else but its Is. *Oh petty Lucy.* Does this belong in your poem? *Oh petty Lucy.* Are these words just meant for you? Write them. Try it. Oh petty Lucy. 'Oh petty Lucy.' *Oh petty Lucy.* You're done, now. Be done.

So Ariel had been out of the bath, for awhile. Lucy probably had noticed, had overheard the metallic push of the drain opening, the sloshing glug of Ariel easing herself up and out - Lucy can almost imagine that Ariel had asked for help, come to think of it, probably had peeked in to find Lucy writing and so tip-toed about her business, leaving the artiste in peace. And here, Ariel can be found taking a just finished pizza out of the oven. 'Ariel, you're the bloody Bronze Age - I'd be nowhere without you.' Ariel takes this to mean Lucy thinks Lucy gets some of the pizza and has to sadly inform her of the contrary. 'But I thought you loved me.' 'I'm also the one who cooked this.' 'But I bought it!' 'But I put it in the oven and now took it out - you see how all of your arguments, however well-worded, will wind you up in the same ditch? So I'd give it up and say you gave it up while you were still ahead.' 'You mean give myself dignity?' 'I mean give that a try, sure - what have you got to lose?' Lucy opens the fridge and selects something microwaveable, hoping to stir pity in Ariel, but finds instead that Ariel is pouring Parmesan cheese over the still sizzling round - an addition Lucy cannot abide, a clear piss of territory-marked. 'How was your friend today, by the way?' Lucy looks up from reading the *Heating Instructions* - wondering if these things would be better if conventional-ovened, but deciding against doing that because they only need to be heated to three-fifty while Ariel's pizza was heated at four-fifty so Lucy doesn't know if she'd trust the oven to cool down so precisely if she re-pushed buttons and told it to heat up to that. A long pause there, Lucy - but Ariel is still waiting. 'She was actually kind of okay. Eventually she decided to head in to work. I think it all just threw her for a loop.' Ariel asks 'It was sudden?' Lucy rips the perforated tab of her box-top and drops the two cellophaned calzones to the counter - thud thap - nodding. 'And before you chew me out, I - of course - did try to stop her - but she said stepping out of her routine would make everything seem somehow worse.' 'Are you going to the funeral?' Lucy gets a plate from the cabinet, tears open the calzones, and puts them into their crisping sleeves while she, first blowing a breath out, says 'No - I didn't know this person, I just know the friend.' Beep beep beep Lucy enters the cook-time and then nuclear-whir goes the sound of preparation. 'I saw someone get hit in the face, though.' 'Just today?' 'Yeah - when I stopped to get you doughnuts. One guy just whacked the other guy with his motorcycle helmet and then fled the scene like a full-fledged movie-star! I kind of went weak at the knees.' 'Is the guy okay?' Lucy admits that she did not get a very good feeling from the victim, had been figuring he likely deserved the assault, as far as such things go, and now that it's just an anecdote she doesn't feel like revisiting it as an exercise-in-conscience. 'Meaning: I hope he isn't okay. It makes me feel better to assume that he's not. I refused to be a witness for him - told him I hadn't seen a thing.' Ariel approves of this - so adorable in her hatred of eating hot food, touching the pizza-top every fifteen seconds, set to devour it as soon as she feels that to do so would not lead to so much as the slightest sting. The microwave - that seemed quick - sounds off that Lucy's food is ready and, yes, the snapping hiss of the calzones where the insides have leaked out through the holes made for breathing confirms it must be so. 'You should cut that in half' Ariel says, holding the pizza-cutter across after - Lucy feels a flush of desire to lean in and kiss Ariel, but doesn't - rinsing it at the sink-tap, toweling it, and turning it this way and that, rotating the blade once around with her finger to be certain not a crumb of Parmesan remains. 'Otherwise those things take forever to cool.' Lucy takes the blade, applying it rapidly in and across, surprised that the innards don't burst out like ink from a harpooned octopus.

Lucy, innocuous, is realizing it's still daytime - not because of the well-lit of the apartment, the clear sun warming her studiously through the window to her left, but due to the particular game-show they are finishing an episode of, both her own and Ariel's plates on the floor - when Ariel clears her throat and says 'I need to ask you something, really specific.' No, neither turns the volume of the television down. Lucy sweeps the air as though her table is clear of all other saws and traps of books - though is still kind of thinking about at least two other things - and Ariel asks 'So: you're basically scared of everything, right?' 'Basically' Lucy says, levity-colored, but actually now focusing and showing she is ready to give sober response. 'Are you afraid of me?' 'Of you? No.' But Ariel had noticed the tilt of pronunciation given to *Of* - spoken like an italic. 'Then how are you afraid, vis-a-vis me?' Lucy regards Ariel, who both looks and does not look like Ariel, who could have been a separate Ariel on at least several occasions between meeting, meeting-again, and coming-to-be-on-this-sofa. Lucy says 'I don't know how to explain it. But I will tell you that I am afraid *for* you.' '*For me?*' 'Not *of*.' They stare at each other for a few moments and now Ariel turns off the television. And now Ariel kisses Lucy Jinx. And now Ariel tells Lucy Jinx 'Kiss me.' 'We just kissed.' 'But this time you kiss me, first.' 'But, this would be second.' 'Only if I do it, again.' 'But you are doing it, again.' 'But that's only second for me - you're like flirting with a thirteen-year-old and I'm too old for it!' So 'Fine' Lucy says and then kisses Ariel. And then they kiss - Lucy wondering if Ariel is somehow keeping track of who is doing it when to who and how many times - until Ariel pulls back and touches at her hair, though her hair is not out of place. 'I told them to tell me, yesterday. What it is.' Lucy narrows her eyes - it honestly does take her a moment, she thinks of three quips before landing on what to actually say - then smiles '*It* being *that?*' and two-finger points at Ariel's belly. '*It* being *that*. I broke down. I wanted them to tell me so I could come home and tell you something. There was something I just wanted to say beforehand and figured I needed to know in order to say it.' 'Sounds complicated' Lucy says, Ariel's smile - frightened, eager, stern, lost - almost too intoxicating not to slap - and obviously something that had to be flirted with. 'It is complicated.' '*It* being *that*?' Lucy points. Ariel smiles more by biting a thack sound. 'No. That's pretty simple. That is a girl. Which I knew it would be. I just wanted to know how much I was right.' Lucy does not know what to say here and says so, but Ariel laughs and says 'There isn't anything to say.' Adds: 'Yet - not yet.' And a moment passes in which a car out in the lot honks its horn and someone makes an annoying sounding greeting to someone and Lucy and Ariel both roll their eyes. 'Why did you ask about Leopold?' 'What do you mean?' 'You thought he would be at the thing, yesterday.' 'I just thought' Lucy is off-balanced now 'because Kayleigh. Kayleigh was there, right? I guess I just thought.' Then there is nothing. Lucy is more foreign here than anywhere else - which later on, likely, she will wax poetic-philosophical on, but right now is merely a bay that got overrun by an ocean and doesn't quite know what that makes it. 'What if I just wanted us to leave, Lucy?' Ariel takes Lucy's hand and places it on her belly - first over shirt, then under shirt, whispering 'Shhhh.' Nothing. Nothing. 'What if I asked you, Lucy: *Could we just leave?* You and I.' Lucy is still watching Ariel's face, but Ariel has turned her head sideways, ears cocked as though listening to the apartment below them. Ariel whispers 'Shhh shhh' and presses Lucy's hand a bit harder. Now, Lucy almost looks down, but Ariel meets her eyes and the colorless grey of the irises holds Lucy as firm as a sin. 'Her name is *Lucy* - is what I wanted to tell you. Her name is *Lucy Ariel Jinx*.' Lucy chuckles and kind of goofball says 'Oh - alright. That's easy. Let's go, then.' And Ariel says 'Shhh' as her belly undulates just the meagerest knead. 'Did you hear that?' Lucy answers by flashing her unclosing eyes just a tap so they sting more. The flesh under Lucy's palm moves, again. 'Listen to how she kicks.' Ariel's head drifts to the side and Lucy tries not to blink, straining to hear. 'Listen to how she kicks, Lucy. She kicks just exactly like you.'

*Lancaster, Pennsylvania*
*September 24, 2015 - May 19, 2016*
*(revised January 2019; July 20 - August 19, 2019)*

CPS... ...formation can be obtained
at www....Testing.com
Printed in the USA
LVHW080234... ...919
634236LV00003B/82/P

9 781646 692217